OTHER BLOOM BOOKS BY JENNIFER L. ARMENTROUT

COVENANT SERIES

Half-Blood (includes the novella "Daimon")

Pure

Deity (includes the novella "Elixir")

Apollyon

Sentinel

FRIGID SERIES

Frigid

Scorched

SENTINEL

SENTINEL

JENNIFER L.
ARMENTROUT

Bloom books

Cover design by Nicole Hower and Antoaneta Georgieva/Sourcebooks
Cover images © Jose A. Bernat Bacete/Getty Images, serikbaib/Getty Images

Published by Bloom Books, an imprint of Sourcebooks
P.O. Box 4410, Naperville, Illinois 60567-4410
(630) 961-3900
sourcebooks.com

Originally self-published in 2013 by Jennifer L. Armentrout.

Cataloging-in-Publication data is on file with the Library of Congress.

Printed and bound in Germany.
BPG 10 9 8 7 6 5 4 3 2 1

PRONUNCIATION GUIDE FOR SENTINEL

Aether: EE-ther
Agapi mou: ah-GAH-pee moo
Akasha: ah-KAH-sha
Apollyon: ah-POL-ee-on
απόλυτη εξουσία: ah-POL-ee-tee EX-shoo-shee-ya
αήττητο: EYE-tee-toe
Daimon: DEE-mun
Deimos: DEE-mohs
Δύναμη: TZEE-nah-mee
Hematoi: HEM-a-toy
Ixion: ICKS-zee-ahn
Phobos: FOE-bohs
Θάρρος: THA-roesh

"Some people say when life gives you lemons, you make lemonade. But I say when life gives you one seriously ticked off god gunning for your ass, you prepare for war and you hope for paradise."

—Alex (Alexandria) Andros

CHAPTER ONE

Feeling came back in my feet first, and then my legs. A pins- and-needles tingling rushed over my skin, causing my fingers to spasm. The sweetness of the nectar still coated the inside of my throat. My body ached as if I'd just completed a triathlon and come in dead last.

Or like I'd had my ass kicked and gotten patched up by a god. Either/or…

Movement beside me brought the whole side of my body closer to a hard warmth, and I thought I heard my name called, but it sounded like it was on the other side of the world from me.

I was moving at the speed of a three-legged turtle, so it took a while to blink my eyes open, and even then it was just a thin crack. When my eyes adjusted to the dim lighting, I recognized the buttercup-colored walls and all the titanium trim of the dorm rooms at the University in South Dakota, the same room Aiden and I had done a whole lot of not sleeping in right before Dominic had brought us news of Deity Island survivors. Things…things were different then; it already felt like years ago.

A terrible heaviness settled like a stone in my chest, pressing all the way down to my spine. Dominic was now dead. So were the Dean of the University and his Guards. It had been a trick played out by Ares, who'd been masquerading as Instructor Romvi. Our enemy had been among us the entire time. My dislike of that man had been epic before I'd discovered who he really was, but now? Every fiber of my Apollyon being loathed him. But my hatred of Romvi/Ares/Asshat wasn't important. So many people were dead, and Ares knew where I was. What was stopping him from coming back for round two? And what was stopping him from killing more people?

I heard my name once more, and now it seemed louder and closer. Turning to the sound, I willed my eyes to open. When had my eyes closed again? I was like a newborn kitten or something. Daimons across the nation shuddered in fear. Gods, I was pathetic.

"Alex."

My heart skipped a whole beat, and then sped up in recognition. Ah, I knew that voice. My heart and my soul *knew* that voice.

"Alex, open your eyes. Come on, baby, open those eyes."

I really wanted to, because for him I'd do anything. Fight a horde of half-blood daimons? There. Tangle with ticked-off furies? Sign me up. Break a dozen or so rules for one forbidden kiss? Done. Open my eyes? Apparently that was asking too much.

A warm, strong hand curved along my cheek; the touch was so different than my mother's, but equally powerful and heartbreakingly tender. My breath caught in my throat.

His thumb traced the curve of my jaw in such a lovingly familiar way that I wanted to weep. I should weep, actually, because I couldn't fathom what he'd gone through when Ares and I had been locked in that room. Come to think of it, I should've cried when I saw my mom. I'd felt the tears, but they hadn't fallen.

"It's okay," he said in a voice gruff with exhaustion and emotion. "Apollo said it could take some time. I'll wait for however long it takes. I'll wait forever, if I have to."

Those words pulled my heart all over the place, twisting it into mushy knots. I didn't want to make him wait for another second, let alone forever. I wanted—no, *needed*—to see him. To tell him that I was okay, because I *was* okay, wasn't I? All right, maybe I didn't fall into the "okay" category, but I wanted to relieve the harsh edge of stress in his voice. I wanted to make him better because I couldn't make my mom better, and I knew I couldn't make myself better.

There was a part of me that felt vastly empty. Dead. That was it. I *felt* dead inside.

Frustration coursed like acid in my blood. My fingers fisted in the soft sheets as I dragged in a deep breath. He stilled beside me, like he held his breath and waited, then let out a ragged exhale.

My heart plummeted.

Gods, all I needed to do was open my eyes, not walk a tightrope.

That frustration quickly flipped to anger—a soul-deep kind of rage that tasted of hot bitterness. My heart rate picked up, and that's when I realized *it* was there—the cord. It had been absent in Olympus, but it was back. I hadn't felt it at first because I'd only been acknowledging the ache in my muscles and bones, but the cord connecting me and the First buzzed like a million yellow jackets, steadily increasing until I swore I could see it in my mind, an amber-colored cord tangling with a blue one.

Seth?

His reply didn't come in the form of thoughts or feelings, but a rush of energy so pure it was like being zapped by lightning. Strength poured into me, a torrential downpour of vitality encasing every nerve ending. Every distinct sound in the room was magnified. My own breathing, more steady now, and the deep and slow inhales of the man beside me. Doors opened and shut in the hallway outside the room, and there were voices, muted but distinct. My skin came alive. Glyphs bled through, swirling across my body in response.

I didn't understand it, but I knew Seth was lending me his power, like he had in the Catskills when I'd fought the furies for the first time. He'd claimed no knowledge of what had happened, chalking it up to adrenaline, but Seth had...he had lied about a lot of things.

But now he was helping me. It didn't make sense, since I was much easier to deal with in my weakened state, but I wasn't going to look a gift horse too closely in the mouth right at the moment.

My eyes flew open. And I saw him.

Aiden was on his side, facing me. His hand still cupped my cheek, his thumb smoothing along my skin, and I could feel the marks of the Apollyon gliding toward his touch. His eyes were closed, but I knew he was awake. Thick, sooty ashes fanned the tips of his broad cheekbones. His dark brown hair was a mess. Waves tumbled over his forehead, brushing the graceful arches of his brows.

An ugly, purplish bruise marred his left eye, and I wondered if he could even open it. There was another violent mark, an astonishing mixture of reds, shadowing the strong line of his jaw. His lips were parted, neck and shoulders tensed.

Without warning, I was thrown back to the very first time I'd seen him.

The Covenant in North Carolina no longer stood, but it felt like I was there again, standing in the training room used for novices. I'd been practicing with Cal and Caleb. I'd done something incredibly moronic, which was nothing new, and the three of us had been laughing. I had turned and seen Aiden by the doors. At that time, I didn't think he really saw us. He was a pure-blood, and they didn't show any interest in halfs, so I had assumed he was just observing. Even then, I'd been captivated by him. To me, he'd honestly been the most alluring male I'd even seen—a face that could be both hard and beautiful. And those eyes, flashing between heather gray and quicksilver, had been permanently etched into my memories from that moment on. That curiosity had been inflamed when he'd shown up in Atlanta, saving me from some really annoying and talkative daimons three years later.

Our love had never been easy.

As a pure-blood, he was untouchable to me even though I was the Apollyon, and even now he risked everything to be with me. He was my strength when I needed him to be, my friend when I needed someone to talk me down, my equal in a world where by law I would always be less than him, and honest to gods, he was the love of my life.

And he would wait forever for me, just as I would wait forever and a day for him.

Except forever will probably end up being fairly short, whispered an insidious voice, and it was right. Even if I managed to get past all the obstacles between me and Seth, and transfer his power to me, there was no doubt in my mind that, even as a God Killer, I was going to have problems fighting Ares. And if, by some miracle, I survived that, there was a really good chance the other gods would kill me.

So why even bother?

Aiden and I could run away together, live as long as we could and *be happy*. He'd do it if I asked. I knew he would. We could hide until we couldn't hide anymore, but we'd be together and we'd be alive. And for a little while, there'd be no more pain and no more death to deal with.

A huge part of me, especially that dark, cold place that had been born when Ares held me down, agreed wholeheartedly with that plan. *Run away.* Nothing seemed smarter or simpler to do.

But I couldn't, because there was too much that had to be done. People relied on me, and the world would descend into absolute chaos if Ares wasn't stopped.

I held onto that needle-thin thread of duty with my life and spoke. "Hey."

His lashes fluttered open, revealing silvery eyes that never failed to make the muscles in my stomach tighten and my heart do a little pitter-patter.

Our gazes met.

Aiden jerked up, his face paling by several degrees, making the bruises along his jaw and left eye stand out in stark contrast.

Fear exploded in my stomach, which was kind of strange since terror typically wasn't my first reaction to sudden movements, but I scrambled against the headboard. My breath stalled out as my body protested the sudden movement.

"What?" I croaked. "What's wrong?"

Aiden stared at me with wide eyes. Color hadn't returned

to his face. He was as pale as a daimon, and while disbelief shattered his gaze, pain churned in them.

He reached out but stopped short of touching me. "Your eyes…"

"What?" My heart beat so quickly I was sure it would jump out of my chest and do a little jig on the bed between us. "I opened them. I heard you asking me to."

Aiden winced. "Alex…"

Now I was really starting to freak out. Why was he reacting this way? Had Ares rearranged my face so badly that my eyes were on my chin or something?

He glanced toward the door and then back to me, his face going stoic, but he could never hide his feelings from me. I could read everything in his eyes. There was so much pain in them that it broke my heart, but I didn't understand why.

"What are you feeling?" he asked.

Uh, what was I *not* feeling? "I'm…I'm going to go with confusion. Aiden, tell me. What's going on?"

He stared at me so long I started to feel a wee bit self-conscious. Several seconds passed, and then I really became convinced that my eyes *were* on my chin, but then it made sense. Panic unfurled in the pit of my stomach and spread like a virus.

Springing from the bed, I hit the floor. Hot slices of pain ricocheted up my still-healing bones. I stumbled to the side, catching myself on the wall.

In a heartbeat, Aiden was off the bed and beside me. "Alex, are you—"

"I'm okay." I bit back a moan.

Aiden reached out, but I pushed away from the wall before he could touch me. Each step hurt like Tartarus. Sweat dotted my forehead, and my legs shook with the effort to make it to the bathroom that joined the two suites together. "I have to see," I gasped out.

"Maybe you should sit down," he suggested, close behind.

I couldn't. I knew what Aiden was thinking. I was connected with Seth, and maybe he even thought this was a trick of some sort and was waiting for me to break free and pull out Deacon's ribcage, but Seth was quiet on the other end of the cord.

Reaching around me, Aiden pushed the bathroom door open, and I all but fell inside. Light flooded the small but efficient washroom when he found the switch on the wall. My reflection formed in the mirror.

I gasped.

This couldn't be me. No way.

Uh-uh, it wasn't, and I refused to believe it, but the damn reflection remained the same. I had changed. Dramatically. The pressure in my chest returned and doubled as I gripped the edge of the sink.

My hair hung an inch or two past my shoulders now, the edges ragged and uneven from the dagger Ares had used. I picked up a strand, wincing as I discovered it was a good deal shorter than the rest. Did the rest of my hair hang in Hades's war room now?

My skin was pale, as if I'd been sick for months and hadn't seen the sun. But it wasn't even that. Hell, it wasn't even the fact that, yes, my eyes were amber-colored. Identical to Seth's in clarity and shininess, they were like two topaz gemstones. And they were glowing, like you could see me in the dark kind of creepy glowing, and I got why that set Aiden on edge. Great, I had glowing, honeycomb eyes. Big freaking deal.

It was *my face* I couldn't get over.

I was as shallow as any other eighteen-year-old girl, so yeah, this…this was major.

Across my cheekbones and nose, faint pink lines criss-crossed over my skin. My forehead was the same. A web-like network of scars covered my face. Only one side of my jaw, where Aiden had been touching me earlier, had escaped the… well, the disfigurement.

Dazed by what I was seeing, I slowly lifted my arm and ran my fingers across my cheek, confirming what I suspected. The lines were slightly raised, like stitching. Apollo and his son had healed me. The nectar was still doing its mojo in my system, but I knew these scars were proof of just how badly I'd needed the gods' help to heal.

Like anything else, there always had to be an exchange.

When anything was gained, something had to be sacrificed.

No one needed to tell me. I knew these scars would never fade. "Oh, my gods…" I swayed.

"Alex, you should sit down." He reached for me again.

"Don't," I snapped, holding a hand up between us. My eyes widened. My hand was also covered with scars. I wasn't even sure what I was saying "don't" to, but my mouth kept moving. "Just don't."

Aiden pulled back, but he didn't leave. Leaning against the threshold of the door, he folded his muscular arms across his broad chest. His jaw set in a hard line.

The pressure moved into my throat, swelling like a balloon and then exploding like a late summer's day thunderstorm. "What are you waiting for? Me to go all Evil Alex on you again?" I swung forward, losing my balance. "That I'm going to use—"

Aiden shot forward, catching me before I cracked my head against the wall. "Dammit Alex, you need to be careful and *sit down*."

I wrenched free, stumbled back a step, and plopped down

on the closed toilet. Air punched out of me. Dear gods, it felt like my tailbone had been cracked. I sat there on the toilet, my butt feeling like someone had literally kicked me in it. Aiden stared at me with warring levels of hope and distrust in the eyes I loved so much. I felt about seven kinds of dejected.

Aiden stepped forward, crouching down so that we were at the same eye level. "You don't want to kill me?"

Most of the rage seeped out of me. Nothing like hearing the man I love ask a question like that to really take the wind out of my sails. "No," I whispered.

There was a sharp intake of breath. "You don't want what he wants?"

"No." My gaze dropped to where his hands rested between his knees. Good gods, the knuckles were bruised and the skin was torn open, as if he'd punched a… Then I got it. Aiden and Marcus had been banging on the titanium doors of the dean's office with their fists.

My heart ached as I watched those battered hands open, close, and then open again. "I don't even feel him. I mean, the cord's there, so I know he's somewhere, but I don't feel him. He's quiet."

His hands unclenched, and even though I wasn't looking at him, I could tell that most of the tension had left him. He believed me for the most part, and I couldn't hold the residual suspicion against him.

"Gods, Alex, when I saw your eyes, I just… They glowed like that when you escaped the basement and…"

When I had almost killed him.

If I lifted my lashes, we'd be face-to-face, but I couldn't bring myself to do it. He shifted closer. "I'm sorry. I should—"

"It's okay." I was so tired. Not the physical kind. Oddly enough, it was more of a…spirit-weary sort. "I understand.

You had every reason to think that. I don't know why my eyes are glowing. Seth's there, but he's not trying to influence me."

"Yet" hung unspoken between us.

"And he's not talking," I added, keeping the fact that Seth had lent me some of his own juice out of the conversation.

I shifted my gaze back to my own hands and the scars that marred them. They hadn't been like that in Olympus, or at least I hadn't noticed.

"It doesn't matter," he said. "It's you, and that's all that I care about—all that matters."

I wanted to believe him. I really did, but the horror in his face when he'd seen my eyes haunted me. I knew Aiden had hated them from the moment they appeared after I'd Awakened, and I couldn't blame him. These eyes would always remind him of Seth and everything I'd said and done back then, especially when they glowed like yellow light bulbs.

"Alex." His much larger hands covered mine. There was a long stretch of silence. "How are you feeling?"

I shrugged a shoulder, then winced. "Okay."

His hands circled my wrists, and I suddenly was on the verge of tears but didn't know why. All I wanted to do was curl up in a ball, right there, on the bathroom floor.

"I've never been more scared in my life than when you forced me and Marcus out of the room."

"Me too." I swallowed hard. I don't know what made me do it, but I pulled my hands free and slipped them between my knees. "How is Marcus?"

"He's hanging in there, but he's going to be relieved once he learns you're awake." Aiden leaned in, his breath warm against my cheek. Every instinct insisted that I lift my chin a fraction of an inch to meet his lips, but I couldn't move.

There was another pause, and the words he spoke next were heavy. "I know why you made sure Marcus and I were out of that room when Ares attacked. It was incredibly brave, and so like you."

My fingers dug into my stiff denim jeans. Gods, were they the ones I'd worn during the fight? Patches of dark dried blood covered the legs like paint. Squeezing my eyes shut, I was sickened to find that the images of what had caused the stains lingered.

Aiden took a deep breath. "But if you ever do anything like that again, I will strangle you. Lovingly, of course."

I almost cracked a smile at the same thing I'd thought about him not too long ago, but the smile never made it to the surface.

He wasn't done. "We promised each other we'd face this stuff together."

"Ares would've killed you," I said, and it was the truth. Ares would've killed him and Marcus if they had stayed in that room, and he would've relished doing so.

"But I would've protected you," Aiden countered. "I would've done every godsdamn thing there was to save you from having to go through what you went through in there. When I came into the room and saw you…" He broke off, cursing under his breath.

"You would've died trying to protect me. Don't you get that? I had to do it. I couldn't live with myself if you or Marcus died—"

"And do you think either of us can live with ourselves knowing what that bastard did to you?" Anger snapped through his voice. So did frustration. "Look at me."

At a loss of how else to explain the obvious to him, I shook my head.

"Godsdammit, Alex, look at me!"

Startled, my head jerked up and my eyes met his. They were a furious shade of gunmetal gray, and they were so *open.* Raw pain flowed from them, and I wanted to look away from that, to take the coward's way out.

"My heart stopped when that damn door closed on me. I could hear you two fighting. I could hear him taunting you, and I could hear him *breaking* your bones. And there wasn't a damn thing I could do about it." He placed his hands on the sides of my legs. Tension rippled through the muscles in his arms. "You never should've faced something like that alone."

"But you would've died."

"And because I love you, I am willing to die to save you from that. Don't you dare take that decision away from me again."

My mouth opened, but there were no words. So much was going on inside my head and chest. What he said had split my heart wide open and then stitched the wound closed. But what would I have left if he'd died? I would've been beyond heartbroken, and I couldn't even bear to think about his death without hurting. If I had to do it over again, I would make the same decision because I loved him. So how dare he expect me to do anything less?

I knew I needed to say those words to him, but they…they just couldn't get past the ball in my chest or pop the lid on the pressure inside me. I shivered, numb and chilled to the core.

Aiden went to grasp my shoulders, but he stopped, his fingers curling around air. "You have my heart, and you also have my strength. Make no mistake, I am willing to die for you, but you have to trust that I don't want to leave your side. Ares wouldn't have taken me out easily, because I would've fought to stay alive and be there for you."

I heard him, and I felt what he said, but all I saw were the Guards that Ares hadn't even touched. Dominic, whom he'd snapped in two with the twist of his hand. The dean he'd tossed out the window with a wave of his arm. All the wanting and needing in the world wouldn't have saved their lives.

He let out a ragged breath when silence filled the bathroom. "Say something, Alex."

"I…understand."

He stared at me, dumbfounded.

The numbness had seeped into my muscles. "I want to take a shower. I need to get out of these clothes, and I need to bathe."

Aiden blinked, and then his gaze dropped. Some of the color brought back by anger drained as if he'd just realized I was in the same blood-splattered clothing I'd worn when I faced Ares. "Alex…"

"Please," I whispered.

He didn't move for the longest time, and then he nodded. Rising fluidly, he stopped halfway and pressed his lips to my forehead. My heart thumped heavily, but then I realized his lips were touching those scars and I winced.

Aiden pulled back immediately. Concern etched into his striking face. "Do they—did I hurt you?"

"No. Yes. I mean, it's tender." Truth was, it hadn't hurt at all. Not like the rest of my body did. At first, it had actually felt nice. "I just need to shower."

He hesitated, and for a moment I thought he wasn't going to leave, but then he nodded again. "I'll get something for you to wear when you're finished."

"Thank you," I said as the door closed behind him.

I stood slowly, feeling like I was ninety as my joints popped and my muscles stretched. Stripping off the soiled clothing took an indecent amount of time, and as I turned the water on and steam filled the bathroom, I stepped in. Hot water doused me from head to toe, pricking my raw skin.

The water coursed through my hair and down my body, filling the tub with red and circling the drain like a grotesque raspberry swirl. I washed my hair twice, going through the mind-numbing mechanics until I was satisfied when I didn't see a hint of pink in the bottom of the tub.

Only then, as I turned off the water and felt the spray lessen until it dripped down the plastic walls, did I look down at my body. From my toes to my collarbone, with only a few places where there were no bones to break, I was covered in a thin lacing of pink scars.

Good gods…I'd never seen anything like this before. I looked like one of those patchwork dolls. I stepped out of the shower, legs shaking as I twisted to the side. My back was much worse. The coloring was darker along my spine, where many of the vertebrae had been smashed. Had all these bones broken the surface, or had the injuries burst blood vessels? There had been too much pain when it'd happened for me to tell.

Apollyon or not, I couldn't believe I'd survived this. None of it seemed real.

The numbness in my chest spread like a weed. Maybe I was struck stupid by what I saw, because I had known it was my body that looked like this, but the knowledge had only sunk through a layer or two.

A strange mark on my back, near my hip, caught my attention. Colored like a pale pink rose, it didn't follow the typical pattern of the rest of the scars.

Swiping the mist off the mirror, I twisted to get a better look at the mark on my lower back. My mouth dropped open.

Holy Hades holding hockey sticks, it was the shape and distinct form of a *hand*. "What the hell?"

"Alex?" Aiden's voice came from the bedroom. "Are you okay in there?"

Heart pounding, I grabbed a towel off the rack and wrapped it around me. That was the last thing I wanted Aiden to see. Opening the door, I forced what I hoped was a reassuring expression. "Yeah, I'm fine."

The look on his face said he didn't believe me, but then his gaze dropped. It wasn't the towel that had caught his attention or the fact that so much flesh was exposed. Deep down, I knew why he stared and why his lips thinned. I knew that, when he saw me, it wasn't my body that held him immobile.

It was the patchwork of web-like scars that now covered almost every inch of me, and it was the first time he was really getting to see them in all their glory.

Embarrassment flooded my cheeks with heat. There'd been scars before—daimon tags and, of course, the stab wound—but never like this. It was ugly, really ugly. No way around that.

His gaze flicked up, meeting mine, and I couldn't stand to see the emotion churning in his silver eyes or go through another conversation like before.

Hurrying across the room, I grabbed the fresh set of clothing he'd set on the bed and stumbled around, nearly falling into the bathroom. "I'll be right out."

"Alex—"

I shut the door on whatever he was going to say, which would be something ridiculously supportive and typical Aiden, but I knew better.

It wasn't okay. This body sure as hell wasn't beautiful anymore, and I wasn't stupid enough to believe that.

Tears clogged my throat as I ripped the towel away and threw it to the floor. It was stupid to get upset about this, because it surely didn't make the Top Ten List of Messed-Up Problems right now, but damn, it burned like a fire in my chest.

Once dressed, I stared at the door. The tears never fell, but the invading numbness spread, leaving behind the worst of emotions: anger and pain.

And fear and anxiety.

CHAPTER TWO

Who knew glowing eyes could set an entire roomful of people on edge?

Everyone, even my uncle, couldn't stop staring. Or maybe it was my face that held them morbidly fascinated. From a distance, the scars weren't so noticeable, but after Aiden assured the group that I wasn't psychotic, everyone got all up close and personal.

The hugs were…uh, awkward.

Even Deacon's embrace was stilted, and crap was serious if he wasn't cracking jokes or messing around. I didn't know if it was because they were worried about my injuries or because they feared I was going to Apollyon-out on them and snap their necks when they least expected it. I wished Lea were here. She would've just come out and said what everyone was really thinking without having qualms about it.

But Lea wasn't going to stride into the room. Lea was dead, and the sharp pang that accompanied that thought hadn't lessened one bit.

We were in the common room near the main academic campus building. It was almost identical to the one I'd found Caleb in the day I returned to Deity Island, except this one was outfitted with nicer furniture and a much bigger TV.

Olivia's caramel-hued cheeks were a shade paler than normal as she stepped back from me, her curly hair pulled back in a tight ponytail on top of her head. "How are you feeling?"

"I'm okay." It was my standard answer, changed out with "all right" and "fine."

Her gaze met mine and quickly flitted away. "We've all been so worried. I'm glad that you're…okay."

I didn't know what to say to that.

Laadan was a lot more tactful, but while she'd always remained a picture of cool collectiveness, the linen pants she wore looked like she'd slept in them and strands of raven-colored hair had escaped her twist. She met my stare and somehow managed to keep the sympathy in her expression to a minimum.

Aiden stayed close to my side, either as my own personal bodyguard or just wisely within tackling distance. He was unusually quiet while everyone settled into chairs or took spots against the wall. Unable to stand still, and figuring I needed to work the ache out of my legs, I paced, and Aiden never strayed more than a step or two away from me.

I asked the first question that popped into my head. "How long has it been since Ares was here?"

"Almost three days," answered Marcus, and he made talking look painful. Half his face was a swollen array of blues and purples.

From the sofa, Diana, one of the Head Ministers from the Catskills and my uncle's potential kissy-kiss interest, followed my movements with wary eyes. "Apollo removed you immediately afterward. You were gone for maybe an hour, and you've been…asleep since then."

I glanced at Aiden. My stay in Olympus had felt much longer than that, but time worked differently there, like in the Underworld. Minutes here were hours, if not days, there. "Has Ares returned?"

Aiden shook his head. "No. Apollo threw up wards to keep him out."

"Why didn't he do that before?" I asked.

"Apollo didn't know it was Ares until it was too late," Aiden answered patiently. "And I believe he assumed the University was safe."

"Yeah, and we all know what assumptions do." I passed by the TV again, vaguely aware that it was on a news station. "I thought the talisman was supposed to prevent the gods from discovering where…" I reached for the necklace and found that it was gone.

"Ares must've taken it," Aiden said, a muscle spasming along his jaw. "The only thing that we can come up with is that those Guards and Sentinels on the highway had made some sort of contact with Ares, Lucian, or Seth, and they put two and two together."

"Or someone is working with him." No one in the room looked like they wanted to believe it. "Ares said he has many friends."

Marcus's eyes followed me warily. "That is something we've taken into consideration, but…"

"But how would we know who it is?"

He said nothing, because what could he say? Anyone could be a traitor, but believe it or not, we had bigger problems at the moment.

I took a deep breath and kept my eyes trained on the minuscule space between Deacon and Luke on the couch. "There's a good chance Seth knows where I am."

No one in the room made a sound. Not even the guys in the back of the common area. There were twenty or so Guards and Sentinels from the University. I recognized a few from the group that had been led by Dominic, the ones who had met us at the walls when we arrived here. I truly hoped there were more where they came from.

"Besides the fact that Ares had to have told Seth where I was, I…I let the shields drop when I was fighting Ares." Shameful heat flooded my cheeks as I now stared at a tiny tear in the rug.

"We figured Seth would be aware of your location by now," Marcus said quietly. "I'm not an expert when it comes to the whole Apollyon connection, but Seth was able to feel what you were experiencing before you Awakened. That's how we were able to find you in Gatlinburg when you… when you…"

When I'd left to find my mom when she'd become a daimon. I felt several sets of eyes on me, especially a pair of silver ones. "Yeah."

"Does that mean he felt exactly what you were feeling when you fought Ares?" Aiden asked, and his voice was deceptively even. That was also known as the calm before the apocalyptic storm.

"Do you really want the answer to that?"

"Yes."

Glancing at him, I wished I hadn't. Aiden looked like he already knew the answer and was ready to murder someone, and that someone was Seth. I started pacing again. "Yes."

Aiden swore loudly. His brother jumped to his feet and

went to his side, saying something too low and quick for me to make out. Aiden's hands clenched at his sides, drawing my attention to his busted knuckles.

I wanted to go to him, but I felt rooted to the floor, near where Olivia sat on a black chaise lounge. I willed my legs to move toward him, but nothing happened. Frustration and uncertainty poured into me, overriding the numbness, and my anger skyrocketed.

My gaze locked with Aiden's, and a godsawful sensation lit up my chest. I yearned to run to him but a cold primal fear, a need to run *away* from him, was equally powerful.

"Alex," Olivia whispered.

I looked at her and saw her eyes widened with anxiety. Actually, *everyone* was staring at me with the same expression. What the…? My gaze dropped.

Oh—my feet weren't on the floor.

My heart tumbled over. Closing my eyes, I forced myself back down. Relief crashed into me when my sneakers hit the carpet. "Sorry," I said, putting some distance between me and those in the room. "I didn't mean to do that. I'm honestly not even sure how that happened."

"It's okay," Laadan reassured me with a small smile.

With wide eyes, Deacon remained by Aiden's side. "If your head starts spinning…"

"Shut up, Deacon," Aiden growled.

He made a face but remained quiet, and I really felt like a freak.

I remembered what it felt like when the shields came down between Seth and me. So much fury had burned through the connection. Seth had been epically pissed, but I wasn't sure if it was because of what Ares had been doing or if it was something more than that. The connection had fed him everything:

all the pain and the hopelessness I'd felt when Ares had gotten the upper hand. And when I'd wanted to die instead of facing another second of soul-shattering pain, Seth had gotten a taste of that bitter, rotten emotion.

How could he have been okay with that? Did the means really justify the end for him? I'd experienced way too much at Ares's hands to hope that Seth had changed. It seemed more believable that his anger was associated with me not submitting to Ares more than anything else.

Another random thought formed. The prophecy of Grandma Piperi, oracle extraordinaire, came back like a cold sore. *You will kill the ones you love.*

Part of me did love Seth—pre-jackass, of course. He was a part of me. We were yin and yang, and Seth had been there for me for a lot. I'd never forget that, but I was no longer so blinded by how he used to be that I couldn't see what needed to be done. If I couldn't get the power of the God Killer to transfer to me, I *would* kill him.

Or go down trying.

But that prophecy didn't mean just my loved ones would die by *my* hand. Kain, a half-blood Guard who'd helped Aiden train me, had been turned by my mom in an attempt to reach me and had died by Seth's hand. Caleb had been murdered by a daimon because I'd been so emo over Aiden that we'd snuck out to get food and drinks, even knowing that there could be daimons on campus. And my mom had been turned into a daimon—her true death—because of me. Then I *had* killed her. Even though I couldn't claim to love Lea, I'd respected her a great deal toward the end, and her death was also linked to me.

And more people I loved would die.

I crossed my arms, ignoring the way my bones cracked

from the movement. "The University isn't safe with me here."

Aiden whirled toward me, his eyes narrowing into thin slits, but before he could speak, Marcus stepped in. "There is no other place safer, Alexandria. At least here, we have Sentinels and—"

"Sentinels and Guards are nothing if Ares finds a way in. And let's say he doesn't—we still have Seth to worry about."

"We can't leave here." Luke leaned forward, dropping his arms onto his knees. "Not until we've rallied the troops and you've fully recovered—"

"I'm fine!" My voice cracked on the last word, a humiliating lie detector. Luke raised a brow.

"Whatever," I said. "I need to leave."

"You. Are. Not. Leaving."

Everyone in the room turned to Aiden, including me. His words hung in the air, and challenge seeped out every pore. "I have to," I said.

"No." Stalking forward, his powerful muscles rippled under the black shirt he wore. The black shirt of a Sentinel, and gods, he was a Sentinel through and through at that moment. "We already had this discussion. All of us know the risks, Alex."

Challenge accepted. "But that was before Ares went all god badass on us."

His eyes turned a furious shade of silver as he stared down at me. "Nothing has changed."

"Everything has changed!"

"The technicalities have, maybe, but nothing else."

I stared at him, dumbfounded. "It was one thing when we thought it was Hephaestus or Hermes, but it's *Ares*. In case you don't remember, he's the mother-fu—"

"I know who he is," Aiden gritted out.

"Children," Marcus admonished.

We shot him mutual death glares.

Marcus ignored it. "Aiden is right, Alex." Of course, he took Aiden's side.

"We all know what we're getting into." He gestured at his battered face. "Trust me, we all know, and like we said before, we are in this together."

"What about them?" I totally remembered when everyone had stood up and announced that they had my back. And one of them was dead now. I gestured at the back of the room. "What about every person at the University—the students, and all the people who came here for the safety it once offered? Are they willing to take that risk?"

A Sentinel next to the young one who'd been with Dominic the day we'd arrived here stepped forward and said, "If I may speak?"

Aiden sent him a look that a wiser person would've run from. Apparently this Sentinel wasn't used to running. Then again, none of them were.

"What is your name?" Diana asked.

"Valerian," he answered, and I pegged him to be in his late twenties. A half-blood, of course.

"Like the root?" Deacon asked. Luke rolled his eyes.

The man nodded. "Most people call me Val."

"What do you have to say, Val?" Diana spoke again.

"Everyone here has been affected by what is happening. I can't name one person who hasn't lost a friend or a loved one. Not to mention we lost our dean and our friends when Ares attacked. I can't speak for everyone, but you will find that the vast majority of those who reside here are willing to do just about anything to see an end to this."

Then they all were idiots.

I shook my head as I turned around. None of the Sentinels or Guards here could stand against Seth, let alone gods knew what else Ares could throw our way.

Aiden caught hold of my arm in a firm but gentle grasp, as if, even in his anger, he was aware that my body was still healing. "Stop being so stubborn, Alex."

"You're the one who's being pigheaded," I shot back, and I tried to pull free, but Aiden held on, a warning flaring in his eyes. "I'm trying to protect them."

"I know." His voice lost a fraction of its edge. "And that's the only reason I'm not throwing you over my shoulder and locking you in a room somewhere."

My eyes narrowed. "I'd like to see you try."

"Is that a challenge?" he asked.

Someone in the back of the common area cleared his throat. "So, I'm assuming these two have some sort of past?"

Deacon choked on his laugh as he plopped down on the sofa. "That would be an affirmative." Aiden's gaze slid to his brother, and he took a long, nice, deep breath.

"Wow." Deacon elbowed Luke. "This would be awkward if it weren't so entertaining. It's like watching our parents—"

"Shut up, Deacon," both Aiden and I snapped at the same time.

"See!" Deacon grinned. "They're like peas and carrots."

Luke turned to him slowly. "Did you just quote *Forrest Gump*?"

He shrugged. "Maybe I did."

And just like that, some of the tension seeped out of Aiden…and me too. He let go of my arm but was like Velcro on my hip. "Sometimes I worry for you, Deacon," he said, his lips curving up on one side.

"I ain't who you should be worrying about." Deacon jerked his chin at me. "Little Miss 'I Gotta Be a Martyr' over there is the one you should be concerned with."

I made a face, but everyone in the room, even the bulk of Sentinels in the back, stared back at me with determined expressions. There would be no convincing them otherwise. I knew I wouldn't be leaving here alone, and I really didn't want to. Honestly, the thought of facing Ares or even Seth alone scared the bejesus out of me.

And I would need an army—a really big one. Hopefully, the Sentinel who'd spoken up was right that the vast majority of people here wanted to make a stand, because we were going to need them.

Letting out a long breath, I looked up at Aiden. "Okay."

"Okay, what?" he prompted.

He was so going to make me say it. "I will stay here."

"And?"

Dear gods… "And I accept everyone's help and whatever."

"Good." He bent down, swiftly kissing me on the cheek. "You finally see the light."

I flushed and then really turned beet red when half of the room—half-bloods so unaccustomed to seeing a pure and a half together—stared at us open-mouthed. Even though they'd suspected there was something between us, seeing the proof had to be shocking.

In the lull of conversation, I caught a bit of what was on the news. A full-scale war had broken out in the Middle East. Entire towns were leveled. One of the countries had access to nuclear weapons and was threatening to use them. The U.N. was calling for global intervention, and the U.S. and U.K. were sending thousands of troops overseas.

I had a real bad feeling about this.

"It's Ares," Solos said, speaking for the first time since this whole meeting of the minds began.

I turned toward him and was reminded that my scars were nothing compared to the jagged mark covering his handsome face. "Do we know for sure?"

Marcus nodded. "His presence in the mortal realm causes discord, especially when he's not masking what he is."

"And we saw something very interesting on the telly yesterday," Deacon added.

"Yep," Luke chimed in. "One of the commanders of the attacking army was sporting a very fashionable arm band with a Greek shield on it. I have no idea what Ares hopes to gain by starting a war."

It seemed obvious to me. "He just…loves war. He feeds on it like the gods used to feed on mortals' belief in them. And if there's a huge war that splits a bulk of the world, he can swoop in and subjugate mankind."

"Very true," Diana said softly. "Ares's love for war and discord is well-known. He grows stronger in times of great strife."

"That's exactly what we need." Aiden folded his arms. "Ares growing stronger."

Moving a few steps over, I leaned against an air hockey table. It was hard seeing one and not thinking of Caleb. "Ares wants to rule. He thinks it's time for the gods to reclaim the mortal realm as their own, and I wouldn't be surprised if there are other gods supporting him." Namely Hermes, but other than Marcus and Aiden, no one knew that Hermes had helped Seth contact me.

There was a round of artistic uses of four letter words from those in the back, ones that would've brought a smile to my face at one point in the past.

"Well, at least we know what Ares wants. He's looking

for a war," Aiden said, addressing the room like the leader he was and I so obviously hadn't quite learned to be. "And we're going to give him one."

CHAPTER THREE

As a group, we decided we would hold a meeting in two days for anyone on campus who wished to join what Deacon had named the "Army of Awesomeness." Diana and Marcus, who apparently had jointly taken over the day-to-day operation of the campus after the dean's death, picked the Council's coliseum as the location of the meeting. All twelve of the University's Council members, plus a handful from other locations, were on campus, and Diana swore they would have no problems with us making use of what was considered one of the most sacred buildings on campus.

I had a hard time believing it.

But the day before that wouldn't be about recruitment for the A.O.A. or battle strategies. That day would be the day the dead were given their rightful burial.

After the meeting had ended, I quickly skedaddled out of the common area and headed outside, needing the fresh air. The oxygen in my lungs felt stale, my brain full of holes. Once the anger had faded, all that was left were the dull ache of my healing body and the odd numbness in my core.

Night had begun to fall, and although it was the middle of May, cool air brushed my cheeks and made me grateful for the long-sleeved shirt Aiden had dug up.

I strode past the main building and looked up, sucking in a gulp of air when I got a good look at the top floor. The window facing the courtyard had been boarded up. My gaze fell to the marble pathway below. It was cracked.

Shuddering, I hurried around the wrought iron fence separating the courtyard from the walkways. Like the one that had been on Deity Island, flowers and trees from all around the globe blossomed here, despite the climate. The clean scent of roses and the sweeter scent of peonies mixed with the heavier scents of grapes and olive trees.

Stopping near the entrance, I stared up at a marble replica of Zeus. With his curly hair and beard, he looked more like a mountain man than the all-powerful god he was.

Couldn't he have stepped in at some point, put the smackdown on Ares, and ended all of this? Surely Zeus could find a way to get around Seth and take out Lucian. But even if Zeus did, that still left Seth for him to deal with…and me.

Farther into the courtyard, a statue of Apollo glowed, lit by a small lamp at its base. His face was turned toward the sky.

"Where are you?" I asked.

Once Apollo had blown his cover as Leon, he wasn't able to stay in the mortal realm for long periods of time without weakening. I wondered if it was the same for Ares, and if so, did he hang out in Olympus with the other gods or did he have a hidey-hole somewhere?

Turning from the statue, I started back down the path, because it wasn't like the hunk of rock was going to answer any of my questions. Passing several smaller buildings that looked like miniature Greek temples, I skirted the Council building. Busts of the Olympian Twelve were carved into the four sides of the building, which closely resembled an ancient temple. Like always, a measure of dread knotted in my stomach as I hurried past.

Council buildings had never held good memories for me.

Beyond the Council building, I looked back. Dorms rose into the sky behind the main academic buildings. The University really was its own city, but other than the patrolling Guards, I hadn't seen a student yet.

It was probably a good thing they were keeping the students in their rooms. The last thing anyone needed was a bunch of pures running amok, feeding off hysteria.

Gods, I sounded like an old fart. I *felt* like an old fart.

Coming to the end of the pathway, the marble walls in front of me rose into the night. Spotlights situated every few feet atop the walls cast light throughout the campus. In the shadows of the twenty-foot monstrosity surrounding the University, Guards and Sentinels were stationed where sections of the wall had taken some damage.

I sat down on a bench and stretched my legs out, working the healing muscles and tissue as I watched the men. Even from where I sat, I could tell that they were all half-bloods. Every damn one of them, and I couldn't help but think of my father. I'd given up hope that he was here because Laadan would've found him by now. He could still be at the New York Covenant in the Catskills. He could be anywhere, or he could be dead.

Rubbing my hands down my face, I told myself not to think that, but man, I was so rocking a Negative Nancy vibe like there was no tomorrow. Or maybe I was just being a

Realistic Rachel? How could he have survived? How could Ares not know that my father had been at the Catskills? Surely he would use my father against me if he could.

And what would he have chosen for his life if he'd had a choice to be something other than a Sentinel, Guard, or servant? What would any of these men out by the walls have chosen? Did any of them ever think about that?

I'd thought about it, at one point in my life, when I'd been living among mortals, way before I knew what I was or had even heard that stupid prophecy. I'd wanted to work at a zoo. Not the biggest aspiration for one to have in life, but I loved animals, and because all creatures could be controlled by compulsion—therefore by pure-blooded daimons—I'd never had a pet. The few times I'd visited a zoo, the workers had always seemed to enjoy their jobs, and I wanted that. I wanted to be happy with what I was doing with my life. I used to think becoming a Sentinel would fulfill that need.

Funny thing was, when I'd been living among mortals, all I'd really wanted was to be back at the Covenant among my own kind. Now I wasn't so sure I wanted to be a Sentinel if I survived this. Glancing down, I put my hands on my stomach, like a pregnant woman would. The cord buzzed along, a constant open connection. I closed my eyes and focused, like I had the night before I went toe-to-toe with Ares. Gods knew I probably looked as much an idiot now as I did then.

Seth?

There was no answer—nothing on the other side. Like the cord went out into space and just ended.

Footsteps crunched over the gravel, and I didn't need to look behind me to know who it was. Aiden had been following me the whole time.

The footsteps stopped behind the bench.

"I'm not going to run off," I said, and I wasn't planning to.

There was a pause. "I know."

A few seconds later, he came around the bench and sat beside me, his hands resting on his thighs.

Neither of us spoke for what felt like forever. He was the one to break the silence first. "I'm sorry for yelling at you back there."

I choked on a laugh as I slid him a glance. "No, you're not."

One side of his lips tipped up, but it wasn't a real smile that showed off those dimples. I hadn't seen one of those since I'd woken up this afternoon. "Okay," he conceded. "I'm not sorry for what I said, but I am sorry for raising my voice."

"It's okay."

"I wish you'd stop saying that."

I stood a little too fast, and my knees backhanded me in the form of sharp bursts of pain. "But it *is* okay."

My back was to him, but I could *feel* the frown in his voice. "Everything is not okay, Alex. I'm pretty sure the world is coming down around us. It's all right for things not to be okay."

I placed one foot in front of the other as if walking a balance beam, but my equilibrium hadn't caught up with the healing, and after three steps I could've easily passed as a drunk.

"It doesn't mean you're weak if you admit that things are pretty screwed up right now," he continued.

I stood still. "This isn't a very motivating speech."

Aiden laughed dryly. "It's not meant to be. More like a dose of reality."

"I think I've had enough doses of that recently."

He let out a heavy sigh. "You don't have to be okay with what happened to you, Alex. No one expects that. I sure as hell don't."

Turning around slowly, I opened my mouth to tell him that was the last thing I wanted to talk about, but that wasn't what came out. "If I'm not okay with that, then what am I supposed to be?"

His eyes met mine. "Angry."

Oh, there was a whole lot of that.

"You can be upset—scared—and you can rage that it wasn't fair, because it *wasn't*. A lot of this stuff hasn't been fair for you, but especially this. Nothing about it was right, and you've got to let yourself experience those emotions."

"I am." Kind of. Strange thing was that I felt all of those things, but it wasn't enough. Like a cap on a bottle unscrewed just enough to let a little bit of air in.

A sad look crossed his face as he shook his head. "You're not. And you've got to let it out, Alex, or it will rot you from the inside."

My chest rose sharply. I was already rotten on the inside. "I'm trying."

"I know." Aiden leaned forward, his eyes never leaving mine. "I'm sorry I doubted you this morning."

"Aiden—"

He raised a hand. "Hear me out, okay? The last thing you needed when you woke up after something like that was to have me react that way. I know that didn't help."

It wasn't the choir-singing, romantic reunion I imagined, but I also understood. "My eyes…"

"That's not a good enough reason for how I acted."

"It's not that big of a deal, Aiden, but I forgive you."

Aiden stared at me a moment longer and then sat back. His gaze drifted over my face and then to the sheared locks. I wanted to hide. "Come here," he said gently.

The coldness seeped into my chest, and I stayed in place,

but the words burst out of me as if my mouth had been hijacked by inner Alex. "I look like Frankenstein."

"You're beautiful."

"I look like Frankenstein with a beauty-school-dropout haircut."

Our eyes locked again. "You've never been more beautiful to me than you are right now."

"You need your eyes checked."

He smiled a little. "And you need your head examined." I bit down on my lip. "Come here," he said again, raising his hand.

This time, I didn't think about the numbness and the coldness in my chest. I pushed past them and forced my legs forward. In three uneven steps, my fingers curled around his.

Aiden tugged me into his lap, fitting me against his chest so I could hear his heart thunder in it. His arms swept around me, holding me in place. A breath shuddered through him, and gods, I loved it when he held me like this.

His lips brushed my forehead. "Agapi mou."

I smiled against his chest, and in the dark, I could almost pretend that everything was normal.

And in that moment, I needed that. I really did.

Just as the sun began to crest the horizon, thousands of students, hundreds of staff members, and those who had sought refuge converged on the cemetery that rested beyond the dorms, nestled against the fortress-like wall surrounding the back of the Covenant.

The cemetery was a lot like the one on Deity Island. Statues of the gods oversaw the massive mausoleums and graves, and hyacinths bloomed year-round. To me, those flowers had always served as a twisted reminder of what could happen if you were favored by a god.

I wondered if there'd be a flower named after me one day. *Alexandrias* had a nice ring to it. Hopefully they would be beautiful, like a dense spike of vibrant red flowers, and not look like something you'd find growing up from a crack in the pavement.

In death, a half and a pure were treated as equals, and like my mom had once said, it was the only time the two races would rest side by side. But things were still segregated among the living, even when there was no greater time than now for halfs and pures to come together as one.

Pures took center stage, situated in front of the funeral pyres. It didn't seem to matter that only one of the linen-wrapped bodies had belonged to a pure, and the other three bodies belonged to halfs. Ritual and law decreed that pures got first-row seating, and so they did. Behind the pure-blooded Council members, students, pure Guards and Sentinels, and civilians, stood the half-bloods. I knew they could barely see the pyres or hear the memorial speech being given by Diana and another Head Minister.

Our group stood off to the left of the masses, there but separate. We had followed the somber procession through the campus just before dawn, and the eight of us had moved as a collective group to the side, as if we all agreed without words that we would be a part of this but would not separate into the class structure.

One would think most of the eyes would be faced forward at a funeral, but they weren't. A lot of people stared at our group, namely Aiden and me. Some of the stares were openly hostile. Others looked disgusted. Those looks came from the pures. The halfs just seemed shocked and awed.

Aiden's hand tightened around mine.

I glanced up at him, and he gave me a faint smile. There was no way he didn't know half the congregation was staring at us, but he held onto my hand. I think he knew I needed that connection.

It was funny how things were so different. Before everything had happened, whenever Seth was around large groups of halfs, he got stared at in wonder.

I got stared at because I was holding hands with a pureblood. How messed up was that? Looking over the crowd, I caught the eye of a pure-blooded student. Pures looked just like halfs, but all of us had this gods-given, wonky ability of sensing the difference between the two. He stared at us like he wanted to rip my hand out of Aiden's and then take a day's worth of time to explain why we shouldn't be holding hands.

My eyes narrowed on him as I raised my free hand and scratched the bridge of my nose…with my middle finger.

The pure's head whipped forward. Back in the day, I probably would've been beaten for that, but I was the Apollyon, so I doubted he'd go tattle. And honestly, there were much bigger problems than a half and a pure being naughty.

Tightening my grip on Aiden's hand, I forced my gaze to the pyres. The words spoken were in ancient Greek, and for one of the first times in my life, it didn't translate into "wha-wha-wha." I understood the language, and the words were powerful and moving, prayers and accolades truly fit for those who'd died by Ares's hand, but there was something missing. Not that Diana or the other minister was doing anything wrong. I didn't understand it at first, but then I got it.

What was missing…it was *inside* me.

The words spoken meant something, and I felt the somber pall hanging over the campus. As the torches were placed along the foot of the pyres, I even thought about Lea and how she deserved this kind of burial, not a hastily dug grave out in the middle of nowhere. My chest ached for her and all those who were being mourned.

I mourned.

But while I felt these things, I really didn't *feel* them. The sharp pang of grief, a feeling I'd become well familiar with over the past year, was numbed. When the orange flames licked into the air and covered the bodies like blankets, I didn't turn away like I always did. The finality of it was muted. There was this ball of coldness deep in my chest, sharp shards of ice in my veins, and every so often fear spiked like the flames.

Fear and pain were things I did feel—they were real, and tangible enough that I could taste them. Everything else was dulled, like I was disconnected and detached from the rest of the human scale of emotions, and I didn't understand why.

Realizing this caused that very fear to skyrocket, bringing along a nice little dose of anxiety, and it figured that, since fear and apprehension were like two peas in a messed-up pod, it made sense that if I felt one, I'd feel the other.

My heart was pounding like a jackhammer, and my palms were sweaty by the time the funeral was over and the sun was directly overhead. The crowd started to move back toward the campus. There'd be a feast in memory of those who were lost, and most of the group was attending it. Marcus had left to join Diana. Solos was chatting it up with Val, and Luke and Deacon were walking ahead with Olivia.

Air sawed in and out of my lungs at an alarming rate, and I only became aware of how slowly we were walking because there was a good distance between us and the crowd ahead.

The cord was snapping out. Maybe it was a reaction to my anxiety levels or something, but sights and sounds were amplified. The calls of the birds were shrill. Leaves rustled like a thousand papers crinkling. The sun was too bright, conversation from the mass of people too loud. Gods, the pressure came out of nowhere, clamping down on my chest—holy crap, it was hard to breathe—like someone had put vise grips on me. A sharp, hot tingle swept up my spine and spread along my head.

There was something definitely wrong with me, and it wasn't of the panic attack variety. Running through my head on repeat was one thought: why couldn't I really *feel* anything other than this? Where was the grief? Why did my chest feel empty and cold unless I was angry or scared? But last night, when I'd been in Aiden's arms, the numbness hadn't felt so bad, like the lid had been unscrewed just a bit more. And I was normally a pretty emotional person. In any given day, I experienced a hundred different things like I was trying ice cream flavors.

This wasn't right or normal, and it terrified me.

I stopped suddenly, and so did Aiden. Holding onto my hand, he looked over his shoulder at me. "Alex?"

My chest hurt. "I can't feel anything."

Facing me fully, he cocked his head to the side, brows lowered. "What do you mean?"

I placed my free hand on my chest. "I can't feel anything *in* here."

Aiden started to let go of my hand, but I held on for dear life. "What's happening?"

"I don't know." I took a shallow breath. "I can't feel anything except—except fear and pain. Everything else feels muted. I can't cry—I didn't even cry when I saw my mom."

Shock flickered across his striking face. "You saw your mom?"

"See!" Panic dug in with rotten claws. "I didn't even tell you about that, and I tell you everything. I haven't even *thought* about it, not really. I'm like meh. Everything is meh."

Concern replaced the surprise as he shifted closer. "Do you think it's Seth?"

I shook my head so fast the choppy hair smacked my cheeks. "He's not talking to me."

"But that doesn't mean it's not him," he reasoned, and anger flashed among the concern.

"It doesn't make sense. What does he have to gain from doing this? Then again, does it have to make sense?" I pulled free then, tugging the hair back from my face. "What if I'm broken? What if this is how I'm always going to feel? What—"

"Whoa. Slow down, Alex." Aiden cupped my cheeks. "You're not broken. You're not going to always feel this way. You've been through some crazy stuff. It's going to take time for you to process everything. Take a deep breath. Come on, just a deep breath. Inhale, and let it out slowly."

I gripped his wrists, barely able to get my fingers around them, and did what he said. "Okay. I'm breathing."

"Good." The silver hue of his eyes was my entire world. "Keep breathing with me."

I kept breathing, but I also started moving. I don't know why I did what I did next. Maybe it was because if I didn't really feel this, I was screwed six ways from Sunday. Rising up on the tips of my toes, I kissed Aiden.

Yeah, totally not appropriate after-funeral behavior. But I kissed him.

I needed to feel something other than numbness, pain, and anger, if only for a little bit. And when Aiden kissed me, I'd always felt so many emotions I was dizzy from them.

Aiden lifted his head slightly. "Did you feel that?"

"Yes," I breathed, shivering as our lips brushed.

His lips curved into a one-sided smile. "I was kind of hoping you'd say you didn't, so I'd have a really good excuse to kiss you again."

My fingers dug into his arms. "You don't need an excuse."

And I didn't have to wait long. His lips were on mine again, an incredibly gentle sweep that sent another tremble through me. It was slow and soft, kicking my heart rate up. The tingling in the back of my neck resided and returned, spreading across my belly and lower, but it was a different sensation. I *felt* Aiden—I *felt* love in his arms, and I didn't want to lose that feeling.

Desperate to keep the numbness and colder, darker feelings at bay, I pressed against him, practically stepping on his shoes. He was so much taller than me, but we made it work. Well, Aiden did. The arm around my waist tightened, and I was lifted onto the tips of my toes. He supported most of my weight as I reached a hand up, threading my fingers through the hair resting against the nape of his neck. Heat swept through my veins; it felt like it had when Seth lent me his energy. Like I was opening my eyes again and coming alive. Glyphs rushed to the surface and spread across my skin.

So all I needed to do was kiss Aiden to feel something real and good? Sign me up for that.

But in the back of my mind, I knew that wasn't normal, or right, or half a dozen other things. I ignored that annoying voice because, seriously, that voice wasn't helping right now. I deepened the kiss, parting his lips and sweeping my tongue inside his mouth. A deep, sexy sound rose up from his chest, and his other hand wrapped around the back of my head.

"Alex." There was a soft warning in his voice.

"What?"

His head tilted to the side, causing his nose to brush mine. "You don't know what you're doing."

I almost laughed. "I know exactly what I'm doing."

"Gods..." Aiden cradled my cheek as he shifted my hips closer to his. My stomach dipped in such a pleasant way. "You've been through a lot. You're still healing and—"

"And what?"

"I'm not perfect. I only have so much control." His eyes were like heated quicksilver. "And if you keep kissing me like that, we won't even make it somewhere private."

Oh, me likey the sound of that. "And there's something wrong with that?"

"No. Yes." He pressed his forehead to mine, and the once-wonderful dipping motion suddenly twisted. "You've been—"

"I'm okay. I'm better than okay when I'm like this with you." A desperate edge rose to my voice as I clutched his arm. "I need this. I need *you*, Aiden. Please don't—"

Aiden's mouth crashed into mine. Whatever I had said was like finding the map to a treasure. Bam. Right there. His kiss swept me up into a place where I wasn't thinking. There was no Ares. No looming battle to plan for. No Seth. No pain or fear. All I felt was warmth and love and *Aiden*.

All I felt was him.

We made it into the closest building—the training center. Aiden opened the first door he found unlocked. A supply closet. It would work.

Our gazes locked. His eyes were like liquid pools of silver, and his chest rose sharply. "We need to talk about what you told me," he said.

"I know."

"But not right now."

A breath caught in my throat.

In one powerful lunge, he was on me. Our mouths came together as he backed me up. My hip bumped into a cart. Folded white towels toppled to the floor. There was an ache in my bones, but a deeper one drove me to ignore the pain. "When you were in that room, I thought..." He kissed me again as his hands dropped to my hips. They trembled. "I thought I'd never have this with you again. Gods, Alex, I..."

I brought our mouths together, silencing both our fears. Aiden's fingers were tight on my waist as he lifted me up, placing me on the now-cleared cart. My heart skipped a beat as his lips trailed across my forehead and my cheek. There was a lot we should be doing, but at the moment, nothing seemed more important than this.

We kissed like it was the last time we'd have the luxury of drinking each other in. My breath caught again. Coldness seeped into me like a chilly, rainy day. My insides numbed. The moment that thought formed, I realized how true it was. There was no promise of tomorrow or the next hour. Ares could find a way in. Seth could show up. Aiden could—

"Hey, where'd you go?" Aiden asked softly, holding my cheeks with the tips of his fingers. When I didn't answer, he brushed his lips over mine, coaxing them open with infinite patience.

He pulled me back into the moment, away from the coldness building in my chest.

He gently tilted my head back. "Stay with me. Okay? Stay with me."

I curled brittle-feeling fingers into the front of his shirt, grounding myself in the feel of him. His lips touched mine, pushing away the invading numbness. He tilted his head, deepening the kiss and—

A shrill, eardrum-bursting alarm went off from somewhere

within the campus, starting as a low hum that increased, causing Aiden and me to jerk apart.

Sliding off the cart, I glanced up at the flashing red light above the doors. I recognized the sound, knew what it meant. My muscles tensed as my wide eyes met Aiden's.

There was a security breach, and just like at the Covenant in the Catskills, I knew this wasn't a false alarm.

We were under attack.

CHAPTER FOUR

Aiden flipped from sex god to warrior god in about two seconds flat while I just sort of stood there, rooted to the floor like one of the many statues outside. My lips still tingled in a pleasant sort of way, but the ball of ice was back in my chest, spreading like a winter storm.

He spun toward me, dipping his head and kissing me quickly. "We'll have to pick this back up later."

Then he started for the door.

I forced myself to follow him out of the supply closet and down the empty hall. Sirens continued to scream, and the whole time all I could think was that Ares was back and trying to get past whatever wards Apollo had thrown down. It couldn't be Seth because I didn't feel him.

My steps were slow, but Aiden's were long, purposeful strides. He was ready to face whatever waited outside. I wasn't. In my chest, my heart was throwing itself against my ribs, and my palms were sweating again. The rush of nervous energy made me feel sick. An image of the shattered aquarium and the vibrant-colored fish flopping on the floor filled my head, followed by the sound of Ares's cold, taunting laugh.

I can't do this again.

Air punched from my lungs in an unsteady rush as Aiden pushed open the heavy double doors. I had to do this. Battle was what I'd prepared for, and as a Sentinel, we could be walking into a fight at any given moment. That was why two Covenant daggers were attached to Aiden's legs, hanging from his black tactical pants. The same were secured to my thighs, their weight so familiar that I'd forgotten them.

A Sentinel never left home without them.

Reaching down, I curved my fingers along their slender handles. This was what I'd trained for.

Well, kind of. I'd trained to face daimons, not a cray-cray God of War.

I have to do this.

Outside, we headed toward the front of the campus. Several Guards had taken up defensive stances outside the coliseum-style building that held the common rooms and cafeterias. Most of the campus would be in there right now for the feast, but as we rounded the building, pure-blooded students were being ushered inside, their faces pale and fearful.

I wondered if I had the same look on my face. If so, I bet that wasn't very reassuring to them.

"What's going on?" Aiden asked one of the Guards.

The half-blood shook his head. "Something's going down at the wall. We've been ordered to get all the pures into one safe area."

"It can't be what they said," another Guard said, eyes wide as he gripped the handle of his Glock, his attention being pulled toward a group of pures who appeared from the side of the building. "Hey! You all need to get inside. Now!"

"What did they say?" I asked, happy to hear my voice didn't crack, but there was no answer. The Guards were distracted with the lagging group of pures. "Never mind, then," I muttered.

Before I could start forward, though, Aiden turned to me, putting his hands on my shoulders. "You should stay back."

"Huh?" It was the only thing I could come up with.

Determination flashed in his gunmetal gray eyes. "Alex, you're not completely healed, and we have no idea what the hell is happening up there."

A big, really irresponsible part of me wanted to say "okay" and skip into the building to join the frightened masses, but no matter how scared I was, I would not fall apart. "I'm fine, Aiden. I—"

"You are a lot of things, Alex. Strong. Brave. Beautiful. Incredibly sexy," he said with a quick grin. "But you are *not* fine. You and I both know that."

Okay. He had a point. "You're right, but you don't understand. I can't hide. If I do..." I took a deep breath and decided to be honest for once. Go me. "If I don't go out to that wall and face whatever's there, I never will. You get that? And I can't let myself do that. I have to...I have to get over this."

And that was true. So much was riding on me. I needed to face Seth and transfer the power of the God Killer from him to me, and that was going to require a major throwdown between us. Then I'd have to face Ares. I couldn't wimp out because I got my ass handed to me. I needed to pick myself up and get going. I'd done it before.

But this time is different, whispered that annoying voice that sounded so much like me. I ignored the voice. "I have to do this or..." Or I would hide forever.

Aiden looked away, drawing in a deep breath. His shoulders

tensed, and I knew he was going to argue with total Aiden logic. He let out the breath. "Okay. But stick close to me. If it gets out of hand, and if I think you can't handle it, I'm throwing you over my shoulder. Do you understand?"

Color me surprised—and a little annoyed—about the high-handed statement, but I got that it was coming from a good place, and the sirens weren't shutting up anytime soon. I nodded.

"Deal?"

I sighed. "Deal."

"Then let's do this."

Picking up my pace, I forced my tired muscles to work as we jogged down the pathway. As we got closer, we were joined by several more Sentinels, and I could already see a couple dozen near the wall.

The sirens eased off, but the thick, unnatural tension hanging in the air like heavy clouds told me that whatever had happened hadn't ended. Scanning the grounds, I felt my stomach dip. To our left, a small group of Guards and Sentinels crouched, circling something. I recognized Luke, Olivia, and Solos, and I wasn't surprised to see them in the thick of things. They didn't hesitate. Even though Luke and Olivia hadn't technically graduated, they were Sentinels.

I, on the other hand, was a poser in black.

Solos straightened, tucking back a strand of shoulder-length brown hair that had escaped his low ponytail. He turned at the sound of Aiden's voice, and the jagged scar stood out against his abnormally pale cheek.

I didn't hear what he was saying. My gaze was fixed on what the other Sentinels were staring at. A body was on the ground, totally unrecognizable. Male? Female? No clue. It had been a Sentinel, that much I could tell from the tattered remains of the black uniform. The skin and clothing looked like they had been *pecked* away until only thin slices of flesh and muscle remained. Even the eyelids and eyeballs were removed.

My stomach turned. "Good gods…"

Olivia rose, smoothing her hands along her thighs. That's when I saw the other Sentinel on the ground, knees bent and hands clenching over her stomach. Blood streamed across them. Deep, vengeful cuts tore through her cheeks. Her left eye was a bloody mess. Moaning softly, she was trying to stay still as another woman wrapped white gauze around her face, covering her destroyed eye.

"They were out doing rounds, down by the burnt-out cars. They're saying they came out of nowhere," Olivia told me in a hushed voice. "She almost got taken out by them when she pulled him back to the gate."

I tore my gaze from the body. "*What* came out of nowhere?"

Olivia opened her mouth, but the eeriest high-pitched squawk I'd ever heard cut her off. It was a constant crescendo of harsh screeching.

Several shots boomed and my chin jerked up. Beyond the wall, a dark cloud zoomed across the horizon, heading straight for us. Except it wasn't a cloud.

I took a step back, my hands going to the daggers.

The cloud arced up and shattered into hundreds of mother-freaking crows. My jaw dropped open. "Holy crows…"

"There's a couple of eagles mixed in there," Luke commented.

"And a few hawks," Aiden added.

I rolled my eyes. "Okay. Holy birds of prey! Is that better?"

"Much," Aiden murmured.

The birds blanketed the sky, so thick they eclipsed the sun

for a moment. I'd never seen anything like it. They swirled overhead, a dark, ever-expanding funnel. They changed course suddenly, flying down toward us like little, winged torpedoes with sharp claws and beaks. I thought of the flayed body and almost hurled.

"They're possessed!" shouted a Guard. Dirt streaked his white uniform.

I wanted to thank the guy for the obvious. I wasn't an animal specialist, but I knew birds didn't go psychotic for no reason, which meant there had to be daimons nearby...either them or a god. A god could influence our feathered friends. But my smartass response died on my tongue when the birds from hell swooped.

They were on us in seconds.

Dipping down, Olivia shrieked as she batted one away. "Ah! Birds! Why did it have to be birds?" I smacked one before it got its gross little claws in my already jacked-up hair. How in the hell were we supposed to fight a swarm of birds? Talons grazed the back of my hands, and the pain was sharp and quick.

Solos spun around, his arm arcing gracefully. A dagger flew across the space, tip over handle, and embedded deep into the back of an eagle that had attached to a Guard's shoulder.

Well, that was one way—a little time-consuming but effective. However, I had a better idea. Waving my arms like a deranged crossing guard, I darted toward Aiden. He'd grabbed a hawk off a fallen Sentinel. Tiny red scratches bled on his cheeks.

"Fire!" I yelled. "Light the sky up!"

Luke was swinging at the sky with his blades like a cracked-out chef. "Olivia and I will cover you two!"

Sheathing the daggers, Aiden raised his hands, brows

lowered in concentration and the line of his jaw tightened. Sparks flew from his fingers, and a second later, his hands were on fire. I reached over, wrapping my hands around his wrist. I took a deep breath, ignoring the wings that came awfully close to my cheek and the willies they gave me.

Closing my eyes, I used the air element and pictured the flames moving up in a steady stream and then spreading like a ceiling of fire. Aiden could get the fire into the sky, but not at the same magnitude and not as quickly as he could with my help.

"That's it," Aiden said, his skin hot under my fingers.

I opened my eyes. For a moment, I was awed. Using the elements was still new to me. Fire, a vibrant shade of blood-red, pulsed over Aiden's hand and exploded outward in a massive ball. Wind blew my hair back from my face as the inferno licked into the air, rolling toward the wall and back to the campus, consuming the birds in its path. The blaze wasn't natural, but a product of the aether that Aiden carried inside him. It ate the crows up, leaving nothing but a fine sprinkling of dust behind.

When most of the birds were destroyed and only a few were left to dive-bomb us, Aiden closed his hands into fists and I let go of his wrists. Only then did I see the faintly glowing glyphs on my hands. No one but Seth could see them, but they still made me feel a little weird when they came out to say hello.

"That was so *Resident Evil*," said Luke, his eyes wide. "Awesome."

I cracked a grin, a little breathless. "It was kind of Alice awesome, wasn't it?"

Luke started to nod but stilled when a Guard flew past us, arms flailing as he tried to get one of the remaining birds off his back. He frowned. "I'll never look at a bird the same way again."

Shooting him a look, Aiden stepped forward, snatching what I guessed was a hawk off the back of the yelping Guard. The hawk twisted in his grasp, and I got a good look at its face. The thing's eyes were all black—no pupils or irises, just like a daimon's.

I turned away from the sickening crack that followed. Once the animals were that far under the control of a daimon or god, there was just no undoing it.

Several Sentinels staggered to their feet, battered and cut, but no one had gotten it as bad as the two who'd been by the burnt-out cars on the access road and were most likely blindsided by the birds. A shiver snaked its way down my spine, and my hands automatically went to the daggers on my thighs. Tiny hairs rose on my body. All around me, halfs and pures reacted to the peculiar tension seeping into our skin. My glyphs swirled, changing patterns and forming new ones.

"They're coming!" yelled a Guard near the top of the wall. His white robes flapped like wings in the wind.

I was kind of expecting a griffon to come out of nowhere, but that's not what slammed into the iron gate with enough force that it rattled the massive structure and split open the skin of the assailant.

It was a daimon.

Face as white as the Guards' robes and veins as thick as black snakes, the daimon backed up and charged the gate again.

Wiping blood off her hand, Olivia shook her head. "What is it doing?"

"Other than rearranging its face?" I flinched as it slammed the gate once more. "Maybe it's really hungry."

Daimons were pure-bloods that had become addicted to the aether in the blood of pures, and only within the last year we'd learned they could also turn halfs. They were what originated the whole vampire myth, though they weren't nearly so hot. It started eons ago—something Dionysus had done, most likely when he'd been bored.

Most of our problems stemmed from the gods' boredom.

Another daimon joined in, then another, and another. Each time they whacked into the gate, I flinched. Their exposed flesh was mangled and bloody.

Solos was at the gate, able to pick off two of them by shoving daggers through the gaps. Daimons were highly allergic to titanium. It cut through their flesh as though it were water. They burst into shimmering blue clouds, one after another, but more joined in, bouncing off the gate. My gaze went to the sides. The hinges were weakening.

I moved, seeing dozens and dozens of daimons behind the ones at the gate. Aiden summoned fire, catching several of them ablaze, but they kept coming at the gate until the fire consumed them.

This was *so* not good.

But a frightening realization occurred. When I'd been all Team Seth after I'd Awakened, I'd learned he and Lucian were working with daimons, feeding the monsters pures who weren't siding with them. The daimons could be here because of Ares, or they could be here because Seth was coming. Either way, it was unlikely that this many would just show up in the middle of nowhere, like it had been during the Council meeting in the Catskills.

"We have to do something." Luke unhooked his daggers, eyes narrowing as he turned to me. "Can you do your Apollyon thing? Like you did with the automatons?"

Figuring I should do the same as Luke, I unsheathed my daggers. My hands shook, and I hoped no one noticed. "I can't promise I won't take the gate out in the process. Maybe if I could get outside, slip up behind them."

"Not happening." Aiden stalked forward. "They'd be on you in seconds."

With all the aether in my veins, it would be like ringing the dinner bell, but if I did get out there, I could do something. I could end this before it got out of hand. My mouth stayed closed, though, which was so unlike me that I wasn't sure I *was* me anymore. A week ago, I would've been scaling those damn walls.

Sentinels don't show fear.

All I knew right then was fear.

More slammed into the gate, causing the center to bulge dangerously.

"Open the gate!" shouted Aiden, grabbing the shoulder of a Guard. "If they break the gate, then we will have an open wound to protect."

"That's insane!" argued the Guard. "If they get past us—"

"They won't get past us. Have half of us form a line several yards back," Aiden ordered. "The rest of us will stay here."

Luke shook his head and muttered, "That would be the oh-shit line."

Beside him, Olivia snorted. Her fingers opened and closed around the handles of the daggers. "You know, this isn't too bad."

"It's not?" I asked.

She shook her head. "This could've happened during the funerals."

The gate rattled like dry, angry bones once more, and then the Guard sprang into action, shouting orders. Letting the daimons in sounded crazy, but Aiden was right. Even if we stopped this attack, we would be vulnerable with a giant hole where the gate should've been.

Half the Sentinels and all the Guards moved back, forming the oh-shit line. Olivia and Luke remained by the gate, ready for battle. I forced my lungs to inflate as two Sentinels volunteered for the near-suicidal mission of opening the gate.

Aiden stalked to my side, lowering his head and speaking low enough for only me to hear. "This is about to get crazy. I know you don't want to hear this, but you should go back to the common area. Find your uncle and—"

"I can do this," I said, and then repeated it in my head about five times. "And you guys need my help. I can do my Apollyon mojo without worrying about the gate."

His eyes turned into a dark, tumultuous gray. "Alex, I really—"

"Too late," I interrupted as the Sentinels threw open the gates.

Aiden whirled, and before I could take another breath, the daimons were inside the gate, swallowing the two Sentinels in a massive wave. He cursed and glanced back at me. I didn't need him distracted. Daimons couldn't kill me, but they could kill him.

"I'm okay." I tightened my grasp on the blades. "Go do your thing."

He appeared to want to protest more, but there really was no time. Dipping down at the last possible second, he caught a daimon in the stomach with his shoulder. The force of the blow flipped the daimon over onto his back. Aiden spun, thrusting the dagger deep into the daimon's chest. Within seconds, it was nothing more than a shimmery pile of dust. Aiden whirled, shoulders taut and mouth pressed into a slash of a line. He took out another daimon and then another. If Leon/Apollo had been here, they would have been keeping count.

I turned at the sound of pounding feet. A daimon was

gunning for me, eyes as black as midnight oil and skin leeched of color. My muscles tensed the way they did in the seconds before engaging in battle, but it was different this time. They locked up completely. My mouth dried. My heart went straight into cardiac arrest territory. It was like when I'd seen my mom in that alley back on the island. I was immobile.

You can't fight. You can't do this anymore. You're broken.

My internal voice was *such* a shit-stirrer. I was frozen. Around me, the sounds of metal clattering and grunts of those fighting amplified until it was all I heard.

The daimon drew to a halt, sniffing the air, and then its mouth dropped open, revealing a row of shark-like teeth. It howled.

My mind…something was wrong with it. I knew it was a daimon before me, and I knew I didn't even have to use my daggers. I could use fire or wind. I could tap into akasha, the fifth and final power that only that gods and the Apollyon could wield, but I didn't see the daimon. In its place, I saw one pissed off, seven-foot god. I saw Ares.

My breath burst from me in short pants. I took a step back, swallowing down the rise of bile. "No."

The daimon slammed into me, knocking me flat onto my back. The daggers flew from my hands, skidding along the dry dirt, kicking up plumes of dust.

"I gave you the easy way out," Ares said, digging his fingers into my shoulders. "But you chose this, and everyone you love will die because of it."

Someone shouted my name, and the image of Ares blurred around the edges. Ropey black veins bled through in his cheeks. Jagged teeth appeared behind a cruel mouth. A powerful shudder worked its way down my body, and the glyphs on my skin started to go crazy, like there was a god…

A flash of white light blinded me, and then the daimon exploded into a cloud of blue dust. A silver arrow plopped down on my chest.

"What the…?" I picked it up, squeaking as it stung my fingers.

"I'll be needing that," came a soft, musical voice I'd heard only once before. The arrow was plucked from my fingers. "Thank you!"

I looked up and discovered why my glyphs were doing a cracked-out version of the electric slide on my skin.

Decked out in her bubble-gum-pink camo, she stood above me, silver bow propped against a shapely hip. Her red hair was pulled up in a ponytail, but the long, curly mass fell to her waist. Static crackled from her all-white eyes. "Are you trying to get a tan?"

Sort of stupefied by her appearance, I pushed myself to my feet. "What are you doing here? Is Apollo—?"

"My brother is currently getting chained to some rock by our father because of Ares." She loaded another arrow. "Zeus is mighty upset, and of course is blaming Apollo for the mess. Like how was he supposed to know what Ares was up to?" She let go of the arrow, and it zinged past my head. A fleshy grunt told me she had hit her mark. "It's not our fault Ares got hit with the wildstick about a hundred times."

Another arrow flew from her nimble fingers. This time it blew past my head, and I was pretty sure I was centimeters from having my ear pierced.

"And you need to buck up, buttercup," she said, her full lips tipping up into a megawatt smile. "Loverboy is about to be taken down for the count."

"What the—?" Her words sank through, and I spun around. My heart dropped.

Aiden was surrounded, two daimons at his back and two at his front. No other Sentinels were around. The daimons were going straight to the pures because they, like Artemis and me, were chock-full of aether. This was good for the halfs, since it gave them the advantage. But not Aiden. Blood trickled from the side of his throat. A female daimon in front of him had blood on her pink, chapped lips.

He'd been tagged.

Aiden had been tagged.

Oh, that flipped my bitch switch from meh to pure "I'm going to cut a bitch" rage.

Whatever funk had invaded my system was overshadowed by my fear *for* him. Forgetting Artemis and her sudden, unexpected, and really bizarre appearance, I launched forward. My muscles and body knew what to do. Brain clicked off. Instinct kicked in. Finally.

I came up behind the two daimons and slammed my dagger into one of them. The other sensed my aethery goodness and whirled on me.

It screeched. "Apollyon—"

"Shut up," I said, dipping down as it swung on me. I sprung up, kicking and swiping the legs out from underneath him. "I know I smell good. I'm sure I taste good too."

Thrusting the dagger down, I took the daimon out, and then popped up. Slipping under Aiden's arm, I went straight for the female with *his* blood on *her* ugly face. Flipping the blade back, I swung my arm, catching the female daimon in the jaw. Her head smacked back, and the pleasure I felt would worry therapists across the nation.

"Damn," Aiden said under his breath, and then took down the other daimon.

The female daimon charged me, practically impaling herself on my dagger. Blue dust blew into my face. "Gross."

Artemis was making short work of the daimons and looking disgustingly beautiful doing so. With her cheeks slightly flushed and her lower lip sucked between her teeth, she darted around, popping the daimons off one after another. And once the Sentinels began to realize that a god was in the mix, everyone pretty much stopped what they were doing.

The legion of daimons wasn't going to kill us. Nope. Artemis was here.

She sprang onto a tree trunk, spinning like a ballet dancer. Sun glinted off her silver bow. Three arrows flew from her bow, zipping between Sentinels and smacking into daimons.

Holy Hades's butt crack…

I did not want to piss Artemis off.

Within a minute, over a dozen daimons were nothing but shimmery blue piles of dust, and Artemis hadn't even broken a sweat. Not a strand of hair was out of place. Slipping the bow into the harness strapped across her back, she winked at Solos before blinking out and reappearing like right in my face.

"Good gods," I gasped, taking a step back. "Was that necessary?"

She cocked her head to the side. "Ares is playing dirty. These," she waved her arm around, "are from him. He led them here, and more will come. The First is on the move."

"Seth?" Aiden swiped his hand over his neck. "He's coming here?"

Artemis's creepy god eyes shot all kinds of static when she looked at him. A fine shimmer surrounded her, like she'd been dipped in glitter, and then the camo get-up disappeared.

My eyes widened.

A true goddess stood before us, dressed in white, nearly

transparent linen that hugged her curves and revealed more skin than a thong. A silver band covered her upper arm. A moon hung from it, shining as if it had been dipped in light.

Her lips curled in a smooth, seductive smile as she eyed Aiden. "Hey there, how about you ditch the little Apollyon over there and get with—"

"Hey." I folded my arms, trying to keep my own eyes on her face. "Aren't you supposed to be a *virgin* goddess?"

A soft, tinkling laugh came from her. "Honey, have you ever heard of kiss and don't tell?"

"Have you ever heard of a bra?" I demanded. "Because I can see your…you know. *Everything*."

Aiden cleared his throat as he averted his gaze, brows raised. Artemis laughed again as she turned her attention to me. "I will aid you when I can, as will the others, until Apollo can return to your side. We cannot allow Ares to continue. You must transfer the power of the First to you."

How she went from hitting on my boyfriend to all serious war-death-blah talk was beyond me. "It's at the top of my to-do list, along with—*hey*!" I leaned back from her suddenly outstretched hand. Her fingers grazed my cheek. "Stop it!" I jumped back as she went to touch me again. "Man, you gods are so weird."

Artemis wrinkled her nose at me. "There is something wrong with you."

"Uh…" That didn't seem very polite. I glanced at Aiden. He was staring at Artemis, but not in the way every other guy except Luke was staring at her. Correction. Even Luke was checking her out. "Care to explain?" I asked.

Her eyes narrowed, and then her hand snaked out again. I forced myself to stand still and let her feel me up, because seriously, she didn't appear like she was going to stop until she did. She cupped my cheek and placed her other hand below my breasts, between my ribs.

"Um…" I was really starting to feel a bit wigged out. "I really hope this has a point, because half the guys are staring at us like they're hoping we're going to make out."

Aiden coughed.

The goddess's lashes swept up. "There's something inside you."

"Well, I do have organs and…" I trailed off, remembering how Apollo's son had said the same thing. Concern swelled. "Like something that doesn't belong there?"

"I don't know." She removed her hands—thank the gods. "You should do something with your hair."

And then she blinked out of existence. Really gone this time because the marks of the Apollyon calmed down. I reached up, self-consciously patting the jagged ends of my hair as I glanced at Aiden. He stared at me, looking like someone had punched him in the gonads. He opened his mouth to say something, and then he pivoted on his heel.

Having no idea what that was about, I took in the carnage of battle. Blood pooled over sparse grass, and bodies littered the ground, some dying and others already dead. There would be more funerals. I saw that my friends still stood. Somehow, the relief of not facing another day without any of them was just one drop less in the bucket of suckage.

Fighting was a desire and need that had been bred into me, as it was into all halfs who didn't go into servitude. Except somewhere between when Poseidon destroyed the Covenant on Deity Island and I woke up after Apollo returned me from Olympus, fighting had lost its appeal.

An entire life of this?

I thought about when I told Aiden I wasn't sure I wanted

to do this anymore, but that was back before Ares. Everything was different now.

My gaze found Aiden.

He was kneeling beside a fallen Sentinel, one who couldn't be much older than me. The wind picked up strands of Aiden's hair, tossing them off his forehead. He looked up, his somber gaze meeting mine, and I thought I saw the same weariness in his stare.

We both were so…so over this.

CHAPTER FIVE

Long after the sun had set and the campus was calmed as much as it could be after a nearly disastrous attack, I fell into bed. Freshly showered, I'd stolen a pair of sweats and a T-shirt from Aiden.

I was exhausted but antsy. I knew I should sleep, because I would wake up to the big day to recruit for the A.O.A., but I stared at the ceiling, wiggling my feet until Aiden slipped in, tugging a shirt over his head.

My eyes dropped to those finely designed stomach muscles. Did it make me a bad person that, despite all the terrible stuff happening, I was staring at those indents on either side of his hips?

Aiden let the shirt fall, covering up all that gloriousness as he came to the bed. He bent down, placing his hands beside my head. His lips pressed against mine, and warmth flooded me, like it had before the Hitchcock movie came to life.

The way Aiden kissed me, well, it never ceased to affect me. Every time was like the first time. Butterflies buzzed in my belly the second our lips touched. My chest always fluttered, and I could never get used to the fact that he was kissing me. That we were together in spite of the laws forbidding it and everything that stood in our way, including each other. When he lifted his head, I let out a little sigh, and he kissed the corner of my lips.

Stretching out on his side, he leaned over my stomach, putting his weight on his elbow. "You should be asleep."

"I know."

"But you're not."

"Neither are you."

One side of his lips tipped up. "How are you feeling?"

"Okay." I reached down, my fingers brushing just below the tag he'd received. The skin there would always be a few shades paler than his natural tone. The bite had been so close to his jugular. Although he was a pure-blood, the bite could've taken him out of commission for a while, or even killed him. "What about you?"

He wrapped his hand around mine, pulling it away from his neck. He pressed a kiss to my palm. "I'm okay."

I tried not to let it show, but fear spiked in me. "You've never been tagged before."

"There's a first time for everything." He lowered my hand but kept holding it. "It's really not that bad."

I disagreed. "I want to kill that daimon all over again."

Aiden smiled then. A real one, showing off those deep dimples. It seemed like it had been so long since I'd seen him smile like that. "It was kind of hot how you popped out of nowhere and owned her."

"I need a shirt that says, 'I owned her.'"

"I can do that for you, but I like seeing you in my clothes."

A flush crept across my cheeks. "I probably should've asked."

"You never need to ask." He squeezed my hand gently. "Are you hungry?"

I groaned. "No. Gods, no. My stomach feels like it's going to burst from all you made me eat earlier."

He didn't say anything to that and closed his eyes. Thick lashes fanned his cheekbones, and I got a little lost staring at him. A year ago, I never thought we'd be where we were now. A year ago, I never thought I would've frozen in the middle of a fight, either.

Aiden's eyes had opened, and he was staring back at me. "What's going on inside your head?" Sometimes his ability to read me was frightening.

"I hesitated out there."

"It happens, agapi mou."

The endearment almost broke me. "Not to Sentinels," I whispered, staring over his shoulder. "I completely froze, Aiden. I couldn't move. I didn't want..."

"What?" he prodded when I didn't continue.

I wet my lips and said quietly, "I didn't want to be out there."

"Who would?"

Pulling my hand free, I shifted my gaze to him. "You don't understand. I didn't want to be there. I didn't want to fight. I wanted to be anywhere but where I was, and when I saw that daimon, I thought I saw—" I cut myself off. I couldn't admit that I thought I saw Ares. He would think I was insane. "I just locked up. What if I do that again and more people get hurt or killed?"

"Alex, you're not responsible for those who died today." He shifted so that his face was right over mine. "Don't put that kind of crap on yourself. It's not right."

But it IS right, whispered that voice. "People expect me

to fight and kick ass. You can't tell me the people out there didn't expect me to take out those daimons. And if Artemis hadn't shown—"

"You would've snapped out of it. Just like you did," Aiden said, cupping my cheek and forcing my gaze to his. "You're being too hard on yourself. What you've been through is going to affect you, and you're not giving yourself any time to deal with what *just* happened. You're not okay, Alex, but you're not broken and you're not damaged."

My breath shuddered from me. "Then what am I?"

"You're someone who is incredibly strong and brave, and who has been through way too much. Too many people expect too much from you. And it's not because you're weak. You're eighteen, Alex. Even if you were twenty-eight, all this crap would be too much." His fingers trailed down my cheek, the path slightly uneven from the raised scars. "You're the Apollyon, but you're only one person. And you're not alone. You have me. You have Luke, Olivia, and your uncle. You have Solos, and you have my brother, although he's a little wild." A small, quick grin appeared on his lips. "And tomorrow, you'll have a whole army. You're not alone in any of this. You'll never be alone."

I blinked back the wetness gathering in my eyes. "I think you spend your spare time studying a book full of the right things to say."

He chuckled softly, and then his lips brushed mine in a quick kiss. "Nah. I just love you, Alex."

Raising my hands, I placed them on his smooth cheeks. The tiny scratches from the birds had healed over already, leaving behind faint marks. "I think I'd go out of my mind without you."

He kissed my cheek and then stretched out beside me,

snaking an arm around my waist. In the quiet moments that followed, I didn't feel numbness or fear. I was content, warm, and I felt a little like my old self. Tomorrow was going to be a big day, and who knew what was waiting for us beyond that. I didn't want to think about any of that. Not right now.

I rolled onto my side and stretched up, bringing our lips together. The kisses started off slow, nothing like this morning when they'd quickly reached fever pitch, but then they deepened and my heart kicked up, thumping in my chest. His hand curled around my hip, tugging my body to his. Pressed together, a shiver danced down my back as his fingers slipped under my shirt, skimming the bare skin of my waist. My hand moved across his chest, and I wished I had some kind of Apollyon power that made clothing disappear. That would've been really handy right about now.

He eased me onto my back and slid a leg between mine. His tongue swept in, scattering my thoughts and pulling me in. A delicious tension built in my lower stomach, and when his body shifted against mine, I gasped. My reaction was immediate, rocking against him.

Aiden shuddered as he lifted his head. Those eyes were heated silver. "We need to press pause for a second."

I knew I couldn't have heard him correctly, because he moved his leg in a way that had me trembling, then kissed me again, nipping at my lower lip.

"Seriously, we need to talk for a second," he said, his voice thick.

A small grin pulled at my lips. "Then stop kissing me."

"That's an excellent idea." He pressed his lips to the sensitive spot under my ear. "Yet so incredibly hard." But then he did sit up, cross-legged beside me. "I want to talk to you about something."

The way he said that made my stomach dip. And he was rocking the "Aiden is being serious" face.

"Okay. About what?"

"About what Artemis said to you out there today."

"About my hair?"

He shot me a bland look. "No. When she said there was something inside you."

"Oh. That? Weird, right? Apollo's son—Hippo-whatever—said the same thing when I was in Olympus." I sighed, trying not to be too freaked out by it. "I have no idea what they're talking about."

"You don't?" Surprise flooded his voice.

"No." I frowned. "Do you?"

Aiden opened his mouth and closed it. Several seconds passed, and then he thrust his hand through his hair, scratching his head. "Think about it, Alex."

Crossing my ankles, I gave a lopsided shrug. "Enlighten me, wise one."

"You're really going to make me say it?" He swore under his breath as his hand fell to his lap. "Of course, you are. Don't you think there could be a possibility that whatever Artemis felt, or saw or whatever, means you're…pregnant?"

I stared at him. "*What*?"

His dark brows lowered. "Pregnant."

"No." I coughed out a laugh and rolled my eyes. "No way." Aiden looked at me like I was half-stupid. "What?" I made a face. "There's no way it could be that, because that just isn't possible. I would, like, know if that was it, and I would totally be…"

Wow. I sounded kind of stupid, because it really could be *that*. I'd had my shots, but I honestly couldn't really say when the last one was, and who knew if they were really a hundred percent effective, or if they even worked on Apollyons, and when *was* my last period? And…

Oh my gods in Olympus…

I sat up, nearly knocking Aiden off the bed. My eyes were wide. "Pregnant? Bun in the oven? A little Alex or Aiden running amok? Okay. A little you would be so adorable, but preggers? Oh gods, have I told you how much I hate the word 'preggers?' Like, is 'pregnant' such a long word that you have to shorten it? I feel the same way about 'hubby.' Seriously? Hubby and preggers are the stupidest—"

"Alex, whoa." He chuckled. "Slow down. Take a breath."

I tried to take a breath, but I couldn't get it around the word *pregnant*. It formed a ball of *holy crap* in my throat. "It can't be that, can it?"

His chest rose, and then he nodded. "It could be, Alex."

Whoa, I was blown away by the prospect. Pregnant? Me? I wanted to laugh, but if I did, I was pretty sure I wouldn't stop, and it wouldn't be the cute kind of laughter. It would be the hysterical kind of laughter.

"That…" I let out a stuttered breath as I glanced down. I was half-tempted to pull up my shirt and start pressing on my stomach. I didn't, though, because that would cause me to have an absolute nervous breakdown.

"That changes everything."

I lifted my gaze, meeting Aiden's. His eyes were a bright silver, and my heart skipped a beat. When they were that color, Aiden was feeling something strong, something good, but I didn't know what to think. Pregnant with Aiden's baby? I could *not* be a mother. Seriously. I barely remembered to brush my own teeth in the morning. Being responsible for a child, especially in the mess that was my life? That kid wouldn't have a chance. It would end up getting eaten by wild coyotes or something.

One side of Aiden's lips tipped up. "What are you thinking?"

"What are *you* thinking?" My heart was pounding.

"I'm thinking…a lot of things, but if this is what the gods are feeling in you, we need to really think about what we're doing." He reached over, tugging on my bottoms. "I know this isn't happening at a good time."

I did laugh at that. "Yeah, that would be horrifically bad timing."

"But would it be so bad?" he asked.

The look on his face, the open honesty, and—*dear gods*—the hint of acceptance startled me. "You would be okay with this?"

Aiden lowered his gaze for a moment and then shifted so he was sitting in front of me. He took my hands in his, and I suddenly realized how serious this was. I was a little slow on the uptake. "This isn't the right time for us," he started, threading his fingers through mine. "Not with everything going on, but…but how could I not be okay?"

I was actually speechless. Someone needed to record this moment.

"I love you, Alex. That's never going to change, and although neither of us is ready for this, I can *get* ready for this. Both of us can, and we will face this together. I can't be that bad at being a father. I mean, I basically had to raise Deacon, and he's still alive." He laughed softly as a slight flush spread across his cheeks. "But if you are, we really have to think about what we're doing. I know neither of us can walk away from what we have to do—what *you* have to do—but we need to make some adjustments."

I couldn't even fathom what kind of adjustments we'd need to make. If I was pregnant, could I really go out there and fight? Could I transfer power from Seth? And good gods, what kind of kid would I be popping out? Part half, part pure, and part Apollyon?

This kid could destroy the world.

But Aiden… Gods, I wanted to cry. I wished I could get those tears to fall, because I was so lucky to have him. So many guys would be in another state by now.

The tears didn't fall, but I could move. I scrambled onto my knees, and he knew what I wanted. His arms opened, and I crawled into his lap, wrapping my arms around his neck and clinging to him like an octopus.

"You're perfect," I said, my face buried in the crook between his neck and shoulder.

"I'm not perfect." His hand sifted through my hair, resting against the back of my skull. "I just can't be that upset over the fact that we might be having a baby."

I squeezed my eyes shut as a sharp pang of unbridled emotion shot through me. Among the hailstorm of fear and confusion, a fine, barely there sliver of…of *happiness* filled me like a wisp of smoke. Halfs were products of pures and mortals and not allowed to procreate. Besides that, Sentinels didn't have kids—not even the pures who chose that kind of duty. They simply didn't live long enough to raise them. So I had never really even considered the idea of having a child, but this—if this was what this was—would be Aiden's child, and how could I not want that? Especially because, even as unprepared as both of us would be for something so major, Aiden would be right there with me. Not out of any sense of duty, but because he loved me and would love our child.

And *me*? On every day that ended with a Y, I'd probably be the most irresponsible parent known to exist, but I'd love it with every breath I took.

My gods, my brain felt whacked, because I never thought the day would come that I would even think that.

Aiden pressed a kiss against my temple. "We need to see one of the doctors here soon and find out so we're a hundred percent sure either way, and then…well, we'll handle this together."

Oh, wow. Making a quick trip to the infirmary for a pregnancy test? That was going to be so awkward. A thought occurred. "Marcus is going to kill you."

A deep, rich laugh rumbled up from his chest. "Good gods, you're right."

I started to smile, but then reality smacked me upside the head and that little wisp of happiness was extinguished. "I can't be pregnant, Aiden."

"Alex—"

"You don't understand." I pulled back and slid off his lap, scooting toward the head of the bed. I sighed as I tucked my knees close to my chest. "It's not like I'm denying the way that male and female bodies work, but we haven't done *that* since Ares came, and there's no way, if I was pregnant, a baby could've survived the fight."

The silver flare dulled a little. "I hadn't even thought of that. Oh gods," he said, rubbing his jaw. "How could I not have thought of that? It would be…" He shook his head, jaw locking down.

I didn't know what to say to that, because the chance that I was pregnant would be so insanely slim. An ache pierced my chest. When his eyes dulled, so did the brimming excitement that had been in them. I hated to take that from him.

Aiden moved so that he was stretched out onto his side, then patted the spot next to him. Biting my lip, I wiggled down so I was lying beside him. Neither of us said anything, because I don't think either of us knew what to say. At some point, Aiden turned off the light beside the bed and then settled back beside me.

Long after I'd believed Aiden had fallen asleep, I took a deep breath, closed my eyes, and did something that felt incredibly insane.

I placed my hands on my lower belly.

My heart jumped in my chest even though my stomach didn't feel any different. Could I be pregnant and it—no, not *it*. It was a baby. It was Aiden's baby. Could *our* baby have survived the fight with Ares? Crazier things had happened. And in my life, I could almost expect that the impossible could and would happen. So even though I shot it down, there was a chance. I recognized that. I just didn't know what to think or do.

In the darkness, Aiden placed his hand over where mine rested on my stomach, and it stayed that way through the night.

CHAPTER SIX

Aiden left in the morning to scrounge up some breakfast. I offered to go with him, but he insisted I stay in bed and get some more rest. Nightmares had plagued me most of the night. Daimons breaking through the walls. Ares finding a way in past the wards. Loved ones dying all around me. My constant tossing and turning had kept Aiden up most of the night, but it was more than that. In the back of my head, I knew why Aiden had wanted me to stay. There was still a part of him that believed I could be pregnant. Hell, there was a small part of *me* that wondered the same thing.

Every time I thought there might be a chance, my stomach dropped and my heart jumped. I couldn't focus on that today, but it was the only thing I really thought of as I took a quick shower and got changed.

I caught sight of my reflection in the foggy mirror and winced. Even wet, my hair hung in way too many lengths. I needed to do something about it. Heading into the small kitchen and living room area joining the two dorm rooms together, I found a pair of scissors. Immediately, I remembered holding them before, after Caleb had died.

You should cut your hair.

Romvi/Ares had said that to me, and in my despair over losing my best friend, I had tried to cut my hair. Weird reaction then, but now?

I stared at the scissors, feeling a lump grow in my throat. Seth had stopped me. He'd been there for me the whole time after Caleb's death, and even when I'd taken all my hurt and anger out on him, he'd remained by my side. We'd been two sides of the same coin, and if it hadn't been for him, the depression and self-loathing would've dragged me down.

What happened to you, Seth? I asked, but there was no answer through our connection. Nothing but the soft hum of the cord, and it really didn't matter what had happened. Everything that he'd done overshadowed the good things. And he was on Team Ares. After what Ares had done to me, I couldn't forgive Seth for that choice.

Sighing heavily, I left my room and headed across the hall to knock on Olivia's door. "Hey," she said as she opened the door, but her smile faded a bit when she glanced down and saw the sharp instrument in my hand. She didn't take a step back, but the look on her face said she wanted to. "What's up?"

"I was hoping you could do something with my hair before the meeting today." I started to wave the scissors but decided I'd look pretty aggressive doing so. "I kind of don't want to look like a weed whacker got hold of my head before meeting a bunch of people."

Her smile returned, lighting up her brown eyes. "Sure! I can do something." She took the scissors with deft fingers. "I'm actually glad you came to me because I wanted to offer, but I figured that would be kind of rude."

"It wouldn't have been. I know my hair is jacked up." I followed her into her dorm. "Thank you, though."

"No biggie. Come into the bathroom." Olivia had me sit on the rim of the bathtub, feet inside. She draped a towel around my shoulders and then picked up a comb. We were silent as she combed the tangles out, and then she finally said, "Yesterday was crazy, wasn't it? I've never seen anything like those birds. And all of those daimons?"

"I know. You and Luke were awesome, though." I stared at a bottle of shampoo as Olivia made a couple more soothing strokes with the comb. "Artemis said they'd been led there by Ares."

"I cannot believe a god would stoop to using daimons. There is something so inherently wrong with that." She picked up the scissors. "Keep still, okay?"

Sitting still was not my forte, but I tried. "Seth and Lucian were doing the same thing."

Olivia's hand stilled over my head. "I remember you saying that. I…I just don't understand any of this. I get that Ares wants war. Duh, he's the God of War. He thrives on this stuff. And Lucian? Power-hungry pure-blood? Check. But Seth? I don't get it. I don't know what they could be offering him that would make him do this stuff."

"Everything. He thinks he's going to get everything." Scissors snipped.

"You?"

"I don't think it has anything to do with me, not like that." I wanted to move, but I also didn't want my hair to end up being more uneven. "I'm just a…means to an end."

Olivia was quiet for a few moments as she maneuvered the scissors above my shoulder blades. "You know him better than I do. Seth always freaked me out, but I just never thought we would end up here. I never could have imagined any of this."

I don't think any of us ever thought we'd be sitting here with the entire world on the verge of collapse.

"Are you nervous about today?" she asked, running the comb through my hair again.

"Yeah, a little. I mean, I have no idea what to say. I'm not the rah-rah kind of leader, and I'm not…very motivational."

"Just tell the truth." The scissors were back, and I sighed. "If Ares gets control of the God Killer and goes after Olympus, the gods will destroy everything in their path to stop him, including every pure and half out there."

"And if he manages to enslave mankind, pures will be next on his list." I frowned. "The whole thing sucks."

Olivia laughed softly. "That would be the understatement of the year."

"True."

She finished up the impromptu haircut, and I took a deep breath before I stood and checked myself out. "Wow." I leaned back, surprised. "It actually looks good."

Olivia rolled her eyes. "Did you think I would cut it badly?"

I shrugged.

"And you still came to me?" She shook her head as she backed out of the bathroom. "You've must've been desperate. Luckily, the shortest lengths were in the front, so it kind of blends in with the cut. You'll be able to pull it back and whatnot."

While my hair used to reach the middle of my back, it now rested on my shoulders, and without all the weight it was wavier than before. I actually felt sort of normal again.

I smiled tentatively as I left the bathroom. "You did a really great job. Thank you."

"You're welcome. I'm glad I could do something." She patted the spot beside her on the bed. "Chill with me."

I shuffled over to her, sitting down. I thought about how Caleb had asked me not to tell Olivia anything about him and his life in the Underworld. It wasn't fair, because I knew Olivia still cared for him deeply, but Caleb wanted her to move on. It made it difficult, though, not being honest with her.

Olivia reached over, running her fingers over the back of my knuckles. "Does it still hurt?" she asked, looking up.

I fought the urge to pull my hand away. "It doesn't really ache today."

She sucked her lower lip between her teeth and slowly pulled her hand away. "I'm sorry."

My brows shot up. "For what?"

"For what happened to you," she said, clasping her slim hands together. "I didn't see you. Not until Apollo brought you back, but the way Aiden and your uncle were afterward. They were so..." She cleared her throat. "Anyway, I'm sorry."

I didn't know what to say at first, but then the words sort of blurted out. "I look that bad, don't I?"

"What?" Her eyes widened as she twisted toward me. "I didn't mean it like that! Oh my gods, I'm such a douche. I didn't even think before I said that. You don't look bad, Alex. The scars are so faint and I'm sure—"

"It's okay, Olivia. Honestly, it's the last thing I should even be thinking about." Especially considering what Aiden and I discussed last night and what might lie ahead. The urge to tell her about what could be a possibility hit me hard, but I really didn't know how to branch out into that conversation. "And

I hate thinking about it because it makes me feel so shallow. Like, not even the acceptable level of shallowness."

"It's not shallow." She nudged me with her knee. "It's fine to worry about stuff like this. And if anyone says you're shallow for worrying about it, let's cut up their face and see what they think afterward."

I coughed out a dry laugh. "Wow."

"I'm serious." She winked. "So—" A knock on the door cut her off. She jumped up. "If it's Deacon, I'm going to body-slam him. He woke me up in the middle of the night because he couldn't sleep and Luke was out on the wall." She stopped at the door, twisting to me. "He made me put his hair into braids. And I mean those little tiny braids, and then he made me take them out."

A laugh bubbled up my throat. "Deacon is so bizarre."

"No joke." She reached for the door. "I swear to the gods, I could—oh! *Not* the annoying brother." I looked up, spying a confused-looking Aiden, and I grinned.

"I'm looking for Alex," he said, carrying a plastic bag. "But I'm curious to know what my brother did now."

"You don't even want to know." Olivia stepped aside. "She's here."

"I see." Aiden lingered at the door, a slight smile on his full lips. "Like the hair."

I picked up a few strands. "Olivia did a kick-ass job."

"She did." He turned that half-smile on Olivia, and her cheeks deepened with color. "I brought some breakfast."

Hopping up from the bed, I headed toward the door. "Food is calling." I stopped in front of Olivia. "Thank you again."

"No problem." She sprang forward and hugged me. At first, I sort of froze. It felt weird, but good.

I hugged her back, and for some reason, that felt like a huge step to me.

Aiden shoved about half a pig's worth of bacon at me. I mean, I could eat someone out of house and town on a normal day, but he watched like a hawk until I finished it all off.

"I really do like the hair," he said, after I returned from washing the greasy goodness off my fingers. He tucked a strand back behind my ear. "But you could be bald and I'd still think you were hot."

I made a face. "My ears are huge. That would not be attractive."

Aiden chuckled and pressed a kiss to the corner of my mouth. "Mmm, you taste like bacon."

"That's hot."

His hands settled lightly on my hips, and I leaned forward, resting my cheek against his chest. "Do you want anything else to eat?"

"Oh, gods, no. I'm stuffed."

"Sure?"

I turned into his chest, rubbing my cheek against him much like a cat might when it wants to be petted. "I'm sure." I closed my eyes, knowing why he was suddenly all about stuffing my face. "Aiden…"

"I know." He circled his arms around me, dropping his chin to the top of my head. "I know what you're going to say, and I know what we talked about last night, but I think, before we completely rule out anything, we should be careful. You need to get checked out."

Once more, the idea of skipping down to the infirmary and asking for a pregnancy test was tantamount to sunbathing nude in front of a pack of daimons, but Aiden was right. Lifting my head, I met his gaze. "I will. I promise."

"Good." He lowered his head, kissing me to the point where I almost forgot what I had to do. "You ready? Marcus will be waiting for us at the Council."

I wasn't ready, but I said yes. I quickly changed into a Sentinel uniform. The thrill I normally got from donning the all-black uniform was gone.

Completely gone.

You're not a Sentinel anymore.

Had I ever really been a Sentinel? The first time I'd put the uniform on and left to face my mom, I'd felt like one. The badass rush had filled me when I'd donned one after I broke the connection to Seth and prepared to enter the Underworld with Aiden.

I shouldn't be wearing this uniform now. The inner-annoying-Alex voice agreed.

But I kept it on, because I needed to look the part even if I didn't feel it. Strapping the daggers onto my thighs, I slipped the Glock Aiden handed me into the side holster. He patted my rear as I walked past him and, well, that made me feel a little better about the uniform.

My uncle was with Diana, waiting in one of the side rooms. There was a decent crowd out there, and the bacon I'd eaten was doing funny things in my stomach. Standing in the wings of the raised dais reminded me of when Lucian and Seth had turned on the Council.

Marcus still looked rough, but like all pures, he healed quickly. The bruises were fainter, and the swelling had gone down. "How are you feeling, Alexandria?"

One of these days, he would consistently call me Alex, and people would also stop asking how I was. "Okay. You?"

He gave me a tight smile. "Better."

Solos entered, and Aiden immediately started questioning him about the walls. The gate was holding. There'd been no more attacks, and scouts had been sent out, like the party that had met us at the wall before we entered the University. Luke was among them.

Deacon had been chatting with Olivia, but he'd quieted at that and sat up straight on the bench. His gaze shifted from his brother to Solos, and I was grateful Deacon hadn't seen the two Sentinels who'd been down by the burnt-out wreckage. His eyes, the only feature he shared with Aiden, were a bright silver. Worry etched into his features.

I made my way over to him. "Luke will be okay. He's an awesome Sentinel."

His lips tipped up in an uneven smile. "I know. It's just…"

No one, no matter how good they were, was truly safe, especially not a Sentinel. I wished there was something more I could say, but if Deacon and Luke were serious about each other, he was going to have to get used to the dangers Luke faced. It was a harsh reality.

"He'll be okay," I reassured him, and Deacon nodded, exhaling softly.

Val entered from the main room, a hand on the hilt of his dagger. His blue eyes were extraordinarily bright against his swarthy complexion. "Everyone's ready if you are."

My uncle turned to me and nodded. Full of nervous energy, I stepped forward, relieved when he and Aiden followed.

Walking onto the Council dais was freaky. After all, Head Minister Telly, the leader of all the Councils, had once tried to place me under the Elixir and commit me to servitude during a Council session. So, yeah, I wasn't a big fan of walking before the twelve thrones. All I could think, as I stopped in the center, flanked by two pure-bloods, was that I wished I had prepared a speech or something.

A lot of people were staring at me—well over three hundred, if I had to hazard a guess. In the back were all the Guards and Sentinels not on patrol, and the numbers were disheartening—maybe a hundred to a hundred and fifty. And most of them had to be from the University, meaning most of the others didn't make it here…or they had joined with the other side.

So not good.

Council members who resided at the University were easy to pick out. They were in their ceremonial robes: red, blue, white, and green, representing the different houses of power. Fire. Water. Air. Earth. Council members who had taken refuge here weren't dressed in their finery, but the cool disdain of seeing a half-blood standing where they belonged was written all over their faces, as well as on the faces of many students and staff members.

One would think in a time of war that prejudice wouldn't be strengthened, but it seemed to only fortify the age-old beliefs that halfs were less than pures.

A Council member in the front curled her lips as she leaned over to another member, whispering what was probably a very flattering observation.

And then, before I could even open my mouth and make a single, embarrassingly inept attempt of unifying the masses, a Council member in red robes stood and the real fun began.

"She should not be standing before the thrones of *Ministers*," he said, his hands forming fists against his robes. "This is not what the Council chambers should be used for. And a traitorous pure-blood stands there, too! One who used compulsion on his own kind. It's a disgrace." Aiden arched a brow, looking wholly unrepentant.

I sighed and folded my arms.

A low murmur started from the back of the room. A student shot to her feet. She was a pure-blood, a beautiful redhead who reminded me of Dawn, Lea's sister. "People are dying outside these walls, mortals and pures and halfs alike, and the first thing you have to comment on is the fact that there's a half-blood standing on the Council stage?"

The Council member whipped around. "As a pure-blood, you should respect the laws of our society!"

"Laws of our society?" The girl's eyes widened as she laughed. "Are you insane? I heard that daimons almost broke through the walls yesterday, and that a god was controlling them. Who gives a shit about our laws right now?"

I kind of really liked this girl.

Marcus stepped forward, clearing his throat as he tipped his chin up. "You may not agree with the use of the Council chambers, Minister Castillo, but that is not the point of this meeting."

As the Minister clearly stated why he felt this was the perfect moment to discuss his opinions, my gaze met Laadan's. I immediately thought of what she'd told me about my father while we were in Illinois. I'd hoped I'd find him here, but deep down, I knew I wouldn't. He'd most likely stayed in the Catskills with the other half servants, protecting and leading them. Head Minister Telly had enslaved him, placed him on the Elixir, and even cut out his tongue, but my father…he was a leader.

And I was his daughter.

"This is stupid," I said, loud enough that it shut up the over-talkative Council member. All eyes were on me. I took a step forward. "We're arguing over whether or not I belong on this stage—this *stupid* stage. That's all this is. And these thrones? They're just chairs. Who cares? They mean nothing to me or to the rest of the world. They only mean something to you because you made them so."

The minister turned the color of his robes. "How dare you?"

"Oh, I dare." Tapping into some of the anger that simmered in my stomach like a poison, I pulled it to the surface. "Yes, I am a half-blood. I am one of *many* trained to give their lives so you can sit in your precious *chairs*. So how about you show the halfs a little bit of respect?"

"Alexandria," Marcus said in a low voice, stepping up beside me.

I was on a roll, and there was going to be no stopping me. "But I am also the Apollyon. If I wanted to, I could blast your asses into next week, or use compulsion to gain everyone's agreement here, but I don't believe in forcing people to do things they don't want to. You could learn from that." Several heads turned to one another. Whispers grew. The Minister tipped his chin up defiantly.

"I see what you're getting at, but that does not change the blatant rape of our laws!"

"Rape of our laws? Whoa. That isn't insulting or anything." I shook my head at all of those nodding. "You people are being irrational. You don't get it. When Ares gets through the wards, which he will, he will be sitting on one of your precious thrones. None of you will be. And he will do with you as he pleases."

"He is a god," another Minister argued, a woman in her late forties. "We are their servants. If he—"

"Oh, yeah, you'll definitely be his *slaves*. Maybe we should stop right here and invite him in. Karma is a big, fat—"

"Alex," Aiden said, shaking his head slightly.

I rolled my eyes, but took a deep breath and forced my gaze away from the Minister before I made him start squawking like a chicken. Honestly, that would make just as much sense as the words he was saying.

I scanned the crowd. "I watched Ares kill people without lifting a finger. I heard his plans. He doesn't care about any of you. He sees pures just as you see the halfs. He will enslave you along with the mortals. He believes the gods should rule over the mortal realm once more, and that's a dangerous desire. He will make war on the mortals, on you, and any god who stands in his way. There will be no Council to argue over. There will be new rules and new laws to follow, and all of us will still be on the same level. I can promise you that. And if he succeeds in turning the First into a God Killer, then the other gods will rip this world apart to stop him. They've already begun."

Some stared back in disbelief, others wore masks of fear. One of the Sentinels in the back spoke up. "Can we even stop Ares?"

No, whispered that voice. *No one can stop Ares.* Pressure clamped down on my chest.

Swallowing hard, I struggled to ignore the now-familiar anxiety rising within me.

"He defeated you. That's what I heard," said a student. "And you're the Apollyon. If you can't defeat him, how can any of our Sentinels or Guards do anything?"

"Maybe we can reach some sort of agreement with him," suggested an older pure. "Fighting is not the only answer."

One of the Guards scoffed loudly. "Ares is the God of War, not the God of Treaties."

"He *is* the God of War," argued the pure. "How can we defeat him?"

"So, we do nothing?" asked Val from the side of the dais. "We let the fear of falling in battle lead us into surrendering? Is that how a Sentinel or Guard behaves?"

There were several shouts of disagreement, and all were from the Sentinels and Guards—soldiers who would never leave their posts.

"I don't know," I said, and again, the mass quieted. "I don't know if we can stop Ares. And you're right, he did kick my ass every which way from Sunday, but I know that no one is safe if he succeeds. I also know that we're not alone. We have Apollo, and Artemis, and other gods behind us, and we…we have…"

A strange feeling unfurled within me, sending a series of shivers like icy fingers all over my skin. I shook my head, causing a sharp pain to crack down my neck. I suddenly found it hard to breathe. It was like waking up unexpectedly and realizing I was already late for something.

"Alex?" Aiden stepped up beside me, his brows knitting. His eyes searched over my face. He placed a hand on my arm. "What's wrong?"

I saw him and Marcus, but every fiber of being was focused on *someone* else, outside this building and so very close. The crowd shifted nervously. A tremor coursed through my body. Deep inside my core, the cord snapped alive, thrumming frantically. The marks of the Apollyon bled to the surface, swirling over my skin. My heart hammered as tiny hairs rose all over my body.

"He's here," I said to Aiden, my voice a thready whisper. "Seth's here."

CHAPTER SEVEN

There were no sirens, and I knew there'd be none. Seth was too cool for that. "Alex, hold up." Aiden grabbed my arm, pulling me to a stop just outside the Council building.

Marcus was behind him, as was Val. "What are you doing? You just left in the middle of your speech."

"He's here. I know he is. I can *feel* him." Seth wasn't talking to me, but I could feel him in every cell. The cord was buzzing along happily, in a way it only did when he was near. "Tell Val to make sure everyone is safe, but I have to go."

"Something is happening at the gate," Val said, placing his hand over an earpiece. "I can't get a definite response from them, but something's going on."

"You don't have to go." Aiden's eyes turned a thunderous shade of gray. "We need to take a minute—"

"And what? Give him more time? No."

"He's right." Marcus stood at our shoulders. "What is our plan? Go out there and shake Seth's hand?"

My eyes narrowed on my uncle. "Actually, my plan was more to stab him in the eyeball and then decide what to do."

Marcus's jaw locked down. "I think you're missing the point. If he transfers your power or gains control over you, it is all over. We must think about this."

"He can't get control over me." My eyes flicked to Aiden's, and I willed him to understand what I didn't even really understand myself. I didn't want to face Seth, but I *had* to see him. I had to know that my instincts were right, that he was here and I wasn't wrong. "We are so beyond that phase."

Aiden shook his head. "There have been no sirens, and Val can't get the Guards at the gate to respond. Think about that. We could be walking into a trap. *You* could be walking into a trap."

Seth could keep dozens of Guards quiet with a compulsion. That fact didn't change anything. I pulled my arm free, done with this conversation. Spinning around, I cut through the campus, heading for the gates. I didn't even look to see if Val was doing anything. Each step made the cord tighten. My skin felt stretched to the point of ripping by the time I passed the courtyard and inhaled the sweet scent of peonies.

"I swear to the gods, Alex, I will pick you up and throw you over my shoulder. You cannot go out there. Think for a second." Aiden was right by my side, head down low and his voice a low warning. "Remember what we talked about last night. If you're—"

"I remember," I shot back, picking up my pace. "And *that* has nothing to do with this."

"*That* has everything to do with this!"

I blinked, sort of stunned that he would yell at me, but how could I be surprised? Aiden would do anything to keep me—and the baby, if there was one—safe, but if Seth was here, there was no hiding. Nothing was safe.

Marcus appeared on my other side. "What did you two talk about last night? And yes, I know this isn't the appropriate moment for this discussion, but you two really need to find separate beds so there aren't any 'late night' chats."

I almost laughed, because wow, if only he knew how late in the game that advice was. "This isn't the right time for that talk. Trust me."

"That I don't find reassuring." Marcus thrust a hand through his wind-tossed brown hair, his bright-green eyes narrowed. "Alexandria, please listen to us. This isn't safe or smart. We have to *think* about this."

Aiden stepped in front of me, forcing me to skid to a stop. His hands landed on my shoulders. "You're starting to scare me. Okay?" He cupped my cheeks gently, forcing my eyes to his. "You're not ready for this—ready for *him*."

Alex?

I sucked in a sharp breath as I pulled away. Aiden's fingers trailed off my cheeks. The cord coiled tightly, straining inside me, and then expanded, yearning for its other half at the sound of Seth's voice. He came right through the shields. Was it because he was so close? Or was I truly unprepared because this was the first time that we had been near each other since I'd Awakened?

My gaze shifted beyond Aiden to the walls in the distance.

Seth?

There was a pause, and then the cord snapped inside me. *We need to talk.*

I don't know what it was about those four words that set me off, but rage poured into me, so potent and so quick that I almost screamed in fury. "We need to talk." That, after everything, was what he had to say? I wanted to drop-kick that question into his face.

I took off, my boots digging into the loose dirt. Aiden shouted, and I heard him coming after me, but I was fast when I wanted to be, faster than him. I flew past the last of the statues and almost ran into a pack of Guards crowding the entrance to the wall. They didn't move, didn't speak.

They were *enthralled*.

"Move," I shouted, shouldering the Guards aside. "Get out—"

The words died on my lips. I came to a complete standstill, but it felt like the ground was moving under my feet. "Oh, my gods…"

He stood a foot away from the closed gates, separated from me by iron and titanium. His hair was longer than it had been when he'd come back from the Catskills, falling over his forehead in a mess of blond waves. He was dressed as a Sentinel; all the black was a contrast against his golden skin. His impossibly perfect features were devoid of the typical, ever-present smirk, but the inky black marks of the Apollyon glided across his skin, and his iridescent amber eyes were fixed on mine.

Seth was beautiful. It was like the gods themselves had pieced him together, and in a way, they had. There'd always been a lack of humanity in his beauty, the whole time I'd known him. As I stared at him now, seeing him for the first time in months, there was something brimming in his eyes and etched into his features that had never been there before.

It made me uneasy in my own skin.

Movement behind him drew my attention. Luke stepped forward as if in a daze. He didn't even blink as he unlocked the gate. Hinges groaned, and then the heavy gate swung open. It was just Luke with Seth, but I knew there were others. Every instinct in my body told me an *army* waited over the crest, just hoping for the signal to attack us.

Seth stepped forward, his eyes only leaving mine to take in my altered appearance. That emotion strengthened in his eyes and face, and I refused to believe what I was seeing. In that moment, I wanted to kill him *and* I wanted to touch him. Weird, but I figured it had something to do with what we were.

"Alex," he spoke out loud, shattering the trance.

The very thought of him made my skin crawl. I wanted to find a wool brush and scrub all the memories of him out of my head. I hated him for what he'd become, for what he'd allowed, and I hated him for the fact that a part of me still loved him, because he was a part of me—a part that had turned on me like a venomous pet snake.

Aiden skidded to a stop beside me, breathing raggedly. He was talking, but I wasn't hearing him or my uncle shouting at the immobile Guards.

My brain clicked off—never a good thing for me and definitely not a good thing for Seth. I shot forward, sidestepping Aiden who tried to get between us as I drew my Glock.

"Make one move I don't like, and I'll put a bullet right between your eyes." My hand didn't shake. Whatever fear lived inside me was vanquished by the growing, nearly out-of-control rage. "I know it won't kill you, but I sure as hell know it will hurt."

Emotion flashed in Seth's eyes. It wasn't surprise. More like a lick of pain or regret, but then again, I was probably giving the douchebag more credit than he deserved. He slowly lifted his hands.

"Release them from their compulsion," I ordered, my finger steady on the trigger. "*Now*."

His amber gaze shifted to where Luke stood motionless with the Guards. He didn't say anything, but I felt the ripple of power brush over my skin like a smooth caress.

"What the…?" Luke stumbled back a step, placing his hands on the sides of his head. He looked up, saw who was standing there, and sucked in a breath. "Holy shit."

Seth's stare swung back to meet mine. The tension in the air increased as the others came out of their compulsion and, for the first time in their lives, saw two Apollyons together. "We need to talk," he said again.

My head cocked to the side. I hadn't forgotten the musical lilt of his voice, but hearing it in person was nothing like the voice that came through our whacked-out connection. The cord hummed along, but out of the corner of my eye, I saw Aiden moving around to Seth's back, leveling his own gun on the First. I knew that, if Seth took one step toward me, Aiden would pull the trigger.

And I also knew Seth could disarm us both before either of us blinked.

"There's nothing you could possibly say that I want to hear." I took a breath, forcing myself *not* to pull the trigger for the fun of seeing him go splat. "And if you think you're going to be able to convince me to side with you after what Ares did, you can go screw yourself."

"That's not why I'm here."

"Bullshit."

His head tilted to the side, a near mirror image of what I had done. Again, his stunning amber gaze traveled over my face. He shook his head, and then he dropped onto his knees and closed his eyes.

Okay. Sure wasn't expecting that.

I opened my mouth, but there were no words. Glancing at Aiden, I saw he looked as dumbfounded as I felt. A keen wariness kept me from lowering my gun. Seth could be a tricky little devil, but this? I didn't know.

Seth's arms fell to his sides. He didn't speak out loud. *You're right. This won't kill me, but I deserve it. So do it.*

So stunned by what he said, I spoke out loud. "What?"

Do it. A breath shuddered from his body. *If it wipes out the memory of what Ares did to you, then do it. Do it!*

Taken aback, I stared down at him. *You felt everything, right? Everything that he did to me?*

Seth's eyes fluttered open, and I didn't want to believe what I saw in them. Regret was too late for both of us. "Everything," he said out loud, voice hoarse.

"What's he talking about?" Aiden demanded.

I shook my head as my stomach plummeted. *You know how I felt? What I wanted?*

He squeezed his eyes shut. *Yes.*

And you want me to take those memories from you? You really think a bullet will do that? Fuck that. I lowered the gun, hand shaking. Violent anger rushed to the surface. *I can't get rid of those memories, so neither can you.* "Fuck you."

On guard, Aiden shifted behind Seth. "Come on, Alex, talk to me. What's going on?"

"I never meant for any of this to happen," Seth said before I could answer. His eyes were open again, and there was no denying the pain in them. And there were only two things that waited behind that kind of sharp-edged hurt: anger and the truth. "I would never be okay with what happened. I didn't know he was going to do that to you."

"Is he talking about Ares?" A misleading, deadly calmness entered Aiden's voice as he stepped forward, the muzzle of his gun coming awfully close to the back of Seth's head. "That he didn't know what Ares was going to do?"

Seth turned his head to the side, looking over his shoulder. "I know it doesn't change anything or make it right, but I didn't know, and I would never be okay with anyone hurting Alex."

"*You* hurt Alex, you son of a bitch." A dangerous glint filled Aiden's gray eyes.

The First bit down on his lower lip as his lashes lowered. "Well, you have a good point there, *Saint* Delphi, but I love her—"

"Don't shoot him!" I warned Aiden, catching how Aiden's finger spasmed on the trigger. "Whatever you do, don't shoot him."

A muscle popped in Aiden's jaw. "I can't make any promises." A weak, barely there smirk appeared on Seth's lips.

"Don't," I said, slipping my gun into its holster, unwilling to take my eyes off Seth. Shock rippled through me. "Other than trying to piss you off, he's not trying to trick us."

Aiden's eyes widened. "How can you be so sure?"

How could I be? It was something I just *knew*. "Seth wouldn't bow to anyone unless..." I couldn't even finish, because Seth turned back to me and our eyes met again.

I'm so sorry, he said, and although it wasn't out loud, the apology rocked me to my core. Seth never apologized. That wasn't his thing. *I'm so, so sorry.*

Blood drained from my face, and then quickly returned, spreading along my cheeks. "He's not trying to trick us."

Aiden stared. "Alex—"

"He's not. I...I just know." My hands suddenly felt weak. "Why are you here, Seth? You know we can't trust you. And you can't be near me." Even now, the cord stretched tight between us, drawing me to him like a moth to an Olympus-made bug zapper. Part of me yearned to get closer to him in spite of whatever common sense said, how I felt about him, and about a dozen other things.

"I know you won't take my word or hear me out. You don't have any reason to. That's why I brought you something."

My stomach roiled, because the last time he brought me a gift, it had been an obliterated Head Minister Telly. "You brought me something? You bring me some bat-shit crazy stuff, Seth."

"You're going to love this." A little bit of his dark humor crept into his glowing eyes, but it quickly dulled. "Can I stand since you're not going to shoot me?"

"Like I said, I'm not making any promises," Aiden replied, his lips tipping up grimly.

Seth's chest rose. "I wasn't asking you."

"And I'm the one with a gun still pointed at the back of your head."

"Well, then," Seth murmured.

I sighed. Even though I didn't believe Seth was trying to trick us, I didn't fully trust him. And when he said I would love something, I would rather spin-kick myself in the face than see what he had up his sleeve. "Stand *very* slowly."

Seth rose to his feet fluidly, keeping his hands raised at his sides. Daggers and a Glock hung from his waist and thighs. I caught Marcus's eye, and while I'd prefer someone else to get closer to Seth, he nodded. He moved forward quickly, removing the visible weapons, and it was clear Seth allowed him to. We couldn't do anything about his deadliest weapons—the control of the elements and akasha.

"What, Seth?" I asked.

He tilted his head back to the gate. "Give them a second."

"There's movement outside the gates—Sentinels." A

Guard gripped the handle of his gun. He took a step forward, head tipping to the side. "There's a Minister with them."

"What?" My gaze darted back to Seth. "Who is it, Seth?"

His gaze locked with mine. "The one person you want to see dead more than me." I held his stare. "Let them in, but be ready for a Trojan Horse."

Seth gave a little grin as he turned his gaze to the gate. Aiden kept his eyes trained on him, and I was sure if baby Apollo walked through that gate and shook his baby butt, he still wouldn't look.

My heart pounded as the first Sentinel came through the gates, followed by another. They exchanged wary stares with the Sentinels on our side as they stepped aside, revealing who stood between them.

"Holy crap on a cracker," I whispered.

Between the two Sentinels stood a completely out-of-it Lucian—my stepfather and the pure-blood responsible for Seth turning on the Council. I *did* hate that man more than I hated Seth. He'd used Seth's need for a family, for acceptance, against him, twisting it into some kind of sick familial bond. Lucian had never been a fan of mine, not since he'd married my mother, and one of the few reasons he'd paid any attention to me was because I was the second Apollyon. As long as he controlled Seth, I could give him what he wanted—absolute power.

His long, dark hair looked oily and unkempt, and those obsidian-colored eyes were glazed. He was definitely under a compulsion, but that didn't explain why he was here. I took a step to the side, my fingers hovering over the handle on my gun. "What is this?"

"He knew," Seth said simply. My head jerked toward him.

He knew, he repeated, taking our conversation private.

We were at the Catskills, and I knew…I knew that Ares had left, but I didn't know that he'd gone for you. He didn't tell me that. He promised that you would never be hurt in any of this and…so did Lucian. I believed them. I completely believed them.

I started to feel like I was going to hurl. I didn't want to hear any of this, but I had to.

But then I connected to you, and I knew something was happening. You were in so much… Seth trailed off, his eyes drifting shut. His face tensed. *I went to Lucian, and I told him what I'd felt on your end. I told him how bad it was and how I hadn't agreed to this and never would. That I couldn't be okay with what Ares had done, and Lucian, he knew. He knew why Ares had left. He knew what Ares would do if you didn't submit.*

My gaze shifted to my stepfather. He stared back at me blankly. I didn't know what to feel as Seth continued, or maybe I was feeling too much. This man may've loathed the ground I walked on, as I was a constant reminder of my mother's only true love, but to know what Ares planned to do and be okay with it? Had he not felt even a sliver of compassion for me? Nothing?

Lucian had once told me I needed to be broken. Well, if he agreed with what Ares had done, he had succeeded. I had been broken.

Lucian laughed. Seth's voice twisted up my insides. *He laughed, and in that moment, I couldn't do this any longer. When Ares returned, I told him I was going to find you and transfer your power to me. That you'd be weak enough for it to work, and that I was bringing Lucian to talk to those who were here and sway them to our side. Ares believed me.*

Seth laughed out loud, the sound as dry and shattered as broken twigs. "I'm a lot like him."

"Ares?" I whispered, aware that everyone who had cognitive control was staring at us.

He gave a curt nod. "I get my…*blinding* arrogance from him. He wouldn't dare think that I'd disobey him. Well, he will soon, very soon. I doubt he'll be happy."

"Wait," Marcus said, stepping forward. "You two need to stop with the covert conversations. What the hell is going on?"

Seth ignored him and took a step toward me. He didn't make it very far before Aiden's gun pressed against the back of his head. "One more step," Aiden warned, eyes flashing. "And we'll find out how an Apollyon survives a head wound."

"You have no idea how badly I want to find that out myself," Seth replied, one side of his lips curling up. "Did I tell you about the time I slept—"

"Seth," I snapped, drawing his attention back to me. "Can you take Lucian out of the compulsion, or did you fry his brain?"

"I didn't fry him." His eyes met mine again. "I figured I'd leave that to you."

I didn't need to ask Seth to release Lucian, because a second later, Lucian stumbled forward, dragging in air as if he'd been underwater. His dark eyes cleared as his gaze took in his surroundings. "What is going on?" he demanded, pulling himself away from the two Sentinels. His hands pressed into his chest. "Seth?"

"How many Sentinels do you have with you?" I asked Seth, staring at my stepfather.

"Hundreds," he replied, his voice weary. "An army of them, all loyal to me."

Lucian's head swung toward Seth. "What? Yours? Seth, what are you doing?"

"And he laughed?" Tears filled my eyes, but they did not fall.

The hurt inside me twisted into something ugly and violent.

"Yes," came Seth's reply.

There was always a chance Seth was playing me, but I had no doubt in my mind that what he had said about Lucian was true. My stepfather had known what Ares was going to do. And he had *laughed*. To me, there was nothing more evil than that. Seth wasn't a completely innocent bystander. He'd made his own decisions, but Lucian had aided that process. He'd led Seth down that road. Maybe he hadn't held his hand, but who knew where all of us would be if Lucian hadn't had *friends* in higher places and hadn't used Seth the way he did.

I didn't feel calm, but there was an acceptance that slipped into my bones, mixing with the coldness inside of me. The only thing that was warm as I stared at my stepfather was the cord connecting me to the First.

In my head there were two outcomes. Being the bigger person was one. Revenge was the other. Two options, and that cold voice inside me told me there really wasn't any choice between the two.

Aiden shifted warily. "Alex, what's going on?"

Moving lightning-fast, I drew the Glock and fired one round.

Lucian didn't make a sound.

Falling over backward, he landed in a motionless heap—his black eyes fixed sightlessly on the cloudless sky and his dark hair spilling out around him like an inky puddle of blood—with one small, titanium-laced bullet hole in his forehead.

Grandma Piperi had said I'd kill the ones I love. She'd been right and wrong in this case. I did kill Lucian, but I'd never loved him. I would've, maybe at one point in my life, if he hadn't treated me like the Antichrist or, later on, an object.

Aiden swore under his breath, but he kept his gun leveled on Seth.

"Gods." Marcus exhaled hard as he stared at the Minister. "Alexandria…?"

I stepped back, legs shaking. "That takes care of one problem, doesn't it?"

My uncle shook his head slowly, and in those deep, forest-green eyes, there was fear. I couldn't bring myself to be that affected by it.

Seth stared at me, almost like he hadn't really believed I'd do what I did. I don't know what he thought I *would* do. Pat Lucian on the head? Smack him, and have that be all? But that tortured tautness to Seth's expression deepened until I felt stronger stirrings of unease.

"Alex," Seth whispered, and that single word was heavy and sad.

Had I done the wrong thing?

It was a little too late now to be questioning that, I supposed.

The gun was still hot in my hand as I slipped it back into the holster. I turned to Seth. "I still don't completely trust you."

"I didn't think you would." The glyphs seeped into his skin, disappearing. "So, what do we do now?"

Aiden snapped forward, cracking the butt of the pistol off the back of Seth's head with enough force to kill a mortal. Seth slumped over. Apollyon or not, that was going to take him out for a couple of hours. Aiden met my wide eyes. "I'm not taking any chances, either."

CHAPTER EIGHT

Seth was taken to one of the cells under the main Council building. The bars were made of titanium and the Guards stationed to watch him were pure-bloods, but if Seth wanted to get out, he was going to get out. We didn't have Titan blood or Hephaestus to build an Apollyon-proof cell, so we were taking a huge risk by housing Seth. But we really had no other option. We also had hundreds of Sentinels loyal to Seth on the other side of the gate, and who knew how long they'd remain there if they didn't hear from him. Only good news was that he'd be out for a while, but when he came to, well. I'd deal with that when I had to stampede that bridge.

Right now, I needed to shower.

Sweat slicked my skin like leftover residue from the adrenaline that had coursed through my veins upon seeing Seth, but it was more than that. I felt grimy and grubby inside and out, like I hadn't bathed for days.

I felt *dirty*—like, morally corrupt.

My heart was pounding a little too fast as I scrubbed until my skin turned a bright pink. I squeezed my eyes shut and took several breaths.

Had I been wrong?

Had killing Lucian been the wrong thing to do? Morally speaking? Duh. It was wrong, but hadn't he deserved it? Hadn't he had it coming to him?

"As a Sentinel, I'll kill daimons. That's not the same as playing jury and executioner."

The spongy loofah fell from my suddenly limp fingers, landing with a wet thud against the shower floor. My stomach roiled as I bent at the waist, nauseated. Water beaded across my back, but I barely felt it.

When I pulled that trigger, I hadn't felt a damn thing. There had been anger right before that, even a brief welling of sadness in response to Lucian's cruelty, but nothing when my finger squeezed. As if taking a life was an insignificant action.

There was something wrong with that—wrong with *me*.

It seemed like yesterday when Seth had wanted to kill Head Minister Telly and I'd told him it was wrong. That even as the Apollyons, we couldn't make those kind of decisions.

But I had.

I had killed Lucian.

In cold blood, whispered that nasty little voice. *You didn't even blink*.

True. I hadn't felt a damn thing as I'd pulled that trigger, nothing beyond anger, but even then that fury hadn't felt tangible. Gods knew I totally had an anger management problem, but I had never snapped like that. Throwing apples was one thing. Shooting people in the head was taking it to a whole new level.

What was wrong with me? Better yet, what was I turning in to?

Forcing several deep breaths into my lungs, I straightened and let the suds rinse off my body. I turned off the shower and grabbed a fluffy towel, wrapping it around me.

The numbness was inside me, seeping through the pores, coating my skin. I felt like I needed to take another shower and keep taking them until it washed away whatever this was.

I didn't check myself out when I opened the door and stepped into the adjoining room.

Aiden sat on the edge of the bed, hands resting on his knees. The Glock was next to him, and the daggers were unhooked, placed in a neat line beside the gun. He lifted his head, his dark gray eyes slowly moving over me until centering on mine. My heart jumped in my chest, and I felt the muscles in my lower stomach tighten.

When I was around Aiden, I wasn't numb. I felt so much.

Crossing the distance between us, I stopped between his spread legs. Aiden sat up straighter, his gaze questioning. Air hitched in my throat as he lifted his arms. I moved forward, placing my knees on either side of his hips. He folded his arms around me, sealing my chest to his as I rested my cheek against his shoulder. Minutes ticked by in silence. His hand trailed up and down my back in a soothing gesture that beat away at the numbness, but I wanted to feel more. *Needed* to feel more.

I rocked back in his lap and placed my hand on his cheek. A jolt of awareness ran from my palm up my arm. Unseen to him, the marks of the Apollyon bled through my skin, swirling down my arm until they reached my hand.

His lashes lowered. "We need to talk about what happened, Alex."

Talking was the last thing I wanted, right next to thinking. Feeling was the only thing I was interested in at the moment. I leaned forward, pressing my forehead against his. Our mouths lined up perfectly, and Aiden's chest rose sharply.

His hand tightened into a fist against the small of my back. "This isn't talking."

"I don't want to talk." I brushed my lips across his. Nothing more than a quick sweep of our mouths, but Aiden's embrace tightened. "I want to feel you."

"Alex—"

I pulled back a little and dropped the towel, surprising even myself since I was definitely on the body-conscious side of things at the time.

Aiden held my gaze for a moment, and then it dipped, and I felt his stare as if it were a heated touch. Warmth rose to my skin as he dragged his eyes back up. Knowing Aiden, he wanted to do the right thing. There was a lot we needed to talk about—the numbness I felt, the fact that I'd frozen in battle the day before, the meeting with the Council, Seth, the fact that I'd just shot my stepfather in the head, and the possibility of us becoming very unprepared parents. The Aiden I *knew* would want to hash all that out, because every single item was important, but the Aiden I *loved* wouldn't ever turn me down again.

He placed his hands on the sides of my face and guided my head to his. The moment our lips touched it was like waking up after a too-long sleep. Sensation raced through my system, pouring into my bloodstream and chasing away the coldness. The kiss deepened, and I knew that Aiden was right where I was. We would talk, but it would be later. Much later.

"What is this?" Aiden asked, his voice deep and husky.

"What?"

His fingers skimmed over my hip and lower back. He was touching the oddly shaped scar. I stiffened. Grabbing his hand, I moved it away. I kissed him deeper, harder, drawing his attention from it until I knew he wasn't thinking about it any longer. His hands slid across my shoulders and then down to my waist, leaving a shivery wake behind. He tugged me to his chest and, though he was still in his uniform, his skin seared mine. Kissing Aiden was like taking a deep breath of fresh air after not being able to breathe. His kisses chased away all the what-ifs and strange feelings that had twisted inside me.

Aiden's lips blazed a path down my throat, and my head tipped back. He wrapped an arm around my waist as his other hand drifted up my stomach and then farther up, eliciting a sharp gasp from me. A deep, nerve-frying sound came from within his chest, and every muscle under my hands knotted in response. His lips neared the sensitive spot, and his breath rasped in my ear. There was a painstaking moment when neither of us moved and it was just our hearts pounding in our chests, thundering in our veins, and then in an instant, the exquisite feel of his lips against my pulse wasn't enough.

I pulled back to get my hands on that annoying shirt of his and opened my eyes.

All-white eyes stared back into mine. Lips were twisted into a cruel smirk. The face was frighteningly familiar—chillingly handsome and devoid of compassion. "You can never win."

Icy terror froze the scream building in my chest as I jerked back, breaking the hold around my waist. I thumped onto the floor. Ignoring the burst of dull pain across my backside,

I rocked to my feet and lurched to the side, grabbing Aiden's pistol. It was only as my fingers closed around the handle when I realized how fruitless shooting Ares would be.

I swung the gun around anyway, because I figured it had to sting at least, but I froze because it wasn't Ares standing there.

It was Aiden, his eyes wide and the color of the sky before a violent summer storm. His hands were at his sides, and his chest rose and fell sharply. "Alex? What…what are you doing?"

I drew in a ragged breath, but it never reached my lungs. A boulder had landed on my chest, crushing me as I took a step back. I didn't understand what I was seeing. It had been Ares—it had been him! His face—his voice.

"Agapi mou, talk to me. Tell me what is going on," he said, his voice hoarse but his eyes still holding mine. "What's happening?"

"Aiden?" I whispered, my hand shaking.

He nodded slowly, and the one word he spoke was hoarse. "Yes."

The pressure turned into slicing fear and confusion as I stared at him. The logical part of me screamed that this was Aiden standing before me, that Ares couldn't get inside the University, but I couldn't let my guard down, because if it was him…

"It wasn't you," I whispered, my finger spasming dangerously over the trigger. "It wasn't *you*." Tension pulled at his lips.

"What do you mean? Because it's me. I'm here with you, agapi mou. I'm right here."

A tremor coursed down my arm as uncertainty spread into my chest like a gulp of too-cold water. I knew I should probably lower the gun before I accidentally did shoot Aiden, because it had to be him standing before me, but I couldn't do it.

"Is it Seth?" he asked, his fingers curling into his palms. "Is he doing this?"

"Seth?" I blinked. "No. It wasn't you. It was…it was Ares."

An immediate pain flickered across his face, spreading sorrow into his brilliant silver gaze, and I didn't like the look because it was such a deep hurt. "I'm here with you. I've been here with you this whole time, agapi mou."

The next breath I took scalded my throat. "I think…I think I'm going crazy."

"Oh, Alex…"

Those two words broke my heart in a way nothing ever had before. The ache in them settled in my bones like lead. I shuddered.

"Look at me," he said in a low voice. "You know it's me."

Then Aiden stepped forward, and he was the bravest being in this world to do so with a gun pointed at his heart. Slowly, as if not to frighten me, he reached out and gently pried my fingers off the gun. My heart turned over heavily. Without taking his eyes off mine, he placed the gun back on the bed and picked up a quilt. He draped the soft material over my shoulders, pulling it closed in the front as he pressed a small, tender kiss against my forehead.

That tiny show of affection broke me.

"I'm sorry," I said as my body shook. I'd almost shot Aiden. I could've seriously hurt him, if not *killed* him. "Oh my gods, I'm so sorry, Aiden."

"Shh," he murmured, wrapping his arms around me and gathering me close. He sat down on the bed, and I pressed my cheek to his chest above his thundering heart. I squeezed my eyes shut. "It's going to be okay, Alex. Whatever is going on, we're in this together, remember? And it will be okay. I promise you."

A new terror flooded my senses as Aiden held me, one hand curled around the nape of my neck and the other smoothing up and down my back. He rocked slowly, murmuring something that I really wasn't hearing because all I could focus on was one thing.

It was quite possible that I'd taken a detour straight into Crazyville, which would explain a lot. Would anyone be surprised? People cracked under stress all the time, and half-bloods, even though we were trained to keep our heads together, weren't any different. But did it matter? Not really, because one thing was true.

Aiden wasn't safe around me.

Aiden and I didn't talk.

I think he was worried about pushing things too far for the time being since I was obviously rocking a first-class ticket to certifiable. After all, a few hours ago I'd shot someone in the head, then I'd hallucinated Ares and pulled a gun on Aiden… while I was buck-ass naked.

Talk about an awkward mood killer.

Somehow, we ended up stretched out on the bed, and Aiden finally drifted off into a fitful sleep. It was late, but I couldn't sleep. My mind raced with everything. If I was crazy, which I had a good feeling I was, how could I lead the Army of Awesome against Ares? This had trouble written all over it.

And Seth was awake.

He wasn't trying to communicate with me, and the fact that I knew anyway was freaky on a whole new level, but his consciousness existed on the fringe of mine. He was up, and he was antsy.

And so was I.

As quietly as possible, I pulled myself away from Aiden and dressed in the dark. I figured if I ended up putting my shirt on backward, I could blame it on my lunacy. Going crazy had to have some benefits, right? Maybe I'd just go fully crazy.

I crept from the room and closed the door behind me. I tried to tell myself I didn't know what I was doing, but I did. Every part of me knew where I was heading, especially the annoying cord inside me. It was buzzing around like an over-eager puppy.

Moving through the shadows, it took no time at all to make it to the Council building. The entrance to the catacombs housing the cells was heavily guarded.

None of the Guards looked thrilled with the idea of stepping aside and allowing me access to the First. Not that I blamed them. Everyone knew what would happen if Seth transferred my power to him, but he was here, and that fact alone was risky.

Solos moved up the narrow stairwell, his eyes narrowing as he spied me standing before the Guards. "What's up, Alex?"

"I need to talk to Seth."

He positioned himself in front of me. "Do you think that's a good idea?"

"Do you have any suggestions other than knocking him out every couple of hours?"

His lips quirked into a grin that lessened the severity of the jagged scar running from his right eye to his jaw. "I really don't see a problem with that."

I laughed, but it felt and sounded forced. "Neither do I, but I need to talk to him to figure out what the hell he's really doing here and if the Sentinels on the other side of the gate are going to be a problem."

"They're probably going to be a problem," Solos replied.

He was a fountain of reassuring comments. I shifted my weight impatiently as I tucked the shorter strands of hair behind my ear. "I'm not here to connect with him," I said in a low voice. "He doesn't hold that kind of power over me anymore. And besides, I won't let him get close enough to even try." Solos looked away, his jaw working overtime.

"I don't like this. Don't get me wrong. I don't think you're going to turn Evil Alex on us, but it's the middle of the night and Aiden isn't with you."

My brows rose. "And what does that have to do with the Apollyon locked in our cell?"

"I just feel a hundred times more comfortable when Aiden is around, especially if you're chit-chatting with Seth," he admitted.

"Aiden's asleep, and he needs to rest. Besides, I don't need a babysitter." Of course I did, but I sure as hell wasn't admitting that. "Come on, Solos, don't make me *make* you do this."

He regarded me closely and then exhaled through his nose. "*Don't* make me regret this."

"What faith you have in me," I muttered as he stepped aside and I walked past.

"It has nothing to do with faith." Solos was right on my heels as I went down the steep stairway. A wave of cool air seeped through my jeans. Putting on the tactical pants of a Sentinel had felt wrong, all things considered. "And no offense, I don't trust anyone. I learned the hard way many years ago, and I see the reminder of that every time I look in the mirror."

I bent under the low archway and stepped into a wide

chamber. Seth wasn't here. My gaze fell to the titanium door across from me, and then I glanced over my shoulder. "Your scar?"

Solos leaned against the wall and folded his arms. "I didn't get it shaving."

"I thought you got it fighting daimons."

He gave a slight shake of his head. "I got it when I was nineteen."

As wrong as it might be, I was morbidly curious. "How did it happen?"

There wasn't an immediate response, and the cord inside me tightened with impatience. "I was out one night patrolling, and toward the end of my shift, I met this woman. She was the most beautiful woman I'd ever seen. One thing led to another and, well, I *was* a nineteen-year-old guy. It was a one-night stand, no commitment or exchange of names, and all that was her idea, not mine. Sign me up for that."

"Of course," I said, figuring out where their meet-and-greet had ended up, but not how a hook-up had resulted in such a scar.

"But she wasn't an ordinary woman, Alex. She was a goddess." My mouth dropped open.

"Aphrodite," he said, tipping his chin down. "Apparently, she was bored and decided to pay a visit to the mortal realm. Wrong place, wrong time kind of thing. Or right place, depending on how you look at it, and who was I to turn that down?" One side of his lips tipped up as I gaped at him. "As you can imagine, good old Hephaestus wasn't too happy about that."

"I would think not," I said slowly.

"He gave me this scar." He gestured at his right cheek. "And he would've killed me if Aphrodite hadn't intervened.

I pretty much had to make myself nonexistent when Apollo brought him to build that cell for you, but I have to say a couple of hours with her was worth it."

A surprised laugh burst from me, and Solos's uneven grin spread. "But I learned to never really trust someone when they say things will be cool, you know? And I learned to never, ever trust a god—or anything they create. They're the snakes in the grass that you never see coming."

Solos remained in the circular chamber, and as I walked down the narrow hall lit by torches on the walls, I couldn't help but feel like *I* was a snake in the grass. So was Seth. We both were dangerous beings created by the gods, and we could and had turned on everything and everyone around us at one point or another.

Maybe our violent natures were the product of those who created us. No one else in this world was more off their rocker than an Olympian god.

I tucked away Solos's story as I rounded a corner and saw the cell several feet in front of me. The light from the flames flickered across the titanium bars. A darker shadow was pressed against the bars, and it took me a second to realize it was Seth, his back to the hall.

Stopping a few feet from where he sat, I ignored the near-intoxicating pull of the cord—of our connection.

"Are you coming to knock me out again?" he asked, his voice oddly absent of the lyrical lilt.

I crossed the remaining distance, stopping just out of his reach. "I haven't quite decided yet."

"You can save yourself the effort. I'm not plotting a daring escape, and I don't have any plans to rain down chaos and destruction."

"That's good to know."

"Is it?" He turned his head, and his profile came into view. His eyes were closed, and the long lashes, darker than his blond hair, rested against the tops of his cheekbones. "Does St. Delphi know you're down here, Alex?"

My eyes narrowed. "I'm not talking about him."

One side of his lips curled up in a quick grin and then vanished. "Good, because I really don't want to hear about how happily in love you two are. I'd rather you knock me out."

Considering I'd just pulled a gun on Aiden, I wouldn't say there was a "happily" in that equation right now, but his comment took me aback. I inched to the side and knelt down out of his reach. "Let's be real with one another. You never loved me like that. You know that, right?"

Seth didn't respond for a long moment, and then he tipped the side of his head back against the bars and let out a weary sigh. "You're right, but I never had the chance."

Again, I was knocked off guard by his candidness. Seth was like the king of vague and unhelpful responses, worse than a god most of the time. I stared at his profile for a long, tense minute; the words sort of just burst from my mouth like a dam breaking under pressure.

"I loved you. It's not the same way I feel about Aiden, but I *loved* you, and you betrayed me. You sided with Lucian and practically held me hostage so that I would be forced to connect with you! And I still had hope for you. I *still* defended you. And then you turned me into Evil Alex and started a war alongside Ares! People have died, Seth." My voice rose and cracked as my legs weakened. I sat down, my hands limp between my knees as I stared at him through the bars. "And not just recently. How far does all of this go back? To my mom? To the daimons that were at Deity Island and killed

Caleb? To all of those who died at the Catskills? Were you and Lucian using daimons then? You were, weren't you?"

There was another pause, and then his eyes opened. The bright amber glow startled me. "I'm sorry."

My chest tightened with pressure. "People are dead. People I loved. People I've never met, and for what?"

"If I could go back and change it all, I would. I'd never take that post guarding Lucian," he said quietly. "I would've gone AWOL if I'd known this was how it was going to play out, Alex."

My mouth opened as I shook my head. This Seth—this regretful, apologetic creature—was not the Seth I knew. "Your personality issues are starting to show."

His lips tipped up in a wry grin. "Look who's talking."

"You have no idea," I muttered, and then louder, "Where did all of this go wrong, Seth?"

"When I was born."

My shoulders tensed. "That's not true, Seth."

"Actually, it is. You were supposed to be the First, Alex. All the Apollyons came from Apollo. I was created for this—for what Ares wanted. It was the same with Solaris and the First. So, yes, it's true. Everything went wrong at that moment." He laughed, but it was like all my laughs after Ares. There was no warmth behind it. "Hell, things went wrong hundreds of years ago when Ares decided he wanted to rule the world."

"No," I said, swallowing. "You've always done what you wanted, Seth. And you didn't know about any of this when we met. You made these decisions. You went—"

"Have you ever tasted aether, Alex?" He flipped around so quickly that my heart thumped. Facing me, Seth gripped the bars until his knuckles bleached. "Not like how a daimon feeds, but to have so much aether in you that you could do *anything* you wanted and feel *everything* you never could before? Did you know that it feels like lightning in your blood? Have you experienced the taste of supreme and ultimate power? Have you?"

I shook my head slowly.

"Sure, Lucian promised me a lot of things, and so did Ares when I met him in the Catskills, but those promises were nothing in comparison to what it felt like once you had Awakened. It was like tapping into pure power." A feverish glint brightened his eyes as they latched onto mine. "After that, I didn't need their promises, because I knew—*I knew* I could get whatever I wanted, I had the power to do so. And that power..." He let go of the bars and rocked back. "There's nothing like it, Alex. I became addicted to it, and it blinded me to everything else. It was my weakness. It *is* my weakness."

I didn't say anything to that, because a part of me had always known the power wasn't his strength.

"You have no idea how hard it is to even be near you right now. The connection calls to me—your aether, everything." He shot forward, wrapping his fingers around the bars once more. "It's all I think about, and if I did manage to transfer your power to me, I don't think even Ares could control me. It would all be over."

I lowered my gaze. "You're better than that."

"I'm not, and you know that, so cut that shit out." He laughed that cold laugh again. "But *you* are."

"I'm not better than you."

"You are," he insisted quietly. He shifted, and I looked up. His forehead was resting against the bars. A haunted look crept into his face. "You are."

The back of my eyes burned. "In case you don't remember, I shot a man in the head earlier just because I wanted to."

"He deserved it."

I flinched. "I didn't feel a damn thing, Seth. Not an ounce of remorse or regret. Nothing. That's…that's not right."

"He deserved it, Alex. You have no idea what he was doing, what he abused with his power." Our gazes locked, and he took a deep breath. "But I never wanted to see you do something like that. Maybe I did before, but after what Ares did to you? After seeing what *I've* done to you? I don't want any of this. I want it to be over, and the only way we can finish this is if you take on the power of the First. You need to become the God Killer."

I gaped at him. There was no way he knew our plans.

"It's the only way to stop Ares, Alex." His throat worked as he swallowed heavily. "And I can't do it. If I take on that power, I can't promise what I'd do. It has to be you, and I know it can be done. You have to—"

"I know," I said, cutting him off as I scooted forward. "I know how to do it, Seth, but…"

His lips parted. "But you can't do it until it's damn close to time—until we are face-to-face with that son of a bitch, because the longer the power is in you, the crazier you get. Trust me."

"I'm already crazy," I whispered.

"What?"

I repeated myself, and I don't know what made me admit what I said next. Maybe because, in a way, Seth and I were the same person whether I trusted him or not. "I'm not the right person to be doing any of this. There's *something* wrong with me. Ever since I fought Ares, I haven't been right. I don't feel things the way I used to. I don't feel anything half of the time. I froze in a fight, and I mean really froze. I thought I saw Ares earlier and pulled a gun on Aiden."

His brows rose. "What's wrong with the last part?" My shoulders slumped. "Hey, I'm kidding. And I'm also curious why you'd do that. The sun rises and sets out of Aiden's ass, according to you."

Nice imagery. "I thought…I thought he was Ares."

"Like you saw Ares in place of him?"

I nodded numbly. "I don't know if I can do any of this, and then there's also this chance I could be…" I trailed off before I said too much and totally let my guard down.

"You could be what?" he asked. When I didn't answer, he turned sideways and settled down next to the bars. *What, Alex?*

Having him switch to talking that way was always unnerving. *I don't know. I think…Aiden thinks I'm…* I shook my head. *It doesn't matter. It doesn't change anything.*

Seth stared at me so long I started to worry that he could read my thoughts. Then his eyes widened slightly. *Are you…?* A strangled sound came from his throat. "I can't even think it. Are you pregnant?" Unable to confirm or deny, I said nothing, and that must've been answer enough because Seth swore under his breath. Squeezing my eyes shut, I dropped my head into my hands. My fingers curled into my hair, and the thin, raised scars on my face felt rough against my palms.

Alex? His voice was a thready whisper, and then out loud, he said, "I'm sorry, Alex, for everything I had a part in."

I shook my head without lifting it or removing my hands. I was unsure of why he'd apologize after that. It wasn't like he had anything to do with my potential baby making shenanigans with Aiden. That was all us.

We sat like that for a few minutes, neither of us speaking. I searched inside of me for…for something more than a twinge of sadness, an emotion beyond anger and confusion, anything more substantial than vast emptiness.

There was nothing.

Seth's sigh shuttled through my thoughts. "I saw your father, Alex."

CHAPTER NINE

I didn't think I heard Seth right at first.

Slowly, I lifted my head and locked my gaze with his. "What?"

"I saw your father when I was at the Catskills," he repeated quietly. "Not before you Awakened. I didn't see him when I was there at that time, but when we arrived about a month ago, he was there—is still there."

My mouth worked, but there was no sound. I scooted forward, coming closer to Seth than I probably should have. I drew in a breath, but it got stuck. "Did you… How is he?"

"I didn't talk with him, but he's there with the other servants. The Elixir isn't working, and he seems to be keeping them safe. He can't leave. None of them can with Ares there." He paused, and my heart dropped. "He appears to be okay, but Ares knows who he is, Alex."

I stared at him as those words sunk in. "But he's okay for now?"

For now. Seth reaffirmed silently.

Closing my eyes, I squirmed under the sudden pressure in my throat. *And Ares knows he's my father?*

"Yes."

"Does he have any plans to use him against me?" I asked, already knowing and fearing the answer.

"I would like to give you the answer that would make it better." There was a pause, and then I felt his fingers graze my arm. Electricity passed from his skin to mine, and my head jerked up. I backed out of his reach, watching the marks of the Apollyon glide up his arm and onto his neck. Seth pulled his arm back through the bars. "He will use any means necessary, Alex. He can't get to you right now, but the moment he can, he will dangle your father in front of you."

I looked away, pressing my mouth closed until my jaw ached with the effort. I knew I wasn't feeling everything I should be considering how much danger my father was in. I let out a ragged breath. "It's not just me he's going to come at. It's you, too."

"I know." Seth laughed dryly, and my gaze fell back to him. "But what does he have to hold over my head other than you?"

And I got it then. Once Ares realized Seth was batting for the opposite side, he'd force Seth's hand by forcing mine, and he'd use my father and everyone I cared about to make that happen.

"Shit's bleak, isn't it?" Seth said.

I huffed. "You have no idea."

"Then why are we doing this? Seriously? We could leave."

I pinned him with a look.

He laughed again, and this time, he sounded more like himself. "You could bring St. Delphi along."

"I'm sure he'll appreciate the invite." Truth was, the idea

of running away was tantalizing as hell. It wasn't like I hadn't considered it before, and we could hide for as long as we could, but it wasn't right. "There's enough of me left inside that knows I can't do that."

Seth cocked his head against the bars but said nothing.

"I especially can't after what Ares did, but it's more than that. There are so many innocent people who will end up enslaved by him or dead. I couldn't live with myself."

"I could." One side of my lips tipped up.

"Of course."

There was a stretch of silence, and then he said, "You're so different."

I didn't know what to say.

"It's not because you're crazy, but I know what you went through."

The muscles along my back tensed. "I wanted to die." There. I said it out loud, and it sounded just as horrible as when I thought it.

Seth lowered his gaze. "I know."

"Part of me wishes—"

"Don't say it." Seth stood quickly and backed away from the bars. A niggle of shame rose like a weed, and he looked away. "I know you're not going to let me out. It's probably better if you don't until we have a plan that we can act on immediately. It will make everyone else feel better."

"Would it make you feel better?" I pushed to my feet.

Seth backed farther into the shadows of his cell. "It should make *you* feel better." I was pretty sure I belonged in a cell too, like the one Seth was in.

"You don't," Seth said. I must've thought that at him. "You're not crazy, Angel."

"Don't call me that."

Seth didn't respond. The conversation was obviously over. I lingered for another moment, unsure if there was anything else to say at this point. I ended up not saying anything as I turned around and headed toward the titanium door I'd left cracked open.

One thing I knew for certain: Seth wasn't going to trick us. And if he came after me, it would be like a daimon going for aether and for no other reason. It didn't mean he was safe, but it was better than him working with Ares.

Opening the door, I spied a lithe form leaning against the wall. It wasn't Solos. Crap.

I closed the door behind me, took a deep breath, and faced Aiden. Locks of dark hair fell over his forehead in uncontrollable waves. His hair was starting to curl like Deacon's, and I favored that wilder look. Right now the edges of that hair brushed equally dark eyebrows—eyebrows that were currently slammed down. His lips were in a taut, tight line, and his eyes were a gunmetal gray. He was not a happy camper.

"Hi?" I said pathetically.

The muscles in his folded arms rippled under the black shirt he wore. He was so still he was almost a part of the wall. "You left in the middle of the night."

I shifted my weight from one foot to the other. "I did."

"Without saying a damn thing," he added in voice that was too calm. I knew him well enough to know how misleading that was. I was entering the danger zone. "Especially after what happened between us? Did you stop and consider what I would think when I woke up and found you gone?"

He had a point. "I'm sorry, but I'm okay."

"Obviously, you're *not* okay."

I opened my mouth, thinking he was referencing the

whole gun thing, but then I realized something else. Knots formed in my stomach. "How much did you hear?"

Aiden unfolded his arms. "Enough."

My brain winced. Didn't sound possible, but it was. "Aiden—"

"Hearing you say that you loved him was…well, there aren't many words for that."

Heat rushed my face. "I said not in the same way I feel for you."

"Wait." He held up his hand, silencing me. "For days I've been trying to get you to talk to me about everything. I figured you weren't ready, so I haven't pushed it, but then you leave me in the middle of the night to go talk to *him*."

Uh. Oh.

"And then you tell *him* what's going on in your head when you've barely told me anything?"

Backed into the corner, I reacted the only way I knew how—the only way the old Alex, the Alex before Ares, would've reacted. "Maybe you shouldn't have been eavesdropping." The moment those words left my mouth, I wanted to drop-kick myself in the face, because Aiden had a right to be pissed. "It's rude," I finished weakly.

"Are you serious?" Aiden pushed off the wall, and his eyes flashed quicksilver. Double uh-ohs. "You *went* to him."

Whoa. Wait a second. "It's not like that. I didn't go, *go* to him."

"It's not like that?" Aiden stopped directly in front of me. He lowered his chin, and his eyes flashed with anger. "You told him how you were feeling—what you haven't been feeling—"

"I've told you that!" My hands clenched into fists as my own anger surfaced like an old friend.

Yes. I grabbed onto that anger. At least it meant I was feeling something.

"You told him you wanted to die." His voice broke on the last word, and the quick burst of anger inside me vanished. Pain poured into his expression, paling his face. "And I know you were about to say that part of you still wishes you had died that day."

I took a step back, wanting to deny that, but words left me and the shame came again, stronger this time. I wrapped my arms around my waist, trying to stop it from spreading. Aiden was the last person I'd wanted to know how weak I'd been—how weak I still was.

"It kills me to know you think that." A muscle ticked in his jaw as his gaze locked with mine. "Why wouldn't you come to me with that?" He shook his head, his throat working. "Why would you go to him of all people? After everything he's done?"

"You don't understand." And he didn't. No matter what, Seth and I were the same person. That didn't mean he was all forgiven, but Seth knew what I'd been through without me telling him, and I never wanted to share that with Aiden. I knew I needed to tell him that, but the words wouldn't come out.

Aiden drew in a shallow breath. "You told him you thought you were pregnant." He looked like I had stabbed him in the chest with a Covenant dagger. "How could you even trust him with something like that? What if he's playing us? What if he takes that knowledge back to Ares?"

"He's not playing us."

His eyes widened as his stance shifted. "How can you be so sure, Alex? We all saw what Seth was like way before you did, and none of us had a connection with him. He has control over—"

"He doesn't have any control over me! I know he's not playing us. I *know*."

"Maybe you're right," he said, the heat dying in his eyes. "But that's not a risk I'm willing to take, and you didn't stop to take that into consideration. You..." He stopped and looked away, thrusting his hand through his hair. "You didn't take how I would feel into consideration."

"I...I'm sorry. It's just..." I shook my head helplessly.

He then did something I honestly couldn't remember him ever doing to me before. Aiden walked away from me.

I went back to the room I was sharing with Aiden, but he wasn't there, and by the time I'd drifted off to sleep waiting for him, he hadn't returned. And when I woke up, there was no sign of him, but he had made an appearance at some point while I'd slept.

The quilt that had been pushed down to the edge of the bed had been spread over me.

I knew that wasn't a white flag, and Aiden had every reason to be upset with me. I wished I had explained why I told Seth what I had. Not that I really believed Aiden would've been a hundred percent understanding, but it would've been better than apologizing or saying nothing.

Or telling him not to eavesdrop.

I pulled myself out of bed and took a quick shower. My empty stomach growled as I pulled on a pair of jeans and a shirt that belonged to Aiden. It swallowed me, but it smelled like him. Before I left the room, I scrubbed my hands down my face.

I would find Aiden, and somehow I would make this up to him.

Going to Seth had been wrong when Aiden had been with the one person who had always been and always would be there for me. My intentions hadn't been malicious or shady, but they still stung like a hundred bees. The only good thing to come from it was that I knew Seth wasn't playing us.

Convincing everyone else would require nothing short of a miracle.

The first place I checked for Aiden was the common area in the dorm. He wasn't there, but Luke was sitting at one of the tables along with Deacon and Olivia.

And there was a mammoth plate of bacon and sausage links in front of them.

Lured by the wonderful, greasy scent, I drifted over to their table, my mouth watering at the sight.

Bacon made everything better.

"Want some?" Deacon offered, knocking a mess of blond curls out of his face. "Because you look like you're about to start eating our faces if we don't give you some."

Olivia's nose wrinkled. "Ew."

I sat beside Aiden's brother and helped myself to a heap of the crispy goodness. "Thank you." I was munching away on my fourth slice when I felt eyes on me. Glancing up, my gaze met Luke's. His cheeks were red, as if he'd been kissed by the sun. "What?" I asked around a mouthful of bacon.

"I don't know how he did it—Seth." He sat back in his chair, rubbing his hand along his jaw. "I remember being out by the cars and seeing a few Sentinels I didn't recognize, and then the next thing I know, I'm standing inside the gate and there you two were."

"Compulsion," Deacon said, turning to me. "I've been telling him that all morning."

"He has," Olivia threw in.

Luke frowned. "I know it was a compulsion, but damn, I never felt something like that before."

"I have." Olivia looked at me pointedly, and my appetite vanished at the reminder. "You weren't responsible, Luke." She speared a link with her fork. "And now we have another crazed Apollyon—no offense, Alex—locked in a cell."

"None taken," I muttered, and then sighed. "It really isn't your fault, Luke. Deacon could do a compulsion, but one from an Apollyon packs a punch."

Luke didn't look relieved by that, but he grabbed a handful of bacon, so I figured if he was eating, he wasn't too traumatized.

"So, what are we doing with Seth?" Deacon asked after a few moments.

A shudder coursed through Olivia. The girl had never been a fan of Seth, and I remembered what Aiden had said last night. Everyone had seen what Seth was really like, but not me. Well, and not Caleb, because Caleb had been a major fanboy when it came to Seth.

Oddly, there was no slicing pain when I thought about Caleb.

"We aren't going to do anything right now," I said finally. Everyone at the table stared at me. My gaze lowered to the half-eaten plate of bacon. "Seth isn't working with Ares anymore. I'm not saying we should welcome him with open arms or invite him in for breakfast, but he's not our big enemy right now."

"What?" Olivia's voice was an octave higher. "How can anyone be sure of that?"

"That's a good question." Deacon slid me his unopened bottle of OJ. "Thirsty?"

I murmured my thanks and took a drink. "Well, for starters, that cell is only holding him because he's not trying to escape. If he wants out, he'll get out faster than any of us could, including me. Secondly, he doesn't want to become the God Killer anymore."

Luke rocked back on his chair, eyes widening. "Come again?"

Olivia stopped with another sausage link halfway to her mouth and gaped at me. Shifting in my seat, I felt heat spread across my cheeks, but I wasn't sure why. "He doesn't want to be the God Killer. He wants me to transfer the power from him."

"How did he find out that was our plan?" Deacon asked. He was suddenly serious, which was a rarity for him.

"He didn't. He suggested it without me saying anything. Seth's got… Well, like I said, he no longer wants anything to do with Ares and Lucian…" My brows pinched. "Lucian is no longer an issue."

"I'd say," Luke said under his breath and then louder, "Not to beat the dead-and-buried horse, but how can anyone, including you, trust anything that Seth says? I mean, if he changes his mind…"

We were all screwed.

I got that, but I couldn't really vocalize why I trusted Seth. His issues with his twisted addiction were his own business. No longer hungry or in the mood to convince them when I had Aiden and a whole slew of other people to talk to, I pushed up from the table. "I'll see you guys later."

I made it to the door before I realized Deacon was following me. He fell in step beside me as we walked out of the dorm. "You know they were just vocalizing their concerns, right?" he said, shoving his hands into his jeans. "They didn't mean to upset you."

"I know." I squinted against the bright glare of the sun. "And they didn't upset me."

"You sure about that?"

I was. Like always, I really wasn't feeling much of anything. We continued down the pathway in silence, passing a few pure-blood students. They stared.

"Aiden is in a mood. Like an 'if you breathe in my direction, I will nunchuck you into next week' mood," Deacon announced as we passed one of the training centers.

My stomach sank a little. "Nunchuck? I don't think he knows how to use them."

"My brother knows how to use every weapon known to man. Nunchucks are no exception."

A small grin tugged at my lips. "I'll take your word for it."

"So, are you gonna tell me what crawled up his ass, besides the fact a fleet of potentially enemy Sentinels is poised outside our gates and his archnemesis is chilling in a cell right under his nose?"

"Have you seen Aiden?" I asked instead.

He nodded. "He's in the dean's office with Marcus."

Veering toward the main Covenant building, I didn't look forward to going to the room where I'd last seen Ares.

"So, you're not going to talk to me about Aiden?"

"Are you going to follow me all the way to the dean's office?"

"Yep." Deacon shot me a quick grin.

"There's a lot of steps."

"I need my exercise."

I sighed. "Aiden's mad at me."

"I doubt that."

"Oh no, he's definitely mad at me." I tucked my hair back behind my ear and glanced at Deacon. He elbowed me gently in the arm, and the corner of my lips pulled up a little, but it quickly slipped away. "He's mad because I went to see Seth."

Deacon raised a brow. "He's mad over that?"

"Well, I left in the middle of the night, didn't tell him what I was doing, and there's other stuff, but…" I shook my head, not wanting to really get into it. "So, he's a little perturbed at the moment."

He didn't respond as we stepped into the main building and passed the Guards, waiting until we reached the stairwell. The cord inside of me strained since we were near Seth.

"Well, considering all the crap with Seth, I can get why Aiden isn't happy."

"I know." I rounded the second floor. "I'm not mad at him. He has every right to be upset."

Deacon hopped up the stairs, chock-full of energy. I hated him. "He'll get over it. My bro loves you, like *really* loves you. Like, he's *in* love with you, Alex."

I cast him a smile. "I know. I just hate that he's mad."

He looked at me, his eyes a brilliant silver. "I think that's the first time I've seen you really smile in a while." He spun around, opening the door to the top floor. "You doing okay?"

"No." I stepped through the doorway. "But I will be."

Deacon dropped his arm over my shoulder as we headed down the long hall. There were no Guards at the dean's door, because there was no dean to protect, not really. "We'll be okay," he said, squeezing me. "I'm all into positive thinking these days."

The door to the dean's office was cracked open, and without a second of hesitation, Deacon slid around me and opened the door, pulling me in behind him. "Hello!"

Marcus looked up from the desk, brows raised. Over his shoulder, Aiden straightened. His gaze went from me to Deacon, and then back to me. There was nothing to be gained from his expression, but the tips of my ears burned.

"What's going on?" Marcus asked.

Deacon dropped his arm and plopped into one of the leather chairs. "I have no idea. I just have nothing better to do."

Aiden folded his arms as he pinned his brother with a look.

Well aware that we probably weren't welcome at this moment for a multitude of reasons, I inched my way over to the other seat and sat.

Taking a quick inventory of the room, I was happy to see that, with the exception of the boarded-up window, everything had been repaired. The aquarium was gone and the desk had been replaced, as had the carpet. But I knew, if I pulled up the carpet, there'd be bloodstains underneath.

Some of them would be mine. "Alex."

My chin jerked up at the sound of Aiden's voice, and our gazes collided for a brief second. I'd come to talk to him, but I'd lost my courage the moment those thundercloud-colored eyes had focused on mine. "I don't have anything better to do, either."

"So, what are you two doing?" Deacon asked, batting impossibly long lashes.

Marcus leaned back in his chair, and his cool emerald gaze drifted over us. "We were discussing what to do with the Sentinels outside the gates. They haven't caused any problems yet. In fact, it appears they are now guarding the gates from outside."

My gaze flicked over to Aiden. He was staring at me in that intense, consuming way only he could pull off. It was the same way he used to watch me while I was in grappling class. I shifted in my chair. "Well, um, that's good news, right?"

"We hope." Marcus scratched his chin. "Aiden was telling me you talked to Seth last night?" Oh.

Oh crap.

I squirmed some more. "Yeah, I did."

"And you believe him?" he asked. "He's turned over a new leaf?"

"I'm not sure I'd say he's completely turned over a new—" A quick fissure of energy rolled down my spine, and the marks of the Apollyon raced across my skin. Electricity filled the room, and my senses flared. I knew the feeling. A god was here. I shot to my feet and started to turn.

Apollo stood behind me. "Hi."

I jerked back, smacking my hand over my pounding heart. "Good gods..."

One side of his lips curved up. He looked completely unrepentant, but he was rocking those baby blue eyes instead of the creepy god ones.

"Why must you keep doing that?" Aiden shook his head. "Gods."

The god shrugged. "How else should I do it? Ring a bell first?"

"That's actually a great idea," Aiden replied dryly. Deacon was on his feet, eyes wide, and he immediately started to backpedal out of the room. "I think I need...to, um, go find something else to do. Yeah."

Momentarily distracted from Apollo's sudden appearance, I narrowed my eyes at Aiden's brother. "What *is* it between you two?"

Deacon froze near the door.

The lopsided smile on Apollo's face spread. "Well, I would never kiss and tell."

My mouth dropped open as Deacon's face turned bloodred. Oh jeez. Suspicions confirmed.

Wow.

"What. The. Hell." Aiden stepped around the desk, glaring at Apollo. "Have you—?"

"Wait." Apollo held up a hand, his voice brooking no argument. He stared at me for a second. "Come here, Alex."

"Uh…" I didn't move, and I sure as hell didn't want to get between Aiden and Apollo. "No, thank you. Find another diversion tactic."

Apollo's head moved to the side. "Alex—"

I sensed Seth the second before I heard a shot outside, and then he barreled through the door, skidding to a halt a few feet behind Apollo. There were daggers in his hands.

Amber eyes dilated, Seth took a deep breath and let it out slowly as his gaze landed on Apollo. "Oh. It's you."

Well, now we knew Seth most definitely could get out of that cell when he wanted to. Out of the corner of my eye, I saw Aiden draw his gun. Deacon crept back to our side.

"Yeah, it's me." Apollo seemed to grow in height, which was a bit frightening considering he was already Godzilla-sized.

A handful of Guards appeared behind Seth, all of them out of breath and a bit banged up. Seth shrugged and turned, handing the pair of daggers back to an empty-handed Guard. Several of them began talking at once.

"He just got out. No warning," one Guard said. "We tried to stop him."

"Sorry," Seth said. "I thought it was another god, one more annoying than this one." My eyes widened.

Apollo smiled tightly. "Oh, you're so cute."

Seth smirked. "I am fabulously sexy, the last time I checked, but I'll go back to my cell now. Breakfast would be nice, by the way. I'm starving."

"This isn't a hotel," Aiden said, his gun leveled on Seth.

The Apollyon eyed the gun in Aiden's hand and then arched a brow. "You really like pointing that thing at me."

"You have no idea how much joy it gives me."

Seth got that look on his face—the one that said he was tossing out bait and knew Aiden was about to bite. "Don't let me forget. I do owe you for the knock over the head yesterday."

"You want that again?" Aiden smirked. "Keep talking."

"Oh, for the love of gods everywhere, stop it," I said. "This is ridiculous." Everyone turned to me. "Obviously, you don't think he's tricking us, Apollo, or you'd have blasted him with some god juice by now."

"Just because I haven't doesn't mean I won't."

Seth opened his mouth, but I jumped in before he could make the situation worse. "And it's rather pointless. He can get out if he wants to. So what's the point of making him go back into the cell?"

"I can knock him out again," Aiden suggested calmly. "He'll stay put for a while after that."

"You're really starting to annoy me." Seth turned to Aiden, his eyes glowing faintly. "You know what your problem is?" I rolled my eyes.

"Do tell." A muscle spasmed in Aiden's jaw.

"One word." Seth took a small step forward, a grin playing across his lips. "Jealousy."

I threw my hands up. "I give up. Not like we don't have real problems to deal with, but let's continue the boy-fight."

"Actually, as entertaining and long overdue as this boy-fight is, Alex has a point for once. Surprising, huh?" Apollo earned a death glare for that. "Aiden, put your gun away. Marcus, there's no need for daggers." Then he eyed Seth. "If you have nothing to hide, you aren't going to run from me."

Seth's spine straightened. "I would never run."

I had no idea what was going on, but Seth held himself still as Apollo took two long strides and placed his hand on the center of the First's chest. Surprise flickered across Seth's face, and then Apollo stepped back.

"He's telling the truth. He's no longer working with Ares, but that doesn't mean he's not still a threat," Apollo announced, and I had a feeling I knew what the god was referencing. And then he turned to me. "We need him here anyway. He's not the problem. You are."

"What?" He was staring at me. "Why me? I'm, like, the voice of reason for once."

"It's not that." Apollo faced me completely. "Guards, leave the room and close the door behind you."

They didn't even hesitate. They scattered like cockroaches. Unease formed little knots in my belly as I glanced at Aiden. He hadn't put the gun away and looked like he was going to aim it at Apollo next. Deacon had successfully pinned himself against the wall, out of everyone's path.

"Have you been marked?" Apollo asked, his nostrils flaring.

I shook my head, taking a step back. Sweat dotted my brow as I eyed the door. I wanted out of this room really badly. "I have no idea what you're talking about, but you're starting to freak me out."

Apollo's eyes flipped from blue to white—no pupils, no irises. Static crackled in the air. "Come here," he repeated.

I needed to get out of here. Blood pounded in my veins. Every ounce of my being screamed for me to leave. Apollo wasn't—

He shot forward—over the roaring in my head, I heard Aiden shout—and clamped his hand down on my shoulder. I staggered under the weight.

"Did he mark you?" Apollo demanded, his expression furious. "Did Ares mark you?" Those all-white eyes became my whole world.

"What is going on?" Marcus asked, but he sounded far away. Apollo reached around me and grabbed the hem of my shirt.

By the time I realized what he was doing, it was too late. He yanked up the shirt, exposing my back. Aiden exploded, yelling at the god as I tried to twist away.

"There it is." Apollo's hand landed on the oddly shaped scar, and my entire body jerked as if I'd been shocked. "Phobos! Deimos! Show yourselves!"

Seth cursed.

I started to think Apollo might've lost his damn mind, but then, without any warning, there was a deep wrenching inside me. I broke the god's hold and stumbled back a step. A tremor worked its way through my body, rippling through every muscle. The room tilted.

"Oh, gods," I whispered, doubling over and clutching my stomach.

"Alex?" shouted Aiden.

"Don't touch her!" Apollo got in between us, holding Aiden back with nothing more than a raised hand. It was like an invisible shield appeared between us. "Deimos! Phobos! Σε διατάζω να σου αφήσει αυτό το πλήθος!"

The skin…oh gods…the skin under my hands *moved*, pushing out against my shirt and my palms, and formed…*fingers*. Pressure expanded my stomach, and I dropped to my knees. Something slithered through my chest, into my throat. I couldn't breathe. Aiden's voice sounded farther and farther away as a sensation like icy, sticky fingers crawled under my scalp. It slipped down to the base of my skull, joining the mass in my throat.

Tears streamed from the corners of my eyes as I threw my head back. I opened my mouth to scream, but thick, white smoke poured out of me, steaming to the ceiling. Through the haze of tears, I saw the smoke spread and then drop into two separate pillars. There was a final tugging motion deep in my chest, as if something was digging in and not wanting to let go, and then it broke. The last of the smoke slipped out of me.

I fell forward, catching myself with my hands. Breathing raggedly, and with trembling arms, I lifted my head.

"Holy crap," someone whispered.

The pillars of white smoke spun like mini-tornados, taking shape with each dizzying pass. Two sets of legs. Two sets of arms.

An ear-piercing cry reverberated through the room. A burst of wind rattled the chairs and the desk, and then there was nothing.

Silence.

Two gods stood in the room, their forms translucent, but there was enough mass to them to make out their identical features. They weren't as tall as Apollo, but I had a feeling they weren't fully formed.

One of them drifted toward me, too quick for me to react. Through his eerily handsome face, I could see Seth's legs coming forward. "You're prettier on the inside..." the god said, his voice slick like a snake.

"Than you are on the outside," the other said.

The first one gave a mocking smile. "Then again, you're not..."

"All there, are you? It's nothing but rot," the twin finished, chuckling. It sounded like ice falling.

"What a shame," the first spoke again.

The second floated closer, his wispy lower body dissipating. "And who's really to blame?"

"In the end?"

"When there's nothing left to defend?"

I shrank back, horrified. They were like the twisted Oompa-Loompas of the Olympian world. More and more, their forms faded out, but their words were clear.

"You're all destined to die. Taste the fear…"

Strong arms encircled me from behind, pulling me back from the gods and against a hard chest.

Aiden turned, using his body to shield mine, but it didn't stop me from hearing their final words. "It will all be over by the end of this year…"

A loud sigh swept through the room as the smoke dispelled. The twins were gone. "Well," Apollo drew the word out. "That made absolutely no sense."

Muscles weak, I slumped over and would've face-planted on the carpet if Aiden hadn't caught me. He gripped my arms, but my skin felt too sensitive, too raw as he gently lowered me to the carpet. I crawled away, dragging in deep breaths.

"What…what was that?" Deacon asked, his voice hoarse.

Shaking, I sat back and lifted my head. There was a balloon expanding in my stomach, moving up my chest.

Apollo stood in the middle of the room with his hands on his hips. "*That* was Phobos and Deimos. The Gods of Fear, Dread, Panic, and Sheer Terror. They are Ares's sons. When you fought him, he marked you, giving them access to your psyche. I knew something was off about you while you were in Olympus, as did Artemis when she was here, but I didn't see it until now."

I blinked slowly. "What?"

"Phobos and Deimos have been riding you, feeding off

your emotions, and choosing and amplifying which ones you feel."

Seth paled as he took a step back. His eyes met mine. "I didn't know." He raised his hands. "I had no idea."

"That's what Artemis meant by something being inside of her?" Aiden was kneeling beside me. Horror whipped through his voice. "They were *inside* her?"

"Yes." The white light dimmed in Apollo's eyes and blue irises appeared.

"I thought...I thought I was going bananas. I thought I was pregnant. I didn't think..." I was too shocked, too *everything* to care about what I had just admitted to everyone in the room, to even acknowledge Aiden's sharp inhale or how broken it sounded, or the way Seth turned his back, like he couldn't bear to look at me. "They were inside me this whole time?"

"Since you fought Ares," Apollo confirmed. "I'm sorry. If I could've come sooner, I would've known."

Staring at the god, I had a hard time accepting what he said. I got it. I believed it, but to think another god—*gods*—were inside my head and my body, tinkering around, messing with me and being with me the whole time floored me. A floodgate broke, and the balloon in my chest burst. Rage flooded me, burning like lava through my veins. It tasted like blood and acid.

The room tinted amber.

Seth whirled around. "Uh, guys..."

The hair lifted off my shoulders and neck. Aiden called my name, but I was beyond hearing. I was beyond listening.

I lost my shit, right then and there.

CHAPTER TEN

I don't remember leaving the dean's office, but I must have, and I assume no one tried to stop me. I needed to be alone. I needed space.

I made it to a room down the hall.

I stood inside, the door swinging shut behind me, my chest rising and falling rapidly. I was feeling too much—anger, hurt, loss, hate, love, and everything else that had been muted while Ares's sons had been camped out *inside my body*. All the emotions at once were a poison in my blood. The lid on the bottle inside me had been completely unscrewed. Emotions broke the surface in a rush, and it felt like I had been drowning this whole time.

A burst of power left me.

The heavy oak desk in the corner, as well as a line of chairs and small tables, lifted into the air. They rose to the ceiling. My fingers curled in, nails digging into my palms. Wood creaked and groaned, then splintered. The furniture shattered like dry, brittle bones.

A volcano erupted inside me.

I opened my mouth and screamed. I didn't recognize the sound. Windows cracked. Shards of glass fell and stopped before they hit the floor.

It wasn't enough—the destruction wasn't enough. It could never be enough. Every cell inside me had been violated on a level I couldn't begin to comprehend.

The room shook and the building shuddered as I took a step forward. My feet lifted off the floor. Below me, the tile warped and peeled up, breaking apart in large, uneven sections that rose into the air. Another shock wave of akasha rolled out from me. Blue light pulsed, incinerating the flooring.

In a flash, I felt the rage and shame of being so broken by Ares.

I hadn't mourned all those who'd died at the hands of Ares until that moment.

I hadn't felt the loving embrace of my mother's arms or the loss of her all over again until that very second.

I felt the damage that'd been done to my body and head all over again.

I tasted the bite of fear and the tang of fury when I remembered waking up and seeing the condition of Aiden's hands, and again when I remembered seeing Marcus's mangled face.

I felt the horror of pulling the trigger and killing Lucian. I felt it all.

I felt *alive*, as if I was finally *awake*, and it was too much. Another scream tore through me, and the walls trembled.

The door opened behind me, and I slowly turned around, breathing through my nose. Seth stood there. My feet touched the floor.

"You need to try to calm down," he said. "Or you're going to bring this whole building down."

Calm down? Oh, shit was about to get real up in here.

I flew toward him, my arm snaking back. My fist cracked against his jaw, snapping his head back. Seth stumbled a step and bent over, clutching his face. The burst of pain flaring across my knuckles felt damn good.

"*Gods*," he grunted.

Jerking my leg up, I slammed my knee into Seth's stomach. A harsh expletive exploded from his mouth as I grabbed fistfuls of his shirt and shoved him backward. He caught himself against the wall with one hand.

"Okay." He spat out a mouthful of blood. "I'll admit I deserved that."

The stupid cord in me didn't understand the violence, but it liked that I was touching him. For that reason alone, I dropped down low and spun. I took his legs out from underneath him. Seth folded like a paper sack, hitting the destroyed floor on his side.

I vaulted to my feet and then dropped into a crouch.

Seth was back up in record time, his golden brows slammed down. "Okay. You want to work out your aggression. I'm all for that, *Angel*."

"Don't." I dipped under his arm and sprang up behind him. "Call." I slammed my hands down on his shoulders and brought my knee up. "Me. That!"

Seth twisted away before I could say hello to his spine. He faced me, pushing the longer strands of hair out of his gleaming eyes. "Come on. Bring it, Angel."

The sound that came from me would've sent most people scurrying for the hills.

He lifted his hand and gave the universal "come get some" sign. "Work it out of your system. You can't kill me."

I wasn't sure if my anger was directed at him or if he just made for a very convenient punching bag, but I launched myself at him. I hit him in the midsection, knocking him backward. We crashed into what was left of the desk and toppled over it. In a rather impressive feat, Seth shifted and hit the floor under me, taking the brunt of the fall. I was on top of him, straddling him. My arms rose up and I brought them down on his chest, over and over. I hit him, and I *kept* hitting him. His face blurred through the sudden wetness in my eyes. What the hell? The dampness rose and spilled over. My hands ached, but I couldn't stop. Tears streamed down my face and the whole time…the whole time Seth let me hit him. He didn't raise a hand. He didn't stop me.

My body shook and my arms ached. The sobs came from deep within me, from that dark and rotted-out place that had cropped up when Ares shattered my bones. My fists landed against Seth's chest once more, weaker this time, and I couldn't lift them. I hunched over, my chin dropping to my chest, and I cried so many tears I was sure I was going to drown the whole world with them. "Stop." Seth gripped my arms. "Come on, Angel, stop."

I wished I could, because crying on top of Seth wasn't my ideal way of licking my wounds in private. It was a whole lot of pathetic and awkward, but it was like the seal that kept me from crying had been broken. There was no turning back now.

Seth made a sound, and then he rolled. A second later I was lying on my side. For several long minutes, we were stretched out on the floor like two idiots, his arms like a vise, restraining me from doing any more damage to him or the poor, unsuspecting room. It took more time than usual for the tears to finally ease off, and for me to calm down enough to speak.

"Why you?" I asked, my voice thick and gross-sounding.

Seth sat up slowly, pulling me into his lap, my back against his front. "And why not Aiden?" I didn't answer because it was obvious.

"You would've killed anyone else who came into this room."

My head hung limply. "That wouldn't have stopped him."

"I had to tie him up and stash him in a closet." When I stiffened, he tightened his arms and laughed. "I'm just kidding. I didn't do anything other than use my deadliest weapon—logic. Apollo may've had to restrain him a bit, but he's right outside this room waiting."

"Logic?" I laughed, and although the sound and feel of it didn't hurt, it sounded strange to me. "You never used that before."

"I know." He was quiet for a long moment. "But I'm very familiar with this kind of rage, Alex, and I know what you felt. And you haven't really dealt with everything until now. Aiden thinks he knows how you feel, and maybe he has an idea, but I *know* what you felt and I *know* what you went through."

I was still ashamed that anyone had been privy to those horrible, wretched moments when I'd prayed for death and wanted it more than I'd ever wanted anything. It was so weak, and I had been so broken, flayed open to the core.

Seth rested his head on mine and sighed. "I wasn't lying. I *never* wanted something like that to happen. Out of everything I have done and caused to happen…it's the one thing I can never ask forgiveness for."

And I wasn't sure I could ever truly forgive him. I knew he hadn't done this to me, but he'd played a significant part in all of it. But I was too tired and just…too done with everything to hold onto the anger anymore, because it was doing what Ares and his sons wanted. It was chipping away at me, killing me.

I relaxed and closed my eyes, concentrating on the steady rise and fall of Seth's chest. A little part of me still felt lost, and I wasn't sure when I'd feel whole again or if I ever really would, but I knew what was happening right now. It was that connection between us and the calming effect it had.

Seth had done this before. He'd used it to calm me down when I'd had nightmares, and he'd used it to connect and control me, but now, when I was at my most vulnerable, he didn't twist the connection back on me. He used it to help me.

Some time passed before I was in any condition to stand and face things. My legs and arms felt strangely weak. I glanced over my shoulder at Seth and cringed. A deep crimson stain was already spreading across his jaw. "Sorry about your...face."

Our eyes met, and an uneven grin appeared on his face. "No, you're not."

"You're right."

Seth stepped forward, and I eyed him wryly. "You know you can take a time out, right? Take the rest of the day to just, I don't know, deal with it all. Get some rest."

I was exhausted in the way one felt only after going through an emotional upheaval. The idea of laying my little head down on a soft pillow was more appealing than eating cheese fries loaded with bacon. "I'm sure Apollo has a reason for showing up other than yanking those freaks out of me."

"He can wait." Concern flickered in Seth's eyes, and it was odd seeing that. As long as I'd known Seth, it was rare to see him genuinely care about someone other than himself. Then again, I wasn't giving him credit. I'd changed. He'd changed.

"No. I'm fine." I turned to the door. "We don't have time for me to take a nap."

"We have time." Seth followed me. "Not like tomorrow is going to be any different than today."

Who really knew if that was true? Denying the urge to agree and go find the nearest bed, I opened the door. It was slightly off its hinges, so it scraped the floor and opened only halfway. I sighed as I squeezed through. I wasn't surprised when I saw Aiden and Marcus leaning against the opposite wall. Both seemed to relax a little when they saw me standing and obviously not looking like I'd stuck my hand in an electric socket.

Though I did come to an abrupt halt when my gaze centered on Aiden again. It was like seeing him for the first time—the broad cheekbones; the full, expressive lips; his dark, unruly hair; and those brilliant smoky-gray eyes. A veil had lifted from my vision, and I couldn't—didn't want to look away. How much had Ares's sons affected? Everything, it seemed.

Marcus's gaze shifted over my shoulder, and his brows rose. A small grin tipped up the corner of Aiden's lips. No doubt he was happy to see that I was unscathed while, on the other hand, Seth looked like he'd run into a wall.

My uncle recovered first, stepping forward. "Are you okay, Alexandria?"

"Other than the fact I just spewed out two gods like a drunk college chick? I'm feeling *fabulous*."

Relief shuttled across his face. He clapped a hand on my shoulder. "There's my niece."

I cracked a grin at that while I kept an eye on the two guys. Aiden and Seth were eyeballing one another like they were about to start boy-fight, round two.

Marcus squeezed my shoulder and then dropped his hand.

For him, that was a whole exercise in bonding, and I was okay with that. I turned, catching Seth's attention. My eyes narrowed and his rolled. Raising his hands in surrender, he pivoted around and headed into the dean's office. Marcus was right behind him. Before I entered the room, Aiden caught my arm and stopped me. We were alone in the hall.

"Alex," he said, his voice low and rough.

Turning to him, I looked up and met his gaze. My mouth opened, but a sudden knot clogged my throat. I threw myself forward, pressing my forehead against his chest and breathing him in. He shuddered, and then he wrapped his strong arms around me. He dropped his head, pressing his cheek to the top of my head as he held me in a tight, heart-melting embrace. I clung to him like a deranged baby monkey, soaking in his warmth and the absolute feel of him. There was *a lot* we needed to talk about, but this hug? Gods, I needed this hug.

I needed this hug from Aiden. "Shit, Alex..."

Squeezing my eyes shut, I let out a choked laugh. "It's funny when you cuss."

"Only you would laugh at something like that," he said, and I heard the relieved amusement in his voice. Fingertips appeared under my chin, and Aiden lifted my gaze to his moonlight-colored one. "You're with me now?"

I blinked back tears. "Yes. Yes, I am."

"Good." His thumb smoothed over my jaw as his intense gaze searched my face. "I'm happy to have you back."

Turning my cheek into his palm, I swallowed hard. "I'm sorry."

"I'm the one who should be apologizing, especially for last night. I was jealous, and that was stupid, I know, but I'm—"

"No." I shook my head slightly. "No, you were right to be

upset, but that's not what I'm talking about. That's not what I'm apologizing for."

His brows rose.

My chest ached. "I know...I know there was a part of you that was okay with the idea of us having a baby. I know there was a part of you that was excited in spite of everything else, and I'm sorry that's not what was going on. I'm sorry that it was *this* and not—"

"Stop." Aiden dropped his forehead to mine and slid his strong hands up to cup my cheeks. "You do not need to apologize. Ever. Do you understand me? None of this is your fault. And you haven't done anything wrong. What we thought? It doesn't matter."

"You have to be disappointed," I whispered, curling my fingers around his wrists.

"Never," he swore. "If anything, I'm upset this happened to you. I'm freaking pissed that it did, but, Alex, we have a lifetime ahead of us to have that conversation and feel that way again."

My breath caught. "You're perfect."

"And you know that's not true."

"It is."

A throat cleared behind us, and then Apollo said, "Seriously, you two? It's not like you're keeping a god waiting or anything."

Aiden drew back with a soft groan. "Sometimes I hate him." My lips curved up. "Sometimes."

"I heard that," Apollo said. "And I'm pretty sure there's someone else you hate more than me. I'll give you two clues. Starts with an S and ends with an H." There was an audible huff from inside the office.

I started to grin.

"Well, you got that right." Aiden's eyes were fixed on me. "You want to do this right now?"

I nodded, and then Aiden lowered his head once more, kissing me in a way that truly felt like the very first time. When he lifted his head, his eyes shone with everything he was feeling in that moment. I knew what he'd said moments before was the truth. He believed we had a lifetime to feel that odd little burgeoning of hope again, and I latched onto that.

Together, we turned and headed past Apollo. He followed us in and stood in the middle of the room. "Well, the gang's all here. Almost. We are missing a few, but this will do."

We were missing Solos, Luke, and Olivia, and it didn't feel right that they weren't here. And it felt really weird that Seth was here. He was leaning against the wall where the daggers had once hung. He arched a brow at me.

"Your mark should be gone, which means the twins won't be able to get back into you," Apollo said, and I resisted the urge to yank my shirt up and check right then. Then he turned to Seth. "And don't think you and me are okay. It's great you're no longer Ares's little bitch-boy, but you're still a punk ass."

Aiden snickered.

"And I hope your jaw really hurts," Apollo added.

Seth smirked. "Hey, if you want to go a few rounds again, Golden Boy, we can do it."

"This is an awesome start to our Army of Awesome meeting number two," Deacon murmured. The air around Apollo crackled, and I let out a loud sigh and propped myself against a chair.

"So, I'm assuming you had a reason for coming here besides helping me and arguing with Seth."

"That's right."

I waited, and when Apollo said nothing, I crossed my arms. "And that would be?"

"We need a plan," he replied.

"Wow." Seth folded his arms. "That's a unique concept."

"Seth," I hissed, shooting him a look.

"That's okay," Apollo replied, smiling at Seth in a wholly creepy "hide your kids" kind of way. "When you least expect it, I'm going to turn you into a pink flower that smells like cat pee."

I choked on my laugh. "Oh, my gods..."

Seth's eyes narrowed into thin, amber slits, but before he could volley back, a whole different conversation sprouted out of the depths of my very own personal hell.

"I'm sorry." Marcus was leaning against the desk, looking a bit green. "Am I the only one stuck on the fact that *these two* thought they might've been...that you could've been...that there might have been...?"

"That we could've made you a great-uncle," I supplied since he'd obviously run out of words.

His eyes narrowed, and heat spread across my cheeks. "Can we not talk about that right now?"

"I second that," Aiden muttered, shifting awkwardly.

"I disagree." Apollo's "hide your kids" smile was now spreading across his face. "This conversation is going to be epically entertaining."

"For you." Aiden cut him a dark look.

"Exactly," the god replied.

Marcus ignored that. "I don't know how many times I've told you two that you shouldn't be sharing a room." He turned to me. "I don't care how old you are or that you're an Apollyon, Alexandria. You're my niece; therefore, I am responsible for you. And you?" He spun on Aiden, whose eyes widened. "You know better."

“Oh my gods,” I moaned. I would rather have run naked through the quad than had this conversation both with my uncle and with an audience. Especially with *this* audience.

“Don’t ‘oh my gods’ me.” The color had returned to Marcus’s face. It was red. “Do I really need to have a conversation with you about responsible sexual activity?”

Seth looked like he wanted to shove a dagger in his eye.

“I think you do,” Apollo suggested.

“Oh! You’re one to talk!” I whirled on Apollo. “Seriously? If I was to Google ‘irresponsible sexual activity,’ it would be your picture staring back at me!”

Apollo made a face at me—actually *made a face* at me like he was ten years old or something.

Marcus was now staring at Aiden like he wanted to take his dagger and use it on Aiden in an area much lower than the eyeballs.

“Okay, can we move on to the important stuff?” I demanded, losing my patience. “If not, then this is wasting my time, and I’m going to bed. That just might include irresponsible sex, because I’ve had a really crappy day!”

Five sets of eyes settled on me. One set was particularly interested in what I had just said.

“What?” I rolled my eyes, scowling. “Get on with it.”

Apollo sent Seth one more scathing look, which I was sure wouldn’t be the last one directed at the First. “As I said, we need a plan, and although I have many talents…”

For some reason, I couldn’t help but look at Deacon. He flushed. “I am not a strategist, not like Ares.”

The look on Seth’s face said he was wondering why Apollo was here then, but before he could vocalize that opinion, another fissure of energy whipped through the air. The aether in my veins hummed, and the marks raced to the surface. Seth and I stiffened in anticipation.

A shimmery blue form appeared and then solidified beside Apollo. A second before, there had been nothing but a glittery waterfall, and now there was a tall brunette woman dressed in a tailored business suit. Her hair was pulled up in a tight bun, which did nothing to lessen the ethereal beauty of her face. In her slim, almost delicate-looking hands, she held a rolled parchment.

Gods were like opossums. You could go your whole life without seeing one, but once you found one of them, you found the whole freaky family.

Every pure in the room bowed, leaving Seth and me standing straight like two douches. We apparently were a little slow on the show of respect. The goddess didn't seem to notice or care.

"Athena, please meet the, uh…Army of Awesome." Apollo arched a brow. "Or whatever they are calling themselves."

The Goddess of Wisdom, Strategy, and a whole slew of other things inclined her head. "Nice title."

"Nice suit," I said, my gaze dipping to her pointy heels.

Her all-white eyes centered on me, and one side of her lips tipped up. "I picked it up at Saks along with this amazing leather satchel and these to-die-for shoes."

"Oh." I slid Aiden a glance. He studiously ignored me. "They're very nice, too."

She strode forward, placing the parchment on the desk. Marcus swallowed and stepped to the side, giving the goddess a wide berth. It was a map. A really crudely drawn map of trees, mountains that looked like upside-down Vs, and stick people. Apparently, drawing was not one of Athena's skills. "The plan, and I assume that has not changed," she paused, passing an arched look between Seth and me, "will require the God Killer to get close to Ares. Currently, he's camped out—"

"In the Catskills," Seth interrupted, and I thought of my father. He was *there*. Seth came forward, eyeing the map. "He's got around the same number of Sentinels that I have here with me, plus mortals. All of them are under compulsion."

"Ares's compulsion?" Marcus asked, and when Seth nodded, my uncle sighed. "There's no way to break a compulsion from a god, is there?"

"Not unless you take out the god, or so we assume," Apollo said. "Dionysus has confirmed that the mortal encampment is several miles out from the Catskills."

"We would have to get past them, and then get through the walls of the New York Covenant, which are guarded by Sentinels." Seth tapped his finger along what appeared to be an uneven brick wall, squinting. "But that's not all. Ares is heavily guarded."

"Guarded by what?" I asked.

"Daimons," Seth said, looking away. "And you know how he's controlling them."

My stomach roiled. I did. He was feeding them pures and probably halfs—dinner in exchange for loyalty. I remembered the days when the Council didn't believe daimons could reason. Now the daimons had most likely drained those Council members dry.

"And the automatons." Athena glanced at Apollo. "Hephaestus has completely lost control of them."

The god sighed. "Don't start."

Her eyes narrowed. "I warned all of you that using them was a bad idea. We had no idea what god was responsible for this, and using a creature designed for war without such knowledge was a poor plan."

It was. The half-machine, half-bull, fire-breathing creatures had turned on us and were now under Ares's control.

"So, not only will your…" Her nose wrinkled. "Your Army of Awesome have to get past the mortals, they will have to face Sentinels, daimons, and automatons before even reaching Ares."

Aiden folded his arms. "That is, if he doesn't come after us the moment we set foot out of the University."

"He won't." Athena tapped her finger down on a square, which I assumed was the Covenant building. "He knows how heavily entrenched he is, and moving an army would make him vulnerable to attack. Before the First left him, he would've risked it. But not now that he knows the God Killer is coming for him. He will remain where he is and wait for you to come to him. He knows you will suffer losses in the process."

The truth weighed heavily. We *would* suffer losses.

"Getting past the mortals will not be hard," she continued. "The loss of their lives will be unfortunate, but we have to sacrifice the few to save the many. Then there are the Sentinels, daimons, and automatons, but it is fighting Ares that will take everything."

"We can't just zap him with a God Killer bolt and call it a day?" I asked.

Athena arched a brow. "It's not like he's going to stand still and allow you to do that, and we know what happened last time you faced off with him."

"Thanks for the reminder," I muttered.

"It is only to serve a much-needed point. None of you are trained to battle a god, let alone Ares. Even I can't prepare you, not effectively. He can and will outmaneuver and outplan you, and he knows that." Athena waved a hand over the map, and it disappeared. Neat trick. I was jealous.

"So are you saying that we cannot defeat him, not even with the God Killer?" Marcus asked, and the crinkled skin around his eyes appeared more noticeable.

"No." She faced us and hopped up on the desk, demurely crossing her legs. "War is partially strength, partially skill, and partially psychological. We have the strength in the Apollyons and the Sentinels, but we do not have the skill, and we do not have anything that will put Ares in a state of unease. Without the last two factors, we will not succeed."

I frowned. "Are you also the goddess of depressing facts?" Apollo snorted.

"I am just being realistic," she stated coolly. "But I do have an idea."

Here we go. A bit of excitement thrummed through me. An idea was better than everything else she'd been spouting, because right now, I didn't need Phobos and Deimos inside my head to believe we were embarking on a suicide mission.

"It is a risky idea, but we really have no other choice. If the God Killer fails, it will be an all out war, and we know what happened the last time the gods went to war," Athena said.

Aiden shifted his weight. "Hundreds of thousands died."

"And it will be millions this time." Apollo studied the goddess. "What is your idea?"

A small smile appeared. "We use Perses."

Apollo stiffened, and I didn't understand the reaction. "The demigod? Are we going to go slay Medusa or something?"

"No. Not Perseus. *Perses*."

I stared at her. "Okay. I'll admit, I slept or doodled through most of my classes. I have no idea who you're talking about."

"That is a lovely discovery." Marcus pierced me with his

Dean of Academics stare. I withered like a poor little flower left out in the sun without water.

"Perses is the God of Destruction and War," Apollo explained, eyes wide. "He was nearly indestructible and nearly unstoppable."

I shook my head as I glanced at Aiden, relieved to see he looked just as clueless as me. "Okay. Is there another god of war that I'm unaware of?"

"You guys populate like rabbits," Seth added, grinning slightly. "It's possible we haven't heard of him."

Deacon's lips twitched, but Athena's next words knocked the smile off his face and silenced the entire room.

"No," she said. "Perses is not an Olympian. He is the Titan God of Destruction."

CHAPTER ELEVEN

I gaped at the goddess in what must have been the most unattractive manner known to man.

"A Titan?" I squeaked out. "A mother-freaking Titan?"

Athena nodded. "A Titan."

"Whoa." Aiden ran his hand through his hair before clasping the back of his neck. He turned sideways, shaking his head. "Wasn't expecting that."

"I don't think anyone was expecting that." Apollo stepped toward Athena. "Let's break down this idea step-by-step. How would we be able to use Perses? The last time I checked, he was in Tartarus."

"He is still there." Athena tipped her chin up. "And as you know, he is not dead. He is only entombed."

"And how do you think we're going to release him?" Apollo demanded, brows slashed. "Zeus would never agree to this."

"I *am* Zeus's favorite child." Her smile beamed.

Apollo's blue eyes rolled. "That's something to be proud of?"

She tsked softly. "I can get him to agree to anything, and he's desperate, Apollo. You know that's true. The last thing he wants is a full-out war."

"The last thing he wants is to do anything. That lazy son of—"

"True." Athena raised her hands. "But I will get his backing."

"Okay. So if you get his backing, what about Hades? He will never agree to releasing Perses," Apollo argued.

"He will if Zeus demands it."

Apollo laughed deeply, and the sound shook the chairs. "Hades controls the Underworld. He will deny it just *because* Father demands it."

"I'm sure you can get Hades to understand and agree. That will be up to you." She tapped her manicured fingers on her bent knee. "And you know how Hades likes to make a deal."

Last time I'd seen Hades, he'd wanted to kill me. This idea was going downhill fast.

"All right, let's say we get Hades to agree to release Perses. How in the world would we be able to control him?" Apollo asked.

"Perses is just one Titan. He is powerful and a bit… wild, but Ares nearly died by his hands during the war, if you remember correctly. Perses can train the God Killer. He could train hundreds of our people to fight. We will have the skill, and we will have the psychological upper hand." She smiled again. "Besides, Perses will do anything to be free. Any of the Titans would. Put the fear of gods in him, or whatever it is the mortals say. Make him behave, and in return, Hades can give him better accommodations."

"Oh, this is rich." Apollo laughed.

"You're serious about releasing a Titan?" Seth blinked slowly, as if coming out of a daze. When Athena simply nodded, he turned to me. "Ares would never expect it."

There were honestly no words.

From what I remembered about the Titans, those who stood against Zeus had been imprisoned since they could not truly be killed. Titans were badass, like "they put the 'bad' in badass" kind of badass. The last time they were topside, it had been a bloodbath. No one, not even the Olympians, messed with the Titans. And now we were talking about unchaining one and working with him? And hoping for the best?

Oh, this had apocalypse written all over it. And people thought I made bad decisions?

But Seth was right, and so was Athena. Ares would never expect something as wild as this. Perses was the Titan God of War and Destruction. If anyone could prepare us for coming face-to-face with Ares again, it would be him and no one else.

"Okay," I said, letting out a deep breath. "Let's unleash a Titan on the unsuspecting world." The others agreed, and plans were made to meet with Hades. The atmosphere was much better, and that probably had to do with the absence of Phobos and Deimos and the fact that we had something, no matter how wild, to work with. Still, I couldn't help but think we might be making the whole situation worse.

I knew Seth wasn't being housed in the cell anymore, but I also knew he wasn't in this dorm. There were others, and he'd wisely chosen one that didn't house a decent number of people who wanted to commit an act of homicide when they were around him.

And it had put some much-needed distance between us.

The stupid cord in me wasn't happy about the separation, but it had ceased its incessant buzzing and humming. I liked to think that I was gaining some control over the obsessive need to be near Seth, and if both of us survived this, it was something we both needed to work on.

We *would* survive this.

I couldn't allow myself to think anything else. When Deimos and Phobos had been inside me, it was all I could think about. We would fail. I would die. Those I loved would die. Now that their influence was gone, I felt like myself again. Things weren't all rainbows and puppy tails. I could still lose people, and after I discovered there was a good chance the Olympians would take out my rosy-red behind after fighting Ares, there had been moments when I wanted to find a corner to rock in.

But I was a born fighter, and I would fight. That's who I was at the core.

Alone in my room, I stripped out of my clothes and kidnapped another one of Aiden's shirts to sleep in. The soft, well-worn cotton slipped over my head and ended at the thigh. I wasn't sure if he was truly okay with me hijacking his clothes, but he wasn't there and I simply liked his shirts.

Dragging myself to the bed, I tucked my legs under the covers and rolled onto my side, facing the door. The last I'd seen of Aiden, he'd left with Marcus to go over the newest developments with Solos and the crew. As exhausted as I was, I had bowed out of the third meeting with the Army of Awesome. There was just too much going on in my head to face everyone.

Lying there, waiting for Aiden to return, I told myself again that we were actually planning to release a Titan. Crazy pants right there. Obviously, I'd never met a Titan, and a part of me was excited by the prospect of coming face-to-face with such a legendary being.

A freaking Titan.

I gave a sleepy snort.

My eyelids grew heavier as the minutes ticked by. I didn't want to fall asleep, because there was so much I needed to talk with Aiden about, but I was sinking through the bed. After Deimos and Phobos had been yanked out of me, the emotional storm that had followed had been a cleansing of sorts, but it had also tuckered me out.

I realized then that I hadn't thanked Seth.

That was the last thing I remembered thinking before I felt something warm and slightly rough graze my cheek. Stirring restlessly, I forced my eyes open.

"Aiden," I whispered.

A slight smile appeared on his full lips. His hand stilled on my cheek. "I didn't mean to wake you up."

"It's okay. I didn't mean to fall asleep. I was waiting for you."

"You need to sleep, but I..." His thumb smoothed my cheek again. "I couldn't stop myself from touching you."

A wealth of warmth blossomed in my chest at those words, and then spread when I realized that Aiden was under the covers and he was shirtless. Maybe even pantsless. "I'm not complaining."

In the soft light from the nightstand, his eyes were a luminous silver. "How are you feeling?"

Wiggling closer, I bit back a sigh as his hand slid around the nape of my neck. "I feel...I feel good. I mean, hurling up those gods changed things. That was wild, right?"

His lashes swept his cheeks and then lifted. The intensity in his gaze was consuming. "It isn't something you see every day."

My lips tipped up at the corners. "It's a relief to know that a lot of what I was feeling wasn't coming from me."

"I have to agree." His knee rose under the covers, and soft flannel brushed my bare legs. Damn. He did have pants on. "Want to talk?"

What I really wanted to do was cross the scant distance between our mouths, but I did need to talk to him. There had been so much I'd held back while the gods had been squatting in my head, and there was so much Aiden needed to know, so I told him everything from how I'd felt when I fought Ares to what it was like the moment all those violent emotions rose to the surface.

When I was done, he smoothed his hand over my cheek. His hand had stayed on me the whole time. "Do you feel that way now—the way you felt with Ares?"

I met his gaze as I placed my hand against his warm chest. "I think there will still be moments when it…well, when it sucks, but I don't want to die. I'm glad I didn't." I laughed, a little embarrassed. "I don't feel that way anymore."

"Good." Aiden inched his head over and kissed me so softly, like he was being cautious, and then pulled back. He slipped his hand off my cheek, placing it over where mine rested against his chest. "It killed me, Alex, when I heard you admit that to Seth. All I wanted to do was go in there and hold you, figure out some way to make it better."

"I'm okay now." I turned my hand over and threaded my fingers through his. "But I'm still scared."

"That's normal."

"I know. And I know it's okay to be scared."

He squeezed my hand. "Damn. I should record that statement."

I laughed, and it was a real sound. It was good. "I never

thanked Seth, and I need to, Aiden. He helped me calm down. He didn't try to manipulate me. If it hadn't been for him, I would've brought that building down."

His eyes latched onto mine. "About Seth…"

Swallowing heavily, I prepared myself. "I can't blame the gods for that. I knew what I was doing when I went to see Seth. I should've woken you and told you where I was going. That was my fault."

"He was right," he said, as if he hadn't heard me.

I blinked. "What?"

"The little bastard was right." He let out a heavy sigh. "I was jealous when I found you with him. I was jealous afterward. I am *still* jealous."

"I—"

"I heard what you said," he stated quietly, not looking away. "I heard you say that you loved him."

My eyes widened and my stomach dropped as a horrible feeling opened up in my chest. How had I forgotten that he'd overheard me saying that, too? For a moment, I didn't know what to say. Awkward didn't even cover it. "I did say that, but it's not the same—"

"Same way you feel about me." His eyes shut briefly. "I know. I honestly know it's not, but hearing that…? I wanted to punch him. I still do for various reasons, but mostly because I know that there will always be a part of you that does love him. That you two will have this connection for the rest of our lives, and that's something I can never compete with."

An ache opened up in my chest, and I closed the distance between us, practically crawling onto him. "I'm sorry."

His brows rose as he rolled onto his back, wrapping an arm around my waist. "For what, Alex? *I* should say I'm sorry. I was a dick to you because of my stupid jealousy. You shouldn't have to apologize."

"But you shouldn't have to deal with a freaky Apollyon connection." I peered down at him. "What normal couples have to deal with that?"

"We deal with a lot of things normal couples don't deal with," he replied dryly.

"I know! That's why I'm sorry you have to deal with… with Seth and me on top of everything else. If it was me, and you were connected to someone, I'd probably stab her in the eyeball every time I saw her."

Aiden's lips quirked up lazily. "Really?"

"It's not funny." I smacked his chest lightly. "I would. I wouldn't be able to deal with it, so I totally get your jealousy. I just don't want you to feel that way, because I love you. I'm *in* love with you. Forever and ever, and all the corny things I can attach to that."

He chuckled deeply, and the sound brought a smile to my face. "I know you do. And I have to work on not hating him for this. I have to remember that there are other reasons to want to kill Seth."

I laughed, and he rewarded me with another tender kiss that curled my toes. It didn't go any further than that. He guided my head down to where his heart beat steadily in his chest. I wanted to take that kiss further, but the moment my cheek hit his skin, I found my head too heavy to lift.

Aiden told me how the rest of the group had taken the news about releasing Perses. He also had explained to them that Apollo had checked Seth out, and the First could be trusted…as far as anyone could really trust Seth. Then he explained to them about the evil god twins, and for that I was eternally grateful. That was the last thing I wanted to explain all over again.

It didn't take long for me to drift back to sleep as Aiden talked, not with the rise and fall of his chest luring me off or with his hand playing in my hair. I wasn't sure how comfortable it was for Aiden, considering I was sprawled half on top of him, but when I woke in the morning, neither of us had moved. I was still on my side, one leg thrown over his and my cheek on his chest.

Pleasant pressure built inside me. I wanted a million mornings of waking up like this. I was going to have those mornings. I stayed there for a little while, feeling and listening to Aiden breathe. My mind started to wander over so many things—Seth, my father, my friends, the state of things for half-bloods, the future if we defeated Ares, and what would happen if we failed. By the time I got tired of where my mind had gone, half his body had to be numb. I started to push off.

Aiden's other arm swung around with startling quickness, and his hand landed just above my knee. "Where do you think you're going?" he asked, voice gruff from sleep and from… from something else.

A flutter started in my stomach as I raised my head to look down at him. His dark waves were going in every direction. His eyes were heavy lidded, and his lashes were thick. The slight stubble on his jaw pushed me over the edge into dangerous territory. Only Aiden could look so sexy sleep-ruffled. "Nowhere?"

"Sounds about right." One hand curled around the edges of my hair while the other crept up my thigh, causing me to shiver. "How long have you been awake?"

"Not long." My gaze dropped to his mouth. Those lips were perfect.

He made a deep sound in his chest, and that flutter picked up in my stomach. "What time is it?"

"No clue." I couldn't tear my gaze away from his lips. "But I think we might've slept in."

"Maybe." The hand slipped up to my neck, and he guided my mouth to his. There was a quick flash of concern over brushing my teeth and kicking morning breath, but that worry went out the window the moment our lips touched.

The kiss was slow, lazy, and never-ending. It felt like forever since he'd kissed me like that when, in reality, it had really only been a handful of hours, but I lost myself in that kiss, in Aiden. And kissing him now was nothing like it had been those hours before. I felt the pressure, the intense sweetness, and the love behind every stroke of his tongue and sweep of his lips, to my very soul. The hand in my hair tightened while the other traveled north, up my thigh, and then over the curve of my hip.

Aiden's hand stilled and then swept back down, causing me to suck in a sharp breath. He pulled his mouth away from mine and opened his eyes. They were a pure, heated silver. "You're not wearing anything under this shirt, are you? Like, at all?"

I giggled. "I think you know the answer to that." He had to, especially considering where his hand drifted to in that moment. I wasn't giggling anymore. I was barely breathing.

He made that sound again, that absolutely sexy male sound that rumbled through him and then me. "You're killing me, agapi mou."

"I'm sure that's *not* what I'm doing to you."

Aiden moved lightning-fast. He rolled me onto my back and was above me, on me, pressing his leg between mine. His lips found mine like they'd been born to do so. This kiss was different. Hungry. Starving. My hands slid up the hard sides of his stomach and then onto his back. Those sculpted muscles flexed under my hands as the kiss deepened until my senses were spinning.

There was probably a lot to do today.

Some would also say there were a lot more important things we could be doing at this very moment.

I would argue against that point adamantly because there was nothing more important than this. Not when those wonderfully rough hands skimmed under the borrowed shirt. His hips rocked against mine, and a fire raced throughout my blood. I wrapped my fingers around the band of his pajama bottoms.

"Agapi mou, I've missed you." His lips moved across my jaw and trailed a heated, shivery path down my throat, and then back to my lips. "I need you."

My heart stuttered. "Yes."

Who knows what I was really saying yes to? Anything at that point. Karate chop a few daimons while I was naked? Sure. Do trig formulas for fun? Okay. As long as he kept kissing me, kept calling me agapi mou, and kept touching me, I'd say yes to a lot of things. Too bad we weren't doing this while I was still in school. I could've used his kisses as an amazing studying incentive.

His hand hooked around my hip, urging me to wrap my leg around his, and I stopped thinking.

If only I got these damn pants off—

A sudden pop and crackle preceded the overwhelming and very unwelcome presence of a god. Aiden's lips stilled against mine. My eyes popped up, latching onto his quicksilver ones. No way. I refused to believe it. No freaking way.

"Hades will be here in twenty minutes," Apollo announced from somewhere way too close to the bed. "Either speed this up or pick it up later, kids."

"Oh my gods," I whispered, horrified.

"Oh, and I hope you two are being *responsible*," Apollo added.

And then he was gone. There was a muffled, hoarse shout from a room nearby.

"Damn him," Aiden muttered, dropping his head onto my shoulder. He shuddered. "Damn him to the Underworld and back again."

My cheeks burned. "A bell—the first chance we get, we are buying him *a bell*."

CHAPTER TWELVE

A god popping in and out of your bedroom was, unsurprisingly, a major mood killer.

After Apollo vanished, neither of us was willing to risk him coming back with a ten-minute warning. Aiden had offered to speed up the get-ready-together process by sharing a shower.

From the bed, I raised my brows. "I don't think that would be a quick shower."

"You're right." He backed toward the bathroom door, his pajama bottoms hanging too low on his hips to be legal. "Can't blame me for trying."

He disappeared, and I flopped onto my back, groaning. I was going to ninja-kick Apollo in the face when I saw him.

Today, I didn't put jeans on. I wore my Sentinel uniform.

My hair was still damp when we headed to the dean's office. I don't know why we had to keep meeting in there. It wasn't so much because of what Ares had done in that room but because there were a lot of stairs to climb.

A lot.

The whole crew waited inside the office, and I knew Apollo was in there with Hades. I ran my hand over my arm, watching the marks glide seamlessly across my skin.

"Itchy?" Aiden asked.

I shrugged a shoulder. "The marks always go crazy when there are gods nearby."

As we walked toward the dean's office, he reached over, trailing his fingers along my arms. "Do they still react when I touch you?"

Heat crawled through my veins, and I nodded. The marks had followed the path of his touch. "Yeah, they still like you."

One side of his lips curled up, and a look of male pride crossed his face. I shook my head. Boys. We entered the office, and all the godly power in the room, plus Seth's presence, was a bit overwhelming at first. I clenched my hands into fists to keep myself from bouncing off the walls or monkey-climbing Seth.

The two gods stood a good head taller than everyone else. They were shoulder to shoulder, but they couldn't have been more opposite of one another. Where Apollo was all golden skin and sunlight, Hades was dark as night.

Aiden sent Seth a downright frightening glare as he strolled toward the people clustered around the two gods. At least he didn't punch Seth, so that was a start in the right direction.

I guessed.

Seth lingered in the back, leaning against the wall as he eyed the two gods with an edge of distrust. I took a deep breath and approached him. A new wariness crept into his expression. "What's up?" he asked.

"I didn't say thank you."

One golden brow rose. "For what?"

"For helping me out yesterday," I explained, turning so we stood side by side. "I didn't say thank you, so thank you."

"You've said 'thank you' three times now."

"Yeah." I leaned against the wall. "I can say it again, if you want."

Seth turned sideways, facing me. When he spoke, his voice was low and held a biting, hard edge to it. "I don't want you to say it at all."

I arched a brow, but before he could elaborate, Marcus cleared his throat, drawing my attention. Two gods stared at us.

I swallowed. Eerie. At least Apollo had normal eyes. Hades, on the other hand, looked like someone had forgotten to give him irises and pupils.

Seth pushed off and went to stand by the opposite wall, his back stiff and shoulders tensed. The gods tracked his movement like lions watching a gazelle. Then Hades turned to me.

The god's lips spread into a tight smile. "Nice to see you again, Love."

With the exception of wanting to kill me that one time, Hades was an exceptionally gorgeous man. And he had a British accent, which made him that much hotter. I had no idea why Hades had an accent, and I'd yet to hear another god with the same accent.

"No puppies this time?" I asked.

His eyes narrowed at the reminder. The last time we'd met, it had been in a convenience store in Middle of Nowhere, West Virginia, and I'd taken out a few of his prized three-headed hellhounds.

"No puppies. *Yet.*" Dressed in a sleeveless tunic, Hades's biceps flexed as he folded his arms. "So, it's true?" He swept the rest of the room with an arched look. Olivia shrank back, her normally caramel-colored skin pale. Hades's grin spread. "You all have a favor to ask of me?"

Marcus glanced at Apollo. "You haven't told him?"

"Oh, he has. I was hoping that someone in here had used their intelligence and changed their minds." Hades smirked. "Although, I see that is highly unlikely."

Luke elbowed Deacon, who kept his face perfectly blank.

"Does everyone in this room understand the danger of releasing Perses?" Hades asked, standing in the middle of our loose circle. His leather-clad legs were spread wide, thighs like tree trunks. The silver cuffs at his wrists glinted in the light. "I'm not talking about a slight risk of him killing someone we don't want dead. He will, mark my words. Perses is what you would call…"

"Unpredictable," Apollo threw out, grinning. "We are well aware of that, as is Zeus, and from what I hear, he has sanctioned Perses's release."

Athena *was* his favorite child.

"That means squat to me, and you know that. Zeus has no power over my realm. And before this conversation proceeds any further, I want everyone to fully grasp what they are agreeing to."

"We understand," Seth said, gaining the boss of the Underworld's attention.

"Do you?" Hades turned to him, head cocked to the side. "You've been around Ares. Let me ask you a question. What does Ares thrive on the most?"

"More than one thing—war and fear," Seth responded blithely, and I flinched. "But most of all, he loves winning."

"Correct, but Perses thrived on the bloodshed of battle. He used to bathe in the entrails of those he'd defeated."

Olivia turned green.

"Not only that, Perses fought to destroy—not to win. There's a big difference there." Hades paused, and it felt like cold wind had circled its way down my spine. "And what has happened since Ares decided to play in the mortal realm?"

Aiden shifted his weight, his jaw set in a tight, grim line. "There's been conflict—countries everywhere on the verge of war. His presence affects mortals. We know."

"And what do you think will happen if you add Perses to the mix?" Hades asked. "His influence is stronger than Ares's. Those countries on the verge may make war just because we've released him. Is that another risk you're willing to take?"

No one answered, because seriously, we could be exchanging one apocalyptic situation for another.

"We have to take that risk," I said finally, meeting the all-white eyes of Hades. "And we'll make sure he behaves." Hopefully.

"You think he'll behave because I'll release him into the Elysian Fields afterward? Do you have any idea what crimes Perses was responsible for?"

I could only imagine.

Apparently Hades didn't want me to use my imagination. "He created the term 'rape and pillage.' He wiped out entire generations and civilizations for the *fun* of it. He killed our brethren just to hear them scream and plead for their lives. He took our children and ripped them apart because he *could*. That is what you are releasing into the mortal realm. That is what you're asking me to give paradise to."

My heart rate kicked up. I got what Hades was saying. It was like allowing Hitler into Heaven or something, but I wondered if Hades had ever heard of the whole throwing stones and glass houses thing. "And how is that any different than what you guys have been responsible for throughout history?"

Hades took a step toward me, and over his shoulder I saw Aiden and Seth stiffen, but I didn't need them. I held my ground and lifted my chin. The god stopped a few feet in front of me.

Akasha, the fifth and final element, simmered in the pit of my stomach. The marks on my skin tingled in warning, but I refused to look away from his unflinching stare. "What? It's the truth. How is a Titan truly any worse than an Olympian running amok? Any worse than what Ares is already doing?"

A slow, almost-reluctant smile graced Hades's lips. "You want to know the difference?"

"Yes." Did he know how creepy his eyes were? Probably.

Hades leaned down, coming so close that we shared the same breathing space. "A God Killer can kill an Olympian. Not a Titan. And a Titan can kill an Apollyon."

My brows shot up. "Oh." Well, then…

"Yeah, 'oh.'" Hades wheeled around, eyeing Aiden, who had made it halfway across the room before Apollo had intercepted and blocked him. "So does everyone still want to hold a welcoming party for a bloodthirsty Titan that no one can kill if he decides to not play along?"

Unrest filled the room. Luke and Solos shifted their gazes, no doubt having second thoughts. Deacon looked like he had no idea how he'd ended up in this room, and Olivia was slowly shaking her head. Only Aiden, Marcus, and Seth looked resolute.

"You've stopped the Titans before," Aiden said, voice level and calm despite the rising tension. "And there were many more than one at that time."

"It took all of us to stop the Titans, one at a time. And if we manage to stop Ares, we will be down one," Hades responded. "So it wouldn't be easy."

Apollo squared his shoulders. "You offer him paradise. He will behave."

"You think?" Hades folded his arms again. "And I thought you weren't really down with this plan?"

"It's not the best thing, but it is all we have, and you know that's true, so stop posturing. What do you want in return for releasing Perses?"

Hades's jaw worked like he was crunching bone. "And for offering him paradise?"

The Sun God looked like he wanted to toss Hades *at* the sun. "Yes. And for that."

Here it comes, I thought. What could Hades possibly want that we could give him in return for his assistance? The souls of our firstborn children? A giggle rose, but I squelched it, because it seriously could be that.

Seconds turned into an eternity, and then Hades finally spoke. "You."

I blinked, at first having no idea who he was speaking to, but then I saw his attention fixed on Aiden. My heart thumped against my chest like a caged bird.

"What?" I demanded, my voice too thin.

Hades's lips curled into a smirk. "I want him."

A flash of bewilderment raced across Aiden's features. "You want me?" I had no idea where this was going, but I did not like it.

"He doesn't swing that way," Apollo commented, his blue eyes alive with amusement. "And I didn't think you did, either."

Someone, I suspected Seth, choked on a laugh.

Hades shot the other god a scathing look. "I want his soul."

CHAPTER THIRTEEN

I was seconds away from discovering what would happen when an Apollyon hit a god with a bolt of anger-fueled akasha. Seth sensed my fury. Hell, he had to be drowning in it. He was edging along the wall, coming closer and closer to me.

Or the exit.

"No," I said, and then louder, "Hell to the no, you cannot have his soul."

Hades whipped toward me, and the tense pull to his lips told me he didn't like my tone. Well, he wasn't going to like my foot up his ass, either. "I would've asked for yours, but Apollo wouldn't have allowed that."

I so did not care. "You cannot have his soul. I don't care what we need you for."

Apollo heaved a heavy breath. "Alex."

"No!" I spun on the god. "No way."

Hades's smirk infuriated me. "But you haven't even heard the details."

I stormed up to the god, already tasting his blood.

"You can take your details and shove them up your fake British—"

"Alex!"

Clamping my mouth shut, I tensed my shoulders as I turned to the one person in this world who could get me to shut up. Aiden stood to my right, and the moment our gazes locked, I saw it. He wanted to hear Hades out. Knots spiraled tightly in my stomach.

"No," I said again, my voice a pitiful whisper. "I don't want to even hear it."

He held my gaze for a second longer and then turned to Hades. "What are the details?"

The god oozed smugness. "I want your soul."

"I think we've covered that," I snapped.

Hades ignored me. "Your soul would belong to me once you've died to use however I see fit."

I took a breath, but it got stuck. However he saw fit? My hands itched to get around his thick neck.

"I could always use a guard with your boldness and skill," Hades continued.

Images of the guards of Hell, in leather and astride giant warhorses, flashed through my mind. I couldn't—wouldn't picture Aiden as one of them.

"And I wouldn't take your life," Hades went on while I started to picture myself lopping his head off with a giant sword. "When you die, not by my hand or through any trickery on my part, I will have your soul. I give my word."

I thought of what Solos had told me. Snakes. "And we're supposed to believe that?"

"He's not lying," Apollo said, eyes narrowed. "He gave his word. It's unbreakable."

I laughed, and the sound was coarse. Trust a god's word?

Were they on meth? I twisted halfway and saw Deacon's expression as he stared at his brother. Stark. Accepting. Oh gods, he knew. I whirled on Aiden. "No! We'll find another way."

"There is no other way." Aiden crossed the short distance between us and gently placed his big hands on my cheeks. "You know that."

"No." I gripped his wrists. "There has to be something else."

"Is there? Minutes ago, Perses was our only option," Hades oh-so-pleasantly reminded me.

Outrage caused the akasha in my veins to start begging to be used. Loudly. "It's your *soul*, Aiden. When you die, you will have to go to work for him or worse. You won't go to the Elysian Fields. You..." I broke off, unable to say what was so selfish but true.

We wouldn't have eternity together.

When I died, barring I didn't kill Hades right now, I'd go to Elysia, and Aiden would not be there.

He'd never be there, not until Hades allowed it. And he would never allow it.

Tears filled my eyes as Aiden lowered his forehead to mine. "I don't plan on dying for a long time, agapi mou. We have today, and we'll have many tomorrows, but only if we get Hades's help. We won't have any of that if we don't stop Ares."

"But—"

"This is bigger than both of us." His thumb caught a tear that had snuck out, wiping it away before anyone besides Seth noticed. And there was no hiding how I felt from the First. He was standing close to us, his expression devoid of its usual smirk. Aiden smiled, but it *hurt*. "We have to do anything and everything to stop this."

"I don't care," I whispered.

"Yes, you do."

I shook my head. "Not if it means this, I don't. I don't care."

It wasn't fair. It wasn't fair that we had to keep making sacrifices. We could possibly face losing a mortal life together, and now we wouldn't even have an afterlife? Sorrow rose in me swiftly. "You wouldn't want this for me."

"I wouldn't," he admitted, "but that's not the situation, and we need this."

"You do," Hades cajoled, and I wanted to claw his face into tiny, bloody pieces.

Seth shifted closer. I didn't see him, because I couldn't look away from Aiden, but I felt him. "Aiden is right," Seth said quietly, but it was still intrusive. "You know there's no other choice."

"I don't want you to have to make this choice," I insisted. Yes, I was being selfish, but it didn't just affect me. It also affected his brother and his family. If Hades didn't allow it, he'd never see his mother and father again. This was too much.

Aiden's striking face blurred through the haze of tears. "I know." His lips brushed the corner of my lips. "But we have to."

I opened my mouth to protest more, but he took advantage of that moment. He deepened the kiss and kissed me like we were the only two people in the room, in the world. Tingles shot up and down my spine in a wave of electricity. I leaned into him, kissing him back with everything I felt. Aiden tasted of salt, of mint, and of love.

Someone, maybe my uncle, cleared his throat.

Aiden slowly lifted his head, and the room came back

into focus. My cheeks burned. "By doing this, we are giving ourselves a future together. Okay? We have to do this. I have to do this, and there's nothing that can be done to change that."

"Oh, this conversation is *so* not over," I promised, blinking back tears. "I'm going to spin-kick you in the head for this one later, but okay. Okay."

Aiden chuckled, but he wisely stepped back and turned to Hades. "Okay. You have my soul when I die."

"See?" Hades eyed me over Aiden's shoulder. "Was that so hard?"

"I hate you," I hissed.

"It's nothing personal, Love."

"Yeah, and the last time you said that to me you wanted to kill me." My hands curled into fists.

The God of the Underworld shrugged. "Okay."

"That's it?" Seth asked, the hollows of his cheeks more pronounced. "You're not going to even shake on it? He says 'you can have my soul' and you say okay?"

I shot Seth a glare.

Hades smiled again. "That's all I need."

Seth's amber eyes rolled. "That's anticlimactic."

The god was unbothered by that as he settled his attention on Aiden and me. "You two will be responsible for Perses, meaning you will come with me and take him out of Tartarus."

My spine stiffened. "We have to go to Tartarus?"

Static crackled around Hades's eyes. "I think showing you two what could possibly lie in store for your pure-blood may incline both of you to work extra-hard to ensure that Perses sticks to the plan."

I gasped.

"Wait." Seth stepped forward. "I'm going with them."

Aiden opened his mouth, most likely to passionately disagree, but Hades cut him off. "I think that is a great idea. Then the *three* of you will be responsible for Perses and what role Aiden takes on in the afterlife."

My stomach dropped, and I felt like I was falling. Before I could protest, Hades was already making plans. We would leave for Tartarus within the hour. He would take us straight there, no need for finding a gate or facing any of the guards. It was all happening too fast. Aiden was talking to Deacon in low, hushed tones, and Solos was with Marcus, surrounded by Olivia and Luke.

My unease about the deal settled in me like sour food. My heart pounded in my chest way too fast, and if I didn't know any better, I would've sworn Phobos and Deimos were back, but they weren't. Fear formed an icy knot under my breastbone.

Alex…

I didn't turn to Seth. *What if Perses doesn't do what we need him to? What if he runs off and slaughters an entire nation? Hades will put that on Aiden. He'll have his soul and—*

We'll make sure that won't happen. The confidence in Seth's words pushed through our bond. *St. Delphi won't end up in Tartarus, I promise you.*

The fact that Seth would promise something like that didn't go unnoticed. *Either way, he'll own Aiden. No matter what happens. Aiden will be like a half-blood, nothing more than…*

Air leaked out of my lungs. Aiden would be like a slave, like every half-blood was now and would be, even after we took care of Ares. Aiden's own words came back to me in that moment. *This is bigger than us.* Realization whirled, and an opportunity presented itself. Hell, the opportunity had always been there, but I'd been too self-absorbed to realize it, too caught up in my own problems to…

To use the power I held in my hands to change things.

"Wait!" I called out.

"Alex," Seth said in a quiet voice.

I shook my head, breathing deeply. Apollo turned to me, inclining his head. I readied myself. "Wait. There's something I want before we do this."

Hades chuckled deeply. "What position are you in to bargain, Love?"

If he called me "Love" one more time… I reeled in my temper and focused on Apollo. "You want us to go down into Tartarus and fetch Perses, watch over him while he helps us, and then you want me to become the God Killer and take out Ares, right?"

Apollo shifted his weight. "That sounds about right."

My heart turned over heavily. "I will only do this if you do something for me."

Hades scoffed. "Again, Love, what position are you in to bargain with us?"

I slid my gaze toward Mr. Tall, Dark, and About to be Missing an Eyeball. "Without me, you don't have a God Killer. You can't make me become it, and you can't make me fight Ares."

"We can be very persuasive," Hades growled.

"Yeah, and Ares tried to be persuasive, and I still didn't give in." I looked at Apollo. "I know you guys can't make Seth or me do it. We could leave you guys to this mess. You need us *willing*."

Apollo's lips twitched as if he wished to smile. "What do you want, Alex?"

"I want you to free the half-bloods. I want you to get rid

of the laws requiring them to either become Sentinels, or Guards, or servants. I want you to give them the same rights as pure-bloods. I want the Breed Order revoked."

Silence.

It was so quiet that you could hear a fly run into a wall. Everyone was staring at me like I'd just pulled up my shirt and asked for some beads.

And then Seth chuckled deeply. "Clever, Angel."

I ignored the nickname. I also ignored the way Aiden's eyes went from the purest color of gray to silver in a nanosecond. "I know you can do it, Apollo. I know you can make the other gods agree. You do this for me, and I'll be all about taking a tour of Tartarus."

Apollo stared at me as he slowly shook his head. "There was so much more you could've asked for, Alex."

My brows knitted. "Like what? What could be more important than that?"

His gaze held mine, and suddenly I knew what he meant. I could've asked for his protection, because once I took care of Ares, it would be open season on my arse. I knew Apollo would already do what he could to ensure that I walked away, but it seemed useless to waste this opportunity on something that Apollo might not be able to stop.

The god nodded curtly. "Okay. Once everything has settled, we will change the laws and the Elixir will be no more. You have my word, no matter the outcome."

No matter the outcome. Meaning if Ares kicked our asses into the next generation. I wanted Apollo to do it now, because I had the patience of a hyena, but I could understand why he couldn't. The last thing we needed was more half-bloods, thousands of them, coming off the effects of the Elixir in the middle of this mess.

My gaze traveled across the room, skipping over the shocked expressions of Luke and Olivia. I think, in that moment, they realized the same thing Solos must have by the look in his wide eyes. After all this was said and done, they would have something they'd never had before.

Complete and utter control of their future.

CHAPTER FOURTEEN

Olivia hugged me so hard I thought my lungs would deflate. She held on, her lithe form trembling. It was a good hug, reminding me of the ones my mother used to give me. "The whole evil-twin god thing is so messed up. I'm sorry, but I'm glad they're out," she said, and then in a lower, hoarser voice, she added, "Thank you."

I knew why she was thanking me—for the deal. I squeezed her back and then leaned away. I kept my voice low. "So what are you going to do?"

"After this craziness with Ares?" When I nodded, a far-off look crept into her pretty eyes. She dropped her arms, shaking her head. "You know, I don't know. I never thought about it, but now I do have something to think about, and it's…"

"Amazing," Luke said, dropping a quick kiss on my cheek. "I think I'm going to enroll in college."

Both Olivia and I stared at him.

"What?" A flush spread across his cheeks. "I actually like school."

"Freak," I muttered.

Hades was growing impatient. *Surly bastard.* I said goodbye, giving my uncle a stiff and somewhat awkward hug. Tension and elation warred in the room. The agreement made with Apollo, who was actually going to remain here instead of popping back to Olympus, was obviously a big deal, but what the three of us were about to embark on could quickly become dangerous.

Perses could kill us all and make a run for it.

Continuing that line of thought wasn't what I wanted to focus on as I made my way over to where Hades stood between Aiden and Seth. My eyes bounced between the two guys. Then again, I wasn't so sure that Perses was going to be the problem.

Aiden and Seth were sizing each other up like they were ready for a caged death match. Sidling up to Aiden, I elbowed him in the side.

He glanced down at me, eyes the color of the ocean during a storm. "I'm proud of you."

Oh, the swelling in my chest could've lifted me right up to the ceiling. I smiled up at him, smiled so widely my cheeks ached.

"I would've used that favor more intelligently, Love." Hades smirked.

Aaand Hades burst my bubble with a quickness I should have expected. "Thanks for your input," I muttered.

"You're welcome," he replied. "Is everyone ready for our little field trip?"

With Apollo's seal of approval, Seth was given his toys back, so all of us, even Seth, were decked out in our Covenant daggers and Glocks. Our eyes locked for a moment. There was something in his amber gaze that unsettled me.

Aiden reached down, threading his fingers through mine. "We're ready." Without any warning, the floor dropped out from under us.

"Holy daimon babies!" I gasped, stumbling back as the world righted itself once more. "Good gods..."

Aiden patted his hands over his chest as if checking to make sure he was all there. Seth looked a little out of it. None of us had been prepared for that method of traveling.

The God of the Underworld watched us. Amusement bled into the air around him. "It's easier that way, don't you think?"

I smoothed my hand over my hair, relieved to find it still attached to my head. When the floor had moved under us, it had felt like we'd fallen a million feet. "Did you just...just *teleport* us?"

"Something like that." Hades turned, putting his hands on his hips. Tipping his head back, he let out a loud, ear-piercing whistle, causing me to jump.

"So, this is the Underworld?" Seth turned, taking in his surroundings.

Forcing myself to get over the fact that I wasn't exactly sure how Hades had managed to teleport us, and the whole science behind that concept, I looked around. I recognized where we were.

"Thank the gods it's not the Vale of Mourning, huh?" Aiden said.

I nodded. That vast, depressing stretch of the Underworld was not a place I wanted to visit again. We were just outside the Vale, several feet from the congested road that led to the Plain of Judgment. Seth watched the recently departed making slow progress with a troubled look. A lot of the deceased were Sentinels, their black uniforms in various stages of distress. Seeing them…well, I had to think it was a painful reminder of what he'd been a part of.

The sound of pounding hooves drew my attention from the First, and I turned. "Holy gods…"

I jerked back, bouncing off of Aiden's chest. An arm circled my waist, steadying me. Good gods in Olympia, the horses were the size of elephants. Four of them. Their coats were as dark and shiny as midnight oil, their manes glossy and groomed. They looked like extremely large horses with the exception of the all-white pupils behind their black-leather eye shields. "I don't remember them being this big."

"Me, neither."

Seth neared one, head cocked to the side. The horse whinnied. "They're like the Hummer of the horse world."

I almost laughed, but then I noticed the saddles on each of them. I glanced at Hades as he ran a large hand down one of the horses' manes. "These *are* bigger than what you saw last time. They are from my personal stable." He grabbed the saddle and swung himself up with astonishing ease. "It is not a quick journey to Tartarus. We will ride there."

Glancing at one of the horses near me, I hesitated. "Why didn't you just pop us into Tartarus?"

"Tartarus is an ever-changing landscape, adapting to its… newest arrivals." He shrugged. "I would hate to pop my newest acquisition into a lake of fire."

My eyes narrowed.

Hades smirked at me as he wrapped a meaty hand around the reins. "We don't have all day. There's a mean game of Mario Kart waiting for me when I get back."

Resisting the urge to run up to Hades and knock him out

of the saddle, I wheeled around. Seth had already found his horse and was in the saddle, looking very proud of himself. Then Aiden was on his, swinging a leg over the horse, which left me staring at the last one, the one that reminded me of a T-Rex.

It sniffed at me.

"You might want to get used to these magnificent creatures." Hades's smile was cold and pleased as he looked at Aiden.

An ache hit me in my chest at the reminder of Aiden's deal. I turned, ready to lay into him for agreeing, but drew up short. I was face-to-face with a massive horse head.

Walking up, I awkwardly patted its nose. "Nice horsey."

Its lip curled up, revealing oddly sharp teeth. Did horses have sharp teeth? Or just Underworld horses? My gaze traveled over the massive chest and leather saddle. How in the hell was I supposed to get on this thing? The stirrup was so far off the ground I was going to need a stepladder to access it.

"You put your foot in the stirrup," Seth said, tipping his chin down.

"I know," I snapped. But I didn't move any closer. The horse turned its elegant head back away from me and snorted. "I've never ridden a horse before."

Hades sighed.

Heat crept into my cheeks. Honestly, I was sort of afraid of horses. Normal ones could break your bones. These could eat you.

Aiden guided his horse toward where I stood, smiling slightly as he looked down. "Come on." I stared at him.

The slight smile spread, revealing a dimple in his right cheek. "There's room for both of us up here. Ride with me."

Okay. I was scared of horses, and that made me a wuss, but

I thought about all those romance novels my mom used to read with the hero astride a horse, and then there was Aiden, larger than life astride a horse, and that was…well, that was hot.

"I really don't care if you ride alone or with Loverboy here, but can we move this along?" Hades tightened his hand on the reins, turning the horses. "I am not known for my patience."

I shot him a scathing look, which was ignored. Crossing the distance between Aiden and me, I reached up, putting my hand in his. With astonishing ease, he hauled me up into the saddle in front of him. After a few seconds of awkward fumbling, I was seated on the horse, clenching the edge of the saddle.

Well aware that both Hades and Seth were staring at us, I remained stiff as Aiden snaked an arm around my waist and tugged me back between his thighs. His heat immediately seeped into my tense muscles.

"How cute," Seth drawled.

"Shut up," Aiden said, and then much lower, directly in my ear, "This is the greatest idea I've ever had."

I shivered.

We started off then, galloping along the crowded road. It took a little while to get used to the jarring motion of the horse and even longer to get familiar with the stagnant, sweet-scented air blowing in my face. About half an hour in, four guards suddenly flanked us, their faces pale and somber. I tried desperately not to picture Aiden becoming one of Hades's henchmen, but I couldn't help but wonder why Hades had even asked for Aiden. It wasn't like there was any shortage of people who had some kind of penance to pay, and wasn't that what these guards were doing? Working off their sins in the afterlife? Or was it something else?

I knew it was punishment. Hades knew we'd snuck into the Underworld to see Solaris, and he obviously wasn't happy about that. In a twist of irony, our journey had been rather pointless now. Seth wanted me to become the God Killer, and he knew how to make the transfer. We'd ended up not needing Solaris.

The barren landscape turned lush as we neared the crossroads. The bare, brown ground gave way to thick, bright-green grass. The congestion of those recently deceased grew as the spired tips of Hades's stone palace finally came into view.

And so did Tartarus.

The eerie red glow off in the distance was hard to ignore. So was the very faint, almost untraceable scent of sulfur. I couldn't believe we were actually going there willingly.

My unease grew with every passing moment. I was waiting for it to happen, and when it finally did, Seth swore loudly.

A loud *pop* thundered through the air, followed by a *whoosh* as the ground trembled under the hooves of our horses. The sky lit up, bleeding red and orange as a ball of flames shot up, spreading first into fiery wings, and then the jaws of the dragon opened, emitting the horrifying scream that stuck with us. The fiery dragon swooped back down, its tail flaming as the ground shook once more. "Holy shit," Seth said, eyes wide. "What in the hell was that?"

"Tartarus's welcoming party," Hades replied. "Get used to it. I have a feeling you'll see it up close and personal more than once."

Seth snorted, as if the very real possibility of him ending up in Tartarus wasn't a big deal, but my stomach roiled at the thought. I looked at him as we rode on, remembering quite clearly where Solaris's First was currently located.

Did Seth deserve eternal damnation for his actions?

He glanced over at me, his expression unreadable. Our gazes locked. His perfectly pieced face was emotionless, but something churned in his eyes. *Seth?*

There was no answer. Instead, those amber eyes, so much like my own, flicked back to Aiden. "Hey, Saint Delphi."

Oh, Lord.

Aiden stiffened behind me. "Yes?"

Seth guided his horse beside us, and I wondered where both of them had mastered horseback riding. "If you find yourself needing some extra space on that horse, I have more than enough room on mine." Seth's tight smile grew as I stared at him. "We could…share."

Heat roared off of Aiden. He hadn't missed the innuendo. "Not going to happen."

One shoulder rose in response. "It was just an offer."

"Can you not talk?" Aiden retorted.

"Hey, all I'm saying is, for a while there, we really did share—"

"Seth!" I hissed, my cheeks burning.

"What?" he replied innocently, and if I wasn't so afraid of being stomped to death, I would've jumped off this horse and beaten him senseless.

Our little quarrel hadn't drawn the attention of Hades or his guards, and I sure hoped it stayed that way. Besides being annoying, this was as embarrassing as the time I nearly broke someone's neck doing a take-down incorrectly in class. Mainly because I had messed up then, and I also had messed up when it came to Seth and Aiden.

Aiden's voice was deceptively calm when he spoke. "You never had her, Seth. We weren't sharing anything."

"Hmm. That's not how it seemed to me. You know, there's a reason why I call her Angel."

"Oh, for the love of the gods," I muttered, glaring at Seth. I was damn sure he'd been calling me that long before any parts of our bodies had touched. "Knock it off. Both of you."

Seth winked.

He finally quieted down, but Aiden was stewing. I could feel the tension in him as we rode on, but there was nothing I could do, because I had a feeling anything I said to calm him down would only instigate the butthead beside us. Besides, my mind went elsewhere.

A huge part of me had hoped to see Caleb, but as we galloped past the Plain of Judgment, heading straight for the eerie red glow of Tartarus, I knew I wouldn't get to see him this time. As if sensing my thoughts, Aiden dipped his head and kissed my cheek. Squeezing my eyes shut, I allowed myself to fully relax into him since it didn't appear like the mammoth beast underneath us was about to eat us.

Tracking time in the Underworld was difficult. What felt like an hour here could be only a half-second above ground, and it seemed like we'd been on the damn horses for longer than an hour. But the scent of sulfur grew, and the sky darkened into an ominous mixture of orange and deep blue, like the sky before a violent storm at dusk.

As we traveled on, the grass was replaced by a fine trail of fire that smoldered along the ground, following the road to Tartarus.

The group of people traveling along the road was heavily guarded, and I wondered if that was why Hades's guards had appeared.

Those on this road wore ragged, torn clothing. Their chins were tipped down, and their progress was slow as they shuffled along, chained at the ankles and wrists.

The dragon made another appearance, and this time I

could feel the heat of the morphing fire. A heaviness permeated the air as we passed under a crudely built stone archway, and I shuddered.

Bare trees stood, their branches thin like bones, stretching toward the sky. Up ahead, a rocky hill rose sharply, and beyond the crest, the glow of orange was stronger. Aiden's arm tightened around me as the horses slowed, whinnying softly. The atmosphere shifted dramatically, and it was more than the fact that night had descended like a heavy, suffocating blanket. The only light was from the thin rows of fire and the glowing torches posted along the road. A sour tang of bitterness coated the inside of my mouth, and a fierce bite of hatred choked my heart.

Seth was staring at something to our left, and my gaze followed his. The River Styx had reappeared, its murky waters flowing swiftly, but it wasn't the river he was staring at.

Dozens of women in bloodied white gowns were near the bank of the river. Some were bending, reaching into the dark waters. Others carried jars away. The jars were leaking. By the time they were a few feet from the road, the jars were empty.

The women silently turned back to the river. "Who are they?" I whispered.

"They are the daughters of Danaus," Aiden said. His hand rested over my stomach, and his thumb moved in absent-minded, smoothing circles.

"They murdered their husbands on their wedding nights, at their father's request. This is their punishment."

I wanted to look away from them, because I couldn't comprehend an eternity of fruitless labor, but I couldn't tear my gaze away as our horse rode on. I craned my neck, watching the women turn back to the Styx, slowly, sadly, their jars empty. Their appearance was significant.

We had entered Tartarus.

CHAPTER FIFTEEN

Tartarus wasn't very scenic.

Imagine the worst section of any town, and then imagine that neighborhood on fire and throw in some random torture scenes between the run-down shacks. That was Tartarus.

Fire was everywhere. Bushes on fire. Trees burning. The Styx at some point had turned into a river of flames as it slithered between stone buildings. Some were standing and, of course, on fire. Others were halfway destroyed, large sections crumbling to the ground.

It was like the apocalypse happened and then stayed around.

The stench of sulfur and blood was almost unbearable, but the heat…oh, dear gods, I was seconds away from pulling my shirt off. Sweat beaded on me, rolling between my breasts.

"This would make a lovely vacation spot," Seth muttered.

I started to respond, but my eyes latched onto a flaming…a flaming wheel? "What the hell?"

Hades glanced over his shoulder at me, those freaky eyes

doing the static thing. "That's Ixion." As we grew closer to the tragedy, I could see that there was a man in the center of the large wheel.

"Oh, my gods." I clamped my hand over my mouth.

"Don't make a pass at Hera," Hades remarked, moving along. "Zeus doesn't take kindly to another man making a move on his wife."

That was absolutely ridiculous if you took into consideration the fact Zeus couldn't keep it in his pants.

"Stop staring," Aiden murmured in my ear, and when I still didn't look away, he reached around and turned my cheek. "I thought Ixion was located in the lowest part of Tartarus?"

I made a face. Only he would know who Ixion was. Aiden had to have been such a Goody Two-shoes in school—the kind of kid who'd raised his hand with the answer to every question. *Dork.* I loved him.

"We took a shortcut, so we're several levels down." Hades stopped his horse and swung down. We'd hit a dead end consisting of dark, slick-looking boulders. "There is another portion of Tartarus that isn't spoken of in myths."

Seth dismounted with the grace of a feline. "And that's where we're heading?"

"Yes. We're going into the Tombs of Tartarus."

"The Tombs of Tartarus?" Aiden repeated, sliding his arm off my waist.

Ha! Something he didn't know. I cast him a look over my shoulder and then slid off the horse. I stumbled a step when my feet landed. The ground was oddly...*soft* and buoyant.

Hades snorted. "It amazes me that you're an Apollyon with all your agility."

My mouth opened to fire back, but I squinted. Something was up with the ground. I took a step and my feet sank about an inch in. Aware that Aiden had landed behind me, I bent down and ran my hand over the pale pink ground. It felt like…

I jerked my hand back and looked up, horrified. "The ground feels like skin!"

A slow smile crept onto Hades's face. "Zeus got bored with the whole rock and eagle bit."

Rock and eagle bit…? Then it hit me. "Prometheus?"

"You're standing on him," Hades remarked.

My stomach turned. "Oh gods, I think I'm going to vomit."

"Perfect," the god said.

Seth's brows rose, but he remained quiet. I forced myself to walk forward, desperately ignoring my gag reflex with each cushiony step. Behind us, several guards dismounted as Hades strolled toward his right. He stopped in front of a smoothed section of the rock and placed his palm to it.

Beside me, Aiden cocked his head to the side. His dark hair was damp and curled around the temples. The wall before us trembled quietly, and then the slab of stone glided open, beckoning us into the darkness.

One of the guards stepped forward, a torch in hand. He handed it to the god and then moved back, hands on his daggers—big, wicked-looking daggers.

"We keep the Titans in the tombs," Hades explained as he stepped forward. "They're separated from the rest and have to be handled delicately. Their damnation comes in the form of eternal sleep."

Cool air washed over my sticky skin as I followed Seth and Hades, and even though it was freaky to be walking into tombs, I welcomed the colder temps. My eyes adjusted quickly. The stone walls were covered in glyphs, much like the ones that appeared on Seth's and my skin.

"Sleep doesn't sound like damnation," I said.

"We couldn't handle them if they all were awake." Hades continued down the narrow hall. "Their powers are weakened in the Underworld, but if all of them were up and moving about, it would be a problem."

"So it works the same way as it does for the Olympians?" Aiden asked, staying close behind me. "They feed off each other's power."

"Yes." Hades came to a split in the hall and hung a left. The temp dropped another couple of degrees as we headed down roughly carved steps. "Once Perses gets topside, he's going to get some of his power back. He won't be at a full charge, but he'll be as powerful as any lesser god."

"Any lesser god" meant Perses was going to be powerful. Maybe not at the same level as Hades or Ares, but he wasn't going to be any weakling. The next hall was wider, opening up into a circular chamber. In the center was a small pool that smelled faintly of jasmine, which made me think of the pool Aiden and I had gone swimming in the last time we were in the Underworld.

I caught Aiden's stare and knew he was thinking the same thing I was. The corner of his lips tipped up, and I flushed.

"Seriously? Could you guys go longer than five minutes without making googly faces at one another?" Seth walked between us, scowling. "It's distracting."

Aiden smirked, and then opened his mouth. I cut him off before we got into another battle of wits that ended with me wanting to crawl under Prometheus's skin. "How many of the Titans do you have down here?"

"All of the ones who want to cause problems." Hades disappeared into another corridor, and I sighed, hurrying to catch up to him. "Very few are in the Elysian Fields. Cronus and his cronies are all here."

Cronus was the father of Zeus, Hades, and who knew how many other gods. A shudder snaked down my spine. Hades kept his own father imprisoned in a hell-tomb. The hallway was a tight fit. Luckily, we weren't in it for very long. We entered another chamber, but this one was different.

We were in the tombs.

Twelve tombs, to be exact. I thought it was odd—the number. Twelve Olympians. Twelve entombed Titans. They were in some kind of capsule-like containers, embedded deep into the stone wall. A thick layer of reddish ice covered them, revealing only a humanoid shape beyond the barrier. But from the looks of it, Titans were tall.

Like gargantuan-size.

"Do you know that I'm actually older than Zeus?" Hades asked as he placed the torch into a sconce in the wall. "As are Poseidon, Demeter, Hera, and the rest? But because Cronus was a dick—and he was a *huge* dick—and our momma only saved Zeus, the world thinks baby brother was the first to be born."

"Didn't Cronus eat you guys?" Seth asked. I made a face.

Hades laughed. "The whole 'swallowing us' crap was symbolic for hiding us. He held us in captivity until our baby brother set us free." He walked along the iced-over tombs, and his eyes narrowed as he stopped in front of the tomb in the center. "Screw you, Dad."

I passed a look to Aiden, who slowly shook his head, but then Hades stepped to the left and let out a heavy sigh. "There was a time when Perses wasn't so bad, and maybe the years have changed him, but I'm not holding my breath." He turned to me. "Are you sure you want to do this, Love?"

My gaze crawled to the tomb in front of him, and my pulse picked up. "Like I've said, we really don't have any other choices."

Hades stared at me for a long moment and then turned back to the tomb. "You don't." He placed his hand on the center of the tomb. I wanted to step back, but I forced myself to stand where I was. I was pretty sure running through the tombs would only end up with me being lost, and then Seth would make fun of me for the rest of my life.

The ice shuddered, and a spiderweb of cracks formed underneath Hades's palm, rapidly spreading across the front of the tomb. Seth and Aiden flanked me, and for once, both boys were quiet and not picking at each other.

Ice slipped away, shedding from the tomb, and hit the floor, making tiny sounds like a distant wind chime. Within seconds, the Titan was revealed.

Perses *was* tall—almost seven and a half feet, maybe more. And he was unnaturally still inside his tomb. Thick lashes fanned cheeks the color of supple brown leather. His skull was smooth, free of hair, and his features were angular and exotic—full lips, sharp cheekbones, and a well-defined brow. He was beautiful in the way all the godly creatures were: inhumanly perfect.

As still as the Titan was, he looked dead. Not even his chest moved, but an air of danger surrounded him nonetheless. I couldn't imagine what it would be like once he was released.

Leather pants and a tunic stretched over broad, thick muscles. There were cuffs on his wrists, adorned with odd symbols I didn't recognize.

"What is it with gods and leather?" I muttered.

Hades slid me a long look. "We make it look good."

They did. Couldn't argue that, but the gods' hotness didn't compensate for their overall creepiness and deranged thought processes.

"Last chance," Hades said, looking over his shoulder at us.

There was a pause, and then Aiden said, "Do it."

With a slight shake of his head, Hades turned back to the Titan and placed his hand on the center of his chest. A red glow radiated from the god's palm and then washed over Perses. No words were spoken or rituals completed. It appeared that Hades alone had the special touch.

Hades stepped back and folded his arms. We didn't have to wait long.

The Titan shuddered once and then opened his eyes. I tried to squelch the gasp but couldn't. Unlike the Olympians, his eyes were pitch black. The whole eye—the exact opposite of the Olympians. And if I'd thought the gods' eyes were messed up, it was nothing compared to the Titan's.

Perses's gaze landed on Hades and his lip curled up. "You've got to be kidding me."

My brows shot up at the sound of the deep voice. So wasn't expecting that to be the first thing for the Titan to say when he came out of the deep freeze.

Hades tilted his head to the side as a slow, lazy smile spread across his lips. "Hello, Perses, how was your nap?"

"It was great, asshole." Oh. Dear.

The spine of the god stiffened. "I can see your attitude is the same as it was when we chained you into this tomb."

"*Barely* chained me," he sneered. The Titan raked our little group with a passing look and then swung his head back toward us. The violent curl of his lips slipped away as his eyes narrowed. "I'm awakened to find an asshole, a child of a demigod, and two Apollyons before me? I must admit, I am curious."

I was surprised by how well Hades was handling the insults being flung his way.

"We need your help," I forced myself to say. "That's why you've been awakened."

One dark eyebrow rose into a perfect arch. "You need *my* help?" The Titan tipped his head back and laughed so deeply I thought I felt the ground under my feet tremble. Laughing was good, though. At least he wasn't trying to kill us. "My help? I cannot imagine what ludicrous situation you all have gotten yourself in if the Olympians are coming to a Titan for help."

"Well, you see..." I cleared my throat and gave him the quick and dirty version of events. The whole time he stared at me until I felt like my insides were spread across my clothing. "We know you can prepare us and you can—"

"Cause Ares to lose some of his confidence? Make him uneasy?" Perses's chuckle echoed throughout the cavern. "You need me as the psychological ace up your sleeve."

"Basically," Aiden replied evenly.

The Titan didn't even look at him. "Ares must really be making a mess of things if Zeus has given permission to release me."

"It is bad. He has the mortals on the brink of an all-out war. The gods have practically torn the world apart. Innocent people are dying..." I trailed off as a look of boredom crept into his expression. "You don't care about any of that. Okay. That's cool. We don't need you to care."

"That's a good thing, child, because I don't care."

I took a deep breath. What if Perses refused? Would he really willingly go back to being an oddly colored ice cube? "We need you to help us defeat Ares. You know, the God of War."

Perses huffed. "He is not the true god of war. I am."

"That's not what *he's* saying," Seth added, picking up where I was heading with this.

"He says no one, past or present, can defeat him," Aiden threw in. "Maybe that's the truth."

I forced a casual shrug. "If you don't want to fight him or—"

"If you say I'm afraid, you obviously do not value your life, Apollyon." Perses took a step forward, and ice slipped down my spine. "It has nothing to do with fear."

"I don't think it does." My gaze bounced to Hades, who was being oh-so-helpful through all of this. "But don't you want the chance to go toe-to-toe with Ares again?"

A muscle popped in his jaw. "The only reason any of us were enslaved was because I was tricked." He growled low in his throat as he spared a brief glance at the quiet god. "Ares is no match against me. He never was and never will be."

"Then you could prove it. You don't have to care about any of us to prove it," I said, close to begging. "If you help us, Hades will not put you back here. He'll release you into the Elysian Fields."

Perses stared at me for a long moment and then turned to Hades. "Is that true?"

"I don't like it. Frankly, I think you should be in Prometheus's place."

The Titan's eyes narrowed. "That is not an answer."

Hades folded thick arms across his chest. "If you do as you are told and don't cause any problems, you will be released into the Elysian Fields. If not, we will chain your ass to a rock and strip your skin from your body, one tiny section at a time."

"Is that so?" He raised a brow. "Seems to me you'll have your hands full with Ares and won't have time to spend an eternity torturing me."

Hades stepped up, unfolding his arms. "You forget Ares has no power in my realm unless I grant it, and he cannot enter without my permission. Ares can rip the mortal world apart, but if you betray us, we will take the time to track you down, and I will spend eternity getting my jollies off on your suffering."

"Poor Persephone." Perses stared down his nose at the god. "It must be hard on her if that's what gets you off."

I wrinkled my nose.

"If her name drips from your forked tongue one more time, I will rip it out," Hades promised, his voice deadly low.

Was his tongue really forked?

Perses's lips curled up on one side. "What? You don't like me talking about your wife?" He looked over at us. "Is abduction as a means of marriage still all the rage these days?"

"Uh…no," I said, shaking my head. "It's really frowned upon."

Hades's cheeks deepened in color. "You're really pushing me."

"I haven't even begun to push."

Aiden sighed and said under his breath, "Well, this conversation has really digressed."

"Yeah," I muttered, crossing my arms as I watched the two try to out-snark each other.

This is going smoothly. Seth's voice filtered through my thoughts.

I kept my eyes on the Titan. *He's not that…bad. I mean, all things considered, right?*

His answering chuckle tugged at my lips. *I sort of like him.*

Of course you do.

"So, let me make sure I understand this clearly." Perses was apparently done antagonizing Hades. "I help you prepare for war and lead the charge against Ares, and I will be returned to the Elysian Fields in one piece? I must clarify that. You Olympians can be oh-so-tricky."

“Yes,” I said, shifting my weight when his heavy gaze landed on me. “In one piece, happy and whole.” I frowned. He didn’t look like the happy type. “Or in whatever mood you prefer.”

Perses moved forward so fast I hadn’t even seen him move. One second he was in front of Hades, and the next he was towering over me. Neither Aiden or Seth had a chance to react. “Swear it,” the Titan said. “And you will have my word.”

“We promise.” The words tasted like ash on my tongue. “We swear it.”

“I agree—” Hope swelled in my chest. Well, this wasn’t *too* hard. Perses smiled. “On one condition.”

Oh. I tried not to show my distrust. “What is your condition?”

His smile returned, and it was hungry. I wished he’d take a step back. “I need something strong to drink, and I need a woman. Maybe two.”

CHAPTER SIXTEEN

Vegas.

I was in Vegas with a Titan who needed to get drunk and get laid.

What in the holy Hades? Like, at what point in my pretty short time on Earth had my life veered so off course that I would end up here?

If someone said this was going to happen a few hours ago, I would've told them to get off the drugs, but Hades had poofed us just outside Palms Place, a colossal shimmery hotel near a million glittery casinos. It felt like my stomach was still in the Underworld as I gazed at the Sky Tube connecting the Palms to a casino.

I'd never been to Vegas. I remembered not too long ago, before I'd Awakened and the world went to hell, Aiden and I had made plans to get assigned to a place like Vegas. There was a huge—or used to be a huge—community of pures out here, and that meant there'd be daimons to stab and all that jazz. But I wasn't sure if the community still existed here or if they'd fled to one of the Covenants.

"Vegas," Perses's deep voice rumbled. "It's like an Olympian playground?"

A wry grin pulled at Aiden's lips as he twisted toward us and ran a hand through his hair. "Vegas is basically a playground for adults."

The Titan smiled. "Then it is my kind of place."

"We need to get a place for the night." Seth looked up at the lighted hotel. "This should work."

Hades had given us explicit orders to meet him back here at noon the following day, which hopefully was enough time for Perses to do, uh, his thing. As the four of us headed toward the front entrance of the Palms, we passed several mortal tourists. The world had gone to hell in a hand basket, but by the teeming streets and crowded sidewalks, nothing had really changed here.

Mortals had a wonderful ability of sticking their heads in the sand, even as the entire world came down on top of them.

I envied that.

Perses strode past two laughing college guys. They immediately quieted when they spied the nearly eight-foot-tall man in leather. Although I'm sure there were stranger things to see in Vegas, he was sure going to draw a lot of attention.

We'd made it about a foot when a string of curses exploded behind us. I whipped around, as did Aiden. The two college guys were pushing each other, dangerously close to the curb. Under the glowing street lamps, their faces were red with anger.

Perses chuckled.

A shiver ran down my spine. "It's you, isn't it? Already, you're affecting mortals." He shrugged and kept walking.

I glanced at Aiden, and we shared the same thought. *This is not going to go well.*

The lobby of the Palms was opulent and wildly calming compared to the glitz of outside. I lingered back as Seth strode to the registration desk. I knew he was using compulsion, and I couldn't bring myself to feel bad about it. I looked up, awed by the size of the dazzling crystal chandelier.

Aiden smoothed his thumb over my cheek. At the same time, he was keeping an eye on Perses, who was keeping an eye on a cluster of young women dressed in short, sexy dresses—the kind of dress I'd wear if given a chance.

Then again, I'd seen the scars on my legs. I doubted the world wanted to witness that hot mess.

So here we were, standing in Vegas in our Sentinel uniforms next to a giant Titan, looking like damn fools among all the fancy-dressed patrons of the hotel and casino.

Correction.

The guys could have been wearing used garbage bags, and they would still have looked hot. Every female around us openly gawked at the trinity of hotness. I, on the other hand, looked like I belonged in a paintball arena.

Aiden's hand slipped to my shoulder as Seth returned, several key cards in his hand. He grinned. "I got us Penthouse A."

"Penthouse A?" I took the card, curious.

We left the lobby and headed for the elevator just as I thought I heard a fleshy smack, like one of the women had just slapped another across the face.

Penthouse A took up almost half the top floor. It had three bedrooms and a game room. The place was completely decked out. It was the kind of room that catered to the filthy rich—lush furniture, stocked bar and fridge, Jacuzzi tub, TVs in the bathroom mirrors, and a breathtaking view of Vegas from the all-glass wall.

Perses and Seth each picked out rooms, and the Titan

immediately disappeared into one of the bathrooms. I couldn't imagine what he thought of modern technology, but he seemed to figure it out, because as I neared the open door, I heard the shower running.

Glancing over my shoulder, I saw Aiden disappear into the last bedroom. I tucked my hair back and walked forward, hesitating just inside the door. Seth was sprawled across one of the plush white couches, glass in hand. Man, he'd found the liquor quick enough. He arched a brow when he spotted me, and the cord tightened within me.

"Want a drink?" he offered. "It's scotch. Found it in the bar."

Getting liquored up was probably the only way I was going to make it through this night, but I shook my head. "What are we going to do with him?" I nodded back toward the hall that led to the bathroom.

"Let him get what he needs for the night." Seth laughed to himself as he swished the golden liquid around in his glass. "Ladies and liquor—the fundamental L's of life."

"We can't just let him roam Vegas by himself. He walked past two guys and they nearly had a wrestling match."

"I wasn't suggesting that." Seth finished off his drink and stood. "I'll watch him."

Yeah, I wasn't so keen on that. "Do you think that's a good idea?"

"Better than staying here with you two." He strolled up to me. "There's only a thin wall separating our rooms. I think I'd rather spend my night frolicking in high-priced strip clubs."

I rolled my eyes. "Nice."

"Just being honest."

"You don't have any money," I felt the need to point out.

He chuckled. "Do you really think *I'll* need money?"

If any guy could get attention in a strip club without money, it would be Seth, but that was beside the point.

"Aiden could go with him," I argued.

Seth cocked his head to the side. "Aw, Angel, are you trying to spend time with me?"

Hearing the shower turn off, I winced. I so did not want to be in here if Perses decided to walk out with no clothes on. I doubted he cared about privacy. "Look, I'm just making—"

"You don't trust me." Seth leaned against the wall in front of me. Close. Very close. "I wouldn't if I were you."

I frowned. "Well, that's a reassuring statement, Seth." He shrugged one shoulder as he stared down at me.

Growing frustrated, I looked behind me when I heard a door close somewhere in the suite. "You know he's right inside your room, waiting. And he's probably doing push-ups or something to keep himself from coming in here and stopping me…" He bent his head, so that his mouth was inches from mine. "From getting this close."

I sucked in a breath as the cord in my belly jumped.

His lips formed a half smile. "So, why don't you help out the *Saint* and go back to him before we make another scene."

Taking a step back, I met his gaze. "Don't be a douche."

"Don't be a pain in my ass."

He reclaimed the distance, crowding me, and for a second, unease gave way to a spark of fear. "It's better if I go out with Perses."

I didn't understand the sudden shift in mood with him. While he'd been in the cell, and after the evil god twins had been yanked out of me, Seth had been understanding and repentant. Now he was back to the Seth I wanted to shank with a rusty spork.

What's up with you? I tried the whole mental path thing,

hoping it would help. The last thing anyone needed was the two of us going at each other's throats.

His eyes flared. "Nothing is up."

Bull. You're incredibly moody.

"Incredibly moody?" Seth tipped his head back and laughed. *You have no idea.*

"Then tell me."

Seth blinked and then he leaned in again, speaking loud enough for everyone and their mother to hear. "I'm really not interested in talking with you. Other things? Maybe. You know, for old times' sake."

"You were wrong," Aiden announced from behind me, appearing in the doorway like a damn ghost. "I wasn't doing push-ups to stop myself. I was just visually entertaining myself with all the different ways I could break your jaw. So back the hell off."

Seth snickered as he pushed off the wall, raising his hands. "Look, all I was doing was telling her I would pull babysitting duties. She wanted me to stay and you to go. Don't hate on me."

My nails dug into my palms. *I'm on to you, jerk face. You're trying to piss me off on purpose.*

Seth winked, but then the door behind him swung open and Perses swaggered out, dressed in a white suit.

Momentarily distracted, I moved so I could see around Seth. "Where did you get the suit? Wait. I don't even want to know."

Perses laughed as he checked himself out in a gilded mirror. He wasn't wearing a shirt under his jacket, and when he turned, the cut of his broad chest really drew the eyes. Speaking of eyes, they looked mortal now. "So the male Apollyon is *babysitting* me." He walked up, clapping a large hand on Seth's shoulder. "That will work."

Remarkably, Seth had no reaction to the Titan getting all hands-on. "We'll have fun."

There was something in Seth's voice that said he wouldn't be having that much fun. I folded my arms, feeling like a mother who knew her child was about to go out and raise all kinds of holy hell but couldn't prove it. It wasn't that I thought Seth was going to try to take out Perses and run back to Ares. I believed with every cell in my body that he hated Ares as much as I did, but there was something going on.

"What happened to your face?" Perses asked, startling me as he twisted back to the mirror and straightened his jacket.

Aiden stopped whatever he was doing behind me, which probably involved giving Seth "I'm going to kill you while you sleep" looks, and placed a hand on my lower back. "That's none of your business," he snarled.

The Titan simply laughed deeply. "The pure-blood is touchy, isn't he?"

Seth snorted as he headed for the door. Apparently he was going to wear his Sentinel uniform for his night of hell-raising. The daggers and gun were no longer visible, but I knew he still had them on him. "You have no idea," he replied.

"You know..." Perses faced us once more, and his brand spanking-new irises shone like polished obsidian. "I could end you in half of a second."

I shifted so I was standing in front of Aiden. The knot of unease between my breasts grew and then doubled when Aiden somehow ended up in front of me.

"I know you can end me with a snap of your fingers," Aiden said, his body tense. "But it is still none of your business."

The smile on Perses's face widened.

I forced my muscles to relax as I stepped to stand side by side with Aiden. "Ares did it."

Perses cocked his head to the side as his gaze moved from me to Aiden and back. "I assume those are not your only scars?"

I shook my head.

At the door, Seth had paled visibly. He looked like he wanted to bolt. I couldn't blame him. So did I.

"How bad was it?" Perses asked.

While I had no desire to discuss this with anyone, let alone Perses, we needed to keep the Titan somewhat happy. And if that meant strolling down Awkward Lane, then so be it. "It was really bad. He kicked my ass."

The Titan was unaffected by the statement, but he tipped his chin toward Seth. "Where were you when this was happening? Aren't Apollyons bonded if there are two at the same time?"

Seth didn't answer immediately. "I wasn't there for her," he said, and those words were like a cold wind.

"Interesting." Perses shrugged his broad shoulders, stretching the material of his suit jacket. "It's a shame."

I frowned, not following where he was going with that statement. "What is?"

"What was done to you," Perses replied. "I bet you were beautiful at one time."

Sitting on the most comfortable couch known to man, I picked at the dinner Aiden had ordered from room service after Perses and Seth left to go do things it was best not to think about. Aiden sat beside me. The TV was on, and we were trying to be normal, but my mind was elsewhere. I felt edgy, restless.

Aiden laughed softly, drawing my attention. A small smile pulled at my lips. "What?"

"You haven't heard a word of what I've been saying, have you?"

My cheeks flushed as I shook my head. "Sorry. I'm just distracted. What were you saying?"

"It honestly wasn't anything important." He put his empty plate on the glass coffee table and twisted toward me. Taking the plate from my hands, he also set that aside, and then faced me. "Are you okay?"

With anyone else I'd get annoyed with that question, but coming from Aiden, it made me love him more. "I'm fine. Really, I'm not lying."

"Something is on your mind." He reached out, gently clasping my cheek and causing a delicate shiver to skate over my skin. "You're still beautiful. You know that, right?"

A wider smile pulled at my lips.

"What Perses said isn't true." He bent his head, brushing his lips over mine. The touch was barely there, but I felt it in every part of my being. "You are still as beautiful as you were the night I saw you standing in that warehouse in Atlanta."

I placed my hand on his chest, kissing him back as his heart jumped under my palm. "Thank you, but it's not what Perses said that's bothering me." I pulled back, running my teeth over my tingling lower lip. "I mean, yeah, I'm as shallow as the next girl, and hearing that kind of sucked, but it's not like I haven't accepted that I'm not going to be entering beauty pageants any time soon."

"What's going on in there, then?" Aiden tapped his forefinger on my temple.

At first, I wanted to say nothing and just enjoy this quiet time with Aiden, because I doubted we would have many more moments like this for a long time, but there was no reason to keep things to myself. No matter how small it was, I owed that to Aiden.

"It just seems bizarre to be sitting here while everything is going on." I shook my head, frustrated for a hundred different reasons. Unable to sit still, I stood, and the floor was cool under my bare feet as I padded over to the window. Vegas at night was like seeing the stars on the ground. "It's not like we have endless time on our hands. Ares is doing gods-know-what right now. Our friends are back at the University, where we're not."

"Apollo is with them. He'll keep them safe."

"I know." I pressed my forehead against the window and blew out a breath. "And who knows what Seth and Perses are getting themselves into. You saw it outside, right? He walked past two guys and they started fighting. That and Seth's charming personality is a winning combination."

"You're worried about what kind of trouble they're getting into?" he asked, and I heard him stand.

"Yes. No." I sighed and turned toward him, leaning back against the glass. "It's just ridiculous that we're doing this. Perses *is* going to cause trouble. And Seth? I doubt he's really going to try to stop him."

Aiden stopped a few feet in front of me. "You want to go see if we can find them? Maybe tail them?"

Tipping my head back, I closed my eyes. That seemed like a reasonable idea, but… "No. Seth will feel me the moment we get near him, and it's not…" I stifled a groan. "There's something going on with him."

Even though he didn't say anything at first, I felt his sudden shift in interest. Tension poured into the air, and the cord tightened deep inside me. "Do you think he's up to something?"

"Seth is always up to something." I let my arms fall to my sides and squeezed my eyes shut until I saw little white dots. "I know it's not anything to do with Ares. It's something else. I can feel…" I trailed off as it hit me. I did groan out loud then. "Dammit."

"What?" Aiden's voice was closer.

"I feel frustrated, restless, and pissy, but I didn't know why. It's not me. I'm picking up on Seth through our bond. And I know that's weird and you probably didn't ever need to know that, because it's worse than having PMS—"

Without warning, I felt Aiden's lips touch the center of my throat, and I gasped. Opening my eyes, my gaze locked with his. "Gods, you're as quiet as a ninja."

One side of his lips tipped up, and his hands settled on my hips. "So, you're telling me that Seth's not in a good mood, therefore you're feeling the effects of it?"

"Yeah." My mouth was suddenly dry. Trapped between his body and the glass window, I felt my pulse kick up. "It's been awhile since we've been around each other. I forgot that it does that."

Truth was, I knew that was part of the reason why I was feeling antsy, but I also knew there was something else going on with Seth. I couldn't put my finger on it, though, and I didn't want Aiden to worry needlessly.

His hands slid up my hips and settled on my waist. "So how do we fix this?"

"Fix it?"

Aiden dropped his forehead to mine. "Seth can be in whatever mood he wants to be in, but there's no reason for you to have to feel it if there's something we could do."

I was about to tell him that it really wasn't that big of a deal, but then he tugged me forward, watching me as he did so, and I didn't say a word.

"Maybe you need a distraction," he murmured, lashes dipping but not quick enough to shield eyes that were now a heated silver.

What I needed to do was to stop whining and enjoy the downtime. Maybe we could go out and sightsee. I almost laughed, because seriously, that would be so inappropriate given everything, and I honestly didn't want to be anywhere that required me to share Aiden's attention.

Because the kind of attention Aiden was giving me right now was the stuff dreams were made of.

Forcing myself to let out a long breath, I shook it all off—Seth, Perses, and Ares. I pushed away the fact that Aiden would be employed in the afterlife, and thoughts of the battles that lay ahead, and the uncertainty of our futures no matter what happened. I wanted to be *here* with Aiden, because he was *here* with me. I focused on those pink, bedazzled walls in my head, hopefully cutting off Seth's access to what I was feeling. So didn't need a peeping Seth for this.

"A distraction would be nice," I agreed in what I hoped was a serious voice.

His fingers curled around my side, tightening. He pulled me into the warmth of his body, and I tipped my head back. "Any ideas?"

My mind produced some really naughty ideas like rapid fire.

So many, so quick, I was actually worried for myself. "Maybe you could kiss me? That seems to always distract me."

"Hmm, I could do that." He lowered his lips to mine, and electricity zinged through my veins. It was that spark—the spark I only had with Aiden. When he lifted his mouth from mine, I almost whimpered. The kiss wasn't nearly long enough. "I'm not sure that worked at distracting you."

I shook my head, my heart racing. I placed my hands on his chest, fisting his black shirt. "Try again?"

"I can do that." He moved his hands to my back, and then his lips were pressing against mine, coaxing them open. The kiss was deep, shattering in the way it completely took me over. I clung to him as one hand flattened against the small of my back and the other caught the ends of my hair. "Did that distract you?" he asked, his voice thick.

I was barely breathing or standing on my own. "A little."

"A little?" he said, and his chuckle caused me to shudder. "I'll have to try harder."

Aiden's hand drifted down my lower back and around the curve of my waist. His long fingers slipped under the hem of my shirt, and I jerked when they touched my skin.

"Still trying," he said, using the hand in my hair to guide my head back and expose my throat. He pressed tiny, hot kisses against my throat as his hand slipped up, curving over my breast. I moaned his name, and he made this deep sound in his throat.

"Keep trying," I said, letting my eyes fall closed as his lips pressed against my pulse.

Aiden murmured something and shifted his body against mine, wringing another breathy moan from me. In this moment, everything was about us and only us, and I welcomed it. A second later, my shirt landed somewhere on the floor, and the glass against my back was cool. He snaked an arm around my waist and lifted me up. I wrapped my legs around his hips as he brought my mouth back to his.

There was something raw and feral in the way he kissed me then. It was a possessive kiss, a welcome one that staked a claim on my heart and soul. He turned, and in one powerful surge he trapped my back against a nearby wall and pressed the entire length of his body against mine. I wanted to feel his skin against mine, but with the way he was sealed to me, that wasn't happening.

Our mouths collided, hungry and demanding as I threaded my fingers through his hair. His lower body rocked against mine, sending sharp pulses through me. The marks of the Apollyon raced to the surface, causing my already sensitive skin to tingle. We kissed like we were drowning in one another, and each time he rolled his hips, I felt like I'd shatter apart.

"Gods, Alex," he said between kisses. "You'll never know what you do to me, how you make me feel."

I had a pretty good idea. I brought his mouth back to mine, and I don't know how he could obliterate my senses with his kisses and still manage to walk, but he did. He stalked toward the bedroom, his hands tight on my hips. My back parted the gossamer canopy over the bed, and then he laid me down, his mouth trailing off my lips and gliding down my heated skin, followed by his hands.

Sitting up, I tugged his shirt off, and he laughed when I tossed it outside of the bed, outside of our little world. The sound brought a smile to my lips, and he froze over me, his knees planted into the bed on either side of my thighs.

"I love seeing you smile," he said, cupping my cheek. "And I miss it when it's gone."

A knot formed in my throat as my fingers traced the hard lines and rises of his chiseled stomach. "I missed this."

He smiled as he lowered himself, putting most of his weight on the elbow next to my head. When he kissed me again, it was much slower but no less intense or soulful than the ones before. He kissed me until my body burned under his, and then he moved south, slipping the straps of my bra down my shoulder and then getting rid of it completely. Those lips sought out every scar, and there are many, and I never felt more beautiful than I did in that moment.

Or when he flicked open the button on my pants, and then hooked his fingers under the band, slipping them plus another very important article of clothing down my legs. The air was cool, but not for long. Aiden returned to me, and I got the top button of his pants undone before he starting moving down.

It wasn't like the first time, when Aiden had stopped to ask permission. He didn't hesitate. He dropped a sweet kiss against the inside of my thigh, and then there was lightning in my body. Even tapping into akasha couldn't compare to the feeling. I broke apart into a million, dazzling pieces.

When he lifted away from me and leaned out of the canopy, I whimpered.

"Condoms," he said, reaching into the drawer of the nightstand. I heard clothing hit the floor, and I rose halfway up. "Found them earlier."

I laughed, relieved that we were playing this safe since it was doubtful the shot was still working. "Nice how they keep those stocked."

"You should've seen the rest of the stuff in here." He came back to me, and my breath caught as my gaze dropped. He was absolutely beautiful. "Maybe later I'll show you."

My curiosity was piqued, but then Aiden kissed me again, and I wasn't thinking about what could be in that drawer. He nipped at my lip, and I opened to him. His tongue slipped inside, curling my toes as he settled between my legs. His mouth left mine, traveling down my throat and between my breasts. He hovered there, my body arching against his until he traveled back to my mouth. "Agapi mou," he murmured, capturing my lips in a searing kiss as he thrust his hips.

There were no more words, not with our bodies moving together, our tongues twisting and our hearts pounding. I rolled him onto his back. His muscles tensed and rippled under my hands.

The sweetest fire burned through me as I leaned down, whispering against his lips. "I love you."

Aiden shifted me so I was on my back once more, his body shaking as he moved over me, *inside* me. A powerful tension curled within me, and I coiled my body around his. My chest swelled so much, warring with the other intense feelings inside of me so that when I cried out, it was almost too much. Sometime later, our breathing still rapid and heavy, Aiden pressed kisses to the lids of my eyes, to my cheeks, and then to my parted lips. He threaded his fingers through mine, holding them down beside my head, kissing me softly. "I love you."

And then he started all over again.

CHAPTER SEVENTEEN

Something crashing to the floor jarred me awake. I shot up in bed, clutching for the sheet as my eyes adapted to the darkness. The canopy was still, but my heart was racing and I felt…I felt ridiculously happy. Like everything in the world was right.

What Aiden and I had done into the late hours of the night had been earth-shattering, but this was different.

Aiden stirred, rising halfway up on his elbows. "What is it?"

Before I could utter a word, what sounded like a heavy body hitting the floor broke the silence. "What the hell?" Aiden swung his legs off the bed.

I stood, finding his shirt in the darkness. It fell to my knees when I slipped it on. I grabbed the dagger off the nightstand, and by the time I made it to the bedroom door, Aiden already had his pants on and gun in hand.

But the pants were unbuttoned and hung low, and well, with his sleep-tousled hair and his cut abs all on display, I got a teeny tiny bit distracted for a second.

Aiden caught my stare and his lips tipped up. I forced my gaze away so I didn't say screw it and jump him.

Outside the bedroom, we headed for the door to the living room. He unlocked it and entered first, which was stupid considering I was the Apollyon, but he was a guy.

Flipping on the light, he drew to an abrupt halt and laughed—laughed deeply and loudly. Tension eased out of my muscles. Whatever was going on couldn't be bad if he was laughing.

I peeked around him and my mouth dropped open.

Perses was sprawled on the floor, missing his jacket. There were red marks on his white slacks, some a dark crimson. Others were a deep red and more like smudges along the zipper.

A basket of meatballs was on his chest—half were in the carton, and half had rolled down his twenty-pack abs.

The Titan reached down, picked up a meatball from somewhere near his belly button, and popped it into his mouth. "These things are so damn good."

There were no words.

Seth leaned against the couch. No shoes. No shirt. His amber eyes were glassy and unfocused.

Now the half-stupid happiness I felt upon waking made sense. "You two are completely trashed," I said, eyes wide.

Seth raised a hand, busted knuckles bruised and raw. "We are…not drunk."

"Really," Aiden drew out the word.

Fighting the smile on my face, I loosened my grip on the blade. "What happened to your hands?"

"Nooothing," Seth replied, chuckling. Perses chewed loudly on another meatball.

I glanced at Aiden. "Is that blood on your pants, Perses?"

"Among other bloodily fluids," he replied, and then he snorted.

"Gross."

Aiden shoved the gun in the back of his pants and folded his arms. "I'm assuming it's not your blood?"

The Titan laughed.

Okay. I was starting to get a little worried. "It's not a mortal's blood, is it?"

Seth pushed to his feet and swayed to the side. He sat—er, fell back—onto the couch. "No. We ran into some daimons."

I stared at him. "And you decided to get into a hand-to-hand bitch fight with them? You could've just used one of the elements or akasha."

"Your buddy has a lot of pent-up aggression," Perses said, picking up a meatball. He sat halfway up and tossed the meatball. "I like him."

Even drunk, Seth had ninja reflexes. He caught the meatball with a laugh. I had no idea what to say.

"All right, as entertaining as this is, make sure you two are sober enough by noon." Aiden turned, catching my free hand. "Have fun."

At the door to our room, I glanced over my shoulder. Seth was leaning way to the side, eyes drifting shut, expression slack. It was then when I noticed that, like Aiden, his pants were unbuttoned. Between him and Perses, I wondered how they'd even made it back to the hotel room.

Back inside the bedroom with the door locked, Aiden pulled the gun out and placed it on the nightstand.

"Wow," I said, grinning.

He laughed. "Wasn't expecting that."

"Me neither."

After relieving me of the dagger, he stepped back and

eyed me. Even in the darkness, I could feel his intense stare. "I know I've said this before, but I like seeing you in my clothes."

Warmth spread over my cheeks, and heat flooded my veins. "Good. I like wearing them."

"But you know what I like better?"

I didn't get a chance to say anything before he hooked his fingers under the hem of the borrowed shirt and tugged it over my head. The material fluttered to the floor as he clasped my hips, lifting me up.

Aiden's lips brushed mine as he spoke, eliciting a series of shivers. "I like taking them off."

Hades appeared exactly at noon, not a second early or late, and didn't ask any questions. He popped us back to the middle of the University, and while I was a little woozy on my feet from the method of travel, Seth looked like he was going to hurl up everything he'd drunk the night before. That explained the way my stomach was churning. Bastard.

Which was confirmed a second later when Seth said, "I think I'm going to vomit."

Aiden cast him an amused look. "Lightweight."

"Shut up," Seth moaned, clutching his stomach.

The air in front of us shimmered, and then Apollo appeared, startling me enough that I took a step back. My eyes narrowed on him. Couldn't any of the gods just walk somewhere?

Okay. If I could pop in and out and avoid stairs, I'd do it, too.

And I'd probably get the same amount of sick pleasure Apollo got out of doing it.

Hades stepped forward, eyeing Perses before he turned to

Apollo. "I hope you're right and this idea works." He tossed a sneer at the Titan, who scoffed loudly. "The son of a bitch doesn't deserve a chance, and you know it."

The sun seemed to soak through Apollo's skin as he leveled a stare on the other god. "As I recall, you had no other suggestions."

Hades smirked. "I did. Shut down the Underworld and let you guys battle it out." He shrugged. "You didn't like that idea." With that, the god disappeared.

"I have never been a fan of Hades. Over-pompous asshole," Apollo muttered. I arched a brow. That was something coming from him.

The Titan's lips curled up. "You're still a glowing bundle of fun, Apollo."

Apollo narrowed a gaze on Perses. "Do not start with me. You know what has to be done. And I promise you, if you cause us any problems, you'll end up on Prometheus's rock, except it won't be an eagle pecking away at you."

"What would it be, then?" Curiosity marked Seth's tone.

Apollo's smile was chilling. "I'll do it. Personally. Strip by strip with a dull blade dipped in cobra venom. And then, when I'm done at the end of the day, I will sew you back together to just start all over the following day."

"Wow," I murmured. "Inventive."

Perses didn't look impressed. "I've heard worse threats."

My eyes widened. Beside me, Aiden hid his smile while scrubbing at his chin with his palm. Seth had a far-off look on his face, as if picturing what Apollo had said. Didn't think it was possible, but he turned even more pasty.

"Are you okay?" I asked.

Seth waved one hand. "Yeah, perfect."

"So, where is the army I'm to train?" Impatience filled

Perses's tone. "All I see are buildings and a few children of demigods peeking around corners. I hope they aren't your warriors."

I snorted. "No, they're not. They're students. Our army is trained. They're—"

"Trained as Guards and hunters, right?" Perses chuckled mockingly, and I sort of wanted to see Apollo break out the dull blade. "They may be skilled when it comes to hunting daimons, but are they skilled enough to fight?"

"They won't be fighting Ares," Aiden explained, earning an interested look from the Titan. "Ares is heavily guarded by mortal soldiers, daimons, and automatons."

Perses's brows knitted. "Your army should be able to defend themselves against two of them. The automatons would be a problem, but they'll just have to be quicker. I do not see what you need me for."

"As Sentinels and Guards, we've never tried to work together in groups larger than three or four. We were never trained on war tactics. And *I* need you," I said, hating myself for having to say that. "I need you to prepare me for facing Ares. You have already seen how that went the first time."

Seth's eyes tightened. "You also have to prepare me to fight Ares."

The likelihood of me letting Seth near Ares was right up there with me actually cooking myself a dinner that was edible. I opened my mouth, but Aiden jumped in.

"And I need to be trained on how to fight him as well."

"Guys, the last time I checked, I was becoming the God Killer, which would make me pretty badass as it is. And with Perses's training, I'm going to also be kick-ass."

"That doesn't mean you don't need backup," Seth retorted.

I wished he'd just go puke somewhere. I swallowed hard against the sick feeling leaking through the bond.

"And you're not facing Ares alone," Aiden added. And I wished Aiden would go hold his hair for him.

Apollo rolled his eyes. "Children, really, Alexandria is a big girl and doesn't need two boys rushing to defend her."

I smiled broadly. "Exactly."

Neither Aiden or Seth looked like they agreed, and the look Aiden sent me promised that we'd talk about this later. Oh, we would. He wouldn't like the outcome. There was no way in holy Hades Aiden was getting within a city block of Ares.

Perses exhaled roughly. "I can spend the mornings training your army and the afternoons working with one or three of you. I really don't care how many, but I can tell you this. Ares would've sensed my presence the moment I stepped into the mortal realm. He knows I'm here. He will be unnerved by it, but the longer we take, the more time he will have to rebuild his confidence or bring in more reinforcements. We attack immediately, within the week, or we lose our advantage. Because if you have spies, so does he."

I glanced at Apollo. Perses had a point. We couldn't string this out. We would need to move fast, but would we be ready? Would *I* be ready?

Apollo's jaw tensed, and then he nodded curtly. "A week from now, on Monday, we move on the Catskills. We take on Ares."

Training with Perses was like running into a brick wall, getting back up, and face-planting into it again just for the fun of it.

We'd started immediately with our training. Of course,

Aiden and Seth took part. It was a waste of breath to try to convince them otherwise.

Just like when Seth and I used to train, we drew an audience of Sentinels, students, and staff. Word got out quickly that there was a Titan on campus, something that most people never thought they'd see. I couldn't blame them for gawking. Among those crowded around the largest training room in the athletics building were my friends.

Which was great, because there was nothing like having friends and strangers around to watch you get your ass kicked.

And we were getting our asses kicked.

I'd hit the padded floor more times than I could count, taking turns with Seth and Aiden, who were doing no better than me.

It was Seth's turn, and I eased myself down, biting my lip when my tailbone hit the mat. "I think I broke my butt," I moaned.

Sitting beside me, Aiden reached over, rubbing his hand along my lower back. The touch ached at first, but the steady burn started to ease my muscles. "Yeah, that was a pretty nasty landing you took."

It had started out so perfect. I'd gotten behind Perses, who, by the way, was weaponless, and had sprung up and spun out, about to land a beauteous spin kick when he whipped around and caught my leg, throwing me down like a rag doll.

My butt had broken my fall.

Seth was currently backed into a corner by Perses, dodging the Titan's vicious strikes. In theory, we had a week to train before leaving for the Catskills. It was a twenty-three hour drive, and Marcus was currently rounding up a billion vehicles for the trip.

The army mostly needed standard tactical training, but

us? We had to actually knock Perses down and gain the upper hand before our training would be complete. Sounded easy until I realized that Perses was like Ares on steroids. Either way, by Monday morning, we were leaving, prepared or not. I glanced over toward the door. Deacon spotted my gaze and winked. I grinned at him, and my gaze moved on. Several pures were staring at Aiden and me. Apparently, a pure-blood touching my back was more shocking than a Titan kicking an Apollyon's ass. I rolled my eyes and turned back to the match in front of us.

Dipping under Perses's outstretched arm, Seth came up behind the Titan, and just like I had, he prepared to deliver a vicious kick. Perses turned and dipped, catching Seth's foot. Unable to keep his balance, Seth hit the mat on his side.

Perses tipped his head back and laughed. "Next."

When one of us went down, it was the next one's turn. Aiden dropped his hand and pushed himself up. Passing Seth on the mats, the two idiots exchanged smirks.

Seth dropped down beside me. I glanced at him. "I don't know why you two are giving each other that 'I'm superior' look. Both of you are getting your asses kicked."

He shrugged one shoulder. "Doesn't mean we have to hug it out."

Turning my attention back to Aiden, I watched him beautifully execute an uppercut that did absolutely nothing to deter Perses's brutal punch to the stomach. "You know this is pointless, right? Neither of you needs to be subjecting yourself to this. I'm going to become the God Killer. You won't be fighting—"

"We will be fighting with you," Seth argued, his voice low. He too watched Aiden and Perses. "Just because you're the God Killer doesn't mean you can go in there alone."

"I won't be." I winced as Perses's kick caught Aiden in the thigh. "I'll be with Perses."

"And that's not really backup. Who knows what he'll do in the end? You need someone there with you." Seth leaned back, stretching out his legs. "And you and I both know Aiden would be a distraction."

I clenched my jaw. "Aiden will not be with me."

He snorted. "Does he know that?"

"He will." I looked at him. "Seth, we need to talk about when we'll transfer power."

"That's not what we're talking about now. There's no way I'm letting you go face-to-face with Ares with just Perses. It's not going to happen, and I'm not going to argue with you. You'll need me there to run interference, if anything," he said, returning my stare. "Besides, we shouldn't make the transfer until we're in the Catskills."

I opened my mouth, but Aiden hit the floor on his back and Perses yelled out, "Girl! Your turn!" Sending Seth a quick glance, I pushed to my feet. "We'll talk about this later."

He arched a brow.

As I passed Aiden on the mats, he reached over, tugged on the hem of my shirt, and then kept going. I stopped in front of the Titan, muscles locking up. Over at the door, Deacon whistled and shouted, "Show him what a girl is capable of!"

I took my eyes off Perses for a second to smile at Deacon, and that was all it took. Out of the corner of my eye, I saw Perses's hand zooming for my face. At the last moment, I dropped down. The speed at which Perses's fist shot past my head, stirring wisps of my hair—*gods*. If that had connected with my head, he would've probably knocked me out cold.

"Never take your eyes off the opponent," Perses said, chuckling.

How many times had Ares said that when we knew him as Instructor Romvi? Nothing flipped my kill-and-maim switch like hearing those words.

I rolled forward and popped to my feet behind Perses. Spinning around, I dodged his second punch and dipped under his arm. I knew I was fast—faster than Aiden, who was like a freaking ninja, and faster than all other half-bloods. But Perses was like Ares. Fighting was bred into their blood. There was no one in this realm better than them. I could only hope to be their equal.

But I wasn't Perses's equal at the moment.

The second I shot up in front of him, he anticipated the move and kicked out, his booted foot connecting with my midsection. Pain exploded along my stomach, and I doubled over. His hand slammed into my shoulder, and I lost my balance. Toppling backward, I hit the mats on my back, hard.

Perses was suddenly in my face, looming over me. A smirk graced his lips. "God Killer or not, girl, he will own you if you fight like this. And as you know, he can't kill you, but he can make you beg for death. Is that something you want to experience again?"

Anger burned through my veins like poison. "My name is not 'girl,' and no, that's not something I want to experience again."

The smirk slipped off his face. "Then get back up, *girl*."

Meeting his stare, I rolled into a sitting position. Ignoring the slice of pain, I got back up.

CHAPTER EIGHTEEN

By Wednesday, I was sure my entire back was an array of violets and blues. I was, literally, one giant walking-and-talking bruise. Aiden and Seth hadn't fared any better. Last night, when Aiden and I had gone to bed, we'd been too sore and too tired to take off our pants.

Needless to say, Marcus had given up on the separate bedrooms thing. Not that there was any point now. Neither of us could do anything even if our body parts touched.

The Army of Awesome was faring a lot better than us. Numbering near a thousand, they were learning basic tactical maneuvers. It was like the videos of boot camp I remembered seeing on TV. If anything, I think Perses was just trying to harden them instead of teaching them any real skills. He was worse than any Covenant Instructor I'd ever seen.

The Titan was a cesspool of insults.

Later that night, after a long soak in some kind of herbal mixture Laadan had provided, I sat on the bed, too tired to make my way back to the common area for food.

Thankfully, Aiden was possibly the most wonderful man in the whole universe. He brought a plate full of chicken tenders and fries to the room.

"Nice shirt," he commented, nudging the door shut with his toe.

I glanced down at myself, grinning. "Sorry."

He laughed as he eased down beside me, placing the tray between us. "As I've said a hundred times before, I like seeing you in my clothes."

A flush covered my cheeks. "I was too tired to put pants on."

Peering up through his lashes, he grinned. "And I'm not going to complain about that." He picked up a can of soda, popped the tab, and handed it to me. "I lost the battle of wills with Deacon."

"Uh-oh."

Deacon wanted to travel with us to New York. He felt, since he'd christened the name of our army, he was some kind of official mascot or something. Of course, Aiden wasn't happy with that, and I couldn't blame him. Deacon was safer here. Who knew what we'd meet on the road and what we'd find in New York once we got there?

"I've told him about a million times that I'd feel better with him staying here." He picked the breading off his tenders, causing me to smile. "But I'm not winning this battle."

"He'll probably just sneak out with us, anyway." I bit off half of my tender, breading and all. "And he's worried, you know. Not just about you, but Luke, too."

"I get that." He tossed the breading onto the plate. "Doesn't mean I have to like it."

I watched him meticulously remove more breading and then took a deep breath. "Speaking of not wanting people to get hurt and the whole keeping them safe thing. We need to talk about that."

He peeked up, his fingers stilling. "Details?"

Finishing off my tender, I took a drink before I continued.

"I'm not asking you to stay behind here, because I want you to go with me. And I know you wouldn't do that anyway."

Aiden lowered the chicken piece, his head tilting to the side. "Damn straight."

"But I need you to know that I can't face Ares with you by my side." I rushed on, so that the words that were forming on his tongue couldn't get out. "I know why you want to be there, and I respect that. Hell, I love you for that. But Ares is going to go after you just to get to me."

He dropped the tender. "Alex, you're asking the impossible."

"No, I'm not." I met his thundercloud-gray stare. "I love you, Aiden. I love you more than anything. And the fact that you want to be there for me is amazing. But I can't have you there. Ares knows how much you mean to me, and you'll be a distraction. I hate to say that, but it's the truth."

A muscle began to throb in his jaw. "I'm not sure if I'm supposed to feel insulted by that."

"You're not!" I resisted the urge to throw a piece of chicken in his face. "Look, I get that the idea of me going in there without you—"

"Makes me freaking sick to my stomach?"

"Well, yeah, that, but you have to understand that, because I love you, I don't want to have to worry about Ares getting a hold of you."

The muscle was really ticking now. "And because I love you, that's why asking me to let you do this by yourself is insane."

Striving for patience, I shoved a handful of fries in my mouth before continuing. "I'm not going to be by myself. Seth will be there."

"Oh, and that's supposed to make me feel better?"

"Not like I haven't tried to get him to change his mind, too." My eyes narrowed. "But he's an Apollyon."

"And I'm a trained Sentinel who can handle myself," he shot back. "And besides, you think I'll be safer with the army?"

"If I could have my way, you wouldn't be there at all, but I'm not asking you to do that. I'll feel better knowing that you're not near Ares." Wiping my hands off, I folded my arms. "And I know, deep down, you understand that."

Silent, he picked up the tray and stood, placing it on the small desk. He turned to me and scrubbed both of his hands down his face. A wince creased his features as he lowered his arms. "Alex…"

"It's the same reason why you don't want Deacon with us, but I'm hoping—I'm praying—you'll listen to me." I tucked my legs under me and pulled down the hem of the shirt. "And seriously. You owe me."

"I do?" He moved toward the bed.

I nodded. "Yeah. The whole soul and Hades thing? I don't need you possibly dying next week and ending up as Hades's henchman for eternity."

"I'm not going to die, but you do realize being with the army isn't exactly safe."

Hope sparked in my chest. "But I know you will get through that. I know you will." I couldn't believe anything else. Truth was, being a part of that army was dangerous, but being there against Ares was suicidal.

Aiden eased down on the bed beside me. "I don't like this."

"You don't have to like it. Just like I didn't like the idea of you giving up your soul to Hades. All you have to do is understand it."

The moment those words left my mouth, I internally patted myself on the shoulder. There were moments when my maturity surprised me.

He shifted onto his back, resting his hands on his flat stomach. His eyes were closed, and thick lashes brushed the tops of his cheeks. The muscle in his jaw thrummed along like a hummingbird, but as I watched him, it slowed down. Aiden took a deep breath, the ticking stopped, and he finally opened his eyes.

They were the softest shade of gray as they locked with mine.

"I don't agree with this. I *hate* it, Alex, but I get it. If it were the other way around, I wouldn't want you near him. Hell, I *don't* want you near him, but you have to. So, yeah, I'll stay with the army."

Relief eased the tense muscles in my shoulders and neck. I leaned over him, kissing his cheek. "Thank you. I know it wasn't easy for you, so thank you."

He rolled onto his side, resting his head on his curved elbow. Reaching over, he skimmed his hand up my leg, swerving to miss a nasty bruise. "When are you and Seth going to do the whole transfer of power thing?"

"Good question." Now that I'd worked this one thing out, it was time to figure out the next problem. "He wants to wait until we're in the Catskills."

His dark brows knitted. "Why?"

I shrugged a shoulder. "I really don't know. He said something earlier about the power being hard to handle, so maybe he thinks I'll crack and, I don't know, start zapping everyone in sight."

Aiden laughed. "That's ridiculous."

"Yeah, I don't know, though. My only other option is to hold him down and do it, and I don't see that going well."

He arched a brow. "I have no problem with that idea. I'll gladly hold him down."

A grin pulled at my lips. "You're terrible."

"Just being helpful."

I kissed his cheek again and then sat back. "I'm going to try to talk to him again. I think we need to do it soon, before we leave for New York."

"I agree." His fingers toyed with the hem of the borrowed shirt.

In the quiet moments that followed, I leaned over again and kissed him for a third time. "For good luck," I whispered. "We're going to war."

His lashes fluttered closed. "We are."

"Did you ever think you'd be in this position?" I placed my hand on his smooth cheek, and he pressed into it. "I never did. Not in a million years," I admitted.

"Me, neither." He pressed his hand over mine, holding it there. "I don't think any of us would have predicted this."

I bit down on my lip. In that flash of a second, I felt incredibly...young. I wanted Aiden's reassurance. "And you think it will get better afterward? Go back to normal?"

"I do." He kissed my palm again. "Let's talk about less depressing things. Do you still think there's something up with Seth?"

I laughed. "Is that really a better conversation for you?"

"Maybe." He grinned a little, and my heart toppled in my chest. "So?"

I started to respond, but there was a knock on the door. By the time I tugged the quilt over my legs, the door swung open and Deacon popped in, not even waiting for an invite.

The mop of blond curls bounced as he jumped to the foot of the bed. "Hi, guys!"

Aiden sat up slowly. "Hi, Deacon. Are you aware that it's customary to wait until someone answers the door or says 'come in'?"

"Not like I was interrupting anything. Both of you still have your clothes on."

I laughed. "He has a point."

Aiden shot me a "you're not being helpful" look. "So, what's up, Deacon?"

"Marcus is looking for you. He's in the common room, so I figured it would be better if I was the one who checked in on you two, just in case you were naked." He winked, and I smothered another giggle. "You're welcome."

Groaning, Aiden sat up. "Okay. You do have a point."

"Thought so." As his brother stood, Deacon dive-bombed the bed, causing me to bounce. He flicked my hand lightly. "Marcus wants to talk about the Council or some boring shit like that. His ladylove wants to talk plans about rebuilding. Then again, I sort of zoned out for half of the conversation."

My brows rose. There was an open seat on the Council that had belonged to Aiden's father. Since Aiden had never taken the seat, it was left open, something that had ticked away at Aiden. He knew that his father would've wanted him to follow in his footsteps rather than become a Sentinel.

Aiden ran a hand through his hair. "All right. Well, this should be interesting."

His brother snorted. "I'll stay here and keep Alex company."

"You do that." Aiden moved around the edge of the

bed, swooped down, and kissed my cheek. "I'll be back in a few."

I waved goodbye to him and watched him leave. Then I glanced at Deacon. My brows rose as his fingers flew over his cell phone. "Whatcha doing?" I asked.

"Just wait." No more than a few seconds later, the door opened again and Luke and Olivia poked their heads in. Deacon grinned up at me. "Slumber party?"

I laughed as I waved them in. "Sounds like a great idea."

Olivia scooted in next to me, while Luke stretched out across the head of the bed. She reached over, grabbing the remote control. "We may be leaving in a few days to fight in a war, but that doesn't mean we're too old for a slumber party."

"So very true." I took the pillow Luke handed me and snuggled down.

The four of us watched a bad movie well into the night. It was one of the most relaxing moments I'd had in a long time. When they got up to leave, I sat up, holding the pillow to my chest.

"Let's make a promise," I said.

Three sets of eyes settled on me. "What?" Olivia asked.

I felt kind of corny about what I was about to say, but oh, what the hell. "After all of this is done and over with, let's promise to do this at least once a week. No matter what we're doing or where we are."

A wide smile spread across Olivia's face. "That's a promise I'd love to make."

"Same here," agreed Luke, dropping his arm over Deacon's shoulders.

Feeling good about making plans to do something normal, I dozed off and didn't wake up until I felt Aiden sliding into bed behind me. I tipped my head back toward him as he slipped an arm around my waist. "How was everything with Marcus?"

"Okay." He kissed my cheek and tugged me back against him. "He wants me to take my Council seat once everything is...settled."

I'd figured as much. "What do you think?"

Aiden was silent for a long time. "There are things that I could do on the Council, things that I could help make right, especially when the Elixir stops working for the rest of the half-bloods. It's just..."

He didn't finish. The Council seat was a lot of things to Aiden—more than just responsibility. I turned so I was facing him and cuddled up close, wiggling so that my head was under his. "You don't have to make a decision now. You have time."

"You're right." His hand slid up my spine and settled there. "We have time."

After another grueling training session on Friday, I found myself limping into the dean's office. Our A.O.A. was leaving in the late morning on the following day. There was a lot to be discussed, and I had scored an invite. So had Seth. The only other times we'd been called to the dean's office in the past were because I'd done something I was about to get in trouble for, and those meetings usually ended in insults being slung back and forth.

Like when I'd threatened to cut Seth with one of Marcus's daggers. I had to smile at that memory.

Easing down into an empty chair, I glanced around the room. Marcus was behind the desk, because where else would he be, with Diana alongside him. Aiden and Solos hovered by the desk like two hawks, both wearing intense expressions that told me this was going to be a serious conversation. Even Apollo was there. He'd been hanging around a lot, watching over the training. Right now, he was holding a Newton's cradle like he'd never seen one before, his hand hovering over one of the small, silver balls. I looked around again, frowning.

Looking for Perses? Seth glanced at me from where he was leaning against the wall. *Last I saw him, he was heading into an empty room with two pure girls.*

"What?" I screeched out loud before I could stop myself.

Several sets of eyes landed on me, and Seth smirked. Aiden's gaze narrowed between the two of us, and I began to suspect that we were about to have a repeat performance of threatening Seth.

Apollo let go of the silver ball and it swung sideways, knocking into the next ball and creating a chain reaction. A wide smile broke out across his face.

"Did no one ever tell you two that it is not nice to communicate telepathically with one another while others are present?" Marcus said, folding his hands on the desk.

I pursed my lips. "No, actually, no one has said that."

He smiled tightly. "Well, I am."

Busted, Seth said.

Gripping the edges of the chair, I stared straight ahead. *I hate you*. "So, what's up?"

Other than the fact Perses is getting some instead of being here?

Apollo picked up a silver ball from the other side and let that one go. Oh my gods…

Marcus's look turned suspicious as his gaze bounced between Seth and me. "Solos was talking battle strategy with Perses. We figured, since you two play an intricate role in this, it would be smart to bring you in on these meetings."

Seth strolled forward and dropped down in the seat beside me. "What's to discuss? From what I understand, it's fairly simple. The army will attack the front gate while Alex and I sneak in with Perses."

Perses had discussed his plan with us the previous day between rounds of kicking our butts. Aiden was still taking part in the additional trainings even though he'd agreed to remain with the larger group once we launched our attack against Ares.

Propping his hip against the desk, Solos pointed down at a map of the New York Covenant, a much better map than the one Athena had created. "It's really not that simple. We have to find a way to sneak you in. I'm sure you remember how well-guarded the Catskills is. Getting past the preliminary fences will be no problem. The wall is another story."

An insolent smile twisted Seth's lips. "There was a breach in the east wall. I've already told Perses. It's not a huge hole, but it is large enough for a person to slip through. Unless Ares is interested in masonry work, I doubt it has been repaired."

"It's unlikely that Ares would leave the breach unguarded," Aiden said, his eyes a steely gray. "You won't just walk in there."

That smirk on Seth's face grew. "I wasn't planning to just walk in there."

"Okay," I said, interrupting before a battle of wills erupted. "So we will have to scout the wall first. We can—*Apollo*!"

The god looked up. In his hands, the Newton balls knocked off of each other once more. "What?" he asked.

"*What?*" I shot him an annoyed look. "Seriously. Have you never seen a Newton's cradle before? Every time you move the first ball, it's going to move the rest of the balls."

"No." His gaze dipped to the cradle. "Physics is cool."

"Oh my gods," I moaned, slumping in my seat. "My brain hurts."

Apollo let go of the silver ball once more and then placed

the cradle on the edge of Marcus's desk. "I imagine you're leaving with the army on Saturday?" he said to Solos. When the half-blood nodded, he glanced at Aiden. "And you will travel with Alex?"

"Do you need to even ask that question?" Aiden replied, placing his hands on the desk and leaning in.

Apollo shrugged.

"I will leave with the army, as well," Marcus announced, sitting back in the chair.

Diana cleared her throat delicately. "If I may make a suggestion?" My uncle nodded, and she smiled. "I think you are needed here more, Marcus."

His eyes immediately sharpened into green crystals. "I'm needed in the Catskills."

"I know you feel that way," she started again, patient and understanding. "You are a Sentinel at heart, Marcus, but there is so much we have to do. More than just fighting."

"She's correct," Apollo said, apparently ready to contribute to the conversation. "Rebuilding is just as important as war, and that process starts long before the war is over."

Marcus's jaw tightened. "You are here, Diana, plus other surviving members of the Council."

"The Council is in ruins, Marcus. We need you here, and we need you alive to help rebuild after all this is said and done," Diana argued, and I couldn't help but wonder if something deeper drove her conviction. If so, I didn't blame her. I would cut off my left arm to convince Aiden to remain behind. "We need you here."

Several agreed, and Marcus stiffened in his chair. "I'm a trained Sentinel. I have assets that will be of—"

"We know that." It was Aiden who spoke. "But I have to agree with Diana. We have this covered."

"We do," Solos confirmed. "Defeating Ares means nothing if we can't deal with the chaos afterward. And there will be chaos. We have Covenants that are destroyed or heavily damaged, and entire Councils have been wiped out. And we will have half-bloods coming off the Elixir and out of servitude. We will need leadership—strong leadership."

A proud grin crossed my lips. Marcus would make a great leader. He already was. And I could easily see him taking the role of Head Minister. Marcus might act like he had a stick shoved in a very unmentionable place half the time, but he'd be righteous and fair. Strict, but he would always do the right thing by pures and halfs.

Our eyes met, and I don't know what he saw in my expression, or if my smile had anything to do with what he did next, but I liked to think it did.

Marcus rubbed a hand across his brow, sighing heavily. "I want to be there, but...you're right. I need to stay here."

"Well, now that's settled, I think I'm going to find something soft to lie on." Seth popped up from his chair, his movements not nearly as fluid as normal. He glanced at me, and a mischievous glint filled his amber eyes. "Want to join me?"

I rolled my eyes.

Annoyance flashed into Aiden's eyes, turning their hue into a stormy gray as he pushed off the desk and straightened. "Very amusing."

Seth winked as he backed away. "Hey, just being gentlemanly."

"Go somewhere else, then," Aiden replied.

Chuckling, Seth dipped out the door as I shook my head. While Seth and I had been more than friends at one point and our feelings for one another did run deep, I was a hundred percent certain that Seth was just trying to cause Aiden to stroke out.

Once Seth exited, the conversation moved back to the Council, and my interest also exited. Pushing up from the chair, I limped out of the office after telling them I was heading back to my room. I foresaw another herbal bath in my future. I had two more training sessions with Perses, and while each of us was getting better, none of us had taken him down.

Yet.

One of us had to take him down before we left for the Catskills.

I'd made it halfway down the stairs before Apollo poofed in front of me, startling me. I jerked to the side and lost my balance. Teetering on the edge of the step, visions of bones crunching rang in my head. He caught my arm, stopping my fall.

"Gods," I gasped, grasping the handrail with my free hand. "Is it necessary to do that?"

"You're okay." He dropped my arm. "We need to talk."

I leaned against the railing, eyeing him wryly. "What? You got bored with the Newton's cradle?"

His lips tipped up at the corners. "Why haven't you transferred the power from Seth yet?"

"He wants to wait until we get to the Catskills." I paused as his eyes narrowed. "Look, I'm going to try to get him to do it before we leave, but—"

"Seth doesn't want to do it, and I bet it's because he's not sure he can let you do it." Apollo cursed, and unease blossomed deep in my belly. "This could be a potential problem."

The unease gave way to irritation. It pricked at my skin and poked holes in my insides. "You know, I love how you just pop in and out whenever you want to and offer little to no answers. Nothing really helpful either, but boy oh boy, there may be a problem!"

Apollo's expression slipped into a scowl, but I was on a roll. No stopping me now. "You know, all of this is bullshit. I said it before, and I'll say it again, Ares is *your* problem. He's the gods' problem." His mouth opened, but I kept on going. "And don't you dare say it's Seth's problem! Ares created this mess ages ago when he started this crap with Solaris and the First. But you guys didn't really do anything then, did you? You sent the Order in to kill them instead of getting to the bottom of what was happening."

"Alex—"

"And now it's happening again. We are going to war for you—for the gods. People will die. My friends and the people I love could die! I could die!" My voice cracked, and I took a step down. My throat felt like it was on fire. "I haven't forgotten that, Apollo. I know I could die in the end."

He clapped a heavy hand on my shoulder and squeezed. "I promise you, Alex, that no matter what happens, I'll take care of you. I told you that, and I *always* keep my promises."

A knot in my throat made it difficult to speak. The probability of my inevitable death at the hands of those who needed my help wasn't something I'd forgotten about. In reality, it was just something I couldn't fixate on. Since the hellboy twins had been exorcised from me, I had refused to dwell on it, and the reason why descended in startling clarity in that moment. In the end, no matter what Apollo wanted, he would not disobey the other Olympians. Doing so would further split them, and it could become disastrous.

Blinking back tears, I looked away, working my throat until I was sure that, when I opened my mouth, it wasn't a sob. "I don't want to die."

"I know," Apollo said, and his voice was surprisingly

gentle. "I will do everything in my power to make sure that doesn't happen. I haven't let you down yet, have I?"

My gaze crawled over the gray cement walls, finally settling on his. Had he? He'd skirted the truth and divulged information only when he felt like it, but had he let me down? I didn't answer the question. "The gods should be fighting. You know that, Apollo. They should be a part of this."

Seconds passed. "You're right."

Wow. I was stunned into silence. Next thing I knew, Aiden and Seth would start to make out and profess their undying love for one another. "I'm right?"

"You are. They do need to be involved. They need to fight."

It took me a couple of moments to remember how to use my tongue. Hope kindled in my chest like a fledging, delicate fire. If the gods would fight, then the losses on our side would be less. "And you can make this happen?"

Apollo lowered his chin. "I will do everything I can to get them involved."

"You should. This is their fight."

"This is everyone's fight," he corrected. "Because it's everyone's future."

CHAPTER NINETEEN

Saturday had been a day full of pain.

While we were getting better at fighting Perses, we still were getting our butts handed to us. Seth had come close to taking Perses down with a kick. The Titan had stumbled, but he hadn't fallen. He'd come back at Seth, and within seconds the First was on his back.

But Sunday got worse.

"Mats are for the weak," Perses announced as I bounced across the blue butt-saver, and that comment took the happy right out of my step. He raised a hand, and the mats flipped up on their own, starting to fold like accordions. "Warriors do not need mats."

Jumping back, I missed being smashed and folded by less than a second. Under the mats was nothing but cold, hard floor. I sighed, knowing this was going to sting, and as usual, we had a crowd watching. Three pures had mixed among my friends. Solos was already cringing.

Perses motioned me forward. "Come on, girl."

I took a deep, calming breath before I stalked toward him. Attacking in anger seemed like a good idea. The gods knew I was known to do so from time to time, but I made mistakes in the heat of it, and making mistakes with Perses or Ares wouldn't end well for me.

He immediately launched at me, swinging a meaty hand at my head. Easy. I dipped down, avoiding the attack. Springing up, I twisted to the left as he kicked out with a booted foot. I blocked him at the knee, and then struck out for his throat. Perses countered, sneaking a punch that caught my arm and spun me. I tried to twist out of it into the fall, but as I turned, he threw his arm out, hitting me across the chest. Air exploded out of my lungs. Stumbling back, I was unprepared when he kicked out, sweeping my legs out from underneath me. I hit the hard floor on my back, knocking the oxygen out of my cells this time.

"Ow," I moaned, bending my knees. I blinked the ceiling back into focus, clearing the white flecks of light from my vision.

Aiden's curse rang loudly.

Hovering over me, Perses's laugh grated on my nerves. "I hope, when you become the God Killer, Ares stands still for you."

I flipped him off.

The Titan tipped his head back and laughed. "Charming."

Rolling to my feet, I limped over to the side, passing our little audience. Olivia caught my eye and smiled sympathetically. *Almost*, she mouthed.

Almost didn't really count. I joined the guys by the wall. "Well, that was a fail."

"It wasn't." Aiden tucked a stray piece of my hair back behind my ear. "You did well."

"She looked like a pancake when she hit the floor," Seth remarked, earning a pissy look from both of us. He laughed as he jogged off toward Perses.

Sitting down, I took the bottle of water Aiden handed me and gulped it down. As Seth squared off against Perses, I readied myself for another round. When Seth ate floor, Aiden took his place. Half of my bones felt brittle, as if they were about to break, and I couldn't fathom why Aiden was subjecting himself to this when he didn't have to. Not that Perses was complaining. The more butts he was kicking, the happier he was. I stretched my legs out, easing the sore muscles. Every time I went up against Perses, I wanted to tap into akasha and just give a good old, aether-fueled bitch-slap in the—

"Holy daimon butts," I whispered.

Seth glanced down at me, frowning. "Uh, what?"

Popping up to my feet, a smile split my lips. "I got it."

He shook his head as he studied me. "Got what? Milk?"

"No." Excited, I couldn't wait until Aiden went down. Not that I really wanted that, but I wanted at Perses. "I know how to take him down."

Seth snorted.

I ignored his lack of faith in my ability. Never once during our training had Perses told Seth and me that we couldn't use our Apollyon abilities. We'd just assumed that we couldn't. After all, we were treating these training sessions like we were back in class, fighting instructors. But we weren't. We also weren't normal students.

Aiden caught a kick in the middle of the back, taking him to his knees. "We're so stupid," I said to Seth, grinning.

His brows rose. "Speak for yourself, Angel."

As Aiden started back toward us, I passed him halfway, brushing my fingers down his arm. "I got this," I told him.

He smiled down at me, and as I continued forward, I saw the pures gathered at the doors exchange looks of disgust and disbelief. I flipped them off.

Perses yawned. "Back so soon, girl?"

"I can't wait to see your face when you hit the floor." I shook my arms out, letting the rush of power in my veins make it to my skin.

His gaze flickered over me, and I knew that he, like the gods, could see the marks of the Apollyon.

A smooth brow rose. "Well, let's do this."

Backing off, we circled one another, eyeing each other for that fine, slim moment of weakness. Springing forward, he twisted in midair, kicking out, but I spun to the side. He landed in a crouch, shooting up. Summoning akasha, I welcomed the rush of power as I threw my hand out. Shock flickered across his face. A pulse of light arced across the short distance between us, smacking into his chest. It wouldn't kill him, but it definitely did the trick.

Perses stumbled back, his body bending at the waist. There were only a few seconds to complete this. Spinning around, I aimed my knee for his stomach. He tried to avoid the kick, but he wasn't fast enough. I caught him in the midsection. He went down on one knee as I straightened. Bringing my arm down, I slammed my elbow into his back, between his shoulder blades. He planted his hands on the floor to catch himself. Moving lightning-quick and putting every muscle into the motion, I brought my leg up. The toe of my sneaker connected with his solar plexus. Perses flipped.

He hit the floor on his back, his eyes wide. Silence.

It was like the sound had been sucked out of the room. And then I heard Aiden yell, and then Luke, and then Olivia. I'd done it.

I'd taken down a mother-freaking Titan. Ares could suck it.

Standing over Perses, a ridiculously large smile crossed my face. "I don't think you'll be calling me 'girl' anymore."

He grunted.

"What the hell?" Seth stalked up to us. "You used an element—akasha. How was that fair?"

Rocking back on my heels, I resisted the urge to start jumping around and clapping. "He never said we couldn't use our abilities. We just assumed we couldn't."

Seth stared at me.

Perses shifted to his feet. "She's right. It's only taken a week for you idiots to figure that out. Even that one," he said, gesturing to where Aiden waited. "He could've used fire, but he never did. To defeat Ares or any god, you will have to use every weapon you have. That was the lesson."

I almost giggled with glee—actual *glee*.

Seth's mouth dropped open. "If that's the case, I could've taken you down the first day."

"But you didn't." Perses smiled as he tapped a long finger against his head. "You need to start using this as well as your muscles." Okay. I felt like clapping.

Seth rolled his eyes, but he turned to me. *Nice work, Angel.*

My smile spread, and I let my pride consume me for a moment. Perses ended the session shortly after that, and Seth disappeared out the door, parting the crowd like he was our version of Moses. I watched him go, knowing I needed to track him down. We had to do the transfer tonight.

Aiden hugged me when I joined him, resting his chin atop my head. "Brilliant."

I laughed as I squeezed him. "Not really. Think about how long it took me to figure out that we should've been using our abilities the whole time."

"Seth and I didn't figure it out at all, so you're one step ahead of us." He stepped back, sliding his hands off me. A shiver coursed through me, something that didn't go unnoticed. His eyes switched from gray to sliver. "What are you doing now?"

A flutter started in my stomach. "I'd love to do what you're thinking."

"But?"

"I need to talk with Seth." Stretching up, I kissed his cheek. Part of me might have done it because the gaping pures were still at the door even though our friends had disappeared. The other part did it because I liked kissing Aiden. "See you in a bit?"

Aiden nodded, but the tense line of his jaw said he wasn't happy. "You want me to go with you?"

I laughed under my breath. "No. That's not going to help."

He grumbled something and then said louder, "You did well today, you know that?"

A wide smile crossed my face. "Yes, I do."

Aiden chuckled. "Modesty?"

"Bah!" I started to turn, but stopped. "Hey, can we, like, chill tonight? Watch a movie with Olivia and the guys? Deacon and Luke?"

He nodded. "If that's what you want."

It was what I wanted. Tomorrow, when we left for New York, things would get, well, they would get *real*. And I wanted the night before to not be stressful.

With the exception of trying to convince Seth to transfer power and hoping I didn't turn into the Terminator Apollyon afterward.

That would ruin our movie plans. "Alex?"

I spun back to Aiden. "Yeah?"

"Be careful," he said, swiping up his water bottle.

"Always."

He smiled, but it didn't reach his eyes. I knew he was worried about what I was about to do, and I knew he wanted to be with me, but having Aiden and Seth in the same room wasn't going to help.

Walking toward the door, I raised an eyebrow at the remaining pures. They shifted to the sides, allowing me to pass.

I stopped in the hallway, facing them. "Hi."

The three pures exchanged surprised glances, but none of them spoke.

"Ah, you have nothing to say." I popped my hands on my hips and rocked back on my heels. "I know it's shocking to see a pure and a half together. And yes, we're together in the biblical sense."

Their eyes widened.

I smirked. "And seriously? That's not a big deal. So, why don't you three douche canoes go find something else to gawk at? Or, I don't know...get a hobby. Or better yet, there's this huge war that's about to start. You guys could go figure how to help instead of standing around like a bunch of bigoted asshats. Okay? Buh-bye."

Spinning around, I left them staring at me for a much better reason than age-old prejudices.

Back in the day, if I were looking for Seth, I'd probably have found him in the girls' dorms or somewhere where a lot of single females were mingling, but now? I wasn't so sure. With the exception of his wild night in Vegas, I hadn't seen him pay attention to anyone, really.

Troubled, I sighed.

All of us had changed so much in the last year. Sometimes

I didn't recognize myself when I looked in the mirror, and not in the physical sense. It had to be the same for Seth—probably even more so for him.

Using the freaky connection between us, I headed down the marble pathway leading beyond the high-rising dorms. The cord began to tighten as I rounded the last dorm and the cemetery came into view.

A shudder snaked down my spine. Seth was in the cemetery. Yeah.

Picking up my pace, I reached the titanium-encased gates quickly. Among the mausoleums and a statue of Thanatos, the red and purple hyacinths swayed softly in the breeze. They caught my attention for a few moments as I walked to the center of the cemetery. Under the peaceful gaze of the stone Thanatos, I scanned the tombs.

There he was.

Sitting on a stone bench, Seth's back was to the path. He sat straight, his gaze focused on the olive trees. It was so weird seeing them here in South Dakota, but like the gardens, the cemeteries had a godly green thumb. But what was even weirder was seeing Seth out here. Hanging out in places where tombs were built to remember the dead wasn't his thing.

"Are you following me?" His voice carried on the wind.

I made my way over to him and sat beside him. "Maybe."

One side of his lips tipped up. "Did you come to gloat about taking out Perses?"

"No." A tiny grin fought to make its way onto my lips. I lost. "Maybe a little."

He chuckled. "Figured."

"I did damn good."

Casting me a sidelong glance, he arched a brow. "You did. I almost had him."

"So did Aiden," I reminded him. "'Almost' being the key word."

"Whatever." He turned back to staring at the trees. I wondered what was so interesting about the clusters of leaves.

"What are you doing out here?"

"It's weird, right? To be hanging out here?" He bent forward, resting his arms on his thighs. "I don't know. It's quiet. I like to come out here and think."

It was quiet, too quiet. Granted, we were sitting in the middle of cemetery. Not a very happening place. "What are you thinking about?"

He chuckled again, but the sound was weak and strangely hollow. "Like you really care."

I blinked and opened my mouth. His tone was light, but there was a coating of frost to his words. "If I didn't care, I wouldn't ask. You of all people know that."

Moments passed, and then a breath shuddered from him. "Do you know what I think about when it's quiet, Alex? I think about all the bad things I've done."

My breath caught in my chest like someone had punched me. I didn't know what to say at first. What I had seen Seth do and what I knew he'd been a part of was enough to earn him a trip to Tartarus. Then there were the things I didn't know about and really didn't want to find out.

Shifting on the bench, I rubbed my hands over my sweats as a chill danced along my skin. It was cooler in this part of the campus, unnaturally so for the time of year. It seemed like forever passed before I spoke. "We've all done bad things."

"Ah," he said, scrubbing his hands down his face. A smile peeked through every few seconds, but when he finally dropped his hands, it was gone. "Have you ever killed an innocent person?"

Dropping my gaze, I shook my head. "No."

"That's the level of bad things I've done. Maybe you've kissed a boy you shouldn't have. Maybe you acted out when you should've thought more clearly about something," he replied. "Maybe you hurt someone's feelings or did the wrong thing, but nothing you've done will ever touch what I'm responsible for."

"I don't know what to say," I admitted quietly. "I can't tell you that any of that is okay. You'd know I was lying. But Seth? You weren't completely responsible for everything."

"When an addict kills someone to get money for drugs, are they not responsible? Or is it the drug dealer's fault?" When I didn't answer, he laughed dryly. "Anyway, obviously I'm not thinking about those things right this second. You're here. And I know there's a reason for you being here other than stalking me."

Now I felt kind of bad for why I had come looking for him. In spite of everything that Seth had done to others and to me, a part of me still cared for him and considered him a friend—and something more that could never quite be labeled. He needed someone to talk to. He needed someone to help him make things better. He needed someone who cared for him—cared for him more than I did.

Swallowing, I turned my gaze to the trees. I felt like an uber-bitch for my next words. "I want to do the transfer of power now. That's why I came here." He was silent, but I could feel his eyes drilling holes through the side of my head. "I don't want to wait until we get to the Catskills. We should do it now. Get it over with so we—"

"No." Steel poured into that one word. "We wait until we're about to face Ares. Not a moment sooner."

I turned my head toward his. "Why not? And don't you say 'because I said so.'"

His lips twisted wryly. "Damn, there goes my only explanation."

My eyes narrowed.

"We wait," he said, his eyes narrowing, too. "It's not up for discussion."

"How can you say it's not up for discussion? You're not the only person who has a say in this."

"I'm the only person whose say matters," he replied.

Pushing off the bench, I stood in front of him. "Oh, now you're just pissing me off."

Seth smiled. "So?"

"This isn't funny, Seth. Why in the hell are you so adamant on waiting? I'm ready. You should be ready, too. This isn't just about you, buddy."

The infuriating smile remained fixed. "Like I said before, you have no idea what it's like to be the First, how hard it is. So you can't even imagine what it will be like when you become the God Killer."

Anger flooded my system. "Oh, come off it, Seth! All you do is whine about how 'terrible the need' is and—"

In a nanosecond, Seth was in my face. He moved that fast, causing my heart to jump. I jerked back. Apollyon or not, he *was* the First, and when he moved like that, it didn't create a happy feeling. "All I do is whine?" Anger flushed his cheeks, and his amber eyes glowed. "You have no idea, Alex. You're just the Apollyon. That's all you have to deal with."

I stepped back, trying to rein in my own anger. "I have to deal with our connection and the stupid cord inside me freaking out all the time."

"Oh, you poor little thing." He took a step forward, and the marks seeped into his skin. He was not happy. Perhaps I didn't know when to keep my mouth shut. "You have a cord to deal with while I have to deal with the fact that, every time I'm around you, all I can even *think* about is transferring the power."

The anger coursing through my veins immediately switched to the acidic burn of unease. I sidestepped him and the bench, thinking space might be good right about now.

Seth advanced, following me back up the path. "Every fucking time, Alex. I'm the First. It's what I'm supposed to do. It's what I was built to do. So resisting that is bad enough, but after having had a taste of that power? Oh, you have no idea."

My eyes widened. When Seth had pulled on my power to take out the Council and kill the furie, he'd tapped into just the tiniest bit of it that existed in the God Killer, and that tiny taste had been enough.

I swallowed hard as I stopped under the wing of a marble Thanatos. *Seth?*

"Don't," he spat, drawing in a deep breath. "I fight the need every single second of the day. I'm trying here, so I'm sorry that it comes across as whining."

Widening my stance, I prepared myself just in case Seth went completely wild. "I'm sorry. I didn't mean it that way. It's just that—"

"It doesn't matter!"

His eyes flashed an intense shade of amber a second before sparks erupted from his bare arms. A bolt of intense light—akasha—flew out from him, smacking into the center of the statue.

Marble cracked like a whip of thunder. Stone splintered as I turned, sending chunks into the air. Throwing my arms up, I shielded my face as shards blasted through the air and dust thickened around me. Tiny chunks pelted my back and arms.

When it settled, I slowly lowered my arms. My heart pounded insanely fast as my gaze locked with his.

"Shit," Seth muttered, his chest rising and falling rapidly. "Just stay…stay away from me."

I didn't have a chance to respond. He spun on his heel, leaving me standing there among the remains of the ruined statue. There was no way we could stay away from each other. Right now, we needed each other, especially to transfer the power, though it was more than that.

But I didn't chase after him. I let him go. He won. We would wait, but we couldn't wait forever.

CHAPTER TWENTY

The skies were gray and overcast. Clouds were thick. A fine drizzle coated the ground and our vehicles. The slight chill in the air warned that autumn was well on its way. Perses had wanted to travel with the rest of the army, but none of us trusted him enough to let that happen. Gods only knew what he'd get himself into between here and the Catskills.

Luke and Olivia were also traveling with us, mainly because Deacon and I demanded that they did.

"Do you think Deacon will talk the entire trip?" Olivia asked, hoisting a small bag of weapons and tucking several small coins into a pocket on her leg. It was a depressing necessity after what had happened to Lea, and we all carried them now. Just in case. "I'm betting at least fifty bucks that he does until he passes out."

I laughed. "I'm not betting against that. On the way here, I thought Marcus was going to strangle him."

"I would've if he hadn't fallen asleep," Marcus said, coming out from behind us. "Or at the very least, I would've knocked him out."

Olivia giggled. "Want me to get that?" She gestured at my own bag of things made to stab and dismember.

"Nah," I said. "I got it."

Smiling at Marcus, she headed toward where Luke and Deacon stood behind a black Expedition. Deacon spun around and pulled Olivia into a dance you'd see in a ballroom while Luke took the bag of weapons from her. A laugh escaped my lips as I watched him dip Olivia over his arm.

"He's something else, isn't he?" Marcus folded his arms. "In spite of everything, he's…" He trailed off, shaking his head. "He's just Deacon."

"That's what I love about him."

Marcus glanced at me, his expression unreadable. Several seconds passed. "Are you ready for this, Alexandria?"

"As ready as I'll ever be," I admitted, wiping the fine sheen of rain off my forehead. Seth appeared with Perses. They headed toward another vehicle. My stomach tipped over. I hadn't seen Seth since he'd left me in the cemetery last night.

Seth glanced over to where Marcus and I stood. Our eyes met for a second and then he looked away, saying something to Perses.

"You haven't transferred the power yet," Marcus said.

My lips pursed. "No. We're going to do it when we get to New York." *I hope*, but I didn't add that last part. Taking a deep breath, I forced my gaze away from Seth and turned to my uncle.

The lines around his eyes appeared deeper than they had been yesterday. Gray hairs liberally sprinkled his chestnut-colored hair. I hadn't noticed them before, but they had to have been there. His eyes were sharp with keen intelligence and clear with foresight, as usual.

In a second, I saw him as he'd been the first day I'd returned to the Covenant. He'd sat behind that shiny desk of his, full of stiff, unyielding authority, and his displeased stare had made me dislike him immediately. A lot had changed since the day he'd almost kicked me out of the Covenant. He'd changed. So had I. Somewhere in the last year, he'd gone from being the dean to becoming my uncle. And I never would've believed that last year. I honestly hadn't believed that he cared one bit about me, but I knew now he always had. He may've had a hard time showing it, and I'd just made it even harder for him to do so. I'd been such a brat.

His lips tipped up at the corners. When he spoke, it was as if he knew what I was thinking. "I'm not sure I've ever told you this, Alexandria, but I am proud of you."

My eyes misted over, but I blamed the rain. "You never thought you'd say that, huh?"

"No, I always knew that one day I would say that," he replied, his slight smile softening his features. "I'd just hoped it would've been when you graduated from the Covenant."

"Same here." I sighed.

"You make sure you come back here." His voice thickened. "After all, you haven't technically graduated yet, and there are a few courses you need to finish up before you can."

I laughed, but the sound caught in my throat. "Okay. Deal."

Marcus nodded and unfolded his arms. He started to turn, but he stopped. An emotion I couldn't quite pick out flickered across his face, and a second later he hugged me. My uncle gave the most awkward hugs in history. But in a way, they were the best.

Closing my eyes, I inhaled the faint scent of his cologne and hugged him back.

"I know you will look for your father when you get there," he said, his voice low. "I know how much finding him means to you, but you need to be careful. There will be time afterward to find him."

"Okay," I said, even though I wasn't sure I meant it. As much as I wanted to believe that Apollo would hold to his promise, I couldn't be a hundred percent sure that there would be an afterward for me.

Marcus pulled back, and I swore his eyes were shiny. He muttered something about helping Luke and stalked off. After saying my goodbyes to Laadan and Diana, I waited off to the side while Aiden spoke to my uncle. No doubt he was getting some overprotective warning, because when Aiden joined me, he was a shade or two paler.

My brows rose. "You okay?"

His gray eyes shifted to mine. "Marcus can be really scary when he wants to be."

I grinned. "Yeah, he can."

He took my bag from me, placing it in the back as Deacon shimmied across the seat and situated himself between Luke and Olivia.

"You haven't seen Apollo, have you?" I asked, chewing on my lower lip.

Shutting the door, Aiden shook his head. I'd told him about Apollo's promise to bring in the rest of the gods, and I'd also told him that, obviously, I hadn't transferred the power from Seth, but I'd left out the blowing up the statue part. "I wouldn't hold my breath, Alex. While I think Apollo wants to help and get involved, I don't think the others will."

"That's such crap." Familiar anger simmered in my stomach. "It's taking the absentee landlord theory to a whole new level."

"I know." He dug the keys out of his tactical pants. "But throughout history, they've all really only gotten involved once before, and that was with the Titans. Any other time, most of them don't get involved."

"This is different," I grumbled, beating the horse dead and then bringing it back to life to beat again. "This is one of their own—their problem."

"Maybe Apollo will surprise us." He bent down, brushing his lips over my forehead. "Either way, we have this."

Car keys dangling from his fingertips, Seth passed by us. "If you two can stop making doe-eyes at each other for a few minutes, we're all ready to go." Behind him, Perses inspected the vehicle with a distrustful scowl. One of the other SUVs in our little section of the convoy revved an engine, and the Titan transferred his scowl to the other vehicle.

Aiden straightened, his gaze narrowing on Seth's back. "Jealousy is an ugly thing."

"So is blind ignorance," Seth shot back, rounding the front of a Hummer.

Tension rolled off Aiden as he turned to me. "I really do dislike him most of the time."

"Yeah, well..." What could I say? The two of them would never be friends. "Ready?"

"We are!" Deacon shouted from inside the Expedition. "I've already got the first road game picked out, so freaking hurry!"

Shaking his head, Aiden smiled. "This is going to be the longest twenty-three hours of our lives."

Turned out, the next twenty-three hours of our lives weren't the longest, even when they turned into closer to twenty-six hours after our caravan hit a traffic snarl outside of Chicago. I switched places with Aiden and then Luke, giving all of us time to rest up.

As expected, while awake, Deacon kept us somewhere between entertained and five seconds away from pulling the SUV over and duct taping his mouth shut.

When we entered New York, we followed Seth's vehicle, keeping to the back of the massive group of Sentinels and Guards. Solos checked in periodically with Aiden from where he rode in one of the lead vehicles. They hadn't run into any problems, but there was no way Ares didn't know we were coming. Any number of people we passed on the way here could've been spies, mortal or not, even though we were traveling in small clusters of SUVs and cars so as not to stand out. Not to mention that Ares was a god, so it wouldn't be hard for him to figure out what we were up to.

But the fact that we reached the Catskills without incident had me squirming in my seat, restless and unnerved. When we'd first traveled to South Dakota, we'd been intercepted by Ares's Sentinels, and that had basically been out in the middle of nowhere. How could it be this easy?

Upon entering the mountainous back roads, my unease tripled to paranoid levels when the vehicle in front of us rolled to a stop. I exchanged a nervous look with Aiden. Ahead, Perses's arm appeared out the window, waving us forward.

"Why don't they use a cell?" Luke asked, peering over my seat.

"Does Perses even know to use a cell phone?" Olivia asked.

I snorted while the knot of anxiety worked at giving me an ulcer in record time. "He seems like a quick learner."

Aiden slipped the Expedition into park and glanced back at his brother. "Stay in the car."

Deacon rolled his eyes. "Yes, Dad, because I couldn't possibly be of any help."

That statement was ignored as Aiden and I stepped out of the SUV and made our way over to Perses's side. Three Sentinels from the other vehicles joined us—I recognized them as halfs I'd seen in South Dakota, but I didn't know any of their names.

"What's going on?" Aiden asked.

Perses stepped out of the vehicle, his all-black eyes fixed on the thick tree line ahead. "Something's not right."

"Other than the fact we're stopped?" I asked, folding my arms. The air was chilly in the mountains, especially where the sun didn't break through the trees, and my black shirt didn't offer a lot of warmth.

His lips curled up at the corner in a sardonic twist. "I sense something abnormal among us."

I peered in through the car at Seth. He just shrugged. "Details?"

"There's violence in the air; the smell of battle that has yet to begin," Perses said, stretching his arms above his head. Bones cracked. The twist of his lips spread into a real smile. "Bloodshed is pending."

My brows rose as I glanced at Aiden. "Well, that's not freaky or anything."

"Yeah," he said, his gaze darting over the tree line and the empty, narrow south lane.

Seth shut the Hummer down and climbed out. "I don't feel anything, but then again, I'm not a Titan."

Perses chuckled deeply as he walked toward the front of the vehicle. "I am never wrong about these things."

Doors opened and closed behind us. "What's going on?" Luke called, joined by Olivia. Both had daggers in their hands. Sentinels from the other cars were close behind them. "Are we just taking a potty break or something?"

Aiden turned toward them, his mouth opening to respond just as the ground beneath our feet trembled. He looked down, brows furrowing. "What the…?"

The vibration continued, growing in intensity, shaking the vehicles and rattling the trees that crowded the road. Asphalt cracked like an ear-piercing gunshot. A fissure cracked along the side of the road, spreading toward the guardrail. I whipped around, following the progress of the crevice as it widened along the land, splitting open. Loose soil pebbled and rolled as giant elms shook until thick roots poked up from the ground.

"Deacon!" Aiden shouted, spinning. His brother was already out of the car, his eyes wide. "Stay near Luke!"

"Earthquake?" Olivia asked, one hand braced on the hood of the Expedition.

I shook my head. "I have a really bad feeling about this."

"Ditto," Seth said, joining us.

The trembling eased off and the earth seemed to settle, along with my stomach. The reprieve lasted seconds. From the wide crack in the ground, rich, dark soil spewed into the air like from a volcano. The earthy scent was overpowering as the dirt arced up and shot back down, landing in twenty or so different piles.

"Yeah," Luke drawled the word out. "That crap ain't normal."

The piles of dirt swirled along the ground in circles, then rose up, rapidly taking form. Legs appeared, thick and well-muscled, followed by torsos, broad chests and shoulders, and finally heads.

I blinked once and then twice. "What in the hell?"

The things resembled human males—human males who could've easily been pro wrestlers in another life. Soil traveled down their arms, taking shape over the hands. Axes appeared in their palms, blades sharpened into deadly edges. Like, axes bigger than what I imagined Vikings used to carry once upon a screwed-up time.

These things...they were made of dirt, but the axes were very, very real. "The *Spartoi*!" shouted Perses. "Warriors born of soil—sons of Ares!"

"Oh, shit," Aiden said, eyes flaring with recognition.

I had no idea what the Spartoi were, but seeing that full-grown men made of dirt had just popped out of the earth heavily armed, and hearing they were sons of Ares, I was going to assume this was a very bad situation.

Their mouths opened in unison, letting out a heart-stopping battle roar that was matched only by the sound that came out of Perses's mouth. He launched himself forward, over the crack in the road, and met the first Dirt Man head-to-head.

"Yeah, screw this," Seth said, lifting his hand. The marks on his skin brightened and akasha blasted from his palm, striking one of the manifestations in the chest.

Dirt Man Two exploded outward, but all the tiny, million particles froze and then snapped back, reforming. The thing laughed, spewing tiny pebbles from its open mouth.

"Oh crap," I said, my mouth dropping open.

"The heads," Perses grunted, engaging his sickle blade. "You must remove their heads!"

I unhooked my sickle blade as Dirt Man Two threw his ax. It whipped through the air, narrowly avoiding Aiden, and smacked into a tree across the road, embedding deep. A second later, a red film covered the majestic elm tree, completely and utterly swallowing it whole. When the red haze disappeared, nothing of the tree remained.

"Holy crap," Luke said.

Another ax appeared in Dirt Man Two's hands.

Perses whirled, cleaving the head off of his Dirt Man's body. The creature collapsed into itself, the ax disappearing along with it. The Titan's laugh was disturbingly joyful.

Dirt Man Two charged forward, and I used the air element to fling him back against the trees. The thing shattered and came back together within seconds. Seth shot forward, avoiding the broad sweep of the ax as he brought the sickle around sharply, catching it under the chin.

"Two down," Aiden said, springing to the side as another ax flew by our heads.

Luke grunted as he shoved Deacon back toward the rear of the Expedition. "Stay back, pretty boy."

Deacon responded, but it was lost in the invasion of the Spartoi. One was heading straight toward me, a trail of soil chasing after it. I dipped down, engaging the sickle part of the weapon with a shake of my wrist. I sprung up behind Dirt Man Three. The thing twisted as it swung the ax down. Heat flew off the weapon, causing me to jump back.

The Dirt Man lurched at me. Darting to the side, I reached up and caught his arm. It fell apart under my hand, crumbling in a sheet of dry dirt. Ignoring the grossness of that, I swung it down and twisted hard, causing the creature to lose its grip on the ax. As it fell to the ground, I brought the sickle blade against the back of its neck.

"Three down!" I shouted, feeling a familiar adrenaline rush inside me. Olivia spun gracefully, relieving another Dirt Man of its head. "Four!"

Was it twisted that we were counting? I guessed not, because within a few minutes, we were down to ten. Even Perses was calling out numbers, but he seemed to be having a hell of a lot more fun than we were. A wide smile was on his face as he stalked a Dirt Man, easily avoiding the axes lobbed at him. It was like Christmas morning for the freak.

Turning at the waist, I found myself nearly losing my own head when one of them swung an ax. I had two of them, coming from both sides. I started to summon the air element again, but Aiden appeared in front of me.

In a graceful move, he spun and lopped off the head of one of the Spartoi. I wanted to take a moment to recognize the beauty of the way he moved, but another was running straight for me. Rushing forward, I met it with the sharp side of the sickle.

Drop! Seth's voice shouted in my head.

Without thinking twice, I hit the ground half a second before Seth's blade cut through where I'd been standing, taking out a Dirt Man that had been really close to putting the hurt on me. None of these things could kill Seth or me, or at least that was what I was banking on, but they could put us down long enough for Ares to swoop in.

Rising, I nodded at Seth. "Thanks."

He said nothing as he joined Luke in cornering two more of the creatures. Looking around, I saw that Deacon was safe and Aiden was now a few yards in front of him. Nothing would get past him.

I started toward another Dirt Man when a ball of flames landed about two feet from me. Fire licked over the ground. Startled, I spun, and my stomach dropped. Cresting the hill above us was one of the worst possible things we could've seen at this moment.

Horns, dark matted hair, and long, flat snouts that sloped into mouths full of strong teeth came into view. Their thick thighs and large hooves made of titanium were next.

Automatons.

Perses shouted another battle roar, and the rush of adrenaline coiled tight around my heart. I spun and darted out, reaching the Dirt Man closest to me. The thing dove forward, but I ducked under its arm. Swinging around, I swung the blade down, dispatching another one of the freaky creations.

Something inside me clicked off as I ran toward the cars, dodging the axes and fireballs. We had to get rid of the Spartoi first. There were only a few left, so that was completely doable, and Perses was charging toward the bulls to keep them at bay for a while.

Hearing pounding footsteps behind me, I whirled and jerked to the side, narrowly avoiding another ax. Springing into the air, I spun and delivered a nasty kick that would've been so damn good if my foot hadn't sunk through the thing's chest.

We went down in a burst of dirt and rocks. Dust flew into my mouth and nose. I gagged, trying not think about the fact that I just swallowed some of the Dirt Man as I rolled away from him. He swung his ax through the air and brushed my thigh. A slice of pain shot down my leg as a thin slit formed in the pant leg. The Dirt Man roared to its feet, heaving the ax like a Viking straight from Valhalla.

Summoning air, I blew the SOB back, slamming it into the Hummer. I popped to my feet and raced after it, taking it out. Through the smoke and clouds of dirt, I saw Aiden engaging an automaton. Like the Spartoi, the heads had to be removed.

One of the automatons lit up from the inside, like a blue X-ray, before exploding in a shower of sparks.

Or Seth could use akasha. That would work, too.

With the automatons coming closer and closer, our group was scattered. Perses was making short work of the monsters, but the falling flames were making it difficult to pay attention to any one thing. A burst of flames shot from where Aiden and Deacon were, smacking into the nearest automaton.

Flames spread across the ground, and I darted around the blaze. Springing up, I caught a Dirt Man before it launched its ax at Luke.

Perses slammed the pointed end of the weapon into the chin of an automaton. Silvery blood sprayed the Titan in the face and chest. He didn't even blink as he yanked the blade to the side. He turned, and his smile was gory with blood.

In that moment, I understood the Olympians' distaste for Perses. To enjoy battle and war was one thing. Twisted, yes, but there were a lot of aggressive people out there. Perses didn't just enjoy it, though. The Titan got off on the violence and bloodshed.

For a moment, the Titan transfixed me. The way he dispatched the enemy with that level of glee would make serial killers across the nation happy.

A little sickened, I joined Seth and tapped into primitive, raw energy. Power rushed through me, and my skin tingled with the appearance of the marks. Using akasha, intense blue light erupted from me. Arcing through the air, it struck its target, reducing it to nothing but a pile of shimmery dust.

Out of the corner of my eye, I saw Olivia dart to the side to avoid an incoming fireball. My heart kicked in my chest as a Dirt Man let loose his ax. I shouted at her—at least, I thought I did as I rushed toward her. In my head, I was screaming, but

I wasn't sure any sound was making it past my lips. A horrible, terrifying feeling of déjà vu settled in my stomach. In a split second, I saw Lea in my head, but this wasn't Lea.

No—no no no. This couldn't be happening again.

A flicker of recognition shot across Olivia's face a second before the Dirt Man's ax struck her in the chest. She hadn't even tried to move. I think, in that tiny second, she knew it was already too late.

"No!" I screamed, and then I screamed again.

Olivia stumbled back a step. The red film spread out from her chest, quickly slipping over her.

In a heartbeat, she was gone.

Another hoarse scream tore through me, scratching my throat and darkening a part of my soul.

Olivia was gone. She was gone. Just like that. Nothing in this world left of her.

Luke shouted as he spun on his Dirt Man, dispatching it, and then whirled back to where Olivia had been. He kept saying the same word over and over again—the same word that was repeating itself in my head.

No. No. No. No.

Deacon rushed forward, but Aiden caught him around the waist. Tears streamed down the younger St. Delphi's face as he struggled against Aiden's hold. He was saying her name—screaming it, really.

My heart split open as my gaze returned to the spot. This wasn't fair. Oh gods, it *hurt*. How could someone be there one second and be gone the next? It didn't matter how many times people had died. I still couldn't fathom the quick and unforgiving end of existence on Earth.

And there was nothing left of her. Not a speck of flesh or clothing. Not even a weapon remained.

No body to bury or mourn.

I hit the scorched earth on my knees, slowly shaking my head back and forth. All around us, the fight raged on with Seth and Perses taking on the remaining automatons. Flames burst a few feet from me, but I didn't flinch, and I didn't move.

Olivia was gone.

CHAPTER TWENTY-ONE

Things were a blur after that. Seth and Perses destroyed the automatons, and when they returned, the Titan hadn't given a damn that we'd lost someone.

That we had lost Olivia.

"We don't have time for this. We must move on."

I looked at him, searching for a fleck of sorrow, or compassion, or anything, but there was nothing. He stalked forward, walking right through the spot where Olivia had last stood.

Luke started toward the Titan, his hands curling into fists, but Aiden grabbed his arm, shaking his head as he all but dragged the half-blood to the Expedition.

"Get inside," Aiden ordered.

His eyes were still trained on Perses, and he wasn't budging. "Luke," Aiden warned.

It was Deacon who got through to him. "Come on. Get in with me. Please?"

Luke blinked, and anger, hurt, and a dozen other violent

emotions still infused his cheeks, but he climbed into the back seat with Deacon.

Alex?

I didn't respond as Seth passed me. I turned, opening the passenger door.

I'm sorry, he said.

My breath caught as I hauled myself into the seat. *I know.*

No one spoke as the vehicles ground into gear, easing around the fissure in the road, with the exception of Aiden checking in with Solos. He shared what'd happened in a low voice. I sat unnaturally still, with my cheek pressed against the window, watching the trees as we continued up the mountain. My heart was heavy, and my eyes burned. Pain lanced my jaw from how tight I was clenching my teeth. I was barely holding it together, but I knew we had to forge on. We had to, but it didn't seem right. I wanted to yell, "STOP!" and I wanted to make everyone, including the Titan, acknowledge that we had lost someone important to us, someone who was too young to die.

A tear streaked down my cheek, and I squeezed my eyes shut as I pressed my hand against the pocket that held several small coins—the ones I'd brought in case…in case we had to bury someone. We couldn't even bury Olivia, but she had the coins with her. She'd have them in the Underworld.

Olivia would get to be with Caleb now. He would find her, and she would be okay. Olivia was with Caleb now. I kept repeating that, because it helped to know that they would be reunited. They would be back together for eternity, and that was something to be happy about, because Olivia had never truly gotten over Caleb's death. Knowing that still didn't make this any easier to accept. At some point, Aiden reached over and found my hand. He squeezed.

I squeezed back.

We reached the heavily forested outskirts of the Catskills just before dusk. We parked the dusty SUV in front of a sprawling house at the base of the mountains; Solos had directed us to the address, so we assumed it was full of allies. I stretched my tight muscles, then opened the door.

Behind us, Seth and Perses had already sprung free from their vehicle and were rounding ours. Up ahead, I could see a mass of Sentinels in front of the house, and there were several lights on inside. It seemed like more than what we'd left with, and sweet relief coursed through me. They had somehow made it around the automatons. Maybe they'd just been waiting for the Apollyon-Titan carpool.

"Ares has to know about this," I said, hopping down and walking toward the stone fence separating the gravel road from the yard.

Seth fell in step beside me, folding his arms. "I'm sure he does, but this kind of warfare reminds him of his glory days."

"He's right." Aiden hefted the bag of weapons onto his shoulder. "There's no way two enemies would be stationed this close together in modern warfare, but this..." He waved his arm in the direction of the waiting Sentinels and Guards. "This is like trench warfare."

In high school, before I'd returned to the Deity Island Covenant, I had read *All Quiet on the Western Front*. That was about all I knew about trench warfare, and that was enough for me to want to sneak into the Covenant and act like a nuclear missile.

I couldn't bear to lose anyone else.

Perses strode ahead of us, tall and silent, and I watched him for a moment. He'd relished the skirmish that had cost Olivia her life. The Titan thrived on the bloodshed and death.

I didn't want to hate him, because it was what he was, but there was still no trace of remorse or sorrow for the lives lost.

Deacon stumbled past us, rubbing his red-rimmed eyes wearily. "I don't want to see the inside of a car again for as long as I live."

"I'll remind you of that the next time you have to walk any real distance and start whining," Luke replied, the words light but the look on his face grave.

He had been so close to Olivia, closer than me. An ache pierced my chest as I stepped through the narrow opening in the stone wall. The only thing I could console myself with was that I knew—*I knew*—she was with Caleb. She was with the boy she had loved so fiercely, had never stopped loving.

I was still holding onto that thought like it was a life jacket.

Solos jogged across the clearing, slowing down as he passed Perses. He cast the Titan a look before continuing toward us. He stopped in front of Luke, placing his hand on the half-blood's shoulder.

"I'm sorry," he said, and those two words carried so much weight.

Luke nodded and said something in a low voice before he walked past. Deacon's hand went to his lower back, and a small smile tugged at my lips when Luke moved closer to him as they followed Perses.

Aiden clasped Solos's hand as we met him. "How are things here?"

"Better than what you had to face," Solos replied. "I should've—"

"There's nothing you could've done," I interrupted, shifting my weight. I wanted a pillow—stat. "It seems like there are more Sentinels here than there were with us."

"There are." His eyes gleamed with excitement. "Come

on. I'm sure you guys could use something to eat. I'll explain on the way."

My stomach rumbled in response, and Aiden sent me a quick grin. I was too tired to be embarrassed. "So, what's going on?"

"Our advance scouts met up with a group of about fifty Sentinels outside of the city. They're from the New York Covenant and were out scouting beyond the line of the automatons. They showed us a way around. We had a minor run-in with a few automatons, but we didn't lose any numbers."

They were lives, not numbers.

He knows that. Seth's voice startled me. I hadn't realized I'd projected those thoughts anywhere.

But looking at them that way helps keep the mind clear.

I guess, I responded without much conviction.

"They brought us back here. There are at least a hundred more. They've been here since Ares took over. They made it out after he did." Purpose filled his voice. "They know the set-up inside, where Ares has been holing up, how many he has beyond the walls, and so on."

All of that was valuable knowledge, necessary knowledge, and that was what Aiden was telling Solos, and then they were talking about more important stuff. But all I could think was that, if there were Sentinels here that had gotten out after Ares took over, was my father among them? Solos wouldn't know if he was, but Seth and Laadan had said that my father had stayed behind with the servants.

"Are there servants here?" I asked, interrupting them.

Solos glanced back at me. "Yes. There are quite a few. Most of them aren't under the effects of the Elixir anymore."

My heart tripped up in my chest, and my wide eyes met Aiden's. There was reluctant hope in his gaze. I knew he wanted my father to be somewhere among those up ahead or in the house, but he was wary of that fragile dream and the crushing disappointment that was sure to come if he wasn't.

He was behind the walls when I was last here. Seth's words were as heavy as Solos's apology. *He could've made it out since then, but…*

But Ares knew that my father was there. I sighed. *It was stupid to hope, wasn't it?*

"Never," Seth said out loud.

Aiden glanced back, brows furrowed, but then he turned back to Solos.

Stones sat in my stomach. Man, that disappointment wasn't far behind. I tried to shake it off, because we had such huge things to accomplish. We would have to move on Ares quickly, probably by the following nightfall, but I wanted to see my dad. I needed him to know that I knew who he was.

If things went south fast, I wanted to see him before I…

I didn't allow myself to finish that thought. I had to trust that Apollo would find a way to stop the Olympians from snuffing me out once I became the God Killer. He'd said he would take care of me. He'd sworn, and supposedly gods kept their promises.

Except in Solos's case, and just about every other story I could think of. Sigh.

As we crossed the lawn, the Sentinels that had been gawking at Perses did the same as Seth and I neared. Several muttered curses when they laid eyes on the First, their gazes cold and unfriendly.

"Friends of yours?" I asked, watching one of them rest his hand on his gun.

Seth gave a lopsided shrug. "I'm sure we may have exchanged a few words before…"

"Before you pulled your head out of your ass?"

A laugh burst from him. "Exactly."

"You should sleep well tonight."

He stepped around a bag full of what looked like rifles. "I doubt any of us will really be sleeping." I recognized some of the faces from the University, but there were a lot of strangers in the crowd, and many of them were my age. Young. I didn't feel young, not anymore, but I guessed technically I still was, and so were they.

Solos introduced us to the Sentinels who were in charge of the group from inside the Covenant. They looked battered but hopeful as they saw with their own eyes what Solos must've been telling them.

The Apollyons were unified, and we'd brought a Titan with us.

It sounded kind of badass, but then again, we *were* going up against Ares.

We headed into the house, which was really a mansion. Someone said it'd once belonged to a mortal in the government, but they had abandoned it when Ares brought in the mortal troops. Food was given to us, and I tried to eat quietly while Aiden conversed with the different Sentinels. I didn't see where Luke and Deacon had roamed off to, but I hoped, wherever they were, Luke was doing okay.

I picked at my sandwich, my stomach too full of knots to be hungry. Part of me worried that I was throwing way too many vibes at Seth, but I suspected he was blocking me. After all, he was a hell of a lot better at it than me.

Giving up on the food, I set the plate aside, left the large sitting room, and investigated the house. I lost count of how many rooms were downstairs after I walked through what looked like the third sitting room. Who needed this many rooms? And why were there so many short halls? It was like a maze.

Sighing, I pushed the shorter strands of hair that had escaped my ponytail out of my face. I knew I should be back in that room with Aiden and Solos. They had been talking about plans for tomorrow. I should've been leading those conversations—or at least paying attention. Or pretending to listen by being in the same room as them.

"You shouldn't feel guilty."

I jumped at the sound of Seth's voice, surprised that he was able to sneak up on me. Turning toward him, I found him under the archway. Well, there went the idea that he was blocking my feelings.

"Are you following me?" I asked instead of acknowledging his statement.

"Yes."

"Shouldn't you be following Perses?"

"Why?" He tipped his head down, and a lock of blond hair fell across his forehead. "He's behaving. Right now, he's outside with the Sentinels, getting them all wound up."

I sat on the edge of an antique couch that had the hardest, most uncomfortable cushions ever. "Do you think that's a good idea?"

"I think so. He'll get them ready to battle. We're going to need everything we have to get past the army Ares has inside those walls."

I nodded slowly. "You think we can do it?"

"Most definitely." One side of his lips quirked up.

"And you think we can take out Ares?"

"I do." Seth strode over the couch and sat beside me. My initial reaction was to get up, especially since he was having so many problems ignoring the allure of the power that rested inside of me, but I stayed put. "Perses will make sure we get to him, and then he will weaken Ares, giving us time to make the transfer. You remember how to do it?"

"Yes." I clasped my hands together in my lap and peeked at him. The amber hue of his eyes was deeper. I decided to take a stab at the argument again. "Waiting until the very last minute is risky."

"Doing it now is risky, Alex. You don't know what it's like. I know—"

"I believe you," I said, and I really did. The power had corrupted Seth, and he was only the First. Becoming the God Killer was apparently going to turn me into an aether-crazed Terminator. Besides, yelling at him hadn't worked last time. "If I can't handle it after I take out Ares, you've got to get away from me. Quickly."

His frown did nothing to lessen his beauty. "I don't think I've said this to you right." My brows rose.

His frown deepened. "You *can* handle it."

Now I was confused. "That's not what you said before."

"Like I said, I'm saying it wrong." Seth twisted toward me. "And I'm not being honest."

The knots in my stomach tightened, and I resisted the urge to hit him before he spoke, because I figured whatever he was about to say would deserve a five-finger hello to the face. "*Seth*."

"Alex—"

"What in the hell could you possibly have to not be honest about now?" I demanded as a rush of anger rose inside me. "That you're waiting until the thirtieth hour to divulge?"

Seth looked away, his chin jutting out stubbornly. "You could lay off the attitude."

I flipped him off.

A reluctant-sounding chuckle parted his lips. "Okay. Do I think you're going to go a little power-crazy? Probably."

My eyes narrowed.

"But you'll handle it. You always handle everything, and I..." He trailed off, shaking his head. "We have to wait until the last minute because I'm not sure I won't try to stop you. I'm not sure I won't try to take the power myself."

I stared at him, the scowl slipping off my face as his words sank in. Holy gods, this was a big deal. Apollo had been right. I had wanted to believe Seth that night at the University, but Apollo had been right.

Two pink spots appeared in his cheeks. "You're looking at me like...like I said the worst thing possible."

"Well, that is pretty...um, well, it's something." I shook my head. "Seth, if you think you're going to stop me and try to do it yourself, how in the hell is waiting to the last minute to do it a good idea?"

He didn't answer. Instead, he looked away, focusing on a really creepy deer head hanging from the wall.

Seth?

Lowering his chin, he rubbed the palm of his hand over his cheek. *I'll let you do it then. I know I will.*

How? What if you don't? What if—?

"I will," he snapped, lifting his head. His eyes were glowing. "I know I will then."

"Excuse me if I'm not reassured by that!" I started to stand, but he grabbed my arm. The tiny hairs on my body rose.

"I know I will, because too much will be riding on me to let you do it."

Was he saying that he'd perform better under pressure? That somehow having our heads on the line would ensure he wouldn't suck me dry? What the hell was that? I tried to pull my arm back, but he held on. "I think we should do it now."

He closed his eyes.

"I'm serious. We could do it now." My heart was trying to come out of my chest. "I'll get Aiden, and then we'll do it. Afterward, he'll make sure we're separated and—"

"I'm not going to fail you or anyone. Not again. We'll do it then, as planned."

"Seth…"

The marks of the Apollyon went wild, spinning and twirling across my skin, reaching his. His face contorted, and I felt the cord jump inside me. My pulse kicked into overdrive as every warning sensor went off. The last time, he'd said—

Suddenly, the tip of a Covenant dagger was under Seth's chin, pushing into the delicate skin of his throat. My gaze dropped to where Seth's hand was wrapped around my forearm and then back to the tip of the dagger. Definitely a silent way of saying "let go." Seth released my arm, finger by finger.

I looked up, and my gaze locked with eyes the color of warm chocolate. Air halted in my throat, and my voice cracked on one word. "Dad?"

CHAPTER TWENTY-TWO

The huge, potential problem of Seth taking the God Killer power from me at the last and possibly worst moment known to mankind was suddenly insignificant.

I was staring at my dad.

My father.

He looked just like I remembered—a classically handsome face lined by the weather and his life, but his brown eyes were lively with intelligence and awareness. He was thinner, gaunter than before.

And he was wearing a Sentinel uniform.

Something in my chest came unhinged, like a door had been thrown open too fast and too hard.

Tears poured out of my eyes. He was in a *Sentinel* uniform.

My father also held a dagger against Seth's throat.

"It's okay," I said, my voice hoarse. I glanced at Seth, who looked as surprised as I felt. "Seth?"

Standing slowly, Seth raised his hands. His amber gaze was locked on my father. "I'm not going to hurt her."

My father didn't look convinced. His lips curled in a sneer as he kept the blade against Seth's throat, but he let Seth back away. The First headed for the door, stopping once to look at us, and then he disappeared through the archway.

I stared up at my dad, too afraid to look away because I feared he might actually vanish, too scared to stand because I knew my legs wouldn't hold me. My throat clogged with emotion, and his face blurred. This whole time, from the moment I first received Laadan's letter, I had hoped that I would see him again, but I never really thought that I would.

And here he was, on the night before battle, standing before me.

"Dad?" I croaked. It was all I could say. It was like I'd lost my ability to speak in comprehensible sentences.

He expertly sheathed the Covenant dagger the way we'd been taught in training. For a whole minute, he didn't move or look away. His gaze crawled over my face, and the lines around his eyes deepened, as did the furrow between his brows. I knew it was the scars, and even though he had never been in my life—couldn't have been—they had to affect him deeply.

Letting out a breath that he seemed to have been holding for years, he sat beside me on the couch.

I didn't know what to say. There was so much pressure in my chest and my throat.

He reached out with one hand and cupped my cheek. His hand was cool, but I didn't care. I squeezed my eyes shut to stop the tears. The pressure increased, pushing at the seams. My dad didn't say anything, because he couldn't, but his touch…it was better than any words that could be spoken.

I struggled to pull myself together, waiting until I was sure I wouldn't start sobbing all over him before I spoke. And of course, I said the stupidest thing possible. "It's really you?"

He nodded, a slight smile appearing.

Taking in a shuddering breath, I blinked a few times. "Did you…did you get my letter?" Another nod.

"Okay. Okay." I took another breath. "How long have you been here?"

He held up a finger, and then leaned back. Reaching into the side pocket of his tactical pants, he pulled out a small notebook and pen. He wrote something quickly and handed it to me. His handwriting was neat and small, so unlike mine.

"Two days?" I read out loud and then waited while he scribbled something. "You heard that a group of Sentinels had arrived." My heart tripped up as I glanced at him. "You left the Covenant to see if I was among them?"

He nodded.

"How?"

My dad wrote: *I knocked out the guard he had watching over me. He thinks I don't know that he knows who I am.*

I laughed, and his lips twitched into another small smile. "Gods," I said, smoothing my hands over my thighs. I wanted to hug him, but I wasn't sure what he'd do. "When I was at the Covenant before, I didn't know it was you. If I had, I would've done something. I swear I would have."

His pen flew across his little notepad. Two sentences. *I know. Not your problem.*

"But you're my dad. It *is* my problem."

He shook his head no, and then wrote quickly. *You look so much like your mother.*

I smiled widely, blinking back another rush of tears. "Thank you."

There was a pause as he stared at me, and then he started scribbling away, faster than before.

Your mother and I wouldn't have wanted this kind of life for you.

"I—"

He held up a finger and finished his note. *Laadan kept me updated on you, telling me what she could. I would've wanted anything but this for you, but I am so very proud of you.*

I sucked in a sharp breath as the tears welled up again. He was proud of me. How many times had I wondered if he was? There had been so many stupid things I'd done in my past, things that had gotten me in a world of trouble, and the gods knew I had a lot of stupid left in me, but my father was proud of me, and that was all that mattered after everything was said and done. The pressure expanded until it was too much.

Springing forward, I wrapped my arms around him and held on like he might disappear in front of me. He dropped the pen and notepad, enfolding me in a powerful hug. The kind of hug I'd been missing my entire life. A hug that hadn't come too late, but just in time.

The tears came. There was no stopping them, but they were happy tears.

I stayed with my dad for hours, me talking and asking questions and him answering with a shake of his head or with his notepad. On and off, I cried. I kept thinking this was a dream, but the longer he remained by my side, the more I began to realize this was real.

Maybe an hour into our reunion, something else amazing happened. Something that I had never thought would.

Dad met the other most important man in my life.

He met Aiden, who'd come looking for me, and then I got to see what it was truly like to have a father in my life. He regarded Aiden coolly; he looked like he was thinking about using the dagger the same way he had with Seth.

Aiden was as polite as ever, and he started to make a quick escape to give us privacy, but I captured his hand. Our eyes met and he nodded. I wanted him there, to share this with me, because none of us knew how much time we really had left and there was no point in missing an opportunity like this. Aiden sat on the floor by my feet, his hand and thumb smoothing over the back of my calf.

I would've loved to have met my dad under better circumstances. Maybe where the three of us could go out to dinner like normal people, but this…this was perfect in its own way.

Honored that he would leave those who were still behind the walls to see if I was among the Sentinels that had arrived, I fought the pain and the panic when he showed me the message I'd been dreading.

I have to go back to them. They have no one else.

My heart turned over heavily. "But Ares knows you're my father."

I won't be strolling in the front door, he wrote. *I know my way around in there, and I stay out of Ares's way. If Ares was going to use me, he would've done so by now.*

"How can you be so sure?"

Aiden continued the soothing gesture. "He may be right. Maybe Ares has some sort of code he operates by."

I doubted that. My chest seized at the thought of him falling into Ares's hands.

My father tipped his chin down as he scribbled on the pad. *I don't want you doing what you're planning.* I opened my mouth, but he wrote on. *But I know you have to. Like I have to.*

He was right. Damn my father for actually being the logical parent. My wildness came from my mom, but apparently I got my stubbornness from my dad.

When the morning was only a few hours away, my father

hugged me goodbye, and I knew he was heading back to the Covenant. I didn't want to let go of him, and I didn't for several minutes. I held onto him, squeezing him as tightly as I could, and when we broke apart, there was a stinging pain deep in my chest. Seeing him go was one of the most painful things I'd ever experienced.

In a small room with a pile of blankets as a bed, I stared out the window over the camp. "You should get some rest. We'll have to start out in the afternoon."

My mind wasn't on the battle ahead. "What if I never see him again?"

Aiden came up behind me, slipping his arms around my waist and tugging me into the warmth of his body. "You will see him again."

Clinging to that, I tipped my head back against his chest and closed my eyes. "When this is all over, I want the three of us to go out to dinner."

He kissed my forehead. "Pick a place."

"Anywhere normal. Somewhere like Applebee's."

Aiden chuckled. "I think we can make that work."

Turning in his embrace, I rested my cheek against his chest. He held me as I rambled on about my dad, and then we moved on to less happy subjects. While I didn't want to tell him about Seth, I needed to.

"I don't like the sound of this," he said, resting his hands on either side of my head. "If he doesn't allow you to transfer the power or pulls any crap like he has before, you'll be a sitting duck for Ares." The upcoming face-off with Ares was a constant, low-level hum of adrenaline that was like a pebble in my shoe. Annoying but tolerable. But adding in the possibility of Seth going rogue at the last minute turned that pebble into a shark's tooth.

"I'm going to try again, but I don't think it's going to work. Once Seth has his mind set on something, there's no changing it."

"But that's not acceptable." Aiden dropped his hands and turned, stalking toward the blanket. "It's too risky. If—"

"We don't have any other choice." I followed him. "And I think…I think he needs to do it that way, when the risk is the highest. Like a…"

"Like how an addict stops doing drugs because they're sitting in jail?"

I wrinkled my nose. "Uh, sure?"

"Inmates can still get drugs," he grumbled, reaching down and tugging his shirt off his head. Thick bands of muscle stretched and pulled taut.

"I'm not following this conversation." *For several reasons*, but I kept that last part to myself.

Aiden faced me. "I know the plan is for you and Seth to go with Perses to find Ares, but—"

"But we're not changing the plan, no matter how bananas Seth is." My heart went erratic at the thought of Aiden being with us. "You cannot be there when we face off with Ares! He'll use you—"

"He can only use me if I'm incapable of defending myself, Alex." His brows lowered as his eyes flashed silver. Uh-oh. "I'm not your weakness."

"You're not. You're the opposite of that, Aiden, but I know Ares will go straight for you. He knows I'll be distracted because you're there. And it's what I'd do if I were him."

Aiden looked away as he shoved a hand through his hair. Several seconds stretched out, and then he released a ragged breath. "I know you have to do this, Alex, but it goes against everything in me not to be with you."

Biting my lip, I nodded. I knew it was nearly going to take an act of the gods to get Aiden to not follow us tomorrow. "If it were you asking me to not be with you, I wouldn't want to listen to you."

He let out a dry laugh. "You *wouldn't* listen to me, Alex. You'd go against me, and you'd find a way to be there with me."

"I would." I cracked a grin. "I would do it even knowing that you'd be distracted by me, because I'm selfish like that. You're not."

"I can be incredibly selfish." His gaze settled on me once more, and he placed the tips of his fingers on either side of my cheeks. "I've been nothing but selfish with you."

Confused, I frowned. "How?"

"I was selfish in wanting you, knowing what it could mean for you. I was selfish the first time I kissed you, touched you." The shiver his words brought forth didn't go unnoticed by him. A dimple appeared. "I was selfish the night I came to your bed when you were at my parents' house, and I've been selfish every day since then. The only time I wasn't selfish was when I pushed you away, and that's the day I regret most."

My stomach fluttered like there was a jackrabbit inside it. "Aiden…"

"You're going to be separated from me tomorrow, and it's going to take everything in me to let you face Ares without me standing by your side, so I'm going to be very selfish right now." His finger trailed over my cheek and across my parted lips. "Because it's the only way I can be unselfish tomorrow."

Aiden's lips replaced his fingers then, and the kiss wasn't slow or gentle. It was fierce, consuming, and tasted of soul-burning yearning and desperation. Our clothing came off with a quickness that was rather impressive, and our bodies melded together on the thick blankets. Behind every touch and every kiss there was the knowledge that neither of us wanted to put forth into words. So we used our mouths, our hands, and our bodies to say what both of us were too terrified to speak.

This could be our last time together.

CHAPTER TWENTY-THREE

A cool, calm breeze lessened the effect of the strong afternoon sun beating down on us as we stood at the edge of the forest surrounding the Covenant. The sky was a bright, vibrant bluc with only a few pillow-like clouds floating in it.

It was a beautiful day for a war.

Covenant daggers were strapped to my hips, and a Glock loaded with titanium bullets was holstered on my thigh. With my hair pulled back in a tight bun and my skin tingling from the marks of the Apollyon, I felt pretty badass.

Standing on either side of me were the silent forms of Aiden and Seth. Behind us, Perses and our A.O.A. were ready. Deacon was staying behind, and after what'd happened with Olivia, I wished he'd remained at the University.

I hadn't seen my father among the faces, and I don't even know why I was looking for him. I knew he'd gone back. I *hoped* he'd made it back, but I still looked.

"Warriors know no fear, show no fear." Perses's deep voice boomed, upping the adrenaline in my system. "Many of you will fall today."

My brows rose. That's a motivational statement.

"But you will fall as warriors—the only true, honorable death."

He continued on, and I zoned him out. Motivational war speeches about dying honorably in battle weren't my thing. How about a speech where we were all awesomely alive at the end? I could get behind that. Besides, we had a helluva hike ahead of us, and I was using that time to clear my thoughts of everything that'd happened in the last couple of weeks. There was so much clogging up my head—Olivia, my dad, Aiden, and Seth, and where in the hell was Apollo, and so much more. I needed to be focused.

All those moments were leading up to the here and now, and by the time the sun rose the next day, blood would cover the ground like a crimson river. Blood of our own. Blood of our enemies. And blood of those who'd been manipulated onto the wrong side.

Twigs crunched and snapped under our boots as we crested the second hill. There was one more, and then we would be staring down at the walls. We had the high ground, but they would see us the moment we came down.

"Remember the plan," Perses said, stalking up behind me.

I nodded, because my vocal cords had frozen. The plan had been set into motion before we even left South Dakota, and I had had plenty of time to come to terms with it, but I hadn't.

At the last hill, Perses, Seth, and I would split from our group, leaving Aiden, Solos, and Luke behind with the army. Cannon fodder. No one said that. Instead, Perses had said they would be the distraction needed for us to get inside, but I knew that was what they were. The walls were protected by the automatons, and they would be picking off our guys in bulk. And then, when they made it through the entry gate, there was the mortal army…and gods knew what else.

And where the hell was Apollo?

The Sentinels who'd been inside the Covenant had given us the way in that we needed. The back eastern wall was exposed, a way in and out. There'd be guards, but nothing like what would be seen at the front. I knew in my heart of hearts that Aiden and Luke and Solos would make it. They had to. But the sharp tang of fear was in the back of my mouth.

Alex?

Seth's voice inside my head almost caused me to stumble.

What?

You're having a lot of feelings right now.

My gaze narrowed on his back as he moved ahead of Aiden and me. *And you're not?*

You're afraid, was his simple, two-word response. I contemplated pushing him down the rocky slope but figured I didn't need him bruised before we'd even begun.

There was a pause. *Being afraid isn't the problem, Angel.*

Stop calling me that.

He ignored me. *Use that fear.* Glancing over his shoulder at me, he winked. Aiden cursed under his breath, and Seth smirked. *Use anger. Don't let either of them consume you.*

Yes, sensei.

Seth snorted.

"I hate when you two do that," Aiden muttered.

"Sorry?"

He sent me a long look, but there was no anger in his steely gray eyes. Both of us hadn't been smart about last night. We had gotten just a few hours of sleep, spending those precious hours before and after committing each other to memory…

and in ways that brought a blush to my cheeks in spite of the cool wind caressing them.

Neither of us wanted to admit that we both feared last night would be the final time we were together. I couldn't let myself focus on that, but it was a reality that couldn't be ignored.

We passed the nondescript outer fence and then quickly reached the last hill at dusk. I glanced over my shoulder, my gaze roaming across the assembled throng. All of them were ready. It was time to do this, to end this. Everything came down to this battle, and not just for us, but for the unknowing mortals, too. If we failed, the mortal realm would fall to Ares, and then Olympus would be next on his to-conquer list. The Sentinels and Guards behind us knew this, too. This whole situation was bigger than each and every one of us.

"It is time," Perses said. Excitement practically rolled off the Titan.

Seth nodded and turned to me. Part of me wanted to delay this moment, but this was one of those times when I had to pull on my big-girl panties. What I wanted to do and what I needed to do were two very different things.

I swore in that moment this would be the last time I'd ever have to make a choice between want and need. I spun around and hugged Luke and then Solos. "Be safe," I told them both. "Promise me. If not, I'll find you two in the Underworld and kick your asses. I swear."

Luke chuckled. "You'd actually do that, too. I promise."

"As do I," Solos added, bending his head and pressing his lips to my cheek. "And you do the same."

I nodded and turned away before I got all choked up, coming face-to-face with Aiden. Clenching Aiden by the shirt with one hand, I pulled his head down to mine and kissed him. And it was no chaste kiss. Or tender. Our lips bruised together, our bodies melding into the touch. I drank him up in that kiss, as he did me.

A few low whistles brought me back to reality. I let go, rocking back on the heels of my boots, but he still held on. Aiden's eyes were liquid silver.

"I love you," I said. "I love you so much."

Aiden's lips moved over mine. "Agapi mou, I will be with you in no time."

Nodding slowly, I let out a long breath and slipped from his hold. Turning to walk to where Seth and Perses waited, I couldn't look back. Not even when the three of us started our hike to the east, because if I did, I would run back to Aiden, and we couldn't delay this any longer.

We'd traveled about half a mile when Perses raised his hand, motioning us to stop. He tilted his chin up, expression sharp. Then he smiled wolfishly. A second later, a powerful roar whirled through the tall elms and firs, sending birds flying frantically into the air. It was the sound of rage and determination—a sound of war. I twisted toward the west. The dusky sky brightened in hues of orange and red, intensifying every couple of seconds.

"It has begun." Perses's smile spread as if he'd been presented with a feast of his favorite foods. "We must hurry."

Heart racing, I dug in deep, latching onto the sense of duty and holding onto it for dear life. Along with Perses and Seth, I ran down the hill even though my heart was back at the gates with my friends and Aiden.

Sliding around outcroppings of large boulders and kicking up loose rocks and dirt, we stormed down the rocky slope. The twenty-foot white marble wall came into view and the sounds of battle from the front gate grew.

Perses darted farther to the east, cutting across the sloping hill and heading for the east side of the protective wall. Several fireballs shot into the air, slamming back down to earth by the gate, and I winced with the impact, knowing that, when those flames had landed, lives had been lost.

We reached the bottom of the hill and the corner of the east wall just as that wicked sense all half-bloods had kicked in. Tiny hairs rose on my body, and shivers shot across the back of my neck. "Daimons," I said, skidding to a halt as I pulled out my daggers and hit the button in the middle.

On each side, blades shot out.

Seth did the same, but Perses looked like he wanted to use his hands and get bloody and messy. We rounded the corner, running smack-dab into a cluster of daimons. Their mouths dropped open, letting out eerie, aether-starved howls. Their eyes, black and bottomless, stood out in stark contrast against their pale skin. Among them were daimon halfs, the most deadly of their kind.

It sickened me to see them here, knowing that Lucian, Ares, and even Seth at one point had controlled the daimons by feeding them innocent pures. Anger rose like a violent storm inside me, and I tapped into it.

I threw myself into the fray, taking out the first daimon with a brutal swipe of the sickle blade, cleaving its head clear off its body. Seth slammed a half in the chest with a booted foot, knocking it to the ground before he brought the pointed end of his weapon down into its chest. As I'd suspected, Perses was hands-on, snapping necks and ripping out important body parts.

A female daimon dove for me and I spun, catching the ugly thing in the stomach with my kick. She met the sharp end of my blade before she hit the ground. Dipping down, I sprang back up, whipping the sickle around in a clean sweep.

Another came at me, and I jumped. Landing in a crouch, I flipped the sickle blade over and punched up, catching the daimon in the stomach.

I rose quickly, shaking the blood and gore off my blade as I twisted. Bodies of half-blood daimons littered the ground, but there were still more daimons, at least a dozen. Moving around them, I slammed the dagger end of my blade into the back of a daimon stalking Seth. Unlike the halfs, it exploded into a burst of shimmery dust—right in my face.

Yuck.

Perses kicked a daimon half down and then grabbed it by its legs, lifting it up in the air. The thing screamed its fury, but Perses swung it like a baseball bat against the marble wall. I looked away before I could see that level of splat. There were some things you could never unsee, and that would've definitely been one of them.

Alex!

The sound of Seth's voice in my head spun me around. "Gods."

Rushing toward me, a daimon half howled hungrily and was joined by another and another. All the aether in the three of us had to be driving them wild. They were teaming up, making it more difficult to fight as we had been trained.

A fierce wind blew from Seth, sending his trio of nastiness away from him.

Yeah, screw this.

Hooking the sickle blade to my hip, I threw my hand out, summoning the element of fire. Heat zinged through my veins, warming my skin. Sparks emanated from my palm, followed by an eruption of fire. It hit the center daimon and spread outward to the ones on each side, consuming them.

Three daimons hit the ground, screaming as they rolled

and twisted. The smell of burnt clothes and flesh mingled with the metallic scent of blood.

When all the daimons were down or dust, we wasted no time. Rushing along the side of the east wall, we found the breach—a burnt-out, three-foot-wide section of wall. Wiggling through it was easy for me, but it took Perses and Seth a little finagling to get through the tight fit.

A few steps in and we were met with a set of charging automatons. We so didn't have time for this.

Seth shot past me and raised his hand. The marks of the Apollyon whipped across his skin. Energy seeped into the air around us. In a burst of light, akasha spun from him and smacked into the first automaton, lighting it up. Joining in, I summoned the fifth and most powerful element, hitting my target.

The automatons were no more.

"That does come in handy." Perses stalked back to us, blood dripping from his face. Not his. I wanted to ask if he needed a hanky. "You two should use that more often. It would make this easier."

My eyes narrowed. "You have a god-bolt. Why don't you use that?"

"I prefer my hands in battle. It means more."

That didn't even deserve a response. Shaking my head, I sent Seth a look. *This guy is nuts. But he's good.*

Racing across the now-overgrown lawn of the Covenant, we passed destroyed and shattered statues of the gods. The only ones standing were those of Ares. The guy did nothing to hide his arrogance.

Suddenly, Seth reached out, grabbing my hand and forcing me to make a sharp turn to the left. I looked down, almost mistaking what I saw for dried-out branches. But the brownish-white sticks weren't sticks at all. Nor was the tattered material clinging to it leaves.

"Oh, my gods…"

The remains of once beautifully crafted statues weren't the only things that lay seemingly forgotten on the ground. Every so many feet, there were…bodies in the grass. Some were old and nearly completely decomposed. Others were fresher, their skin a horrible array of purples and browns, their bodies bloated.

Be careful where you step, he said.

When Seth let go of my hand, I looked up to see that Perses hadn't even stopped as he plowed through the remains of someone. Bile rose up the back of my throat, and it took everything I had to push it down. Perses was a necessary evil, but sometimes I really hated the bastard.

The sounds of battle at the gate raged on as we drew near the main Covenant building. Screams of pain mixed with shouts of victory and the sound of weapon fire. The fight had spilled forward, reaching the destroyed row of the Olympian Twelve statues, which was now the Olympian One. I could see many Sentinels and soldiers on both sides, clashing together in hand-to-hand combat. It appeared the automatons were down, but we were close enough to the fight that we now were drawing attention.

Several soldiers shouted, and a large group broke apart, racing toward us.

"The servants' entrance." Seth pointed at the side of the building, where the doors and windows were busted out. "We don't have time for this out here. We have to get to where he's been and—"

A soft, tinkling laugh halted the three of us, and my heart jumped in my chest. I *knew* that sound.

The air shimmered in front of us, taking form, and forcing even Perses to take a step back.

The soft-as-wind-chimes laugh came again.

"You've got to be kidding me," I moaned. "Seriously?"

Two furies floated before us, their translucent wings moving soundlessly through the air. Blond and delicately pale, they were frighteningly beautiful in a way that was deceiving. These creatures were ugly in their true forms. And vicious. Very vicious.

One moved closer, her hair drifting around her slim body. "We're not here for you."

"This time," the other finished.

The closest furie's smile was edged with unimaginable cruelty. "The gods have heard Apollo's pleas and have responded."

Well, color me surprised and call me shocked.

Static crackled through the air, and a low-level hum teased my ears. Turning around, my eyes widened.

"Shit," Perses exclaimed. "I don't believe it."

Across the lawn, about halfway between the group of soldiers and us, a mist gathered, blanketing the overgrown grass. Out of the wispy fog, nine forms took hold. Within seconds, nine Olympian gods stood there.

Artemis yanked the bow off her back and glanced over her shoulder, spotting us. She winked, and then turned, letting loose a silver arrow.

The furies rose into the air, shedding their pearly luminous appearances. Their skin and wings turned gray and scaly. Snapping snakes replaced their hair. They flew above the gods, and I saw one swoop down, catching a man in her talons. A spray of blood spurted into the air and something—oh gods—red and ropey spilled onto the ground, steaming.

The soldier had been torn in half.

Tipping her head back, the furie's laugh tinkled on the wind, prickling the skin on the back of my neck.

Perses's brows rose. "They are as bloodthirsty as I remembered."

I looked at him. "And creepy."

He smiled. "I think they're magnificent."

Of course, he did. One of them had a mortal's head in its hands and looked like it was about to play volleyball with it. *Perses and the furie should hook up*, I thought bitterly.

"Come on," Seth called, motioning to us. He was by the shattered doors. "They got this."

That they did. One last look over my shoulder confirmed it. Apollo had obliterated the soldiers, and the gods were now joining the mess of fighting bodies around front. Hurrying after Seth and Perses, we were inside the Covenant, possibly steps away from Ares.

Stopping in front of us, Perses cocked his head to the side then glanced back at Seth and me, wiping the spray of blood off his cheek. A slow, calculated smile pulled across his face.

He disappeared.

Poof.

Gone. Vanished.

Seth's mouth dropped open. "Shit!"

CHAPTER TWENTY-FOUR

We stood just inside the servant's entrance, the hall splitting into two directions. Gray stains smudged the walls, as if there'd been a small fire.

I couldn't move or speak for several seconds. "I can't believe it!" I exclaimed. "That son of a—" Soldiers poured into the entrance. Their camouflage uniforms were so noticeably mortal, but the armbands with Ares's symbol were anything but mortal. Their guns were raised, and they were ready to fire.

Crap.

Throwing out my hands, I tapped into the element of air. Wind gusted in behind the soldiers. Their boots skidded over the tile floor. The guns shook in their hands. Seth got in on the game. A few soldiers went down. Guns misfired, and one by one, the weapons flew from their hands, sliding across the floors. The soldiers scrambled to their feet as the winds died down.

Can we let them go? I asked.

Seth shook his head and started forward, withdrawing his daggers. *They're under compulsion.*

I wanted to argue, but the soldier closest to Seth engaged, swinging his arm out. There was a wicked-looking knife in his hand, the kind I imagined serial killers would covet. Anyone in their right mind would've run from us, but those under compulsion would fight to the death.

There was nothing we could do.

Seth dipped under the attacker's arm and sprang up, slamming the hilt of one dagger into the back of a soldier while catching another in the chest. Vaulting over the body of the fallen soldier, I dipped down low and spun, taking the feet out from underneath another man. He sat up, impaling himself on the waiting dagger.

I pulled it free, the fleshy suction sound echoing in my head. Wincing, I ignored the stirrings of guilt and threw myself into the fray.

These soldiers were highly trained, no doubt strategically kept inside the Covenant to be the last line of defense if anyone made it inside. Rolling into a kick, I welcomed the sharp slice of pain, then sprang up, arcing the dagger to catch the soldier under the chin. Whipping around, I saw Seth grab one by the head and twist. The crack was lost in the punch thrown at me. I ducked, catching the attacker in the stomach.

Without any warning, my legs were taken out from under me with a brutal swipe, and my training kicked in. Allowing myself to fall, I twisted at the last second and rolled, bringing the soldier around so he was under me.

I saw his face for the briefest second. He was young—too young. Barely out of high school and with his whole life ahead of him. A deeper pain, more intense than any kick or punch, sliced at my heart as I brought the dagger down on his chest, ending his life in seconds. Wet warmth hit my face.

Springing up, I breathed heavily as I wiped the back of my hand under my chin once and then twice. I didn't want any of the boy's blood on me. I turned as Seth caught the last soldier by the neck, slamming him into the floor with enough force to crack the tile, and the man's spine. His last breath gurgled out a moment later.

Seth looked up, his eyes meeting mine. Standing slowly, he hooked his daggers to his thighs and then motioned me forward.

Keeping my eyes off the floor, I followed Seth into the hallway on the right. This close, the aether in us acted like a silent guide, pulling us to where Ares was located. We crept down the wide corridor, silent and watchful for any more surprise attacks. It was the same hall that Seth and I had run down once before, except this time it wasn't littered with bodies. It was disturbingly empty, but there were scuff marks on the once-pristine floors and walls and patches of rust-colored stains every so many feet.

Seth saw me looking at the stains. "It was bad here, when Ares first occupied the Covenant. A lot of people put up a fight."

I raised my gaze, wondering how Seth slept at night.

He seemed to read the question from my thoughts because he looked away, a muscle thrumming along his jaw. "I don't sleep, Alex. Not very well or very long."

Part of me wanted to say something reassuring to him, but what could I say? Who knew how many innocent people Seth had ended? And for what? I had no idea how he could atone for that. Or, if he ever found forgiveness in other people, would he ever find it in himself? Drawing in a shallow breath, I moved in front of him.

We'd taken a few steps when words echoed down the hall.

Familiar ones.

I heard Perses's deep voice taunting Ares, and I almost fell to my knees and started praising every god there was, maybe even a few random celebrities and fictional characters. The relief was that palpable.

He didn't abandon us.

Seth gave a curt nod. *I never thought he did.*

I rolled my eyes. *There was a moment when you did. Admit it.*

Whatever.

Creeping closer, I stuck to the wall. They were in the ballroom, the very same one where I'd faced off against the furies and killed the pure-blood.

How fitting, Seth remarked.

I shot him a death glare, and he grinned—that cocky, insufferably arrogant grin that had been absent for weeks. My lips twitched in response, but I focused. I was happy that Seth had found his mojo or whatever, but I really didn't have time to pat him on the head.

Five doors, all open, lined the hall before the entry to the ballroom. Fingertips tingling, I peeked inside the first room. Nothing. I inched forward, resisting the urge to bum-rush down the hall.

"You can't beat me, Olympian." Perses's voice stopped me for a second.

Ares laughed, but it sounded off. Rattled. "Need I remind you that it was I who wrapped the chains around your wrists?"

"Only with the help of your brethren," Perses responded. "The very ones outside this wall, raging a war on your army. I doubt they will help you this time." He paused. "You're a fool, Ares. An arrogant fool. Make war for the pure bliss of it, but never make war in order to take control."

What the what?

I glanced back at Seth, who shrugged. Why Perses had run off just to lecture Ares was beyond me. Apparently he wanted to get the last word in or something. With gods, it was anyone's guess.

Now two doors away from the ballroom, I was a second from checking the room, when a Sentinel unexpectedly stepped out, startling me.

He opened his mouth, about to give away our location. I didn't stop to think. Springing forward, I grabbed the dagger off my leg with one hand and placed my other over his mouth. Our eyes locked for a brief moment. His blue eyes were unfocused, hazy—a sign of a compulsion. Remorse pricked at my chest, but I slammed the dagger into his chest, above the heart, to the hilt.

Seth caught the body, easing it onto the floor as I sheathed the dagger. He quickly surveyed the room and motioned for me to continue. I stepped carefully around the body, inhaling deeply.

It had to be done, Seth said.

I know.

He glanced over his shoulder, eyebrow arched as if he didn't believe me, and he was right. Killing a Sentinel under compulsion sucked as bad as killing the mortals who were under Ares's control.

All right, I'll tear myself apart about it later, but for right now, I'm fine.

That's my girl.

I frowned. *That's twisted.*

Letting Seth check the next room, I slid around him. My heart pumped fast. The ballroom was next. Somewhere, the imaginary clock stopped ticking.

Seth caught my hand, spinning me around and into an empty, dark room. He pressed me back against the wall, his breath warm against my forehead. Raising my free hand, I was about to punch him in the face when his voice in my head stopped me.

Do it. Transfer the power now.

I'd be lying if I said I hadn't worried about this moment from the time Seth had suggested it. Even before it, when Apollo had said it was the only way, I'd worried. Seeing how Seth struggled with the allure, with the need that existed between us, I was prepared to knock Seth out and then transfer the power, if necessary.

He bent his head quickly, kissing my forehead. *Do it, Alex.*

Full of surprise, I hesitated as I stared into eyes that were identical to mine. *I'm not going to fail you*, he had said, and he hadn't been lying.

Now, he said again, closing his eyes as he let go of me.

My hand trembled as I reached between us, gripping his right hand. "Θάρρος." Courage.

A shock rippled across my hand and shot up my arm, followed by a wealth of warmth. Seth jerked, but remained there, his eyes closed. The tingling ended at my shoulder, and I felt it then, the collapse of fear in my chest replaced by fiery determination. This was right. I would not be stopped.

I cupped my hand around his left hand, squeezing it. "Δύναμη." Strength.

A tremble rocked Seth, and another jolt skittered up my left arm, faster than the one before. The warmth turned to heat, and it spread across my shoulder blades. My body hummed. A thousand little pulses hit my muscles, tearing them down and rebuilding them. I felt like I imagined Aiden did—he was the healthiest person I knew, since he lived off of granola, chicken, and working out.

I pulled up his shirt and placed my hand over the mark on his flat, hard stomach and whispered, "Απόλυτη εξουσία." Absolute power.

Seth gasped, and his eyes flew open. Their amber hue glowed vibrantly, locked onto mine like a laser beam. The rush of pure power almost knocked me back against the wall. Every cell in my body fired up, and the marks on my skin burned.

"One more," Seth said in a low, hoarse voice.

My entire body trembled as I reached up, cupping the back of his neck. "Αήττητο." Invincibility. The air expelled from my lungs at the same moment it did from Seth's, and then it happened. Static charged the room as the amber cord appeared around Seth's upper arm. It spiraled down, entwining over his skin, reaching mine. The blue cord crackled, brighter and more intense than his.

The two cords spun, overlapping, buzzing and spitting licks of blue and amber into the air. My hand fell from his neck, but otherwise I couldn't move. Neither could he.

Inside of me, at the base of the cord, something shifted and pulsed. Behind my eyes, a blinding light burst into an array of vibrant colors, receding quickly.

Under my feet, the floor moved. My lungs seized as Seth's head kicked back, the veins in his throat protruding. A fire lit me up from the inside, rushing through my veins at dizzying speeds. It burned sweetly, cool and hot at the same time. Power poured into my chest, causing my heart to sputter and then speed up.

Shadows danced over the walls as the cords flared, twisting and becoming one, turning into a brilliant, intense white. My other hand slipped away from him, and my arms rose at my sides as the marks on my skin seeped away and reappeared. The now-white cord pulsed once more and then snapped back toward me. Seth lowered his chin, his amber eyes shiny as he met my gaze, and then his gaze dropped.

My feet weren't on the floor. Nope.

I was floating again.

There was at least four feet between my shoes and the floor, and well, I felt damn good. "Wow," I said, grinning.

Seth's throat worked. "Wow, indeed."

Moving my hands in front of me, I watched the glyphs slide over my skin. The color seemed sharper.

You gonna come down from there? He reached up, catching my hand.

Strangely, the cord inside me didn't jump. I willed myself down. *How do you feel?*

He cocked his head to the side. *Okay. I don't feel different, really.*

Which meant he was probably still craving akasha, but at least he wasn't hurt. For a moment there, it hadn't looked fun for him.

How about you?

It was hard to describe—the *power.* I wanted to run straight into a wall because I was pretty sure I could take it on, but I didn't feel uncontrollable since I wasn't running into that wall. *I feel…great. I feel…*

There was no fear in my heart, at least not the paralyzing kind. The strength made my muscles twitchy, and I felt ready in a way I hadn't before. Hours ago, I'd known I had to take on the God Killer power. I'd known I had to face Ares and destroy him, but had I really been ready? No. It had been something I knew I had to do—a duty.

Now I was truly ready.

I smiled up at Seth, my fingers curling into fists. "Let's do this."

CHAPTER TWENTY-FIVE

Each step I took was filled with purpose and steely determination. My hands itched for a fight, but my blood sang for the release of the akasha brimming in my veins.

Ares was *so* about to get knocked down a peg or five.

In the back of my mind, I realized this was how Seth must've felt most of the time—the cockiness, the knowledge that nothing in this realm was more powerful than the First.

Until now.

I stopped in front of the closed ballroom doors and raised my hands, summoning akasha. Releasing it took nothing. Energy pulsed out from me. I blew the titanium doors right off their hinges, throwing them clear across the ballroom.

"Gods," Seth muttered.

Ares and Perses whipped around. Several feet separated them. The Titan's eyes widened. One of the doors hit the floor and slid, tearing up the marble. The other slammed into Ares, throwing him back against the wall.

My lips curled into a wide smile as I stepped into the room. "Whoops. Didn't see you standing there."

Perses chuckled as he tipped his head back. "And here is the God Killer."

With a battle roar, Ares threw the door off him. It winged through the air, catching Perses in the back and smashing him into the opposite wall. The marble cracked, and half of the wall came down, burying the Titan.

I wasn't worried. Perses was a big boy. He'd get back up. Eventually.

Ares wiped his hand over his mouth and scowled, but I could sense the unease in him in that fraction of a second. Perses's presence had done what we needed—knocking him off his game. "Well, look. The girl is the God Killer." His all-white eyes spit electricity. "I always knew you were whipped, Seth."

Seth flipped him off.

The god laughed as he moved his head to the side, cracking the bone. "Oh, I'm going to enjoy killing you, pretty boy."

"The feeling is mutual." Seth stepped forward so that he stood side by side with me.

"You look lovely," Ares remarked, turning back to me. "All juiced up, but oh, your face and body look like a road map. Sexy."

Seth stiffened beside me, but I laughed. "Sticks and stones, Ares. I thought you were more mature than that. And more clever. It's kind of disappointing."

"Disappointing?" Ares gave me a wide smile, but it wasn't as confident as it had been that day in the dean's office. "Oh, little girl, God Killer or not, you can't defeat me. This world will be mine."

"Really?" I took a step forward, skin tingling. "Is there

anything else you want to say? Because I know how you like to give long, boring, and clichéd evil-villain speeches. Can we skip it this time and just get to killing you?"

He snarled and threw out his hand. White light pulsed from his palm, arcing straight for me. I spun, moving quicker than I ever had, avoiding the god-bolt. He sent another at Seth, but he too was quick on his feet.

I was so over the smack talk. My muscles tensed and I charged the god. He averted my attack at the last minute, but Seth was on him, too. He deflected Seth's blow, pushing him back as I sprang up behind the god, shoving my foot into the center of his back with all my strength. That kind of kick would've taken out a demigod or a mortal, but with Ares, he merely stumbled forward and turned.

The look on his face said *bitch, please.*

He swung out and I dipped, but I was an instant too late. His fist caught my jaw, snapping my head to the side. Fiery pain shot across my face. Damn. He could hit. I hadn't forgotten that, but still.

"Ouch," I said. "Hitting girls isn't nice."

"But Ares wouldn't know that, would he?" Seth spun, catching Ares in the leg with a brutal kick. The god stumbled. "After all, I'm pretty sure he's only gotten lucky with Aphrodite, and *everyone* gets lucky with her."

Ares threw his arms out. He didn't touch either of us, but I was suddenly off my feet and flying backward. I caught sight of Seth's shocked expression a second before I slammed into the wall.

I hit the floor on my knees, the air knocked out of my lungs. Before I could recover, Ares's knee collided with my chin, knocking me flat on my back. My head spun as I rolled onto my side.

“Not so badass now, are you? Why don’t—” He stopped, intercepting Seth’s attack.

Lightning erupted from Ares’s palm, and my heart spasmed with the first bite of fear since becoming the God Killer. Ares could kill Seth, just like Apollo could kill me. A cry froze in my throat as Seth drew up short, recognition flaring in his amber eyes. He darted to the side at the last second, and the bolt hit him in the shoulder, flinging him backward.

My relief was short-lived. Ares grabbed hold of the front of my shirt and hauled me off the ground. He snarled in my face, his features contorting inhumanly. “I will have Olympus and I will rule this realm. There is—”

Ares dropped me with a grunt and I hit the floor on my butt, too stunned at first to realize what had happened. Then, I saw it.

Perses had recovered and tackled the god like a linebacker. They slid along the floor, tearing up chunks of marble like it was paper. The Titan’s fists rained down, catching Ares over and over again. His punches were faster than the eye could track.

Rock ’em, sock ’em Titan.

As I staggered to my feet, Ares slammed his palms into the center of the Titan’s chest and yelled. The air snapped with power, and a moment later Perses was several feet away, lying in a bloody, twitching heap.

While he was down, I started toward Ares, knowing I needed one clean shot—one blast of pure akasha when he was at his weakest to end this. I was halfway toward him when my senses fired up.

Seth shouted as he struggled to his feet.

Out of nowhere, a freaking daimon came out at me, ragged teeth exposed and veins like tiny black snakes. I did not have time for this. Engaging the sickle blade, I arced my arm up, catching the daimon at the neck.

That was all she wrote.

Seth rushed forward, hitting Ares at the waist as he fired off a god-bolt at me. Knocked off balance, his aim wasn't spectacular. The bolt caught me in the leg, and pain exploded in a rush of wet warmth.

Holy Hades, *that* hurt…

I staggered back and then fell as the pain ricocheted down my leg. He threw Seth off him like a Frisbee and sprang up fluidly.

On his feet, Ares was a hundred percent focused on me as he stalked forward. I kept my gaze trained on him as I picked myself up, spitting out a mouthful of blood. Red streaked his bare chest, and I felt a surge of satisfaction.

"All I need is you," he taunted. "And you *will* submit to my will."

And all I needed was for him to keep his creepy god eyes on me, so he could keep talking his smack all he wanted.

"Is that so? I think we know where I stand on the whole submission thing."

"We also know how the last time ended when you refused." Ares spared a quick glance at Perses's still-prone body. He laughed. "This time I know how to get what I want from you."

"Do tell." I took a measured step back, drawing on akasha once more. It whipped through my veins like white lightning, boiling my blood and burning my body from the inside. The urge to unleash it was almost too hard to deny, but it wasn't time.

Ares's lips curled into a sneer. "You will do anything to protect those you care for. I could go for that pure-blood of yours. Or how about your father? Both of them are outside, right?"

My fingers straightened. Behind him, Seth was on his feet, a Covenant dagger clutched in his right hand. "If you were going to use them, you'd have pulled that card by now, which tells me you don't quite know where my father is. And you haven't gotten to Aiden."

"I will," he promised. "And it's only a matter of time before they make their way in here. Both will come to your aid, and I know, oh yes, I know you'll do anything to keep them safe," Ares said. "And I will kill one of them, and you'll have to choose. I just need to bide my time." Seth was almost on him.

I allowed myself a smile. "That's the funny thing about time. You never have as much as you think."

Ares opened his mouth, but his words were cut off by Seth's dagger. Shoved deep into Ares's back. The god reared and screamed. "I'm going to kill you!"

"It's a little too late for that," Seth said, yanking the blade out of Ares's back.

I snapped forward at the same moment Ares threw his arm out, sending Seth flying into the air. Seth hit a pillar with a sickening crunch I couldn't allow to distract me. Akasha rushed through me, and my vision tinged with white.

Ares whirled on me, swaying to the side as I unleashed the purest power in and out of the mortal realm. Throwing my arm out, akasha flared from my shoulder, just like the cord that had connected me to Seth. Spiraling down my arm, it erupted in a burst. Ares tried to move, but he wasn't fast enough.

The bolt of akasha hit him in the center of the chest, and I kept the stream of energy up, throwing everything into the attack. Light crackled and spit into the air. Wisps of fine smoke radiated above the cord.

Stalking forward, I kept on him, not giving him a chance

to slip away. I could feel the energy in me waning with each passing second, but I gritted my teeth. This was it. There would be no second chances. When the akasha sputtered out, which it would, I would be down for the count.

But Ares…he was backing away, still able to walk, and I was weakening fast. I had no idea how much more I had in me or what it would take to truly kill an Olympian. But the stream of akasha pulsed, and then the light weakened. My breath expelled from my lungs harshly as an ache started behind my eyes.

Then Seth was beside me, grasping my free hand, and he squeezed. The cord between us reappeared, wrapping around our joined hands. Suddenly, it made sense to me. I drew in a breath, and Seth jerked as if a puppet master had pulled on his strings. The light from the akasha flared intensely, growing until it was too bright to look upon. Pulling from us both, the blast of energy became a white fire.

Ares's fury-filled roar developed into a terror-filled scream. A loud popping sound, like a hundred guns going off at the same time, followed. The akasha faded out, not snapping back to me, but simply fizzling like fireworks vanishing into the sky.

I still held onto Seth's hand, my body shaking as Ares came into view.

The gods' eyes were wide, his arms stretched out at his sides. He tipped his chin down and his mouth opened, but no sound came out. A ball of crackling white light was embedded deep in his chest.

The light spread out, following the intricate network of veins until his chest lit up.

I took a breath, but it got stuck.

Ares lifted his head as the white lines reached across his shocked face, covering his head within a second.

He disappeared under the white light.

The sound of deafening thunder cracked through the room. The air distorted and rippled, and I saw it coming a second too late. The sonic wave rolled across the room at frightening speed, slamming into Seth and me. It broke my hold on him, splitting us apart, and we flew backward, hit the floor, and slid. An explosion rocked the room, and fine, white dust poured into the air like snow. Starbursts flooded my vision like a thousand bombs going off.

And then there was silence.

Hands and arms shaking, I rolled onto my side and lifted myself halfway up. The wall across from me was gone. A hole had been blown straight through it, exposing beams and crumbling brick and sunlight.

I looked over my shoulder and let out a ragged breath.

The spot where Ares had stood was empty. On the floor, the blackened tile formed a perfect circle, like a brand. I knew in my bones that Ares was gone. The blast was a release of his essence, returning it to wherever it came from.

Shifting onto my butt, I winced at the ache that consumed my body as I scanned the room for Seth. The white dust had settled like a fine blanket of snow. Near the entrance of the ballroom, Seth lay face down.

I stared at him for a moment, my brain slowly catching up to my surroundings, and when it did, my heart nearly exploded in my chest.

Seth wasn't moving. Oh gods…

I staggered to my feet and rushed toward him, ignoring the weakness in my limbs. "No. No. No."

Dropping down beside him, I grabbed his shoulders and rolled him onto his back. "Seth," I whispered, shaking him. "Seth, come on."

His eyes were shut. Golden lashes fanned cheeks that didn't move. There was a wrenching feeling deep inside me, a splintering and tearing in my chest that felt so very real.

He *wasn't* moving.

I grasped his cheeks. The marks of the Apollyon—the beautiful blue marks flared under my fingers. No. No. No. I tried our bond to reach him. *Seth?* But there was no answer, nothing but a low hum. Panicked, I shook him again, and when he didn't respond, a broken sob racked its way through my body as I dropped my head onto his chest.

Grief tore through me—the kind I hadn't known would be possible to feel again, because I had felt this when I'd held Caleb as he died. No matter what Seth had done, the terrible things he'd started, he'd made it right in the end. And even if he hadn't, if it had been my hand in the end that brought him down, the pain would've still been there. Seth was a part of me—my other half. And I was losing that part. Forever.

I can't breathe.

"Neither can I. You're squashing me."

Jerking back, I let out a startled shriek. Seth stared back at me, his amber eyes slightly unfocused, but he was breathing. He was alive.

I smacked him. Hard.

"Ow!" Seth rolled onto his side, out of my grasp. "What the hell was that for?"

"Don't ever do that again, you jerk!" I smacked him again, hitting him on the hip. "I thought you were dead!"

Seth chuckled hoarsely as he rose onto his knees. "I was knocked out, Angel. Please don't do that again."

I stared at him, caught between wanting to hit him and hug him. "I hate you."

"I'm going to have to call bullshit on that." Lifting his chin, he squinted as he looked around. "You did it, didn't you? Ares is gone."

Sitting back, I followed his gaze. Pillars cracked. Walls destroyed. I nodded slowly. "*We* did it."

Our gazes locked, and a silly grin appeared on Seth's face as he extended his hand. I took it, and we stood together.

Then I remembered a very important, currently MIA Titan. Dropping Seth's hand, I turned around and scanned the room. Nothing. And Perses was kind of hard to miss, which meant he was gone. The gods weren't going to be happy about that.

"Crap," I muttered. "He bounced."

"There's nothing we can do about that now." Seth pressed a hand against his ribs. A grimace shot across his face. "He's their problem."

Not true. "He's our—"

The air thickened around us, filling with static.

"It's not going to be their first problem," I said, letting out a ragged breath as my heart jumped in my chest.

In front of the massive hole in the wall, shimmery forms appeared like rays of sunshine, one after another after another. I counted the glowing figures once, then twice. "Oh, crap."

Seth wrapped an arm around my waist. "I'm going to admit this. My eyes are kind of blurry, but there are eleven shiny things surrounding us, right?"

I practically plastered myself to him, nodding. There were eleven *shiny things* forming a wide circle around us. The Olympian Twelve—er, Eleven. Would've been twelve if Ares hadn't been obliterated. My breath caught.

Two floated forward, becoming more solid. Lifting my arm, I shielded my eyes. Their light was so bright, so beautiful. For a moment, all I could do was be awestruck by what I was seeing.

"You should have waited before you hit me. I think you broke me," whispered Seth.

"Uh, you'll be okay," I said, and Seth's muscles tensed around me.

"So, you think they're here to congratulate us?"

I lowered my arm, watching as the lights took on human forms. A male and female stood before us, their features not so distinguishable yet, but I knew they weren't Apollo or Artemis.

"I don't think so," I whispered.

"Maybe they're mad because you've been sleeping with a pure," Seth joked, but his voice was laced with unease.

I looked over my shoulder at him. "Really? That's the reason? It couldn't be that you took out an entire Council of pures?"

A wry smile formed on Seth's lips. "You're splitting hairs, Alex."

"Gods, you're so annoying."

He stepped forward, blocking me from the two closest gods. Rolling my eyes, I moved so that we were shoulder to shoulder.

Seth looked down at me. "If I tell you to run, you run."

"No." I grabbed his hand and held on. I didn't have the heart to tell him that they weren't here for him. "We face this together."

The shimmery light faded, revealing the gods around us, but I didn't see past the one in front of us. A million years could've gone by and I never, ever thought I would lay eyes upon *him*.

Zeus was not as I imagined.

I'd always pictured this older guy with a potbelly and bushy, gray beard, but that was not what Zeus looked like. Not in the slightest.

Dressed in some kind of white, linen pants, his chest and stomach were bare. And ripped—ripped like you could cut your fingers on those abs. The curve of his strong jaw was also bare of hair. He was sublimely handsome, his lips wide and eyes tilted. His features were sharp, breathtakingly angular.

I could see a bit of Titan in him.

The only thing my imagination had gotten right was his hair. It was shockingly white.

"You did well," he spoke, his voice as deep and commanding as Perses's. There was no anger in his tone. I knew in that moment, before Zeus even spoke again, that Apollo hadn't come through. My knees suddenly felt weak, and if I hadn't been holding Seth's hand, I would've sunk to the floor. "You will be rewarded greatly."

A shudder rocked through me, but Seth…he didn't understand—he didn't get what Zeus hadn't tacked on at the end. "Well, that's surprising," he murmured.

My gaze darted to the gods, finding Apollo standing next to a somber Artemis. Apollo shook his head *no*, and my heart sank all the way. I took a jerky step back, my skin turning icy.

"Don't," Zeus said, his voice level and calm. "This is the only way."

Seth's grip on my hand tightened. "What's the only way?"

Zeus ignored him. "You know this must be done. We cannot allow a God Killer to exist. The threat is too great, even greater than what Ares posed."

In that moment, I briefly considered trying to take out Zeus, but it had drained everything in me and Seth to kill Ares. It wouldn't work. Maybe I would lay some bruises on Zeus, but in the end, I couldn't defeat another Olympian. All I had was Apollo in my corner. He could walk away from this, refuse Zeus's bidding, because he was the only one who could kill me—besides a Titan, and our Titan had vanished.

But Apollo didn't look like he was going to disobey his father.

Oh, my gods…

Another shiver rocked my body as it really seeped in. This was it. I wanted to run. I wanted to fight, but as I stared back at the gods, I saw that it would all be so very pointless. If I fought, Seth would get hurt in the process. Badly. And who's to say that Zeus wouldn't turn to finding Aiden and my father to make this easier? I couldn't risk them. I couldn't risk anyone else like I'd done with Caleb, Lea, Olivia, and so many more.

It…it was now my turn.

Seth's head snapped back as if he'd been slapped. "No. You can't do this. We helped you! She did everything you wanted her to do!" He dropped my hand, forming his into fists. "You can't do this to her!"

Having not seen Seth this upset in a long time, I sucked in a sharp breath. My heart was trying to come out of my chest again. "Seth…"

"No!" He took a step toward Zeus, but I shot forward, grabbing his arm. His wide eyes met mine. "Alex, you can't—"

"There's nothing either of you can do," Zeus said, taking a step back to stand next to Hera.

She inclined her head to the side, and several strands of russet-colored hair slipped from her elegant coif. "It is for the best of everyone."

An angry flush flooded Seth's cheeks. "Are you serious?"

"Seth!" I tugged on his arm.

"What?" he snapped, turning on me. He gripped my shoulders. "You can't be okay with this. And you're not giving up!"

Was I giving up? I glanced back to Apollo and read the sadness in his expression. "I'm not giving up, Seth, but they won't allow the God Killer to live."

Seth didn't respond immediately, but when he did, he cursed harshly and blanched. "You knew! You knew that this would happen."

I shook my head and whispered, "Could happen. I knew this *could* happen."

"Could versus would? Are you shitting me? You knew this *could* happen, and you still put yourself in this situation?" He shook me as more blood drained from his face. "How could you, Alex?"

Blinking back tears, I shook my head again. How could I say that he couldn't have handled the power of the God Killer and not make him feel worse?

"This is sweet," Hera said, stepping back so she joined the other Olympians. "He cares for her so deeply, and yet she loves another. Tragic."

Really? My gaze slid to her, but then Apollo stepped forward, breaking ranks. Each step was slow, purposeful. A lump formed in my throat. There wasn't enough time. I realized that then. The same crack I'd thrown in Ares's face had now turned back on me.

Karma was a bitch and a half.

And so was Fate, because this was Fate, wasn't it? Either way, I wanted to see Marcus one more time and share an awkward hug with him. I wanted to see my father once more, maybe have dinner with him. I wanted to watch Deacon and Luke laugh, and see Solos's smile.

And, oh gods, I wanted to kiss Aiden, just once more.

But there was no time. This was happening. All those moments, from the second my mother had taken me out of the Covenant, had been leading up to this. She had tried to prevent this—even as a daimon, she had tried to prevent *this*.

Grandma Piperi had said I'd kill the ones I love.

She had forgotten to tell me that I would also die in the end.

Gods, she sucked at the whole foretelling thing. But Solaris had known, hadn't she? She had sounded like she'd be seeing me again soon, and she would be.

This was so not fair.

"Alexandria," Apollo said gently. "It is time."

I turned to Seth, my heart racing. "Please—"

"No!" he yelled, still fighting the inevitable. "This isn't right. They can't do this. You don't deserve this. I do. They—"

"They're not going to take you," I said, tears welling in my eyes. "Listen to me, Seth. They're not. They can't kill you. Ares is gone, and I'm the God Killer. There's nothing we can do."

The full horror of the situation dawned in Seth's expressive face, and he placed his hands on my cheeks. He pressed his forehead to mine. "Oh gods, Alex, I don't want this to happen. Alex..."

I gripped his arms, forcing myself to breathe. "Please take care of Aiden. I know you two don't get along, but *please*. He's going to need someone. So please watch out for him. Promise me, Seth. *Promise* me."

There was a long pause, and I thought I felt his tears mix with mine. "I promise."

Those two words, well, they helped a little, but God Killer or not, I was scared and I didn't want to be alone. "Don't let go," I whispered, closing my eyes.

"I won't," he swore, his lips brushing my cheek. "I will never let go."

I started to shake. I didn't want to be scared. Where was that strength and courage I'd felt earlier? I wanted to be the one who faced Fate with her head high, but I *was* scared. I knew there was no coming back from this. I would never see my father, my friends, or Aiden again through living eyes. My breath caught again, and each time I took a breath, I feared it would be the last one. "Don't leave me. Please? I don't want to be by myself."

"You're not." Seth slipped his arms around me, holding me close. "You're not alone." His tears *were* mingled with mine. "You're not alone. You'll never be alone, Angel. I promise you. You'll never—"

I took a breath and never heard his next words. There was a harsh expletive from Seth, and then the world ended for me on the heels of a burst of beautiful bright sunlight.

CHAPTER TWENTY-SIX

Dying the second time was nothing like the first time. When I opened my eyes, I knew I was in the Underworld, and I knew I was dead. Not like when I was stabbed by Linard. Nope. I was as dead as everyone else around me.

I also didn't end up on the banks of Styx waiting for Charon with all the other dead folks; there would've been a lot of them after all the fighting.

My death was just all kinds of special.

When I opened my eyes, I was standing in the middle of Hades's palace. There had been no pain, no feeling of suffocation—a blink of an eye and my life was over, and I was staring at the translucent, shimmery dress of Persephone.

The first things I saw upon dying were Persephone's breasts and nipples. Or at least one nipple, but there was definitely *a* nipple.

Something seemed wrong about that being the first thing I saw in the afterlife.

I was too dumbstruck by the whole dying thing to do

or say much of anything. Hades was already back, and when Persephone dropped her arm over my shoulders, I was too out of it to be freaked out about her being so close to me.

"Where's Apollo?" I asked, because I wanted to see him, needed to see him.

The arrogance that was typically present on Hades's face was gone as he shook his head. "He will come when he can."

I didn't like that answer. Apollo should be here, not Hades. Apollo had promised to take care of me, but I had ended up dead in Hades's palace, staring at Persephone's nipples. This was not what I'd expected when he'd sworn to make sure I was okay.

Hades strolled up to me and clasped my cheeks. I flinched out of habit. "You did an amazing thing today. We will forever be in your debt."

I jumped on that. "Then bring me back to life."

He shook his head and smiled sadly. "I cannot grant such things."

So I jumped on it again. "Then release Aiden from his promise."

And he shook his head once more. "I cannot grant that either, Love."

"You can't do anything?" I demanded. "You're a god and you're—"

"It all is done, Alexandria. It is over." Looking at his wife, he nodded. "Take her to her final resting place."

Her final resting place?

I shuddered.

Yep, that sounded just as disturbing as one would think.

Persephone ushered me out the back of the palace, and at first I was absolutely stunned by what I saw. It wasn't like any part of the Underworld I'd seen before.

"It's beautiful, isn't it?" Persephone asked. "This is the beginning of the Elysian Fields, and they go as far as the eyes can see. Like Tartarus, they are ever-changing, fitting to each person's version of paradise."

The Elysian Fields were…they were striking, and they looked so real, so normal, that my heart ached at the sight. The sky was beautiful—cloudless blue and bright. The air was warm, and the light scent of jasmine reminded me of…

I didn't let myself finish that thought.

"Your paradise will be what you decide, Alexandria, and you can share it with others," Persephone explained as I stared over the lush rolling hills and, beyond, the rooftops of many homes. In the valley below, the tips of exotic-looking trees swayed, playing peekaboo with crystal clear waters below them. "It will be your choice."

My choice?

My choice had been not to die.

Persephone took my hand, and the ground seemed to swallow us up. A second later, we were standing in an empty field cluttered with white and yellow daisies.

"This will be your paradise," she said and vanished. And that was…that. She'd left me in an empty field.

I stood there for an ungodly amount of time, until the sky overhead started to darken and tiny, brilliant stars appeared to blanket the deep blue of night. I learned a couple of things about being dead during that time.

My lungs worked like they had when I was alive, because I kept feeling the air catch in my throat. I could still cry, because quiet tears tracked my cheeks. I'd always thought the sobbing, body-shaking tears were the worst, but I was wrong. Quiet tears fell in a way that scarred my soul and seemed to never end.

I'd also learned that, in death, I could still feel lonely.

But finally, after what already felt like an eternity, I found my paradise. I closed my eyes, willing the tears to stop, and for some reason, I thought about Deity Island, of the rolling waves and the clean, warm sand. In my head, I heard the seagulls and felt the wet spray of the ocean against my cheeks. And I thought of the small but perfect cottage that had sat at the edge of the marsh.

Opening my eyes, I let out a little yelp of surprise.

I was back in North Carolina. I had to be, because the ocean rolled calmly before me, its waves a deep, dark blue in the night, and sand was under my feet. I could smell the marsh and feel the dampness on my cheeks. I spun around and cried out when I saw the cottage—a light was on in the window, glowing a soft yellow. I took off, slipping over the sand at breakneck speed. The door was unlocked, and the wood was warm and real, so *real*, in my hand. I threw the door open and realized that, even dead, my heart beat in my chest like I'd downed dozens of energy drinks.

Upon seeing the living room, I pressed a hand to my chest. It was exactly how I remembered: a small, efficient kitchen to the right, a large couch and TV, and very minimal design. In a daze, I walked down the short, narrow hall, passing a bathroom and then entering into the spacious bedroom.

The bed was *his*—the black sheets, the pillows, and the scent of the sea and something earthy, of burning leaves and man.

But *he* wasn't here.

Because *he* was alive and I, well, I was dead.

I spent hours in that bedroom, soaking up his scent, before I pulled myself away. I opened the back door at the end of the hall and saw the garden—an exact replica of the one on Deity Island, the very one where I had met Grandma Piperi.

Ripe blossoms and rich soils, trees I couldn't begin to even name, and enough flowers to start a botanical garden. There was even an old stone bench.

I turned back around, staring at the cottage.

Once I'd found my paradise and the sun came back up the following day, the others around me had become visible—houses and apartment buildings of all different sizes, farms, and sprawling cities. And sunny palm trees and snow-capped mountaintops. It was a smorgasbord of every place in the world.

But that wasn't all.

Paradise was simplistic, centering around needs but not wants. Over the course of time that seemed longer than normal days and nights, I learned how paradise operated.

What you needed, you got. It was as simple as that.

If I needed to be hungry, I would be hungry. And if I needed a juicy steak, it would simply appear after closing my eyes. If I didn't need to eat, there were no stomach pains. If I needed to wear jeans or a dress, all I had to do was open the closet, and there they would be.

There was more.

Apparently when you died and you were scarred up like I was, you got an afterlife makeover. My hair was long again; it was the length it had been before Ares had given me the beauty-school-dropout haircut. Reaching the middle of my back, the ends were neat, and the strands were shiny and soft. At first, I'd been obsessed with my hair—touching it to make sure it was still there, picking it up and waving it across my face.

When you're dead, it's not like you have much else to do.

Up until that very moment, I was still surprised by what I saw. Leaning in until my eyes almost crossed, I studied my reflection in the mirror. The fine network of faint pink scars was gone. They were also gone from my body. I'd been restored, but the afterlife makeover had gone farther than that. The daimon tags I'd received when I was in Gatlinburg, those patches of pale white skin on my neck and arms, were healed completely. And when I pulled up my tank top, I saw the jagged scar left behind from Linard's blade and the first time I'd died was gone, too.

Underworld was like a scar-be-gone.

I rocked back on my heels of my bare feet, sighing.

Strangely, what took the most for me to get used to were my eyes. They were different. The irises were brown, like they had been before I'd Awakened, but there was a thin line of amber around the pupils. I didn't know what that meant or why they were like that.

He...he would've been so happy to see my eyes brown again.

The inside of my throat thickened immediately, and I squeezed my eyes shut. *I will not cry. I will not cry.* Crying was bad in the Underworld, I'd discovered. Once you started, it was hard to stop and could become a one-way ticket to the Vale of Mourning. And that didn't sound like fun.

Tears pricked at my eyes nonetheless.

I knew I shouldn't cry, but it was hard because I missed my uncle and my dad. I missed Luke, Deacon, and Solos. I missed Seth and how easy it was for him to infuriate me. But I yearned for Aiden something fierce. With each passing second, it only got stronger, more intense. It didn't fade, my longing for him, and I didn't think it ever would.

"Alex?"

Looking away from the mirror, I turned to the boy lying on my bed. His shoulder-length blond hair was pulled back into a ponytail, but shorter strands had escaped, falling across his tanned cheeks. Every day since the first day after I'd died, Caleb had been here for me. I'd spent time with my mom, with Olivia, and even with Lea, but I'd seen Caleb the most. I felt bad for sucking up so much of his time, because I was sure he and Olivia were trying to discover if you could make a baby in the Underworld every free moment they had, but I didn't know what I would do without him. "Come here," he said, patting the spot next to him.

I shuffled over and sat beside him. "Olivia's going to cut me if you keep hanging out in my bed."

Caleb laughed, and each time he did, I had to smile. I'd missed that laugh as much as I now missed life. "She's not going to cut you."

"I'm sucking up all your time."

"No, you're not." He reached over, tugging on the hem of my jeans. "And she understands. Dying isn't easy, Alex. Not for anyone, and definitely not for you."

I arched a brow.

Caleb tugged on the hem again. "Why don't you come with me tonight? Me. You. Olivia. There's this club I found a few weeks ago, near the palms. I think it belongs to some pure whose idea of a 'happily ever after' is a nonstop party."

The Elysian Fields were as close to living as you could get, and there were a lot of things to do, people to meet, and whatnot. Lea had already hooked up with some half-blood *and* one of Hades's guards.

I shrugged a shoulder.

"I think it would be good for you, Alex. I mean it."

"I know." And I also knew where this conversation was heading.

Caleb didn't disappoint. "You need to get out and be

happy. I know it's hard, but I'm worried about you. I'm scared. You could end up in the Vale, and there's no coming back from that."

"I don't want you to be scared," I said, staring at my fingernails. They'd never been this smooth and buffed in life. "But Apollo lied to me. He said he would take care of me."

Caleb didn't say anything because this wasn't the first time I'd said it to him. I'd been saying it every day.

"And where has he been?" I asked, lifting my gaze. Sympathy crossed Caleb's boyishly handsome face. "Not once has he visited me. I feel like he used me, which was stupid, because he's a god and that's all they do, but I..." I trailed off, shaking my head. "I'm sorry. It's the Alex twenty-four hour whine channel."

"It's okay. Don't apologize." He patted the spot again. "Lie down with me?" Stretching out beside him, I stared at the ceiling. "This reminds me of our..."

"Last time together topside?" he supplied, and then laughed when I cringed. "At least you don't smell this time around."

I laughed as I shot him a glare. "You jerk. I didn't smell then."

"The hell you didn't. You hadn't showered in days." He rolled onto his side, grinning. His blue eyes literally glimmered. "You were stinky."

"That's so wrong."

"Love you," he replied.

My smile spread, and honestly, if I could spend eternity with Caleb, I might be okay. I might not go into the Vale, but that wasn't fair to put that on him. He had made a life for himself...in the afterlife, but I snuggled closer to Caleb, into his open arms, and closed my eyes.

"It'll get easier," he promised, resting his forehead against mine. "It does."

I wanted to believe him, but I wanted Aiden and I wanted life, and paradise simply could not provide those two things.

CHAPTER TWENTY-SEVEN

I wasn't big on the Covenant garden when I was alive, but I kept finding myself in this one now. There was something calming and peaceful among the roses and peonies. I kept coming back to the old stone bench, especially in the mornings. Maybe I thought Grandma Piperi would magically appear and give me another messed-up prophecy for old time's sake. That would be fun.

Or not.

Making my way down the marble pathway, my gaze skipped over the intricate designs in the sidewalk. Somehow I hadn't noticed this before, but the carvings were the marks of the Apollyon. Interesting.

I rounded the thick nightshade bush and lifted my gaze. I drew up short, my eyes widening. The bench wasn't empty today.

Apollo sat there, hands clasped between his knees. "It's about time," he said. "I've been waiting for about an hour."

I stared at him, my mouth hanging open. "I…I slept in."

He cocked his head to the side. "I hear you've been sleeping a lot."

I snapped out of it. "Where have you been?"

"I've been busy." He stood, towering over me. "I came as soon as I could."

"As soon as you could?" I repeated dumbly. "It's been more than a week!"

Apollo folded his massive arms. "Time moves differently here, Alexandria. An hour or two here is a second in the mortal realm. It hasn't been that long."

"Since I died?" I crossed my arms, mimicking his stance. "I thought you were supposed to take care of me."

"I did."

My eyes narrowed. "I'm dead. I'm not quite sure how that's taking care of me."

Apollo unfolded his arms and strolled up to me. "You need to get over that tiny fact." Then he patted me on the head. Actually patted me on the freaking head. "Come on. We have something we need to do."

I turned, half-tempted to spin-kick him in the head, and while I was sure I could break out some of the moves, I didn't have any leftover, supercool Apollyon powers. Spin-kicking him probably wouldn't end well.

Apollo glanced over his shoulder, exasperated. "Are you coming? Time is ticking."

"Oh, I think I have, like, an eternity worth of time." I wanted to stay where I was, because I was feeling pretty damn childish, but I groaned and then followed him. "Where are we going?"

"You'll see."

I made a face at him as I struggled to keep up with his long-legged gait. Pissed as I was at him, I remained sullenly quiet as we walked. We made it to the edge of the garden before I couldn't hold back my questions.

"How is everyone?"

He looked at me sideways. "How do you think?"

My palms tingled, and anger heated my cheeks. "A part of me knew that this would be the outcome, but I hoped it would be different. I hoped because of what *you* said and what I was being asked to do. You let me down, Apollo. So the least you could do is give me a straight answer."

His blue eyes deepened, turning the color of the sky before a storm. I knew I'd struck a chord, but I didn't care. What could he do? Kill me? A quiet voice whispered in the back of my head that he could drop my unhappy ass in Tartarus, but I doubted he'd ever do that, no matter how much I ticked him off.

Apollo sighed. "They're not happy. Your uncle holed himself up in a room and drank himself into a stupor. Your friends? Inconsolable. I think you know how Seth feels. Maybe you don't—not to the full extent, anyway. And Aiden?" He paused, and the back of my eyes burned. "I have never seen a man break the way he did. And he broke. Set half the damn Covenant on fire. If his brother hadn't showed up when he had, I'm *positive* that he would've stayed in the burning building. Is that what you wanted to know? Did it make you feel better, Alexandria?"

"No," I whispered, my chest aching as if someone had split me wide open. Tears welled up and spilled down my cheeks. I wiped at them hastily. "That didn't make me feel better at all."

"I didn't think it would, but you insisted." He headed around the front of the cottage—the cottage I wasn't sure I could even look at now. "People loved you—still love you. Mourning is never easy. But they will heal, and they will continue to live."

And I wanted that—I wanted them to move on. Even as badly as I wanted to see them again, I didn't want them here. They deserved to live.

"The Elixir is no more," Apollo said. "I thought you'd like to know that."

I looked up at Apollo as we crossed the beach, the sand warm under my bare feet. Since I'd died, I'd boycotted shoes. "Thank you."

"Some of the servants will have lasting effects from being on the Elixir for so long, but many are functioning well. Many are presented with options they've never had before." He stopped, several feet from the edge of the lapping waves. "After Ares's defeat, an emergency Council meeting was called. Solos was given a spot on the Council."

My mouth dropped open. "Are you serious? A half-blood on the Council? Oh my gods, that's…wow, that's awesome. How did it happen?"

A small grin appeared on his lips. "Only a few days have passed, but a lot has happened. Aiden took his spot on the Council as well."

I sucked in a shallow breath as pride swelled through me. "He did? His parents…"

"He did. With his vote, among others, they officially revoked the Breed Order and gave those rights I promised you back to the halfs."

Oh, my gods galore, I felt like I needed to sit down. This was major. "He also gave up his seat afterward. He gave his seat to Solos."

My eyes widened. "He did what? I mean, that's great about Solos, but why would he do that?" Then fear poured into my chest like ice. "Oh gods, he's going to be okay, right? He's not going to do anything stupid—"

"He's not going to do anything stupid. He will be okay," Apollo responded. "Change is coming for our society, Alexandria. It will take some time, but it will happen. Just like you will come to accept your new path."

Thrown off by that last statement, I took a step back, away from Apollo. "My new path?"

"Yes, it's time that you start to move on."

I gaped at him. "I just died!"

"And apparently, enough time has passed for you to get ticked off about me not coming to visit you immediately." Apollo smiled widely at my death glare. "Remember what you did with Caleb to honor your mother and those who died last summer?"

"What?" The change of subject left me spinning.

"You used spirit boats as a way of moving on, didn't you?"

I frowned. "Were you peeping on me then, Apollo?"

He ignored that. "I think you need to do the same thing for yourself."

"What the what?" I stared at him, stunned into stupidity. "You want me to set a spirit boat into the ocean that's meant for me?"

Apollo nodded once more. "I think it's the perfect idea. It will be symbolic and hopefully a new start for yourself."

Several seconds passed while I waited for him to yell "just kidding" and slap me on the shoulder, but he didn't. "You're serious."

"Do I look like I'm joking?"

Actually, he looked like he wanted to hit me. "But that is so…weird."

"It is not weird." His gaze dropped over me. "But you should be dressed nicer than this, like you were when you did it before."

My mouth opened, but before I could utter a word, Apollo snapped his fingers, and my clothes changed. They changed while on my body. Jeans and tank top, my choice of afterlife attire, turned into the black tube dress I'd worn the day Caleb and I had set the little spirit boats free.

Smoothing my hands over the soft material, I lifted my gaze. "That's…that's creepy, because there had to be a split second when I was naked, so don't do that again."

He shrugged and then held out his once-empty palm. Not so empty now. A spirit boat rested in his hand, candle and all.

I hesitated. "You're really going to make me do this."

"Yes."

Fighting the urge to roll my eyes, I recognized that Apollo wasn't going to be swayed on this matter. And it was strange. Ever since Apollo had killed me, I'd imagined letting loose on him hundreds of times, but now that he was here, holding a damn spirit boat in his hands, I didn't have it in me.

Maybe because I had agreed to become the God Killer, knowing how it would probably end.

Shaking my head, I took it from Apollo. The moment my fingers wrapped around it, a tiny flame encased the wick of the white candle. I held the fragile spirit boat in my hands. "You know this is twisted and morbid, right?"

"You need to let go of your old life, Alexandria."

"My only life," I muttered.

Apollo didn't respond to that.

Exhaling harshly, I turned toward the ocean. Sun glinted off the waves, and I knew the water would be warm and foamy, because that was how I liked it. But walking out to those waves with a spirit boat meant for myself wasn't as easy as anyone would think.

I stood there for several moments, so many thoughts

racing through my head as a soft breeze rolled off the ocean and stirred my hair. Could I really do this without laughing or crying? Because I wasn't sure if it was funny or just really sad. And was I ready for this? Contrary to Apollo's annoying opinion, I did just die. Was I ready to move on? Did I want to?

That was a tough question.

The pain, the longing, and the yearning had become familiar to me. Letting go seemed like I was giving up, but that wasn't right. Even in my darkest moments, I knew that wasn't true. The truth was, I didn't want to be like this forever. I didn't want to be like this for another week. And I sure as hell didn't want to end up in the Vale.

I wasn't sure that a spirit boat would be the answer, but it wouldn't hurt to try. And who cared if I felt a little stupid for doing it? I was dead. Not like anyone was going to judge me here.

Taking a deep breath, I forced my legs forward. The sand gave way under my feet, and water tickled my toes. I kept going until the water foamed just below my knees. I stopped, staring down at my boat. I'd done this before. Hadn't I said that Mom was in a better place? She was—I saw her yesterday. We pulled weeds in the garden together. So wasn't I in a better place now? No more looming threats of death or dismemberment. No more messed-up Fate or duty. No more loss.

There was just the loss I'd already suffered.

But maybe that too would fade one day. And I'd see my friends and family again. I knew that. And maybe when it was time for Aiden, Hades would take pity on us. After all, the rotten SOB owed us. He most definitely owed me.

Letting out a sigh, I bent down and placed the spirit boat in the ocean. My fingers lingered for a second, and I said the only thing I could think of saying. "Goodbye."

And so I let the boat go.

Straightening, I watched the waves carry it off, farther and farther out until I couldn't see the boat anymore. I wasn't sure I felt any better, but I thought it was a step in the right direction. It was something, which according to my own personal motto was better than nothing.

I turned around, about to yell back at Apollo and ask him if he was happy now, but as my gaze flickered over the god, something else caught my attention.

My heart stopped.

Air froze in my lungs. I couldn't blink, because I was *terrified* that if I did, what I was seeing would vanish, because it couldn't be real.

He couldn't be real.

Aiden stood at the shoreline, the water curling around his ankles, dampening the hems of the jeans he wore. The breeze caught the edges of his white shirt, lifting them slightly, and played with his locks of dark, wavy hair. Rays of sun kissed his broad cheeks, and from that distance, I could see that his eyes were a breathtaking, fierce silver. He was smiling.

He was smiling at *me*.

"Hey," he said, and oh my gods, it was his voice. A voice I thought I wouldn't hear again for a very long time—or maybe never again.

I placed my hand against my chest as my throat worked. "Is this…is this real?"

His smile spread, revealing those deep dimples in his cheeks. "This is real, agapi mou." I couldn't move.

"Alex," he called, laughing softly.

"How are you here? Oh my gods…" My gaze darted to Apollo. "Is he dead? You said he would be okay! That he wouldn't do anything—"

"I'm not dead," Aiden interrupted, stepping forward. Waves lapped up his calves. "Come out of the water and we'll explain. Come on, agapi mou."

I was held immobile for another second or two, and then it seemed to sink in. *Aiden* was here. A cry parted my lips as I sprang into action. Holding my hair back from my face, I half-stumbled and half-ran toward the beach. He came forward, meeting me halfway.

Throwing myself at him, I nearly knocked him down, but he regained his footing, wrapping his arms around my waist as he pulled me against his chest. The feel of him, warm and real, against my chest was wonderful and sent a thrill through me. His scent, the mixture of sea and soap, filled me.

It also ripped me right open.

Tears fell from my eyes as I burrowed against his chest, squeezing him so tightly I was surprised I wasn't hurting him. Though he held me the same way, whispering in my ear words I couldn't understand above my sobs. And I was speaking, but the words didn't make much sense.

But finally, his hand slid up to my cheek, leaving a trail of fire in its wake, and he made this deep sound in his chest a second before his lips brushed across mine. Another cry came from the depths of my soul, and the kiss deepened. The kiss reached into me, wrapped its way around my heart, and jump-started it in a way that it never had when I was alive. And I kissed him back, tasting the salt of my tears and of the sea on his lips.

Apollo cleared his throat.

As if we had all the time in the world and didn't have an audience, Aiden slowed the kiss down at his own pace, nipping at my lower lip as he lifted my head. I was breathless as I opened my eyes.

He kissed my forehead and then eased me down onto my feet. Keeping an arm around my waist and tucking me close to his body, he turned us toward Apollo and we waded back to the sand.

The god was smiling. Not the creepy smile that he usually graced the world with, but a real one. "How?" I asked, clutching the front of Aiden's shirt as if I planned to hold him there. "How is this possible? Is he visiting me? Is he—?"

Aiden chuckled as he smoothed his free hand under my chin. "I'm not visiting." My heart almost imploded at that, but I didn't understand.

Apollo took pity on me. "Remember when I told you that I would take care of you? It was a promise I wasn't going to break, but this—this is not all me."

"It's not?" I still held onto Aiden's shirt.

"I knew that this could be the outcome long before you agreed to it," he explained. "A lot of things in life aren't fair, and there are lessons to be learned from that, but there was no lesson to be gained in your death. So when I took you to Olympus after your first fight with Ares, I made sure that, no matter what happened, you would be rewarded."

"By giving me Aiden?" I asked, and well, while I really appreciated that, it didn't seem fair to Aiden. The Elysian Fields were nice and all, but they were the Underworld.

"No," Apollo said. "I gave your mother a drink to give you. Remember? I told her it would help you heal?"

I remembered that. "It tasted good, but…strange."

That smile was back, tipping his lips up at the corner. "It wasn't a normal drink. It was ambrosia."

My lips slowly parted as I stared at him. Ambrosia? The nectar of the gods? Those who were gifted with ambrosia became immortal. "I don't understand. I'm dead. That couldn't—"

"You had a mortal death, Alexandria, but you are not truly dead, not like those around you. By setting the spirit boat free, you set the next stage of your existence into play. You are immortal. To get technical, you are now a demigod."

My jaw was on the sand. There were no words. None at all.

"But for every gift, there has to be an exchange," Apollo continued. "You did have a mortal death, and my brethren were not aware of what I'd done. They say it will upset the strands of Fate if there is not an exchange. Follow me?"

Uh, *no*, but I nodded.

"You will have to spend six months in the Underworld—six months Underworld time—and then you will be allowed to spend six months—six months mortal time—in the mortal realm."

"Like Persephone?" He nodded, and I shook my head. "Holy gods, I don't know what to say. Thank you and—wait!" My heart jumped as I looked up at Aiden. "If I'm immortal, then what about Aiden? He can't stay in the Underworld for six months. I don't understand." Not that I was ungrateful. If I could see him and my dad and friends just for six months topside, I'd take that, but I was thoroughly confused. Aiden had said he wasn't visiting, and I knew I was missing something. "Someone help me out here."

"That's the other half," Aiden said, dropping his chin and kissing the top of my head.

"And that had nothing to do with me," Apollo said. "I would've made sure that Aiden could visit you when he could and for however long he could be here, but this…this is all because of Seth."

I blinked. "*Seth?*"

"If you're surprised, just imagine how I felt." Aiden's arm

tightened. "Seth made a deal with Apollo and Hades before I even knew what was going down."

"What deal?" I looked at Apollo. "What deal did Seth make?"

"First, you must understand that Seth never should've been, Alexandria. You were always meant to be the Apollyon, and Seth knew that. To him, for you to be the one who died, he couldn't live with that," Apollo explained, and my skin chilled. "When he came to me, I told him that you would be fine. I told him that you'd been given ambrosia, and I explained the exchange to him. I even told him that you would see Aiden again, and that in the end, you were being taken care of and you would be happy, but that wasn't enough for him.

"He knew that, when Aiden died, his soul would go to Hades, and who knows what mood Hades would be in when that day came. And in the end, you would outlive Aiden. You would have to watch him grow old and die while you stayed the same during those years he aged. Seth didn't want that for you."

Aiden's hand smoothed over my hip as he spoke next. "Seth offered an exchange. He offered his servitude to the gods, which is needed, since no one can find Perses and none of the Olympians can kill Seth."

"We need him on our side, so we were willing to deal," Apollo confirmed. "He offered his servitude and obedience in exchange for ambrosia for Aiden. And then he offered to Hades to take Aiden's place once he died. And as you would guess, Hades was over the moon with the prospect. We accepted."

My eyes widened. I didn't know what to say. Seth…oh my gods, that little punk…that wonderful little punk. "He gave up his life to the gods, basically? You'll be able to call on him whenever."

And knowing Seth, that would drive him absolutely wild. "And when he dies?" I shook my head, beyond words.

What Seth had done was unbelievable. He'd sacrificed so much. My heart was pumping fast. I wanted to cry again. I probably would. And I wanted to laugh, and I wanted to find Seth and shake him because he hadn't needed to do this. He shouldn't have. My future with Aiden wasn't more important than his future, no matter how badly I wanted that.

I was blown away.

"Seth didn't want you to know he did this, and while I have honored most of his requests, I felt you needed to know what he has done for you. He gave you this, Alexandria. He gave Aiden this. And I know it is hard for you to accept. And it was hard for Aiden to fully accept, surprisingly," Apollo added dryly. "But it was Seth's decision, and it cannot be undone. And when you go topside in six months, you should find him and thank him."

I was actually going to hug and squeeze and love the dude. Then smack him. And then hug and squeeze and love him again.

"We are not sure what it does with your connection. You are no longer the God Killer, as you did die a mortal death, but this has never been done before." Apollo shrugged. "You may still be connected once you're in the mortal realm. You may not be. We don't know."

There was so much I wanted to say. My head was spinning. I hadn't expected any of this, especially not what Seth had done. He had given us everything. I couldn't imagine how I could repay him, but I would find a way one day.

Apollo's smile was soft then, the most human thing I'd ever

seen from the god. "His journey is not over, Alexandria. And neither is yours. Or Aiden's. Remember that."

Choked up in a ridiculous way, I nodded and then, without any warning, Apollo faded out. I stared at the spot where he'd stood for a long moment, then turned into Aiden's embrace.

One side of his lips curved up, and a dimple appeared in one cheek. "We owe Seth a lot."

"Everything," I agreed, my fingers still digging into the front of his shirt. "We owe him everything."

Aiden lowered his head, brushing his lips over mine. My mouth immediately opened to his. I sank into him, ready—

"Oh. I almost forgot."

I jumped a good four inches off the ground at the sound of Apollo's voice, which was right in my ear. "Oh, my gods, will you ever stop doing that?"

"No. Make sure you give Hades some hell while you're down here." He winked, and then he disappeared again.

Aiden looked from where Apollo had been, then to me, and laughed. "Do they have bells in the Elysian Fields?"

A laugh bubbled up in my throat. "Yeah, I'm sure they do. You kind of need something, and it appears. Like, if you want to eat some coconut shrimp, you get coconut shrimp."

"Really?" He laughed again, looping his arm around my waist. "What about Big Macs?"

"Yep. Even Big Macs."

"Wow. This must really be paradise for you, then."

The knot of emotion was back in my throat again. "It… really isn't. I've missed you terribly. I…" I stopped myself.

He pressed his lips together as he smoothed his thumb along my jaw. Then he glanced over his shoulder. "Is that what I think it is?"

I bit down on my lip, hoping this didn't make me come across like a total creeper. "It made me happy, and it felt…it felt like you, so it turned out to be a part of my paradise."

Aiden's hand slipped down my arm, and he threaded his fingers through mine. When he spoke, his voice was rough with emotion. "Show me?"

I led him into the cottage, and as he looked around, seeing the familiar living room and kitchen, his hand tightened around mine. I felt my cheeks flush. "It has a bedroom and a bath, like yours, but there's a garden in the back. I know it's not—"

"It's perfect. You're perfect." His silvery gaze landed on me. "I'm sorry I couldn't get here sooner. I know—"

"Don't," I said, placing my fingers over his lips. "You have nothing to apologize for. Apollo told me about the Council and the Breed Order. What you were a part of was amazing. Solos on the Council, and how the Breed Order was revoked, and—"

Aiden swooped down, silencing me with a lingering kiss that left me breathless when he lifted his head. "Nothing that I did was truly amazing, Alex. It was just what needed to be done. I only wish it hadn't taken so long from your perspective."

He told me then that Seth had made his deals before the Council meeting, within hours of my death, but that he had taken care of the Council seat and spoken with his brother before he'd left with Apollo.

"Deacon," I gasped. "Oh gods, you won't see him for six months. And it will be even longer for him with the time-moves-differently thing."

"It's okay."

I shook my head. "But he's your family, and I know he means the world to you."

"He does mean the world to me, and I'm going to miss him, but he'd try to kick my ass if I didn't come to you." Aiden grinned. "He knows how I feel about you. He saw how I was…afterward. He understands, and he's happy. Besides, we'll see him again."

Then it struck me. Excited, I almost started bouncing. "Oh, Aiden! You'll get to see your parents. I haven't seen them, but they're here. Somewhere."

"I know, but as terrible as this sounds—and gods, it probably is—right now, I don't care." Using my hand, he turned me around and hauled me against his chest. "That's not what I want right now, *or* what I need."

Grandma Piperi's prophetic words came back to me. There is want and there is need… To her, those two things had been very different entities, but right now, they were one and the same.

He placed the tips of his fingers on my cheeks, the hold heartbreakingly tender as his gaze moved on my face. "Look at you," he said. "Your eyes…"

I stood still, letting his fingers trail an unseen path across my face. "I look a lot better half-dead or whatever, huh?"

"You've always looked beautiful to me, Alex." He trailed his fingers over the line of my jaw and down my neck. His hands trembled as he slid them down my shoulders. "Gods, Alex, I thought after what happened with Linard, I'd never face losing you again. Even when you were connected with Seth, you were still alive. And even if you didn't want to be with me, you were living, and in the end, that was all that mattered."

Aiden took a deep breath. "But when I came into that room and saw Seth and Apollo, but didn't see you, my heart stopped. It broke me," he admitted with quiet honesty. "Because all I wanted was a future with you, and it had been taken from me *again*."

I closed my eyes against the rush of tears.

"But here we are," he murmured.

"Here we are." I blinked open my eyes, my chest swelling with the emotion I read in his gaze. We'd been given that future because of Apollo and Seth. And there was no way I was going to dishonor that gift by not living every second of that future. "I love you."

"Agapi mou, you are my everything."

Aiden kissed me. Words weren't necessary at that point. He'd experienced every moment of loss that I had, every second of desperation, and it was reflected in every touch, every sweep of the lips, and every soft moan. We were greedy with one another, finding ourselves in the bedroom. In no time, our limbs were tangled together, and when our bodies joined, everything slowed down. Our want for one another was all-consuming, but for the first time since we'd locked eyes in Georgia, we had all the time in the world to enjoy our love. And we did.

Long after our breathing returned to normal, Aiden hovered above me, his hand slowly tracing the line of my jaw. I smiled as something occurred to me. "We're demigods now." I laughed as a wealth of emotion built in my chest. "We're actually *demigods*."

His lips responded, curving upward and spreading until deep dimples appeared, and my heart melted in the way only he could make it. "Yeah, we are," he said.

"You know what that means?" I stared into those silver

eyes. I had an infinite number of moments like this ahead of me to share with Aiden. "They're going to tell stories about us."

Aiden lowered his head, kissing me softly, deeply, and so lovingly that tears pricked my eyes. "They already are."

READ ON FOR A SPECIAL BONUS SCENE

BONUS SCENE FROM "THE RETURN" (AIDEN'S POV)

Brilliant white light exploded from the Council building, blow-ing out windows. Glass shattered, flying in every direction. The deadly shards mowed down Sentinels on both sides. An entire side of the building crumbled like it was made of nothing but dust.

Yanking the sickle blade back, I sucked in a breath that went nowhere. In an instant, I knew. I knew. An icy ball formed in my gut and then traveled up, fisting around my heart. A crack rocked down the center of my chest. I stumbled back a step and glanced down, half expecting to find a Covenant dagger shoved deep. Nothing was there, but the pain…

"No," I whispered.

My legs were moving before my brain even caught up with what was happening. I took off across the lawn, heading for the blown-open doors. Someone shouted my name, but I didn't stop, couldn't stop. I raced into the building, instinct guiding me to the right, all the way my heart pounding and refusing to process what my brain was telling me.

It was too late.

We'd won.

But it was too late.

I flew into the room and saw him standing there in the middle, his head thrown back, his hands closed into fists at his sides. Blood and dirt caked his cheeks. His shirt was torn. An odd scent permeated the room, along with leftover vibrations of power.

"Where is she?" My voice sounded raw to my ears.

Seth lowered his chin and when he looked at me, he didn't really see me. He shook his head.

My heart stuttered and skipped a beat. "Where is she, Seth?"

"I'm sorry." His voice cracked, and the sickle blade slipped from my fingers, clattering on the marble floor. "She's gone."

I didn't move. There was a good chance I stopped breathing as raw, burning pain lit me up, tore deep into me with razor sharp claws and ripped me apart. I opened my mouth, but there were no words, and that pain kept digging in. I doubled over, resting my hands on my thighs.

Alex couldn't be gone.

No. No way. She'd done everything the gods had asked. She had sacrificed so much already. Time and time again. She couldn't be gone. No. No. No. I straightened and started toward Seth, but stopped halfway. He wasn't even looking at me, his gaze cast to the cracked floor, his expression etched in a deep sorrow that nearly matched what I felt. No. No. No. This wasn't happening.

"Is there not…?" My voice cut off, because I couldn't even bring myself to ask it.

Seth's shoulders shook once and then twice, and when he

spoke his voice trembled. "There's nothing…there's nothing left of her."

"Oh gods." The blow staggered me and I stepped back. A second later, my knees gave out. The pain of them cracking against the floor didn't even measure. "No, man. No."

Seth lifted his hands, pressing the palms against his face. His voice was muffled. "We did what they wanted. We defeated Ares, but…there can only be one of us. Not the God Killer. She knew." His hands dropped to his sides. "She knew."

I wanted to deny that. I wanted to scream from the top of my lungs, but then I'd be lying to myself. Gods, Alex did know there was a chance she wouldn't walk away from this, but I couldn't let myself believe that. I couldn't let myself believe that she wouldn't be in my arms again, that I wouldn't go to sleep tonight holding her, that I wouldn't wake up in the morning and be able to touch her, kiss her.

There was nothing left to hold.

Nothing left to even fucking see.

The pain exploded, a hurt so intense I threw my head back and an unholy sound erupted from me, and that sound kept coming up until my throat was raw, and I didn't stop. Heat burned from within, the powerful element of fire. It fed the rage, buzzing under my skin and demanded to lay waste to everything around me.

"Aiden." Seth's voice was nearer.

I couldn't breathe around the burn. The heat came from the center of my chest and my palms. It became a living, breathing, tangible thing.

"Get out," I warned, voice low and guttural.

Sparks flew from my widespread hands. Flames dripped like liquid, hitting the floor and scorching the marble. I latched onto the fury, slamming my hands down on the floor. Purplish flames erupted and then turned blue. Rising to my feet, I let the fire erupt from me. It was unnatural.

"Aiden—"

"Get out!" I shouted, and then I didn't see if Seth left. My vision turned red and blue. I wanted to burn this whole place down. I wanted to find the gods and take out each of them. I wanted to cut a path of destruction through all of them. Most of all, I wanted Alex.

I wanted to tell her that I loved her once more.

I don't know how much time had passed. I didn't care. The walls were burning all around me. The air was on fire. Above, the ceiling collapsed and fell to the floor. Embers twinkled like sparklers.

I wanted to look into those whiskey brown eyes once more.

My cheeks were damp. My eyes blurred. My chest was an empty cavity.

Something else crashed to my right. I didn't care. The whole building could come down around me. I didn't—

A hand touched my arm. "Aiden."

My head jerked up at the sound of my brother's voice. At first it didn't compute. He shouldn't be here.

"Aiden, what are you doing?" Soot covered his pale cheeks. Some of his curls were singed.

I stared into my brother's eyes. "She's gone."

Deacon flinched as his hand tightened on my arm. "You've got to leave."

Shaking my head, I closed my eyes. "She's gone, Deacon."

"I know. I'm sorry. Gods, I'm so damn sorry, but you can't stay in here. The whole building is about to come down. You've got to get out of here."

My shoulders shook as another blast of pain pounded into me. Lifting my fists, I slammed them into the marble.

"Please, Aiden, you've got to get out of here. I can't do it on my own and if you don't…" His surprisingly cool hands curved around my face. "Then I'm staying. I'm not leaving you."

My eyes flew open. "Get the hell out of here, Deacon."

His gaze met mine. Tears filled his eyes. "I'm not leaving you."

Anger flashed through me. "Deacon, for once in your godsdamn life, listen to me and get the hell out of here!"

"You listen to me!" he shouted back as somewhere, the fire popped, exploded in a rush of heat. "Do you think Alex would want this? Do you think she'd be okay with you allowing yourself to burn to death? Do you?"

Part of me didn't want to acknowledge that question, but I couldn't ignore the truth. Alex would kick my ass. Gods. A sob rattled out of me. Gods, she would kick my ass for doing this to myself, to Deacon…mainly to myself. She would be so disappointed.

"I'm sorry," Deacon's voice cracked as he slid an arm around my neck. "Please. Don't do this."

Calling on strength I didn't know I had, I pushed myself to my feet. I felt like I had when I made the decision to put Alex on the Elixir after she had connected with Seth and things had gone horribly wrong. I was a dead man walking.

How Deacon and I got out of the inferno, I had no idea. Maybe a god was watching over us, but then again, they would not have my thanks. I wanted nothing from them.

I hit the damp, cool grass outside and I sat down. Maybe I fell down. I didn't know. I sat there and watched the Council building burn, barely aware of Deacon sitting beside me, his forehead resting on my shoulder. At some point, I heard Luke and then I heard Marcus come and go. Luke remained, but I had no idea what he was saying.

Deacon was crying.

Gods, I was cracked, broken wide open, and that was never going to be fixed. No amount of time was going to heal this. I'd lost my heart and my soul.

I'd lost the most beautiful treasure.

As I lowered my head to my hands, I curled my fingers into the ends of my hair and pulled hard. A great and terrible shudder rocked me. I didn't know how I was going to deal with this. Didn't know if I could move on without Alex. I don't think she ever realized just how much strength she gave me. Knowing her, she probably thought it was the other way around. It wasn't. She was my everything.

And she was gone.

"Gods." My breath caught.

A fissure of power trickled down my spine and before I could look up, I heard him speak. "Aiden."

Lifting my head, I stared into the all-white eyes of a god—a god I trusted to keep Alex safe. Rage took over. I popped to my feet, and before a single thought could even form, I cocked back my arm and punched Apollo in the jaw, snapping his head back.

"Holy crap," gasped Deacon, and out of the corners of my eyes, I saw Luke step in front of him.

A sick sense of satisfaction filled me. The impact of my fist caused a burst of real pain, and even though Apollo was looking at me like a kitten smacked him, I welcomed the external pain.

"You know, I deserved that. And I'm not going to hold it against you." He held up his hand as I started toward him again. "But if you hit me again, I'm not going to be able to tell you why I'm here."

"I don't give two fuc—"

"Yes. Yes, you do. I'm here because of Alex."

I stopped moving and it was then I noticed that Seth was behind Apollo. He wasn't looking at either of us, but staring at the sky. I shifted, my hands opening and closing at my sides.

Apollo said nothing more, almost like he was waiting, and I cracked again. "She's gone." The god's face blurred as my voice rose to a hoarse shout. "She didn't deserve that!"

"You're right," he replied calmly. "She deserves an eternity and I have given her that."

I opened my mouth as his words tried to make it through the haze of pain and raw sorrow.

"What?" Deacon asked. "What does that mean?"

Apollo stepped toward me, and I stiffened. For once, I saw true sympathy etched into his features. "I told Alexandria and I told you that I would protect her. I did."

I stared at him. "How…how is this protecting her? She's…" Wetting my lips, I looked away. I couldn't say it.

"She's not dead, Aiden. Not really. When she was in Olympus, I gave her ambrosia. That is what healed her then. That is what has already brought her back from a mortal death."

I turned my head to him slowly. A kindling of hope sparked in my chest as I stared at the god.

He exhaled softly. "She's alive. She's still in the Underworld, and there she will have to remain for a time, because…well, let's just say some of the other gods aren't too keen on what I did, but she's alive."

"I…" Too much rose in me. I took a step to the side. My legs were suddenly weak. I felt my brother get close and then his slender arm curled around my chest. "When…when can I see her?"

Apollo arched a brow. "A thank-you would be nice."

I stared at him. "How about a go fu—"

He sighed. "I'm always so underappreciated. And you know who else is underappreciated? Seth."

My head was spinning, not really following any of this.

"I had to make a deal for Alex to retain her shiny new immortality. She must remain in the Underworld for six months. You can't go there, but you'll be able to see her when she comes up here. But that's not the only problem," he went on. "She won't age anymore. She's a made demigod. Not one made from birth, but for all intents and purposes, that is what she is. She will never grow old. You will. She won't die. You will, and because of the deal you made with Hades, your soul will be his."

I didn't care about any of this. "Alex is alive? That is all that matters." The tiny spark in my chest grew, and I suddenly wanted to laugh. I did, and it sounded wild. "Alex is alive?"

"Get to the point, Apollo," Seth's rough voice ordered.

Apollo's eyes narrowed. "Boy, you better watch your tone."

Seth sighed.

Drawing in an aggravated breath, the god looked seconds away from throwing a major hissy. "Seth has also made a deal. It was done quick and it has been accepted. He, among other things, will take your place when your time comes. You are no longer indebted to Hades."

Shock floored me as my gaze darted to the Apollyon. "What?"

"But Seth was smart in the deal he made. He has some things we want. We can use. He bartered not just for your soul, but for your immortality. His deal was granted."

I was going to pass out.

Apollo raised his chin. "You will become as Alex, if that is what you choose. You will spend six months with her in the Underworld and then six months here."

I was seriously going to pass out.

"I won't take your answer now," he continued. "This is something you must seriously consider. I will be back."

And just like that Apollo was gone. I couldn't believe I was still standing. Shock and happiness warred in me, mixing with confusion and the bone-deep fear that this was all a hallucination born of desperation.

I glanced at my brother and whispered, "Is this real?"

"I think so."

"It is," Seth spoke, voice void of emotion. "And if I was you, I'd take it. You…you need her and she…she has always needed you."

My gaze tracked over to him, and I think…I think I saw him for what he really was for the first time. All the hate and the jealousy and the general distrust I felt toward him were an odd companion to carry for the man who was handing me my forever. But he wasn't the Apollyon as he stood there. He wasn't the Seth I'd taken great pleasure in beating the ever living shit out of.

Seth was something else now, something broken.

"You did this for us?" I asked.

He said nothing, just continued to stare at the sky.

"Seth, I—"

"Don't thank me." He backed away, flinching as he lifted his arm, thrusting his fingers through his hair. "Don't ever thank me for any of this."

How could I not? He didn't just give me time with Alex. He had handed over an eternity with her, but Seth wheeled around and strode across the lawn, appearing oblivious to the destruction he passed, just as I had been unaware of the blood and gore littering the field when I came out of the building.

A light touch to my arm drew my attention. Shadows from the raging fire danced over Deacon's face. "This is good, right? You're going to get Alex back. You're going to be able to be with her."

"Shit," Luke said from behind me. "You're going to be immortal."

The hope that had exploded in my chest still kindled as fiercely as the fire.

"And don't you dare think about not taking this because of me. I don't want to even hear you bring it up. I'll be fine. I'm always going to be fine." Deacon straightened his shoulders. "And you're going to do this. When Apollo comes back, you're going to do whatever you need to be with her. You understand me, right?"

My lips twitched at the burgeoning authority in his voice. I glanced over at Luke and I knew beyond a doubt that my brother was going to be okay. "Yes." Then I said it louder and I was free of any ties. "Yes. There's just some stuff I need to take care of first."

I threw myself into tying up all the loose ends, not allowing myself to think beyond what needed to be done. An emergency meeting had been called for the Council. I took my seat, and through the course of a heated session, the Breed Order was abolished, done so in Alex's and every half-blood's honor.

And then I gave my seat to Solos, making him the first half-blood to serve on the Council. The world was in a drastic upheaval. The Council needed someone like Solos, even if he didn't realize it yet.

I spent the time I had left with my brother, and when Apollo appeared again, I looked the god straight in the eye and answered his question before he could speak it.

"Yes."

The sweet taste of ambrosia lingered long after I'd taken the drink. Strange thing was I didn't feel any different, but then again, I wasn't allowing myself to feel much. All Apollo had explained before he disappeared again was that I would be summoned soon. As I sat with Deacon, watching him demolish a box of doughnuts, there was a part of me that feared this was all some kind of joke. That Apollo wouldn't bring me to Alex. Although Apollo had never been so cruel to me, the gods made screwing with people an art form.

"You sure you don't want the last one?" Deacon pointed with his pinky at a glazed ring of fat.

I arched my brow. "Help yourself."

"Don't mind if I do." He picked it up. "I love my fat and calories."

"I can…" Trailing off, I stiffened in the chair. A sudden fissure of power rolled down my spine. Across from me, Deacon felt the same thing. He had to have, because there was no other reason as to why he wouldn't have half the doughnut in his mouth yet.

A burst of light momentarily blinded me and when it receded, there was a titanium door in the wall where the fridge had been.

Deacon gaped. "Holy crap…"

My legs trembled as I stood. Deep down, I knew what that door led to. My heart started pounding. "It's time." I looked at my little brother and swallowed.

Dropping the doughnut back in the box, he popped up and came around the table. Our embrace was tight. "Take care of yourself," I told him. "And for gods' sake, stay out of trouble."

"I always stay out of trouble."

I laughed hoarsely. "I love you, Deacon."

"I love you." He pulled back, smiling. "Tell Alex I expect a lot of Underworld gossip in six months."

"Will do." Smoothing my hand over his head, I pressed my lips to his forehead.

Walking away from my brother was one of the hardest things I'd ever had to do. He was all grown up now, but that knowledge didn't make it easier. Glancing back at him, I smiled when I saw Luke enter the kitchen. The half-blood Sentinel came to a complete stop, mid-step, as his wide gaze bounced between Deacon and the door.

"I'll be back in six months," I told them.

The pull of power grew as I neared the door and opened it. There was nothing but thick blackness on the other side, and stepping forward was more than a leap of faith. More like a leap of love, because I had no idea what I was walking into, but Alex was worth whatever risk I had to face.

I stepped through.

The door slammed shut behind me and the darkness seemed to vibrate all around me. There was a popping sound and another flash of light, followed by the scent of the sea. I was facing the cabin I'd stayed in while at the Covenant. I knew it had to be a replica, because that island no longer existed. I blinked, finding myself standing on the beach—the Deity Island beach. The sand was gritty under my bare feet, the sun warm on my face, and the breeze soft and alluring. The ocean hummed from behind me.

Slowly, I turned around and my heart…it had to have expanded in my chest three times its normal size.

I saw her.

She was standing in the ocean, the foamy water bubbling around her calves as the breeze played with the hem of her dress and tossed her hair around her shoulders. Even from where I stood, I could tell she was different. Her hair was back to the length before Ares had cut it. Her bare arms and legs were free of the fine webbing of scars. None of that really mattered, though. I loved her just the same.

I opened my mouth to call her, but my voice was choked off. I knew Apollo was there. I didn't look at him, couldn't pull my eyes off Alex to check to see what he was doing. I could just feel him.

Alex straightened, watching something for a few moments, and then she turned around, her gaze flickering across the beach. Seeing her was like a sucker punch in the chest. She was there. She was real. For the first time in what felt like forever, I smiled.

I felt the exact moment she saw me. She was frozen, so still she could be mistaken for a statue.

"Hey," I called out.

Her hand fluttered to her chest. "Is this…is this real?"

My smile spread in response to her voice. "This is real, agapi mou."

She didn't move.

"Alex," I called out again.

"How are you here? Oh my gods…" She looked at Apollo. "Is he dead? You said he would be okay! That he wouldn't do anything—"

"I'm not dead." I stepped forward, into the ocean. "Come out of the water and we'll explain. Come on, agapi mou."

Alex's wide gaze darted back to me and then she cried out. Springing into action, she raced toward the beach, toward me. I met her as she all but threw herself at me, nearly knocking me down. My arms closed around her, and to feel her again, to feel how so very warm and real she was, I almost lost it then. But I held her, sucking in her warmth and her scent as she held me just as tightly.

I held her as the tears began to fall, telling her how much I loved her, how much I missed her. She was speaking, but I couldn't understand the words, but the words really didn't matter in that moment.

We were together.

I slid my hand to her cheek, gently guiding her head back. Our gazes locked, and the wealth of love in hers nearly cut me at the knees. There was so much I needed to explain—about Seth and what he had done for us, about the Breed Order and Solos, and I needed to tell her that she was stuck with me for an eternity, and most importantly, I needed to tell her how much I loved her, but again, there were no words powerful enough. Words were not what I wanted in that moment.

I didn't even care if Apollo was there, watching us.

A sound came from deep within my chest as I lowered my mouth, brushing my lips over hers. The simple touch was like a jolt of electricity, a benediction, and when she cried out, her hands clenching my shirt, I deepened the kiss. I reveled in the pure beauty of it, an act I never thought I'd ever get to experience again. Our tongues danced and tangled, and that kiss said everything that needed to be said.

Nothing in this world or any of the worlds beyond would keep us apart. We were together now and always, and we had an eternity.

DISCOVER THE COVENANT SERIES FROM THE VERY BEGINNING.

READ ON FOR A SNEAK PEEK OF *HALF-BLOOD*.

CHAPTER ONE

My eyes snapped open as the freakish sixth sense kicked my fight-or-flight response into overdrive. The Georgia humidity and the dust covering the floor made it hard to breathe. Since I'd fled Miami, no place had been safe. This abandoned factory had proved no different.

The daimons were here.

I could hear them on the lower level, searching each room systematically, throwing open doors, slamming them shut. The sound threw me back to a few days ago, when I'd pushed open the door to Mom's bedroom. She'd been in the arms of one of those monsters, beside a broken pot of hibiscus flowers. Purple petals had spilled across the floor, mixing with the blood. The memory twisted my gut into a raw ache, but I couldn't think about her right now.

I jumped to my feet, halting in the narrow hallway, straining to hear how many daimons were here. Three? More? My fingers jerked around the slim handle of the garden spade. I held it up, running my fingers over the sharp edges plated in titanium. The act reminded me of what needed to be done. Daimons loathed titanium. Besides decapitation—which was *way* too gross—titanium was the only thing that would kill them. Named after the Titans, the precious metal was poisonous to those addicted to aether.

Somewhere in the building, a floorboard groaned and gave way. A deep howl broke the silence, starting as a low whine before hitting an intense shrill pitch. The scream sounded inhuman, sick and horrifying. Nothing in this world sounded like a daimon—a hungry daimon.

And it was close.

I darted down the hallway, my tattered sneakers pounding against the worn-out boards. Speed was in my blood, and strands of long, dirty hair streamed behind me. I rounded the corner, knowing I had only seconds—

A *whoosh* of stale air whirled around me as the daimon grabbed a handful of my shirt, slamming me into the wall. Dust and plaster floated through the air. Black starbursts dotted my vision as I scrambled to my feet. Those soulless, pitch-black holes where eyes should have been stared at me like I was his next meal ticket.

The daimon grasped my shoulder, and I let instinct take over. I twisted around, catching the surprise flickering across his pale face a split second before I kicked. My foot connected with the side of his head. The impact sent him staggering into the opposite wall. I spun around, slamming my hand into him. Surprise turned to horror as the daimon looked down at the garden spade buried deep in his stomach. It didn't matter where we aimed. Titanium always killed a daimon.

A guttural sound escaped his gaping mouth before he exploded into a shimmery blue dust.

With the spade still in hand, I whirled around and took the

steps two at a time. I ignored the ache in my hips as I sprinted across the floor. I was going to make it—I had to make it. I'd be super-pissed in the afterlife if I died a virgin in this craphole.

"Little half-blood, where are you running?"

I stumbled to the side, falling into a large steel press. Twisting around, my heart slammed against my ribs. The daimon appeared a few feet behind me. Like the one upstairs, he looked like a freak. His mouth hung open, exposing sharp, serrated teeth, and those all-black eyeholes sent chills over my skin. They reflected no light or life, only signifying death. His cheeks were sunken, skin unearthly pale. Veins popped out, etching his face like inky snakes. He truly looked like something out of my worst nightmare—something demonic. Only a half-blood could see through the glamour for a few moments. Then the elemental magic took over, revealing what he used to look like. Adonis came to mind—a blond, stunning man.

"What are you doing all alone?" he asked, voice deep and alluring.

I took a step back, my eyes searching the room for an exit. Wannabe Adonis blocked my way out, and I knew I couldn't stand still for long. Daimons could still wield control over the elements. If he hit me with air or fire, I was a goner.

He laughed, the sound lacking humor and life. "Maybe if you beg—and I mean, really beg—I'll let your death be a fast one. Frankly, half-bloods don't really do it for me. Pure-bloods on the other hand..." He let out a sound of pleasure. "They're like fine dining. Half-bloods? You're more like fast food."

"Come one step closer, and you'll end up like your buddy upstairs." I hoped I sounded threatening enough. Not likely.

"Try me."

His brows rose. "Now you're starting to upset me. That's two of us you've killed."

"You keeping a tally or something?" My heart stopped when the floor behind me creaked. I whirled around, spotting a female daimon. She inched closer, forcing me toward the other daimon.

They were caging me in, giving no opportunity to escape. Another one shrieked somewhere in the pile of crap. Panic and fear choked me. My stomach rolled violently as my fingers trembled around the garden spade. Gods, I wanted to puke.

The ringleader advanced on me. "Do you know what I'm going to do to you?"

I swallowed and fixed a smirk on my face. "Blah. Blah. You're gonna kill me. Blah. I know."

The female's ravenous shriek cut off his response. Obviously she was very hungry. She circled me like a vulture, ready to rip into me. My eyes narrowed on her. The hungry ones were always the stupidest—the weakest of the bunch. Legend said it was the first taste of aether—the very life force running through our blood—that possessed a pure blood. A single taste turned one into a daimon and resulted in a lifetime of addiction. There was a good chance I could get past her. The other one…well, he was a different story.

I feinted toward the female. She came right at me. The male yelled at her to stop, but it was too late. I took off in the opposite direction like an Olympic sprinter, rushing for the door I'd kicked in earlier in the night. Once outside, the odds would be back in my favor. A small window of hope sparked alive and propelled me forward.

But then, the worst possible thing happened. A wall of flames flew up in front of me, burning through benches and shooting at least eight feet into the air. It was real. No illusion. The heat blew back at me, and the fire crackled, eating through the walls.

In front of me, *he* walked right through the flames, looking every bit like a daimon hunter should. The fire did not singe his pants nor dirty his shirt. Not a single dark hair was touched by the blaze. Those cool, storm-cloud-colored eyes fixed on me.

It was him—Aiden St. Delphi.

I'd never forget his name or face. The first time I'd caught a glimpse of him standing in front of the training arena, a ridiculous crush had sprung alive. I'd been fourteen and he seventeen. The fact that he was a pure blood hadn't mattered when I'd spotted him around campus.

Aiden's presence could mean one thing only: the Sentinels had arrived.

Our eyes met, and then he looked over my shoulder. "Get down."

I didn't need to be told twice. Like a pro, I hit the floor. The pulse of heat shot above me, crashing into the intended target. The floor shook with the daimon's wild thrashing, and her wounded screams filled the air. Only titanium would kill a daimon, but I felt confident that being burnt alive didn't feel too good.

Rising up on my elbows, I peered through my dirty hair as Aiden lowered his hand. A popping sound followed the movement, and the flames vanished as fast as they appeared. Within seconds, only the smells of burnt wood, flesh, and smoke remained.

Two more Sentinels rushed the room. I recognized one of them: Kain Poros, a half-blood a year or so older than me. Once upon a time we had trained together. Kain moved with a grace he'd never had before. He went for the female, and with one quick swoop, he thrust a long, slender dagger into the burnt flesh of her skin. She too became nothing but dust.

The other Sentinel had the air of a pure blood to him, but I'd never seen him before. He was big—steroids big—and he zeroed in on the daimon I knew was somewhere in this factory but hadn't seen yet. Watching how he moved such a large body around so gracefully made me feel sorely inadequate, especially considering I was still lying sprawled on the floor. I dragged myself to my feet, feeling the terror-fueled adrenaline rush fade.

Without warning, my head exploded in pain as the side of my face hit the floor *hard*. Stunned and confused, it took me a moment to realize Wannabe Adonis had gotten ahold of my legs. I twisted, but the creep sank his hands deep into my hair and yanked my head back. I dug my fingers into his skin, but it did nothing to alleviate the pressure bearing down on my neck. For a startled moment, I thought he intended to rip my head right off, but he sank razor-sharp teeth into my shoulder, tearing through fabric and flesh. I screamed—*really* screamed.

I was on fire—I had to be. The draining burned through my skin; sharp pricks radiated out through every cell in my body. And even though I was only a half-blood, not chock-full of aether like a pure blood, the daimon continued to drink my essence as though I were. It wasn't my blood he was after; he'd swallow pints of it just to get at the aether. My very spirit shifted as he dragged it into him. Pain became everything.

Suddenly the daimon lifted his mouth. "What are you?" His whispered voice slurred the words.

There was no time to even think about that question. He was ripped off me, and my body slumped forward. I rolled into a messy, bloody ball, sounding more like a wounded animal than anything remotely human. It was the first time I'd ever gotten tagged—drained by a daimon.

Over the small sounds I made, I heard a sickening crunch, and then wild shrieks, but the pain had taken over my senses. It started to pull back from my fingers, sliding its way back to my core where it still blazed. I tried to breathe through it, but *damn*...

Gentle hands rolled me onto my back, prying my fingers away from my shoulder. I stared up at Aiden.

"Are you okay? Alexandria? Please say something."

"Alex," I choked out. "Everyone calls me Alex."

He gave a short, relieved laugh. "Okay. Good. Alex, can you stand?"

I think I nodded. Every few seconds a stabbing flash of heat rocked through me, but the hurt had faded into a dull ache. "That really...sucked something bad."

Aiden managed to get one arm around me, lifting me to my feet. I swayed as he brushed back my hair and took a look at the damage. "Give it a few minutes. The pain will wear off."

Lifting my head, I looked around. Kain and the other Sentinel were frowning at nearly identical piles of blue dust. The pure blood faced us. "That should be all of them."

Aiden nodded. "Alex, we need to go. Now. Back to the Covenant."

The Covenant? Not entirely in control of my emotions, I turned to Aiden. He wore all black—the uniform Sentinels wore. For a hot second, that girly crush resurfaced from three years ago. Aiden looked sublime, but fury stomped down that stupid crush.

The Covenant was involved in this—coming to my rescue? Where the hell had they been when one of the daimons had snuck into our house?

He took a step forward, but I didn't see him—I saw my mother's lifeless body again. The last thing she ever saw on this Earth was some god-awful daimon's face, and the last thing she'd ever felt… I shuddered, remembering the body-ripping pain of the daimon's tag.

Aiden took another step toward me. I reacted, a response born out of anger and pain. I launched myself at him, using moves I hadn't practiced in years. Simple things like kicks and punches were one thing, but an offensive attack was something I'd barely learned.

He caught my hand and swung me around so I faced the other direction. In a matter of seconds, he had my arms pinned, but all the pain and the sorrow rose in me, overriding any common sense. I bent forward, intent on getting enough space between us to deliver a vicious back kick.

"Don't," Aiden warned, his voice deceptively soft. "I don't want to hurt you."

ACKNOWLEDGMENTS

Acknowledgments are never easy to write. There's always this stress when it comes to writing them, because you fear you'll forget someone. But the acknowledgments for this book are pretty damn important to me. It's the end for Alex, and there have been so many people with her from day one, all the way back in late 2007 and early 2008, who helped shape her into the Alex we've all come to love...or hate.

The Covenant Series has had a lot of beta readers during its time that lent their insightful advice and knowledge. Chu-Won Martin was literally the first person to ever read *Half-Blood*. She holds the first reader's card, and because she didn't laugh in my face after reading it, we're here where we are today. A big thank you to Lesa Rodrigues for always being eager to delve back into the Covenant world and for reading early manuscripts that were nothing more than chicken scratch. Thank you to Carissa Thomas, Julie Fedderson, and Cindy Thomas for reading these books before they ever reached the hands of a reader. Thank you to the peeps over at Query Tracker for helping shape up the query letter that landed the contract back in 2010. A big thanks to Molly McAdams, who has probably read the last couple of books in the Covenant Series months and months ahead of release and always makes me feel good about the story. A huge thank you to Stacey Morgan for critiquing *Sentinel* and many other books one chapter at a time and suffering through all the changes I end up going back and making and not telling her about.

Of course, a big thank you to Kate Kaynak for taking a chance on *Half-Blood*. To Kevan Lyon for always being the uber-amazing agent that she is, to Rebecca Mancini for introducing the Covenant Series into the foreign markets, and to Brandy Rivers for well, being awesome in general. Big thanks to my amazing personal assistant Malissa Coy, and my second edition editor Wendy Higgins.

Now here comes the hard part, because there will inevitably be people I forget to mention, but I do want to name all those that I can remember off the top of my head. These are the readers and the bloggers who've done AMAZING things for the Covenant Series and were there since the very beginning. Thank you to Vee (and yes, I'm going to spell your name the way I say it. Or Vi. Or Vivian.), Valerie from Stuck in Books, Momo from Books Over Boys, the entire crews over at Books Complete Me, Mundie Moms, Good Choice Reading, all the sisters at YA Sisterhood, Kayleigh from K-Books, all the peeps who take part in the Covenant Read Along, the Greer family—especially Papa Greer—Reading Angel, Amanda from Canada, and oh goodness, my brain has not run out of names because *Ghost Adventures* is on the TV and I'm drawn in by the douche-tastic-ness of it all.

Of course, none of this would be possible without my

family and friends, who put up with the fact I spend more time writing than speaking to any of them in real life.

And finally, to all the readers, I can never thank you enough. I'm so honored to have taken this journey with you. This may be it for Alex, but you know…stories never really, truly end.

ABOUT THE AUTHOR

#1 *New York Times* and #1 international bestselling author Jennifer L. Armentrout lives in Shepherdstown, West Virginia. All the rumors you've heard about her state aren't true. When she's not hard at work writing, she spends her time reading, watching really bad zombie movies, pretending to write, hanging out with her husband, her Border Jack Apollo, Border Collie Artemis, six judgmental alpacas, two rude goats, and five fluffy sheep. In early 2015, Jennifer was diagnosed with retinitis pigmentosa, a group of rare genetic disorders that involve a breakdown and death of cells in the retina, eventually resulting in loss of vision, among other complications. Due to this diagnosis, educating people on the varying degrees of blindness has become a passion of hers, right alongside writing, which she plans to do as long as she can.

Website: jenniferlarmentrout.com
Facebook: JenniferLArmentrout
Instagram: @jennifer_l_armentrout

OTHER BLOOM BOOKS BY JENNIFER L. ARMENTROUT

COVENANT SERIES

Half-Blood (includes the novella "Daimon")
Pure
Deity (includes the novella "Elixir")
Apollyon
Sentinel

FRIGID SERIES

Frigid
Scorched

APOLLYON

APOLLYON

JENNIFER L. ARMENTROUT

Bloom books

Cover design by Nicole Hower and Antoaneta Georgieva/Sourcebooks
Cover images © Daniel Grizelj/Getty Images, stockcam/Getty Images, powerofforever/Getty Images, Nerthuz/Getty Images, Ivan Yarovyi/Getty Images, Jose A. Bernat Bacete/Getty Images, kjpargeter/Freepik

Published by Bloom Books, an imprint of Sourcebooks
P.O. Box 4410, Naperville, Illinois 60567-4410
(630) 961-3900
sourcebooks.com

Originally self-published in 2013 by Jennifer L. Armentrout.

Cataloging-in-Publication data is on file with the Library of Congress.

Printed and bound in Germany.
BPG 10 9 8 7 6 5 4 3 2 1

To my friends who help me keep sane while
I'm playing in imaginary worlds.

PRONUNCIATION GUIDE FOR APOLLYON

Aether: EE-ther
Agapi: ah-GAH-pee
Akasha: ah-KAH-sha
Apollyon: ah-POL-ee-on
απόλυτη εξουσία: ah-POL-ee-tee EX-shoo-shee-ya
αήττητο: EYE-tee-toe
Chlamys: KLIM-is
Daimon: DEE-mun
Eíste pánta mou: EAST-ah PAN-da moo
Hematoi: HEM-a-toy
Ισχύς: ISH-heez
Θάρρος: THA-roesh

CHAPTER ONE

My blood itched for a fight. Muscles screamed to engage. My thoughts were covered in a heady, amber haze of power. I was the Apollyon. I wielded control over the four elements, and the fifth and the most powerful—*akasha*. I fueled the God Killer. I was his power-up—the ace up his sleeve. I was the beginning and he was the end. And together, we were *everything*.

Yet, all I could do was pace back and forth. Caged and made helpless by the markings etched in the cement above me and by bars crafted by a god.

"Alex."

Of course, I wasn't alone. Oh no. My own personal hell was a party for two. Well, it was really a threesome…foursome of sorts. Sounded more fun than it was. Voices…there were so many voices in my head.

"Do you remember?"

I tipped my head to the right, feeling the muscles stretch and the bones crack. Then I repeated the movements to the left, my fingers moving—pinky, middle, pointer…over and over.

"Alex, I know you can hear me."

I looked over my shoulder, my lip curling at what I saw. Boy, did I have a T-Rex-sized bone to pick with that pure-blood. Aiden St. Delphi stood on the other side of the bars. There, he was an immovable force. But without the protections from Hephaestus or Apollo between us, he would become an inconsequential nothing.

No. No. No.

My hand flew to the crystal rose on its own accord, feeling the smooth and delicate edges. *He* was everything.

Sharp pain sliced between my temples, and I snarled. Sending him a hateful look, I faced the bare cement wall. "You should have kept me on the Elixir."

"I should have never put you on the Elixir," he countered. "That wasn't the way to get to you."

I laughed coldly. "Oh, you got to me all right."

There was a pause. "I know you're still in there, Alex. Underneath that connection, you are still you. The woman I love."

I opened my mouth, but there were no words—only memories of standing by the stream and telling Aiden I loved him, and then an endless stream of thoughts and actions centering on him.

Months, if not years, of them cycling over and over again until I couldn't distinguish between the past, the present, and what was to become of my future.

As if sensing where my thoughts had gone, he said, "A few days ago you said you loved me."

"And a few days ago I was high as a kite and hiding in closets, thanks to you." I whirled around, just in time to see him flinch. Good. "You put me on the Elixir."

Aiden sucked in a sharp breath but didn't look away in shame or guilt. He met and held my gaze, locked onto eyes I knew he loathed with every fiber of his being. "I did."

I took a deep, heavy breath. "I will get out of here eventually, Aiden. And I will kill you. Slowly."

"And you'll murder everyone I care for. I know. We've been here before." He leaned against the bars. There wasn't a hint of stubble on his smooth face this time around. He was in his Sentinel uniform—all black. But there were dark shadows under those striking eyes of his.

"I know you won't hurt me if you get out," he continued. "I believe in that."

"Sad."

"What is?"

"That someone as good-looking as you is so incredibly stupid." I smiled as his eyes narrowed. The moment they flashed silver, I knew I'd hit a nerve. That made me all warm and fuzzy for about three seconds, and then I realized I was still in a freaking cage. Pissing Aiden off helped pass the time, but it didn't change anything.

There were better things I could be doing.

I just needed to wait and bide my time. The low-level static was in my head. Constant. All I needed to do was tap into it, but the moment Aiden even thought I was doing that, he started talking. Going to the mattress on the floor, I sat down and tucked my knees under my chin. I watched Aiden watch me. And I tried to keep the voice that popped up whenever he was around quiet. I didn't like or understand that voice.

Aiden ran a hand through his hair, and then pushed back from the bars. "Do you know what's happening out there, right now?"

I shrugged. Was I supposed to care? All I cared about was getting out of here and connecting with my Seth. Then, if my father was still enslaved in the Catskills, we would free him. My Seth had promised me.

"Do you remember what Poseidon did to Deity Island?"

How in the hell was I supposed to forget that? Poseidon had wiped out the Covenant there.

"Well, it's going to get worse, Alex. Half of the Olympian Twelve want to make war on Seth and Lucian," he continued. "And I'm sure he knows that. Maybe that's what *he* wants, but is that what *you* want? Do you know how many innocent lives will be lost—*have* been lost? Both mortal and half? Is that something you can live with?"

I really wasn't living right now, considering I was *in a cage*.

"Because I know deep down you couldn't live with yourself, knowing you helped cause the death of thousands, if not millions—especially those halfs. You were questioning becoming a Sentinel because of how they were being treated. If Seth goes through with this, they will die." The conviction in his voice was annoying. So was the passion that fueled the words. "Caleb—do you remember how you felt after Caleb—"

"Don't talk about him!"

His dark brows shot up. Shock splashed across his face and then he darted toward those damn bars, grasping them. "Yes, *Caleb*, Alex! Do you remember how you felt when he died? How you blamed yourself?"

"Shut up, Aiden."

"Do you remember being so torn up that you stayed in bed for five days? Your heart was broken when you lost him. Do you think he'd want to see you do this to yourself? His death was a wrong-place-at-the-wrong time thing, but this? There will be thousands of Calebs, and they *will* be your fault."

I pressed my head against my knees and clamped my hands over my ears. But that did nothing to stop the rising tide of emotion beating at me or the ache in my temples that was quickly turning into a sharp, stabbing pain.

And it didn't stop him. "What about your mother, Alex?"

"Shut up!" I screamed.

"This wasn't what she wanted!" The bars shook as he hit them with what I guessed were his fists. *That* had to hurt. "This is what she died to protect you from. How dare you just roll over and let him do this to—"

My entire body snapped like a rubber band pulled too tight. "Shut—"

The buzzing in my ears roared, drowning out Aiden and everything else. In an instant, *he* was there, slipping through my veins like warm, rich honey.

Listen to me. The words were in my thoughts, soothing like balmy summer air. *Listen to me, Alex. Remember what we will do together once we connect. Free the halfs—and your father.*

"Alex," Aiden snapped.

Good gods, doesn't he have anything better to do? Seth's exasperated sigh shuddered through my body. *Close him out. He doesn't matter. We do.*

My fingers tightened in my hair.

"He's in there now, isn't he?" Anger deepened Aiden's voice. The bars shook again. At the rate he was going, his knuckles were going to be mush. Just like my brain. "Don't listen to him, Alex."

Seth's laugh was like chips of ice. *Is he coming in there? Lay him out, Angel. Then make a run for it. No one will be able to stop you.*

I pulled my hair until tiny needles stabbed at my scalp.

"Alex, look at me." The desperate edge in Aiden's voice reached a part of me I wasn't entirely familiar with. My eyes opened and latched onto his. They were silvery, like moonlight. Beautiful eyes. "Together we can break the bond between you and Seth."

Tell him you don't want to break the bond.

Amazing…and creepy how much my Seth could see and hear when we were connected. It was like having another person living inside me.

"Alex," Aiden said. "Even if you make it to him, he'll drain you just like a daimon would. Maybe he won't mean to, but he will."

My heart tripped up. I'd been warned before—by my mother, months ago. It was one of the reasons she'd wanted to change me into a daimon. A messed-up reason full of failed logic, but still…

I'd never do that to you, Alex. All I want is to keep you safe, to make you happy. Freeing your father is what you want, isn't it? Together we can do that, but only together.

"I'm not going to give up," Aiden said. Blessed silence stretched out for a few heartbeats. "Do you hear that, Seth? It's not going to ever happen."

He's annoying.

You're both annoying. Then I said out loud, "There's nothing to give up on, Aiden."

His eyes narrowed. "There is everything."

Those words struck me as odd. "Everything" was a ghost of what was and never could be. Everything had changed the moment I'd connected with my Seth. It was hard to explain. Months ago, when I'd had trouble sleeping, and the connection between us had eased my body and mind? Well, this was like that, times a hundred.

There was no *me* in this. Sort of like there'd been no Seth in this before I'd Awakened. I understood that now. How much he'd struggled being around me, fighting to not get sucked into what I had going on. Now there was just us—a single being existing in two separate bodies. One soul split apart. Solaris and the First—

Sharp pain exploded behind my eyes.

Don't. His whisper carried in my veins. *Don't think about them.*

I frowned.

And then my Seth kept chatting. So did Aiden. But he wasn't stupid enough to come into the cell. Even tired and held back by the wards on the walls, I was sure I could take him. Minutes went by, maybe hours, while the two of them slaughtered my brain cells.

When it was all over, I sagged against the mattress. One hell of a headache thumped. Aiden only left because someone—my uncle?—had opened the door from above, which usually meant something was going on. I rolled onto my side, slowly stretching out.

Finally, Seth sighed.

I unfurled my fingers. The joints ached. *He won't stay gone for long.*

We don't need forever, Angel. We just need to figure out where you are. And then we'll be together.

A faint smile curved my lips up. If I concentrated hard enough, I could feel my Seth at the end of the buzzing cord that was always present. Sometimes he hid himself from me, but not now.

My memory pulled together his image. His golden complexion and slightly arched brows formed in my thoughts. The strong curve of his jaw demanded to be touched, and the smug grin on his full lips spread. Gods, his face was unearthly beautiful—cold and hard as the marble statues that used to line the Covenant building.

But there…there were no more statues on Deity Island. There was nothing. Poseidon had ripped it all apart and pulled it back into the ocean. Buildings, statues, sand, and people—all of it gone.

I lost the image of my Seth.

Unease formed in the pit of my stomach. Aiden had been right earlier—sort of. Something about that whole situation bothered me, made me feel helpless, and I wasn't helpless.

I was the Apollyon.

Go back to thinking about how good I look. I liked that.

Some things never changed. My Seth's ego was as big as ever.

But my Seth's image blossomed before me. His hair was curly around his temples and the color of spun gold. He reminded me of the paintings of Adonis. But Adonis wasn't blond. Through the knowledge of the previous Apollyons, I knew his hair had been brown.

Where are you? I asked.

Heading up north, Angel. Are you in the north?

I sighed. *I don't know where I am. There are woods around me. A creek.*

Not helpful. There was a pause, and I imagined the feel of his hand on my cheek, tracing the curve of the bone. I shivered. *I miss you, Angel. Those weeks when you were hidden from me drove me crazy.*

I didn't respond. I hadn't missed my Seth. While I'd been under the influence of the Elixir, I hadn't even known he existed.

Seth chuckled. *You do wonders for my self-esteem. You're supposed to say you missed me, too.*

Rolling onto my back, I tried to work out the kink in my leg. *What will it be like when I transfer my power to you?*

There was a pause and I started to get nervous. *It won't hurt,* his voice whispered. *It will be like when we touched before, when the runes appeared. You liked that.*

I had.

There are a few words spoken, nothing huge, and then I will take your power. I won't drain you, Alex. I'd never do that.

And I believed him, so I relaxed. *What is the plan, Seth? You know what the plan is.*

He wanted to take out the Olympian Twelve before they found a way to take us out. Legend said we were only vulnerable to another Apollyon, but neither of us was secure in that belief. Loopholes and lesser-known myths were something all the Apollyons had sought to discover. But once the gods were out of the picture, we would rule. Or Lucian would rule. I didn't know or care. All I wanted was to be near my Seth. I was having a mad case of separation anxiety.

No. What's the plan so we can be together?

Seth's approval washed over me like I'd just stepped out into the summer sun. I basked in it, like a good little puppy with a full tummy. *Eventually, they will show a weakness. They always do. Especially St. Delphi. You are his weakness.*

I squirmed. *I am.*

And when you are presented with a chance to escape, take it. Don't hold back, Angel. You're the Apollyon. Once free, they can't stop you. Trust that. And the moment you get an idea of where you are, I'll be there.

I trusted my Seth.

There was that pleasant and heady fog again, invading me. *Have you seen Apollo or any other god recently?*

No. Not since I'd come out of the Elixir high, and that

was odd. Apollo had been up my butt from the moment I'd Awakened, but I hadn't felt or seen him—or any god.

I opened my eyes and stared at the bars. Would Hephaestus need to reinforce the bars soon?

Gods, I hoped so. If they weakened, then so would the wards. Then I could get out.

Seth said something that caused my toes to curl so I would pay attention to him again. *Where did you go?*

I showed him the bars and my thoughts. He was doubtful. Hephaestus's work rarely weakened, but I was hopeful… for a hot second. This…this bond wasn't the real deal. Even though my Seth was inside me, he really wasn't here. I was alone—alone in a cell.

He'll never let me out. Aiden will never let me near you. Tears burned my eyes as an endless gulf of hopelessness ripped open. *And I'll never see my father.*

Yes, you will. It doesn't matter what he does. I will get to you. The gods say there can only be one of us, but they're wrong. A strange coiling, and then relaxing, filled me. *You're mine, Alex—always have been and always will be. We were created for this.*

Part of me warmed in response. And part of me, the source of the other voice whenever Aiden was around, tucked away and hidden from my Seth, recoiled as I fingered the crystal rose around my neck.

CHAPTER TWO

Sometime later—I had no idea if it was night, day, or how long I'd slept—I was alone. There was no Aiden sitting in the chair watching me. No Seth at the end of the amber cord. This was a treat.

My head was somewhat clear.

I stood and stalked toward the bars. They looked normal—silvery titanium—but it was the fine mesh circling them that was the problem.

Hephaestus's chain was a real bitch.

Taking a deep breath, I grabbed the bars and squeezed. A flash of blue light volleyed up the bars, billowing along the ceiling and over the mark like smoke full of glitter.

"Dammit," I muttered, backing away.

I tried calling on akasha. Nothing stirred inside of me, not even a flicker. Lifting my hand, I opted for something smaller. Well, small to me.

I called upon fire.

Aaaaaand…there was nothing.

When I'd Awakened, the power that had broken open and flooded my veins had been a rush—a high so great I could have licked the ceiling, a high of no equal. I got why daimons yearned for aether. I'd had just a taste of it. And I hadn't felt it since Apollo had knocked me into next week with a freaking god-bolt.

Jerk.

He was also on my to-kill list.

I went to the bathroom and cleaned up. Freshly showered and attired, I returned to testing out the bars. The shimmering blue light was sort of pretty. At least it was something to stare at.

I sighed, about ready to put my head through the wall. I searched for my Seth at the end of the cord—still gone. I could call out to him and he would respond, but I was sure he was busy trying to free me. With nothing left to do, I returned to testing sections of the bars.

What seemed like hours later, a door opened upstairs. There were voices. One of them was Aiden's, but the other…

"Luke?" I called out.

"Leave," was Aiden's harsh reply.

The door shut, and one heavy set of footsteps came down the stairs. I swear to the gods the sound that came out of my throat was an animalistic growl.

Aiden came into view, holding a plastic plate of eggs and bacon. One eyebrow was arched. "Do you really think I'm going to allow a half-blood near you?"

"A girl can hope." Halfs were more susceptible to compulsions, and I now packed one on steroids. He held the plate through the space in the bars. The last time I'd done the whole not-eating thing, it hadn't worked. I'd pretty much starved and ended up on the Elixir because of it. Food was my friend this time around.

I reached for the plate.

Aiden's empty hand snaked out and wrapped around my arm. His hand was so large it swallowed my wrist. He said nothing, but his thundercloud eyes willed me to do *something*. What? Remember us together? Remember how much he'd consumed my thoughts? How I'd ached to be with him? Did he want me to remember what it was like when he'd told me about the night the daimons had attacked and massacred his family? And what it felt like being in his arms, being loved by him?

I remembered all those things in detail.

But the emotions that belonged to those events and memories weren't there. They were cut off completely. Gone with the whims of the past… Aiden was my past.

No. No. No. That small voice was back again. *Aiden was the future.* For some reason I thought of that damn oracle—Grandma Piperi. *Know the difference between need and love*, she had said. There was no difference. Couldn't she have tried to educate me on how to break out of these bars?

Aiden let go, his eyes as hard as the cement walls. He backed away while I took my food to the mattress. Surprisingly, he let me eat in silence.

Afterward, not so much.

Today Aiden wanted to talk about our first training session and how much I'd apparently annoyed the crap out of him because I hadn't stopped talking. When he got to the part when I'd mimicked his voice, I started to smile. He *had been* irritated and unsure of how to handle me.

Aiden's eyes flared the same moment my lips twitched. "You said I sounded like a father." I had.

"You also said you were going to have to drop your crack habit when I went over the rules." Aiden smiled.

My lips almost answered in kind. And I didn't like that. Time to change the topic. "I don't want to talk about this."

Aiden leaned back in the metal folding chair. The thing had to be uncomfortable. "What do you want to talk about, Alex?"

"Where has Apollo been? Since he's my great-whatever, I'm feeling unloved."

He folded his arms. "Apollo won't be around."

Oh, interesting development. My little old ears perked right up. "And why not?"

His stare was level. "And do you really think I'm going to tell you when you'll run right back to tell Seth?"

I put my bare feet on the cold floor and stood. "I won't say a word."

Aiden shot me a bland look. "Call me crazy, but I don't believe you."

Making my way to the bars, I kept an eye on his expression. As I neared, it lost the insipid look. His jaw hardened as if he worked his molars. His eyes turned sharper, lips thinning. When I touched the bars, the flare of light was weak. Somehow it knew the difference between when I was just touching it and when I was trying to escape. Clever chains.

"What are you doing?" Aiden asked.

"If you let me go now, I swear that you and all those you care for will be untouched." He didn't say anything for a heartbeat.

"But I care about you, Alex."

I tilted my head to the side. "But I will be unharmed."

"No. You won't be safe." Sadness crept into his eyes right before his thick lashes swept down. My stomach shifted in warning. Recalling the bits of information I'd picked up while under the Elixir, I knew there was more to what he said.

"What do you know, Aiden?"

"If you leave here still connected to Seth...you will die." The last bit came out ragged.

I laughed. "You're lying. Nothing can harm—" *Myths and legends, Alex. Duh.* What had I thought earlier? There were *always* checks and balances of sorts. That was why the Apollyon had been created in the first place. "What do you know?"

His lashes swept up, revealing startling silver eyes. "It doesn't matter. All you need to know is that it's the truth."

My mouth opened, but I snapped it shut. Aiden was trying to get under my skin. That was it. If Thanatos and his Order hadn't found the Achilles's heel of the Apollyons in all their centuries of trying, one pure-blood wouldn't have succeeded. The Order hadn't...

Or had they?

But they didn't count. My Seth and his Sentinels had systematically wiped them off the Earth.

I lifted my gaze and found Aiden staring at me. The inexplicable urge to stick my tongue out was hard to deny.

"Can I ask you something?"

I shrugged. "If I said no, you would still ask."

"True." There was a tight smile. "When you were with Lucian, before the Council meeting? He took you to his house against your will, didn't he?"

"Yeah," I said slowly, growing uncomfortable already.

"How did that make you feel?"

My hands tightened on the bars. "What are you? A psychologist now?"

"Just answer the question."

Closing my eyes, I leaned against the bars. I could lie, but there really wasn't a point. "I hated it. I tried to kill Lucian with a steak knife." Obviously, that hadn't gone as planned. "But I didn't understand then. I do now. I have nothing to be afraid of."

Silence, and then Aiden was right in front of me, his forehead touching mine through the bars. His larger hands were above mine and when he spoke, his breath was warm. I didn't pull back, and I didn't understand why. Being this close to him wasn't right on so many levels.

"Nothing has changed," he said quietly.

"I have."

Aiden sighed. "You haven't."

I opened my eyes. "Will you ever get bored with this? You have to, eventually."

"Never," he said.

"Because you won't give up on me, no matter what I tell you?"

"Exactly."

"You're incredibly stubborn."

Aiden's lips tipped up in a half smile. "I used to say the same thing about you."

My brows knitted. "And you can't now?"

"Sometimes I don't even know what to say." He reached through the bars and the very tips of his fingers grazed my cheekbone. A moment later, he placed his entire palm against my cheek. I flinched, but he didn't remove his hand. "And there are moments when I almost doubt everything I do."

He tilted my head back so my eyes met his. "But I don't doubt for one second that what I'm doing right now is the right thing."

Many retorts rose to the surface, but they faded away as the little voice inside me piped up. *I'd give it all up for you…*

A knot formed in the back of my throat. Suddenly, this

cell was too small. The basement was constricting and the little distance between Aiden and me suffocating. Heart turning over heavily, I searched for the cord—

"Don't," Aiden whispered. "I know what you're about to do. Don't."

I jerked back, breaking the contact between us. "How do you know what I'm doing?"

His hand was outstretched, as if he could still feel my cheek. "I just do."

Anger rose, fueled by frustration and a good mix of what-the-hell. "Well, aren't you special?"

Shaking his head, Aiden lowered his hand. He watched me stomp over to the mattress and plop down. I glared back at him, willing almost every ill thing on him I could think of. And there were things I knew I could say that would hurt him, that would strip away his control and break him down into little pieces. Things that my Seth had whispered and things I'd told him I wanted to do. I could lash out—oh yeah, I could *destroy* Aiden. But when I opened my mouth, all those hurtful, destructive things got stuck around the lump in my throat.

Sitting here, I didn't feel right in my skin, as if I really wasn't a part of it. And the only time I felt comfortable was when I was connected to my Seth. Without him, I wanted to shed that skin, or rip at it until I bled.

I wanted to hit something. Hard.

Drawing in a shallow breath, I focused on the mark on the ceiling. There were two moons drawn, interlocking. Since so many gods were tied to the moon, I didn't know what it represented or how it had the power to strip me of mine.

"What is that?" I asked, pointing at the ceiling.

Part of me didn't expect Aiden to answer, but he did. "It's Phoebe's symbol."

"Phoebe? Obviously you don't mean the one from *Charmed*." He snorted.

Whoa, they'd brought out the big guns. I felt all kinds of special as I squinted at the markings.

They held an odd bluish-red tint to them. "So, a Titan…"

"Yes."

"And that's a Titan's blood, isn't it?" I tilted my head toward Aiden. "Care to explain how it's possible that a Titan's blood is on this ceiling? Do the Olympians just keep jars of it around?"

Aiden let out a dry laugh. "When the Olympians overthrew the Titans, most were imprisoned in Tartarus. Phoebe wasn't one of them. And she has a fondness for her children."

Racking my brain for who she'd popped out, I came up empty. "Who?"

"Leto," he answered. "Who in turn gave birth to Apollo and Artemis."

I groaned. "Of course. Why not? So Apollo asked his grandma for some blood? Great. But I don't get how it works." I gestured around me. "How is it negating my powers?"

"Titan blood is very powerful. You know that blades dipped in Titan blood can kill an Apollyon." When I sent him a *duh* look, his smile was tight. "Mix that with blood of your own lineage and, well, it has the ability to keep you from hurting yourself."

"Or from hurting you," I snapped. Aiden shrugged.

Anger pumped through my blood like poison; with no way to expel it, I was seriously seconds away from going stir-crazy. I stretched my legs, then my arms. In my head, I pictured myself running up and kicking Aiden in the shin.

There was a sigh from the other side of the bars. Sometimes I wondered if he had the ability to read minds.

"I hate this," Aiden admitted so quietly I wasn't sure I'd heard him. He twisted around, giving me his back. "I *hate* that Seth has done nothing but play you—lie to you—and you trust him. I hate that this connection is more important than everything else going on out there."

I was about to argue, but my Seth *had* lied to me. He'd probably been playing me right from the moment he'd discovered I was the second Apollyon. No doubt Lucian had.

Unease slithered up my spine, leaving cold shivers in its wake. "It…it doesn't matter now," I said.

Aiden whirled toward me. "What doesn't?"

I met his stare. "That Seth lied to me. It doesn't matter. Because what he wants, I want. If I—"

"Shut up," Aiden growled.

Surprised, I blinked. I couldn't recall a moment when Aiden had told me to *shut up*. Wow. I so didn't like that for a multitude of reasons.

Aiden's eyes glowed a fierce silver. "*You* do not want what Seth wants because there is *no you* in any of that. There is only him."

Shock rippled through me, stealing any response I could come up with. There was no me. There was only us. That freaking little voice deep inside me roared in fury, then threw itself around.

There was no *me*.

CHAPTER THREE

When my Seth decided to show up on the other side of the rainbow, I was grumpy and he was…well, he was wound up. There were, uh, *things* he said through the connection that just weren't right.

Distracting? Yes.

Acceptable in the mood I was in? No.

I want out of here, I told him, mentally shaking him off. *I can't take it any longer. Aiden…he…*

Seth's disapproval was like razor blades knocking around in my skull. *Aiden what?*

What could I tell my Seth? That Aiden was making me think? *Aiden talks a lot.*

His laugh tickled the back of my neck. *That he does. Angel, it won't be much longer. Lucian has done us a great favor.*

With who? White Robe of the Month Club?

Another pleasant laugh curled through me. *Let's just say he's given me an endless supply of bait and leverage.*

I gave him a mental eye roll. *Yeah, I don't get it.*

There was a pause, and I could feel what Seth was wanting through the bond. He was in a playful mood, but this conversation was too important for screwing around. Finally, he answered. *The pures that have stood against us have proven to be useful.*

How so?

Do you remember how Telly refused to accept that the daimons could play nice and work together to form a cohesive attack against the Covenants?

Yeah…and Marcus didn't believe it was just them working against us.

And neither had I. At the emergency Council meeting Lucian had called before my Seth had leveled the Council members, I'd suspected that Lucian had been behind the daimon attacks somehow, but there hadn't been any real proof. Besides, my hatred for Lucian probably had led to that idea.

Well, Telly was obviously half-right. Without the right motivation—say, an endless supply of aether—they are likely to settle for whatever pure they can get their hands on.

There was another gap, and the intensity of what he was feeling, what he wanted, roared through the connection. For a moment, I really believed I could feel him, and the emotion swamped me, draining my thoughts and filling me with the bliss of the connection.

Alex. His voice was chiding, self-satisfied. *Are you paying attention?*

Yes. Daimon…aether…stuff…

Good. Let me ask you a question, Angel. Do you really think daimons orchestrated those attacks all by their little selves?

Some of the lovely fog my Seth was creating faded as if icy wind had blown down the nape of my neck. *What? What do you mean?*

Even reasonable daimons couldn't pull off what they did in the Catskills. They had to have help, don't you think?

I couldn't think as my pulse kicked up. So I'd been right? A sour taste filled the back of my throat.

Don't be upset, Angel. Lucian needed discord for all of this to happen.

Thinking back to the attack in the Catskills, I tried to remember where Lucian had been in the chaos. I'd assumed that he'd been in the ballroom with the rest of the pures, but I hadn't seen him. All I knew was that my Seth had contacted him...

All those dead half-blood servants, the Guards, and Sentinels...all innocent... I jerked up, almost losing the connection with my Seth.

Angel, how do you think the daimons got into Catskills in the first place? You saw the security there. And the ballroom? There were only two entrances, and both were guarded. One of the doors belonged to Lucian's guard.

Suspecting that Lucian had been behind these attacks was one thing—I didn't put anything past that man—but my Seth? He couldn't be okay with that. Believing he was a part of all those innocent people dying was accepting something horrific. What my Seth wanted, I wanted, but the daimons...they were and always would be the enemy.

Foes can be allies in war, Angel.

Oh, my gods. A huge, freaking, crater-sized part of me couldn't process what my Seth was saying.

I fought the pull of his emotions, resurfacing as if I were drowning, then gulping in air.

There were so many innocent people, I reasoned. Appalling images of the slaughter came one after another—the servants in the hall with their throats ripped open, the Sentinels and

Guards who'd been eviscerated and then thrown through windows.

They don't matter, Angel. Only we matter, only what we want matters.

But those people *did* matter. *We could've been killed, too, Seth. My father could've been killed.*

But he wasn't, and I would never let anything happen to you. Nothing did.

We'd been separated during the attack. And if I remembered correctly, I'd come very close to being trampled to death. Not to mention I'd had to fight the furies alone. Not sure how he'd exactly prevented my death in all of that.

Angel, we need this to happen. The daimons will help me get to you. Don't you want that? For us to be together?

Yes, but—

Then trust me. We want the same things, Angel.

Aiden's words came back to me, and I squirmed in my own skin. *Seth? You…you aren't making me want anything, right? You're not influencing me?*

He didn't respond immediately, which caused my heart to trip over itself. *I could, Angel, if I wanted to. You know that, but I'm not. We just want the same things.*

I bit my lip. We did want the same things, except the thing with the daimons… I stopped those thoughts. As if two strong arms were pushing down on my shoulders, I was on my back. And then I was drowning in what Seth was feeling again.

Aiden returned with food, and he brought company with him this time—my uncle, Marcus. The man was actually being sort of decent toward me now. Ironic. I ate and drank my water like a good captive.

And I didn't even yell anything insulting.

I figured I deserved a reward, like time out of the cell or something, but that was asking too much. Instead, Marcus left to go see what the others were up to. As soon as the door closed upstairs, Aiden sat with his back pressed against the bars.

Brave, brave man…or really stupid—it was a total toss-up. I could easily fashion the bed sheet into a noose and slip it around his neck before he'd have a chance to react.

But I sat down, my back almost against his. The flare of blue from the chains appeared weaker. Silence stretched out, oddly comforting. Minutes passed and the taut muscles in my back relaxed. Before I knew it, I was leaning against the bars… and Aiden's back.

My earlier conversation with my Seth had left a weird taste in my throat and a ball of knots in my stomach. Maybe that's why I wasn't indulging in my murderous intentions with the bed sheet and Aiden's neck? Missed opportunity, I supposed.

Lowering my chin, I sighed. What my Seth wanted, I wanted, but…daimons? I rubbed my hands on my bent knees and sighed again—louder, like a petulant child.

Aiden's back twisted as he turned his head. "What, Alex?"

"Nothing," I mumbled.

"There's something." He leaned back, tipping his head against the bar. "You have that tone."

I frowned at the wall. "What tone?"

"The *I have something I want to say but shouldn't* tone." A little bit of humor seeped into his voice. "I'm well familiar with it."

Well…damn. My gaze dropped to my hands. The fingers were okay, I guess. But my nails were chipped and short. Hands of a Sentinel—a Sentinel who killed daimons. I pushed up the sleeve of my sweater. Pale-white bite marks covered my right arm. The crescent-shaped marks were a pain to hide and they were on both arms, as well as my neck. They were so ugly, a vile reminder of being trapped by them.

And no matter how hard I tried, I couldn't wipe the faces of all those slaughtered halfs in the Catskills out of my head… or forget the look on Caleb's face when he'd seen the blade embedded in his chest—a blade that had been wielded by a daimon.

Caleb would be so…*disappointed* didn't even sum it up.

But my Seth would be pissed. He'd go snooping in my memories, and I wanted him to be happy with me. I wanted—

I didn't want to *work* with daimons. That was a slap in the face to all those who'd died at their hands—my mom, Caleb, those innocent servants—and my scars.

My Seth…he'd just have to understand that. He would, because he loved me.

Mind made up, I took a deep breath. "Just so you know, I'm not telling you this because of anything to do with you. Okay?"

He laughed darkly. "I would never think such a crazy thing."

I made a face. "I'm only telling you this because I don't think it's right. It goes against something…inherent in me. I have to say something."

"What, Alex?"

Closing my eyes, I drew in a deep breath. "Do you remember how Marcus thought there was more to the daimon attacks, especially the one in the Catskills?"

"Yes."

"I sort of thought it was Lucian, especially at his Council meeting. It made sense. Creating chaos and whatever makes it easier for people to overthrow and take control." I ran a finger over the tag on the fleshy part of my elbow. "Anyway, the daimon attacks have apparently been orchestrated by Lucian and...Seth."

Aiden's spine went stiff against mine. No response. He was quiet for so long I scooted around. "Aiden?"

"How many?" His voice was gruff.

"All of them, I think," I said, guilt chewing at my insides. I was betraying my Seth, but I couldn't stay quiet. "They've found a way to control the daimons."

His head lowered and his large shoulders rolled. "How?"

Climbing onto my knees, I grasped the bars and ignored the weak pulse of blue light. "They...they are using pures as motivation. The ones who are against them—us, I mean us."

Aiden twisted so fast, I let go of the bars and jerked back. His eyes burned silver. "Do you know where they're keeping these pures?"

I shook my head.

His lashes dipped. "Do you know why they would do something like this?"

The disgust in his voice was understandable. I rubbed my palms over my thighs. Why *were* they doing this? To create discord was obvious. With daimons attacking left and right, the Council had been distracted. The gods had developed doubts about the pures' ability to control the daimon hordes and had sent furies as a result. And now, it would serve as a distraction for me to escape. How they'd work that one out I didn't know. And if the fading blue light was any indication, it wouldn't be necessary.

"No. I don't know."

His eyes met mine and our gazes locked. "Why did you tell me this? I'm sure Seth won't appreciate it."

I looked away. "I told you. It's not right. Those pures…"

"Are innocent?"

"Yeah, and Caleb…he was killed by a daimon. My mom was turned by one." My breath shuddered through me and I stood. "I want what Seth wants, but I cannot get behind that. He'll understand."

Aiden tipped his head back. "Will he? You know I will forward this information on. It will hinder his plans."

I wrapped my arms around my waist. "He'll understand."

Sadness flowed into his expression and his eyes turned down. "Thank you."

For some reason, anger bubbled up and I wanted to lash out. "I don't want your thanks. It's the last thing I want."

"You have it." He stood in one fluid motion. "And you have my thanks for more than you realize."

Confused, I stared back at him. "I don't understand."

Aiden's smile was tight, tinged with that ever-present sadness whenever he looked at me, as if I was this unfortunate creature who provoked sorrow wherever I went. Behind that sadness though, there was steely determination.

"What?" I said when he didn't answer.

"You've given me the hope I need."

My Seth wasn't mad that I'd blabbed. I hadn't even tried to hide it from him. As soon as we connected, I told him what I'd done. If anything, he seemed to have expected it. And *that* I didn't understand, but either way, he didn't want to talk about it.

Telling me about his childhood, he was a different Seth—a side of him I'd rarely seen. When he started to talk about his mom, vulnerability seeped through the bond, as if speaking about his mother unnerved him.

What was her name? I asked.

Callista.

Pretty.

She was very beautiful. Tall and blond, regal like a goddess. His words drifted off for a moment. Considering the past tense reference, I assumed she'd died. *But she wasn't kind, Angel. She was cold and unapproachable, and most of all, when she looked upon me, there was always hate in her eyes.*

I flinched as my suspicions were confirmed, and I wanted to make him feel better. *I'm sure she didn't hate you. She—*

She hated me. His sharp reply was like being doused with ice water. *I was a constant reminder of her shame. She'd gotten a taste of the forbidden fruit, and then regretted it.* Halfs and pures were forbidden to mingle. Only recently had I discovered this was because the offspring of a male half and female pure made the Apollyon.

When he spoke again, his voice was soft like a down blanket. *She was nothing like your mother, Angel. There was no great love affair. She used to tell me the only reason why she'd kept me was because a god had visited her after my birth. The most beautiful man she'd ever seen, or so she said. That god told her that she must protect me at all costs, that I would become a great power one day.*

As he talked, I recalled the glimpses of Seth's past that I'd seen when I'd Awakened. Of Seth as a small child, all golden skin and blond curls, playing by a creek or hunched over a toy in a large room stuffed with uncomfortable looking furniture. He was always alone. Nights when he'd awoken crying from a bad dream and no one would come to comfort him. Days when the only person he saw was a nanny who was just as uncaring as his mother. He'd never met his father. To this day, he didn't even know his name.

My heart wept for him.

Then at age eight, he was brought before the Council to

determine if he would enter the Covenant. His experience was nothing like mine. There was no poking or pinching. He didn't kick a Minister. They had taken one look at him and seemed to know what he would become.

It was the eyes.

The tawny, amber eyes that held wisdom that belonged to no child—eyes of an Apollyon. Things got better for him once he was sent to the Covenant in England, and then to the one in Nashville. So odd that we'd been so close to one another for so many years and had never crossed paths.

But something was off. When I'd Awakened, I'd learned all of what the previous Apollyons had discovered during their lifetimes, like being plugged into a computer and booting up. And none of them had been born with the eyes of the Apollyon. All of their eyes had become golden *after* they'd Awakened.

My Seth had been different.

But right now, that raw hurting in his chest was eating at him. *Where were you born?* I asked, hoping to take the topic away from his mother. *You've never told me.*

He laughed and I smiled. Happy Seth was a better Seth. *You won't believe this, but you know how Fate loves to mess with people?*

Boy, did I ever know that.

I was born on the island of Andros.

A shiver danced down my spine. *How...ironic.* No large leap of faith to consider that my ancestors had also hailed from that island, since many took the name of where they were born. Or, in some cases, the islands were named after the founding families.

Either way, that was ironic. And something gag-worthy surfaced. Andros was a whopping 147 square miles. *You don't think we're related?*

What? Seth burst into laughter. *No.*

How can you be so sure? Because if we're pulling a Luke and Leia, I'm going to barf.

My family isn't linked to yours in any way. Besides, your lineage is to Apollo.

And who is yours? There was no answer, only a wealth of arrogant silence. *Why do you keep that from me?*

Seth sighed. *I will tell you when we're together. I'll show you everything, Angel. And all the questions you have, you'll have your answers.*

CHAPTER FOUR

After lunch was served the following day, I roamed my cell alone. Something was going on upstairs—doors opening and slamming shut, pounding feet, and happy shouts.

Curious, I went to the bars and strained to hear more. The conversation was too muffled to make heads or tails of who it was, but someone had arrived. And it wasn't a god. I would know it if it were. Their essence was strong, something I could feel *inside* me.

Touching the bars, I measured the response. The blue shimmer *was* fading. Take that, Seth. Did that mean the mark above would also fade without a booster? Good gods, I hoped so. I searched for the cord, wanting to tell him about the new development. Seth was there but not talkative. He was with Lucian, at least that much I got. Whatever was being discussed was muted to me.

Immediate dislike rose in response to Lucian's presence. I'd obviously have to get over it, but it was going to be difficult. I would never be a fan of my stepfather.

Unhooking from the connection, I wondered what Aiden was doing. He usually spent the greater part of his day sitting in that folding chair, brooding at me.

You've given me the hope I need.

Hope for what? A "happily ever after" for us?

I found myself in the tiny white bathroom, staring into the sucky plastic mirror above the sink. The thing was practically cemented into the wall, lightweight plastic so I couldn't fashion it into some kind of weapon.

Leaning against the sink, I all but plastered my face against the mirror. My reflection was wavy, distorted by the cheap quality, but it was my eyes I was staring at.

They were amber, just like all the other Apollyons after they'd Awakened. It was kind of strange seeing my eyes like that, but it also felt right. Like I'd come into something I was destined to become. Which, duh, I had.

I cocked my head to the side. What would my Seth think when he finally saw me—really saw me—all Apollyoned-out? He would be pleased, so unlike Aiden, who hated my eyes…

A sudden sharp feeling speared my chest. *Holy crap…* I was lightheaded as I gripped the sink. This wasn't a physical pain, more like the kind when the world drops out from underneath my feet. Or when there's really sucktastic bad news.

It was the sensation of a heart being annihilated with no possibility of repair.

The breath I sucked in was shrill. The feeling didn't make sense. My heart wasn't broken. It was whole and it belonged to my Seth. And he loved me in return. He'd never told me that he did, but he had to. We were destined for each other, and once together, we would be perfect. We would rule over both Olympus *and* the mortal world.

"We will be gods," I whispered.

"Oh, Alex, even I'm amazed by how inflated your ego has become. Gods, if I was fully corporeal, I'd so kick your ass right now."

I whirled around, fully expecting to find Caleb standing in the bathroom, because that was *his* voice. But no one was there. Heart racing, I peeked into the cell. Empty. "Caleb?"

No response.

I inched into the cell, willing Caleb to appear if he was really here. Silence stretched out, and just when I was about to admit that I might've lost my damn mind, warmth passed through me.

Did Caleb just…walk *through* me? "Uh…"

There was a light chuckle from behind me. Whipping around, I just…I could only stare.

Caleb stood there, dark-blond brows arched in such a painfully familiar way. He was wearing a tunic-style shirt and white, linen pants. It was Caleb, but…not.

I could totally see the bars through him. Freaky. "Caleb?"

He glanced down at himself. "Yeah, it's me, in shade form for your viewing pleasure."

"Are you really here, or have I lost my mind?"

A slow, easy grin pulled at pale lips. "I'm here. Well, as here as I can be."

I drew in a breath, but it got stuck. "Can I touch you?" My legs were moving me forward in jerky motions. No graceful Apollyon here. "Can I hug you?"

His brows lowered. "No, Alex, you can't. You'd go right through me." He grinned. "Though you seemed to enjoy it the first time around."

I laughed, stopping short of touching. "Gods, I want to hug you so badly."

"I know." His grin faded. "But we don't have a lot of time."

We never did. I rocked back on my heels, smiling. "You're here to break me out, aren't you?"

"Ah, no, I'm not here to break you out."

My smile slipped off my face. "Why? I don't understand. I need to get out of here. My Seth needs—"

"I'm here as a last-ditch effort, Alex." He reached out as if to touch me but stopped. "Apollo sent me."

I folded my arms and scowled. "What does he have to do with this?"

"He hopes that I can reach you, Alex."

"Do you know he hit me with a god-bolt?"

Caleb winced. "Yeah, I heard. Everyone in the Underworld sort of heard, but Alex, you kind of had it coming." When I opened my mouth, he silenced me. "Apollo would be here if he could."

"And why can't he?" I turned away, trying to push down my anger, which was like screwing a lid on a box—it wasn't working. "He's afraid of me, isn't he? He should be. Apollo is totally on my shit list."

"Do you hear yourself? A god afraid of *you*?" He sounded dumbfounded. "Apollo's not here because Aiden, the love of your life, banned him from here."

I spun around, eyes narrowing. "He's not the love of my life."

Caleb shook his head. "He has always been yours, Alex. And you've always been his."

My mouth puckered as if I had tasted something sour. "Is this why you came from the great beyond? To talk about my love life?"

"Well, the love of your life banned Apollo from entering this house because Aiden's afraid Apollo will harm you." Oh, yeah, Caleb got an eyeful of my shock. "And Apollo had one of his nymphs come down to the Underworld, pulled me right out from underneath Hades's nose to help you. Both of them—Aiden and Apollo—are doing crazy things to save you."

"But…I don't need anyone to save me."

"Exactly!" Caleb threw his arms up in the air. "That's what I said!"

Okay, I wasn't following this conversation. "Then why aren't you helping me escape? You could go shade yourself right up to wherever the keys are. I'm sure Aiden has them."

He rolled his eyes and they disappeared for an instant. Yikes. "You can save yourself. Only you, and you need to get a-crackin' on it."

My lips pressed together. Here Caleb was, my best friend—my *dead* best friend, but whatever—I hadn't seen in what felt like forever, and we were arguing. I didn't want to argue with him.

"What are you doing, Alex? This isn't you. None of this is what you ever wanted."

I took a deep breath. "It's what I want now."

Caleb growled low in his throat. He looked like he wanted to strangle me. "What you're doing is going to get you and Seth killed. Yeah, that's right—you aren't invincible. Neither of you are! And there's a war brewing in Olympus and it's going to rain all kinds of holy hell down on Earth. Do you want to be responsible for that?"

Squeezing my hands into fists, I glared up at him. "We want to change things, Caleb! You of all people have to understand that! Together, Seth and I can free the servants—my father! We can overthrow the Council. We can—"

He barked a mad sort of laugh. One that usually meant he was close to pushing me into a corner.

"Do you really think that's what's going to happen once you succeed in wiping out all the Councils? That Lucian is going to free the halfs and everyone is going to love one another?"

I opened my mouth, but he kept going. "And let's pretend that's not absurd and we'll all be high on happy pills. The gods are never going to allow it. They will risk exposing themselves to the whole mortal world to stop you. Innocent people will die. *You* will die."

My heart tripped up a little. "So I should do nothing?"

"No. Don't you know? The supreme art of war is to subdue the enemy without fighting."

"And whoever came up with that was a complete and utter idiot. To win the war, the enemy must be stripped down to their bare bones and destroyed."

His eyes narrowed. "You're an idiot."

My lips twitched. "Shut up."

Caleb drifted over to me. "Alex, you have to break the bond with Seth. Break it and you will understand everything."

"No." I backed up, running my hands along my hips. "You told me to not give up on Seth. And now you want me to?"

"I don't want you to give up on him," he said, voice taking on a pleading edge. "There's still hope for him, but only if you can truly reach him. And being the head of Seth's fan club isn't going to do it."

I laughed then. "That was so you when you were…you know, around. You totally had a boy crush on him."

"And I still do. He's pretty awesome, but right now he's high on power. Like a meth-head. No. Better yet. A crack-head and a meth-head rolled into one. He's out of control. Good gods, he's working with daimons! And if you get out of here and connect with him—transfer your power to him? It's all over, Alex. He will drain you dry without even meaning to."

I gasped. "He would never do that."

"He wouldn't mean to, Alex. But he would. And once he has, he'll become the God Killer and no one needs you." He shook his head sadly. "That's if you even make it to him. Apollo will stop you. *Every* god will come down here to stop you."

Shaking my head, I refused to believe this. My Seth would never drain me. He needed me like I needed him. And together, we would be unstoppable. We could change things. As the Apollyon, I wouldn't lose people like I'd lost Caleb and my mom.

I shook my head.

"Alex," he pleaded softly.

"No. No! Because I'm powerful enough now that no one I love will ever die again!"

"Alex—"

Stupid, weak tears burned my eyes. "If I had been the Apollyon when we were attacked, I could've saved you!"

His form flickered. "No, Alex, you couldn't have."

"Don't say that. Don't *ever* say that." My chest was too tight. He faded a little. "What's happening?"

"I have to go." Caleb looked stricken. "Break the connection, Alex. It's the only way to save you both."

I shook my head so fast my hair slapped my cheeks. Before I could utter a word, he flickered out and was gone. I stood there for minutes, maybe hours, staring at the spot where he'd stood, fighting tears and everything he'd said. I didn't—couldn't believe what he'd said.

Caleb didn't get it. He'd never lost people like I had—people like him. While he was in the Underworld playing

Mario Kart, I was up here, knee-deep in the pain and anguish of losing him and my mom. I was dealing with the fact that my father was a damn servant.

He didn't get it!

Being connected with my Seth was the only way to save us. By the time my Seth and I were done, there would be no more pain.

CHAPTER FIVE

I had the distinct impression that Caleb had failed somehow after he'd left, and I hoped he wasn't going to get punished. I didn't think Apollo would do anything to him, but then again, what did I know?

Caleb's visit left me tattered. Keyed up and with no way to expel the nervous energy, I paced the cell. Part of me wanted to rage and scream. A whole other side of me wanted to sit down and cry like a little baby. Seeing Caleb was like a gift, but all we'd done was argue. It left a stone in my stomach that just kept pulling me down, down.

When Aiden appeared with a bag of takeout food, I almost threw it back at him, but I was starving. And I…had the strangest urge to tell him about Caleb.

"Who's here?" I asked between mouthfuls of mystery meat and soggy buns. He didn't answer.

I rolled my eyes, finishing off the burger. Rummaging around in the bag, I pulled out an extra-large order of fries. With all the exercise I was getting, my escape would involve me rolling out of here. "I know someone has shown up."

A handful of fries went into my mouth, and then another. Salt and grease coated my fingertips. Yum. "Are you not going to talk? Just sit there and stare at me like a creeper?"

Aiden cracked a half-smile. "You called me that once before."

"Yeah, because you *are* a creeper." I frowned at my almost-empty carton. There were never enough fries.

"Actually, I'd been watching to make sure you didn't sneak off the island."

I remembered. It had been the night of Zarak's house party, back when things had at least seemed simpler. Zarak... I wondered what had happened to Zarak. I didn't think he'd been on the island when Poseidon had pitched a fit, but I didn't know.

Finished with the fries, I licked the salt off my finger as I lifted my gaze.

Aiden's eyes flared silver, and something warm unfurled in my stomach. I put my other finger to my lips—

Holy baby daimons everywhere, what the hell was I doing? I grabbed a napkin, wiping furiously at my fingers. Across from me, heat roared off Aiden.

By the time I finally looked at Aiden again, he was all kinds of coolness—the master of impassivity. He even arched his brow at me. Good for him. Whatever. He'd totally checkmated me, but now I knew who was upstairs—Laadan and Olivia. I remembered then that while I'd been on the Elixir, Deacon had told Aiden they were coming. Then I'd hid in the closet because Aiden had raised his voice.

I'd actually hid in *a closet*.

"You look happy," Aiden commented as he unwrapped a chicken sandwich.

Man, who scraped the mayo off and only ate a sandwich on one bun? Aiden. That's who. "Oh, I was just reminiscing about learning how to play chess and hiding in closets."

He'd only taken two bites, but tossed the remainder in his bag. A muscle worked in his jaw. "Alex, I hated seeing you like that. As much as I hate seeing you like this. So if you want me to feel guilty, I do. If you want me to hate myself for making that decision, I do."

I should've been doing a celebratory dance or something, because I'd gotten a nice little jab in there, but my shoulders sagged. Words were on the tip of my tongue, words I shouldn't say. So I said nothing. We spent the rest of whatever time of day it was in silence. When he left, I didn't reach out to Seth. Between Caleb's surprise visit and the thing with Aiden, I was too out of it.

Sometime later, maybe a couple of hours, I heard the door open and shut quickly—way too quickly and quietly to be Aiden, who always came down the stairs like a warrior preparing for battle.

I popped up from the mattress, holding my breath.

Two slender, denim-clad legs came into view, and then a billowy white shirt tucked into the front of jeans. The knee-high boots gave my visitor away. They were *great* boots.

Olivia.

Opportunity had just come a-knocking.

She came to a halt at the bottom of the stairs, her tight curls pulled back from her face. Olivia's caramel-colored complexion was beautiful, even when it was pale. She looked like she was staring down a horde of daimons right now.

"Alex," she whispered, swallowing.

Slowly, so I wouldn't send her scurrying back up the steps, I approached the bars. I knew the moment she got a good look at my eyes, because she backed up, hitting the bottom step.

"Don't go," I said, gripping the bars. Pale blue light flickered. "Please don't go."

Her throat worked again, and she glanced behind her quickly before her gaze swung back to me. "Dear gods, it's true. Your eyes…"

I smiled wryly. "They take a little getting used to."

"No doubt." She took a deep breath and stepped closer. "Aiden…he's going to kill me if he finds out I'm down here, but I just had to see you for myself. He…they're saying you have to stay down here—that you're dangerous."

For once, someone else's impulsivity was a benefit to me. "I'm not dangerous."

"They've said you've threatened to make a crown out of Deacon's ribcage."

Aw, hell… "I haven't done anything."

She looked doubtful.

"Okay. You know me. I say mean things when I'm mad."

Her lips twitched. "Yeah, you do. Alex…" Her gaze flickered over the bars. "Damn…"

I had to proceed with caution, but I had to do it quickly. Who knew how much time we had before Aiden realized Olivia was down here and ruined all my fun? Using a compulsion would be easy and the quickest way to deal with this, but…but a part of me, that stupid, *stupid* part of me, wanted to talk to her…my friend.

And there was something I hadn't gotten a chance to tell her, something important. Olivia inched closer to the cell. "You look…you look terrible."

I frowned. "I do?"

"Have you been sleeping?" Her gaze drifted over me. "You've lost weight."

Sort of relieved to hear I hadn't packed on the pounds, I shrugged. "You look great."

She touched her cheek. "I don't feel great. You have no idea what's going on out there. Everyone is freaked out, because of..."

"Because of us."

"Us?"

"Seth and me." I leaned my head against the bars. "You went to New York, right?"

Olivia shook her head. "We started to, but it's real bad there. They're not letting anyone in. The place is on lock-down, but there's a lot of fighting inside, I hear."

The Elixir had stopped working there, courtesy of Lucian, and my father...my father was there. "The gods, they have these *things* surrounding the Covenants." She shuddered and wrapped her arms around her slender waist.

My interest piqued. "What things?"

"I don't know. They're like half-bull, half-man—but machines. We ran into them when we were heading to New York. My mother continued on, but she didn't want me there. She sent me here with Laadan."

A foggy memory resurfaced, one of Apollo and Aiden talking about those creatures. I wondered if my Seth knew about them. Probably. I let go of the bars and tucked my tangled hair back. The ends curled halfway down my chest and probably were in need of a cut. Around Olivia, I couldn't help but compare myself.

"Alex, things are going to get worse. You—"

"I saw Caleb."

Her mouth dropped open, and whatever sales pitch she had was forgotten. "What?"

"I've seen Caleb twice since he...passed." I needed to get

this out, and then I'd do what I had to. My Seth would call this need a weakness and it was, because I was wasting precious time, but Olivia needed to know. I'd promised Caleb I'd tell her, and after I escaped I had no idea if I would see her again. "The Order attacked me while I was still at the Covenant. One of their members killed me. I went to the Underworld—"

"You *died*?"

I winced at the shrill pitch. "Yeah, I was dead, and then I wasn't. Long story. But I saw Caleb."

A hand fluttered to her chest. "Are you messing with me, because I swear to the gods, Alex, I *will* hurt you."

Cute, considering she couldn't touch me, but I grinned. "Caleb's okay. He's really okay. He spends most of his time playing Wii, and he looked great. Nothing like..." The back of my throat burned. "He's really good."

Her eyes glistened in the dim light. "You really saw him?"

I nodded. "He wanted me to tell you something. I didn't get a chance, with everything that's going on."

"Understandable." She choked out a laugh. "What...what did he tell you?"

Olivia had always had manicured hands, but the nail polish was chipped and old. I kept my eyes on them. "I don't know what this means, but he said to tell you that he would've picked Los Angeles." There was a sharp inhale, and the silence stretched out so long I eventually had to look, and when I did, I almost wished I hadn't.

Tears streaked down Olivia's cheeks, running over the fingers now pressed to her lips. An answering emotion rose in my throat and I bit down on my lip. Los Angeles must've meant something really important. I wished I were on the other side of these bars, not to escape, but to hug her. But I needed to be on the other side of these bars, and I needed to escape. There was no more time.

"Olivia," I said, and my voice was different, even to my own ears—softer, lyrical. Power hummed.

She stiffened, and then her hands left her mouth as her eyes locked onto mine. Tears clung to her thick lashes, but they weren't what made her eyes glassy now. It was the compulsion in my voice, an ability that had become innate upon Awakening. Part of me abhorred what I was doing. Olivia was my friend. Using a compulsion on her was wrong, but there was no other way. I had to get to my Seth. She would understand eventually.

"Do you know where the keys are, Olivia?" She nodded slowly.

"Good. That's really good." I reached through the bars, motioning her toward me. When she placed her cool hand in mine, I squeezed gently. "Where are they?"

"With Aiden." Her words were slow.

Dammit. That wasn't good. "And where is Aiden?"

"He's with your uncle and Laadan." A soft sigh leaked from her lips.

Crap. There was no way she could get the keys. My gaze slipped to the cage door and an idea took hold. Letting go of her hand, I gripped the bars and watched the flare of light. It was weak and didn't reach the Titan mark on the ceiling.

"Olivia, will you help me?" I threw as much power as I had into my voice, and her eyes widened. "You'll help me, right?"

"Yes."

"Great." I smiled as I hurried to the door. The weakest point was where the lock was; if both of us worked it at the same time, it might just be enough. "I need you to pull on this door, Olivia, as hard as you can."

She walked to the door in a daze, obediently placing her hands on the handle. "Put everything into it," I urged softly. "Pull. Pull hard."

And she did. Half-bloods were unbelievably strong, and metal ground as the bars rattled. Olivia bent at the waist, digging in with her boots. I stepped back, wishing I had some shoes, because this was seriously going to hurt.

"Keep pulling," I ordered, and then I took a deep breath.

Turning halfway, I spun and planted my heel into the bars around the lock. Pain splintered into my foot as shimmery blue light flared and faded quickly. An inch-wide gap appeared between the door and the bars.

"Pull really hard, Olivia." She grunted, bearing down. Caleb was going to haunt me for this.

Leaning back, I hit the door again. Another gap appeared. With my foot going numb, I gave it one more kick. Metal groaned and gave way. The sudden force sent Olivia to the floor and the door…it was open.

Not wasting time, I bolted through the gap, half-expecting to be cut down by some unknown defense, but then I was on the other side of the bars.

I wanted to do a victory dance and shout, but I dropped down and clasped Olivia's cheeks. She stared into my eyes, completely under my control. "Stay here, okay? Stay here until someone comes and gets you."

Olivia nodded.

I started to let go, but paused. "You won't blame yourself for this. You will blame me."

"Okay," came the soft, sleepy reply.

I let go and started for the stairs. A bitter taste was in the back of my mouth as I glanced over my shoulder. Olivia remained on the floor, her eyes fixed on the spot where I'd stood.

"Thank you," I said, not that it mattered. She didn't hear me or understand. She wouldn't do anything until someone came down here, and then it would be like waking from a dream.

I'd see her again. Once my Seth and I changed things, I'd see her again and I'd apologize.

Reassured by that, I slipped up the narrow stairs, pausing at the door. There were no voices on the other side. Taking a second, I tested the bond for Seth. He wasn't there, and I didn't have time to wait around for him to show up. As soon as I was outside and knew where I was, I'd call for him.

Inching the door open, I checked out the hallway. Empty. It was narrow, and paintings hung on the walls. It split two ways. Toward the right, natural light streamed in through a small window, beckoning me. I slid through the door, closing it behind me quietly as I took in my surroundings. I'd been on the Elixir the last time I'd been upstairs—the only time, actually—and I vaguely remembered that this hall led to the kitchen and a living room of sorts. Off the kitchen was the sunroom, which led outside. A strange feeling unfurled inside me, and there was a flash of Aiden and me in that sunroom. I pushed it out of my head and crept down the hallway. I seriously wished someone had left a dagger or something lying around. No such luck. Come to think of it, I should've asked Olivia where we were. I rolled my eyes. Gods, I sucked sometimes, but I'd been so concerned with getting free.

As I neared one of the closed doors, I thought I heard Deacon laughing, and then Luke. Biting down on my lip, I slipped around the staircase that led upstairs—

The door swung open and I came face-to-face with Lea. Crap.

Mouth dropping open, Lea blinked and took a step back, bouncing into the wall. "Don't—"

Her high-pitched, shrill battle-roar cut me off, and then she swung at me. She actually freaking swung at me. Gods. With no time for a compulsion, I deflected her blow with a brutal swipe that sent her spinning. She caught herself on the wall and grunted. Before she could regain her balance, I swiped her feet out from under her just as Deacon's shocked face appeared in the doorway.

"Oh crap," Deacon said, and he backed up quickly as Luke shot forward.

Luke grabbed for me, but I was quick. "Alex, you don't want to do anything—"

Down the hall, the last door flew open, slamming into the drywall. I caught sight of black pants. *Sentinel.* Without thinking twice, I threw up my arm and the one closest to me took the brunt of the air element.

Luke flew backward, his eyes wide and stunned. He crashed into Lea, who had moved in front of Deacon as if to protect him. There were several grunts, a yelp of pain, and then someone yelled my name.

Spinning around, I took off for the kitchen. My bare feet slapped off the floor as I skirted the table and entered the sunroom. I reached the door in seconds, tugging then realizing it was locked. Cussing under my breath, I unlocked the damn thing and threw the door open.

Aiden barreled into the kitchen. "Alex! No!"

He was too late. I was out. I was free.

CHAPTER SIX

The moment the sunlight touched my skin, I faltered a step. It felt like years had passed since I felt the warmth of natural light. My senses came alive. Grass was cold under my feet and damp. Thick, tall elms blurred as I darted across a small dirt driveway, around a Hummer, and into the heavy woods surrounding the cabin.

Legs and arms pumping, I kept running. My hair streamed out behind me, and I pushed hard, paying attention, looking for any sign of where I was. There was nothing.

A seedling of panic took root. I hurdled a fallen tree, my feet skidding over sharp pine needles.

How was I supposed to tell my Seth where I was when I had nothing but freaking trees—

"Alex! Stop!"

My breath hitched and I dared a look back. It was him—Aiden.

"Crap," I spat, picking up speed.

Up ahead, there was a creek—*the* creek. I remembered

that. Thousands of years of Apollyons and their abilities rushed through me. Tapping into that ability was so easy, like slipping into well-worn jeans, which was irritating considering the heinous training I'd gone through in preparation for Awakening, and of course, my Seth would have known that. Punk.

Extending one arm, I summoned the water, willing it to respond to me.

Water stirred, and then a stream jetted into the air, arcing high above me. The wall of water kept coming, draining the shallow creek within seconds. It spun into a funnel, slamming into the earth behind me. A curse was drowned out. That should've bought me some time.

Racing over the creek bed, mud splattered my feet and jeans. Low-hanging branches tore at my hair, snagging strands and my shirt. Cloth ripped, but I kept going. Sunlight peeked through the thick branches as I headed deeper into the forest, away from the cabin…away from *him*.

Without warning, the bond snapped alive. *Alex?*

I'm out. I leaped off a boulder over a small gulley and landed in a crouch. Springing up, I took off.

I don't know where I'm at, but I'm out. Seth, I'm—

I could hear Aiden. He was close and fast, powered by something stronger than aether and I knew, even as fast as I was, I wouldn't have been able to outrun him this long if a wall of water hadn't stopped him. I'd have to fight. But I wouldn't be alone. My Seth was here.

Skidding to a stop, I turned. Wind blew my hair back as I dragged in fresh, mountain air. Aiden cleared the small gulley, landing in a nimble crouch several feet away from me. Water streamed from the dark waves plastered to his head, and his black shirt clung to the hard muscles of his chest and stomach. Under the thin, soaked material, his shoulders tensed.

Our eyes locked.

He rose gracefully, hands open at his sides.

"You don't want to do this," I warned. "Turn away."

Aiden came forward. "I'm not going to leave you. I'll never do that."

There was a flutter in my chest that didn't belong there. I took a step back, feeling heat radiating from my fingers.

My Seth's voice hummed through the bond and I knew what he wanted me to do; therefore, I understood why I had to do this.

I took a shallow breath and raised my chin. "Then it's your funeral."

"So be it."

I launched myself at Aiden.

He was prepared for it. He darted to the left, avoiding my attack. He was fast and also very skilled. I knew, because he had trained me, but I was better than him now. I was something *else*.

Moving lightning fast, I dipped and went for his legs. Aiden jumped, and I shot up, slamming my fist into his stomach. He stumbled back a step but quickly regained his footing. My next punch was deflected. The third one caught him in the jaw, snapping his head back.

Sunlight reflected off the daggers attached to his thighs, and I went for them.

Aiden spun to the left at the last second, and my fingers only grasped the handle of one. He took a hold of my wrist, twisting only enough that I yelped and let go. My head jerked up at the surprise burst of pain, and it reflected in his gunmetal gray eyes. For some reason, I hadn't expected him to hurt me. I guess...I didn't know what I thought.

He pushed me back, and as if he could read my thoughts, he said, "I don't want to."

Fury blasted through me like a rocket. "You *can't* hurt me."

Aiden jerked out of the way as I shot forward. I whirled, delivering a spin kick to the kidneys. I moved to deliver another, but Aiden caught my leg and tossed me back. I hit the ground and popped up, throwing my head back.

Energy slammed into me. Akasha simmered beneath the surface, waiting to be called upon, demanding it.

I flew at Aiden and we went at it—brutally. Mostly on my end, because Aiden was more about the defensive instead of the offensive, but bruises were traded, one after another.

Memories of training together surfaced. I wasn't sure if that was a benefit to either of us, because we anticipated each other's moves and neither of us could gain the upper hand. I dropped and he'd be there to deflect. He moved for a submission hold and I escaped before he could lock me down. Blow for blow we went, and in the back of my head, I knew I could've called upon the elements, but I didn't. Maybe it was all the pent-up rage from being caged for so long, and I needed the physicality of fighting. Maybe it was something else.

Blood trickled from Aiden's lip. A red mark bloomed across his jaw. His shirt was torn along the midsection, exposing a row of taut abs, but he didn't show any signs of slowing down.

Frustrated, I pushed off the tree, gained some air and twisted, realizing my mistake an instant after it was too late. As I spun, Aiden stepped into it, catching me around the waist and spinning me around. In training, I'd never been able to get past him this way. I should've known better.

I tipped my weight forward and we both went down on our knees. I tasted blood, but Aiden hadn't hit me. Not once. But my face had connected with his more than a few times.

"Give up," I growled, throwing my head back.

His arms tightened around me. "You should know by now I'm not going to give up on you. You're not that stupid."

"Can't say the same thing about you." I spread my thighs and gathered my strength. "You can't win."

His breath danced over my check. "You want to bet on that?"

I ground my teeth. "You can't have me. I'm not—"

"You're not his, Alex. You don't belong to anyone but yourself!"

He was wrong, so wrong. I belonged to my Seth. I was created for him, only him, and Aiden was in the way.

Rocking forward, I put enough space between us and powered to my feet, breaking his hold. Throwing my arm back, I caught him across the cheek with a closed fist. The impact bruised my knuckles.

Aiden went down on one knee and spat out a mouthful of blood. "*Gods*."

Spinning around, I started running, ignoring the sharp pebbles digging into the soles of my feet. I made it about five feet before I was tackled from behind.

Aiden pulled me up so that my back was pinned to his chest. "Leaving so quick? When the fun is just getting started?"

"I hate you!" I struggled wildly, trying to dig into the ground. Loose dirt kicked up as I thrashed, becoming more like an animal caught in a net. Hours of training slipped away. "I hate you!"

"You can hate me all you want, but it doesn't change a thing." He made it to his feet and started dragging me backward, and I knew he'd drag me all the way back to the cabin, to the cage. "I'm not going to let you do this to yourself."

I wiggled and threw myself from side to side, but we were back to the cluster of trees within seconds. "You can't stop me! You can't do this!"

"You don't understand, Alex. You can't be out here." I elbowed him. He grunted but didn't let go. "They'll kill you. Do you understand?" He shook me. "They'll come to kill you!"

"I don't care!" I screamed myself hoarse. "I need to go. I need to be with him."

Aiden sucked in a sharp breath and his grip loosened a fraction.

Using my core, I pulled my legs up and the combined effort toppled us over. Aiden hit the ground first and rolled before I could break free, shoving his hands into my back, forcing me down. I got a mouthful of mud and grass.

"Stop it!" he hissed in my ear. "This isn't going to work, Alex. You may not care about dying, but I care enough for you."

"I don't care! All that matters is Seth. If I can't be with him, then I'd rather be dead."

"Do you even hear yourself?" His hands pressed into my shoulders. "You'd rather die than not be with him? Do you know how weak that is? The Alex I know would never feel something like that!" What he said reached deep and broke *something* inside me. Enraged, I planted my hands in the rich soil and felt the earth tremble. A great roar started below, and the ground buckled under us, rolling like stormy seas. We were thrown apart. I smacked into a tree and hit the ground on my hands and knees.

Lightning pierced the sky, blinding me for an instant. Clouds rolled in, blocking the sun, and darkness fell. The skies opened and a torrential downpour pounded us.

I didn't know if it was me or something else. I was beyond caring. A giant ball of messy emotion settled in my stomach, unraveling with dizzying speeds. Anger. Frustration. Fear. All of it rushed me.

Air whipped under me and I rose off the ground. Static charged. Sparks flew. The world was colored in amber tones. I wasn't me. I wasn't anything anymore.

Aiden stood a few feet away, his silvery eyes fixed on me. A look of horror and awe marked his striking features.

I was a god, like Seth had said. We were gods.

Do it. Seth's whisper penetrated my blood. *It's time.*

My feet touched the ground and I took a step forward—one, and then another. And Aiden didn't move. He waited. It was in those eyes of his, the finality of this. He wouldn't win, he couldn't and he knew it. Aiden accepted it.

As I reached him, the rain stopped and the clouds parted. The sun followed my footsteps. "Alex." Aiden's voice was broken.

Like a cobra striking, I took Aiden's legs out from under him, and he was on his back before another breath could be taken. Straddling him, I placed my hands on his shoulders. The marks of the Apollyon glowed a vibrant blue and raced over my skin.

I leaned in, placing my lips above his, and the words that came out of my mouth were mine…but weren't. "All moments end, St. Delphi. And now yours has." I pressed my lips to the corner of his and he flinched. "You are weak because you love."

Aiden stared up at me, unblinking. "To love is not weak. Love is the strongest thing there is."

My lips curved into a smile. Idiot.

Akasha raced to the surface. My skin was on fire, *I* was on fire. Bright blue light formed over my right arm, circling it as it climbed down to my fingers. Light flared, as intense and beautiful as it was destructive.

Sunlight fell over us, and I reared back. Akasha covered

my right hand. When I let it go, it would snuff out the life of everything in its path. There was death in that beauty. And Aiden made no move to defend his life.

His eyes fixed on mine and he reached up slowly. The tips of his fingers, calloused over from years of training and fighting, grazed my cheek tenderly. "I love you, Alex. I always will."

I blinked. My heart stuttered. I couldn't wrap my head around how he could say that, touch me so…so lovingly, seconds from death.

Do it, Alex, and then we can be together. We'll free the halfs—your father. We'll change the world. You and me, Angel, we'll be together always.

My gaze fell between us. The rose necklace had slipped out, exposed by the torn collar of my shirt. A ray of light caught the deep-red crystal edges of the rose in bloom—such a delicate thing, crafted by the hands of a true warrior.

Air left my lungs and my arm started to shake.

We're in this together, Alex, to the end. Those words weren't Seth's, but this *was* the end. My eyes burned like it was raining acid, but the skies were clear. I was seconds from freedom… but so much, so many memories started flipping through my head.

I couldn't stop staring at the rose.

Images of the first time I'd seen Aiden while I'd been training with Caleb, then again when he'd come through the wall of fire and saved me—saved my life. Memories of his patience, his support, even his frustration with me.

Seth called to me, but I swatted him away. These memories were important. They meant something—everything—to me, right? There hadn't been any feelings attached to them before, but now they were soaked in emotion. I focused on them, remembering how he'd cared for me after Gatlinburg, how he'd been there for me when I broke down after Mom…*my mom.* The first time he'd held me—kissed me. There was never any judgment in Aiden's eyes, like I was his equal.

I'd always been Aiden's equal.

My chest rose sharply. The day at the zoo washed over me, and then Valentine's Day. The love we had shared. It had to mean something.

I couldn't breathe.

I'd give it all up for you.

Seth called for me again, but I was breaking apart. Shattering. Everything was coming undone. Pieces of who I used to be were repelled by what I'd become. The past and the present couldn't coexist with the future.

I was torn in two.

Seth yelled now, his voice roaring in my head, and there was no escaping him. He was everywhere, in every cell and thought, pulling at me. But I couldn't breathe and under me, *he* was under me, and I couldn't think straight. There were so many voices again. So many different ones, some were my own…and I couldn't *think.*

I focused on the mental shields Seth had taught me. I needed a moment, just a second of silence to think this through, to understand why *he* wasn't defending himself and how *he* could love me.

Seth was furious. Pain sliced through my skull as if someone had taken an ice pick and started slamming it into my head, and I knew he hated this, but I needed *time.* He screamed for me, but I pictured those walls. They were neon-pink, bedazzled walls, and they went up, stacked higher and higher. I made them thick and full of titanium, topped them off with barbed wire and threw a nice little electrical fence over them, and all of that was backed by the power of the gods. A film of shimmery blue light draped over the walls.

The cord snapped inside me, recoiling like whiplash, and then it was gone.

Except for a low hum, there was silence, and it was just me now, alone with everything I had done.

Tipping my head back, I screamed.

Unlocked from the depths of my soul, it kept coming and coming. I couldn't stop it. I couldn't comprehend what I'd become—the things I had done. And when I stopped, it was only because my throat was raw.

I scrambled off of Aiden, unable to look at him, because I…the things…

Body trembling, I crawled over the muddy ground and tucked into a ball against a tree. Pressing my face to my knees, I dragged in breaths, but my chest ached and the pressure kept building.

"Alex?" Aiden called out, his voice hoarse and ragged.

I shied away, wanting him to leave. He needed to leave me, to run away as fast as he could. Strong hands landed on my shoulders and then slid over my arms, gently wrapping around my wrists. He pried my hands away, and even though I couldn't bear to look at him, my eyes opened.

It was like seeing Aiden after months of separation. He was clear to me. The curve of his broad cheekbones, the hint of dimples, and the strong line of his jaw—features I'd committed to memory eons ago. Dark waves curled over his naturally tan skin…skin marred by bruises and streaks of crimson. Bruises I'd given him, but he still held that masculine beauty that always undid me.

Aiden shuddered, and then clasped my cheeks. His silver

eyes searched mine. They were covered in a fine sheen—like tears, but Aiden never cried. "Alex...oh, gods, Alex, are you here?"

I burst into tears.

CHAPTER SEVEN

Yeah, I wasn't going to stop crying anytime soon. These were the big, body-shaking, embarrassing kind of sobs. The ones I really couldn't think or see around—hell, even breathe around. Aiden held me through it, his arms a strange and grounding contact. He murmured words in ancient Greek. I picked up agapi mou several times, and the rest made as much sense as the words I tried to speak around the sobs. I knew that I'd be able to understand them now if I weren't choking on my tears, but I could barely understand English at the moment.

I soaked Aiden's shirt.

And he still held me against his chest as he leaned against the tree, smoothing back my hair, pressing his cheek against the top of my head. He rocked us. We both needed it, I think.

There were footsteps and voices at some point and I stiffened in his arms. I didn't know who came, but I felt Aiden shake his head, and then the footsteps retreated.

Gods, I could think—really think—after what felt like forever. But every thought was overshadowed by the pain inside me. The sharp spearing I'd felt in the bathroom—I understood it now. My heart and my soul had been screaming out, trying to reach me. That pain was everywhere now, clamping down on me from all sides.

I couldn't escape all the things I'd said and done since I Awakened. From the moment I'd connected with Seth, I'd turned into a living, breathing embodiment of my worst fear and I hadn't even realized it. Seth and what he wanted had consumed me until there had been nothing left, and I'd thought I was stronger than that.

Oh gods, the things I'd said to Aiden horrified and sickened me. The things Seth had said he wanted to do to me—that I'd wanted him to do, back when we'd been connected… now I wanted to crawl out of my skin, to shower for years, and I didn't think I'd ever feel the same again even then.

How Aiden could still hold me was beyond my comprehension. I clearly remembered threatening to kill Deacon about twenty times. My behavior had forced him to do the unthinkable—place me on the Elixir. I knew that had to have killed a part of him.

I remembered all the little things. *My Seth?* Oh, yuck. I wanted to scrub out my brain with detergent. And those things I'd yelled when I fought Aiden—actually fought *Aiden*? Scrub my brain? Add mouth and soul to that laundry list.

"Shh," Aiden murmured, smoothing a hand along my back. "It's okay. Everything is okay, *agapi mou*. You're here now and I have you."

I gripped the collar of his torn shirt with my aching hands. "I'm so sorry. I'm sorry, Aiden. I'm sorry."

"Stop." He leaned back, but I followed him, keeping my face pressed to his chest. "Alex." I shook my head, my breath catching on another sob. "Look at me."

Tears streamed down my face, and he carefully cradled my cheeks, forcing me to look up. I wanted to squeeze my eyes shut, but I also needed to see him, even if it was just his blurry face right now.

"How can you look at me?" I asked. "How can you stand to touch me?"

His brows furrowed and he became very serious. "How could I not, Alex? I don't blame you for what happened. The things you did and said weren't you. I know that. I've always known that."

"But it *was* me."

"No." His voice was firm, eyes pure silver. "It was a shell of you, Alex. You were there, in the background, but it wasn't you. It wasn't the Alex I love, but you're here now and that's all that matters. That's it. Nothing else does."

His blind faith in me, his acceptance and forgiveness, brought forth another round of waterworks. I cried so much that I didn't think I could ever cry again, and when it was finally over, I couldn't lift my head from his chest.

The sun was starting to set, and the temperature was dropping when Aiden pressed his lips against the top of my head. "Are you ready?"

No, I wanted to say, because I wasn't sure I'd ever be ready to face everyone. Besides turning into Evil Alex, I'd also been dopey, hiding-in-closets Alex.

But I drew in a breath and it felt okay, good even. "Okay."

"Okay," he repeated, and he stood, keeping me nestled close to his chest, my cheek resting on his shoulder.

Aiden took one step, and a fissure of unnatural energy rolled down my spine—godly energy. The marks of the Apollyon roared to life, whipping over my skin. His arms stiffened around me as he turned, lifting his head to the sky.

Gods could shield their presence if they wanted to—Apollo had for months—but we both felt the ripple of power.

"This isn't good," I said, stirring in his arms.

He placed me on my feet, his hands on my hips. One look into his stormy eyes and I knew he was thinking the same thing.

Before he could open his mouth, a high-pitched wail rattled the branches overhead. Air around us stilled, and then the sound of wings beating pulled the breath from my lungs in a painful rush.

Aiden shoved me behind him—actually shoved *me* behind *him*. "Go back to the house now, Alex. The wards will keep them out."

What? And leave him? He was insane. Heart leaping into my throat, I shook my head. "No. No—"

Another shriek turned my blood ice-cold. Then a great howl barreled through the trees, blowing my hair back from my face.

The furies arrived, darting down to Earth like heat-seeking missiles with "Alex" written all over them. Each hit the ground in a crouch, knocking up plumes of dirt and small pebbles.

They were beautiful—the two furies. All pale and shimmering skin and long, flowing blond curls as they rose simultaneously, their bodies moving sinuously as one stepped forward, her bare feet sinking deep into the soil.

Thunder cracked the air and a flash of blinding light exploded. Throwing up my arm, I stumbled back and reached out for Aiden. Pulse pounding, my fingers wrapped around his thick forearm.

When the light receded, a god stood between the two furies, and my heart felt like it stopped right then and there. I'd seen him before. Oh, gods, I'd seen him.

Honey-colored hair brushed his shoulders, framing a square, defiant chin and features that were angelic and pure—peaceful, even.

Thanatos.

Electricity sparked from his all-white eyes. "I may not be able to kill you, Apollyon, but I can make sure you cannot reach the First."

"Wait!" Aiden yelled, one hand curling around the hilt of the dagger. "She's broken—"

The furies flew forward, luminous skin shedding away to reveal ghastly gray complexions that resembled corpses that had been floating in the water waaay too long. Long, glowing hair shriveled up and turned into tight coils that snapped at the air with vicious fangs around their skeletal faces. Claws formed—talons that could rip through bone and tissue like they were paper.

They came right at us.

Aiden lurched to the side and twisted toward me. "Alex!" He threw one of the daggers.

Leaping up, I caught the dagger as the first furie reached Aiden, its razor-sharp nails aimed right for his throat. He spun around, whipping out a sickle blade. In one smooth, elegant motion he brought the sharp edge of the blade down, severing the arm of the furie.

It keened a mixture of a baby's scream and a hyena's as it arched up, clutching its bloody stump. Damn.

With absolutely no time to run over to Aiden and give him a high-five, I pivoted and dipped as the second furie made a grab for my hair. Shooting up at the same moment the furie dive-bombed me, I shoved the blade deep into its sunken stomach.

Its distorted face inches from mine, the furie opened its mouth, revealing a row of serrated teeth, and laughed.

I bit back a gag. "Gods, your breath is kicking." I pulled the blade free, revolted by the sucking sound. "For real."

Cocking its head to the side, it blinked. "Kicking?"

"Yeah." Spinning around, I planted my left foot and kicked out, catching the furie in the stomach.

It flew back, smacking into the tree. "See? Kicking."

The other furie was going at Aiden with its one good arm, backing him up while avoiding the dangerous sickle. He glanced over at me and that tiny moment cost him.

She knocked the sickle out of his hand with a cackle. "Pretty pure-blood…"

Forgetting about the god and the other furie, forgetting about everything other than Aiden, I raced forward, ignoring the ache building in my legs.

Aiden dipped under the furie's sweeping arm, popping up behind her, but she turned wicked fast and swung out, hitting Aiden along the chest with the broad side of her arm.

He went down on one knee, staggered by the blow.

Swiping the sickle off the ground, I yelled his name and repaid the favor by tossing the sickle to him. Aiden snapped it out of the air and rolled, narrowly missing the furie. It flew up and flipped over him, reaching down, grabbing a handful of his hair. She yanked his head back.

"No!" My heart stopped—my world stopped.

Akasha surged under my skin and the marks brightened. Each and every one of them burned and tingled with the power of the fifth element.

Something snapped inside me; my vision dimmed, and then brightened. I heard nothing but my own thundering heart and the hum in the back of my head.

Throwing my arm out, a bolt of intense blue light flared from my open palm and arced. My aim was off since I was going for the bitch's head, but the bolt of energy clipped the furie's wing, whirling her around.

Absolute insanity broke out.

Thanatos roared his rage. The furie shot into the air, but sputtered out with one wing and came spinning back down. Aiden darted to the side, but not fast enough. He was weary from fighting me, just like I was from fighting him, and she crashed into him. They rolled in a tangle of arms, blades, and deadly sharp claws.

Out of the corner of my eye, I saw forms cresting the hill—Solos and Marcus bearing sickle blades.

Marcus? What the…?

I shot toward the wrestling forms before me.

Thanatos whipped around and extended an arm. He didn't physically touch Solos, but boy did he fly like he'd been smacked with a cannonball. The half-blood Sentinel hit the tree with a loud grunt and dropped to his knees.

The god turned his creeptastic eyes on my uncle and raised another hand. "Stand down, pure-blood, or you shall meet an untimely fate."

Marcus lowered his chin. "Sorry, but that's my niece, so that's not going to happen."

Something with sharp claws and rank breath caught hold of my hair and pulled hard. I hit the ground and in a heartbeat, air punched from my lungs. Scrambling to my knees, a second passed and the furie's bare foot connected with my chin, snapping my head back.

A metallic taste flooded my mouth. The dagger flew from my hands as pain radiated down my spine, exploding out over my nerves.

Panic dug in—raw, unbridled panic.

All around me the sounds of fighting escalated. There

were grunts and yelps of pain. The furie that had kicked me into next week reared up, her fingers splaying. I stared, numb and unflinching as death…

Death? It struck me then. They couldn't kill me. Yeah, they could put a serious hurting on me, but kill me? No. I was the Apollyon. I wielded control over the four elements and the fifth and the most powerful—akasha. I fueled the God Killer. I was his power-up—the ace up his sleeve. I was the beginning and he was the end. And together… There was no together.

There was just me.

My eyes locked with the furie's and I smiled. She hesitated. I snapped to my feet. "Bitch, please."

The furie's mouth gaped open, and I summoned the air element, letting it go. The hurricane-force winds smacked into the furie and sent her flying back through the trees as if she were connected to a rope and Zeus himself had given a good old pull.

"One down," I said, turning around. "Who's ne—?"

Thanatos tossed Marcus to the ground, deflected Solos's attack, and turned on me in a nanosecond.

It was pretty epic.

A bolt of white light flew from Thanatos's hand and there wasn't a single thing in this world that could move fast enough to avoid it. Not even Seth, I was betting.

It hit me just below the chest, and my legs collapsed from underneath me. Red-hot, searing pain sliced through my skin and my face smacked on the ground. I didn't even feel it. There was nothing but the razing pain locking up my muscles.

God-bolts *sucked*.

Aiden yelled my name, and then I thought I heard my name called again, but it was inside my head, loud, and so very angry…and it sounded like Seth.

Without any warning, the ground trembled under my twitching body. A flash of golden light cascaded through the clearing. Warmth stole over my body. Weakly, I lifted my head.

Two leather-clad legs stood before me.

"That is enough, Thanatos." Apollo's voice was calm, but it was that creepy, deadly calm I never wanted to be on the receiving end of.

"N-n-nice of y-you to s-show up," I gasped.

"Shut up, Alex." Apollo strode forward. A ray of light followed his steps.

Thanatos held his ground. "She must be neutralized if we cannot kill her. Let me take care of this, Apollo. We must do something to prevent war."

"She broke the bond, you idiot."

The other god huffed. "Like that matters. Time will pass and she will connect with him again."

"It does matter!" Apollo roared. "If she is not connected with the First, we are not to harm her! You—" Apollo growled at the increasingly close sound of hissing. "Call your two furies off or they will join their sister. I promise you."

"We must—"

Too weak to hold my head up, I rested my forehead against the ground, but I didn't need to see what happened to know that Apollo had lost his patience. Wind picked up and the ground shook. The two gods collided with a crack.

I closed my eyes and hoped that Apollo had won this round, because there was no way I was fighting anymore. No way at all.

Someone was body-slammed into the ground, followed by a quick succession of pops. The air crackled with electricity, and then silence, blissful silence.

Strong hands gripped my arms and gently rolled me onto my back. I stared up into silver eyes. "Alex?"

"I'm okay. Just...just a little twitchy. You?"

Aiden had seen better days. Blood trickled out of the corner of his mouth. A bruise shadowed his jaw and the front of his shirt was torn, but he was alive and he was okay.

His gaze scanned over me and then he lifted me up, not even bothering to put me on my feet.

Holding me close, he turned and I surveyed the damage.

Solos and Marcus stood near Apollo, who held one of the Covenant daggers in his hand. Blood dripped from the edge, making me stare.

Apollo glanced down at it and shrugged. "He'll get over it." I changed focus and stared at him.

"But I'm going to have to answer for that, I think." Apollo handed the dagger to a bruised Solos.

"And it may take a few days..."

Apollo stalked forward, stopping in front of us, and Aiden placed me down and stepped between us. The god smirked. "I know she's broken the bond. Good to have you back, Alex."

"Yeah," I breathed.

He turned his attention to Aiden. "Keep the wards on the house until I can return. In the meantime, prepare for battle."

Battle? What the hell did he think we'd just done? Aiden nodded.

The god took a breath and flexed his hands. "And you were right. I was wrong."

"I know," Aiden said, and I glanced up, confused.

Apollo turned to the other men and nodded. His form started to fade.

"Wait," I called out. There were so many questions I had, but all he did was look over his shoulder and smile.

CHAPTER EIGHT

I don't remember much of the trek back to the cabin. At some point, I'd wiggled enough to get free and walk, but I was moving so slowly and so pathetically that Aiden had finally stopped grumbling under his breath and picked me back up.

I didn't fight it after that. On my feet, I was more of a hindrance.

The cabin was quiet upon our return. Marcus and Solos had limped off, no doubt to tend to their injuries. Somehow the rest of the occupants knew that right now wasn't time for a welcome back to the world of the sane and logical. Aiden carried me up the stairs and down the narrow hall, toward the bedroom he'd slept in when I'd been on the Elixir. I remembered that, even when I'd been high on the happy drink, I'd sought out his presence and snuggled against him on the couch. My heart tripped up.

Aiden started toward the bed, but I stopped him. "Shower," I said hoarsely. "I need a shower."

"Yeah, you kind of do—we both do." Pivoting around,

he headed for the bathroom. There he placed me on my feet, his eyes shadowed with concern when I swayed a little. "Are you okay?"

"Yeah, I'm just tired. There's nothing seriously wrong with me." And that was true. I was bruised and sore, but that was all. And I was lucky, considering we'd just been in a death match with a God of Death and two furies. "Are you…?"

"I'm fine." He stared a moment, then pressed a kiss on my cheek. "I'll be right back."

"Okay." I was a zombie on my feet.

His eyes searched my face with such stark relief that I gripped the sink. "Don't hog all the hot water, all right?" he said.

That brought a small smile to my lips. As soon as he left, I turned slowly to the shower and twisted the faucets. Pulling off my ruined clothing was a painful experience. Every muscle ached, and it took a few minutes. By the time I stepped into the stall, steam filled the bathroom.

I was probably going to use a week's worth of hot water while Aiden most likely was rallying the troops and convincing them that I wasn't a sociopath anymore.

I shivered under the stream, pressing my face to my hands. They shook. I shook. I moved them to the chain around my neck, slid my fingers to the rose. Something so small had been the one thing to break the connection.

It wasn't the rose itself, but what it symbolized—Aiden's love for me and how I felt for him—something pure and natural, an emotion not forced. Seeing that had broken the bond between Seth and I.

Bringing the crystal to my lips, I pressed a kiss against the rose.

The bond *was* broken, but Seth was still there…at the end of the cord slumbering in the pit of my stomach. Gods, he'd been so furious, murderous really, but shock had rippled through our bond the second before it had ended. And then again, when Thanatos had hit me with the god-bolt, he had been *there* like a creepy stalker with a one-way ticket to my brain.

Seth hadn't believed I'd be capable of breaking the bond. And how far would this have gone if I hadn't?

They'll come to kill you. And although Thanatos didn't have the juice to carry it out, he sure as hell didn't have a problem putting a hurting on me—or anyone who defended me. People could've died today because of me.

I sucked in a sharp breath.

And why had Aiden blocked Apollo from the cabin? What happened to that love-fest?

Gods, there were so many questions, and I was too weary for this right now. I needed a moment to regroup. I *needed* a bed after this shower.

Water streamed over my body, over skin that was as bruised as my insides, and plastered my hair to my back. Closing my eyes, I lifted my chin and let the showerhead do its thing, erasing the tears that had clung to my lashes with a death grip, clearing my mind of everything.

There would be time to ask those questions, to plan Seth's very painful death, and to find my father, but right now, I just couldn't do it. I couldn't think about anything other than right now, right this moment, because everything was too raw and too fresh to delve into.

I heard the bathroom door close and I kept my eyes screwed shut, but my heart rate skyrocketed into uncharted territories. I folded my arms around me and held my breath.

There was the slightest movement behind me. Skin brushed against mine. A fine shiver rolled up my spine. An infinite spark transferred between us, something that couldn't be replicated or forced. How could I've forgotten that when connected with Seth? My heart turned over heavily.

Aiden brushed the mass of thick hair over one shoulder and his lips met the space between my neck and shoulder. His hands slid down the slick skin of my arms, cupping over my elbows and then to my wrists. Gently, slowly, he eased my arms to my sides.

I bit down on my lip and my legs started trembling. But he was there. Like always, holding me up when I couldn't stand and letting me go when he knew I needed him to. He was more than just a shelter. Aiden *was* my other half, my equal. And he needed no weird Apollyon connection.

Aiden waited, still as a statue, patient as ever, until my muscles unlocked, one by one. Then his hands dropped to my waist and he turned me toward him. A heartbeat passed and he placed his fingers on my chin, tipping my head back.

I opened my eyes, blinking the wetness off my lashes, and the air hitched in my throat. Faint, purplish bruises shadowed his jaw. There was a cut over the bridge of his nose. No doubt injuries I had given him.

"I'm so sorry, Aiden." My voice cracked. "I can't say it enough. I know, but I'm so—"

He dipped his head and his mouth brushed mine, silencing my words. My lips opened to his, as did my heart and everything else. The sweet and tender kiss, well, it lessened the heaviness, eased some of the guilt and shame. My skin—my insides—were scraped and aching, but his touch soothed the frayed edges. I imagined it was the same for Aiden. Gods, it was probably worse for him, considering everything I had done and said. What he'd had to do, to sacrifice, to keep me safe.

The kiss deepened, flipping and twisting my insides into a pleasant mess, and it was like the very first time we'd kissed.

Sensations raced over my skin, my heart sang, and the feeling unfurling in the pit of my stomach was better than tapping into akasha, stronger and more addicting. He kissed me like he'd never expected to do so again, as if he could somehow kiss away the weeks.

I placed my hands on his upper arms. His muscles coiled under them as he lifted me up and I wrapped my legs around him. Desire wasn't the only thing between us. There was so much more: forgiveness, acceptance, relief, and most importantly, love.

Not the kind of love that was fueled by need and that destroyed cities and entire civilizations, but the kind that rebuilt them, that much I knew.

Keeping an arm around my waist, his other hand tangled in my wet hair. And we didn't stop kissing, because this was *right* and that was all that mattered. My heart was pounding way too fast, but it was perfect, like coming home after never believing I'd be able to.

I don't know how we made it to the bed or if the water was ever turned off in the shower. But we were together, our bodies slippery, our wet hair soaking the sheets we were tangled in. And then *we* were tangled, our legs and arms. His hands were everywhere, paying reverence to the many scars on my body. His lips followed, and I grew reacquainted with the hard muscles of his stomach, the feel of him.

I glanced down at my body, surprised to see the marks of the Apollyon glowing faintly as they swirled across my skin, forming one rare symbol and then another.

"What?" Aiden cupped my cheek, drawing my eyes back to his. "Is this too fast? I should—"

"No. No, it's…it's the marks of the Apollyon. They're kind of doing their thing right now."

"Should I be worried?"

I laughed self-consciously, feeling like one of those venomous snakes that warned of its poison in its vibrant colors. "I think they like you."

Aiden's hand slid off my cheek, down my throat, to right below my chest. The marks slid toward his hand, as if drawn to him. Maybe they were. I wasn't sure how the marks worked. The answer probably lay in the thousands of years of memories, but that was like digging for a needle in a pile of needles.

"I saw them," he said, his voice raw and deep and his eyes like pools of liquid silver. "When you Awakened, and when you went on the Elixir." His brows drew tight as he smoothed his hand over my hip. "They were beautiful."

"Really?" I felt beautiful when he looked at me, even all tattooed up.

"Yes. It was the most beautiful thing I'd ever seen."

A long, agonizing moment passed as he hovered above me, his eyes locked onto mine, his body coiled tight like a rope ready to snap. And when he did, his lips found mine and there was a sound that came from the back of his throat that seared me. Our bodies met and for a few moments, neither of us moved, and then we did, our voices soft whispers in the dark room.

Sometime later, we lay facing each other, his hand wrapped around my smaller one. Our bodies were pressed close. Exhaustion dogged me now, and Aiden, too—it had been for weeks. The fighting and everything else had tipped us over the edge. Sleep claimed me first. I only knew this because I could feel Aiden's gaze on my face, and seconds before I slipped away I felt his lips on my forehead.

I heard him whisper, "Eíste pánta mou…"

You are my everything.

CHAPTER NINE

No matter how convoluted my life got, one thing remained consistent—my hair looked like a baby opossum had taken refuge in it, invited some friends over, and thrown a party. That's what I got for sleeping on it wet.

I wrangled it into a thick braid and took a deep breath.

Admittedly, I'd seen better days. Well, my face at least. Most of the damage I'd done to myself. Aiden hadn't raised a hand against me the entire time we'd fought. He'd only defended himself. But we were both lucky to be standing after facing Thanatos and the furies.

My reflection winced.

Aiden was gone by the time I had crawled out of bed. I'd wanted to stay among the covers, inhaling his unique scent of sea and burning leaves, holding the pillow he'd used close to my chest. I'd wanted to wait there until he returned, so I could wrap myself around him, doing a replay of last night.

But reality wasn't going to pause or wait for us. There was way too much to be done, and I needed to face everyone. I took a long breath and pushed away from the mirror. Staring at my face for hours wasn't going to fix anything.

I found the bag of clothes I'd brought with me when I'd stayed at Aiden's parents' house and Aiden had the sense to take when we left Deity Island. There were some items in there I hadn't packed or noticed before—one of them being a Sentinel uniform. That brought a smile to my face. I tugged on a pair of jeans, surprised to find how loose they were. Slipping on a pair of boots that were nothing like Olivia's, I went to the doorway and flinched. *Olivia.* Oh, dear gods, I'd used a compulsion on her. I seriously hoped she wasn't still in the basement.

I crept down the silent hall, scrubbing at the itchy bruise on my cheek. I didn't even know what month we were in. It had been cool but not freezing when I'd been outside yesterday. Hell. I didn't even know where I was.

Grabbing the middle of my braid, I went down the steps, fiddling with the ropey sections. At the bottom of the stairs, I caught sight of a tall Sentinel with brown hair pulled into a low ponytail. Solos. As far as I recalled, I hadn't threatened him with bodily harm—at least, not to his face.

He turned at the waist. "Well, look who's back."

My cheeks flushed and I stopped on the landing, wholly unsure of what to say.

Solos smiled, and it distorted the scar that cut deep into his cheek. "I'm not going to bite, little one."

Heat now swept over my body and I raised my chin. Gods, what was wrong with me? "Good. Because I bite back."

"That's what I hear." His blue eyes glimmered. Now I flushed for a whole new reason. "I'm sure you're hungry. You've slept for almost a whole day. Everyone's in the kitchen now."

My stomach growled at the thought of food, but then soured. "There's not sharp silverware or anything?"

Solos's laugh was deep and rich. "No. It's a takeout night, so you're in luck."

Finding my courage, I followed him down the hallway. He went into the kitchen first, and I peeked around the corner. Deacon and Luke sat on one side, several cartons of Chinese spread out in front of them. Laadan was beside them. Marcus, Lea, and Olivia were across the table. I had no idea where Aiden was.

"We have company," Solos announced, grabbing one of those yummy dumplings and popping it into his mouth.

Everyone turned. And everyone stopped eating and stared.

I let go of my braid and gave the group the most awkward wave ever. "Hi."

Luke dropped his chopsticks into his noodles. There was a nasty bruise on the side of his face, disappearing into his hairline.

"Did I do that?" I stepped into the kitchen. "The bruise?"

"Yeah," he said slowly. "When you slammed me into the wall...without touching me."

I winced. "I'm really sorry about that."

"Aw, don't worry about it." Deacon smiled as he leaned back in his chair, rocking it up on two legs. "He's okay."

"My ego's not." He shot Aiden's brother a dirty look. "She didn't even touch me."

Deacon shrugged. "Well, she *is* the Apollyon. Duh."

A chair scraped over tile and my head jerked toward the sound. Marcus walked around the table and stopped in front of me. Now, I had threatened him quite a bit to his face, but he'd still come to fight yesterday, as had Solos.

I felt horrid.

Marcus placed his hands on my shoulders. There was a fine tremble to them. "Alexandria…"

My uncle had always refused to call me by my nickname, and I'd always called him Dean, due to his position at the Covenant, but things…things were different now. "Marcus?"

There was a long, terse moment, and then he gathered me in a fierce hug. For once, it wasn't an awkward one with my arms stuck out at my sides. I hugged him back, just as tightly, and tears burned the back of my throat.

Marcus and I…well, we'd come a long, long way.

When he pulled back, I bit back a gasp. Those emerald-colored eyes were normally cool, but they weren't now. They were like staring into my mother's eyes.

He inhaled sharply. "I'm glad to have you back."

I nodded, swallowing thickly. "I'm glad to be back."

"Hell, we all can agree on that." Luke picked up a donut. "There's nothing creepier than having a psychotic Apollyon caged in the basement."

"Ha," I said.

Luke winked and then tossed the donut to me. I caught it. Sugar flew everywhere.

"Or waiting for her to break loose and run amuck," Deacon added as I took a bite. He glanced across the table. "Or waiting for someone, no names mentioned, to not listen to us and go say hi."

Olivia's cheeks reddened as she stood. She approached slowly, waited for me to finish chewing.

I started to apologize. "I'm really sorry—"

She socked me in the stomach. *Hard*. I doubled over, gasping for air. "Gods."

Solos and Marcus both stepped forward, but I waved my hand at them. "That's okay. I deserved that."

Then I realized they weren't moving in to protect me, but to guard Olivia. I guessed no one was a hundred percent relaxed around me. Guess I couldn't blame them when I wielded the most powerful weapon on Earth, and only a day ago I'd been willing to use it against them.

"You totally deserved that." Olivia's voice shook. "Do you know how terrible I felt when Marcus came down and found me sitting there like a turd? I helped you escape!"

I thought she might hit me again, so I took a step back.

Olivia smoothed her hands over her tight curls. "But I'm better now, especially since I got to hit you." Then she sprang forward and hugged me.

Standing there, I patted her back, hoping she didn't change her mind and snap my spinal cord. "I'm really sorry."

"I know." She pulled back, smiling. Her eyes were misty.

Laadan was next. The raven-haired beauty was as elegant as ever. Dressed in a form-fitting red turtleneck and white slacks, she enveloped me in a warm hug. She smelled of spring roses, and when she pulled back, I didn't want to let go.

"We'll talk later. Promise," she said, and I knew she was talking about my father. Taking my hand, she pulled me to the empty spot next to Olivia. "Sit. Eat."

Glancing around the table, I watched as a plastic plate was passed around, each person slopping a helping of food on it. Even Lea, who hadn't said a word to me yet, placed some shrimp on the plate.

When it came back to me, my mouth watered, but I had to say something first.

"Guys, I'm really sorry for everything." I glanced down at my plate, but forced my eyes back up. "I know I was a terror and I wish…I wish none of you'd had to go through that."

Marcus returned to his seat. "We know you weren't yourself, Alexandria. We understand."

Beside him, Lea cleared her throat. "I actually preferred the crazy Apollyon version to the Elixired up one, to be honest." She glanced at me, thick lashes hiding amethyst eyes. "That was kind of freaky watching you hide behind Aiden."

"You were pretty different," Luke agreed, and then shuddered. "Man, the Elixir is no joke."

"You hid in a closet," Deacon felt the need to inform me.

Poking at my noodles, I frowned as fragments of my time on the Elixir slid into place. "I bet that was amusing to watch."

"I don't know if I would call it amusing," a new voice added.

My head jerked up and my heart toppled over itself. Aiden stood just inside the kitchen door, dressed as always—as a Sentinel. He stalked toward the table and picked up the carton of brown rice. He leaned against the counter, the curve of his jaw hard, eyes like flint.

They met mine. He gestured at my plate with his carton. "Eat. You need to eat."

Everyone stared at their plates as I picked up the fork I hadn't even realized I'd dropped. I dared a peek at Aiden as I twirled my fork around the noodles. He was watching, always watching.

Deacon offered me a pair of chopsticks. "You shouldn't be using a fork."

I shot him a bland look. "Do I look like I know how to use chopsticks?"

He grinned. "Poser."

"Punk," I retorted.

His eyes rolled. "It's not that hard. Here, let me show you."

Deacon's impromptu chopsticks lesson and my absolute

failure at mastering them eased the sudden awkward tension around the table. Laughing, I gave up when Aiden finally ordered his brother to let me eat in peace.

Digging in, I listened to the conversation around me. The talk was of nothing important, and I figured they were waiting for me to finish eating before the real, necessary conversations took place.

I finished off everything I'd been given, ate the remaining rice that Aiden had dumped on my plate as he prowled around the table, and then finished off the sugary goodness of the donuts.

Stomach full, I leaned back in my chair and sighed. "That hit the spot and then some."

Olivia patted my stomach. "You need it…and probably a couple of Big Macs, too."

My eyes widened. "Mmm, Big Macs…please tell me there's a McDonald's around here? Actually, where am I?"

Everyone grew silent, and no one looked at me.

"What? *What?*" I sat up, looking around the table. And then it hit me. "You guys don't trust me, do you?"

Lea was the first to meet my eyes. "Okay. I'll rain on this happy parade. How do we know you're still not connected to Seth?"

"She's not," Aiden said, picking up the empty cartons and tossing them in a black trash bag he carried. "Trust me, she's not connected to him anymore."

Deacon snorted. I glared at him.

Lea settled back in her chair, folding her arms. "Is there any concrete proof, other than you telling us to trust you?"

Aiden glanced at me and I quickly looked away. I doubted Lea wanted to hear about that kind of proof. "I'm not connected to Seth. I promise you."

"Promises are weak; you could be faking it," she shot back.

"Lea, dear, she has no reason to fake it." Laadan smiled gently. "If she was connected to the First, she wouldn't be sitting here."

"And my brother wouldn't be cleaning up after us, right?"

Deacon slumped back, as if it had just occurred to him that Aiden had been seconds away from death. I wanted to hide under the table as Deacon shook his head, dumbfounded. "Gods, we'd have to get a maid then or something."

Aiden smacked the back of Deacon's head as he passed by. "I feel the love." His brother tipped his head back, grinning.

Taking a breath, I stood and clenched the back of my chair. "I'm not connected to him, and I'm pretty sure he can't get through the shields. But I know he's there. I can feel him."

Aiden stopped and turned to me.

Whoops, better clarify that. "I mean, I can feel him, but he can't reach me, not really. There's just a low-level buzz. Nothing like before. He can't get to me. I'm pretty sure."

"Pretty sure?" Marcus asked, throat working.

I nodded and took another breath. "Look, I can't say that something freaky won't happen. I don't know what he's really capable of, but he's going to have to try really hard to get past these shields."

"You'll be okay," Aiden said. Tying off the garbage bag, muscles popped in his arms. "He won't break through."

Forcing a smile, I knew Aiden believed that. "And you'll know the second he does. I don't think I have the patience to try to fool anyone."

Luke barked out a short laugh. "Don't I know that."

"Let's take the conversation to a more comfortable place,

then." Marcus stood, grasping his glass of what I assumed was wine. I eyed the crystal longingly. "I'm sure all of us have a lot of questions."

The group followed Marcus, but I stayed behind. Picking up the empty cans, I brought them over to the trash can Aiden was placing a fresh bag in.

"Cleaning up?" he asked, fitting the bag to the can. "This is unexpected."

"I'm a new girl." I dumped the cans. "Are you okay?"

Aiden hooked a finger into the belt of my jeans and led me over to the sink. Then he rolled up my sleeves, turned on the tap and picked up the hand soap.

I rolled my eyes, but shoved my hands under the warm water. "Aiden?"

"What? You're going to have sticky hands and be touching everything." He squirted the apple-scented soap on my hands. "You'll leave little fingerprints all over the place."

I watched my hands disappear under his larger ones and sort of forgot about what I was asking. Who knew washing hands could be so…distracting? "Are you concerned about CSI visiting the place?"

"You never know."

I let him finish and then I dried my hands. "Are you okay?"

"Are you?"

I balled my freshly cleaned hands into fists. "Yes, I'm okay. Answer my question."

He tilted his head to the side. "What did you mean earlier about being able to feel Seth?"

So was this what had him suddenly uptight? "You know what it's like when you're in a house with a TV on mute? There's that weird frequency you can feel?" When he nodded, I smiled. "It's like that. He's just there, but he can't reach me."

There was a pause. "Have you had any headaches?"

Confused, I shook my head. "No. Why do you ask?"

"Nothing," he said, and he smiled. "And I'm okay, Alex. I'm the last person you should worry about."

"But I do worry." There was so much to worry about. Turning back to the fridge, I stretched up to grab a bottle of water. As I pulled one down, it revealed another bottle, but it was different.

The contents had been emptied out and replaced with vibrant blue liquid. Aiden's sharp inhale was like a blast of cold air. "Alex—"

Ignoring him, I dropped my bottle and reached for the other one. Hands shaking, I wrapped my fingers around the plastic. I knew what was in the bottle. I knew what harmlessly sloshed around inside would carry a sickeningly sweet aroma and could rob me of who I was in minutes.

Aiden swore under his breath.

Facing him, I held the bottle. "This is the Elixir, isn't it?"

His hand clenched at his side. "It is."

I glanced down at the water bottle. Two fears in life: losing myself to Seth and losing myself to the Elixir. Both had happened, and somehow I'd come back out of those rabbit holes. But holding it in my hands, I couldn't deny the raw taste of fear building in the back of my throat.

It was like holding a bomb—a bomb designed to decay my mind.

Aiden looked like he wanted to rip it from my hands, and I gave a weak smile. "Should we keep it?"

"What?" Tension rolled off him, and something else.

Disgust? Bits and pieces of memories of when I'd been under the Elixir weren't pretty.

"What if we need it again?" I asked, fighting that cold lump in my throat. "Isn't that why you…you all were keeping it?"

"No. I'd placed it there and forgot about it." Then he did take it out of my hands. Moving stiffly, he brought it back to the sink and unscrewed the lid.

"Aiden?"

Without saying a word, he dumped what was left of the Elixir. Sweetness filled the air, rinsed away when he turned on the tap. I hoped he wasn't making a mistake.

I placed my hand on his arm.

Muscles tensed as he stepped into me, placing the tips of his fingers on my chin, but before he could do anything, someone cleared their throat behind us. I turned, spying Solos in the doorway.

"Just making sure you two are okay," he said, a single eyebrow arched.

A rush of shame and guilt smacked into my stomach. "I'm not going to kill him and stash his body in the fridge."

"That's good to know," Aiden muttered.

"One can never be too safe." Solos pivoted. "Chop, chop, kids; people are getting antsy."

I sighed. "Gods, I kind of miss Apollo. At least he didn't think I wanted to kill you."

"Yeah, well, about that…"

I faced Aiden slowly, remembering that Aiden had somehow banned Apollo. "What did you do? You banned him, right? How? Why?"

His brows arched. "I'm not sure you really want to know what provoked that."

Crossing my arms, I waited.

Aiden cocked his head to the side, jaw clenching. "Apollo wasn't completely honest about a lot of things, namely how an Apollyon can be killed."

I had a real bad feeling about this.

"Apollo can kill you, Alex. He was planning to if I took you off the Elixir and you connected with Seth again. And whoever is responsible for Seth can do him in, but it seems like that god may be working with them." He paused, grimacing. "So, I banned Apollo from the house."

My stomach lurched. Yeah, maybe I should've waited on that explanation until after my food had settled.

CHAPTER TEN

After I forced Aiden to drop that little bomb, we went into the large sitting room. I was numb. Apollo could kill me? Apollo had *wanted* to kill me? Then why had he shown up and put a smackdown on Thanatos? Gods, why was I trying to be logical about this? Apollo was a god. Who knew?

I sat beside Deacon and decided to push the Apollo issue aside for right now. "Okay, can I start small? What is today's date?"

Marcus leaned against a desk. I realized then he was in jeans and I couldn't think of a time when I'd ever seen him so casual. "Today is April 5th."

Blinking a couple of times, I sat back. A month…I'd basically lost an entire month. Gods, what was going on in the world outside this cabin? I cleared my throat. "And where am I? If it makes you feel better, you can just tell me the state."

"Apple River," Aiden said, keeping watch by the large picture window.

I folded my arms, which kind of hurt. "Okay, I know you have to be making that name up."

A slight smile formed on Aiden's lips. "It's real. You're in Illinois."

"Illinois?" My brain was stuck on the name Apple River being real.

"And it's about as empty and boring as it sounds," Deacon said, tipping his head at Luke. "And really backwoods. I went out once. Scary. Lumberjacks, enough said."

Solos scoffed. "This is my father's hunting cabin—one of many—and it's not that scary."

I nodded slowly. "Okay. So the gods? How many of them are ticked off right now?"

"All of them." Marcus laughed, swishing the contents of his glass. The smile quickly left his face. "All of them, Alexandria."

"We haven't seen many of the gods, but Hephaestus reinforced the bars," Lea said, studying her nails. "He was kind of scary."

I guessed I'd been out of it when he'd showed. "I can't believe Apollo hit me with a god-bolt."

"I can't believe Aiden punched him," Marcus said, downing the rest of his wine.

"What?" My mouth dropped open. "You did not."

The half grin spread until a dimple appeared in his left cheek. "I did."

"All those times you yelled at me for hitting people, and you hit a *god*?" I couldn't believe it.

That half-grin turned into a full smile. "This was a different situation."

Oh. Okay. Shaking my head, I moved on. "All right, have there been any more attacks like...like what happened to the Covenant?"

Laadan stared at me. "He...he didn't tell you?"

I figured by "he" she meant Seth. "I'm not sure. He kept me out of a lot of stuff."

"Except for telling you that they were working with daimons," she said, and I nodded. She glanced at Marcus and sighed. "A lot has been happening out there, dear. And very little of it is good."

Steeling myself for the worst, I wrapped my fingers around the crystal rose. "Tell me."

"We really don't have to tell you." Lea picked up a slim remote control and twisted, pointing it at a flat-screen on the wall. "We can just show you."

Lea picked one of the nationwide news stations. I didn't think there'd be anything happening right this instant, but apparently so much had happened, it was always on the news.

An image of destroyed buildings and toppled cars streamed over the screen. It was Los Angeles. Three days ago, there had been a catastrophic earthquake, a magnitude 7.0. A day later, another had hit the Indian Ocean, triggering a destructive tsunami that had wiped out an entire island.

And there was more.

Devastating wildfires plagued the Midwest and portions of South Dakota—near the University. I figured Hephaestus's automatons had something to do with that, considering they breathed balls of fire or whatever. There were various skirmishes in the Middle East. Several countries were on the brink of war.

Scrolling along the bottom of the screen was a breaking news announcement—seismic activity had begun below Mount St. Helens. Fears of a full volcanic eruption had people fleeing nearby towns.

Holy baby daimons…

The news anchor was interviewing a doomsday fanatic.

I sat back, soaking it in, horrified by what was happening. All of this because of Seth—and me—and there were so many innocent lives that had been lost, so many more that hung in the balance. There was a good chance I was going to hurl noodles all over the floor.

Lea turned the TV off.

"The gods are responsible for all of that?" I asked. Laadan nodded.

Man, the gods *were* pissed.

"There is more," she said gently, and a mad laugh bubbled up in my throat. How could there be more? "So many Sentinels have been killed by Lucian's…by his army. And many pure-bloods have simply disappeared. Those who have reached the Covenants are holding strong, but no one is safe. Then there are the occurrences with mortals that look like wild animal attacks, but we believe them to be the work of the daimons. It appears they are trying to provoke the gods."

At some point, Aiden had moved to stand behind the couch. His hands were on the back of the cushion. His presence was comforting, but I was shocked to the core. Apollo could have appeared in front of me and done a naked jig and I wouldn't have blinked an eye. Seth hadn't mentioned any of this, but Aiden *had* tried to tell me while I was in the cage.

And I'd told him I didn't care.

I started to stand, but my legs wouldn't cooperate.

"It's a lot to swallow, huh?" Luke said as he stared at his black boots. "The world's gone to shit in about a month's time."

"It's not too late. The gods are showing us what they want." Lea sounded entirely too mature to be the girl I'd thrown an apple at a couple of months ago. "They want Seth dead."

I knew that wasn't so much the case. They wanted one of

us dead, preferably before we came within hugging distance. I racked my brain for something useful. After I'd Awakened, I'd learned the history of all the Apollyons, but none of that was useful. None of it except something with Solaris…

"It's just not as simple as killing Seth." Solos scratched at the stubble on his chin. "There is the problem of getting close. Dionysus said that Lucian had many Sentinels and Guards, mostly halfs."

Dionysus? How in the world had he come into the picture? Wasn't he the god of drunks or something?

"And if we get too close—if Alex gets too close, then…" Marcus trailed off.

Then he would take my power, possibly even drain me, because I now wasn't sure Seth could stop if he wanted to. No matter what he'd said to me while we were connected, I couldn't rely on his promises—his sales pitch—because I really didn't believe Seth knew what he was doing.

I stood then, because I couldn't sit anymore. Walking to the window, I stared at the shadowy landscape as I twisted the necklace between my fingers. Night had fallen and, even with my souped-up eyesight, the trees were dark and ominous. My reflection stared back at me, pale and unfamiliar. It was me—Alex, slightly rounded cheeks and wide lips. With the exception of the freaky amber eyes, I looked the same.

But I felt different.

There was a stillness *in* me that had never been there before. I didn't really know what it meant yet.

"Then what do we do?" Luke asked. "Hide Alex forever?"

My lips twisted into a grim smile. That wasn't going to work.

"I could get behind that as long as someone brings in a game system," Deacon joked, but it fell flat. "Or not…"

There was a pause, and then Lea said, "Please gods, tell me you're not still against killing Seth."

"Now is probably not the best time to go there," Marcus said.

"What?" I heard her come to her feet, and her anger blasted the room. "Alex, you have to understand, especially after everything he's done to you."

"Lea," Aiden snapped, finally getting involved in the conversation.

"Don't 'Lea' me. Seth has to die, and Alex is the only person who can do it!"

Dropping the necklace, I faced them. "I know...he needs to be dealt with. I understand that." Everyone, including Aiden, stared at me. He started to speak but closed his mouth.

Truth be told, I loathed the idea of killing anything at this point. Didn't mean I wouldn't do it when I faced a daimon again, and even though Seth had been a real bastard about things, I knew that deep down he was nothing more than an unloved little boy who wanted acceptance. And yeah, he had a major akasha addiction, but he was a victim in all of this, too. The only person I'd probably enjoy taking out, just a little bit, was Lucian. Yeah, I could get behind that.

But getting to Lucian wasn't going to happen.

"Alex," Marcus said softly.

I took a breath, unable to put forth the words necessary for what needed to be said. "What do we do?" I glanced at Aiden and then Solos. They were the skilled Sentinels here. Time for some battle strategy, which wasn't my strong suit, because I was more of a "run into things headfirst and face-plant a wall" type of fighter. "We have to stop Seth and Lucian, but we can't just walk up to them. We need to be able to get close without them knowing, and we—*I* need to know how to fight Seth without transferring my power to him."

Aiden looked like he didn't like the sound of that, but he turned to Solos and nodded. "Apollo said that it may take a few days for him to come back, but he asked that we don't lift the wards until he can come to us. Those wards prevent them from finding us, and right now they are the *only* thing stopping the gods from finding us."

"How did Thanatos find me?" I asked, curious.

"You went outside, beyond the wards," Aiden said. "Hopefully Apollo can tell us more when he returns."

"So we wait in here until then and do nothing?" Lea slumped against the cushion, crossing her arms. A petulant look crossed her face.

"We don't sit and do nothing," Solos said, eyeing the girl. "What we need to do is train and prepare for what…for what's coming. That's what Apollo wanted."

Because something *was* coming, and it was a war.

"Hopefully Apollo can convince the gods to lay off," Aiden said, jaw working. "Right now, we need the gods on our side."

"Agreed," half the room said.

Hope flickered in my chest. "Do you think they'll stop this…zombie-apocalypse-in-the-making if they realize I'm back on Team Not-Insane?"

No one really looked hopeful, but Aiden smiled at me, and I knew he did it to make me feel better, because it was what I wanted to hear. It took everything in me not to cross the room and jump him.

Priorities, Alex, priorities…

Everyone agreed on starting training as soon as possible. And it made sense. Fighting was not like riding a bicycle.

Muscles weakened, reflexes slowed. Honestly, we had no other choice. Hopefully no other gods showed up, dishing out some good old god wrath.

I sat on the edge of the couch and started fiddling with the rose again. I knew everyone was waiting to hear any plans Seth had shared with me. They were going to be disappointed. "The only thing Seth told me about was the daimons, and he knew I'd told Aiden afterward. I don't think he was too concerned. He really didn't tell me anything else. The plans he… the plans we made were about freeing my father."

Laadan's eyes dampened, and I hoped we could talk soon. There was so much I had to ask her.

Solos didn't even try to hide his displeasure. "Well, that's not really helpful."

"It's not her fault," Aiden shot back.

The Sentinel cracked a distorted smile. "Simmer down, lover boy."

My mouth opened to deny that Aiden was my lover boy. The response was immediate, inherent in nature. I forced my mouth closed before I could say anything. Everyone in this room already knew that Aiden and I were *together* together. Hell, everyone in the world probably guessed, courtesy of Lucian's announcement before Seth blew up the Council, which had made Aiden Public Enemy Number Two.

It was odd being so open about it, though—not odd in a bad way, but something that would take me a little while to get used to. I wasn't Aiden's dirty little secret.

I'd never been his dirty little secret.

Deacon laughed. "Oh, you're *so* going to be the next person who gets hit. I'm putting money on that."

"You need to add yourself to that list." Aiden looked about seventy-percent serious.

"And I'm putting money on *that*," Luke threw in.

I shot forward, gripping my knees. "I do remember something! It's not major, but Seth was heading north. He's probably heading to the Catskills."

"That's something to go on." Marcus glanced at his glass, as if he couldn't fathom how it was empty. "He won't reach it. Not with the Khalkotauroi surrounding the place."

Olivia shuddered. "You think they can actually stop him?"

"They'll slow him down." Marcus pushed off the desk, heading for the door. "Anyone else in need of refreshments?"

"You sharing?" Deacon perked up.

Surprisingly, Aiden didn't caution him. Perhaps a little underage wine drinking wasn't our biggest concern at the moment. Our group scattered, some following Marcus on the wine run. Only after they left did I realize that the Dean of the Covenant was supplying alcohol to minors.

This really was an alternate universe.

After a few minutes, it was just Aiden and me. He sat beside me, exhaling a long breath. "You doing okay?"

Wondering how many times he was going to ask that in twenty-four hours, I turned to him. "I'm fine, really."

He looked like there was something he wanted to say, but he leaned forward and kissed my forehead instead. "I'm going to go check the grounds."

"I'll come with you."

"Stay here and take it easy, Alex. Just for tonight, okay?"

I felt the urge to pout. "You shouldn't have to do that alone."

"I'm not." He flashed a grin. "Solos will be with me."

"He wasn't with you earlier. That's what you were doing when everyone was eating, right? Checking the grounds, making sure no daimons were sneaking up on us?"

"I doubt there are any daimons out here."

But he was still patrolling, because that's what Sentinels did, and I thought about how he was willing to leave this life… leave it for us. I bet, if we lived in some place like Apple River, he'd still check the yard every night. Thinking that brought a smile to my lips.

"I've missed your smiles," he said, standing.

I looked up, wanting to grab his hand and make him stay. "I'll be here waiting."

"I know."

He looked at me strangely and then he left, and I was alone…alone except for the low buzz in the back of my head. I tried not to pay attention to it, because it symbolized a whole truckload of potential problems. That damn buzzing meant that Seth was still there, and I didn't know what that really meant in terms of him contacting me.

Glancing at the window, I took a breath but it got stuck. What if Seth could reach me? Would I be able to fight off what he wanted? If I did, could I somehow reason with him? Or would I just lose myself again, and this time there'd be no reaching me? An ache pierced my chest.

Unable to think about that, I reached for the remote and turned the TV on. The news still focused on the horrific earthquake in Los Angeles and the developing story coming out of the Pacific Northwest.

Taking in the destruction the gods were wreaking, I knew only one thing—and it hurt in a way that it shouldn't have, in a way I couldn't really explain. Seth had to die, but I had no idea how to do it…or if I really could, when it came down to it.

CHAPTER ELEVEN

I stayed in front of that TV the entire night, tired but not sleepy. Aiden passed out in the recliner beside the couch around three in the morning. I doubted that he was cool with leaving my side for long stretches of time. I didn't know if he was worried that I'd turn into Evil Alex again, or if he just needed to be near me. Either way, I was comforted by his soft snores. I think he was waiting for me to give up on my morbid fascination with the news, but I didn't.

Every newscaster had something different to add. More pictures streamed in from all around the globe. Mortals poured into the L.A. streets, rioting and looting, but in the Middle East, they dropped to their knees in the streets and prayed.

Clutching the remote until my knuckles ached, I tried—really tried—to imagine what it must be like to be these mortals. To be caught in something so much bigger than them while having no idea that, at any given second, everything could be ripped away from them.

I had more in common with them than I realized.

It really did seem like the end of the world. No mortal could explain the series of catastrophic events that, in their limited knowledge, couldn't be related to each other.

What was happening out there was beyond horrifying, and the destruction was because of Seth and me. Maybe it wouldn't have come to this if Seth hadn't attacked the Council. Maybe the gods would've left us alone to live our lives.

Maybe they would've found a way to kill us anyway.

I didn't know and it really didn't matter. This was where we were now, and things were screwed up. While all the knowledge of the Apollyons was floating around in my head, none of it was useful when it came to fixing this.

Laadan appeared in the doorway, dressed in slacks and a white sweater today. Her hair was perfectly coifed, in spite of the fact that the world had donned its banana pants. The woman was awe-inspiring.

She glanced at Aiden and smiled. "Care to join me for some coffee?"

How could I ever turn down caffeine? Nodding, I started out of the room, but backtracked to where Aiden rested and fixed the quilt I'd draped over him a few hours ago. The man must have been exhausted, because he didn't wake up, which was rare.

I followed Laadan into the kitchen and watched her make quick work of the coffee. With our steaming cups in hand, we went into the sunroom for the privacy it offered. We sat on the window seat, our legs tucked toward each other. Finally, we were going to talk about my father, and I had no idea what was going to come out of her mouth.

I was even a little scared, as stupid and weak as that was, and my stomach was flipping all over the place. I knew nothing of my father, only discovering that he was a half-blood and alive a few months ago.

Laadan took a sip of her coffee and blinked several times. "First, I want to apologize for what happened to you at the Council. I—"

"You don't have to apologize. That wasn't your fault." And it wasn't. Laadan had been compelled to give me the Brew—like a souped-up roofie of the gods—by one of Telly's Guards, probably the one I'd killed…

"What they tried to do to you was horrid." Tears filled her eyes, shining like crystals. "I wish—I wish I had known. I am so sorry—"

"Laadan, seriously, you don't have to apologize. I know you would never willingly do something like that. And I know you don't remember who did it. It's okay." And gods, I did not want to talk about that night. Beside the fact that it made me think about the Guard I'd killed, if I hadn't ended up puking my guts out, Seth and I…we would've done it, and after everything now, I don't think I'd ever get over that.

I sat my coffee on the small wicker table as my stomach roiled. "I want to know about my dad."

A remarkable change occurred in Laadan. A different kind of sheen misted in her eyes. She took another drink, her pointer finger tapping on the glass. The anticipation was killing me.

"Your father is a…an incredible man, Alex. You should know that above all else."

My breath fell short. "I know." I did know, because he had to be to break the rules and love my mother. "The Elixir didn't work on my father, did it?"

Laadan smiled wistfully. "Your father—Alexander—well, he always had a strong will, much like you. The Elixir has taken its toll on him, but he never completely fell to the compulsion. I do not know how, but he resisted it from the beginning."

I clasped my hands together. "I think I saw him on the stairs once, and then toward the end, during the attack. He was fighting..."

"You did see him." Her gaze moved to the window behind us. Early-morning sunlight sliced over the frost-covered glass. "He was in the library the night we spoke of your mother and him."

I could only stare. I knew someone had been in there. "The books that fell over—that was him?" She nodded.

How many times had I been close to the man—to my father—without knowing? A hurricane of disappointment swelled inside me. "And...and he knows I'm his daughter?"

"Yes, he knows." She reached out with her free hand, gently touching the skin of my face, near a bruise that was already starting to heal. "He would recognize you anywhere. You look so much like your mother."

That bite of sadness strengthened me, and I pulled back. "Then why didn't he talk to me?"

Laadan looked away, her chin lowering.

"I tried talking to him, Laadan. In the stairwell, but he just...stared at me. And why didn't he come up to me in the library? I know he couldn't just announce who he was, but why..." My throat tightened. "Why didn't he want to talk to me, at least?"

Her head snapped toward me. "Oh, honey, he wanted to talk to you more than anything, but it's not that simple."

"Seems simple to me. You open your mouth and talk." I struggled to sit still. Had he heard of my escapades? Gods know rumors of my problems with authority had traveled far and wide. Had he been embarrassed as a trained Sentinel? Worse yet, as a father? "I just don't understand."

She took a breath. "He was close to you a lot when you were there and you didn't know, but it was also very dangerous for him to be seen around you. The truth of what he is, what your mother was, and what you are, was too much of a risk. You already had too many eyes on you."

The conversation Seth and I had overheard came back to me. *We already have one here.* Anger sparked and was quick to ignite a fire inside me. Marcus…Marcus had known, and now that it was all out in the open, we were so going to talk about that.

"What I told you in the library that night? That he would be proud of you because of who you have become and not what you will become?" She clasped my fisted hand in her gentle grip. "That is the truth. From the moment you arrived back at the Covenant last summer, I did my best to keep him up-to-date on how you were. Your mother…she didn't know what had happened to him and Alexander wanted it that way. In a way, death was easier than the truth."

I blinked away sudden tears and wanted to pull my hand free, but like always, Laadan's calming nature was disarming.

"Things are more complicated than you realize, Alex. He couldn't talk to you."

Shaking my head, I tried and failed to understand that. I'd think that a father would've done anything to speak to his daughter just once.

Laadan squeezed my hands and let go. "The Masters always suspected that your father was different, and that perhaps he was influencing other servants. They treated him quite cruelly. He cannot talk to you, Alex. They removed half his tongue."

I balked at what she said. I'd heard her wrong. There were

no other options. "No. I saw him talking with another servant in the dining hall."

She shook her head sadly. "If anything, you saw a servant talking *to* him."

Forcing myself to remember the morning after I'd been slipped the Brew more clearly, I tried to see my father and the younger servant. Things had looked tense and his back had been to me most of the time. I'd assumed that he'd been talking by the reaction of the other servant.

I *hadn't* seen him talk.

Shooting to my feet, I heard Laadan's little gasp of surprise. Even I was a little shocked by how fast I moved. The marks of the Apollyon appeared on my skin and tingled as they glided in various directions. She couldn't see them, but some innate sense coaxed her to scoot back.

"They cut out his tongue?" Power surged over my skin.

"Yes."

That was it. I was going to take out the Council and every freaking Master on this planet. Bad, dangerous thoughts, but gods, how could they do something like that?

"How can I be so surprised?" I said out loud, and then laughed. "How am I surprised by this, Laadan?"

There was no answer.

Turning away, I struggled to control my fury. Already I could hear the branches slapping along the side of the cabin. Knowing my luck, I'd probably cause an earthquake. Controlling the elements was easy, but I'd learned through the Awakening that my emotions affected them, made them violent and unpredictable.

As did the amount of aether, the essence of the gods, that coursed through my veins.

Our society had always been cruel to the half-bloods.

Pures had always taken a role of dominance, and the things that I knew went on behind the closed doors of some of the pures—things no one talked about, things I wanted to rage about—happened every day. And like every other half, I'd been in a subservient role my entire life. I'd grown up being taught to accept these things, because there was no other choice for me, or for any other half. Even after living in the mortal world, I'd come back into the fold, barely missing a step when I'd seen the servants.

And only once had I intervened. I'd received a punch in the jaw for it, but stopping a Master from striking a female servant was nothing compared to what those halfs went through.

Stepping away, I ran my hands down my outer thighs. The breath I inhaled was harsh. This was bigger than me and my own problems with becoming a Sentinel and continuing on while others of my kind were enslaved. This was more than my father. It was the Breed Order.

"This has to change," I said.

"I agree, but…"

But now, right this instant, there was nothing I could do. Believe it or not, we had bigger problems. The Breed Order and how halfs were treated wouldn't matter if we were all dead.

Facing Laadan, I realized something huge—huge to me, at least. Old Alex would've probably stormed off somewhere and kicked a Master in the junk. A huge part of me wanted to do that, but the new Alex—this girl/woman/whatever who came out of nowhere knew that some battles had to be planned.

The new Alex waited.

I sort of struck myself speechless.

Laadan, more observant than I realized, smiled and patted the spot beside her. "You're growing up."

"I am?" Seemed late in the game for that sort of nonsense. I sat, and when she nodded, I sighed and sounded ten years older. "Growing up sucks, then."

"There is a naïveté to young selfishness."

My brows rose. I was itchy, like I had slipped on more responsible and mature skin and a part of me didn't like that. Shaking it off, I went back to my dad. "You talk to him a lot?"

"As much as I can. Communication is one-sided at times, but he can write, obviously. I know he got your letter, but unfortunately, with everything happening, I do not know his response or if he had the chance."

I nodded in a jerking motion. "Do you know where he is right now?"

She fingered the lace on the edge of her sweater. "Alexander is at the New York Covenant."

"He's still there?" When she nodded, I wanted to get up and figure out how to get to New York, but logic seeped in. It would be near impossible to get to him. And with Seth out there, looking for us? It would just be plain stupid to go running off.

"When the Elixir stopped working, there was a lot of confusion among the servants. There are very few like him who resisted the compulsions. Those who are going through their own Awakening of sorts need a leader, and that is your father. There is a lot of turmoil there, with the recent attack and with what the First is doing."

But I wanted to scream that I needed him here with me. Wasn't I more important? His long-lost daughter? I frowned. Well, good to see some of my *naïve selfishness* was still present.

"Does he still love my mother?" I asked, peeking at her.

Her expression was guarded. "I think a part of him will always love her."

"Do you love him?" I blurted out.

Laadan swallowed and a long pause followed. In the gap, I heard someone moving around in the kitchen.

I started to grin. "You like him."

Looking away, her lips pursed.

I nudged her with my elbow. "You like him *a lot*."

She drew herself up. "Your father—"

"Is the love of your life?"

"Alexandria," she snapped, but there was no real heat to her tone.

I laughed as I leaned back against the cool windowpane. I knew that my parents had this wondrous, forbidden love affair that started long before Stepfather Douchey had come into the picture. And if it hadn't been for the Breed…the gods-damn Breed Order, they'd still be together. Gods, so many things would be different. Namely my mother…she'd still be alive, because I bet my dad was like Aiden. He would've never allowed anything to happen to my mom.

Laadan's lips curved up at the corners. "You are so much like your father. Your stubbornness and tenacity." Her gaze went to the closed door. The smell of fresh coffee grew. "And just like your father, you dared to love a pure-blood."

My mouth opened. *Touché.* "Well, I kind of walked into that one."

I thought she snickered, but I had to be wrong, because that would be so unladylike of her.

For some odd reason, some of the weight lifted from my shoulders and I went from vengeful, albeit more mature Alex, to girlie-girl in less than two seconds flat. "I do love him. I really do. More than…more than I probably should."

She patted my hand. "You can never love someone more than you probably should." I wasn't sure about that.

"He loves you just as strongly. It was obvious to me from the beginning."

"It was?"

"The Aiden I knew, the one before he went to Atlanta to find you, had always respected and viewed halfs equally, but he never would've taken time away from his Sentinel duties to help any half."

Knowing what had been done to his parents in front of him while he was a small boy, I could see why she would think that. Becoming a Sentinel and avenging his parents had become everything to him.

"And then I saw the way he was around you in New York." Her smile turned wistful again. "It's all in the way he looked at you—the way he *constantly* looked at you. You were his world, probably before either of you realized that."

"You could tell all that by the way he looked at me?" I may've sounded skeptical, but oh, wow, that girlie-girl was jumping and shrieking inside me.

Laadan laughed then, the sound like wind chimes. "He watched you like a man starved for the only thing that could fulfill his hunger."

My eyes popped out and my body flushed about a thousand shades of red. "Oh, wow..."

That was TMI. How come more people hadn't noticed that? And then it hit me. Laadan would know, because it was how she looked at my father...and probably had witnessed my father looking at my mother in the same manner.

I was suddenly very sad for her.

Scooting closer to her, I wrapped my arms around her

slender shoulders. It was awkward at first, because I seriously gave the worst hugs. "Thank you."

Tears filled her eyes again. "Talking to you about your father is the least I could do. If you like, there are many stories I can tell you. It will be a…joy to speak openly about them."

"I'd like that," I whispered.

Laadan rested her cheek atop my head, and in that moment, she reminded me so much of my mom that it was almost too much to keep the tears at bay, but I couldn't stop the question that formed on the tip of my tongue.

"Do you think I'll ever get to meet him?"

Her embrace tightened. "You will. Both of you are determined enough to make it happen. I have no doubt."

Closing my eyes, I latched onto her words. I wanted to believe them—I needed to—but doubt swelled like bitter wisps of acrid smoke. A lot stood between me and my father—years of rules and secrets existed, an army of half-man/half-bulls, and most importantly, Seth.

CHAPTER TWELVE

A few hours later, I stood in the warded-up clearing by the cabin, covered in mud and chilled to the bone. All around me, the sounds of grunts and hard falls echoed through the otherwise silent forest.

I glanced down at my dirty hands and sighed. I was filthy. Maybe I'd get a repeat of that shower later. My gaze found Aiden's lithe form. He was fighting Luke. In other words, he was repeatedly kicking Luke's ass.

I doubted a shower repeat was on the menu.

A sharp pang of dissatisfaction formed in the back of my throat. I'd really thought that, since I was supposed to be training, I'd end up with Aiden and it would be like old times with a lot more touchy-feely stuff going on. Boy, was I wrong.

Solos exhaled loudly. "How long are you going to stare at your hands? I'm not getting any younger over here."

But oh no, the moment we stepped outside, Aiden had paired up with Luke and Olivia, Lea with Marcus. Deacon and Laadan were inside, supposedly making dinner.

Now I was in full internal whine mode.

I moved forward, wincing as my cold jeans chafed my skin. "I don't think this is the kind of training Apollo had in mind."

Solos tucked a loose strand of hair back behind his ear. "When's the last time you trained?"

I honestly couldn't remember. "I was fighting, like, two days ago."

"One day in the span of many means nothing." Broken branches crunched under his booted feet. "Our muscles need to be used daily."

I caught the tail end of Luke ending up on his butt. "I think they could use your help more. I could be working on using akasha right now. Seth has years of practical experience on me."

"And you will work with that, but not right now." Solos was nowhere near as patient as *some* of my previous trainers had been. He ranked up there with Romvi.

Eyes narrowing, I raised my hand. "I could just use the air element and knock—"

"Alex," Aiden snapped, stopping Luke's vicious kick with one hand. He gently pushed him back as thundercloud eyes sharpened on me. "I also doubt Apollo meant for your mouth to be the only thing getting a workout."

So many inappropriate comments rose to the tip of my tongue and danced around, but I snapped my jaw shut and glared at him.

"He's trying to help you." Aiden swiped up a titanium dagger from where it was implanted deep in the ground. "The least you could do is go along with this without torturing those who are helping you."

Embarrassed and angry, I was two seconds from raining my wrath down on Aiden when I stopped. Aiden *was* right. I was being whiny and bitchy and flat-out annoying.

Our eyes met, and there wasn't much heat behind his words, but he was frustrated with me and I hated that, because I was being a brat. I wasn't sure what was wrong with me. Ever since Laadan and I had spoken, my mood had plummeted. Lack of sleep, maybe?

The sting of Aiden's admonishment forced me back to Solos, who, by the way, had mud splattered on him like gore at a gruesome crime scene. No one in this world could get me to do what I was supposed to be doing as quickly as Aiden.

Part of me hated that. The other part respected and thanked him for it.

Cheeks burning, I dropped into stance. Solos launched at me. We went at it, blow for blow. He dipped. I spun. More times than not, he ended up sprawled on the ground, kicking up dirt and loose grass on me. My muscles were a little out-of-use, but I was fast—faster than I ever remembered being. When I'd been fighting Aiden the other day, I hadn't been aware of what I was really doing, not the mechanics of it. But now? Whoa, I felt like a superwoman.

Solos picked himself off the ground, exhaling out his nose. We moved on to disarming one another, which usually had been a weak area for me.

I darted under Solos's outstretched arm, caught both of his elbows and pulled back, running my hands down to his wrists as I planted a foot in his back. He released the blades and I caught them.

Waving them in his face, I grinned. "I kind of rock at this."

He turned, brows furrowed. "I don't even know what that move was."

I flipped the dagger in my right hand. "It's called being awesome and it worked."

"There's a difference between skill and speed." He

snatched the dagger out of my other hand. "You won't always have speed."

"But I have the elements," I reminded him.

"That you do." He gave a lopsided grin that didn't stretch his scar. He was handsome when he smiled like that. Hell, he was handsome even with the scar—kind of like a pirate. "But correct me if I'm wrong—doesn't using the elements tire you out?"

"That's what I hear." Olivia dropped down onto a tree stump and stretched out her long legs slowly. "Well, I heard Seth say that once."

With only one dagger left in hand, I pointed it at Solos. "Using the elements can tire us out, but not as much as akasha. That's why he doesn't use it all the time. Zaps him—us, I guess."

Aiden threaded his fingers and stretched, bowing his back. My gaze followed the movement quite obsessively. Everything he did looked fluid and graceful. "That's why it's important not to rely solely on those abilities."

As long as I'd known Aiden, I could count on one hand how many times he'd used the fire element. Each pure had an affinity to a certain element, while the Apollyon could wield control over all of them. Aiden liked to fight hand-to-hand.

Or titanium-to-titanium.

Lea was leaning against a large oak, her hair a mess as Marcus retrieved the fallen blades they'd been practicing with. My uncle handled them expertly. Sometimes I forgot he had trained as a Sentinel, once upon a time.

Our little recess was over, and under the cloudy April skies we continued until the sun began its descent in the west. Only then did we shuffle back into the cabin, and I guessed practicing akasha was on the schedule for tomorrow. The smell of roasted meat teased my taste buds. I was so hungry I could eat a daimon, but a shower came first.

And as I'd expected earlier, I was all by my lonesome in that endeavor.

All of us sat at the kitchen table and dug in. Someone thanked Laadan for the meal and Deacon about had a coronary.

"Who tenderized the meat? Who marinated and watched it dutifully?" His blond brows lowered as he held his fork like Luke held a dagger. "That would be *me*."

Laadan nodded. "I peeled potatoes. That was about it."

"I didn't know you could cook," I said to Deacon, surprised.

Freshly showered, Aiden dropped into the seat beside his brother. His dark hair was damp and swept back, revealing his broad cheekbones. He clapped his brother on the shoulder. "Deacon is one hell of a cook."

"Hmm." Olivia grinned as she chased a scalloped potato across her plate. "Learn something new every day, right?"

Not even trying to hide his proud smile, Deacon glanced at Luke. "I'm full of surprises."

I arched a brow, but shoved a piece of succulent meat into my mouth rather than saying anything.

For a little while, sitting at that table with everyone, things were, well, they were nice and warm.

Aiden remained mostly quiet while everyone traded stories, cracking a grin every once in a while, but still slightly apart from the boisterous group. More than once, our gazes met. Something churned in his gray eyes. I could easily see the sharp slice of sorrow mixing with regret before he looked away.

After dinner, bellies full, the group split into different sections of the house. Lea disappeared with one of the books

Laadan had brought with her. Olivia and the boys set up in the living room with a deck of cards. Solos and Marcus went out to check the perimeter with Aiden. It was getting late, and I was trying to stay up for when they came back, but eventually I said goodnight to the group and dragged myself upstairs.

I stopped in front of Aiden's bedroom, suddenly unsure of where I was supposed to be sleeping. There was another bedroom adjoining the bathroom, which was supposed to be mine, but I couldn't recall ever sleeping in there. Was I supposed to be in that room? And if I made myself at home in Aiden's, was I overstepping something?

Shifting my weight wearily, I chewed on my bottom lip. Gods, this shouldn't be this complicated.

Come on, Alex, you're being stupid. And I did feel stupid.

Heading to my room, I discovered I was severely lacking in the nightclothes department. Going back through the bathroom, I found a few of Aiden's longer shirts folded separately from the rest of his clothing, as if they'd been purposefully left aside.

I changed into one of the thin cotton shirts that reached my thighs, and there was no way I wanted to go back to the cool, untouched room that was supposed to be mine. Slipping under the covers, I snuggled down, inhaling the earthy scent that blanketed the bed.

It didn't take long to drift off to sleep. Probably only minutes, and I was floating in a comforting haze, but something made me open my eyes. And when I did, I was staring right into a pair of amber-colored ones.

CHAPTER THIRTEEN

Seth.

Oh gods, I was staring at *Seth*. He was here. Impossible, but he was here with me.

My heart raced in a chaotic rhythm as I pressed away. So afraid, so terrified by his sudden appearance, I couldn't catch my breath.

His arms formed a cage around me. I didn't dare move, for his skin was too close to mine, his lips a fraction of an inch away. His amber eyes glowed under thick, dark-blond eyelashes. Marks of the Apollyon raced up his neck, spreading over his cheeks in a vibrant wave of blue over his golden complexion. My own marks responded to his proximity, causing my skin to tingle. The cord snapped alive.

The force of Seth's presence was everywhere, invading my body and thoughts, but when I finally breathed in, the scent was all wrong. It was earthy with a hint of sea salt. *Aiden*.

Seth's lips curved into a satisfied smile and he placed his mouth near my ear. "I told you, Alex. I'd find you anywhere."

My mouth opened, but my scream was strangled by the lump of terror in my throat as I twisted to the side and jerked awake…*awake.*

Pulse pounding, I sat up and the bedroom slowly came into focus. My frantic gaze traveled the room, searching out the shadows for any sign of Seth. A sliver of moonlight seeped in under the blinds, spreading across the floor, its fingers brushing over the antique dresser. Under the bathroom door, a slit of yellow gleamed. Other than the tingling marks, there was no sign of him.

It was just a dream—a nightmare. Nothing more, but the adrenaline kicking around inside me begged to differ.

The bathroom door opened and Aiden filled the doorway. Lit by the soft glow of the light behind him, he was a study of shadowy contrasts—shirtless and wearing only a pair of pajama bottoms that hung low on his hips.

That didn't help my heart *or* breathing problem. The light behind him flipped off.

"Alex?" He moved silently to the bed, dipping down beside me. "I didn't wake you, did I?"

I shook my head.

His head tilted to the side and dark hair fell over his forehead. "Are you okay?"

"Yeah," I croaked out, feeling ridiculous now for overreacting to a stupid nightmare.

Aiden reached out, stopping with his hand a hairsbreadth from my cheek. He pulled away, settling onto his back. One arm stretched out, beckoning me. Stretching out beside him, I placed my head on his shoulder, my hand on his chest above his thundering heart. His skin was warm, comforting.

Several heartbeats passed in silence while his heart slowed down. Why it had been beating so fast, I didn't know. I snuggled closer, fitting my body to his side, and his arm curled around my waist. I felt his jaw graze the top of my head, and then his lips pressed against my forehead.

I squeezed my eyes shut, wanting to tell him about the dream, but instead, something else came out. "They cut out my father's tongue, Aiden. He can't talk. *They* did that to him."

He seemed to hold his breath for a moment.

"Why would they do something like that?" I asked, and my own voice sounded incredibly small and fragile.

"I don't know." His hand came up, pressing between my shoulders, moving in a soothing circle. "There isn't any justification for something as horrific as that." There was a pause. "I'm sorry, Alex."

I nodded, squeezing my eyes shut. We needed to do something about the Breed Order, and I knew Aiden would agree, but discussing something so political at two in the morning seemed out of place. Stretching up, I placed my lips to Aiden's, but the kiss turned out more chaste than the hot and steamy action I was going for. His arm tightened, though, and a fine tremor coursed through his body as if he was fighting the pull between us.

Confused, I ceased my attempt at seducing him, since it really wasn't working, and settled back down, heart racing again. Why hadn't he kissed me back? Was he still upset over my bratty display earlier while training with Solos? If so, then geez, there was nothing I could do to fix that. Or was it something else? Like the regret and sadness that flashed in his gray eyes?

Out of the silence that had fallen in the room once more, Aiden said, "I love you."

There was no missing the heavy thread of emotion in his voice. My breath caught. Even with my failed seduction attempt, hearing him say those three little words was something I'd never get tired of. "I love you, too."

Very little time later, the steady rise and fall of Aiden's chest deepened. I stayed in his embrace, staring through the darkness at the empty wall across the bed for what seemed like hours before I carefully disentangled myself from his arms and crept out of the bed.

Unable to sleep or stay put, I found a pair of sweats in the darkness and drew them on, rolling the cuffs at the bottom. My bare feet padded on the wood floors as I slipped out the door and headed downstairs.

The house was tomb-quiet and chilly. Folding my arms, I piddled around in the kitchen, even though I wasn't hungry or thirsty. Restless and wide awake, with no idea of what to do, I made my way to the sunroom.

It was colder in there, but in a weird way, surrounded by all the plants and windows with nothing but darkness looming outside, it was peaceful.

Sitting at the window seat, I tucked my legs against my chest and stared out one of the windows. Too much was running through my head: my father, training again, the Breed Order, Aiden and his sudden resistance, everything that was happening outside these walls, and…

And I was thinking about Seth, courtesy of the nightmarish visit.

A sharp slice of panic pierced my belly. What had happened had to have been a nightmare. Which was completely understandable considering Seth was pulling a Dr. Evil right now. It couldn't be anything else, so I needed to stop freaking out over it. But that low buzz in the back of my head—it was still there and it signified that, no matter what I did or how strong I was, I would always be connected to him.

And that he could possibly still reach me.

That anxious pang was back, spreading to my chest. I squeezed my eyes shut. Fear was a sour taste on the roof of my mouth. Could that nightmare really have been Seth reaching out to me?

I checked my mental shields. Almost like running my tongue over my teeth after Jackson had stomped me in the face during class, I poked and prodded at the shield, making sure nothing had been knocked out of place or loose. The shield was sturdy, but the traces of alarm lingered.

When I'd been connected to Seth after I'd Awakened, I could hear his thoughts as clear as my own.

I rocked back a little, squeezing my legs until my arms ached.

Seth had really seemed like he'd been here tonight, leaning over me and whispering his warning. Even my nightmares from what had happened in Gatlinburg hadn't been that real, and they'd been pretty damn visual.

Footsteps neared the sunroom, and my head snapped up. "Marcus."

He was still dressed like he'd been at dinner, jeans and a tailored flannel shirt—a sure sign he hadn't gone to bed yet. "Up a little late?" he asked, leaning against the doorframe.

I gave a lopsided shrug and kept my arms locked around my knees. "I'm not sleepy."

"You were dragging all evening. I figured you'd sleep another day away."

It wasn't like I could tell him the truth, so I said nothing. Marcus hesitated in the doorway and then strode forward, sure and strong. I watched him wearily as he sat beside me, taking the same spot Laadan had when we'd spoken. Several tense, uncomfortable minutes passed, and although Marcus and I had come a long way, we still had mountains to climb before things weren't so epically awkward between us.

He placed his hands in his lap and sighed. "Are you feeling well, Alexandria?"

So formal…"Yeah, like I said, just not sleepy. How about you?"

"Was out patrolling and just switched out with Solos." He cast me a quick sidelong glance. "I'm not sleepy, either."

I turned back to the window. "Do you guys think it's necessary to patrol?"

"Some of it may just be out of habit, especially for Aiden and Solos, but strange things have been known to happen."

Surprised that he answered honestly, I faced him. With my Apollyon sight, I could make out the lines of his face in the shadows. Another shocker came when I found his expression was open. "And even though the gods might not be gunning for us this very second, that could always change," he said. "So we watch…and we wait."

I didn't say anything for a long moment. "I hate that."

"What?" Curiosity marked his tone.

My hands curled into themselves, balling next to my thighs. "That people would so willingly give their lives away to protect me. I hate that."

Marcus twisted toward me and then leaned his head back against the window. "Don't take this the wrong way, but it's not just you that we're protecting, Alexandria. There's Lea and Deacon, Olivia and Luke. Three of them are trained to a certain extent, but not against gods or a horde of daimons. Even though a daimon attack out here seems unlikely…"

Stranger things had happened. I nodded.

His vibrant eyes slid closed. "It's not always about you."

My mouth worked on a refusal. I didn't think it was always

about me, but wait… I kind of sort of did by assuming that everyone was throwing themselves in front of a bus for me. My cheeks burned.

"I didn't…I didn't mean it like that." I took a breath. "Well, I kind of did, but I know you guys are protecting them, too. And that's…that's a good thing."

His shoulders relaxed. "And I didn't mean that how it came out."

I laughed and the sound surprised me. It wasn't forced or snarky, just amused. "Yeah, you did, and I get it. I've been riding the Alex-Is-Important train for quite some time."

One eyebrow arched.

The urge to laugh came again, but I stopped it and placed my cheek on my knees. "I've been…uh, I've been a handful. I know that. Most of the time it was on purpose."

"I know," was all he said.

"You did?"

Marcus nodded. "You're like any child—"

"I'm not a child."

His lips curved up at the corners. "You *were* like any child who was seeking a place to fit in. It's especially hard with you halfbloods. Many of you come from unhappy homes, or no homes at all. The environment you're raised in is violent and aggressive. I've seen so many…" He shook his head slightly. "Anyway, you were different."

"Why?"

"For starters, you're my niece."

"Wow." I blinked, loosening my grip on my legs. "I'm surprised that the first thing wasn't that you knew I was the Apollyon."

Marcus's eyes opened and met mine. "That was never first, second, or third. You are my niece. You are my sister's daughter. And you are so much like her..." He exhaled through the nose, his jaw locking. "You were so much like her that when you came back to the Covenant...and even now, I have a hard time looking at you without seeing my sister."

Something...something came unhinged in my chest. Never had Marcus been this open with me. And it'd seemed more likely for me to waltz around the living room with a daimon before Marcus would talk to me about my mother, but here he was.

Holy daimon butt, we were climbing that mountain.

The breath I inhaled was a bit raspy. "You loved my mom a lot."

"Rachelle was my little sister and I...I loved her dearly." His eyes closed again. "Rachelle was full of life—vibrant. We were opposites. She drew people to her in droves, and I pretty much repelled them."

My lips quirked at the corners.

"She was probably the only person who could get me to relax." He sat up suddenly, dropping his hands onto his knees. "When you were really little, she used to bring you over to my home, and if you behaved, which wasn't always likely, she'd take you for ice cream afterward." A pensive smile formed. "You were such a tiny thing then, but my gods, I knew immediately you would look just like her. Everything except the eyes..."

Searching my memories, I found I could recall nothing of him from when I'd been a little girl, only the few visits when I was older, and they had been cold and impersonal. Marcus had been like every other pure.

"She always claimed that your father was a mortal, but that one Sentinel was always with her, always following her... and you."

"What?" My head snapped up.

Marcus focused on something I couldn't see. "You were too young, Alexandria, to remember your father."

Hearing Marcus mention my father stopped the world.

"You were just a baby. Your mother couldn't so much as walk outside without Alexander not too far behind her, especially if she had you with her. Looking back, it seemed obvious, but Sentinels and Guards were always around. And they'd attended the Covenant together, two years behind me. I just thought they were friends. But I think I always knew, deep down, and I couldn't see past that. Every time I looked at you, I saw my sister's downfall."

My eyes widened. "Ouch."

"Yeah," he sighed. "Sounds terrible, but you of all people know what happens to halfs and pures that mix. I was so angry with my sister for putting herself into that position and for bringing a child into it." Marcus paused, pensive. "I took it out on you. It was wrong."

Pigs had just officially sprouted wings and were flying alongside airplanes. Instead of jumping around and pointing out what he just admitted and acting like a general douche about it, I focused on something else. Sometimes I amazed myself with my own maturity.

"Did…did you know my father personally?"

His lips thinned. "I trained with your father before I decided to go a more political route. He was a damn good fighter. Like you."

I stared. Once upon a time, hearing something like that would've have filled me with pleasure, but now it wasn't the compliment that had drawn me in; it was hearing that *my father* had been a damn good Sentinel that did.

"I think your mother hoped she wouldn't be paired. I

wasn't. Neither was Laadan. But when your mother was paired with Lucian, Alexander...you just knew, if you knew the man behind the uniform."

Again, I had no idea what to say.

"There was nothing he could do but stand back and let the woman he loved marry someone else. And he had to live with that someone else raising his child." Marcus cleared his throat. "And I'm sure Alexander knew that Lucian wasn't kind to you, but there was nothing he could do. Coming forward would have put both your mother and you in danger. He was helpless."

My muscles were tensing and relaxing at the same time. "What happened? How did he end up a servant?"

Marcus faced me. "When you were three years old, Alexander disappeared. It wasn't uncommon. We were told he'd been killed by a daimon."

I shook my head, brows furrowing. "How did you not know where he was? He was in the Catskills, under Telly's thumb."

"I didn't see him there until about a year prior to your return." The sincerity in his words rocked me. "I'd believed that he was dead, and I didn't know that a male half and a female pure made an Apollyon. Even when Rachelle came to me before she took you away, I didn't suspect what that truly meant. Not until I saw Alexander in the Catskills, and then what could I do?"

"You could've helped him!"

"How? How was I to do that? What do you think would've happened if everyone realized that your father was a half-blood? Halfs and pures have mixed before and have been caught. Those children were not allowed to live."

Sickened, I swallowed. "That's so wrong."

"I don't disagree." He ran his fingers over the leaf of a nearby plant. "Your father didn't seem to recognize me. Only recently did I learn from Laadan that that must've been an act."

Then it hit me—smacked me right upside my ever-loving head. The conversation that I'd overheard between him and Telly resurfaced. Marcus had been furious with Telly. "Telly wanted you to hand me over, didn't he? He even offered you a seat on the Council."

He looked at me sharply.

I grinned. "I overheard you guys."

Staring at me a moment, he shook his head. "He did."

"And you refused."

"Yes." His look said, *How could I do anything else?*

Wow. Things kind of made sense now, after all this time. I reminded him of Mom and he missed her, which probably made him uncomfortable around me. And Marcus wasn't really a people person, anyway. He hadn't known about my father until it was too late. I believed that. *And* he hadn't handed me over to Telly. I remembered how he'd picked me up and carried me after Seth had attacked the Council and I'd been sick.

How, like Aiden, he hadn't given up on me.

Marcus…he cared about me. And that meant a lot. Beside my father, who was out of reach to me, Marcus was the last of my family—my blood.

"Thank you," I said. And then, impulsively, even though he wasn't a hugging man, I sprang forward before he knew what was coming and hugged him. It was quick, though—I didn't want to freak the man out.

I settled back in my spot as he stared at me, eyes wide. Guess I *had* freaked him out.

"Why are you thanking me?" he asked slowly.

I shrugged.

"You are a strange girl."

Laughing, I leaned back against the cushions on the window seat. "I bet Mom was a strange girl."

"That she was."

"Will you tell me what you know about my dad? I mean, if you're not tired or anything?"

"There're some stories I could tell you." He mirrored my position. "And I'm not tired. Not at all." His smile was tentative, but real, and I couldn't think of any other time that he had smiled like that.

My lips responded in kind. "That would be really nice."

It wasn't until dawn came and the sun rose, chasing away the murky shadows, that I thought about how happy my mom would be, knowing that Marcus and I had sort of patched things up.

And I couldn't help but believe that she did know. And maybe she was smiling upon us now. Just like the sun filtering through the windows, warming our backs.

CHAPTER FOURTEEN

Over the next three days, our little band fell into a rhythm of sorts. Things had settled down in the world. There'd been no more natural disasters, and Mount St. Helens seemed to have quieted. Apollo was still a no-show, and the cabin out in the middle of nowhere had become a god-free zone. A good thing, but I figured one would just pop in, most likely in Deacon's bed or something, where we'd least expect them. But even though there'd been no godly interference, it was like watching the countdown clock on a time bomb. We all were just waiting.

Each day had been filled with training, training, and more training. Parts of it were worse than any days at the Covenant, because *everyone* stopped and watched when it came time for me to break out the akasha.

Marcus and Solos had lined up several large rocks they'd found scattered about, and my job was to make itty, bitty pebbles out of them. And that worked—up close. Say, like a few feet away. But the farther away I got, the worse my aim became.

Sweating under Aiden's loose thermal, I grunted as I pulled from where akasha rested just below my ribcage. The power of the gods mark tingled as the fifth element crackled across my knuckles.

Under the canopy of trees, Aiden and Olivia stopped their sparring to watch.

Focusing on the element, I felt my senses sharpen. Using akasha was like being connected directly with the earth—like run-and-hug-a-tree connected. I could feel the vibrations of the grass and soil under my feet, as well as the dozens of scents carried on the low moan of the wind, and I could *feel* the air gliding over my skin with ghostly fingers.

Akasha crackled over my right arm as I threw my hand out. A bolt of lightning erupted from my palm, shooting across the ten feet and smacking into the right edge of the boulder. With a loud *crack*, the thing splintered.

Luke darted out of the way, but he was still pelted with rubble. He doubled over, about to kiss the ground.

"Whoops." I winced. "Sorry?"

Rubbing his back, he waved it off and limped toward where Deacon was trying to hide his laughter. "Shut up," he grumbled.

"You should've known better than to be that close," Deacon replied.

I sighed and turned to Solos. "I have terrible aim."

Solos nodded. "It's slightly off."

"Slightly?" My brows lifted.

"You're hitting the target, and I suppose that's all that matters."

Peeking at Aiden, I found that his attention was now on the sparring Lea and Olivia. The two girls were marvelous fighters and equally matched, and Aiden was in full Instructor mode, calling out commands in his deep, oddly musical voice. I found myself missing that one-on-one attention.

Heck, I was missing a lot of attention.

One thing had been certain over the last three days—something was definitely up with Aiden. It wasn't that he avoided me. Every night he joined me in bed, pulled me close, and held me. Nothing progressed further than that, even though I could sense he wanted more. He just didn't make a move, and I had no idea why. I was pretty sure the way I ended up curling all around him was evidence I was down for some happy times.

I bit my lip as I turned to the last boulder, shaking out my shoulders. There hadn't been another nightmare of Seth, thank the gods. Part of me suspected it had something to do with the fact that I didn't go to sleep until after Aiden did. Maybe just knowing that he was there helped, but he didn't go to sleep until late, which usually meant it took another couple of hours for me to drift off, and when he awoke at the crack of freaking dawn, so did I. Since I was tapping into akasha daily, I was drained like a daimon victim.

But I pushed away the fatigue. Like Marcus had once said, I was a lot of things, but not stupid. I knew why Apollo wanted me working with akasha. He was preparing me to fight Seth. And I would need everything in my arsenal to avoid the power transfer that would end everything.

There was an inherent problem with training for a face-off with Seth. How was I supposed to fight him when all it would take from him was a touch and a few whispered words in Greek?

Yeah, we were doomed to failure.

Panic hammered me in the chest as my gaze drifted over those around me. If anything went wrong, which it most likely would, all of them were at risk. Lea could end up like her sister, Olivia like Caleb, Luke and Solos like every Sentinel that had been slaughtered by Lucian and his army. Marcus could end up like my mom.

My eyes settled on Aiden.

Deacon had gotten up and was standing next to his older brother. Under the sunlight, his blond curls were a pale platinum. The brothers shared the same striking eye color, but that was all. They were like yin and yang, night and day, standing side by side.

Deacon's hands were cupped around something, and as he lifted his head, a genuine smile spread across his lips and those gray eyes glittered. Aiden laughed at whatever Deacon had said.

They could end up like their parents.

Fear made my skin tight as it replaced the panic. I rubbed at my temple, forcing my breath to saw in and out evenly. No one was going to die. There would be no more deaths. There couldn't be. *Everyone* had suffered enough already.

But there was Fate. There was no such thing as paying dues when it came to Fate. It simply did not care or recognize past experience.

Knowing that made me want to plop down in the cold, damp grass and cry like an angry, fat baby.

"Alex?" Solos's soft voice drew me out of my troublesome thoughts.

I nodded and focused on the last rock. What I didn't like about using akasha was the fact that the buzzing in my head was always the strongest then, like tapping into the most powerful element somehow affected the bond. None of the Apollyons had ever thought or discussed that in the past, so I had no idea if that was true.

Calling upon akasha, I let it go. The bolt of blue lightning was incredibly intense, shattering in its power. Silence and then another loud *crack* followed. This time it hit the rock in the middle and the thing didn't explode, but was reduced to a pile of dust.

Solos let out a low whistle as he stared at the dust and the scorched soil below. "Remind me to never piss you off."

I cracked a smile as I backed off, letting the buzz of akasha settle back down. Bending at the waist, I snatched up my water. Over the rim, I watched Olivia deliver a spin kick that knocked Lea back several feet.

Aiden clapped. "Perfect, Olivia." And then to Lea, "You hesitated. If you hadn't, you would've blocked that kick."

Nodding, Lea stood up and dusted herself off. She quickly fell back into stance and went at it again.

A low, annoying ache blossomed in my temple, making my right eye all twitchy. I tossed the bottle back down and turned to Solos. Out of rocks to destroy, I was handed off to Marcus to work on elements.

Off a little from the main group, he raised his hands. A gust of wind picked up. Branches rattled, and fresh, tiny leaves swirled in the air as the wind barreled toward me.

I raised my hands, and unlike before I'd Awakened, I met the air element with my own. His sputtered out weakly under the force of mine. Amazing how the air element had been my greatest enemy before, but now was only a mild annoyance.

Deacon and Laadan even got involved in the later part of the day. Laadan worked with the air element and Deacon set about creating small fires and controlling them. I couldn't picture those two fighting, but at this point, everyone had become a warrior.

Aiden watched his brother with narrowed eyes and a tight

jaw, so tight I wondered if he had any molars left. Finally, he left the halfs and stalked over to where Deacon had several piles of twigs burning.

"What are you doing?" Aiden demanded.

Deacon looked up from under the mop of curls. "I'm becoming a fire bug."

The humor was lost on Aiden. "I know what you're thinking."

"Ah, hell, well if that's the case, then that's embarrassing."

Aiden's back went rigid. "Unless you're practicing starting campfires, you're wasting your time."

"But—"

"You don't need to do this." Aiden waved his hand over the piles of burning twigs and the flames fizzled out. "I don't want you involved in any of this."

Deacon drew himself up to his full height, which meant he only came to Aiden's shoulders. "You can't stop me, Aiden."

Ah, wrong thing to say.

"You want to bet on that?" Aiden growled, his head dropping so that he was eye level with his brother.

Undaunted, Deacon held his ground but dropped his voice. "Do you expect me to sit back and play card games while everyone else is doing something important?"

"Yes, I do, actually."

Deacon laughed humorlessly. "I can help."

"You're not trained." His hands formed into fists at his sides. "And before you say it, you're not like everyone else."

"I know I'm not trained, but I'm not freaking useless, Aiden. I *can* help." They were in an epic stare down I hadn't seen before, especially not from easygoing Deacon. "And asking me to sit back and watch everyone else—people that I care about, people like *you*—prepare to risk their lives while I do nothing isn't fair."

Aiden opened his mouth, but his brother rushed on. "I know your over-controlling behavior comes from a good place, bro, but you can't protect me forever, and you can't continue babying me. It's a waste of time, because even if you forbid me to get involved, it won't matter. You can't stop me." Deacon took a deep breath. "I need to help, Aiden."

Something in what Deacon said caused Aiden to string together an atrocity of f-bombs. My brows flew up. Aiden rarely cussed or lost his cool, but boy, he was a grenade whose pin had just been pulled.

He took a step back, placing his hands on his hips. I almost expected him to drag Deacon into the cabin and lock him in there, but instead, he jerked his head in a curt nod. "Okay. If this is what you…need, then okay."

I was stunned into silence. So was Deacon. Without another word, Aiden returned to where the halfs waited.

Deacon's eyes met mine and he shrugged.

Shocked that Aiden had given in—and somewhat pleased that he was seeing Deacon as something more than his little brother who partied too much—I followed Marcus over to the rest of the group.

We practiced with the air element for the rest of the day and even went as far as to use it against the rest of the halfs, forcing them to break my hold. I hated doing that, because I knew how helpless I'd felt when the air element was used to pin me down, but air users were the most common, which meant over half of the daimons used air. It was one of the reasons so many halfs died in battle against them.

So we had to deal with it.

Fire and earth were rare among pures. Aiden and Deacon were the only two I knew who wielded fire, and I hadn't met a pure who controlled earth, although I'd seen it used once, in the New York Covenant. The water element came in handy if the user was near water or in the rain. Some thought they had gotten the crappy element, but I knew it wasn't true. They could pull water from pipes—from *anything*.

I was squared off against Lea. Not that long ago, I would've experienced a twisted sort of satisfaction at taking her down, but things…things were so different now.

We stared at each other for a few seconds, and then she nodded.

Slowly, reluctantly, I raised my hands and drew the air around me. A vicious stream of wind formed just behind my fingers, and then slid through them. Like with akasha, my aim wasn't great, but it struck Lea below the chest, knocking her right on her back.

I moved forward, my arms shaking as I forced the element on her. It was hard to look at her, hard to not see myself struggling and thrashing on the ground, unable to gain footing.

Aiden crouched behind her, barking out orders in his own soft way, but the best she could do was draw her legs up.

Her body trembled as her lips pulled back in a snarl. She fought to just sit up, and I wanted her to, because from there, it was easier to break the hold, but the element pinned her shoulders down to the grass.

Wave after wave of air beat down on her, and she threw her head back and screamed as she raised one hand, her fingers clawing at the invisible enemy.

"Lea, come on. Use your core muscles," Aiden said, lifting his lashes to pierce me with concrete eyes. "Push through it…"

I hated this, hated this so much. My entire body shook.

Another scream as she slammed her hands down into the short blades of grass. Her fingers dug in, tearing through dirt. Clumps came up as she pushed up into a sitting position. I started to smile, but Lea powered up quickly and rushed me.

She cut through the element, arms wrapping around my waist as she smashed into me. We went down, a tangle of arms and legs. The back of my head smacked on the ground. Starbursts exploded behind my eyelids. Air rushed from my lungs in a painful gasp.

The sound of applause was thundering, and I think Deacon yelled, "Girl fight!"

And then there was silence. No one moved. I liked to think everyone was preparing for a massive Apollyon bitch-smack from my end.

"Damn," I grunted, blinking several times. Through Lea's coppery hair, the sky was a light color of blue.

Using her arms, Lea lifted up and grinned at me. "Let's just call that a little bit of payback." She rolled off and sprang to her feet, still grinning broadly. "Well, that was fun."

I remained sprawled on the ground, the throbbing in my right temple now spreading to the back of my skull. Quite possible she'd knocked something loose—hopefully nothing important.

A strong, tan-colored hand appeared in my vision. "Up?"

Placing my hand in Aiden's, I let him haul me to my feet and stood there while he brushed clumps of dirt off my aching shoulders. On second thought, my whole body ached. A small smile played over his full lips. Our eyes met, and while everyone milled about around us, in that moment, it was just him and me.

Aiden leaned over me, his breath warm against the curve of my neck. A fine shiver scuttled over my skin, and the ache in my right temple eased off. I inhaled deeply, surrounding myself in his masculine, earthy scent. Everyone around us disappeared.

"I know what you did," he whispered.

I jerked back, eyes narrowing. Not the sweet nothings I'd been hoping he'd whisper. "What?"

Arching a brow, he then turned and swaggered off to join the congratulatory group forming around Lea. I popped my hands on my hips, shaking my head. There was no way he could know. No way at all.

CHAPTER FIFTEEN

Later that night, I was on the hunt and Aiden was my prey. After training, he'd *disappeared*. After dinner, he'd *disappeared* again, and hours had gone by since then. It was a few minutes past midnight, and I knew he wasn't on rounds. Solos was, and the niggling suspicion that Aiden was avoiding me was turning into full-blown paranoia.

Prowling through the lower floor, I hoped to burn off most of the nervous energy and stave off the beginnings of a headache. Right now, it was just a dull ache behind my eyes, but I had a feeling it was going to turn into a head-splitter.

There was another long night ahead, made worse by where my thoughts were. Of all things I should've been worried about at the moment, I knew this wasn't it, but I hated that there was this wall that had come out of nowhere. And it was a weird wall that…

I weathered a sudden, terrible memory of Aiden staring at the bottle of Elixir I'd held in the kitchen after my first dinner back in the land of the sane. Had seeing that Elixir reminded him of what he'd taken part in? He couldn't be...feeling guilty over placing me on the Elixir, could he? I'm pretty sure everyone in the world would agree that had been necessary.

"You look pissy." Lea's voice rattled me out of my thoughts.

I stood outside a small study that held only a couch and a desk. Bookcases lined the wall, but most of the shelves were empty. The only light came from the little lamp peeking over the back of the couch.

"I'm not pissy." I was confused, frustrated and paranoid, tired and...okay, I was a tiny bit pissy.

She tucked a stray strand of hair back. A moment of silence passed and then, "I know what you did."

That was the second time someone had said that to me in a few hours, and honestly, neither of them could really know. Could they? Wasn't like I wore a sign on my forehead.

I stared at Lea blankly. "I have no idea what you're talking about."

She made a show of slowly closing her book and putting it aside. Biting back a groan, I walked into the room and leaned against the desk. "What?" I demanded, folding my arms.

My archnemesis stared back at me unflinchingly. Whatever I'd dished out at her over the years, she'd always returned. In some ways, we were a lot alike. We were two alpha females, constantly at one another's throats.

But it was more than that.

In a flash of disturbing insight, I knew why we'd become sandbox enemies so very long ago. When I was younger, before Mom had yanked my butt out of the Covenant, before Lea and I hated each other, we used to be decent. That is, until one day, I'd said something terrible to her.

Even at the age of ten, Lea had loved her pure-blooded stepmother and half-sister—to the point that the rest of us halfs thought something was wrong with her. Most of the pures ignored their half-blood children, especially the ones who hadn't birthed or sired the half-bloods. Stepparents in our world were truly step-monsters. But in Lea's world, her pure-blooded stepmother must've loved her dearly. Every Monday, after spending the weekend with her stepmother, Lea would talk about all the wonderful things they'd done together—shopping, watching movies, and getting ice cream. None of us had that with our step-monsters. Lucian used to lock me in my bedroom when Mom wasn't home.

So naturally, we'd been jealous.

We'd dogged her constantly about her love of her stepmother. Destroyed the dress she had bought Lea by spilling cranberry juice on it. Hid the tiny photo album Lea carried with her all the time. It had been polka-dotted with pink stripes, full of these pictures of her and Dawn, her pure-blooded half-sister. Once I'd found a card Lea's stepmother had written to Lea, tucked away in one of her textbooks.

I had ripped it to shreds in front of Lea, laughing as she cried.

Then one day, while we were all running laps, Lea had stopped to stare at a visiting pure-blood Council member. Her face had taken on this glow that none of us understood. It looked like respect and wonder. But that couldn't be right. Because, as halfs, we didn't stare at pures in open admiration, like we'd cut off our left arm to be like them.

After class, I had found Lea sitting in the courtyard with her friends. Followed by Caleb and a few others, I'd stormed their circle and stood in the middle. And I'd said the biggest, meanest thing I could ever say to another half-blood.

"You have more pure-blood in you than half." The same thing Seth had said to me once before.

Come to think of it, I think I may have spit on her, too.

Lea pretty much hated me after that, and honestly, I don't know how I had forgotten that. Then again, I probably chose to forget what'd started our sandbox hate. I always chalked up Lea's animosity toward me as a product of her general bitchiness, when in reality I had been nothing more than a bully.

It seemed too late to apologize now, and knowing Lea, it wouldn't change anything, not that I expected it would.

Lea watched me now, head tilted to the side as if she knew where my thoughts had gone. She smiled tightly. "You let up on the air element while we were fighting." My mouth dropped open, but she rushed on.

"I wouldn't have broken your hold if you hadn't let up. I felt it lessen—the pressure—and I didn't realize right away that you did it, but I figured it out," she said, as if she wanted to prove that she'd been smart enough to see through it. "What I don't get is why you did it. You could've pushed me straight through the ground. Gods know you never had a problem coming after me before. What's so different now?"

Unfolding my arms, I gripped the edge of the desk. I had no idea what to say. Lea was right. I *had* let up on the air element, and that wasn't the only thing she called me out on. A few months ago, if I'd had control over the element then, I would've tossed her around the forest for the fun of it, maybe even thrown another apple at her face. Anything was possible.

I tugged on my hair, pulling the thick braid over one shoulder. Lea waited for my explanation, and I felt my cheeks redden.

Her amethyst eyes narrowed.

Blowing out a low breath, I rolled my eyes and tossed my hair back over my shoulder. "Okay. You got me. I did let up, and I did it because I remember how much it sucked to be held down like that and be helpless. I *hated* it when Seth did it to me."

She paled under her ever-present tan. "He…he did that to you?"

"In training," I said, dismissing where her mind was obviously going with that. "Anyway, I just couldn't do that to someone else, even if that person *is* a stuck-up, tan-as-leather hooch."

Lea watched me a moment, then cracked a smile. "And that's coming from Alex, Covenant dropout extraordinaire and psycho Apollyon."

My lips twitched. "Ow. Burn."

Turning her head, she hid her grin but quickly sobered as she faced me. "You've changed so much, Alex."

Part of me wanted to deny it, but it was true. As I stared back at the copper haired girl, I realized we'd both irrevocably changed. There was no going back to the girls we'd been over the past summer.

Lea sighed and her nose wrinkled. "So…this is awkward."

I laughed. "Yeah, it is. I feel like I need to insult you some more."

She leaned back in an arrogant sprawl as she raised her hands. "Do your best."

"It's too easy," I said, letting go of the desk, feeling the blood rush back into my fingertips. "I'll just wait for you to do something to tick me off. I'm sure it won't take long."

"Probably not," she replied. "I'm surprised you're not all up Olivia's butt."

I arched a brow. "Trying to tick me off so soon? I'm surprised."

Lea shrugged and then there was a pause. "Olivia told me that you saw Caleb twice. Was that…was that true?"

I nodded. "I saw him when I went to the Underworld, and he visited me right before I escaped."

Her thick lashes swept down. "Was he okay?"

And then it hit me. It wasn't concern for Caleb or anything, but the reason she was asking had to do with her half-sister. "Yeah, he was more than okay. He was happier than he was before he passed." A lump formed in my throat and I focused on the empty bookshelves. "He said my mom was there too, so I'm sure your parents and Dawn are there…and they're okay."

She drew in a choked breath, and like me, she suddenly became focused on the frayed edges of the couch arm. All half-bloods had been trained to show no pain, and gods forbid we cried. The whole show-no-weakness mantra was hard to leave behind.

I dropped down on the cushion beside Lea and picked up the book she'd been reading. Turning the book over, my brows flew up as I got an eyeful of the hottie on the cover. "Wait. Is this book about aliens?"

She snatched it back from me. "Yes."

"Really?"

"But they're hot aliens." She tapped on the guy's face with one thin finger. "And he can be my E.T. any day."

I laughed outright, and it did feel a little odd to be laughing with Lea of all people, but she smiled a little. Lea and I would never be BFFs, but I wondered if, one day, we'd actually consider each other friends.

A sharp slice of pain shot from behind my eyes and across my temples. Wincing, I stood and took a deep breath. "Do we have any Tylenol around?" Another shot of pain, like fire streaking through the vessels in my brain, caused nausea to rise in my throat. "Or a sledge hammer? Something?"

"I'm sure there's something—hey—*hey*—are you okay?" Lea's voice suddenly sounded so, so far away, but her hand was on my arm.

"Yeah, I'm…okay." I took a step and felt a tremble in my legs. Muscles twitched, gave way.

An explosion flashed white in the dimly lit room, blinding me temporarily. I thought I screamed a warning. I thought I turned to move in front of Lea, but when the intense white light receded, I wasn't in the little room anymore.

The circular chamber was made of sandstone and lined with marble pillars. Strange glyphs covered the walls, runes that matched the ones gliding over my skin. There was nothing in the room—no couch or bookshelves or Lea—but I wasn't alone.

"What the hell?" I demanded.

Standing before me was a god, one who looked like he wasn't much older than me. The winged cap he wore hid most of his hair, but light brown wisps poked out from underneath. He wore a white chlamys cloak.

The god gave a little smile. "Don't kill the messenger." And then he blinked out.

"What the fu—"

Then I saw him. He leaned against one of the pillars, his back to me. The familiar black garb, the wave of blond hair—now slightly longer… Recognition sent a terrible, icy shock wave of disbelief through me.

"Seth?" I whispered.

A heartbeat passed and he turned his head to the side. "I am not very happy with you, Alex." Horror rose quickly and I took an involuntarily step back. Before, I never would've feared him—would've laughed at the thought. But now I was terrified—not of him, but what he could do.

Seth turned to me and his face was as I remembered—strong jaw and expressive lips, eyes like liquid amber and a beauty that was too perfect. It always reminded me of sculptures done in the images of the gods.

He arched a mocking brow. "What? Are you struck speechless? That would be a first."

"How?" I croaked, heart racing painfully.

"We're still connected, and I've been waiting for the right moment to…how should I say this? Make a long-distance call via our bond?" He smiled that smug half-grin. "Shield or not, I can still reach you…with a little help from friends in high places."

The god… "Hermes?"

Seth nodded. "He's always been a fave of mine. Bringing you to me will surely piss off some of the other gods, which was all it took to convince Hermes to do it. And before you jump to the wrong conclusion, Hermes is not the god responsible for me."

The fact that Seth had gotten Hermes to swoop in ticked me off, but it didn't make sense. How had Hermes found me? Confusion swamped me, but there was something that tasted like blood behind it. "I don't understand. Where am I?"

"You're where I want you to be." He took a calculated step forward.

I inched backward. "That's not much of an answer."

Seth cocked his head to the side, eyes narrowing as he kept coming forward. "Do you think you deserve an answer?"

Now I knew what tasted like metal in the back of my throat. Anger. "Am I dreaming, Seth?"

He laughed; while we'd been connected, he had laughed a lot, but now I realized there was a difference between real Seth and the ghost version of him. His presence was potent;

his voice held a husky, musical quality to it with the slightest accent. And his laugh…his laugh was deep and smug. "You're not dreaming, Alex. Like I said, I used our connection, and Hermes helped. This…" He spread his arms out, and the golden skin was covered in moving symbols. "This is in here." He tapped a finger on his skull. "It's like Skyping."

My hand itched to knock that smile off his face. "So this isn't real?"

"Oh, it's real to a certain extent."

I found that I'd kept backing up and now my back was against the warm sandstone wall. "This can't be real."

Seth stopped in front of me and leaned in, coming so close that I turned my head, my fingers curling helplessly at my sides. His breath danced over my cheek. "If you're worried that I can transfer your power in this state, I can't. Neither can I really get anything out of our bond. Your shields"—he rolled his eyes—"are still intact. I probably shouldn't have taught you how to do that, but anyway, you're not really here. Hermes rode our connection to your subconscious and pulled you into mine."

Gods, that sounded so entirely messed up. "I missed you. So relax."

Relax? I was supposed to relax when I was here, wherever here was, with banana pants Seth? My head jerked toward him. Our faces were mere inches apart. "You missed me?"

"I miss the Alex who lived to make me happy." He laughed at what I was sure was an *I'm going to murder you* look that crossed my face. "Okay. I wanted to see if this would work and it did."

"So if I touch you, then nothing will happen?"

"Correct." His amber eyes flared. "Wait. You want to touch me? I like where this is going."

I smiled, and then a second later I planted my fist in his stomach with everything I had in me. Doubling over, Seth grunted and let out a low curse. Moving forward, I brought my knee up, slamming into the same spot my fist had connected with seconds before.

"Dammit, Alex, I can *feel* that." Seth straightened, rubbing his stomach.

Sweet satisfaction tasted like sugar on my tongue. "Good! Because there's more where that came from, you douchebag!" I swung again.

Seth reacted quickly, capturing my hand in his. He pushed back, snatching my other wrist, which was heading for his face. Less than a second later, he had both my wrists pinned above my head.

Smiling like I hadn't just kicked the air out of his stomach, which totally ticked me off, he pressed in. "How many times have I told you, Alex? Hitting isn't nice."

I pushed off the wall, but all that succeeded in doing was bringing our bodies flush. Anger deepened the hue of his eyes, as did something else—interest and lust. And even though that made my skin crawl, I realized something important. The cord wasn't snapping alive like it usually did when I was around him, especially when he was practically on top of me. It rested dormant in the pit of my stomach.

This was real…but it wasn't real. Still, I wasn't thrilled with what was happening.

"You're in my personal space." My jaw ached from how hard I was grinding my molars. "Let go."

"No." His eyes widened. "You might hit me again."

"You can count on it!" Rage boiled inside me, swallowing the confusion and terror that had held such a tight grip on me. "How could you do that to me?" I kicked off the wall, but

Seth pushed back. "You promised you wouldn't use our bond against me, and you did! You turned me into the president of the Seth Fan Club."

His lips twitched. "I see nothing wrong with that."

I seethed. "I referred to you as *my* Seth!"

"Again, I see nothing wrong with that."

Hands curling into fists, I glared at him. "It was wrong, Seth! What you're doing is wrong! Don't you understand that? Dammit!" Throwing my hand back, it cracked against the wall. Very real pain exploded up my arm. "Shit!"

"Now, calm down. You're just going to hurt yourself." Mischief sparkled in his golden eyes, and for an instant, I was reminded of Seth—Seth before he went crazy on aether power, who ticked me off just as much as he made me laugh—the boy who had stolen a piece of my heart.

I stared into his eyes, feeling some of the rage seep away. "What happened to you?"

He blinked. "What?"

Slumping against the wall, I lowered my gaze. "You've always been arrogant as hell, but..."

"Thanks," he said dryly, but the grip around my wrists loosened.

"But you never would've done this to me—used the bond against me." I lifted my gaze. "You never would've attacked the Council or sided with Lucian. *What* happened to you?"

A muscle popped out in Seth's jaw. "I got smart, Alex. What happened to *you* is the better question. The girl I met would've gone against the Council without a second thought. She would've still hated Lucian, but she would've seen that what he was trying to do was the right thing."

"No." I turned my head, swallowing hard.

"Yes!" Moving my wrists to one hand, he caught my chin

in his other, forcing me to look at him, and I hated the near-feverish gleam to his eyes. "He wants to change the world."

"He wants to rule it, Seth! There's a big difference. And you're nothing but a pawn." I dug into that fury in me, clinging to it. "He's *using* you, Seth. You used to be stronger than that, but you're weak—weak on power."

Anger flashed across his face like lightning as his grip tightened on my chin. "I am not weak."

"You are! You're so weak that you can't even see what Lucian is doing to you! Don't you even care about what's happening to the world? Innocent people are dying, Seth." Meeting his furious gaze, I willed him to understand, to see where everything went wrong. "How can you be okay with that? You have to stop this."

His silence was stony.

"Do you understand what I'm going to have to do?" Tears welled in my eyes at the same moment I heard the whisper of my name being called from what sounded like miles away.

Seth heard it too, and he recognized the voice. His lips pulled back in a snarl.

"I'm going to have to kill you, Seth." My voice gave out.

He jerked back, letting go of me so quickly that I nearly fell. Something a lot like disbelief flickered across his features, and there was more. A look I couldn't figure out, and then his expression went cold. "You can't kill me."

The sound of Aiden's voice calling for me tugged at every cell in my body. "I will find a way, because I can't let you do this."

Seth folded his arms. "You'll fail."

My heart tripped over itself. "What do I have to do to make you stop? Tell me!"

His lips twisted in a cruel smile. "There is nothing you

can do, Alex. You need to accept what's happening—accept our Fate. You were made for me, and I *will* find you. And if anyone stands in my way, I won't think twice about taking them down."

I gasped, sickened, saddened, and a whole lot disturbed to hear him say that. He'd done so many hideous things, but to hear that, to see how truly far gone he was, cut deep into me. "Seth..."

He shot forward, clasping the sides of my head. "So go ahead and shield me out all you want. As you can see, I can still get to you." Pressing his forehead against mine, he dragged in a deep breath. "We'll be seeing each other again real soon."

Seth shifted again and I felt his lips brush my forehead a second before light exploded in and around me.

CHAPTER SIXTEEN

Lungs burning as if I'd been underwater, I sucked in a deep breath and jerked. When the light receded this time, gunmetal gray eyes stared into mine.

"Alex?" Relief tinged Aiden's tone, making his voice deep and tight. His eyes were shadowed by concern, but there was a twinge of anger way in the back of them. "Gods, Alex, I thought..."

I blinked a couple of times as the small den came into focus around me. It was the one Lea and I had been in. Aiden's arms were around me, and I was half on the floor, half in his lap. I started to sit up, but he placed his hand on my cheek, pressing my head against his own.

"Hold on there for a few minutes," he said, shifting so that his back was against the lower part of the couch. "Are you okay?"

"Yeah." I cleared my throat, willing the pounding of my heart to slow. "That...that was trippy. Where's Lea?"

"Outside the room with everyone else." His thumb traced

a soothing circle over my cheekbone. "She came and found me when you passed out. She said you complained about a headache before you dropped. It…it freaked her out. Are you sure you're okay?"

I dropped? Geez, not only could Seth just reach out and touch me, but he could cause me to faint like a wuss? "Yeah, the headache is gone. I just feel a little out of it." Pushing into a sitting position, I twisted to face Aiden in his embrace. "How long have I been out?"

"A few minutes." His eyes searched mine. "Alex, you… you said Seth's name. I thought…" He shook his head and his lashes swept down, hiding his eyes.

"What?" I placed my hand on his smooth cheek, and then it hit me. My breath hitched in my throat. "You thought I connected with Seth again?"

He didn't immediately respond. "I thought it—yes, especially when I heard you say his name. I got everyone out of the room." Aiden looked up, his gaze meeting mine. "I didn't know what I was going to do…"

Elixir wouldn't have been an option. He'd tossed the last of that down the drain. What would he have done? The look in his eyes shattered me.

I leaned in, pressing my forehead against his. The act reminded me of Seth, but it was so much different, meant so much more. "I did see Seth, but I didn't connect with him."

Aiden reached with both hands, placing them on either side of my face. There was a faint tremble in his powerful arms. Neither of us spoke for a long second. My heart raced in a different kind of pounding. "What happened?" he asked finally.

"Hermes—freaking Hermes," I said. "I really don't understand how he did it, but he followed the connection between

Seth and me and pulled me into Seth's subconscious, or some kind of junk like that."

I was sure Aiden was quiet because he was so angry he couldn't form words.

Taking a deep breath, I wrapped my hands around his wrists and told him everything. With each word, Aiden's fury increased until it became a tangible thing in the room, thick like smoke.

I ended up lowering his hands, keeping mine wrapped around his. "It was real…but not real. I don't know if he'll be able to do it again, or if Hermes will help him again. Or if there was something I was doing or not doing that made it easier."

"You got a headache before it happened?" When I nodded, his eyes turned as cool as steel. "When you were on the Elixir, do you remember getting headaches?"

I shook my head.

He let out a low curse. "You would get a headache when the Elixir was starting to wear off. You would also start to hear Seth's voice. It was him trying to connect with you. I think the same kind of thing is happening here with Hermes."

"Crap," I said, stunned. Then I thought of the nightmare. Moving faster than Aiden could track, I stood and backed away. "I had a nightmare a few nights ago."

He rose fluidly. "I remember."

"I dreamt that Seth was in the room, but maybe it wasn't a nightmare. Maybe it was him testing out our freaking long-distance calling feature with Hermes?" I cursed, fighting the urge to pick up and throw something. "Well, the good thing is he couldn't get anything through the bond. He can't pick at my thoughts or take control."

"There's nothing good about this," Aiden all but growled.

"Well, I *was* trying to be Positive Polly."

His hands clenched at his sides. "You could hit him, so that means he can hit back, Alex. Yeah, he may not find out where you are, but that is a huge violation."

I nodded numbly. Aiden was right. There was no telling if Seth could do it again.

"And there's nothing I can do if he does this again. I swear to the gods..." Spinning quickly, Aiden picked up a small figurine and threw it across the room. It shattered off the wall, an explosion of plaster and glass.

The door to the room swung open and Solos peeked in, brows raised. "Is—"

"Leave us!" Aiden ordered sharply, then he took a shuddering breath. "Alex is fine. We're both fine."

Solos looked like he was about to disagree, but he took another look at Aiden and decided against it. He shut the door.

I slid Aiden a look. "Did that make you feel better?"

"No," he shot back, taking a deep breath as he gestured at the dent in the wall. "I wish that was Seth's head."

Seeing Aiden lose his control was something I always found nothing short of awe-inducing, mainly because he *never* lost control, but sometimes I forgot that he was far from perfect or saintly. He had a temper—nothing as crazy as Seth's or mine, but fire hummed in his blood.

I crossed my arms, suddenly feeling chilled. "But there has to be a reason why he was only able to do this now. And—*and*—he heard you calling my name." Hope sparked inside me. "His hold on me wasn't that strong."

"I bet he was thrilled about that."

Recalling the way Seth had appeared when he heard Aiden's voice, I was sure he'd been damn near murderous.

"There has to be something, Aiden. We just need to figure it out."

Aiden cut me a dark look as he stalked across the room, stopping before the window. I bit my lip. "We will. We always do."

He said nothing, his back unnaturally stiff. "Are you sure you're fine?"

"Yes," I said, exasperated. "Can you stop asking me that? I'm fine. I'm okay. Tonight was a small setback, but—"

"I know." He looked over his shoulder, his voice measurably lower and even. "I know, Alex. I'm sorry."

"You don't have anything to apologize for."

He let out a short laugh. "I have a lot to apologize for, Alex."

I stared at him. This was about something more than what had just happened with Seth. Yeah, he was ticked off, mostly for my benefit and I appreciated that, but this was more. I thought of the weird gap between us in the last few days.

Irritation pricked my skin. "What is your deal?"

"I have no idea what you're talking about."

"You don't?" I stalked up to him and reached up to place my hand on his face. He flinched away, and I felt a pang in my chest. "That! That's what I'm talking about."

He scowled.

Like with any other situation in my life, when I was annoyed or frightened by one thing, I pretty much turned all that energy on something else. "You've been acting weird for days and practically hiding from me."

"I haven't been hiding from you, Alex." A muscle worked in his jaw as he stared out the window. "Do you really think this is the time to be talking about this?"

I took a deep breath and felt my famous temper rise to the occasion. "Is there a better time?"

"Maybe when you haven't just been sucked into gods-know-where by Seth and we're not planning on going out there and coming face-to-face with gods-know-what." He glanced over his shoulder, eyes a cool gray. "Maybe then."

Oh, I was two seconds from jumping on his back and strangling him from behind…with love, of course.

"Do you think we're going to get a better time to talk about this? That sometime in the near future everything is just going to pause for us to have a heart-to-heart?" Aiden had turned back to the window, but I didn't need to see his face to know he wasn't a happy camper. "Okay. I don't get this. You were fine when we came back. We—"

"We shouldn't have done that."

Pain sliced into my chest like he'd socked me. At once, I felt the marks respond, bleeding across my skin.

Aiden's head tipped down and he cursed. "I didn't mean it like that. That night—it was the best night of my life. I don't regret it, but I should've waited until you'd had time to come to grips with everything. I lost…I lost control."

I stepped forward. "I like when you lose control." He shook his head mutely.

"I was okay, Aiden. I wasn't damaged. I'm not damaged now. So why are you hiding from me?"

"I'm not hiding from you."

"Bull! You avoid spending any time alone with me, except at night."

Aiden faced me, thrusting his fingers through his hair. "At night, when I'm sleeping, is the only time I don't think about it—what I did. You…don't understand. What I did to you—putting you on the Elixir? I don't deserve anything else."

"You—"

"I didn't have to, Alex. It was weak of me. I didn't trust

that eventually you'd break the bond. And seeing what it did to you? I can't forgive myself for that."

My mouth dropped open. "You can't blame yourself for that! You did what was right."

Anger flashed in his eyes. "It wasn't right."

"Aiden—"

"The Elixir was one of your greatest fears, Alex! And I did that to you!"

Surprised, I took a step back. Rarely did Aiden ever raise his voice, but I knew his anger and frustration weren't directed at me. It was his own guilt—guilt he shouldn't be carrying around with him.

"How..." He came forward, lowering his voice as his eyes locked with mine. "How is what I did any different than what Seth did to you—is still doing to you?"

I gaped. "Putting me on the Elixir isn't the same thing as Seth twisting me into a violent Apollyon!"

"But I stripped you of *who* you are, Alex. It's the same." Heat rolled off him in waves, intensifying as the seconds passed. Most people would've been terrified of him like this.

I was mostly annoyed—and saddened.

"I held you down and forced your mouth open as Marcus gave you the Elixir." He shook his head a little, as if he was dumbfounded by his own actions. "You begged for me to stop and I didn't. I watched the Elixir take hold, and it was *me* who became your Master. I can't..." He cut off and turned away.

Tears filled my eyes. Wanting nothing more than to take that guilt away, I was at a loss as to how I could. I stepped behind him, wanting to just hug him until he understood I didn't blame him. If there was anyone else more stubborn than me in this world, it was Aiden. If the tables were turned, Aiden would've had something ridiculously supportive to say. He would use an eloquent mash-up of words that meant something, and when that didn't work, he would just tell me how it was.

I didn't have pretty words, so I settled on second—er, third best. "Look, I hate to cut through your self-pity with a big dose of grow-up."

Turning around, Aiden's brows shot up and he opened his mouth.

"No." I placed my hand over his lips—his warm, warm lips. My entire arm tingled from the contact. "You had to make a tough decision. All of you did. I was Evil Alex. And I remember threatening to pull out Deacon's ribcage. I can understand why you did it."

He wrapped his fingers around my wrist and gently removed my hand, though he didn't let go. Score! "Alex, this isn't about you forgiving me."

"Then what's it about?" I moved closer, my thighs knocking into his locked knees. "I forgive you. Hell, there's nothing to forgive. And if anything, I should be thanking you."

Dropping my hand, he looked away and shook his head as he moved to the couch, sitting heavily. "Don't *ever* thank me for putting you on the Elixir."

"Ugh!" I threw up my hands. I was *this close* to knocking him off the couch. "I wasn't thanking you for that. I was thanking you for not giving up on me. For still being there for me when I was acting like a psycho." He stared up at me, stony as ever. "I want to strangle you."

Aiden arched a brow.

I let out a long breath. "We've all done things that we regret. I'm living with the fact that I threatened everyone that I care about. You have no idea the things I thought—the things I believed in—when I was connected with Seth. Or maybe you do, but it's not the same. And if I can get over it, then by gods, you need to get over it."

His mouth opened, but I wasn't done. "I need you right now, more than ever. And I don't need you to just hold me at night." I paused, frowning. "Even though that's really nice and all, I need you to really be here."

Hurt flashed in his silvery eyes. "I am here for you."

"You're not." I shook my head. "You can't be when you're sulking around here, blaming yourself for something you had to do. I need you to man up, Aiden."

"Man up?" He sat back in a lazy, arrogant sprawl, but the coiled tension was in every muscle in his body. "It's a good thing I love you or I'd find that particularly insulting."

"If you love me, you'd get over this. You'd deal with it, accept that you had to do it, and get past it." My breath got caught. "Because I'm scared out of my mind, Aiden, and I don't know how any of us are going to survive what's happening. Right now, I need you—*all* of you. We—*we*—are more important than your guilt, or at least I thought so, but apparently I'm wasting my breath."

I was really close to tipping the couch back and dumping him off it, but he shot up and was in front of me before I could blink an eye. He wrapped an arm around my waist and our eyes locked. Everywhere our bodies touched, heat rushed to the surface. It wasn't like I had forgotten what it was like to be in his arms, I just wasn't prepared for it.

I could never be prepared for it.

Neither was Aiden. His eyes were burning a liquid silver and his arm tightened around me. "I would *never* give up on you, Alex. Never."

"Then why are you being such a—"

"What?" His voice dropped low. "I'm being what?"

Infuriating. Stubborn. Thick-skulled. Freaking sexy. "Good gods, can we stop arguing and just, I don't know, make out?"

A deep, husky laugh rumbled through his body and teased mine. "Is that what you want?"

More than the air I breathed. "What do you think?"

He moved forward, backing me up until I was pressed against the closed door. "That I'm seriously in love with your one-track mind."

I opened my mouth to point out that my multitasking skills had drastically improved, but Aiden took advantage. His mouth was on mine, and the kiss—oh, the kiss killed that freshly acquired skill. Blew it right out the window.

When he lifted his head, just by the slightest, I gasped.

"Okay. You may have a point," he said.

"A point?" I thought I'd made several.

"It's hard, Alex, remembering how you were," Aiden admitted quietly. He slid a hand through the mess of hair at the nape of my neck, sending shivers dancing over my skin. "I hated it. Hated every moment of it."

I placed my hand on his cheek. "I know."

"And all I could think about was getting you back." He pressed his lips to my temple and then the hollow of my cheek. "But you're right. I haven't been *here* completely."

"You're not going to feel guilty over that, too?"

He grinned against the side of my neck, his lips moving against my wildly pounding pulse. "You always have to be such a smart-ass."

Looping my arm around his neck, I smiled. "Maybe…" Hope dared to spark. "Are you okay, now? Are we okay?"

"We're okay." Aiden kissed me softly and kept on kissing me as he lifted me just by one arm and turned me around.

Within seconds, my back was pressing into the cushion and he was over me, fully clothed and covered with weapons. "I'm okay."

"You are?"

He smiled and revealed those dimples. "I will be."

I started to say something, but his hand drifted down my side, tracing the line of my ribcage and then higher, and I totally forgot what I was going to say. I felt dizzy with expectation, of want and need, and a hundred other things as my heart pounded and my breath grew short.

"Thank you," he whispered, and then brought his lips to mine again, pressing me closer, until our hips fitted together tightly. Crazy-insane sensations rushed over my body. "Thank you."

I wasn't sure how we went from arguing to this, or what he was really thanking me for, but I wasn't complaining, and in a really twisted way it seemed normal. Aiden worshipped me as if I'd been born worthy of such a beautiful, complicated man, and over the course of that night, he truly showed me that *we* were okay, that *he* was okay. For now, that was all I needed to face tomorrow.

CHAPTER SEVENTEEN

I had a stupid grin on my face for most of the next day. Even though I was chilly, covered in mud from training in the warded area, and tired from using akasha and the elements, I looked like I'd been smacked with a silly stick.

Only a few times did it slip, and that was when I thought about Seth and the stunt he'd managed to pull yesterday. After Aiden and I…well, when we'd started actually using our mouths for words again, we agreed to keep what had happened between us and Marcus. There was no reason to freak everyone else out, and going by the way Marcus had reacted, it'd been a smart decision.

Marcus hadn't thrown anything, but he'd been as angry as Aiden.

And I knew that was why Marcus had switched out with Solos when it came to training today.

But it was weird beating up my uncle.

Whenever our ragtag group took a break, Aiden was by my side. There were moments when he'd become unbearably quiet and Broody McBroodsters, and I knew he was thinking about what he had done with the Elixir. He was trying, though, and that was what mattered.

We ended the day and hobbled back inside, greeted by the scent of the stew Laadan and Deacon had cooked up. I went upstairs to wash the day's worth of grime off, and Aiden followed.

Once inside the room, I tossed him a coy look over my shoulder. At least, I thought it was coy, but I probably looked like I had something in my eye.

Aiden grinned nonetheless.

"Are you following me?" I asked, kicking off my boots.

He prowled forward, moving like one of those caged panthers we'd seen at the zoo. "I'm just being here for you, and I think you really need me right now."

"Ha. Ha." Out of my shoes, Aiden towered over me, I felt like a hobbit standing in front of him. Aiden's grin spread and a dimple in his left cheek appeared.

He tucked a strand of my hair back, then his hands dropped and he tugged the shirt out of my cargos. "I think you called it 'manning up.'"

This wasn't the kind of manning up I'd been talking about the night before, because even with my limited knowledge of such things, he excelled in that department. But I said nothing as I stared up at him.

He lowered his head, and his lips brushed over mine. I was sure I tasted of dirt and sour apple, courtesy of the Blow Pop I'd been nursing earlier, but he made this sound against my mouth, part growl and part something deeper. As the kiss deepened, like he could just devour the taste and feel of me, I melted against him.

"I really like your idea of manning up," I murmured, clutching at the front of his shirt.

Aiden chuckled as the tips of his fingers skimmed over my stomach. Heat followed, chasing away the chill in my skin. I reached up, wanting more, always needing more—

"Don't stop on my account."

I shrieked at the sound of Apollo's voice and jerked back, tripping over my feet. Aiden caught my arm, steadying me before I face-planted the floor.

"Gods," I muttered, placing a hand over my pounding heart. I'd been so caught up in Aiden I hadn't even sensed Apollo's presence.

Apollo sat on the edge of the bed, head cocked to the side, one leg crossed over the other. His blond hair was loose, framing a face that was eerily perfect. Vibrant blue eyes stared back at me instead of the creepy all-white eyes of a god. I was surprised that he remembered how much they freaked me out.

Aiden recovered first, moving to stand in front of me. He stiffened at the sound of Apollo's amused chuckle. "How did you get in here?"

"The wards on the house faded about three hours ago. Luckily, none of the other gods have realized that and, for the most part, they don't want Alex dead." And then he tacked on, "Right at this moment."

I looked at him blandly. "Good to know."

"Maybe next time you'd want to knock?" Aiden suggested, relaxing a fraction of an inch.

Apollo's shoulders lifted. "Where is the fun in that?" But he stood, his head inclining to the side. "We need to talk, but both of you look like you've been wrestling in mud."

"We've been training," I pointed out. "Like you suggested."

If he was grateful that we'd actually followed instructions, it didn't show. "I will be waiting downstairs. Try not to take ten years."

With that, he simply blinked out of existence. A moment later, I heard a startled yelp downstairs.

Glad we weren't the only ones he liked to do that to.

I slumped against the wall. "I think he took a few years off my life."

Aiden's brow arched. "I still think we need to put a bell on him."

My lips twitched. "And I still think that's a good idea."

He glanced at the door and then took my hand, tugging me toward the bathroom. "We only have a few minutes. Let's make them worth our while."

More than a few minutes later, Aiden and I stood in the large living room with everyone else. Apollo was busying himself with a bowl of the stew Laadan and Deacon had made.

"Hungry?" I asked, after several moments of awkward silence stretched out.

He looked up. "Not really, but this is delicious."

Laadan all but beamed from the couch. "Thank you."

"We wouldn't know," Aiden said. He was leaning against the wall, arms crossed.

Apollo's lips spread into a smile. "Sorry. I'll try to come after dinner next time." The bowl disappeared from his hands, and I wondered where it went. "Well, it's good to see the Scooby gang all in one piece. Warms my heart and all that jazz, but let's get to the point."

"Let's do that," I murmured as I hopped up on the desk, letting my feet dangle off the edge. "You said we needed to talk."

"We do." Apollo drifted toward where Olivia and Deacon sat primly beside Laadan. He looked at them a long moment, as if he could see something beyond what our eyes were capable of, and then turned around. "First, I need you to fill me in on everything the First has shared with you."

Kicking my legs off the side of the desk, I gave him the quick and dirty version of events. There wasn't much to tell, and Apollo didn't pass over that fact.

"That's it?" He didn't even attempt to hide his irritation and disappointment. "You two have this unbreakable bond that nearly destroyed the entire world, and all you can tell me is that you *think* he's heading north, which is something I already know?"

My lips pursed. Way to make me feel like an epic failure of an Apollyon.

"It's not her fault," Aiden snapped, eyes flashing like quicksilver. "He kept most of his plans to himself."

"Probably because he feared that she might eventually break the bond," Marcus said. "So the question remains—what do we do with the knowledge that we have?"

"And hopefully you have some knowledge to bring to the table?" I fixed an innocent look on my face. "That would be a nice change of pace."

His eyes narrowed.

"Can you tell us how Thanatos was able to discover us?" Marcus asked.

"Yes, that's rather easy. Alex's little display of akasha while fighting Aiden drew Thanatos to her."

I frowned at the reminder. "But I've been practicing with it since then."

"Practicing with akasha is one thing, Alex. It doesn't even register on our scale, especially if you stayed within the wards I sensed outside." His eyes slid toward Aiden. "Using it to try to kill someone is like throwing up a homing beacon."

Flinching, I looked away. "So you're saying not to use akasha, then?"

"I have a work-around for that." Apollo held out his hand

and the air around it shimmered an electric blue. A second later, a small medallion appeared in his palm, connected to a chain that dangled from his fingers. A smug, satisfied grin stretched Apollo's lips. "I took Hermes's helmet, melted the mother down, and here you go. An invisibility charm just for you."

Apollo dropped the necklace into my palm. It was a reddish-gold color, and a crudely shaped wing was etched into it. "Ha," I said. "It's like Harry Potter and the invisibility cloak."

Everyone stared at me.

I rolled my eyes. "Whatever. So I'm invisible if I wear this?"

Apollo laughed like I'd asked the stupidest question ever. "No. Your energy will just be hidden from the gods—all except me—even if you use akasha."

"Oh," I said, holding up the necklace. "Handy."

As Aiden came over and helped clasp the necklace, he asked, "What else have you been able to find out?"

"Oh, you know, I've been doing nothing." Apollo glared at us. "I've managed to convince my brothers and sisters to stop their destruction long enough to give us a chance to make this right, but they will not be held back for long. With every moment, Lucian and the First draw closer to overthrowing the Council. And with daimons attacking humans in droves, they will risk millions of innocent lives to put a stop to it."

"Not because they're actually concerned about the mortals." I tucked the necklace under my shirt, ignoring how oddly warm the metal was. It hung about an inch below the crystal rose. "But because if Lucian and Seth overthrow the Council in the Catskills, then they'll be one step away from overthrowing the gods, right? Because whoever controls those seats are the rulers."

Apollo said nothing.

"You know, that's what I don't get." Deacon stretched out his long legs from the chair, wiggling his toes. "I know that if Seth and Lucian overthrow the Council, it's a big deal for the Hematoi, but the gods can't be that frightened."

Without saying a word, Apollo faced Aiden's brother. I knew that he was probably giving the boy one of his Leon/Apollo looks that said, *Do I really need to explain this?*

Deacon fidgeted. "I mean, you guys can just hide in Olympus and call it a day."

"He has a point," Luke said carefully. "Not like Seth can storm Olympus—not really."

I rifled through the memories of the other Apollyons, and nervousness moved through me, quick and slithery like a snake.

"Well..." Apollo sighed. "There *is* a way to get to Olympus."

My jaw smacked on my knee. "Portals?"

He nodded. "They are headed there. It's how we move between Olympus and the mortal world."

"You know," Aiden said. "This kind of information would've been helpful weeks ago. We could have had Sentinels we trust guarding these portals."

"And what Sentinels can you truly trust?" Apollo asked evenly. "Lucian's offer is enticing enough to sway them to his side. Most of the Sentinels have turned on the Council, turned on the gods. Besides, it wasn't necessary for any of you to know that."

Aiden looked like he wanted to say more but wisely remained quiet.

"And luckily, we've kept their locations secret, even from the previous Apollyons." Apollo's gaze flickered to me. "What have you learned from the Awakening?"

I was sort of surprised by Apollo's faith in my ability to block Seth. I doubted that faith would remain if I told him about Seth and Hermes.

Still kicking my legs, I shrugged. "A lot of it is about their lives, and there are so many. It's like watching every episode of a TV series that has been on for a millennium. It's hard to sort through all of it. Sometimes something is said and it wiggles a memory free."

An unsympathetic look crossed Apollo's features.

Well, it wasn't like I was expecting a hug from him. "Most of it is how to use the elements and akasha. And Greek—I can read Greek now."

Most of the room looked unimpressed by that, but Aiden caught my eye and smiled reassuringly.

I grinned back. Reading Greek was a pretty big damn deal to me.

"Well, that's all fine and dandy," Apollo said, letting out an exaggerated sigh.

I kicked off the desk extra hard, my leg bouncing.

Aiden slid me a look. "What do we do from here? Obviously the gods expect us to do something."

"The gods expect *her* to do something." Apollo jerked his chin at me.

"But how can she fight him without touching him?" Aiden pushed off the wall and strode to the middle of the room. "The gods have to understand that."

"They do." Apollo's eyes narrowed on me. "I was hoping there was something knocking around in her brain that held the answer to that little problem. But—"

Apollo smacked a hand down on my leg. "Must you always be moving some part of your body?"

I glared at him as I not-so-gently removed his hand. The

contact of his flesh on mine brought the marks of the Apollyon out like nothing else. And I knew he saw them by the way his eyes darted over my face. "It's not hurting you," I said.

"It's annoying."

"*You're* annoying," I shot back.

To our left, Aiden rolled his eyes. "All right, children, back to the important stuff."

"Think, Alex, there has to be something that can help us—possibly with Solaris." Apollo leaned in, planting his hands on either side of my now-still legs. Over his shoulder, I saw Aiden move toward us, but then Apollo moved his head so that he blocked him. "Alex."

"What?" I gripped the edge of the table. "Look, it's not like I'm being stubborn or stupid. If I could remember something useful, I would. It's not like I'm stopping myself—" *Stopping myself from seeing or remembering something very important*—that was what I was going to say, but like it was with other things, that wave of familiarity washed over me again, raising the hairs on the back of my neck.

When I'd been connected to Seth, there had been something that he hadn't wanted me to think about, and it had to do with Solaris—probably just the whole morbid ending of the two Apollyons. But going back further, there was something that I'd seen, something that Solaris had done, or… tried to do.

In the moments before I'd connected with Seth, I had seen her turn on the First. "Alexandria?" Apollo said.

I held up my hand, resisting the urge to shush him. "There's something with Solaris, but it's weird. Almost like I wasn't meant to know, but I can't…"

Slipping off the desk, I brushed past Apollo. Without realizing what I'd done, I had moved toward the shelter of

Aiden's body. Completely at ease, he slipped an arm over my shoulders, the look on his face daring anyone to say a word.

I looked up at him, remembering how much Solaris had cared for the First. The love I saw in Aiden's silvery eyes had been reflected in the First. And I felt—remembered feeling—the terrible decision Solaris had made—protecting others by destroying the First. Piece by piece, it came together.

"Solaris tried to stop the First, and there was something she did…or was trying to do. Something that would've worked, but the Order of Thanatos made their move before she could complete it." I let out a frustrated sigh. "She knew how to stop the First—kill him, somehow—but I don't know what it was. It's like that information was shielded or erased somehow." Frustrated, I bit out a groan. "Too bad I can't talk to Solaris."

Laadan cleared her throat. "But that is something, dear. At least we know there is something out there."

"Wait," Marcus said. "Solaris would be in the Underworld, right?"

Apollo's eyes were suddenly sharp. "She would be, but I can't travel to the Underworld. Hades still has his panties in a bunch."

Solos smirked as he leaned over the back of the couch. "Well, that's another dead end."

"Not really," Apollo said.

I suddenly got a real bad feeling about this.

"What do you mean 'not really'?" Aiden asked, his arm tightening around my shoulders. Apollo moved to stand in front of the window. Pale moonlight cast a strange glow around him.

"Well, if Alex thinks Solaris can help us, then it's an avenue we want to check out. And who better than Alex?"

Aiden stiffened. "What?"

"She could have some Apollyon girl-talk," Apollo said, his blue eyes dancing with amusement. "Actually, I'm not really suggesting that Alex—"

"Wait." I slipped out from under Aiden's arm. "There's a possibility that we could reach Solaris?" When Apollo nodded, optimism took hold. The rush was like getting buzzed off of wine coolers—harmless at first, but packing a hell of a downer the morning after. "And I could get to the Underworld?"

Apollo's gaze flickered beyond me, settling on Aiden for a moment, and I knew that, if I went down there, Aiden would come too. An old part of me would've protested, but now I understood why he wouldn't allow me to do something like that alone, and I wasn't insane enough to try it. I'd need help.

"You could," Apollo answered.

I could barely contain my excitement. Little Alex wanted to do cartwheels across the living room. I knew in my marrow that Solaris knew how to stop the First. That she held the knowledge to stop this, because she'd planned on doing it before.

But then the one big problem surrounding going to the Underworld surfaced.

"Do I have to die again?" I added quickly, because I was pretty sure Apollo might be thrilled with the idea of killing me at this moment. "Because the whole dying part of going to the Underworld sucked butt last time."

Apollo's eyes rolled. "Dying isn't the only way into the Underworld, but it's the safest." Well, that sounded like an oxymoron if I'd ever heard one.

"There are several entrances to the Underworld in the mortal realm," Apollo continued. "The closest to our location would be the one in Kansas."

"If you say Stull Cemetery, I'll probably hug you," Luke

said, and then he shrank back when the Sun God turned to him. "Or not—no hugging necessary."

"Stull Cemetery?" I asked, glancing around the room. Something about the name did sound familiar. "I cannot be the only person who has no idea what that is…other than a cemetery."

Aiden shook his head. "I'm right with you."

"How cute," Apollo murmured.

I ignored him. "So?"

"Go ahead," Apollo said to Luke. "Tell them what it is, since it's obviously hugging material."

Crimson stained Luke's cheeks. "Legend goes that one of the gates to hell is in Stull Cemetery in Kansas."

"Oh, gods," I muttered, remembering where I'd heard this before. "Wasn't that a season finale on *Supernatural*?" When the boys nodded, my eyes rolled. "Seriously? Are Sam and Dean going to be there?"

Luke and Deacon looked way too happy about that idea, and then Deacon threw out, "Luke has a theory."

"I do." Luke flashed a grin. "Stull Cemetery is a freaky place with a lot of unexplained things happening, just like other places labeled 'gates to hell.' I think that the gates to hell are actually gates to the Underworld."

"You're correct." A ball of golden light appeared above Apollo's hand and he started tossing it up in the air, over and over, reminding me of Seth. "The gateway was actually inside a church there, but Hades came through one night on Halloween and everyone thought the idiot was the devil. Kind of blew our cover—we tore the church down."

"Nice," I said, watching the ball. He was inches from smacking it into the light fixture.

"But the gateway is still where the church stood." Up went

the ball of golden light. "And we've taken some precautions, after a few mortals accidentally stumbled upon it."

My brows rose.

"So, what happens to mortals when they find one of the gates?" Aiden asked.

Apollo caught the ball of light. "Oh, you know. They tend to become one of Hades's dogs' chew toys. Anyway, the gates only show now to someone of godly descent."

"Pures?" Marcus asked.

"Ah…no." The ball vanished and Apollo looked straight at me. "They'll appear to gods, original demigods, those created by taking ambrosia, or the Apollyon."

I elbowed Aiden. "I feel so special."

"That you are." He grinned when I shot him a look. "So, we find the gate and go through it. Sounds easy."

Apollo laughed. "It's not that easy. The gate is guarded now, even to those it appears to." My stomach sank. "Do I even want to know?"

He flashed a smile, and my tummy hit my toes. I so did not like when Apollo smiled like that. "There are hellhounds and guards."

"Oh, goodie."

"And then there are spirits—most don't get past the spirits." Apollo stepped back. "But if you do, the gate appears and you're in the Underworld; however, going into the Underworld without a guide is not only dangerous, but stupid."

So I needed to play with some dogs, beat up a company of guards, *and* call Ghostbusters?

And I needed a guide? Okay. This didn't sound too bad. I smiled. "I know just the person."

CHAPTER EIGHTEEN

"Caleb," Olivia whispered, speaking for the first time. When I nodded, she shot to her feet. "I want to go."

Apollo arched a brow. "Two people sneaking into the Underworld trying to find one soul among millions is insane and dangerous. No one else can go."

Olivia turned her wide, pleading eyes on me. "I have to go, then. It has to be me. I need to—"

"And that's why it cannot be you," Apollo said before I could respond. "You will be focused on finding Caleb instead of the mission at hand."

Her hands curled into fists at her side. "How is that any different than Aiden? He'll be focused on Alex!"

I slid the person in question a look, but Aiden had the same expression that Apollo did. There might be a lot of tears and pleading, but there would be no debate.

"And that's what we need," Apollo said, almost gently. For a moment, I was almost convinced that he pitied her. Not in a bad way, but like he could sympathize with her, which would be amazing since gods were really lacking in the empathy department. "There's no guarantee that they will even find Caleb, but either way, Alex must return from the Underworld with the information we need. Alive."

Some of the other gods probably didn't feel that way.

Apollo's gaze settled on Aiden again. "You would give your life for her?"

I didn't like that question at all and I opened my mouth, but Aiden answered without hesitation. "Yes."

The god nodded. "I know you would too, Marcus, but Aiden would…"

Marcus looked less than pleased but nodded. "I know what you mean."

A bitter taste crawled up my throat as my heart turned over heavily. Going into the Underworld would be insanely dangerous, and the idea of Aiden risking his life scared the crap out of me, but as my gaze fell over the room, I knew that out of everyone there he was the most skilled.

Realizing that she wouldn't be able to change anyone's mind, Olivia said nothing as she walked out of the room, head high. Sorrow panged in my chest, as potent as the fear. It wasn't fair. I wished that Caleb and Olivia could have had one more moment together before all their future moments were stolen from them.

After Olivia's exit, plans were quickly made for our departure. The group would stay behind, as was safest for them, and Aiden and I would leave in the morning for Kansas. Other than an apparent Underworld gate, I had no idea what was in Kansas. Hay bales? Dorothy?

"There's something else," I said to Apollo after the group scattered. Aiden remained behind, closing the door, seeming to know what I intended to tell Apollo.

"I can't wait to hear," Apollo said dryly.

I took a deep breath. "I saw Seth yesterday."

Apollo's brows slammed down as he opened his mouth, but no words came out.

Maybe I should have clarified. "What I mean is," I said quickly, "kind of."

"Kind of?"

I nodded. "He was able to pull me…inside my own head. It looked and felt real, and it was like I was dreaming…but I wasn't."

His eyebrows began to lift. "That makes no sense, Alex."

"She was talking with Lea and started to get a headache right before it happened, like before, when she was on the Elixir," Aiden explained, since obviously I couldn't form a coherent sentence. "Alex fainted—"

"I didn't faint," I grumbled, feeling my cheeks flush.

Aiden's lip curved up on one side. "Okay. She was suddenly not walking or talking anymore. During that time, she saw Seth. Apparently, he used Hermes to pull her in."

"Hermes?" Apollo hissed—actually hissed like an angry lion. "That little punk-ass bitch."

My brows rose.

"I actually felt somewhat bad about stealing his helmet and melting it down." Apollo sounded indignant. "Hermes won't be helping Seth anymore."

It was hard not to laugh when Apollo got all butt sore, but somehow I managed. "By the way, when did you steal his helmet?"

Apollo shrugged. "A couple of days ago."

"Do you think that's why he might have helped Seth?"

"Hmm…" Apollo's face screwed up. "Good point. Anyway, did Seth tell you anything?"

Geez. "He didn't really say anything important. I have this feeling he was really just testing it out, but if you can stop Hermes from helping, then it shouldn't be a problem."

A muscle flexed in Apollo's jaw. "Can he transfer power in this state?"

"No. And he can't read my thoughts." I leaned against the wall, smothering a yawn. "It seems more like an annoyance than anything else."

"It's more than an annoyance." Aiden's eyes flashed silver.

"He sees it as a 'violation,'" I explained, upon seeing Apollo's puzzled look. "But it could be worse."

"As in him doing something like that when you're in the middle of a battle or in the Underworld?" Apollo asked.

"Well..." I frowned.

"I've been thinking," Aiden continued. "We know Hermes helped, but it has to be more than that or Seth would have done this the moment you broke the connection. When you were on the Elixir, he seemed to be able to reach you when it started to wear off, and when it wore off, you were exhausted. Maybe that has something to do with it—how tired you are."

"Makes sense. I guess I just need to get my beauty sleep."

Aiden looked unimpressed. "That's the best theory I can come up with."

"It does make sense." Apollo stretched his head to the side, his striking face tense with annoyance. "You two are still connected, and even though you've shielded out the bulk of that connection, he may be able to get to you when you're weakened, with or without Hermes."

"Like a crappy two-way radio," I muttered.

"Exactly. And especially if Hermes created a path to you."

I did not like the sound of that.

Apollo smiled at Aiden then. "Needless to say, I think you know how important it is to stay close to Alex."

"Like you even have to point that out," Aiden responded.

Apollo smirked. "The trip to the Underworld isn't going to be easy, and that's not even taking into consideration Alex's newly acquired narcoleptic tendencies."

I rolled my eyes. What part of "wasn't asleep" did they not understand?

"And if this happens again, you may not believe he can glean any important information, but you need to be careful that you do not let on to what you are doing, especially your new mission."

"I know," I said, staring at the worn chair next to the god. "I'm pretty sure he doesn't know what Solaris was planning to do with the First, but he knew there was *something*. And maybe we'll get lucky. Seth may not be able to pull it off again."

Neither of them looked convinced.

"Okay, back to the bigger problem at hand. The one I can sort of help you with." Apollo strode over to the desk, finding a piece of paper and pen. "The Stull portal should place you beyond the entrance to the Underworld, at the beginning of Asphodel Fields. They might not really be fields, or they could be." He paused, glanced over his shoulders. "They have changed every time I've been there. Sometimes they are vacant. Other times they are not. Souls that you encounter there will be…relatively harmless."

I crept closer, peering over his shoulder. He was drawing a map. I recognized "Styx." The rest I figured I'd have recognized if I'd paid attention in class.

"There will be tunnels you will enter. You should be able to find a place to rest there for a few hours since the souls are unable to travel through them. Get there before night falls and stay there until the sky is golden. If you don't make it there before night, you'll find out why souls don't travel there."

I waited for him to elaborate and when he didn't, I exchanged a look with Aiden.

"You do not want to be roaming *any* part of the Underworld at night." Apollo's pen swept over the paper. "From there, you will cross into the Vale of Mourning."

"Oh, that sounds fun," I said.

Apollo smirked. "You will eventually come to a crossroads. One way will lead you to Tartarus, and the other will lead you to the Elysian Fields—this will be the Plain of Judgment. You'll want to make yourself as invisible as possible. And I don't mean necklace-invisible."

He set the pen down and handed the map over to Aiden. "I can call in a favor and get word to Caleb, have him meet you there. But from that point..."

"We're on our own." When Apollo nodded, I bit on my lip. "Okay."

"Wait," Aiden said, eyes narrowing on the map. "Isn't the Plain of Judgment near Hades's palace?"

"As I said, you two will want to make yourselves as invisible as possible. I have it on good faith that Hades will be at Olympus, but he has many eyes guarding the palace." Apollo's folded arms were the size of tree trunks. "I need you both to understand that the Underworld will be dangerous. Caleb could be anywhere, and it won't be like the last time, when your arrival was noted. You will see things you cannot understand. Things that you will want to intervene in, but you won't be able to."

I swallowed at the seriousness in his tone. "I understand."

"Do you? You have shown very little impulse control in the past, Alex. You will be unwelcome there. And it's not just the Underworld." His cold, steely gaze moved to Aiden. "The gates are well-protected."

"We understand," Aiden responded calmly.

Keen knowledge flared in the god's eyes. "Be careful. Most who enter the Underworld do not leave, and those who do are irrevocably changed by what they experience."

Apollo started to fade out as we stared at him, no doubt our expressions mirroring the seriousness of what he'd said. Just before his body was enveloped in shimmery blue dust, he said, "I'll owe you two for this, and everything else."

It was way too early to be up and moving around, but here I was, standing beside one of the Hummers, glaring up at the morning sun.

Aiden was saying goodbye to his brother, and I was trying to give them some space while maintaining my balance on one foot. It was the only thing keeping me from falling over on my face. Last night, Aiden had called an "early night" and literally forced me to bed like he was my babysitter. "You need to be well-rested," he had argued, and then sat watch until I went to sleep. And even after about eight hours of shut-eye, I still didn't want to get up at the crack of dawn. We had a long drive ahead of us—about nine hours and nearly five hundred miles. A plane would've been quicker, but there was no way we were getting the weapon stash past mortal security without using a compulsion on half the TSA. And it would've been harder to explain why Aiden was painting runes in Titan blood inside a 747. With that and the talisman Apollo had given me, at least it should be a relatively uneventful road trip.

"Alexandria?"

I turned at the sound of my uncle's voice and headed toward where he stood just off the porch. "Hey."

He tried to smile, but it was forced. "I know you'll be careful, but really—be careful. Okay?"

"I'm always careful."

Marcus's expression turned bland.

Unable to help myself, I grinned. "I'll be careful. I promise."

At the sound of Aiden's approaching footsteps, he stepped back and pinned the other pure with a dark look. "If anything happens to her, it's your ass."

My mouth dropped. "Did you just cuss? I've never heard you cuss before. Wow."

Instead of responding, Marcus hugged me. He let go quickly and looked away, swallowing hard.

Within seconds, we'd said our goodbyes to the rest of the group. "Try not to let any souls free," Luke said, grinning.

"Unless it's Sam's or Dean's souls, right?" When they laughed, I gave them each a quick hug and then trotted over to where Aiden was packing the Hummer.

Once I got a look at the heavy sack of weapons and provisions, I said, "Not it."

Aiden chuckled. "I got it." He lifted it with one arm—impressive—and tossed it in the back. "I've already stashed a few daggers in front. You ready?"

"Yeah." I glanced over my shoulder, taking in those waiting on the porch. An odd ache filled my chest. For a moment, everything was peaceful, though. Birds called. Rays of bright light sliced through the thick trees. It was almost like Aiden and I were going on a vacation or something.

Not going to the Underworld.

Aiden placed a hand on my arm. "We'll see them again."

"I know." I smiled, but it felt all kinds of wrong. "It's just..."

"What?" He closed the trunk.

Shaking my head, I tore my gaze from my friends—my family. As I turned to Aiden, a flash of movement caught my attention. Near the edge of the oak trees stood a doe on thin, elegant legs, and I'd swear our eyes met. There was something intelligent in the gaze—something foreign. Then it shot off, disappearing into the abundant foliage.

"Do you think they'll be okay?" I asked, meeting Aiden's eyes.

"I wouldn't leave my brother behind if I didn't think so."

There was truth in those words. Nodding, I headed to the passenger side, my gaze drifting to where the doe had stood. I thought of Artemis. The gods shouldn't be able to find us, but it took no stretch of the imagination to assume that Apollo would've told his twin where we were.

A small smile played at my lips as I climbed in. They would be okay. Over half of them were trained and damn good with a dagger. Not to mention that all of Deacon's playing around with fire was paying off. With Laadan and Marcus capable of controlling air, they could protect themselves. And if Artemis really was hanging around, they had one badass goddess on their side.

Belting myself in, I placed my hands in my lap. They balled into fists. I glanced over at Aiden as he started the engine. The Hummer rumbled to life. "You know I suck at long car rides, right?"

A half-grin appeared. "I remember."

"You'll need to entertain me. A lot."

He laughed as he coaxed the massive vehicle down the narrow, one-lane dirt road that was all new to me. "By the way," Aiden said, casting me a long look that had me totally forgetting about the seriousness of our mission. "You look damn good in a Sentinel uniform."

A hot flush that had nothing to do with embarrassment spread over me. "So do you."

"I know."

I laughed outright. "Wow. Healthy ego there."

Aiden's eyes were light, a heather gray, as they focused on the rural road. "Check out the glove box."

Curious, I leaned forward and threw the latch. Inside were two black, shiny objects. I pulled one out carefully, turning the heavy thing over. It was a specially designed Glock. Feeling like a badass, I checked the clip—titanium bullets.

The gun felt weird in my hands, though. "I've only held one of these once outside the Covenant."

Aiden was quiet as he waited for me to continue. Of course, he knew when. "I didn't use it. I hesitated."

"You were facing down your own mother, Alex. It's understandable."

I nodded, ignoring the lump in my throat as I placed the gun back in the glove box. "What else is stashed away?"

"Look under the seats," he murmured as the Hummer's tires evened out on pavement. Under the seat were two daggers and a sickle blade. "The same under yours?"

He nodded.

"What are you expecting? A daimon siege?"

"Safe than sorry, Alex. We have no idea what or who we're going to run into out here."

I straightened. "Seth's nowhere near here and we're protected." I tapped a finger on the talisman I wore, and then gestured at the mark above our heads.

Aiden grunted something unintelligible.

My brows rose, but I dropped it. Not like I was bothered by the things designed to stab, shoot, and otherwise kill. "Man, I wish we had coffee."

"Like you need more caffeine."

"Ha. Ha." I stared out the window, nibbling on my lower lip. "Caffeine is my friend."

"And red meat—can't forget red meat."

I grinned at his teasing tone. "Whatever. Eat your bland chicken breast, but soon...very soon, I shall sway you to the dark side of red meat."

We went back and forth for a while, distracting ourselves, and it worked. My muscles relaxed with each passing mile, and we weren't bombarded by daimons dropping from the sky from the moment we hit civilization, otherwise known as the interstate. When we took a detour to grab a quick lunch from the drive-through, I ordered a hamburger.

Aiden got a grilled chicken sandwich...and took one of the buns off.

Rolling up the wrapper, I laughed. "Why do you do that? It's like you have something against two-bun sandwiches."

"One bun is enough." He glanced down at his lap, one hand on the steering wheel and the other covered with specks of seasoning. Looking up, he sighed. "Did you take all the napkins?"

I looked at him sheepishly. "Maybe, but I saved you...half of one." Digging into my bag, I pulled out a napkin and tore it into two. Then I dabbed at his hand, not as graceful as he'd been when he'd washed my hands the night in the kitchen.

I think I may have rubbed his skin raw.

Snatching the bag out of his lap, I pulled out the other bun, wiggling it near his mouth. "Alex..." He leaned toward the window, avoiding the dangerous second bun. "Come on."

"Eat it," I ordered, holding it with two hands now, making it dance in the air. "It's begging you. 'Eat me.'"

He arched a brow.

"Perv," I muttered.

Aiden pressed his lips together, but when he glanced at me and my dancing bun, he burst into laughter. "All right, give me the bun."

Grinning, I watched him eat the bun, and then pulled out the small order of fries. "Want some?" Surprisingly, he didn't turn them down. But after the food was gone and neither of us could find anything remotely worth listening to on the radio, I started to get twitchy. Four hours in, we hit a convenience store a few miles beyond Des Moines, where we refilled the tank and stocked up on what looked like gerbil food. Considering my run-in with Hades last time I was in a convenience store, I stayed in the car and asked for some Doritos, but apparently nacho cheese wasn't appropriate Underworld food.

"Want to drive?"

I shook my head as I buckled in. "If I was driving this, I'd take out a family of four."

"What?" He laughed.

"I've only driven a car, like, once. And it was a bug compared to this thing. I mean, I know how to drive, but I don't think you want me on the interstate."

Aiden reached over, wrapping his hand around mine. "When all of this is over, I'll get you up to speed. You'll be driving one of those trucks over there."

I laughed as I eyed the eighteen-wheeler. "You might want to add 'small town' to the list of casualties."

"You'll do okay—more than okay." He slid the Hummer between two trucks. "Anything you set your mind to, you succeed at it. So no worries."

Tipping my head back against the leather seat, I smiled. "You always say the right things."

Aiden's brows furrowed. "Nah, I don't think so."

"You do," I said quietly, holding his hand tighter. "I don't think you even try. It just comes natural to you."

Two points on his cheeks flushed, and I found it terribly cute. So I leaned over the center console and kissed one of those flaming cheeks. I settled back, grinning at the bemused look he sent my way. The rest of the trip was uneventful, and I actually dozed off about an hour or so from Stull. At first I didn't realize I was dreaming. Everything was foggy, like I was staring down a narrow tube filled with mist. As it cleared and the glimpse of images settled into place, I thought the circular chamber and its sandstone walls looked vaguely familiar. But it wasn't the place that caught my attention.

It was what was on the floor.

Apollo was on his knees, his hands outstretched, and he wasn't alone. Aiden was there, his back to me as he held something—*someone*—to his chest, his body bowed over the still form as he rocked back and forth, his broad shoulders trembling. There was another person in the room, but their form and image were too hazy to make out.

Unease slithered through me like murky fog as I focused on Aiden, wanting to reach out to him. I called his name, but I had no voice. The anxiety grew and I felt cold—too cold. Something wasn't right. I felt like I was there but detached, as if I was watching what was happening from a great distance.

Aiden was saying something, but it was too low for me to make out. All I heard was Apollo's response.

"I'm sorry."

Without warning, Aiden straightened and threw his head back, letting loose a roar full of pain and fury.

I jerked awake to the low sound of Aiden singing along to The Maine's "Saving Grace," slamming my knee into the dashboard.

"You okay?" he asked.

Dragging in a deep breath, I nodded as I pushed loose strands of hair out of my face. My heart pounded in my chest. I'd seen the lifeless body Aiden had been holding and I understood the scream that tore from the depths of his soul.

It had been me in his arms.

I slumped back against the seat, staring out the window. It was just a dream—only a dream. And could I be surprised that I was having messed-up dreams like that? All the stress and unusual stuff going on had to foster some whacked-out nightmares, but…

There had been something to the dream that made it hard to shake, that had left behind a chill deep in my bones. It took a lot to push the dream out of my thoughts. I settled back against the seat, watching Aiden from behind my lashes, picturing us going somewhere else—anywhere other than a freaking cemetery. Like maybe if we were driving to Disney World. Okay, maybe not. Maybe a beach for a sunny, romantic weekend, and I could almost see it. I could *taste* it.

Us being normal, living among mortals like we'd talked about, having a future where we weren't doing stuff like this, where I wasn't connected to a controlling Seth. We'd have a house, because I couldn't picture Aiden in an apartment or a townhouse. He'd want space—a yard—and even though a dog was out of the question because of the power daimons had over animals, it was my perfect future, so we had a Labrador that ran along the fence.

And I'd have a cat that curled in my lap, a fat tabby that ate Aiden's leftover sandwich buns. We'd have a deck where we'd sit out in the evenings. Aiden would be reading a comic or some boring historical text written in Latin, and I'd be doing everything in my power to distract him.

I could get behind a future like that.

"What are you thinking?" Aiden's quiet voice startled me.

"How did you know I was awake?"

There was a pause. "I just did. So tell me…?"

Feeling a bit foolish, I told him about my fantasy future. Aiden didn't laugh. He didn't poke fun at it or ask why a cat would be eating sandwich buns. He looked at me—looked at me so long I started to worry about crashing. Then he looked away, a muscle popping along his jaw.

"What?" I asked, squirming in the seat. "Did I divulge a little TMI?"

"No." That single word was hoarse.

"Then what?"

Aiden's eyes were so bright and luminous when they met mine again—shiny and strong like the titanium daggers we wore. "Only that I love you."

CHAPTER NINETEEN

Kansas was...flat and grassy.

As far as the eye could see, there was nothing more than flat fields with yellowish grass and tall reeds. In the distance, the horizon seemed to meet the land, a dark and ominous blue-gray as night neared, bleeding onto the brownish tall grass and white wildflowers.

"Prairie land," according to Aiden's impromptu history lesson, but what I picked up was that we were driving straight into Tornado Alley. All things considered, probably not the best place to be, especially when I got an eyeful of some of the most recent destruction caused by the unpredictable gods.

Entire towns leveled. Debris-strewn fields and streets. The aftermath of so many lives uprooted, and knowing that it had something to do with me—the response to my initial inability to fight Seth's influence.

It was hard to look past that, but I knew I couldn't drown in the guilt right now or analyze the dream I'd just had. I needed my A game. We were too close to Stull Cemetery.

Nervous energy hummed through both of us. Even with Apollo's insight on the gates and the Underworld, neither of us really knew what we were going to face.

About ten miles west of Lawrence, we came upon the small, unincorporated town of Stull. I sat up straighter, eyes glued to the window.

At dusk, the main street, which appeared to be the only street, was completely abandoned. None of the businesses were open. People didn't stroll down the sidewalks. There was nothing. Man, we were definitely in rural Kansas.

"So creepy," I whispered.

"What?"

"There's not a single soul on the street." I shivered in full heebie-jeebies mode.

"Maybe they're all in the cemetery." When I shot him a dirty look, he laughed. "Alex, we're about to go to the Underworld. A seemingly empty town can't scare you that much."

We came to a three-way stop and Aiden hung a right. "You know, Luke was saying that there's only like twenty people who live here and that it's believed they aren't from Earth," I said, glancing at Aiden. "Do you think they're gods?"

"Could be. Maybe Stull is their summer home."

I took another look at the squat, ancient-looking houses. "Pretty odd vacation spot, but hey, the gods are weird."

"That they are." Aiden leaned toward the steering wheel, eyes squinting. "There it is."

Following his gaze, I sucked in a soft gasp. A dozen or so feet down the road, up on the right hand side, was Stull Cemetery. Not a gateway to hell, but one to the Underworld.

And in the fading sun and gathering darkness, it was creepy as hell.

"I hope no one tries to kick us out," I murmured as Aiden coaxed the Hummer through the narrow entrance in the chain link fence. We were planning to leave the Hummer inside the cemetery. It wouldn't be there very long; time in the Underworld moved differently. Hours there were half-seconds here. Days would be minutes. Weeks would be hours.

"For some reason, I don't think we'll have a problem." Aiden pulled the vehicle to the side and killed the engine. Off went the lights.

Staring at the tombstones, I shuddered.

"Are you going to get out?" Aiden already had his door open.

A tumbleweed rolled down a walkway that had seen better days, and my eyes widened as I followed it until it came to a rest against the fence. "Do I have to?"

Aiden chuckled as he closed the door, disappearing around the back of the Hummer. Not wanting to reenact a scene from *Night of the Living Dead*, I hopped out and quickly followed him. I found him sliding his arms through the straps of the heavy backpack.

By the time he closed the Hummer and hit the security system—*who in the hell was going to steal the car here?*—the cemetery had been plunged into dark shadows. Thick, dark-as-oil clouds blocked the moon, but my eyes adjusted quickly and I almost wished they hadn't.

Thrusting out of the swaying weeds and overgrown prairie grass were fewer than a hundred gravestones. Scattered among the newer tombstones were ancient ones whose inscriptions had faded long ago. Some were square; others reminded me of mini-Washington Monuments, and a few were old crosses that tipped heavily to one side or another.

At the very cusp of the cemetery was a crumbled stone

foundation edged by a few trees. Two mounds of sandy brick marked where the church had once stood, before the gods had burned it down due to Hades's untimely midnight showing.

The pathway was nothing more than a dirt track about a foot wide, and I was almost a hundred percent positive I was strolling on unmarked graves.

"Gods, I hate cemeteries."

Aiden placed a hand on my back. "Dead people can't hurt you."

"Unless they're zombies."

"I doubt there are any zombies around here."

I huffed, hitting the button on the sickle blade. It extended, one end forming a sharp point, the other a nasty, reaper-looking scythe. "One can never be too safe."

Aiden shook his head but kept on trekking up the narrow path. Eventually the walkway faded, overgrown by brush weeds and itchy grass that clung to my cargos. A prickly feeling skated across my neck and down my spine as we neared the foundation of the church. I wanted to look behind me, but I seriously expected to find a horde of brain-eating zombies standing there.

I edged around one lonely looking tombstone and stepped beside Aiden. We were no more than a foot away from the crushed stone.

Aiden straightened the straps on the bag as he cocked his head to the side. "So, you see anything—?"

Suddenly, the wind stopped. Like, completely.

An unnatural stillness permeated the air, raising the tiny hairs at the nape of my neck. Under the black thermal, tiny bumps stole across my flesh. A stale, musky scent seeped in from nowhere. I let out a ragged breath and a small, frothy white cloud formed.

"Okay," I whispered, tightening my hold on the blade. "Not normal."

Aiden's breath lingered in the air, too. Holding a hand between us, he nodded toward the thick stand of trees crowding the remains of the church. Two darker shadows stood a few feet in, almost indistinguishable among the foliage.

My muscles tensed. Guards? Ghosts? I wasn't sure which was worse.

"Showtime," Aiden said, silently slipping off the backpack. He placed it near a rickety stone cross.

I nodded. "Yeppers peppers."

The two figures drifted forward. They were hooded and shapeless, and I realized that their feet—if they had feet—didn't touch the ground. Their dark-red robes trailed an inch above the grass.

Slowly, their arms rose and the material slipped back. A weird creaking noise followed the motion. Slender, pale-white fingers reached for the hoods, drawing them back.

Oh…oh, wow.

Under the hoods was nothing but bones. Pale-white bones and empty, vast blackness where eye sockets and nostrils would've been. The mouths…the jaws hinged on loose joints, so the mouths gaped open. There was no skin, no meat or hair. They were skeletons—floating, freaking skeletons.

Not as frightening or dangerous as zombies, but still, they were creepy.

I stared at them, wanting to look away but unable. It was eerie…their eyes. They were just holes, but the longer I stared at them, something…something moved deep inside them, teeny, tiny dots of flickering light.

My fingers loosened around the sickle blade. "I could just…blast them with akasha."

"Your idea has been noted and discarded."

"Oh, come on."

"Using akasha tires you out, right?" he said evenly, keeping his eyes on the things. "Why not save it for something other than a bag of bones?"

"Oh. Good point."

Those "bags of bones" reached into their robes at the same moment.

I arched a brow. "I hope they don't flash us. Really don't want to see a skeleton pe—"

And then they withdrew two thick and shiny handles. Wondering if they were going to chuck the handles at us, I admitted I was quite disappointed by the guards. No wonder mortals had discovered the gateway when all that stood between them and the portal were two walking Halloween decorations.

"Alex," Aiden murmured.

My chin jerked up, just as sparks flew from the handles, bright and intense in the darkness. Fire spread rapidly, fiery red and powerful, each forming a shape of a long, deadly blade.

"What the…?" My eyes widened.

They flew at us, bones rattling and knocking in a gruesome chorus. Aiden ducked under the first burning blade. Pivoting around cleanly, he planted a foot in the back of one skeleton.

The other lurched toward me, swiping the blade so close to my neck that I felt the heat. Darting to the side, I swung the sickle in a wide arc. The deadly sharp blade sliced through the robe and bone.

In a flash of light, the sword fizzled out and the bones collapsed into a smoldering heap. Taking a step back, I caught sight of the same thing happening with Aiden's opponent.

The fire-sword disappeared, and then nothing remained but bone and wisps of smoke.

I waited for them to get back up and do something, maybe even an entertaining jig, but nothing.

Lowering the sickle, I frowned. "That was way, way too easy." Aiden stalked toward me, his eyes darting over the landscape.

"You're telling me. Stay close, because I have a feeling they were just meant to distract us."

A low growl rippled through the silent cemetery, and my stomach dropped all the way to my toes. Together, Aiden and I turned. I don't know who reacted first. Whether it was Aiden's explosive curse or my groan, it didn't matter.

Crouched in the ruined remains of the church was one big, mean, ticked-off-looking hellhound. Stone crumbled under meaty paws the size of Aiden's hands. Claws, as sharp as the blades we held, gleamed like onyx. The body was huge, about the size of one of those energy-efficient deathtrap cars, but the heads—those were three of the biggest, ugliest things I'd ever seen. It was like taking a mutant sewer rat and mixing it with a pit bull. And the teeth…they belonged in a shark's mouth—white, wet, and very, very sharp. Drool foamed under pink gums and dripped onto the ground, where the soil burned as if splashed with acid.

Six ghoulish yellow eyes settled on us.

"Damn," I muttered, falling into a crouch. "Don't cut the heads off. It's the hearts that we need to hit."

"Got it." Aiden flipped the dagger in his hand, like a total badass.

"Show-off."

Aiden smirked. "Wonder what this one is called?"

The hellhound's ears twitched as the massive body

lowered, preparing for attack. I slid my hand to the middle of the blade, feeling my heart pound and the adrenaline kick my system into overdrive. In the pit of my stomach, the cord started to unravel.

I swallowed. "Let's call this one...Toto."

Three mouths opened in a growl that sent a cold chill down my spine, and a wave of hot, fetid breath smacked into us. Bile burned the back of my throat.

"I guess it doesn't like the name," I said, moving slowly to the right.

Aiden's powerful body tensed. "Here, Toto..." One head snapped in his direction. "That's a good Toto."

I slipped around the ancient cross, creeping up on the hellhound from the right. The middle and left head focused on me, snapping and growling.

Aiden clucked his tongue. "Come on, Toto, I'm pretty tasty."

I almost laughed, but the damn thing lurched from the pile of rubble, landing between us. The ground shook from the impact. Behind us, a few tombstones shuddered loose and toppled over. For a brief moment, it looked like Toto was coming straight for me, but at the last second, it lunged at Aiden.

Caught off-guard, Aiden stumbled back a step, his foot snagging on a fragment of stone. My heart leaped into my throat as I spun toward them, throwing out my free hand. There was a spark, a strong scent of burnt ozone, and then a ball of fire shot forward, more violet than red, unnatural and consuming. It smacked into the belly of the hellhound.

Toto reared back, shaking his three heads, about as affected as if a bee had stung its paw. Well, apparently the fire element didn't hurt it. Good to know.

Then Toto powered off the ground, launching into the air. There was only a second, if that, before it came crashing down on me. I hit the ground, inwardly cringing because I was sure I was atop a grave, and rolled, shoving the pointed end of the sickle up.

I hit the gut, missing the heart by a mile.

"Dammit." Pulling the blade free, I scrambled back. Toto's claws dug into the earth between my spread legs, twisting around so fast it left my head spinning. I jerked back, but the hellhound was huge. Rotten breath blew my hair back. Acid drool dripped, splattering off my shoulder. Clothing burned, and red-hot pain seared my skin. Panic was an icy wind in my veins.

Aiden's hoarse shout of my name was warning enough. Screw this.

Tapping into the cord, I felt it come alive, sparking into a low, steady hum that rushed through me. Marks of the Apollyon bled through my skin, churning into glyphs. Something flared in the hellhound's eyes, as if it could see the marks and understood them for what they were.

Toto snarled. All three heads snapped down on me with the precision and deadliness of a king cobra. Thrusting my hand up, my fingers dug into the matted, coarse hair. Supreme power rushed down my arm. Blue light crackled.

Without any warning, Toto's heads whipped back in a yelp.

The big body tensed, and then shuddered. It flopped to the side, legs twitching. The sharp end of the sickle jutted out from its chest, coated in slick darkness. A moment later, Toto was nothing more than a pile of shimmery, blue dust.

Stunned, I looked up as akasha settled back into the cord, unused.

Aiden stood above me, legs widespread and shoulders back, dark hair falling in messy disarray, eyes the color of steel and just as hard. Power—natural, trained power that came from years of dedication—radiated from him. He was a tall, looming force to be reckoned with, and here I was, the Apollyon, laid flat out on my rear while he stood.

He was a warrior, and I was awed.

Aiden extended his arm. "Are you okay?"

"Yes," I croaked, placing my hand in his. He carefully hauled me to my feet. "Thank you."

"Don't—"

Clasping the sides of his face, I kissed him. Long. Deep. Hard. When I pulled back, his eyes were pools of silver. "Just say you're welcome. It isn't hard. Say it."

For the longest moment, Aiden said nothing and then, "You're welcome."

My lips split into a wide smile. "That wasn't hard, was it?"

Aiden's gaze drifted over my face and then lower. He sucked in a sharp breath. "You're hurt."

"It's nothing." I dodged the hand that reached for my shoulder. The burn had already dulled. "I'm fine. It's just doggy slobber. Don't come too close; I smell like wet hellhound. I'm really—"

"Lexie."

The name—the sound of the voice—wasn't Aiden's, but I recognized it in my heart and soul. It couldn't be, but it was. My breath stalled in my lungs. My legs felt suddenly weak as I turned from a shell-shocked Aiden. My heart—*my heart* already knew the source of that wonderful, soft, and beautiful voice.

I stumbled back a step, suddenly swamped in emotion that tightened my chest and stole my breath. Confusion followed as

I shook my head in a daze. Tears sprung to my eyes. My chest cracked wide open, because this couldn't be real.

"Mom?"

CHAPTER TWENTY

She didn't look like I remembered.

When I'd seen her last—when I'd killed her—she had been a daimon, with black holes where her eyes should've been and a mouth full of razor-sharp teeth, set in skin so pale and translucent that inky veins had shown through.

That image had tarnished my memory of her. Something I'd been too ashamed to really delve into. The fact that I couldn't recall how beautiful she'd been horrified me, but she…

She was beautiful now.

Dark brown hair fell past her shoulders, framing her oval face. Her skin was slightly darker than mine, more olive in nature. She looked like me, but better—more refined and beautiful—and her eyes were a bright, emerald-gem color. Even in the darkness, I could see them, was drawn to the warmth in them.

I staggered a step forward, pulling free of Aiden's grasp. "Mom?"

"Baby," she said, and a little of my world shattered in response to her voice. "You shouldn't be here. You can't be here."

I didn't care about "here" or whatever. All that mattered was that it was my mom, and I *needed* her—needed to feel one of her hugs, because they made everything so much better and I'd been needing one for so, so long.

I stumbled up the incline, dropping the sickle in the prickly weeds. "Mom. *Mommy*..."

"Alex," Aiden called out, his voice pained, and I couldn't understand why.

He should've been happy for me. To get to see my mom again was something I'd secretly hoped would occur while we were in the Underworld, so to see her so soon, before we'd even made it through the gates, was so...

Then I remembered Apollo's warning. There would be spirits, but my mom? I drew up short, standing a few feet from her. That...that was too cruel, even for the gods.

She cocked her head to the side, a small and very sad smile forming on her lips. "You shouldn't be here. Turn away before it's too late."

I blinked, unable to move. Was it really her? Or was it some kind of ploy? Heart racing, I opened my suddenly dry mouth, but then her form flickered, much like Caleb's had in the cell. She was a shade—so there'd be no hugs—but was it her?

Aiden came up the hill behind me, stopping short of standing by my side. "Alex, it's..."

"Don't say it." I shook my head, because I couldn't deal with this right now. I tried and was failing to see this objectively. "*Please* don't."

My mom's form flickered again. "You must turn away.

Leave this place before it's too late. You can't go there. You'll never come back."

My throat worked to let a sob loose. Lowering my chin, I squeezed my eyes shut. It was her, but it…it wasn't. *Déjà vu*, I thought bitterly. I could almost see it—Mom and me standing there, me holding the gun pointed directly at her, my arm trembling, unable to do what needed to be done.

And we could've died right then or over the course of the time in Gatlinburg. Caleb could've died then, instead of months later, within the false safety of the Covenant. I had failed then and was on the verge of failing again. And this time, would it be Aiden who died because of my inability to see past what was the truth?

This wasn't my mom. This was just an *it*—a ward to keep us from reaching the gates. Chest constricting, I lifted my damp lashes.

"You're not my mom," I said, voice hoarse.

Her delicate brows furrowed and she shook her head a little. "Baby, don't do this. Whatever reason you think you have to do this, you don't. Turn away, before you lose everything."

It sort of felt like I'd already lost everything.

Aiden placed his hand on my back and I drew strength from the simple gesture. I sucked in a deep breath and let it out slowly. "This isn't going to work. You're not my mom. So…I don't know. Go do whatever you're supposed to do."

An exasperated sigh, so much like my mom, came from her.

For a moment, I doubted myself.

Maybe this was her and I was making a terrible ass out of myself. But then she changed.

Face fish-pale, veins slithered under her papery skin like baby snakes. Her eyes were sunken, black pits, and when her mouth opened, razor-sharp teeth filled them. "Is this better?" she asked in that sweet voice of hers.

"Gods," I whispered, horrified. "That's so wrong."

Her lips formed a twisted smile. "You're going to have to go through me, and baby, we know you don't have it in you to do it again."

My stomach sank with understanding. "Crap..."

Aiden moved to stand in front of me. I saw him raise the dagger and I knew that he was going to do this—take care of this for me. As much as I appreciated that and really wanted him to do it, I couldn't.

I placed my hand on his arm, stilling him. "I...I have this." My mother's cold laugh was like a shock wave.

"Are you sure?" Aiden asked.

The grim set to his jaw told me he didn't want to listen, but when I nodded, he stepped back and handed me the sickle blade I had dropped. I felt cold as my fingers wrapped around the handle. I hated the fine tremble in my arm and the heavy weight of the weapon.

Most of all, I hated what I had to do.

Mom watched me curiously. "Aw, baby, you really want to do this?" She took a step straight *through* the rubble, stopping in front of me. She laughed again. "Kill your mother twice? Wait. It's actually three times."

"Shut up," Aiden growled.

But this thing—whatever it was—was on a roll. "She died—at least in all ways that mattered—in Miami. And that was to keep you safe. So, that was also your fault. Three's a charm, eh? And you think you can do it? So what? Doesn't mean anything. You haven't seen anything yet."

The back of my throat burned as I took a wobbly step forward, lifting my arm.

"You bring nothing but death to those around you," she continued. "You should've never been born, because you will kill the ones you love, one way or another."

Those words dug in deep, shattering in the depths of my heart. Without saying a word, because I knew it wouldn't matter, I brought the blade down.

It swept clean through her. There was a dull flash of light, and then her form faded away as if she was nothing more than smoke and mirrors. Within seconds, it was like she'd never been there, and only the cruel, punishing words lingered.

"Well," I said a bit unsteadily. "Can't get any worse than that." And then it did…within a heartbeat.

Two forms appeared beyond the broken foundation, quickly taking shape. Having no idea what or who the gate was going to throw at us now, I stood by Aiden and waited as the ghostly shadows became two people.

Aiden sucked in a breath and went ramrod straight. I didn't realize the significance at first. The two shades were strangers to me, a male and a female. Both were tall and elegant-looking, carrying the air of pure-bloods. The woman had springy, curly hair the color of spun corn silk, and the man was dark-haired, with shockingly familiar silver…

I *had* seen them before…in a photo frame back in the room in Aiden's home—his parents' home. The man and woman were his father and mother.

"Oh, gods," I whispered, lowering the sickle blade.

Seeing Aiden's parents—the appearance of our deceased loved ones—suddenly made sense. It wasn't a physical fight that guarded the gates, not like with the guards and hellhound. This was on an emotional and mental stage—a different tactic to get us to turn away, because if we didn't, we had to face the unthinkable.

Aiden said nothing as he stared at them. I'd never seen him so still—not even after the first time he'd seen me cleaned up, after I'd punched him in the face, and then kissed him. Or even when the furies attacked the Council, or after he realized I'd killed a pure-blood. Not even when he stood above my bed, waiting for me to wake up after Linard had stabbed me.

I'd never seen Aiden like this—his face utterly devoid of emotion, but his eyes churning in gray and silver. Tension radiated from every locked limb. After witnessing what I had just gone through, he knew this wasn't going to be good.

And I wanted to stop it before it even got started—spare him the pain of brutal, hurtful words that would lance open old wounds. But when I stepped forward, he snapped alive.

"Don't," he said, his voice thick. "I want to hear this." I stared at him like he was crazy.

"Of course he does," Aiden's father spoke. "My son is no coward. Foolish, but no coward." I jerked toward the sound of his voice. I couldn't get over how much he sounded like Aiden.

His mother's smile seemed warm enough. "My son, you do not want to do this. The answers you seek do not exist where you wish to tread."

"I have to," Aiden replied stonily.

The father tipped his chin up. "No. What you have to do—the right thing to do—is turn around and leave this place." When Aiden didn't respond, his father drifted closer and his voice was stern, relentless. "You must do the right thing, Aiden. We raised you to always do the right thing."

Aiden nodded stiffly. "You have, and that is why I have to do this."

The man's eyes narrowed, and I knew I was about to witness some epic family drama. "The right thing would've been to take your place among the Council, as you were raised to do."

Oh no…

A muscle popped in Aiden's jaw.

"Do you think you can accomplish anything as a Sentinel?" his father asked, and I wondered if he'd been this way in real life. Cold. Disciplined. Was that where Aiden's near-rigid control came from? But Aiden had never let on that that was the case.

His father wasn't done. "You're wasting your life, and for what? A sense of revenge? Justice? You shirk your duties while our family's seat remains empty?"

"You don't understand," Aiden said. "And…none of that matters right now."

The change that came over his mother was nothing short of dramatic. Gone was the warmth and elegance. "You shame us, Aiden. You *shame* us."

I blinked. "Wait a second—"

"You have no control." Disgust dripped from his father's voice.

"We taught you to never take advantage of those who are under your charge. Look at what you have done."

The mother clucked her tongue. "You risk her, knowing she could be harmed because of your lack of control. How could you be so reckless? How could you do this to someone you claim to love?"

My mouth dropped open. "Oh, now that's not—"

"You can't protect her." His father gestured toward me. "You couldn't protect us. You're a failure. You just don't see it yet, but you will just keep on plowing forward until you can't go any more."

His mother nodded. "I'm surprised that Deacon has made

it this far. But then again, look at my baby boy—a drunk and an addict, all before eighteen. I'm so proud."

I whipped toward Aiden and pleaded, "You don't need to listen to this! You can stop this."

She smiled coldly, continuing as if I hadn't even spoken. "And her—look at what you did to her. Placed her on the Elixir, stripped her of her will. You're less than a man."

"You *bitch*," I spat, readying to throw my blade at her, ninja-style.

"Go now," his father said. "Leave this place. Or her blood will be on your hands."

Never in my life did I want to exorcise some ghosts more than I did right then. Anger hummed like venom through me. "Aiden, don't listen to them. They aren't real. What they're saying is bull. You—"

"What they are saying is real." Aiden swallowed hard, sparing me a brief glance. "But it's not them saying it."

I didn't get it at first, because I so doubted his parents were such big douchebags in life, but then it sank in.

"What my mom had said . . . it's us."

I turned to him slowly.

"What they are saying? It's what you really think?"

When Aiden said nothing, I think I was more horrified by that than anything else that'd happened so far. He thought those terrible, horrific things about himself? And how long had he been carrying that with him? Years?

"And your brother?" his father said, shaking his head as concern pinched his face. I was going to gut both of his parents.

"He is unprotected right now," added the mother. "You should be there, not here, chasing a fool's errand. He will die too, like us, and it will be your—"

"Enough!" Aiden roared, shooting forward.

I hadn't even seen or felt him take the sickle blade from my fingers, but he had. The blade arced through the dark sky.

"You'll be sorry," his mother said, a second before the blade sliced through both his parents. Like my mother, they broke apart into thin, wispy strands of color and smoke and then vanished, scattered into the air around them. And like with my mother, their words lingered.

Aiden stood with his back to me. Wordlessly, he hit the release on the sickle blade and with a soft, sucking noise it disappeared into the tube of the handle. There was no danger now. Three wards had come to pass—guards, hellhounds, and spirits.

But I couldn't control my pounding heart. "Aiden…?"

His shoulders tensed and he turned his head to the side. His profile was grim, the line of his jaw hard. "I have thought those things for a long time. Becoming a Sentinel was the right thing for me, what I wanted and needed, but was it really the right thing?"

I didn't know how to answer that. "But you're not shirking your duties or whatever. You are still doing something so important, Aiden. And one day, if you wanted to take your seat…you could." The words hurt to say more than they should've, and for a purely selfish reason. If Aiden took his seat, there'd be no chance of us ever being together. No future with the house, the dog, and the cat.

But I wouldn't stop Aiden if he felt he needed to take his seat.

And his parents or inner voice could be right in some sense. With a seat on the Council, he could do more in regards to changing things, but…

Hell, nothing mattered if Seth was successful.

"I could," he said almost to himself, and I winced. "My brother—"

"Isn't an addict." I paused. "Okay. He was a bit of a drunk and stoner, but he's not an addict. Seth's an addict. A daimon is an addict. Deacon is at the cabin making marinated steaks." That brought a faint half-smile to his face. "He's safe."

"Yes."

He faced me and exhaled roughly. "I really don't think I'll get you killed."

"That's a relief to hear."

Aiden closed his eyes briefly. When they reopened, they were a soft gray. "I have to say, it was kind of nice to shut those damn voices up, if just for once."

Stepping forward, I placed my hand on his arm and squeezed. "Are you okay?"

"I am." He bent his head, placing his lips on my forehead. "Let me grab the bag and then we'll enter the church together. Okay?"

I nodded, waiting outside the foundation. Aiden returned with the bag and knelt. Reaching in, he pulled out a dark, shapeless material and offered it to me. Another followed as I took mine.

"A cloak?" I slipped it over my head. "Where you'd get two of these?"

Aiden stood, throwing the backpack onto his back. "You'd be surprised by what Solos's father has stashed away in his cabins, but I actually picked these up when we were in Athens. Figured we might need them."

"You're so smart and organized."

Laughing, he pulled his on and then reached over, grasping the edges of my hood. He tugged it up. "We have to hide that pretty face of yours."

I flushed. "Same for you."

"I have a pretty face?" Aiden pulled up his own hood, which cast his face in shadows. "I'd like to go with handsome instead of pretty."

"Handsome" wasn't a strong enough word, but I nodded. He extended his hand, and I took it, comforted by the steady, warm grasp.

"Are you ready?" he asked.

"Yeah."

Together, we moved down the line of the fallen stones and found the opening. Together, we stepped through where a door had once stood. There were no more warnings or wards. We moved through the patches of crumbling cement and overgrown weeds.

We waited.

After about ten seconds, a fissure of energy coursed down my spine. Aiden felt it too, for his hand tightened around mine. Anxious energy built in my stomach, forming a tight ball of dread and even a little bit of excitement.

Hopefully, my visit to the Underworld would be different this time.

Toward the back of the foundation, the air rippled, reminding me of heat rolling off hot pavement in the summer. The veil that separated the truth from the mortal world simply slipped away.

"Do you see it?" I asked.

Aiden squeezed my hand. "Yes."

The wrought-iron gate encased in titanium was huge, latching into something neither of us could see. Instead of bars, there were two-pronged spears decorated with images of black bulls and ewes. Where the two gates joined, a replica of the invisible helmet was engraved into the iron. The musty scent grew stronger.

With his free hand, Aiden pushed the gate open. It swung backward, making no sound, revealing nothing but darkness—not the kind associated with night, but a black void. A portal. And together, hand in hand, we stepped through the gates to the Underworld.

CHAPTER TWENTY-ONE

I almost expected that, when we stepped into the void, we'd fall flat on our faces. But the ground remained under our feet as we continued into the darkness, which eventually gave way to fog as thick as soup.

Glancing over my shoulder, I sought to find the gate before the fog swallowed us whole, but it was gone and the fog was even heavier. I gripped Aiden's hand as tendrils seeped between us, wrapping a different kind of cloak around us. I couldn't even see Aiden…or two feet in front of me. A pang of panic unfurled in my chest.

"I'm right here." Aiden's deep voice parted the veil and he squeezed my hand. "Just keep hold."

I briefly considered using the air element to dispel some of the fog, but if the fog was supposed to be here, that could be potentially bad news if it suddenly up and disappeared.

The farther we moved into the fog, the more unnerving it became to be so blind. And then there was a sound other than my own pounding heart—a shuffling type of sound, like feet and cloth dragging all around us, and a low hum, like a soft, never-ending gasp of a moan, and I didn't even want to know what it was. Following the path on Aiden's arm, I stepped closer to him, so close that I was surprised I didn't trip him up.

After several minutes of nothing but blindly walking through fog and that terrible dragging and moaning sound, the fog started to break apart until the path was revealed before us.

I sucked in a breath, unable to stop from clutching his arm. What little part of the Underworld I'd seen before hadn't prepared me.

The fog gave way to a sky that was the color of the fading sun, a cross between red and orange. But from what I could tell, there was no sun. And all around us were people, moving about aimlessly. Dressed in bland, tattered clothing, they shuffled to-and-fro. Many stayed silent; some moaned quietly, while others muttered under their breath from behind their own cloaks, but all had their gazes trained to the ground. They were young and old, from the smallest child to the most aged crone.

This…this holding place continued as far as the eye could see, to the cusp of the hills Apollo had spoken of. I didn't understand what this place really was. It wasn't limbo—that much I knew—as I had been there before.

None of the souls looked up as we navigated around them. There were no guards on horses, like I'd seen in limbo. It appeared as if these people had been placed here, left alone to their own devices and boredom.

"Why?" I asked in a hushed voice.

Aiden knew what I was asking. "The majority of the dead reside here." He led me around a group of three huddled together on the dirt. "Those who have been buried, but haven't gone on to face their judgment. Some of them may have done something in their lives to make them fear their judgment. Others are…"

A woman moved in front of us, her gaze glued to the ground as she wrung her hands. She muttered under her breath, "Where's my baby?" over and over again.

"Some are confused," I answered. "They don't know they're dead." Aiden nodded solemnly.

And then the sad woman simply vanished, as if she had walked through an invisible portal—there one moment and gone the next.

I halted. "What the…?"

"I'll explain, but we must keep moving." Aiden tugged me forward. "Legend says that some of these souls leave limbo and have turned shade. They go back to the mortal world, and then return here again. I don't think they can even control it."

I swallowed. "They're ghosts."

"Thought you didn't believe in ghosts." Humor laced his tone.

Now was a pretty good time to change my mind. As I peered out from beneath my hood, there was something ghastly to some of the souls. Many of them looked solid, and from how they'd brushed against me, I knew they had mass, but others had that wonky fuzziness to them. And the more I paid attention, the more others simply vanished.

This place was creepy, like walking through a maze of the hopeless and forgotten. And we hadn't even reached the Vale of Mourning yet. Yee haw, this was going to be fun.

A sudden damp coldness clung to the air around us. I lifted my head, eyeing the burnt orange sky. One drop of water fell, splashing on my cheek. Then the sky opened up, drenching us in cold rain within seconds.

I sighed. "Really, it has to rain?"

"At least it's not acid."

That was Aiden, always looking on the bright side of things.

Tugging my hood down closer, I trudged forward. The souls paid no heed to the heavy rainfall. Perhaps they'd grown used to it. I wanted to stop and yell at them to go to judgment, because whatever waited for them couldn't be worse than this.

Especially for the little ones who were all alone—there was nothing they could have done to warrant them eternity in Tartarus.

One small boy sat alone in a large puddle the rain had already created. The child couldn't have been more than four or five. He moved his chubby fingers in the mud, drawing a circle and then wiggly lines all around it.

The sun—he was drawing the sun.

I started toward him, not sure what I'd do, but I had to do something—maybe convince him to go to judgment. Gods knew how long he'd been here. His family could already be in the Elysian Fields.

"No," Aiden said softly.

"But—"

"Remember what Apollo said. We cannot intervene."

I stared at the little boy, fighting the urge to break free. "It's wrong."

Aiden's grip on my hand tightened. "I know, but there's nothing we can do."

My heart ached as I watched the little boy carve a moon beside the sun, heedless of the rain or the other souls practically trampling him. I wanted to be angry and I was—even at Aiden, because he was right. There was nothing we could do. And there would be more like this little boy—more forgotten souls.

Fighting back the sting of tears, I pulled my hand free from Aiden's but didn't run off. I fell in step beside him as we passed the poor child, navigating the endless field of souls that had been either left behind or cast aside.

It took hours to pass through the Asphodel Fields. By the time we left the ankle-deep mud and our boots touched scattered patches of grass, we were drenched and cold, our cloaks weighted down and heavy. Rain had somehow snuck into my boot and, with each step, my foot sloshed back and forth. Exhaustion dogged me, and probably Aiden too, but neither of us complained. Traveling through the fields of all those souls had served as a reminder that things could always be worse.

The rain had let up a little, turning to a constant, steady drizzle. The sky was now a darker orange, signaling that night was close at hand. Ahead, the rolling green hills led up to a thick, nearly impenetrable slate wall. It was going to be a steep climb.

"Do you want to take a breather?" Aiden asked from behind his cloak as he surveyed the hills. "It looks relatively safe. We could take a—"

"No. I'm fine." I stepped around him, slowly climbing the first hill, ignoring the dull ache taking up residency in my temples. "Besides, the faster we can get into the tunnels, the sooner we can rest, right? We'll be safe there at night."

"Yes." Aiden was beside me in a second. His hand came out from the cloak and slipped inside my hood. His palm was warm against my cheek. The gesture was brief, and gone all too quickly.

We traveled on in silence, but worry nagged at me. The

headache wasn't severe, nothing like what I'd experienced before Seth had paid a call, but I had no idea how long it would take for it to progress. The only hope was that we would reach somewhere safe—preferably dry—where we could bunk down for the night. Sleep was what I needed, and the sooner the better.

The odd sky darkened with each hill we crested, forcing us to pick up our pace. We crossed a field of narcissus that rose to our knees, petals a luminous white and carrying an incredibly sweet scent. The slate wall drew closer as the flowers gave way to trees.

At least that's what I thought they were.

They rose into the sky, their branches bare for the most part, like slender fingers reaching for the ever-increasing darkness. Around the lower branches, ruby-red fruit hung in the air. Pomegranates.

Curious to how they tasted, I reached for one.

Aiden's hand snatched mine in a near painful grasp. I let out a startled gasp.

"No," he said harshly. From behind the cloak, his eyes were a bright silver. "Do you know nothing of Persephone?"

I glared at him. "Uh, she's the Queen of the Underworld. I'm not stupid."

"I didn't say you were stupid." His grip loosened as he led me through the trees, toward the last mound. "Though, I'm really starting to think you should've spent less time in class sleeping or doing whatever you were doing."

"Ha. Ha."

"Persephone ate from the pomegranate trees here. If you eat anything from this world, you can never leave."

All my smartass responses faded away. Boy, did I feel like an idiot for not recalling that. "Okay. Maybe I should've paid attention in class."

He chuckled. But all humor left him when he got a good look at the hill. "Gods…"

It was steep, covered with grassy patches, exposed roots, trees with enormous black, teardrop-shaped fruit hanging from their branches, and what I seriously hoped were fragments of pale rock—not bones, like they appeared. At the very top, a ledge butted up to the thick gray wall.

Sighing, I sidled past Aiden. "We better get going."

We climbed the hill, using the roots to gain purchase and to keep climbing. I don't know how Aiden did it, carrying the heavy pack on his back, but he moved a hell of lot quicker than me.

Halfway to the top, a twittering sound rose above the canopy of odd fruit. I stopped, lifting my head. The heavy hood slipped back as I stared through the drizzle, beyond the trees, to the now dark-blue sky.

Night had fallen, and I recalled Apollo's warning. "Come on," Aiden called. "We need to hurry."

Grabbing a root, I hauled myself up. "That noise—do you hear it?" Aiden said nothing, just kept on climbing.

The branches above us began to shudder, rocking the giant fruit. The twittering grew louder. "I…I think…it's coming from the fruit."

Above me, a black teardrop the size of a beanbag chair shook—and then it spread open, one…one long, black and hairy *leg* at a time. The center of the mass twitched—and then a row of ruby-red eyes peered down at me.

"Oh, my gods…they're not fruit." And I *so* got why the souls didn't travel near the tunnels now.

The giant spider dropped from the tree, hitting the ground on six of its eight legs. Its squeal turned my blood to ice. Another smacked onto the grass…and then another and another. Their sick chorus drowned out the sound of everything else.

Aiden slid down the hill, kicking up loose pebbles and bones as he came to my side. He grabbed my hand as one dropped beside us, fangs gleaming, raised two of its legs, and made a fingers-on-a-chalkboard screech.

Shrieking, I jumped back, knocking into Aiden as the huge spider scuttled over the ground. Aiden shoved me to the side and whipped out a dagger. Jerking up, he slammed the blade to the hilt into the center of the spider.

I rolled to my knees and scrambled up, catching sight of thousands of black legs scurrying across the ground.

Weight slammed into my back, pushing me face-first into the loose dirt and wet grass. Sharp pain sliced across my lip and I tasted blood in my mouth, but that was a nonissue when I felt the heavy, hairy weight of the spider on my back.

Its legs dug through the cloak as it hissed in my ear. Summoning the power that rested inside me, I felt…felt nothing.

Crap.

Digging my knees in, I powered off the ground and threw the spider. It landed on its back a few feet away, legs thrashing in the air as it hissed.

"Gods, I hate—I *hate* spiders."

Aiden leaned down, hooking his hand around my arm. He hauled me to my feet and pushed forward. "This would be a good time to use akasha."

Hundreds of beady red eyes stared at us. "I can't. I don't think it works down here."

With his hands on my back, he pushed me up the hill, swearing under his breath. "I can still feel the fire element. Can you?"

Lifting my muddy hand, I was surprised and relieved to find a tiny spark. "Yes."

"Good. At the count of three, we'll clear a path to the rocks ahead—" He cut off, swiping the sickle blade at a spider that ventured too close. Legs flew in every direction. "See the break in the rock there?"

I saw it. I also saw about a hundred spiders between us and the slim crack. "Uh-huh."

"On the count of three, light it up and run. Do not stop. Okay?"

"Yeah."

"One…two…*three*!"

Concentrating on the fire element, I extended my hand, as did Aiden. Balls of violet-colored flame hit the ground on both sides, spreading rapidly as they formed a wall.

"Go!" Aiden ordered, pushing me upward.

I scrambled over the ground, not surprised when I saw some of the hairy bastards leaping over the fire. Others rammed straight into it, but they fell to the side, hissing in pain. Aiden grabbed hold of my arm as we climbed the last of the rain-slick hill. Behind us, the spiders overtook the flames. The sound of their legs scuttling across the ground would haunt me right into group therapy. Reaching the top of the ledge, my fingers smacked on rock and I almost cried out in joy.

One of the quicker monsters lurched from below, latching onto my leg. My grip slipped and my heart leaped into my throat as the weight of the spider and the heavy cloak dragged me right back over the edge.

I let out a hoarse shout as my fingers continued to slip, but then Aiden was suddenly there, threading his arms under mine. He threw himself back, powerful muscles tensing and popping under the cloak as he pulled me over the ledge, spider and all. Pulling my free leg up, I twisted and rolled, slamming the heel of my boot into one of the spider's eyes. Letting out a hiss, the spider slipped off my leg and tumbled down the hill, taking out a few of its friends with it.

Staggering to our feet, we slipped through the narrow crevice just as the mass of spiders breached the ledge and hit the wall.

CHAPTER TWENTY-TWO

We traveled for what felt like hours through a cramped tunnel so dark that even my eyes were having a hard time adjusting to it. Aiden sent out a tiny ball of flame every few minutes, but neither of us wanted to risk the light for long—who knew what might be down here? Those spiders couldn't fit into the narrow crack, but, knowing our luck, they probably had babies that would be more than eager to find us in the labyrinth of tunnel work.

Exhausted and soaked to the bone, we stopped as the tunnel widened into what appeared to be an entrance to a cavern. Aiden inched toward it, peering into the blackness. He held up a hand as I moved forward to check it out.

"Let me see what we got first, okay?" he asked.

I checked my urge to push him aside and help out. "Be my guest. If there's an Underworld bear inside, let him gnaw on you first."

Shooting me a wry grin, he shook his head and crept forward, dagger in hand. The tiny ball of flame he sent out was swallowed by the dark. Staying outside the cavern literally took all my self-control.

I leaned against the unseen but probably slimy rock, numb in my soaked clothing. I wasn't even sure I still had all my fingers. It was a good thing that Aiden loved me and could look past my appearance. I didn't doubt I looked like last week's prom queen after a hellish night.

Aiden returned, his daggers sheathed for now. "All clear. We should be good for the night."

Pushing off the rock, I followed him inside. It was a narrow fit for a few steps, and then it opened into a circular chamber—definitely drier inside, so that was a plus. Rain pelted the rock bed from a few relatively small holes in one part of the ceiling, but the rest was dry and suitable.

There was also something else inside…

Toward the left of the chamber was some kind of natural spring. Well, down here, I wasn't sure what it was. For all we knew, it could be a vat of acid, but it smelled like…

"Jasmine," I said.

"I know." Aiden appeared at my side. He eased the hood back on my cloak and gently smoothed his thumb under my lip that no longer throbbed. "Strange, huh?"

"Everything is strange down here." Moving closer to the pool of scented water, I held my hand out. Warmth tickled my palm. "It's heated but doesn't seem too hot."

Aiden had removed his hood. "I doubt we'd get lucky enough for a bath—Alex, don't!"

Too late. I'd already knelt down and gingerly placed a finger into the water, figuring I could spare one. Water fizzled.

Air stirred around me as Aiden shot forward, grasping my shoulders.

"It's okay," I told him. Other than the sudden frothy

bubbling, the water actually felt pleasant. It was so clear I could see the floor of the rock pool.

"Gods, Alex, you don't just stick your finger into things."

I arched a brow.

He rolled his eyes. "Your mind scares me."

I grinned. "You like how my mind works."

Instant heat darkened his eyes to silver. "Most of the time, yes." He relaxed, letting go of my shoulders. "I'm not sure if we should start a fire."

Straightening, I glared at my itchy, wet clothing. Damn.

His lips twitched. "It may draw unwanted attention."

"Spiders," I whispered. Aiden nodded.

I shuddered.

"You're so fierce." He came to stand before me, cocking his head to the side as he placed the tips of his fingers on my chin. "And so brave, but spiders send you into a fit."

"Those spiders were twice the size of Rottweilers, Aiden. They were not normal spiders."

"Still, spiders," he murmured, lowering his head. His lips brushed mine. The gentle sweep was all too quick but powerful. "But if you take off your clothes, I'm sure I can get them dry."

My eyes went wide. "Wow. Are you trying to get me naked?"

His silvery gaze met mine. "Do you really need me to answer that?"

A hot, sweet flush stole across my cheeks. When he was like this—open, flirty, and downright sexy—I was at my lamest. I wasn't used to this side of him. I don't think I ever would be, and there was something thrilling in that. But I stared at him, caught between the images playing out in my head and the very real *man* standing before me.

Aiden chuckled. "You should see yourself right now."

Snapping out of it, I hoped my expression now looked like Alex the Sex Goddess and not Alex the Goof. "What do I look like?"

His grin was small and secretive. "Cute."

"Cute?"

"Mmm hmm." He prowled toward the edges of the cavern, searching the shadows for gods-know-what. "But seriously, if you get out of those clothes, I can dry them."

But I'd be totally naked. There was no need for me to be shy around him, but something about that, here…

He took off the cloak and shrugged off the backpack. As if he read my mind, he raised his brow. "I packed two blankets. They're not much, but they're big enough to cover you."

My lips spread into a smile. Yep, Aiden thought of everything. "You're awesome."

The look he cast over his shoulder said he knew. "I know the clothes are bothering you."

"Are not." The last thing I wanted was to be whiny and weak in front of Aiden.

His gaze dropped. "They're not?"

"Yeah…" My gaze followed his to where I was scratching at my hip. I stilled. "Okay. They are bothering me."

"Delicate skin?" He stalked over, then knelt and unzipped the bag.

I stared at his wet, dark curls as he rummaged through the bag. "Yep, I have sensitive skin. Did you pack any lotion?"

"No," he laughed. "But we have some trail mix."

"Yum."

"Also some mixed nuts…"

"Double yum."

"And some water." He tipped his chin up, eyes dancing. "Sorry. I couldn't pack McDonald's for you."

"Well, no one's perfect."

Aiden laughed again. Gods, I loved that deep, husky sound, and I'd never grow tired of hearing it. Not too long ago, Aiden hadn't laughed enough. So, every time he did, I cherished it like a most prized possession.

He placed the blanket on a dry spot and then stood. "I'll go check the entrance just to make sure we're okay for the night."

I nodded, and he turned without a word, disappearing back into the crack in the wall.

Feeling oddly giddy, considering where I was, I turned to the pool. Just thinking about slipping into the warm water had my chilled, dirty skin begging.

But Aiden so wouldn't approve.

Tugging off the cloak, I kicked off my boots, eyeing the water like it was a slab of filet. If the water was dangerous, it surely would've peeled the skin off my finger by now or had me running around, squawking like a chicken. Mind made up, I quickly stripped down and slipped my toes into the water. I sighed as the pool frothed and bubbled, and carefully made my way down the natural steps. Water lapped and fizzled at my hips as I moved farther out. Warmth, heady and pleasant, seeped through my skin, into my muscles. It didn't sting the numerous bruises or cuts—if anything, the water seemed to soothe them. The soft, seductive scent appeared to soothe the dull ache in my temples, too.

In the middle of the spring, the water reached just below my chest, but my presence stirred the water and the white-tipped foam reached my collarbone, bubbling around the talisman.

Closing my eyes, I let out a low breath. The water felt too good. I could stay in here all night, feeling the little bubbles teasing my toes, sliding up my legs.

It was heaven in the Underworld.

I smiled, thinking Hades had the good stuff when it came to spas and relaxation.

"Alex..."

Aiden's voice pulled me out of my musings. I glanced over my shoulder, smiling sheepishly. "I couldn't resist. Sorry."

He didn't look angry. Surprisingly, he didn't look exasperated, either. I couldn't say he looked thrilled, but...

Oh...

Aiden looked hungry.

My breath hitched in my throat, and it took me a few tries to find my voice. "Is everything clear outside the cave?"

Eyes hooded, he nodded.

I bit my lip. Of course it was fine. We were safe for the night, but resting wasn't on my mind. What *was* was wholly inappropriate and I seriously had my priorities mixed up, but we were facing the unknown. This trip was dangerous and both of us could be hurt. Worse yet, Aiden could die.

Raw panic punched through my chest at the thought of losing him. I simply could not bear his loss. And because of that, I wanted to press pause. I wanted to live, to really live in the moment, and with Aiden, that was always possible. It was magical, actually.

I took a deep, long breath. "You...you should join me."

Part of me expected that I would have to do a decent amount of begging. Aiden was "on the job," and I was prepared to deploy every technique I knew, including whining.

So when he stepped back and slid off his boots, I was

pretty damn surprised. Shock splashed over me as he quietly tugged his shirt out of the waistband of his tactical pants and pulled the wet cloth over his head.

I bit back a gasp.

His stomach was some serious perfection, a product of years of rigorous training. It looked like someone had placed paint rollers under his taut skin. And his chest…

Yeah, I couldn't stop staring.

And the whole time, he watched me with an intense gaze like heated silver. I felt the flush return to my cheeks as my breath quickened.

When his hands moved to the top of his pants, I did turn away. Only because I was sure I'd pass out and drown if I kept staring, and well, that would so kill the moment.

Clothing hit the rock bed and there was a second, too long, of silence, and then the water stirred in the pool, bubbling even more. Pulse pounding everywhere, I twisted toward him and lost my breath and my heart all over again.

Aiden stood there like a god.

So much taller than me, water grazed his navel. White foam lapped at the ribbed planes of his stomach, and I was struck by the image of Poseidon rising from the ocean.

Poseidon had nothing on him.

He glided through the fizzing water, hands out to his sides. I had to tip my head back to meet his gaze. "Hey," I said.

One side of his lips curved up. "This probably isn't a good idea."

"Why?"

"I have a feeling I'm going to be very distracted here in a few seconds." He reached out, though, finding the band that kept most of my hair up. "Actually, I'm already distracted."

My heart was trying to come out of my chest. "But we're safe here. Apollo said so."

"We are, but..." He gently pulled the band out and then set about rearranging the thick strands around my shoulders. A great deal of it sank below the surface. "But we should be careful. I should be paying attention."

I stepped into the loose circle his arms created as he played with my hair. Placing my hand on his chest, I was thrilled by the way he jerked and sucked in a breath. "Can't you multitask? I can."

Aiden lazily tossed a damp strand over my shoulder and moved to another. "You're such a liar. Your multitasking skills suck."

"Do not. And we're not talking about *my* multitasking skills." My hand slid down, having a mind of its own. "I think you can handle doing two things at once."

He'd gathered all my hair now, twisting it around his fist. "You do?" He placed a finger on my bottom lip, slowly tracing the curve. His lashes lowered even more, and only the thinnest sliver of silvery eyes shone. "You should be resting."

"I will." I took the last step forward. The bubbles fizzled and gave way. Stretching up, I looped an arm around his neck. "But you should rest, too."

Aiden's free hand drifted down my neck, over my shoulder, and then his arm was around my waist, holding me tight against him, our bodies touching length to length. It was maddening, and when his lips brushed over the curve of my jaw, my eyes fluttered shut. Every muscle in my body tensed, and then I felt the marks gliding over my skin.

"We can take shifts," Aiden said against my chin, and then on the other side of my jaw. "You sleep first. Get a couple of hours in and I'll wake you up." He paused, pressing a kiss to the sensitive spot below my ear. I shivered. "Okay?"

I'd have agreed to anything at that point, so I did.

"Then we head out first thing." Aiden lowered the hand wrapped tightly in my hair, arching my back. The chilled air of the cavern spread goose bumps over my exposed skin. I sucked in a breath when I felt his lips return to where my pulse pounded and then lower, over the rise of my collarbone, and still lower.

Then he pulled back, letting go, his chest rising and falling unsteadily as he moved toward the edge of the pool. "And you should be resting right now. This—"

"Stop talking." I pushed through the water, well aware that as I moved closer to him, the cloak of water slowly receded.

Aiden was well aware, too. A muscle flexed in his jaw as his gaze dropped. "Did you just tell me to shut up?"

"No." I followed him as he kept backing up, until he had no other place to run to, until his back was against the edge of the rock pool and he was trapped. Placing my hands on either side of him, I looked up. "Okay. I did tell you to shut up, but I did so nicely."

He took a deep, long breath. "I may be able to overlook it."

I floated in, letting my legs tangle with his. "For someone who doesn't talk a lot, you sure do talk a lot when I'd rather you not be talking."

Aiden's laugh sounded choked. "That makes very little sense, Alex."

Grinning, I leaned in and pressed my lips to the strong curve of his jaw, repeating what he had done until my pulse thundered in every part of me. "Making sense is overrated."

"I think you believe a lot of things are overrated." Aiden's head fell back, the thick cords of his muscles in his neck and shoulders tensing as his hands dug into the edge of the pool.

For a moment, I froze in awe of him. It wasn't often that anyone got to see Aiden like this, completely vulnerable to someone else. I touched his cheek, wanting to remember this moment. The enormity of what lay ahead was a cold draft on my skin and deeper, on my soul. There was no telling what my future held—what Aiden's would end up being. So many things were still so uncertain.

Apollo's words intruded. *There can only be one.*

I shuddered, understanding what that meant more than I wanted to. Even Seth had understood it.

I thought about the damn dream I'd had on the way here.

There might not be years for Aiden and me—maybe not even months or weeks. There might not even be days. And what time we had left, we'd be spending in constant danger. The next hour wasn't even guaranteed, and I didn't want to spend every moment racing toward the end time.

Aiden's eyes opened. "Alex?"

I blinked back the sudden tears. "I love you." It was all I could say.

His head lifted, eyes searching mine, and maybe he saw what I was thinking. Maybe he too knew that, in the end, there would be more lives lost—ones that would be nearly impossible to overcome and move on from, losses that would steal a part of us. That this moment together, we might never have again.

He was done talking.

Aiden came off the wall so fast the water reacted in a frenzy of bubbling. He—*we*—were in a frenzy. His arms crushed me to him, his mouth demanding, saying those three little words over and over again without speaking them. Aiden lifted me up, one hand burying deep in my hair, the other pressing into my lower back, fitting us together. He turned and my back was against the edge and he was everywhere all at once, stealing my breath, my heart, my soul. There was no coming up for air, no control or limits. There was no tottering on the edge. We both fell headfirst. In his arms, in the way the water bubbled and moved with our bodies, I may've lost track of time, but I gained a little part of me. I gained a part of *him* that I would hold close for the rest of my days, no matter how long or short that turned out to be.

CHAPTER TWENTY-THREE

While I'd slept, Aiden had managed to dry our clothes without turning them crispy. If it'd been left to me, I probably would've turned them into torches. I slept for a little over four hours, waking before he told me to. I changed, and then settled back down beside him on one of the two thin blankets. Both of us smelled of jasmine, which was better than the dank smell of the Underworld.

Aiden lay on his side, one heavy arm over my waist. "You could've slept longer."

I idly played with the hand that rested on my stomach. "I'm fine. It's your turn. I'll keep an eye on things, make sure no spiders run off with you."

He pressed his lips to my cheek and let out a little chuckle. "I'm worried if it comes to you saving me from a spider, I might be screwed."

"I'd face down a horde of spiders for you, baby." I grinned at the sound of his laugh again. "For real."

"That's true love there. Some serious stuff," he teased.

"It is."

There was a pause and then he said, "While you were sleeping, I was thinking about what Apollo said about there being another god involved."

Curiosity piqued, I tipped my head back so I could see his face. "Yeah?"

"I know Seth hasn't let on to who it could be, but Marcus has his bets on Hermes, and since he did help Seth..."

"It's always Hermes. He's like the gods' punching bag. The big joke."

"Exactly." Aiden brushed a damp strand of hair off my forehead. "It seems too obvious that it would be him. And even though Hermes has been known to pull some stunts, his actions are usually relatively harmless. This—what has been done to the whole world, Olympus included—is bigger than him, almost like it's personal."

He had a point. "I bet being the butt of Olympus's jokes could make things personal after a few thousand years."

"True, but I don't know..." He yawned. "I keep thinking about Seth—about his personality."

"Oh dear..."

A tired smile appeared. "Whether you want to admit it or not, you carry some of Apollo's traits. So, logically, Seth would carry some from his own lineage."

There were worse things than being compared to Apollo. "Seth is arrogant and smug. That really doesn't narrow down the list." At Aiden's tired nod of agreement, I squeezed his hands. "Go to sleep. We'll figure this out in the morning."

Aiden insisted he wasn't that tired, but it didn't take more than a few moments before his breathing became deep and steady. I stayed in his arms, eyes glued to the entrance. I was still tired, and the headache had kicked back up the moment I'd awakened, spreading from my temples, but it was manageable.

Mulling over what Aiden had said, I had to give the idea that there was something personal behind this some cred. But the only problem with that was the fact that all the gods probably had a damn good reason to cause discord. Apollo had even said once before that, after thousands of years of being together, they had nothing better to do than tick each other off.

We needed to figure out who it was behind this, but what could we do? Taking out a god was unheard of. Even the Titans had been entombed, not killed. The loss of any god carried cosmic consequences. The world wouldn't stop spinning, but all the gods would be weakened if one fell. It was probably the only thing that kept them from outright killing one another, but…

One massive problem at a time…

Seth and Lucian were our biggest problem. Hopefully, we'd find Solaris and she would hold the answer to stopping him. Part of me hadn't given up on the tiniest sliver of hope that somehow Seth could be saved—that he could be fixed. I sincerely believed that, without Lucian's and the aether's influence, he wouldn't have done the things he had.

But who was I to say that absolved him of his sins? If a drug addict killed someone while under the influence, he was still guilty. Seth had done what he had done, and it felt like there was no going back from that.

Sorrow was like slush in my blood, dirty and messy, because it felt misplaced. As if I felt bad for a killer…

Pushing thoughts of Seth aside, I stroked the length of Aiden's fingers and wondered if I'd ever hear Aiden play the guitar again. I hoped so. Maybe even get him to sing, because he had a nice voice. I wasn't sure how much time passed, but it couldn't have been more than an hour. The sky peeking through the holes in the roof of the cavern was still a deep blue and my headache had steadily increased. Now it throbbed behind my eyes.

There was no fooling myself. I knew what it meant. Seth was on the other end of the bond, and he was trying to reach me. The venom of panic gave me a sharp bite. Now was so not the time for him to pull this kind of crap. A freaking army of spiders could descend on us while I was with him. Worse yet, we could be discovered by Hades.

Carefully wiggling free of Aiden's embrace, I pushed to my feet and went to the pool, scooping the jasmine-scented water up and splashing it over my face. It had seemed to help before, but I had a feeling I was beyond help.

I sat down, concentrating on my breathing. I could feel the cord now. It still slumbered, but the hum was louder, more powerful. Placing my head in my hands, I squeezed my eyes shut and waited. Part of me already knew there was no stopping this.

Seth was incredibly strong and hellishly determined when he wanted to be.

So I waited for pain to come, but it never did. Instead, the hum of the cord became louder and stronger, until it felt like my entire body vibrated. Then out of the white noise filling my head, a whisper grew until I made out the words and recognized the voice.

Nice to see…or hear you again, Alex. Seth.

My eyes snapped open and, unlike last time, I wasn't mentally transported somewhere by Hermes. The spring was still in front of me. I could hear Aiden's deep breaths and feel the slight chill in the air of the cavern.

I know you can hear me, Alex. I can feel it.

I groaned. *I'm really starting to get annoyed with this.*

Through the bond, I could feel his smugness. It was like before, when we'd been connected. His emotions flowed through to me and vice versa. I bet, if I closed my eyes, I could see him as clearly as he stood in front of me, but we weren't connected.

Deep down you love it, he said.

Uh, no. Tucking my damp hair back, I let out a low breath. *I don't understand how you're able to do this. We're not connected.*

After our last little social call, it's easier to tap into the connection. Whenever you're feeling really worn down or emotional, I can reach you. I guess it would be the same if you were in pain. There was a pause, and I swore I felt a flicker of concern. *Are you in pain?*

I rolled my eyes. Good news was that Apollo must've had a little talk with Hermes. *No, but you're a pain in my ass. Does that count?*

Seth's laugh still had that weird, warm feeling. *At least this way you can't hit me.*

Hitting Seth still felt like a viable option. *I don't have time for this right now.*

Curiosity filtered through the connection. *What is it that you're doing right now, Alex?*

What are YOU doing right now, Seth?

There was that laugh again. It was a nice laugh. It didn't have the same effect as Aiden's, but it was rich and deep and it reminded me of Seth.

Pre-killing-rampage Seth, that is.

You tell first.

Yeah, that's not going to happen. Glancing over my shoulder, I saw Aiden stir a little. Then I closed my eyes and focused on the connection. I figured I might as well glean some information from this.

A split second later, Seth took form in my thoughts. For some reason, he only had half his clothes on. I wasn't sure if that was me doing that or if he really was shirtless. Either way, it was way too much golden skin exposed. Treading lightly, I tested out the connection and the emotions it fed to me. I didn't know if I could somehow get sucked into him this way, so I proceeded with a great deal of caution.

The only thing I felt was...calmness, which was really—

A sudden cold chill snaked down my spine, and then Seth said, *Whatever you're looking for, you're not going to find it.*

What do you think I'm looking for? With you, one can never be too sure.

Oh, that's the pot calling the kettle black.

Amusement flowed through the connection as Seth said, *Or it's the pot calling the pot a pot.*

I made a face. *What?*

Seth laughed. *Ah, I've sort of missed this, Alex.*

Opening my eyes, I resisted the irrational urge to admit that I too missed the banter, the out-snarking battle that neither of us won. It was weird—the dynamics of my relationships with Seth and Aiden.

Aiden complimented me; he was the yin to my yang, the "*now, now*" to my smartass. But Seth and I were too much alike, and in a way, we really were the same person. Together for too long, we probably would murder each other.

But yeah, there was a part of me that missed this—missed him.

Why haven't you started yelling at me yet? he asked.

I choked out a laugh. *Only you would ask that question.*

What?

Do you want me to yell at you? I doubt that it would do any good. It's not going to change you.

But that's never stopped you from doing anything before. Even if you knew the outcome and it was pointless, you'd still do it.

Like now? Staying away from you is pointless?

The smugness was back, settling over me like a second skin. *Very pointless*, he added.

Frustrated now, I closed my eyes and sighed.

Maybe you don't know me as well as you think you do.

I know you don't care about anyone but yourself, but I really need to go.

Pricks of irritation overshadowed the warmth of amusement and arrogance. *I want to talk.*

Immediately wary, my hands opened and closed. *What do you want to talk about?*

How wrong you are.

It was a good thing Hermes hadn't showed up, because my hand itched to connect with his face.

Oh, gods...Seth, I can't do this—

I care about you, he said, surprising me.

I shook my head, wanting to deny it, because stripping my ability to make my own decisions was a hell of a way of showing he cared, but it was the truth. I remembered that night in Telly's house, that moment I'd seen the indecision in his eyes, the vulnerability. He hadn't wanted to hurt me then, but I believed that what he *needed* overwhelmed what he *wanted*.

I know, I said, because, deep down, I knew he did care.

Even more shocking, there was a sudden opening in the connection. Not that I could read any of Seth's thoughts, but there was a vulnerability that hadn't been there before. *It wouldn't have been bad between us, even if you never connected with me. It wouldn't have been terrible.*

My chest felt heavy and it ached, because there was also some truth to that.

But it never would've been enough, he added, and in a weird way, he felt closer now, like he was right beside me. *I'm man enough to admit that. Even if I fought for you fairly—and trust me, Aiden has nothing on me when I'm determined—in the end, whatever you felt for me would've been leftovers. I would've been a leftover. You would've never really been mine. I've always known that.*

I squeezed my hands until my joints ached. *Then why did you want to be with me—in the Catskills, you asked me to give it a try. Or was that a huge part of your master plan?*

Master plan? Seth laughed, but it was humorless. *Why wouldn't I have asked? I'm attracted to you, Alex. Doesn't take much to figure that out. And there's more. I've been drawn to you, ever since I first saw you. It's just the way it is for our kind.*

A distant, almost sad feeling crept through the connection. *That pull between us—I don't think you've ever understood, or even felt it, as much as I do. But anyway, like I said, I do care about you, too.*

There was a physical thing between us, partly due to the Apollyon bond and our own attraction to each other. I was grown-up enough to admit that it still was there, but it was watered down in comparison to how I felt for Aiden. But some things didn't change.

I care about you. The words were whispered and sounded broken to me.

For a moment, we said nothing. It was like a stalemate, a really weird, awkward, and sad one.

Please don't do this, Seth.

He sighed. *Alex…*

I can help you.

The pricks of irritation soured my stomach now. *I don't need help.*

You do. I took a deep breath. *You're like an addict—the aether, whatever love and approval you're seeking from Lucian. You need help.*

I knew the moment I'd said the wrong thing. Irritation flipped to anger and it was like standing too close to a fire. *I don't need your help, Alex. What I need is for you to understand that you can't escape Fate. That everything will be different—it will be better—if you just let Lucian do what needs to be done.*

Seth—

And I need you to understand, Alex, if you can, that maybe—just maybe—Lucian actually cares for me, that I'm worth that, and he wants the best for me—for us. Do you think you can do that?

My throat worked on the lump that had formed there. *You are worth someone caring about you, but—*

But what? His voice snapped fire, daring me to say what he knew I was going to say.

I drew in a stuttered breath. *But I can't do what you're asking. You are worth it—worth so much—but not Lucian. He's using you. And it'll be too late—*

It's not too late. In the end, no matter what, I will have everything that I want. And then he pushed back and broke the connection.

CHAPTER TWENTY-FOUR

When I opened my eyes again, Aiden was still asleep, and although the cord hummed softly in my stomach, Seth was gone for now. I climbed to my feet and quickly scanned the cave. Everything was the same—not exactly the Hilton Hotel, but safe.

Swallowing down the lump that felt like a permanent fixture in my throat, I shuffled over to Aiden and sat beside him, pulling my knees to my chest. Gods, I didn't know what was worse—if Seth was completely gone and there was no hope for him, or if there was a part of him still in there somewhere. Either way, wondering about it was hopeless. Right now I was on a mission to discover a way to destroy Seth. So did it matter? In the end, I couldn't allow him to transfer power from me. Too many lives rested on stopping him.

Aiden must've been the proud owner of an internal clock, because when the sky started to turn orange beyond the irregular holes in the roof of the cavern, he stretched like a jungle cat coming awake from an afternoon nap.

He sat up fluidly and leaned over, placing his hands on either side of my bent knees. Heat rolled off his bare chest. He pressed his lips to the sensitive space beneath my ear and murmured, "Good morning."

"Good morning."

"I'm guessing we weren't overrun by spiders?" Aiden popped to his feet and stretched again, raising his arms, his back bowing.

"No."

He sent me a look over his shoulder and then bent down, grabbing his shirt off the bag. "You hanging in there?"

I nodded.

As we ate a quick breakfast of gerbil food and got ready to head back out into the tunnel, I debated what to tell Aiden. I couldn't hide the fact that I'd had some sort of interaction with Seth again, but I wasn't sure how to put what I was feeling into words that anyone could understand.

When he handed me the musty-smelling cloak, I finally said something. "I saw Seth last night."

Aiden stilled, hands clenching his own cloak. "Okay."

I focused on his shoulder. "I know I should've said something earlier."

"Yes. You should have."

A flush stained my cheeks. "I didn't really see him. Not like last time. He talked to me through the connection. He doesn't know what we're doing. He asked, but I didn't say anything."

"Of course." He slipped on the cloak with quick, stiff movements. "What did he want?"

I shifted my weight uncomfortably. "I think he just wanted…to talk."

"To talk?" Disbelief colored his tone.

"Yeah, he… I think there's a part of him still there. You know, a part of him that's confused, but that really believes that Lucian cares for him." I trailed off, shaking my head. "It doesn't matter. You ready?"

Aiden studied me a moment, then nodded. With our hoods in place, we left the little slice of peace behind and ventured out into the dark, narrow tunnels, traveling them in silence. Since I couldn't see Aiden's face or his eyes, I wasn't sure what he was thinking, but I was sure it had something to do with Seth. It was what I was thinking about as we navigated the darkness, with only our footsteps echoing in the silence.

I wished that I had seen what was happening to Seth before it had become too late, noticed how the aether and akasha had been affecting him. Most of all, I wished I had seen how badly he needed someone—someone who accepted him, even loved him. Instead, I had been so wrapped up in my own problems I hadn't seen what everything had been doing to him.

What I'd been doing to him.

In a way, I had seriously failed Seth.

After two hours of nonstop walking in the dark, a small speck of orange light shone ahead, and the closer we got, the larger the spot became until we could see the world outside the cavern.

"Finally," Aiden muttered.

He stopped at the rough, irregular opening and peered out over the sloping hill that led into a thick mist that blanketed the orange sky. "The Vale of Mourning," Aiden said. "We're close to the Plain of Judgment."

"Hopefully Apollo got word to Caleb." I stepped out. The drab grass crunched under my boots. "It shouldn't take long."

And it didn't, taking only half an hour to get down the

hill and to enter the mist, which gave way like stirred smoke, revealing the Vale.

The place was as depressing as it sounded.

Bare trees dotted the landscape. Their branches curled down at the ends, as if weighted by the suffering that seeped into the air. Slabs of gray rock rose from the dull grass and a small creek, its water dark and moody, parted the plain.

People were everywhere.

Some were by the creek, lying listlessly on their sides. Their fingers trailed into the water, their bodies shuddering over and over again with deep, heavy sighs. Others were perched upon rocks, sobbing openly, hands clutched to their chests. A few sat at the bases of trees, tucked into balls as they cried out.

The Vale of Mourning was a cesspool of heartbreak and suffering—the final resting place of those who'd died unhappily in love.

I couldn't get past these people fast enough. Although no one approached us, as they seemed too lost in their misery to even notice us, the lump that had been in my throat all morning grew rapidly. Depression was the air that was breathed here. Sorrow filled the river. Grief rooted the dead trees in place.

Even Aiden's steps seemed heavier, as if we were walking through the rain-soaked Asphodel Field.

"I don't want to be here," I said finally, drifting closer to him.

Aiden reached out, finding my hand under my cloak. "I know. We're almost through."

A man turned his tear-streaked face to the sky, letting out a hoarse cry. Near him, a woman collapsed onto the ground, sobbing and spitting hysterical, unintelligible words that no one was listening to. That was probably the suckiest part about the Vale. All these souls were here because of unhappy love, but no one cared. They were alone in their misery, as they probably had been in life.

But we weren't a part of the Vale, so we traveled on, able to do what these poor souls had been unable to do in life and death. We moved on, past the wants and needs that never had come to fruition, beyond love that had been lost, or never had been theirs to hold.

Some of the weight lifted along with the mist, and before us was a cobblestone road that honestly came out of nowhere as the skies cleared to the odd burnt orange. But we weren't alone. Hundreds, if not thousands, of souls traveled the same path as us. All kinds of people—young and old, pure and half—traveled toward their Judgment. Picking out the Sentinels and Guards was easy, even though their uniforms weren't covered in gore like they had been when I'd been in limbo. These souls all had been buried.

Aiden and I stuck out.

Very few of the souls traveling wore cloaks of any kind, since obviously that wasn't the fashion trend above ground. If anyone had passed away in a cloak, I'd be curious as to how and why. Most were in street clothing. Some had ball caps on, and maybe we should've stashed away some of those. Someone was even rocking a cowboy hat.

Anyway, this wasn't good.

Hades's guards were posted along the road, atop their black warhorses. They kept the travelers in order and the path moving. It was probably an endless, boring job.

We moved toward the center of the group, hoping to get lost in the masses of tall Sentinels. Some of them passed cursory glances at us, but no one spoke to us. At the sound of a low nicker and approaching hoofs, my heart tripped up as I placed my hand on the dagger under my cloak. I felt Aiden move to do the same thing.

But the large warhorse blew past us, the guard riding low over the back. People darted out of the way; if they hadn't, they'd have been trampled under the powerful hoofs.

Unease blossomed in the pit of my stomach, but it wasn't like we could turn back now.

Nearing the Plain of Judgment, it was hard not to notice the low reddish glow spreading across the horizon, and the farther we traveled, the larger the…the *fire* grew.

Tartarus.

Whoa, I so didn't want to be anywhere near that place. And I really hoped that we wouldn't get caught and tossed into Tartarus.

My heart was throwing itself against my ribs by the time we entered the open Plain of Judgment. The mass of people crowding the crossroads was enormous, and guards were everywhere, positioned just in case someone doomed for Tartarus tried to make a run for it.

Aiden stayed close to my side. "You don't happen to see Caleb?"

I laughed dryly as I scanned over the people. The crowd was so thick I had no idea how I could see anyone in the throng. And I had a hard time not staring at the palace, which seemed way too close. More of a medieval fortress than a home, Hades's palace rose like the mountains we'd traveled through, casting a dark shadow across the Plain of Judgment. Four turrets reached into the orangey sky, one from each corner of the stronghold.

Although I hoped the Elysian Fields offered better scenery, I couldn't imagine waking every morning and looking out one of the many windows to see…all of this.

Focusing on the important stuff, I joined Aiden in the search to find the familiar blond head.

There were a lot of blonds, but none of them were Caleb.

"What if word hasn't gotten to him?" I asked Aiden, afraid to say Apollo's name down here.

"He has to know," he assured me, scanning the rapidly increasing pile of people.

"Gods, how many people do they process here in a day?" Thousands, it appeared.

Proceeding forward, I realized I was pretty useless in the search for Caleb. Being so short, all I could see were backs of heads. My unease grew unchecked. The longer we were here, the more dangerous it was. I thought back to the guard who had raced ahead. My mouth went dry. We needed to find Caleb and we needed—

A heavy hand landed on my shoulder.

Sucking in a sharp breath, my fingers twitched around the handle of the dagger as I spun around, ready to use the blade if need be.

"Geez, don't stab me. I think we've had enough of that going on between the two of us."

I stumbled back as the familiar voice sunk in. He wore a baseball cap pulled low and a hoodie tucked over it, but wisps of blond hair poked around the edges. A wild grin shone from underneath the shadow of the cap.

"Caleb." My voice sounded hoarse.

Seconds away from tackling him to the ground, I was stopped when Aiden gripped my shoulder. "I know you want to," he said in a low voice, "but it would draw attention."

"Yeah, it would." Caleb nodded. "So let's keep the hugging and crying to a minimum."

I was already on the verge of crying, so thank the gods the

hood hid that. Stepping away from Aiden, I stopped in front of Caleb. "I am so glad to see you again."

"And I'm happy to see you…" He lifted his hand, as if he would touch me but stopped. "It's also good to see you back to normal."

I winced. "Yeah, about that…sorry?"

Caleb chuckled. "It's all good in the hood. Come, we've got to do this quickly." He gestured toward the road leading to Hades's palace. "I'm surprised you guys even made it this far without getting caught. The whole Underworld is in a tizzy over what's been going on topside."

"I imagine that's why they're so busy down here," Aiden commented.

"Yep." Caleb shoved his hands deep into the pockets of his jeans. "A lot of Sentinels and pures coming through here. Sort of blows, you know?"

"Yeah, it blows real bad. So why would we—?"

Without warning, the ground trembled violently and a great, terrible roar cracked overhead, shaking me to the bone.

I turned, as did everyone else, toward Tartarus. The smell of sulfur grew until it was thick and choking. Fear exploded in my gut. Aiden was beside me in an instant, his hand pressing into my back.

"What's happening?" I asked.

"You'll see," Caleb responded, totally nonplussed.

I shot him a look, but then a ball of fire flew straight into the air over Tartarus, twisting and churning as embers flew in every direction. The fire shifted, morphing as it continued to stream into the sky.

The funnel of fire stilled for a moment.

On each side, the fire grew, spreading into giant wings that seemed to reach all corners of the Underworld. In the center, a dragon's head appeared. The mouth opened, omitting another bloodcurdling scream, and then it swooped down. The impact shook the ground as the fiery tail whipped through the air.

Then it quieted.

"Holy Hades," I mumbled.

"It's like the welcome party for those sentenced to Tartarus," Caleb explained. "Happens every time a group arrives in there. You get used to it after a while."

"What the hell..." I muttered. There was no way I'd grow used to seeing *that*.

"Come on, we've got to go." Caleb slid in front of us. "It could take years to find Solaris, but I know just the thing that—"

Four black stallions parted the crowd, their riders tall and imposing, garbed in leather. *Swords—freaking swords*—were leveled out from their sides. They surrounded us in seconds, herding the three of us until our backs pressed against one another.

Aiden reached for his dagger and ended up with the business end of a sword pointed at his throat.

The look on the guard's face screamed he was neither above nor afraid of using it. "Crap," I muttered.

We were so screwed.

CHAPTER TWENTY-FIVE

The guard's arm didn't tremble. "Move, and you will not move again."

Aiden froze, and I don't think I breathed. I was pretty sure Caleb wasn't breathing either, but then again, he didn't need to breathe, being that he was dead. But that didn't mean he would go without punishment. We were caught. *He* was caught, and all I could think of was the dragon we'd seen. Guilt tore through me like wildfire.

The guard eyeballed Aiden. "Raise your hands."

"You told me not to move, so I'm not sure how I can raise my hands," was Aiden's dry response. I bit back a laugh that wouldn't have been appreciated.

Not amused, the guard slipped the sword inside Aiden's hood. The sword tipped up, easing the material back. The guard smiled when Aiden's face was revealed and a thin trickle of blood seeped down his cheek.

Hot and fiery rage burned, and I wanted nothing more than to knock the ass off his horse, but the sword was too close to the skin of Aiden's neck.

"Raise your hands," the guard repeated.

A smirk crossed Aiden's lips as he slowly raised his hands. "Is this good enough?"

"The three of you are to come with us," another guard announced as he sheathed his sword. "If you do not obey, we have been given permission to use any method needed. Please be assured that a death in the Underworld is the same as topside."

The guards turned pale eyes beyond me to Caleb. "And there are things worse than death here, boy. You should have thought about that."

Caleb said nothing, but we had to do something. We couldn't let them take us wherever they planned to take us. Problem was, only Caleb knew how to get Aiden and me out of the Underworld, and it wasn't like we could really ask him that right now. And I wasn't leaving Caleb to face this alone.

So yeah, like I said, we were screwed.

A guard on foot came between the two horses and headed straight for me. Aiden moved only a fraction of an inch, and the tip of the sword pricked his skin.

"We're back to the not moving part again." The guard smirked. "Is that good for you?"

Aiden glared at the guard and heat poured off him. The guard's smile tipped up in response.

The one in front of me grabbed a fistful of my hood and wrenched it back. His ice-blue eyes narrowed. "It's them."

My heart dropped to my toes. He said it like someone had been expecting us, and that was so not good. I tried to keep the panic out of my face, but it must have been evident, because the guard laughed as he turned back.

"Disarm them all," he said. "And then we must go."

The disarming part took seconds. Our cloaks were

removed, daggers stripped away. Aiden's backpack was taken hostage. I passed Aiden a glance, but he stared ahead, his jaw set in a rigid line. Crap on a cracker, this was bad. Caleb seemed resigned, though, his shoulders slumped, as if he knew what punishment was coming.

Watching the backs of the guards, I wondered how quickly I could take them all out so the three of us could make a run for it. But that would probably require akasha, and where would Caleb hide down here? Where would we go? And to come this far, only to lose it all? I couldn't even come to grips with it. A cold knot of fear sat heavy in my stomach.

With dread raking deeper and deeper with each step, we could do nothing else but follow the guards to Hades's palace.

"I'm sorry," I whispered to Caleb.

He shrugged. "Like old times, though."

"Yeah, but this is different. There's a dragon made of fire that will—"

"No talking." The guard who liked to play with his sword rode up beside us. "Or I will make it so that none of you can talk again."

Like my father? Sweet, hot rage exploded. My mouth opened, but Aiden's warning glare closed it. We were herded toward the palace in silence. Two guards on horses in front of us, two behind us, and one on the ground made it impossible to do a damn thing.

And then the gates to the palace were swinging open and we were ushered in across a sparse courtyard. Everything was happening so fast. My heart pounded; sweat dotted my brow. I felt naked without the damn cloak, and there was a freaking hellhound sleeping on its back by the entrance, its meaty paws kicking in the air as it dreamt of chasing souls or whatever hellhounds dreamt of.

Guards dismounted from their horses and strode toward the entrance, pulling open the palace doors. The guys on either side of me seemed to be handling all of this better than me, or they were just better at pretending not to be one step from freaking out, but Caleb probably wasn't blown away by Hades's palace like I was.

After all, he played Wii with the gods here. But Hades's palace was…opulent.

Gold and titanium plated everything—the walls, ceiling, furniture, and even the floor. Hades's symbols were everywhere. The bull and the two-prong spears were engraved into the floors, stitched into the elegant tapestries. Black velvet chaise lounges filled the great hall, but it was the covered thrones occupying the dais that caught and held my attention. They were truly fit for a king and queen, but it was also what was near them.

Slumbering beside them were smaller hellhounds—maybe puppy hellhounds. Their multiple heads rested on their paws, and acid drool pooled under the lolled tongues.

The guards stopped and, without any words, dropped onto one knee and lowered their heads. A second later, the floor-to-ceiling gold and titanium doors next to the thrones swung open. Even though Hades was supposed to be in Olympus, I fully expected the god to come strolling through the doors, ready to toss the three of us into the fiery pits of Tartarus.

Weak in the knees, I forced myself to keep my eyes trained forward. Sentinels didn't feel fear…my rosy half-blood butt.

But as the figure drew nearer, I knew it wasn't Hades. It wasn't even a guy. It was a female—and it was a goddess.

She was beautiful—tall, damn near seven feet. Waves of curly red hair fell to an impossibly narrow waist. Her eyes were all white, cheekbones high, lips plump, and nose pert.

And she was practically naked.

Her white gown was gauzy and completely see-through. I got a good idea of her bra size…if she'd been wearing one, which she wasn't. Underwear must be optional down here.

Aiden was staring. So was Caleb, although he looked like he was quite used to all this…woman on display. Hell, even I was staring.

She crossed the great hall, her long legs parting the chiffon of her skirt, playing peekaboo. Dear gods, I felt my cheeks start to burn, but I still couldn't look away. As she neared, her all-white eyes flared, and then dimmed. Two bright, emerald-colored eyes appeared.

Caleb relaxed beside me, a slow smile creeping across his handsome face—the face I'd missed so much. "Hello, Persephone."

My eyes widened at the beautiful goddess. So this was the infamous Persephone. Even though I was Team Boy, I could see why Hades had become so enamored with her, going as far as to pluck her away and bring her down to the Underworld.

The first guard, not the one who'd cut Aiden, lifted his head. "We apprehended them as you wished."

"Apprehended" was so not a warm and fuzzy word.

"You three look surprised." Persephone's lush lips were tilted with mischief. "These are my personal guards and they've been keeping an eye out for you. I've been expecting you."

"How?" I asked, stunned.

Persephone smiled. "Caleb and I play Mario Kart every day at one, and when he cancelled on me I knew something was up."

I looked at Caleb slowly.

He shrugged. "It's not my fault she's observant."

"And very bored when my husband is in Olympus. Caleb keeps me company."

I so hoped it was the platonic type of company, because Hades wasn't known for his forgiving nature.

"Guards, you may leave us now." When they hesitated, she laughed. "I am fine. Please leave and do not speak of this to anyone."

One by one, they filed out of the room, sword guy eyeing Aiden like he wanted to slice his other cheek. Aiden held his stare as a smirk crossed his lips.

Men. Sigh.

Once the palace doors closed behind them, Persephone clapped her hands together. "I asked a few questions of a little nymph who had come into the Underworld just a few days ago—one of Apollo's nymphs. And it doesn't take a weather scientist to figure out it had something to do with his lineage."

"It's rocket scientist," Caleb corrected as he tugged down his hood and pulled off his cap.

She frowned. "Anyway, I figured it had something to do with you…and I had a choice. Call my husband and he'd come rushing home, but then he'd be in a tizzy, and he's such a pain like that. Or I could just find out what you all needed. I'm sure it will prove very interesting."

Aiden shifted beside me, clearly caught as off-guard as I was. I glanced at Caleb and whispered, "Can we trust her?"

Caleb nodded. "She's pretty cool, and actually this makes my job so much easier."

The goddess raised a delicate eyebrow. "Do tell?"

"I need to see the Calling Waters."

Calling Waters? I had never heard of such a thing, and from the look on Aiden's face, neither had he.

"And why would you need to use the Calling Waters?" she

asked, folding slender arms under her breasts, like she needed help drawing attention to them. "If you would like to see someone, Caleb, you only have to ask."

"I know." He dropped an arm over my shoulders, and the gaping hole in my heart that had been there since he'd died filled. "But it's not for me. It's for them. They need to use it."

Persephone was quiet for a long moment. "Who do they wish to call upon?"

"Solaris," I answered. The Calling Waters suddenly made sense—call a soul to you. "We need to talk to Solaris."

"Because of what is happening topside with the First?" she asked.

I nodded.

Her bright gaze slid to Caleb. "And what did you plan to do? Sneak them in here to use it?"

"That was the plan."

The goddess shook her head. "If my husband were home and you were to do something so unwise, I would not be able to stay his hand."

A shiver danced down my spine. The last thing I wanted was for Caleb to get into eternal-damnation-type trouble.

"I know," Caleb replied, squeezing my shoulders. "But they are worth the risk, and Solaris could possibly hold information to stop the First. And that's what Hades wants, right? That's what the gods want?"

"Most of them," she murmured, her gaze slipping back to me, and then to Aiden. "But not all, it appears."

Something struck me. "Do you know who the god is—the one who's helping Seth and Lucian?"

She picked a glossy red curl and twirled it around one elegant finger.

"If I knew such a thing, then that god would be taken care

of. But I am rarely on Olympus and have little interest in the politics of who pissed off whom enough to end the world as we know it this time around."

Aiden cleared his throat. "This happens quite a bit, then?"

Persephone smiled, and when she smiled, even I lost my breath. "More than you will ever know. The world has been on the brink of total devastation several times over for one reason or another. But now…it is like when we faced the Titans. It has gone beyond a few pretty words used to gloss over a perceived insult." She let out a little sigh. "But anyway, I have very little to do, and if this Solaris can be of some help to you, then she will be of some help to my husband. Follow me."

As she turned gracefully on her heel, I was too shocked to move at first. Persephone helping us was not something I'd planned on.

Aiden smiled. "This is good."

"Way good." I turned to Caleb. "You rock."

"I know." He pulled me in for a quick, tight hug. "Missed you."

Holding him close, I swallowed the happy tears. "I missed you, too."

Caleb kissed the top of my head, and then pulled away. "Come on. Let's get this show on the road."

The three of us followed behind the goddess. Poor Aiden was trying to look everywhere but at her, but underneath it all, he was a guy. Strangely, I wasn't jealous—probably more amused than anything else, because he was doing his hardest to keep his eyes north.

Slipping my hand around his, I squeezed. When his gaze flicked to mine, I grinned and he gave me a lopsided smile of apology.

As we headed down a long, dark hallway covered with black velvet tapestries, Caleb watched Aiden and me, a strange look on his face.

"What?" I asked.

He shook his head. "You guys are really doing this—the relationship, out in the open and all?"

Aiden's hand wrapped more firmly around mine. "I think right now the world has bigger problems than a pure and a half being in love."

My heart did a happy dance at the last part. Just hearing him say that—the L-word—could chase away all the dark shadows and expectations.

Persephone's throaty chuckle drifted back to us. "Isn't that the truth? Besides, they are not the first, nor will they be the last."

Caleb's sky-blue eyes settled on Aiden. "And you're not going to try to hide the relationship once everything settles down?"

The challenge in his tone had me smiling.

"Not going to happen," Aiden told him. "It won't be easy, but we'll find a way."

"Good." Caleb's eyes hardened. "Because if you do her wrong, I will haunt your ass until you die."

I burst into laughter and so did Aiden, even though we both knew Caleb was being serious.

Letting go of Aiden's hand, I wrapped my arm around Caleb. "That won't be necessary."

The goddess stopped in front of a bronze door. With a wave of her hand, it sprang open. Good thing she was helping us out, because I had no idea how Caleb would've pulled that off.

At the rush of cold air, we stepped into the circular

chamber. There were so many weapons on the wall: battle axes, spears, swords, and pikes. There were morbid items too, like the heads of long-forgotten animals slaughtered in the hunt and an entire section dedicated to cutoff ponytails.

I cleared my throat. "Nice…room."

"It's Hades's war room." Awe filled Aiden's tone. "Damn."

"The weapons are my husband's, but…" Persephone slid a dismissive glance around the war room. "These are mostly Ares's trophies, not my beloved's. Hades does have a tendency to swing a little on the morbid side, but the hair…" She gestured at the sheared ponytails tacked onto the wall. "Those belong to Ares. He likes to cut the hair of those he's conquered and then string them up for all to see. It disturbs most of the other gods, so he keeps them here."

Caleb's brows rose. "Nice decorative touch, I guess."

There was something eerily familiar about the hair. Not the whole cutting it off and hanging it on walls, because, thank the gods, that was strange to me. But there was something that poked at my memory.

"You know Ares," Persephone said, drawing us further into the war room. "To him, everything is about war and its spoils. Peace practically emasculates him. He believes one should never turn his back on war…" She trailed off and gave a dainty shrug. "He should be thrilled now, with everything on the brink."

"He's probably a happy camper," Caleb said, sliding a WTF glance my way.

I shrugged, but that weird sensation was there, nagging at me. Did Persephone mean never turn one's back on *Ares*, a.k.a. "Mr. War," or just on war itself?

"Here we are." She stopped in front of a marble pedestal. Demonic faces were etched into the marble of the basin and ruby-red water filled it. "All you have to do is stand before it and call for the soul you wish to speak to—any soul—and they will be summoned here."

"Any soul?" My breath caught as an image of my mother filled my head.

"Yes, but I can only allow you to use it once. So choose wisely." Persephone giggled. "I feel like I'm in Indigo James and the Lost Ark."

Aiden cast his gaze to the floor, jaw flexing to hide his grin. Caleb rolled his eyes. "It's *Indiana Jones and the Last Crusade*."

"Oh." She shrugged. "Same thing."

My gaze dipped to the basin. My mom's name was on the tip of my tongue, and I knew without looking at Aiden that he was thinking about his parents. Either of us would probably give anything to see them, especially after how wrong the spirits had been at the portal.

Persephone's gaze turned knowing. "Ah, the chance to see a loved one is a hard one to pass over."

"You would know," Aiden said quietly.

Her smile slowly faded. "I would. Perhaps some find me selfish for the decisions I have made and the impact they have had."

Recalling the myth of Persephone, I shook my head. "No. You were smart. You made sure that both could have you—Hades *and* your mom."

If she felt smug for how it all turned out in the end, the whole splitting of time and the seasons, she didn't show it—surprising, since the gods weren't a humble bunch of folks.

Turning back to the basin, she clasped her hands in front of her. "It is time to make your choice, and then you must leave."

I looked at Aiden, who nodded. There was a hint of sadness in his eyes, reflecting what I knew shone in mine. Caleb placed his hand on my shoulder. As much as I wanted to see my mom, as much as I wanted to gift Aiden with the chance to see his parents, neither of us could be that selfish.

Stepping up to the basin, I stared into the still red water that reminded me of blood. Actually, it was thick like blood, and there was a faint metallic scent. Ew.

A second passed, and then I said, "Solaris."

Nothing happened at first, and then the water rippled as if I had blown a soft breath upon it. Part of me expected her face to appear in the basin, but the water settled again. Then there was a sudden fissure of energy that crawled up the walls and rolled over the floors. Tiny hairs on my body rose and a shudder worked its way across me. There was a soft gasp of surprise and I turned.

Solaris had arrived.

CHAPTER TWENTY-SIX

When I'd stepped into the Underworld, I really hadn't known what to expect. The same could be said for Solaris. I'd really had no clue, and I was blown away.

Solaris stood directly in front of Caleb, and she looked a lot better than I'd thought she would. For some reason, I'd expected that she and the First would be serving it up in Tartarus, but her white gown was pristine and intact. Silvery-blond hair, long and wispy, settled over thin shoulders. She was tall and willowy and her eyes were like mine—a bright amber color. Her delicate, porcelain features reminded me of a frail, exotic flower, which I hadn't been expecting. Maybe I was rocking one hell of an ego or something, but I'd thought she'd look like me.

She was the complete opposite of me.

Solaris looked around the room, her pale brows rising as she took in where she was. Surprise and a little bit of fear flitted across her face, but when her gaze landed on me, a keen understanding seeped into those ashen eyes. A sense of familiarity washed over me, mirrored in her expression.

Striding forward, Solaris stopped a mere foot from me, her head tilted inquisitively. When she spoke, her voice was soft. "You are the Apollyon."

There wasn't much time for me to figure out how she knew what I was. "I'm one of them."

Another flicker of surprise shot across her face, quickly followed by sorrow. "So there are two again?"

I nodded.

She glanced over her shoulder. "And neither of these are he. I can tell. One of them is dead. One of them is a pure-blood."

I ignored Caleb's offended look. "No. The First isn't here."

Solaris faced me, brows knitted. "You have Awakened. I can see the marks of the Apollyon."

"You can?" I glanced down, surprised to find that my visible skin was all marked up. I hadn't even felt them.

"How can you be Awakened and not be with the First? You are not dead."

Yet. "It's complicated. That's why we've come to talk to you."

"Oh." The sorrow deepened and her lashes swept down. "He is like mine?"

Everyone in the room, even Persephone, was fixated on Solaris, but she seemed wholly unaware of them now. I took a breath and fought the sudden tightening in my throat. The grief rolling off Solaris was palpable.

"Yes." My voice sounded hoarse. "He's like yours."

Twisting away, she wrapped her arms around herself. "Then there is nothing that I can do for you."

I stared at her. "But we haven't asked anything."

"If he has lost himself to the aether, to the call of akasha, there is nothing to be done." Her chin tipped down, causing her hair to slip forward, shielding her face. “And there is nothing to be done for you. I tried…but the power transferred.”

“Wait.” I stepped toward her, pushing down on the frustration roaring inside me. “I haven’t transferred my power to him. He’s only the Apollyon. Not the God Killer.”

Solaris stiffened. “That’s not possible.”

“It is. I haven’t been near him since I Awakened. There is something about the aether and akasha with him, but he’s still just the Apollyon.” I paused, drawing in a long breath. “I need to know how to stop the transfer.”

She remained quiet.

“And I think—*I know*—that you know how to do it.”

Her head swung toward me. “There is no way. I blocked that knowledge so no other Apollyon could learn it.”

“Well…I saw something when I Awakened. You turned to him, tried to stop him. You knew how, but the Order found you first.”

Solaris laughed a dry, brittle laugh. “Is that what history tells you?”

I glanced at the goddess, figuring she’d know, but she looked as confused as I felt. “But I saw it—”

“Did you? The Awakening is what the previous Apollyons wish for you to see. At the moment of your death, when it does come, you will implant your memories. Some of them may be as you wished to see them, but not how they truly existed.”

Well…daimon butt. Did Seth know that? “What happened, then?”

Her lashes swept down again. “When I first met him, he wasn’t like he was in the end. He was a beautiful, kind man who just happened to be the Apollyon.” A small, sad smile pulled at her lips. “We really didn’t understand any of it.

We were the first to exist in the same generation. He didn't even understand why he came to find me. It was like he was drawn, and I didn't understand what was happening when I Awakened. The pain…I thought I was dying."

I winced, unable to imagine going through that without Aiden and without any knowledge of what was happening.

"But when we met, it was like it was destined. For many months, we got…we got to know each other. I do not think even the gods knew what could happen." A distant look crept into her eyes, not quite overshadowing a pain that still hadn't healed. "He seemed to grow more powerful the longer we were around each other, able to harness akasha with little effort, and he would not grow tired. But he was more unstable. Never toward me, but I knew…I knew that it was because of me. There was a situation…"

My stomach sank as my gaze flickered to Aiden.

"A large group of daimons had attacked one of the Covenants and during the battle, he…pulled from me. The power he displayed was unimaginable. The Council grew concerned and then…then I met the oracle."

Ah, the oracle strikes again.

"She told me what would happen. That he would pull all of my power from me and he would attack the Council. I didn't believe her, because that would be insane." Solaris laughed softly. "But she was insistent that I stop him. That if I could not find it in my heart to kill what I loved most, then I must take the power."

My breath caught, and the walls seemed to do a Tilt-A-Whirl.

"I never thought he would act, but the Council moved against us. They wanted us separated, and neither of us, in our naïve selfishness, could bear such a thought. We left the safety of the Council and we went out on our own." Solaris shook her head. "They followed, sending their most skilled Sentinels. When they didn't succeed, the Order of Thanatos came."

She swallowed thickly. "He threatened the Council then, and I knew what the oracle had said was all coming true. She had given me the means to stop him, but it was too late."

I bit my lip. "What did he do?"

Her eyes met mine. "He would've never done it if the allure of the power—the draw of supreme power—hadn't overtaken him. But it did. Before I could stop him, he drew from me. There was a moment, immediately after he took my power, when he was not yet able to channel it. Like an Achilles's heel, so to speak, and the Order attacked. The rest… the rest is history."

I didn't know what to say. Sorrow rode the back of my throat. It was obvious that Solaris had loved her First, so much so that not once did she speak his actual name. I couldn't bring myself to ask just to quench my own curiosity, because I knew speaking it would only bring her more pain.

"I'm sorry." It was all I could say.

Solaris nodded. "What is your First doing?"

I told her everything—the destruction, the impending war, and the hope that somehow we could stop history from repeating itself. If she was surprised, she didn't show it. Solaris simply walked up to me.

"I blocked it from him and from the other Apollyons," Solaris said again. "I'm not sure how you even saw it. Perhaps it was Fate?"

Gods, for once Fate wasn't trying to force me to take one for the team. Nice change. "Perhaps."

"It's simpler than you think." Solaris reached out, placing

her cold hand over my right one. "You must follow the order of the marks as they appeared on you. The original." Solaris squeezed my right hand, "Θάρρος." *Courage.*

Then she cupped her hand around my left. "Ισχύς." *Strength.*

Letting go of my hand, she placed hers below my rib-cage, over my navel, "απόλυτη εξουσία." *Absolute power.* Then finally, she reached up and cupped the nape of my neck. "αήττητο." *Invincibility.*

The air went out of my lungs, and Solaris nodded. "You will need to press your flesh to his and call upon each mark by its true name."

"Wait," Aiden said. "Isn't that how he would transfer her power to him?"

I already knew, so when Solaris stepped away and turned to Aiden, I could barely look at him. "Yes," she said. "She will have to do it before he does."

Aiden opened his mouth, but there were no words. We had learned how to transfer power and that was something, but it would also be damn near impossible.

"Is that all?" she asked. "I wish to leave."

Persephone cleared her throat. "I believe so."

For an instant, Solaris's eyes met mine, and I thought I'd be seeing her again. *And sooner than I'd probably expect.* I didn't know where that thought came from—if it was rooted in any real possibility or just paranoia.

"Are you sure this is what you want to do?" she asked, voice low enough for only me to hear. "For the power of the God Killer will transfer to you. And though you may feel strong and you may think you can control it, it can warp you, too."

Looking terribly sad, as if she knew this great secret, she

sighed. "And for whatever purpose the gods seek to use you for, once they do, will you be left standing in the end? As the oracle warned me, there cannot be two of our kind in any generation."

And then she was gone, but her parting words lingered deep, wrapping their way over my heart and soul. Her words weren't a warning, but more a statement of fact. I glanced down at my left hand, and I felt as if my fate had been sealed long before I even knew what I was.

I let out a shaky breath.

"Well, that was depressing." Caleb ran a hand through his hair. "If I wasn't dead already, I'd feel a tad bit suicidal."

"No doubt," Persephone murmured. "But dead people—no offense—tend to be on the depressing side of things."

Caleb shrugged. "No offense taken."

Each time that I'd seen Caleb, he hadn't seemed depressed. As if he read my mind that moment, he smiled and I remembered what he'd said when I'd been in limbo. "You told me there was still hope for him."

Caleb swaggered over to me, seeming so alive it was painful to see. Wrapping his arms around me, he held me tight. "There's always hope. Maybe not the kind of hope you're thinking about, but there *is* hope."

I didn't understand at first, so I snuggled closer, knowing our time was quickly coming to an end. As I inhaled the fresh scent of Caleb, I realized I needed to know something that would probably slice me into tiny ribbons.

Pulling away, I turned to Persephone. "Where is her First?"

A whole minute passed before she answered. "He is in Tartarus."

I pressed my fingers to my mouth before the lump came all the way up. It wasn't so much the fate of the First, but what it signified. If I succeeded and was able to kill Seth, his fate would be the same. And so would mine.

I was like Velcro on Caleb for the next fifteen minutes or so, while Aiden busied himself studying the weapons and Persephone filed her nails or whatever. While we sat on the floor of the war room, our knees pressing together, Caleb told me about some of the stuff he was doing down here to pass time and I told him how much Olivia had wanted to see him. We didn't talk about what would happen next. I was pretty sure that Caleb was aware of all the unusual stuff going on, and neither of us wanted to tarnish these precious minutes.

"Did you tell her what I asked you to?" he asked.

I nodded. "She cried, but I think they were happy tears."

Caleb's smile was broad. "I miss her, but can you do me another favor?"

"Anything." And I meant it.

"Don't tell Olivia that you saw me again."

I frowned. "Why? She would—"

"I want her to move on." Caleb grasped my hands and stood, pulling me to my feet. "I need her to move on, and I think hearing about me is stopping her. I want her to live, and I don't want to be shadowing every step she takes."

Gods, I hated the idea of lying to Olivia, but I understood what Caleb was saying. Olivia would never move on, knowing that, in a way, Caleb was conscious and as alive as he could be in the Underworld. It was like he was there, not reachable, but still *there*. Knowing that, how could she really move on?

So I agreed. I promised to tell everyone that it had been only Persephone who had found us. Even if Apollo knew the truth, it wouldn't matter as long as Olivia didn't. In a way, this was his gift to her. "Thank you," Caleb said, and hugged me once more. Part of me wanted to stay in Caleb's arms, because he'd always had this grounding effect on me. Caleb was my rational side. He was more than that; other than my mother, he was the first person I'd ever truly loved.

Caleb would always be my best friend.

"It's time," Persephone said quietly, and when I pulled away and looked at her, there was sympathy in her gaze. A god who could empathize was an abnormality.

Aiden returned to my side, swinging the backpack onto his shoulders before handing me back the weapons that the guards had stripped off me, as well as my yucky cloak. Persephone drifted toward the center of the war room and waved her hand. A black void appeared, completely opaque. "This gate will take you back to the one you came through."

"Thank you," I said to Persephone. She nodded gracefully.

As I said goodbye and looked over my shoulder one last time, my chest squeezed as I met Caleb's blue, blue eyes. I knew then that death could stop a lot of things, but it could never cut the bond of friendship.

Caleb smiled, and I returned it with a watery one of my own, and then I turned back to the void waiting for us. Threading my fingers through Aiden's, we stepped back through the gate, armed with the knowledge we needed, but bearing the burden of needing to accomplish the impossible.

CHAPTER TWENTY-SEVEN

The Hummer was where we'd left it, and according to the clock on the dashboard, only three hours had passed—three hours in the mortal realm, forty-eight hours in the Underworld, and a lifetime for Aiden and me.

I offered to drive back, but Aiden insisted that he was fine and I knew he wanted me to sleep. I knew I should—to avoid Seth using the connection—but it didn't seem fair. Aiden had to be exhausted.

But it was a battle I wasn't winning anytime soon, so I snuggled into the passenger seat and tried to get some sleep. The only problem was that my brain would not shut down. Ever since I'd stood in the war room, something had nagged at me. What Persephone had said, the sheared ponytails on the wall—all of it seemed familiar, but I couldn't place how or why. And it was more than that. Solaris's parting words were unsettling, and they poked around in my head.

What I could never figure out was why Apollo had kept me alive once Seth had gone all banana pants on the Council.

Or why Artemis had stopped Hades from taking me into the Underworld. The gods—or at least all of them except one—feared the transfer of power, because when that happened there'd be no stopping Seth. Taking me out of the picture before I'd Awakened, or putting me out of commission afterward, made sense.

Keeping me alive didn't.

But I remembered what Artemis had said in that convenience store as she'd faced down Hades. Prophecies could change, and it didn't take a leap of logic to know that, if I became the God Killer, the prophecy would change.

Unease blossomed in my chest. Had Apollo and the others known that this was possible? Then I felt dumb for even questioning that. The oracles belonged to Apollo, and even though he didn't know all of their visions, the portion of what the oracle had told Solaris could've been shared with Apollo. Which made sense since Apollo had been oh-so-supportive of me going down to see Solaris.

Part of me was naïve enough to hope that wasn't the case, because that meant Apollo had some explaining to do. The other part was more analytical about it, more reasonable. Apollo had said before that they needed to stop the god who was obviously working with Lucian. And how else would they stop him?

They needed the God Killer.

The real kicker of this whole crappy situation was that Lucian controlled Seth, and this god—whoever it was—controlled Lucian, and therefore he/she controlled Seth and all of those who were following Lucian. So if Seth succeeded and transferred my power to him, this god would then control the God Killer. Risky, because Seth could always turn on him, but in the end, once the god had Seth do what he wanted, I was sure he'd be creative enough to somehow keep him under control. Possibly that meant keeping a member of the Order stowed away, safe and sound.

My muscles tightened in reflex as I worked this out. None of it looked good. And Seth was being manipulated from every direction and he had no idea. Hell, he refused to even think that was the case.

As the miles between Kansas and Illinois disappeared, I couldn't shake what Solaris had said about the gods using me, and what it would mean. Neither could I let go of the feeling that, by learning how to transfer the power to me, I had sealed my own fate.

The sudden weight of Aiden's hand on my knee drew my attention to him. His eyes were on the dark highway. "You're not sleeping."

I smiled as I placed my hand over his. "How did you know?"

"I just do." He sent me a brief grin. "What are you thinking about?"

Everything was on the tip of my tongue—my suspicions, my concerns about what Solaris had said, and what I now knew Apollo was hiding—but when Aiden glanced at me again, I found I couldn't tell him.

He hadn't heard what Solaris had said, and I didn't want to burden him with this on top of everything else. If my suspicions were correct, if everything was leading to one thing...

Taking a deep breath, I focused on the white lines parting the darkness. "I was just thinking about how I'm supposed to get close enough to Seth to transfer his power to me. Seems impossible, right?"

"I don't like it, Alex. I'm going to be honest; I think it's wild. To me, it's like sneaking up on a cobra. It's not going to work."

"I know, but what choice do we have? Besides, we don't just have to figure out how to get close enough to him. There're all the Sentinels and Guards who are backing him."

Aiden squeezed my hand. "We're going to need an army."

Slowly, I looked at him. "And where are we going to dig up one of those?"

"Good question." He barked out a short laugh. "What we need to find out is exactly how many Lucian has backing him—"

"I can always ask Dionysus to do some scouting," Apollo's voice boomed from the backseat.

Shrieking, I sprang forward, knocking my knees off the dashboard. Aiden's hand jerked on the steering wheel, swerving the Hummer into the left lane, which was, thankfully, empty.

Aiden cursed under his breath. "You need a freaking bell."

I twisted around in the seat, ready to knock the grin off the god's face. I was already pretty pissed off at him without him giving us a heart attack. "You could've caused an accident!"

Apollo leaned forward, resting his arms on the back of our seats. "But I didn't. Aiden has the reflexes of a hellhound."

Making a face, I shook my head. "How did you just… pop in here?"

He gave me a very ungodlike *duh* look. "These wards make your power invisible to the gods; they don't keep us out. You carry my bloodline. I can find you when I want."

"Well, that's not creepy."

Aiden glanced in the rearview mirror. "You want to know what we found out?" When Apollo nodded, a scowl appeared on Aiden's face. "And you couldn't have waited until we got back to Apple River?"

"Let's see..." Apollo tapped a finger on his chin. "The whole world is on the verge of a god apocalypse. Should I wait another six hours?"

"Six hours isn't going to change anything," Aiden replied, eyes turning a steely gray.

"I hope not." Apollo turned his gaze to me. "What did you learn?"

I debated telling him that I hadn't learned a damn thing, but that was pointless. "I learned how to transfer the power to me."

Apollo showed no reaction, and I really think I hated him right then. "And do you think you can do it?"

I glanced at Aiden. "There's the tiny problem of getting to Seth."

"Like I said, I can have Dionysus do some scouting. See what they have going for them," he replied.

"We still don't have an army." I flipped in my seat, facing the front and feeling all kinds of bitchtastic.

"Actually..."

I refused to turn around and take the bait. "What?"

When he didn't answer, Aiden growled deep in his throat. "What, Apollo?"

"About an hour after you guys left, one of the Sentinels who had been using Solos's cabin before you not-so-nicely kicked them out showed up. He brought news."

Aiden had gone completely motionless, and I wondered how he could still manage to drive like that. "And you trust this Sentinel?"

The god laughed darkly. "Let's just say I made sure he was playing on our team."

Curious, I started to ask how, but Apollo grinned at me. "Use your imagination," he said, and my imagination went to some really weird places.

"Anyway," he continued, "most of the pures are fleeing the Covenants and their communities, heading to the University in South Dakota. So are their Guards. Makes sense—the location of the University is pretty remote and almost certainly cannot be breached. The Sentinels who haven't fallen in with Lucian have left their duties and are en route to the University."

"What about the daimons?" I asked.

"What about them? They will go where the pures are, and the pures will be well-protected. Then there are the daimons that Lucian is feeding the pures to. Nothing we can do about that." Apollo sat back, eyeing the roof of the Hummer like he'd never seen one before. He tapped the internal light once and it flicked on, then he turned it off. Shiny things must be distracting for gods, too. He did it again, brows furrowed.

"Apollo," I snapped.

His gaze settled on me. "There is a good chance that Lucian and the First will overtake the New York Council, so Council members and Sentinels are being secreted out of the Covenant."

My heart tipped over. "My—"

"I don't know if your father is among the ones who have already arrived at the University, or if he is en route, or even if he is alive.. I'm sorry."

My shoulders slumped. "So what are they doing? Moving the base of operations to there?"

"Yes. So there will be hundreds, if not thousands, of Sentinels and Guards there. Those who have seen their friends and other Sentinels killed by those who have sided with Lucian. Those who want nothing more than to get a piece of him."

Aiden nodded slowly. "An army—our army."

"Marcus and Solos are already making plans to travel to the University. The sooner you all get there, the better."

I could get behind this plan. And yeah, there was a bit of a selfish reason behind it. Any chance that my father might be there was enough for me.

"It would be safer there for Deacon and the others," Aiden said. "It would be best."

Now I felt like a douche for only thinking of what I could gain. "How early can we leave?"

"As soon as possible," Apollo responded. "Once at the University, we can appeal to those who wish to put an end to this. Then we could move against Lucian—"

"And the god who's pulling the strings?" I threw in, unable to help myself. "We'll want to move against him or her, right?"

Apollo's vibrant blue eyes met mine and he held my gaze. "Yes. We will."

Right then I wanted to call him out, but the only thing stopping me was Aiden…and that part of me, the tiny part that Laadan had claimed was growing, becoming more mature. *She* sort of understood.

"But I need to check in with Dionysus." Apollo was still looking at me, and I knew I'd be seeing him real soon. "Check you guys later." And then he was gone.

Aiden slid me a sidelong glance. "Sometimes I really hate him."

"You and me both," I muttered.

We arrived back at Apple River just as the sky overhead was turning from black to a dark blue. The cabin was dark as we climbed out of the Hummer and the distant call of birds was the only sound.

Aiden stretched, bowing his back as he worked out the kinks. He stopped, catching me watching him from the other side of the vehicle. "Come here."

He was probably the only person in the world who could demand that of me and I'd listen. All too obediently, I headed around the front of the Hummer and stopped in front of him. "What?" I asked, stifling a yawn.

Aiden cupped my cheeks and tilted my head back. "You didn't sleep at all."

"Neither did you."

A tired grin appeared. "I was driving."

I placed my hands on his wrists. Our eyes locked. "I can't believe we went to the Underworld and came back out."

"Me, neither." His thumbs traced along the curve of my cheekbones. "You were perfect."

"Except for the spiders…"

His head dipped and his nose brushed mine. "I wasn't talking about the spiders."

"You weren't?"

Aiden laughed and his breath was warm and tantalizing. "No. I was thinking about what came after the spiders."

"Oh…oh!" I sucked in a sharp breath and my legs suddenly felt weak. "*That.*"

"Yes." His lips brushed mine. "That."

I started to smile, because that really had been perfect, but then Aiden kissed me and I melted into him. There was strength in that kiss, along with love and a taste of what a future would be like with him. I loved—*loved*—that in the midst of everything, we could still have moments like this. Where it was just us and there weren't any walls between us. The kiss deepened, his tongue slipping past my lips, and my fingers dug into his wrists. A low, sultry growl came from Aiden, and I wanted—

"You two should really get a room," Apollo said from out of nowhere. "My poor eyes…"

I groaned. Even in his true identity, he still had impeccable timing.

"Gods," Aiden spat. He pulled back, casting Apollo a disgusted look over my head. "Do you get off on sneaking up on us?"

"You probably don't want to know what I get off on."

I made a face. "Ew."

Aiden kissed my forehead as his hands slipped off my cheeks. Dropping an arm around my shoulders, he pulled me into the shelter of his body and I went, resting my cheek against his chest. "Did you already talk to Dionysus?"

Apollo leaned against the bumper. "Yes. He's on it as we speak."

"How can we trust that Dionysus isn't the god behind this?" I smothered another yawn. "And that he won't lie to us?"

"Dionysus cares little for war, and he doesn't have the motivation to engineer something like this."

"How long until he lets us know?" Aiden asked.

"We should hear from him by the end of the day." Apollo's gaze flickered to the deep blue sky. "It's almost morning. You two should rest."

Aiden glanced down at me. "Let's head in."

I pulled away, glancing at Apollo. "I'll be in in a few seconds. I want to talk to Apollo."

He hesitated, sending me a questioning look. I hated keeping him in the dark about this, but there was no other way, because if Aiden knew, he would stop it, and then the world would go to crap.

"It's okay." I smiled. "I'll be right in."

Aiden looked at Apollo and let out a low breath. "Okay. I'll go…wake up Deacon or something."

"I'm sure he'll appreciate that," I said.

A brief smile appeared. "True."

At the sound of the front door shutting behind Aiden, I looked at Apollo and felt the mask I'd been wearing slip away.

Our gazes met and Apollo sighed. "Alexandria…"

"I knew there was something you'd been keeping from me. That there was a bigger reason for why you all would want to keep me alive when it would be so much easier to just kill me. It would fix the problem with Seth, so I just didn't get why you'd risk it."

He looked at a loss as to what to say. Good—I'd struck a god speechless. Score one for me. I was going to go for point two. "You need the God Killer."

A long moment passed. "We need to stop this from happening again."

"You need me to kill the god responsible." Anger grew inside me, but so did hurt, and that hurt had been festering since we'd left the Underworld. I didn't know why. Apollo might be related to me by blood, but he was a god and they'd missed out on the whole empathy train, sort of like a bunch of sociopaths. It still hurt something fierce, though.

It cut deep.

Because in the end, I was the lion *and* the lamb; I would slaughter and then be slaughtered. Apollo didn't say it, but I saw it in what he wouldn't say.

"We cannot risk this kind of destruction again, Alexandria. Thousands of innocent people have died, and there *will* be more. And even if we stop the First, this will happen again." He placed his hand on my shoulder and it was heavy. "We cannot kill one another. We need the only thing that can kill us. We need the God Killer—we need you."

I stared at him, dumbfounded. "You don't want me to kill Seth, then."

He snorted. "On most days I do, but you must take his power, and he has to be alive for that. I need you to be able to defeat him and transfer his power to you."

My hands balled into fists and it took everything in me not to grab hold of those golden locks and rip them out. "You've been lying to me this entire time."

"No, I haven't." He didn't even blink.

"Bull! You told me before I Awakened that you wanted me to kill Seth! You know, over grape soda and Spider-Man cake?"

"I *wanted* you to kill Seth, but it's not what I *need*."

My mouth dropped open. "That's not even semantics!"

"And I didn't know for sure then that there was a way to transfer his power to you," he argued calmly. "I had my suspicions. So did my sister, but we couldn't be sure. Either way, he cannot be allowed to take your power. If you cannot defeat him and take his power, then you must kill him."

Apollo made it all sound so simple, like he was asking me to go to the store and pick up Crunchy Cheetos and if they didn't have them in stock, to get Cheetos Puffs. Insane.

"I don't want it to end like you fear, but there is only so much I can do to stay the hands of others."

"Yeah, because after I take out this god—if we figure out who it is—there's a good chance the gods will turn on me, because I will be a threat. And I bet they have an Order member just lying around, right? Even if I don't do anything, they will act as judge and jury on a crime I haven't committed?"

There was that damn pause again and then he said, "Everyone dies, but in the end it comes down to what you are willing to die *for*, Alexandria."

Gods, there was a part of me—a huge part of me—that wanted to kick Apollo in the balls, but I got it. As messed up as it was, I got it. And maybe that was why I wasn't flipping out on him. The loss of one life, maybe two, was worth the safety of billions. I could see that, and if I was totally impartial about this—say, if they weren't talking about *me*—then I'd probably even support it.

But it was me. It would be me.

That was a lot to swallow. It was something that I couldn't really even begin to process. I felt too selfish, but I also knew what had to be done.

Gods, I was so not old enough or mature enough to be making these kinds of decisions.

It grew so quiet between us that the gentle winds stirring the branches seemed too loud. If I didn't have my freaky god-sensing abilities right now, I'd have thought he'd left. But he was still there, waiting.

"And there's no other way?" I asked.

He didn't respond, and I took his silence as a no.

Heart heavy, I lifted my head. "What will happen if I die?"

Apollo didn't answer immediately. "You will have a warrior's death. There is pride in that and you will want for nothing."

Except to live, but I figured that was a moot point. "Will you make sure that…that Aiden will be okay?"

The god's eyes met mine and he nodded.

Throat burning and tightening, I focused on the dark gravel. "He…he had to see his parents afterward, Apollo. I don't want him to see me, okay? Can you make sure he doesn't?"

"If that is what you wish."

I pressed my lips together, relieved a little that Aiden would be spared that horror—maybe not the bulk of it, but some of it. "And will you make sure Marcus and the rest of them are okay?"

"Yes."

"Okay." I swallowed, but I still felt like I was choking. "I want to be left alone for a while."

"Alex—"

I looked then, meeting his gaze. "Please leave."

He looked like he was going to say something, but then he nodded and simply vanished. I don't know how long I stood there, but eventually I shuffled over to the porch and sat down on the steps.

The night air was still cool and it stung my hot cheeks. Tears burned my eyes, but I refused to let them fall. Crying served nothing. It wouldn't change what would happen. If I somehow managed to get to Seth, transfer his power to me before he took mine, and destroy the mystery god, I'd still be put down like a rabid animal. Possibly even Seth would be, as well, although he'd no longer be a threat. Maybe without me around to influence him, he'd get better. He'd just be the Apollyon then, like it was supposed to be—only one of us and all that jazz.

I rubbed my eyes until they ached.

What day was it? Sometime in April? Less than a month from now, I was supposed to be graduating from the Covenant. That was so obviously not going to happen. So much had changed, and so much would never be the same. I wondered if my Fate had changed too, or if this had always been a part of it and no one had thought to clue me in.

An idea occurred to me. It was insane, but I thought about

letting the wonky connection with Seth happen. The ache was in my temples. Maybe I could tell him what I knew. Maybe there was a part of him that still cared enough.

I shook my head and lowered my hands.

Seth would probably just use it as another reason for me to jump ship.

Taking several deep breaths, I pushed thoughts of Seth out of my head and, for some reason, I thought about my father. Features roughened by a hard life fell into place. Broad cheekbones and a strong chin spoke of a warrior's face. We really didn't look too much alike, but it was his eyes…they were mine.

I tried not to think about my dad. Perhaps that was wrong, but it was hard sitting here knowing that he was in the Catskills. And it was even harder acknowledging that there might be a good chance we'd never meet face-to-face, aware of what we were to each other.

Squeezing my knees together, I thought about the sacrifice he was making—had made—for so many years. Deep down I knew he probably wanted to be here with me, but he had a job to do. Through and through, my father was a Sentinel.

I respected him for that.

I don't know how long I sat there, but it couldn't have been that long before the door behind me eased open. Boards creaked as the footsteps drew near.

Aiden sat beside me, still in his Sentinel uniform. He stared straight ahead and said nothing. I looked at him. The dark waves were messy, going in every direction. A slight shadow was forming on his jaw.

"Didn't wake up Deacon?" I asked.

"Nah. If I did, then I'd probably never get to bed. He'll need entertainment or something, and you know how that goes." Aiden tilted his head toward me. "When did Apollo leave?"

"A little while ago."

Aiden was quiet for a moment. "Is there anything I should know?"

My heart skipped a beat. "No."

His eyes met mine and I couldn't tell if he believed me, but he extended his arm. I scooted over, fitting myself against the side of his body as he locked his arms around me. He rested his cheek against my hair and I felt his breath.

Minutes passed, and then he said, "We're in this together, Alex. Don't ever forget that. We're in this together to the end."

CHAPTER TWENTY-EIGHT

By the time Apollo reappeared later that night, I hadn't really come to terms with everything. I mean, how could I? Going through all of this, facing only gods-knew-what, knowing there was a 99% chance I'd die in the end really didn't help with the whole motivation factor. So I decided to do the only thing I could do.

Forget about the end result.

Probably not the wisest method, but it was the only way I could do this and keep sane, because right now I didn't know how to change any of it.

Apollo didn't return alone. When he popped into the living room, he brought along Dionysus. It was the first time I'd seen the god. He looked like a frat boy in his Hawaiian shirt and cargo shorts.

Dionysus dropped onto the couch in a lazy, arrogant sprawl. His heavy-lidded gaze moved over the females in the room, sizing them up like one looks at a menu. When his freaky eyes landed on me, I arched a brow.

He grinned. "So, this is the Apollyon?"

"That would be me."

"For some reason, I expected you to be taller."

What the hell? Folding my arms, I shot him a bland look. "I don't know why people keep saying that."

Aiden leaned against the desk I sat on. "You *are* pretty short."

My height wasn't our biggest problem. Thankfully, Marcus reined the conversation in, bringing it back to more important things. "Do you have news of Lucian?"

The god stretched, folding his arms behind his head. "Well, I got as close as I could. Something's different this time around." Apollo frowned.

I didn't like it when gods frowned—usually it meant something really, really bad. "What do you mean?"

"I could only get *so* close. Something barred me from getting among them, even barred my nymphs." He wiggled his toes. "No ward can do that. Only another god."

"I don't understand," I said. "How could another god block you?"

"A powerful one can, little Apollyon." Dionysus winked one all-white eye. "It would be like hitting an invisible wall. The First and the pure-blood are well protected."

"Hermes?" Marcus said, rubbing his jaw thoughtfully.

Dionysus snorted. "Hermes couldn't pull off something like that."

"Who could?" Solos asked, gaze shrewd.

"One of the core," Dionysus answered with a smirk.

"What do you mean?" Luke leaned forward in his chair, dropping his arms over his knees. "'One of the core'?"

The god spared him a brief glance. "There's a social…or political structure to things in Olympus—a ranking by power."

Across the room, Laadan cleared her throat. Beside her, Olivia remained quiet. She hadn't spoken since asking about Caleb earlier. I had kept his promise, as much as it sucked.

"Can you give us a little more detail?" Laadan asked politely. "I believe this is something that we are unaware of."

"Not really," Apollo answered. "You modeled your Councils after Olympus, with each Council having a leader, so to speak. Olympus is the same."

My curiosity swelled. "So, who is the core?"

Dionysus might not have had pupils, but I was pretty sure that, when his head swung back to me, he was staring at my chest. And I was also sure that Aiden believed so, too, considering the way he stiffened.

"Zeus and Hera, followed by the ever-popular Apollo and his sister Artemis, then Ares and Athena," Dionysus answered. "Last but not least, Hades and Poseidon. They are the most powerful gods and the only ones who could pull that off."

"Well, it's not Hades. He wanted to take me to the Underworld. And I doubt it was Poseidon since he went all water-god on Deity Island."

Aiden slid Apollo a look.

The Sun God's eyes narrowed. "Yeah, like it's me."

"Could really be any of them," Dionysus said, and then yawned loudly. "They'd have to be fooling everyone, so they could've fooled even us." He shrugged as if none of this was a big deal. "It is what it is."

"Did you sense anything?" Apollo's hands closed at his sides when Dionysus shook his head. "Did you see *anything* that might tell us who the god was? Anything?"

"Really wasn't looking for that. You told me to see how many Guards that idiot pure-blood had with him, and I did."

A muscle popped in Apollo's jaw and he all but growled, "So, what did you see?"

"Nothing good."

"Details," Apollo said, exhaling through his nose. "Details."

I wondered if Dionysus was drunk or high. My gaze caught Deacon's on the other end of the couch, and I could tell he was thinking the same thing. Even Lea, who was sitting on the arm beside Deacon, was giving Dionysus a *what the hell* look.

"He has damn near close to a thousand half-blood Sentinels and Guards, maybe more. Plus, he's surrounded by some sort of inner circle—other pures. And it gets even better." He paused, and I knew it was for dramatic effect. "There were mortals with him."

My mouth dropped open. "*What?*"

"Soldiers," Dionysus replied. "Mortal soldiers—like the 'Be all you can be' kind of soldiers. There were probably about five hundred of them."

I almost fell off the desk.

"How is that possible?" Lea demanded. Then she squeezed her eyes shut, features pinched. "He's using a compulsion."

"No." Marcus shook his head as he turned to Apollo. "No pure-blood could control that many mortals. Not even if he had a hundred pures surrounding him."

"It's the god." Apollo looked disgusted.

My stomach heaved at the thought. Using mortals like that was wrong on so many levels. They'd never survive a fight against a Sentinel or Guard, no matter how many guns they had. We were simply so much faster and better trained. Mortals would be cannon fodder and nothing more. It was revolting.

Anger filled the room, so thick I could practically taste it.

"I don't get it." Deacon ran a hand over his head, clasping the back of his neck. "How is the mortal world not paying attention to something like that?"

"One of the mortals must be high up in the army, someone who can make that kind of call and give some sort of reason." Apollo's lips thinned. "At least that's what I'd do."

"And they could've called some sort of state of emergency," Marcus added. "No part of the U.S. has gone completely unscathed, and I'm beginning to wonder if this god even cares about exposure."

Aiden gripped the edge of the desk. "I think it's obvious that the risk of exposure isn't important. Hell, maybe it's even planned." All eyes turned on him. "Think about it. Why else would a god be orchestrating all of this? Or going along with what Lucian wants?" Aiden asked. "To take out the gods and then what—rule Olympus? Or rule Olympus *and* the mortal realm?"

A shiver raced across my shoulders. My wildest imagination couldn't even fathom what it would be like if the world knew that gods did exist—and on top of that, if the world ended up being ruled by one.

"We can't let that happen," I said.

Apollo's eyes met mine. "No. We can't."

I averted my gaze, because right now I didn't want to think about what stopping this god meant.

I cleared my throat. "I wonder if Lucian and Seth even know."

"Does it matter?" Lea asked, snotty as ever.

My lips quirked at her tone. "I guess it doesn't, but you have to wonder who's using who. And what will happen to them in the end if the god is successful. Does he plan to keep them around or get rid of them? Do they even have a clue?"

Most of the people in the room couldn't care less—that much was apparent—but Marcus strode over to where I sat and leaned against the desk on the other side of me. "I doubt they know. In a way, no matter what they have been responsible for, it is tragic."

"It will be tragic if they succeed." Dionysus stood and stretched his arms over his head. "Well, I'm out."

Apollo nodded and Dionysus bowed to the room, sweeping his arms out to the sides with a flourish. And then he was gone.

I shook my head. "Okay. Who else thinks he was high as a kite?" Hands went up across the room and I grinned.

"So, we're leaving tomorrow morning for the University?" Olivia asked as she pulled on a springy curl. "Don't you think that, if this god is so conniving and smart, he's figured out that Alex will be going there? I mean, even if he's using Lucian and Seth for his ultimate evil plans, he's still going to need Alex, right? Because he's probably controlling Seth, or wants to."

Everyone grew quiet, and I felt like a little ant under a magnifying glass. I glanced at Apollo, but he was staring at the globe on the desk.

"Making any move is going to be as dangerous as sitting here," Marcus said finally. "But in South Dakota, we will be safer."

"Alex will be safer there, too," Luke murmured, staring at his hands.

I opened my mouth, but Lea spoke. "Well, I think our job is to make sure that Seth and this god don't get to Alex."

My mouth really dropped open.

She smiled smartly at me. "Can't have you going all psycho-Alex again and ending the world as we know it."

"She has a point." Deacon grinned.

I narrowed my eyes. "Wait. Guys, I don't want—"

"What?" Aiden nudged me with his elbow. "You don't want us having your back?"

"That's not what this is." I stared at Apollo, but damn, that globe *fascinated* him. "If there's going to be a god gunning for my butt—"

"It is a nice butt," Aiden murmured as he studied the toes of his boots. A small grin was on his face.

I stared at him a moment. "*Plus* Seth is out looking for me. This…this is going to be really dangerous. I don't want you guys risking your lives for me."

Lea snorted. "Damn, Alex, your ego is out of control. You know me. I'd sooner throw you in front of a daimon any other day, but if keeping you away from them means saving millions of lives, then I'm on your team. So this is bigger than you."

"I *know* this is bigger than me." My cheeks burned, and Deacon's idiot grin wasn't helping. "And I know you'd toss me in front of a daimon, but I don't want to see any of you get hurt."

"Everyone here knows the risks, Alex." Marcus's voice was stern, reminding me of the days back in the Covenant when he'd spent the majority of his time yelling at me. "No one is being forced to do this."

"And none of us would do anything else." Olivia offered a tentative smile. "All of us have lost people because of what's happening. We all have reasons to make sure this stops and doesn't happen again."

"Even me," Deacon said. "I haven't gotten my regular twelve hours of sleep since all of this went down, and that is damn tragic."

Aiden rolled his eyes.

"Everyone is ready to fight." Laadan crossed the room,

smiling as she stood next to Marcus. "This isn't just your battle."

"It was never just your battle," Solos corrected.

"In other words," Marcus said, his jade-colored eyes meeting mine, "you're not in this alone. You never were."

"And you're not going to be," Aiden finished quietly.

Wow. I think I sort of loved everyone in that room right then, even Lea. Tears burned my eyes, and I tipped my head forward so no one could see. The thing was that, ever since I realized how all of this could end—probably would end—I'd never felt more alone. But sitting here, hearing them…

"Group hug time?" Deacon suggested.

"Shut up," I said, but I laughed.

Aiden slid an arm around my shoulders and tipped me toward him. Right in front of the entire room full of halfs, pures, and a god, he kissed my temple. "You're just going to have to accept that this isn't going to just be you. It's going to be all of us."

I lifted my head and looked at all of them, at a loss as to what to say.

Luke smiled. "I know. We're awesome."

I laughed again.

"And we were born to do this," Olivia said, shrugging. "We'd be doing this in a month or so, anyway. We're ready."

Lea slid Olivia a grin that said she was more than ready. "Bring it."

CHAPTER TWENTY-NINE

I'd only gotten a few hours of sleep by the time the sun broke through the blinds the next morning. Listening to everyone tell me they were ready to face whatever was thrown our way… Even hours later, I still couldn't find the right words for how much it meant. But an unseen weight had settled on my shoulders and it'd grown overnight, pressing me straight down through the mattress. I couldn't stop any of them—and I wouldn't, just like they wouldn't stop me—but a thousand things raced through my head.

And the main thoughts centered on any of them losing their lives in this. So many had already perished, and no matter how Positive Polly I tried to be, I knew deep in my core that something terrible, something violent, waited in the future. Death had come long before they'd pledged to see this through, and it was on the other side of the door, or in another state, waiting patiently, because nothing was as unwavering as Death. It probably had the most time in the world.

Even though I knew what awaited them—awaited us

all—in the Underworld, I couldn't bear the idea of seeing any of them fall. If I could, I'd seal them all up in the cage downstairs, even Aiden. No doubt that wouldn't go over well, but I knew that, between what Apollo needed of me, what Solaris had warned, and how far gone Seth seemed to be, this would end in disaster.

When Aiden shifted beside me and dropped an arm over my waist, I grimaced. "Sorry."

He snuggled closer. "About what?"

"I kept waking you up." I pressed back against him, looking over my shoulder. Two silvery eyes peered from behind a mess of dark hair. "I know I did."

"Not that much." Aiden rose up on one arm. His body was relaxed, but concern radiated in his gaze. "How much did you sleep?"

I thought about lying, but I shook my head, and then wiggled onto my back. "We're leaving in a few hours."

Aiden nodded as his eyes searched mine.

Twisting my fingers together, I tried to smile. "How long will we be on the road?"

"We're looking at about ten hours."

Yikes. "Deacon's riding with us?"

"Yes. So are Luke and Marcus. Solos is taking the girls."

Something stirred restlessly in the pit of my stomach. I didn't want to name it. "You think that's okay?"

Aiden placed his hand over mine, stilling them. "Olivia and Lea are very good. You know that." They were. Especially Lea—she was like She-Ra. And Solos and Marcus had gone out earlier, picking up two throwaway cell phones to help us keep in communication.

"And you know Solos will never let anything happen to them. Neither will Laadan." As he spoke, he eased my hands apart and threaded his fingers through mine. "We have six hundred miles of no-man's-land to get through. We're going to be okay."

That thing in my stomach tipped over. "I'm not afraid."

"I didn't say you were."

My eyes narrowed.

Aiden cracked a grin. "But you are."

"I'm—"

"Do I need to find a sensory deprivation chamber again?" When my cheeks flushed at the memory, his grin spread into a full smile. Deep dimples appeared and, instead of my stomach tumbling, my heart did. "It's okay, Alex."

"What is?" My voice sounded terribly fragile, and normally I would've hated that, especially considering I was this big bad Apollyon, but with Aiden, I didn't need to pretend. Sometimes I forgot that, though.

"To be afraid, Alex, it's okay. What we're facing is some scary...shit."

I smiled then. "You cussed."

"I did."

My smile quickly faded, though, because we *were* facing some scary shit. Crap that Aiden didn't even know the half of. "Are you scared?"

For a moment, he didn't answer. All that could be heard were the slow, steady ticking of the ancient wall clock and the distant chirping of the birds outside the rustic log walls. "Yes."

Hearing him admit that was both relieving and frightening. "You're never afraid."

Aiden shook his head, his smile slipping into a wry one. "You know that's not true. There're a lot of things that terrify me, Alex."

I met his eyes. "Tell me."

Stretching out beside me, he tugged me over so my cheek was pressed against his chest. "I'm afraid that Deacon is going to get hurt…or worse. I'm afraid that we will lose more people." There was a pause and his heart picked up under my cheek. "I'm terrified of what you're going to face—what you have to do and how it's going to affect you."

My breath caught around a denial as I curled my fingers into the sheet tangled around his hips. "I'll be okay." Those words were bitter on my tongue.

His chest rose sharply. "I don't want you to be okay."

I lifted my head so I could see his eyes. They were a dark gray and shadowed. He tried for a smile, but like mine earlier, it looked pained.

"I want you to be more than okay." Aiden cupped my cheek gently. "I don't want you to have nightmares for the rest of your life, and see Seth's face instead of your mother's. I don't want *this* to haunt you."

Suddenly, everything felt too real, and I was too close. Sitting up, I put some space between us, but I still felt hot and suffocated. "I know what has to be done."

And I also knew what that likely meant for me.

He followed, capturing the newly gained distance. His face, those beautiful lips were only inches from mine. "I know, Alex. I also know that you're going to do it, because I cannot even think for one second that you will fail. You can't. You *won't*."

At the pain and determination in his voice, I pressed my lips together. Failing and succeeding kind of ended the same.

"Look at me," he ordered.

I hadn't realized I'd looked away, but I felt his hand on my cheek.

He guided my chin up until our eyes locked and I couldn't

move. "But I also know that killing Seth isn't going to be easy, and I don't mean on a physical level. I know deep down you care for him. Maybe a part of you even loves him."

Horrified of what he must think, because he'd nailed it right on the head, I shook my head. "Aiden—"

"I understand." The small grin that played on his lips was real. "I know it's not the same as what you feel for me, but it doesn't make it any less strong or important."

"He..." I didn't know what to say. Aiden was right. Part of me still loved Seth, and it wasn't in the way I felt for Aiden, but it wasn't any less real or powerful. Even after all that Seth had done, I couldn't forget all that he had done *before* that. It had been the same with my mom, but in the end, I had taken her life like it had been fated all along.

You'll kill the ones you love...

Aiden's forehead pressed against mine. "Seth was there for you when you needed someone. You guys share this bond that...that is more than him connecting with you. We broke the connection, but there's something else underneath that. He's a part of you."

I drew in a surprised breath. "He's...he's done such terrible things."

"He has." Aiden pressed a kiss to my temple. "But he has done some good things, and I know you can't forget how he used to be. I know none of this will be easy for you."

Killing Seth would break a piece of me, and no matter how long I walked this earth afterward, it couldn't be repaired. He was a part of me—a part that was a bit insane—but still. It would change me in a way I couldn't fathom. Just as facing down my mom had. But this time was different.

Apollo didn't want me to kill Seth; he wanted me to strip him of his power. Knowing Seth, he'd probably prefer death.

And if Seth figured out what I was up to, he'd come after me. So I would have to stop him—kill him. Killing Seth would be the only way I walked out of this alive.

"Alex?" Aiden whispered. "Talk to me, *agapi mou*."

"Don't be afraid." My voice was hoarse. "I'll be...okay."

His hand slipped to the nape of my neck, and he held on as if he could keep me there forever. "You'll tell me that you'll be okay. And you'll act like you're okay, but..."

I squeezed my eyes shut. Aiden would know better. Seconds passed in silence. The truth was on the tip of my tongue, burning me from the inside out. I wanted to tell him what could happen—I really needed to—but putting that on him wasn't fair. Time stretched out, but it wasn't enough.

"'You will kill the ones you love.'" My laugh was dry and brittle. "I hate that damn oracle."

Aiden's fingers splayed across my cheek. "If I could change this, I would. I'd do anything to save you from this."

"I know." I tipped my head a little to the side and kissed him softly. "But Fate is a bitch."

"Or a bastard," he said lightly.

I laughed, because whenever Aiden cussed, I couldn't help it. It sounded wrong rolling off his tongue, but still elegant, somehow. Like a British person cussing. Anyway, I just couldn't talk about this anymore. I didn't even want to think about it, but I'd need a brain scrub to fix that.

Leaning forward, I looped my arms around his neck and all but climbed into his lap. "Can we talk about something else?"

Aiden looked like he was going to argue, but he nodded.

Staring into his eyes, I thought back to the days when he used to pop in and watch me train. That made me smile. "I used to think you were the source of my failure."

"What?" He arched a brow as he wrapped his arms around my waist.

"I could never get things right when you were around, especially when you used to watch me in class." I shrugged. "I wanted to be perfect in your eyes. I wanted you to be proud of me."

"I am."

I beamed at him, smiling for real for the first time since this conversation began. "But you're kind of like my source of strength, even when I couldn't concentrate because of you."

Aiden tilted his head to the side, causing his lips to graze my cheek. "We had the same problem, then."

"Doubtful."

"You have no idea how hard it was." Aiden sighed against my lips. "To train you—to be so close when all I wanted…"

There was a flutter in my chest. "What did you want?"

He leaned in, his warm breath becoming my world. "How about I show you?"

Oh, I so liked where this was heading. So much better than the doom and gloom crap that wanted to pull me under, bringing Aiden along with me. "I'm down with that."

Laughing softly, he erased that minuscule distance and I let out a little sigh. If he kissed me like that every couple of hours, it would keep the darkness at bay. It would obliterate everything I feared and would probably come to regret. My world would be close to perfect.

There was a knock, and we drew apart an instant before the door swung open and Deacon's mop of a head popped in. Aiden groaned, but his eyes lightened by several shades.

"Good morning!" Too much cheer rang in his voice for this time of the morning.

My cheeks burned as I mumbled, "Morning."

Before either of us could say another word, Deacon darted from the door and launched himself onto the bed, soaring through the air like a human projectile. I jerked to the side with a split second to spare. He landed with his legs on his brother and the upper part of his body between us.

Deacon threw his arms behind his head, folding them as he tipped his head back and grinned at us. "It's like a puppy pile."

"A puppy pile?" Aiden arched a brow. "You are so weird."

"Whatever." Deacon's gray eyes flicked to me. "Was I interrupting anything?"

Aiden rolled his eyes and I fought a grin. "Not at all, brother."

"Good, because you guys better get your butts in gear. We're leaving in an hour." Deacon crossed his ankles, letting out a content sigh. "Time to hit the road."

I tucked my hair back, wondering how much coffee he'd had to be up this early and already this hyper. "You're so unnaturally wound up."

"I'm excited," he replied. "I'm looking at this road trip like a real life game of Oregon Trail."

My brows rose. "Are you going to catch typhoid fever?"

"Actually, I was thinking about breaking a leg or drowning."

"There's always starving to death." My lips split into a grin. "Or you could get kidnapped by terrorists."

Deacon's eyes widened dramatically. "They'd want me for my glorious blond locks."

"It's about time someone cut your hair." Aiden mussed the already unruly curls and then threw the covers back. "I'm taking a shower."

The look Aiden sent me said he hadn't planned on doing

it alone, and my stomach did all kinds of crazy twists and turns. It didn't help that he strode across the room in all his bare-chested glory. The heat that zinged through my veins was hard to deny, but Deacon apparently wasn't going anywhere.

I waited until Aiden closed the door and I heard the hiss of the shower before I glanced down at his younger brother. "What?"

His lips tipped up on one side. "We need to chat."

Having no clue what was going to come out of his mouth, but positive it would be entertaining, I wiggled down and stretched out beside him. "Okay. About what?"

"You need to stay alive."

Okay, so not what I was expecting. "I'm not planning to off myself, Deacon."

"No, but you have that look of someone who is facing down death, practically even expects it." Deacon paused and his gaze went to the bare rafters in the ceiling. "I know what that looks like. I saw it in the mirror for a long time."

My mouth opened, but I couldn't find any words.

He laughed dryly. "I hated living after seeing what'd happened to my parents and those other people. If it hadn't been for Aiden, I wouldn't have survived. I shouldn't have survived. Neither should he." He gave a lopsided shrug. "I guess I had a mad case of survivor's guilt or something like that. Every time I drank or got high, I secretly hoped that I would overdo it, you know?"

As his words sank in, my chest ached. I reached over, placing my hand on his arm. "Deacon..."

"Ah, I'm okay now. I think I am, at least. But you know why I never really went there?" Deacon turned his head toward me, and I knew what he meant. "I wasn't scared of death, but I was scared of what me dying would do to him."

Deacon nodded at the bathroom door and my gaze followed his. I couldn't see Aiden and I knew he couldn't hear us, but my heart was pounding like I'd just run up a thousand steps.

"He wouldn't get past losing you," I said, swallowing hard. "He's so strong, but..."

"It would kill him. I know. Losing you would kill him."

A cold chill washed over me, like I'd stepped into a freezer. Sitting up swiftly, I tugged my hair over one shoulder. "Why are you telling me this?"

"You've had that same look ever since you came back from the Underworld." There was a pause, and he looked at me with all the seriousness no one ever gave him credit for. In that moment, he reminded me so much of Aiden. "Whatever you do, don't break my brother's heart. You are his world. And if you leave it, it will destroy him."

CHAPTER THIRTY

Our Hummer was the party car—the cool one. Or at least that's what I believed. Between Luke and Deacon, the ten-hour drive to the wilds of South Dakota wasn't turning out to be that bad. Poor Marcus looked like he wanted to duct tape the two boys' mouths shut after two hours of their nonstop rundown of the last season of *Supernatural*. I wasn't complaining. Then, Luke moved on to this new show about thrones and dragons, which he tried to explain to Aiden. Considering that Aiden was a fan of old black-and-white TV shows, Luke wasn't getting very far.

Marcus looked like he had a headache, which mirrored how I felt. It had nothing to do with the boys' chatter or the ridiculous—but hilarious—car games they insisted on playing. And I was pretty sure that, if Deacon leaned between the seats and punched Aiden on the arm again the next time he saw a Beetle, Aiden was going to pull the car over and strangle him.

I was also sure Marcus would hold Deacon down. The man had to have a wicked bruise on his leg from the last punch Deacon had delivered.

But after the fourth hour, restlessness set in. Minutes from turning into the kid who makes their parents threaten to turn the car around, I tried to get some rest. It wasn't like the scenery was much to look at. Lots of fields. Then lots of hills. Then lots of trees. Boredom itched at my skin as I stared at the wards, drawn in Titan blood throughout the car, that kept the gods from sensing me. But the fact that I was stuck in the vehicle for the foreseeable future wasn't the worst part. The steadily increasing throbbing in my temples sent a nervous rush through my system.

Seth was there, pecking away, waiting for that moment he could pop in and have a chat. Part of me almost welcomed it, because it would be something to do, but that was so stupid. Talking to Seth wouldn't help anything. He was on one side of the fence and I was clear on the other side.

I didn't want to think at all.

Twisting in the seat, my eyes met my uncle's. I smiled as he nodded at Deacon. The pure had finally passed out, with his cheek plastered against the window. Beside him, Luke was staring out the window, jaw locked down tight.

Not wanting to wake the talkative beast, I said nothing and turned back around. My booted foot slid over the sickle blade resting on the floor. We were just as stocked and well-armed as we'd been when we drove to Kansas.

I settled in the seat, carefully stretching out my legs when I really wanted to flail about. Out of the corner of my eye, I caught Aiden's amused grin. I made a face at him and he laughed softly.

Time slowed down to a crawl. Every time I looked at the clock on the dashboard I would've sworn two hours had gone by, but it was only twenty minutes later. When we hit the halfway point, Solos called Aiden. They needed to get gas.

Aiden wasn't thrilled about it. "We're too close to Minneapolis."

In other words, we were too close to a heavily populated area. Nearly every major city in the U.S. had communities of pures on the outskirts. Where there were pures, there were daimons. And that also meant there would be Sentinels and Guards—those who might be working with Lucian.

But we didn't have any choice. Both vehicles were running low on gas, and it was either stop now or run out of gas in the middle of nowhere and get eaten by wild coyotes and bears.

We pulled into a decent-sized travel area, and I immediately reached for the door handle. "I prefer you'd stay in the car," Aiden said, unbuckling.

I frowned. "Why? I have the talisman."

"I know." He shot me look. "But knowing our luck, someone will recognize you."

"But I have to use the bathroom."

"Hold it," Luke said, opening the car door. "I'll get you something to snack on, and some water—lots of water."

I glared at him. "That's so wrong."

Everyone but me rushed from the Hummer and I flung myself back against the seat, folding my arms. I got that we didn't need another god smackdown in the middle of the gas station, but damn… Aiden headed toward the other Hummer while Marcus pumped gas. Here I was, the freaking Apollyon, and I couldn't even go inside to get a bag of beef jerky by myself. Geez.

A few moments later, Aiden came around to my side of the car. I debated leaving the window up, but I rolled it down. He leaned in, resting on his forearms.

"Hey," he said, grinning.

I knew I was pouting, but I couldn't feel my butt.

"Olivia and Lea are checking out the bathroom. Looks like it's outside and around the back."

"Oh, thank the gods." I slumped in my seat.

His grin spread on one side. "I'll make sure Luke gets you something other than water."

"You're the best." I popped forward and kissed him quickly. "I mean it."

On his way past us, Marcus's eyes narrowed. "I feel like I'm going to need to separate you two." Aiden's cheeks flushed as he pulled back and cleared his throat.

Marcus stopped beside him, folding his arms. "Especially the sleeping arrangements. And I'm not naïve enough to—"

"Whoa!" I cut in. "Not a topic that I'm willing to delve into."

Marcus gave me a bland look. "You are my niece and I'm your guardian."

"I'm eighteen."

"And you're still too—"

"Olivia! Bathroom break!" I threw open the door, nearly knocking Marcus over. Shooting my uncle a quick grin, I darted around him.

Aiden grabbed my arm. "Be careful."

"Of course. Other than dying of fumes and wanting to hurl, it's just a public restroom."

He still looked like he wanted to escort me in there, but Marcus was also eyeing Aiden like he wanted to punch him again. Aiden let go and I joined the girls at the sidewalk.

"What's going on over there?" Olivia asked.

I looked over my shoulder. Marcus's mouth was flying a mile a minute, and Aiden stood there, stiff and silent. I grimaced. "You don't even want to know."

"Probably has to do with the fact that you and Aiden are having sex," Lea announced, crossing her arms.

My jaw dropped.

"Nice." Olivia swatted her on the arm. "Way to just throw that out there."

Lea shrugged. "Hey, it is what it is. He's a hottie. I'd be doing it with him every five seconds."

"Okay. Thanks for sharing."

Olivia eyed the other half. "Speaking of having sex like a horned-up rabbit, have you heard from Jackson? He wasn't at the Covenant when…" She looked around and lowered her voice. "He wasn't there when Poseidon went nuts."

"No. My cell died and I don't have a charger." Her eyes narrowed on the overcast sky. "I don't know what he might be doing. We weren't really as close as you guys think. At least, we didn't talk a lot."

Olivia snorted.

"I don't think he's with Seth and Lucian," I said as we started around the corner of the cement building.

"Why?" Olivia tucked a tight curl back.

"Remember when Jackson got his face rearranged?" We'd stopped outside the bathroom door, and I could already smell the funk. The girls nodded. "I'm pretty sure Seth did that to him."

"Holy crap," Olivia murmured as she slid the key into the door. "Because of what Jackson did to you in class?"

I nodded. Jackson had taken sparring too far, planting his boot in my face—I had a tiny scar to prove it—and I was sure that Instructor Romvi had goaded him into it. As we headed into the bathroom and I looked for a somewhat decent stall, I wondered if Romvi was still alive.

Romvi had disappeared after Linard delivered Head

Minister Telly's ultimatum, and Seth had had members of the Order hunted down, as they were the only real threat to us. As terrible as it sounded, if he had met his end, I wouldn't be too torn up. Romvi'd had it out for me from day one.

The trip to the bathroom turned out to be uneventful, since I didn't consider the risk of catching hand, foot, and mouth disease to be an event.

Back in the Hummer, with my lap full of Skittles and other assorted goodies, I was surprised by the fact Medusa hadn't appeared in the toilet and tried to eat me. Perhaps this trip wouldn't be so bad. I glanced behind me, past where Deacon and Luke were sharing nachos. Marcus's arms were spread along the back of the last seat. His gaze was focused on the back of Aiden's head like he could somehow bore holes through it.

Okay. Perhaps this trip wouldn't be so bad for *me*. Aiden on the other hand…

Flipping to the front, I caught Aiden's gaze and offered a sympathetic smile. "Skittles?"

"Please."

I dumped some into his open palm, then picked out the green ones. Aiden grinned at me. "You know I don't like the green ones?"

Shrugging, I popped them in my mouth. "The few times I've seen you eat them, you leave the green ones behind."

Deacon popped his head between our seats. "That's true love right there."

"That it is." Aiden's gaze flicked to the road.

I flushed like a little schoolgirl and focused on the remaining pieces of candy until Deacon drifted back into his seat. I handed all the red ones to Aiden.

A couple of hours after we'd hit the traffic apocalypse

outside of Sioux Falls, the open skies had darkened and night was only minutes away. Knots formed in my stomach as I thought of the distance between me and the University evaporating. We were still about four hours away, but that was nothing after being in the car this long.

The University was nestled deep in the Black Hills of South Dakota. Not near Mount Rushmore, but in the part known as the Northern Hills. It was a heavily protected wilderness, only reachable in vehicles such as the one we were in. People had to know what they were looking for to even see the entrance to the school.

I'd never seen the University in person, but I knew it looked like something straight out of Greece. Like all the Covenants, the mortals believed the school to be a part of an elite, invitation-only education system. Even though I was sort of excited to see the school, my nerves hummed for a different reason.

My father could be there—or he could be on his way there.

Hope soared in my chest and I felt giddy for a few seconds. I didn't know what I'd do if I saw him—probably something along the lines of pouncing and tackling the man, and I so hoped I wouldn't bawl like a baby and embarrass myself.

I knew I shouldn't get my hopes up. My father might not be there. He might never show up there.

He could be dead.

My stomach tumbled, and for a moment I thought I was going to hurl.

The thing was—and what I kept trying to tell myself—I didn't know. And there was no reason to get worked up either way. And I had more important things to concentrate on, like how in the hell I was going to convince a bunch of

Sentinels and Guards to risk death by warring against Seth and a god.

Aiden's cell went off, and the look on his face as he listened wasn't good.

"What?" I asked, feeling my stomach drop again. I wondered if I had an ulcer...or if that was even possible.

"Got it," he said into the phone, and then snapped it shut. "We're being followed."

I spun in my seat, just like Marcus and Luke did. The headlights from Solos's Hummer were right behind us. I squinted. Several car lengths behind there was another set of headlights. I wasn't an expert on those things, but it looked an awful lot like another Hummer.

Sentinels and Guards loved to drive Hummers. The bigger the better and all that jazz—probably making up for something else. Mortals drove Hummers too, but every instinct was telling me it was Covenant-issued and not friendly.

Crap.

"How long?" I asked.

"Since we passed Sioux Falls," Aiden replied, eyes flicking to the rearview mirror.

"There's an exit coming up—take it. We need to get off the main highway." Marcus cursed as he leaned back, pulling out a Glock. "Good news is that the road will be clear of mortals. Bad news is that the roads will be clear."

There would be no one around for either side to worry about exposure, if they even cared about that anymore.

"Tell Solos to follow," Marcus said. "And to stay close to us."

As Aiden relayed the message to Solos, I kept my eyes glued to the stretch of highway behind us as we hit the ramp and flew down the dark back road. Then I saw what Aiden hadn't said, and what Marcus must've realized once Solos had moved into the other lane.

It wasn't one Hummer; it was two, and I was sure both were packed. Double crap.

Luke was straining to get a better look. "We can't let them report back, guys. If they haven't already. We're too close to the University."

"So, you really think they're his—Lucian's?" Deacon asked, gripping the back of my seat.

Aiden nodded. "Everything's cool, though. We've got this."

The strength in his words—the determination to get everyone through this—was so like him. No matter what, he held it together. He might falter a step or two, but he weathered the blows and he never gave up. Not on me. Not on his brother. And never on life. Gods, no wonder I loved this man. As I stared at him and saw the steely resolve in the lines of his striking face, I realized something.

Actually, it was like being hit by a seven-ton truck.

I needed to put my big-girl panties on—like, for real.

Deacon had been right. A part of me had accepted that my death would be inevitable since I'd left the Underworld, that in the end Fate would find a way to win. Me—I'd felt this way—believed it. *Me?* The girl who pretty much said F.U. to everything, especially Fate.

Holy crap…

Sort of stunned, I faced the front of the vehicle. I was better than this—better than wallowing in my own pity. And I was a hell of a lot better than letting Fate control me. I wasn't weak. I'd never been a quitter before. I was born to be the ultimate warrior. So if anyone could walk out of this situation unscathed, it should be *me*.

It *would be* me.

Because I was a fighter. Because I didn't quit. Because I was strong.

As the front end of Solos's Hummer reached the midway part of ours, there was a distinct popping sound and their car suddenly jerked to the left.

"Holy crap," Deacon gasped. "They're shooting at them—"

Our back window exploded. Glass shattered and rained through the car. I spun in my spot, finding that Luke had Deacon plastered against the seat. I didn't see my uncle.

"Marcus?"

"I'm okay," he called out.

"Alex, get down." Aiden kept a tight grip on the steering wheel with one hand as he reached for me, grabbing my arm and yanking me down.

Marcus popped up and returned fire in a quick succession. Tires squealed; the Hummer next to us jerked again, and then flew ahead in a roar. I couldn't believe they were actually shooting at us. And then it struck me. They didn't care about anyone else in the vehicle. They knew I'd survive the crash one way or another.

They were going to keep shooting until they made us crash.

Another pop, and the window beside Aiden blew out. Shards of glass flew sideways, pelting Aiden and me. He winced, and I was so over this.

"Stop the car," I said.

"What?" Aiden's hand pressed down on my back as he sped up, putting some distance between us and the vehicle full of our enemies.

I struggled up. "Stop the car!"

He glanced at me, and gods-know-what he saw in my eyes, but he cursed under his breath and veered onto the shoulder. The other vehicles shot past us, the sound of their tires squealing on the pavement.

Before Aiden could stop me, I threw the door open. Another curse exploded from him, and I heard Marcus yell out, "What the hell?"

I slipped out of the Hummer, keeping low. There was one dagger attached to my thigh, but that wasn't what I needed.

Aiden slid out the passenger side, eyes narrowed on me. He had a gun in one hand. "What are you doing?"

"Good question." Luke shoved Deacon onto the embankment. "Stopping doesn't seem like the smart thing to do."

"I can't believe they are actually shooting at us. *Us?*" Deacon started to stand up. "What is wrong—?"

"Stay down!" Aiden twisted around, pointing at Luke. "Keep him alive or—"

"I know." Luke yanked Deacon down and behind him. "Nothing will happen to him."

Up ahead, Solos had pulled over and everyone spilled out of the car, keeping to the passenger side.

I breathed a sigh of relief and then edged toward the front of the Hummer. "Alex!" Aiden followed in a crouch. "What are—?"

The two vehicles had turned around and were nearly on us. There was really no time to think about what I was doing. Using the speed that all halfs have, and the extra oomph of the Apollyon, I darted around the bumper and into the lane.

Aiden let out a ripe curse.

I was bathed in headlights as I threw up my hand, summoning the element of air. It was like unlocking a door inside me. Power rushed from the inside then spread out, slipping over my skin.

Air barreled down the highway, blowing past me, faster and stronger than what a pure could wield. Hurricane-force winds slammed into the first Hummer.

It went up on two wheels, tires spinning in the air as the headlights pierced the night sky. The Hummer hovered there a second, and then flipped over the second vehicle. Through the air, it tipped over and over until—something was flung from one of the windows, perhaps a person.

Seat belts save lives.

The first Hummer landed on its roof. Metal crunched and groaned, then gave way. The one behind it spun to the right to avoid a direct collision. Amber-colored sparks flew.

The doors on the second opened, and I counted six Sentinels garbed in black. They were halfs, playing on the wrong side of the field.

One charged forward, and I flung him into the thick elms that crowded the roadway with a flick of my wrist. There was a sickening crunch upon impact that said that tool would be out of commission for a while.

A second brandished two Covenant daggers as he headed straight for me. "Come with us and we'll let your friends live."

I tipped my head to the side and smiled. "Well, isn't that cliché as hell? How about this—turn away and I might let *you* live."

Apparently the Sentinel didn't understand English, because he lurched at me. I stepped to the side, reaching up and catching his arm. I swung it down as I brought my knee up, making contact just above the elbow. Bones snapped and the Sentinel yelped. Swinging behind him, I caught his other arm and twisted. His back bowed and the dagger fell to the pavement.

Marcus appeared in front of us. Without blinking an eye,

he shoved a dagger into the chest of the Sentinel I'd dropped. The man didn't even make a sound.

I let go, and his body fell to the street.

My eyes met my uncle's. A second later he had the Glock raised and aimed. I was so close I saw the tiny spark as the trigger pulled. Gasping, I spun around.

The bullet smacked between the eyes of a female Sentinel.

"Geez," I said, stumbling back.

"They know they can't kill you." Marcus grabbed my arm and shoved me back toward the Hummer. "But I do believe they wish to take you in, no matter what your condition is."

"I'm starting to see that."

Solos and Aiden were working on two Sentinels. Looking behind me, I saw that Olivia and Lea had two more cornered. My attention swung back to the crumpled Hummer.

There were halfs in that car, and as expected, they weren't down for the count. Another six piled out. Feeling the rush of adrenaline coiling tight around the cord, I shot forward with Marcus right behind me.

I reached a Sentinel, gripping the dagger in my right hand. He dove at me, but I ducked under his arm, faster than the half-blood's eyes could track. Swinging around, I caught him in the back with my boot and he went down on one knee. Something inside me turned off as I gripped his hair and yanked his head back. These weren't Sentinels. They were enemies, like daimons. I couldn't think of it any other way. I brought the dagger down in a clean and quick kill.

Hearing pounding footsteps behind me, I whirled and jerked to the side, narrowly missing a meaty fist to the face. Springing into the air, I spun and delivered a nasty I-hope-someone-sees- this-spin kick.

The Sentinel hit the ground, clutching what was most

likely a broken jaw. Flipping the dagger over, I started forward. Man, I sort of missed fighting with Apollo. We'd be keeping count—

Hands grabbed my shoulders and yanked me back. I hit the pavement and slid. Pain burst along my spine and I stared up, stunned.

A dark-skinned Sentinel stared down at me. "You could make this—" His words were choked off. Something wet and warm sprayed into the air. His body went in one direction and his head went in the other.

I rolled onto my knees, clamping my mouth shut against the urge to hurl.

Olivia stepped back, her gaze flicking from me to the dagger. "That…that was nothing like what they teach you in class."

Pushing to my feet, I shook my head. Was this the first time Olivia had fought? For her first kill to be another Sentinel… I didn't know what to say. And we didn't have time for a therapy session.

Broken Jaw was standing. He spun around, his dagger arced low. I felt the hiss of the sharp blade along my stomach. Material split, but that was as close as he got.

Aiden appeared behind him and gripped the sides of his head. There was a quick twist, another sound that would creep back in and replay over and over again later, and then the Sentinel dropped.

Aiden's eyes met mine and they were the color of steel. "Even though that display of power was hot as hell, try not to run out in traffic anymore."

I started to respond, but a shadow slipped up behind him. My heart stopped. "Aiden!"

Before I could even raise a hand, he spun around like the

wind, letting go of the dagger. It smacked into the chest of the white-garbed Guard sneaking up on him. Darting forward, he pulled the blade free before the Guard collapsed, and then threw it again, taking out the other Guard who'd cornered Solos.

Damn. Aiden was a badass ninja.

Only a couple of minutes had passed and we'd been lucky so far, but approaching headlights warned that we were out of luck.

"Olivia, get Lea and go around to the other side of the car."

Her gaze dipped to the fallen Sentinel once more and then she nodded, taking off. She grabbed Lea's arm and pulled her toward where Luke and Deacon started to emerge from the embankment.

A sedan stopped behind the crumpled Hummer. Sheathing the dagger, I jogged up to the car just as the driver's window rolled down. A middle-aged mortal surveyed the scene with growing horror.

"Oh, my God," he said, holding a cell phone. "I can call for help—is that a body?"

I knelt down, forcing the mortal to look me in the eye. "There's nothing to see here. You will see nothing as you drive past. You will go home and…kiss your wife or whatever."

The mortal blinked slowly and then nodded. "I'm not married."

Whoops. "Uh, do you have a girlfriend?"

He nodded, eyes trained on mine.

"Okay…then go kiss her and tell her…that you love her?" Gods, I sucked at compulsions. "Anyway, go. There's nothing going on here. Move along."

As the car drove past, I turned to find Solos gaping at me. "What?" I demanded.

"Did you just Jedi mind trick him?"

A small grin pulled at my lips. "I've always wanted to say that."

"Dear gods," he mumbled, turning back.

Shrugging, I followed him and passed Aiden. He was stopping at each body, placing two fingers on the still forms. I watched as sparks flew from his fingers and traveled over the bodies with an unnatural quickness. Violet-hued flames covered the fallen, and within seconds nothing remained but ashes. The air was thick with the scent of juniper, blood, burnt flesh, and metal.

South Dakota had never smelled more gross.

When Aiden headed toward the two Hummers, I turned and saw a body near the rear of our car. Swallowing down the bitter taste building in my throat, I went to the Sentinel and knelt. As weak as it sounds, I couldn't look at his face as I placed my hand on the motionless shoulder. It too became nothing but ashes.

Heart heavy, I stood. "Sorry."

Aiden reappeared, taking my hand. "Are you okay?"

I nodded. "You?"

"Yes." His gaze moved to the pile of ashes and his hand tightened. "We need to get going."

On the other side of the Hummer, two Sentinels were on their knees before Solos in the dirt and gravel. I recognized one of them as the guy I'd flung into the tree. Both were bruised and bloodied.

"Who is the god behind this?" Solos demanded.

One lifted his head and spat a mouthful of blood. Tree Guy laughed.

"Did I say something funny?" Solos knelt before them. "I didn't think so. I'll ask one more time. Who is the god behind this?"

"Kill us now, because we aren't going to talk." Tree Guy lifted his head and his gaze settled on me. "You guys can't win in this. They are going to change the world, and if you stand in their way, they will destroy you."

I stepped forward. "By 'they' you mean Seth, Lucian, and this god? You do realize that not a single one of them gives a flying monkey's ass about halfs, right?"

Tree Guy laughed again, the sound broken and chipped. "And you do realize that you can't escape him, Apollyon?"

Anger flared. "I think I'm doing a pretty good job at staying away from Seth, jerk-face."

The other Sentinel arched a brow. "Do you think we're talking about the First?" He laughed. "You have no idea what you've stepped into, little girl. This is bigger than you and the First, bigger than a simple Council seat."

A shiver shot straight down my spine, and I took an involuntary step back. "What is?"

Neither of the men answered. They said nothing as Solos questioned them about Lucian's plans.

Marcus stepped in then, but when he used compulsion on them, they remained silent.

"They're not going to talk," Marcus said, hands clenched at his sides. "Either it's a stronger compulsion than a pure can do, or it's blind loyalty. Either way, we are wasting precious time and risking too much."

"We can't let them go," Aiden said quietly.

My heart sank a little in spite of the fact that, if given the chance, these two men would slit the throats of those standing next to me. They were young, maybe a few years older than me—too young to be out here, about to die. But Aiden was right; we couldn't let them go.

Marcus quickly rounded up Deacon and the others, taking

them back behind the damaged Hummer Solos had been driving. It was still drivable, but it would draw attention if we had the thing out during the day.

Placing my hand on Aiden's arm, I twisted toward him. "I can—"

"No." He used that voice that I'd come to loathe and respect—the *no argument* tone. "You will not do this."

Laadan, who'd stayed out of the fight with Deacon, turned away.

I wanted to, because an execution was the last thing I wanted to see, but as Aiden broke free of my side and headed toward them, I forced myself to stand still. If he had to do this, then I had to witness it. It was the most I could do, and the least.

Aiden moved lightning fast. The kills were clean and quick. They hadn't felt it. Their bodies slumped forward, separated from their heads.

No matter how quick and painless Aiden had made it, I knew that he would feel this in the dark corners of his soul for a long time to come.

CHAPTER THIRTY-ONE

Back on the highway, I tried not to let the chilly wind blowing in my face get on my nerves. Things could be worse. People I cared about could have ended up dead. They could've been like those unfortunate souls we'd put down like rabid dogs.

Right now, we all had it pretty good, with the exception of that creeptastic warning the Sentinel had given us—or me.

Glancing at Aiden for like the hundredth time since we'd gotten back into the car, I chewed on my lower lip.

"Penny for your thoughts?" he said, not taking his eyes off the road.

I took a deep breath. "So, we know that the god is a 'he,' and apparently I don't know what I'm stepping into."

"Do any of us know what we're stepping into?" Luke commented dryly.

"I don't think we do," I said, staring at the dark stretch of highway. "Was it just me, or did it sound like they were loyal to the god, and not Lucian or Seth?"

"That's the way it sounded to me," Aiden said.

"Unless even their loyalty came from a compulsion." Marcus sounded bone-weary. "But it doesn't matter. Loyalty is just as bad as a compulsion. The end result is the same."

I nodded. "I wonder if Lucian or Seth know. I mean, I know it doesn't matter, but Seth and Lucian both have egos the size of a god's. If they think they have complete control over their army or whatever, but they really don't? That isn't going to be pretty."

"Who knows how much they really know?" Aiden gripped the steering wheel so tightly that his knuckles bleached. "This god could be promising Lucian the head of the Council or gods-know-what else. And Seth, well he...he will have everything he wants."

Hot and uncomfortable knots twisted my insides. Seth had said the same thing, but what he wanted—love and acceptance—he'd never get this way. It would be a caricature of the real thing. One day he might realize that, and it would be too late...for all of us.

And gods, he did deserve better than this. I knew I shouldn't think that, but I did.

Letting out a low breath, I tipped my head toward the passenger window and watched the blur of dark trees. Most of South Dakota was prairie land, but the Black Hills were something else entirely. Trees clustered together, so thick that no one could see what rested beyond. Somewhere up ahead, the University was spread across one of the largest mountain meadows.

"Do you think Apollo is telling you guys everything that he and the other gods know?" Deacon's voice broke the silence.

I snorted. "I think Apollo tells us what he thinks we need to know when he wants to."

"Gods are such douchebags," Deacon muttered, sitting back.

Marcus actually laughed, and I thought the world was coming to an end. "They are arrogant," he said. "That's the problem. With arrogance comes great blindness."

It was kind of funny hearing that —mostly because I pictured Lucian, Seth, and the mystery-god as the three blind mice—but it was true. All of the parties involved were pretty arrogant. Gods knew I had a healthy dose of it myself.

"None of them think anyone will truly step up against them, not even one of their own." Marcus sighed. "Their arrogance led to this."

Everyone fell quiet after that, lost in their own thoughts. I was doing a mental rundown of all the gods, trying to figure out who won for Most Arrogant. Seriously, it could be any of the male gods: Hades, Poseidon, Zeus, Ares, and even Apollo. Despite what Dionysus said, it might not even be one of the core, but a lesser deity tired of being pushed around. It was like looking for an especially drunk guy at a party full of drunk guys—impossible. Good news was that we at least knew it was a "he," unless the Sentinel was messing with us.

Closing my eyes, I breathed out slowly and winced. My temples throbbed something fierce. It was like having a toothache in my entire face, and I had no idea how long I'd last before it was time to have another chat with Seth.

I stared. "Holy..."

"Crap," Deacon whispered over my shoulder.

Silence fell, thick and heavy, as we all sat in the car and stared. I knew the same thing was happening behind us in the other Hummer. None of us knew what to say.

Horror engulfed me. This…none of this had been expected.

About an hour earlier, Aiden had found the narrow lane that looked like a fire access road, but was really the five-mile-long entrance to the University. We'd made it up the rocky road about a half mile when the scenery changed from clusters of juniper trees to…a scene straight out of *Red Dawn*.

The headlights from our cars cast light on a gruesome scene. Burned-out Hummers crowded the sides of the road, resting against equally charred trees and scorched ground. There were half a dozen crispy car skeletons. I couldn't tell if there were bodies in them, not from this distance.

I swallowed. "Aiden…"

He placed a hand on my arm. "It could've been Sentinels trying to infiltrate the University."

Blinking rapidly, I shook my head. I had a bad, bad feeling about this. Call it a Spidey sense or whatever, but this wasn't good.

"Can we, like, call ahead?" Deacon said in a hushed voice. "I mean, they're expecting us, right?"

"They are." Aiden glanced back at his younger brother. "It's okay. I promise. Nothing is going to happen."

"I can't get a damn signal at all." Marcus glared at his cell phone like he could wish it into Tartarus. "Nothing at all." He glanced up, eyes hard as gems. "Any of you?"

Aiden checked his phone. "Nope."

I wet my lips as my gaze fell back to the scorched vehicles. My heart pounded and my head ached. "There must be a lot of firebug pures in there…"

"No doubt," Aiden muttered, both brows rising.

Solos appeared on Aiden's side of the car, running a hand through the dark strands of hair that had escaped his ponytail. In the shadows, his scar was less visible. "You think the Covenant did this?" He gestured at the vehicles. "Their version of torch security?"

"It's possible," Aiden replied, but I wasn't sure he believed it.

"I can't get ahold of them, so I'm assuming you can't either, right?" When Aiden nodded, Solos folded his hands behind his head and stretched so that his back bowed. "I guess we can make it through."

"We can from what I can see." Aiden sat back, thrumming his fingers on the wheel. "We'll have to go slow."

As I watched the two Sentinels, I knew in my core that Aiden and Solos didn't want to do this. We were blind to what lay ahead. It could be a murderous band of grizzly bears, or a legion of Sentinels waiting to make s'mores out of us. We just didn't know.

Solos sighed and dropped his arms. "Well, I guess we do this."

"We really don't have any other option." Aiden shifted the gears back into drive. "Let's do this." With a curt nod, Solos loped back to his vehicle. I squirmed in my seat as the Hummer lurched forward. Easing around the torched cars wasn't an easy feat. It was like driving a boat through a china shop. Thank the gods that Aiden was driving because I would've plowed through the wreckage on the first narrow turn.

More burned-out cars lay by the side of the road every so many feet, and with each one we passed, the scorch marks looked fresher, the acrid smell hung thicker…as if each time someone had tried to reach the University, they'd made it a little farther than the group before them. And farther up, deep orange flames crawled across the hood of a Hummer, licking at the smoke-filled air.

Oh, this was so not good.

"How will they know we're friends?" Deacon asked, thinking along the same lines as me. He leaned between the seats, face pale. "Aiden, we should stop—"

Aiden suddenly did stop, but not because of what Deacon was saying. Debris was strewed across the access road, choking the lane. As far as I could see were scattered skeletons of cars. Many of them still smoldered, glowing hellish red in the predawn dark. The apocalyptic landscape was something straight out of nightmares.

"Gods," Aiden muttered darkly.

My stomach twisted into knots as I undid my seat belt. "This isn't good."

No one said anything for several moments, and then Marcus spoke, "We're going to have to walk it from here."

"How many miles?" I asked.

"We're about three miles out." Aiden killed the engine, leaving the headlights on.

All of us climbed out of the Hummer, casting anxious looks at all the burned-out cars surrounding us, feeling like we'd been driving around with a giant bull's-eye on us.

Quickly, we weaponed-up with daggers, sickle blades, and Glocks. As I strapped a gun on, I looked over my shoulder and saw that the crew with Solos was doing the same thing.

We looked like we were preparing for war as we came together between the two Hummers. In a way, we were—we had been this whole time. We were at war.

A chill suddenly snaked its way under my skin. We stood in a circle, the nine of us, silent with the exception of titanium clips clicking into place, daggers snapping onto our sides. We were nine. But somehow—in a way I couldn't explain but knew to be the truth—I knew we weren't going to return as nine. At that cold realization, I looked at the faces of those around me. Some had been virtual strangers, others enemies until recently, and a few I'd considered friends from day one.

And then there was Aiden.

I took a breath, wishing I could forget the fatalistic feeling taking up residence around my heart. But the somber faces of those around me pretty much told me that I wasn't the only one who was thinking the same thing at that moment.

As a unit, the nine of us turned. Ghastly, flickering flames lit the road ahead. The weight of the daggers and guns was sobering and grounding. We had no idea what waited ahead of us, other than the big, fat unknown, and most likely a big, fat kick in the face. The gravity of that was killing me—killing *us*.

I squared my shoulders. "Release the Kraken!" Several sets of eyes settled on me.

"What?" I gave a lopsided shrug. "I've always wanted to yell that since I saw that movie. Seemed like the perfect moment."

Aiden laughed.

"See! That's why I love him," I told the group. "He laughs at the stupid crap that comes out of my mouth."

In response, Aiden leaned over and pressed his lips against my temple. "Keep talking about loving me," he murmured, "and we're going to scar some of these guys for life."

I flushed beet red.

Someone cleared their throat. Another groaned, but I was grinning as I lifted my gaze back to the road. Jokes aside, everyone was waiting for one person to take the first step, so I did. And then we all did.

Our eyes adapted to the darkness, but I stayed beside Aiden, who stuck close to Deacon and Luke, as we carefully made our way around the shells of vehicles. I didn't look inside them, absolutely refused to, because there was a certain stench in the air…

The night was eerily silent with the exception of our footsteps. In South Dakota, I expected to hear the chilling call of the mountain lion, the scurry of tiny creatures, and the squawking of birds that could probably snatch up a baby, but there was nothing.

Dead silence.

The creeped-out vibe didn't go away after we started making quick progress, covering well over two miles. The destroyed cars littering the roadway didn't help. There were so many of them.

"Gods," Lea whispered, stopping beside one of the char-broiled piles. "Oh, my gods…"

I told myself not to look at what so obviously horrified her, but I rarely listened to that little voice of common sense. I turned and almost lost the Skittles.

Behind the charred wheel of a Hummer was a body…or what was left of one. Burnt, blackened fingers still clutched the steering wheel. Nothing else about the body was distinguishable. It could've been a male, female, or a hydra. And it wasn't alone. Charred remains were in the passenger seat… and in the rear seats.

Someone sucked in a sharp breath. "The plates are crispy, but these are New York tags."

"Gods," someone else said.

People were moving backward, checking the plates on cars that'd received less damage, but I already knew in my heart. These weren't Lucian's Sentinels coming to fight. These were people—innocent pures and halfs—seeking sanctuary.

In the farthest seat of the Hummer, some of the clothing remained, just bits and pieces of singed material, but the color was a deep forest-green. Council robes, I realized slowly.

Mother-freaking Council robes.

It dawned on me suddenly that it was a really good thing that we'd gotten out of those damn Hummers, because these people—they'd been trapped. And this whole road was nothing but a graveyard.

"We need to get out of here," Aiden ordered, and my heart dropped. "We need to go now."

Lea whirled around. "But where are we going to go? This has—"

A ball of fiery light split the darkness ahead, casting an eerie glow over the debris and the burnt, twisted ground. It flew past the car I stood by, smacking into a small juniper tree, enveloping it in flames and thick, bitter smoke.

I jumped. "Holy..."

Everything happened so fast. Balls of fire seemed to come from the heavens, raining down on us. Everyone scattered, splitting into smaller groups as we moved off the road and into the uneven terrain. A hand found mine—*Aiden*—and I was running with him and his brother. Luke was behind us. In seconds, I lost sight of everyone else.

CHAPTER THIRTY-TWO

We were running, running away.

Fire still fell, splattering on the earth, shaking the ground. It was chaos as we scrambled over the small hills, hitting the ground each time the sky lit up and another volley of fire filled the air.

And where in the hell was popping-in-when-you-least-expect-it-Apollo when we needed him? Sure, he could poof in when I was about to get some kissy-face time with Aiden, but oh no, when we actually *needed* him, he was nowhere to be found.

I started to push up, but Aiden held on. "I have to find Marcus! And Olivia! Laadan—"

"No." His grip tightened. "You're not running out in the middle of this!"

On the ground beside me, Luke moaned. "I think…my arm is on fire."

"*What?*" I rolled toward him, grabbing at the back of his shirt, aware of Deacon trying to scramble past his brother.

Flipping him onto his back, I winced as another blast hit far too close. "Gods…"

His right arm was an unnatural, bright shade of red from the elbow to the wrist. Patches had already begun to bubble. He offered a wobbly smile. "Well, I've been wanting a tan."

I stared at him, and then Deacon shot around us, grasping the front of Luke's shirt. Before the bronze-haired half could utter a word, Deacon planted one on him. I fell back on my side, breathing heavily.

Then Deacon lifted his head, eyes wide. "Don't ever scare me like that again. Okay?" Luke nodded slowly.

"What is it with the St. Delphi brothers and their attraction to halfs?" Solos grunted, hitting the hill near us. Laadan was with him, her hair falling loose from her neat chignon, pants dirtied and singed. "Don't get me wrong," he went on. "Being a half and all, I totally support equal love, equal rights, down with the Breed Order, and blah, blah, blah."

"We just have good taste," Aiden replied, as he glanced over his shoulder at the half-blood Sentinel. "Unlike some…"

Solos snorted.

"Do you know where Marcus and the girls are?" I asked, eyeing the calm-for-now sky. "Did you see them?"

He nodded. "They're on the other side of the road, down in a ditch. They're okay." Solos glanced over at Laadan. "She saved my rosy red butt, you know? A ball of fire was heading straight for my head, and she just lobbed it away with air."

Laadan shook her head. "It was nothing."

"It was something—"

A deep shout shattered the air, like a chorus of battle cries. A sound I'd never heard before. It wasn't human; it wasn't animal, but a twisted and revolting mixture of both. Suddenly it became all too obvious what was coming.

Hephaestus's automatons.

It didn't make sense. They were supposed to be *protecting* the Covenants. Had they deemed us a threat? Well, obviously, since they were trying to turn us into crispy critters. But those people in the cars…no way would they attack first and ask questions later. It defeated the whole purpose of having them here and moving Council members to the University unless…

I looked at Aiden. "The god… Is it Hephaestus?"

Aiden opened his mouth, but the ground trembled under the weight of the approaching storm. Over the rise of the hill, no more than a few yards away, tall and imposing shadows marched out from behind the stand of trees. When they stepped under the slice of moonlight, I sucked in a shrill breath.

Holy daimon butt…

Their thick-as-tree-trunk thighs and large hoofs were made of titanium. Dark, matted hair covered their broad chests and muscular arms. Each head was that of a bull—two horns and a long flat snout that sloped into a mouth full of strong teeth and jaws.

"Dear gods," I heard Laadan whisper.

There were over a dozen of them forming an unbreakable line between us and the University, and I doubted they were acting as sentries like they were supposed to be.

One of the larger automatons opened its mouth and snorted loudly. "I bet his breath stinks," I muttered.

Deacon nodded. "No doubt."

Then it opened its mouth once more and a stream of fire shot forth. A ball formed, heading straight for the ditch on the other side of the road. The girls scattered over the hill.

The first gunshot came from Solos, directed at the monstrosities. Then Marcus was on his feet and so was Aiden, their guns blazing. Titanium bullets ripped through the air, smacking into the automatons but doing little to stop them.

Fire streamed toward our group and we broke apart. My hand was on the trigger, systematically squeezing at anything that looked like a whacked-out version of a minotaur. And they returned fire with…uh, fire.

Flames spread across the ground and I darted around the blaze. The automatons raced toward us, spitting fire, then fighting.

The first one reached Marcus, hitting him with the broadside of its beefy arm. Marcus flew back several feet, landing in a groaning heap. Another was before me and I dipped under its flying arm. Springing up, I leveled the gun at the back of the automaton's head and let loose. Silvery-colored blood and gore splattered the low bushes as the automaton dropped and then turned to dust.

Well, that was one way to kill them. Sort of like zombies…

I swung around, realizing the daggers were absolutely useless and the Glocks were only helpful if we were able to sneak up behind one. Heart pounding, I hit the ground as another fireball shot straight at me. Crap. This was bad—beyond bad. This was a nightmare come to life. Horrified to the core, I froze for an instant on the dry, burnt ground. Tiny stones prodded my stomach and thighs. Oddly, I felt every one as if it were the prick of a hot knife.

Everything slowed down, and the air halted in my lungs.

Marcus was back on his feet and he fought back-to-back with Lea, darting forward with their sickles blades, lobbing off an automaton's arms. But the thing kept coming at them. Solos was trying to keep Laadan out of the line of fire. Soot covered Aiden's flushed cheeks as he delivered a blast of fire at the creatures. Deacon actually had a gun in his hand as he stayed near Luke. Olivia was cornered in some trees.

In a rush, I recalled the premonition I'd had earlier. They were going to die, all of them. Like those well-done bodies in the cars, they would be charbroiled and that would be the end of them.

Something snapped inside me—something primitive and absolute. Power rushed through me and my skin tingled with the appearance of the marks. The shadowy battlefield was suddenly tinted with shades of amber. I welcomed the almost-foreign surge of energy, even though it was like poison in my veins. My brain clicked off and I was no longer Alex.

I was the *Apollyon*. I was the beginning and the end.

Loose strands of hair began to rise above my head, and I'd swear that for a moment time really did stop as I rose to my feet. The sickle blade and dagger fell from my fingers, and then I curled my hands into fists.

Oh, it was on like Donkey Kong.

I flew over the barren land toward Olivia as she tried to fend the thing off. I dipped under the automaton, springing up between it and Olivia, slamming my foot into its hairy stomach. He went down on one knee, rattling the nearby trees.

Absolute power—unforgiving and hard, pure as it was deadly—coursed over my skin. I reared back, summoning the fifth and final element. Intense blue light erupted from my palm.

Akasha ripped from me, arcing through the air like cloud-to-cloud lightning, homing in on its target and striking true. The sky crackled and heated. One second, the automaton was on his knee, and the next he was nothing but a pile of shimmery dust.

"Good gods," came Olivia's hoarse whisper.

Another automaton took the fallen one's place, swinging out with a metal hand that clinked and clicked. Fire sparked from its open mouth. I spun, catching the broad side of his arm and twisting. The hoarse shout of pain was lost in the clash of metal, the thunder of bullets finding another automaton.

It raised its bull face and snapped at me with massive jaws.

"*Please.*" I placed my hand on the massive forehead.

Blue light coursed over the head and down the body, lighting up the metallic skull and bone structure. For a moment, it was like a pretty X-ray or a jellyfish—a really disturbing jellyfish—and then cobalt light radiated from its eyes and open mouth. It *imploded*—caved in on itself, turning to nothing but dust.

And then the crap really hit the fan.

The automatons—every last one of the freaky bull things—turned on me. They moved quickly, metal legs rattling and clinking. Fire spewed from their mouths like the poor man's version of a dragon. They came from all directions, Apollyon-seeking missiles with "Kill Alex" stamped all over them.

Fire came from them, blinding and intense. Nothing existed outside the flames. No sound. No sight. My world was red and orange.

Alex? His voice came through the thrumming connection.

I ignored him and the way his consciousness slid in alongside mine.

What are you up to?

Still I ignored the pull of the First. Instinct on a deep, ancient level I wasn't familiar with had taken over. The marks of the Apollyon flowed across my skin as I lifted my hands. The fire stopped inches from me, forming a fiery circle. Heat fell back on me but did not burn. I blew out a soft, steady breath and the fire flickered once, twice, and then faded out.

The automatons drew up short, puffing and snorting loudly.

My arms rose to my sides, my fingers splayed out, and the air hummed with power and anticipation. Blue light crackled over my fingertips, waiting…wanting…

One of the automatons, the biggest of those remaining, charged. At the sound of the dark roar, akasha pulled tight and constricted just like the bond between Seth and me.

I let it go.

The blast of power rushed from me, rolling like storm-tossed waves. The surge smacked into the automaton nearest me. Blue light flared from the creature's eye sockets and open jaws. A second later, it imploded. The swell crashed into four more, taking them out before the outpouring of akasha eased off.

As the shimmering dust settled onto the dry soil, exhaustion swept through me. The bond to Seth still felt open, even though the world was shaded in deep blue and black again. Being that this was my first time using akasha like a flyswatter, I wasn't prepared for the exhaustion that followed. My legs trembled under my weight as I struggled to hold myself up. I reached for my daggers and realized, like a total tool, I'd thrown them somewhere over yonder in a fit of an "I am so awesome" and "Who needs daggers when I have akasha fingers of power?" ego trip.

Luckily, others still held their weapons, and the automatons were distracted with me. Marcus took out one with a point-blank shot to the back of the skull. Aiden wielded his sickle blade like an executioner, lopping off the head of another.

One of the automatons reached for me and I darted—er, stumbled—to the side and plopped down on my rear. And once I was down on my butt, I really didn't want to get up. I was like a toddler, all tuckered out. Pathetic—I needed to learn to pace myself.

The automaton uttered a guttural growl.

I crab-walked backward, putting very little distance between us. Just when I was pretty sure I was about to end up with a deep tan, Lea came out of freaking nowhere, shoved the sharp end of her Covenant dagger through the back of the automaton's neck, and then wrenched her arm to the side.

My eyes widened as the shimmery dust fell near the toes of my boots. "Wow."

Lea cocked her head to the side as she frowned at the gore dripping from the blade. "Well, that was gross."

"Yeah," I said slowly, looking around. I counted eight and then Lea. Nine. All of us were still standing. Bruised and exhausted, but we were still fighting. I let out a weak laugh. "Gods."

The sound of metal crunching, along with the wet, fleshy give of bone and muscle, continued as the rest of the automatons were taken out in less explosive displays.

Lea reached down and wiggled her fingers. "You gonna sit there the rest of the night or get up? Because I'm sure as hell not carrying your ass."

Grinning weakly, I lifted my hand just as a dark shadow appeared behind Lea. My heart leaped into my throat as fear balled in my chest. The extreme burst of emotion had Seth in a tizzy, and I could tell he was paying close attention even though he was put-out from me ignoring him.

"Lea!" I shouted out as my fingers brushed hers. She turned halfway, sucking in a breath.

Finding a reservoir of energy, I shot to my feet but—*oh, gods*—it was too late. I summoned akasha, but it was like tapping a dry well. There was nothing left, but I was the Apollyon and there should have been something that I could do—there had to be, but before I could use the air element to move Lea out of the way, it had happened.

The automaton grasped the sides of her head and twisted. The crack of bone was deafening, as loud as thunder. Her fingers spasmed and the dagger slipped from them. The sound… it whipped through me, stealing my breath and twisting my insides into raw painful knots. The sound…it would stay with me forever.

Lea was on the ground before me, a boneless, motionless heap of nothing more than flesh. My brain couldn't reconcile what'd just happened. Like with Caleb, denial rose and it was so strong, so potent that I *refused* to believe it.

Someone came up behind the automaton and there was an explosion of shimmery dust, but I didn't know who it was and I didn't care. At that moment, automatons could rain down on us and I wouldn't care.

There had been nine of us…

My heart stuttered and then sped up way too fast. The world whirled around me, a kaleidoscope of muted shades with flashes of intense amber. Someone was calling my name, the deep, near-frantic voice mixing with the low hum of Seth's.

I wanted them to shut up—both of them, because this wasn't real. It couldn't be, and then in a moment of painful and stark reality, I couldn't understand how I could be so surprised. As if I hadn't expected death. As if death couldn't touch us. How could I be so surprised? Every one of them had set out knowing that this was dangerous, that any moment could be their last. And a few miles ago I had known death was coming, so much so I could taste the sorrow on the tip of my tongue.

I dropped to my knees, hands shaking as I placed them on Lea's shoulder and gently rolled her onto her back. From the odd angle of how her head lay, to the pale color bleeding under her tan skin, to the way her eyes…

My fingers trembled as I brushed the coppery strands off her cool forehead. Gods, how could the body cool that fast? It didn't seem possible or right. It definitely wasn't fair.

Lea's beautiful amethyst eyes—eyes I had envied as a kid—were fixed on the dark sky. There was no shine to them, no inner light. There was nothing.

Lea was gone, like Caleb and Mom, like all those people back in those cars. She was… I couldn't finish the sentence. That one little word couldn't be taken back.

I jerked my hands away, folding them under my chin. Others were nearing us. Someone was crying softly. Voices rose, uttering denials, and then there was silence. My breath caught again.

Someone knelt on the other side of Lea. A Covenant dagger was carefully placed on the ground and soft words were uttered in ancient Greek. A prayer for a warrior's death—a hymn delivered during burial.

I lifted my gaze and my eyes locked with dark, tumultuous gray ones. Aiden's face was so pale; the horror etched into his features mirrored my own. His eyes were dry, but anger and sadness burned from within them. He shook his head. My lashes felt damp.

I couldn't sit here. I just couldn't.

Pushing to my feet, I stumbled past Marcus and Olivia. I went past Luke and Deacon, beyond where Laadan and Solos stood. I kept walking, having no idea where I was going or what I was going to do.

Alex?

My hands curled at the sound of Seth's voice. Red-hot anger roared through me like a train derailed. He hadn't snapped Lea's neck like it was nothing more than a twig, but his hands were bloody, weren't they? *I don't want to talk to you right now.*

There was silence—for now.

Stomach churning, tears coursed down my cheeks. Part of me was still in shock, as stupid as that was. The nine of us had been *alive*. We all had been still standing. I had laughed. And then Lea was gone. Just like that, with no real warning.

Gods, Lea and I had never been best-friends-forever, but we'd come so far. I'd respected her, probably for longer than I'd realized, and the same went for her. There was so much between us that needed to be addressed—to be repaired—but there would be no more time. And even though we'd spent the better part of whatever time we'd been together hating on one another, she'd come to my aid and she'd stood her ground.

Realizing that cut so deep it matched the pain of Caleb's loss.

"Alex," Aiden said from behind me.

I shook my head. "I can't...I can't do this right now." My voice cracked. "I need a few minutes."

He hesitated, and then I felt his hand on my shoulder. I pulled free and walked ahead, dragging in deep breaths even though they didn't seem to be pulling enough air into my lungs. I couldn't afford to lose it like I had after Caleb's death. I couldn't disconnect from this or self-destruct. I had to deal, but...

Godsdammit. I bent over, placing my hands on my

knees. The urge to vomit was strong, but there was nothing coming up.

Had I apologized to her about what a douchebag I'd been to her when we were kids? I didn't think so. I squeezed my eyes shut and saw her body lying on the ground back there.

Alex? There was a pause and the bond pulled taut. *What's happening?*

I sat down—probably fell down—for the second time that night. Keeping my eyes closed, I kept the shields up but followed the bond to Seth. I didn't know how to feel about that. Maybe it was all the anger taking up too much room to feel anything else. *Is this what you wanted?* I asked.

Seth didn't respond immediately. *I'm not sure what you mean. I can feel your emotions. Something has happened.*

Shut up! I'm not sure what did it—the almost-sincere quality to his voice, or the fact that he had taken Lea's sister and my mom had taken her family and, because of what Seth and I were, she had lost her life. I broke wide open in an instant. *Shut up! Just shut up! Are you happy, Seth? Is that what you wanted from this?*

Tears tracked down my cheeks, fast and furious. My arms shook—my entire body trembled to keep the shields up. I couldn't let them down, not when Seth was inside my head like this. He'd know where I was and there'd be more death.

I threw my head back and there were no words, just sorrow, guilt, and rage. They poured from me in a scream that made no sound outside my body.

Stop, he said, and there was a pressure around me, almost like Seth was wrapping his arms around me, holding me still. *You need to calm down because you're bursting a lot of my brain cells. Take a couple of deep breaths. Just calm down. Okay?*

Several moments passed, and I breathed heavily through

them. I sat there, eyes closed, seeing nothing and feeling nothing. None of this seemed real.

Who's dead? Seth asked, and I could tell by his tone that he expected the worst.

Lea. Even the voice inside my head sounded numb. *She's dead, like her whole family.*

Seth said nothing. Maybe he knew the significance. After all, when we'd been connected before, he'd seen a lot of my past, and he probably could guess that I had no idea how to deal with this. Perhaps he was even thinking the same thing I had—that our connection had taken everything from Lea, including her life. I doubted that, even if he was thinking that, it would make any difference. Seth would continue doing what he was doing. And so would I. He didn't say anything as I pulled my legs to my chest and balled up, desperately not wanting to feel the biting loss again. And he said nothing as the odd pressure inside me increased.

We were enemies to the core, more so now than ever, but my loss was his. When I suffered, he suffered. It was the way we were built, and even the death that he had indirectly caused couldn't breach that or shatter what lay between us.

Nothing could.

CHAPTER THIRTY-THREE

I don't know how long I sat there, but when I opened my eyes again, the sky was still dark and Seth's presence was gone. At some point, I'd felt him ease away. I thought he had whispered something before the connection faded, but I had to be hearing things, because it couldn't be right.

I'd thought I'd heard him say he was sorry.

Obviously, I was losing my mind. Seth rarely apologized, and given his needs for power and acceptance that had driven him toward this endgame, I doubted he felt remorse.

Taking a deep breath, I almost choked on the bitter remnants of smoke. I knew what I needed to do—pick myself up and get moving. Sitting out here in the open, waiting for more automatons to come along, wasn't safe.

I stood and turned, brushing the dirt off my tactical pants. The group was still around Lea's body. Olivia was sitting beside the fallen half-blood, her head in her hands. Deacon and Luke flanked her, the half cradling his injured arm.

Wiping my hands across my cheeks, I stopped beside Aiden.

Olivia looked up, her eyes shiny in the moonlight. "She didn't feel it, right?"

I shook my head. "No. I don't think so."

She nodded, and then picked up Lea's blade, holding it close as she stood. "What do we…what do we do from here?"

It was Solos who spoke. "We need to move quickly. There's no telling if more will come along, and we're sitting ducks out here."

"Do you still think the University is a safe place?" Marcus asked, rubbing his chin. The palm of his hand came back red. I realized then he was bleeding.

I started toward Marcus, but he waved me off. "I'm okay. It's just a scratch," he said gruffly. "How do we know that the University is still standing? The automatons could've torched it and…"

And all those people. My head swam as I glanced down at Lea. Someone had closed her eyes.

Mine burned.

"We have to find out." Aiden thrust a hand through his hair. "We're about a mile from the campus."

Luke shook his head. "There could be more of them. Hell, there could be a dozen or more over the next damn hill and we'd be walking into that blind."

"Or there could be nothing but open land and the damn University," Aiden countered, his jaw set hard. "As far as we know, these automatons may've been here to stop anyone from reaching the campus…or to stop people from leaving."

"Or the campus could be gone." Deacon backed up, running his hands down his sides.

Solos stepped forward, clapping a hand on Deacon's shoulder. "I cannot believe the whole campus is gone."

"With all those automatons, anything is possible." Luke

straightened his injured arm as he stared in the general direction of where I assumed the campus was. "But we have to see. We've come this—"

"Wait!" Olivia's voice rose above the guys'. "I wasn't asking about going to the University or not. I was talking about what we're going to do with Lea."

Silence fell again and I turned to Aiden. "We can't leave her here."

Pain flickered in those deep gray eyes. He reached out, extending his hand, and I went, pressing myself against his side. My fingers dug into his singed shirt, finding tiny burnt holes in the material. "We can't," I whispered.

His arm tightened around me. "I know."

"We can't…take her with us," Solos said. "We have no idea what we'll be facing."

Olivia went off like a nuclear bomb, holding that dagger like she was considering impaling it between Solos's eyes. "We can't leave her here like this. That's so wrong I don't even need to explain."

Sympathy shone in Solos's scarred face. "I know, but we—"

"We bury our dead—our warriors." Olivia's lower lip trembled. "We don't just leave them here to rot."

Laadan placed a pale hand on Olivia's arm, but Olivia was beyond consoling. "I don't care what we have to face or what is waiting for us! We can't just leave her here." Her gaze swung to me. "We need to bury her."

"With what?" Solos asked gently. "We don't have shovels and this ground is rock hard."

Olivia sucked in a sharp breath and turned. Her slim shoulders shook as Luke wrapped his good arm around her.

"Aiden, we have to do something," Deacon pleaded. "I don't know what, but something."

Pulling away from Aiden, I glanced down at my hands. I wasn't sure how much juice I had left in me, or even if I could use the earth element to create…to create a grave, but I would try. There was no way we could leave Lea out here.

"I don't know if this will work." I tucked my hair back, having no idea what'd happened to my ponytail.

Aiden's brows slammed down as concern flared. "Are you sure you're up to it?"

I nodded. "Where do you think we should do it, Olivia?"

It took her a couple of seconds to pull away from Luke and process what I was asking. She looked around and seemed to recognize that there really wasn't a suitable place. She headed off and I followed her. We stopped near two juniper trees that had remained unscathed from the fire and battle, their sweet scent so at odds with the lingering acidic and metallic smells.

"This should work," she said, clearing her throat. "It's not much, but the trees…she'd like the trees."

I looked at her.

Olivia slowly turned to me and she let out a choked, hoarse laugh. "Okay. Lea really wasn't big on nature or trees."

"No." I smiled and it *hurt*. "She's probably thinking *what the hell* right now."

She blinked. "You think?"

"Yeah, I mean, when I was down there waiting, I couldn't tell what was going on up here, but maybe it's different for her." I thought of the oracle I had met, and then the old woman. "It seemed different for everyone, but I know she's not in pain."

Olivia nodded slowly. "That's the thing about death, I've realized. They're gone to us, but not really, you know? There *is* life after death, just a different kind of life." There was a pause. "I wish we'd become friends before all of this crap. Lea…she was pretty cool if you got past the bitchiness."

I rubbed my temple, feeling an incredible empty place in my chest. "I wish I hadn't been such a bitch to her."

"What?"

Shaking my head, I lowered my gaze. "It's a long story."

Olivia looked like she wanted to push it, but didn't. "She'll see her family again."

"Yeah, she wanted that." My eyes were starting to burn again, and I knew if I let the tears fall once more, they wouldn't stop and I'd be utterly useless. "Okay. I can do this."

Taking a deep breath, I got down on my knees and placed my hands on the dirt. I closed my eyes, wiggling my fingers into the leaf litter until I found the topsoil. I'd made the ground move before, when I'd fought Aiden, so I imagined I could do this.

I pictured the soil loosening and giving way under my fingertips. The ground trembled slightly and my confidence bloomed. I created an image of the ground cracking open, deep—deep enough for a decent burial. In my head, the soil was darker—a rich brown—the deeper I went. Inhaling, I caught the damp, earthy scent of disturbed soil.

When I opened my eyes, the ground really was split open. Mounds of fresh dirt lay on either side of the circular six-foot hole. Seeing that it was deep enough, I sat back and wiped my shaking hands along my thighs. I felt dry inside and a little brittle. And I was definitely not going to stand anytime soon.

Everyone started doing their own part. Someone found a blanket in one of our backpacks and Lea was wrapped in it. When her body was lowered into the grave, Marcus helped me up. He handed me a bottle of water, along with the daggers I'd dropped.

"Thanks," I murmured, gulping the water down before

sheathing the daggers. And then something struck me. "Wait. Does anyone have any coins?"

Aiden patted his pockets, as did the rest of the guys. They came up empty and my stomach sank. "Burying her doesn't really make a difference," I said. "That's for us. But she needs passage for Charon or she'll be stuck there."

"We can bring back coins," Solos suggested.

"No." Panic bubbled. "We have to have something. Trust me, she needs the coins now."

Laadan stepped forward, reaching behind her neck. "I have this," she said, unclasping a necklace and pulling it from underneath her shirt. "The embellishments are gold coins, ancient ones. They will be worth more than enough."

My muscles relaxed, full of relief. "Thank you."

She smiled as she handed the necklace to Marcus, who then snapped off two of the gold coins.

Parting the blanket, he placed them in Lea's hands.

I took a breath, trying to ease the burning and the ever-increasing knot in my throat. Aiden came to my side, wrapping his arms around my shoulders. I turned into him, resting my cheek against his chest. The steady rise and fall of his breathing soothed my frayed edges.

Solos had found two thick branches, and shoved them into the ground above the disturbed earth after Laaden and Marcus had used air to push the dirt back into the grave. Deacon and Luke had gathered up a few rocks, which they placed around the branches. It wasn't much of a tombstone, but it would have to do for now.

We stood around Lea's makeshift grave as Laadan murmured a prayer in the old language. I didn't realize I was crying until I felt Aiden's thumb brushing the tears away. I couldn't help but wonder how many more times we would be doing this before it was over—and who would brush Aiden's tears away if it were my grave they ended up standing over.

The sun had begun to rise by the time we reached the outer wall of the University campus, casting a sliver of orangey light that stretched across the mountain meadow. We'd spent the last mile of the trip in solemn silence. There was no conversation, no joking or laughter. Talking seemed inappropriate after the loss we'd all suffered. I knew I wasn't alone in convincing myself that Lea was, or would be, in a much better place—a place where the fighting could no longer reach her, where the future was no longer precarious, and where she was reunited with her loved ones.

It helped a little.

But when the outer stone wall came into view, we pretty much knew things were going to suck daimon butt.

Entire sections of the marble-encased outer structure were either gone completely or in the process of crumbling down. It looked like someone had brought in a wrecking ball and played yo-yo with it.

"Gods," Marcus muttered. "This could be a problem."

I arched a brow at my uncle. "Really?"

The eeriest part of it all was the hundreds of trees just inside the outer wall. They were all tipped over at the trunks, the limbs reaching the ground, roots exposed and ash-white, like they had succumbed to a powerful wind.

"I've never seen anything like this," Laadan said, her head moving slowly from side to side. "It's like a great unseen hand forced them all to the ground."

I walked up to one, placing my hand on it. I half-expected the tree to fall over, but it was stable. "So weird." I turned to Aiden. "Any idea what could've done this?"

"No clue." He frowned at the rising sun. "But hopefully we'll get an answer to this. We need to move on."

We continued on, the eight of us weary and desperately hoping that the University was safe and in one piece. It almost seemed like too much to ask.

The second wall looked better. Damage showed in places, but the gate was still standing and locked. Kind of good news, I guessed. But how in the hell were we supposed to get over a twenty-foot wall?

I folded my aching arms. "Before anyone gets any ideas, I am so not knocking a hole through this."

Aiden sent a wry grin over his shoulder as he joined Marcus and Solos approaching the titanium gates. The sharp spikes along the top caught my eye, and my imagination placed decapitated heads on the things.

I shuddered.

Luke dropped an arm over my shoulders. "You hanging in there?"

"Of course."

His brows rose. "You've been running like the little Apollyon Energizer Bunny."

I almost laughed. "Hopefully, we'll all get to recharge soon. How's your arm?"

"Not as bad as I initially thought." Luke squeezed my shoulders and let go. "I think Deacon's getting blisters on his feet."

At the sound of his name, Deacon scowled over his shoulder. "My feet *are* covered in blisters."

"Your poor precious feet," Luke teased.

From the gate, Solos raised his hand, silencing us. My heart sped up as I grabbed the daggers strapped to my thighs. Luke moved Laadan and Deacon behind us as I inched forward.

"What's going on?" I asked in a low voice.

Dawn had yet to crack the darkness beyond the gate, and all I could see were the shadows of more twisted trees.

Marcus cleared his throat. "Hello!" he called out, and his voice echoed on for what seemed like forever. "We…we come in peace."

I rolled my eyes and muttered, "Wow."

My uncle shot me a dark look and then continued. "I am Marcus Andros, the Dean of the Deity Island Covenant. I have Sentinels with me and the—"

The sound of guns being locked into place was a rat-a-tat-tat that shut Marcus up and probably stopped everyone's hearts. Not a single shadow had moved beyond the gate.

"Turn around and lower your weapons now," came a dark voice from behind us. Oh, crap on a cracker.

My eyes flicked up, meeting Aiden's for a brief second, and then, because I really didn't want to be pumped full of titanium, I turned and hoped I hadn't tapped that well of power inside me completely dry.

Two Sentinels stood behind Deacon and Laadan, guns pressed against their pale cheeks. But there were more than two Sentinels. Over a dozen surrounded us, forming a half-circle. They all held Glocks and looked more than ready to use them.

We were surrounded.

CHAPTER THIRTY-FOUR

"Lower your weapons," the one Sentinel said again. He was tall and older, maybe in his forties, and apparently was used to being listened to.

Gods, it was truly possible for a crappy situation to get even crappier.

Aiden was the first to lower his daggers, placing them on the ground beside his feet. Then he rose slowly, lifting his hands. I knew he carried more weapons on him, and I hoped the other men didn't realize that. Following suit, I got rid of my daggers, but left the gun shoved in the back of my waistband just in case.

The Sentinel in charge stalked forward, keeping his gun leveled on Solos, which I thought was kind of funny. Out of the four of us, he really should've had that gun pointed on me.

Then I realized he didn't know who I was. Part of me relaxed, because if they were playing for Team Evil, I was sure they would have had pictures of my face plastered across their bedroom walls. Marcus prepared to speak again, but the

Sentinel's eyes narrowed in warning. "I heard where you said you were from and that you mean no harm, but please tell me how we're supposed to believe that."

Good question. I glanced at my uncle, brows raised.

"We were a part of the group that escaped Deity Island," Marcus said.

"Well, obviously," replied the Sentinel.

I sort of liked this dude, gun pointed in our faces notwithstanding. A muscle flexed in Marcus's jaw. "We are not working with Lucian or the First. I am not sure how to prove that to your standards, but we have traveled far to come here and have lost one of our own, courtesy of the automatons guarding this place. We are not your enemy here. We want the same thing, to stop Lucian and the First. Sentinel Mathias was on his way here. He should've arrived with news of our travels."

"If this Sentinel was set to reach here within the last twenty-four hours, then he's among the poor souls beyond the wall." The leader's gaze drifted over us. "No one has made it past them for over a day, which makes me curious how your group has."

I hadn't met the Sentinel who'd arrived while Aiden and I had been in the Underworld, but it sucked to hear that he was now among the dead.

"They turned on you, then?" Aiden asked calmly. "They weren't guarding the campus?"

At first I didn't think the half-blood was going to answer, but he did. "The automatons were guarding the campus up until about a day ago, and then they started firing upon those seeking sanctuary here. We tried to stop them, and we ended up losing half of the first wall and many lives. So again, I am curious to how a group consisting of teenagers and two untrained pure-bloods could've made it past them."

"I'm the Apollyon," I said, squaring my shoulders. "That might have something to do with it."

Every damn gun went straight to me, and I wondered if that'd been the best thing to say. Out of the corner of my eye, I saw Aiden start to move toward me.

"It's okay," I added quickly, keeping my hands out in front of me. "I'm the good Apollyon, as in the one who *doesn't* want to take out the Council and kill the gods."

The Sentinel in charge didn't look relieved or awed. Instead, he appeared ticked off and like he really wanted to put a bullet between my eyes. Which wasn't good, because I was pretty sure Aiden was already calculating the time it would take for him to pull his gun and take out this Sentinel.

Bullets were about to fly—just as the sun started to crest too, and wouldn't that really gore up a beautiful sunrise?

"Half of the Sentinels and Guards who have sided with the First are looking for you, and you came here?" Anger flashed in the Sentinel's eyes. "Do you have a death wish?"

Good thing I hadn't mentioned that Seth and I were still sort of connected. "Actually, I don't have a death wish. And you can shoot me if it makes you feel better, but it's not going to kill me."

He looked like he was seconds away from finding out.

I took a deep breath, trying to keep a grip on my temper. "Look, I get your unwillingness to house me. I understand that, but you need me—you need *us*—because we took out those automatons and we can protect you. Not to mention I'm the only one who can stop any of this. So if you throw us out to the wolves, you're sealing your own fates."

The Sentinel stiffened but said nothing.

"And you have to realize this isn't about a pure-blood's thirst for power. This is bigger than that. Only a god could've turned those automatons. Not Lucian, and not the First. And that god is going to wipe out anyone who stands in his way."

I gave my best smile, the one that usually got me out of trouble or ticked off those on the receiving end of it. "And that god isn't the only one you're going to have to worry about. There's another one who goes by the name Apollo—yeah, *that* Apollo—and he's going to be pretty pissed if you turn us away. See, we're kind of related and he sort of likes me."

Someone swore under his breath.

My smile tipped higher. "Just one more thing—you hurt any of my friends, you're going to seriously regret doing so. Get my drift? So let's all play nice and become best friends forever."

"I think we should let them in," one of the Sentinels said.

"Sounds like a smart idea." Dark humor laced Aiden's tone. "You might want to get your gun off my brother's face while you're at it."

No one moved for a second, and I seriously hoped this guy didn't call my bluff. I wasn't sure I could do much in terms of the Apollyon thing, but luckily he raised a hand and the guns disappeared.

I let out a relieved breath.

"I hope I don't regret this," the Sentinel said, slipping his gun back into his holster. Then he extended a hand, much to my surprise. "My name is Dominic Hyperion."

My brows rose as I took his hand. He had a firm shake.

"Hyperion?" said Marcus. "Interesting last name."

Dominic grinned wryly. "I guess someone had a sense of humor, taking the surname of a Titan."

"I guess so," I murmured, relieved to see my friends no longer had guns pointed at their heads. Stalking past me, Dominic stopped at the gate. "So you guys really took out the automatons?"

"Unless they send more, you should be free of them," Solos answered.

"That is good." The half paused. "You say you lost one?"

Olivia cleared her throat. "Yes. She was only eighteen, training to be a Sentinel. Her name was Lea."

Dominic's chin tipped down. "I am sorry for what you all have lost. The gods know we can sympathize with what you're feeling." With that said, he turned back to the gate. "Please follow me."

"So you really can stop the First?" another Sentinel asked. He was younger than Dominic, around Aiden's age. A certain gleam filled his eyes when I nodded. "Well, I'm sure there're a lot of people beyond these gates who'll be happy to hear that."

"Do tell?" asked Aiden, who suddenly was by my side. He placed an arm over my shoulders, and I sent him a curious look.

The Sentinel's eyes about popped out of his face as they landed on Aidan's overly possessive arm. "You're a—and you are a—"

Oh, dear.

Aiden smiled, his eyes a dark gray. "We're what?"

"No. No. It's just..." The Sentinel looked back at equally flabbergasted halfs. No one came to his aid. "It's nothing. Never mind. Bigger problems, eh?"

"Yeah, *bigger* problems..." There was a clear, cold warning in Aiden's voice as he steered me around.

The gate was opening as Aiden's arm slid off my shoulder, drifting across my back, leaving a wave of shivers in its wake. Dominic went through first, followed by Marcus and then Solos.

I stopped, twisting back to the bug-eyed Sentinel. "You said others would be happy to hear that I knew how to stop the First? Who would that be?"

Dear gods, the guy looked at Aiden first before answering. "Before the automatons turned on us, a handful of groups made it in from other locations, including the Catskills."

My heart stopped. "Council members and Sentinels?"

When he nodded, I was close to doing the Muppet arm-thing. I hadn't let myself consider that my father could have been one of those burnt corpses lining the road, but knowing that some had made it to the University safely sparked hope deep in my chest. It didn't ease the tight pain of Lea's loss, but it was something to go on.

It was something, and that was better than nothing.

As dawn crept across the lush meadow, throwing light over the tiny blue wildflowers, we reached our destination. The University campus was large, spreading between two mountain peaks like its own little town in a hammock. I imagined it was like any other college in size and atmosphere, but that was where the similarities ended.

Early-morning light reflected off the large sandstone buildings modeled after the ancient coliseums. Courtyards were filled with what seemed like every flower and tree known to man, scenting the air. Statues of the Muses guarded one academic building, while sculptures of the Olympian Twelve lined the road. Dorms that looked like mini-skyscrapers rose in the background, housing potentially thousands of students.

It was so like Deity Island, but on a much larger scale, that there was a pang in my chest.

In the center of the campus was what I assumed was their Council building, and that was where we were heading. Muscles in my legs ached, and visions of beds were dancing in my head, but I forced myself to keep going instead of sitting down in the middle of the road and going to sleep.

Busts of the Olympian Twelve were carved into the marble and sandstone structure. It was circular, like an indoor amphitheater, and a cold shiver rolled down my spine. I don't know what it was about the Council buildings that always freaked me out, but they did.

As we climbed up the steps, I saw the statue of Themis and almost laughed. Her scales were balanced, but in whose favor?

There seemed to be no one else moving around as we entered the brightly lit lobby. Students were probably still asleep, if they were even continuing with classes. Hell, I didn't even know what day it was. It might've been the weekend for all I knew.

Dominic led us around another cluster of statues, but by then I was getting tired of seeing them and, of course, we headed up a never-ending flight of stairs. Not even the damn University could throw some money at an elevator.

It was when we were heading down a wide hallway, and I saw the Guards standing before double doors sheathed in titanium, that I knew where we were heading.

"The dean's office," I said.

Dominic nodded at the Guards, and then they moved as a unit, opening the heavy doors. My first glimpse of the office really struck home. It was nearly identical to Marcus's. Lush. Spacious. Tons of expensive-looking leather furniture, including a big old desk that probably made someone feel powerful and all kinds of special. There was even an aquarium built into the wall behind the desk, with vibrant fish zooming back and forth.

I glanced at Marcus and saw that his face was impressively blank. Months ago I would've believed that Marcus just didn't feel anything, but now I knew better. Seeing this office had to bring forth memories both good and a buttload of bad, and I sincerely felt for him.

A door opened to our left, and a tall man with ice-blond hair and startling blue eyes entered the room. He was dressed like Marcus used to—a poster child for Golf Club of the Month. Behind him, a smaller figure entered and my mouth dropped open.

"Diana," Marcus gasped, and then shot forward.

A wide, beautiful smile spread across the Minister's face. I'd met her while I'd been at the Covenant in the Catskills, and she had been the Minister to stand against Telly by voting against me being placed into servitude.

So, yeah, I liked the woman.

Marcus clasped her hands in his, and it seemed like he wished to do more—maybe pull her into his arms, hug her and kiss her like a man who'd never expected to see her again.

"I am so…thankful to see that you've made it here safely."

Marcus's voice was gruff and heavy with unspoken emotion. He so had a thing for this woman. "So very thankful."

Pink stained the woman's cheeks. "As I am to see you here."

The Dean cleared his throat. "I was unaware that you were familiar with my sister, Dean Andros."

Sister? Oh…*oh*, awkward.

Marcus let go of Diana's hands and faced the man. "We are…friends, Dean Elders. She's a lovely woman, but as much as I'd like to list her glowing attributes, that is not why we are here."

My brows inched up my forehead.

The Dean's lips twitched as if he wished to smile. "I am also grateful to see that you have made it here safely. Not many have recently."

"That is what we have heard and seen." Marcus clasped his

hands behind his back, throwing me headfirst into memories of him in an office very similar to this, where he'd been about to lay into me for something stupid that I'd done.

He made a quick round of introductions. The Dean seemed measurably surprised when Marcus announced Aiden's name. His head cocked to the side. "I have heard that name before—a pure-blood who used a compulsion against another pure to protect a half-blood?"

Crap. With everything going on, we'd forgotten that Aiden was Public Enemy Number Two.

My fingers inched toward my daggers, but Aiden spoke, his voice even and calm. "That would be me. And make no mistake, if you're looking for remorse or guilt, I have none. I'd do it again."

The Dean smiled then. "Ease yourself, Sentinel. At this moment, I could not care less what you have done. It is not an issue…now. As I am sure most of the members of the Council would agree."

The way he tacked on *now* did not make me all happy face.

"Thank you for your hospitality," Marcus said, obviously trying to diffuse the building tension. "Hopefully we will be able to repay you in some measure."

My uncle was such a diplomat.

The dean of the University nodded. "Please start by explaining how you made it past the automatons."

Between Marcus and Dominic, they filled the Dean and Diana in, for the most part, on how we made it here in one piece. The conversation quickly turned, though, when Dominic announced that I could stop the First.

I shifted restlessly, surprised to be so uncomfortable with all the eyes on me. Usually I loved being the center of attention. I had no idea when that had changed.

"I can stop Seth," I said finally. "It won't be easy, but I know how."

"And how can you?" the Dean asked. "From what our history teaches us, the First has complete control over the Second, and if you two are around each other, he can transfer your power to his, therefore becoming the God Killer."

Folding my arms, I met Dean Elders's curious stare. "Well, obviously the First doesn't have complete control over me. And there is a way for me to reverse the transfer, stopping him from becoming the God Killer. And if he's not the God Killer, then Lucian has no real weapon protecting him."

Diana leaned against the oak desk, her brows pinched. "But you would have to be near him to do this, correct?"

I nodded. "Yes. We came here hoping there would be others who would be willing to…to fight for this. There's no way that just the eight of us can breach the army that Lucian has surrounding him, so that I can reach Seth. We need our own army."

Dean Elders looked at Dominic, who shrugged. "We have many Sentinels and Guards here, plus half-bloods who are receiving advanced training. And we also wish for the same outcome. This needs to be stopped before more innocent people are lost, so you may recruit whomever wishes to join you."

Well, that was surprisingly easy.

"There will be some, maybe even many," the dean continued, "but none will be forced to join the cause, Apollyon."

I found that funny considering how an entire race of halfs had been forced into either servitude or a certain early death, but somewhere along the line, I'd learned to keep my mouth shut. Kind of.

"Understood," I said. "As a half-blood, I would never force people into something that would risk their lives."

The dean's brows rose. "Point taken." He gazed over the rest of my group. "I imagine you all wish to meet with the Sentinels and Guards here as soon as possible, but all of you look like you could use showers, food, and clean beds. While you rest, Sentinel Hyperion and I will have time to set something up for you."

"Okay," I said, wondering when whether or not I agreed had started to matter. I wanted to talk to the Sentinels now, but I knew if I did, so would Aiden and most of the others. We all needed to rest; we were barely standing. "That will be fine."

"There are many rooms available for your rest," the dean said. "Sentinel Hyperion will show you to them."

Unable to hold back the question any longer, I turned to Diana. "The Sentinels who have arrived from the Catskills… do you know any of their names?"

"Some I am familiar with," she said.

Then it struck me. My father probably wouldn't be known as a Sentinel, at least not any longer. "What about the servants?"

I couldn't tell by Diana's pained expression if she knew what I was getting at or if she was aware that my father had been a servant at the Catskills. "Things were in a state of chaos when we left there. Some servants were brought here, and those who no longer appeared to be under the influence of the Elixir escaped into the woods. Some remained behind. The servants could be anywhere."

"Oh," I whispered. They could be anywhere—my father could be anywhere. I felt Laadan's hand on my back and I drew in a sharp breath. "What was the state of the Covenant when you left?"

A dark shadow crossed Diana's face. "The walls had not been breached, but it was only a matter of time. Lucian and the First wish to take the Catskills. It does not matter that the bulk of the Council no longer resides there. It is the seat of power, and whoever sits upon the throne rules our society. It is the law."

It was an incredibly stupid law that didn't mean a damn thing to me.

"May I ask a question?" Diana countered. When I nodded, she went on. "If you were to succeed in transferring the power to you, what would happen?"

At the unexpected question, I blinked. "What would happen to Seth? He would still be alive. I guess he'd still be the Apollyon, but weaker. The tables would turn. The prophecies…" I shook my head. "The prophecies would change."

"And what would it do to you?"

I could feel the eyes on me again, mainly Aiden's. "I would become the God Killer."

Her brows knitted in confusion. "Please do not take offense to this, but isn't the God Killer the last thing the gods want?"

"I imagine so, with the exception of the god who is working with Lucian. That god obviously wants the God Killer for his own reasons. Speaking of which, it must be Hephaestus, considering he created the automatons," I threw that out, hoping the topic would change. "I don't know why he'd do this, though. I mean, he helped keep me away from the First, right?"

Aiden nodded. "He did."

"It doesn't make sense, but when do the gods ever make sense?" I forced out a laugh. "I guess he was tired of being the butt of every joke."

"But what about the other gods?" she persisted. "They cannot be pleased with the idea."

Seeing no way around this other than ignoring her question, I sighed. "It is what Apollo wants. And it is what the gods want."

Aiden turned completely toward me, as did half the room. I felt like slinking under the desk. "After I become the God Killer, they want me to take out the god responsible." I looked up, my gaze settling on a marble bust of Zeus. "The Olympians want me to kill one of their own."

CHAPTER THIRTY-FIVE

That little ditty went over like the Titanic. Everyone was pretty stunned. There were a couple of ripe curses from Aiden and Marcus, and some surprised gasps from the rest of the peanut gallery.

I got the whole "Holy crap-a-roo" thing going on. The gods had fought on and off for millennia, but had never seriously wanted one another dead, not since the Titans fell. But things were different now. This god, surprisingly one whom no one would've expected, had gone too far. Although many mortals had died, the gods were most likely more concerned with the fact that Hephaestus hoped to use the God Killer against them.

So, yeah, things were different now.

Once the shock died down, Dominic led us to the first dorm and showed us inside. It was nothing like the ones on Deity Island. This dorm had suites—two bedrooms joined by a shared living room and bathroom.

We were left to figure out the sleeping arrangements

ourselves. Before Marcus could go all parental on us again, Aiden claimed one of the suites for the two of us, practically dragging me inside. Before he'd even shut the door, he leaned down so that our faces were only inches apart. I knew he was mad—the steely, thundercloud-colored eyes, the rigid line of his jaw, and his stiff movements pretty much gave him away. That and the fact he hadn't so much as looked in my direction since we'd left the Dean's office.

"Take the shower first, and then we need to talk," he said, his voice low, leaving no room for argument. He disappeared into his room before I could even agree.

Olivia's lips pursed. "Someone's not a happy camper."

"Can I bunk with you?" I was only half-joking.

She leaned against the door of the suite across from mine, smiling slightly. The tight curls drooped around her face. Shadows bloomed under her eyes. "My room is your room, but seriously, you do need to talk to him. It's obvious he didn't know about what you'd been asked to do. None of us did."

I scrubbed my grimy cheek. "I…I wasn't even sure I was supposed to say anything."

"Does that matter?"

"I guess not. I just didn't want anyone to worry."

"I get that. I'm sure he does too, but there are some things you shouldn't keep from those who love you." Olivia turned, opening her door. "Talk to him."

Not like I had a choice when it came to talking to him. "Thanks."

She nodded and then slipped into her room. Letting out a loud and largely obnoxious sigh, I went into my room. My gaze immediately went to the full-size bed and I groaned.

"Shower first. Epic bitch-out session second, sincere apology third, and then sleep."

Freshly showered, I was thrilled to find someone had dug up a pair of jeans and a clean shirt that fit me. Most likely Aiden had done so while I was hogging all the hot water. It was so like him, even when he was mad at me. Alone for a few moments, I sat on the bed and crossed my legs. The bedroom walls were a nice shade of buttercup, while the door and window frames were trimmed with titanium, as were the headboard and the small end table. On the far wall, a picture of Artemis hunting with her bow and arrows was framed in titanium as well.

It was like these people expected daimons to pop out from under their beds.

But studying the décor wasn't the whole point of me sitting on the bed like a Buddha knockoff. Ever since Seth's appearance after Lea's death, he had been oddly quiet. As if he was gone, actually. The cord was still there, but his unmistakable presence was absent. Like before I'd Awakened, when my head and body had been my own.

Closing my eyes, I concentrated on the cord. It was there, humming softly and barely discernible. But there was no Seth.

I screwed my face up in concentration. This wacky long-distance internal phone call crap should be able to work both ways. Maybe I was crazy to be the one initiating contact, but a quiet Seth made for a really nervous Alex. It wasn't like him. He was up to something. He had to be.

Seth? I called his name again…and again. At some point, I heard the low hiss of the shower and then it turned off. The muted sound of a door closing followed minutes later. That was how long I sat there, looking like an epic fail at meditation.

The door to the living area opened, and Aiden came in carrying a plate of fruit and roasted turkey slices. "I bring gifts in the form of food—what are you doing?"

"Nothing." I flushed as I patted the spot beside me. "I'm starving. Thank you." And I was also surprised that he was bringing me food.

Aiden sat beside me, placing the plate between us. He smelled of clean soap and spice. Moving a few slices out of the way, he found a thick piece of dark meat.

"Aiden—"

"Eat first."

I frowned at him, but he held the turkey way too close and my mouth watered. Taking it from him, we spent the next several minutes gorging on the meat and fruit. As I chased a ripe strawberry across the bowl, he leaned over and tucked a damp strand of hair back behind my ear. I looked up and our eyes locked. All the air fled my lungs. Aiden was probably ready to throttle me, but that look in his silvery eyes…wow, simply wow.

Aiden leaned back, observing me, studying the blush I knew was spreading like a fever across my cheeks. "Before this goes any further, what you did with the automatons was nothing short of amazing. I haven't had a chance to tell you, but I wanted you to know."

I blinked. "Really?"

"Yes. That kind of power—it was epic and graceful. It was pretty amazing."

My gaze fell to the empty plate. "If I hadn't worn myself out, I could've saved Lea."

His fingers found my chin, tipping it up. "Don't blame yourself for what happened to her. Her death was not your fault. And if you hadn't used your power, all of us would've died."

I nodded. Those words weren't as easy to swallow as they were to say.

"Done?" Aiden gestured at the plate and bowl. He placed them on the table when I nodded again. There was a stretch of silence where he just looked at me until I squirmed. He sighed. "How could you not tell me, Alex?"

"I didn't want you to worry," I said. His eyes narrowed.

"That's bullshit." I jumped, eyes going wide. "We're in this...this screwed-up situation together, right? Both of us would do anything for each other, am I correct?" He didn't give me a chance to answer. He was really on a roll. "We love each other. And call me stupid or old-fashioned, but I think all of that means we don't keep secrets from one another, especially potentially dangerous secrets that the other party really should know about."

My cheeks were burning for a whole different reason now. Everything he said was true. Keeping him in the dark had sprouted from the best of intentions, but he was right.

"I'm sorry and I mean it. I should've told you when I figured it out."

His brows lowered. "When did you figure it out? Wait. While we were in the Underworld, right? You were different when we came back."

Damn. He was good. "It was when I was talking with Solaris. Things sort of clicked, and then I confronted Apollo. He confirmed that the gods wanted me to become the God Killer so that I could stop the god responsible."

Aiden cursed under his breath. "Sometimes I want to hit that bastard."

"Join the club."

He was silent for a couple of moments. "They expect you to fight Seth and have the power transferred to you. Then they expect you to fight this god?"

I nodded.

"I don't like this—I don't want you to do this." Anger burned in his gaze. "This is too dangerous—every part of it. Besides the fact that Seth could transfer the power from you, no god is going to go down easy. It's insane."

It was, but when had anything in my life been completely sane? I wiggled closer to him. "But it has to be done, Aiden. Even if we manage to stop Lucian and Seth, this god will try something again. Look at all the people who have died."

"I don't—" He cut himself off.

"You don't what?"

He looked up, features rigid. "I was going to say that I don't care. Not when you could die doing this. I don't care."

I had no idea what to say to that, and I knew that it took a lot for Aiden to admit that. Hell, it would take a lot for anyone to admit that. But it was the truth, and sometimes the truth wasn't pretty or ethical or fair. It just was.

Aiden tipped his head back and sighed. "What if I asked you not to do this?" My mouth opened in surprise, but no words came out.

He shook his head. "I know I can't ask you that. I know it's incredibly selfish. Don't answer it, okay?"

Tears moved up the back of my throat so quickly I didn't think I'd be able to hold them back. By some miracle I did. I knew I needed to tell him that there was a good chance I wouldn't survive this in the end. It wasn't like I was giving up, because Deacon had sort of given me the kick in the rear that I needed, but it didn't change the possibility.

Aiden made a sound in the back of his throat and he reached for me. I went, climbing into his lap. As his arms circled me, squeezing me so tight against him that I could feel his heartbeat, I couldn't tell him that now. I didn't think I could ever tell him.

And that was the thing about truths and secrets. Sometimes the truth didn't need to be known. The lie was healthier than the truth and, while some secrets could set people free, other secrets could destroy them.

I didn't feel good about it as I closed my eyes. Guilt settled in my stomach like a handful of sharp stones, but this secret wasn't meant to be shared.

Finally, Aiden's grip loosened and his hands moved from my shoulders. He held me back, his gaze searching my face. "Have you been having any headaches recently?"

Grateful for the change in topic, I shook my head. "Not since…Lea died. Seth was there afterward, but he's gone. I mean, I can still feel the cord, but it's weird. It's like he's taken a vacation."

Aiden arched a brow. "He's up to something."

A small grin pulled my lips. "Exactly what I was thinking."

"Great minds think alike." With one hand, he smoothed his thumb over my lower lip. "You have to be exhausted."

I shrugged. "So do you."

"We should get some rest." His hand fell back to my shoulder. "Marcus isn't going to be happy with you sleeping in here."

"I know."

He leaned back against the headboard, his eyes hooded. "We're probably going to have to cut the whole sleeping together thing back."

I pouted.

Aiden chuckled. "I said sleeping together, Alex. What I have in mind doesn't involve sleeping."

"Oh." Warmth spread through me like I was back in the steaming shower. "*Oh.*"

A slow grin tugged at his lips as his hands spread down my arms to my hips. That dizzying warmth stole into the marrow of my bones. "Little slow on the uptake, huh?"

I laughed and it felt…okay to laugh. Bending forward, I pressed my forehead to his. "Sorry. My mind isn't in the gutter, like some people I could name."

"So you say." His hands tightened. "We'll just have to see about that."

Aiden moved so quickly that one second I was in his lap, and the next I was on my back and he was hovering above me. He lowered his head so that his lips brushed mine softly. That one all-too-quick touch nearly undid me.

"I love you," he said, and those were the last words spoken for quite some time.

CHAPTER THIRTY-SIX

Aiden hadn't left the bed, so I guess cutting back on the whole sleeping arrangement thing wasn't going to start today. Not that I was complaining. After…well, not sleeping and then sleeping for several hours, and some more of the "not sleeping" thing, we were summoned by a knock on the door.

We exchanged a quick look. "Uh, should I be answering the door, since this is my room?"

Aiden nodded and I started to rise, but he caught my arm. "You might want to put some clothes on first."

"Oh. Ha." I giggled as I started searching for my clothes. "Good call."

"Uh-huh."

Hopping around the room, I shoved my legs into the jeans. "Be right there!"

I was sure Aiden got an entertaining eyeful, and my face was blood-red by the time I reached the door. Opening it wide enough for me to slip through, I saw Dominic.

"Hey," I said, hoping I didn't have a mad case of naughty-in-bed hair.

His expression remained bland. "I'm sorry that I've woken you, but we have new arrivals. One of them, I do believe, was an Instructor at Deity Island."

"Really? Wow. Where are they?"

"Currently with the Dean," he replied. "Your uncle is already aware. I stopped by Sentinel St. Delphi's room, but..."

"Oh. Yeah, um..." I was pretty sure I matched a fire truck. "He's a heavy sleeper."

"I'm sure he is." Dominic stepped back. "If you wish to join your uncle, I'll be waiting outside. You should have time to get ready. Your uncle is a...heavy sleeper, also."

Whaaaa...and then it hit me. Ew. Ew. Ew.

Hurrying back into the room, I closed the door, and then leaned on it. "Dear gods, that was awkward. You heard?"

Aiden stood beside the bed, buttoning his pants. My eyes got hung up on his fingers and then that stomach. "Yes. He didn't say who it was?"

I wasn't thirsty, but my mouth sure was dry. "No. Just that it was an Instructor. Do you think we should check it out?"

"Sure." Muscles popped as he reached over his head, pulling a shirt on. "I think it'll be good to see a familiar face."

I thought it would be good for him to take off that shirt, but what did I know? After running a brush through my mass of hair, I grabbed a slender dagger, slipped it into my back pocket, and tugged my shirt down over the handle.

Daggers. Never leave home without them.

It was late evening and the air seemed unseasonably chilly when we joined Dominic and my uncle. Then again, we were pretty high up in the mountains, but I was pretty positive it was the beginning of May and made a mental note to find a calendar pronto.

"I wonder who it is," I said, feeling a little high-strung.

"I do not know," Marcus said.

I increased my step to stay in line with the long-legged freaks. "Do you know of any Instructors who had escaped?"

"Many were not at the campus when Poseidon attacked."

"That's right. They were away on break." I shoved my hands into my jean pockets. "So it really could be anyone."

Marcus glanced down at me, a single brow arched. "It really could be."

I pulled my hands out of my pockets. "Why didn't Diana come?"

My uncle shot me a look and I grinned.

"Anyway, I hope it's someone I know." I started to shove my hands back into my pockets, but Aiden grabbed my wrist.

He frowned. "What is your deal?"

"What do you mean?"

"You're acting fidgety right now."

I pulled my hand free. "I don't know. I'm just hyper."

"Oh, great," Marcus muttered.

Shooting him a look, I tried to keep my jittery movements to a minimum. It wasn't hyperactivity. More like nervousness, but I didn't have any reason to be nervous. Well, besides the obvious, but this was different. The marks of the Apollyon were bleeding though my skin, moving sluggishly into glyphs.

The stairs weren't as killer this time around. As always, two Guards were posted at the end of the hall, outside the Dean's doors. They stepped aside as they opened the door and in we went. Curiosity had begun to outweigh the edginess somewhere on the stairs.

My gaze drifted over the room, finding Dean Elders first, and then to the far side of the room, to the oval-shaped window and the figure who stood in the light, his back to us.

Aiden and I hung back as Marcus strode to the desk. I wasn't sure if Dean Elders really wanted us here.

"Dean Andros," Dean Elders said, bowing slightly. "Thank you for joining us. Our newest arrival was most pleased to hear that some of his colleagues from the Deity Island Covenant had reached our campus."

The man by the window turned slowly, and I recognized the thinning dark hair, olive skin tone, and near obsidian-colored eyes. My mouth dropped all the way to the floor.

"You have got to be freaking kidding me," I said.

Instructor Romvi smiled tightly. "I am happy to see you too, Miss Andros."

Well, I guess I knew my suspicions about some Order members escaping Seth and the Sentinels were correct.

One of them was now standing in front of me.

Aiden and Marcus both moved toward me, withdrawing daggers. The poor Dean of the University looked like he was about to have a coronary.

"Guards!" he yelled, moving behind his desk as if that could somehow protect him in case the poo was about to hit the fan.

The doors behind us flew open and the two stepped in, eyes darting around the room. Dominic held his dagger out, too. "What the hell is going on?"

All of this wasn't necessary. I was no longer the student in class. I was the Apollyon and fully charged. Let Romvi try something. I'd seriously look forward to throwing his monkey ass out the window.

"He is a member of the Order of Thanatos, which tried to kill Alex." Fury rolled off Aiden, and I expected something to catch fire. "He is not what we'd consider a friendly acquaintance."

Instructor Romvi clasped his hands in front of him. "As I remember, I was not the one who carried out the deed, which was successful, might I add."

Oh, that was the wrong thing to say.

Aiden's stance said he was about to break all kinds of bad. "That is correct, but you are a member of the Order and you—"

"Have the ability to kill the Apollyon?" interrupted Romvi. "Yes. I do. But I am many things. Stupid is not one of them. It appears Miss Andros has many gods on her side, and the Order's only real mission is to serve the gods."

"And that meant killing me?" I said, folding my arms.

His eyes met mine. "It did at the time."

"And not anymore? We're supposed to believe that?"

Romvi cocked his head to the side. "We are on the same side, Miss Andros."

That nervous, too-much-caffeine feeling was back, tying my stomach up in knots. The runes were really going crazy now. "And what side is that, Romvi?"

"The only side there is to stand on," he replied. "In war, there is only one side to truly stand on, and that is on the side that wins. And make no mistake, Miss Andros, we are at war."

"You never seemed like the philosophical type," Aiden said.

Romvi's smile didn't slip. "I'm sure I didn't seem like much to you, St. Delphi."

Aiden replied, but I wasn't listening. I was getting a weird feeling again, the one I had had while standing in the war room in Hades's palace. That odd, nagging feeling, like there was something I should remember, that I should see. It was much stronger now.

"In times like these, we must let go of mutual dislike." Romvi still hadn't moved closer, but I felt…choked by his presence. "We must work together."

"We are always at war," I murmured, feeling very, very odd.

Romvi arched a cool brow. "You remember my teachings. That pleases me."

I thought of the strangest thing then. When Romvi and I had sparred once, what had he told me? I should cut my hair. Something to do with vanity, but I recalled that war room all too easily and what Persephone had said.

He likes to cut the hair of those he's conquered and then strings them up for all to see.

I slowly unfolded my arms. My heart sped up. Romvi was watching me curiously, as if he was waiting for something. Memories of what Persephone had said pieced themselves together rapidly. *To him, everything is about war and its spoils…* What had she said about him? Without war, there was nothing.

"One should never turn their back on war," I said, moving my hand behind me. "I also remember you saying that."

And I also remembered Persephone saying that about…

Romvi's gaze dropped. "No. One should never turn his back on war. I believe that is why we are where we are today. The fools have turned their back on it, even though war always exists."

Suddenly, the weird, edgy feeling and the marks made sense. It wasn't nervousness or hyperactivity. No, not at all. And the automatons. There was one other god who could wield control over them—they were creatures created *to fight*. There were the mortal armies that were backing Lucian. That made sense now.

Son of a daimon donkey.

Moving lightning quick, I pulled the Covenant dagger from my back pocket. With speed and perfect precision, I threw the blade across the room.

The pointy end embedded deep into Romvi's chest before he could take his next breath. "What the hell?" Marcus exploded, whirling on me. "What is wrong—?"

Aiden turned wide eyes on me. "Alex…? Holy crap…"

The Dean of the University started toward Romvi, but drew up short. And Marcus and Aiden quieted down, because Romvi was still standing.

And he was laughing.

Marcus took a step back. "What the…?"

The Guards and Dominic exchanged looks, and then moved toward the Dean, surrounding him and edging him toward the door.

Romvi's laughter faded. "I was beginning to think you weren't that clever, Miss Andros."

Then a blue shimmery cast surrounded Romvi's body, swirling around him until we couldn't see the man behind the eerie, godlike glow. Then it receded, revealing what stood behind it.

Ares was impressive.

Well over seven feet tall, he neared Godzilla-size with his height and bulk. He had more muscles than a pro wrestler, like Apollo on steroids.

He wore leather pants and a tunic that was punctured by the Covenant dagger still in his chest.

Snakelike bands covered his biceps, but as he lifted an arm, I realized they weren't bands at all.

They were bronze snakes, pulsing and slithering around his arms. "Holy crap," I whispered.

Reaching up, Ares wrapped a meaty hand around the handle of the hilt and pulled the dagger free. It turned to dust in his hands. "That wasn't very nice, Miss Andros. The gods and the Council fear the First, but who's the one lobbing daggers at a god?"

To say I wasn't scared would be a bald-faced lie. Ares was the god of war and discord. Armies trembled at his feet and nations fell under his wrath. His children were gods of terror and misery. There wasn't a single thing about him that didn't send a spike of fear straight through me or any other living, breathing creature.

This must be the god who was a part of Seth's bloodline, the one who'd been working behind the scenes with Lucian.

We were so screwed.

At least now I could understand how Romvi could kick my ass day, night, and on Sundays. It struck me then. I'd been sparring with *Ares*. Dear gods...

His cold, apathetic gaze drifted over us. "Silence? No one is going to cower before me? Beg for mercy, like thousands have before you? How disappointing. But there will be time for that in the future."

"How?" Marcus choked out.

"How what?" Ares's dark brows rose. "How have I been right under your noses this entire time? The same way Apollo apparently was, I assume. I avoided him whenever he was around, and therefore he never sensed me. The Golden Boy had his suspicions, I am sure, but...well, he just isn't that smart, is he?"

"What do you want?" I was proud that my voice didn't shake.

Ares brushed the dust off his hand. "Oh, you know. Just... everything. And to get everything, I need you to connect with the First."

Aware that Marcus and Aiden were moving in behind me, I tipped my chin up. "That's not going to happen."

He sighed. "I was really hoping I wouldn't have to tack on the always cliché *or else* at the end of that, but I see that I do. You can make this very easy, very painless. You know what I am, what I am capable of. Apollyon or not, you cannot even begin to hope to defeat me. I am the God of War. Connect with the First or else."

I held my ground. "Or else what? You're going to stand there and glare me to death? You can't kill me. And you can't force me to connect with the First."

The smile that etched over his lips sent an icy shock wave through me. "You are right *and* wrong. I may not be able to kill you, but I can bend you to my will and I can make you wish for death. And I can kill all those you love."

Ares threw out his arm, and several things happened within a matter of seconds. The Guard closest to him was flung across the room and through the window I'd wanted to toss Romvi/Ares out of. The second Guard moved toward him and Ares closed his fist. The Guard crumbled to the floor, blood streaming from his nose, mouth, and ears. Dominic was next. He was thrown back, his body contorting and twisting in air. Bones snapped through skin. He was nothing but a mangled mess when he hit the floor. Then, Ares turned on the Dean of the University.

Ares turned his wrist and the man's head twisted to the side.

The crack of bone echoed through the room.

Aiden started around me and true terror stole my breath. In a flash of horror, I saw him taking the place of Dominic, as would Marcus. Ares *would* kill them. Everything was happening too fast, but there was no way I could allow this.

I did the only thing I could do.

Throwing my arm toward the door, I summoned the element of air and I used it against Aiden and Marcus. The gust of wind was so strong there was nothing they could do but submit to it.

There was a second when my eyes met Aiden's, before he was pushed through the door along with Marcus, when I saw the stark horror in his silver eyes and I knew there was a good chance he'd never forgive me for this.

The heavy doors swung shut and locked from the inside.

"Aren't you a killjoy," Ares said, chuckling softly. "I was really looking forward to ripping the heart out of St. Delphi in front of you. But there's always later."

I turned around slowly, my breath catching in my throat. Ares winked. "Now it's just you and me."

"Well, that's not freaky or anything."

"Ah, that's so like you. To joke when you're afraid." His large boots thumped as he took a step forward. "Or what do they call it? Being *snarky*?"

My chest rose sharply as fists pounded on the door behind me. The thick titanium muted their voices. "That's what some people say."

"Hmm..." Ares tilted his head to the side, brows raised. "You know what I think about this snarky thing you have going on? It's a poor attempt to mask how affected you are by things. What?" He grinned. "You look so surprised. Do you think I don't know you? That I haven't watched you just as long as Apollo has? See, I'm just smarter than him. After all, I am a great strategist."

"The God of War has been stalking me? Wow, I feel all kinds of special. Usually the other gods are known for such creepy things, but you? Wow."

He laughed again, the sound deep but flat. "You are amusing. Very pretty, too. I see why Seth is quite fond of you."

"I'm guessing, since you're here, Seth won't be too far behind." Ares just smiled, and the fists on the door continued.

"How did you find me, by the way?" I asked, buying time—time for what, I wasn't sure.

"Oh, I have comrades everywhere, little girl. Ways to get around stupid talismans." One more step and he was only two feet away from me. "You're shaking," he whispered.

I was?

"You went to the Underworld recently. Pray tell, what for?"

My throat felt like it was closing up. "Well, I guess you don't have comrades *everywhere* if you don't know."

Ares smirked. "Charming. You will tell me what you were doing there, or this will end with you not being able to talk. It's your choice."

I refused to back up even though every instinct screamed that I do so. "I thought I was going to end this begging for death. How can I do that when I can't talk?"

He laughed again. "You are so simple, little girl. There are other ways to beg for death than with words."

"Are there?" My voice cracked a little and I winced.

His all-white eyes gleamed. "I've seen it all in battle. The way the body curls into itself when it wants death. The silent scream for release. There are the eyes, and they speak even when the tongue no longer works. And then there is the soul that rots so poorly when death is wanted but withheld that it carries a certain stench."

Ice shot through my veins, turning my blood to slush. At that moment I knew, no matter how much I fought, this… this was going to suck.

"So unless you want to experience these things firsthand, you will tell me why you were in the Underworld, and then you will submit."

I swallowed, wincing as fists hit the door behind me again. "I'm not big on the whole submission thing."

"You may want to rethink that." He sounded civil as he suggested it. "Look at this rationally, little girl. All that I ask is that you connect with Seth. Allow him to do what he was made to. That is all. He will take care of you. You know that. How is that so bad?"

"He will strip me of who I am."

"So what? You'll be happy and alive. You will want for nothing." He tipped his chin down almost playfully. "I'll even let the ones you love live. It's a win/win situation."

"Except for the gods you want taken out, and the thousands, if not millions, of people who will die."

He shrugged. "Consequences of war."

"Sickening," I said.

"It is the truth."

My stomach churned. "Why…why are you doing this?"

"Why not?" He tapped a long finger on my chin. "For too long the Olympians have sat on their thrones doing nothing. Letting the entire world be overrun with the children of demigods and mortals while we are sequestered on Mount Olympus. The world should be ours."

I shook my head. "The world belongs to humankind."

"The world belongs to the gods!" he roared, eyes crackling. "To me and any other god who sees the truth. That is who the world belongs to."

My fingers curled helplessly. "Why don't you just take me to Seth? Why try to convince me?"

"Well, I can't really just pop you there, now can I?"

"You didn't think this through, did you?" I forced out a laugh. "You could just knock me out and stuff me in a car. Why go through this?"

His brows slammed down and a muscle ticked in his jaw.

"There's something. You *can't* force me to go with you." My pulse sped up. "Can you?"

The god was seething. "You are the Apollyon. Therefore I cannot force you, but keep in mind, little girl, I can and will hurt you."

"This 'little girl' is having a hard time believing that." Courage fed my bravado, which usually was never a good combination. "Or are you like those villains who insist on giving a long, unnecessarily boring speech? Too bad. I'd have figured you were a more-action-and-less-words kind of god."

Ares's lips parted. "You have no idea. The rules that protect the Apollyon are like all things in nature—balanced. While you cannot be forced with compulsion or by hand, you can be persuaded by certain other means."

"You suck as a salesman, so you aren't persuading crap."

He let out a low, deep growl. "Submit, or so be it."

I met the eerie all-white eyes. "Go to hell."

For a moment, he almost looked disappointed, like the kind of disapproval parents feel when their kid is too stupid to figure something out, but then he smiled broadly. "I don't think Seth will like this, but oh, well."

"What do—?"

Ares shot forth, in my face in half a second. All thoughts of Seth fled, and instinct kicked in. I summoned forth akasha, knowing it wouldn't kill but hoping it would send him back to Olympus with his tail between his legs, but that wasn't what happened.

He caught my arm by the wrist and squeezed with what

was probably the slightest pressure, but the spike of pain caused me to lose my concentration. "You will not like my persuasion, little girl."

Then he pushed, and I hit the door with enough force to knock the air out of me. Unfortunately, his Dr. Evil speech hadn't been all pomp. But if he could hurt me, I could take it. I wasn't submitting. Too much was at stake. Too many lives. I could deal with this, and all I could hope was that he forgot about Aiden and Marcus when he was through, or they got with the program and got the hell out of Dodge.

I can deal with this.

Pushing off the wall, I spun to the right and extended my arm, but where his chest had been was empty space, and I stumbled into it.

"Missed me."

I whirled around, finding him behind me. Dropping down, I swept my leg at his…and hit nothing but air.

"You can keep this up if you want."

Looking up, he was leaning against the door, arms crossed. Now I was starting to get pissed off. Launching to my feet, I gained momentum and pushed into the air, twisting into the perfect butterfly kick that—

Arms snagged me out of the air from behind and I let out a surprised gasp.

He held me like I was nothing more than a sack of rice. "I am the God of War, little girl. There is no move that you know, no method of battle or maneuver that I do not."

Crap.

"I will always be one step ahead. I will always outthink you. You cannot fight me."

Throwing my head back, I hit his broad, hard shoulder.

Then I swung my legs, but Ares dropped me. Stumbling to my feet, I saw he wasn't in front of me.

Double crap.

Whirling around, I kicked out into nothing. I spun back and suddenly—*dear gods*—his hand was on my throat, lifting me off the ground as I kicked and clawed at his hand, too panicked and distracted to try to summon akasha again.

"You will wish for death by the time I am through." His fingers dug in deep, cutting off my air supply. "You will beg for it in all the ways I listed. You had your choice. You had your fun. Game over."

For a terrifying second, I thought he'd crush my windpipe, and I told myself again that I could deal with this. But then I was suddenly flying backward through the air. I crashed through the aquarium. Sharp glass sliced through my back as water and fish poured out around me.

I hit the floor on my side. Vibrantly striped pink-and-blue fish flopped on the marble floors. Sucking in a sharp inhale against the pain, I put my hand down and pushed up. I grunted as glass sliced open my palm. Blood mixed with water.

I can deal with this.

I stood up, breathing raggedly as I lifted my head.

Ares stood in front of me. Without a single word, his backhand hit the side of my face. Starbursts flooded my vision like a dozen firecrackers going off at once. I smacked into the leather chair behind the desk. Blood pooled in my mouth as I caught myself on the edge of the desk. Something had split. My cheek? Entire face? I had no idea. And over the pounding pain, I could hear them at the door.

I can deal with this.

Grabbing the keyboard, I ripped it free and swung around,

aiming for his head. Ares caught the keyboard, yanked it free, and then snapped it in two like it was a twig.

I stumbled back, reaching blindly for something. Daggers and swords hung from the wall, but he was on me before I could go for them.

Ares picked me up like I was nothing more than a helpless kitten. Before I could wiggle free, before I could taste the raw fear building in the back of my throat, he flipped me over, slamming my back into the corner of the upturned desk.

There was a crack I *heard* and felt. Sharp pain came in a flash of light, and then every nerve ending fired at once. My senses overloaded as I slipped to the ground, eyes fixed on the ceiling.

Something had come unhinged inside me. I could feel it. A searing hurt roared through me like a gunshot blast. I was wet and warm on the inside, and if I hadn't been the Apollyon—if I had been only a half-blood or a mortal—I knew whatever Ares had done would've been fatal.

But I wouldn't die and I couldn't move. Something bad was broken. The tips of my fingers were numb, and I couldn't feel my toes, but I felt *everything* else. And I figured that, if anyone knew the right place to snap the spine to immobilize someone but ensure they could still feel everything, it would be Ares.

I can deal with this—oh gods, I can deal with this.

He loomed over me, smiling, eyes all-white. "This can all end now, little one. Just say the words."

My throat worked, and my tongue felt way too heavy. It took everything to get the words out.

"Fuck…you…"

The smile slipped from his face, and then he moved lightning fast. Pain…it was everywhere. Another bone cracked—maybe my leg, or a kneecap, but I couldn't be sure. My mouth opened to scream, but a wet, warm whimper came out instead.

I…I can deal with this. I had to…I had to.

When he snapped my other leg and then each rib, one at a time, the pain became my world. There was no escaping it—no breathing around it or hiding. Consciousness was slipping away from me and I fought the fog, because when he was done with me, if he'd ever be done with me, he would move on to Aiden and Marcus, to the whole University. He was the God of War and he would lay waste to everything.

But that pain…it rotted me from the inside. It reached down into the tiny part where I was still a person, where I was still Alex, and the pain took over. I couldn't take it. I couldn't deal with it. My shields crashed down and the cord roared, but the growing hum was overshadowed by the terrible pain, and the growing hopelessness dug in deep with razor-sharp claws and pulled away my entire sense of being.

I wasn't as strong as I thought I was, or maybe I'd just hit my limit, because I wanted out—I wanted to *die*. There was no pride in this. There was no purpose. My soul fragmented and I broke wide open.

Ares grabbed hold of my broken arm, dragging me to the center of the room, over broken glass and dead fish and the blood of those who'd already died in here. That fresh burst of pain seemed like nothing in comparison to everything else, but out of the corner of my eye, I saw Ares pick up a dagger. He knelt over me, lips curled back. There was a blade in his hand, and this was about to get much, much worse. "Say the words."

I was shattered and I was weak. He had won, and I wanted to die, but I couldn't, and there was no way—I screamed as the first strike of the blade sank deep.

With another sharp slice, my vision flashed amber momentarily and then reverted, but something…something was different. A foreign sensation wiggled around the broken bones and severed muscles. It wasn't from me, but it was a part of me. It was cold and it felt like steel and it was fury, dark and endless.

It wasn't from me, because what little part of me that was left had curled up in a ball and was waiting and praying for this to be over. It had given up, cowering away from more pain like an abused dog. It wanted this to be over. It wanted to taste the peacefulness of death.

But that fury built and, as Ares bent over me holding the red-tipped dagger, I knew that the anger was filtering through the connection between me and the First.

It was Seth.

Was he angry that I hadn't gone with Ares? Or was it because I was so weak that I wished for death? Or was it something else, something deeper than which side we stood on, because Seth…Seth had to feel this now. He had to know, and that last little shred of my being refused to believe that he would condone this. I suffered, and so he suffered.

The god laughed coldly. "I wonder, if you cut the head off the Apollyon, does it grow back? Guess we could find out, huh? You'd like that."

Part of me died right then, maybe not a physical death, but on some mental, some emotional level, I was good as dead. When all of this was over, I wouldn't be the same.

Wood and metal splintered, and I knew the door had finally been breached. As the god brought the dagger down, a body crashed into him. The blade impaled the floor harmlessly beside my neck. Before I could take my next painful breath, the three of them moved above me, engaging in a sick, macabre dance of sorts. Ares. Aiden. Marcus. They moved too fast for me to track. The three of them were too close together.

Light exploded, casting the room in white light as bright as the sun. The presence of another god filled the room, and I was blinded. I tried to take my next breath and wheezed. Wet warmth spread along the left side of my body, pooling across the floor like red rain. My blood? Someone else's? Gods… gods didn't bleed like us.

There was an inhuman roar and Ares spun around, his attention on whatever was behind me. In an instant, the God of War threw out his arms. A shock wave rolled through the destroyed room. Shattered wood and broken furniture flew into the air, along with prone, lifeless bodies…and Marcus and Aiden.

Red rain seemed to pour from the ceiling now.

My name was called, but it sounded so far away. I struggled to sit up, to see Aiden and Marcus, to know that they were okay, but I couldn't move and I couldn't breathe. Hands landed on me, but my skin felt detached. There was screaming in the background, and I wanted them to shut up—*to just shut up*. My entire body felt slippery as I was lifted, my head flopping loosely to the side.

Where were they—where were Aiden and Marcus?

The mounting horror took over the pain and it mixed with Seth's rage. The marks spread across my skin and the cord hummed violently. There were voices, so many voices, and one came through so clear, and I didn't know if it was spoken out loud or in my thoughts. "Let go, Alex."

Then there was nothing.

CHAPTER THIRTY-SEVEN

There was nothing, and then the pain came back, starting with the cracked bones in my toes and then crawling up my shattered calves and knees, licking over my pulverized pelvis in waves of white-hot, fiery pain. When the fire reached my head, I tried to scream, but my jaw wouldn't unhinge. The scream tore through me still, silent but full of rage that tasted of the blood that pooled in my mouth.

Death…oh gods, I begged for death over and over in my mind. A relentless, steady stream to whatever god was listening to take this away, because the pain was splitting the seams of my sanity.

But the pain didn't lessen. It burned. It remained. It continued to rot me from the inside until I willed my eyes open.

My vision didn't focus as first. What I saw was a hazy blur of blue, but when my sight cleared, I didn't understand what I was seeing.

Maybe I'd already gone insane.

I was staring at a sky—the brightest blue I'd ever seen. Like the deepest ocean water, untouched and pure. No sky was that color. And I'd been in the Dean's office, where Ares… where he…

I couldn't think of that. I couldn't think of anything.

The air smelled of jasmine, like…like the pool in the Underworld, when I'd been with Aiden.

Aiden…

Oh gods, I didn't know what'd happened to him, if Ares had hurt him or Marcus. I didn't know where I was, or how I had gotten here. All I knew was pain. It was in every fiber of muscle, every splintered bone and burst vessel, but that…that wasn't true. There was one thing that I did know.

The cord—the connection between Seth and me—it was gone.

There was no humming. No rage. No outside presence mingling with mine. Oh gods, I was nothing now but pain.

"Alexandria."

I didn't realize my eyes were closed again until I forced them to reopen at the sound of the vaguely familiar voice. At first, I didn't see him, or anything other than that beautiful, unreal sky.

A shadow fell over me and then a form appeared, blocking out the sky. Seconds later, the man pieced together. Tall and broad and a head full of honey-colored hair, the man had the face of an angel.

Oh for the love of gods, I couldn't catch a freaking break. Thanatos.

The god's lips tipped up a little on one side, as if he knew what I was thinking, and I wondered then if I was actually dead, if someone had lied about the whole Apollyon-death thing, because I was staring at the God of Peaceful Death.

Then again, my death, if that was what this really was,

had been anything but peaceful. Had he come to answer my prayers? To take this pain away?

Easing down, Thanatos tipped his head to the side as he leaned over me. "Can you hear me?" I tried to open my mouth but couldn't.

"Blink if you can," he said with surprising gentleness. I blinked.

"We may have been foes in the past, but I am not here to harm you now. I'm watching over you until Apollo can return with his son, Asclepius."

Apollo? His son? Confusion swamped me and I dragged in a deeper breath I immediately regretted. Pain arced across my chest.

Thanatos moved to place his hand on my forehead, but stopped short. "It's okay. You're in Olympus."

Olympus? How in the world was *that* okay?

"Well, just outside of Olympus, if you want to get technical." He glanced over his shoulder, sighing softly. "What you did by standing up to Ares? Not many would—no mortal, demigod and surely not even the Apollyon. You could've submitted to him. You would've saved yourself so much pain."

Thanatos leaned in close, focusing on me with white eyes that held no pupils or irises. "You held your ground, and I can respect that. I can also admire that."

Maybe, if it didn't feel like my body had been shattered into a million pieces, I could really appreciate that statement. The jasmine-scented air stirred, and two more shadows fell over the spot where I lay…in the grass, I realized dumbly. My entire back felt wet and I wasn't hopeful enough to think that it was dew instead of my own blood…or someone else's. No. It couldn't be someone else's, because that would mean that Aiden or Marcus…

Apollo came into focus, and instead of showing off those creepy god peepers, he stared down at me with eyes that matched the sky over his shoulder. A small, almost sad smile tugged at his lips, which I found so strange since it was rare that Apollo showed any real emotion.

"There was no way I could heal you in the mortal realm. The damage is too extensive," he said, and for the first time, he cut right to the chase. "I had to bring you here, as close to Olympus as possible. All the aether surrounding my home will help Asclepius."

I wanted to ask about Aiden and Marcus, but when I finally managed to open my mouth, only the smallest whimper leaked out.

"Don't try to talk," Apollo said. He leaned back, making room for another god. "My son is going to heal you." A wry grin twisted his lips. "And I know if you could, you'd say something like 'how many kids do you have?' and my answer would be 'many.'"

Yeah, I was kind of curious, and I also wondered if it meant that Asclepius was related to me, but what I really wanted to know was what had happened to Aiden and Marcus.

Asclepius took the place of Thanatos. This god barely resembled Apollo. A full beard covered his face, making it difficult to gauge his age, but the fine lines spreading out from the corners of his white eyes made him look much older than his father. My eyes moved to Apollo, and I was comforted to find that he was still there. He hadn't left me with Thanatos and a stranger.

Finally, Apollo took pity on me. "The last I saw of Aiden and Marcus, they were fine. But I haven't been back since I brought you here."

I closed my eyes and swallowed hard. It wasn't a hundred

percent confirmation that they were okay, but it was something that I could hold onto.

"Do you know the story of my son?" Apollo asked.

When I did nothing, Asclepius laughed. "He loves to tell this story."

"His mortal mother died during childbirth, and while she was on the funeral pyre, I cut him from the womb." As Apollo spoke, his son eyed the numerous injuries with a mixed look of disgust and challenge. "I gave him to the centaur Chiron, who raised him in the art of medicine. Of course, having my genes, he already had a knack for healing."

Of course.

"But my sister had asked Asclepius to bring Hippolytus back to life, and between Hades being pissed off about that, and Aphrodite's whining, Zeus killed my son with a thunderbolt." A muscle popped out in Apollo's jaw. "So I killed Cyclopes, ensuring that Zeus would have no more thunderbolts."

Oookay…

"I ended up banned from Olympus for a year," Apollo continued blithely. "But in the end, Zeus resurrected my son to ensure there would be no future feuds with me." He paused. "You're wondering what the moral of this story is? I *always* find a way to take care of my own."

Before I could process what that meant, his son placed his hands on my chest. Under normal circumstances, I wouldn't have been thrilled with the idea of being felt up, but incredible warmth swept through me. From the tips of my aching toes to the top of my fractured skull, dizzying, wonderful warmth invaded every pore.

The god closed his eyes. "This may sting."

What? *No*, I wanted to scream, because I couldn't take

anymore, but then the warmth blistered my skin and I *did* scream.

Fire raged through me, spreading out of control and searing every cell. My broken body reared off the ground.

Asclepius's face blurred into a severe frown. "There's something else here..."

For the second time in however many minutes, I was pulled into the void, lost in a black sea of nothingness.

When I opened my eyes, my vision was clear and I'd been moved into a circular chamber with marble walls. Birds shrilled in a soft, lyrical verse from somewhere outside the room. A table sat in the middle of a raised dais. Resting atop the table was a pitcher full of honey-colored liquid. Heavy, scented air flowed through a small opening in the wall, stirring the white canopy hanging from the posts at the foot of the bed I rested in.

A bed? Obviously it was a step up from lying in grass, but confusion pinged at me. I pushed up onto my elbows and winced as an ache rolled through my entire body.

I'd been healed, but...

Memories pieced back together of Thanatos, Apollo, and his son. Holy crap, I was in—or near—Olympus.

Never in my life did I think I'd breathe the aether-enriched air of the gods, but here I was. A low hum of excitement trilled in my veins. I wanted to race off the bed and investigate. Olympus was rumored to be the most beautiful place in existence, even more so than the Elysian Fields. Creatures of myths roamed freely here, and plants that no longer flourished in the mortal realm grew to staggering heights in Olympus. This was a once-in-a-life...

The excitement gave way to unrest. I wasn't here for sightseeing. It wasn't like I was on vacation and Apollo would pop in and give me a tour along with keepsake mouse ears. This wasn't Disney World, and I was here because Ares…

In the back of my mind, and in the center of my very being, there was a dark and ugly thing that had been born and taken root, a distinct coldness that no amount of warm air could quell. My thoughts swung to Ares and my heart turned heavy. Raw terror formed in the back of my throat, tasting like bile.

But, oh gods, it wasn't just Ares, or the thought of facing him again. It was the pain that had festered and rotted me, the pain that had shattered me into pieces and caused me to beg for release—for death. Even though I had never spoken the words aloud, I knew that Ares had felt it. It had been in my eyes; my very soul had been laid bare.

Ares knew. Seth knew.

Shame and something dark rose inside me, twisting and choking like a vile weed. I'd begged for death.

Me. Alex. The all-powerful Apollyon. The girl who got knocked down only to jump back up and ask for more. I'd been training to be a Sentinel, a warrior bred to disregard fear. I'd known pain before this, both physically and mentally. I'd even come to expect it.

But Ares had broken me wide open.

A raw vulnerability inched through me. Feeling sick, I tugged the soft blanket up to my chest. Gods, I felt…I felt like a poser in my own skin. What would Aiden think if he found out? He would never have begged or given up like I had—oh gods, what if Aiden really wasn't okay? What if Apollo had lied?

I started to throw the blanket off, but stopped. Indecision

smacked into me. What was I doing? Where was I going to go to demand answers? My hand tightened around the blanket until I thought I was going to undo Asclepius's hard work.

I couldn't move.

I was frozen by…by what? Fear. Distress. Shame. Confusion. Anxiety. A hundred or so emotions whirled through me like an F5 tornado. My breath sawed in and out painfully. Pressure blossomed out of nowhere, clamping down on my still-tender chest. This was worse than how I'd felt after Gatlinburg, magnified by a million.

I couldn't breathe.

Images of the fight in the dean's office flipped through my head like a twisted photo album. The maneuvers that always had been too late. The kicks and punches that'd never landed. Being picked up and thrown like I was nothing more than a sack of rice. The breaking of my spine and every bone thereafter and then the knife…

The sound of Aiden and Marcus banging on the doors, desperately trying to get in, haunted me. So many memories of Ares owning my ass kept on coming in a continuous onslaught of how-not-impressive-I-really-was. How could I have thought I could stand against Ares—the God of War? How could any of us?

And I'd begged for death. I couldn't breathe.

The pressure constricted my chest again and I let go of the blanket, pressing my hand to my clammy skin. I stumbled out of the bed, falling on the chilled granite knees-first, and then I pressed my forehead to it. The cool floor seemed to help, like the night I'd been slipped the Brew.

I don't know how long I stayed like that—minutes or hours—but the floor had this wonderful grounding ability. A bone-deep exhaustion set in, the kind a warrior feels at the end of the final battle, when they are ready to turn in their sword and fade into eternity.

Somewhere in the room, a door opened, scraping against marble. I didn't lift my head or try to sit up, and I knew how I looked to whomever was in the room—like a dog cowering in the corner. That was me.

"Lexie?"

My heart stopped.

"Lexie? Oh my gods, baby."

I was frozen again, too afraid to look and discover that the voice didn't really belong to my mom, that it was some kind of messed-up illusion. A different kind of pressure fisted in my chest. Fragile hope swelled.

Warm arms surrounded me in a gentle, painfully familiar embrace. Inhaling a ragged breath, I caught her scent—*her scent*. Vanilla.

Lifting my head, I peered through the strands of hair and lost my breath, along with any ability to form a coherent thought.

"Mom?"

She smiled, sliding her hands up to my cheeks. It was her—the oval face and complexion slightly darker than mine, lips spread in a wide smile and eyes the color of the brightest green. She looked like she had the last time I'd seen her in Miami, the night before the daimon attack that had changed her into an aether-addicted monster, before I had killed her.

That fist squeezed down until I couldn't breathe, couldn't think, and couldn't see anything other than her.

"Baby, it's me, it's really me." Her voice was as I remembered—soft and melodious. "I'm here." I stared at her until her beautiful face began to swim. Part of me couldn't allow myself to accept this—this *gift*—because, if it wasn't real, it would be too cruel. The spirits guarding the gates to the Underworld had almost fooled me.

But her hands were warm and her eyes were full of tears. It smelled like her and sounded like her. Even the dark hair fell in waves past her shoulders the way it had before.

Then she came to her knees and leaned forward, pressing her forehead against mine. Her voice was tight with tears. "Do you remember what I said to you that night?"

I struggled to get the words out. "That you loved me?"

"Yes." Her smile was watery. "I told you that, with or without purpose, you were a very special girl."

Oh gods…

"And you told me that, as your mother I was obligated to tell you that." She laughed and it seemed to catch in her throat. "Even I didn't know how special you truly were."

It was her—really her.

Clamoring forward, I threw my arms around her, nearly knocking her backward. With a soft laugh, she enveloped me in a strong hug—the hug I'd been missing and needing for so long. Mom gave the best hugs ever.

She squeezed me tight, and I clung to her while she smoothed my hair back with one hand. Tears burned the back of my throat and welled in my eyes. Emotion poured into my chest until it felt like my heart would explode. I'd been waiting for this moment for what felt like forever, and I never wanted to let her go.

"How is this possible?" My voice was hoarse and muffled. "I don't understand."

"Apollo thought it would be good for you after what happened." She pulled back a little. Tears glistened in her eyes, and I hated that. "He called in a favor with Hades."

Apollo must have a lot of favors at his disposal.

"I've missed you so much." She placed her hand to my cheek and smiled. "And I wish I could've been there for you when you lost Caleb and faced the Council. I wish for that more than anything else."

A red-hot lump filled my throat. "I know. Mom, I'm… I'm so sorry. I—"

"No, baby, don't you dare apologize for anything that happened to me. None of it was your fault."

But it *was* my fault. Sure, I didn't turn her into a daimon, but we'd left the safety of Deity Island because of what I would become. She sacrificed everything—her *life*—for me, and I'd still connected to Seth when I had Awakened, spurring horrific, catastrophic events across the globe as the gods retaliated. How was that not my fault?

"Listen to me," she said, clasping both sides of my face now and forcing my gaze up. "What happened to me in Miami wasn't your fault, Lexie. And you did the right thing in Gatlinburg. You gave me peace."

By killing her—my mother.

She pressed her lips together, and then took a shaky breath. "You can't hold on to that kind of guilt. It doesn't belong to you. And what happened after you Awakened wasn't something you could control. You broke the connection in the end. That is what matters."

Her words were so sincere that I was *almost* convinced, but I didn't want to spend this time with her talking about all the terrible things that had happened. After everything that had happened, I just wanted her to hold me.

Pushing down the guilt was like taking off a pair of too-tight pants. I could breathe now, but the marks were left behind on my skin. "Are you happy?" I asked, scooting closer.

Mom gathered me close again, resting her chin atop my

head, and I closed my eyes, almost able to pretend that we were home and that a heart actually beat under my cheek. "I miss you, and there are other things I miss, but I am happy." Pausing, she tucked my hair back. "There is peace, Lexie. The kind that erases a lot of the negative stuff and makes it easier to deal."

I was sort of envious of that kind of peace.

"I watch over you when I can," she said, pressing a kiss on the crown of my head. "It's not something they suggest for us to do, but when I can, I check in. You want to tell me about this pure-blood?"

My eyes popped open, and heat flooded my face. "*Mom.*"

She laughed softly. "He cares for you so much, Lexie."

"I know." My heart squeezed as I lifted my head. "I love him."

Her eyes lit up. "You have no idea how happy that makes me to know that you've found love among all of this…"

Tragedy, I finished silently. Wrapping my hands around her slim wrists, my gaze fell to the window. Thin branches swayed in the breeze. Bright pink flowers were open, their teardrop-shaped petals moist with dew. I stared at them for an obscenely long time before I spoke.

"Sometimes I wonder if it's right, you know—if I should feel happiness and love when everyone is suffering."

"But *you* have suffered, too." She guided my gaze back to hers. "Everybody, no matter what is happening around them, deserves the kind of love that man feels for you, especially you."

Flushing again, I wondered just how much Mom had seen. Awkwardville, dead ahead.

"And that kind of love is more important than anything right now, Lexie. It's going to keep you sane. It's always going to remind you of who you really are."

I took a deep breath, but it got caught. "So many people have died, Mom."

"And people will, baby, and there'll be nothing you can do about it." She pressed her lips to my forehead. "You can't save everyone. You're not meant to."

I wasn't sure how to feel about that. Was being the Apollyon all about death and destruction instead of saving lives?

"Can you stand?" she asked.

Nodding, I pushed to my feet and winced as pain splintered down my legs. Concern pinched my mom's features, but I waved it off. "I'm fine."

She stood, keeping a hand on my arm. "You should sit. Apollo said that it would take a little while for…you to feel normal."

Feeling normal wasn't possible, probably never again, but I sat on the edge of the bed and watched my mom glide toward the raised dais and the table. She didn't walk—never had. My mom had this innate grace I always wished I'd been born with. Instead, I stomped around like a cow most of the time.

She picked up the pitcher and a glass that had been behind it. "He wants you to drink this."

My brows rose in suspicion. If I'd learned anything over the last eighteen years, drinking or eating something from the gods warranted a hefty amount of misgiving. "What is it?"

Mom poured the contents into an ancient-looking glass cup and headed back to the bed. Sitting down, she handed it over. "It's a healing nectar that Apollo's son concocted to aid what he had done. You can't stay here the amount of time that it will take you to heal completely, but this will help. Even for you, there's too much aether in the air. It will suffocate you."

Suffocation sounded sucktastic, but I stared at the chalice warily.

"It's okay, Lexie. I understand your hesitation, but this isn't to trick you."

With a great deal of trepidation, I took the glass and sniffed it. The aroma was a mix of honey and something weedy. Because I knew this was my mom, and I could feel that truth deep inside me, I drank from the glass. I was relieved when I discovered it tasted sweet and not like butt.

"Drink it slowly," Mom cautioned. "It's going to make you sleepy."

"It is?" I frowned down at the chalice.

"When you wake up, you'll be back in the mortal world."

A cold wind filled my chest. "This isn't a dream, is it?"

"No." Mom smiled as she reached out, catching that piece of hair that always fell forward and tucking it back. "This isn't a dream."

Letting out a stuttered breath, I took another sip. There was so much I wanted to say. Many times since she'd died, I'd fantasized about seeing her again and had created this massive list of things I wanted to say to her, starting off with a whole slew of apologies for sneaking out, cussing, fighting, and being a general round-the-clock nuisance. And then I'd move on to how great of a mom she'd been. Now, it was funny and strange. When I opened my mouth, emotion choked out that list, erasing it completely. The words I spoke were, "I miss you so much."

"I miss you too, but I am with you as much as I can be." She watched me drink the healing nectar. "I want you to promise me something."

"Anything," I said, and I meant it.

A small smile appeared. "No matter what happens, and

no matter what you have to do, I want you to absolve yourself of guilt."

I stared at her. "I—"

"No, Lexie. You need to let the guilt go, and you need to let what Ares did go."

Lowering the glass, I looked away and gave a little shake of my head. Let go of how badly Ares had broken me, how I had begged for death? Impossible. "Did you…did you see it?"

"No." She placed her hand on mine and squeezed. "But Apollo told me."

The laugh that came out of me sounded incredibly bitter. "Of course he did. And where was Apollo when I was getting my ass handed to me, by the way?"

A pained look crossed her face, and I immediately regretted saying that. "I'm sorry," I whispered. "He was probably off doing important god stuff." Or chasing nymphs.

"It's okay." Her hand swept across my cheek, and I was surprised to find that my face no longer ached. "Apollo is very concerned about you. So am I."

"I'm okay." The lie rang false in my own ears.

She tilted her head to the side and sighed. "I didn't want this life for you. I wanted to spare you this darkness."

"I know." Looking at her, I soaked in her features. Gods, my mom was beautiful. It was more than good godly DNA. It was what was inside that bled through—her goodness, love, and everything I aspired to be. In my eyes, she shone. And her life had ended way too early. She deserved so much more, and I wished I could give that to her. But I couldn't, so I gave her the only thing that I could.

"I promise," I told her. "I promise to let it go."

Her lips curved up at the corners. "I want to kill Ares for what he did to you."

I choked on my drink. I don't think I'd ever heard my mom say she wanted to kill anyone, except after she'd turned into a daimon. Then, she'd wanted to kill everyone. A different kind of ache filled my chest. Not wanting to think about that, I swatted those thoughts away.

Smothering a yawn that came out of nowhere, I finished what was left of the sweet drink. Mom took the cup from me and stood, replacing it on the table. By the time she'd turned around, I was lying flat on my back.

"Damn," I murmured. "That stuff…it's strong."

Hurrying to the bedside, she sat beside me. "It is. I wish we had more time, baby."

"Can't we?" I tried to lift my arm, but it felt cemented down. Panic clawed at my chest. I wasn't ready to let her go. It wasn't fair. I *needed* her now more than I'd ever needed her. There was something inside me and it scared me. "There are so…many things I still have to tell you, that I want to ask."

With a smile that wrenched at my chest, she cupped my cheek. "There'll be time later."

"But I'm not ready. I don't want to leave you. Please…" Strange. I forgot what I was saying.

Apparently, the nectar was taking over.

As my lids became too heavy to keep open, I heard her say, "I'm so proud of you, Lexie. Always remember that I'm proud of you and that I love you." There was a pause and then her sweet voice said, seconds before I slipped away, "Don't give up hope, baby. Paradise is waiting for you in the end."

READ ON FOR A SNEAK PEEK AT THE NEXT BOOK IN THE COVENANT SERIES

SENTINEL

CHAPTER ONE

Feeling came back in my feet first, and then my legs. A pins-and-needles tingling rushed over my skin, causing my fingers to spasm. The sweetness of the nectar still coated the inside of my throat. My body ached as if I'd just completed a triathlon and come in dead last.

Or like I'd had my ass kicked and gotten patched up by a god. Either/or…

Movement beside me brought the whole side of my body closer to a hard warmth, and I thought I heard my name called, but it sounded like it was on the other side of the world from me.

I was moving at the speed of a three-legged turtle, so it took a while to blink my eyes open, and even then it was just a thin crack. When my eyes adjusted to the dim lighting, I recognized the buttercup-colored walls and all the titanium trim of the dorm rooms at the University in South Dakota, the same room Aiden and I had done a whole lot of not sleeping in right before Dominic had brought us news of Deity Island survivors. Things…things were different then; it already felt like years ago.

A terrible heaviness settled like a stone in my chest, pressing all the way down to my spine. Dominic was now dead. So were the Dean of the University and his Guards. It had been a trick played out by Ares, who'd been masquerading as Instructor Romvi. Our enemy had been among us the entire time. My dislike of that man had been epic before I'd discovered who he really was, but now? Every fiber of my Apollyon being loathed him. But my hatred of Romvi/Ares/Asshat wasn't important. So many people were dead, and Ares knew where I was. What was stopping him from coming back for round two? And what was stopping him from killing more people?

I heard my name once more, and now it seemed louder and closer. Turning to the sound, I willed my eyes to open. When had my eyes closed again? I was like a newborn kitten or something. Daimons across the nation shuddered in fear. Gods, I was lame.

"Alex."

My heart skipped a whole beat, and then sped up in recognition. Ah, I knew that voice. My heart and my soul *knew* that voice.

"Alex, open your eyes. Come on, baby, open those eyes."

I really wanted to, because for him I'd do anything. Fight a horde of half-blood daimons? There. Tangle with ticked-off furies? Sign me up. Break a dozen or so rules for one forbidden kiss? Done. Open my eyes? Apparently that was asking too much.

A warm, strong hand curved along my cheek; the touch was so different than my mother's, but equally powerful and heartbreakingly tender. My breath caught in my throat.

His thumb traced the curve of my jaw in such a lovingly familiar way that I wanted to weep. I should weep, actually, because I couldn't fathom what he'd gone through when Ares and I had been locked in that room. Come to think of it, I should've cried when I saw my mom. I'd felt the tears, but they hadn't fallen.

"It's okay," he said in a voice gruff with exhaustion and emotion. "Apollo said it could take some time. I'll wait for however long it takes. I'll wait forever, if I have to."

Those words pulled my heart all over the place, twisting it into mushy knots. I didn't want to make him wait for another second, let alone forever. I wanted—no, *needed*—to see him. To tell him that I was okay, because I *was* okay, wasn't I? All right, maybe I didn't fall into the "okay" category, but I wanted to relieve the harsh edge of stress in his voice. I wanted to make him better because I couldn't make my mom better, and I knew I couldn't make myself better.

There was a part of me that felt vastly empty. Dead. That was it. I *felt* dead inside.

Frustration coursed like acid in my blood. My fingers fisted in the soft sheets as I dragged in a deep breath. He stilled beside me, like he held his breath and waited, then let out a ragged exhale.

My heart plummeted.

Gods, all I needed to do was open my eyes, not walk a tightrope.

That frustration quickly flipped to anger—a soul-deep kind of rage that tasted of hot bitterness. My heart rate picked up, and that's when I realized *it* was there—the cord. It had been absent in Olympus, but it was back. I hadn't felt it at first because I'd only been acknowledging the ache in my muscles and bones, but the cord connecting me and the First buzzed like a million yellow jackets, steadily increasing until I swore I could see it in my mind, an amber-colored cord tangling with a blue one.

Seth?

His reply didn't come in the form of thoughts or feelings, but a rush of energy so pure it was like being zapped by lightning. Strength poured into me, a torrential downpour of vitality encasing every nerve ending. Every distinct sound in the room was magnified. My own breathing, more steady now, and the deep and slow inhales of the man beside me. Doors opened and shut in the hallway outside the room, and there were voices, muted but distinct. My skin came alive. Glyphs bled through, swirling across my body in response.

I didn't understand it, but I knew Seth was lending me his power, like he had in the Catskills when I'd fought the furies for the first time. He'd claimed no knowledge of what had happened, chalking it up to adrenaline, but Seth had...he had lied about a lot of things.

But now he was helping me. It didn't make sense, since I was much easier to deal with in this state, but I wasn't going to look a gift horse too closely in the mouth right at the moment.

My eyes flew open. And I saw him.

Aiden was on his side, facing me. His hand still cupped my cheek, his thumb smoothing along my skin, and I could feel the marks of the Apollyon gliding toward his touch. His eyes were closed, but I knew he was awake. Thick, sooty ashes fanned the tips of his broad cheekbones. His dark brown hair was a mess. Waves tumbled over his forehead, brushing the graceful arches of his brows.

An ugly, purplish bruise marred his left eye, and I wondered if he could even open it. There was another violent mark, an astonishing mixture of reds, shadowing the strong line of his jaw. His lips were parted, neck and shoulders tensed.

Without warning, I was thrown back to the very first time I'd seen him.

The Covenant in North Carolina no longer stood, but it felt like I was there again, standing in the training room used for novices. I'd been practicing with Cal and Caleb. I'd done something incredibly moronic, which was nothing new, and the three of us had been laughing. I had turned and seen Aiden by the doors. At that time, I didn't think he really saw us. He was a pure-blood, and they didn't show any interest in halfs, so I had assumed he was just observing. Even then, I'd been captivated by him. To me, he'd honestly been the most alluring male I'd even seen—a face that could be both hard and beautiful. And those eyes, flashing between heather gray and quicksilver, had been permanently etched into my memories from that moment on. That curiosity had been inflamed when he'd shown up in Atlanta, saving me from some really annoying and talkative daimons three years later.

Our love had never been easy.

As a pure-blood, he was untouchable to me even though I was the Apollyon, and even now he risked everything to be with me. He was my strength when I needed him to be, my friend when I needed someone to talk me down, my equal in a world where by law I would always be less than him, and honest to gods, he was the love of my life.

And he would wait forever for me, just as I would wait forever and a day for him.

Except forever will probably end up being fairly short, whispered an insidious voice, and it was right. Even if I managed to get past all the obstacles between me and Seth, and transfer his power to me, there was no doubt in my mind that, even as a

God Killer, I was going to have problems fighting Ares. And if, by some miracle, I survived that, there was a really good chance the other gods would kill me.

So why even bother?

Aiden and I could run away together, live as long as we could and *be happy*. He'd do it if I asked. I knew he would. We could hide until we couldn't hide anymore, but we'd be together and we'd be alive. And for a little while, there'd be no more pain and no more death to deal with.

A huge part of me, especially that dark, cold place that had been born when Ares held me down, agreed wholeheartedly with that plan. *Run away.* Nothing seemed smarter or simpler to do.

But I couldn't, because there was too much that had to be done. People relied on me, and the world would descend into absolute chaos if Ares wasn't stopped.

I held onto that needle-thin thread of duty with my life and spoke. "Hey."

His lashes fluttered open, revealing silvery eyes that never failed to make the muscles in my stomach tighten and my heart do a little pitter-patter.

Our gazes met.

Aiden jerked up, his face paling by several degrees, making the bruises along his jaw and left eye stand out in stark contrast.

Fear exploded in my stomach, which was kind of strange since terror typically wasn't my first reaction to sudden movements, but I scrambled against the headboard. My breath stalled out as my body protested the sudden movement.

"What?" I croaked. "What's wrong?"

Aiden stared at me with wide eyes. Color hadn't returned to his face. He was as pale as a daimon, and while disbelief shattered his gaze, pain churned in them.

He reached out but stopped short of touching me. "Your eyes..."

"What?" My heart beat so quickly I was sure it would jump out of my chest and do a little jig on the bed between us. "I opened them. I heard you asking me to."

Aiden winced. "Alex..."

Now I was really starting to freak out. Why was he reacting this way? Had Ares rearranged my face so badly that my eyes were on my chin or something?

He glanced toward the door and then back to me, his face going stoic, but he could never hide his feelings from me. I could read everything in his eyes. There was so much pain in them that it broke my heart, but I didn't understand why.

"What are you feeling?" he asked.

Uh, what was I *not* feeling? "I'm...I'm going to go with confusion. Aiden, tell me. What's going on?"

He stared at me so long I started to feel a wee bit self-conscious. Several seconds passed, and then I really became convinced that my eyes *were* on my chin, but then it made sense. Panic unfurled in the pit of my stomach and spread like a virus.

Springing from the bed, I hit the floor. Hot slices of pain ricocheted up my still-healing bones. I stumbled to the side, catching myself on the wall.

In a heartbeat, Aiden was off the bed and beside me. "Alex, are you—"

"I'm okay." I bit back a moan.

Aiden reached out, but I pushed away from the wall before he could touch me. Each step hurt like Tartarus. Sweat dotted my forehead, and my legs shook with the effort to make it to the bathroom that joined the two suites together. "I have to see," I gasped out.

"Maybe you should sit down," he suggested, close behind.

I couldn't. I knew what Aiden was thinking. I was connected with Seth, and maybe he even thought this was a trick of some sort and was waiting for me to break free and pull out Deacon's ribcage, but Seth was quiet on the other end of the cord.

Reaching around me, Aiden pushed the bathroom door open, and I all but fell inside. Light flooded the small but efficient washroom when he found the switch on the wall. My reflection formed in the mirror.

I gasped.

This couldn't be me. No way.

Uh-uh, it wasn't, and I refused to believe it, but the damn reflection remained the same. I had changed. Dramatically. The pressure in my chest returned and doubled as I gripped the edge of the sink.

My hair hung an inch or two past my shoulders now, the edges ragged and uneven from the dagger Ares had used. I picked up a strand, wincing as I discovered it was a good deal shorter than the rest. Did the rest of my hair hang in Hades's war room now?

My skin was pale, as if I'd been sick for months and hadn't seen the sun. But it wasn't even that. Hell, it wasn't even the fact that, yes, my eyes were amber-colored. Identical to Seth's in clarity and shininess, they were like two topaz gemstones. And they were glowing, like you could see me in the dark kind of creepy glowing, and I got why that set Aiden on edge. Great, I had glowing, honeycomb eyes. Big freaking deal.

It was *my face* I couldn't get over.

I was as shallow as any other eighteen-year-old girl, so yeah, this…this was major.

Across my cheekbones and nose, faint pink lines

crisscrossed over my skin. My forehead was the same. A web-like network of scars covered my face. Only one side of my jaw, where Aiden had been touching me earlier, had escaped the…well, the deformity.

Dazed by what I was seeing, I slowly lifted my arm and ran my fingers across my cheek, confirming what I suspected. The lines were slightly raised, like stitching. Apollo and his son had healed me. The nectar was still doing its mojo in my system, but I knew these scars were proof of just how badly I'd needed the gods' help to heal.

Like anything else, there always had to be an exchange.

When anything was gained, something had to be sacrificed.

No one needed to tell me. I knew these scars would never fade. "Oh, my gods…" I swayed.

"Alex, you should sit down." He reached for me again.

"Don't," I snapped, holding a hand up between us. My eyes widened. My hand was also covered with scars. I wasn't even sure what I was saying "don't" to, but my mouth kept moving. "Just don't."

Aiden pulled back, but he didn't leave. Leaning against the threshold of the door, he folded his muscular arms across his broad chest. His jaw set in a hard line.

The pressure moved into my throat, swelling like a balloon and then exploding like a late summer's day thunderstorm. "What are you waiting for? Me to go all Evil Alex on you again?" I swung forward, losing my balance. "That I'm going to use—"

Aiden shot forward, catching me before I cracked my head against the wall. "Dammit Alex, you need to be careful and *sit down*."

I wrenched free, stumbled back a step, and plopped down on the closed toilet. Air punched out of me. Dear gods, it felt like my tailbone had been cracked. I sat there on the toilet, my butt feeling like someone had literally kicked me in it. Aiden stared at me with warring levels of hope and distrust in the eyes I loved so much. I felt about seven kinds of dejected.

Aiden stepped forward, crouching down so that we were at the same eye level. "You don't want to kill me?"

Most of the rage seeped out of me. Nothing like hearing the man I love ask a question like that to really take the wind out of my sails. "No," I whispered.

There was a sharp intake of breath. "You don't want what he wants?"

"No." My gaze dropped to where his hands rested between his knees. Good gods, the knuckles were bruised and the skin was torn open, as if he'd punched a… Then I got it. Aiden and Marcus had been banging on the titanium doors of the dean's office with their fists.

My heart ached as I watched those battered hands open, close, and then open again. "I don't even feel him. I mean, the cord's there, so I know he's somewhere, but I don't feel him. He's quiet."

His hands unclenched, and even though I wasn't looking at him, I could tell that most of the tension had left him. He believed me for the most part, and I couldn't hold the residual suspicion against him.

"Gods, Alex, when I saw your eyes, I just… They glowed like that when you escaped the basement and…"

When I had almost killed him.

If I lifted my lashes, we'd be face-to-face, but I couldn't bring myself to do it. He shifted closer. "I'm sorry. I should—"

"It's okay." I was so tired. Not the physical kind. Oddly enough, it was more of a…spirit-weary sort. "I understand. You had every reason to think that. I don't know why my eyes are glowing. Seth's there, but he's not trying to influence me."

"Yet" hung unspoken between us.

"And he's not talking," I added, keeping the fact that Seth had lent me some of his own juice out of the conversation.

I shifted my gaze back to my own hands and the scars that marred them. They hadn't been like that in Olympus, or at least I hadn't noticed.

"It doesn't matter," he said. "It's you, and that's all that I care about—all that matters."

ACKNOWLEDGMENTS

It takes a village to write a book—thank you to Kate Kaynak, Rich Storrs, Marie Romero, Traci Inzitari, Anna Masrud, and Rebecca Mancini. Without you guys, Alex would just be a sparkle in my eyes. Thank you to Kevan Lyon for being the best agent, and to my PA Malissa Coy, and editor Wendy Higgins.

A big thank you to my friends and family for putting up with my crazy writing deadlines, which means I pretty much don't do anything other than write. Thank you to Cindy Husher and Stacey Morgan for talking me off the writing ledge many times over. To Molly McAdams for giving me an awesome sauce blurb, and a huge thanks to my beta/crit team for telling me it sucks…when it sucks.

None of this would be possible without my readers. Thank you for reading and enjoying the Covenant Series. I know a lot of authors say this, but I have the best readers ever. You guys rock.

ABOUT THE AUTHOR

#1 *New York Times* and #1 international bestselling author Jennifer L. Armentrout lives in Shepherdstown, West Virginia. All the rumors you've heard about her state aren't true. When she's not hard at work writing, she spends her time reading, watching really bad zombie movies, pretending to write, hanging out with her husband, her Border Jack Apollo, Border Collie Artemis, six judgmental alpacas, two rude goats, and five fluffy sheep. In early 2015, Jennifer was diagnosed with retinitis pigmentosa, a group of rare genetic disorders that involve a breakdown and death of cells in the retina, eventually resulting in loss of vision, among other complications. Due to this diagnosis, educating people on the varying degrees of blindness has become a passion of hers, right alongside writing, which she plans to do as long as she can.

Website: jenniferlarmentrout.com
Facebook: JenniferLArmentrout
Instagram: @jennifer_l_armentrout

OTHER BLOOM BOOKS BY JENNIFER L. ARMENTROUT

COVENANT SERIES

Half-Blood (includes the novella "Daimon")

Pure

Deity (includes the novella "Elixir")

Apollyon

Sentinel

FRIGID SERIES

Frigid

Scorched

DEITY

DEITY

JENNIFER L.
ARMENTROUT

Bloom books

Cover design by Nicole Hower and Nicole Lecht/Sourcebooks

Published by Bloom Books, an imprint of Sourcebooks
P.O. Box 4410, Naperville, Illinois 60567-4410
(630) 961-3900
sourcebooks.com

Originally self-published in 2012 by Jennifer L. Armentrout.

Cataloging-in-Publication data is on file with the Library of Congress.

Printed and bound in Germany.
BPG 10 9 8 7 6 5 4 3 2 1

To Kayleigh-Marie Gore, Momo Xiong, Valerie Fink, Vi Nguyen, and Angela Messer for being über Covenant Series fans…and the first to respond on Twitter. And to Brittany Howard and Amy Green of YA Sisterhood, for just being, well, awesome. And to the Greer family, for being the official first family of the Covenant Series.

PRONUNCIATION GUIDE FOR DEITY

Aether: EE-ther
Agapi: ah-GAH-pee
Akasha: ah-KAH-sha
Apollyon: a-POL-ee-on
Daimon: DEE-mun
Hematoi: HEM-a-toy
Zoi mou: ZOY moo

CHAPTER ONE

Red silk clung to my hips, twisting into a tight bodice that accentuated my curves. My hair was down, silky around my shoulders like the petals of an exotic flower. The lights in the ballroom caught each ripple in the fabric so that, with every step, I looked like I was blooming from fire.

He stopped, lips parting as if the mere sight of me had rendered him incapable of doing anything else. A warm blush stole over my skin. This wouldn't end well—not when we were surrounded by people and he was looking at me like that, but I couldn't make myself leave. I belonged here, with him. That had been the right choice.

The choice I…hadn't made.

Dancers slowed around me, their faces hidden behind dazzling bejeweled masks. The haunting melody the orchestra played slipped under my skin and sunk into my bones as the dancers parted.

Nothing separated us.

I tried to breathe, but he had stolen not just my heart, but the very air I needed.

He stood there, dressed in a black tux cut to fit the hard lines of his body. A lopsided smile, full of mischief and playfulness, curved his lips as he bowed at the waist, extending his arm toward me.

My legs felt weak as I took the first step. The twinkling lights from above lit the way to him, but I would've found him in the dark if necessary. The beat of his heart sounded just like mine.

His smile spread.

That was all the reinforcement I needed. I took off toward him, the dress streaming behind me in a river of crimson silk. He straightened, catching me by the waist as I looped my arms around his neck. I burrowed my face against his chest, soaking in the scent of ocean and burning leaves.

Everyone was watching, but it didn't matter. We were in our own world, where only what we wanted—what we'd desired for so long—mattered.

He chuckled deeply as he spun me around. My feet didn't even touch the ballroom floor. "So reckless," he murmured.

I smiled in response, knowing he secretly loved that part of me.

Placing me on my feet, he clasped my hand and placed the other on the small of my back. When he spoke again, his voice was a low, sultry whisper. "You look so beautiful, Alex."

My heart swelled. "I love you, Aiden."

He kissed the top of my head, and then we spun in dizzying circles. Couples slowly joined us, and I caught glimpses of wide smiles and strange eyes behind the masks—eyes completely white, no irises. Unease spread. Those eyes...I knew what they meant. We drifted toward a corner where I heard soft cries coming from the darkness.

I peered into the shadowy corner of the ballroom. "Aiden…?"

"Shh." His hand slipped up my spine and cupped the nape of my neck. "Do you love me?"

Our eyes met and held. "Yes. *Yes.* I love you more than anything."

Aiden's smile faded. "Do you love me more than him?"

I stilled in his suddenly lax embrace. "More than who?"

"Him," Aiden repeated. "Do you love me more than him?"

My gaze fell past him again, to the darkness. A man had his back to us. He was pressed against a woman, his lips on her throat.

"Do you love me more than him?"

"Who?" I tried to press closer, but he held me back. Uncertainty blossomed in my belly when I saw the disappointment in his silvery eyes. "Aiden, what's wrong?"

"You don't love me." He dropped his hands, stepping back. "Not when you're with him, when you chose him."

The man twisted at the waist, facing us. Seth smiled, his gaze offering a world of dark promises. Promises that I'd agreed to, that I'd chosen.

"You don't love me," Aiden said again, fading into the shadows. "You can't. You never could."

I reached for him. "But—"

It was too late. The dancers converged and I was lost in a sea of dresses and whispered words. I pushed at them, but I couldn't break through, couldn't find Aiden or Seth. Someone pushed me and I fell to my knees, the red silk ripping. I cried out for Aiden and then Seth, but neither heeded my pleas. I was lost, staring up at faces hidden behind masks, staring at strange eyes. *I knew those eyes.*

They were the eyes of the gods.

I jerked straight up in bed, a fine sheen of sweat covering my body as my heart continued to try to come out of my chest. Several moments passed before my eyes adjusted to the darkness and I recognized the bare walls of my dorm room.

"What the hell?" I ran the back of my hand over my damp and warm forehead. I squeezed my watery eyes shut.

"Hmm?" murmured a half-awake Seth.

I sneezed in response, once, and then twice.

"That's hot." He blindly reached for the box of tissues. "I can't believe you're still sick. Here."

Sighing, I took the tissues from him and cradled the box to my chest as I pulled a few free. "It's your fault—*achoo*! It was your stupid idea to go swimming in—*achoo!*—forty-degree weather, jerk-face."

"I'm not sick."

I wiped my nose, waiting a few more seconds to make sure I was done sneezing my brains out, and then dropped the box on the floor. Colds sucked daimon butt. In my seventeen years of life, I'd never gotten a cold until now. I hadn't even known I *could* get one. "Aren't you just so damn special?"

"You know it," was his muffled response.

Twisting at the waist, I glared at the back of Seth's head. He almost looked normal with his face planted into a pillow—*my* pillow. Not like someone who'd become a God Killer in less than four months. To our world, Seth was sort of like any mythical creature: beautiful, but usually downright deadly. "I had a weird dream."

Seth rolled onto his side. "Come on. Go back to sleep."

Since we'd returned from the Catskills a week ago, he'd been up my butt like never before. It wasn't like I didn't understand why, with the whole furie business and me killing a pure.

He probably was never going to let me out of his sight again. "You really need to start sleeping in your own bed."

He turned his head slightly. A sleepy smile spread across his face. "I prefer your bed."

"I prefer that we actually celebrate Christmas around here, and then I'd get some Christmas presents and get to sing Christmas songs, but I don't get what I want."

Seth tugged me down, his arm a heavy weight that pinned me on my back. "Alex, I always get what I want."

A fine shiver coursed over my skin. "Seth?"

"Yeah?"

"You were in my dream."

One amber-colored eye opened. "Please tell me we were naked."

I rolled my eyes. "You're such a perv."

He sighed mournfully as he wiggled closer. "I'll take that as a no."

"You'd be correct." Unable to fall back to sleep, I started chewing on my lip. So many worries surfaced at once that my brain spun. "Seth?"

"Mmm?"

I watched him snuggle farther down into the pillow before I continued. There was something charming about Seth when he was like this, a vulnerability and boyishness missing when he was fully awake. "What happened when I was fighting the furies?"

His eyes opened into thin slits. This was a question I'd asked several times since we'd returned to North Carolina. The kind of strength and power I'd displayed as I'd faced the gods was something only Seth, as a full-blown Apollyon, should've been able to accomplish.

As an un-Awakened half-blood? Yeah, not so much. I

should've gotten my rosy rear handed to me when I fought the furies.

Seth's mouth tightened. "Go back to sleep, Alex."

He refused to answer. Again. Anger and frustration rushed to the surface. I flung his arm off me. "What aren't you telling me?"

"You're being paranoid." His arm landed on my stomach again.

I tried wiggling out of his grasp, but his grip tightened. Grinding my teeth, I rolled onto my side and settled next to him. "I'm not being paranoid, you asshat. Something happened. I've told you that. Everything…everything looked amber. Like the color of your eyes."

He blew out a long breath. "I've heard that people in high stress situations have increased strength and senses."

"That wasn't it."

"And that people can hallucinate while under pressure."

I swung my arm back, narrowly missing his head. "I didn't hallucinate."

"I don't know what to tell you." Seth lifted his arm and rolled onto his back. "Anyway, are you going to go back to class in the morning?"

Instantly, a new worry surfaced. Classes meant facing everyone—Olivia—without my best friend. Pressure built in my chest. I squeezed my eyes shut, but Caleb's pale face appeared, eyes wide and unseeing, a Covenant dagger shoved deep in his chest. It seemed I could only remember what he'd really looked like in my dreams.

Seth sat up, and I felt his eyes boring holes in my back. "Alex…?"

I hated our super-special bond—absolutely loathed that whatever I was feeling fed into him. There was no such thing as privacy anymore. I sighed. "I'm fine."

He didn't respond.

"Yeah, I'm going to class in the morning. Marcus will have a fit when he gets back and realizes I haven't been to class." I flopped onto my back. "Seth?"

He inclined his head toward me. Shadows cloaked his features, but his eyes cut through the darkness. "Yeah?"

"When do you think they're coming back?" By *they* I meant Marcus and Lucian…and Aiden. My breath caught. It happened whenever I thought about Aiden and what he'd done for me—what he'd risked.

Easing down on his side, Seth reached across me and grabbed my right hand. His fingers threaded through mine, palm to palm. My skin tingled in response. The mark of the Apollyon—the one that shouldn't be on my hand—warmed. I stared at our joined hands, not at all surprised when I saw the faint lines—also the marks of the Apollyon—making their way up Seth's arm. I turned my head, watching as the marks spread across Seth's face. His eyes seemed to brighten. They'd been doing that a lot more lately—both the runes and his eyes.

"Lucian said they'd be back soon, possibly later today." Very slowly, he moved the pad of his thumb down the line of the rune. My toes curled as my free hand dug into the blankets. Seth smiled. "No one's mentioned the pure-blood Guard. And Dawn Samos has already returned. It appears Aiden's compulsion worked."

I wanted to pull my hand free. It was hard to concentrate when Seth messed with the rune on my palm. Of course, he knew that. And being the tool that he was, he liked it.

"No one knows what really happened." His thumb now traced the horizontal line. "And it'll remain that way."

My eyes drifted shut. The truth of how the pure-blood Guard had died would have to remain a secret, or both Aiden and I would be in deep trouble. Not only had we almost hooked up over the summer—and then I'd had to go and tell him that I loved him, which was *totally* forbidden—I'd killed a pure-blood out of self-defense. And Aiden had used a compulsion on two pures to cover it up. Killing a pure meant death for a half-blood, no matter the situation, and a pure was forbidden to use a compulsion on another pure. If *any* of it came out, we'd both be totally screwed.

"You think so?" I whispered.

"Yes." Seth's breath was warm against my temple. "Go to sleep, Alex."

Letting the soothing sensation of his thumb against the rune lull me away, I drifted back to sleep, momentarily forgetting all the mistakes and decisions I'd made in the past seven months. My last conscious thought was of my biggest mistake—not the boy beside me, but the one I could never have.

On a good, normal day I hated trig class. The whole subject seemed pointless to me. Who cared about Pythagorean Identities when I was attending the Covenant to learn how to kill things? But today my hatred of the class had hit an all-time high.

Almost everyone had their eyes on me, even Mrs. Kateris. I sank low in my seat, shoving my nose into the book I wouldn't read if Apollo came down and demanded that I do so. Only one set of eyes really affected me. The rest could suck it.

Olivia's stare was heavy, condemning.

Why, oh why, couldn't we change seats? After everything that'd happened, sitting next to her was the worst kind of torture. My cheeks burned. She hated me, blamed me for Caleb's death. But I hadn't killed Caleb—a half-blood daimon had.

I'd just been the one who snuck out with him on a campus that'd been under curfew for what'd turned out to be a really good reason.

So in a way, it was my fault. I knew that, and gods, I'd do anything to change that night.

Olivia's outburst at Caleb's funeral was probably why everyone else kept sneaking peeks at me. If I remembered correctly, I think she'd yelled something like, "You're the Apollyon" as I stared at her.

Back at the New York Covenant in the Catskills, the half-blood kids had thought I was pretty damn cool, but here...not so much. When I met their gazes, they didn't look away fast enough to hide their unease.

At the end of class, I shoved my book in my backpack and hurried out the door, wondering if Deacon would talk to me next period. Deacon and Aiden were poles apart on almost everything, but both Aiden and his younger brother seemed to view halfs as their equals—a rare thing among the pure-blood race.

Whispers followed me down the hall. Ignoring them was harder than I'd imagined. Every cell in my body demanded that I confront them. And do what? Jump on them like a crazy spider monkey and take them all out? Yeah, not going to win me any fans.

"Alex! Wait up!"

My heart sank at the sound of Olivia's voice. I picked up my pace, practically barreling through a few younger half-bloods who stared at me with wide, frightened eyes. Why were they afraid of me? I wasn't the one who was going to go all God Killer soon. But oh no, they stared at Seth like he *was* a god. Just a few more doors and I could hide in Technical Truths and Legends.

"Alex!"

I recognized Olivia's tone. It was the same one she used to get whenever she and Caleb were about to have one of their quarrels—determined and stubborn as hell.

Crap.

She was right behind me now, and I was only a step away from my classroom. I wasn't going to make it. "Alex," she said. "We need to talk."

"I'm not doing this right now." Because really, being told that it was my fault Caleb was dead was not on the top of my list of things to hear today.

Olivia grabbed my arm. "Alex, I need to talk to you. I know you're upset, but you're not the only one who's allowed to miss Caleb. I was his girlfriend—"

I stopped thinking. Whirling around, I dropped my bag in the middle of the hall and caught her by the throat. In a second, I had her against the wall and on the tips of her toes. Eyes wide, she grabbed my arm and tried to push me off.

I squeezed just a little bit.

Out of the corner of my eyes I saw Lea, her arm no longer in a brace. The daimon half that'd broken her arm had also killed Caleb. Lea stepped forward like she wanted to intervene.

"Look, I get it," I whispered hoarsely. "You loved Caleb. Guess what? So did I. And I miss him, too. If I could go back in time and change that night, I would. But I can't. So please just leave me—"

An arm the size of my waist shot out from nowhere and tossed me back a good five feet. Olivia slumped against the wall, rubbing her throat.

I whirled around and groaned.

Leon, the King of Impeccable Timing, glared at me. "You are in need of a professional babysitter."

I opened my mouth, but then I closed it. Considering some of the things Leon had interrupted in the past, he had no idea how true his statement was. But then I realized something more important. If Leon was back, then my uncle and Aiden were also back.

"You," Leon gestured at Olivia, "get to class." He turned his attention back to me. "You are coming with me."

Biting my tongue, I grabbed my bag off the floor and commenced my walk of shame down the now-crowded hallway. I caught a glimpse of Luke but looked away before I could gauge his expression.

Leon took the stairs—gods know how I loved them—and we didn't speak until we stood in the lobby. The furie statues were gone, but the empty space left a cold hole in my stomach. They'd be back. I was sure of it. It was just a matter of when.

He towered over me when he stopped, nearly seven feet of pure muscle. "Why is it every time I see you, you are about to do something you shouldn't?"

I shrugged. "It's a talent."

Reluctant amusement flickered across his face as he pulled something out of his back pocket. It looked like a piece of parchment. "Aiden asked me to give this to you."

My stomach dropped as I reached out and took the letter, hands shaking. "Is…is he okay?"

His brows furrowed. "Yes. Aiden is fine."

I didn't even try to hide my sigh of relief as I turned the letter over. It was sealed with an official-looking red stamp. When I looked up, Leon was gone. Shaking my head, I went over to one of the marble benches and sat. I had no idea how Leon could move such a massive body around so stealthily. The ground should tremble in his wake.

Curious, I slid my finger under the crease and broke the

seal. Unfolding the letter, I saw Laadan's elegant signature at the bottom. I quickly scanned the parchment once, and then I went back and read it again.

And I read it a third time.

I felt unbearably hot and cold all at once. My mouth dried, my throat seized. Fine tremors racked my fingers, causing the paper to flutter. I stood and then sat back down. The four words replayed before my eyes. It was all I could see. All I cared to know.

Your father is alive.

CHAPTER TWO

Heart racing, I took the steps two at a time. Spying Leon near my uncle's office, I broke into a sprint. He looked mildly alarmed when he saw me.

"What is it, Alexandria?"

I skidded to a halt. "Aiden gave this to you?"

Leon frowned. "Yes."

"Did you read it?"

"No. It wasn't addressed to me."

I clutched the letter to my chest. "Do you know where Aiden is?"

"Yes." Leon's frown turned severe. "He's been back since last night."

"Where is he *right now*, Leon? I need to know."

"I don't see how there could be any reason you'd need Aiden badly enough to interrupt his training." He folded thick arms across his chest. "And shouldn't you be heading to class?"

I stared a moment before I spun around and took off again. Leon wasn't stupid, so he hadn't accidentally told me where

Aiden was, but I didn't care enough to look into the reason behind that.

If Aiden was training, then I knew where to find him. A cold, damp breeze sprayed my cheeks as I burst through the lobby doors and headed toward the training arena. The milky gray sky was typical for late November, making summer seem so long ago.

Classes for lower-level students were being held in the larger training rooms. Instructor Romvi's impatient barking from behind one of the closed doors followed my quick footsteps down the empty hall. Toward the end of the building, across from the med room where Aiden had brought me after Kain had handed my ass to me in training, was a smaller room equipped with the bare necessities and a sensory deprivation chamber.

I had yet to train in that thing.

Peeking through the crack in the door, I saw Aiden. He was in the middle of the mat, squaring off with a punching bag. A fine sheen of sweat coated his ropey muscles as he swung, knocking the bag back several feet.

Any other time I would have admired him rather obsessively, but my fingers spasmed, crunching the letter. I slid through the gap and crossed the room.

"Aiden."

He whipped around, eyes flaring from a cool gray to a thunderous shade. He took a step back, wiping his arm across his forehead. "Alex, what...what are you doing here? Shouldn't you be in class?"

I held the letter up. "Did you read what was in this letter?"

He had the same look as Leon. "No. Laadan asked me to make sure you got it."

Why had she trusted Aiden with such news? I couldn't

even begin to figure that out unless… "Did you *know* what was in this letter?"

"No. She just asked me to give it to you." He bent, swiping a towel off the mat. "What's in the letter that has you chasing me down?"

A stupid, totally unimportant question rose to the surface. "Why did you give it to Leon?"

He averted his eyes, growing still. "I thought it would be best."

My gaze dropped from his face to his neck. There was that thin, silver chain again. I itched to know what he wore, since he wasn't a jewelry type of guy. I dragged my eyes back to his face. "My father is alive."

Aiden tilted his head toward me. "What?"

A bitter feeling settled in my stomach "He's *alive*, Aiden. And he's been at the New York Covenant for years. He was there when I was there." The swirling emotions I felt when I first read the letter picked up again. "I saw him, Aiden! I know I did. The servant with the brown eyes. And he knew—he knew I was his daughter. That must be why he always looked at me strangely. It's probably why I was so drawn to him whenever I saw him. I just didn't know."

Aiden looked pale under his natural tan. "Can I?"

I handed him the letter and then dragged shaking hands through my hair. "You know, there was something different about him. He never looked doped-up like other servants. And when Seth and I were leaving, I saw him fighting the daimons." I paused, drawing in a deep breath. "I just didn't know, Aiden."

His brows furrowed as he scanned the letter. "Gods," he murmured.

Turning away from him, I hugged my elbows. The

sickening feeling I'd been staving off flowed through my stomach. Anger boiled the blood in my veins. "He's a servant—a freaking *servant*."

"Do you know what this means, Alex?"

I faced him, shocked to find him so close. At once I caught the scent of aftershave and saltwater. "Yes. I have to do something! I have to get him out of there. I know I don't know him, but he's my father. I have to do something!"

Aiden's eyes widened. "No."

"No what?"

He folded up the letter in one hand and grabbed my arm with the other. I dug in my heels. "What are you—?"

"Not here," he ordered quietly.

Confused and a bit startled by the fact that Aiden was actually touching me, I let him lead me to the med office across the hall. He shut the door behind him, turning the lock. An uncomfortable heat flooded my system as I realized we were alone in a room with no windows, and Aiden had just locked the door. Seriously, I needed to get a grip because this was *so* not the time for my ridiculous hormones. Okay, there really *wasn't* a time for them.

Aiden faced me. His jaw flexed. "What are you thinking?"

"Uh…" I took a step back. No way was I admitting that. Then I realized he was angry—furious with me. "What did I do now?"

He placed the letter on the table I'd once sat upon. "You will not do something crazy."

My eyes narrowed as I snatched up the letter, finally catching onto why he was so angry. "You expect me to do nothing? And to just let my father rot in servitude?"

"You need to calm down."

"Calm down? That servant in New York is my father.

The father I'd been told was dead!" Suddenly, I remembered Laadan in the library and how she talked about my father as if he was still alive. Rage socked me in the stomach. Why hadn't she told me? I could've spoken to him. "How can I calm down?"

"I…I can't imagine what you're going through, or what you're thinking." He frowned. "Well, yes, I can imagine what you're thinking. You want to storm the Catskills and free him. I know that's what you're thinking."

Of course I was.

He started toward me, his eyes turning a brilliant silver. "No."

I backed up, clutching Laadan's letter to my chest. "I have to do something."

"I know you feel like you need to, but Alex, you cannot return to the Catskills."

"I wouldn't storm it." I edged around the table as he grew closer. "I'll think of something. Maybe I'll get in trouble. Telly said all I needed to do was make one more mistake and I was being sent to the Catskills."

Aiden stared.

The table was now between us. "If I could get back there, then I can talk to him. I have to talk to him."

"Absolutely not," Aiden growled.

My muscles locked. "You can't stop me."

"You want to bet?" He started around the table.

Not really. The fierceness in his expression told me he'd do everything to stop me, which meant I needed to convince him. "He's my father, Aiden. What would you do if it was Deacon?"

Low blow, I knew.

"Don't you even dare bring him into this, Alex. I won't

allow you to get yourself killed. I don't care who it's for. I won't."

Tears burned the back of my throat. "I can't leave him in that kind of life. I can't."

Pain flickered in his steely gaze. "I know, but he's not worth your life."

My arms fell to my sides and I stopped trying to outmaneuver him. "How can you make that decision?" And then the tears I'd been fighting broke free. "How can I not do something?"

Aiden didn't say anything as he placed his hands on my upper arms and guided me to him. Instead of pulling me straight into his embrace, he backed up against the wall and slid down, bringing me along with him. I was nestled in his arms. My legs curled against him, one of my hands fisting his shirt.

The breath I took was shallow, filled with a kind of hurt I couldn't let go. "I'm tired of people lying to me. Everyone lied about my mom, and now this? I thought he was *dead*. And gods, I wish he were, because death is better than what he has to live through." My voice broke and more tears spilled over my cheeks.

Aiden's arms tightened around me, and his hand smoothed a comforting circle over my back. I wanted to stop crying because it was weak and humiliating, but I couldn't stop. Discovering my father's true fate was horrifying. When the worst of the tears subsided, I pulled back a little and lifted my teary gaze.

Damp silky waves of dark hair clung to his forehead and temples. The dim light of the room still highlighted those high cheekbones and lips I'd memorized so long ago. Aiden rarely ever fully smiled, but when he did, it was breathtaking.

There'd been a few times I'd gotten to bask in that rare smile; the last time had been at the zoo.

Seeing him now, truly seeing him, the first time after he'd risked everything to protect me—I wanted to start crying again. Over the last week, I'd replayed what had happened over and over again. Could I have done something differently? Disarmed the Guard instead of shoving my blade deep into his chest? And why had Aiden used a compulsion to cover up what I'd done? Why would he risk so much?

And none of that seemed important right now, not after learning about my father. I wiped under my eyes with my palms. "Sorry for…crying all over you."

"Never apologize for that," he said. I expected him to let go of me at that point, but his arms were still around me. I knew I shouldn't, because it would just bring a world of hurt later, but I let myself relax against him. "You have this knee-jerk reaction to everything."

"What?"

He lowered an arm and tapped my knee. "It's the first initial response. The immediate thought when you hear something. You act on that instead of thinking things through."

I burrowed my cheek against his chest. "That's not a compliment."

His hand moved to the back of my neck, fingers tangling deep in the mess of hair at the nape of my neck. Wondering if he was aware of what he was doing, I held my breath. His hand tightened, holding me so I couldn't pull back too far. Not that I would—no matter how wrong it was, how dangerous or stupid.

"It's not an insult," he said softly. "It's just who you are. You don't stop to think of the danger, only what is right. But sometimes it's not…right."

I mulled that over. "Was using a compulsion on Dawn and the other pure a knee-jerk reaction?"

He took what seemed like forever to answer. "It was, and it wasn't the smartest thing to do, but I couldn't do anything else."

"Why?"

Aiden didn't answer.

I didn't push it. There was a comfort in his arms, in the way his hand traced a soothing circle along my back, that I couldn't find anyplace else. I didn't want to ruin it. In his arms, I was calmer—strangely. I could breathe. I felt safe, grounded. No one else offered that. He was like my very own prescription of Ritalin.

"Becoming a Sentinel was a knee-jerk reaction," I whispered.

Aiden's chest rose and fell under my cheek. "Yeah, it was."

"Do…do you regret it?"

"Never."

I wished I had his kind of resolve. "I don't know what to do, Aiden."

His chin tipped down, brushing over my cheek. His skin was smooth, warm, thrilling, and calming all in one. "We'll figure out a way to get in touch with him. You said he never seemed like he was under the Elixir? We could get a letter to Laadan; she could pass it to him. That would be the safest step."

My heart did a stupid, happy dance. Hope was spreading out of control inside me. "We?"

"Yes. I can easily get a letter to Laadan—a message. It's the safest way for right now."

I wanted to squeeze him but refrained. "No. If you get caught… I can't have that happening."

Aiden laughed softly. "Alex, we've probably broken every

rule there is. I'm not worried about getting busted over passing on a message."

No, we hadn't broken *every* rule.

He pulled back slightly, and I could feel his intense stare on my face. "Did you think I wouldn't help you with something as important as this?"

I kept my eyes closed, because looking at him was a weakness. *He* was my weakness. "Things are…different."

"I know things are different, Alex, but I will always be here for you. I will always help you." He paused. "How can you ever doubt that?"

Like a fool, I opened my eyes. I was sucked right in. It was like everything that'd been said, everything I knew, didn't matter anymore. "I don't doubt that," I whispered.

His lips tipped up on one side. "Sometimes I just don't get you."

"I don't get myself half of the time." I lowered my eyes. "You've already done…too much. What you did in the Catskills?" I swallowed the lump in my throat. "Gods, I never thanked you for it."

"Don't—"

"Don't say it's not worth thanking you for." My gaze flicked up, locking with his. "You saved my life, Aiden, at the risk of your own. So, thank you."

He looked away, his eyes focusing on a spot over my head. "I told you I'd never let anything happen to you." His gaze came back to me and amusement sparkled in those silver pools. "It seems more like a full-time job, though."

My lips quirked. "I've really been trying, you know. Today was the first day I even did anything remotely stupid." I left out the part where I'd been sequestered in my room with a nasty head cold.

"What did you do?"

"You really don't want to know."

He laughed again. "I figured Seth would be keeping you out of trouble."

Realizing I hadn't even thought about Seth since the moment I'd read the letter, I stiffened. I hadn't even thought about the bond. Dammit.

Aiden drew in a deep breath and dropped his arms. "You do know what this means, Alex?"

I struggled to pull myself together. There were important things to deal with. My father, the Council, Telly, the furies, a dozen or so pissed off gods, and Seth. But my brain felt like mush. "What?"

Aiden glanced at the door, as if he was afraid to say it out loud. "Your father wasn't a mortal. He's a half-blood."

CHAPTER THREE

I didn't go back to my classes. Instead, I went to my dorm room and sat on my bed, the letter resting in front of me like a snake ready to spread its venom. I was reeling from learning that my dad was still alive and…I felt so stupid for not figuring it out right away. Laadan's letter didn't come out and say it. Obviously, I understood why she skirted the true bomb she was dropping in the brief letter. How else would the Council have been able to get my father under control? And I'd seen him fight. He was like a ninja with those candleholders.

My father was a freaking half-blood—a *trained* half-blood. Hell, he'd probably been a damn Sentinel, which totally explained how my mom had known him before she met Lucian.

A half-blood.

So, what in the holy Hades did that make me?

The answer seemed too simple. I flopped on my back, staring blindly at the ceiling. Gods, I wanted Caleb to talk this through with, because this couldn't be what it was.

A pure-blood who had children with other pures made happy, little pure babies. A pure-blood who got it on with a mortal created the ever-useful half-blood. But a pure-blood and a halfblood getting together—which was so forbidden, so taboo that I couldn't think of one situation where a child was actually produced—made…what?

I jerked straight up, heart thundering. The first time Aiden had been in my dorm room and I'd looked at him—well, I'd been ogling him, but whatever—and wondered why relationships between halfs and pures had been forbidden for eons. It wasn't the fear of a one-eyed Cyclops, but it kind of was.

A pure-blood and a half-blood made an Apollyon.

"Shit," I said, staring at the letter.

But it had to be more than just that. There was typically only one Apollyon born every generation, with the exception of Solaris and the First, and Seth and me. Which would mean a half and a pure only produced a child a handful of times since the time the gods had walked this earth. There had to be more times when it happened. Or were those babies killed? I wouldn't put it past the pures or the gods to do such a thing if they knew what could come from the joining of a pure and a half. But why had Seth and I been spared? Obviously, they knew what my father was since they'd kept him around. My heart clenched, as did my fists. I pushed the anger down to revisit later. I'd promised Aiden I wouldn't do anything reckless, and my anger always led to something idiotic.

A shiver inched its way down my spine. A sound came from my door, much like a lock being turned. I glanced at the letter, chewing my bottom lip. Then I looked at the clock beside the bed. I was way late for training with Seth.

The door opened and shut. I grabbed the letter, quickly folding it. I knew the moment he stood in the doorway without looking up. A level of awareness danced over my skin and the air filled with electricity.

"What happened today?" he asked simply.

There was very little I could hide from Seth. He would've sensed my emotions from the moment I read the letter and everything that I had been feeling while I'd been with Aiden. He wouldn't know exactly what was causing my feelings to be all over the place—thank the gods—but Seth wasn't stupid. I was a little surprised that he'd waited this long to come find me.

I lifted my gaze. He looked like one of those marble statues that adorned the front of every building here, except his skin was a unique golden color—otherworldly perfection. Sometimes he looked cold, impassive. Especially when his shoulder-length blond hair was pulled back, but it hung loose now, softening the lines of his face. His full lips were usually curved in a smug smile, but now they were pressed together in a hard, tight line.

Aiden had suggested that I keep the letter and its contents to myself. Laadan had broken gods know how many rules by telling me about my father, but I trusted Seth. We were, after all, fated to be together. A couple of months ago I would've laughed if someone had said that we would be doing whatever it was that we were doing. It'd been a case of mutual dislike when we first met, and we still had some epic moments. It wasn't too long ago that I'd threatened to stab him in the eye. And I'd seriously meant it.

Silently, I held out the letter.

Seth took it, quickly unfolding it with long, agile fingers. I tucked my legs underneath me, watching him. There was nothing in his expression that gave away what he was thinking. After what seemed like forever, he glanced up. "Oh, gods."

Not exactly the response I was shooting for.

"You're going to do something incredibly stupid in response to this."

I threw up my hands. "Jeez, does everyone think I'm going to Sparta-charge the Catskills?"

Seth's brows rose.

"Whatever," I grumbled. "I'm not going to attack the Covenant. I have to do something, but it won't be…reckless. Happy? Anyway, do you remember the half-blood we passed when we were watching the Council the first day there?"

"Yes. You were staring at him."

"That's him. I know it. That's why he looked so familiar to me. His eyes." I bit my lip, looking away. "My mom always talked about his eyes."

He sat beside me. "What are you going to do?"

"I'm going to send a letter back to Laadan, a letter for my dad. From there, I don't know." I looked at him. Thick strands of hair shielded his face. "You know what this means, right? That he's a half-blood. And this—" I gestured at us. "We're the reason why relations of the fun kind are forbidden between halfs and pures. The gods know what'll happen if a pure and half hook up."

"It's probably more than that. The gods like the idea of subjugating the halfs. What do you think they did to the mortals during their heyday? The gods subjugated the mortals until it went too far. They still treat the half-bloods like dirt worthy only of being walked upon."

Man, was Seth on a god-hating kick or what? I stared down at my right palm, at the faint rune that only Seth and I could see. "It was him—my father—in the stairwell. I can't explain it, but I know it was."

Seth looked up then, his eyes a strange shade of yellow. "Who knows about this?"

I shook my head. "The Council has to know. Laadan

knew because she was friends with my…my mom and dad. It wouldn't surprise me if Lucian and Marcus knew, too." I frowned. "Do you remember when we overheard Marcus and Telly talking?"

"I remember dropping you on your butt."

"Yeah, you did that because you were staring at Boobs."

His eyes widened and he let out a shocked laugh. "Boobs? What?"

"You know—that girl who was all over you in the Catskills." When his brows rose, I rolled my eyes. So like Seth to have trouble remembering *which* girl. "I'm talking about the one who had, well, huge boobs."

He stared off into the distance for a moment and then laughed again. "Oh. Yeah, that one—wait a second. You named her Boobs?"

"Yeah, and I bet you don't even remember her name."

"Ah…"

"Glad we're on the same page now. Anyway, remember how Telly said that they already had one there? That they could keep them together? Do you think he was talking about my father and me?" If Marcus and Lucian knew, I wanted to bash their heads together, but confronting them would place Laadan in danger.

Seth glanced down at the letter. "That would make sense. Especially considering how badly Telly wanted you to be placed into servitude."

Minister Telly was the Head Minister of all the Councils, and he'd had it out for me from the get-go. My testimony about the events in Gatlinburg had been a complete ruse to get me in front of the entire Council so they could vote me into servitude. And I truly believed that Telly was behind the compulsion that'd been used on me the night I almost turned into a human Popsicle. If Leon hadn't found me, I'd have frozen to death. Then there was the night the equivalent of an Olympian roofie had been given to me in a coarse attempt to catch me in a compromising position with a pure. It would've worked if it hadn't been for Seth and Aiden spotting me with the drink.

My cheeks burned as I remembered that night. I'd pretty much molested Seth—not that he'd complained. Seth had known I was under the influence of the Brew, and he'd tried to control himself, but the bond between us had spewed my revved-up lust all through him. I would've lost my virginity if I hadn't ended the night by puking up my guts. I know the whole situation bothered Seth. He felt guilty for giving in. And Aiden's fist had done a number on Seth's eye after discovering me on the bathroom floor…in Seth's clothing. Aiden couldn't understand how I'd forgiven Seth, and sometimes I couldn't, either. Maybe it was the bond, because what linked us together was strong. Maybe it was something more.

Then there was the pure-blood Guard who'd tried to kill me, saying he needed to "protect his kind." I suspected Minister Telly had been behind that, also.

"Who else knows about this?" Seth dragged me from my musings.

"Laadan asked Aiden to give me this letter, but Leon did instead. Leon claims he didn't look at the letter, and I believe him. It was sealed. See." I pointed out the broken stamp. "Aiden didn't know what was in it, either."

Seth's jaw flexed. "You went to Aiden?"

I knew I needed to proceed with caution. Seth and I weren't together or anything, but I also knew he wasn't messing around with anyone else now. The hot flashes I'd picked up on since returning from the Catskills had only been when he was around me, mostly during our hands-on training sessions. Seth was foremost a guy. It happened…a lot.

"I thought maybe he knew, since Laadan entrusted him with the letter, but he didn't," I said finally.

"But you told him?"

There was really no point in lying. "Yes. He knew I was upset. Obviously, he's trustworthy. He's not going to say anything."

Seth was silent for a heartbeat. "Why didn't you come to me?"

Oh, no. I focused on the floor, then my hands, and finally the wall. "I didn't know where you were. And Leon told me where Aiden was."

"Did you even attempt to find me? It's an island. It wouldn't have been hard to do." He placed the letter on the bed, and out of the corner of my eye, I saw his feet point to me.

I bit my lip. I didn't owe him anything, or did I? Either way, I didn't want to hurt his feelings. Seth might act like he had none, but I knew differently. "I just wasn't thinking. It's not a big deal."

"Okay." He leaned over and his breath warmed my cheek. "I felt your emotions this afternoon."

I swallowed. "Then why didn't you come looking for me?"

"I was busy."

"Then what's the big deal about me not looking for you? You were busy."

Seth brushed the thick hair off my neck, tossing it over my shoulder. My muscles locked up. "Why were you so upset?"

I turned my head. Our gazes locked. "I just found out that my dad's alive, and that he's a servant. That's kind of emotional."

His eyes deepened to a warm amber. "That's a good point."

There wasn't much space between our mouths. A sudden nervousness took over. Seth and I hadn't kissed since the day in the labyrinth. I think my cold had grossed him out, and it wasn't like I'd been pushing it, but I hadn't sneezed or sniffled since early this morning. "You know what?"

He smiled slightly. "What?"

"You don't seem very surprised about my father. You didn't know, did you?" I held my breath, because if he did, I didn't even know what I'd do. But it wouldn't be pretty.

"Why would you even think that?" His eyes narrowed. "You don't trust me?"

"No. I do." And I really did…most of the time. "But you just weren't surprised at all."

Seth sighed. "Nothing surprises me anymore."

I thought of something else. "Do you know which of your parents was a half-blood?"

"I guess it had to be my father. Mother was a pure through and through."

I didn't know that. Then again, there was very little I knew about Seth. Sure, he liked to talk about himself, but it was all on a superficial level. Then there was the greatest mystery of all. "What's your last name?"

"Alex, Alex, Alex," he chided softly, rising to his knees.

I squeezed my hands together, recognizing the calculated edge to his gaze. He was *so* up to something. "What?"

"I want to try something."

Since we were on my bed and Seth was a pervert most of the time, my suspicion level was pretty high. It showed in my voice. "Like what?"

Seth pressed me back until I was lying flat. He hovered above, a slight tilt to his lips. "Give me your left hand."

"Why?"

"Why are you so damn inquisitive?"

I arched a brow. "Why do you always have to invade my personal space?"

"Because I like to." He patted my stomach. "And deep down you like it when I do."

My lips pressed together. I was pretty sure the bond between us liked it when he did. I could feel it right now. It practically purred. Whether I liked it was something I was still trying to figure out.

"Give me your left hand," he ordered again. "We're going to work on your blocking technique."

"And we have to be holding hands to do this?" *In my bed*, I wanted to add.

"Alex."

Sighing loudly, I gave him my hand. "Are we going to sing songs now?"

"You wish." He straddled my thighs, placing a knee on either side. "I have a lovely singing voice."

"Do we have to do this right now? I'm not really feeling it after everything." Practicing blocking techniques of the mental kind required concentration and determination—two things I was lacking right now. Well, to be honest, concentration was something I usually lacked on most days.

"Now is the best time. Your emotions are all over the place. You need to learn how to push through that." Seth grabbed my other hand, threading his fingers through mine. He bent so far that the edges of his hair brushed my cheeks. "Close your eyes. Picture the walls."

Closing my eyes was something I did not want to do with Seth sitting on me. The bond between us had been growing stronger every day. I could feel it moving low in my tummy, thrumming to the surface. My toes curled inside my fuzzy socks. The same feeling I'd had the day I blew up the boulder swamped me. I wanted to touch him. Or the bond wanted me to touch him.

Seth tipped his head to the side. "I know what you're feeling right now. I totally approve of it."

My cheeks burned. "Gods, I hate you."

He chuckled. "Picture the walls. They're solid, cannot be breached."

I pictured the brick walls. In my mind, they were neon pink. With sparkles. I gave the walls sparkles because they gave me something to focus on. Seth had said the technique could work against compulsions if done correctly, but when dealing with emotions, the walls weren't built around the mind, they were built through the stomach and over the heart. The walls formed in my mind first and then I shifted them down, giving myself a body of armor.

"I can still feel it," Seth said, shifting restlessly above me.

This really must suck for him, I realized. He could tell I was still obsessed with Aiden, upset over my dad, and conflicted over him. And the only thing I got to pick up from him was when he was feeling randy.

The damn cord inside me—my connection to Seth—started to hum, demanding that I pay attention. It was like an annoying pet…or like Seth. I wondered if I could use the cord to block my emotions. Opening my eyes, I started to ask but then shut my mouth.

Seth had his eyes closed, and he looked like he was really concentrating on something. His lids fluttered every so often, lips drawn into a tight, tense line. Then the marks flowed over his skin, moving so fast that the glyphs were nothing more than a blur as they raced down his neck, under the collar of his shirt.

My heart jumped. So did the cord inside me. I tried to pull my hand free before those marks reached my skin. "Seth."

His eyes snapped open, glazed over. The marks glided over his skin. A burst of crackling amber light radiated from his forearm. Struggling to get out from underneath him and away from that damn cord, I only succeeded in having my hands pinned down.

Panic unfurled, ripping through me. "Seth!"

"It's okay," he said.

But it wasn't okay. I didn't want that cord to do what I knew it was going to do. And then it was doing it. The amber cord wrapped around our hands, snapping and sparking, spreading down my arm. I jerked back, trying to scoot sway, but Seth held on, his eyes locked with mine.

"The cord—it's the purest power. Akasha," he said. Akasha was the fifth and final element, and it could only be harnessed by the gods and the Apollyon. The hue of Seth's eyes turned luminous. They almost looked crazy. "Hold on."

He wasn't giving me much of a choice. My gaze fell to our hands. Pulsating, the cord tightened and flared a brilliant amber. A blue cord wiggled out from underneath the amber cord, spilling drops of incandescent light onto the bedspread. Vaguely, I hoped we didn't catch the bed on fire. That would be hard to explain.

The blue cord flickered in and out, fluttering. Vaguely, I realized it was mine and weaker than the amber one. Then the blue jumped and pulsed. My left hand started to burn as the skin pricked. Recognizing the feeling, I freaked.

I squirmed, trying to scoot back. I didn't want another rune, and we hadn't held on this long last time. Something was very different about this. "Seth, this doesn't feel—" My body jerked, cutting off my own words.

Seth's body tensed. "Good gods…"

And then I felt it—akasha—shifting through the cords, leaving me and entering Seth. It was kind of like a daimon tag, but not painful. No…this was nice, heady. I stopped struggling, letting the glorious tug and pull lift me away. I didn't think about anything. There were no concerns or fears. The pain in my hand melted away, leaving only a dull ache that was spreading elsewhere. There was just this…and Seth. My eyes drifted shut and a sigh leaked out. Why had I been so afraid of this?

There was a flash of light that I could still see even though my eyes were closed. Seth dropped my hand and it fell limply to my side. The bed dipped beside my head from where he placed his hands. I felt his breath on my cheek, and it felt like warm, salty air rolling off the ocean.

"Alex?"

"Hmm…?"

"You okay?" He placed his lips to my cheek. I smiled.

Seth chuckled, and then his mouth was making its way to mine, and I opened for him. The edges of his hair tickled my cheeks as the kiss deepened. His fingers drifted down the front of my blouse and then they were sliding over the bare skin of my stomach. I wrapped my leg around his, and we were moving together on the bed. His lips were dancing all over my flushed skin as his hands slid down, fingers finding the button on my jeans.

A second later, there was a knock on my door and a booming voice. "Alexandria?"

Seth stilled above me, panting. "You have got to be freaking kidding me."

Leon knocked again. "Alexandria, I know you're in there."

Dazed, I blinked several times. The room slowly came

back into focus, as did Seth's disgruntled expression. I almost laughed, except I felt…off.

"You better answer him, Angel, before he barges in here."

I tried but failed. I took a deep breath. "Yeah." I cleared my throat. "Yeah, I'm in here."

There was a pause. "Lucian is requesting your presence immediately." Another gap of silence followed. "He is also requesting to see you, Seth."

Seth frowned as the gleam in his eyes faded. "How in the world does he know I'm in here?"

"Leon…just knows." I pushed at him weakly. "Get off."

"I was trying to." Seth rolled over, running his hands down his face.

I scowled at him and sat up. A wave of dizziness swept over me. My gaze moved from Seth to my curled hand. Slowly, I opened it. Glowing in iridescent blue was a glyph that was shaped like a staple. Both of my hands were marked.

He leaned over my shoulder. "Hey, you got another one."

I swung at him and missed by a mile. "You did that on purpose."

Seth shrugged as he straightened his shirt. "You didn't mind now, did you?"

"That's not the point, you douche nozzle. I shouldn't have these."

He glanced up, brows arched. "Look, I didn't do it on purpose. I have no idea how or why it happens. Maybe it's happening because it's supposed to."

"People are waiting," Leon called from the hallway. "Time is of the essence."

Seth rolled his eyes. "They couldn't have waited another thirty or sixty minutes?"

"I don't know what you think you were going to get accomplished in that extra time."

Still feeling a little dizzy, I swayed when I stood and looked down at my unbuttoned shirt and bra. *Now how did that happen?*

Seth grinned at me.

I fumbled with the buttons, turning a thousand shades of red. My anger with Seth smoldered inside me, but I was too tired to get into a verbal smackdown. And then there was Lucian. What the hell could he want?

"You missed one." Seth sprung to his feet and clasped the button above my navel. "And stop blushing. Everyone is going to think we weren't training."

"We were?"

His grin spread, and I wanted to smack him upside the head. But I took the time to smooth my hair and tug out the wrinkles in my shirt. By the time we met Leon in the hall, I felt like I looked pretty decent.

Leon eyed me like he knew exactly what had been going on in the dorm. "Nice of you two to finally join me."

Seth shoved his hands into his pockets. "We take training really seriously. Sometimes we get so caught up in it, it takes a few minutes for us to come down."

My mouth dropped open. Now I really wanted to hit him.

Leon's eyes narrowed on Seth then he turned stiffly, gesturing for us to follow him. I trailed behind the two, wondering why Leon would care what I was doing in the room. Everyone wanted us to embrace our Apollyon goodness. Then I thought of Aiden and my heart seized.

Well, probably not *everyone*.

A weird, twisty feeling took over my stomach. What'd just happened in there? We'd gone from talking to full-on making out when nothing like that had occurred since the Catskills. I glanced down at my hands.

The super-special cord had happened.

I felt sort of sick when I looked up and watched Seth swagger down the hall. Cheeks glowing, he looked like he could barely contain the energy rushing through him. Confusion swept through me. The whole energy transfer thing had actually felt good, and so had the stuff afterward, but Aiden's face haunted me.

Seth glanced over his shoulder at me as Leon opened the door. Darkness had already started to fall, but the shadow that crept over Seth's face was no product of the night.

I tried to build up the wall around me. And I failed.

CHAPTER FOUR

I was exhausted by the time I dropped into the seat farthest from Marcus's desk. Those stairs had been a bitch, but I was grateful that I hadn't been expected to walk to the adjoining island where Lucian lived. I didn't believe I'd have made it. All I wanted to do was curl up and go to bed—go anywhere other than this brightly lit room.

"Where is everyone?" Seth asked, standing behind me. His hands rested on the back of the chair, but his fingers, shielded by my hair, were pressed into my back. "I thought time was of the essence."

Leon looked smug. "I must have mistaken the time."

A tired smile tugged at my lips as I pulled my legs up, tucking them under me. Like I said, Leon was the King of Impeccable Timing. Maybe I'd get a nap before everyone showed up. I closed my eyes, scarcely paying attention to Leon and Seth trying to out-snark one another.

"Most training doesn't occur in a dorm room," Leon said. "Or have they drastically changed methods?"

Snark point two to Leon.

"The kind of training that we have to do is unconventional." Seth paused and I knew he had that horrible smile on his face. The one I'd wanted to drop-kick off so many times. "Not that a Sentinel would fully understand the amount of effort that goes into preparing an Apollyon."

Snark point three to Seth.

I yawned as I scooted down in the chair, resting my cheek on the back of it.

"Is something wrong, Alexandria?" Leon asked. "You look awfully pale."

"She's fine," Seth answered. "Our training was rather… exhausting. You know, there's a lot of moving around. Sweating, thrus—"

"Seth," I snapped, reluctantly handing over snark points four, five, and six to him.

Thankfully, the doors to Marcus's office opened and an entourage of people entered. First was my pure-blood uncle, the Dean of the Covenant in North Carolina. Behind him was my pure-blood stepfather Lucian, the Minister of the North Carolina Covenant. He was in his ridiculous white robes, his stark black hair hanging down his back, secured in a leather thong. He was a handsome man, but there was always a level of coldness and fakeness to him no matter how warm his words might be. He was flanked by four of his Guards, as if he expected a fleet of daimons to jump on him and suck out all his aether. I suppose, given the recent events, he couldn't be too careful. And behind them were Guard Linard and Aiden.

I averted my eyes and prayed Seth actually kept his mouth shut.

Marcus glanced at me as he sat behind his desk, brows rising curiously. "Are we keeping you from a nap, Alexandria?"

No, *how are you?* or *good to see you alive*. Yeah, he loved me lots.

Leon retreated to the corner, folding his arms. "They were *training*." He paused. "In her room."

I wanted to die.

Marcus frowned, but Lucian—oh, dear Lucian—had a typical response. Sitting down in one of the chairs across from Marcus, he spread out his robes and laughed. "It is expected. They are young and drawn to one another. You cannot fault them for seeking privacy."

I couldn't help it. My eyes found Aiden. He stood beside Leon and Linard, his gaze flitting over the room, stopping and lingering on me before passing on. I let go of the breath I'd been holding and focused on my uncle.

Marcus's eyes were like emerald jewels, just like my mother's, but harder. "Fated or not, the rules of the Covenant still apply to them, Minister. And from what I've heard, Seth has a hard time remaining in his own room at your house during the night."

This seriously couldn't get any more embarrassing.

Seth leaned over the back of my chair and, lowering his head, whispered in my ear. "I think we've been found out."

There was no way Aiden could've heard Seth, but anger rolled off him in waves, so much so that Seth tipped his head up, met Aiden's stare, and smiled.

I'd had it. Sitting up straight, I knocked Seth's arm off the back of my chair. "Is this why we're having a meeting? Because, seriously, I could really use a nap instead."

Marcus eyed me coolly. "Actually, we are here to discuss the events at the Council."

Ice drenched my stomach. I tried to keep my face blank, but my eyes darted to Aiden. He didn't look too concerned. In fact, he was still eyeballing Seth.

“There are several things that we have discovered regarding our trip,” Lucian said.

Marcus nodded, his fingers forming a steeple under his chin. “The daimon attack is one of them. I know that some have been able to plan attacks.”

My mother had been one of them. She’d been behind the attack on Lake Lure during the summer, the very first proof some daimons could form cohesive plans.

“But that type of large-scale attack is unheard of,” Marcus continued, glancing at me. “I know…I know your mother had insinuated that such was coming, but to pull something off of that nature seems improbable.”

Aiden cocked his head to the side. “What are you saying?”

“I think they had help.”

My heart tripped up. “From the inside—from a half or a pure?”

Lucian huffed. “That is absurd.”

“I do not think that is entirely out of the question,” Leon said, eyes narrowing upon the Minister.

“No half or pure would willingly assist a daimon.” Lucian folded his hands.

“It may not be willingly, Minister. The pure or half may’ve been coerced,” Marcus continued, and where I should’ve felt relief, something ugly still sat inside me. What if someone had actually let them in past the gates?

No. No way could that have happened. If Marcus’s suspicions were right, it had to be under duress.

Marcus glanced at me. “It’s something we need to keep in mind for Alexandria’s safety. The daimons were there for her. They could try it again. Capture a half or pure Guard or Sentinel, have them lead the daimons right to her. It is something to be aware of.”

I grew very still, and I imagined so did Seth and Aiden. The daimons hadn't been after me. It'd been a lie that we told so that I could leave the Catskills immediately after…after I'd killed the pure-blood Guard.

"I agree." Aiden's voice was remarkably even. "They could make another attempt."

"Speaking of her safety"—Lucian twisted in his seat toward me—"Minister Telly's intentions were painfully clear, and if I'd been aware of what he'd planned, I never would have agreed to the Council session. My utmost priority is to see that you remain safe, Alexandria."

I shifted uncomfortably. Growing up, Lucian hadn't even pretended to care about me. But since I'd returned to the Covenant at the end of May, he'd acted like I was his long-lost daughter. He didn't fool me. If I weren't the second coming of the Apollyon, he wouldn't be sitting here right now. Who was I kidding? I'd probably have been eaten by daimons in Atlanta.

His eyes met mine. I'd never liked his eyes. They were an unnatural black—the color of obsidian and cold. Up close, there didn't seem to be any pupils. "I'm afraid that Minister Telly may have been behind the compulsion and the unsavory act of giving you that drink."

I suspected as much, but to hear him say it left me queasy. As the Head of all the Ministers, Telly exerted a lot of control. If it hadn't been for Minister Diana Elders's vote, I would've been cast into slavery.

"Do you think he will attempt something else?" Aiden's deep, melodic voice was hard not to respond to.

Lucian shook his head. "I would like to say no, but I fear that he will attempt something again. The best we can do at this point is to ensure that Alexandria stays out of trouble and does not give the Head Minister any excuse to place her into servitude."

Several pairs of eyes landed on me. I smothered another yawn and tipped my chin up. "I'll *try* not to do anything crazy."

Marcus arched a brow. "That would be a nice change."

I glared at him, rubbing my left palm over my bent knee. The skin still felt weird and tingly.

"Isn't there a more proactive method?" Seth asked, leaning on my chair. "I think we all can agree that Telly will try something again. He doesn't want Alex to Awaken. He's afraid of us."

"Afraid of you," I muttered, then yawned again.

Seth tipped my chair back in response, causing me to grasp the arms. He grinned at me, which was so at odds with his next words. "He almost had Alex. He was one vote shy of servitude. Who says he won't build some trumped-up charge against her and sway their votes in his favor?"

"Diana will never compromise her position to serve Telly's wishes," Marcus said.

"Whoa. On a first name basis?" I said.

Marcus ignored my comment. "What do you suggest, Seth?"

Seth pushed off the back of my chair and moved to stand beside me. "How about removing him from his position? Then he has no power."

Lucian watched Seth with an approving look in his eyes and I'd swear Seth beamed. Almost like he'd brought home his report card with all A's on it and was about to get a pat on the head. *Weird*. Weird and extraordinarily creepy.

"Are you suggesting a political coup? That we rebel against the Head Minister?" Marcus turned his disbelief on Lucian. "And you have no response to this?"

"I would never want to stoop to something so distasteful, but Head Minister Telly is rooted in the old ways. You know that he wants nothing more than to see us regress as a society," Lucian replied smoothly. "He will go to great extremes to protect his beliefs."

"What are his beliefs, exactly?" I asked. The leather made unattractive squishing noises as I sank back in the seat.

"Telly would love to see us no longer intermingling with mortals. If he had his way, we'd do nothing but dedicate ourselves to worshipping the gods." Lucian smoothed a pale hand over his robes. "He feels it is the Council's duty to protect Olympus instead of leading our kind into the future and stepping into our rightful place."

"And he sees us as a threat to the gods," Seth said, crossing his arms. "He knows he can't come after me, but Alex is vulnerable until she Awakens. Something has to be done about him."

I made a face. "I'm not vulnerable."

"But you are." Aiden's eyes were gunmetal gray when they settled on me. "If Head Minister Telly truly fears that Seth will be a threat down the road, then he will seek to take you out of the equation. He has the power to do so."

"I understand that, but Seth isn't going to go crazy on the Council. He's not going to try to take over the world once I Awaken." I glanced at him. "Right?"

Seth smiled. "You'd be by my side."

Ignoring him, I wrapped my arms around my legs. "Telly can't want to take me out just on some idea of a threat." I thought of my father. I knew beyond a doubt he was behind that, too. "There has to be more to it than that."

"Telly lives to serve the gods," Lucian said. "If he feels they may be threatened, that is all the reason he needs."

"Do you not live to serve the gods?" Leon asked.

Lucian barely looked in the direction of the pure-blood Sentinel. "I do, but I also live to serve the best interests of my people."

Marcus rubbed his brow wearily. "Telly is not our only concern. There are also the gods themselves."

"Yes." Lucian nodded. "There is also the issue of the furies."

I ran my hand over my forehead, forcing myself to concentrate on this conversation. It was a big deal that they were even including me in this. So, I guessed I should pay attention and keep the snark to a minimum.

"The furies attack only when they perceive a threat to the pure-bloods and to the gods," Marcus explained. "Their appearance at the Covenants before the daimon attack was solely a precautionary act from the gods. It was a warning that if we could not keep the daimon population under control, or if our existence was exposed to the mortals through the daimons' actions, they'd respond. And when the daimons launched their attack on the Covenant, the furies were released. But they went after *you*, Alex. Even though there were daimons they could've fought, they perceived you as the biggest threat."

The furies had ripped through daimon and innocent alike in those bloody moments after the daimon siege and had come after me. Not going to lie—I'd never been more terrified in my life.

"They will be back," Leon added. "It is their nature. Maybe not immediately, but they will."

My head was spinning. "I figured as much, but I haven't done anything wrong."

"You exist, my dear. That is all they need," said Lucian. "And you are the weaker of the two."

I was also the sleepier of the two.

Seth rocked back on his heels. "If they come back, I'll destroy them."

"Good luck with that." I closed my eyes, giving them a break from the harsh light. "They'll just burn up and come right back."

"Not if I kill them."

"With what?" asked Aiden. "They are gods. No weapon made by man or demigod will kill them."

When I opened my eyes, Seth was smiling. "Akasha," he said. "That would put them down permanently."

"You don't have that kind of power now," Leon stated, jaw tensed.

Seth just continued to smile until Lucian cleared his throat and spoke. "I never did get to see the furies. It would have been…something to witness."

"They were beautiful," I said. Everyone turned to me. "At first, they were. Then they changed. I've never seen anything like that. Anyway, one said that Thanatos wouldn't be pleased with their return after…I got rid of them. She said something about the road the Powers had chosen and that I would be their tool. The oracle had said something like that too, before she poofed."

"Who are 'the Powers'?" Leon asked.

Aiden nodded. "That's a good question."

"That is not a concern. The furies are," Lucian responded, dismissing the concept with a flick of his slender wrist. "Like Telly, they are operating on old fears. The furies are loyal to Thanatos. If the furies come again, I fear that Thanatos will not be far behind."

Marcus dropped his hand to the top of the glossy mahogany desk. "I cannot have the gods attacking the school. I have hundreds of students I must keep safe. The furies show no discrimination in their kills."

Not once had he mentioned keeping me safe. That kind of stung. We might be related, but it didn't make us a real family. Marcus hadn't even smiled at me—not once. I really didn't have anyone left. That made getting to my father all the more important.

"I suggest we move Alex to a safe place," Lucian offered.

"What?" My voice squeaked.

Lucian glanced at me. "The furies know to look for you here. We could move you someplace safe."

Seth sat on the arm of my chair, crossing his long legs at the ankle. He didn't seem surprised by any of this.

I tapped his back, gaining his attention. "Did you know about this?" I whispered.

He didn't answer.

The look I gave him promised trouble later and not the fun kind. Seth could've at least given me a heads-up about this.

Aiden frowned. "Where would you take her?"

My eyes went to him again. The muscles in my chest clenched when our gazes locked momentarily. At the moment, if I concentrated hard enough, I could still feel his arms around me. Not the best tactic when everyone was discussing my future like I wasn't even sitting here.

"The fewer people who know, the better," Lucian replied. "She would be well protected by my best Guards and Seth."

Marcus appeared to consider this. "We wouldn't have to worry about the furies attacking here." He looked in my direction, his expression guarded. "But if she leaves the Covenant now, she will not graduate and become a Sentinel."

My stomach turned over. "Then I can't leave. I have to graduate."

Lucian smiled, and I wanted to punch him. "Dear, you do not have to worry about becoming a Sentinel now. You will become an Apollyon."

"I don't care! Being an Apollyon isn't my whole life! I need to become a Sentinel. That's what I've always wanted." Those last words sat oddly on my chest. What I always wanted was to have choices. Becoming a Sentinel was the lesser of two evils in reality.

"Your safety is more important than what you desire." Lucian's voice was hard, throwing me back to when I'd been the little girl who'd ventured into a room I wasn't supposed to be in or dared to speak out of turn. That was the real Lucian and it snuck through his facade.

No one else noticed.

I squeezed my thighs until they ached. "No. I need to become a Sentinel." I looked at Seth for help, but he was suddenly interested in the tips of his boots. "None of you understand. Daimons took my mom from me and turned her into a monster. Look at what they did to me! No." I struggled for breath, knowing I was two seconds from losing it. "Besides, no matter where you take me, the furies will find me. They're gods! It's not like I can hide forever."

Lucian faced me fully. "It would give us time."

Anger rushed through me. I almost came out of the chair. "Time for me to Awaken? Then what? You don't care what happens to me?"

"Nonsense," Lucian said. "Not only will you have power, Seth will be able to protect both of you."

"I don't need Seth to protect me!"

Seth glanced over his shoulder at me. "You know how to make a guy feel useful."

"Shut up," I hissed. "You know what I mean. I can fight.

I've killed daimons and I fought the furies and lived. I don't need Seth to be my babysitter."

Leon snorted. "You do need a babysitter, but I doubt he's qualified for the job."

Aiden coughed, but it sounded an awful lot like a choked laugh.

"Do you think you can do a better job?" Seth's voice was casual, but I felt him tense. I also knew he wasn't talking to Leon. "Because you're more than welcome to try," he added.

Aiden's eyes went from gray to silver. His full lips tilted into a smirk as he met Seth's stare. "I think we both know the answer to that."

My jaw hit the floor.

Straightening, Seth squared his shoulders. Before he could say something, which I felt sure would be very bad, I jumped from the seat. "I can't leave the—" Bright dots danced before my eyes, making everything a blur as my stomach tilted dangerously. "Whoa..."

Seth was at my side in an instant, an arm around my waist. "Are you okay?" He lowered me back into the chair. "Alex?"

"Yeah," I breathed, slowly lifting my head. Everyone was staring at me. Aiden had stepped forward, eyes wide. My cheeks burst with heat. "I'm fine. Seriously. I'm just a little tired."

Seth knelt beside me, taking my hand. He squeezed gently as he glanced over his shoulder. "She's had a cold all week."

"She's had a *cold*?" Lucian curled his lip. "How...very mortal."

I shot him a hateful look.

"But we...halfs do not get sick," Marcus said, eyes narrowing on me.

"Well, you can tell that to the box of Kleenex I've been

living with." I dragged my fingers through my hair. "Seriously, I'm fine now."

Marcus suddenly stood. "I think we are done for the evening. We all can agree that nothing needs to be decided at this moment."

Lucian, who had grown quiet and docile, nodded.

The discussion ended and I got a momentary reprieve. I wouldn't be leaving the Covenant now, but I couldn't shake the dread gnawing at my stomach that, eventually, the decision wouldn't be mine to make.

CHAPTER FIVE

I overslept the following morning and missed my first two classes. It kind of worked out, since I didn't have to face Olivia after trying to choke her the day before, but the exhaustion from the previous night continued to drag at me. I spent the break before my afternoon classes arguing with Seth.

"What is your deal?" He pushed his chair back.

"I've already told you." I glanced around the sparsely populated common room. It was better than eating in the cafeteria where everyone stared at us. "I know you knew about Lucian's plan to put me in the Apollyon Relocation Program."

Seth groaned. "Okay. Fine. He may have mentioned it. So what? It's a smart idea."

"It's not a smart idea, Seth. I need to graduate, not go into hiding." I looked down at my barely touched cold-cut sub. My stomach turned over. "I'm not going to run."

He leaned back in the chair, lacing his hands behind his head. "Lucian does have your best interests in mind."

"Oh, gods. Do not start with the Lucian crap. You don't know him like I do."

"People change, Alex. He may have been a giant douche before, but he's changed."

I leveled a look at him, and suddenly, I didn't even know why I was arguing. My shoulders slumped. "What is the point, anyway?"

Seth frowned. "What do you mean?"

"Nothing." I toyed with my straw.

He leaned forward, nudging my plate. "You should eat more."

"Thanks, Dad," I snapped.

He held up his hands, sitting back. "Simmer down, Cuddle Bunny."

"All of this is your fault, anyway."

Seth snorted. "How is this my fault?"

I scowled. "No one wants to kill you, but you're the one who'll have the potential to wipe out the entire Olympian Court. But everyone is like, 'Let's kill the one who isn't doing anything!' And you can just skip off into the sunset while I'm dead."

His lips twitched again. "I wouldn't skip off if you were dead. I'd be sad."

"You'd be sad because you wouldn't be the God Killer." I picked up my sub, turning it over slowly. "Olivia hates me."

"Alex..."

"What?" I looked up. "She does, because I let Caleb die."

His eyes narrowed. "You didn't let Caleb die, Alex."

I sighed, suddenly wanting to cry. It was official: I was certifiably whacked out today. "I know. I miss her."

"Have you tried talking to her?" His eyes widened at my look. He motioned at the sub. "Eat."

Grudgingly, I took a huge, sloppy bite.

Seth arched a brow as he watched me. "Hungry?"

I swallowed. The food formed a heavy lump in my stomach. "No."

We didn't talk for a few minutes. Without wanting to, I turned over my left hand and looked at where the staple-shaped rune glowed softly. "Did…did you do this on purpose?"

"What? The rune?" He took my hand, holding it so my palm faced up. "No, I didn't do it on purpose. I've already told you that."

"I don't know. You looked like you were concentrating really hard when it happened."

"I was concentrating on your emotions." Seth ran his thumb around the glyph, coming close to touching it. "You don't like this, do you?"

"No," I whispered. Another mark meant one more step toward becoming someone—something else.

"It's natural, Alex."

"It doesn't feel natural." My eyes flicked to his. "What does this one mean?"

"Strength of the gods," he answered, surprising me. "The other one means courage of the soul."

"Courage of the soul?" I laughed. "That doesn't make sense."

His hand slid to my wrist, resting his thumb over my pulse. "They are the first marks the Apollyons receive."

My wrist seemed so small in his hand, fragile even. "Did yours come early?"

"No."

I sighed. "What happened…between us last night?"

A wicked grin played over his lips. "Well, most kids call it making out."

"That's not what I meant." I pulled my hand free and rubbed my palm over the edge of the table. "I felt it—the energy or whatever you want to call it—leaving me and going into you."

"Did it hurt you?"

I shook my head. "It kind of felt good."

His nostrils flared as if he smelled something he liked. Then, without any warning, he leaned over the table between us, clasped my cheeks and brought his mouth to mine. The kiss was soft, teasing, and felt really weird. Kissing last night really hadn't counted—or at least I'd convinced myself of that. So, this was the first real kiss since the Catskills, and it was a totally public display. And I was still holding the sub in my right hand. So yeah, it felt bizarre.

Seth pulled back, smiling. "I think we should do that more often, then."

My cheeks were burning because I knew people were staring. "Kissing?"

He laughed. "I'm all about kissing more, but I meant what happened last night."

Out of nowhere, anger crept over me. "Why? Did you feel anything?"

One brow arched. "Oh, I felt something."

I took a deep breath and let it out slowly. "I meant when you were holding my hand and the mark appeared. Did you feel anything?"

"Nothing you apparently want me to talk about."

"Gods." I squeezed the sub. Globs of mayo splattered off the plastic plate. "I don't even know why I'm talking to you."

Seth slowly exhaled. "Are you PMSing or something? Because your mood swings are killing me."

I stared a moment, thinking, *Wow, did he really just go there*?

And then I cocked back my arm and launched the sub across the table. It hit his chest with a somewhat satisfying plop, but it was the look on his face as he jumped out of his seat that almost had me smiling. A cross between disbelief and horror marked his features as he knocked pieces of lettuce and ham off his shirt and pants.

There were only a handful of people in the common room, mostly younger pure-bloods. All of them stared, eyes wide.

Throwing a sub at the Apollyon probably wasn't something that should be done in public. But I couldn't help it; I laughed.

Seth's head jerked up. His eyes were a heated, angry ocher. "Did that make you feel better?"

My eyes watered from laughing so hard. "Yeah, it kind of did."

"You know, let's cancel training after class for today." His jaw flexed, cheeks flushed. "Get some rest."

I rolled my eyes. "Whatever."

Seth opened his mouth to say something else but stopped. Brushing off the last of the ham and cheese, he pivoted around and left. I couldn't believe I'd just thrown my lunch at Seth. That seemed a little extreme even for me.

But it was funny.

I giggled to myself.

"Are you going to clean that up?"

Jumping a little in my seat, I looked up. Linard stepped out from behind one of the columns, eyeing the mess on the floor. "Are you, like, watching me?"

He smiled tightly. "I'm here to make sure you are safe."

"And *that* is kind of creepy." I pushed out of my seat, grabbing a napkin off my plate. I picked up what I could, but the mayo was stuck to the carpet. "Is this Lucian's idea?"

"No." He folded his hands behind his back. "It was Dean Andros's request."

I stilled. "For real?"

"For real," he replied. "You should get going. Your next class will begin soon."

I nodded absently, tossed my trash, and grabbed my bag. Marcus's order surprised me. I expected Lucian to sic his Guards on me. He wouldn't want anything to happen to his precious Apollyon. Maybe Marcus didn't find me as distasteful as I thought he did.

Linard followed me out of the common room, keeping a discreet distance. It reminded me of the day I'd bought the spirit boats that Caleb and I had released into the sea. The memory tugged at my heart and worsened my foul mood. I was like a zombie in the rest of my classes. After a quick change into my training clothes, I walked into Gutter Fighting. Instructor Romvi looked absurdly pleased with my appearance.

I dropped my bag and leaned against the wall, pretending that I wasn't bothered by the fact that I had no one to talk to. The last time I'd even been in this class, Caleb had still been alive.

Pressing my lips together, I let my gaze roam over the wall where the weapons were kept. I'd grown so used to this room during my practices with Aiden that it was like home to me. Standing near the wall of things meant to kill daimons, Jackson grinned at something another half-blood said. Then he looked straight at me and smirked.

Once upon a time I'd found him hot, but somewhere between my daimon mom murdering his girlfriend's parents—if he was actually still with Lea—and the last time I squared off with him, I'd stopped thinking so highly of him.

I held his stare until he looked away. Then I continued my perusal. Olivia stood next to Luke, tying her curly hair into a ponytail. Bruises marked the caramel-colored skin of her neck. I glanced down at my hands. I'd done that.

Gods, what had I been thinking? Guilt and shame tore through me. When I looked up, Luke was watching me. His stare wasn't hostile or anything, just…sad.

I looked away, chewing on my lip. I did miss my friends. And I really missed Caleb.

Class quickly began, and even though I was tired, I threw myself into it. I got paired with Elena for a series of cinch work and holds. Going through the various techniques, my brain was finally able to shut down. Here, in training, I didn't think of anything. There was no sorrow or loss, no fate to deal with or father to save. I imagined this was what being a Sentinel would be like. When I'd eventually go out hunting, I wouldn't have to think about anything other than locating daimons and killing them. Maybe that was the real reason behind wanting to be a Sentinel, because then I could go through life…and do what? Kill. Kill. And kill some more.

That wasn't what I really wanted, deep down inside. I was just realizing that now?

Even slow on my feet, I was a bit faster than Elena. When we moved into takedowns and reversals, which consisted of getting thrown down and trying to get out of it, I was able to keep her pinned, but I was slowing down, growing weary.

She broke my hold and tipped her hips, rolling me onto my back. Staring down at me, she frowned. "Are…are you feeling okay? You look really pale."

I really needed to Google how long the lingering effects of a cold lasted, because this was seriously getting annoying. All I wanted was a bed. Before I could respond to Elena's question, Instructor Romvi appeared behind us. I bit back a groan.

"If you're able to talk, perhaps you are not training hard enough." Romvi's pale eyes were like glaciers. He loved to terrorize me in class; I'm sure he'd missed me. "Elena, off the mats."

She stood and slinked off, leaving me with the Instructor. Around us, students were sparring. I rolled to my feet and shifted my weight restlessly, preparing myself mentally for whatever he was going to throw at me. I turned away, placing my hands on my hips.

His hand smacked down on my shoulder. "One should never turn their back in war."

Shrugging his grip off, I faced him. "I didn't realize we were at war."

Something gleamed in his eyes. "We are always at war, especially in my class." He looked down his hawkish nose at me, which was a common practice since he was a pure-blood who'd once been a Sentinel. "Speaking of which, it is nice of you to finally join us, Alexandria. I was beginning to believe you thought training was no longer necessary."

Several responses rolled to the tip of my tongue, but I knew better than to let them out.

He looked disappointed. "I heard that you fought during the daimon siege."

Knowing fewer words usually ended with less of my butt being kicked, I nodded while I pictured Pegasus landing on his head and biting him in the neck.

"You also fought the furies and survived. Only warriors could claim such a feat."

My gaze slid past him to where Olivia and Luke now stood watching me from the edge of the mats. How many times had we been in this position? But this was different because Caleb used to be among them.

"Alexandria?"

I focused on him, mentally cringing. I should never take my eyes off Romvi when he was talking. "I did fight the furies."

Interest sparked in his eyes. "Show me what you did."

Caught off-guard, I took a step back. "What do you mean?"

A small smile tugged up one side of his lips. "Show me how you fought the furies."

I dampened my lips nervously. I had no idea how I'd fought the furies and survived—only that everything had turned amber, like someone had splashed the tawny color over my eyes. "I don't know. Everything was happening so fast."

"You don't know." He raised his hand and the sleeve of his tunic-style shirt slipped up his arm, revealing the downward-turned torch tattoo. "I find that hard to believe."

I experienced a momentary lapse of sanity. "What's up with the tattoo?"

His jaw clenched, and I expected him to attack. But he didn't. "Jackson!"

Loping onto the mats, Jackson came to a stop and rested his hands on his narrow hips. "Sir?"

Romvi's eyes held mine. "I want you to spar."

I glanced at Jackson's smiling face. What Romvi wanted me to do was show him how I'd fought the furies and survived, using Jackson to do so. It didn't matter who I was fighting; I couldn't show what I didn't know.

As Romvi headed off the mats, he stopped and whispered to Jackson. Whatever he was saying brought an easy grin to Jackson's face right before he nodded.

Wiping my hand over my clammy forehead, I slowed down my breathing and tried to ignore the fine tremors running through my legs. Even tired I could take Jackson. He was a good fighter, but I was better. I had to be better.

"You're going to be hurting by the end of class," Jackson taunted, cracking his knuckles.

I raised a brow and motioned him forward with one hand. I may've had a serious hankering for a pillow, but I could take him.

I waited until he was only a foot away before I launched a brutal offensive. I was fast and light on my feet. He would feint in one direction to avoid a sharp thrust and end up with a sideways kick in his back. Before long, he ended up on his back, panting and swearing from a fierce spin kick.

"I'm going to be hurting?" I said, standing above him. "Nah, I don't think so."

Breathing harshly, he jumped onto the balls of his feet. "Wait and see, baby."

"Baby?" I repeated. "I'm not your baby."

Jackson didn't respond to that. He flew into a butterfly kick, which I dodged. Those kicks were brutal. Blow after blow, we went after each other—each hit more vicious than the last. Admittedly, I was taking this a little too seriously myself. I wasn't going easy on the douchebag. A weird kind of darkness rose in me as I blocked a series of kicks and jabs that would have brought even Aiden down. I grinned in spite of the sweat pouring off me and the way my forearms ached. I channeled all of my earlier anger into fighting Jackson.

Our sparring eventually drew the attention of the other students. I was only slightly surprised when Jackson's fist glanced off my jaw and Instructor Romvi didn't call the fight off. If anything, he looked like he was getting his jollies by watching the brutal fight.

So, Jackson didn't want to play by the rules and Romvi didn't care? Whatever. He swung his fist around again, but this time I caught his hand and twisted it backward.

Jackson broke the hold too easily, which showed that I was reaching my own limits. I turned on my heel, saw that the overhead lights flickered—or was it my eyes? — and with one powerful roundhouse kick, I took Jackson's legs right out from under him. There wasn't a moment to celebrate his obvious defeat. I saw Jackson move for my legs. I tried to jump like we'd been taught, but worn down, I was too slow. His leg caught mine, and I landed on my side, immediately rolling out of range.

"I'm sure that's not how you defeated the furies." Instructor Romvi sounded smug.

I didn't have a second to think about how much I wished I could drop-kick Romvi. Jackson whipped around. I scooted to the side, but his kick caught me in the ribs. Pain exploded, so unexpected and so intense, that I froze.

Sensing that Jackson wasn't done yet, I brought my hands up, but that teeny, tiny second cost me. Jackson's heel slipped past my hands, hitting my chin and cutting my lip right open. Something warm gushed into my mouth, and I saw flashes of light. Blood—I tasted blood. And beyond the flashing lights, I saw Jackson's boot come up one more time.

CHAPTER SIX

Jackson was going to stomp my head in.

That was so not a part of training.

At the last possible second, someone caught Jackson by the waist and tossed him to the mat. My hands flew to my mouth. Something sticky and warm covered them immediately.

All I tasted was blood. Hesitantly, I ran my tongue along the inside of my mouth, checking to make sure I hadn't lost any teeth. When I figured that I still had a full set, I pushed to my feet, spitting out blood. Then I lunged at Jackson.

I came up short. Shock nearly brought me to my knees.

Jackson was already preoccupied with fending off someone else, and that someone was Aiden. Pain was momentarily forgotten as I vaguely wondered where *he* had come from. Aiden didn't watch my classes anymore. He didn't even train me, so it wasn't like he had a reason to be hanging around these rooms.

But he was here now.

Entranced by the odd blend of grace and brutality, I

watched Aiden pull Jackson off the mat by the scruff of his shirt. Their faces were inches apart. The last time I had seen Aiden *that* angry was when he'd gone after Seth the night I'd been slipped the Brew.

"That is not how you spar with your partner," Aiden said in a cold, low voice. "I'm sure Instructor Romvi has taught you better than that."

Jackson's eyes grew impossibly large. He was on the tips of his toes, arms dangling at his sides. It was then that I realized Jackson's nose was bleeding—bleeding worse than my mouth was. Someone had hit him—that someone most likely being Aiden. Because only a pure would be able to do that and have no one intervene.

He let go of Jackson. The half fell to his knees, cradling his face. Aiden spun around, his eyes quickly assessing the damage. Then he turned to Instructor Romvi, speaking too low and quick for me or the class to understand.

Before I knew what was happening, Aiden crossed the mats and caught hold of my arm. We didn't speak as he walked me from the training room. "My bag," I protested.

"I'll have someone retrieve it for you."

In the hall, he grasped my shoulders and turned me around. His eyes went from dark gray to silver when his gaze fell to my lip. "Instructor Romvi never should've allowed it to go that far."

"Yeah, I don't think he cared."

He swore.

I wanted to say something. Like "these things happen," or at least, about how it could be expected since I didn't have a lot of friends here. Or maybe I should thank Aiden, but by the warring emotions playing out across his striking face I could tell he wouldn't appreciate it. Aiden was furious—furious for all the wrong reasons. He'd reacted as if a common *guy* had hit me, and not a half-blood. As a pure-blood, there had been no reason for him to intervene. That was the Instructor's job. Aiden had forgotten that in a moment of complete, unbridled rage.

"I shouldn't have done that—lost my temper," he said quietly, sounding and looking terribly young and vulnerable for someone I believed to be so powerful. "I shouldn't have hit him."

My eyes flicked across his face. Even though my face throbbed, I wanted to touch him. I wanted him to touch *me*. And then he did, but not in the way I wanted. Placing his hand on my lower back, he steered me toward the med office. I wanted to touch my mouth to see how bad it was. Actually, I wanted a mirror.

The pure-blood doctor took one look at my face and shook her head. "On the table."

I hoisted myself up. "Is it going to scar?"

The doc grabbed a cloudy-looking white bottle and several wads of cotton. "Not sure yet but try not to talk right now. At least until I make sure there is no damage inside the lip, okay?"

"If it scars, I'm gonna be so pissed."

"Stop talking," Aiden said, leaning against the wall.

The doc shot him a smile, apparently not curious as to why I had been escorted by a pure. She turned back to me. "This may sting a bit." She dabbed the cotton over my lip. *Sting?*—it burned like crazy. I nearly jumped off the table.

"Antiseptic," she said, offering a sympathetic look. "We want to make sure you don't get any infections. Then you would scar."

Burning? I could deal with that. It took the doc a couple

of minutes to clean up my lip. I waited, somewhat impatiently, for the verdict.

"I don't think you're going to need stitches on the lip itself. It's going to swell and be a bit tender for a while." She tipped my head back and gently poked at my mouth. "But I think we're going to need a stitch right…under your lip here."

I winced as she started poking there too and focused on her shoulder. *Show no pain. Show no pain. Show no pain.* The doc dipped her fingers in the brown jar and pressed the torn skin together. I yelped as a scalding pain radiated from the skin under my lip and spread across my face.

Aiden started forward, stopping when he seemed to realize there was nothing he could—or should—do. His hands fell to his sides, and his gaze met mine, eyes an endless thundering gray.

"Just a little bit more," she said soothingly. "Then it will all be over. You're lucky you didn't lose any teeth."

Then she squeezed the skin once more. This time I didn't make a sound, but I squeezed my eyes shut until lights danced behind my closed lids. I wanted to jump off the table and find Jackson. Hitting him would make me feel better. I believed in that.

The doc stepped back to the cabinets. Returning with a damp wipe, she started to clean the blood away, mindful of the stitch. "Next time you train her, be a little more careful. She's only this young and pretty once. Don't ruin it for her."

My eyes snapped to Aiden. "But—"

"Yes, ma'am," Aiden interrupted, cutting me a stern look. I stared back at him.

The doc sighed, shaking her head again. "Why do you halfs choose this? Surely, the alternative is better. Anyway, do you have any other injuries?"

"Uh, no," I mumbled. The doc's words surprised me.

"Yes," Aiden said. "Check the left side of her ribs."

"Oh, come on," I said. "It's not that bad—" My words were cut off when the doc tugged up the hem of my shirt.

The doc pressed on my ribs, running her hands along the side. Her fingers were cool and quick. "None are broken, but this..." She frowned, leaning closer. Inhaling roughly, she dropped my shirt and faced Aiden. It seemed to take her a moment to collect herself. "Her ribs aren't broken, but they are bruised. She should take it easy for a few days. Also, she should limit talking so the stitching is not pulled."

Aiden looked like he wanted to laugh at the last suggestion. When he agreed with the doctor, she left the room pretty quickly.

"Why did you let her believe you did this?" I asked. "You're not even training me anymore."

"Aren't you supposed to be limiting your speaking?"

I rolled my eyes. "Now she thinks you're some great and terrible half-blood beater or something."

He pointed to the door. "It wouldn't be a far stretch of the imagination. Your Instructor allowed it to happen. The doc sees more cases like this than she probably cares to."

And she probably saw very few pure-bloods who even cared enough to make sure the half was okay. I sighed. "What were you doing over here, anyway?"

There was a ghost of a smile. "Didn't I tell you that making sure you stay safe is a full-time job?"

I started to smile, but quickly remembered not to. "Ow." I ignored his amused look. "So why were you here, for real?"

"I just happened to be over here and looked in the room." He shrugged, staring over my shoulder. "I saw you sparring and watched. The rest is history."

I didn't really believe him, but I let it go. "I would've had Jackson, you know? But this damn cold has kicked my butt."

Aiden's gaze settled on me again. "You shouldn't be sick." He stepped forward, reaching out and carefully placing his hand under my chin. He frowned. "How did you get sick?"

"I can't be the first half to get sick."

His thumb moved over my chin, careful to avoid the tender spot. That was Aiden, always so careful with me even though he knew I was tough. My heart jumped. "I don't know," he said, dropping his hand.

Unsure of how to respond, I shrugged. "Anyway, thanks for, um…getting Jackson to stop."

A hard, lethal look flickered across his face. "I will make sure Jackson is punished for what he has done. The Covenant has enough on its shoulders without halfs trying to kill one another."

I lightly touched my chin and winced. "I don't know if it was his idea."

Aiden grabbed my hand and pulled it away from my face. "What do you mean?"

Before I could answer, a fine shiver went down my spine. Seconds later, the door to the room flew open. Seth came through, eyes wide and lips thinned. His gaze went from my lip to where Aiden held my hand. "What the hell happened?"

Confusion and then understanding dawned on Aiden's face.

He released my hand and stepped back. "She was sparring."

Seth shot Aiden a scathing look as he made his way to where I sat on the table. He clasped my chin with two slender fingers, just like Aiden had. My heart didn't flutter, but the cord did. "Who were you sparring with?"

"It's no big deal." I felt my cheeks start to burn.

"It doesn't look that way." Seth's eyes narrowed. "And you hurt elsewhere. I can feel it."

Gods, I really needed to work on that shield.

"Thank you for keeping an eye on her, Aiden." Seth didn't take his eyes off me. "I have it taken care of."

Aiden opened his mouth to say something, but then he closed it. He turned around and left the room quietly. The urge to jump off the table and run after him was hard to ignore.

"So, what happened to your face?" he prompted again.

"I broke it," I muttered, straining away from him.

Seth tilted my chin to the side, frowning. "I can tell. This was really done while sparring?"

"Yeah, well, it was done to my face in class."

His frown deepened. "What is that supposed to mean?"

I knocked his hand away and slid off the table. "It's nothing. Just a busted lip."

"Busted lip?" He caught me around the waist, pulling me back. "I swear I see a boot print on your chin."

"Really—is it that bad?" I gingerly touched my chin, wondering what he'd think if he saw the boot print on my ribs.

"So vain." Seth grasped my hand. "Who were you sparring with?"

I sighed and tried to wiggle free, but it was no use. Seth—and the cord—wanted me to be here with him. I placed my cheek against his chest. "It doesn't matter. And aren't you still mad at me for throwing food at you, anyway?"

"Oh, I'm not too happy about that. I think mayo stains." His embrace loosened a little. "Does it hurt?"

Lying was pointless, but that's what I did. "No. Not at all."

"Yeah," he murmured against the top of my head. "So, who did you spar with?"

I closed my eyes. Being this close to him, with the bond and everything, it was easy to stop thinking. Just like it had been while fighting. "I always get paired with Jackson."

After class the following day, I piddled around the training center. I found myself walking into the smaller room Aiden had been in when I'd found out about my father. Of course, he wasn't in there now. No one was. Dropping my bag just inside the door, I approached the punching bag hanging in the middle of the mats. It was an old, raggedy thing that had seen better days. Sections of the black leather had been knocked off. Someone had taken duct tape and patched it up. I ran my fingers over the edges of the tape.

Restlessness inched over my skin. The idea of going back to my dorm and spending time alone wasn't appealing. I hadn't seen Seth since he'd dropped me off yesterday. I guessed he was still pissed about the sub issue.

I pushed the bag with my palms. Then I flipped my hands over. Two softly glowing glyphs stared back at me.

My gaze went back to the punching bag. Had my father trained at this Covenant? Stood in this very room? It would explain how he'd known my mother so well. Again, melancholy crept over me.

The door to the room opened. I turned, expecting Guard Linard. But it wasn't him. My heart did a brief, stupid happy dance.

Aiden stepped inside the training room, the door sliding shut behind him. He wore the garb of a Sentinel: a black long-sleeved shirt and black cargos. I just stared at him like an idiot.

The way my body responded to him—to a pure-blood—was entirely unforgivable. I knew this, but it didn't stop the way my breath caught or the warmth that stole over my skin. It wasn't just how he looked. Don't get me wrong—Aiden had the whole rare masculine beauty thing going for him. But it was more than that. He got me in a way very few people did. He didn't need a bond to do so, like Seth. Aiden figured me out through his unwavering patience...and not putting up with any of my crap. During the summer we'd spent hours together training and getting to know one another. I liked to think something beautiful had grown out of it. After what he'd done to protect me in New York...and then with Jackson, I could no longer really be angry with him about the day he'd told me he couldn't love me.

Aiden watched me curiously. "I saw Seth entering the main part of Deity Island and you weren't with him. I figured you'd be here."

"Why?"

He shrugged. "I just knew you'd be in one of the training rooms even though you were told to take it easy."

Whenever he was dealing with something, he hit the mats. I was the same way, which reminded me of the night I'd accosted him after learning my mom's true fate. I turned away, running my fingers down the center of the bag.

"How are you feeling—your ribs and lip?"

Both were sore, but I'd felt worse. "Good."

"Have you written the letter for me to give to Laadan?" he asked after a few moments.

My shoulders slumped. "No. I don't know what to say." It's not like I hadn't thought about it, but what do you say to a man you'd believed dead—a father you'd never met?

"Just tell him how you feel, Alex."

I laughed. "I don't know if he wants to know all of that."

"He would." Aiden paused, and the silence stretched out between us. "You've seemed...out of it lately."

I still felt out of it. "It's the cold."

"You looked like you were going to faint in Marcus's office and, let's face it, there is no reason why you couldn't have taken Jackson down yesterday…or at least moved out of the way. You've been looking exhausted, Alex."

Sighing, I faced him. He was slouched against the wall, hands shoved deep in his pockets. "So, what are you doing here?" I asked, seeking to take the focus off me.

Aiden's expression was knowing. "Watching you."

Warmth fluttered in my chest. "Really? That's not creepy or anything."

A teeny tiny smile appeared. "Well, I'm on duty."

I glanced around the room. "Do you think there're daimons in here?"

"I'm not hunting right now." A lock of wavy, dark brown hair fell into his gray eyes as he tipped his head to the side. "I've been given a new assignment."

"Do tell."

"Along with my hunting, I'm guarding you."

I blinked and then I laughed so hard my ribs hurt. "Gods, it must suck to be you."

His brows furrowed. "Why would you think that?"

"You just can't get rid of me, can you?" I turned back to the bag, eyeing it for a weak spot. "I mean, not that you want to, but you keep getting saddled with me."

"I don't consider it being *saddled* with you. Why would you think that?"

I closed my eyes, wondering why I'd even said that. "So, Linard also has a new assignment?"

"Yes. You didn't answer my question."

And I wasn't going to. "Did Marcus ask you to do this?"

"Yes, he did. When you're not with Seth, it will either be

Linard, Leon, or myself keeping watch. There's a good chance that whoever meant you harm—"

"Minister Telly," I added, balling up my fist.

"*Whoever* meant you harm in the Catskills will try something here. Then there are the furies."

I punched the bag, immediately wincing as it pulled the sore muscles over my ribs. Should've wrapped them first. Stupid. "You guys can't fight the furies."

"If they show up, we will try."

Shaking my hand, I took a step back. "You'll die trying. Those things—well, you saw what they are capable of. If they come, just step out of the way."

"What?" Disbelief colored his tone.

"I don't want to see people die for no reason."

"Die for no reason?"

"You know they'll just keep coming back, and I don't want someone to die when it all seems…inevitable."

The breath that he sucked in was sharp, audible in the small room. "Are you saying you believe your death is inevitable, Alex?"

I pushed the punching bag again. "I don't know what I'm saying. Just forget it."

"Something…something is different about you."

A desire to flee the room filled me, but I faced him instead. I glanced down at my palms. The marks were still there. Why did I keep checking on them like they'd go away or something? "So much has happened, Aiden. I'm not the same person."

"You were the same person the day you found out about your father," he said, eyes turning the color of a thundercloud.

Anger began low in my stomach, humming through my veins. "That has nothing to do with this."

Aiden pushed off the wall, hands coming out of his pockets. "What is *this*?"

"Everything!" My fingers dug into my palms. "What's the point in all of this? Let's just think hypothetically here for a second, okay? Say Telly or whoever doesn't manage to send me into servitude or kill me and the furies don't end up tearing me apart, I'm still going to turn eighteen. I'm still going to Awaken. So, what's the point? Maybe I should leave." I stalked to where I'd dropped my bag. "Maybe Lucian will let me go to Ireland or something. I'd like to visit there before I be—"

Aiden grabbed my upper arm, turning me so that I faced him. "You said you had to stay at the Covenant so you could graduate, because you needed to be a Sentinel more than anything else." His voice dropped low as his eyes searched mine intently. "You were passionate about this. Has that changed?"

I yanked on my arm, but he held on. "Maybe."

The tips of Aiden's cheekbones flushed. "So, you're giving up?"

"I don't think it's giving up. Call it…accepting reality." I smiled, but it felt icky.

"That is such bull, Alex."

I opened my mouth, but nothing came out. I'd argued to stay at the Covenant so I could become a Sentinel. And I knew, deep down, I still wanted to become one for my mom, for me, but I wasn't sure it was what I needed anymore. Or what I could agree with if I was honest with myself. After seeing those servants slaughtered on the floor and no one cared…no one came to help them.

I wasn't sure I could be a part of any of this.

"You've never been one to wallow in self-pity when the odds are stacked against you."

My jaw snapped. "I'm not wallowing in self-pity, Aiden."

"Really?" he said so softly. "Just like you aren't settling for Seth?"

Oh, good gods, not what I wanted to hear. "I'm not settling." *Liar,* whispered an evil voice in my head. "I don't want to talk about Seth."

He looked away for a second and then settled on me again. "I cannot believe you've forgiven him for what…for what he did to you."

"That wasn't his fault, Aiden. Seth didn't give me the Brew. He didn't force—"

"He still knew better!"

"I'm not talking to you about this." I started to back away.

The hand beside him clenched. "So, you are still…with him?"

Part of me wondered what had happened to the Aiden who held me in his arms when I'd told him about my father. That version had been easier to deal with. Then again, obviously I wasn't behaving like the person I was before, either. And a part of me liked the way he said "him"—as if the very name made him want to punch something. "Define 'with,' Aiden."

He stared.

I tipped my head up. "Do you mean am I hanging out with him or are we just friends? Or did you mean to ask if we're sleeping together?"

His eyes narrowed into thin slits that shone a fierce silver.

"And why are you asking, Aiden?" I pulled back, and he let go. "Whatever the answer is doesn't even matter."

"But it does."

I thought about the marks and what they meant. "You have no idea. It doesn't. It's fate, remember?" I grabbed for my bag again, but he caught my arm again. I looked up, exhaling slowly. "What do you want from me?"

Realization crept over his expression, softening the hue of his eyes. "You're afraid."

"What?" I laughed, but it came out sounding like a nervous croak. "I'm not afraid."

Aiden's eyes drifted over my head and determination settled into his eyes. "Yes. You are." Without saying anything else, he turned me around and pulled me toward the sensory deprivation chamber.

My eyes shot wide. "What are you doing?"

He kept pulling until we stopped in front of the door. "Do you know what they use this for?"

"Um, to train?"

Aiden glanced down at me, smiling tightly. "Do you know how ancient warriors trained? They used to fight Deimos and Phobos, who used the warriors' worst fears against them during battle."

"Thanks for the daily weird god history lesson, but—"

"But since the gods of Fear and Terror have been off the circuit for a while, they created this chamber. They believe that fighting using only your other senses to guide you is the best way to hone your skills and face your fears."

"Fears of what?"

He opened the door and a black hole greeted us. "Whatever fears are holding you back."

I dug in my heels. "I'm not afraid."

"You're terrified."

"Aiden, I am two seconds from—" My own surprised shriek cut me off as he hauled me into the chamber, shutting the door behind him, casting the room in utter darkness. My breath froze in my throat. "Aiden...I can't see anything."

"That's the point."

"Well, thanks, Captain Obvious." I reached out blindly,

but only felt air. "What do you expect me to do in here?" As soon as the question left my mouth, I was assaulted with totally inappropriate images of all the things we could do in here.

"We fight."

Well, that blew. I inhaled, catching the scent of spice and ocean. Slowly, I lifted my hand. My fingers brushed against something hard and warm—his chest? Then there was nothing but empty space. Oh gods, this wasn't going to be good at all.

Suddenly, he grasped my arm and spun me around. "Get into stance."

"Aiden, I really don't want to do this right now. I am tired and I got kicked in the—"

"Excuses," he said, his breath dangerously close to my lips. I locked up.

His hand was gone. "Get into stance."

"I am."

Aiden sighed. "No, you're not."

"How do you know?"

"I can tell. You haven't moved," he said. "Now get into stance."

"Jeez, are you like a cat that can see in the dark or something?" When he didn't respond, I groaned and moved into the stance: arms halfway up, legs spread, and feet rooted in place. "All right."

"You need to face your fears, Alex."

I squinted but saw nothing. "I thought you said I was fearless."

"You usually are." Suddenly, he was in front of me and his scent was driving me to distraction. "Which is why being scared now is so hard for you. Being afraid isn't a weakness, Alex. It's only a sign of something you must overcome."

"Fear is a weakness." Expecting him to still be in front of me, I decided to go along with him. I threw an elbow out, but he wasn't there. And then he was at my back, his breath dancing along the back of my neck. I swung around, grasping air. "What are you afraid of?"

A whoosh of air and he was behind me again. "This isn't about me, Alex. You're afraid of losing yourself."

"Of course not. What was I thinking?" I whipped around, cursing when he was gone. This was making me dizzy. "So why don't you tell me what I'm afraid of, oh-fearless-one?"

"You're scared of becoming something you have no control over." He caught my arm as I swung toward the sound of his voice. "That scares you to death." He let go, backing off.

He was right, and because of that, anger and embarrassment flooded me. Out of the darkness surrounding me, there was a patch thicker than the rest. I threw myself at him. Anticipating the move, he caught me by the shoulders. I swung out, catching him in the stomach and chest.

Aiden pushed me back. "You're angry because I'm right."

A hoarse sound moved up my throat. I clamped my mouth shut and swung again. My elbow connected with something. "A Sentinel is never afraid. They'd never tuck tail and run."

"Are you tucking tail and running, Alex?"

The air stirred around me, and I jumped, narrowly missing what was probably a perfect leg sweep. "No!"

"That's not what it sounded like earlier," he said. "You wanted to take Lucian up on his offer. Visit Ireland?"

"I…I was…" Dammit, I hated it when he was right. Aiden laughed from somewhere in the darkness.

I followed the sound. Going too far, too caught up in my anger, I lost my sense of balance when I attacked. Aiden caught my arm, but neither of us could gain our footing in the darkness. When I fell, he came with me. I landed on my back, with Aiden right on top of me.

Aiden caught my wrists before I could hit him again, pinning them above my head and down on the mats. "You always let your emotions get the best of you, Alex."

I tried to push him off, not trusting myself to speak. A sob was rising in my throat as I wiggled under him, managing to get one leg free.

"Alex," he warned softly. He pressed down, and when he breathed in, his chest rose against mine. In the utter darkness of the sensory deprivation room, his breath was warm against my lips. I didn't dare move. Not even a fraction of an inch.

His grip around my wrists slackened and his hand slipped over my shoulder, cupping my cheek. My heart was trying to come out of my chest in those seconds and every muscle locked up, tensed with anticipation. Was he going to kiss me? No. My lip was busted, but if he did, I wouldn't stop him and I knew that was so wrong. Chills went down my spine, and I relaxed under him.

"It's okay to be afraid, Alex."

I threw my head back then, wanting to be far away from him as much as I wanted to be right where I was.

"But you have nothing to fear." He guided my chin down with gentle fingers. "When will you learn?" His voice was heavy, gruff. "You're the only person who has control over who you become. You're too strong to ever lose yourself. I believe that. Why can't you?"

My breath came out shaky. His faith in me was nearly my undoing. The swelling in my chest would've lifted me off the mats. Several moments passed before I could speak. "What are you afraid of?" I asked again.

“I thought you said I was afraid of nothing once,” he threw back.

“I did.”

Aiden shifted slightly and his thumb caressed the curve of my cheek. “I’m afraid of something.”

“What?” I whispered.

He drew in a deep, shuddering breath. “I’m afraid of never being allowed to feel what I do.”

CHAPTER SEVEN

The air hitched as I tried to breathe. I wished I could see his face, his eyes. I wanted to know what he was thinking right at this moment, to touch him. But I lay there, my heart the only part of me that was moving.

His thumb brushed my cheek once more. "That's what scares me." Then he lifted himself off me. He backed up, the mats rolling under his unsteady step. "I'll be in the other training room when you're ready…to walk back to your dorm."

There was a brief flash of light from the outside training rooms when he slipped out the door and then darkness covered me again.

I didn't move but my brain raced on. He was afraid of never being allowed to feel what he did. Gods, I wasn't stupid, but I wished I was. I knew what he meant and also knew it didn't mean a damn thing. Part of me was angry, because he dared to say it when all it did was make my chest heavy with an aching want—a want so intense that it felt like it could crush me under its weight. And why admit it now, when I'd begged him before to just tell me he felt the same and he'd denied it? What was so different now?

And he was right about the other thing. I was terrified of becoming something I couldn't control, of losing myself to the bond, to Seth. It seemed like, even if I got past all the other obstacles in my way, there was *that* one—the one I couldn't hurdle over with good ol' Alex recklessness.

The door opened again and the soft murmur of two male voices floated through the room. There was a deep, husky chuckle as the mats dipped under their feet. I could've said something, but I was too lost in my own thoughts to even utter a single word.

A second later, feet tangled with my legs and a surprised yelp sounded. The mats gave way as a body crashed down, half-sprawled atop me. I let out an *"oomph"* and pushed the hands off my chest.

"Gods, Alex!" exclaimed Luke, rolling off me and sitting up. "Holy Hades, what are you doing in here?"

"How'd you know it was me by just feeling up my boobs?" I grumbled, throwing an arm over my face.

"It's a superpower."

"Wow."

Luke snorted. I felt the mats roll as he faced his silent mystery partner. "Hey," Luke said. "Can you give us a few minutes?"

"Sure. Whatever," the guy responded, dipping back out the door. The voice was super familiar, but as much as I tried, I couldn't place it.

"Pervert," I said. "What have you been using these rooms for, Luke? Naughty."

He laughed. "I'll go with something a hell of a lot more entertaining and normal than what you've been using them for. You're the one lying in a dark sensory room like a little freak. What are you doing in here? Plotting to take out the Covenant? Meditating? Self-pleasuring?"

I made a face. "Don't you have something better to do?"

"Yeah, I do."

"Then go. This room is already occupied."

Luke sighed. "You're being ridiculous."

I thought that was funny considering he had no idea why I was being a "little freak" in the sensory room. Luke had no idea what had just gone on in here. He probably thought I was hiding from everybody or having some sort of mental breakdown. That last part was still up in the air and could be a strong possibility. If it'd been Caleb who'd stumbled upon me, he would've known. I sucked in a sharp breath.

Missing him wasn't getting any easier, I realized suddenly.

"It sucks not having any friends, doesn't it?" Luke asked after a few moments.

I frowned. "You know, it's a good thing you can't become a therapist, because you really suck at the whole 'making people feel better about themselves' thing."

"But you do have friends," he continued as if I hadn't said a damn thing. "You just seem to have forgotten us."

"Like who?"

"Like me." Luke stretched out beside me. "And there's Deacon. And Olivia."

I snorted. "Olivia hates my guts."

"She does not."

"Bullshit." I dropped my arm, facing him in the darkness. "She blames me for Caleb's death. You heard her at his funeral and in the hallway yesterday."

"She's hurt, Alex."

"I'm hurt, too!" I sat up, crossing my legs.

The mats shook as Luke rolled onto his side. "She loved Caleb. As impractical as it is for any of us to love someone, she loved him."

"And I loved him. He was *my* best friend, Luke. She blames me for my best friend's death."

"She doesn't blame you anymore."

I smoothed back the tiny hairs that had escaped my ponytail. "When did that happen? In the last twenty-four hours?"

Undaunted, Luke sat up and somehow found my hand in the darkness. "The day she came up to you in the hallway, she wanted to apologize to you."

"That's funny, because I remember her saying something like I needed to rein in my grief." I didn't pull my hand away from his, because it did feel kind of nice for someone to touch me and nothing freaky happen. "Is that a new form of apology I'm unaware of?"

"I don't know what she was thinking. She wanted to apologize, but you wouldn't stop to talk to her," Luke explained softly. "She lost it. She was a bitch about it. Olivia knows that. Then you owning her ass in front of everyone didn't help, either."

The old Alex would have snickered at that, but it didn't make me feel good.

"You need to talk to her, Alex. You both need each other right now."

I pulled my hand free and came to my feet swiftly. The room suddenly felt stifling and unbearable. "I don't need her or anyone."

Luke was standing beside me in an instant. "And that was probably the most childish thing you've ever said."

I narrowed my eyes in his general direction. "And I have something even more childish to say to you. I'm like two seconds from hitting you."

"That's not very nice," Luke teased, stepping around me. "You need friends, Alex. As hot as Seth is, he can't be your only friend. You need girl time. You need someone you can cry to, someone who isn't trying to get into your pants. You need someone who wants to be around you not because of what you are, but who you are."

My jaw hit the mat. "Wow."

Luke must have sensed my stunned response because he laughed. "Everyone knows what you are, Alex. And most people think it's pretty damn cool. What they don't think is cool—the reason why everyone is avoiding you—is your attitude. Everyone gets that you're hurt over Caleb and what happened with your mom. We understand that, but that doesn't mean we have to tolerate your constant bitchiness."

I opened my mouth to tell Luke that I wasn't the one being the bitch, that it was all of them who'd been treating me like a three-headed dog since I'd returned—and even before then—but nothing came out. Besides spending time with Seth, I *had* isolated myself from everyone.

And sometimes I was a terrible person. I had reasons—good reasons, but they were just excuses. Weight settled over my chest.

In the silence and darkness surrounding us, Luke found me and wrapped his arms around my stiff shoulders. "Well, maybe we do have to tolerate it a little bit. You are an Apollyon after all." I could hear the smile in his voice. "And even though you've been a giant bitch, we still love you and we're worried."

A lump formed in my throat. I fought it, really, I did, but I felt tears stinging my eyes as my muscles started to relax. My head somehow found his shoulder and he patted my back soothingly. For a moment, I could believe that Luke was Caleb, and in my head, I pretended that I told him everything that had happened. My make-believe Caleb smiled at me, held me closer, and ordered me to pull my head out of my ass. That no matter what had happened and everything I learned, the world hadn't ended and wasn't going to.

And for the time being, that seemed to be enough.

Aiden was waiting for me when I finally pulled myself out of the sensory room. He didn't say anything as we headed outside. Both of us had said and probably thought too much as it was. There wasn't any awkwardness between us, but there was this vast sense of...uncertainty. Although, it could have been that I was projecting my own feelings onto him.

We made our way up the walkway, heading toward the dorms. The wind kicked up sand and there was a cold, damp feeling in the air as we neared the garden.

Two pure boys were staring at the marble statue of Apollo reaching for Daphne as she changed into a tree. One elbowed the other. "Hey, look. Apollo is getting wood."

His friend laughed. I rolled my eyes.

"Alex." There was something about Aiden's voice, a roughness that told me that whatever he was about to say was going to be powerful. His gaze moved to my face, then behind me. "What the hell?"

Not what I was expecting.

Aiden brushed past me, solely focused on something other than me. Dammit. I whirled around. "You don't—*oh*."

Now I saw what had cut Aiden off.

Two half guys carried a barely conscious Jackson between them—a hardly recognizable Jackson. He looked like he'd woken up on the wrong side of an ass kicking. Every visible inch of his skin was bruised or bloodied—eyes swelled shut, lips split wide open—and the deep, angry mark smeared across his left cheek suspiciously resembled a boot print.

"What happened to him?" Aiden demanded, taking the place of one of the halfs and practically supporting all of the boy's weight.

The half shook his head. "I don't know. We found him like this in the courtyard."

"I…I fell," Jackson said, blood and spit trickling from his mouth. I think he was missing some teeth.

A dubious expression crossed Aiden's face. "Alex, please go straight to your dorm."

Nodding mutely, I stepped out of the way. I was still pissed at Jackson. He had tried to stomp my head in, but what had been done to him was horrific and calculated. Compared to the fist Aiden had planted in his face when Jackson had…

My wide eyes met Aiden's for a second before he carried Jackson off toward the med building. My conversation with Seth came back to me.

"So, who did you spar with in class?" he'd asked.

"I always get paired with Jackson."

My gods, Seth had done this.

It appeared that Seth was avoiding me for the most part, probably because of the whole ham sandwich incident. Our practices were either canceled or consisted of working on my mental shields. For a whole week, whenever I saw him, I asked him about Jackson. With a look of complete innocence, he'd told me he hadn't done it. I didn't believe him, and I'd told him just that.

He'd looked at me, expression beautifully empty, and said, "Now why would I ever do such a thing?"

I didn't want to believe that he had, because whoever had done that to Jackson had put him out of commission for a long time. Jackson wasn't talking, literally. His jaw was wired shut, and I'd heard he needed a lot of dental work. Even though he'd heal a lot quicker than a mortal, I knew he still wouldn't talk. The boy had had the ever-loving crap scared out of him.

And even though I didn't want to believe it was Seth, I couldn't shake my suspicions. Who else would do such a thing to Jackson? Seth had motive—a motive that made me feel ill. If he'd done it, it'd been because of what Jackson had done to me in class. But how could he do something so…violent, so unstable? That question haunted me.

The one good thing was that the weird funk that had settled over me like an itchy blanket faded. A tiny part of me missed Seth's company in the evenings and the way he always managed to turn me into a human body pillow during the night, but there was another part of me that was sort of relieved. Like there wasn't anything additional expected from me.

Even though no one tried to drug or kill me, Linard and Aiden still followed me around. And when they were busy, it was Leon's massive shadow that lurked behind me. I'd taken to hanging around the training rooms even on the days Seth and I wouldn't practice. I knew that Aiden would eventually find me there. We didn't talk about being afraid again, but we sort of just…hung out…in the training room.

It sounded lame, but it was like the old times, before everything got so incredibly screwed up. Sometimes Leon popped in on us. He never seemed surprised or suspicious. Not even the last time, when we'd been sitting with our backs against the wall, arguing about whether or not ghosts existed.

I didn't believe in them.

Aiden did.

Leon had thought we were both idiots.

But damn, I looked forward to it. Just sitting there and talking. No training. No trying to tap in and use akasha. Those moments with Aiden, even when Leon decided to join us, were my favorite part of the day.

I hadn't choked Olivia again, but things were super-awkward when I did see her—no big surprise there. But I did start eating my lunch in the cafeteria with Seth. After the second day, Luke joined us, then Elena, and finally Olivia. We didn't talk, but we also didn't yell anything at each other.

Some things didn't change, though. The mortal holidays of Christmas and New Year came and went, along with most of January. Most of the pures still seemed to expect every half to turn into an evil aether-sucking creature and jump them. Deacon, Aiden's brother, was one of the few who braved sitting next to us in class or talking to us around campus. Another thing that hadn't changed was my inability to write a letter to my father. What was I supposed to say? I had no idea. Each night that I'd been alone, I'd started a letter, and then stopped. Paper balls littered my floor.

"Just write what you're feeling, Alex. You're overthinking it," Aiden had said after I'd complained. "You've known that he's been alive for two months now. You need to just write without thinking."

Two months? It hadn't felt that long. And that meant I had a little over a month before I Awakened. Maybe I was trying to slow time down. Either way, my feelings were all over the place, and if my father was as competent as I believed him to be, I didn't want him to think I had issues.

So, after practice with Seth, I gathered up my notebook and headed over to one of the less crowded rec rooms. Curling up in the corner of a bright red sofa, I stared at a blank page and chewed on the end of my pen.

Linard took up position at the door, looking bored. When he caught me watching him, I made a face and returned to gazing at the blue lines on the paper. Luke interrupted a few times, trying to lure me into a game of air hockey.

When his shadow fell across my notebook again, I groaned. "I don't want to…"

Olivia stood in front of me, wearing a thick cashmere sweater I immediately started lusting after. Her brown eyes were wide.

"Uh…sorry," I said. "I thought you were Luke."

She smoothed a hand over her curly hair. "He's trying to get you to play Skee-Ball?"

"No. He moved on to air hockey."

Her laugh was nervous as she glanced over at the group by the arcade games. Then she squared her shoulders as she gestured at the spot beside me. "Can I sit?"

My stomach turned over. "Yeah, if you want."

Olivia sat, running her hands over her jean-clad legs. Several moments passed without either of us speaking. She was the first to break the silence. "So, how…how have you been?"

It was a loaded question, and my laugh came out choked and harsh. I brought the notepad to my chest as I glanced over at Luke. He was pretending not to have noticed us together.

She let out a little breath and started to rise. "Okay. I guess—"

"I'm sorry." My voice was low, words hoarse. I felt my cheeks burn, but I forced myself to keep going. "I'm sorry for everything, especially the thing in the hallway."

Olivia squeezed her thighs. "Alex—"

"I know you loved Caleb, and all I've been thinking about is my own hurt." I closed my eyes and swallowed down the lump in my throat. "I really do wish I could go back and change everything that night. I've thought a million times about all the things we could've done differently."

"You shouldn't…do that to yourself," she said quietly. "At first, I didn't want to know what really happened, you know? Like the details. I just couldn't…deal with knowing for a while, but I finally got Lea to tell me everything about a week ago."

I bit my lip, unsure of what to say. She hadn't accepted my apology, but we were talking.

She drew in a shallow breath, eyes gleaming. "She told me that Caleb saved her. That you were fighting another daimon, and if he hadn't grabbed her, she would've died."

I nodded, clenching the notebook. Memories of the night surfaced, of Caleb streaking past me.

"He was really brave, wasn't he?" Her voice caught.

"Yes," I agreed passionately. "He didn't even hesitate, Olivia. He was so fast and so good, but the daimon…was just faster."

She blinked several times, and her lashes looked damp. "You know, he told me what happened in Gatlinburg. Everything you guys went through and how you got him out of the house."

"It was luck. They—my mom and the others—started fighting. I didn't do anything special."

Olivia looked at me then. "He thought the world of you, Alex." She paused, laughing quietly. "When we first started dating, I was jealous of you. It was like I couldn't live up to everything you guys had together. Caleb really loved you."

"I loved him." I took a breath. "And he loved you, Olivia."

Her smile was watery. "I guess I needed to blame someone. It could've been Lea, or the Guards who failed to keep the daimons out. I don't know. It's just that you're this unstoppable force—you're an Apollyon." Springy curls bounced as she shook her head. "And—"

"I'm not an Apollyon yet. But I get what you're saying. I'm sorry." I squeezed the wire on the notebook. "I just wish—"

"And *I'm* sorry."

My head jerked toward her.

"It wasn't your fault. And I was a total bitch to blame you. That day in the hallway, I wanted to apologize but it just all came out wrong. And I know that Caleb would hate me for blaming you. I shouldn't have in the first place. I was just so hurt. I miss him so much." Her voice cracked and she turned away, taking a deep breath. "I know those are just excuses, but I don't blame you."

Tears clogged my throat. "You don't?"

Olivia shook her head.

I wanted to hug her but wasn't sure if that would be cool. Maybe it was too soon. "Thank you." There was more I wanted to say, but I couldn't find the right words.

Her eyes closed. "Want to hear something funny?"

I blinked. "Yeah."

Turning to me, she grinned even though her eyes glistened with tears. "After the day you and Jackson had that fight, everyone was talking about it in the cafeteria. Cody was walking by and said something ignorant. I don't remember what—probably something about how great being a pure-blood is." She rolled her eyes. "Anyway, Lea got up all casually and dumped her entire plate of food on his head." A giggle broke free. "I know I shouldn't laugh, but I wished you'd seen that. It was hilarious."

My mouth dropped open. "Seriously? What did Cody do? Did Lea get in trouble?"

"Cody threw a fit, calling us a bunch of heathens or something lame like that. I think Lea got written up and her sister wasn't too happy with her."

"Wow. That doesn't sound like Lea."

"She's kind of changed." Olivia sobered up. "You know, after everything? She's not the same. Anyway, I have some stuff I need to do, but I'm…I'm glad we talked."

I met her gaze and felt some of the tension leak away. It wouldn't be like before, not for a while. "Me, too."

She looked relieved as she smiled. "See you in the cafeteria for lunch tomorrow?"

"Sure. I'll be there."

"I'm leaving for winter break next week with my mom. Some kind of Council business she has to attend to, and she wants me to go with her, but when I get back, can we do something? Like maybe watch a movie or hang out?"

While mortals had winter break over the Christmas holiday, we had ours the entire month of February, in celebration of Anthesteria. Back in the old days, the festival was only three days, and everyone pretty much got drunk in honor of Dionysus. It was like All Souls Night and Carnival rolled into one giant, drunken orgy. At some point the pures had extended the festival to an entire month, calmed it down, and filled it with Council sessions. Slaves and servants used to be able to participate, but that had also changed. "Yeah, that would be great. I'd love to."

"Good. I'll keep you to that." Olivia got up to leave but stopped at the door. Turning around, she gave me a small wave and a tentative smile before dipping out.

I glanced at my notebook. Some of the hurt and guilt

that had lingered after Caleb's death had lifted. I took a deep breath and scribbled a quick note to Laadan, telling her not to worry about the drink incident and thanking her for telling me about my father. Then I wrote two sentences under the brief paragraph.

Please tell my father that I LOVE him. I will fix this.

Later that night, I sealed the letter and handed it over to Leon, who was hovering outside my dorm, with explicit instructions to give it to Aiden.

"May I ask why you're passing notes to Aiden?" He eyed the letter like it was a bomb.

"It's a love note. I'm asking him to circle 'yes' or 'no' if he likes me."

Leon pinned me with a bland look but shoved the letter in his back pocket. I gave him a cheeky grin before shutting the door. It felt like a semitruck was lifted from my shoulders now that I'd written the letter. Spinning away from the door, I darted toward the computer desk. My bare toes smacked against something thick and heavy.

"Ouch!" Hopping on one leg, I looked down. "Oh, my gods, I am so stupid."

The Myths and Legends book stared up at me. I bent quickly and grabbed it. Somehow, during all the craziness, I'd forgotten about it. Sitting down, I cracked open the dusty thing and began searching for the section Aiden had mentioned in New York.

I had no luck in the part written in English. Sighing, I flipped to the front of the book and started skimming the pages covered in what looked like gibberish to me. My fingers stilled about a hundred pages in, not because I recognized any of the writing, but because I recognized the symbol at the top of the page.

It was a torch turned down.

There were several pages written in ancient Greek, completely useless to me. They should be teaching that instead of trig at the Covenant, but what did I know? Then again, the pures were taught the old language.

Aiden knew the old language—kind of nerdy, in a totally hot way.

If I could find out more about the Order, then maybe we could get the evidence needed to prove that something crazy was up with Telly and Romvi. I wasn't a hundred percent sure that it had anything to do with what had happened, but it was much better than Seth's suggestion.

The last thing we needed was an uprising…or one of us killing *another* pure-blood.

CHAPTER EIGHT

Later that night, when I was half asleep, I heard the familiar click of my door unlocking. I rose onto my elbow, pushing the mess of hair out of my face. The fine shiver tiptoeing down my spine told me it was Seth. Locks didn't stand a chance against him. He either melted them or used the element of air to unlatch them from the other side.

He stopped just inside the doorway. His eyes were a soft, tawny glow in the dark.

Surprised to see him, it took me a few moments to say anything. "You're not supposed to be in my dorm this late, Seth."

"Has that ever stopped me before?" He sat on the edge of my bed, and I could feel his gaze on me. "You've been in a much better mood this evening."

"And here I thought I was getting better at blocking you."

"You are. You did really well at practice today."

"Is that why you're here?" I heard him kick off his shoes. "Because I'm less likely to throw food at you right now?"

"Maybe." I could hear the smile in his voice.

"I was beginning to think you found your own bed more appealing."

"You missed me."

I shrugged. "Seth, about Jackson—"

"I've already told you. I didn't have anything to do with that. And why would I do such a bad, bad thing?"

"I don't know why. Maybe because you're psychotic?"

Seth laughed. "'Psychotic' is such an extreme term. That would suggest I don't feel guilty about my actions."

I arched a brow. "My point exactly."

When he pulled back the covers, I scooted over and watched him slide his legs under them. He eased onto his side, facing me. "You do realize I have a guard detail. They'll know you're in here."

"I passed Linard on my way in." He brushed back a strand of hair that had fallen across my cheek, tucking it behind my ear. His hand lingered. "He told me I was breaking the rules. I told him to bite me."

"And what did he say to that?"

Seth's hand dropped to my shoulder, covering the thin strap of my tank top. The cord inside me started to hum softly. "He didn't look too happy. Said he was going to report me to Marcus." My heart dropped a little. There was no doubt in my mind that meant Aiden would hear about this; Aiden had to be aware of Seth's sleeping habits. Knots formed in my stomach as I stared at Seth. *I'm not with Aiden. I'm not with Aiden. I'm not doing anything wrong.* Tension still dug into my muscles.

"Not that Marcus can really do anything about it." He leaned over, gently guiding me down so that I was lying on my back. His fingers glided under the strap, and I shivered as his rough knuckles brushed over my collarbone. "He's just the Dean."

"And my uncle," I pointed out. "I doubt he likes the idea of boys sleeping in my bed."

"Hmm, but I'm not just any boy." He tipped his head down. His hair fell forward, shielding his face. "I'm the Apollyon."

My chest rose sharply. "The rules…still apply to you and me."

"Ah, I remember this girl who couldn't follow a simple rule even if her life depended on it." He angled his head, which caused his nose to brush mine. "And I think what we're doing, right now, is the least shocking rule you've broken."

I flushed as I put my hands on his chest, stopping him from overcoming that last inch or two that separated us. "People change," I said lamely.

"Some people do." He placed his arm beside my head, supporting himself.

The cord was really starting to go crazy, demanding that I pay attention to it. My toes curled. "Did you come here to talk about the rules I've broken or what?"

"No. I actually had a reason for coming."

"And that is?" I shifted uncomfortably, trying to ignore the way my skin, especially the palms of my hands, started to tingle. Thank the gods he had a shirt on.

"Give me a second."

I frowned. "Why do—"

Seth dipped his head, brushing his lips over mine, and being caught between wanting to clamp my mouth shut and wanting to open for him was a frustrating feeling. I ached to be near him as equally as I did to be away from him.

"That's…that's why you came here?" I asked when he lifted his head.

"It wasn't the main reason."

"Then why are you—" His mouth cut my words off, and the kiss deepened, stealing my protests. The cord tightened as his hand slipped down my arm, over my stomach and under the hem of my shirt.

He smiled against my lips. "I have to travel with Lucian over winter break. I won't return until the end of February."

"What?" The cord's buzzing was getting excessive, making it hard to concentrate. I was kind of surprised that he'd leave so close to my eighteenth birthday, since I'd figured he'd camp inside my room in the weeks leading up to my Awakening. "Where are you going?"

"To the New York Covenant," he answered, sliding his other hand into my hair. "There have been some problems that demand the Council's attention."

Some of the fuzziness receded. "I want to go with you. My father is—"

"No, you can't go. It's not safe for you there."

"I don't care. I want to go. I have to see my father." By the look on Seth's face, I could tell I wasn't gaining any ground. "You'll be there. Nothing will happen. And I'd be less safe here without you." The last words physically hurt to say, but I threw pride under the bus. Seeing my father was that important.

Seth's lips tipped up, enjoying that little ego stroke. "Marcus has assured Lucian that you'll be well protected. Your darling pure-blood would slit his wrists before he let anything happen to you."

I gaped.

"What?" He moved his hand up until it rested under my

rib cage. "It's the truth. And Leon and Linard will be here, watching over you. You'll be fine."

I wasn't scared of being left behind. I just wanted to see my father. "Seth, I have to go."

He kissed my lower lip, which had scarred just a little. "No, you don't. And you're not going. Not even I could get Lucian to agree to take you back to that hellhole."

My mind raced frantically, trying to find a way to convince him.

"And don't even think about sneaking off because everyone is expecting you to do that. I don't think I'll be able to sense much from you when we're that far apart, but from the moment I leave, someone will be watching you. So don't even think it. I'm serious."

"I don't need a damn babysitter."

"Yes, you do." His lips found my chin next. "The girl who can't follow rules to save her own life is still inside you."

"You're an asshole."

"Been called worse by you, so I'll take that as a compliment." He grinned even though I knew he felt the fury rising in me.

"When do you leave?" I asked, trying to keep my voice steady.

"I'm leaving Sunday night, so you're completely stuck with me until then." He kissed the hollow of my throat.

"Great," I muttered. Classes would be suspended on Wednesday. Almost all the pures left for super-posh vacations, which meant most of the Guards would be gone, protecting them. Some of the halfs would be out of here—anyone who still kept in contact with a mortal parent or was on good terms with a pure-blood one. There was still a chance I could sneak out, but how in the hell would I get to New York? I didn't even have a driver's license, but that was the least of my problems.

I'd have to get to New York without getting killed in the process.

Seth kissed me again, and I debated pulling his hair out by the fistful while the bond between us tried its best to choke the living crap out of me.

"Why do you have to go, anyway?" I asked when he took a breather. I needed something—anything—to focus on that would take the edge off the cord that was tightening and tightening.

He twined strands of my hair around his fingers. "There's a problem with the...servants in the Catskills."

"What?" Dread blossomed in my stomach, growing as quickly as a weed. "What do you mean?"

"Some of them disappeared after the attack. Their bodies weren't found and no daimons escaped." Another quick, deep kiss before he spoke again. "And something appears to be wrong with the Elixir."

"Do you know anything about the ones who disappeared?" I caught his wrist before the hand crept any higher under my shirt.

"I don't believe your father is among the missing, but as soon as I can confirm that I'll let you know." He lowered himself down, and since I'd grabbed his wrist, there was nothing to stop him. "I don't want to talk anymore. I'm going to be gone for weeks."

His weight made the cord extremely happy, and I struggled to pay attention. "Seth, this...this is important. What happened with the Elixir?"

He sighed. "I don't know. It doesn't appear to be working as strongly."

"As strongly?"

"Yeah, the halfs…are becoming self-aware. Kind of like the computers in *The Terminator*."

Odd comparison, but I got what he meant. And whoa—that was some serious stuff right there. The Elixir was a mix of herbs and chemicals that worked to keep a half-blood compliant and dazed. Without it, I doubted the halfs in servitude would be thrilled with their lot in life. "It seems to be working here."

"That's the thing. It's working everywhere but there. The Council wants us there to make sure nothing happens in New York, especially after the attack."

"But why do you have to go?"

"I don't know, Alex. Can we talk about this later?" He looked down at me, eyes glowing. "There are other things I want to do."

The cord buzzed its approval. "But—"

Seth kissed me again and the hand against my stomach pressed down. I let go of his wrist, intending on pushing him off, but then I was gripping his shirt. The air around us seemed to crackle. There was something building inside me, a warning that the damn bond was up to no good.

I felt the cord rushing to the surface before I actually opened my eyes. Amber and blue lights cast strange shadows across the wall of my bedroom. I was transfixed by them for a moment. It was so bizarre that we were responsible for them. That they even came from within us.

It freaked me out a little.

But Seth's free hand was everywhere, skimming down my arm, over my leg, and our cords were spiraling together, connecting us. My fingers clenched his shirt, and I was pulling him down one second, then pushing him away the next.

Suddenly, my skin under his palm burned. Tiny pricks of pain stole my breath. I felt the rushing building in my stomach, akasha passing through the cords. A brief flicker of sanity reminded me of what had happened the last time we'd held on. Us, moving together on the bed, and there were fewer clothes to be removed this time.

Panic dug its claws deep in me. I wasn't ready for this—with Seth. Letting go of his shirt, I pushed him hard enough that I was able to wiggle out from underneath him, breaking the connection. I scrambled onto my knees, clutching my stomach. "That…hurt."

Seth looked dazed. "Sorry, it kind of just happened."

Hands shaking, I pulled my shirt up far enough to see what I suspected was going to be there. Centered above my navel, right under my rib cage, was a glowing mark that looked like two check marks joined at the top.

"The power of the gods mark," Seth whispered, sitting up. "Damn Alex, that's a big one. Tomorrow, we should try blowing something up. I know you completely sucked at it when you did it the first time, but I bet it would work now."

I couldn't believe how quickly he went from wanting to get it on to wanting to blow something up. Seth seemed more excited about the rune than the other thing. Hell, his eyes had that crazy look again.

He placed his hands around the mark reverently. "There are four marks that appear first: courage, strength, power, and invincibility. But the power one, that's akasha. See how it's placed here?" He went to touch the mark, but I scooted back. He frowned. "Anyway, that's where you pull power from."

It was also where the cord slumbered when it wasn't trying to turn me into one giant, raging hormone. "What happens when I get the fourth mark?"

Seth ran a hand through his hair, tugging it back from his face. Moonlight cut through the blinds, slicing across his features. "I don't know. Mine came all at once, but they appeared in that order: on both of my palms, my stomach, and then on the back of my neck. Then everywhere else."

My mouth suddenly felt dry. I dropped my shirt and backed up to the edge of the bed. "Do you think I'll Awaken early if the fourth one appears?"

He lifted his eyes. "I don't know, but would it be such a bad thing?"

Dizziness swept through me. "Maybe we should stop… touching or whatever until I turn eighteen."

"What?"

"Seth, I can't Awaken ahead of schedule."

He shook his head. "I don't understand, Alex. Things will be so much better once you Awaken. You wouldn't have to worry about Telly or the furies. Hell, the gods won't even be able to touch us. How is that not a good thing?"

It wasn't a good thing, because once I Awakened, there was a strong chance I'd lose myself in the process. Seth had warned me long ago that it would be like two halves coming together, that whatever he wanted would color my choices and decisions. I'd have no control over myself or my future.

And Aiden had been right that day in the sensory deprivation chamber. It terrified me.

"Alex." Seth took my hand carefully, gently. "You Awakening now would be the best thing for…us. We could even try it. See if we can get the fourth mark to appear. Maybe nothing will happen after that. Maybe you'll Awaken."

I pulled my hand free. The eagerness in his voice creeped me out. "Are…are you doing this on purpose, Seth?"

"Doing what?"

"Trying to get me to Awaken early by touching me or whatever?"

"I'm touching you because I enjoy it." Then he reached for me again, but I knocked his hand away. "What is your deal?" he asked.

"I swear to the gods, Seth—if you are doing this on purpose, I will destroy you."

Seth's brows furrowed. "Don't you think you're being a tad bit melodramatic here?"

"I don't know." And I really didn't. My palms tingled, my stomach burned, and the cord was finally settling down. "You haven't done anything with me except training in weeks and then you show up tonight, all touchy and feely. Then this happens?"

"I was all touchy and feely because I'm going to be gone for weeks." Seth slid off the bed, standing in one fluid motion. "And I wasn't really avoiding you. I was just giving you some space."

"Then why did you come here tonight?"

"Whatever the reason was, clearly it was a mistake." He bent, grabbing his shoes. "Apparently, I'm just here to use you for my nefarious plans."

I climbed off the bed, hugging my elbows. Was I being paranoid? "What are you doing?"

"What does it look like? I don't want to be where I'm not wanted."

An uncomfortable feeling started to twist my insides. "So why did you come here if it…wasn't because of that?"

His head snapped up, eyes a furious shade of ocher. Like a lion that'd been cornered, caught between wanting to run and attack. "I missed you, Alex. That's why. And I'm going to miss you. Did that ever cross your mind?"

Oh, oh gods. Guilt brought a hot flush to my face. That hadn't even crossed my mind. I felt like the worst kind of bitch.

A moment passed and something flared in his eyes. "It's Aiden, isn't it?"

My heart tripped over itself. "What?"

"It's always about Aiden." He laughed, but there was no humor there.

This wasn't about Aiden—had nothing to do with him. It was about Seth and me, but before I could even say a word, Seth looked away.

"I guess I'll see you when I get back." He started toward the doorway. "Just…just be careful."

"Crap," I muttered. I darted around the bed, blocking the door. "Seth—"

"Get out of the way, Alex."

His words irked me, but I took a deep breath. "Look, this whole marking and Awakening thing freaks me out. You know that, but…but I shouldn't have accused you."

There was no change in his expression. "No, you shouldn't have."

"And this has nothing to do with Aiden." It didn't, or at least that's what I kept telling myself as I grabbed his free hand, and he flinched. "I'm sorry, Seth."

He stared behind me, lips thin.

"I really am sorry." I let go of his hand and placed my head against his chest. Carefully, I wrapped my arms around him. "I just don't want to become someone else."

Seth inhaled sharply. "Alex…"

I squeezed my eyes shut. Bond or no bond, I did care about him. He was important to me and maybe there was more to how I felt about him than what the bond was making me feel. Maybe it was just that I cared for him like I'd cared for Caleb. Either way, I didn't want to hurt his feelings.

He dropped his shoes and swept his arms around me. "You drive me crazy."

"I know." I smiled. "The feeling is mutual."

He laughed and then brushed his lips over my forehead. "Come on." He started pulling me back to the bed.

I stalled a little. Not hurting his feelings did not equal me ending up with a mark on the back of my neck.

Seth dropped down, tugging me forward. "To sleep, Alex. Nothing more…unless…" His gaze dropped to my tank top. "You know, you should wear that more often. It leaves very little to the imagination, which is something I like."

Flushing to the roots of my hair, I quickly climbed over him and pulled the covers up to my chin. Seth laughed as he lay down. He threw an arm around my waist, snuggling close. His breathing was steady. Nothing like mine, which seemed to be racing. And he was smiling easily, as if we hadn't just argued.

"You're such a perv," I said for the hundredth time.

"You've called me worse."

And I had a feeling I probably would in the future, too.

CHAPTER NINE

"Wow. Look who's smiling. The world is going to end." Two silvery eyes peeked out behind a mop of curly blond hair, and Deacon St. Delphi smirked as he dropped into the seat beside me. "How's it going, my favorite half-blood?"

"Good." I glanced down at my textbook, lips pursed. "Sorry I haven't been real chatty."

He leaned over, nudging me in the side. "I understand."

Deacon did. That's probably why he hadn't pressured me into talking with him since I'd been back. He'd just sat beside me in class, not saying a word. I hadn't realized he'd been waiting for me to come around.

I glanced at him again. That's the thing about Deacon. Everyone, including Aiden, saw him as a lazy party-boy who didn't pay attention to anything, but he was far more observant than anyone gave him credit for. He'd had a real hard time growing up without his parents, and I think he was finally coming out of the "party-boy who doesn't care about anything" stage.

"Are you doing anything for winter break?"

He rolled his eyes. "That would require Aiden taking time off, since he won't let me off this island without him. He's been super-paranoid ever since the whole thing in the Catskills. I think he's expecting daimons or furies to drop in here any minute."

I cringed. "Sorry."

"Whatever," he replied. "It's not your fault. So, I'm not going to be doing anything exciting. I hear my esteemed older brother is playing guard for you."

I rolled my eyes.

"You know, I overheard him and the Dean talking when he visited the house."

"What house? Aiden's cabin?"

Deacon arched a brow. "No, like *the* house." He saw my dumbfounded look and took pity on me. "Our parents' house? Well, it's really Aiden's house now. It's on the other side of the Island, near Zarak's."

I had no idea that there was another house. I'd just assumed that Aiden had the cabin and Deacon stayed in the dorm. Come to think of it, why in the hell was Aiden living in that tiny shack if he owned one of those huge, opulent houses on the main island?

As if he knew what I was thinking, Deacon sighed. "Aiden doesn't like to stay at the house. Reminds him too much of our parents, and he hates the whole lavish lifestyle thing."

"Oh," I whispered, glancing at the front of the classroom. Our teacher was always late.

"Anyway, back to my story. I overheard them talking." Deacon's chair and desk made a terrible scratching noise as he scooted closer to me. "Want to know?"

Luke, who had been sitting on Elena's desk, faced us. His brows rose when he saw us. "Sure. Spill it," I said.

"There's something going on with the Council—that has to do with the half-bloods."

"Like what?" I asked.

"Don't know exactly. But I know it has something to do with the New York Council." Deacon looked away, focusing on the front of the class. "I figured you might know, since you were just up there."

I shook my head. There was always something going on with the Council, and it probably had to do with the Elixir. Then I realized Deacon was still staring at the front of the classroom. I followed his gaze. He was staring at Luke.

And Luke was staring back at him.

Like in the really intense way I sometimes stared at...Aiden.

My eyes darted back to Deacon. I couldn't see his eyes, but the tips of his ears were pink. After several moments, like too long for one dude to be looking at another dude casually, Deacon leaned back. I thought about the phantom voice I'd heard with Luke in the sensory room. It had sounded familiar...but no way.

"Anyway." Deacon cleared his throat. "I think I might throw a party for those left behind during winter break. You think Aiden will be game?'

"Uh, probably not."

Deacon sighed. "It's worth a try."

I glanced at Luke again. "Yeah, I guess so."

"It's not working."

Seth made an impatient sound in his throat. "Try concentrating."

"I am," I snapped, pushing the windblown hair out of my face.

"Try harder, Alex. You can do it."

I hugged myself, shivering. It was freezing out by the marshes. The cold, damp wind beat against me, and the heavy sweater was no help. We'd been at this for the better part of Saturday. When Seth had suggested I try to blow something up, I'd assumed he'd been joking.

I'd been wrong.

Closing my eyes, I pictured the thick boulder in my mind. I already knew the texture, the sandy color, and its irregular shape. I'd been staring at the damn thing for hours.

Seth moved behind me, taking my hand and placing it against the spot where the latest mark had appeared. "Feel it in here. Do you?"

Feel the cord? Check. I also liked the fact that he was now blocking the worst of the wind.

"Okay. Picture the cord unraveling, feel it coming alive."

I had a feeling Seth was enjoying this way too much, considering how he was pressed against me.

"Alex?"

"Yeah, I feel the cord." I did feel it opening up, slithering through my veins.

"Good. The cord is not just us," he said softly. "It's akasha—the fifth and final element. You should feel akasha now. Tap into it. Picture what you want in your mind."

I wanted a taco, but I doubted akasha could serve me up some Taco Bell. Gods, I'd do some terrible things for Taco Bell right about now.

"Alex, are you paying attention?"

"Of course." I smirked.

"Then do it. Blow up the rock."

Seth made it sound so easy. Like a toddler could do this. I wanted to elbow him in the stomach, but I pictured the rock and then pictured my cord shooting from my hand. I did this over and over again.

Nothing happened.

I opened my eyes. "Sorry, this isn't working."

Seth moved away, brushing back the shorter strands of hair that fell out of his ponytail. He popped his hands on his hips and stared at me.

"What?" Another gust of biting wind had me shuffling to stay warm. "I don't know what you want me to do. I'm cold. I'm hungry. And I saw that *National Lampoon's Christmas Vacation* is on TV for some odd reason, and I must watch it since you soaked up all the time it was on TV during Christmas."

His brows inched up. "Watch what?"

"Oh, my gods! You do not know of the trials and tribulations of the Griswold family?"

"Huh?"

"Wow. That's kind of sad, Seth."

He waved his hand. "It doesn't matter. Something must trigger your ability to tap into akasha. If only..." A thoughtful look crept over his expression and then he clasped his hands. "The first time you did it, you were pissed. And then when you went all crazy ninja on the furies, you were angry and scared. You have to be *pushed*."

"Oh, no no no." I started backing up. "I know where you are going with this, and I'm not doing this with you. I mean it, Seth. Don't you—"

Seth raised his hand and the air element smacked me in the chest, knocking me flat on my back. Fighting the use of the elements was something I had gotten a bit better with. I did tap into the power then and I felt the cord tense, then snap. I buckled, breaking through what felt like hurricane-force winds. Rising up, my hair blew straight back.

I was going to maim Seth.

Then he was on me, using his weight to force me back against the coarse, dead grass. Small pebbles dug into my back as I squirmed under him. "Get off, Seth!"

"Make me," he said, lowering his face to mine.

I tipped my hips, wrapped my legs around his waist and rolled. For a second, I had the advantage and I wanted to wrap my chilled fingers around his neck and choke the living crap out of him. I didn't like being pinned or the ensuing feeling of helplessness. And Seth knew that.

"Not like that," Seth grunted. He grasped my shoulders, flipping me onto my back. "Use akasha."

We struggled, rolling through the small bushes. He was growing more frustrated each time he slammed me back, and I was feeling murderous. Rage, sweet and heady, rushed through me, twisting around the cord. I felt it building. My skin was tingling. The marks of the Apollyon seared and pulsed.

Seth's lips curved. "That's it. Do it."

I screamed.

And then Leon was above us, grabbing Seth by the scruff of his neck and tossing him several feet back. He twisted in midair like a cat, landing in a crouch. The marks of the Apollyon came out all at once, blurring across his skin in dizzying speed. He zeroed in on Leon. There was something deadly in his eyes—the same look he'd given the Master after he'd hit me. I thought of Jackson.

I jumped to my feet, rushing Seth. "No! No, Seth!"

"You really shouldn't have done that." Seth advanced, his intentions clear.

Leon arched a brow. "You want to try that, boy?"

"You want to die?"

"Stop it," I hissed, squirming between them. I looked over

my shoulder at Leon. The pure-blood Sentinel didn't even look concerned. He was crazy. "Leon, we were training."

"That's not what it looked like to me."

Over Seth's broad shoulder, I saw several Guards and Aiden heading our way. I hoped they picked up their pace and got here before one of these idiots did something stupid.

"Leon, he wasn't hurting me," I tried again.

"What do you think you're going to do?" Seth demanded. "To me?"

He stared down at Seth. "You really think you can take me, don't you?"

"I don't think." Akasha, brilliant and beautiful, surrounded his right hand. The air crackled around the ball. "I know."

This was insane. I grabbed Seth's arm and a rush of anger hit me. *I* wanted to attack Leon, needed to show him that he was messing with the wrong person, that I was better than him. He wouldn't dare touch *me* again. I was going to show him.

"Bring it," Leon said, his voice low.

"Hey!" yelled Aiden. "That's enough!"

Seth and Leon moved at the same time, both of them knocking me aside. The combination of their arms sweeping out and hitting me sent me flying backward. I hit the boulder I'd been trying to blow up, tumbling over the top. Twisting so I didn't hit the soggy marsh face-first, I landed on my hands and knees. Icy muck saturated my jeans and splashed my face.

Stunned more by the pure rage than anything else, I lifted my head and peered through my hair. What the hell had just happened? The whole pushing me thing had been an accident, but the violence I'd felt had not been my own.

It had been Seth's. It wasn't like those times I'd had those hot flashes. This had been different. I'd *felt* what he'd felt, *wanted* what he'd wanted. Had that happened before? I didn't think so. My hands shook.

The Guards had reached Leon. I wasn't sure if they were trying to protect Leon or Seth. Aiden, though, went after the Apollyon, like I should've known he would the moment I spied him stalking across the wind-tossed sand.

I was sure Aiden knew what had happened had been an accident, but he looked like he wanted to pummel both guys. By the sounds of their arguing and shoving one another, Leon blamed Seth. Seth blamed everyone but himself. The Guards looked increasingly worried.

Staggering out of the marsh, I headed toward them just as Seth tried to sidestep Aiden.

Eyes flashing, Aiden grabbed him by the collar of his shirt and pushed him back several feet. It was like he didn't even see the strongest and deadliest element known to the gods inches away from his body—or he didn't care.

"That's enough," Aiden said, shoving Seth as he let go. "Back off."

"You really want to get involved in this?" Seth asked. "Right now?"

"More than you would ever know."

Akasha fizzled out and Seth pushed Aiden. "Oh, I think I do. And you know what, it's something I think about…*every time*. You get what I'm saying?"

"That's the best you got, Seth?" Aiden went toe-to-toe with the Apollyon. And suddenly, I knew this wasn't just about what had just happened. This was more. "Because I think you and I both know the truth about *that*."

Oh, dear gods, this was turning into a boy fight.

Seth moved so fast it was hard to see him. An arm cocked

back, aiming right for Aiden's jaw. Reacting just as fast, Aiden caught Seth's arm and threw him back again.

"Try it again, and I won't stop," Aiden warned.

A second later they were crashing into each other. Both hit the ground, rolling and throwing punches—a blur of black garb as each one gained and lost the upper hand. I started forward but stopped short. They weren't even fighting like Sentinels. There was nothing graceful in their punches or blocks. They brawled like two idiots high on testosterone, and I had the strongest urge to walk up and kick them both in the heads.

I threw my hands up. "You've got to be kidding me."

The Guards and Leon shot forward, grabbing for the two guys. It took several tries to get Aiden off Seth. A cut marred his right cheek. Blood beaded. There was a split in Seth's lip.

"Are you done?" demanded Leon, shouldering Aiden back a few steps. "Aiden, you need to *stop*."

Aiden wiped the back of his hand over his cheek as he shrugged Leon's hand off. "Yeah, I'm done."

The Guards were saying the same thing to Seth, but when they let go of him, Seth shot around them. "You think I'm scared that you'll turn me in for fighting? Any of you? They can't touch me! I'm the fu—"

"Stop it!" I screamed. "Just stop!" Seth froze, and several sets of eyes centered on me. "Gods! We *were* training. There's no reason to kill each other over this." I glanced at Aiden. "No reason to do *any* of this. Just freaking stop."

Tension still ripened the air, but Seth pulled back and spat out a mouthful of blood. As he straightened his shirt, the marks started to fade. "Like I'd been saying, but apparently all of you are too stupid to understand, we were—"

"Shut up, Seth." I clenched my hands. His brows rose.

Aiden still looked furious. His eyes were like pools of silver, consuming his entire face.

"It's done and over, okay?" I said, mostly to him. "I'm fine. No one is dead. And if you three can manage not to kill each other, I'm going to go and take a shower, because now I smell like ten-day-old butt."

Leon's lips twitched as if he wished to smile, but after the glare I cut his way, his expression returned to the stoic one I was familiar with.

I headed around them, shivering. Icicles were forming on my jeans.

Seth wheeled around. "Alex—"

"No." I stopped. There was no way he was coming back with me. I needed to be away from him, putting some distance between his anger and me before I started throwing punches. I needed to figure out what'd happened back there, why I'd felt what Seth wanted so strongly.

"Alex!" Seth called out. "Come on."

"Leave me alone right now." I started walking again. "I'm done with this for today. I mean it. I'm *done*."

CHAPTER TEN

Seth knew better than to seek out my company Saturday night. I was grateful for that because I didn't want to see his face. I did, however, answer the door Sunday evening when he actually knocked. That's how I knew he was feeling apologetic. Seth never knocked.

His hands were shoved into the pockets of his dark cargos. The right side of his lip was swollen. "Hey," he said, staring over my head.

"Hey."

He shifted from one foot to the next. "Alex, I'm…sorry about yesterday. I didn't—"

"Stop," I cut him off. "I know you were just trying to get me to use akasha and you didn't mean to knock me over, but you guys were insane. Not in a good way, Seth."

A sheepish look crept across his face. "I know, but Aiden pissed me—"

"Seth."

"Okay. You're right. It's over and done. And I don't want

to argue with you. I'm getting ready to leave." He looked at me then. "I thought it would be nice if you walked with me to the bridge."

"Just let me grab something to put on." I needed to talk with him, anyway. After I grabbed a hoodie, we walked out of the dorm in silence. The campus was dark; only the shadows of the patrolling Guards moved. When I let out my breath, it formed small puffs in the air. "I felt your anger yesterday."

"I'm sure anyone within a ten-mile radius felt my anger yesterday."

"That's not what I meant." We followed the marbled pathway around the dorms, heading toward the bridge by the main Covenant building. "I *really* felt it. I wanted to knock the crap out of Leon. It was like…like it was my anger."

Seth didn't respond as he stared ahead, eyes narrowed.

"It went away as soon as I wasn't touching you, but it was pretty weird." I stopped walking as the bridge came into view. A black Hummer was being loaded with luggage. Exhaust filled the air, and several Council Guards stood post. "You don't have anything to say about that?"

He glanced down at me. "You were so close to tapping into akasha, Alex. If Leon hadn't interfered, it would've happened."

As if that was the most important thing that'd happened. "Seth, did you hear a word I said?"

"I did, and I don't know why you felt my anger so clearly." He took his hands out of his pockets and folded his arms. "Maybe it was because you were tapping into akasha. It made you more in tune with what I was feeling."

What I had felt didn't seem to bother or really surprise Seth. But to me, it was a pretty big deal. "When I Awaken, I'll feel and want what you want. Don't you get what I'm saying? I *wanted* what *you* wanted already."

"Alex." He dropped his hands on my shoulders and pulled me against his chest. "You're not Awakening. Stop worrying."

I frowned and pushed off. He let me go. "But it's really starting to happen, isn't it? With the marks and now this? And I'm only like a month away."

"It's not such a—"

"Alexandria, I am so glad you've come to see Seth off," said Lucian. I turned and was immediately enveloped in a weak hug. The smell of incense and cloves choked me. "I wish it was safe to bring you along. It would ease my worries to have you by Seth's side."

My arms stuck out from my sides awkwardly. Ugh. I hated when Lucian did this.

He patted my back and stepped away, addressing Seth. "How many Guards do you think we should bring?"

Lucian was asking Seth for his opinion? What. The. Hell. I turned to Seth in disbelief.

Seth stood straighter. "At least five, which would leave four behind to help keep guard in case something should arise here."

"Good. You have an eye for leadership, Seth." Lucian patted his shoulder. "If we had more Sentinels like you, we wouldn't have such a serious daimon problem." He paused, smiling. "If we had more men like you on the Council, then our world would be far better."

I wanted to gag. There was no way Seth could be falling for this epic level ass-kissery. It was so obvious from the way Lucian simpered and cooed. It was blatant, but by the gods, Seth looked like he'd just been handed a million dollars and been told he could spend it all on girls and liquor.

"I'd have to agree." Seth's smug smile spread.

I wanted to shake Seth. I was seriously considering it.

Lucian faced me. "You, my dear, are lucky in more ways than most half-bloods. Being blessed as an Apollyon and having this fine young man as your other half."

I scrunched up my face. Beside me, Seth went still.

"I'll leave you two to say goodbye. We shall be leaving in a few moments, Seth."

I stared at Lucian's retreating form. The white robes flowed out, never quite trailing on the ground. I thought about how he'd stared at Minister Telly's throne while I'd given my testimony in the Catskills. No one loved power more than Lucian.

"You know," drawled Seth, "you don't have to look so shocked by what Lucian said. It could be worse."

I laughed. "Are you serious?"

Seth glowered. "I happen to think I'm a pretty damn good catch."

"You happen to think you're the greatest thing that ever breathed, but that's not what I'm talking about. He was kissing your ass, Seth. He's up to something."

"He wasn't kissing my ass." He folded his arms again. "Lucian happens to think I know what I'm talking about. He also happens to appreciate what I have to say."

"You have got to be kidding me." I tried to not roll my eyes.

"Why is that so hard for you to believe?" Displeasure radiated from his voice and stance. "Let me ask you a question, Alex. If that was Lucian or your uncle saying good things about Aiden, would you find it so hard to swallow?"

"What the hell is that supposed to mean?" And where had that come from? "Aiden is a Sentinel. His ability to make decisions or lead is—"

"What do you think I am?" Seth leaned his head forward, brows lowered. "A joke instead of a Sentinel?"

Yikes. I saw my mistake. "That's not what I meant. You're a Sentinel. A damn good one, but please tell me you don't trust him." I grabbed his forearm and squeezed. "That's all I meant to say."

"I do trust Lucian, and you should, too. Out of everyone around you, he's the only one who's trying to make our world different."

"What?"

"Seth?" Lucian called. "It's time."

"Wait." I held onto his arm. "What do you mean?"

Agitation blew off him as he stared at me intently. "I have to go. Please be careful and remember what I said the other night. Don't even think about trying to make your way to New York."

I glared at him.

A bit of a smile peeked through. He started to turn away but stopped. "Alex?"

"What?"

His mouth opened as he ran his hand over his head. "Just be careful, okay?" When I nodded, he reached into his pocket and pulled out something small and slim. "I almost forgot. I picked this up so we could talk while I was gone."

I took the cell phone. It wasn't one of the cheap versions, and I hoped it had a lot of games preloaded on it. "Thanks."

Seth nodded. "My number is programmed in there. I have yours."

There was nothing else to say. When Seth reached the Hummer, Lucian clapped him on the back *again*.

Leon suddenly appeared beside me—my escort back to the dorm, I realized.

Seth climbed into the Hummer, leaving to board a private jet at the airport on the mainland. He glanced back at me as the vehicle began to move.

I forced a smile before Leon guided me away from the bridge, but under the overhead lamps, I saw the brief look of disappointment on Seth's face. And the satisfied smile that was on Lucian's.

It was weird with Seth being gone. The cord in me settled down, and I was pretty sure if a god appeared in front of me, Seth wouldn't have felt a flicker of surprise. It had only been one day since he'd left, but I already felt...*normal*. Like a weight had lifted off my shoulders.

And that was odd, because my backpack was ridiculously heavy with the Myths and Legends book in it. I was carrying it around, hoping to corner Aiden with it whenever he took up babysitting duties. Right now Leon was trailing behind me at a not-so-discreet distance.

I stopped in the middle of the pathway by the garden and turned around. "Aren't you cold?"

Leon glanced down at the short-sleeved shirt he was wearing. "No. Why?"

"Because it's freezing." And it was. I had a tank top, a long- sleeve thermal, and a sweater on, and I was still cold.

Leon stopped beside me. "Then why are you outside if you're so cold?"

"Unfortunately, going outside is the only method of traveling to other parts of the campus, unless you know something I don't."

"You could just do us all a favor and stay in your dorm," he suggested.

Shivering, I hugged my elbows. "Do you have any idea how nice it is to be able to do something other than train or stay in my room?"

"Or spend time with Seth?"

I looked at him closely, trying not to smile. "Was that a joke? Oh, my gods. It was."

His features remained expressionless. "There is nothing about that boy that is a joking matter."

"Okay." I turned around and started walking. This time Leon walked beside me. "You really don't like Seth, do you?"

"Is it that obvious?"

I peeked at him. "No. Not at all."

"Do you?" he asked as we rounded the corner of the training center. The wind off the ocean was unnaturally brutal. "I've heard rumors…that two Apollyons share a powerful bond. It must be hard to know how you truly feel about someone if that's the case."

Now this was awkward. There was no way I was discussing my relationship troubles with Leon of all people.

He sighed deeply as he stared up at the statue of Apollo and Daphne, a distant look on his face. "Emotions that are forced always end in tragedy."

That was deep. Another gust of frigid wind cut through me. The look on Daphne's face was tragic. "Do you think Daphne knew that the only way she could escape Apollo was by dying?"

He didn't answer immediately, and when he did, his voice was thick. "Daphne did not die, Alex. She still remains as she was the day…she was lost. A laurel tree."

"Man, that sucks. Apollo was such a freak."

"Apollo was struck by a love arrow and Daphne was struck by a lead one." He looked down as he gestured at the statue.

"Like I said, love that is not organic in nature is dangerous and tragic."

Tucking my hair back, I glanced at the statue again. "Well, I hope I don't have to turn myself into a tree."

Leon tsked. "Then pay attention to what is need and what is want."

"What?" I looked at him sharply, squinting. The sun had begun to set, casting an eerie golden halo over him. "What did you just say?"

He shrugged. "Your other babysitter is here."

Distracted, I turned around. Aiden was strolling up the walkway. I'd kill to see him in jeans again. I winced. Okay, maybe not *kill*, but close. I twisted back around. Leon was gone.

"Dammit," I muttered, scanning the growing shadows creeping across the beach and garden.

"What?" Aiden asked.

My chest fluttered like always as I faced him. There was a slight bruise along his jaw from his scuffle with Seth. "I was talking to Leon and he just up and disappeared on me."

Aiden smiled. "He has a habit of doing that."

"It's just that he said something—" I shook my head. "It doesn't matter. Are you my babysitter for now?"

"Until you decide you're staying in for the evening," he responded. "Where you headed?"

"I was going to the rec center, but I have something I want to show you." I tapped the bottom of my bag. "You up for it?"

His brows rose. "Should I be concerned by what's in your bag?"

I grinned. "Maybe."

"Well, what is life without taking risks? Do we need privacy?"

"Probably."

"I know just the place." He shoved his hands into the pockets of his cargos. "Follow me."

Grasping the strap of my bag, I ordered myself to pull it together. I wasn't talking to him just so I could ogle him or flirt. Or do anything I wasn't supposed to be doing. I had a purpose for this, so there was no reason for my heart to be racing as fast as it was.

No reason at all.

Aiden nudged me with his elbow after a few moments of walking in silence. "You look different."

"I do?"

"Yeah, you look more like..." He fell quiet. By the time he spoke again, the ocean was a golden red as the sun slowly disappeared over the horizon. "You just seem more relaxed."

"Well, I have some time to myself. That's relaxing." I wondered if I did look different. Didn't seem that way when I got ready this morning. The only thing I really noticed that was different was that the marks hadn't burned or tingled once since Seth left.

"Oh, I almost forgot. Your letter was sent to New York, ahead of the crew that just went up there. Laadan should've received it yesterday or today."

"Really? I hope my father isn't one of the ones who are missing."

"How do you know about that?" He shook his head. "Never mind. Seth?"

I nodded. "He told me that some of the half servants were missing, and that the Elixir wasn't working."

A troubled look darkened his eyes. "How much did he tell you?"

"Not much at all."

Aiden nodded curtly. "Of course not. Some of the halfs aren't responding to the Elixir. There've been outbreaks of fighting among the servants; they're refusing Masters' orders and disappearing. The Council fears there will be a rebellion, and the New York Covenant has been weakened since the attack. And no one knows exactly how or why the Elixir stopped working."

I thought of my father. Was he one of those who'd disappeared, or was he fighting back? I knew he had to be one of the ones the Elixir had stopped working on. "I should be there."

"You should be anywhere but there."

"Now you sound like Seth."

His eyes narrowed. "For once, I have to agree with him."

"That's shocking." My gaze fell on the main academy building, and I knew immediately where we were going. "You're taking me to the library."

The smile returned. "It's private. No one is ever in there at this time, and if anyone spots us, you're studying."

I laughed then. "And someone is going to believe that?"

"Stranger things have been known to happen," he replied as we headed up the wide steps.

We passed two Guards posted at the entrance. Ever since the attack here that had taken Caleb's life, and the subsequent one in the Catskills, security had gone through the roof. Back in the day I would've bitched about this because it made sneaking around so much more difficult. But now, after everything, I was relieved to see the increased numbers.

Toasty air greeted us as we entered. Silently, I followed Aiden down the hall toward the library. Several Instructors still lingered in their offices, and we passed a few students heading out.

Aiden stepped forward and opened the door to the library, forever the gentleman. Smiling my thanks, I stepped inside and came to a complete standstill.

Luke and Deacon were emerging from one of the tall stacks, shoulder to shoulder. When they saw us, I'd swear they jumped at least three feet apart.

"Deacon?" Aiden sounded shocked. "You're in the library?"

"Yeah." Deacon brushed the mop of curls off his forehead. "We were studying for trig."

Neither of them had a single book in their hands. I looked at Luke expectantly. He looked away, but his lips twitched.

Aiden eyes widened. "Wow. I'm sort of proud of you. Studying?"

I clamped my mouth shut.

"Turning over a new leaf and all." Deacon bumped into his older brother. "Taking my education seriously."

My tongue was literally burning to say something. Aiden nodded at Luke. "Keep him out of trouble, Luke."

Oh jeez. By the way Deacon was shifting back and forth on his feet and the size of Luke's grin, I figured Aiden had no idea what kind of "trouble" those two were probably getting into. It wasn't that same-sex relationships were taboo—they weren't. It was the fact that Deacon was a pure and Luke was a half.

And of all the half-bloods in the world, I knew just how stupid and dangerous their relationship was. I glanced at Aiden. He caught my eyes and smiled. My belly flopped. Stupid and dangerous, but it didn't change how I felt.

CHAPTER ELEVEN

I was still struggling to keep my mouth shut when Aiden found an empty study room in the back of the library, somewhere near the Books-I've-Never-Read and the Books-I've-Never-Heard-Of section. He left the door cracked open, which relieved and disappointed me in the same breath.

Sitting down, I dropped my bag on the table. "That's really cool that Deacon is studying and all."

Aiden took the seat beside me, turning so that his knee pressed against mine and he was facing me. "Can I ask you a question?"

"Sure." I pulled out the massive book and placed it between us.

"Do I look stupid?"

My hand froze over the edge of the book. "Uh, is this a trick question?"

He arched a brow.

"No. You don't look stupid."

"I didn't think so." He reached over, taking the book

away from me. His hand brushed mine as he did so, sending little shivers through my fingers. "They were doing the same amount of studying that we're doing."

I wasn't sure how to proceed with this. So, I said nothing.

Aiden stared at the book, brows lowered. "I know what my brother is doing, Alex. And you know what? It pisses me off."

"It does?"

"Yes." He looked up, meeting my gaze. "I can't believe he thinks I'd care if he was into guys or whatever. I've always known he's been that way."

"I didn't."

"Deacon is good at hiding it. What am I looking at?" he asked. I reached over, opening the book to the section about the Order of Thanatos. Understanding dawned. He turned a couple of the pages before going back to the beginning of the section. "He's always pretended to be interested in girls, and maybe he is, too. But he never had me fooled."

"He had me fooled." I watched a wavy lock of hair fall over Aiden's forehead. An insane urge to brush it back hit me hard. "So, he's never said anything to you about it?"

Aiden snorted. "No. I think he believes I'd be upset or something. And trust me, I've wanted to tell him I don't care, but I think it makes him uncomfortable. You know, talking about it. So, I just pretend like I don't see it. I guess he'll talk to me about it eventually."

"He will." I bit my lip. "But…it's Luke."

A muscle popped in his jaw. "I don't like the fact that he may be…involved with a half, but I trust that he won't do anything—" He broke off, laughing. "Yeah, well, I'm not the person to be lecturing on the whole pure and half business."

A flush crept over me. Aiden looked up, and our eyes

locked. He opened his mouth but shut it quickly. He turned back to the book, clearing his throat. "So, the Order of Thanatos? Not exactly fun reading material."

Finding safe ground, I nodded. "Telly had this symbol tattooed on his arm." I pointed at the torch, careful not to touch him. "And so does Romvi—who, by the way, still hates my guts, in case you're wondering. And I remembered in the section that talked about the Apollyon, it mentioned that Thanatos killed Solaris and the First. Maybe this Order business is still going on and they have something to do with what…what happened in the Catskills."

The hand beside the book curled into a fist, but Aiden didn't look up. "As far as I know the Order doesn't exist anymore, but you never know."

"Maybe this can tell us something? But I can't read it."

He smiled briefly. "Give me a few minutes. Reading this isn't exactly easy."

"Okay." Beyond the crack in the door, the library was dark and silent. There was no way I was going out there. I pulled out a notebook and pen. "I'll…pretend to study or something."

Aiden chuckled. "You do that."

I smiled as I started doodling on a blank page of notebook paper. It was hard, because his knee was still touching mine, and it may have been my imagination, but we seemed to be getting closer. His entire lower leg was against mine.

While Aiden read, I sketched a really bad version of the Apollo and Daphne statue outside. Several times, Aiden glanced over and made comments about the drawing. He offered to pay for art classes at one point. I punched him in the arm for that.

Giving up on my masterpiece, I checked to see what page he was on. As I stared at the symbol on each page, I felt a tightening in my throat. Instead of thinking about Telly or Romvi, I thought of the pure I'd killed in the Catskills. Leaning back in the chair, I rubbed my hands over my thighs. The feel of shoving a blade into a pure was very different than shoving one into a daimon, even a half daimon.

There were always choices, and once again, I'd made the wrong decision. Actually, I'd made a string of bad decisions over a short period of time, but that one kind of took the cake. I could've disarmed the pure-blood Guard. I could've done something other than what I had done. I'd killed him and still didn't even know his name.

"Hey," Aiden said softly. "Are you okay?"

"Yep." I lifted my head, forcing a smile. "Find anything out yet?"

He was watching me intently. I could feel it, even after I returned to staring at my hands. "Just why the Order was established," he said. "It appears that they were created by us—the pure-bloods—as an organization to keep the old ways alive and to protect the gods. And it looks like even a few chosen half-bloods were initiated into the Order."

"Great." I smoothed my hands over the table. "Do the gods need protection?"

"It doesn't seem to be in the way you'd think, but more like protecting their existence from mortals and those who might be a threat to the gods." Aiden turned back to the book, flipping several chapters ahead. "It does say the members are marked, which would explain the tattoo if they do belong to the Order. But there is something else."

"What?" I glanced at him. "What is it?"

He took a deep breath and slid the book toward me. "We've all misread it. Understandable because of how it's phrased. Look at this."

Aiden was pointing at the section on the Apollyon. "'The reaction from the gods, particularly the Order of Thanatos, was swift and righteous. Both Apollyons were executed without trial.'"

I sat back, understanding sinking in. "It wasn't Thanatos who killed them, but the Order of Thanatos."

Aiden nodded as he turned back to the section on the Order. "That's what it looks like."

"But how? Both Solaris and the First would have been fully Awakened. The way Seth talks, once that happens, we become indestructible."

He shook his head. "The Order is very mystical, or at least, that's how it reads in this section." He tapped his finger on something that looked like chicken scratch to me. "The Order is said to be 'the eyes and the hand of Thanatos.' There's something here about the Order being gifted with 'daggers dipped in the blood of the Titans.'"

"Daggers dipped in the blood of the Titans? Like, literally? Is the Apollyon somehow allergic to Titan blood?" I shook my head. "What I don't get is, if the gods and the Apollyon can both use akasha, then why would the gods—Thanatos—need anyone else to kill the Apollyon? They could just use akasha."

"I don't know," he said, looking at me. His eyes were gunmetal gray. "And I have a hard time believing that Seth wouldn't know, either. Didn't he tell you that, once you Awaken, the knowledge of the previous Apollyons will pass on to you?"

"Yeah, he did. Seth would have to know." An uncomfortable feeling clawed for my attention as I rested my chin on my palm. If Seth knew everything that the previous Apollyons knew, then wouldn't one of them, in all these years, have figured out that they were a product of a union between a pure and a half? And wouldn't one of the Apollyons have to know about the Order, especially if the lives of Solaris and the First had passed to Seth during his Awakening?

"What is it?" Aiden asked quietly.

Anger stirred, poking at the cord. "I don't think Seth is being completely honest with me."

Aiden didn't respond.

I drew in a deep breath. "I don't understand why he would lie about this. Maybe…maybe he just never put two and two together." That sounded lame even to me, but my brain had a hard time accepting that Seth could be hiding something like this. Why would he?

A few moments passed before Aiden spoke. "Alex, if the Order does exist today, then they could be behind the attacks in the Catskills. And if they are the eyes and hand of Thanatos, they've pegged you as a threat."

I thought about what the furie had said before she'd tried to rip my head off—that I was a threat, and it wasn't anything personal. But trying to kill me was very personal. "Do you think the furies were there because of the daimon attack, or because…of me?"

"They didn't react until the daimon attack."

Rubbing my temples, I closed my eyes. This was all giving me a headache. "There are just so many things that don't add up—the Order, the furies, Seth. Why did they go after me instead of him?"

Aiden closed the book. "I need to tell Marcus about this. If the Order is still alive and well, then this is serious. And if Telly is a member, then we need to be careful."

I nodded, prying my eyes open. I could feel his gaze on me again. "Okay."

"And I don't want you going to Romvi's class anymore,"

he continued. "I'll talk to Marcus and I'm sure he'll agree with that."

"That shouldn't be hard. Tomorrow is the last day of classes before break, so I'll skip." I shivered. "Do you think the 'eyes of Thanatos' part is something literal? And daggers actually dipped in real honest-to-gods Titan blood?"

"Knowing the gods, I'd go with a yes." There was a pause, and Aiden reached over, capturing my chin with the tips of his fingers. He slowly turned my head toward him. "What are you not telling me, Alex?"

A spark of heat shot through me. "Nothing," I whispered, and tried to turn my head, but he kept me still.

"You know you can tell me anything, right? And I know there is something you're keeping from me."

Seth's warning to keep the Apollyon marks quiet was overwhelmed by the desire to tell someone what was happening. And who better to tell than Aiden? He was the one person in this world that I trusted, especially considering how much he'd risked to keep me safe. Seth wouldn't be happy if he knew, but then again, I wasn't particularly happy with Seth at the moment.

"It's happening," I said finally.

Aiden's eyes searched mine. "What's happening?"

"This—the freaky stuff." I lifted my hands, palms up. His gaze dropped without releasing my chin, and when his eyes met mine again, they were questioning. "I've started getting the marks of the Apollyon. You can't see them, but they're there, on both of my palms. And there's one on my stomach."

He seemed taken aback by this, releasing my chin but not moving away. "When did this start happening?"

I looked away. "The first happened while we were in the Catskills. Seth and I were training one day, and I got mad.

Somehow, I blew up a rock and then the next thing I know there was this cord coming from Seth and I got a rune."

"Why didn't you tell me?"

"Well, we really weren't getting along then, and you were busy. And Seth asked me not to say anything until we knew what was going on." Sighing, I told him about the rest of the times and how I'd seen my own cord. Displeasure rolled off Aiden by the time I finished telling him. "It happens when we're…touching sometimes. Seth thinks that, if I get the fourth mark on the back of my neck, then I'll Awaken. Maybe ahead of schedule, and he's all thrilled by that prospect."

"Alex," he breathed unsteadily.

"Yeah, I know. I'm a huge freak even by Apollyon standards." I laughed. "I don't want the fourth mark. You know, I'd kind of like to ride out the rest of being seventeen and not be the Apollyon. But Seth is all like, 'This would be the best thing ever.'"

"Best thing for who?" he asked quietly. "You or Seth?"

I laughed again, but my weird humor dried up when I recalled how I suspected Seth of doing the rune things on purpose.

"Alex?"

"Seth says it would be best for me because I'd be stronger, but I think he's…I think he's jonesing for a power boost. Reminds me of Super Mario Brothers power up or something, because I can feel it—akasha—going from me to…" My mouth dropped open. "Son of a bitch."

"What?" Aiden frowned.

My stomach rolled. "The second time I got a mark, I was exhausted for days." I sat up straighter, staring at Aiden as it clicked into place. "Remember the night we all met in Marcus's office? Another rune had appeared right before then and that time had been different than any other time." I felt heat crawl over my cheeks as I remembered how much I'd been down with the whole thing while it was happening. "Anyway, I was really tired and just off after that for days."

Aiden nodded. "I remember. You were pretty crabby."

My crabbiness had led to the sensory deprivation room… and Aiden's whispered fear. "Well, you didn't get it as bad as Seth. I threw a sub at him."

He was trying to fight a smile, but his eyes lightened. "He probably deserved it."

"He did, but gods, is that what's going to happen when I Awaken?" Dread traced icy fingers over my skin. "He's going to drain me. I don't even think he realizes that."

Anger flared in his eyes, dispelling the softness that had gathered in them. His hands curled into fists. "Whatever it is that you two are doing that's causing those runes to show up, you need to stop."

I looked at him blandly. "I've already decided that, but that isn't going to stop it from happening eventually. And you know what the really messed-up thing is? My mom warned me that the First would drain me. I just thought she was being all daimon crazy."

Aiden reclaimed the little distance I'd been able to put between us. "I'm not going to let anything happen to you, Alex. That goes for Seth, too."

Whoa. My heart did a crazy thing there. And he really sounded like he believed he could. "Aiden, you can't stop this. No one can."

"We can't stop you from Awakening, but the power transfer will only happen if you touch after you turn eighteen, right? Then you don't touch."

I couldn't possibly imagine Seth being down with the

whole "not touching" part, but he'd understand once he knew what it could possibly do. "He'll understand," I said. "I'll talk to him when he gets back. This is probably something better to discuss face to face."

Aiden didn't look convinced. "I don't like this."

"You don't like *him*," I pointed out gently.

"You're right. I don't like Seth, but there's something more to this."

"Isn't there always?" I moved slightly and felt his breath over my lips. If I moved an inch, our lips would touch. And Aiden was suddenly staring at my mouth.

"I'll talk to Marcus," Aiden said, voice gruff.

"You already said that."

"I did?" His head angled slightly. "We should head back."

I swallowed. Aiden wasn't moving and every muscle in my body demanded that I cross that tiny space between us. But I pushed back the chair, making a horrible scratching noise. I stood. There didn't seem to be enough air in the little room with faded, pea-green walls. I started toward the door but stopped when I realized I'd left my bag on the table. I turned around.

Aiden stood in front of me. I hadn't heard him rise or move toward me. He had my bag in his hand, book already tucked inside. And he was standing so close that the tips of his shoes brushed mine. My heart was racing, and it felt like a dozen butterflies had exploded in my stomach. I was half-afraid to breathe, to feel what I knew I wasn't allowed.

He placed the strap of my bag over my shoulder and then he tucked my hair back behind my ear. I thought that maybe he was going to hug me—or shake me, because that was always a possibility. But then his hand slid over my cheek and his thumb smoothed over my lower lip, careful with the faint scar over the center, even though the pain had long since ceased.

I sucked in a sharp breath. His eyes were liquid silver. My pulse pounded through me. I knew he wanted to kiss me, maybe do other stuff. My skin was tingling with excitement, anticipation, and so much want. And I think he was feeling what I was. I didn't need a stupid cord to tell me that.

But Aiden wouldn't act on it. He had the kind of self-control that rivaled those of the virgin priestesses who'd served in Artemis's temples. And there were all the other reasons why he shouldn't—why I shouldn't.

Aiden closed his eyes and exhaled roughly. When his eyes reopened, he dropped his hand and shot me a quick smile. "Ready?" he asked.

Missing his touch already, all I could do was nod. We walked back to my dorm in silence. I kept stealing glances at him, and he didn't look angry, just lost in his own thoughts and perhaps a little sad.

Aiden walked me straight to my door as if some crazy Order member or a furie was going to jump out of a supply closet. The hall was nearly empty since I shared the first floor with a lot of pures. Their parents had pulled them from class on Monday, getting an earlier start on winter break. He nodded curtly and waited until I closed and locked the door.

Dropping my bag by the couch, I sat and pulled out the cell phone Seth had given me. There was only one contact saved in the address book: *Cuddle Bunny*.

I couldn't help but laugh. There always seemed to be two sides to Seth—the funny and charming side, the one who could be patient and gentle. And then there was a whole different side—the Seth I didn't really know, the one who seemed to only tell half-truths and was the physical embodiment of everything I feared.

Taking a deep breath, I pressed on the name and heard the phone ring once, twice, and then kick over to a standard voicemail greeting.

Seth didn't answer. Nor did he call back that entire evening.

CHAPTER TWELVE

I had no clue what Seth could be doing that he was unable to return a call. It wasn't like I was worried about his safety. Seth could take care of himself. But I did wonder if he was still mad at me. Funny thing was, if he wasn't, he was going to be after I got done talking to him. Pushing Seth out of my mind was surprisingly easy as I entered Technical Truths and Legends class.

Deacon glanced up, grinning as I sat beside him. I was surprised to see him on the last day of classes. I figured that, out of everyone, he would have wiggled his way out of class. "How did your library visit go? Get any studying done?"

I peeked at the front of the classroom. Luke was talking to Elena, but he was watching us—Deacon—out of the corner of his eye. "*My* library visit?" I focused on Deacon. "How was yours?"

"Good. Got a lot of studying done." Deacon didn't even miss a beat.

"Wow." I lowered my voice. "Amazing, considering neither of you had any books to study."

Deacon opened his mouth but shut it.

I winked.

The tips of his ears turned bright red. He tapped his fingers on the top of the desk. "Well, then."

Part of me wanted to tell Deacon that Aiden knew and he had nothing to worry about, but that was so not my place. But maybe I could give it a gentle push in the right direction. "It's not a big deal," I whispered. "Honestly, no one here, pure or half, cares about that."

"It's not like that," he whispered back.

I raised a brow. "It's not?"

"No." Deacon sighed. "I like girls, too, but..." His gaze found Luke. "He's different."

Well, at least I hadn't been completely off-base when it came to Deacon's preferences. "Yeah, Luke sure is different."

Deacon cracked a smile. "It's not what you think. We haven't...done anything."

"Whatever." I grinned.

He leaned over the gap between our desks. "He's a half, Alex. Of all people, I think you know just how dangerous that is."

I jerked back and stared at him.

Deacon winked as a sly grin crossed his face. "But the question is: worth breaking the number one rule or not?"

Before I could even open my mouth to respond to that—and honestly, I had no idea what to say—two Council Guards stepped into the class, silencing the entire room. I shifted back in my seat as my unease blossomed, almost wishing I could slide under the table.

The one with cropped brown hair scanned the room, his lips pressed into a hard line. His gaze landed on me. The blood froze in my veins. Lucian wasn't here, and I didn't recognize the two Guards.

"Miss Andros?" His voice was soft, yet full of authority. "You need to come with us."

Every damn kid in the class turned and stared. Grabbing my bag, I met Deacon's wide eyes. I headed toward the front of the class, forcing a "whateva" smile on my face. But my knees were shaking.

Council Guards calling someone out of class was never a good thing.

There was a low murmur radiating from where Cody and Jackson sat. I ignored them and followed the Guards out. No one spoke as we walked through the halls and up the ridiculous number of steps. Dread continued to weave its way through me. Marcus wouldn't have sent Council Guards to retrieve me. He'd have sent Linard, or Leon, even Aiden.

Covenant Guards opened the door to Marcus's office, and I was ushered in. My gaze traveled over the room, quickly seeking out the occupant.

My steps faltered.

Head Minister Telly stood in front of Marcus's desk; hands clasped behind him. Those pale eyes sharpened the moment our gazes locked. The gray seemed to have spread from his temples since the last time I'd seen him, now peppering his hair. Instead of the lavish robes he'd donned during the Council, he wore a simple white tunic and linen pants.

The door shut with a soft click behind me. I spun around. There were no Guards, no Marcus. I was completely alone with Head Minster Douchebag. Great.

"Will you sit, Miss Andros?"

I turned around slowly, forcing myself to take a deep breath. "I prefer to stand."

"But I prefer that you sit," he replied evenly. "Take a seat."

A direct order from the Head Minister was something I

couldn't refuse. But it didn't mean I was just going to bend right over for him. I made my way to the chair as slowly as possible, smiling on the inside when I saw the muscle in his jaw begin to tick.

"What can I do for you, Head Minister?" I asked after I made a show of placing my bag by my feet, smoothing out my sweater, and getting comfortable.

Disgust filled his gaze. "I have some questions for you about the night you left the Council."

Acid was eating its way through my stomach. "Shouldn't Marcus be here? And don't you have to wait till my legal guardian is present? Lucian is in New York, where you should be."

"I see no reason to include them in this…unseemly business." He turned his attention to the aquarium, watching the fish for a few moments while I grew more uncomfortable. "After all, both of us know the truth."

That he was a giant asshat? Everyone knew that, but I doubted that was what he was getting at. "What truth?"

Telly laughed as he turned around. "I want to chat with you about the night the daimons and furies attacked the Council, about the real reason you fled."

My heart stuttered, but I kept my face blank. "I thought you knew. The daimons were after me. So were the furies. See, I was terribly popular by the end of the night."

"That is what you say." He leaned against the desk and picked up a small statue of Zeus. "However, there was a dead pure-blood Guard found. Do you have anything to add to that?"

A bitter taste formed in the back of my mouth. "Well… there were a lot of dead pures and halfs. And a lot of dead servants that no one gave two shits about. They would've been saved if someone had helped them."

He arched a brow. "The loss of a half-blood is hardly a concern of mine."

Anger was a different taste in my mouth. It tasted like blood. "Dozens and dozens of them died."

"As I said, how would that be a concern of mine?"

He was goading me. I knew it. And I still wanted to punch him.

"But I am here about the death of one of my Guards," he continued. "I want to know how he died."

I feigned boredom. "I'd say it probably had to do with the daimons that were swarming the building. They do tend to kill people. And the furies were ripping through people."

The smirk on his face faded. "He was killed with a Covenant dagger."

"Okay." I sat back in the chair, cocking my head to the side. "Did you know that halfs can be turned now?"

The Head Minister's eyes narrowed.

I slowed my speech down. "Well, some of those halfs were trained as Sentinels and Guards. They carry daggers. And I think they know how to use those daggers too." Eyes wide, I nodded. "It was probably one of them."

Surprisingly, Telly laughed. It wasn't a nice laugh—more like a Dr. Evil laugh. "What a mouth you have on you. Tell me, is it because you think you're so safe? That being the Apollyon makes you untouchable? Or is it just blind stupidity?"

I pretended to think about that. "Sometimes I do some pretty dumb things. This could be one of them."

He smiled tightly. "Do you think I'm stupid?"

Odd. That was the second time I'd been asked a version of that question within the last twenty-four hours. I gave the same answer. "Is that a trick question?"

"Why do you think I've waited until now to question

you, Alexandria? See, I know about your little bond with the First. And I know that this kind of distance negates that bond." His smile became real as my hands clenched the arms of the chair. "So, right now, you're nothing but a half-blood. Do you understand me?"

"Do you think I need Seth to defend me?"

The hollows of his cheeks started to turn pink. "Tell me what happened that night, Alexandria."

"There was this giant daimon attack that I tried to warn you guys about, but you ignored me. You said it was a ridiculous notion that daimons could pull off such a stunt." I paused, letting that jab sink in. "I fought. Killed some daimons and brought down a furie or two."

"Ah, yes. You fought magnificently from what I hear." He paused, tapped his chin. "And then a plot was discovered. The daimons were after the Apollyon."

"Exactly."

"I find that strange," he replied. "Considering that they were trying to kill you in plain sight of Guards and Sentinels. Who, by the way, are loyal to the Council."

I yawned loudly, doing everything to show I wasn't afraid while I was shaking inside. If he saw that, then he'd know he was onto something. "I have no idea what goes on inside the mind of a daimon. I can't explain that."

Telly pushed off the desk, coming to stand in front of me. "I know you killed the pure-blood Guard, Alexandria. And I also know that another pure-blood covered it up for you."

My brain sort of emptied as I stared up at him. Terror, so potent and so strong, knocked the air out of my lungs. How had he known? Had Aiden's compulsion worn off? No. Because I'd be in front of the Council, handcuffed, and Aiden…oh gods, Aiden would be dead.

"You have nothing to say to that?" Telly asked, clearly enjoying this moment.

Pull it together. Pull it together. "I'm sorry. I'm just a little shocked."

"And why would you be shocked?"

"Because that's probably the stupidest thing I've heard in a long time. And have you seen the people I know? That's saying something."

His lips thinned. "You're lying. And you're not a very good liar."

My pulse pounded. "Actually, I'm a great liar."

He was losing his patience quickly. "Tell me the truth, Alexandria."

"I am telling you the truth." I forced my fingers to relax around the chair arms. "I know better than to attack a pure, let alone kill one."

"You attacked a Master at the Council."

Crap. "I didn't actually attack him—I stopped him from attacking someone else. And well, I learned my lesson after that."

"I beg to differ. Who helped you cover it up?"

I leaned forward in the chair. "I have no idea what you're talking about."

"You are testing my patience," he said. "You don't want to see what will happen when I lose it."

"It kind of sounds like you *have* lost it." I looked around the room, forcing my heart to return to normal. "I have no idea why you're asking me these questions. And I'm missing the last day of class before winter break. Are you going to give me an excuse or something?"

"Do you think you're clever?"

I smirked.

Telly's hand snaked out so quickly I didn't even have a chance to deflect the blow. The back of his hand connected with my cheek with enough force to snap my head to the side. Disbelief and rage mixed, rushing through me. My brain flat-out refused to accept the fact that he had just hit me—actually dared to hit *me*. And my body was already demanding that I hit him back, lay him out on his back. My fist practically itched to connect with his jaw.

I gripped the edges of the chair, facing him. That's what Telly wanted. He wanted me to strike him back. Then he'd have my ass on a golden platter.

Telly smiled.

I returned the gesture, ignoring the stinging in my cheek. "Thank you."

Anger flared deep in his eyes. "You think you're tough, don't you?"

I shrugged. "I guess you could say that."

"There are ways of breaking you, dear girl." His smile increased, but it never reached his eyes. "I know you killed a pure-blood. And I know someone—another pure or the First—covered for you."

A shiver ran down my spine, like icy fingers of panic and terror. I shoved it down, sure to revisit it later…if there was a later. I arched a brow. "I have no idea what you're talking about. I've already told you what happened."

"And what you've told me is a lie!" He shot forward, gripping the arms of the chair. His fingers were inches from mine, lips pulled back, face red with fury. "Now tell me the truth or so help me…"

I refused to pull away like I wanted to. "I *have* told you."

A vein popped on his temple. "You are treading on dangerous ground, dear."

"You must not have any proof," I said softly, meeting his enraged stare. "If you did, I'd already be dead. Then again, if I were just a half-blood, you wouldn't need much proof. But to take me out, you need the Council's permission. You know, being the *precious Apollyon* and all."

Telly pushed back from the chair, turning his back to me.

I knew I needed to shut up. Taunting him was probably the stupidest thing I could do, but I couldn't stop. Anger and fear were never a good mix for me. "What I don't understand is how you're so certain that I killed a pure-blood. There were obviously no witnesses to his death. No one is pointing a finger at me." I paused, enjoying the way the muscles in his back tensed under the thin tunic. "Why would you…?"

He turned around, face impressively blank. "Why would I what, Alexandria?"

My stomach churned as realization set in. My suspicions had been correct. I stared at his elegant hands. "How can you be so certain unless you ordered someone—a Guard—to attack me? Then I guess you'd be fairly certain if that Guard did turn up dead... But you wouldn't have done that. Because I'm sure the Council would be pretty pissed. You might even lose your position."

So busy gloating, I didn't even see him move.

His hand caught the same cheek. The burst of red-hot pain stunned me. It was no pansy hit. The chair went up on two legs before settling back down. Tears stung my eyes.

"You…you can't do this," I said, voice hoarse.

Telly grasped my wrist. "I can do as I please." Telly hauled me to my feet, his fingers bruising my arms as he dragged me across my uncle's office. He shoved me toward the window overlooking the quad. "Tell me, what do you see out there?"

I blinked back tears, biting down on the fury threatening

to boil over. Statues and sand, and beyond that, the ocean rolled and tumbled with rough waves. People were scattered across the campus.

"What do you see, Alexandria?" His grip tightened.

I winced, hating my moment of weakness. "I don't know. I see people and freaking sand. And the ocean. I see lots of water."

"See the servants?" He gestured toward the atrium, where a cluster of them stood waiting for orders from their Master. "I own them. I own all of them."

The muscles in my body locked up. I couldn't pull my gaze from them.

Telly leaned in, his breath hot in my ear. "Let me tell you a little secret about the true nature of your other half's trip to the Catskills. He's been brought in to deal with any servant who is off the Elixir and is refusing to submit. Did you know that?"

"Deal with them?"

"Take some of that cleverness from your mouth and apply it. I'm sure you can figure it out."

I could figure it out, but I couldn't believe it. There was a difference between those two things. Because I understood that Telly was claiming that Seth would take down any half-blood who was causing problems, but Seth wouldn't actually agree to something like that. And I also knew that Telly was telling me this to rattle me.

It was working.

"I have something else I want to tell you," Telly said. "I do have a favorite of all the servants, you see. One I personally requested many years ago. Did you know I knew your mother and father?"

I closed my eyes.

"What, Alexandria? Has someone already let that little

bird out of the cage?" He let go of my wrist, chuckling. "To think your beautiful mother had tainted herself in that way, to mix with a half-blood. Did they really think they'd get away with it? And do you really think Lucian has forgotten the disgrace she placed upon his head?"

Dad. Daddy. Father. All titles which hadn't really meant anything until I read Laadan's letter. But now they meant everything.

"I know he must mean nothing to you," Telly continued. "You've never known him, but I do know that whoever covered up what you did must mean a lot to you. And what do they say? Like father, like daughter?"

Desperation washed away any relief I felt. Telly wasn't going to use my father against me. He was just going to use Aiden.

Telly left me by the window, returning to the center of the room. "This is your last chance. I will leave the day after tomorrow, before dawn, and if you haven't turned yourself in by then, there will be no more chances. This could end easily."

I didn't even feel the throbbing in my face anymore.

Telly smiled, reveling in my silence. "Admit to killing the Guard, and I won't push on"—his lip curled—"who covered it up. And trust me, I will find out. There are only a few I have noticed who have taken any interest in you, other than the First. What?" He laughed. "Did you think I hadn't been paying attention?"

Air rushed from my lungs so quickly I felt dizzy.

"Let's see." Telly tapped his chin. "There is your uncle, who I think cares for you far more than he lets on. He was in New York. Then there is that one Sentinel—the one who found you that night in the maze. Leon? Then there is the one who graciously offered to train you. I do believe that would be

St. Delphi. And then there is Laadan. All of them are suspects, and I will ensure that all of them suffer. As the Head Minister, I can revoke Marcus's position. I can even remove Lucian. I can file charges against the rest. With all the unrest and recent incidents, it would be all too easy."

A lump of horror and frustration formed in my throat. Tears built behind my eyes at the same moment I wanted to smash Telly's head in.

"You'll go into servitude, and you will go on the Elixir. If you refuse, well, things will end badly."

My hands curled into fists. "You're…revolting."

Telly started toward me, his hand streaking out to hit me again.

I caught his wrist, my eyes meeting his and holding. "I've been hit enough, thank you."

A commotion from the hallway caught Telly's attention and he pulled his wrist free. Marcus's voice rang loud, demanding entry to his office. Telly raised a brow at me. "You have until dawn on Friday."

The walls closed in.

Telly smirked as Marcus's demands grew louder. Neither of us spoke during those moments.

"Why do you hate me so much?" I asked finally.

"I don't hate you, Alexandria. I hate what you *are*."

CHAPTER THIRTEEN

That was what this had come down to—because I was an Apollyon, because I would turn Seth into a God Killer. And I knew then, beyond a doubt, that Telly was a member of the Order. In his mind, he was just protecting the gods from a threat, and he saw no wrong in what he did.

The doors swung open as I turned back to the window, struggling for control.

"What is going on in here?" Marcus demanded.

"I had some…unanswered concerns about the night Alexandria left the Council," Telly replied. "At first, she was not very cooperative when it came to the questions, but I do believe we worked out an understanding. After that, she was surprisingly helpful."

Yeah, he worked it out on my face.

I wondered how quickly I could rip one of those daggers off Marcus's wall and plunge it into Telly's eye before his Guards could react. The tension in the room escalated, waves rippling out in every direction.

"And why was I not involved in this questioning? Or better yet, why couldn't this wait until Lucian's return?" Marcus said evenly, but I recognized the edge to his voice. Gods knew I'd been on the receiving end of it countless times. "He is her guardian and should have been present."

Telly tsked softly. "This wasn't a formal questioning or sanctioned by the Council. I had a few concerns I needed to clear up. Therefore, I had no need for Lucian's or your presence. That is, beside the fact that I am the Head Minister and do not need your permission."

He'd effectively put Marcus in his place.

"Alexandria," called Telly. "Please do not forget what we've discussed."

I didn't respond, because I was still weighing whether or not I could stab him before the Guards took me down.

Head Minister Telly excused himself then, giving out pleasantries in such a calm manner I almost found it hard to believe he'd just pulled the world out from underneath my feet.

"Alexandria?" Marcus's voice broke the silence. "What did he want to discuss with you?"

"He had questions about what happened at the Council." My voice was unnaturally thick. "That's all."

"Alex?" Aiden said, and my heart dropped all the way to my toes. Of course, he was here. "What happened?"

Facing them, I used my hair to shield my stinging cheek from them and kept my gaze plastered to the carpet. "Apparently, I have a bad attitude. We had to work through that."

Aiden was suddenly in front of me, tipping my chin back. My hair slid off my cheek. Rage blasted off him, swallowing up the air like a black hole of fury.

"He did this?" His voice was so low I barely heard him. Unable to answer, I looked away.

"This is unacceptable." Aiden whirled on Marcus. "He cannot do this. She's a girl."

Sometimes Aiden forgot that I was also a half-blood, which pretty much zeroed out the whole "not hitting girls" thing. Like with Jackson. Like with most pure-bloods. Our society—our rules and how we were treated—it sucked. There were no words for it.

And at once, a thousand questions rose up, but one stood out. How could I continue to be a part of this world? Being a Sentinel, in a way, was supporting the social structure, basically saying that I was okay with this, and I wasn't. I hated it.

Shaking my head, I pushed those thoughts out of my head for now. "He's the Head Dick. He can do whatever he wants, right?"

Marcus looked thunderstruck as he continued to stare at me. Was he really that surprised by Telly's violence? If that was the case, he'd just lost some intelligence points. He turned to Leon. "She was supposed to go nowhere by herself. Why was Telly able to reach her?"

"She was in class," Leon responded. "Linard was waiting for her to leave. And no one expected Telly to be here. Not with everything that is happening in New York."

Marcus cut a dangerous look at Linard. "If you have to sit in class with her, then do it."

"It's not his fault," I said. "No one can watch me every second of the day."

Aiden cursed. "Is that all you'll do? She is your niece, Marcus. He hit *your niece* and that's your answer?"

Marcus's eyes deepened to a bright green. "I am well aware of the fact that she is my niece, Aiden. And do not think for one second that I found any of this," he threw his hand toward me, "acceptable. I will contact the Council immediately. I do not care that she is a half-blood. Telly has no right."

I shifted my weight. "The Council is going to care? Seriously? You guys beat the crap out of servants all the time. Why would I be any different?"

"You are not a servant," Marcus said, storming to his desk.

"Does that make it okay?" I shouted, my hands curling into fists. "It's okay to beat servants because of their blood? And it's not okay because I have half—" I cut myself off before I revealed too much. All eyes were on me.

Behind his desk, Marcus took a deep breath and briefly closed his eyes. "Are you okay, Alexandria?"

"I'm just peachy."

Aiden took my arm. "I'm taking her to the clinic."

I pulled my arm free. "I'll be fine."

"He *hit* you," Aiden seethed, eyes flashing.

"And it will just bruise, okay? That's not the problem." I needed to be out of this room, away from all of them. I needed to think. "I just want to go back to my room."

Marcus froze with the phone halfway to his ear. "Aiden, make sure she makes it back to her room. And I want her to stay there until we find out what Telly is up to or until he leaves. I will contact Lucian and the rest of the Council," Marcus said, and his gaze found Aiden's again. "I mean it. She is not to leave the room."

I was too busy going over everything that had happened to care about Marcus sentencing me to my dorm. And if Lucian found out about what'd happened, then that meant Seth would, too. At least there was one bright lining in the cloud of crud. If Seth were here, he'd probably kill Telly.

Marcus stopped me at the door. "Alexandria?"

I turned around, hoping he'd make this fast. Bitch me out for antagonizing Telly, tell me not to do it again, and warn me about my bad behavior.

He met my stare. "I am sorry that I was not here to stop him. This will not happen again."

My uncle had an alien in him. I blinked slowly. Before I could say anything, he went back to his phone call. Sort of stunned, I let Aiden guide me out of the office and down the hall.

Once the door in the stairwell closed behind us, Aiden blocked the stairs. "I want to know what happened."

"I just want to go back to my room."

"I'm not asking, Alex."

I didn't answer, and finally Aiden turned around stiffly and went down the stairs. I followed behind him slowly. Classes were still in session, so the stairwell and the first-floor lobby were virtually empty with the exception of some Guards and Instructors. We walked back to my dorm in silence, but I knew he wasn't going to let this go. Aiden was just biding his time, so I wasn't entirely surprised when he followed me into my room, closing the door behind him.

I dropped my bag and ran my hands through my hair. "Aiden."

He grasped my chin like he'd done in Marcus's office, tilting my head to the side. His jaw tightened. "How did this happen?"

How bad did it look? "I guess I didn't respond correctly after the first time."

"He hit you twice?"

Embarrassed, I pulled away and sat on the couch. I was trained to fight and defend myself. I'd walked away from daimon battles with scratches. This whole situation made me feel weak and helpless.

"You shouldn't be here," I said finally. "I know Marcus said to make sure I stayed in my room, but it shouldn't be you."

Aiden stood in front of the small coffee table, hands on his hips. His posture reminded me so much of our training sessions—the one he got when he knew I was going to push back on something. He was digging in for the long haul. "Why?"

I laughed and then winced. "You shouldn't be around me. I think Telly has someone watching me—us."

There wasn't an ounce of panic in those silver eyes. "You need to tell me what happened, Alex. Don't even think about lying to me. I'll know."

Closing my eyes, I shook my head. "I don't know if I can."

I heard Aiden move around the table and sit on its edge in front of me. His hand pressed against my other cheek. "You can tell me anything. You know that. I will help you always. How can you doubt that?"

"I don't doubt that." I opened my eyes, ashamed to find they felt damp.

Confusion flickered across his face. "Then why can't you tell me?"

"Because…because I don't want you to worry."

Aiden frowned. "You're always thinking about someone else when you should be more concerned about yourself."

I snorted. "That's so not true. I've been really self-centric lately."

He laughed softly, but when the rich sound faded, so did his brief smile. "Alex, talk to me."

The terror and panic returned. I'm not sure they'd ever really left. The words just came out. "Telly knows."

A slight narrowing of his eyes was his only reaction. "How much?"

"He knows I killed a pure-blood," I whispered. "And he knows either Seth or a pure covered it up."

Aiden said nothing.

I really started to freak out. "He's definitely part of the Order, and I think he's the one who sent the Guard to kill me. It's the only way he could know unless the compulsion—"

"The compulsion hasn't faded." Aiden dragged his hand over his head. Dark waves tumbled through his fingers. "We would know. I'd be arrested by now."

"Then the only way he would know is if he sent the Guard to kill me."

Aiden clasped the back of his neck. "Are you sure he knows?"

I laughed harshly as I gestured at my cheek. "He did this when I wouldn't admit to it."

The silver in his eyes burned. "I want to kill him."

"Me too, but that's not really going to help things."

He flashed me a wild smile. "But it would make us feel better."

"Damn, you've gotten dark. Funny, but dark."

Aiden shook his head. "What did he say, exactly?"

I told him the questions Telly had asked. "You know, the only good thing about this is that he didn't think using my father had any pull on me. But he said that, if I turn myself in, he wouldn't push to find the pure who covered for me. If I didn't tell him, then he would go after every pure who seems to tolerate me: you, Laadan, Leon, even Marcus. I guess he doesn't think he can get Seth or he's afraid of him."

"Alex—"

"I don't know what to do." I pushed off the couch, side-stepping him. I prowled the length of the small living room, feeling caged. I stopped, my back to Aiden. "I'm screwed, you know that, right?"

"Alex, we'll think of something." I felt him come up behind me. "This isn't the end. There are always options."

"Options?" I crossed my arms. "There were options when the Guard tried to kill me, and I chose the wrong one. I made a huge mistake, Aiden. I can't fix that. And you know what? I don't even think he cares about that Guard."

"I know," he replied softly. "I think he sent that Guard knowing that you'd be able to defend yourself, that you would probably even kill the Guard. It makes sense."

I turned around. "It does?"

He nodded, eyes narrowing. "It's the perfect setup, Alex. Telly sends the Guard to kill you, knowing there would be a good chance that you'd fight back and kill the Guard out of self-defense."

"And self-defense means nothing in this world."

"Exactly. So, Telly would have you then. No one could stop him from having you killed or at least placing you into servitude. He puts you on the Elixir and you don't Awaken. Problem solved, except Telly didn't expect a pure to use a compulsion and cover it up for you."

I nodded. "But he now knows that someone did."

"It doesn't matter," Aiden said. "He may know but he has no evidence without incriminating himself. Telly may be the Head Minister, but he does not wield the kind of power where he can indiscriminately go after pure-bloods. He can accuse us all he wants, but he can't do anything without evidence."

A tiny seedling of hope rooted in my chest. "He has a lot of power, Aiden. He has the Order, too, and gods know how many people belong to it."

"It doesn't matter, Alex." Aiden placed gentle, strong

hands on my shoulders. "All he has right now is fear. He thinks he can scare you into admitting the truth. He's using that fear against you."

"But what if he does go after everyone? What about you?"

Aiden smiled. "He can, but he's not going to get anywhere with it. And when you don't admit to anything, then he'll go back to New York. And we'll be ready if he tries something again. This isn't the end."

I nodded again.

Aiden looked me straight in the eyes. "I want you to promise me that you won't do anything stupid, Alex. Promise me that you won't turn yourself in."

"Why does everyone think I'm always going to do something stupid?"

His look said he knew better. "Knee-jerk reaction, Alex. I think we've covered that."

I sighed. "I won't do anything reckless, Aiden."

Aiden stared at me for a moment, then nodded. Instead of relaxing like I thought he would, he seemed to grow more tense. He exhaled roughly and then nodded once again. Whatever he was thinking, I knew it wasn't good.

And when his steely gaze met mine, I knew there was a good chance he didn't believe any of the promises I'd made.

CHAPTER FOURTEEN

Later that evening, I held the cell phone two feet from my head and still felt like Seth was yelling in my ear.

"I'm going to kill him!"

"Yeah, you're not the first one to say that." I climbed off the couch, scowling at the door. I didn't need to check to know that Leon stood right outside my room. Thank the gods most of the kids were gone, because having a personal Sentinel guard would make me an even bigger freak. "And it's pretty sad when I'm the voice of reason."

"What else do you suggest?" he asked. "He's the Head Minister, Alex. It's obvious that he ordered that Guard to attack you."

"Yeah." I headed to my bathroom, turning my head to the side. The left side of my cheek was red and slightly swollen. A bit of blue lined my jaw. Jackson had done worse. Telly hit like a weakling. I started to smile. "But Aiden said that he doesn't—"

"Aiden's an idiot."

I rolled my eyes. "Anyway, why didn't you answer the phone last night?"

"Are you jealous?"

"What? No. It was just weird."

Seth laughed. "I was busy, and it was too late by the time I had a chance to call you. Did you miss me or something?"

Not really. I pushed away from the mirror and went into the bedroom. "Seth, what are you really doing up there?"

"I already told you." Static filled the line for a few seconds. "Anyway, is that really important right now? You should be worried about Telly."

I sat on the edge of the bed. "Telly said that you were there to deal with the halfs who were causing problems and weren't responding to the Elixir. Is that true?"

Silence.

Knots started to form in my stomach. "Seth."

He sighed into the phone. "Alex, that isn't the problem right now. Telly is."

"I know that, but I need to know what you're doing up there." I plucked at a loose thread in the bedspread. "My dad…I know he wasn't responding to the—"

"I haven't even seen your father, Alex. Granted, I really don't know what he looks like and Laadan isn't telling. He could be here. He could be gone."

Anger and frustration rushed to the surface. "What are you doing to the halfs who aren't responding to the Elixir?"

A sound of exasperation traveled through the phone. "What I've been ordered to do by the Council, Alex. Take care of them."

Blood froze in my veins. "What do you mean by 'take care of them'?"

"Alex, that isn't important. Look, they're just half-bloods—"

"What the hell do you think we are?" I stood and started pacing. Again. "We are half-bloods too, Seth."

"No," he replied evenly. "We are the Apollyons."

"Gods, I wish you were in front of me."

"I knew you missed me," Seth said. I could hear his smile.

"No. If you were in front of me, I'd kick you in your junk, Seth. You cannot be okay with…*taking care* of those halfs! Wrong doesn't even sum up what that is. It's disgusting—revolting."

"I'm not *killing* anyone, Alex. Gods, what do you really think of me?"

"Oh." I stopped, feeling my cheeks turn red.

A couple of moments passed in silence. It sounded like Seth was walking somewhere fast. "I'd like to be in your head for just one hour." He laughed. "No. Forget that. I don't. You'd kill my self-confidence."

"Seth—"

"Let's focus on the important stuff here, which is Telly. I don't believe he doesn't have a damn thing. He wouldn't hold that threat of going after the pure responsible for the compulsion without having something."

Fear spiked. "You seriously think he has something?"

"Telly is a lot of things, but he isn't stupid. He waited until he knew that neither Lucian nor I were anywhere near you before he made his move. I wouldn't be surprised if Telly didn't screw with the Elixir weeks ago as a fallback plan. He needed a distraction and he got one. And Aiden isn't stupid, either," he said. "He's telling you what you need to hear to stop you from doing something stupid."

Feeling dizzy, I sat back down. "Shit."

"Listen to me, Alex. None of them—your uncle or

Aiden—is important. Stay away from Telly. Let him act on his threat, whether he has proof or not."

"What?" I stared at the phone as if he could somehow see me, which was kind of dumb. "They're important to me, Seth."

"No. Aiden is important to you. In reality, you couldn't care less about the rest," he corrected.

"That's not true!"

Seth laughed, but there was no humor in it. "Alex, you're a terrible liar."

What the hell? Did everyone think I was prone to acts of stupidity *and* a terrible liar? But I wasn't lying. Laadan and Marcus were important to me. Even Leon, though he was kind of weird.

I took a deep breath. "So, you think Telly does have something?"

"I don't think Telly would make idle threats and hope you fall for them. Look at all that he's done so far."

I dropped my head into my open palm. "Seth, I can't let him go after them."

"You can and you will. They. Are. Not. Important. You are. We are."

"I hate it when you say things like that," I seethed.

"Because it's true, Alex. Why? Because once you Awaken, we can change things." Seth paused and then his voice lowered. "You have no idea what the majority of the Council wants done to the half-bloods up here. Luckily, my presence seems to be keeping most of them in line, but they do want them killed, Alex. They see the half-bloods as a problem that they don't have the time or manpower to deal with. Especially now that the daimons have no qualms about attacking the Covenants."

"I thought you didn't care about the half-bloods." I lifted my head and stared at the blank wall across from the bed.

"Not losing sleep over their crappy lives and being okay with exterminating them are two different things, Alex."

"Gods, Seth." I shook my head. "Sometimes I don't even know you."

"You never tried to," he said, without a trace of anger. "And it really doesn't matter right now. All that matters is that you stay safe. Look, I've got to go. Just stay in your room, at least until Telly leaves. I know he has to be back here by Friday because they are having a session."

"All right," I said. "Seth?"

"What?"

I bit my lip, having no idea what I wanted to say to him. There was just so much, and none of it was anything I was willing to get into right now. "Nothing. I'll…I'll talk to you later."

Seth hung up, without making me promise to stay out of trouble. I think he knew my word was just as good as his.

The next twenty-four hours crept by painfully slow. I wasn't allowed to leave my room. Food was brought to me by one of my babysitters. Besides them, I had no visitors. Bored out of my mind, I cleaned my bathroom and started to rearrange my closet, which ended with clothes strewn across the floor.

There was a moment when panic punched a hole through my chest. Was I making the right decision by not turning myself in?

I tried calling Seth a few times, but that was a total bust. He eventually called back just after I'd changed for bed. We didn't talk for long or about anything important. I think he was just surprised that I was still in my dorm and hadn't done anything dumb yet.

It took hours of tossing and turning to drift off to sleep. But I didn't stay asleep for long. I woke up while it was still dark, the comforter twisted around my legs.

I watched slivers of light slice across the ceiling, disappearing when the moon dipped behind a cloud outside my window. My brain immediately kicked into hyper drive, replaying everything that had happened with Telly, then with Aiden and Seth. What if Seth had been right and Telly had a way of finding out that it was Aiden? Or even if he didn't, what if he did go after him? And it wasn't just Aiden I cared about. What would it say about me if I let others be harmed so I skated through until the next time?

Because there would be a next time—I knew it. And who would risk their future and their life then?

It wasn't right or fair.

Sitting up, I swung my legs off the bed and stood. Cool air spread goose bumps over my bare legs. I grabbed a long, chunky sweater off the corner of my bed and slipped it over my tank top. Creeping to the window, I pried the blinds apart and peered outside. I couldn't see anything in the darkness, and I wasn't even sure what I was looking for.

"What am I doing?" I asked myself.

"Absolutely nothing if I have anything to do with it."

Shrieking, I dropped the blinds and spun around. Heart pounding, I squinted at the tall outline taking up the entire doorway to my bedroom. Once I recognized who it was, it did nothing to calm my racing heart. "Holy daimon babies! You gave me a heart attack."

Aiden stepped forward, folding his arms. "Sorry about that."

I pulled the sweater closer, staring at him. "What are you doing in my dorm?"

"You have a problem with guys in your dorm now?"

"Ha. Ha." I hurried over to my bedside table and flipped on the lamp. A soft glow filled the room. "Actually, I never invited Seth in here. He just kind of made himself at home."

A ghost of a smile appeared on his face. As always, he was in his Sentinel garb. Then it struck me. My mouth dropped open.

"You're working, aren't you?" I demanded.

"Well, there was a good chance that you'd try to sneak out and turn yourself in before Telly could leave in the morning. We were taking precautions just in case you did."

"We?" I sputtered. "Is anyone else in here?"

"No, but Leon was in right after you fell asleep. Linard is patrolling the outside." He paused. "I just switched shifts with Leon. I'm sorry if I woke you."

I stared at him, dumbfounded. "You guys have been switching off in here while I slept? Last night, too?"

He nodded. "Thankfully, Marcus suggested the idea. Otherwise, I have a feeling Linard would've been chasing you across the quad and stopping you before you ran off."

"I'm not stupid." My fingers curled around the edges of my sweater. "Do you really think I'd just up and go turn myself in to Telly in the middle of the night?"

He cocked his head to the side. "This is coming from the girl who once snuck out of the Covenant to find a daimon."

Touché. "Whatever. I wasn't planning to do anything like that again."

"You weren't?"

I shook my head. Though there was a part of me that had been considering it. "I couldn't sleep. There's a lot going on in my head."

"That's understandable." His eyes drifted over me, settling on my cheek. "How is it?"

I tipped my head, shielding my face. "It's fine."

He looked away a moment, then his gaze swung back to me. "You've been through worse, I know, but still. You should've never had to deal with what you did…or with Jackson. Any of this really."

"What do you mean?"

"Nothing—I'm just rambling." Aiden's shoulders relaxed as he glanced around the room. "It's been a long time since I've been in here."

I followed his gaze, which had landed on the bed. A warm flush went from my hair to the tips of my toes. A dozen or so vivid images danced in front of my eyes—all of them completely wrong considering everything that was going on.

"It was your first day back here," he said, and a small grin appeared. "There were clothes on the floor then, too."

Surprised, I focused on him—the real, completely clothed Aiden. Of course, he'd been in my living room area, but he was right. He hadn't ventured any further than the couch. "You remember that?"

He nodded. "Yeah, I was lecturing you."

"After I pulled Lea out of her chair by her hair."

Aiden laughed and the sound warmed me. "You finally admit to it."

"She kind of deserved it then." I bit my lip as he looked up, his gaze meeting mine. What was he thinking right now? I sat on the edge of the bed. "I'm not going to do anything, even though I should. You don't have to stay in here."

Aiden was silent a couple of moments, then he made his way to where I was sitting and sat beside me. The air in the room suddenly got heavier, the bed smaller. The last time we'd been on a bed—and I'd been this close to being undressed—had been the night in his cabin. Impossibly, I grew warmer at the memory, and nervous—a lot more nervous. I should've stayed asleep.

"Why do you think you need to turn yourself in, Alex?"

I scooted back and tucked my legs under me. The distance helped a little. "Seth said that there's a good chance Telly can prove that it was you or that he will make a move against everyone he suspects."

He twisted around, facing me. "It doesn't matter if he does, Alex. Going to Telly means the end of you. Don't you understand that?"

"Not going to Telly could mean the end of you—of anyone who he thinks may have helped me."

"It doesn't matter."

"You sound like Seth—like no one else's life is important but mine. That's bullshit." I rose to my knees, dragging in a deep breath. "What if Telly does something to you? Or to Laadan or Leon or Marcus? You expect me to be okay with that? To live with that?"

Aiden's eyes darkened. "Yes, I expect you to live with that."

"That's insane." I climbed off the bed, feeling the spicy rush of anger. "You're insane!"

He watched me calmly. "It's the way it is."

"You can't say that my life is more important than yours. That's not right."

"But your life *is* more important to me."

"Do you hear yourself?" I stopped in front of him, hands shaking. "How can you make that decision for other people—for Laadan and Marcus?"

"Look," Aiden said, his hands rising into the air. "Get mad at me. Hit me. It doesn't change anything."

I moved toward him, to push him but not actually hit him. "You can't—"

Aiden caught both my wrists and hauled me into his lap, switching my wrists to one hand. He sighed. "I didn't mean for you to *actually* hit me."

Too stunned to respond, I just stared at him. Our heads were only inches apart. My legs tangled with his, and then he reached up with his free hand, smoothing the mess of hair back from my face. My breath caught as my heart sped up. Our gazes locked and his eyes turned to quicksilver.

He cupped the nape of my neck. I heard his sharp intake of breath. Then he let go of my wrists and grasped my hips. Before I could blink, I was on my back, and Aiden hovered over me. Using one arm to support himself, he lowered his head and brushed his lips over my swollen cheek.

"How do we always end up like this?" he asked, voice rough as his gaze traveled away from my face and down my body.

"I didn't do this." Slowly, I lifted my hands and placed them against his chest. His heart jumped under my palm.

"No. This was all me." The lower half of his body shifted down. Our legs were flush. His eyes searched mine. "It gets harder every time."

My brows rose and I bit back a giggle. "What does?"

Aiden grinned and his eyes lightened. "Stopping before it's too late."

In a second, everything—the rift that had come between us the day I'd given him that stupid pick, what I'd seen in the Catskills, the mess we were in, and even Seth—everything vanished. The words came out of me in a rush. "Don't stop."

CHAPTER FIFTEEN

Aiden's eyes seemed to glow from within as he stared down at me. Like in the library, I knew he wanted to kiss me. His resolve was cracking, and the hand against my cheek trembled.

I slid my hands down his taut stomach, stopping above the band of his pants. More than anything I wanted to lose myself in him, to forget about everything. I wanted him to lose himself in *me.*

He sucked in air, lips parted. "It probably would be a good idea if Leon or someone else was watching you during the night."

"Probably."

His lips tipped into a crooked smile as his hand drifted away from my cheek, down my neck and under the collar of my sweater. I jumped a little when his hand skimmed over my shoulder. "People say hindsight is always twenty-twenty," he said.

I didn't care about people's eyesight. All I cared about

was his hand on my skin, pushing the sweater down my arm. "When...when does the next babysitter arrive?"

"Not until morning."

Butterflies went crazy in my stomach. Morning was several hours away. A lot of things could go down in those hours. "Oh."

Aiden didn't respond. Instead, his fingers skimmed over the tags on my arm and then he closed his eyes. A shudder rolled through his entire body, shaking me to my core. His head dipped and dark waves of hair fell forward, but not quick enough to shield the hunger in his stare.

I tensed, my chest tightening. His breath was warm and tantalizing on my lips, and then his lips brushed across mine so softly. That simple act stole my breath, my heart. But even as he pulled away, I realized that he couldn't steal something he already had.

Aiden rolled onto his side, pulling me along with him. He eased one arm under me, cradling me to his chest so tightly I could feel his heart thundering. There was something under his shirt that pressed against my cheek. I realized it was his necklace.

"Aiden?"

He lowered his chin to the top of my head and drew in a deep breath. "Go to sleep, Alex."

My eyes snapped open. I tried to lift my head, but I couldn't move an inch. "I don't think I can sleep now."

"Well, you better try."

I tried to wiggle free, but he moved his leg, clamping one of mine between his. My fingers curled into his thermal. "*Aiden*."

"Alex."

Frustrated, I pushed on his chest. Aiden's laugh rumbled

through me, and even though I wanted to smack him, I started to smile. "Why? Why did you kiss me? I mean, you did just kiss me, right?"

"Yes. No. Sort of." Aiden sighed. "I wanted to."

My smile started to turn giddy. It was like there was a part of me that had no perception of the outside world or all the consequences—the part that was completely controlled by my heart. "Okay. Then why did you stop?"

"Can we talk about anything other than that? Please?"

"Why?"

His hand moved up my back, delving into my hair and sending shivers over my skin. "Because I asked you nicely?"

Being this close to him wasn't helping. Every time I breathed, it was full of his aftershave and the scent of sea salt. If I moved, it only brought us closer. There was no way in hell I was sleeping any time soon. "This is so wrong."

"That's the truest thing you've said this evening."

I rolled my eyes. "And this is completely your fault."

"Not going to argue with that." Aiden shifted onto his back, and I ended up pinned to his side. I tried to sit up, but he locked his arms together. My head ended up on his shoulder with my arm trapped against his stomach. "Tell me something," he said after I stopped struggling.

"I don't think you want me to tell you something right now."

"True." He laughed. "Where do you want to be assigned when you graduate?"

"What?" I frowned. Aiden repeated the question. "Yeah, I heard you, but that's such a random question."

"So? Answer it."

Giving up on trying to get free and jump him, I decided to make the best of this weird situation and snuggled closer. I'd probably regret it later when he came to his senses and pushed me away. Aiden's arms tightened in response. "I don't know."

"You haven't thought about it?"

"Not really. When I first returned to the Covenant, I didn't even think I was going to be allowed back in and then I learned about the whole Apollyon thing." I paused because I wasn't sure why I hadn't really given it much thought. "I guess I just stopped thinking it would even be an option."

Aiden unlocked his hands and began to trace an idle circle over my upper arm. It was ridiculously soothing. "It's still an option, Alex. Awakening doesn't mean your life is over. Where would you go?"

Wishing we'd had the foresight to turn off the light before our impromptu cuddle-fest, I closed my eyes. "I don't know. I guess I'd pick some place I'd never been, like New Orleans."

"You've never been there?" Surprise colored his voice.

"No. Have you?"

"I've been there a couple of times."

"During Mardi Gras?"

Aiden picked up my hand that was on his stomach, threading his fingers through mine. My chest fluttered. "Once or twice," he answered.

I smiled, picturing Aiden carrying beads. "Yeah, so maybe some place like that."

"Or Ireland?"

"You remember the weirdest things I say."

His fingers closed over mine. "I remember everything you say."

Warmth stole through me, and I savored it. He'd said the same thing the day at the zoo, but somehow, I'd forgotten in the mess of everything that had happened after that. "That's kind of embarrassing. I say a lot of stupid things."

Aiden laughed. "You do say some pretty weird things."

I couldn't argue with that. We lay there together in a companionable silence for a little while. I listened to the even sounds of his breathing. "Aiden?"

He tilted his head toward me. "Yeah?"

I finally put voice to something that had been nagging me for a while. "What…what if I don't want to be a Sentinel anymore?"

Aiden didn't answer immediately. "What do you mean?"

"It's not that I don't see the purpose behind being a Sentinel and I still have that need, but sometimes I feel like being a Sentinel is agreeing with the way things are." I took a deep breath. Saying this aloud was damn near close to heresy. "It's like being a Sentinel means I'm okay with how half-bloods are treated, and I'm…I'm not okay with that."

"Neither am I," he said softly.

"I feel…terrible for even thinking this, but I just don't know." I squeezed my eyes shut, partially ashamed. "But after I saw those dead servants in the Catskills, I just can't be a part of this."

There was a pause. "I see what you're saying."

"There's a but, isn't there?"

"No. There's not." Aiden squeezed my hand. "I know becoming the Apollyon isn't something you want, but you will be in the position to change things, Alex. There are pures who will listen to you. And there are some who want things to change. If this is something you feel strongly about, then you should do what you can."

"It doesn't mean I'd be shirking my duties as a Sentinel?" My voice sounded tiny. "Because the world needs Sentinels and Guards, and the daimons—they kill indiscriminately. I can't just—"

"You can do what you want." Sincerity rang in his tone, and I wanted to believe him, but that wasn't the case. Even as the Apollyon, I was still a half-blood, and I couldn't do what I wanted. "And it's not shirking your duty," he said. "Changing the lives of hundreds of half-bloods will do more than hunting daimons."

"You think so?"

"I know so."

A little bit of the pressure eased, and I yawned. "What if someone sees us?"

"Don't worry about it." He brushed my hair back over my shoulder. "Marcus knows I'm here."

I doubted that Marcus knew Aiden was in my bed. Maybe all of this was a dream, I decided. But my lips still tingled from the brief kiss. I wanted to ask him why he was here, like this. It didn't make sense, but I didn't want to kill the warmth between us with questions rooted in logic. Sometimes logic was just overrated.

Slowly, I pried my eyes opened and blinked. The dusky rays of early morning sunlight filtered through the blinds. Little dots of dust floated in the stream of light. A heavy arm lay over my stomach and a leg was thrown over mine, as if he'd wanted to make sure I couldn't escape while he slept.

Not that a god could make me move from this bed or his arms.

I delighted in the feel of him pressed against my side, the way his breath stirred the hair at my temple. Last night hadn't been a weird dream. Or if it had been, I wasn't sure I wanted to wake up. Maybe he hadn't been afraid of me running off when he slept. Perhaps he'd hungered for my closeness the way I sought his.

My heart rate picked up even though I hadn't moved. Lying here, staring at the tiny particles of dust, I wondered how many times I'd dreamt of falling asleep and waking up in Aiden's arms. A hundred or more? Definitely more. My throat tightened. It didn't seem right that I'd be teased like this, given a taste of what a future with Aiden could be like, something I could never have.

An ache filled my chest. Being in his arms like this hurt, but there wasn't an ounce of regret. In the silence of the early morning, I admitted that there was no getting over Aiden. No matter what happened from here on out, my heart would remain his. He could settle down with a pure and I could go leave this island forever and it wouldn't matter. Against all odds and common sense, Aiden had slipped under my skin, wrapped himself around my heart and embedded himself into my bones. He was a part of me and...

All of me—my heart and my soul—would always belong to him.

And I was foolish to believe otherwise, to even entertain a different scenario. I thought of Seth then and that ache in my chest spread, turned inward, and burned like a daimon tag. Whatever I had going on with Seth wasn't fair to him. If he truly cared for me, he expected to have some kind of hold on my heart and feelings.

Careful not to disturb Aiden, I reached down to the hand that rested on my hip and spread my hand over his. I'd remember this morning forever, no matter how short or long forever turned out to be.

"Alex?" Sleep roughened Aiden's voice.

"Hey." My smile was watery.

Aiden stirred beside me, lifting up on one arm. He didn't speak as he turned his hand over and clasped mine. His silvery gaze moved over my face and he smiled at me, but it never reached his eyes. "It'll be okay," he said. "I promise you."

I hoped so. Telly would've left by now, without me. I bet he was ticked. There was no way of knowing what he'd do now. And if anything happened to any of them, it was on my head. I rolled onto my side, but the position was a little uncomfortable since Aiden still held onto my hand.

"You hate this—this not doing anything when you feel responsible for what's happened."

I sighed. "I *am* responsible for this."

"Alex, you did it to save your life. This isn't your fault," he said. "You understand that, right?"

"Do you know if Telly has left?" I asked instead of answering.

"I don't know, but I assume so. Before I came here last night, Linard said he hadn't left the main island since he was at the Covenant."

"You guys have been watching him, too?"

"We needed to make sure he wasn't up to anything. The Guards who serve Lucian who remained behind have been an asset. Telly has been watched so closely I know he had steamed lobster for dinner last night."

I frowned. Last night I'd had a cold-cut sub. "You all should start your own spy business."

Aiden chuckled. "Maybe in a different life, and if I got cool gadgets out of it."

I cracked a smile. "The 007 type of gadgets?"

"He has this BMW R1200C motorcycle in *Tomorrow Never Dies*," he said, sounding wistful. "Man, that bike was sweet."

"Never seen it—the movie."

"What? That's sad. We'll have to fix that."

I rolled over. The smile Aiden wore now reached his eyes, turning them a soft heather gray. "I have no desire to watch a James Bond movie."

His eyes narrowed. "What?"

"Nope. Those movies sound boring to me. So do Clint Eastwood movies. Yawn."

"I don't think we can be friends any longer."

I laughed and his smile spread. Those dimples appeared, and oh man, it'd been so long since I'd seen them. It felt like forever. "You don't smile enough."

Aiden arched a brow. "You don't laugh enough."

There hadn't been much to laugh about recently, but I didn't want to focus on that stuff. Aiden would leave soon, and all of this was like a fantasy. One I wasn't ready to let go of just yet. We stayed like that for a little while, talking and holding hands. When the time came to face reality, Aiden climbed out of the bed and went into the bathroom. I lay there with a goofy grin on my face.

This morning had been full of opposites: sadness and happiness, desperation and hope. All of those varying emotions should've left me exhausted, but I felt ready to go…running or something.

And I never felt ready to go running.

A knock at the door drew me from my thoughts.

"That's probably Leon," Aiden said from behind the bathroom door. The rest of what he said was drowned out by a rush of water in the sink.

Groaning, I got out of bed and pulled my sweater around me. The clock in the living room said it was only thirty minutes past seven. I rolled my eyes. Second day of winter break and I was out of bed before eight in the morning. There was something cosmically wrong with that.

"Coming!" I yelled when he knocked again. I opened the door. "Good morning, sunshine."

It was Linard who stood in the hall, his hands clasped behind his back. His eyes drifted over my head, scanning the room. "Where's Aiden?"

"In the bathroom." I stepped aside, letting him in. "Did Telly leave?"

"Yes. He left just at dawn." Linard turned to me, smiling. "He waited, like he offered, but you did not come."

"I bet he was pissed."

"No. I think he was more…disappointed than anything."

"Too bad. So sad." I hoped Aiden hurried up because I really needed to brush my teeth.

"Yes," Linard said. "It is too bad. Things could've ended easily."

"Yeah…" I frowned. "Wait. Wh—"

Linard moved fast, like all Guards were trained to. There was a brief second when I recognized that I'd been in this position before, except that time there'd been adrenaline pumping through my veins. Then red-hot pain exploded just below my ribs, near the power rune, and all thought fled. It was the kind of pain that was sharp and sudden, stealing your last breath before you even realized you'd taken it.

Stumbling backward, I looked down as I tried to pull air into my lungs and make sense of the nerve-racking pain firing through my body. A black dagger was slammed all the way to the hilt, imbedded deep within my body. In a far corner of my mind, I knew that this blade wasn't an ordinary dagger. It was dipped in something—most likely Titan blood.

I wanted to ask why, but when my mouth opened, blood bubbled and trickled out.

"Sorry." Linard yanked the blade free. I slumped over,

unable to make a sound. "He gave you a chance to live, at least," he whispered.

"Hey, I was expecting Leon—" Aiden came to a halt just a few feet from us, and then he slammed into Linard. An inhuman, animalistic sound tore from Aiden as he wrapped an arm around Linard's throat.

My back hit the wall beside the counter and my legs gave out on me. I slid down as I clutched at my stomach, trying to staunch the flow. Warm, sticky blood gushed between my fingers. There was a yelp and then a sickening crunch that signaled the end of Linard.

Aiden screamed for help as he dropped beside me, knocking my trembling hands out of the way and pressing his own down on the wound. Aiden's stricken face loomed over mine, his eyes wide with horror. "Alex! Alex, talk to me. Talk to me, dammit!"

I blinked and his face formed again, but it was fuzzy. I tried to say his name, but a hoarse, wet cough racked my body.

"No! No. No." He looked over his shoulder at the door. Guards had gathered, drawn by the commotion. "Get help! Now! Go!"

My hands spasmed at my sides and then a numbness settled deep in my bones. Nothing hurt really, except my chest, but it ached for a different reason. The way he looked when he turned back to me, his eyes darting to my stomach. He pushed down harder. His gaze was frantic, shocked, and terrified.

I wanted to tell him that I still loved him—that I always had and I wanted to tell him to make sure Seth didn't lose it. My mouth moved, but no words came out.

"It's okay. Everything is going to be okay." Aiden forced a smile, eyes glistening. Was he crying? Aiden never cried. "Just hold on. We're getting help. Just hold on for me. Please, agapi mou. Hold on for me. I promise—"

There was a popping sound, followed by a flash of light, brilliant and blinding. Then there was nothing but darkness, and I was falling, spinning, and it was all over.

CHAPTER SIXTEEN

The ground under my cheek was damp and cold, and a musky, wet scent filled the air, one that reminded me of being deep inside a mossy cavern. Come to think of it, shouldn't I feel cold? This place was dark and dank, the only light being provided by tall torches thrusting out of the ground, but I felt okay. Sitting up, I brushed the hair out of my face as I stood on shaky legs.

"Oh…oh, hell to the no…"

I was on a riverbank, and across from me were hundreds, if not thousands, of people—*naked people*—shivering as they huddled together. The onyx-colored river separating us rippled and the mass of people surged forward, reaching out and howling.

I shuddered, wanting to cover my ears.

People on my side of the bank milled about, some dressed in Sentinel garb and others in casual clothing. Their conditions varied. The ones waiting by the edge of the river seemed the happiest. Others looked confused, faces pale and their clothing splattered with blood and gore.

Men dressed in leather tunics rode black horses, herding the most unfortunate-looking into groups. I figured they were guards of some sort, and by the way a few of them were watching me, I had the distinct impression that I wasn't supposed to be here—wherever here was.

Wait. I turned back to the river, trying to ignore the poor...*souls*...*on the other*—oh, gods dammit. This was the River Styx, where Charon ferried souls to the Underworld.

I was dead.

No. No. No. I couldn't be dead. I hadn't even brushed my teeth, for crying out loud. There was no way. And if I were dead, what would Seth do? He was going to go crazy when he found out—if he hadn't already figured it out. Our bond diminished with distance, but could he have felt my loss? Maybe I wasn't dead.

Pulling open my sweater, I looked down and cussed.

The entire front of my tank top was drenched in blood—my blood. Then I remembered everything: the night before and this morning with Aiden that'd seemed so perfect. Aiden—oh gods—he'd begged me to hold on and I'd left.

Anger rushed through me. "I can't be dead."

A soft, feminine laugh came from behind me. "Honey, if you're here, you're dead. Like the rest of us."

I turned around, ready to clock someone in the face.

A girl I'd never seen before squealed loudly. "I knew it! You're dead."

I refused to believe I was dead. This had to be a bizarre, pain-induced nightmare. And seriously, why was the chick so happy that I was dead? "I'm not dead."

The girl was probably in her twenties, wearing a pair of expensive-looking jeans and strappy sandals. She clutched something in her hand. I pegged her for a pure-blood, but the open and sympathetic look in her gaze told me I had to be wrong. "How'd you die?" she asked.

I hugged my sweater around me. "I didn't die."

Her smile didn't waver. "I was shopping with my Guards at night. Like these shoes?" She stuck out her foot, angling it so I got a good view of them. "Aren't they divine?"

"Uh, yeah. The shoes are great."

She sighed. "I know. I died for them. Literally. See, I decided I wanted to wear them out, even though it was getting late and my Guards were getting nervous. But seriously, why would there be a bunch of daimons on Melrose Avenue?" She rolled her eyes. "They drained me dry and here I am, waiting for paradise. Anyway, you look a little confused."

"I'm fine," I whispered, looking around. This couldn't be real. I couldn't be stuck in the Underworld with Buffy. "How come you don't look like them?"

She followed my gaze and winced. "They haven't been given this yet." A shiny gold coin lay in her open palm. "They can't cross over until they have passage. Once it's placed on their body, they'll look all kinds of fresh and new. And they'll be able to catch the next ride."

"And what if they don't get a coin?"

"They wait until they do."

She meant the souls on the other side of the river. Shuddering, I turned my back to them and realized that I…I didn't have a coin. "What happens if you don't have a coin?"

"It's okay. And some of them just got here." She placed an arm around my shoulders. "It takes a couple of days in most cases. People like to hold funerals and stuff, which totally sucks for us because we have to wait here for what feels like eternity." She paused and laughed. "I didn't even tell you my name. I'm Kari."

"Alex."

She frowned.

I rolled my eyes. Even dead people needed an explanation. "It's short for Alexandria."

"No. I know your name." Before I could question how she knew my name, Kari steered me away from a group of angry-looking Guards who were examining my ruined clothing. "It does get kind of boring down here."

"Why are you being so nice to me? You're a pure-blood."

Kari laughed. "We're all equal down here, honey."

My mom had said that once. Funny. She had been right. Gods, I didn't want to believe it.

"And besides, when I was alive…I wasn't a hater," she went on, smiling softly. "Maybe it was because I was an oracle."

Shock forced my mouth to gape. "Wait—you're the oracle?"

"It runs in my family."

I leaned closer, inspecting the deep hue of her skin and those dark eyes that suddenly looked way too familiar. "You're not related to Grandma Piperi, are you?"

Kari laughed throatily. "Piperi is my last name."

"Holy…"

"Yeah, weird, right?" She shrugged, dropping her arm. "I had this huge purpose in life, but my love for shoes kind of ended it all. Takes the term 'killer shoes' to a whole new level, right?"

"Yeah," I said, totally wigged out. "So, are you the oracle that came into…whatever when Grandma Piperi passed?"

She was silent for a few moments, and then she sighed. "Yes, I did…unfortunately. I was never big on Fate and destiny, you see? And visions…well, they suck most of the time." Kari looked at me, her obsidian eyes narrowing. "You're supposed to be here."

"I am?" I squeaked. Aw, man…

She nodded. "You are. This—I've seen this. Like I knew I was going to meet you, but I had no idea it would be *here*. See, oracles don't know when the passing of their own time will be, which blows." She laughed again. "Gods, I know what's going to happen."

Now, that caught my attention. "You do?"

Her smile turned secretive.

My fingers dug into my sweater. "And are you going to tell me?"

Kari fell quiet, and did it matter now that she was making little sense? She was an oracle, and I was dead. Wasn't a thing I could do about anything, right? Shaking my head, I took in the rest of my surroundings. I couldn't see where the river led to; it flowed to where there was nothing but a deep, black hole. To our right was a small opening, and a strange, bluish glow emanated from whatever was beyond this place.

"Where's that go?" I asked, pointing at the light.

Kari sighed. "Back up there, but it's not the same. You're a shade if you go that way, and that's if you can even get past the guards."

"The guys on the horses?"

"Yep. Going down or up, Hades does not like to lose any souls. You should've been here when someone tried to make a run for it." She shivered delicately. "Gross."

A commotion by the river had us turning around. Kari clapped her hands together. "Sweet gods, finally!" Kari took off toward the ever-increasing throng of people by the river.

"What?" I hurried after her. The guards on the horses were forcing people into lines on both sides of the river. "What's going on?"

She looked over her shoulder at me, smiling. "It's Charon. He's here. It's Paradise time, baby!"

"But how do you know where you're going?" I struggled to keep up with her, but when I reached the fringes of the group, I froze. *Oh, crap.*

"You just know," Kari said, pushing past those who I assumed had no money for passage. "It was nice meeting you, Alexandria. And I'm about ninety-nine percent sure we'll meet again." Then she disappeared into the crowd.

Too busy with the scene unfolding before me, I didn't pay attention to what she said. The boat was larger than they showed in paintings. It was *massive*, like the size of a yacht, and a lot nicer looking than the busted old canoe image I was familiar with, painted a bright white and trimmed in gold. At the helm was Charon. Now, he looked like I expected.

Charon's slight form was swallowed by a black cloak that covered his entire body. In one bony hand he held a lantern. His shrouded head turned toward me and even though I couldn't see his eyes, I knew he saw me.

Within seconds the boat was swarmed and gliding down the river, disappearing through the dark tunnel. I had no idea how long I stood there, but finally I turned away and hurried through the crowd. Everywhere I looked, there were faces. Young and old. Expressions bored or stunned. There were dead people wandering around everywhere, and I was alone, utterly alone. I tried to make myself as small as possible, but I bumped a shoulder here, an arm there.

"Excuse me," an old woman said. A gaudy pink nightgown dwarfed her frail form. "Do you know what happened? I went to sleep and...I woke up here."

"Uh." I started backing off. "Sorry. I'm as lost as you."

She looked perplexed. "You went to sleep, too?"

"No." I sighed, twisting away. "I was stabbed to death."

Once those words left my mouth, I wanted to take them back, because they made everything real.

I stopped outside the throng of people and stared down at my bare feet. I wanted to smack myself. I really was dead.

Lifting my head, my eyes found the strange blue light. If what Kari said was true, then that was the way out of this… holding area. Then what? I'd be a shade for eternity? But what if I wasn't really dead?

"You're dead," I muttered to myself. But I started toward the blue light. The closer I got to it, the more drawn to it I was. It seemed to offer everything—light, warmth, *life*.

"Don't go toward the light!" a voice yelled, followed by laughter—mischievous, beloved laughter. "They lie about the light, you know. Never go toward the light."

I froze and if my heart had still been beating, which I wasn't sure about, it would've stopped right then and there. As if moving through cement, I turned slowly, I couldn't believe—didn't want to believe what I was seeing because if this wasn't real…

He stood only a few feet away, wearing a white linen shirt and pants. His shoulder-length, blond hair was tucked back behind his ears, and he was smiling—actually smiling. And those eyes, the color of the summer sky, were brilliant and alive. Not like the last time I'd seen him.

"Alex?" Caleb said. "You look like you've seen a ghost."

All my muscles sprang into action at once. I took off toward him and jumped.

Laughing, Caleb caught me around the waist and swung me around. It was like a dam bursting open. I turned into a fat, bawling baby in under a second. My whole body shook; I couldn't help it. It was Caleb—*my* Caleb, *my* best friend. *Caleb.*

"Alex, come on." He set me on my feet, but still held me close. "Don't cry. You know how I get when you cry."

"I'm…sorry." Nothing in this world was going to break my boa constrictor hold on him. "Oh, my gods, I can't believe…you're here."

He smoothed my hair back. "Missed me, huh?"

I lifted my head. "It's not the same without you. Nothing is the same without you." I reached up, placing my hands on his cheeks and then in his hair. He was flesh and bone. Real. There were no shadows under his eyes and his gaze didn't hold that weary look it had after Gatlinburg. The tags were gone. "Oh gods, you're really here."

"It's me, Alex."

Pressing my cheek against his chest, I started crying again. Never in a million years did I think I'd get to see him again. There was so much I wanted to say. "I don't understand," I murmured against his chest. "How can you be here? You haven't been waiting this entire time, have you?"

"No. Persephone owed me one. We were playing Mario Kart Wii, and I let her win. I cashed in my favor."

I pulled back, wiping the tears off my face with the back of my hand. "You have Wii down here?"

"What?" He grinned, and oh gods, I'd thought I'd never see that grin again. "We get bored. Especially Persephone when she's down here during these months. Usually Hades doesn't play, thank the gods. He freaking cheats."

"Wait. You play Mario Kart with Hades and Persephone?"

"I'm kind of a celebrity down here, because of you. When I first…arrived, I was taken straight to Hades. He wanted to know everything about you. I guess I kind of grew on him." Caleb shrugged and then he pulled me back in for another one of his mammoth hugs. "Gods Alex, I wanted to see you again. I just didn't think it would be like this."

"You're telling me," I said dryly. "What…what is it like?"

"It's not bad, Alex. Not bad at all," he said softly. "There are things I miss, but it's like being alive, only not."

Then it struck me. "Caleb, is…is my mom here?"

"Yes, she is. And she's really nice." He paused, pursing his lips. "Really nice considering she hasn't tried to kill me this time around, you know."

I felt nauseous, which was strange since I was supposed to be dead. "You've talked to her?"

"Yes. Seeing her the first time was really weird, but what she was when she had us isn't who she is now. She's your mom, Alex. The mom you remember."

"You sound like you've forgiven her."

"I have." He wiped away the fresh tears gathering on my cheeks. "You know, I wouldn't have in life, not really. But once you finally accept the whole dying thing, it kind of enlightens you a bit. And she was forced into becoming a daimon. They really don't hold that against you down here."

"They don't?" Oh, gods, I was going to start crying again.

"Not at all, Alex."

Some of the guards were gathering close to us. I focused on Caleb, hoping they weren't going to pull us apart. "I have to see her! Can you take—?"

"No, Alex. You can't see her. She doesn't even know you're here, and that's probably for the best right now."

Disappointment swamped me. "But—"

"Alex, how do you think your mom would feel if she knew you were here? There's only one reason why you'd be here. It would upset her."

Dammit, he had a point. But I was here, which meant I

was dead. Wouldn't I be seeing her soon anyway? So that logic failed with me.

"I've missed you," he said again, and it brought me back to him.

I clenched the front of his shirt, and the words I wanted to say spilled forth. "Caleb, I'm so, so sorry for everything. What happened in Gatlinburg and…and I didn't really pay attention to what you were going through afterward. I was so stuck on myself."

"Alex—"

"No. I am sorry. Then what happened to you. It wasn't fair. None of it was. And I'm so sorry."

Caleb lowered his forehead to mine, and I swore his eyes glistened. "It wasn't your fault, Alex. Okay? Never think that."

"I just miss you so much. I didn't know what to do after you…left. I hated you for dying." I choked up. "And I just wanted you back so bad."

"I know."

"But I don't hate you. I love you."

"I know," he said again. "But you need to know that none of that was your fault, Alex. This was meant to happen. I understand that now."

I laughed thickly. "Gods, you sound so wise. What the hell, Caleb?"

"Death made me smart, I guess." His gaze searched my face. "You don't look any different. It just seems so…so long since I last saw you."

"You look better." I traced my fingers down his face, pressing my lips together. Caleb looked marvelous to me. There wasn't a hint of all that he'd suffered. He seemed at peace, fulfilled in a way he hadn't been when he was alive. "I just miss you so much."

Caleb squeezed me tighter and laughed. "I know, but we need to stop with this friendship bonding crap, Alex. First, we're tortured by daimons together and now we've both been stabbed. That's taking the 'we do everything together' to an all new high."

Tears streamed down my face, but I laughed again. He felt so warm and real. Alive. "Gods, I really am dead."

"Yeah, you sort of are."

I sniffled. "How can I be sort of dead?"

Caleb pulled back and tipped his chin down. A mischievous smile tugged at his lips. "Well, there's this really big, blond god raising all kinds of hell with Hades right now. Apparently, you're still in limbo or something. Your soul is still up for grabs."

My insides knotted, and I blinked. "What?"

He nodded. "You're not going to be dead for very long."

I wiped under my eyes. "I've been here for hours. I'm so dead."

"Hours here is only seconds there," he explained. "When I came up here I was worried it was too late, that Hades had already released you."

"I'm not going…to stay dead?"

"No." Caleb smiled. "But I had to see you. There's something I need to tell you."

"Okay." A twinge of pain in my stomach startled me. I jerked against him. "Caleb?"

"It's okay." His lanky arms held me still. "We don't have much time, Alex. I need you to listen to me. Sometimes we hear things down here…about what is going on up there. It's about Seth."

A burning kindled deep inside me. "What…what about Seth?"

"He doesn't really know, Alex. He thinks he's in control,

but he's not. Don't…don't believe everything you hear. There's still hope."

I tried to laugh, but the burning was turning into a full-blown fire. "You're still…such a Seth fanboy."

Caleb made a face. "I'm being serious, Alex."

"Okay," I breathed, clutching my stomach. "Caleb, something's…wrong."

"Nothing's wrong, Alex. Just remember what I said. Sometimes people have a hard time remembering everything after these kinds of things. Alex, can you do me a favor?"

"Yes."

"Tell Olivia that I would've picked Los Angeles." Caleb placed his lips against my forehead. "She'll understand, okay?"

I nodded although I didn't understand why as I held onto his shirt for dear life. "I'll…I'll tell her. I promise."

"I love you, Alex," Caleb said. "You're like the sister I never wanted, you know?"

My laugh was cut off by the fire tearing apart my insides. "I love you, too."

"Never change who you are, Alex. It's your passion—your reckless faith—that will save you, save both of you." He held me tighter. "Promise me you won't forget this."

As the pain grew and my vision clouded, I held onto Caleb. "I promise. I promise. *I promise. I prom—*"

I was ripped away from him, or at least, that was how it felt. I was spinning and spinning, coming apart and slamming back together. Pain was everything. It swamped my senses, fueling the terror. My lungs burned.

"Breathe, Alexandria. *Breathe.*"

I gulped in air as my eyelids fluttered open. Two all-white eyes—no pupil or irises—stared back at me. The eyes of a god.

"Oh, *gods*," I whispered, and then I lost consciousness.

CHAPTER SEVENTEEN

People moved around me. I couldn't see them, but I could hear their feet smacking on the tile, their voices hushed. Someone hovered near the bed. Their breathing was even and steady, lulling. I caught the scent of burning leaves and sea salt.

A door opened, and the person beside my bed shifted.

I faded out after that, slipping back into the pleasant haze. When I opened my eyes finally, they felt like they'd been sewn shut, and it took a few tries to get my vision to work. White walls surrounded me—plain and boring white walls. I recognized the med room. There were no windows, so I had no idea if it was night or day. There were faint memories of Linard and pain, then a flash of light and a feeling of falling. After that, things were hazy. I remembered a musty smell and there was more, but it seemed to exist just on the fringe of my thoughts.

My mouth felt as dry as cloth, my limbs wooden. A dull ache throbbed in my sternum. I drew in a deep breath and winced.

"Alex?" There was movement on the other side of my bed, and then Aiden came into view. Dark shadows bloomed under his eyes. His hair was a mess, falling every which way. He sat on the bed, careful not to move me. "Gods Alex, I…I never thought…"

I frowned and reached over to take his hand, but the motion pulled at my stomach. Tender skin stretched, sparking a sharp sting. I gasped.

"Alex, don't move around too much." Aiden placed his hand on mine. "He patched you up, but you need to take it easy."

I stared at Aiden, and when I spoke, my throat felt raw. "Linard stabbed me, didn't he? With damn Titan blood?"

Aiden's eyes flashed to a dark, thunderous gray. He nodded.

"Rat bastard," I croaked.

His lip twitched at what I said. "Alex, I'm…I'm so sorry. This shouldn't have happened. I was there to make sure you remained safe and—"

"Stop. This wasn't your fault. And obviously I'm okay for the most part. I just didn't expect Linard—Romvi, yes. But Linard?" I started to move, but Aiden was faster, gently pushing my shoulders down. "What? I can sit up."

"Alex, you need to lie still." Exasperated, he shook his head. "Here, drink this." He held a cup in front of my face.

I took the straw, glaring at him over the rim of the cup. The peppermint-flavored water did feel absolutely divine, easing the soreness in my throat.

Aiden stared back at me, drinking me in as if he'd never expected to see me again. An image of him leaning over me, stricken and pleading, flashed through me. An array of emotions flickered over his face now: amusement, weariness, but most of all, relief.

He pulled the cup away from me. "Easy."

I pushed the covers down, surprised to find that I wore a clean shirt and the gray sweats that the Covenant usually handed out. Ignoring the twinge of pain, I pulled up the hem of my shirt. "Oh crap."

"It's not as bad—"

My hands trembled. "Really? Because I think this would make your James Bond proud." The angry red line was two inches long and at least an inch wide. The skin around the mark was pink and puckered. "Linard tried to gut me."

Aiden took my hands and pried them away from my shirt. Then he pulled it down and fixed the blankets around me carefully. It never failed to amaze me how…careful and gentle Aiden was with me even though he knew I was tough to the core. It made me feel feminine, small, and cherished. Protected. Cared for.

For someone like me who was born and trained to fight, his gentle handling undid me.

A muscle flexed in his jaw. "He did."

I stared at Aiden, sort of in awe. "I'm like a cat. I swear I have nine lives."

"Alex." He looked up, meeting my eyes. "You used all those lives, and then some."

"Well…" The musty scent came back to me.

Aiden cupped my cheek, and warmth sped through me. His thumb smoothed over my jaw. "Alex, you…you died. You died in my arms."

I opened my mouth but closed it. The bright light and the sensation of falling hadn't been a weird dream and there was more…I knew it.

His hand trembled against my cheek. "You bled out so quickly. There wasn't enough time."

"I…I don't understand. If I died, then how am I here?"

Aiden glanced at the closed door and exhaled slowly. "Well, this is where things kind of get strange, Alex."

I swallowed. "How strange?"

A brief smile appeared. "There was a flash of light—"

"I remember that."

"Do you remember anything after that?"

"Falling—I remember falling and…" I scrunched up my face. "I can't remember."

"It's okay. Maybe you should get some rest. We can talk about this later."

"No. I want to know now." I met his gaze. "Come on, this sounds like it's going to be interesting."

Aiden laughed, dropping his hand. "Honestly, I wouldn't have believed it if I hadn't seen it."

I started to roll onto my side but remembered the whole no moving thing. Staying still was going to be a challenge. "The anticipation is killing me."

He inched closer, his hip brushing my thigh. "After the flash of light, there was Leon crouching over us. At first, I thought he'd just gotten to the room, but he…he didn't look right. He reached for you, and I thought he was going to check your pulse, but he put his hand on your chest instead."

My brows lifted. "You let Leon cop a feel?"

Aiden looked like he wanted to laugh again but shook his head. "No, Alex. He said that your soul was still in your body."

"Uh."

"Yeah," he replied. "Then he told me I needed to get you to the med clinic and make sure the doctors started surgery to stop the bleeding, that we weren't too late. I didn't understand, because you…you were dead, but then I saw his eyes."

"All-white eyes," I whispered, remembering a brief glimpse of them.

"Leon's a god."

I stared at Aiden, unable to come up with any response to that. My brain pretty much shut down with that little piece of information.

"I know." He leaned over me, smoothing my hair back with one large hand. "Everyone pretty much had the same expression when I brought you in here. Marcus had arrived then…and the doctors were trying to get me to leave. Some were closing off the wound. Others were just standing there. It was chaos. You had to have been….gone a couple of minutes—the time it took me to get you from your dorm to the med clinic, and freaking Leon just popped into the med room. Everyone froze. He walked up to you, put his hand on you again, and told you to breathe."

Breathe, Alexandria. Breathe.

"And you breathed," Aiden said, his voice hoarse as he cradled my cheek. "You opened your eyes and whispered something before going unconscious."

I was still stuck on the whole god part. "Leon's a…god?"

He nodded.

"Well," I said slowly, "holy daimon butt."

Aiden laughed—really laughed. It was deep and rich, full of relief. "You…you have no idea…" Averting his eyes, he ran a hand through his hair. "Never mind."

"What?"

Jaw tensed, he shook his head.

I reached up and the moment my hand touched his, he threaded his fingers through mine and looked at me. "I'm okay," I whispered.

Aiden stared at me for what seemed like eternity. "I

thought you were gone—you *were* gone, Alex. You had *died*, and I was…I was holding you and there was nothing I could do. I never felt pain like that." His breath caught. "Not since I lost my parents, Alex. I never want to feel that again—not with you."

Tears rushed to my eyes. I didn't know what to say. My mind was still reeling from everything—total brain overload. And he was holding my hand, which was not the most shocking event of the day by any means, but it affected me just the same. I'd died. And a god who was apparently a Sentinel here had brought me back, and all that jazz. But it was the way Aiden was staring at me, like he'd never expected to talk to me again, see my smile, or hear my voice. He looked like a man who had stood at the edge of despair and had been pulled back at the very last second, but was still feeling all those terrible emotions, still not quite believing that he hadn't lost something—that *I* was still here.

I realized something so important, so powerful then.

Aiden could tell me he didn't feel the same way I did. He could fight what lay between us night and day. He could speak only in lies from here on out. It didn't matter.

I would always, *always* know differently.

Even if space separated us, or a dozen rules were imposed to keep us apart, and we could never be together, I would always know.

And gods, I loved him—loved him so much. It would never change. There were so many things I was unsure of, especially right now, but that I knew. Before I could stop it, a single tear escaped, running down my cheek. I squeezed my eyes shut.

He drew in another breath, this one much sharper, more broken. The bed dipped as he moved, and his hand slid into my hair, where his fingers curled around the strands. His lips were warm and smooth against my cheek, kissing the tear away.

I became very still, afraid that any movement would send him away. He was like some kind of wild creature about to break.

When he spoke, his breath danced over my lips, sending shivers through me. "I can't feel that way again. I just can't."

He was so close, still holding my hand tightly in his while his other slipped out of my hair and traced an invisible line over my face.

"Okay?" he said. "Because I can't lose—" He cut off, looking toward the door. The sound of footsteps grew closer. His lips pressed into a tight line as he turned back to me. He dropped my hand and straightened. "We'll talk more, later."

I sat there dumbly, my heart fluttering erratically, and said the most eloquent thing I could. "Okay."

The door opened, and Marcus walked through. His shirt was half-tucked in, and his usually pressed trousers were wrinkled.

Like Aiden, he looked a mess, but relieved. He stopped beside my bed, exhaling loudly.

I cleared my throat. "You're wrinkled."

"You're alive."

Aiden stood. "That she is. I was just filling her in on everything."

"Good. That's good." Marcus stared at me. "How are you feeling, Alexandria?"

"Okay, I guess, after dying and all." I shifted, uncomfortable with the attention. "So, about this Leon god thing? I don't know of any gods named Leon. Is he like the red-headed stepchild god that no one claims?"

Aiden retreated to the corner of the room, a much more appropriate distance for a pure-blood. I immediately missed his closeness, but he kept his eyes on me. It was like he was afraid I'd disappear. "That's because Leon isn't his real name," he said.

"It's not?"

Marcus sat in Aiden's spot. He reached out but stopped and lowered his hand into his lap. "Do you want some water?"

"Um, sure." Weirded out a little, I watched him refill my cup and hold it for me to drink. The alien in my uncle had obviously taken full control. Soon, it would claw its way out of his stomach and tap dance across my bed.

Aiden leaned against the wall. "Leon is Apollo."

I choked on the water. Wheezing, I clutched my stomach with one hand and waved the other in front of my face.

"Alexandria, are you okay?" Marcus set the cup down and glanced over his shoulder at Aiden, who was already beside the bed. "Go get one of the doctors."

"No!" Eyes watering, I dragged in air. "I'm fine. Water just went down the wrong pipe."

"You sure?" Aiden asked, looking torn between wanting to drag a doctor in and taking my word for it.

I nodded. "Yeah, that just surprised me. I mean, whoa. Are you guys sure? Apollo?"

Marcus watched me carefully. "Yes. He's definitely Apollo."

"Holy..." There weren't enough words in the world to do that justice. "Did he explain anything?"

"No." Marcus tucked the loose blanket back around me. "After he brought you back, he said he needed to leave and that he'd be back."

"He kind of popped out of the room." Aiden rubbed his eyes. "We haven't seen him since."

"And that was yesterday," Marcus added.

"So, I've been sleeping for an entire day?" My gaze darted between the two. "Have either of you slept this entire time?"

Aiden looked away, but Marcus was the one who answered. "A lot has been going on, Alex."

"But you guys—"

"Don't worry about us," Marcus interrupted. "We'll be fine."

Not worrying about them was easier said than done. Both of them looked terrible. "Is…Linard is dead."

"Yes," Marcus said. "He was working with this…this Order."

I glanced at Aiden, now remembering that sickening crunch I'd heard. If I was expecting remorse in his steady gaze, I didn't find it. Actually, the look on his face said he'd do it again. "What about Telly?"

"He never landed in New York. Right now, we have no idea where he is. Instructor Romvi has also disappeared." Marcus dropped his hands into his lap again. "I've made some calls and I have a few trusted Sentinels looking for Telly right now."

"Trusted like Linard?" As soon as those words came out of my mouth, I wished I hadn't said them. My cheeks started to burn. "I'm…sorry. That wasn't right. You didn't know."

Marcus's green eyes flashed. "You are right. I didn't know. There were a lot of things I wasn't aware of. Like the real reason you left New York and the fact that you've already been receiving the Apollyon marks."

Oh, no. I didn't dare look at Aiden.

"It wasn't until a few nights ago that I was even aware that the Order of Thanatos could be involved," Marcus continued, his shoulders stiffening. "If I had known the truth, this could've been prevented."

I squirmed as much as I could. "I know, but if we'd involved you in what happened in New York, then you'd be at risk."

"That doesn't matter. I need to know when these kinds of things happen. I'm your uncle, Alexandria, and when you kill a pure-blood—"

"She did it out of self-defense," Aiden said.

"And you compelled two pure-bloods to protect her." Marcus shot a glare over his shoulder at Aiden. "I get that, but that doesn't change the fact that I needed to know. All of this created a perfect storm for something like this to happen."

"You're not…mad at Aiden? You aren't going to turn him in?"

"Sometimes I doubt his critical thinking abilities, but I understand why he did it." Marcus sighed. "The law requires that I do, Alexandria. It even requires that I turn you in, and by not doing so, I'll face charges of treason. Just as Aiden will face charges of treason if anyone discovers what he did."

Treason equaled death for them. I swallowed. "I'm sorry. I'm sorry I dragged all of you into this."

Aiden softened. "Alex, don't apologize. This isn't your fault."

"It's not. You can't help…what you are. And all of this is because of what you are." Marcus's lips curved into a half smile. "I don't agree with a lot of the decisions you've made or the fact that both of you have kept very important things from me, but I cannot blame Aiden for doing what I would've done in the same situation. I'm your uncle, Alexandria, and I will be tough on you, but that doesn't mean I don't care for you."

Stunned into silence, I stared at him. Could I have totally misinterpreted everything about this man? Because I seriously would've bet my life that he couldn't stand me. But had it just been his version of…tough love? Blinking back tears, I suddenly wanted to hug him.

The look on Marcus's face told me he probably wouldn't be comfortable with that.

Okay. We definitely weren't on hugging terms yet, but this…this was good. I cleared my throat. "So…wow. Leon is Apollo."

Aiden grinned.

Grinning back at him, I suddenly felt panicked, and it took me a second to realize why. "Oh, my gods." I started to sit up, but Marcus stopped me. "I need to call Seth. If he suspects anything, he'll go crazy. You don't even know."

Aiden's grin faded. "If he'd known—felt it through your bond, then he'd have already gone crazy. He doesn't know."

He had a point, but I still needed to talk to him.

"We think it's best that he doesn't know, not until he is here with you," Marcus said. "Right now, we cannot afford for him to lose it. And he did call for you last night. Aiden told him you were sleeping."

Aiden rolled his eyes. "After he complained about *me* answering the phone that *he* gave you, he hung up. If he felt anything, he doesn't know why."

Sounded like Seth. Relieved, I settled back down. "Can someone grab my phone, though? If he doesn't hear from me, he'll suspect something and blow someone up."

"That can be arranged."

"I'll get it," Aiden said, sighing.

"Good. And while you go get it, why don't you take a shower and get some rest. You haven't slept since yesterday morning," Marcus said. "Lucian's Guards are outside the door. No one will get past them."

The only reason I trusted Lucian's Guards was the fact

that there was only one person who wanted me to Awaken more than Seth, and that was Lucian. "Does Lucian know what happened?"

Marcus stood. "Yes, but he agreed that it would be wise to keep Seth in the dark for a little while."

"And you trust Lucian?"

"I trust that he understands that we cannot afford any acts of retaliation from Seth. Other than that, not particularly, but he needed to know about Telly. He has some of his people looking for the Head Minister." He paused, running a hand down the side of his face. "Don't worry about things like that right now. Get some rest. I'll be back later."

There were still a lot of questions, like who were the Sentinels that Marcus trusted? And how in the world could we keep a secret like this from Seth? But I was tired, and I could tell that both of them were, too.

Aiden lingered after Marcus left. He came to my bedside, his silvery gaze drifting over me.

"You haven't left this room, have you?" I asked.

Instead of answering, he bent and placed his lips against my forehead. "I'll be back shortly," he promised. "Just try to get some rest and don't get out of the bed until someone is with you."

"But I'm not tired, not really."

Aiden laughed softly as he pulled back. "Alex, you may feel fine, but you lost a lot of blood and you just had surgery."

And I'd died, but I figured there was no point in adding that. I didn't want Aiden to worry any more than he did, especially when he looked so exhausted. "All right."

He moved away from the bed and stopped at the door. Looking back at me, he smiled. "I won't be gone long."

I eased onto my side carefully. "I'm not going anywhere."

"I know. Neither am I."

CHAPTER EIGHTEEN

I slept longer than I'd expected. When I awoke, the room was empty, and my cell phone had been placed on the bedside table. I hoped that Aiden was getting some rest, and that Marcus was, too. Pushing into a sitting position, I winced as the movement pulled at the skin around the stitches.

Curious, I inspected the jagged scar again. Half-bloods were notoriously fast healers and Covenant blades were designed to cut cleanly, but it had to have done some internal damage. Had Apollo somehow patched me up more? Because I doubted that the doctors could've reversed that kind of damage. Other than feeling lethargic, I felt…okay.

But as I glanced around the room, something poked at the recesses of my memories. I was forgetting something—something hugely important. It was on the tip of my tongue, just like when I'd been under a compulsion before. This was different, though. It was like waking up and not being able to remember a dream.

Sighing, I reached over and snatched up the cell phone.

There was only one missed call from *Cuddle Bunny*. Scooting down, I called him back.

Seth answered on the second ring. "So, you're alive?"

My heart flipped over heavily. "Yeah, why wouldn't I be?"

"Well, I haven't spoken to you in about two days." He paused. "What have you been doing?"

"I've been sleeping, not doing much."

"Sleeping for two straight days?"

I poked at my scar and winced. "Yeah, that's about all."

"Interesting..." There was a muffled sound, like something had been pulled over the phone. "You've been sleeping but Aiden had your phone?"

Crap. "He's been babysitting me. I don't know why he answered the phone when you called." There was another muffled sound, and then Seth grunted. "What are you doing?"

"Pulling on my pants and it's hard when you're holding a phone."

"Um, do you want me to call you back? Like when you're not naked?"

Seth laughed. "I'm not naked now. Anyway, maybe we have some weird Apollyon malaise. I've been exhausted for about two days but feel fine now."

So, he had felt something. I chewed on my lip. "Can I ask you something?"

"Hit me."

"You said that when I Awaken, I'll know what the past Apollyons knew, right?"

There was a pause. "Yes, I said that."

Unease twisted my insides. "Then how did you not know about the Order of Thanatos, and that they'd killed Solaris and the First? Wouldn't you have seen what they've seen?"

"Why are you asking?" Seth asked.

I took a deep breath. "Because it doesn't make sense, Seth. You should've known. And how did you not know that a half and pure made an Apollyon? None of the Apollyons in the past had ever figured that out?"

"Why are you asking about this—" A distinctive, very feminine giggle cut off his words. When Seth spoke again, it sounded far away and an awful lot like the word, "Behave."

I sat up, sucking in air sharply as my stomach screamed in protest. "Who are you with, Seth?"

"Why? You jealous?"

"Seth."

"Hold on a second," he replied, and then there was a sound of a door shutting. "Dammit, it's cold out here."

"Better be careful. Don't want anything to freeze and fall off."

He laughed. "Oh, that was bitchy. I think you just might be jealous."

Was I jealous that he was so obviously with a girl, and he'd been naked? Shouldn't I be? But I wasn't jealous—more like annoyed. Annoyed because I'd been getting stabbed and dying while Seth was screwing around. And how could I be mad? I was the one in love with another guy. I really had no room to talk. But I hadn't gotten naked with that guy, not in several long months. Not since I'd decided to see what could happen with Seth.

Gods, I was so confused, and I had no idea what was going on and why it was happening now.

"I'm not doing anything wrong," Seth said after a stretch of silence.

"I didn't say you were. Wait. You're with Boobs, aren't you?"

"Do you really want to know, Alex?"

Not when he put it like that. I chewed on my lip, unsure of what to say. Suddenly I heard Caleb's voice in my head. *There's still hope.* Weird.

"We never said we were in a relationship, and besides, whatever. You're there. I'm here. And in a week or so, I'll be back. And it's not going to even matter."

I blinked. "Really, it's 'whatever'?"

Seth sighed. "I know he was by your side the minute I left, doing his annoying brooding thing, trying to figure out a way to be with you. And he's answering your phone while you're sleeping? Yeah, it's 'whatever.'"

My mouth dropped open. "That is totally not what is happening here."

"Look, it doesn't matter. I've got to go. I'll talk to you later." Then he hung up on me.

I stared at the phone for several minutes, shocked and a bit disturbed. Had he just given me permission to do "whatever" with Aiden because he was doing "whatever" with Boobs? My gods, had I died and come back into an alternate universe?

The door opened then, and Aiden walked through. Setting the phone aside, I was happy to see that he looked a lot more refreshed. Damp hair curled around his temples and the shadows under his eyes had lessened.

"Hey, you're awake." He sat beside me, and the bed shifted us closer together. "How are you feeling?"

I leaned away from him. "Gross."

Aiden frowned. "Gross?"

"I haven't brushed my teeth or washed my face in days. Don't come near me."

He laughed. "Alex, come on."

"Seriously, I'm gross." I put my hand over my mouth.

Ignoring my protests, he leaned over and brushed my stringy hair back. "You're as beautiful as always, Alex."

I stared at him. He must not get out much. Aiden arched a brow. "Did you call Seth?"

Unwilling to lower my hand, I nodded.

His eyes danced. "Did he seem suspicious?"

"No," I said from behind my hand. "He was actually with Boobs."

He looked confused. "Boobs?"

"It's this girl from New York," I explained.

"Oh." Aiden leaned back. "What do you mean by he was with this girl?"

"What do you think?" I lowered my hand.

"Oh, Alex, I'm sorry."

I made a face. "Why are you sorry? It's 'whatever.' Seth and I aren't in a relationship." But he had been behaving himself since he'd returned to the Covenant with me. Pushing that out of my mind, I focused on something more important. "I need to get out of this bed."

Something flickered across Aiden's face and then he shook his head. "Alex, you really shouldn't."

"I *really* need to."

He held my stare and then he seemed to get it. "Okay, here, let me help you."

The idea of him getting close to me when I felt this gross didn't appeal to me, but there was no arguing with him. Aiden helped me out of the bed and then insisted on guiding me to the little bathroom. I half-expected him to follow me inside.

Closing the door behind me, I did my thing and eyed the shower stall longingly. Aiden would have a fit if I turned it on. I glanced at the door, debating whether or not he'd dare busting in here. Aiden was way too saintly.

I decided to test that theory out.

The second after I turned the water on, he yelled, "Alex, what are you doing?"

"Nothing." I pulled off my clothes, wishing I had something clean to put on.

"*Alex*." Bemused frustration colored his tone.

I grinned. "I'm taking a quick shower. I'm gross. I need to be clean."

"You shouldn't be doing that." The door handle jingled. It wasn't locked. "Alex!"

"I'm naked," I warned.

Silence and then, "Is that supposed to make me not want to come in there?"

A warm flush covered my body as I stared at the door.

There was an audible sigh. "Make it quick, Alex, because I *will* come in there if you are not done in less than five minutes."

I took the quickest shower of my life. Drying off and dressing quickly, I reveled in the feeling of being clean again, but showering had taken whatever energy I'd had left in me. I sat in front of the sink because the toilet seemed too far away, and started brushing my teeth. My mouth no longer felt like a woolly mammoth, but as I eyed the sink and realized that I'd have to get back up again, I kind of wished I'd stayed in bed.

I know he was by your side the minute I left, doing his annoying brooding thing, trying to figure out a way to be with you.

Closing my eyes, I clutched the plastic toothbrush and stretched out my legs.

Whatever. You're there. I'm here. And in a week or so, I'll be back. And it's not going to even matter.

Foamy toothpaste trickled down my chin. It wouldn't matter because Seth would be around? Or it wouldn't matter because in five weeks, I'd Awaken? Was that what Seth was trying to say in between whatever Boobs was doing?

"Alex?" Aiden knocked on the bathroom door. "Are you okay in there?"

I tipped my head toward the closed door. More toothpaste dribbled from my mouth. "I'm tired."

The door opened. Aiden's gaze dropped and his brows went up. A slow smile crept over his face, softening the hard look that had been in his eyes since I woke up. Aiden laughed.

Something fluttered in my chest. "Laughing at a dead girl isn't nice."

"I told you that you should've stayed in bed." The light didn't go out of his eyes as he knelt. He reached over, wiping the toothpaste off my chin with his thumb. "But you never listen. Hold on."

It wasn't like I was going anywhere, so I watched him glance at the sink and then rise. Aiden disappeared back into the room, returning with two small plastic cups and some paper towels a few seconds later.

Prying the toothbrush out of my hands, he tossed it in the sink after filling up the cup. "Here you go."

Cheeks flaming, I took the cup and swished the water in my mouth.

Aiden handed me another empty cup. "Rinse and repeat."

I glared at him, but secretly did a happy dance in my head when he laughed again. Once I didn't have toothpaste falling out of my mouth anymore and my hands were empty, Aiden bent and carefully slid an arm around me. "I can stand without help," I grumbled.

"Sure, you can." Aiden's hair tickled my cheeks. "That's why you're sitting on a bathroom floor. Come on, back to bed."

The door in the main room opened. "What's going on?" Marcus's voice carried through the room. "Is Alexandria okay?"

Crimson stained my entire face.

"She's fine." Aiden easily hauled me to my feet. The tender skin pulled a little, but I kept my expression blank. Didn't want him having a heart attack. "She just wore herself out," he continued, grinning as he let go. "You okay to make it back to the bed?"

I nodded. "It's not my fault. Leon—Apollo—whoever he is—didn't fix me right. Godly powers my—"

"I did fix you, but you were dead. Give me some credit," Apollo said.

I jumped, smacking my hand on my chest. Apollo sat on the edge of the toilet seat, one leg crossed over the other.

Beside me, Aiden bowed stiffly. "My master."

"Oh, my gods," I said. "Seriously. Are you trying to kill me again by giving me a heart attack?"

Apollo tipped his head at Aiden. "I've already told you. You don't need to do the 'master' and bowing business with me." Little sparks of electricity rimmed those all-white eyes. "Why are you out of bed? Doesn't getting stabbed warrant some downtime?" He smiled at Aiden, who was now standing. "She really is hard to take care of, isn't she?"

Aiden looked a little pale. "Yeah…"

"I…I felt gross."

Apollo disappeared from the bathroom and popped up behind Aiden. Marcus took a step back, his eyes wide. He bowed too, and I really thought for a moment that Marcus was going to drop to his knees.

"Good gods," Aiden said under his breath as he led me out of the bathroom.

I stared at the hulking god in the corner of the room as I climbed back into bed. "Did anyone know about this?"

Apollo glided to the bed. It was strange looking at him and seeing some traces of Leon. The face was basically the same, but more refined, sharper. Hair that looked like spun gold replaced the short crew cut Leon had favored, falling just below his broad shoulders. And he seemed taller, if that was even possible. He was achingly beautiful, lacking the rougher edges, but his eyes…they creeped me out. There were no pupils or irises, just white orbs that seemed full of electricity.

The Sun God.

I was staring at the mother effin' Sun God…and yet, it was like staring at Leon. It was bizarre that a god would even be on Earth, but to be as comfortable as Apollo seemed was unreal.

Apollo arched a brow as he slowly turned his head to Marcus. "I know this is a little…shocking, but what I was doing required that I disguise who I was."

Marcus blinked, as if he was coming out of a daze. "Are there more like you here?"

Apollo smiled. "We are always around."

"Why?" Aiden asked, dragging his fingers through his hair. He looked a little out of it also.

"Things are complicated," Apollo said.

"So, was Leon a real person? Did you like, take over his body or something?" I folded my legs under the blanket. "Or have you been Leon this entire time?"

The corners of Apollo's lips twitched. "We are one and the same."

Slowly, I reached over and poked his arm. It felt like real flesh, warm and hard. Disappointed, I poked him again. I was expecting something amazing—celestial—by touching him.

Instead, all I got were weird looks from everyone in the room, including Apollo.

"Please stop touching me," Apollo said.

I jabbed his arm again. "Sorry. It's just that you're real. I mean, I just thought you guys weren't really around here."

"Alex." Aiden sat on the edge of the bed. "You should probably stop touching him."

"Whatever." I dropped my hand into my lap. I still wanted to touch him, though, which was really weird. I kind of wanted to rub all over him like a cat or something…and that was more than weird, and a little uncomfortable.

"Usually we're not," Apollo said, frowning at me. "When we are on Earth, our powers are limited. Everything about this place drains us. We tend to stay away, and if we do visit, it is only for a short while."

"Long enough to hook up with some mortal chicks?"

"Alexandria," Marcus snapped.

Apollo faced me. "No. We haven't spawned any demigods in centuries."

I shuddered when my gaze met his. "Your eyes are really freaking creepy."

He blinked, and in a nanosecond, his eyes were a brilliant, intense cobalt. "Better?"

Not really. Not when he was staring at me like that. "Sure."

Marcus cleared his throat. "I'm really at a loss of what to say."

Apollo waved his hand dismissively. "We've worked together for months. Nothing has changed."

"We didn't know you were Apollo." Aiden folded his arms. "That changes things."

"Why?" Apollo smiled. "I just don't expect you to be as willing to spar with me now."

The skin around Aiden's eyes crinkled as he smiled. "Yeah, you can be sure of that. All of this is just… I mean, how did we not know?"

"Simple. I did not want any of you to know. It made things easier…blending in."

"I'm sorry," I interrupted. Apollo arched a brow, waiting. I felt my cheeks flush. "This is just really awkward."

"Do tell," Apollo murmured.

"I mean, I've like insulted you every which way from Sunday to your face. Multiple times. Like when I accused you of chasing boys and girls and how they turn themselves into trees to get away—"

"Like I said before, some of those things are not true."

"So, Daphne didn't turn into a tree to get away from you?"

"Oh, my gods," Aiden muttered, rubbing a hand along his jaw.

A muscle popped on Apollo's jaw. "That was not all my fault. Eros shot me with a damn arrow of love. Trust me, when you are hit with one of those things, you cannot help what you do."

"But you cut off some of her bark." I shuddered again. "And wore it as a wreath. That's like a serial killer collecting their victim's personal items…or fingers."

"I was in love," he replied, as if being in love explained away the fact that the chick turned herself into a tree to get away from him.

"Okay. What about Hyacinth? The poor boy had no idea—"

"Alexandria." Marcus looked nearly apoplectic.

"Sorry. I just don't understand why he hasn't smote me or something."

"The day is still young," Apollo said, grinning when my eyes widened.

Marcus glanced at me. "You're here because of her."

Apollo nodded. "Alexandria is very important."

This was weird to me. "I thought the gods weren't fans of the Apollyons."

"Zeus created the first Apollyon thousands of years ago, Alexandria, as a way to ensure that no pure-blood would become too powerful and threaten the mortal race or us," he explained. "They were created as a system of checks and balances. We are neither fans nor enemies of the Apollyon, we see them only as a necessity that will be needed one day. And that day has come."

CHAPTER NINETEEN

"Why now?" I asked when no one else spoke. I think the pures were a little starstruck. Apollo was a rock star to them, but even with his otherworldly beauty he was still just Leon to me.

"The threat has never been greater," Apollo answered. Seeing my confusion, he sighed. "Perhaps I should explain a few things."

"Perhaps you should," I muttered.

Apollo drifted over to the bedside table and picked up the pitcher of water. Sniffing it, he placed it back down. "My father has always been...paranoid. All that power, but all Zeus has ever feared is his children doing what he did to his parents. Overthrowing him, conquering Olympia, slaughtering him in his sleep—you know, the same old family drama."

I shot Aiden a look, but he was riveted by Apollo.

"Anyway, Zeus decided that he should keep his enemies close. That is why he called all the demigods back to Olympus and destroyed the ones who didn't heed his call, but he forgot about their children." Apollo smirked. "All that power, but sometimes I wonder if Zeus had been dropped on his head as a baby. He forgot about the Hematoi, the children of the demigods."

I laughed, but Marcus glanced up at the ceiling as if he expected Zeus to strike Apollo with a bolt of lightning.

"The Hematoi"—Apollo looked at Marcus and Aiden pointedly—"are watered-down versions of the demigods, but you are very powerful in your own way. Your numbers frankly outnumber the gods by thousands. If there was ever a cohesive attempt to overthrow us, it might just succeed. And the mortals, they would not stand a chance against the Hematoi."

"I thought you guys were, like, all-knowing. Wouldn't you know if you were about to be overthrown?"

Apollo laughed. "Legends, Alexandria, are hard to separate from the truth. There are things we know, but the future is never set in stone. And when it comes to any creature living on this planet, we cannot see or interfere with them. We do have…tools we use to keep an eye on things."

"That's why the oracle lived here," Aiden said.

Again, there was a tickle in the back of my head. Something about an oracle poked at my fuzzy memories. It stayed out of reach.

"Yes. The oracle answers to me and only me."

"Because you're the God of Prophecy…among five hundred other things," I added, picking back up on the conversation.

"Yes." He came back to the bed, tilting his head to the side. "Once Zeus realized that he had forgotten about the Hematoi, he knew he had to create something that was powerful enough to control the Hematoi but could not populate like the Hematoi did."

Marcus sat in the only spare chair in the room. "And so, the Apollyon was created?"

Apollo sat beside Aiden, which really crowded the bed. "An Apollyon can only be born when the mother is Hematoi, and the father is a half-blood. It is the aether of a female pure combined with that of a half-blood which creates the Apollyon. It is similar to the way a minotaur is born. Apollyons are nothing more than monsters in the scheme of things."

I frowned at his back. "Gee. Thanks."

"Mixing of the two races was forbidden to ensure that there would not be many, and the Hematoi were ordered to kill any offspring of a pure and a half."

My mouth dropped open. "That's terrible."

"That it may be, but we could not have a dozen Apollyons running around." He looked over his shoulder at me. "Two are considered bad enough. Can you imagine if there were a dozen? No. You cannot. And besides, one slipped through every generation as planned. Though, we do make mistakes every once in a while."

I was really beginning to dislike Apollo. "So, I'm a monster and a mistake?"

He winked. "The perfect kind of mistake."

I scooted away from him a little.

The grin reached his vibrant eyes. "As long as the Apollyon behaves himself, he is left alone to do his duty. But when there is a second in the mix, it ups the power of the First. This was something we had not accounted for. Zeus thinks it is a kind of cosmic joke."

Marcus leaned forward. "But why do you even allow the second to live if one is such a threat?"

I shuddered.

Apollo stood again, appearing restless. "Ah, you see, we

cannot touch the Apollyon. The markings are…wards against us. Only Thanatos's Order can carry out a successful attack on the Apollyon and, of course, an Apollyon can kill another Apollyon."

My head was starting to hurt. "And Seth would know this, right?"

"Seth would know all of this."

I exhaled loudly. "I may just kill him."

Apollo arched a brow. "Mankind and the Hematoi have something greater to fear than the daimon…issue. And by the way, the whole daimon problem can totally be blamed on Dionysus. He was the first to discover that aether could be addictive and he just had to show someone. Once Dionysus got so high off the stuff, he actually showed himself to a King of England. Do you know how many problems that caused?"

It was official. The gods were overgrown children. "That's good to know, but can we get back to the whole greater fear thing?"

"The oracle had a prophecy upon your birth, that one would bring the true death to all of us and the other would be our savior."

"Oh geez," I muttered. "Grandma Piperi strikes again."

Apollo ignored that. "She could not tell which one, though. And I grew curious. When Solaris came around, there had been no such prophecy. What made this time so different? So, I checked in on you both throughout your lives. There was nothing particularly remarkable about either of you."

"You're really doing wonders for my self-esteem."

He shrugged. "It is only the truth, Alexandria."

"You did not tell the rest of the gods about Seth and Alexandria?" Marcus asked.

"No. I should have, and my decision not to has not made me many fans." He folded his arms. "But then three years ago, the oracle foresaw your death if you stayed at the Covenant, which led to your mother leaving to protect you, although her prophecy did come true."

It struck me then. "Because I came back to the Covenant…"

"And you did die," Aiden finished, his hands curling into fists. "Gods."

"The oracle is never wrong," Apollo said. "I kept an eye on you up until the night before the daimon attack in Miami. I thought you had sensed me once. You were returning from the beach, and you stopped just outside your door."

My eyes widened. "I remember feeling something weird, but I…didn't know."

"If only I had stayed around…" He shook his head. "When I learned that the Covenant was actively seeking you, I disguised myself as Leon to see what was going on. I had no idea Lucian was aware of your true identity."

"I never told him," Marcus said. "I only knew because my sister confided in me before she left. Lucian already knew by then."

"Interesting," Apollo murmured. "I do believe I am not the only god hanging around."

"Wouldn't you know if there were other gods around?" Aiden asked.

"Not if they did not want me to know," he answered. "And we could be moving in and out at different times. Although, I do not know what any god would have to gain by ensuring that the two Apollyons were brought together."

"Do any of you want revenge?" I asked.

Apollo laughed. "When do we not want revenge against one another? We are constantly irking one another out of boredom. It would take no stretch of the imagination for one to take it all too seriously."

"But what is the fear, Apollo?" Marcus asked. "Why would the Order try to take out Alexandria when she has done nothing?"

"It is not Alexandria they are trying to stabilize."

"It's Seth," I whispered.

Aiden stiffened. His eyes turned a thundercloud gray. "It's always about Seth."

"But he hasn't done anything," I protested.

"Yet," Apollo replied.

"Have you, I don't know, foreseen him doing something?"

"No."

"Then this is all based on crazy Grandma Piperi?" I tucked my hair back. "And that's all?"

Marcus's eyes narrowed. "It does sound extreme."

Apollo rolled his eyes. "You cannot tell me that Seth is not primed for disaster. He already has an ego of a god, and trust me, I would know. The kind of power that a God Killer can harness is astronomical and unstable. He is already feeling the effects of it."

"What do you mean?" Aiden asked.

"Alex?" Apollo said softly.

I shook my head. There were moments when I questioned Seth's sanity and even his intentions. Then there was Jackson. I couldn't prove that it had been him, but… I shook my head. "No. He would never do something so stupid."

"It is sweet—" in a second, Apollo was in front of me and at eye level" —that you would defend him even though I know you do not trust him entirely. Maybe at one point you did, but not anymore."

I opened my mouth but closed it. Lowering my gaze to

my palms, I bit my lip. Once again, something poked at my memory. I swallowed.

"I must leave now," Apollo said quietly.

I looked up, meeting his gaze. Apollo creeped me out and made me really question just how cool I was, but I sort of liked him. "Will you be back?"

"Yes, but I cannot be Leon anymore. My cover is…blown, and I must answer for not informing Zeus of what I have been doing. I will probably be grounded." He laughed at his own joke. I just stared at him. "I am Apollo, Alexandria. Zeus can kiss it."

Marcus once again looked like he wanted to crawl under the bed.

"I will check in when I can." He turned to Marcus. "I will also see if I can track Telly down. Oh, and see if you can have Solos Manolis transfer up here from Nashville. He is a half-blood you can trust."

"I've heard of him," Aiden spoke up. "He's quite… outspoken."

Apollo smiled and then, without so much as another word, disappeared from the room.

"Well, he sure knows how to make an exit." Aiden stood, shaking his head.

Marcus and Aiden made plans to contact this Solos, but I was only half-listening. Curling on my side, I thought about what Apollo had said about Seth. Part of me flat-out refused to believe that Seth could be dangerous, but when I was being honest with myself, I wasn't so sure about that. There were moments he'd proven that I really didn't know what was going on in his head or what to expect from him. I couldn't even figure out why he was so trusting of Lucian—a man who was as plastic as they came.

I hadn't even realized Marcus had left until Aiden sat and placed his hand on my cheek. I wondered if he realized how much he'd been touching me lately. It was almost like an unconscious move on his part. Maybe he did it to remind himself that I was alive…

Suddenly, the fog cleared around my memories. I sat up so quickly that I gasped.

"Alex? Are you okay?" Aiden's eyes were wide. "Alex?"

It took me several seconds to say it. "I remember…I remember what happened when I died."

The look on his face said he hadn't expected me to say that. His hand slid around the nape of my neck. "What do you mean?"

Tears clogged my throat. "I was in the Underworld, Aiden. There were all these people there waiting to pass over and guards on horses. I even saw Charon and his boat—and his boat is much, much bigger and nicer than I expected. There was this girl named Kari who'd been killed by daimons while shopping for shoes and…"

"And what?" he asked, gently wiping away a tear.

"She said she was an oracle. That she knew we'd meet but not like this. And I saw Caleb. I got to talk to him, Aiden. Gods, he looked so…so happy. And he plays Wii with Persephone." I laughed and wiped at my face. "I know it sounds crazy, but I saw him. And he said my mom was there and that she was happy. He told me that a big blond god was arguing with Hades over my soul. He must've meant Apollo. It was real, Aiden. I swear."

"I believe you, Alex." He cradled me against his chest. "Tell me what happened. Everything."

I pressed my cheek against his shoulder, squeezing my eyes shut. I told him everything that Caleb had told me, including what he'd said about Seth. When I asked Aiden to get Olivia's number so I could pass on his message, he shook his head, expression pained.

"I know you want to tell her," he said, "and you will, but right now, we don't want a lot of people knowing what happened. We don't know who we can trust."

In other words, it wasn't Olivia we needed to be worried about, but we couldn't run the risk of things being repeated. I hated the idea of not telling her right now, because it was important, but how could I tell her without giving away what happened? I couldn't.

"I'm sorry, Alex." His hand smoothed along my back. "But it has to wait."

I nodded.

Part of me ached worse after I realized I'd been with Caleb, because his loss was fresh again. But as Aiden held me long after I'd quieted down, the tears that came, in spite of everything, were joyful ones. The pain of Caleb's loss was still there, but it was lessened by the knowledge that he was truly at peace, and so was my mom. And right now, that was all that mattered.

CHAPTER TWENTY

My heart was racing, pumping blood through my body way too fast for someone who'd died and all. I tried and failed not to stare at Aiden as a Guard carried my bags into his parents' house. It was the middle of the night, and I should've felt cold, but I felt ridiculously hot. Especially after Deacon met us in the foyer with a funny little grin on his face.

"This is probably the safest place to stash you until we find Telly and are able to determine if anyone else here is tied to the Order." Marcus dropped his arm on my shoulders. "Once I get back from Nashville, you'll stay with me, or with Lucian, once he returns from New York."

"She should be kept as far away from Lucian's house as possible," Apollo said, appearing out of nowhere. Several of the Guards backed off, eyes wide and faces pale. Apollo grinned at them. "Anywhere Seth will be, I suggest Alexandria should not be."

Every pure and half bowed at the waist. I did too, forgetting the stitches that were healing, and grimaced.

"We need to put a bell on him," Aiden muttered.

I pressed my lips together to keep from laughing.

"Actually," Apollo drawled slowly, "she is probably the safest here."

Deacon sounded like he choked.

Marcus recovered quicker than he had last time. "Have you found something?"

"No." Apollo glanced at Deacon curiously before his gaze settled on Marcus. "I wanted to speak with you privately."

"Of course." Marcus turned to me. "I'll be back in a few days. Please listen to what Aiden tells you and…try to stay out of trouble."

"I know. I'm not allowed to leave his house unless Apollo tells me to." Those were Marcus's exact words. No one else could remove me from this house other than Apollo, Aiden, or Marcus. Not even Lucian's Guards. If anyone else tried, I'd been given permission to kick some butt.

Marcus nodded at Aiden and turned to leave. Passing by, Apollo gave us a two-finger salute that just looked bizarre coming from him. Over the past two days, I'd grown used to his random appearances. It seemed he took great pleasure in scaring the crap out of everyone when he did it.

"You ready?" Aiden asked.

Deacon arched a brow.

"Shut up," I said as I walked past Deacon.

"I haven't said a single thing." He spun around and followed me in. "We're going to have so much fun. It's like a slumber party."

A slumber party at Aiden's house? Oh gods, the images I came up with made me blush.

Aiden closed the door behind the others as they left and shot his brother a look.

Deacon rocked back on his heels, grinning. "Just so you know, I get incredibly bored quite easily and you will be forced to be my source of entertainment. You'll kind of be like my own personal jester."

I flipped him off.

"Well, that wasn't funny at all."

Aiden brushed past me. "Sorry. You're probably going to wish you'd stayed in the med clinic."

"Oh, I'd wager that's not the case." Deacon met my glare with an impish grin. "Anyway, did you celebrate Valentine's Day when you were slumming with the mortals?"

I blinked. "Not really. Why?"

Aiden snorted and then disappeared into one of the rooms.

"Follow me," Deacon said. "You're going to love this. I just know it."

I followed him down the dimly lit corridor that was sparsely decorated. We passed several closed doors and a spiral staircase. Deacon went through an archway and stopped, reaching along the wall. Light flooded the room. It was a typical sunroom, with floor-to-ceiling glass windows, wicker furniture, and colorful plants.

Deacon stopped by a small potted plant sitting on a ceramic coffee table. It looked like a miniature pine tree that was missing several limbs. Half the needles were scattered in and around the pot. One red Christmas bulb hung from the very top branch, causing the tree to tilt to the right.

"What do you think?" Deacon asked.

"Um...well, that's a really different Christmas tree, but I'm not sure what that has to do with Valentine's Day."

"It's sad," Aiden said, strolling into the room. "It's actually embarrassing to look at. What kind of tree is it, Deacon?"

He beamed. "It's called a Charlie Brown Christmas Tree."

Aiden rolled his eyes. "Deacon digs this thing out every year. The pine isn't even real. And he leaves it up from Thanksgiving to Valentine's Day. Which thank the gods is the day after tomorrow. That means he'll be taking it down."

I ran my fingers over the plastic needles. "I've seen the cartoon."

Deacon sprayed something from an aerosol can. "It's my MHT tree."

"MHT tree?" I questioned.

"Mortal Holiday Tree," Deacon explained and smiled. "It covers the three major holidays. During Thanksgiving it gets a brown bulb, a green one for Christmas, and a red one for Valentine's Day."

"What about New Year's Eve?"

He lowered his chin. "Now, is that really a holiday?"

"The mortals think so." I folded my arms.

"But they're wrong. The New Year is during the summer solstice," Deacon said. "Their math is completely off, like most of their customs. For example, did you know that Valentine's Day wasn't actually about love until Geoffrey Chaucer did his whole courtly love thing in the High Middle Ages?"

"You guys are so weird." I grinned at the brothers.

"That we are," Aiden replied. "Come on, I'll show you your room."

"Hey, Alex," Deacon called. "We're making cookies tomorrow, since it's Valentine's Eve."

Making cookies on Valentine's Eve? I didn't even know if there was such a thing as Valentine's Eve. I laughed as I followed Aiden out of the room. "You two really are opposites."

"I'm cooler!" Deacon yelled from his Mortal Holiday Tree room.

Aiden headed up the stairs. "Sometimes I think one of us was switched at birth. We don't even look alike."

"That's not true." I fingered the decorative garland covering the marble banister. "Your eyes are the same."

He smiled over his shoulder. "I rarely ever stay here. Deacon does every once in a while, and visiting Council members stay here sometimes. The house is usually empty."

I remembered what Deacon had said about this house. Wanting to say something, but at a loss for what to say, I trailed behind him quietly. Over the last two days, Aiden had stayed by my side constantly. It had started even before the whole stabby incident, when we'd lain in bed and talked about stupid, inane things.

"Deacon stays in one of the bedrooms downstairs. I'll stay here." He gestured at the first room, drawing my attention.

The urge to see his room was too much to resist. I peeked inside. Like the one in the cabin, there were just the bare essentials. Clothes were folded neatly on a chair beside the full-size bed. There were no pictures or personal effects. "Was this your room when you were younger?"

"No." Aiden leaned against the wall in the hallway, watching me through hooded eyes. "My room used to be the one Deacon stays in. It's hooked up with all the stuff Deacon requires. This was one of the guest rooms." He pushed off the wall. "Yours is down the hall. It's a nicer room."

I tore myself away from his room. We passed several closed doors, but one had closed double doors decorated with titanium inlays. I suspected that had been his parents' room.

Aiden pushed open a door at the end of the carpeted hall and turned the light on. Sliding past him, my mouth dropped open. The room was huge and beautiful. Plush carpet covered the floors, heavy curtains blocked the bay window, and my bags of personal items had been stacked neatly by a dresser. A flat-screen TV hung from the wall, and the bed was big enough for four people. I spied a bathroom with a huge tub and my heart went all fluttery.

Seeing my lovestruck expression, Aiden laughed. "I figured you'd like this room."

I looked inside the bathroom, sighing. "I want to marry that bathtub." I turned around, smiling at Aiden. "This is like going to one of those super expensive hotels, except everything is free."

He shrugged. "I don't know about that."

"Maybe not to you and all your endless wealth." I drifted off to the window and parted the curtains. Oceanside view. Nice. The moon reflected off the still, onyx-colored waters.

"That money isn't really mine. It's my parents'."

Which did make it his and Deacon's, but I didn't push it. "The house is really beautiful."

"Some days it's more beautiful than others."

I felt my cheeks flush. I pressed my forehead against the cool window. "Whose idea was it for me to stay here?"

"It was a joint effort. After...what happened, there was no way you could've stayed in the dorm."

"I can't stay here forever," I said quietly. "Once school is back in, I need to be on the other island."

"We'll figure something out when that time comes," he said. "Don't worry about that right now. It's past midnight. You have to be tired."

Dropping the curtains, I faced him. He stood next to the door, hands curled into fists. "I'm not tired. I was stuck in that hospital room and that bed for what felt like eternity."

He cocked his head to the side. "How are you feeling?"

"Fine." I patted my stomach. "I'm not broken, you know."

Aiden was quiet for a few moments, and then he smiled a little. "Want something to drink?"

"Are you trying to booze me up, Aiden? I'm shocked."

He arched a brow. "I was thinking more along the lines of hot chocolate for you."

I grinned. "And what about you?"

Turning around, he headed out of the bedroom. "Something I'm old enough to drink."

I rolled my eyes but followed him out of the room. Aiden did make me hot chocolate—with tiny marshmallows—and he didn't drink anything other than a bottle of water. He then took me on a quick tour of the house. It was similar to Lucian's—lavishly grand, more rooms than anyone would ever need in a lifetime, and personal property that was probably worth more than my life. Deacon's room was by the kitchen, accessed through a titanium-trimmed door under the stairs.

Sipping my drink, I laughed when Aiden tried to right the bulb on Deacon's MHT tree. I drifted around the room, looking for some sort of personal effects. There wasn't a single picture of the St. Delphi family. Nothing that proved they even existed.

Aiden stood in front of a closed door—a room he hadn't shown me on the mini-tour. "How's the chocolate?"

I smiled. "It's perfect."

He set his water down on the coffee table and folded his arms. "I've been doing a lot of thinking about what Apollo said."

"Which part of crazy are you thinking about?" I watched him over the rim of my mug, loving the way he smiled in response to the stupid things that came out of my mouth. That had to be true love, I decided.

"You shouldn't stay at Lucian's when he returns."

I lowered my mug. "Why?"

"Apollo has a point about Seth. You're in danger because of him. The farther away from him you are, the safer you'll be."

"Aiden—"

"I know you care about him, but you've suspected that Seth hasn't been honest with you." Aiden strode forward and dropped into a chair. His gaze lowered and heavy lashes fanned his cheeks. "You shouldn't be around him—not when he can come and go at Lucian's."

Aiden had a point. I'd give him that, but I seriously doubted that was the whole reason. "And you feel this way all because of what Apollo said?"

"No. It's more than that."

"You don't like Seth?" I asked innocently, setting my mug down.

He flashed his teeth. "Besides that, Alex, he hasn't been honest about a lot of things. He lied about knowing how an Apollyon was created, about the Order, and there's a good chance he's…giving you those marks on purpose."

"Okay, besides all those reasons?"

He stared up at me. "Well, I don't like the fact that you're settling for him."

I rolled my eyes. "I hate when you say that."

"It's the truth," he said simply.

Irritation started to burn below my skin. "That's not the truth. I'm not settling for Seth."

"Let me ask you a question, then." Aiden leaned forward. "If you could have…who you wanted, would you be with Seth?"

I stared at him, somewhat shocked that he'd even throw that out there. And it really wasn't a fair question. What could I say to that?

"Exactly." He sat back, smiling smugly.

A fierce emotion blasted through me. "Why can't you just admit it?"

"Admit what?"

"That you're jealous of Seth." It was one of those times I needed to shut up, but I couldn't. I was angry and thrilled all at once. "You're jealous of the fact that I can be with Seth if I want to be."

Aiden smirked. "There. You just said it yourself. You'd be with Seth *if* you wanted to be. Obviously, you don't, so why *are* you with him? You're settling."

"Ugh!" My hands curled into fists, and I wanted to stomp my foot. "You are absolutely the most frustrating person I know. Fine. Whatever. You're not jealous of Seth or the fact that he's been sleeping in my bed for the last two months, because of course you haven't wished that was you at all."

Something dangerous flared in his silvery eyes.

Cheeks flaming, I wanted to smack myself. Why had I said that? To piss him off or to make myself look bad? I'd accomplished a little of both.

"Alex," he said, voice low and deceptively soft.

"Just forget it." I started past him, but his hand shot out as fast as a snake striking. One second, I was walking and the next I was in his lap, straddling him. Eyes wide and heart thundering, I stared at him.

"Okay," he said, grasping my upper arms. "You're right. I'm jealous of that little punk. Happy?"

Instead of basking in the glory of having him admit that I was right, I placed my hands on his shoulders and basked in something totally different. "I…I keep forgetting how fast you can move when you want to."

A strange, small smile played over his lips. "You haven't seen anything yet, Alex."

My pulse went into cardiac arrest territory. I was done arguing—done talking in general. Other things were on my mind. And I knew he was thinking the same. His hands moved down my arms to my hips. He tugged me forward, and the softest part of me pressed against his hardness.

Our mouths didn't touch, but the rest of our bodies did. Neither of us moved. There was something primal in Aiden's gaze, wholly possessive. I shivered—the good kind of shiver. All I could think about was how good, how right his body felt pressed against mine.

I cupped his face and then slid my fingers through his hair, amazed that the intensity of what I was feeling was stronger than any bond with Seth. Delicious sensations rolled through me as his hands tightened around my hips, and when he rocked against me, the way his hands trembled and the powerful way his body coiled completely undid me.

"There's something I need to tell you," he whispered, his eyes searching mine. "That I should've told you—"

"Not right now." Words would ruin things. They brought logic and reality into the game. I lowered my mouth to his.

A hallway light turned on outside the room.

I sprang away from Aiden as if he'd caught fire. From several feet away, I struggled to catch my breath as my eyes locked with Aiden's. He came out of the chair, his chest rising and falling sharply. There was a second when I thought he was going to say the hell with it and pull me back into his arms, but the sound of encroaching footsteps knocked some sense into him. Closing his eyes, he tipped his head back and exhaled loudly.

Without saying a word, I spun around and left the room. I passed a sleepy, confused-looking Deacon in the hallway.

"I'm thirsty," he said, rubbing his eyes.

Muttering something that resembled good night, I fled

upstairs. Once inside the bedroom, I collapsed on the bed and stared at the vaulted ceiling.

Things just weren't meant to happen between us. How many times had we been interrupted? It didn't seem to matter how strong our connection was—our attraction. Something always got in the way.

Fully clothed, I rolled onto my side and curled up into a ball. I wanted to spin kick everyone who thought me staying with Aiden was a good idea. We—I—had enough problems right now without throwing myself at Aiden.

Not that I'd really thrown myself at him this time…or the last time. *Oh hell…*

I reached under my shirt and felt the scar below my rib-cage. The act served as a painful reminder that my problem with love—or lack thereof—was not the biggest problem I had to face.

CHAPTER TWENTY-ONE

The first thing I did when I woke up was take a nice, luxurious bath in the garden tub. I stayed in that thing until my skin started to wrinkle and even then, it was hard to pull myself out of it.

It was heaven in a bathroom.

After that, I went downstairs and found Deacon sprawled across a couch in the rec room. Knocking his legs aside, I sat down. He was watching *Supernatural* reruns. "Good choice," I commented. "They're two brothers I'd like to meet in real life."

"True." Deacon knocked wild curls out of his eyes. "It's what I watch when I'm not in class or pretending to be in class."

I grinned. "Aiden would kill you if he knew you skip class."

He kicked up his legs and dropped them in my lap. "I know. I've cut back on the skipping class thing."

He'd also cut back on the drinking thing. I glanced at

him. Maybe Luke was a good influence on him. "You doing anything special for Valentine's Day?" I asked.

His lips pursed. "Now why would you ask that, Alex? We don't celebrate V-Day."

"But you do. You wouldn't have that…tree if you didn't."

"Are you?" he inquired, his gray eyes dancing. "I'd swear I saw Aiden at the jewelry—"

"Shut up!" I hit him across the stomach with the throw pillow. "Stop saying things like that. Nothing is going on."

Deacon grinned, and we watched the rest of the shows he'd recorded. It wasn't until the afternoon that I worked up the nerve to ask where Aiden was. "He was outside with the Guards the last time I checked."

"Oh."

Part of me was glad that Aiden was doing his babysitting outside. My cheeks caught fire just thinking about us in the chair last night.

"So, you two were up pretty late," Deacon said.

I kept my expression blank. "He was showing me the house."

"Was that all he was showing you?"

Shocked, I laughed as I twisted toward him. "Yes! Deacon, geez."

"What?" He sat up and swung his legs off my lap. "It was just an innocent question."

"Whatever." I watched him stand up. "Where are you going?"

"Over to the dorms. Luke's still there. You're more than welcome to come, but I doubt Aiden will let you out of this house."

Pures and halfs could be casual friends, especially while they were in school together, and a lot of them were, although not so much since the daimon attacks at the beginning of the school year. Zarak hadn't thrown any of his huge parties lately. But for a half to be hanging out at a pure's house would raise questions.

"What are you two doing?" I asked.

Deacon winked as he backed out of the room. "Oh, I'm sure the same thing you and my brother were doing last night. You know, he's going to show me around the dorm."

Several hours later, Deacon returned, and Aiden finally reappeared inside. Avoiding my gaze, he went straight upstairs. Deacon shrugged and coaxed me into making cookies with him.

When Aiden finally came downstairs, he lingered in the kitchen while Deacon and I made cookies. I sort of gaped at him—dressed down in jeans and a long-sleeved shirt—so long that Deacon elbowed me in the side. Once Aiden loosened up, he joked around with his brother. Every so often our eyes would meet, and electricity danced over my skin.

After eating our weight in raw cookie dough, we all ended up in the living room, sinking into couches bigger than most people's beds. Deacon controlled the TV for four straight hours before ambling off to bed, and Aiden went outside to check in with the Guards—why, I had no idea. I roamed around the house. What had Aiden wanted to talk about before I told him to stop talking? Had he been ready to talk, like he'd hinted when I was still in the med clinic? Restless, I found myself in the MHT tree room.

I poked the bulb, smiling as it swayed back and forth. Deacon was so bizarre. Who had a Mortal Holiday Tree? So weird.

It was late, and I should've been in bed, but the idea of sleeping was unappealing. Full of restless energy, I drifted around the room until I came to a stop in front of the closed door. Curious, and with nothing else better to do, I tried the handle and found it unlocked. Glancing over my shoulder, I pushed open the door and crept inside the softly lit room. At once I realized why Aiden had kept this room off his tour.

Everything personal was crammed into the circular room. Pictures of Aiden lined the walls, chronicling his childhood. There were photos of Deacon as a precocious-looking little boy, head full of blond curls and chubby cheeks that hinted at delicate features.

I stopped in front of one of Aiden and felt my chest tighten. He must've been six or seven. Dark curls fell across his face instead of the looser waves he had now. He was adorable, all gray eyes and small lips. There was a photo of him with Deacon. Aiden was probably around ten or so and he had one lanky arm draped over his younger brother's shoulders. The camera had captured both boys laughing.

Moving around an overstuffed couch, I slowly picked up the titanium picture frame that was on the fireplace mantel. My breath caught.

It was his father—his mother and father.

They stood behind Deacon and Aiden, their hands on the boys' shoulders. Behind them the sky was a brilliant blue. It was easy to tell which boy favored which parent. Their mother had hair the color of corn silk that fell past her shoulders in springy curls. She was beautiful, as all pures were, with delicate features and laughing blue eyes. It was shocking, though, how much Aiden looked like his father. With the almost-black hair and piercing silver eyes, he was an exact replica.

It didn't seem fair that his parents were taken so young,

robbed of watching their boys grow up. And Aiden and Deacon had lost so much.

I ran my thumb over the edge of the frame. Why had Aiden closed off all these memories? Did he ever come in here? Looking around the room, I spied a guitar propped beside a stack of books and comics. This was his room, I realized. A place where he thought it was okay to remember his parents and maybe just get away.

I turned my attention back to the photo and tried to picture my mother and father. If pures and halfs had been allowed to be together, would we have had moments like these? Closing my eyes, I tried to picture the three of us. My mom wasn't hard to remember now. I could see her before she turned, but my father had the mark of slavery on his forehead and no matter what I did, it wouldn't go away.

"You shouldn't be in here."

Startled, I spun around, clutching the frame to my chest. Aiden stood in the doorway, arms straight at his sides. He stalked across the room and stopped in front of me. Shadows hid his expression. "What are you doing?" he demanded.

"I was just curious. The door wasn't locked." I swallowed nervously. "I haven't been in here long at all."

His gaze dropped and his shoulders stiffened. He pried the picture from my fingers and set it back on the mantel. Without speaking, he bent and placed his hands over the kindling. Fire sparked and grew immediately. He grabbed a poker.

Embarrassed and stung by his sudden coldness, I backed away. "I'm sorry," I whispered.

He prodded at the fire, his spine stiff.

"I'll leave." I turned, and suddenly he was in front of me. My heart tumbled over.

He clasped my arm. "Don't leave."

I searched his eyes intently but couldn't gain anything from them. "Okay."

Aiden took a deep breath and let go of my arm. "Would you like something to drink?"

Hugging my elbows, I nodded. This room was his sanctuary, a silent memorial to the family he'd lost, and I'd invaded it. I doubted even Deacon dared to tread in here. Leave it to me to just bust on in.

Behind the bar, Aiden pulled two wine flutes out and sat them down. Filling the glasses, he glanced up at me. "Wine okay?"

"Yes." My throat was dry and tight. "I really am sorry, Aiden. I shouldn't have come in here."

"Stop apologizing." He came around the bar and handed me a glass.

I took the glass, hoping he didn't notice how my fingers shook. The wine was sugary and smooth, but it didn't settle in my stomach right.

"I didn't mean to snap at you like that," he said, moving toward the fire. "I was just surprised to see you in here."

"It's…uh, a nice room." I felt like an idiot for saying that.

His lips tipped up at the corner.

"Aiden…"

He stared at me for so long I thought he'd never speak and when he did, it was not what I expected. "After what happened to you in Gatlinburg, it reminded me of what it'd been like for me…after what happened to my parents. I had nightmares. Could hear…hear their screams over and over again for what felt like years. I never told you that. Maybe I should have. It could've helped you."

I sat on the edge of the couch, clenching the fragile stem.

Aiden faced the fire, taking a sip of his wine. "Do you

remember the day in the gym when you told me about your nightmares? It stuck with me—your fear of Eric and his return," he continued. "All I kept thinking was, what if one of the daimons had escaped the attack on my parents? How would I have gone on?"

Eric was the only daimon to escape from Gatlinburg. I hadn't stopped thinking about him, but to hear his name knotted up my stomach. Half of the tags on my body were thanks to him.

"I thought getting you out of there, taking you to the zoo would help get your mind off things, but I had…I had to do more. I contacted some of the Sentinels around here. I knew Eric wouldn't have gone far, not after he knew what you were and had tasted your aether," he said. "Based on Caleb's and your description, it wasn't hard to find him. He was just outside of Raleigh."

"What?" The knots grew larger. "Raleigh is like, less than a hundred miles from here."

He nodded. "As soon as it was confirmed that it was him, I left. Leon—Apollo—went with me."

At first, I couldn't figure out when he could've done this, but then I remembered those weeks after I'd told him I loved him and he'd ended our training sessions together. Aiden had had time to do this without me ever knowing. "What happened?"

"We found him." He smiled humorlessly before turning back to the fire. "I didn't kill him outright. I don't know what that says about me. By the end, I think he truly regretted ever learning of your existence."

I didn't know what to say. Part of me was awed by the fact he had gone to such great lengths for me. The other part was sort of horrified by it. Underneath the calm and controlled persona that Aiden wore like a second skin was something dark—a side of him I'd only glimpsed. I stared at his profile, suddenly realizing that I hadn't been fair to Aiden. I'd set him up on this incredibly high pedestal, where he was absolutely flawless in my mind.

Aiden wasn't flawless.

I swallowed a sip of my wine. "Why didn't you tell me?"

"We really weren't on talking terms then, and how could I've told you?" He laughed harshly. "It wasn't like a normal daimon hunt. It wasn't a precise and humane kill like we're taught."

The Covenant basically taught us not to play with our kills, so to speak. That even though the daimon was beyond saving, he'd once been a pure-blood or a half-blood. Still, as disturbing as learning that Aiden had most likely tortured Eric should've been, I wasn't disgusted by it.

Gods know what that said about *me*.

"Thank you," I said finally.

His head jerked toward me sharply. "Don't thank me for something like that. I didn't do it just—"

"You didn't do it just for me. You did it because of what happened to your family." And I knew I was right. It wasn't so much that he'd done it for me. It was his way of taking revenge. It wasn't right, but I understood it. And in his shoes, I would've probably done the same thing and then some.

Aiden went still. The flames sent a warm glow over his profile as he stared down at his glass. "We were visiting friends of my father in Nashville. I didn't know them very well, but they had a daughter who was about my age. I thought we were just vacationing before the start of school, but as soon as we got there, my mother practically pushed me in her direction. She was a tiny thing, with pale blond hair and these green eyes." He took a breath, fingers tightening around the fragile stem of the glass. "Her name was Helen. Looking back, I know why my parents arranged that I spend so much time with her, but for some reason, I just didn't get it."

I swallowed. "She was your match?"

A rueful smile appeared. "I really didn't want to have anything to do with her. I spent most of my time shadowing the half-blood Guards while they trained. My mother was so upset with me, but I remember my father laughing about it. Telling her to just give me some time, and let nature run its course. That I was still very much just a boy and that men fighting would interest me more than pretty girls."

There was a lump forming in my chest. I sat back, the glass of wine forgotten.

"It was night when they came." His thick lashes fanned his cheeks as his eyes lowered. "I heard the fighting outside. I got up and looked out the window. I couldn't see anything, but I just knew. There was a crash downstairs, and I woke up Deacon. He didn't understand what was happening or why I was making him hide in the closet and cover himself with clothes.

"It all just happened so fast after that." He took a healthy swallow of the wine and then sat his glass on the ledge. "There were only two daimons, but they had control over fire. They took out three of the Guards, burning them alive."

I wanted him to stop, because I knew what was coming, but he had to get this off his chest. I doubted he'd ever put that night into words, and I needed to deal with it.

"My dad was turning the element back on them, or at least, trying to. The Guards were dropping left and right. Helen was awakened by the commotion, and I tried to get her to stay upstairs, but she saw one of the daimons attack her father—ripped his throat open right in front of her. She screamed—I'll never forget that sound." A distant look crept across his face as he continued, almost like he was there. "My father made sure my mother got up the stairs, but then I couldn't see him anymore. I heard him scream and I just," he shook his head, "stood there. Terrified."

"Aiden, you were just a boy."

He nodded absently. "My mom yelled at me to get Deacon and get him out of the house with Helen. I didn't want to leave her, so I started down the stairs. The daimon came out of nowhere, grabbing her by the throat. She was staring at me when he snapped her neck. Her eyes…just glossed over. And Helen…Helen was screaming and screaming. She wouldn't stop. I knew he was going to kill her, too. I started running up the stairs, and I grabbed her hand. She was panicking and fighting me. It slowed us down. The daimon reached us and he grabbed for Helen first. She went up in flames. Just like that."

I gasped. Tears burned my eyes. This…this was more horrific than I'd imagined, and it reminded me of the boy the daimon had burned in Atlanta.

Aiden turned to the fire. "The daimon went after me next. I don't know why he spared me the fire and knocked me to the ground, but I knew he was going to drain my aether. Then there was this Guard who'd been burned downstairs. Somehow, through what had to have been the worst kind of pain, he made it up the stairs and killed the daimon."

He faced me and there wasn't any pain in his expression. Maybe sorrow and regret, but there was also a bit of wonder. "He was a half-blood. One of the ones I'd been following around. He was probably my age now, and you know, in all that horrific pain, he still did his duty. He saved my life and

Deacon's. I found out a few days later that he had succumbed to the burns. I never got a chance to thank him."

His tolerance of half-bloods made sense. That one Guard's actions had changed centuries of beliefs in one little boy, turning prejudice into awe. It was no wonder that Aiden never saw the difference between halfs and pures.

Aiden made his way over to me and sat. He met my stare. "That's why I chose to become a Sentinel. Not so much because of what happened to my parents, but because of that one halfblood who died to save my life and my brother's."

I didn't know what to say or if there was anything I could. So, I placed my hand on his arm as I blinked back tears.

He placed his hand over mine as he looked away. A muscle worked in his jaw. "Gods, I don't think I've ever talked to anyone about that night."

"Not even Deacon?"

Aiden shook his head.

"I feel…honored that you'd share that with me. I know it's a lot." I squeezed his arm. "I just wish you'd never had to experience any of that. It wasn't fair to any of you."

Several moments passed before he answered. "I had justice for what those daimons did to me. I know it's different from what you dealt with, but I wanted to give you that justice. I wish I'd told you before."

"A lot of stuff was going on then," I said. We hadn't been talking, and then Caleb's death happened. My heart didn't clench as badly as it used to at his name. "I understand what happened with Eric."

He smiled a little. "It was a knee-jerk reaction."

"Yeah." I searched for something to take our minds off everything. We both needed it. My gaze found the acoustic guitar propped against the wall. "Play something for me."

He rose and picked up the guitar reverently. Walking back to the couch, he sat on the floor in front of me. He tipped his head down and locks of hair fell forward as he fiddled with the knobs along the headstock. His long fingers plucked a pick out from the taut strings.

He peered up, his lips tipped in a half smile. "Treachery," he murmured. "You knew I wouldn't refuse you."

I eased down on my side. My stomach rarely ached, but I'd grown accustomed to being careful. "You know it."

Aiden laughed as he thrummed his fingers on the strings lightly. After a few more moments of adjusting the tone, he started playing. The song was as haunting as it was soft, pitching high for a few strands, and then his fingers slipped down the chords. My suspicions were confirmed. Aiden could play. There wasn't one wrong slip or falter.

It entranced me.

Resting my head on the throw pillow, I curled up and closed my eyes, letting the melody filling the room drift over me. Whatever he was thrumming on the guitar was soothing, like the perfect lullaby. A smile pulled at my lips. I could totally see him sitting in front of a packed bar, playing tunes that enchanted everyone in the room.

When the song ended, I opened my eyes. He was staring back at me, eyes so soft, so deep, that I never wanted to look away. "That was beautiful."

Aiden shrugged and gently placed the guitar beside him. He reached up, carefully taking the barely touched glass of wine from my fingertips. His eyes watched me as he took a sip, and then he set the glass aside, too. Minutes could've passed as we stared at each other, neither of us talking.

I didn't know what came over me, but I reached out and placed a hand on his chest, beside his heart. Under my right hand, there was something hard and teardrop-shaped tucked under his shirt. I'd felt the necklace before and never really paid it much attention, but now there was something…familiar about it.

I sucked in a sharp gasp as comprehension shot through me.

Aiden stared back, his eyes incredibly bright. A shiver ran down my spine, spreading across my skin with dizzying speed. I reached up, sliding my fingers under the thin chain.

"Alex," Aiden ordered, pleaded really. His voice was thick, gruff. "Alex, please…"

I hesitated for an instant, but I had to see it. I just had to. Carefully, I tugged the chain up. My breath caught in my throat as I lifted the chain until it was completely out from underneath his shirt.

Dangling from the silver chain was the black guitar pick I'd gotten him for his birthday. The day I had given it to him he'd told me he didn't love me. But this…*this* had to mean something, and my heart was swelling, in danger of bursting.

Speechless, I ran my thumb over the polished gemstone. There was a tiny hole in the top, where the chain threaded through.

Aiden placed his hand over mine, closing my fingers around the guitar pick. "Alex…"

When my eyes met his, there was a brutal level of vulnerability in his stare, a sense of helplessness that I shared. I wanted to cry. "I *know*." And I did. I knew even if he never spoke those words, even if he refused to, I'd still know.

His lips parted. "Couldn't fool you for that long, I guess."

I squeezed my eyes shut, but a tear wiggled its way free, gliding down my cheek.

"Don't cry." He caught the tear with his finger as he

pressed his forehead against mine. "Please. I hate when you cry because of me."

"I'm sorry. I don't want to be all weepy." I wiped at my cheeks, feeling foolish. "It's just that...I never did know."

Aiden clasped the sides of my face, pressing a gentle kiss to my forehead. "I wanted a piece of you with me always. No matter what."

I shuddered. "But I don't...I don't have anything of you."

"Yes, you do." Aiden brushed his lips over my damp cheek. A soft smile filled his voice. "You'll have a piece of my heart—all of it, really. Forever. Even if your heart belongs to someone else."

My heart tumbled over, but I stilled. "What do you mean?"

He dropped his hands, leaning back. "I know you care about him."

I did care about Seth. But he wasn't my heart. When Aiden was there, in front of me, the connection between us was something more than prophecy. My true fate—real and not an illusion. Prophecies are just dreams; Aiden was my reality.

"It's not the same," I whispered. "It never has been. You have my heart...and I only want to share my heart with you."

Aiden's eyes were back to liquid silver. I saw that before he lowered his gaze. Moments passed before his eyes flicked up, meeting mine. There seemed to be some sort of internal battle he struggled with. When he spoke, I wasn't sure if he'd won or lost. "We should go to bed."

A shock ran through me, flushing my skin. But *wait*—was he suggesting that we go to bed together or that we go to bed separately? I really had no idea, I was too afraid to hope, and oddly, I was frightened by the idea. It was like being offered what I'd waited for so long and suddenly having no idea what to do with it.

Or how to do it.

His lips quirked, and then he stood. Clasping my boneless hands in his, he tugged me to my feet. My legs felt weak. "Go to bed," he said.

"Are…are you coming, too?"

Aiden nodded. "I'll be up in a few."

I couldn't breathe.

"Go," he urged.

And I went.

CHAPTER TWENTY-TWO

I was sure I was going to have a heart attack. Rarely did mortal illnesses plague us, but since I'd had a cold already, I figured nothing was impossible.

I still couldn't really breathe.

I brushed my teeth and got the tangles out of my hair. I stared at the obscenely large bed in the middle of the room. I couldn't decide what to wear. Or should I wear nothing? Oh gods, what was I thinking? It wasn't like he said he was coming up to have sex. And if he wasn't and he saw me lying on the bed naked, that would be a whole lot of awkward. Perhaps he just wanted to spend more time with me. Seth issue aside, there was still the whole glaring issue of us not being able to be together.

But he had the pick. He'd had *the* pick hovering over his heart this entire time.

I pulled on a tank top and sleeping shorts, then started toward the bed. Then I looked down at my arms. In the moonlight streaming in through the window, I could still see the patchy, irregular skin. I didn't want Aiden to see that. So, I changed quickly, pulling on a thin, long-sleeved shirt. I kept the bottoms on. Then I jumped in the bed, pulled the covers up to my chin, and waited.

There was a soft knock on the door a few minutes later. "It's okay." I winced at the way my voice croaked.

Aiden came in, shutting and locking the door behind him. He'd changed, too, wearing a pair of dark sleeping pants and a gray tank top that showed off muscular arms. I swallowed nervously and willed my heart to slow down before I freaked out.

He faced me and went rigid. The room was too shadowed for me to see his expression, and I wished I could, because then I could've tried to figure out what he was thinking. Wordlessly, he went to the windows first and drew the blinds. The room was cast into utter darkness, and my fingers dug into the rich comforter. I heard him padding around the room, and then a soft glow appeared. Aiden brought a candle to the bed, setting it down on a small table. He looked at me, expression softened by the candlelight. He smiled.

I started to relax, the blanket easing away from my fingers.

Carefully, he pulled back the covers on his side and climbed in, never once breaking eye contact with me. "Alex?"

"Yeah?"

He was still smiling. "Relax. I just want to be here with you…if that's okay?"

"It's okay," I whispered.

"Good, because I really don't want to be anyplace else."

Oh, the warmth that flooded my chest could've had me floating to the stars. I watched him stretch out beside me. My gaze darted to the closed door even though I knew Deacon was nowhere near us. And it wasn't like he didn't already suspect something. Or like he cared. I bit my lip, daring a quick look at Aiden. His chin was tipped up and his eyes burned silver, bright and intense. I couldn't look away.

Aiden drew in a shallow breath, lifting the arm closest to me. "Come?"

Heart pounding, I scooted over until my leg brushed his. His arm came up, wrapping around my waist. He guided me down so that I was nestled against him, my cheek on his chest.

I could feel his heart racing just as fast as mine. We lay in silence for a little while, and in those minutes, it was like being in paradise. The simple pleasure of being beside him felt so right it really couldn't be wrong.

Aiden brought his other arm across him, cupping my cheek in his hand. His thumb smoothed over my jaw. "I'm sorry for that day in the gym. For how I talked to you, for how much I hurt you. I just thought I was doing the right thing."

"I understand, Aiden. It's okay."

"It's not okay. I hurt you. I know I did. I want you to know why I did that," he said. "After you told me how you felt, at the zoo…it…it shattered my self-control." *Didn't seem that way*, I thought as he continued. "I knew I couldn't be around you anymore, because I knew I would touch you and I wouldn't stop."

I lifted up, staring down at him and opened my mouth to say something that probably would've ruined the moment, but I never had the chance. Aiden's hand found the nape of my neck and pulled me down. His lips met mine, and like every time before, there was this indefinable spark that coursed through us. He made a sound against my lips, kissing me harder and harder.

He pulled back just enough so that his lips brushed mine when he spoke. "I can't keep pretending that I don't want this—that I don't want you. I can't. Not after what happened to you. I thought…I thought I'd lost you, Alex, forever. And I would've lost everything. You *are* my everything."

Many emotions rose in me all at once—awe, hope, and love. So much love that everything outside of us vanished in that instant. "This…this is what you've been trying to tell me."

"It's what I've always wanted to tell you, Alex." He sat up, bringing me along with him. "I've always wanted this with you."

I slid my hands to his cheeks, meeting his heated gaze with my own. "I've always loved you."

Aiden made a strangled sound, and his lips were on mine again. His hand buried in my hair, holding me still. "This wasn't my intention…coming in here."

"I know." My lips brushed his as I spoke. "I know."

As he kissed me again, he eased onto his back. My heart was hammering against my ribs as his fingers left my face and traveled down. He lifted himself up just enough for me to take off his shirt and toss it aside. My hands splayed across each hard ripple, and I kissed my way down until his chest heaved under my lips and he whispered my name in a pleading sort of way. He gripped my arms and pulled me back to his lips.

I shrugged out of his grasp and lifted my arms without speaking. He obeyed the silent command and tossed my shirt aside. Without any warning, I was on my back, staring up at him. His hands slipped over my bare skin as his lips dipped down my throat and over the curve of my shoulder. Each scar was kissed tenderly, and when he came to the one Linard's blade had left, he shuddered.

My fingers sifted through his hair as I held him to me. His kisses were doing crazy, strange, and wonderful things to me. I whispered his name over and over again like some kind of prayer. Then I was moving against him, being guided by some primal instinct that told me what to do. The rest of our clothes ended up in a pile on the floor. The moment our bodies were flush with one another, a sense of wildness came over me.

Our kisses deepened, his tongue swept over mine, and I rocked against him. All of this was wonderful, exquisitely pleasing. Aiden dropped kisses all over my flushed skin. I was lost in the heady sensations, completely unprepared for it. This may not have been what we intended, but this…this was happening.

Aiden lifted his head. "Are you sure?"

"Yes," I breathed. "I've never been more sure."

His hand trembled against my flushed face. "Have you gotten…?"

He was asking if I'd had my shot—the Council-mandated birth control for all half-blood females. I nodded.

The silver eyes flared. His hand trembled against my cheek again and as he lifted up, his eyes roamed over me. My new-found courage all but disappeared under his scalding stare. Somehow sensing my nervousness, his kiss was gentle and sweet. He was patient and perfect, coaxing away the shyness until I wrapped myself around him.

There was a near-panicked edge to him, driven by the knowledge that there was no pulling back, no stopping this time. With a thrusting kiss that left me shaken, his hand drifted with such exquisite detail. His kisses followed the same pattern and when he paused, his eyes begged for permission. That simple moment, that tiny act brought tears to my eyes.

I couldn't—didn't want to—deny him anything.

Aiden was everywhere—in every touch, every soft moan. When I thought I couldn't take anymore, that I would surely break, he was there to prove that I could. When his lips descended on mine again, they did so with a fevered pitch.

"I love you," he whispered. "I have since the night in Atlanta. I always will."

I gasped against his skin. "I love you."

He broke. Whatever control he had wrapped around him finally slipped away. I reveled in it, the pure simplicity of being in his arms and knowing that he felt the same keen madness that I did. Supporting himself with his forearm as his kisses took on the same sense of urgency that I felt, he lifted his mouth to whisper something in a beautiful language I didn't understand. I was nearly over the edge, rushing toward a glorious ending.

We were surrounded by our love for one another. It became a tangible thing, electrifying the air around us until I was sure we both would ignite under its power. Then in a mindless moment of pure beauty, we weren't a half-blood and a pure-blood, we were simply two people madly, deeply in love.

We were one.

I awoke some time later, tucked in Aiden's arms. The candle still flickered by the bed. The sheet had tangled around our legs, and the comforter was pushed to the floor. I realized that I'd been more or less using him as a pillow. I lifted my head and drank him in. I could never grow tired of looking at him.

His chest rose evenly under my hands. He looked so young and relaxed while he slept. Locks of dark waves tumbled against his forehead and his lips were parted. I leaned down and placed a soft kiss against those lips.

His arms immediately tightened, betraying that he was not as deeply asleep as I'd originally thought. I grinned at being caught. "Hello."

Aiden's eyes fluttered open. "How long have you been staring at me?"

"Not long."

"Knowing you," he drawled lazily, "you've been staring at me since I fell asleep."

"That's not true." I giggled.

"Uh huh, come here." He tugged me down. My nose brushed against his. "Not nearly close enough."

I shifted closer. My leg wrapped around his. "Close enough?"

"Let me see." His hands slid down my back and rested over the curve of my waist with the slightest pressure. "Ah, that's better."

I flushed. "Yes…yeah, it is."

Aiden grinned wolfishly and a wicked glint filled his silver eyes. I should've known at that point he was up to something, but this side of Aiden—this playful and sensual side—was unknown to me. His hand glided lower, eliciting a pleased gasp of surprise. He sat up in one fast fluid motion, and I found myself unexpectedly in his lap.

I didn't have a moment to consider much. Aiden kissed me, scattering all thoughts or responses. The sheet slipped away and I melted against him. It was quite some time later, when the sun was about to rise and the candle had long since gone out, that Aiden gently roused me.

"Alex." He brushed his lips over my forehead.

I opened my eyes, smiling. "You're still here."

His hand caressed my cheek. "Where else would I be?" Then he kissed me, and my toes curled. "Did you think I'd just leave?"

I marveled at the fact that I could run my hand up his arm without having him pull away. "No. I don't know, actually."

He frowned as he traced the shape of my cheekbone. "What do you mean?"

I snuggled closer to him. "What happens now?"

Understanding flared in his gaze. "I don't know, Alex. We have to be careful. It's not going to be easy, but...we'll figure something out."

My heart skipped a beat.

A relationship was going to be damn near impossible anywhere we'd go, but I couldn't stop the hope swelling inside me or the tears building in my eyes. Was it wrong to hope for a miracle? Because that's what we would need to make this work.

"Oh, Alex." He gathered me into his arms, holding me tightly against him. I burrowed my face in the space between his neck and shoulder, inhaling deeply. "What we did—it was the best thing I've ever done, and it wasn't just some sort of fling."

"I know," I murmured.

"And I'm not going to let you go—not because some stupid law says we can't be together."

Dangerous words, but I melted along with them, cherished them. I wrapped my arms around him, trying to keep old fears and worries at bay. Aiden was taking a huge risk to be with me—so was I—and I couldn't deny our feelings because of what'd happened to Hector and Kelia. That fear wasn't fair to Aiden or to me.

Aiden rolled onto his back, fitting me to his side. "And I'm not going to lose you to Seth."

The air hitched in my lungs. Somehow, being so lost in Aiden, I'd completely forgotten the unforgettable—the fact that I'd be Awakening in two weeks—and all the ramifications of that. Fear tasted like blood in the back of my throat. What if that changed the way I felt about Aiden?

Crap. What if the bond twisted those feelings back to Seth?

And how in the hell had I forgotten about Seth in the first place? "Out of sight and out of mind" was totally not justifiable. The thing was I did care for Seth—a lot. Part of me even loved him, even though I wanted to hurt him most of the time. But my love for Seth was nothing like what it was for Aiden. It didn't consume me, didn't make me want to do questionable things, be reckless, and in the same breath, be safer and more cautious. My heart, my body didn't respond in the same way.

Aiden's hand skimmed over my arm. "I know what you're thinking, agapi mou, zoi mou."

I took a shallow breath. "What does that mean?"

"It means, 'my love, my life.'"

I squeezed my eyes shut against the rush of tears as I remembered the first time he'd said "agapi mou" to me. My gods, Aiden hadn't lied. He had loved me since the very beginning. Knowing that filled me with steely resolve. I rose up and stared down at him.

He smiled, and my heart jumped. He reached up, tucking my hair back behind my ear. His hand lingered. "What are you thinking now?"

"We can do this." I leaned down and kissed him. "We will do this, dammit."

His arm circled around my waist. "I know."

"Gods, I know this sounds really naive, so please don't laugh at me." I grinned. "But I've been…terrified of this Awakening, of losing myself. But…but I'm not anymore. I won't lose myself, because…well, how I feel about you, it would never let me forget who I am."

"I'd never let you forget who you are."

My grin spread. "Gods, we're crazy. You know that, right?"

Aiden laughed. "I think we're pretty good at crazy, though."

We stayed in each other's arms longer than we should have. I was reluctant to let him leave and he was reluctant to go. Rolling onto my side, I watched him throw his clothes on. He grinned when he caught me. I wiggled my brows. "What? It's a nice view."

"Wicked," he said, sitting beside me. His hand skimmed over my hip. There was something fierce in his gaze. "We will do this."

I snuggled closer to him, wishing he didn't have to leave. "I know. I believe that."

Aiden kissed me once more and whispered, "Agapi mou."

CHAPTER TWENTY-THREE

Everything and nothing changed after having sex. I didn't look any different. Well, there was the goofy smile plastered over my face that I couldn't get rid of. Other than that, I looked the same. But I did feel different. I ached in places I had no idea someone could even hurt. My heart also did that fluttering thing every time I even thought his name, which was so girlie, and I loved it.

Letting my heart instead of my hormones decide when to do it made what Aiden and I'd done special. And when we passed each other throughout the day, the looks we stole suddenly meant more. Everything meant more because we both were risking it all and neither of us regretted that.

I spent the better part of the afternoon and evening playing Scrabble with Deacon. I think he regretted asking me to play, because I was one of *those* Scrabble players—the kind who played three-letter words every chance I got.

There was a part of me that kept expecting the gods to zap one of us for finally breaking all the rules. So, when Apollo popped in on our fourth round of Scrabble, I about had a heart attack.

"Gods!" I clutched my chest. "Can you stop doing that?"

Apollo looked at me strangely. "Where is Aiden?"

Slowly rising to his feet, Deacon cleared his throat and bowed. "Um, I think he's outside. I'll go get him."

I glared at Deacon's retreating form. Left alone with Apollo, I wasn't sure what to do. Should I stand up and bow, too? Was it considered rude to sit in the presence of a god? But then Apollo sat beside me, cross-legged, and started messing with the letters on the board.

Guess not.

"I know what's happened," Apollo said after a few seconds. My brows furrowed.

"What are you talking about?"

He nodded at the board.

My gaze dropped to the game, and I nearly passed out. He'd spelled SEX and AIDEN with those stupid little squares. Horrified, I shot to my knees and swept the letters off the board. "I-I have no idea what you're talking about!"

Apollo tipped his head back and laughed, like, chortled really loudly.

I think I hated him, god or not.

"I've always known." He leaned back against the couch, folding his arms. His blue eyes burned unnaturally, lit from within. "I'm just surprised you two made it this far."

My jaw hit the floor. "Wait. That night Kain came back? You…you knew I was in Aiden's cabin, didn't you?"

He nodded.

"But…how do you know now?" My stomach dropped. "Oh, my gods, have you been doing some kind of creepy peeping-god thing or something? Did you see us?"

Apollo's eyes narrowed as he tilted his head toward me. "No. I *do* have better things to do."

"Like what?"

His pupils started to burn white. "Oh, I don't know. Maybe track down Telly, keep an eye on Seth and, if I get lucky, bring you back from the dead. Ah, and I forgot making a few appearances at Olympus, so that I don't have every one of my siblings curious about what I'm doing."

"Oh. Sorry." I settled down, feeling chagrined. "You are really busy."

"Anyway, I can smell Aiden on you."

My face caught fire. "What? What do you mean, you can *smell* him? Dude, I showered."

Apollo leaned over, his gaze meeting mine. "Every person has a unique scent. If you mix yours enough with that person, it takes a lot to get their smell off you. Next time you might want to try Dial soap instead of those girly body washes."

I covered my flaming face. "This is so wrong."

"But it does amuse me greatly."

"You...you're not going to do anything about it?" I whispered, lifting my head.

He rolled his eyes. "I believe that is the least of our problems at the moment. Besides, Aiden is a good guy. He will always put you first, above all else. But I am pretty sure he will get overprotective at some point." Apollo shrugged while I stared, open-mouthed, at him. "You will just have to set him straight."

Was Apollo giving me relationship advice? This was officially the weirdest moment of my life, and that was saying something. Thankfully, Aiden and Deacon returned then, and I was saved from dying of humiliation.

Deacon shoved his hands into his pockets. "I'm just going

to go busy myself with…something. Yeah." Spinning around, he closed the door on his way out.

There was something really weird about Deacon's reaction to Apollo. For his sake, I seriously hoped he hadn't done anything with Apollo. He might end up a flower or a tree stump.

Aiden strolled into the living room and bowed. "Is there news?" he asked upon straightening.

"He knows about us," I said.

A second later, Aiden hauled me to my feet and shoved me behind him. In both of his hands were Covenant daggers.

Apollo arched a golden eyebrow. "And what did I say about the whole overprotective bit?"

Well, he did call it. Cheeks flaming, I grabbed Aiden's arm. "He doesn't seem to care, apparently."

Aiden's muscles tensed under my hand. "And why should I believe that? He's a god."

I swallowed. "Well, probably because he could've killed me already if he was going to have a problem with it."

"That is true." Apollo stretched his legs out, crossing them at the ankle. "Aiden, you cannot actually be shocked that I know. Do I need to remind you of our special hunt in Raleigh? Why else would a man hunt down someone like that unless it was for love? And trust me, I know the crazy lengths people will go to for love."

The tips of Aiden's cheeks flushed as he relaxed by a fraction. "I'm sorry for…pulling these on you, but—"

"I understand." He waved his hand dismissively. "Have a seat, cop a squat, whatever. We need to talk, and I do not have long."

Taking a deep breath, I sat where I'd been before. Aiden took the arm of the couch behind me, remaining close. "So, what's going on?" I asked.

"I was just with Marcus," Apollo answered. "He's gotten Solos on board."

"On board for what?" I glanced at Aiden. He looked away. Equal parts curious and angry, because I knew that meant he was keeping something from me, I elbowed his leg. "On board for what, Aiden?"

"You have not told her, have you?" Apollo scooted further away. "Don't hit me."

"What? I don't just hit people." Both stared at me knowingly. I folded my arms to keep from hitting them. "Fine. Whatever. What's going on?"

Apollo sighed. "Solos is a half-blood Sentinel."

"Gee. I've figured that part out." Aiden pushed me in the back with his knee. I shot him a death glare. "What does he have to do with any of this?"

"Well, I am trying to tell you." Apollo rose to his feet fluidly. "Solos's father is a Minister in Nashville. He's actually the only son of the Minister; he has been doted on and raised with a lot of knowledge of the politics of the Council."

"Okay," I said slowly. Pures caring for their half-blood children wasn't unheard of. Rare, yes, but I was an example of that.

"Not everyone on the Council is a fan of Telly, Alex. Some would even like to see him removed from his position," Aiden explained.

"And if I remember correctly, he was outvoted when it came to placing you into servitude." Apollo glided over to the window. "Word of what he's involved in will not sit well with those members of the Council, including Solos's father, who, by the way, is a softie when it comes to the treatment of half-bloods. Having them on our side can only help."

"What do you mean, his father is a softie?"

Apollo faced me. "He is one of those who do not believe that half-bloods should be forced into servitude if they do not fit the mold of a Sentinel or Guard."

"Well, you have no one to blame for that rule but yourself." Anger sparked inside of me. "You're responsible for the way we've been treated."

Apollo frowned. "We have had nothing to do with that."

"What?" Surprise colored Aiden's voice.

"We are not responsible for the subjugation of half-bloods," Apollo said. "That was all the pure-bloods. They decreed the separation of the two breeds into castes centuries and centuries ago. All we asked was that pures and halfs not mix."

Those words pulled the world out from underneath my feet. Everything I'd been taught to believe was no longer true. Since I was a small child, I'd been told that the gods saw us as lesser, and our society acted on that belief. "Then why...why haven't you guys done anything?"

"It was not our problem," Apollo responded blithely.

Rage whipped through me like a red-hot bullet, and I shot to my feet. "It wasn't your problem? The pure-bloods are your children! Just like we are. You all could've done something years ago."

Aiden caught my arm. "Alex."

"What did you expect us to do, Alexandria?" Apollo said. "The lives of half-bloods are literally a step—a small step—above those of mortals. We cannot interfere in such trivial things."

The slavery of thousands and thousands of halfs was a trivial thing?

Breaking free of Aiden, I charged Apollo. Looking back, not a good idea, but I was so angry, so shocked that the gods had stood by since the beginning and *allowed* the pures to treat us like animals they could herd. A small, rational part of my brain knew not to take it personally, because this was how the gods were. If it didn't involve them directly, they didn't care. It was as simple as that. But the pissed part beat out the rational part.

"Alex!" Aiden yelled, reaching for me.

I was so much faster when I wanted to be. He couldn't stop me. I made it about a foot in front of Apollo before he held up his hand. I smacked off an invisible wall. The force blew my hair back.

Apollo smiled. "I do like your feisty temper."

I kicked the shield. Pain fired through my foot. I hobbled back. "Ouch! Dammit, that hurt!"

Aiden got a secure grip around me. "Alex, you need to calm down."

"I am calm!"

"Alex," Aiden chided, obviously trying not to laugh.

Apollo lowered his hand, appearing contrite. "I do… understand your anger, Alexandria. The half-bloods were not treated fairly."

I took several deep, calming breaths.

"By the way," Apollo said, "the next time you charge a god, and it is not me, you will be destroyed. If not by that god, then by the furies. You are lucky the furies and I do not get along. They would love to see my entrails strung upon the rafters—"

"Okay. I get the picture." I eased my aching foot down. "But I don't think you really understand. That's the problem with you gods. You created all of this and then just left it. Taking no responsibility for what happened. You guys take 'self-centered' to a whole new epic level. And all of our problems—the daimons and even the Apollyon crap—are the gods' fault. You said it yourself! If you ask me, you guys are freaking useless 99% of the time."

Aiden placed his hand on the small of my back. I expected him to tell me to shut up, because I was yelling at a god, but that's not what he did. "Alex has a point, Apollo. I didn't even know…the truth. Even we are taught that the gods decreed the separation of the two breeds."

"I do not know what to say," Apollo said.

I smoothed my hair down. "Please don't say you're sorry, because I know it wouldn't be true."

Apollo nodded.

"Okay. Now that we've gotten this out of our systems, let's get back to the point of this visit." Aiden pulled me to the couch, forcing me to sit down. "And seriously, Alex, no hitting."

I rolled my eyes. "Or what? You're going to put me in a time out?"

Aiden's grin was daring, as if he was up for the challenge and might even enjoy it.

"Solos and his father will be assets in making sure Telly is removed from the Head Minister position and that an extensive investigation is done to determine how many Order members may be out there. And before you ask me why, as a god, I cannot just see that, I must remind you that we are not omniscient."

"Why were you guys worried about how I'd react to that?" I asked, confused. "Sounds like a good thing."

"It's not everything." Aiden took a deep breath. "Solos's father owns extensive property throughout the states, places where we can hide you until all the Order members are uncovered."

"Not just that," Apollo added. "We can keep you safe until we know how to deal with Seth and your Awakening."

I blinked, positive I hadn't heard them right. "What?"

"The worst thing that can happen right now is for Seth to take on your power and become the God Killer." Apollo folded his arms. "Therefore, we need to make sure you are far enough away that when you do Awaken, the bond is severed by distance, and you cannot connect with him. He cannot be trusted."

"Why? Why can't he be trusted? What has he done?"

"He's lied to you about a lot of things," Aiden pointed out.

I shook my head. "Besides the lying about the Apollyon stuff, what has he done?"

"It is not what he has done, Alexandria, but what he will do. The oracle has seen it."

"You're talking about that whole 'one to save and one to destroy' crap? Why? Why would that be the case with Seth and me, when we aren't the first set of Apollyons?" I tucked my hair back, frustrated and full of the need to…protect Seth's name. Not like he had a good name, but come on.

Suddenly, Apollo was kneeling in front of me at eye level. Aiden stiffened beside me. "I did not waste my time trying to keep you safe, and argue with Hades over your soul, only to have you throw it away based on foolish and naïve trust."

I squeezed my hands into balls. "Why do you even care, Apollo?"

"It's complicated," was all he said.

"If all you can say is that 'it's complicated,' then you can forget that. What about school?"

"Marcus assured us that you'd graduate on time," Aiden said.

"You knew about this?"

He nodded. "Alex, I think it's the smart thing to do."

"Running is the smart thing to do? Since when do you

believe that? Because I remember you telling me that running solved nothing."

Aiden's lips thinned. "That was before you were murdered, Alex. Before I—" He cut himself off, shaking his head. "That was before."

I knew what he meant, and I hurt for that. I ached, because he had to worry about me, but that still didn't completely extinguish my anger. "You should've told me this was what you guys were planning. It's the same as Seth and Lucian planning to whisk me away to some distant country. I should be included in these plans."

"Alexandria—"

"No." I cut Apollo off and stood before Aiden could stop me. "I'm not going into hiding because there's a *chance* that Seth might do something."

"Then forget the issue with Seth." Aiden stood, folding his arms. "You need to be protected from the Order."

"We can't forget about Seth." I started pacing, wanting to pull out my hair. "If I up and disappear, what do you think Seth's going to do? Especially if we don't tell him, which I know is what you guys are thinking."

Apollo rose to his feet and tipped his head back. "This would be so much easier if you had an agreeable personality."

"Sorry, buddy." I stopped, meeting Aiden's steely eyes. "But I can't go along with this. And if you really think that the Order is going to try something again, then we need Seth's help."

Aiden turned halfway; his broad shoulders tensed as he growled under his breath. Typically, I'd be annoyed with the testosterone display, but yeah, I kind of found it hot.

The Sun God sighed. "For now, you win, but if I so much as think that this will end badly—"

"How can things end badly?" I asked.

"Besides the obvious?" Apollo frowned. "If Seth does what is feared, the gods would bring their wrath down upon all pures and halfs to make a point. And as I was saying, if it was even to get to that point, you will have no choice."

"Then why don't you just let the Order kill me? That would solve all your problems, wouldn't it?" Not that I wanted to die, but it did make sense. Even I could see that. "Seth wouldn't become the God Killer then."

"Like I said, it is complicated." Then Apollo simply vanished.

"I hate when he does that." I glanced at Aiden. He stared back at me, brows furrowed, jaw tight. I sighed. "Don't look at me like I've kicked baby Pegasus into the street."

Aiden exhaled slowly. "Alex, I don't agree with this. You have to know that we are only looking out for what is best for you."

Hot or not, there went my tenuous grip on my temper. "I don't need you looking out for what's best for me, Aiden. I'm not a child!"

His eyes narrowed. "I of all people know you're not a child, Alex. And I sure as hell didn't treat you like one last night."

My cheeks flushed a hot mix of embarrassment and something far, far different. "Then don't make decisions for me."

"We're trying to help you. Why can't you see that?" Then his eyes deepened to a tumultuous gray. "I will not lose you again."

"You haven't lost me, Aiden. I promise you." Some of the anger seeped out of me. Fear was behind his fury. I could understand that. It was what drove my tantrums on a regular basis. "You haven't and you won't."

"That's not a promise you can make. Not when there are so many things that could go wrong."

I didn't know what to say to that.

Aiden crossed the room, sweeping me up in a tight embrace. There wasn't a word spoken for several moments, just the ragged rise and fall of his chest.

"I know you're mad," he began, "and that you hate the idea of anyone trying to control you or force you into doing something."

"I'm not mad."

He pulled back, arching a brow.

"Okay. I'm mad, but I understand why you think I should go into hiding."

He led me back to the couch. "But you're not going to go along with this."

"No."

Aiden pulled me into his lap, circling his arms around me. My heart did a flip, and it took me a few seconds to get accustomed to this openly affectionate Aiden who didn't pull away and keep his distance.

"You are the most frustrating person I know," he said.

I rested my head on his shoulder, smiling. "None of you are giving Seth a chance. He hasn't done anything, and I don't have any reason to fear him."

"He's lied to you, Alex."

"Who hasn't lied to me?" I pointed out. "Look, I know that's not a great excuse, and you're right, he has lied to me. I know that, but he hasn't done anything that warrants me running off and hiding. We have to give him a chance."

"And what if we take that risk and you were wrong, Alex? Then what?"

I hoped that wouldn't be the case. "Then I'll have to deal with it."

His shoulder tensed under my cheek. "I'm not okay with that. I've already failed you once and—"

"Don't say that." Twisting in his embrace, I met his gaze and cupped his cheeks. "You had no idea Linard was working for the Order. You are not at fault for that."

He pressed his forehead against mine. "I should've been able to protect you."

"I don't need you to protect me, Aiden. I need you to do what you're doing now."

"Hold you?" His lips twitched. "I can do that."

I kissed him, and my chest squeezed. Never in a million years would I get used to being able to kiss him. "Yes, that, but I just need…your love and your trust. I know you can fight for me, but I don't need you to do that. These problems—they're mine, not yours, Aiden."

His arms tightened around me, so tight, I found it hard to breathe. "Because I love you, we share each other's problems. When we fight, we fight together. I'm going to be by your side no matter what, whether you like it or not. That's what love is, Alex. You never have to face anything alone again. And I get what you're saying. I don't agree with it, but I will support you in any way I can."

I was struck silent. There was really nothing I could say to that. I wasn't that great with words, not those kinds of words. So, I wrapped myself around him like a super-friendly octopus. When he leaned back, I settled over him, not caring that he was still in his Sentinel gear, daggers and all. Quite some time passed before either of us spoke.

"Seth's not really a bad guy," I said. "He can be prone to moments of great douchery, but he wouldn't do something like take out the Council."

Aiden's fingers slipped over my cheek. "I wouldn't put anything past Seth."

I decided not to respond to that. Since the phone call after Linard's attack, I hadn't even heard from Seth. And now that I had calmed down a bit, I started to think logically about what Apollo had said. "Everyone fears Seth—the gods, the pures, and the Order—because he'll become the God Killer, right?"

"Right," he murmured. His hand drifted to my shoulder, brushing my hair back.

"Well, what if he doesn't become the God Killer?"

His hand stilled. "You mean if we stop the transfer of power? That's what we're trying to do by keeping you away from Seth."

"I seriously doubt that's your sole purpose of keeping me away from Seth."

"You got me there," he said, and I could hear the smile in his voice.

Tipping my head up, I decided it was way past time to clear the air. Aiden first...and then Seth, because the last thing I wanted was for anyone to be hurt over this. "I care about Seth—I do. He's important to me, but it's not the same. You know you don't have anything to worry about, right? What Seth and I had... Well, I don't even know what we had. It wasn't a relationship, not really. He asked to try and see what happens. And this is what happened."

Aiden caught a strand of my hair between his fingers. "I know. I trust you, Alex. But that doesn't mean I trust him."

There was no winning this with him. "Anyway, I can talk to Seth and let him know what's going on with the Order and what people fear."

"And you think he'll go along with that?"

"I do. Seth won't force me into anything by using the... connection against us." I wiggled up Aiden's chest and kissed his chin. "Seth once told me that if things ever became too much, he'd leave. So, there is a way out."

"Huh, he actually said that?" His eyes burned silver. "Maybe he's not so bad."

"He's not."

"I don't like this, but like I said, I will support you any way that I can."

"Thank you." I kissed his cheek again.

A sigh shuddered through him. "Alex?"

"What?"

He leaned back, watching me through heavy lashes. "Did you guys eat all the cookie dough last night, or did you actually make some cookies?"

I laughed at the turn in conversation. "We made some. I think there might be a few left."

"Good." He placed his hands on my hips and tugged me forward, pressing our bodies together. "What's Valentine's Day without cookies?"

"I think the mortals put a lot of emphasis on chocolate this time of the year." I placed my hands on his shoulders, and all the stuff with angry gods, Order members, Seth, and everything else took the back seat. "But cookies work."

One hand slid up the curve of my spine, slipping under the mass of tangled hair and sending a fine shiver over my skin. "So, there's no pathetic Christmas tree involved?"

"There's no such thing as a Mortal Holiday Tree." My breath caught as he guided my mouth toward his, stopping just as our lips brushed. "But…but I'm sure the mortals would appreciate the thought of that kind of tree."

"You are?" He pressed his mouth to one corner of my lips and then the other. Eyes drifting shut, my fingers dug into his shirt. When he kissed me slowly, pouring all his unstated passions into that one act, his powerful body tensed under mine.

I couldn't remember what we were talking about. There was just the heady, wild rush of feelings that stormed through me. This was Aiden—the man I'd loved for what felt like forever, in my arms, under me, against me, and touching me.

"Happy Valentine's Day," he murmured.

Aiden held me close and still, and in those moments, he showed rather than told me just how much we were in this together.

CHAPTER TWENTY-FOUR

I'd fantasized so many times about what it would be like to be in a relationship with Aiden. There had been days, not too long ago, that I would've smacked that dream right out of my head because it seemed so hopeless. But for a week, I lived that fantasy to the fullest.

We stole as many moments alone as we could, filling them with deep kisses and quiet laughter. And plans, we actually made plans.

Or at least we tried to.

My back arched and a giggle escaped.

"Oh, so you *are* ticklish?" Aiden murmured against the flushed skin of my neck. "This is a very interesting development."

It seemed that, when we were together, we could never keep our hands off each other for very long. Aiden had to be touching some part of me. Whether it was just a slight contact of skin, his hand wrapped around mine or our bodies flush with our legs tangled lazily, we were *always* touching.

Maybe it was because he'd fought it for so long, or maybe we both were intoxicated by the simple act of just lying together, and we were addicted to it. Our legs pressed together, and our heads rested on the arm of the couch in the room with the family portraits. It was safe in here as no one dared to enter it. What had once been Aiden's sanctuary had become ours.

Today was no different.

But it wasn't all fun. As the days passed and I knew Seth's return was approaching, anxious energy built inside me. There was also barb-tipped guilt that sank in deep. Sometimes, when I thought of him, I remembered those glimpses of vulnerability he'd shown after our midnight swim in the Catskills and the day after I'd been given the Brew. Seth was a lot of things, almost a complete enigma at times, but under it all, he was a guy who…who cared, and he cared about me. Maybe more than I did for him. Maybe not, but I didn't want to hurt him.

I wiggled on the couch beside Aiden, trying to shake the sudden dark cloud that'd settled over me. Talking to Seth wasn't going to be easy. Then again, I had no idea how he would respond. He'd been with Boobs…so maybe it wouldn't be that hard.

"So, tell me," Aiden continued idly, drawing me back to the present—to him. "Where was that spot again? Was it here?" He trailed his fingers over my stomach.

"No." My eyes closed as my heart jumped and tiny shivers skated through me.

"Here?" His fingers danced over my ribs.

Beyond words, I shook my head no.

"Now where was that spot?"

His agile fingers skipped over my stomach and along my

side. I clamped my mouth shut, but my body shook as I tried to restrain my natural reaction.

"Aha! Is this it?" He increased the pressure slightly.

I squirmed, but he was relentless. He laughed when I jackknifed, and I would've tumbled to the floor if it weren't for his quick movement. "Stop," I gasped in between fits of giggles. "I can't take it."

"All right, maybe I should be nice." Aiden pulled me back to his side and leaned over me. He plucked a strand of hair and twisted it around his two fingers. "Anyway, back to the question at hand. What place other than New Orleans?"

I ran my hand down his arm, loving the way his muscles seemed to clench under the skin I touched. "How about Nevada? There're no Covenants nearby. The closest is the University."

He leaned down, brushing his lips over my cheek. "Are you suggesting Las Vegas?"

I fixed an innocent look on my face. "Well, there'd be a lot of daimons, since you pures like to party there, but no real Hematoi establishments of any kind."

"First New Orleans and now Las Vegas?" He brushed his lips back and forth as his fingers tipped my head back. "I'm starting to see a trend here."

"I don't know." My breath caught as he pressed down. "Maybe you can't handle Las Vegas."

Aiden smirked. "I love a challenge."

I giggled, but all humor fled the moment his lips touched mine again. I could go on just kissing him forever. They were gentle kisses at first, soft and questioning. My fingers sank through his hair, clenching him closer, and the kisses deepened. I shifted and wrapped my arms around him, wanting to be able to push the stop button on time. I could stay here forever, feeling his body molded to mine, melting together—I froze against him.

The feeling slithering down my spine was unmistakable. The three runes that had been dormant since Seth left now woke up with a vengeance, burning and tingling. The cord snapped alive, responding to its other half.

His lips moved down my neck, over my collarbone. "What is it?"

There was no stop button for time. Dammit. "Seth's here, like he's right outside."

Aiden lifted his head. "Seriously?"

I nodded stiffly.

He swore under his breath and sprang to his feet. I started to get up, but he held out his hand. "Let me just check this out first, Alex."

"Aiden—"

Swooping down, he clasped my shoulders and kissed me until I almost forgot about the way the cord was unraveling in the pit of my stomach. "Just let me check this out, okay?" he whispered.

I nodded and watched him prowl toward the door. With a quick reassuring smile, he left the room. It was probably a good thing that he was going out to greet Seth. I needed a few moments to collect myself after that last kiss.

Nervous energy rushed me, and the cord thrummed happily. Agitated, I rose to my feet within a minute and crossed the room. Seth was near. I knew it deep in my bones. I stopped in front of the cracked door and held my breath.

They were in the hallway, alone. And of course, they were arguing already. I rolled my eyes.

"You think I don't know?" I heard Seth say in a smug, knowing way. "That I didn't know this entire time I've been gone?"

"Know what?" Aiden sounded surprisingly calm.

Seth laughed softly. "She may be here with you, right now, but that's just a moment in time in the big scheme of things. And all moments end, Aiden. Yours will too."

I wanted to throw open the door and tell Seth to shut up.

"Sounds like something on the back of a twisted Hallmark card," replied Aiden. "But perhaps your time has already ended."

There was a stretch of silence, and I could picture the two of them. Aiden would be coolly looking down on Seth, who would be smiling arrogantly and secretly enjoying the whole confrontation. Sometimes I wanted to smack them both.

"It doesn't really matter," said Seth. "That's what you don't get. She can love you and it still doesn't matter. We belong together. It's fated. Have your moments, Aiden, because in the end, it really won't mean a damn thing."

That was it. I threw open the door and stormed out into the hallway. Neither of them even turned around, and I knew they heard me fly out of the room. Beyond them I could see the shadows of the Guards through the tiny square windows on each side of the door.

"You really think that?" Aiden cocked his head to the side. "If so, then you're a damn fool."

Seth smiled. "I'm not the fool here, pure-blood. She doesn't belong to you."

"She belongs to no one," Aiden growled as his hands flexed by his hips, where his daggers normally hung.

"Debatable," Seth said, so low I wasn't even sure I'd heard him correctly.

I shoved between the two idiots before one of them did some damage. "You don't own me, Seth."

Seth finally looked at me, his eyes a cool amber. "We need to talk."

That we did. I glanced at the furious pure-blood beside me. This wasn't going to be pretty.

"In private," Seth added.

"What can you possibly need to say that you can't say in front of me?" Aiden asked.

"Aiden," I groaned. "You promised, remember?" I didn't need to say any more. Aiden knew. "I do need to talk to him."

"Nothing will happen to her. Not when she's with me."

I spun around. "Just let me get my hoodie. Try not to kill each other."

"No promises." Seth smirked.

Grabbing my hoodie off the back of the couch, I quickly hauled it on and hoofed it back to the hallway. Gods knew a second of those two together was a second too long. I passed Aiden a meaningful look as I followed Seth to the front door. He looked severely unhappy but nodded.

Brutal temperatures sucked away my breath as I stepped outside. I was unable to remember the last time it'd been this cold in North Carolina. Seth wore just a black thermal and cargos. Nothing else. I wondered if I got built-in weather padding once I Awakened.

The Guards immediately stepped aside, revealing the strong winter sun glaring off the still waters. At first I was surprised, but then I remembered whose Guards they were—Lucian's.

Aiden moved uneasily. His hands opened and closed at his sides.

Seth feigned a look of sympathy. "Don't look too happy about this, Aiden."

I kicked Seth in the shin.

"Ouch," he hissed, blasting me with a look. "Kicking is not nice."

"Antagonizing people isn't nice," I shot back.

Aiden sighed. "You have twenty minutes. Then we'll come looking for you."

Backing down the steps, Seth bowed at Aiden and then pivoted around. Wind caught and tossed his hair around. Sometimes I forgot how…beautiful Seth was. He could give Apollo a run for his money. Both of them had this type of cold beauty that didn't seem real, because it was flawless both far away and up close.

I fell into step beside him, shoving my hands into the center pocket of my hoodie. "I wasn't expecting you back so soon."

Seth arched a golden eyebrow. "Really? I'm not surprised by that."

My cheeks flushed. There was no way he could've known what had happened between Aiden and me. The bond didn't work over that many miles. Taking a deep breath, I womaned up. "Seth, I have to—"

"I already know, Alex."

"What?" I stopped, pushing my hair out of my face. "You know what?"

He faced me and leaned in, bringing his face mere inches from mine. The cord went crazy inside me, but it was manageable…as long as he didn't touch me. Oh gods, this wasn't going to be easy. "I know everything."

"Everything" could mean a lot of things. I hunched my shoulders, squinting against the harsh glare. "What exactly do you know?"

His lips tipped into a small smile. "Well, let's see. I know about *that*," he gestured to the St. Delphi house, "back there. I knew that was going to happen."

I went hot and cold all at once. "Seth, I'm really sorry. I don't want to hurt you."

He stared at me a moment, then laughed. "Hurt me? Alex, I've always known how you've felt about him."

Okay. I must've been on crack when I thought I'd seen vulnerability in Seth before. Silly me, he was the boy with no feelings or something. But even for the cocky, annoying version of Seth, he was taking this surprisingly well—too well. My suspicions skyrocketed. "Why are you so okay with this?"

"Am I supposed to be upset? Is that what you want?" He tipped his head to the side, brows slanted. "Do you want me to be jealous? Is that what it takes?"

"No!" I felt my face flush again. "I just didn't expect you to be so…okay with it."

"Well, I wouldn't say I'm okay with it. It is what it is."

I stared at him and then a thought struck me. "You're not going to turn him in, are you?"

Seth slowly shook his head. "How would that benefit me? You'd be in servitude and on the Elixir."

And I wouldn't Awaken, which it always seemed to come down to, and I was a big enough person to admit that stung. I wondered what bothered Seth more—my life being virtually over or my Awakening not happening. I looked away, biting my lip. "Seth, I found some stuff out while you were gone."

"So did I," he responded evenly.

That was cryptic. "You had to know about the Order and how an Apollyon is made."

His expression didn't change. "Why is that?"

Frustration flared. "You once said that when you Awakened, you knew everything from the previous Apollyons. One of them would've known about the Order, and about how they were born. Why didn't you tell me?"

Seth sighed. "Alex, I didn't tell you because I didn't see a point."

"How could you not see a point after everything that

happened to me in New York? If you'd told me about the Order, I could've been better prepared."

He looked away, lips pursing.

"And I asked you while we were there if you knew what that symbol meant," I said. Anger and so much disappointment swamped me. I didn't even try to shield my emotions from him. "You said you didn't know. When I asked if you knew about a half and a pure mixing, you said you guessed your father had to be a half. You knew the truth. What I don't get is why you didn't tell me."

"I was told not to."

"What?" Seth started walking, and I hurried to catch up with him. "Who told you not to tell me?"

He stared up the beach. "Does it matter?"

"Yes!" I practically shrieked. "It does matter. How can we have anything if I don't trust you?"

His brows shot up. "What *do* we have exactly, Alex? I do remember telling you that you had a choice. I didn't ask for labels or expectations."

I remembered that, too. The night in the pool seemed forever ago. Part of me missed that playful Seth.

"And you made your choice," Seth continued softly. "You made your choice even when you said you chose me."

I also remembered that fleeting, satisfied look when I had said that I'd chosen him. Shaking my head, I searched for something to say. "Seth, I—"

"I don't want to talk about this." He stopped where the sand faded into pavement, reached down and brushed his knuckles across my cheek. I jerked back, startled by the contact and the electric shock that followed. Seth lowered his hand, staring at the backs of the small shops lining the main road. "Anything else you want to talk about?"

He hadn't answered a damn question, but I did have one more. "Did you see my father, Seth?"

"No." He met my eyes.

"Did you even look for him?"

"Yes. Alex, I couldn't find him. That doesn't mean he wasn't there." He pushed back the shorter strands that had been blown free. "Anyway, I brought you back a gift."

I wasn't sure I'd heard him right, but then he repeated it, and my heart sank. "Seth, you shouldn't have brought me anything."

"You'll change your mind once you see it." A wicked grin pulled at his lips. "Trust me, this is a once-in-a-lifetime type of gift."

Great. This was making me feel better. If he handed me the Hope Diamond, I was going to throw up. He and I had never been in a relationship, but guilt still twisted at my insides. When I looked at him, I saw Aiden. And when Seth touched me, I felt Aiden. The worst thing of it all was that Seth knew.

"Alex, just come on."

"Okay." I drew in a deep breath and then pressed my lips together. The wind that kicked up from the ocean was shockingly cold, and I huddled down in my hoodie. "Why in the world is it so cold? It never used to be this cold here."

"The gods are pissed," Seth said, and then laughed. I frowned at him.

Seth shrugged. "They are putting all their focus into this little piece of the world. It's because of us, you know. The gods know change is coming."

"Sometimes you really kind of freak me out."

He laughed.

I made a face. We walked in silence after that. I kept expecting him to turn toward the Covenant-controlled island

and when we didn't, then I thought we'd head toward Lucian's house, but he led me straight through town and toward the courthouse, which was used by the Council members.

"My gift is in the courthouse?"

"Yes."

Honestly, I never knew what to expect from Seth. Even with the bond, I didn't have a clue what went on in his head half of the time.

The normal number of Council Guards stood just inside the courthouse, hidden from mortal tourists; beyond them, three of Lucian's Guards blocked a door. They stepped aside, opening the door for us.

I halted, knowing where the door and the stairs led to. "Why are we going down to the cells, Seth?"

"Because I'm going to lock you up and get all freaky."

I rolled my eyes.

Taking my elbow, he tugged me forward. Down we went. My eyes adjusted to the darkness of the stairwell. Old boards creaked under our feet. The cells weren't underground. They were actually on the first floor. The main entrance opened up to the second floor, but it still felt like we were walking down into some dank, dark place.

Dim light lit the hallway. Over Seth's shoulder, I could make out several cells lining the narrow corridor. I shuddered, picturing myself stuck in one of them. Gods, how many times had I come close to that?

Ahead of us, two Guards stood in front of the very last cell.

Seth walked up to them and snapped his fingers. "Leave us."

I gaped as the two Guards left. "Do you have special Apollyon finger-snapping powers?"

He tipped his head toward me. "I have a lot of special Apollyon finger powers."

I shoved him. "Where's my gift, perv?"

Seth backed up, grinning. He stopped in front of the barred door and spread his arms. "Come look."

Okay. I was curious. Stepping forward, I stopped in front of the door and peered through the bars. My mouth dropped open as my stomach hollowed.

Huddled in the middle of the cell, with his hands tied to his ankles, Head Minister Telly stared back at us with blank eyes. His face was battered, barely recognizable, and his torn, dirtied clothing hung off him.

"Oh, my gods, Seth."

CHAPTER TWENTY-FIVE

Stunned, I jerked back from the cell door. Everything Apollo had warned me about rushed to me at once. Everyone had been afraid of something like this happening—everyone but me, and still I had a hard time believing that this was actually happening.

"What have you done?" I asked.

"What? I brought you a gift—Telly."

I turned to him, shocked that I had to explain all the things wrong with this. "Most guys bring girls roses or puppies. Not people, Seth. Not the Head Minister of the Council."

"I know what he did, Alex." He placed his hand over the scar Linard had left behind. "I know he ordered this."

Through the heavy material, I could feel Seth's hand. "Seth, I…"

"I felt something when it happened…like our bond had completely disappeared," he said quietly and quickly. "I couldn't feel your emotions, but I knew you were there…and then you weren't for a few minutes. I knew. Then Lucian told me. My first reaction was to bring just his head back to you, but I did the next best thing."

I felt physically ill as I stared at Seth. And when I looked at Telly in the cell, I saw Jackson's battered face. I should've known. Good gods, I should've known he'd know…and he'd do something like this.

"It didn't take much for me to find him," he continued casually. "And I know people were looking for him. Leon"—Seth laughed—"or should I call him Apollo? Yeah, I beat him to the punch on this one. Those two days you didn't call me? That's all it took for me to find him."

The air flew right out of my lungs. Ice drenched my veins.

He frowned. "He ordered your death, Alex. I figured you'd be happy to know that we have him and he's not going to be a problem anymore."

I turned back to the cell. "Gods, how have the furies not reacted to this?"

"I'm not stupid, Alex." He moved to stand beside me, shoulder to shoulder. "Lucian ordered this and had his Guards carry it out. I was only…along for the ride. Clever, aren't I?"

"Clever?" I gasped, stepping away from the cell—from Seth. "So, this was Lucian's idea?"

"Does it matter?" He folded his arms. "Telly tried to have you killed—he *did* have you killed. For that, he has to be punished."

"That doesn't make this okay! Look at him!" I pointed at the cell, feeling sick. "What *is* wrong with him?"

"He's under a rather strong compulsion not to talk." Seth tapped his chin thoughtfully. "I'm not sure he's even thinking. Actually, I think he's sort of fried."

"Gods, Seth. Hasn't anyone ever told you two wrongs don't make a right?"

Seth snorted. "Two wrongs always make a right in my book."

"This isn't funny, Seth!" I tried to calm down. "Who's going to kill him? The pure-blood Council?"

"No. The new Council will."

"The new Council? What the hell is that?"

Frustration flared in his amber eyes. "You just need to understand why this is happening. This man serves the gods who want you—us—dead. He has to be taken out."

I ran my hands over my head, wanting to pull my hair out. "Seth, was this Lucian's idea or not?"

"Why does that matter? What if it was? He only wants to keep us safe. He wants change and—"

"And he wants Telly's throne, Seth! How can you not see that?" Coldness seized my insides as I stared at Seth. Lucian wanted power and taking Telly out was one way to achieve that, but that didn't mean he could take complete control of the Council…or did it? I shook my head. "There's no way the gods would allow this. They don't want what Telly did."

"The gods are the enemy here, Alex! They don't speak to the Council, but they do speak to the Order."

"Apollo saved my life, Seth! Not Lucian!"

"Only because they have plans for you," he said, stepping forward. "You don't know what I know."

My hands curled into fists. "Then tell me what you know!"

"You wouldn't understand." He turned toward the still form in the cell. "Not yet. I don't even blame you for it. You have too much pure in you—now more than ever before."

I flinched. "That wasn't…wasn't fair."

His eyes closed and he ran the heel of his palm over his forehead. "You're right. That wasn't fair."

Taking the moment of clarity, I seized it. "You can't keep

him here, Seth. You're right. He has to be punished for what he did, but he needs a trial. Keeping him like this, under a compulsion in a cell, is wrong."

Gods, it was a messed-up day when *I* was the voice of reason.

Seth turned to me. He opened his mouth but closed it. "I already have too much invested in this."

Dread inched down my spine. I started toward him but stopped. I folded my arms over my chest. "What do you mean?"

He reached out toward me, but I jerked away. Confused, he lowered his hand. "How can you want him to live?"

"Because it's not our place to decide who lives or dies."

His brows furrowed. "And what if it will be?"

I shook my head. "Then I don't want any part of that. And I know you don't, either."

Seth sighed. "Alex, you're training to be a Sentinel. You'll make life-and-death decisions all the time."

"That's different."

"Is it?" He inclined his head toward me, a smug smile washing away any hesitation.

"Yes! As a Sentinel, I'll kill daimons. That's not the same as playing jury and executioner."

"How can you not see I'm doing what needs to be done, even if you're too weak to do it yourself?"

Who in the hell was this person beside me? It was like reasoning with a lunatic.... Now I knew how people felt when they tried to reason with me. Irony was a cruel, cruel foe. "Seth, where are the keys to the cell?"

His eyes narrowed. "I'm not letting him out."

"Seth." I took a tentative step toward him. "You can't do this. Neither can Lucian."

"I can do as I damn well please!"

I shoved past him, reaching for the handle on the door, and then I was against the opposite wall with Seth in my face. Fear blossomed low in my stomach as the cord hummed madly. "Seth," I whispered.

"He's staying in there." His eyes flashed a dangerous ocher. "There are plans for him, Alex."

I swallowed down the sudden taste of bile. "What plans?"

His gaze dropped to my lips, and a whole new fear took root. "You'll see soon enough. You don't have to worry, Alex. I'm going to take care of everything."

Planting my hands on his chest, I shoved him back several feet. Shock and then anger flashed across his features. "You're freaking insane, Seth. Don't go down this road."

Whirling around, he stormed back to the cell and pointed at Telly. "So, you'd rather see this thing free? Free to enslave half-bloods, to order them killed? Free to continue his assassination attempts on you? And then we are to wait for a trial—a trial rigged to protect the pure-bloods? They'd just slap him on the hand. Hell, they might even order you to apologize for screwing up his plans to kill you!"

Anger flooded me. I stepped forward, toe-to-toe with Seth. "You don't care about what happens to the half-bloods! It has nothing to do with what you're planning! And you know that. What you're doing—what you're agreeing to is wrong. And I'm not—"

"Go," he cut me off, his voice furious and low.

I stood my ground. "I'm not going to let you do this, Seth. I don't know what Lucian's said that's convinced—"

"I said *go*." Seth shoved me—shoved me *hard*. I barely caught myself. "Maybe next time I'll bring you roses or puppies."

That raised my hackles, and so did the smile he gave me. It took every ounce of my self-control to turn and walk away. I hurried up the stairs. Like a thousand times in my life, I didn't plan on listening to what I'd been told to do. But for the first time, it was probably the right thing to do. Aiden and Marcus needed to know what Seth and Lucian were up to. Maybe they could stop this, before it became too late—before Seth took part in killing the Head Minister and sealed both our fates.

There still had to be hope for Seth. Sure, what he was taking part in was crazy, but not *epically* crazy. Technically, Seth hadn't done anything *yet*. Like Caleb had said, there was still hope. Whatever hold Lucian had on Seth, however he was pulling his strings, had to be broken before history repeated itself.

I pushed open the doors of the courthouse and came face to face with the root of all my problems.

Lucian was flanked by several Council Guards, all dressed in those ridiculous white robes. The smile that spread across his face never quite reached his eyes. "I thought I'd find you here, Alexandria."

Before I knew what was happening, his Guards surrounded me. Oddly, the Guards were all pure-bloods. Smart move, I'd give him that. "What's going on, Lucian?"

"When will you call me 'Father'?" He came up the final step, stopping in front of me. Wind blew his robes, giving an appearance that he was floating.

"Um, how about next to never?"

His pleasant smile remained. "One day that will change. We will be one big happy family, the three of us."

Now that was disturbing. "You mean Seth? He's as much a part of you as I am."

Lucian tsked softly. "You will return to my house, Alexandria. There is no need to stay at the St. Delphi residence any longer."

My mouth opened to argue that, but I clamped it shut. There was no way of knowing if Lucian was aware of my feelings for Aiden, or if Seth had told him anything. Putting up a fight would only arouse his suspicions. There was nothing I could do to stop this. Lucian was my legal guardian. Swallowing down my anger and distaste, I stepped forward. "I just need to get my stuff."

Lucian stepped aside, motioning for me to follow. "That will not be necessary. Your belongings will be retrieved by Seth."

Damn him. I stiffened as Seth came out the door. He didn't spare me a glance as he brushed past me.

Lucian clapped Seth on his shoulder. "Meet us back at our house."

Seth nodded and went down the steps. On the sidewalk, he looked up and gave me a sardonic grin before heading off toward one of the Hummers parked along the curb.

"Now, my dear, you will come with me," Lucian said.

Fuming, but unable to do a damn thing about it, I followed Lucian into the other Hummer. Gods forbid that Lucian actually walk to his house. Once he climbed in the back seat with me, I was crawling out of my skin to get out of the car.

Lucian smiled. "Why is it that you're so uncomfortable around me?"

I turned away from the window. "There is just something about you."

He arched a brow. "And that would be?"

"Well, you're like a snake, but slimy."

He leaned back against the seat as the Hummer moved. "Cute."

I smiled tightly. "Let's cut the bull, Lucian. I know about Telly. Why would you do something that even I think is reckless and stupid?"

"The time for change is upon us. Our world needs better leadership."

My laugh escaped before I could stop it. "Are you high?"

"For too long we've been expected to live by the old laws, existing beside mortals as if we are no better than them." Disgust dripped from his words. "They should take the place of half-bloods, serving our every need or whim. And when they do, we— the new gods—will rule this earth."

"My gods, you are insane." There was nothing else I could say. And worst of all, Grandma Piperi had been right, but like always, I hadn't understood. History was on repeat, but in the worst possible way. And evil had hidden in the shadows, acting like a puppet master pulling strings. Grandma Piperi had been referencing Seth and Lucian. I felt sick. If I'd only figured this out earlier, I could've prevented it from going this far.

"I don't expect you to understand, but Seth does. That's all I need."

"How did you get Seth to go along with this?"

He studied his fingernails. "The boy never had a father. His pure-blood mother wanted very little to do with him. I suppose she regretted her relations with the half but had been unable to get rid of him while he was still in her womb."

I flinched.

"It's safe to assume that she wasn't a very kind mother," Lucian continued. "But that boy still managed to impress the Council and gain entrance into the Covenant. He had a tough childhood, always alone. I suppose all Seth has ever wanted is to be loved." He looked at me. "Could you do that? Give him the one thing he's always wanted?"

Suddenly, I knew beyond a doubt Seth hadn't told Lucian about Aiden. But why? Removing Aiden from the equation would only benefit Seth. Could it be that Seth hadn't because he knew it would hurt me? If that was the case, then Seth was still *thinking*. He wasn't a lost cause, after all.

"I do hope so. Seth is a good boy."

My eyes widened. "You sound...sincere."

Lucian sighed. "I've never had a child of my own, Alexandria."

Shock rippled through me. Lucian actually cared for Seth. And Seth saw him as a father. But it didn't change what Lucian was doing. "You're using him."

The Hummer rolled to a stop behind Lucian's house. "I'm offering him the world. The same thing I'm offering you."

"What you are offering is certain death for anyone who goes along with this."

"Not necessarily, my dear. We have supporters in the most...unlikely of places—a very powerful supporter."

My door opened before I could respond. A Guard waited for me to exit, carefully watching me as if he expected me to sprint away, which was what I'd considered but knew I'd never get away with it. I was led into the house quickly and then left in the opulent foyer with my stepfather.

"It's a shame that you have to make this so difficult, Alexandria."

"Sorry to rain on your crazy parade, but I'm not going to go along with this. No one else will, either."

"Is that so? Do you doubt my impassioned words?" His gaze settled on his half-blood guards. "I want to see a better life for the half-bloods."

"Bull," I whispered, and my gaze moved to the Guards. The condemnation that filled their expressions when they looked at me said that they did believe Lucian. And the real question was how many halfs were behind Lucian? The numbers could be astronomical.

Lucian laughed. It was a cold, grating sound. "You really have no control over this."

"We'll see about that." I reached for the doorknob but froze when it turned and locked in my hand. I loathed the air element with all my heart. Slowly, I faced him. "You can't keep me in here. Let me out."

Lucian laughed again. "I'm afraid you will not be allowed any visitors until your Awakening. And do not hope that Apollo will arrive, either. He will not be able to enter my house."

I frowned. "You can't stop a god."

Lucian looked pleased as he stepped aside. My gaze fell behind him and up the wall that Seth had once pinned a Guard to. There was a mark there—a crudely drawn symbol of a man with a snake's body.

"Apollo cannot enter any home that bears the mark of the Python of Delphi. It was created long ago as a punishment for breaching the rules of Olympus. Funny, I never knew that until recently."

I swallowed. The drawing looked like it had been done in blood. "How…how did you figure that out?"

"I have many friends…of great power and consequence." Lucian gazed at the drawing, a slight smile on his angular face. "I have many friends that would surprise you, my dear."

I felt the walls closing in, squeezing the breath out of my lungs. I was trapped here until my Awakening. My breath hitched. I should've listened to Aiden and never left his house. "You can't do this."

"Why can't I?" He drifted toward me. "I am your legal guardian. I can do with you as I please."

My temper stretched and snapped. "Really? When has that worked out for you in the past?"

"In the past I did not have Seth, nor were we so close to the Awakening." He caught my chin, digging his bony fingers in. "You can fight me on this all you want, but in a few days, you'll Awaken. First, you will connect with Seth, and what he desires, you will desire. And then your power will transfer to him. You can't stop that."

I blanched. "I'm stronger than that."

"You think so? Think about that, my dear. Think about what that means and whether or not there is even a point in fighting what's about to happen."

Unease crept over me, but I kept my expression blank. "If you don't release me, I will break your arm."

"You would, wouldn't you?" His breath was warm against my cheek. Bile rose in my throat. "There was only one thing that Telly and I ever agreed on."

"What was that?"

"You need to be broken down." He released me, the same damn smile plastered across his face. "Except he went about it all the wrong way. I will not make the same mistake that I made with your mother. I allowed her too much freedom. As of now, you're mine. Just like Seth is. And you would do very well to remember that."

I recoiled from him. "You're a bastard."

"That may be the truth, but in a few days, I'll control both of the Apollyons. Then we'll be unstoppable."

CHAPTER TWENTY-SIX

Dinner was awkward for several reasons. There were only three of us clustered at the end of the long rectangular table, eating by candlelight as if we'd been thrust into medieval times. Seth alternated between chumming it up with make-believe-daddy Lucian and glaring at me. I refused any attempt Lucian made at luring me into conversation. And I couldn't even bring myself to eat the mouthwatering steak, which really sucked.

This was going to be my last dinner.

I knew it. What I was planning as I watched the two would surely end up with me being killed, but it was either go out this way or be part of something as heinous as destroying those who did not agree with Lucian and enslaving mankind. Because that's what they planned—or at least, Lucian planned. Lucian needed the Apollyons—at least, the God Killer—to achieve this. It made sense. The Apollyons had been originally created to keep the pures in line, but if he controlled the Apollyons then he had nothing to fear. Once I Awakened, Seth could take down any god that went after

Lucian, making Lucian practically invincible. It was a brilliant plan. One that I knew Lucian probably had worked on from the moment he became aware that there were two Apollyons in one generation.

They'd give Council members an option. Stand with them or fall. With Seth at full Apollyon power—the God Killer—he'd be able to zap any god who came gunning for him. Not that Lucian believed any gods would. Once Seth became the God Killer, no god would be stupid enough to come within a mile of him. The only threat would be members of the Order, but they too would have one hell of a time taking Seth down. Lucian already had Sentinels searching for the remaining members. I shuddered at what I knew they would do to them.

And yet, as much as they talked, I felt there was something they weren't sharing. There was more to this, just as I felt there was more to why Apollo had been so adamant about keeping me safe.

"How did the Order kill the First and Solaris?" I asked, speaking for the first time.

Lucian raised his brows at Seth as he twirled the crystal flute.

"They caught them unexpectedly." Seth glanced down at his plate. "At the same moment, they were stabbed through the heart." He cleared his throat. "Why do you ask?"

I shrugged. Mostly because I was curious, since it wasn't like killing two Apollyons was an easy feat. When I didn't give an answer, they resumed their talking. I resumed my plotting.

I was going to do something I never thought I'd do again. I was going to kill a pure-blood—Lucian. My fingers curled around the steak knife. It was the only way to stop this. Take out Lucian and then Seth would be freed from his freakish parental influence. And I'd be dead, but maybe…maybe Aiden and Marcus could prove Lucian's insanity. It was worth a shot. I couldn't let this happen, and it would happen if they kept me here, and then there would be no stopping them.

This was possibly the craziest, most spontaneous and reckless thing I'd ever planned, but what other choice did I have? Lucian already controlled Seth and he could control me through him if Seth willed it. That was everyone's fear—my worst fear.

I had to do something.

"May I be excused?" I asked.

"You haven't eaten anything." Seth frowned. "Are you feeling sick?"

Gee, could it be I'd lost my appetite because I was surrounded by lunatics? "I'm just tired."

"That's fine," Lucian said.

Trying not to think about what I was doing, I placed my napkin over the steak knife and slid it, handle first, up my sleeve. I stood on weak knees. Killing in battle or when I needed to protect myself was totally different than this. Part of me screamed that this was wrong—just as wrong as what they intended to do to Telly, but one life to protect countless more? It seemed worth it.

Okay. Two lives, because I seriously doubted I was going to get away with this. Guards waited just outside the dining room. If they didn't kill me, the Council Lucian sought to betray would. Ironic.

I walked around the table slowly, calming my breathing and blocking my emotions. I had enough strength to shove this knife through his back, severing his spinal cord. It would be easier to go for the throat or eye, but gods, I was grossing myself out just thinking about it.

Just do it. I reached Lucian's side and drew in a deep breath as I let the knife slide out from my sleeve. Then a freight train slammed me to the ground.

I hit the tiled floor with a hard crack. Seth pinned my legs as he twisted my wrist until I cried out and was forced to drop the knife. As I tried to twist out of his grasp, Guards rushed into the room, but Lucian held his hand out, stopping them.

"What is wrong with you?" Seth asked furiously, giving me a little shake when I didn't answer fast enough.

My heart pounded against my ribs. "I'm not the enemy here!"

"Really—you're not the enemy?" His gaze went to the knife. "Do I need to explain this to you?"

"Deal with her." Lucian stood and threw down his cloth napkin, voice eerily calm. "Before I do something I regret."

Seth exhaled harshly. "I'm sorry, Lucian. I'll fix this."

So shocked, I couldn't speak. He was apologizing to Lucian? I was in a different world and there was no escape.

"She needs to accept this," Lucian said. "I will not live in fear of being murdered in my own home. Either she complies or I'll have her locked up."

Seth's eyes met mine. "That won't be necessary."

I glared at him.

"Good." Lucian sounded more disgusted than afraid. It was like I had spit on him instead of trying to kill him. "I'm retiring for the evening. Guards!"

In a rush of activity, they followed Lucian out of the room. Some of them were pures. Had he promised them something worth going against the Council and risking death? I knew what he'd offered the halfs.

Seth still held me to the floor. "That was possibly the stupidest thing you've ever tried to do."

"Too bad it didn't work."

Appearing incredulous, he hauled me to my feet. The moment he let go, I bolted for the door. He caught me before I made it out of the room, clamping his arms around me. "Stop this!"

I threw my head back, narrowly missing his. "Let me go!"

"Don't make this hard, Alex."

I struggled in his viselike grip. "He's using you, Seth. Why can't you see that?"

His chest rose against my back. "Is it so hard for you to accept that Lucian cares for me—for you?"

"He doesn't care about us! He just wants to use us." I kicked my legs out to use the wall, but Seth anticipated this and spun me around. "Damn you! You're smarter than this!"

Seth sighed and started dragging me toward the hall. "You're such a little fool sometimes. You will want for nothing, Alex. Nothing! Together we will be able to change our world. Isn't that what you want?" We had reached the bottom of the steps, and I kicked for the statue of some god I didn't recognize. "Gods! Knock it off, Alex. For someone who's so short, you're freaking heavy. I don't want to have to carry you up these stairs."

"Gee. Thanks. Now you're calling me heavy."

"What?" His arms slackened.

I slammed my elbow into his stomach hard enough that the impact rattled my entire body. Seth doubled over but didn't let go. Cursing wildly, he flipped me around and bent at the waist. He clamped his arm down on my waist and hauled me over his shoulder. Before I could kick him where it counts, he caught my legs and held them down.

"Put me down!" I pounded on his back with my fists.

Seth grunted as he started up the stairs. "Seriously, I can't believe I have to do this."

I continued my assault on his back to no avail. "Seth!"

"Maybe you deserve a spanking, Alex." Laughing, he rounded the landing as I jabbed him in the kidneys. "Ouch! That hurt!"

We were making enough noise to rouse every Guard in the house, but no one intervened. I recognized the upside-down hallway and the door Seth pushed open. It was my old bedroom in Lucian's house.

Seth stormed across plush white carpet that so had not been in my bedroom when I'd stayed in this house. Back then, I'd had bare floors that had been cold in the winter. He dumped me unceremoniously on the bed and then planted his hands on his hips. "Behave."

I sprang to my feet. Seth caught me around the waist and pushed me back down with little effort on his part. An incredible amount of rage filled me with energy, sweeping through me like a rush of roiling waves. And I let the fury swell and spread like the rising tide.

"You're being ridiculous, Alex. And you need to calm down. You're making me wish I had some Valium."

My hands balled into fists. "He is using you, Seth. He wants to control us so he can overthrow the Council. He wants to be greater than the gods. You know they'll never allow that! That's why the Apollyons were created in the first place."

Seth arched a brow. "Yeah, Alex, I know why the Apollyons were first created. To make sure no pure-blood achieved the power of the gods and blah blah. Let me ask you a question. Do you think any of the gods care if you die fighting a daimon?"

"Obviously they care, because they brought me back."

He rolled his eyes. "What if you weren't the Apollyon, Alex? What if you were just a normal half? Would they care at all if you died?"

"No, but—"

"Do you think that's right? That you're forced to be either a slave or a warrior?"

"No! It's not right, but the gods didn't decree that. The pures did, Seth."

"I know, but don't you think the gods could've changed that if they wanted to?" He moved closer, lowering his voice. "Change needs to happen, Alex."

"And you think Lucian is really going to bring that kind of change?" I willed Seth to understand. "That once he takes complete control of the Council, he'll free the servants? Relieve the halfs from their duty?"

"Yes!" Seth dropped to his knees in front of me. "Lucian will."

"Then who will fight the daimons?"

"There will be those who volunteer, just like the pures who do now. Lucian will do this. All we have to do is support him."

I shook my head. "Lucian has never cared about the halfs. All he has ever cared about is himself. He wants ultimate power—to enslave the mortals instead of the halfs. He said so himself."

With a disgusted humph, he stood. "Lucian has no intentions of doing such a thing."

"He told me in the car!" I grasped his hands, ignoring the way the cord jumped. "Please, Seth. You have to believe me. Lucian will do none of the things he's promised you."

He stared at me a moment. "Why would you even care

if enslaving mortals was his ultimate plan? I don't get it. You couldn't stand living among them when you did. Why would you want to protect the gods when the Order killed you—*killed you*—to protect them? And you have a problem with a few pures dying along the way? Look at how they've treated you. I don't get it."

Sometimes I didn't get it myself. The pures treated us halfs like crap. And the gods, well, they were as much to blame as the pures. They'd allowed this to happen. But this was more wrong. "Innocent people will die, Seth. And what do you think the gods will do? They may not be able to touch you and me, but they can be vengeful and downright sadistic. They'll start slaughtering halfs and pures by the busload. Apollo has said so."

He squeezed my hands. "Casualties of war—it happens."

I pulled my hands free. My stomach turned over. "How can you be so uncaring?"

"It's not that I'm uncaring, Alex. It's called strength."

"No," I whispered. "That has nothing to do with strength."

Seth moved away from me, running his hand through his hair, pulling strands free from the leather tie. Had he always been like this? There had always been a degree of coldness to him, but nothing like this.

"It will be okay," he said finally. "I promise. I'll take care of you."

"It's not going to be okay. You have to let me go. We have to be apart from each other."

"I can't, Alex. Maybe in time you'll forget about him and…"

"This isn't about Aiden!"

Facing me, his lips twisted into a bitter, cynical smile. "It's always about Aiden. You don't care about the mortals.

If you could still have him and let us have our way, you wouldn't care."

"I do care. You're going to have to kill innocent people to do this, Seth. Can you seriously live with that? Because I can't."

"What pure is truly innocent?" he asked instead of answering my question.

"There are pures who don't want to see halfs enslaved. And yeah, the gods are a bunch of dickheads, but that's what they are."

"We've already been over this, Alex. We aren't going to agree. Not yet, at least. But your birthday is only days away. You'll understand then."

I gaped. "Seth, please listen to me!"

A cool mask slipped over his face, locking him down. "You don't really get it, Alex. I can't—won't let you go."

"Yes, you can! It's quite simple. You just let me walk out of this house."

Seth was in front of me within a second. He gripped my hands, pressing his palms against mine. "You don't know what it feels like now, but you will. The more marks you take, the more akasha drains into me. Nothing—nothing feels like that. It's pure power, Alex. And you haven't even Awakened! Can you imagine what it will be like then?" His eyes took on that crazed, overly passionate gleam I'd seen and disregarded before. "I can't give that up."

"Gods, do you hear yourself? You sound like a daimon craving aether."

He smiled. "It's nothing like that. It's better."

That was when I realized that between Lucian's influence and the allure of akasha Seth had been twisted into something dangerous. Apollo had been right. Dammit. Grandma Piperi had been right.

And I had been so, so wrong. I was in a precarious, bad position. Anything was possible, and my heart rate doubled. I wanted to smack myself for not letting Apollo stash me away, but when he'd made that suggestion, all I could think was that was what Lucian had wanted to do. I was disgusted with myself for the time I'd wanted to throw the towel in. Running was not something I ever did.

But now I needed to run because that was the only smart thing to do.

"I want you to leave my room." I forced my knees to stop shaking and I stood. "Now."

"I don't want to leave," he replied evenly.

My heart leaped into my throat. "Seth, I don't want you in here."

He cocked his head to the side, eyes heating up a notch. "Not too long ago you had no problem with me being in your bedroom…or your bed."

"You have no right to be in here. You're not my boyfriend."

Seth's brows flew up. "You speak as if what we are can be simplified with little labels. We aren't boyfriend and girlfriend. You're right about that."

I pushed away from the bed, eyes desperately searching for a way out of the room. There was only a bathroom, closet, and one window. And my old dollhouse…what the hell was that still doing here? Perched atop the house was a creepy porcelain doll I hated as a child and still did.

Sneaking up behind me, he whispered in my ear. "We *are* the same person. We want and need the same things. You can love whoever you want, and you can tell yourself whatever you want. We don't have to love one another; we don't even have to *like* each other. It doesn't matter, Alex. We're stuck with one another, and the connection between us is far stronger than whatever you feel in your heart."

Whirling around, I put space between us. "No. This is it. I'm calling on that promise you made me. I don't want to do this. You need to leave. I don't care where you go. Just go—"

"I'm not leaving."

Dread turned into something far worse and far more powerful. Fear snaked its way into me, biting deep and spreading through my veins like venom. "You promised me, Seth. You swore that you would leave if this became too much. You can't take that back!"

His eyes met mine. "It's too late for that. I'm sorry, but that promise is null and void. Things have changed."

"Then I'll leave." I took in a deep breath, but it did nothing to calm the pounding in my chest. "You can't keep me here! I don't care that Lucian is my legal guardian."

He tipped his head to the side, his stare becoming almost curious. "Do you think there is any place in this world that I couldn't find you if I wanted to?"

"Gods, Seth, do you even know how stalkerish that sounds—how creepy?"

"I'm just pointing out the truth," he replied blithely. "When you turn eighteen—in five days—you won't have any control over that."

My hands balled into fists. Gods, I hated when he was right. Especially when he was scary right, and Seth was pretty damn scary right now. I couldn't—I refused to show fear. So, I relied on anger. "You don't have any control over me, Seth!"

Seth arched one eyebrow. A slow, wicked smile spread across his face. Recognizing that look, I shot back, but he was so incredibly fast. His arm snaked out, catching me around the waist.

Instinct took over. My brain switched off and I flipped into fight mode. Letting my legs go limp, I became dead weight in his arms. Seth cussed and as he dipped to catch me, I sprang up, slamming my knee into his midsection. A *whoosh* of air left his lungs as he stumbled back.

Spinning around, I threw out my arm, catching him across the chest. It wasn't a meek hit. I put everything into it and Seth went down on one knee.

I darted toward the door, ready to fight my way out of the house and down the street if necessary.

I never made it—not really.

My fingers wrapped around the doorknob the same second I felt a rush of power in the room that raised the tiny hairs all over my body. Then suddenly, I was off my feet, flying backward. Hair blew around my face, clouding my vision.

Seth's arms went around my waist, and he tugged me against his chest. "You know, I like you better when you're furious. Do you want to know why?"

I struggled in his embrace, but he held on, and it was like trying to move a semitruck. "No. I really don't care, Seth. Let me go."

He chuckled deeply, and the sound rumbled through me. "Because when you're angry, you're always one step from doing something irrational. And that's how I like you."

Seth let go without any warning and I spun around. I saw it in his eyes then, in the way his lips parted. Panic froze the blood in my veins. "Don't—"

Seth's hand shot out, wrapping around my neck. The marks of the Apollyon spread across his skin with dizzying speed. What existed in me, that part that had been created to complete him, responded in a heady rush. The marks flew down his arm, reaching over his fingers. A second later, amber light crackled in the air, and then a weaker sheen of blue. His hand circled, pressing down, burning the skin on the back of my neck, creating the fourth rune.

There was a second, right before my brain overloaded with sensation, an instant where I regretted ever allowing Seth to get close to me, to forge the bond between us into something that seemed unbreakable. He had planned this all along.

And then I wasn't thinking anymore.

CHAPTER TWENTY-SEVEN

Seth's eyes gleamed as the pressure inside me shifted through the cord, leaving me and flowing into him. Suddenly, light flared from four points: my stomach, both palms, and now the back of my neck. Pain pricked along my skin like an angry wasp and then dulled. My head grew heavy, legs weak as the pleasant tug and pull continued.

His free arm caught me just as my legs buckled. I must've blacked out, for how long, I didn't know. I was flat on my back when the room came back into focus. A thick haze settled over me, dragging me down through the bed.

"There you are," Seth said. The hand he smoothed through my hair trembled slightly.

There was a strange, almost metallic taste in the back of my throat. "What…what happened?"

Seth slipped his hand out from my hair. "You didn't Awaken, but…" He grabbed my hand and pressed down on my palm.

The response was immediate. My back arched. It felt like

something had reached down into my core, grabbed hold and then *yanked*. It wasn't painful but not pleasant, either. "Seth..."

When he let go, the invisible strings were cut. I collapsed, boneless and weak, and Seth...he sat back on his haunches, holding his hand in front of his face. An awed, childlike expression filled his face as the bright blue light covered his hand, burning brighter than ever before.

"Akasha... This is good, Alex. This is more...I can feel you under my skin."

Dazed, I watched the ball of light dull, and the excitement went out of Seth's eyes. Somehow I knew, even as he dipped and pressed his lips to my cheek, that Seth had harnessed the kind of power needed to kill a god, if only for a few moments.

Lightning struck outside the window, but still no more brilliant than the glimpse of our power. I knew I needed to get out of here, but when I tried to sit up, I felt like I was glued to my bed.

He smiled as he settled beside me, moving his hand back to my cheek, turning my head toward him. His thumb trailed over my lower lip. "Did you see that?"

I wanted to look away, but I couldn't, and I felt sick to my soul. Thunder drowned out the beating of my heart.

"It was beautiful, wasn't it? So much power. Lucian will be disappointed that you didn't Awaken after the fourth mark, but something happened."

What did that mean? I didn't understand and my thoughts were too fuzzy. The cord jumped as his hand slipped under my head and drifted back to the rune on my neck. "This is the rune of invincibility," he explained. "When you Awaken, it will be activated. Then the gods cannot touch you."

I met his eyes and forced my heavy tongue to work. "I don't...want you to touch me."

Seth smiled and the marks returned, gliding over his golden complexion. I knew the moment our marks touched. He lowered his head till a breath separated our lips. My senses went crazy. Electricity jolted across my skin and down.

"You're so beautiful like this," he murmured, and pressed his forehead against mine.

What was in me, what lay between us, was ugly. How hadn't I noticed that before? There had been signs from the beginning. The night I'd discovered what I was, and Seth had remained behind, with Lucian. Seth's need for power and how my response to him seemed out of my control, even when we first stood beside each other in the courtyard months ago and again, several times over. I thought of that fleeting look of satisfaction I'd seen as I stood by the pool and chose to see what happened with him—I'd chosen him. All that time he'd been spending with Lucian…

I'd been so blind.

Seth's lips pressed against my wildly beating pulse and I shuddered, revolted, angry, terrified, and helpless.

"Don't," I begged, before the twisted connection between us spun so tightly that I couldn't tell where he began and I ended.

"You don't want this? You can't deny that a part of you does need me."

"That part isn't real." My body was tingling, throbbing, and yearning for him, but my heart and soul were shriveling up, growing cold. Tears filled my eyes. "Please don't make me do this, Seth." My voice broke. "*Please.*"

Seth froze. Confusion clouded his eyes, the hard glint of amber fire shattering with pain. "I'd…I'd never force you, Alex. I wouldn't do that." His voice was curiously fragile, vulnerable, and unsure.

I started crying. I didn't know if it was the relief from the fear or that deep down the Seth I knew was still in there somewhere. For now.

Seth sat up, running a hand through his hair. "Alex, don't…don't cry."

My hands felt like blocks of cement as I lifted them and wiped under my eyes. I knew not to cry in front of daimons, to show weakness, and Seth…he was no different.

He reached down but stopped. Several seconds passed before he spoke. "It'll get easier. I promise."

"Just leave," I said hoarsely.

"I can't." He eased down beside me, keeping a discreet distance between us. "The moment I leave this room you'll do something stupid."

Truth be told, I was too tired to stand, let alone stage a daring escape. I managed to roll onto my side, away from him. Sleep didn't come easily that night. The only comfort I took was that, when I closed my eyes, I pictured Aiden. And even though the image did him no justice, his love did the one thing I'd asked for. Not to protect me, but to give me strength to figure a way out of this mess.

Seth rarely left my side the next two days, having food brought to the room, and it took those two days for me to regain any real strength. The last rune had taken more from me than the others, and I knew, just like Seth had said, that something was different.

He'd only pulled akasha from me once more when he'd brought Lucian in to witness.

Seth had been right. Lucian had been disappointed that I hadn't Awakened, but he'd been pleased by the new power Seth gained, even though it had been temporary.

And gods, Seth had beamed like a kid showing his father his prized science fair project. I thought I'd feel sickened by Seth, but during the long afternoons he spent talking to me while I tried to convince him to let me go, I began to feel sorry for him.

There were two sides to him, and the side I had held close to my heart was losing out to the one that craved power like a daimon thirsted for aether. I wanted to fix him somehow, save him.

I also wanted to strangle him, but that was nothing new. During the evening of the second night, a commotion downstairs roused me from the bed. Recognizing Marcus's deep booming voice, I stood on weak legs and ambled toward the door.

Seth was beside me in an instant, placing a hand on the door. "You can't."

I blinked away the dizziness. "He's my uncle. I want to see him."

"Since when?" Seth grinned, and I sucked in a breath, because it reminded me of the other Seth—one who wouldn't hold me hostage. "You hate him."

"I...I don't hate him." At that moment, I realized I'd been a giant douche to my uncle. Granted, he wasn't the warmest of people, but he wouldn't shut me in a room with a potential sociopath. I swore I'd be different...if I ever got to see him again. "Seth, I want—"

"Why would you refuse to let Marcus see his niece? Is something wrong?"

My breath caught in my throat as I pressed my hands against the door, under Seth's. Aiden's voice was like a burst of sunlight and warmth. I was *this* close to kicking Seth in the junk just to make him move, and he must've anticipated that, because the warning in his eyes told me not to even think it.

"She is resting, but fine. There is no need for concern," I heard Lucian say and then his voice faded out.

Drawing in a shallow breath, I closed my eyes. Aiden was so close, and yet I couldn't get to him. I knew he had to be worried, assuming the worst. If I could just see him, let him know that I was okay…it would ease some of the aching around my heart.

"You really love him?" Seth asked quietly.

"Yes." I opened my eyes. His gaze was downcast. Thick lashes fanned his cheeks. "I do."

He slowly lifted his eyes. "I'm sorry."

I seized the moment. "And I care about you, Seth. I really do. Seeing what you're doing—what you're becoming—is killing me. You're better than this, stronger than Lucian."

"I am stronger than Lucian." He leaned against the door, watching through heavily lidded eyes. "I'll be stronger than a god soon."

And that was that. Seth didn't move away from the door, and eventually I went to the window, hoping I could catch a glimpse of my uncle and Aiden. The terracotta roof over the library blocked the view.

We didn't talk again.

Time was running out and I had to do something.

Seth was antsy the following morning, unable to sit still for longer than a few minutes. His constant pacing and jerky movements were so at odds with his normal otherworldly grace. He had my nerves stretched thin and each time he looked my way, I felt a lump of dread and fear inch up my throat. But he never approached me, and he didn't touch me again. Seth would just turn away and stare out the window silently, waiting.

The morning after Marcus's visit, I had to see the rune on the back of my neck again. With my energy at normal levels, I found a handheld mirror and craned my neck, twisting until I caught a glimpse in the bathroom mirror. It was faint blue, shaped like an S that closed at the end. The invincibility rune. I reached back and touched it. The skin on my fingers tingled from the contact.

I lowered the mirror to the counter and turned around. My eyes looked way too wide, scared almost. There were shadows forming under them, dulling the brown irises. Not that my brown eyes were extraordinary in the first place, but *geez*.

The skittish look in my eyes hadn't gone away, even after I'd showered. Weight settled on my shoulders, squeezed my chest. Seth had been trying to Awaken me this entire time, like I'd feared. He'd lied. I pushed my damp hair back. Luckily, he hadn't succeeded, but there was undeniably something different. I could feel it just below the skin.

There was a knock on the bathroom door. "Alex?" Seth called and knocked again. "What are you doing in there?"

Gathering up my strength, I focused on the neon pink walls and reinforced the mental shields, blocking him out.

His sigh was audible. "You're just blocking me to tick me off, Alex."

I gave my reflection a weak smile and then I opened the door. Brushing past him, I tossed my dirtied clothes in the corner.

"So, you're not going to talk to me?" he asked.

I sat in the chair and picked up a comb.

Seth knelt in front of me. "You know, you can't stay silent forever."

Combing out the tangles, I decided I could try.

"Do you know how long we're going to be together? This is going to get boring and old real quick." When I didn't answer, he grabbed my wrist. "Alex, you're being—"

"Don't touch me." I jerked my arm free, ready to turn the comb into a deadly weapon if need be.

He smiled as he stood. "You're talking."

I threw the comb down and shot to my feet. "You've lied to me over and over again, Seth. You *used* me."

"How did I use you, Alex?"

"You got close to me just so you could try to Awaken me! You used this stupid connection against me." I sucked in a sharp breath. Betrayal sat like stones in my stomach. "Did you plan this all along, Seth? Was this what you were thinking when we were in the Catskills? When you asked me to make a choice?"

He whirled on me, eyes a fierce, angry ocher. "That was not the sole reason, Alex. Not that it matters now. You made your choice. You chose Aiden, as pointless as that was."

I didn't even think. Full of rage and sorrow, I swung at him.

Seth caught my fist before it connected with his face. "We are not training, Alex. We are not playing around. Swing at me again and you will not like the consequences." He released me.

I stumbled back, half-tempted to test out his warning with a kick to the face. A knock on the bedroom door interrupted our stare-down. One of the Guards was on the other side, speaking too low for me to understand.

Seth nodded and then faced me. "We're leaving in five minutes."

My heart stuttered. "Leaving? Going where?"

"You'll see." He paused, his gaze dropping over me. "You have five minutes to put something decent on."

"Excuse me?" I was wearing jeans and a black turtleneck. "What's wrong with what I'm wearing?"

"You will be an Apollyon…my mate, so to speak. You should wear something nicer—classy."

I didn't know which part of what he said made me want to punch him again most. "First off, you don't tell me what to wear. Secondly, I am not your 'mate.' Thirdly, there is nothing wrong with what I'm wearing. And finally, you're despicable."

"You now have four minutes." Seth spun around and left the room, locking the door behind him.

A whole minute passed while I stared at the closed door. Then I sprang into action. I raced to the bedroom window and pushed it open. When I'd been younger, I'd used my bedroom window to climb out on the roof above the library and stargaze. I knew I could make the jump. It was actually shorter than the one I'd made in Miami.

Wasting no time, I wiggled out on the ledge. The muscles in my arms screamed as I slowly lowered myself down. Gods, my upper body strength could use some work. My feet dangled about half a foot from the roof. I felt like a ninja spy in that moment. I started to smile, but the familiar tingle spreading over my skin quickly knocked it right off my face.

I let go.

Hands clamped down on my forearms and hauled me up, back through the window. Kicking and lashing out, I struggled like a wild animal until Seth set me back on my feet.

I spun around. "I still had three minutes."

A reluctant grin appeared on his face. "Yeah, and about a minute after I left your room I realized you'd probably try to escape. Throwing yourself out a window is a better choice than putting on something nice?"

"I wasn't *throwing* myself out the window. I was escaping."

"You were in the process of breaking your neck."

My hands curled. "I would've made the jump, asshat."

Seth rolled his eyes. "Whatever. We don't have time. We're needed now."

"I'm not going anywhere with you."

Frustration rolled off him. "Alex, I'm not asking."

I folded my arms. "I don't care."

Groaning low in his throat, he shot forward and grabbed my arm. "You always, *always* have to make everything so damn difficult." He started dragging me toward the door. "I don't know why I expected anything less from you. Part of me—and this is sick, I know—is somewhat excited about the idea of you fighting me. It's amusing. Better than you sitting there not speaking."

I dug at his fingers, but there was no releasing them. "Let go of me."

"Yeah, not going to happen."

We were already to the end of the hall, at the top of the stairs. Below I could see a small army of Guards waiting. "What the hell?" I dug my feet in and grabbed the railing with my free hand. "What's going on?"

Exasperated, Seth grabbed me around the waist. Using brute strength, he yanked me away from the railing. "Now you're just being cute." He started down the steps, carrying me easily even though my sneakers hit every step.

Unease lined only a few of the faces of Lucian's Guards as Seth dragged me past them. Cold, bright sunlight met us outside, and Seth didn't release me until he shoved me into the back of a waiting Hummer. And then, he climbed in right after me and caught both my wrists in one hand.

"Sorry. There's a good chance you'll try to throw yourself out of a moving car."

I glared at him, our faces inches apart. "I hate you."

Seth lowered his head until his cheek pressed against mine. "You keep saying that, but we both know it's not true. You can't hate me."

"Is that so?" I elbowed him in the stomach. It did very little. The Hummer started moving. "What I'm feeling right now is definitely not warm and fuzzy."

He laughed, stirring the hair around my temple. "You can't hate me. You weren't built that way. And soon, we will be the same person. You were created to be mine by the very gods we're going to take down, starting today."

CHAPTER TWENTY-EIGHT

Seth's words stunned me into silence. Fears, never too far away, resurfaced. I had no control in this…fate. No sense of myself. My heart was racing painfully. I couldn't be built for him. He wasn't my existence.

I was my own existence.

I kept telling myself that as Seth led me from the Hummer and into the back entrance of the courthouse on the main part of Deity Island. I had a sick feeling about this, knowing that Telly was in a cell in this building and that something horrific was about to happen. I could feel it, and there was nothing I could do.

Holding my hand in a tight grip, he led me through the narrow halls to the waiting room just outside the glass-domed session area. Through the open door, I could see the place was packed. Every pure who remained on the island during break seemed to be there, as were many of the half-blood Guards and Sentinels. But even more strange was the presence of the halfs who had remained behind at school. Luke sat toward the back with Lea; both of them appeared just as curious as everyone else—even a bit awkward, like they felt out of place. What were they doing here? Half-bloods were never allowed to attend Council unless they'd been summoned to do so.

"What's going on?" I asked.

Seth kept his hand on mine, as if he knew I would bolt if given the chance. "Lucian has called an emergency Council meeting. See?" He gestured toward the front of the square room. "Everyone is here."

The Council filled the titanium-trimmed dais. Easily recognizing Dawn Samos's coppery head in the sea of white robes, I felt my stomach twist.

My eyes scanned over their curious expressions and then I turned to the audience. In the back was my uncle. He was standing, arms folded across his chest. There was a hard, cold look to his emerald gaze. Beside him was a man I'd never seen before, a tall half-blood built like a Sentinel. Lean and coiled muscles flexed under the black uniform. His brown hair was on the longish side, pulled back in a ponytail. His skin was a mix of ethnicities, deeply tanned. He would've been handsome if it wasn't for the jagged scar slicing from above his right eyebrow down to his jaw.

The doors opened suddenly in the back, and more entered the room. Aiden was among them. My heart thundered in my chest as he stopped beside my uncle. He leaned over, his mouth moving quickly. Marcus stared straight ahead, but the stranger nodded. Then Aiden straightened and turned, looking straight at where I was standing.

Seth pulled back before Aiden could see us. I scowled at Seth, and he smiled back at me. "We're special guests," he said.

"That you are, my boy." Lucian strode through the waiting

room. His gaze settled on me and cooled. “Has Alexandria been amicable?”

“What do you think?” I snapped before Seth could respond. Lucian graced me with one of his plastic smiles.

“You’re not as wise nor strong as you think you are, Alexandria, but soon you will be.”

I shot toward him, but Seth pulled me back and slipped an arm around my waist. That left my arms completely free and, boy, did I try to get hold of Lucian’s hair…face…whatever I could grab.

“You are lucky that no one can see what you just tried to do,” Lucian hissed. He stopped by the open door, his Guards blocking the entrance. “Or I’d be forced to do something about it. Make sure she behaves, Seth. And that she understands the consequences of acting rashly.”

Seth held me, my back against his chest, waiting until Lucian and his Guards reached the dais. “Alex, don’t do anything you’ll regret.”

I struggled against him, getting nowhere. “I’m not the one who’s about to do something they’ll regret.”

His chest rose sharply. “Alex, please. If you try to run while we’re out there or if you do anything crazy, I’ll be forced to stop you.”

My movements ceased. Wariness crept over me, and I felt like I could never be warm again. “You would do that…to me?”

It seemed like forever before he answered. “I wouldn’t want to, but I would.” He paused and another breath shuddered through him. “Please don’t make me.”

A lump formed in my throat. “I’m not making you do anything.”

“But you have,” he whispered in my ear. Mixed shivers

ran down my spine. "Since the first time I met you. You just didn't know, so how can I really blame you?"

Lucian was taking center stage, starting the Council session. All eyes were on him. No one knew of the drama playing out just behind the walls.

"I don't understand." I closed my eyes against the rush of tears. "Seth, please..."

"It's this." Seth shifted slightly, pressing his hand on my stomach, above where I felt the cord, close to the jagged scar. "You don't know what it's been like. To feel your power and mine together, to know that it will only grow stronger. It's the aether, yes, but it's also the akasha. It sings to me like a siren."

My breath hitched and I swallowed hard as the cord responded to him.

Seth rested his chin atop my head. "I can even feel it now—I know how to use it. Together, we'll do this together."

I opened my eyes. "Gods, you sound...insane, Seth."

His fingers curled into my sweater. "One man's insanity is another man's sanity."

"What? That doesn't even make sense."

He laughed softly. "Come on. It's starting."

Just like that, Seth changed. He tugged me to the door, where we remained hidden but could hear what was happening. His grip on my hand loosened, but I knew better than to try to make a run for it. I really believed that he'd stop me—painfully, if necessary.

The members of the Council were talking among themselves, and then they quieted.

Lucian glided to the front of the dais, clasping his hands together in front of him. An elderly, stately Minister spoke first, her voice raspy but strong. "Has there been additional evidence indicating more daimon attacks?"

"Or is it the Elixir?" another asked, his hands clasping the arms of a titanium-trimmed throne. "Are we having problems here?"

There was an immediate hum of questions from the crowd and the Ministers. Some of the faces were panicked. Daimon attacks had come too close to home, and the idea of the Elixir not working probably horrified those who relied on halfs to do everything for them.

I stiffened and the worst—absolutely worst—idea took hold.

"What are you thinking?" Seth's voice was low, soothing, and at complete odds with what he was capable of.

Marcus had suspected that the daimons who attacked the Council had help, and Seth had suggested that Telly had messed with the Elixir to cause a distraction, but as I stared at Lucian, I wondered how much Seth really knew.

Lucian, the perfect pure-blood in his pristine white robes, gazed over the near chaotic crowd with a tight, well-practiced smile on his face. Had Lucian been behind all of this? To create chaos? Because I remembered one of my lessons in Myth and Legends about how all the societies that had been on the brink of upheaval were the easiest to control, shape, and manipulate…and overthrow.

"Alex?"

Sucking in breath, I shook my head.

"I did not call this session to discuss those things," Lucian began. "Today is a day of discoveries, my fellow Councilmen. Our world is on the brink of great change. A change that is needed, but feared by some. Today, those who fear change, those who have worked in the shadows to stop it, will be unmasked and prosecuted."

My breath caught. *Telly.* But I didn't see him anywhere.

"What are you speaking of, Lucian?" asked a Minister. Her voice was clear but strained. "What fear and change is so great that we were called back early, away from our families and our vacations?"

I almost rolled my eyes at the last part.

Lucian remained staring straight ahead. It was then when I realized at least half of the twelve were smiling. They knew—they supported Lucian. This did not bode well.

But the others had no idea.

"We have been taught to fear the possibility of two Apollyons," Lucian said. "Taught to see them as a threat against our very livelihood and the gods, but I am here to tell you that, instead of fear, we should feel joy. Yes! Joy that we will have the God Killer to protect us in just a few days."

"Protect them against what?" I muttered. "Crazy-ass Ministers?"

"Shh." Seth glared at me.

My jaw ached from clenching my teeth so hard.

"But first, we must deal with something that is both unsavory and"—he clapped his hand over his chest— "close to my heart. Guards!"

The door on the other side opened, and in an ironic twist of fate, Guards led Head Minister Telly out to the center of the dais. I couldn't help but remember when Kelia Lothos, the half who'd loved pure-blooded Hector, had been brought before him, half-naked and shackled.

Karma was a bitch.

That didn't make what was happening right, though. I itched to run out there and warn all of them what was about to happen, what I could feel building under my skin.

There was a collective gasp from the audience and half of the Council when Telly was forced to kneel. He lifted his head, but his glazed-over eyes didn't focus on any one thing in particular.

"This man has plotted against the Council's own decision and against my stepdaughter." Lucian's voice hardened as his lips pulled back. "And I have evidence."

"What evidence do you have?" Dawn spoke up, her eyes darting from Lucian to the silent Head Minister.

Seth's breath danced along the back of my neck. I tried to step away, but he pulled me back. My temper, my nerves—everything was stretching too thin.

"During the November Council session, my stepdaughter was unfairly targeted. She'd been asked to attend to give her testimony based on the unfortunate events in Gatlinburg. However, Head Minister Telly proved to have nefarious motives."

No one on the Council looked too concerned. I wasn't sure if I was supposed to feel angry or sad about that.

Lucian turned to Telly. A real smile—a satisfied one—appeared on Lucian's face. "My stepdaughter was a victim of several attacks. Some of you"—he glanced over his shoulder at the Council—" may find this of no concern. But she is not just a half-blood; she will be the next Apollyon."

"What attacks?" asked an elderly male Minister. The cane he clutched in his left hand was just as weathered as his face.

"She was placed under an unlawful compulsion and left in the cold to die. When that failed, he attempted to coax the Council of Twelve to have her placed on the Elixir and enslaved," Lucian announced. "When the Council found no reason for doing so, a pure-blood was compelled to give her the Brew."

"Oh gods," I muttered, feeling my cheeks burn.

"Alexandria was unaware of this," Lucian continued, now

appealing to the females on the Council. "It is believed that she was set up to be found in a…compromising position with a pure-blood."

"Son of a bitch," I whispered. The bastard was pulling the family card.

"Not very nice," Seth murmured.

I ignored him.

Dawn looked pale as she watched Lucian. "That…that is most revolting."

"And that is not all." Lucian turned back to the audience. "When all of these things failed, Head Minister Telly ordered a pure-blood Guard to kill her after the daimon attack. If it wasn't for Aiden St. Delphi, who used a compulsion on two pure-bloods, the Head Minister would've succeeded."

My heart slammed against my ribs as my mouth dropped open. I so got what Lucian had just done. He'd let out the cat out of the bag, making it sound like Aiden was some kind of hero to him while knowing what it meant for Aiden.

A Minister eyed Aiden with open disgust. "That is an act of treason against our kind and must be dealt with immediately. Guards!"

No. No. No.

Several people turned toward where I knew Aiden stood. Guards rushed forward, as if Aiden now was the greatest threat. They surrounded Aiden within seconds, daggers out and ready to be used.

Aiden stood remarkably still. There wasn't a flicker of emotion in his face or eyes as the Guards closed in on him.

There was no way I was letting this happen. I started forward, but Seth stopped me. "Don't, Alex."

"How could you? They'll execute Aiden for this." Raw

panic tasted like metal in my throat. "He's turned the *entire* society against him with those words, Seth."

Seth said nothing.

"Wait." Lucian's voice traveled, stopping everyone. "The pure is not a concern at this moment. The Head Minister's attempts in the Catskills failed numerous times, but he did not cease in his actions. He sought her out, leaving the New York Covenant in a state of disarray to continue to threaten her with servitude."

"What happened to the Guard who supposedly attacked her?" asked the female Minister who'd spoken first.

"He has been dealt with," Lucian responded, pushing on before that could be further examined. "Head Minister Telly went against the Council's wishes and still tried to force her into servitude. She was even attacked here, stabbed by a half-blood Guard ordered to do so by him."

"And the proof?" the elderly Minister asked. "Where is the proof?"

Lucian turned back to Telly. "The proof is in his own words. Isn't it, Head Minister?"

Telly lifted his head. "It is true. I went against the majority vote and ordered the assassination of Alexandria Andros."

There were a few stunned gasps. I knew it wasn't for my benefit, but more so that Telly would admit to it so easily. They didn't know what I did—that Telly's brain was most likely fried from a powerful compulsion.

An argument broke out among the Ministers for several minutes. Some immediately wanted Telly impeached. Those were the ones who'd smiled earlier. Others, those who I doubted knew what Lucian was up to, didn't see how what he'd done to me was a crime. There were very few laws protecting halfs.

"There will be no impeachment." Lucian's voice silenced the arguing. "Head Minister Telly will be dealt with today."

"What?" several of the Ministers demanded at once.

"It has come to my attention that the Head Minister is involved in the Order of Thanatos and several of those members are en route to free him." There was another pause. Lucian knew how to shock and awe. "There is no time for anything else. Alexandria's safety is of the upmost importance."

And now I understood Seth's nervousness—all the Guards this morning. Lucian couldn't have the Order ruining his plans. He'd strike first. And my safety? It wasn't about my safety. Lucian was worried that I'd misbehave before he went out on the dais because Seth didn't have full control of me…*yet*.

"This wasn't supposed to happen now, was it?" I whispered.

Seth said nothing.

My mouth was dry. "You all wanted to wait until after I Awakened, but you're doing this because of the Order."

Because wouldn't that suck for Lucian if the Order arrived before I Awakened and ended up killing one of us? All of his plans for nothing.

Lucian motioned toward where we were hidden. "This is a time of change. That change starts now."

"That's us," Seth said, his hand tightening around mine. "And dear gods, please behave."

I didn't have much time to respond to that. Seth started walking, and I had no choice but to follow him out into the session room.

Silence so thick it choked me descended when we appeared. All eyes were on us as we made our way up the marble steps. We stopped just short of Lucian and Telly.

Everyone started talking at once.

The Council quickly grew uncomfortable, shifting in their seats. A murmur swept through the crowd, escalating as the seconds ticked on. Some were standing, their faces showing shock and terror. "No reason to fear two Apollyons," my happy butt. They knew—some out there in the audience recognized the danger.

My heart was trying to come out of my chest, and even though I tried to stop myself, I looked for Aiden. He had gone still. I wasn't sure he was even breathing. Our gazes locked, and in an instant, there was relief and then rage in his steely eyes as his gaze dropped to where Seth held my hand tightly. Then he moved, taking a step forward. Marcus threw out an arm, stopping him. I wasn't sure Aiden was going to pay him any heed, but he did.

I let go of a breath I didn't realize I'd been holding.

"What is this about?" cried a Minister. I'd stopped trying to keep track of them.

Lucian just smiled. I hated that smile. "It is our time to take back what is rightfully ours—a world where we rule and do not answer to a sect of gods who do not care whether we prosper or die. A world where half-bloods are not enslaved, but stand beside us"—several startled gasps cut him off there, go figure— "but where mortals kneel at our feet like they should. We are gods in our own right."

And that was right about when half of the audience came to their feet. Words like "blasphemy," "treason," and "insanity" were tossed around. Some of the half-bloods watched Lucian curiously; his words held a certain appeal to them. But they'd be fools to believe him.

Lucian's Guards and some I recognized from around the Covenant moved to the back doors, blocking anyone from escaping. I almost laughed. We'd thought the Order had infiltrated deep within the Covenant, but Lucian had really outdone himself. It was *he* who had infiltrated the Covenant and Council.

"This is a time for a new era." Lucian's voice resonated through the large courthouse. "Even the lowest half-bloods who stand with us will flourish. Those who do not will fall."

Several members of the Council stood and stepped back. Five of them—the five who supported Lucian—and at least two dozen Guards…and Sentinels.

I caught a glimpse of Aiden and the stranger moving closer to the dais, but then I lost sight of them. Focusing on what was going on in front of me, I felt anger and alarm take hold.

"Seth," Lucian said quietly. "This man has attempted to end Alexandria's life several times. Is he worthy of life?"

The elderly Minister came to his feet, leaning heavily on the cane. "He has no say in this matter! Apollyon or not, he does not decide life or death. If Head Minister Telly has gone against the Council of Twelve's wishes, then he is to be tried by that very Council!"

He was ignored.

I stared up at Seth. "No," I whispered. "No. Don't answer that question."

And I was ignored.

Seth tipped his chin up as the marks of the Apollyon broke out across his face, swirling and moving down his neck, under the collar of his shirt. "He is not worthy of life."

Pride filled Lucian's eyes. "Then he is yours to deal with."

Panic punched a hole straight through my chest. I pulled away from Seth, throwing my entire weight into breaking his grip. He only held on tighter. I knew what he intended to do.

"No!" I cried out, still trying to pull free and break the

contact. "Telly is a douche, but we don't decide who dies, Seth. That is not what we are—not what the Apollyon is."

"Silly girl," Lucian murmured loud enough for only us to hear. "That is not what an Apollyon decides, but what a God Killer does."

"Don't listen to him," I pleaded, and jerked as his mark burned against mine. "You're not like this. You're better than this. *Please.*"

Seth glanced at me. There was a moment—brief but there. Hesitation and confusion flitted across his face. Seth didn't fully believe he was doing the right thing. Hope seized me.

I clutched his arm. "Seth, you don't want to do this. I know you don't. And I know this isn't you. It's the akasha—I get it. And it's him. He's using you."

"Seth," Lucian urged. "You know what you have to do. Do not fail me—do not fail *us*."

"Please," I begged, holding his gaze while wanting to leap over Telly's defeated, hunched form and snap Lucian's neck. "Don't do this to us—to me, to yourself. Don't become a killer."

Seth's lips quirked up and then he turned away from me, facing Head Minister Telly. "He cannot live. That is my gift to you."

Horror stole my breath. And it struck me then. That was the difference between Aiden and Seth. No matter how badly Aiden would want to strike back or how much he wanted something, he would never risk me. And dammit, Seth would.

He did.

His hand tightened around mine. My body snapped inward as he tore akasha right out from underneath me. I doubled over, catching only a flash of amber light as it enveloped Telly. The last I'd seen Seth use akasha, it had been blue, but that was before the four marks, before he could pull the power of the fifth from me.

Shrieks filled the air—not from Telly, but from the Council and the audience. Telly didn't have a chance to make a sound.

Once akasha hit him, charged from both Seth and me, he simply ceased to exist—obliterated.

Glass shattered from the dome overhead. Shards of glass rained down, slicing through the air and through those not quick enough to move out of the way. Three winged shapes came through the opening, howling in rage.

The furies had arrived.

CHAPTER TWENTY-NINE

The furies were in full-out ugly mode. Their skin was gray and milky. Snakes snapped from their heads. Fingers extended into sharp points. Those claws could rip through tissue and bone with ease.

They were headed straight for us.

Only a second or two had passed from the moment Seth had charged up and taken out Telly. One furie broke free from her sisters, arcing over the audience, emitting shrill screams.

Seth raised his arm. Akasha streaked from his hand, streaming through the air at incredible speed. He hit the first furie in the chest before the amber light sputtered out. Shock flickered over her monstrous face and then her jaw slackened. The furie dropped, spinning like a downed bird as her wings sliced through air. The furie landed in a lifeless pile of white chiffon, gray skin, and unmoving flesh a few feet in front of us.

The remaining two furies hovered by the broken window. Their mortal skins slipped over the monsters inside, and horror pinched their beautiful features.

"It's not possible," one shrieked, pulling at her blond hair until strands hung from her clawed fingers. "It cannot be!"

"But it is." The other grabbed her sister's arm. "He has killed one of us."

Weak in the legs, I straightened and swayed unsteadily. Seth's actions had weakened me, leaving me no match for a groundhog, let alone one of the furies, if they attacked. Realizing Seth had released me, I stumbled to the side of the dais. I was going to die. I was sure of it. My screams would join those of the audience…except the furies didn't attack.

"You've made war against the gods," one hissed. Her wings cut through the air noiselessly. "Make no mistake, they will make war against you."

The other spread her muscled arms wide. "You risk them all to gorge yourself with power that never was yours. What a path…what a path *you* have chosen."

And then they were gone.

Chaos reigned supreme below the dais and on it. Telly was gone. There wasn't even a pile of ashes. Bile rose in my throat as I turned away from the spot where he'd knelt.

Toward the back, I heard sounds of fighting as Guards and Sentinels went after the ones blocking the doors. A Guard near us was overtaken. One of his daggers hit the floor. I lurched for it, wrapping my numb fingers around the hilt. I had to stop this—stop Lucian. He was pulling Seth's strings.

I whirled around, finding Lucian speaking to the Council, spouting more crazy stuff that was going to get us all killed.

Seth was on me before I could even take a step toward Lucian. Our eyes met before he wrenched the dagger from my hand. He tossed it aside as he advanced on me. Coldness had crept upon his features. I didn't recognize the look in his eyes.

They glowed violently, nearly luminous. That awe was there again. But it wasn't awe… I'd mistaken that look.

It was a craving, a greed for more. The same thing I'd seen time and time again in the eyes of a daimon.

Weaponless and weak, I knew when to retreat. My spine hit the wall. Desperately, I searched for something and found a titanium candelabrum. I grabbed it and threw it at him using both arms.

Lighting quick, he caught the candelabrum and tossed that to the side, too. "Always throwing things," he said, voice thick and different. Gone was the musical quality. "Such a naughty, naughty Alex."

I inhaled raggedly. "This…this is not you."

"It is me." He reached for me. "And this is us."

Dawn's voice distracted him. "This is treason!" she said. Terror filled her amethyst eyes. She was trembling, hugging her elbows. Other Ministers stood behind her, faces pale. "This is treason against the gods, Lucian. What you ask from us cannot be given."

"Do you think change is not needed?" Lucian asked.

"Yes!" She unfolded her arms and raised them in front of her, as if she was shielding herself. "Change is needed. Half-bloods need more freedom and choice. There is no doubt about that. I have a half-sister. I love her dearly and want a better life for her, but this…this is not the way."

Lucian cocked his head to the side as he smoothed his hands over his white robes. "And what about the gods, my dear?"

Her breath came out ragged as her spine straightened. "They are our only masters."

All my nightmares were coming true, as were the Order's. History *was* on repeat. Seth stepped to the side, facing the Council members who would not bow to Lucian's will.

Lucian smiled.

"No!" My voice came out ragged as I slid along the wall, away from Seth. "Seth, don't!"

But Seth was on autopilot. He grabbed my hand again. Mark pressed against mark. Pressure filled me and then the cord snapped again, pushing akasha through the bond. There was no reaching him when the power took over, no compassion.

Seth was just Lucian's killing machine.

The brilliant amber light erupted from his hand a second time.

Screams rose above the pandemonium. I swore I could hear Lea's above them all. I knew that couldn't be true, because everyone was screaming. I was screaming.

Seth released his hold, and I dropped to my knees, gagging and choking on the smell of burned cloth and…flesh—burned flesh. Where the seven had once stood, only three remained huddled together as they stared at Seth in horror. One whimpered, clutching a blackened arm.

Lea's sister—Dawn—was gone.

He had done it—attacked the Council. My cheeks were damp. When had I started crying? Did it matter? I didn't know.

Lea's sister was gone.

I pressed my hand to my mouth, ordering myself to pull it together. Something had to be done. This was bad—horrendous—but it would get worse once I Awakened. In the chaos, I could escape. I couldn't break down now. Struggling to my feet, I held my breath and edged toward the stairs as Seth's back was to me. I reached the steps and arms went around my waist, lifting me over the edge. Warmth immediately surrounded me, my body—my heart—telling me who it was who'd grabbed me. Sweet relief flooded me.

"I've got you." Aiden set me on my feet. His eyes searched mine intently. "Can you run?"

I heard him as though through a tunnel, and I think I nodded. Within seconds, we were surrounded.

"Shit." He let go of my hand, blocking my body with his. Coiled tension rolled through him.

I wished I'd had the foresight to find the lost dagger, because then I'd at least have something to ward off Lucian's Guards. Not that I'd be able to do much with it. It was taking everything in me to stand, to push through the nearly overwhelming exhaustion that'd come when Seth tapped into my power.

Then Aiden sprang. Spinning around, his boot connected with the jaw of the closest Guard, and then he dipped under the outstretched arm of another. Coming up, his fist struck the second in a fierce uppercut. Without missing a beat, he caught another with a kick to the chest, knocking the Guard back several feet.

It had been so long since I'd seen him fight. Forgetting how graceful and fast he was, I stared in awe. Not a single Guard made it past him. He mowed them down with just his hands and kicks.

One, however, did creep up behind us.

The Guard grabbed me from behind and started to pull me back toward the dais, toward Seth and Lucian. With my arms pinned to my side, I was only able to slam my foot down on his. He grunted and his grip loosened, but that was about it.

Aiden turned, seeing my predicament. Our eyes met for a brief second, and then his gaze dropped. I let my legs collapse. Aiden moved so fast the air stirred around me. A second later the Guard hit the ground, unconscious.

"Nice," I croaked as Aiden tugged me to my feet.

His smile was tight as he grabbed hold of my hand again, and we were running up the center aisle. My uncle and the stranger were making short work of the Guards by the door. On the floor, Luke was holding Lea, rocking her back and forth as he kept an eye on the battle. When he saw us, he stood and pulled Lea to her feet. She was hysterical. I didn't think she even knew what was going on around her, not even when the stranger with the scar threw a dagger and took out a Guard right beside her.

"Who…who are you?" I asked.

He bowed at the waist and grinned. "Most call me Solos."

"Solos from Nashville?"

Solos nodded, spun around, and punched the living crap out of a Sentinel who'd made a run at us. The punch knocked the guy off his feet. It was pretty epic.

"Are we getting out of here?" Luke asked. He held Lea close to him, his movements near frantic. "We've got to get out of—"

The air popped and crackled. Light followed, flashing over the entire room. When it receded, Apollo stood in the middle of the aisle. "Go," he said. "Get off the island now. I will hold him off, give you enough time."

"Alex!" roared Seth.

Cold shivers went down my spine.

"Whatever you all do, do not stop. Do not stay to help," Apollo ordered before he turned around. "Go."

"Come on." Aiden had me again. "We have a car waiting down the street, by the beach."

"You can run, Alex!" Seth's voice carried over the uproar. "Run all you want! I will find you!"

Aiden dragged me toward the front doors. I looked back, seeing Seth standing in the center of the dais, his chest heaving. The body of the furie lay at his feet like a sick trophy.

"Stop them!" Lucian ordered, moving behind Seth. "Don't let her out of here."

The Guards in front of the dais turned and froze. Then they scattered like roaches.

Apollo moved up the aisle. "Yeah, that's what I thought."

"I will find you! We're connected. We are one!" Seth was still screaming. His gaze fell to the god. He sneered. "You want to fight me now, in your true form?"

"I will fight you in any form, you little punk-ass brat."

Seth laughed. "You can't kill me."

"But I *can* beat the living snot out of you."

That was all I heard. We were out of the courthouse, into the sunlight. Pures and halfs streamed out behind us. We kept running. I struggled to keep up with Aiden, breathing harshly. I could barely feel my legs and stumbled more than once, but Aidan caught me each time, urging me on. Then Marcus appeared at my side, and without a word, swooped me up in his arms.

Indignation swept through me. I loathed the idea of being carried, but I was more of a hindrance on my feet. Only then did I realize that my runes were still burning, the skin throbbing. My stomach started to roll violently.

"I'm going to be sick," I gasped out.

Marcus stopped immediately, placing me on my feet. I hit my knees, and the contents of my stomach emptied on the sidewalk outside a coffee shop. It was quick and powerful, over as soon as it started, leaving my insides aching.

"Alex!" Aiden tracked back to us.

"She's okay." Marcus helped me to my feet. "She's all right. Aiden, go ahead. Make sure your brother is there and get those kids to safety."

Aiden hovered. "I'm not leav—"

"I'm fine. Go."

Obviously reluctant to do so, it took Aiden a few more seconds before he spun around and took off.

"Are you okay?" Marcus asked. "Alexandria?"

I nodded slowly. My hands trembled. "Sorry. I'm so sorry."

Marcus's eyes softened, possibly for the first time since I'd known him. He stepped forward, wrapping his arms around me. It was a brief hug, but tight and everything it should've been. And oddly, I discovered it was something I'd been yearning for.

"Good gods, girl," he choked out, releasing me. "Do you think you can run? It's not very far. We have to get back to the St. Delphi house."

Tears clawed at my throat as I nodded. It wasn't far, but the poor man would die carrying me the whole distance. Hoping my stomach didn't decide to jump out of me again, I started running as fast as I could.

The run ended up nearly killing me. When we finally reached the sand, and were running into the wind, my muscles screamed and protested. I kept going, almost crying out when I saw the two black Hummers...and Aiden.

He met us halfway, thrusting a bottle of water in my hands as I slowed down. "Drink slowly."

I sipped the water as Aiden clasped my shoulders. I wanted to tell him that I was okay, that I wasn't who he should be worried about, but we were moving again.

Deacon was pacing at the rear of the Hummer. "Is someone going to tell me what the hell is going on?" He followed us past the first car. "Lea is hysterical. Luke won't talk. What the hell happened?"

"Did you get the bags in the cars?" Aiden asked, taking the

bottle from me before I forgot about the sipping rule. "All of them, like I said?"

"Yes." Deacon ran his hands through his curls, eyes wide and intense. "What happened?"

Solos jogged up to us. "It'll take about eight hours to get where we're going. We should have at least half of that time in before we stop for gas."

"Agreed," Aiden said. He took hold of my limp arm in a gentle grasp, taking on most of my weight. I hadn't realized I'd leaned against the Hummer. His worried gaze kept falling back to me.

"Tell me what happened!" Deacon yelled.

"Seth…Seth attacked the Council." I winced at the words.

Deacon stared incredulously. "Oh, my gods."

I broke free of Aiden and looked inside the Hummer. Piled in the back were suitcases. They'd had it all planned. Pushing away from the back of the car, I watched for Seth. How long could Apollo hold him off?

They were finalizing plans, and I was still staring at the suitcases. Obviously, they'd hoped to grab me at the Council somehow, not knowing the kind of chaos that was going to erupt. What would they have risked to get me out of there? Life and limb, most likely.

The wind picked up.

Aiden headed back to me, all determination and purpose. "We have to leave now."

Solos called out to Marcus. "You ready for this?"

"Let's get out of here," Marcus replied, casting a long look at me. "You holding up?"

"Yeah," I croaked, and then cleared my throat.

"This is crazy." Deacon opened the back door and started to climb in. "Everything is going bat—"

"No!" Aiden pushed Deacon toward the Hummer being driven by Solos. "We're the ones they will target. Go with Marcus. Luke, stay with him."

All business, Luke nodded and gathered a still-sobbing Lea close to him. I wanted to go to her. She'd lost everything… and each time had had something to do with me. First my mother had taken her parents, and now Seth had taken her sister. Razor-sharp guilt dug in.

Deacon stalled. "No. I want—"

Aiden grabbed his younger brother in a fierce hug. Words were whispered between them, but I couldn't hear anything over the wind. Pushing my hair out of my face, I turned back toward the Covenant-controlled part of the island.

Something was happening. I could feel it. Electricity filled the air, raising the tiny hairs on my arms.

Deacon stumbled back from his brother and turned away. Tears had gathered in his eyes. He feared for his brother's life and he should. When Seth came for us, which he would, he wouldn't pay them any attention. Seth would come for Aiden and me, and even as strong as he was, it was doubtful Aiden would walk away from that confrontation.

My heart sank. I couldn't do this to them. "Aiden, you can't go with me. You can't do this."

"Don't start," Aiden growled as he grabbed my arm. "Get in the—"

Lightning erupted from the sky, streaking above us and down, slamming just off the coast of the Covenant. Despite our distance from the impact point, the flash of light still blinded me.

Solos stopped, halfway behind the driver's seat. "What the…?"

The wind just stopped. It was unnatural…and so was the

silence that descended on Deity Island. Then a rush of seagulls took flight, screaming and squawking in a panic. Hundreds and hundreds of them flew overhead, away from the island.

"What's happening?" Lea whispered. "Is it him? Is he coming?"

"No," I said, feeling it in my core. "This isn't Seth."

"We need to go *now*." Aiden started pulling me toward the passenger side of the car.

In a flurry of activity, everyone jumped into their respective cars. Behind us, people were gathering on the decks of their homes. Guards were scattering across the beach. All were staring across the stretch of ocean that separated the two islands.

I had a really bad feeling about this.

Aiden slammed his door shut and threw the Hummer into drive. He grabbed my hand. "Everything is going to be okay."

Famous last words.

A bone-shaking boom blasted around us, rattling the car. A stream of water jetted into the air on the other side of the island, taller than the highest Covenant building, thicker than two of the dorms. The wall of water stilled, reminding me of how Seth had played with the water in the pool.

This wasn't going to be good.

Another stream burst into the sky and then another…and another until over a dozen walls of water dotted the landscape. Power rippled through the air, sliding over my skin, curling around the cord inside me.

And in the center of each of the streams, I could make out a form of a man.

"Oh, shit," I whispered.

Aiden slammed on the gas and the Hummer lurched forward. "Poseidon."

I twisted around in the seat, watching the ocean from the back window. Beyond the formidable Covenant buildings, the walls started spinning into funnels. A shadow of a giant trident fell over the Covenant and the sharpened points touched the main island, spelling doom and death for all who remained. Poseidon, the God of the Sea, the great earth-shaker, was very angry.

"Aiden..."

"Turn around, Alex."

My hands clenched the back of the seat. The funnels formed giant cyclones—tornados over water. "They're going to destroy everything! We have to do something."

"There is nothing we can do." With one hand, Aiden grabbed my arm as we crested the bridge to Bald Head Island. "Alex, please."

I couldn't turn away. From the way the cyclones moved in, it appeared Poseidon would spare the mortal island, but as the first funnel reached the Covenant, my chest seized. "They can't do this! Those people are innocent!"

Aiden didn't answer.

Water crashed through the structures. Marble and wood sliced through the air. Screams from those on the main island crawled deep into my soul where the sound would remain for an eternity.

We flew through the streets of Bald Head, narrowly avoiding the stunned pedestrians watching the freakish outburst of nature. And as we reached the bridge leading to the mainland, I saw the great walls of water recede. No building remained on Deity Island. There was nothing. All of it was gone. The Covenant, buildings, statues, pures and halfs...everything had been wiped into the ocean.

CHAPTER THIRTY

Hours passed in stunned silence. I felt sick, cold. How many had been on the island? Hundreds of servants and Instructors had remained at the Covenant during winter break, and people had been in their homes. Hands shaking, I smoothed my hair back as Aiden fiddled with the radio until he caught a station.

"Meteorologists are saying that the earthquake several hundred miles off the coast of North Carolina produced a wall of water at least thirty feet tall. However, residents on neighboring islands remained unscathed. Some have reported seeing a cluster of up to a dozen cyclones, but those reports have not been substantiated by the National Oceanic and Atmospheric Administration. A state of emergency has been declared..."

Aiden turned the radio off. He then reached over, running his fingers over my arm, my hand. He'd been doing that since we got in the car, as if he was reminding himself that I was sitting next to him, that I was still alive after so many lives had been lost.

I pressed my forehead against the window and closed my eyes. Had Poseidon gone after Seth and Lucian, or had Apollo somehow managed to prevent total destruction? All I did know was that Seth was still breathing because the connection was still there.

Like I'd done during the last couple of hours, I pictured my pink and glittery walls again and reinforced them with all my strength.

"How are you feeling?" Aiden asked quietly.

I peeled my head off the window and looked at him. Everything about him was stiff and tense, from the way he held the steering wheel to the line of his jaw. "How can you even think about how I'm feeling right now?"

"I saw how you reacted when…he pulled power from you." He glanced at me, eyes silvery. "Did they…did he hurt you when you were with him?"

I was exhausted. My head ached and I was pretty sure my toes were numb, but I was alive. "No. He didn't hurt me. And I'm fine. You shouldn't worry about how I'm doing. All of those people…" I shook my head, swallowing against the sudden tightening in my throat. "What Lucian did by telling them you used a compulsion…I'm so sorry."

"Alex, you have no reason to apologize. It wasn't your fault."

"But how can you go back? Being a Sentinel—"

"I'm still a Sentinel. And with everything that's happened, I'm sure what I did is the last thing they'll be thinking about." He glanced at me. "I knew the risks when I did it. I don't regret it. You understand?"

Aiden didn't regret it now, but what about later—if there was a later—and he was tried for treason? Even if he wasn't, he'd be stripped of his Sentinel duties and ostracized.

"Alex?"

"Yes. I understand." I nodded for extra benefit. "Where are we going?"

His knuckles were bleached white. "We're going to Athens, Ohio. Solos's father has a place on the edge of Wayne National Forest. It should be far enough from…him as long as Apollo has given us enough time."

"I don't feel him." We'd stopped referring to Seth by name out loud, like doing so would somehow make him reappear or something.

"Do you think you can shield him, keep him out?"

I glanced at the side mirror; the other Hummer followed close behind. How were they holding up? Lea? "The distance… He shouldn't be able to connect through the bond, if that's what you're worried about. I mean, he couldn't feel anything when he was in New York, so…"

"That's not all I'm worried about," Aiden responded quietly. "It's about an eight-hour drive." He brushed his hair out of his eyes as he squinted into the fading sunlight. "We'll stop along the way, most likely in Charleston, to get gas and something to eat. You think you can hold out that long?"

"Yeah. Aiden…all of those people." My voice broke as my throat tightened. "They didn't stand a chance."

Aiden grasped my hand. "It's not your fault, Alex."

"It's not?" Tears burned my eyes. "If I'd listened to you and Apollo when you suggested that I leave before he came back, this wouldn't have happened."

"You don't know that."

"Yes, I do." I tried to pull my hand free, but Aiden held on. I hoped he was a good one-handed driver. "I just didn't want to believe that he…would do something so terrible."

He squeezed my hand. "You had hope, Alex. No one can ever be faulted for hope."

"You once told me that I needed to know when to let hope go. I was way past the expiration date on hope then." I tried to smile and failed. "I won't make that same mistake twice. I swear."

Bringing my hand to his lips, he placed a sweet kiss against it. "Agapi mou, don't hold this kind of guilt too close. A different path could've been chosen, but in the end, you did what you felt was right. You gave him a chance."

"I know." I focused on the road ahead, willing the tears away. "It's gone, isn't it? The entire Covenant—even Deity Island?"

He took a shuddering breath. "It could've been worse. That's what I keep telling myself. If classes had been in…just a few more days…"

The loss of life would have been astronomical. "What are we going to do? I can't stay hidden forever."

What was unspoken lay between us. In other words, unless Seth came to his senses, which seemed highly unlikely, he would eventually find me.

"I don't know," Aiden said, merging into the other lane. "But we're in this together, Alex, to the end."

Warmth returned to my heart. His hand felt right in mine, and even though everything around us was so incredibly screwed up, we *were* in this together. To the end.

It was the middle of the night when we reached Charleston, West "by gods" Virginia, and it was snowing lightly. The vehicles rolled to a stop by the pumps in front of one of those travel centers that are the size of a small Walmart. We needed gas and food, and maybe one of those 5-hour Energy things, too.

"Hold on." Aiden reached in the seat behind us and pulled out one of the sickle blades. "Just in case."

Collapsed, it fit in my pocket with only half of it sticking out. "Thanks."

His eyes met mine as he slipped me a couple of tens. "Don't take too long, okay? Looks like Solos is going in with you."

I glanced back. He was already waiting by the passenger side. Marcus was fiddling with the gas pump like he'd never used one before. "What do you want?"

"Surprise me." He smiled. "Just be careful."

Promising that I would, I climbed out of the Hummer and nearly ate the pavement as my foot slipped on a patch of ice. "Gods!"

"Alex?" Aiden called out.

"I'm fine." I tipped my head back and closed my eyes, letting the tiny flakes of snow fall upon my face. It had been so, so long since I'd seen snow.

"What are you doing?" Solos asked, killing the moment.

I opened my eyes and forced them to his chest. "I like snow."

"Well, you're going to see a lot of snow where we're going."

We started across the parking lot, mindful of the patches of ice that were bound and determined to take me out. "Probably have a foot or more in Athens."

For a moment, I fantasized about snowball fights and sled rides. Stupid of me to do so, but it helped keep me from freaking out.

"You're not what I expected," Solos said as we reached the snow-covered sidewalk.

I shoved my hands into my pockets. "What were you expecting?"

"I don't know." He smiled, softening the scar. "Someone taller."

A small smile pulled at my lips. "Don't let my size fool you."

"I know. I've heard tales about your many escapades, especially how you fought during the attack on the New York Covenant. Some say it's because of what you are that makes you fight so well."

I shrugged.

"But I say it has more to do with your training than anything." Solos glanced behind him and then his shrewd gaze settled on me. "You and St. Delphi seem to be very close."

I schooled my expression blank as I shrugged again. "He's pretty cool for a pure-blood."

"Is that so?"

"Hey! Wait up!" Deacon hit a patch of thick ice and slid to our sides like a pro skater, eyes wide. "Lea wants to eat something. Luke's going to stay with her."

Saved by Deacon. "How's she doing?"

Solos grabbed the door, holding it open for us. "She slept most of the way here," Deacon answered. "Since she woke up, she hasn't really been talking. Luke convinced her that she should eat something, so we're going to share some Cheetos."

I felt for Lea and understood her pain. So did Deacon. My presence probably wouldn't be the best, but Deacon… he'd be good for her.

I shook off the snow once inside the warm, brightly lit travel center. With the exception of the greasy-haired and scrawny cashier who was reading what looked like a smut magazine, the place was empty. Stomach growling, I headed toward the coolers. Aiden would want water, of course, but I was in need of some caffeine.

Solos stayed with Deacon, because if a random hillbilly daimon appeared, Deacon would be the one needing help. Grabbing a bottle of water and a Pepsi, I scanned the store.

The cashier yawned and scratched his chest, never once looking up. Snow was starting to fall in larger flakes. Sighing, I ignored the desire to watch the snow and shuffled toward the chip aisle. The made-to-order-sandwiches part of the store wasn't open, so our options were severely limited.

A heavy, musky, wet scent flooded the air. I sniffed, finding the smell oddly familiar. I passed Deacon with his arms full.

"You better hurry up. Solos is getting nervous about the mortal."

I glanced back at the front of the store. "What? There's only one guy in here."

"I know."

Shaking my head, I grabbed a packet of beef jerky and a bag of dill-flavored chips. I looked down at my goodies and decided I needed something sweet. After a quick stop in the candy bar area, I returned to the front.

"Nice of you to join us," Solos muttered. A bag of peanuts and an energy drink were in his hands.

I ignored him as Deacon checked out. The cashier glanced up as I handed over my feast of calories but said nothing. People were super-friendly around these parts.

"That will be $10.59," the man grunted.

Good gods. What did I buy? I dug in my pocket for the cash Aiden had given me. Suddenly, the musky smell returned, but much stronger. And then I remembered that smell. It was the same mossy scent from the Underworld. The overhead fluorescent lights flickered once, then twice.

"Oh man," I whispered, and my heart dropped.

Solos stiffened beside me. "What is it?"

"Y'all don't worry," the clerk said, glancing up at the lights. "It happens all the time with the snow. Drivers hit poles in that black ice out there. Y'all must not be from around here."

The air thickened around us, filling with the same electricity that had enveloped Deity Island moments before Poseidon's arrival. The mortal couldn't feel it.

There was a pop and sparks flew. The security camera by the door stopped blinking red as smoke wafted from it.

"What the hell?" The clerk leaned over the counter. "Now I ain't seen nuttin' like that before."

I ain't seen nuttin' like that, either.

Solos grabbed Deacon's arm. "Time to go."

Wide-eyed, Deacon nodded. "Whatever you say, man." Leaving my items on the counter, we started for the door.

Food be damned. There was definitely something going on, something…godly.

"Hey! Where y'all going? You didn't—"

A deep growl cut off his words. We halted about ten feet from the door. My heart leaped into my throat. The smell of wet dog grew strong, and the fine hairs on my body rose. I turned around slowly, my gaze darting over the store. I reached down, wrapping my hand around the handle of the sickle blade.

Beside the display of Twinkies and cupcakes, the air shimmered. Distinctive shapes of large, booted footprints appeared, blackening the vinyl flooring, filling the air with wisps of smoke and sulfur. The white travel star painted on the vinyl bubbled and smoked.

Two leather-encased legs, then narrow hips, and a broad chest appeared out of thin air. By the time my gaze traveled to his face, I think I'd stopped breathing. "Darkly handsome" didn't do him justice. "Sinfully beautiful" wasn't even in the ballpark when trying to describe this raven-haired god. The smell of sulfur and smoke gave away his identity.

Hades was sort of hot for a god, and I was sure he was there to kill me.

A shotgun blasted, deadening my ears, and causing me to jump.

"I don't want none of this bad shit up in here." The clerk cocked the gun again. "Next time I won't—"

Hades raised a hand, and the clerk's eyes rolled back into their sockets. He hit the floor without so much as another word. Hades smiled, flashing a perfect set of ultra-white teeth. The Underworld had a hell of a dental plan.

"Now, we can do this the easy way or the hard way," Hades said, charmingly enough. Weirdly, he seemed to have a British accent. "All I want is the girl."

Solos edged Deacon back against the counter, blocking him in, and casually placed his peanuts and energy drink down. "That's going to be a problem."

Hades shrugged. "Then this will be the hard way."

CHAPTER THIRTY-ONE

The hard way didn't sound or look fun when Solos tried to get Deacon out of the convenience store and found that the doors wouldn't open. On the other side, Aiden and Marcus desperately tried to open the doors, going as far as to try to throw a bench at the reinforced glass, but to no avail.

Things went from bad to really screwed up within seconds. Hades wasn't alone—not that we'd forgotten the smell and animalistic growl from earlier. Behind Hades, the air shimmered before two massive, three-headed dogs appeared.

One was black and the other was brown, but both were as ugly as hell. Matted hair covered everything but their long, hairless snouts. Each head had a mouth on it that could swallow a baby whole and their claws looked vicious and sharp. Six sets of eyes glowed ruby red. At the end of each rat-like tail was what looked like a military flail—a morning star type of weapon, rough and full of spikes.

They flanked Hades, snarling and snapping at the air. We were so screwed.

"Meet Death"—Hades gestured at the black dog— "and Despair. Cerberus is a proud papa to his two boys."

"Nice names," I croaked, and then released the two sharp edges of the sickle blade.

"You wanna play, luv?" Hades cocked his head to the side.

"Not really." I wasn't sure which of them I should keep an eye on.

"It's really nothing personal," Hades said. "But we cannot allow the First to become what has been feared. He's already made his choice, and now we must make ours."

Trying to kill me was as personal as it got. I saw Hades's chin go up about an inch and I jumped to the side just as Despair charged me. Darting down the candy aisle, I hoped that Solos was able to protect Deacon. I grabbed hold of a rack and threw it to the floor. Despair went right over the numerous candy bars, his claws ripping through wrappers and chocolate. Hanging a quick right, I glanced over my shoulder.

Despair lost his balance and slid into the standup cooler, crashing through the glass. Bottles of soda flew through the air, fizzing upon impact. Taking advantage of the situation, I spun around and brought the sickle edge down on the closest head.

The blade went clean through muscles and tissue, and a yelp later, Despair became a two headed dog…until the stump started to grow into another freaking head. Fully restored, Despair bared his fangs and pawed at the ground.

I backed up. "Nice doggy. Good doggy."

Despair crouched, each of his mouths snapping at the air.

"Bad doggy!" I took off running, knocking over cases of beer and anything I could get my hands on. Over the shelves I could see Deacon backed up against the front doors, Aiden and Marcus's horrified expressions on the other side. Solos was squaring off with Death, dispatching heads left and right.

And Hades, well, he was just standing there in his big bad god glory.

"Go for the heart!" Solos yelled over the chaos. "The heart in the chest, Alex!"

"Like I don't know where the freaking heart is!" I just didn't want to get that close to the thing. I picked up speed when I saw the dining area, getting an idea—not a good one, but better than running laps around the store with a mutant pit bull chasing after me.

I leaped over the set of chairs and landed on the table. Spinning around, I grabbed the metal chair and held it, legs up. Despair jumped, clearing the mess of chairs, and landed on top of me. He shrieked and thrashed as the metal legs embedded themselves deep into his underbelly. The impact busted the table and we both went down, his claws narrowly missing my face. All three heads snapped inches from my nose, its hot, putrid breath setting off my gag reflex.

Tipping my hips, I rolled Despair and sprang to my feet. Despair flopped on his back, legs flailing in the air. Pushing down the urge to vomit, I jumped on the seat of the chair. My weight sent the metal spokes down, piercing the protective plate of bone.

A second later the dog was nothing but a pile of shimmery, blue dust. Lifting my head, I whirled around. "One down…"

Hades let out a roar of fury that shook the shelves and sent overpriced items of every shape and size falling to the floor.

And then he vanished.

"Well, that was easy." I flipped the blade, watching Solos dodge one of Death's heads. "Did you see that? Hades totally just chicken—*oh crap*."

Shelves flew through the air, chairs and tables slid across the floor, flung aside by an unseen force. The floor shook under my feet as I backed up. That was about when I remembered that Hades could become invisible. Terror washed through me like a dark, oily wave of heat.

"No fair," I said, and then whipped the sickle blade through what I hoped wasn't empty space.

An invisible hand caught my arm and twisted. Crying out in pain and surprise, I dropped the sickle. Hades reappeared. "Sorry, luv, all is fair in war."

A blinding light filled the store, followed by a popping sound. Then something zinged past my cheek. I caught a glimpse of silver before Hades released my arm and snatched an arrow out of the air.

"Artemis, that wasn't very nice." Hades snapped the arrow in two and tossed it aside. "You could take an eye out with one of those things."

The soft feminine laugh that followed sounded like wind chimes. A few feet behind us, legs widespread and a silver bow in one hand, stood Artemis. Instead of the white chiffon many goddesses were known for, she wore straight up combat boots and hot-pink camouflage pants. A white tank completed her badass ensemble.

She reached behind her, pulling another arrow from her quiver. "Back down, Hades."

Hades's lips thinned.

She placed the arrow on her bow. "You will not catch the next one, Hades. And you will not take her."

I slowly backed away from the god smackdown-in-progress, having no idea why Artemis would come to my aid. Out of the corner of my eye, I saw Death finally go down. I picked up my sickle blade.

Hades stepped forward, tile peeling and smoking under his

boots. “Why are you intervening, Artemis? You know what will happen. All of us are at risk.”

“That is my twin’s lineage standing there and she belongs to us.” Artemis pulled the arrow back, tossing her waist-length blond hair over her shoulder. “Which means she is my flesh and bone. So, I will say it one more time just in case Persephone has befuddled that brain of yours—*stand down*.”

My mouth dropped opened. Apollo’s lineage? *Oh no… oh, hell to the no…*

“I do not care if she is the heir to the bloody throne, Artemis! We must prevent the First from gaining complete power!”

Artemis’s fingers twitched. “She is not to be harmed, Hades. That is it.”

An incredulous look settled over his darkly handsome face. “I would not harm her…not really. I could take her to the Underworld. It would not even hurt. Artemis, we cannot allow this threat to continue. Be reasonable.”

“And I cannot allow you to hurt her. It is not up for discussion.”

“So, you would risk more destruction? Did you see what Poseidon did today? Or were you too busy hunting and playing with your consorts?”

Artemis smirked. “You really do not want to piss me off right now, Hades. Not when I have an arrow pointed between your eyes.”

He shook his head. “You know what Zeus will do if the First becomes the God Killer. You risk it all—the lives of our offspring and the mortals—and for what? Watered-down familial bonds?”

“We will risk it all for everything,” she responded quietly. “You know what the funny thing is about prophecies, uncle?”

"That they are always changing?" Hades sneered. "Or that they are nothing more than a load of rubbish?"

Any other time I would've clapped, but seeing that Hades wanted to kill me, I wasn't about to celebrate our shared opinions when it came to the oracle.

Artemis cocked back her arm. "So be it."

Fury rolled off Hades in swamping waves. Swallowing down fear, I took a step back. I expected an all-out royal rumble between the two.

"I should never have allowed her soul to be released," Hades spat. "Apollo promised me that it would never come to this."

"There is still hope," Artemis said.

Those words sparked something in me. *There is still hope.* Was there? I'd seen the look in Seth's eyes, how far gone he'd been when he'd pulled the akasha from me and taken aim at the Council. Poseidon had leveled the Covenant, and there would be more that would go down. More innocent people would die. People that I loved would surely die—all to protect me.

I glanced back at the doors, seeing Aiden's pale face beside Marcus's. I'd been created, like a pawn, to give Seth complete power. There was nothing that could be done about it. None of us could spend our lives hiding. It wouldn't work. I would Awaken in little over a day. Seth would find me. And everything would be over.

Numbness crept through me as I turned back to the two gods and lowered the sickle. "Wait." My voice came out barely a whisper, but everyone froze.

"No!" Deacon yelled, trying to get past Solos. "I know what she's going to do! Alex, no!"

Tears sprang to my eyes as I took in his horrified expression.

"I can't...I can't let what happened back there happen again."

Deacon struggled against Solos, his eyes burning a fierce silver, like his brother, so much like him. "I don't care. It'll kill..." He swallowed, shaking his head. "You can't do this, Alex."

It would kill Aiden.

Hades clapped his hands together. "See. Even she understands."

My heart cracked.

Artemis's eyes widened. "Alexandria, please, I understand that the mortal part of you demands that you become a martyr, but you really need to shut up."

"People are going to continue to die. And Seth will find me." I pressed the button on the handle, and the blades collapsed. "I saw him. He's..." I couldn't finish. Saying that Seth was lost was too final and, in a way, it broke my heart.

Hades turned those eyes to me. They snapped with electricity. For a moment, I missed Apollo. At least he toned down those eyes around me, making them seem normal. Hades would do no such thing. "You are doing the right thing," he cooed softly. "And I promise you, you will not feel a thing." He held out his hand to me. "It will be easy, luv."

The crack in my chest spread, and I blinked back tears. This wasn't fair, but it was right. It would hurt Aiden—and Marcus and my friends—but it would also protect them. One day I hoped they'd understand. Over the pounding of my blood, I heard Solos yell for me. Slowly, I raised my hand.

"That is it," Hades whispered. "Take my hand."

Our fingers were only inches apart. I could feel their strange mix of heat and bone-chilling cold. I forced my mind empty. I couldn't afford to think about what I was doing because I'd chicken out.

"Hades," Artemis called out.

He turned slightly. "Stay—"

Artemis released the arrow and it struck where she'd intended—smack dab between Hades's eyes. Then he just poofed—like Grandma Piperi had poofed in the garden the day she'd given me her last prophecy. The overwhelming scent of damp walls and caverns vanished, and the arrow clattered onto the linoleum.

I clamped my hand over my mouth to stop my scream. "Is... Did you kill him?"

"No." Artemis scoffed. "I just put him out of commission for a while." She lowered the bow and flicked her wrist. The front doors swung open. Marcus and Aiden rushed in, coming to a halt when they spied Artemis. Neither of the pures seemed to know what to do.

Artemis replaced the arrow back in her quiver and gave Aiden a sexy little grin. "They just keep getting yummier," she purred.

Too stunned to get jealous, I stared at her. "Why? He was right. I'm too much of a risk. I *understand* that."

Artemis focused on me with all-white eyes. "My brother has not risked the wrath of Zeus to protect you, for you to just throw your life away."

I tried to ignore the cyclone of fury building behind me. Dealing with Aiden was not something I was looking forward to. "I don't get it. No one can hide me forever. Seth will find me, and then what? He'll become the God Killer and another god is going to freak out and wipe out an entire city."

Artemis glided toward me, her elegant movements completely at odds with her combat-princess attire. "Or you will turn the tables on the First and all those who think they can overthrow the gods."

"What do you mean?" Marcus spoke, flushing a bright red when Artemis turned to him. He bowed deeply and then straightened. "How can Alexandria turn the tables? If Seth so much as lays a finger on her once she Awakens, he will become the God Killer."

"Not necessarily," she replied evenly.

I blinked rapidly. "Care to explain that?"

Artemis smiled. Impossibly, she became more beautiful… and creepier. "It is true that my brother holds affection for you, but you are a valuable asset to us. Some wish to see you dead, it is true. Hades will be back…eventually, as will the remaining furies. But you will Awaken soon, and you are strong—stronger than you realize."

All my normal smart-ass responses would probably earn me an arrow in the head, so I had no idea what to say.

She stopped in front of me. When she reached out and clasped my chin with smooth, cold fingers, I wanted to flinch away. She tipped my head back. "You have a reckless sort of passion about you. It guides you. Some would see it as a weakness."

"It's not?" I whispered, unable to look away.

"No." She studied me as if she could see into me, through me. "You have the eyes of a warrior." Her hand dropped and she took a step back. "Prophecies always change, Alexandria. Nothing in our world is set in stone. And power never flows just one way. The key is finding a way to reverse it."

Then she just disappeared.

I touched my chin. The skin tingled. Slowly, I turned to Aiden. "You should've seen those dogs."

Aiden grabbed both my arms, his eyes like liquid silver. I

could tell he wanted to shake me. He'd seen through the glass what I'd tried to do, and Artemis had pretty much thrown me under the bus. As he stared at me, it was like he'd forgotten everyone else in the store, that my uncle was there, his brother, and Solos. He was that angry.

"Don't you *ever* think about doing something so stupid again."

I looked away. "I'm sorry—"

"I understand that you thought you were doing the right thing," he said through clenched teeth. "But you weren't, Alex. Sacrificing yourself was not the right thing to do. Do you understand me?"

Marcus placed a hand on his shoulder. "Aiden, this is not the place. We need to go."

My breath caught as my eyes darted between the two. "I just don't know how we're going to win this."

"No one wins if you kill yourself," Marcus said quietly. "We must go."

Drawing in a deep breath, Aiden dropped his hands. His look warned that there would be a later, most likely the moment we stepped back in the car. Solos waited by the door; his sharp gaze narrowed on Aiden as he took a sip of his energy drink.

"Are you okay?" Aiden asked Deacon.

He nodded slowly. "Yeah, I'm great. Nothing like witnessing a death match between gods when I'm trying to get some Cheetos."

My lips twitched. Poor Deacon. He clutched that bag to his chest, too.

The cashier's soft snores were the only sound. Remembering the whole purpose of coming to this place, I hastened back to the counter.

"What are you doing?" Aiden asked.

I dropped some cash on the counter and grabbed my bag. "I'm hungry."

Aiden stared a moment, then a slow smile crept across his face. Maybe I wouldn't get bitched out too badly. On the way out, he picked up a package of Hostess CupCakes off the floor and caught my look. "Me, too," he said.

"At least I paid for my stuff."

CHAPTER THIRTY-TWO

I did get bitched out—a lot. And I deserved it. Aiden had been through the wringer when it came to me lately. He understood why—my motives—but he didn't agree with me. But I knew what I'd been thinking, and it still made sense. I didn't want to die, but I didn't want to see anybody else hurt when handing myself over would stop everything.

Halfway into the second part of the trip, as the tires ate away the miles, Aiden grabbed my hand and held onto it. He hadn't forgiven me, but he didn't want to shake me anymore. That was progress. I still wasn't sure if Artemis shooting Hades in the head was a good move or not by the time we reached Athens.

Tall pines and mounds of snow greeted us when we reached the lodge nestled at the edge of the national forest. Without Marcus and the air element, there would've been no way that we would've made it up the remote road. Even so, it took him over an hour to clear the road.

The lodge was magnificent, made of logs and surrounded

by a wraparound deck. If I hadn't been so exhausted, I would've appreciated its beauty much more.

"Do you know that Athens is one of the most haunted locales in Ohio?" Solos said as he opened the door.

"She doesn't believe in ghosts." Aiden lugged our bags over his shoulder, cheeks flushed from the cold. I could barely feel it. All I wanted was a bed to sleep the rest of the day away in.

"Really?" Solos grinned. "We'll have to take you down to the old Athens Asylum and see if that changes your mind."

"Sounds like fun," I murmured, watching Luke and Deacon usher Lea inside. "How will we be safe here? What's stopping any god from carpet-bombing us?"

Solos's brows furrowed. "We're safe here."

"How so?"

"Look up there." Aiden shifted the bags and pointed above the front door. Carved into the wood was the same S-shaped rune that was on my neck. "Apollo said no god who means ill will against persons in this house can pass through."

"The invincibility rune." I rubbed the back of my neck absently as I stepped over the threshold. "Didn't know you could just rune up a house. That's pretty handy."

Inside was just as beautiful. Wide windows let in the last of the sunset, and the wood floors had been buffed until they shined. It sort of reminded me of the cabin in Gatlinburg. I shuddered.

"You okay?" Aiden whispered, coming up behind me.

I swallowed. "Yeah, I'm just really tired."

Solos showed us to the rooms. Lea was placed downstairs, along with Marcus and Luke. Deacon grabbed the loft above the rec room and the rest of us got rooms upstairs. Everyone huddled in small groups or, like Marcus, stared out one of the windows, appearing lost in deep thought.

Aiden carried my bags into a cozy, rustic-looking bedroom and placed them by the bed. Turning around, our gazes locked. Since the day I'd left with Seth, we hadn't been alone together. The car ride didn't count. We'd been running for our lives after witnessing a tragedy. Kissing and touching hadn't been on our minds.

It kind of returned with a vengeance then.

He crossed the distance, cupping my cheeks in his hands. They were elegant fingers but calloused from years of training. I loved his hands. He angled his head to mine, his lips hovering just within distance. "Later," he promised, and then he pressed his lips to mine.

The kiss was gentle, sweet, and way too quick. My lips tingled awhile after he'd left the room. Later? How could there be a "later" in a house full of people? I took a hot shower and let the water ease my aching muscles once I figured out how to use the three shower heads without drowning myself. Afterward, I changed into sweats and sent the bed a yearning glance on the way out of the room. I had something to do before I rested.

Lea was sitting on the bed, legs crossed as she stared down at her phone. When I knocked on the open door, she glanced up. "Hey," I said.

She watched me for several long seconds and then cleared her throat. "I texted Olivia in Vail, told her we were okay."

"Does she know what she's going to do?" I sat on the bed beside her, running my hands through the wet tangles in my hair. I thought about Caleb's message to her. Hopefully, I could tell her soon.

"No. Her mom…" her voice caught, and she swallowed. "Her mom is freaking out. I think they're going to New York."

Thinking of my father, I felt my chest tighten. Would I

ever see him again? Then I felt bad for even thinking that. Lea had lost all of her family. "Will they be safe there?"

Long, coppery hair I'd envied for years shielded her face as she tipped her head down. "She thinks so. She'll let me know once her mom knows more."

I nodded, dropping my hands to my lap. "Lea, I'm so sorry for what happened."

She drew in a breath of air that seemed to shake her entire body. "We've been here before."

"I know."

Lea lifted her head. Her amethyst-colored eyes glittered with tears. "I know it's not your fault. What your mom did or what...what Seth did. Every death that I've seen or been around has had to do with you. They're not your fault, but they still happened."

I looked away, feeling the weight of the last ten months settle over me. Ten months of death, starting with my mom in Miami, and I knew it wasn't over. With the gods involved as they were, with my birthday tomorrow, and with Seth out there looking for us, it wasn't over. But still, what I was feeling was nothing compared to what Lea was going through.

"And I can't...I can't look at you without seeing all those faces," Lea whispered. "I'm sorry. I don't blame you, but I...I just can't look at you right now."

I nodded stiffly and stood. "I'm sorry," I said again. It was the only thing I could say.

"I know."

Leaving her room didn't diminish the guilt. Crawling into bed didn't make any of what happened disappear. And my guilt wasn't like what I'd felt after Caleb's death. This was like having a child who had done something terrible and everyone was staring at me, wondering where it all had gone wrong. Guilt by association.

I rolled onto my side, facing the window. Snow continued to fall outside. Nature was at its best when it was both beautiful and deadly.

Watching the snow cleared my mind of everything that was happening, leaving behind a thin layer of static until exhaustion claimed and pulled me under.

A feathery light kiss woke me up sometime later, drawing my eyes open. Aiden smiled down at me as his thumb traced the shape of my cheekbone. "What are you doing?" I asked sleepily. "What if someone finds you in here?"

"Solos took Deacon and Luke to the store since the snow has let up a little. Lea is resting and Marcus is keeping an eye on things." He curled around me, finding my hand and threading his fingers through mine. "And I think the cat's pretty much out of the bag on this."

I tipped my head back, my eyes searching his intently. "What do you mean?"

"We're in a house full of halfs, with the exception of Marcus and my brother. Deacon surely doesn't care and Marcus—"

"My uncle's a stickler for rules," I whispered.

Aiden brushed his lips over the tip of my nose. "Marcus knows, Alex. He's not blind."

"He's okay with it?"

"I wouldn't say *okay*." Aiden grinned. "He actually punched me when he figured it out."

I stared. "What?"

He chuckled under his breath. "Yeah, he punched me right in the face when he got back from Nashville—twice."

"Oh my..." I pressed my lips together to keep from laughing. It wasn't funny, but it was.

"The first hit was because you were with Seth and Lucian. The second one was after he figured out about us."

"How did he find out? We were careful." And we had been.

"I think he's suspected something for a while," he mused. "But it was when you were gone he figured it out. I think I was pretty transparent during those days."

I wanted to ease the lines of concern that'd appeared on his forehead. We'd talked about my time spent in Lucian's house on the way here and I'd reassured him a dozen times or more that I hadn't been harmed there, but it still bothered him. Just like when I'd died, it was something that would linger with Aiden.

"What did he say to you?" I finally asked him.

"I don't think you want to know. It was one of the only times I've heard Marcus cuss."

I smiled as I lowered my cheek back to the pillow. Gods knew I was all too familiar with Marcus being angry. "You don't seem too worried about him knowing."

"I'm not. Right now, there are more...pressing issues to focus on."

Wasn't that the truth? "Part of me wishes tomorrow wouldn't come."

He kissed the top of my head. "Everything will be okay, Alex."

"I know." I closed my eyes and snuggled in. "I just don't know what to expect, you know? Will I automatically turn into a super badass tomorrow or something? Or will I be accidentally blasting people with akasha?" Or would I connect with Seth? That I didn't want to put into words.

"Whatever happens, you'll still be Alex…you'll still be agapi mou, my life. Just…just don't ever scare me like you did today, okay? We're still in this together."

"To the end?"

"To the end," he whispered.

Damnable tears rushed to my eyes. Those words were perfect, just what I needed to hear. "Let's make plans again. I liked that." My brows rose when he laughed again. "What?"

"It's just that you are the last person who plans anything."

I grinned because he had a point. "But I like these kinds of plans."

"Okay." He moved his thumb along the inside of my palm. "I've been thinking about the future—our future."

I loved the sound of that: "our future." When Aiden said it, it seemed possible. "What did you come up with?"

"It's more like something I've decided." He pulled his hand free and smoothed back my hair. "Let's say everything blows over with the compulsion thing, okay?"

Not likely, but I nodded.

"I don't want to stay in our world."

I caught his hand, lowering it to where my heart pounded as I twisted around in his embrace. "What? What do you mean?"

Thick lashes shielded his eyes. "If we stayed in this world, the Hematoi world, we couldn't be together. There will be some who don't care, but…it's too much of a risk, even if we did manage to get assigned to the same area."

Air left my lungs as I stared at him. "But if you left, you couldn't be a Sentinel anymore, and you need that."

He looked up, meeting my eyes. "I do need that. Being a Sentinel is important to me, but it's not my world, my life, or my heart. You are. And I want you in my life, really in my life. It's the only way."

I suddenly wanted to cry. Again. I couldn't even form a coherent word, and I knew he could feel my heart slamming itself against his palm, but I didn't care.

Aiden leaned in, brushing his lips over mine. "I love you, Alex. I'd give it all up for you, and I know you've been thinking about it too, but that's up to you."

Could I give it up...this almost inherent need to become a Sentinel? Could I let go of the desire driven by years of having duty ingrained in me, and the need to somehow make up for what'd happened to my mother? Leaving this world would require assimilating back into the mortal world, something I had totally sucked at for three years. Old fears rose in that moment as years of never fitting in, of always being the freak, flashed before me. Mortals, for the most part, were naturally uncomfortable around us and drawn to us in the same breath. It was hard being near them, always pretending.

But I had been thinking about a future that didn't include the Covenant or being a Sentinel. I just never thought it could be possible, but when I looked into Aiden's eyes and saw only love—love for me—I knew I could do it. *We* could do it. Aiden was worth it. Our love was. Living like a mortal had choked me before, but now it could provide the type of freedom I yearned for. And together, anything seemed possible.

Tipping my head up, I met his silvery gaze. I could always tell what Aiden was feeling by the color of his eyes, and right now, he was laying everything out there and still giving me the choice.

"Yes. I could do it," I whispered. "I would do it."

A shudder rocked Aiden's body. "I was almost afraid you'd say no."

Misty-eyed, I cupped his cheek. Day-old stubble grazed my palm. "I could never tell you no, Aiden. Not that I would ever want to. But...but what about Deacon and Marcus? How can we do it?"

"I think they could know. We could trust them."

There were so many "what ifs" with this plan. How could we escape the Covenant and the society that probably would be very unwilling to let either of us go? We needed a plan, a good one if we even had a chance to make it work, but right now, the idea itself flooded me with warmth and so much hope. And hope, it was a fragile thing, but it kept me going.

Aiden lowered his head, bringing his mouth to mine. He made a sound in the back of his throat as the kiss deepened. The tentative touch gave way to something infinitely more. When he rolled his body, fitting it against mine like a warm blanket, my heart thundered. I was feeling so much and not enough—never enough. There was a yearning, devastating and raw, that would never go away. I lost track of Aiden's hands and how many times we kissed as our bodies moved, and in those moments, we finally found a way to make time stop.

CHAPTER THIRTY-THREE

Nothing…amazing happened on my birthday.

All morning, everyone watched me as if they expected me to sprout a second head or start floating to the rafters. And I didn't feel any different from last night. No additional marks of the Apollyon popped up. The existing ones didn't tingle. I tried to levitate a chair in the kitchen—it didn't happen, and I just felt stupid afterward. By the afternoon, the whole Awakening thing seemed very anticlimactic.

"Hey." Aiden popped his head into the bedroom. "You busy, birthday girl?"

I looked up from the magazine Luke had brought back from the store. "No. I'm just sort of hiding."

Aiden closed the door behind him quietly and smiled. "Why are you hiding?"

Shrugging, I closed the magazine and tossed it to the floor. "I kind of feel like an Apollyon failure."

"Why?" He sat beside me, eyes a soft heather gray.

"Everyone keeps watching me, waiting for something to

happen. Earlier, Marcus stared at me so long his eyes crossed. And while Solos was making lunch, he asked if I could heat up the soup with the fire element."

Aiden looked like he was trying not to laugh.

I smacked him on the arm. "It's not funny."

"I know." He drew in a deep breath, but his eyes danced with mirth.

"Okay. It is kind of funny."

My eyes narrowed on him. "I can take you, you know."

He leaned over, lips curving into a wolfish smile. "You can't take what you already have."

A heady feeling came from knowing that, but I socked him on the shoulder anyway. "Stop trying to sweet-talk me."

"I have something I wanted to show you." He reached into his pocket and pulled out a small box. "And then you have to come downstairs and stop hiding."

My eyes were glued to the box. It was plain white, but there was a red bow tied around it. Thoughts of jewelry stores danced in my head. "What is that?"

Aiden placed it in my hand. "It's your birthday, Alex. What do you think it is?"

I looked up, meeting his gaze. "You didn't have to get me anything."

"I know. I wanted to."

I slid off the lid, hooking that soft material of the satin ribbon with my pinky. Upon opening the box, I immediately choked up. "Oh, wow. This…this is so beautiful."

Nestled against more satin, a dark-red crystal had been intricately designed into a rose in bloom, carved as if the petals were reaching up toward the sun. It hung from a delicate silver chain that complemented its beauty. I plucked it from the box. Lights winked and danced off the precious stone, and it immediately warmed to my skin.

"Aiden, it's… Where did you find something like this?"

"I made it." The tips of his cheeks flushed. "Do you like it?"

"You *made* this?" My eyes widened. I breathed a little harder. It was remarkable that he could craft something so astonishing. "I love it! When did you make something like this?"

"A while back," he said, cheeks reddening further. "After you gave me the pick, actually. I wasn't sure I'd ever…get to give it to you. I mean, I just started making it one day and the more it took shape, I thought of you. I was just going to leave it in your dorm, but then everything happened…" He trailed off, looking contrite. "I'm just going to stop talking now."

I stared at him wordlessly.

"Are you sure you like it?"

Climbing to my knees, I threw my arms around his neck. I clenched the rose in my hand as I kissed his cheek. "I love it, Aiden. It's perfect. Beautiful."

He laughed softly, gently untangling my choke hold. "Here, let me help you put it on."

I popped around obediently and held up my hair. Aiden clasped the chain behind my neck, letting the crystal rose settle above my chest. The weight of it felt wonderful. I reached up, running my fingers over the delicate edges. Then I sprang around and tackled Aiden.

Laughing, he caught me before we both tumbled off the bed. "I guess you do like it."

I pushed him down and kissed him. "I love it. I love you."

Aiden reached up, tucking my hair back as his molten stare pierced me to my core. "I know what you're thinking."

"Great minds think alike."

"Later," he growled.

I started to protest, but he rolled me to my feet. "Boo."

He gave me a cheeky grin. "You have to come downstairs."

"I do?"

"Yes. So don't argue with me."

"Fine. Only because you're wonderful and this necklace is beautiful." I paused, nudging him with my hip. "And because you're sexy."

Aiden ushered me out of the room after that. Before I reached the stairs, I tucked the necklace under my shirt. People may know or suspect something, but I wasn't about to broadcast it, even though I wanted to shove the necklace in everyone's face and make them coo over it.

I followed Aiden into the kitchen. My steps slowed as I saw *everyone* gathered around the table. "What's going…?"

Deacon and Luke stepped to the side. "Happy Birthday!" they cried in unison.

My gaze fell to the table. There sat a birthday cake, decorated with eighteen burning candles and…*Spider-Man*? Yep, it was Spider-Man. Red and blue tights and all.

"It was either that or My Little Pony," Luke said, grinning. "We figured you'd appreciate Spider-Man more."

"Plus, he's all wicked cool with the whole climbing buildings stuff," Deacon added. "Maybe one day, when you decide to Awaken, you'll be just as cool."

"I lit the candles," Solos said, shrugging. "All by myself."

"I gave them the money." Marcus folded his arms. "Therefore, I was the key part of all of this."

"And we got grape soda." Luke gestured at the bottles of soda. "It's your favorite."

"This…this is…wow." My eyes found Lea, sitting behind

Solos. Her hair was pulled back from her face, eyes still swollen. She caught my eyes and smiled just a little. "This is great. You guys are awesome. Really."

Deacon grinned. "You've got to blow out the candles and make a wish."

What to wish for? I smiled. That was easy. As I crept to the table, I blew out the candles and wished that all of us made it out of this alive, including Seth.

"I want the spiderweb!" Deacon yelled as I stepped back, producing a supersized knife.

"Yikes." I stepped back into Aiden.

"It's her birthday." Luke took the knife from him. "She gets to pick what piece she wants first."

I laughed. "It's okay. He can have the spiderweb. I'll take the head."

We set about carving the cake and passing around grape soda. I was overwhelmed by everyone. I hadn't expected much of anything on my birthday except weird looks, but this was amazing. It was easy to forget about everything and what today symbolized. Here, surrounded by friends, things were sort of…normal.

Normal for a bunch of halfs and pures celebrating a birthday.

Okay. It wasn't normal at all, but it was just my kind of abnormal.

Huddled around the table, we laughed as we shared cake and grape soda. Lea perked up a little, nibbling on the frosting. The boys continued to give me crap about not Awakening yet, which Aiden tried to put a stop to. It was cute watching him try not to be overly defensive or protective of me. Not like I needed him to, though I think it was just second nature to him. He was the same with Deacon…when Deacon wasn't wielding a six-inch knife.

Toward the end of the birthday celebration, there was a distinctive *pop!* from the rec room. We all twisted around. I prayed the rune worked on the house because there was definitely a god here.

Apollo strolled into the kitchen. The first thing I noticed was that his eyes were blue and not that creepy white. "How is my birthday girl?"

For some reason, I blushed to the roots of my hair. "Doing good, grandpa."

He smirked as he slid into the seat beside me, easily prying the knife from Deacon's fingers. "I do not look nearly old enough to be what I am to you."

That was true. He looked like he was in his mid-twenties, which made it all the freakier. "So, when were you going to tell me that you spawned me?"

"I did not spawn you. I spawned a demigod centuries ago who eventually spawned your mother."

"Can you guys stop saying 'spawn'?" asked Luke.

Apollo shrugged as he carved off an edge of the cake. He handed the knife back to an oddly subdued Deacon. "I did not find it necessary to tell you. It is not like I am going to be bouncing little Alex babies on my knee."

The soda caught in my throat, and I almost spit it back up. Someone chuckled, and it sounded like Luke. "Yeah, that's not going to happen."

"My sister should have kept that to herself." He took a bite of the cake, made a face, and then pushed his plate away. "Our familial tie is not what is important here."

I frowned.

"You know what, guys?" Solos clapped his hands on Deacon's and Luke's shoulders. "I bet I can take you both at air hockey and make you call me 'mama.'"

Luke snorted. "Not likely."

Solos dragged the boys from the room, but Lea sat back in the chair and folded her arms. Her eyes dared anyone to tell her to leave. Now that was the Lea I was familiar with.

"Do you remember when you went to Marcus after Grandma Piperi passed on?" Apollo reached for the bottle of soda.

"Yes." I handed him a cup, wondering where he was going with this. "Kind of hard to forget that day."

"Humph." He sniffed the top of the bottle, shrugged, and then poured himself a small amount. "Well, then you should also realize that there is another oracle."

I glanced at Marcus. He arched a brow as he leaned against the counter. "What does that oracle have to do with this?" he asked.

I thought of Kari. "But didn't she pass on, too?" After a few strange looks, I explained. "I met her in the Underworld. She said she knew what was going to happen."

Apollo nodded. "She had a few visions before her…departure. Probably had something to do with your own untimely visit to the Underworld. See, the thing about oracles is that they…own their visions. What they see is not seen by others, and I can only see what the oracle tells me." He lifted the plastic cup, took a tentative sip, and immediately made a face. Guess grape soda wasn't his thing.

"It is part of how it all works—why we need an oracle at all, instead of me just knowing the future," he continued, looking up at me. "Did she say anything to you while you were there?"

I shook my head. "Just that she knew she would meet me and…and that she knew how it ended. And knowing how it ends doesn't really tell me what to do."

Apollo grimaced. "Figures the dead oracle would know. And Hades is not about to let me go down and talk to her now, not after the thing with my sister. Prophecies are always changing. Nothing is set in stone."

"Artemis said that." Aiden sat beside Lea. "Has the prophecy changed?"

"Not exactly."

My patience was running thin. "So, what's going on, Apollo? Artemis said there was still hope, and she mentioned something about the prophecy. Can you just, I don't know, get to the point?"

"The new oracle has not had any visions, so the last is tied to the dead one. So, all we have to work off of is what we know." His lips quirked into a half smile. "Some of us believe that you will be able to stop Seth. The prophecy—"

"I know what the prophecy says—one to save and one to destroy. I get that, but what I don't get is why any of you would risk Seth going all Godzilla on you guys. Eliminating me does eliminate the problem." I ignored Aiden's dangerous look as I stood. "There's something more to this. You know something else."

"And you know the prophecy says there can only be one of you. There is no way around that." Apollo leaned back, letting his arms drop over the back of his chair. "Do you really think all of this was Lucian's idea? That he knew about you without anyone telling him? That he has gained as much support as he has based on his charm alone?"

I started pacing. "I wouldn't give Lucian that much credit."

"Good. Because he has had help, I am sure of it," Apollo said. "Which means stopping Seth from becoming the God Killer does not fix the overall problem. The god behind this will just find another way to push Olympus to the brink of all-out war, and if that happens, it will spill into the mortal realm. What you saw Poseidon do? That will be nothing in comparison to what can happen."

"That's just great." I was going to wear a path in the kitchen floor at the rate I was going. "Do you have an idea of who this god is?"

"There are many of us who like to cause discord and chaos for the fun of it."

"Hermes," Marcus said. All eyes turned to him. He raised his brows expectantly. "Hermes is known for creating mayhem and mischief—chaos." No one said anything. Marcus shook his head. "Didn't any of you pay attention in your Greek Legends class?"

"Getting Lucian to turn on the Council and the gods isn't mischief," Aiden said. "And why would Hermes want to do that? Isn't he putting himself at risk from Seth?"

"Not if Hermes controls Lucian." I stopped. A sick feeling crawled down my spine. "Lucian controls Seth…completely. He'd be safe."

"Hermes has always been Zeus's personal joke and punching bag." Apollo stood and moved around the table. At the bay window, he grew pensive. "And as of late, Hermes has been…missing. I was unaware of this because I was here so much. You see, we all come and go, never staying away from Olympus for too long."

Marcus tensed. "Do you think it's possible that Hermes has been around us?"

He looked over his shoulder at us. Strands of blond hair fell forward, shielding half his face. "Like I said before, if the other god made sure we did not cross paths, it is possible. Keep in mind, it may not be Hermes. It could be any of us. Whoever it is will need to be stopped."

I stared at him, wondering how Apollo expected any of us to stop a god. Only Seth would be able to, and he wasn't playing for our team right now.

"How can she stop him?" Lea asked, her voice hoarse. "How can she stop Seth? Isn't that the point of all of this?"

Apollo gave her a little smile. "That is the point. Alexandria would have to kill him once she Awakens."

CHAPTER THIRTY-FOUR

I couldn't have heard him right. There was no way. "What?" Apollo turned back to the window. "You would have to kill him, Alexandria. As an Apollyon, you will be able to."

The idea of killing Seth horrified and sickened me. There was no way I could do that. I ran my hand over my face, feeling nauseous. "I can't do that."

"You can't?" Lea stared, her eyes glistening in the light. "He killed my sister, Alex! He killed those Council members."

"I know, but it's…it's not his fault. Lucian has warped his mind." And he'd hesitated before he took out the Council. I'd seen that. For a moment, the Seth I knew didn't want to do it, but afterward…he'd looked thrilled. "It wasn't his fault."

And it sounded like I was trying to convince myself.

Lea's lips thinned. "That doesn't make what he did okay."

"I know that, but…" But I couldn't kill Seth. I sat in the chair heavily, staring at the remains of Spider-Man. "There has to be another way."

"I know a part of you cares for him," Apollo said quietly.

"You were...built to feel that way. A part of him is you and vice versa, but it is the only way."

I met his eyes for a long second, and then Apollo looked away. A shadow passed over his face. A strange, almost-bad taste sprang up in the back of my mouth. "Is there another way, Apollo?"

"Does it matter?" Lea slammed her hands down on the table, causing me to jump. "He needs to die, Alex."

I flinched.

"Lea," Marcus said gently.

"No! I'm not going to shut up about this!" She shot to her feet, coming alive. "I know it doesn't seem fair, Alex. But Seth killed those people—*my sister*. And that wasn't fair."

My throat closed up. Lea had a point. There was no arguing that, but she hadn't seen what I'd seen...and she didn't know Seth. Then again, maybe I didn't even know him.

"And it sucks," Lea continued. Her hands balled into fists that shook. "I even thought Seth was hot, but that was up until he *incinerated* my sister. You like him. That's great. You're a part of him. Awesome. But he killed people, Alex."

"I understand that, Lea." I looked around the room, my gaze settling on Aiden. "Everyone keeps saying there's hope. Maybe we can save him. And Artemis mentioned something about power going both ways. Maybe there is something to that."

Pain flickered in his silver eyes, and then I remembered his words and my own realization. *Sometimes you have to know when to let hope go.*

She sucked in a sharp breath as she clearly struggled to rein her anger and sorrow back in. "You loved your mom, right? You loved her even after she became a daimon."

"Lea," Aiden cut in sharply.

"But you knew she needed to…needed to be stopped." She rushed on before Aiden could shut her up. "You loved her, but you did the right thing. How is this any different?"

I recoiled from the table. Her words were like a punch in the stomach because they were true. How was this any different? I had done the right thing with my mom, so why was it so hard for me to understand why this needed to be done now?

"I think that's enough for today," Marcus interjected.

Lea stood her ground for a few more seconds, but then stormed out of the room. Part of me wanted to go after her and try to explain myself, but I had enough common sense to know that wouldn't be wise.

"She's in a dark place right now," Marcus said. "She hurts. Maybe later she'll understand that this is hard for you, also."

"It's not as hard as it is for her." I tucked my hair back. "I just can't… The idea of killing him makes me sick. There has to be another way."

Apollo glided toward me. "All of this…can wait. Today is your birthday, your Awakening."

"Yeah, well, I don't know what's going on with that." I stared at the runes on my palms. They glowed faintly. Nothing had changed about them. "I feel the same. Nothing's happened."

"When were you born?" Apollo asked.

"Uh, March the fourth."

He arched a brow. "What time, Alexandria? What was the time of your birth?"

I pursed my lips. "I don't know."

A dubious look crossed Apollo's face. "You don't know what time you were born?"

"No. Do people know that?"

"I was born at 6:15 a.m.," Aiden said, trying to hide his grin. "Deacon was born at 12:55 p.m. Our parents told us."

My eyes narrowed. "Well, no one told me…or I forgot."

"Marcus?" Apollo asked.

He shook his head. "I don't…recall."

"Well, you obviously have not hit your time of birth yet." Apollo pushed away from the window. "I think we have had enough serious talk for the day. It is, after all, your birthday. A time for celebration, not making plans for battle."

I shuddered.

"You will be fine." Apollo placed his hand on my shoulder and squeezed. That was the closest offer of comfort I'd probably ever get from Apollo, and that was fine with me. "You do not feel the bond from where we are, so he cannot connect with you. You will be fine."

I kept watching the clock. When had I been born? I had no clue. It was almost 8:30 in the evening, and not a damn thing had happened. Maybe I was doing something wrong?

"Stop it." Aiden grabbed my hand, pulling it away from my mouth. "Since when did you become a nail-biter?"

I shrugged. We were sitting on the couch in the small sunroom. Outside the window, it looked like a winter wonderland. Night had already fallen and moonlight reflected off the untouched snow that covered the deck and trees.

"Do you think I'm weak?" I asked.

"What?" He tugged me over so that I was in his lap. "Good gods, you're one of the strongest people I know."

I glanced at the closed door, but then figured *oh, what the hell.* Allowing myself to relax, I rested my cheek against his chest and pulled the rose out from under my shirt. "I don't feel very strong."

Aiden settled his arms around me. "Because of what everyone was talking about today?"

I traced my fingers over the edges of the rose. "Lea had a point, you know? I faced down my mom, but I can't…do that with Seth."

"Apollo was right." He placed his chin atop my head. "He's a part of you. In a way, it's different than what happened with your mom."

"It is different. My mom was a daimon and there was no coming back from that." I sighed, closing my eyes. I saw Seth's face as I begged him, the indecision in his eyes. "He's still in there, Aiden. There has to be another way. And I think Apollo knows, but he's not telling us."

"Then we'll talk to Apollo. He mentioned the oracle, and maybe something has changed." He shifted slightly, and then I felt his lips against my forehead. "But if there isn't another way…"

"Then I have to face it. I know. I just want to make sure before we decide he needs to be…killed."

Aiden placed one of his hands over mine. "Maybe we need to go see this new oracle. Who knows? She may be able to tell us something, visions or not."

"That is if we can get Apollo to tell us."

"We will."

I smiled up at Aiden. "You're amazing."

He grinned. "What makes you say that?"

"You're easily the most sup—*ow!*" I hissed as I jerked my hand free from his. "Something stung me."

He straightened a bit and grabbed my wrist. "Alex, you're bleeding."

Tiny pricks of blood covered the top of my left hand, but that wasn't what I was staring at. There was a blue glyph taking shape, forming something that looked like a music note.

My pulse pounded as I sat up quickly, scanning the room. A clock shaped like an owl showed that the time was 8:47 p.m. "It's happening."

Aiden said something, but another burst of hot, fiery pain stung just below that mark, and blood beaded on my skin. I pulled free from Aiden, my legs shaking as I stood. "Oh, my gods..."

"Alex..." He came to his feet, eyes wide. "What can I do?"

"I don't know. I didn't—" I gasped as pain shot across my arm. Right in front of my eyes, more blood appeared. Just tiny drops, as if I was under a tattoo needle... "Oh gods, the marks—the marks are like tattoos." This hadn't happened with the other marks—the ones Seth had brought out early.

"*Gods.*" Aiden reached for me, but I backed away. He swallowed as my eyes met his. "Alex, it's going to be okay."

My heart was racing, double-quick. Pure terror flooded my stomach. The marks would be *everywhere* once complete, and it was coming so, so fast. Pain spread up my neck, dampening my skin. When it reached my face, I screamed and hit the floor. On my knees, I doubled over, my hands curling in the air around my cheeks.

"Oh...oh man, this is gonna blow." I struggled for air.

Aiden was beside me immediately, his hands reaching for me but not coming into contact. "Just...take a deep breath, Alex. Breathe with me."

My laugh came out strangled. "I'm...I'm not having a baby, Aiden. This is—" Sharp bites of pain swept down my back, and I screamed again. I placed my hands on the floor, trying to draw in a deep breath. "Okay...okay, I'm breathing."

"Good. You're doing really good." Aiden inched closer. "You know that, agapi mou. You're doing great."

As my back bowed, it didn't feel that way. I'd rather face down a hundred aether-starved daimons plus a legion of Instructors than this. Tears leaked from my eyes as the marking continued lower. My legs gave out, and with Aiden's help, I lay down on my stomach.

The door opened, and I heard Marcus. "What the—oh, my gods, is she okay?"

My face hurt too badly to stay like this, but the skin on my back felt raw. "Shit…"

"She's Awakening," Aiden said, voice tight.

"But the blood…" I heard Marcus move closer. "Why is she bleeding?"

I eased onto my side. "I'm being tattooed by a giant, mother fu—" Another strangled scream cut off my words as a different type of pain settled in, moving under my skin. It was like lightning racing through my veins, frying every nerve ending.

"This is… Wow," Deacon said, and I pried my eyes open. There was a whole audience by the door.

"Get them out of here!" I screamed, jackknifing on the floor. "Gods, this sucks!"

"Whoa," I heard Deacon murmur. "This is like watching a chick give birth or something."

"Oh, my gods, I'm going to kill him." I could feel the beads of blood breaking out under my jeans. "I'm going to punch him—"

"Everyone leave," Aiden ground out. "This isn't a godsdamn show."

"And I think he's like the father," Luke said.

Aiden rose to his feet. "Get. Out."

A few seconds later, the door closed. I thought we were alone until I heard Marcus speak. "She's my niece. I'm staying." I heard him come closer. "Is it…is it supposed to be like this?"

"I don't know." Aiden's voice sounded strained, near panicked. "Alex?"

"Okay," I breathed. "Just…just don't talk. No one—" It moved up my front, searing my skin. I jerked up, hands shaking.

Holy crap. I couldn't breathe. Pain was everything. I was going to kill Seth. Not once had he told me that the Awakening would feel like *this*—like the skin was being filleted from my bones.

My body buckled as another wave of pain rippled through me. I didn't remember hitting the floor or Aiden pulling me into his lap, but when I opened my eyes, he was there, above me. Skin somewhere, where I wasn't sure anymore, caught fire. Another mark was being tattooed. I couldn't hold the cry back, but when it leaked from my lips, it was nothing more than a whimper.

"It's okay. I'm here." Aiden smoothed the hair off my damp forehead. "It's almost over."

"It is?" I gasped as I stared up at him, squeezing his hand until I felt his bones rub. "How in the fuck do you know? Have you ever Awakened before? Is there something—" My own hoarse, weak scream interrupted my tirade. "Oh gods, I'm…I'm so sorry. I didn't mean to cuss at you. It just…"

"I know. It hurts." Aiden's gaze drifted over me. "It can't be much longer."

I squeezed my eyes shut as I curled toward Aiden. His soothing gestures helped ease some of the pain. I stiffened as blinding light flashed behind my eyes. A rushing filled my ears, and I could suddenly see the blue cord so strongly in my mind.

It was like a switch had been thrown.

Information rushed me all at once. Thousands of years of the Apollyon memories dumped into me just like Seth had eventually admitted they would. Like a digital download, I couldn't keep up with it. Most of it didn't make any sense. The words were in a different language—the one Aiden spoke so beautifully. The knowledge of how the Apollyon was born passed onto me, as did the nature of the elements and of the fifth and final one. Images flickered in and out—battles won and long since lost. I saw—I felt—akasha shooting through someone's veins for the first time, igniting and destroying. Saving—saving all those lives. And the gods—I saw them through the eyes of the past Apollyons. There was a relationship there, strained and full of mutual distrust, but there was—and then I saw her. I knew it was Solaris, felt it in my core.

I saw her turning on a beautiful boy, raising her hands as she whispered words—powerful words. Akasha flared from her, and I knew in an instant that she had turned on the First. Not to kill him, because there was infinite love in her eyes, but to subdue him, to stop him. I grasped at the information, but it moved on through the years until the First... *the First*.

The cord was snapping, rushing out through space and distance, seeking, always seeking. I couldn't stop it, didn't know how to. An amber-colored glow covered everything. In a burst of swirling lights, a hazy face came into focus. The natural arch of his golden eyebrows, the wicked tilt to his lips and slant of his cheekbones were all painfully familiar. I couldn't tell where he was. He shouldn't have been there. We were too far apart.

But at the end of the cord, I saw Seth and I wept.

I knew in an instant that the distance between us had meant nothing when it came to our bond. It may have diminished our ability to feel each other, but it couldn't prevent this. Not with the four marks, not when he had pulled on my own power. And I also knew Seth *had* planned this…just in case I fled.

A pulse of light went through my cord and I felt *it*—felt *him*—breaking through my shields, filling me, becoming a part of me. It took just a second—*a second* and I was surrounded by him. I *was* him. There was no me in here, there was no room. It was all about him, always had been.

I couldn't breathe anymore. He was there, under my skin, his heart beating next to mine. His thoughts were mixing with my own until all I could hear was him.

He opened his eyes. A light that had never been there before glowed from behind them.

Seth smiled.

Light crackled and flashed, and the world fell away.

I was shaking—*no*. I was being shaken. The pain receded slowly, leaving behind a raw stinging that covered every inch of my body. That, too, faded as my body was rocked back and forth. There were voices droning in the background, overshadowing the soothing words being whispered.

I inhaled deeply, breathing for what felt like the first time. There was so much in the air around me. The heavy scent of pine tainted the edges. I tasted spice and sea salt on the tip of my tongue.

"Agapi mou, open your eyes and talk to me."

My eyes fluttered open. Everything…everything looked different—sharper and magnified. Lights dazzled, and colors shimmered in amber. I focused on the man cradling me. Eyes the color of heated silver stared down at me. They widened, pupils dilating. Shock shot across his striking features.

"No." That one word sounded like it had been torn from the depths of Aiden's soul.

A popping sound filled the room. Footsteps encroached upon us. Shapes came into focus, one burning brighter than the other.

Apollo peered over Aiden's shoulder and swore. "Let her go, Aiden."

His arms tightened around me instead, holding me close to his chest. *To the end*, I thought…foolishly brave and loyal *to the end…*

"Let her go now." A door slammed shut somewhere behind the shining god. "She's connected with the First."

The First—my whole purpose for existing. Mine. My other half. He was here, waiting. Already inside me, seeing what I was seeing, whispering to me, promising me that he was coming. *Seth.* Mine.

And they all were going to die. I smiled.

ELIXIR

A COVENANT NOVELLA

PRONUNCIATION GUIDE FOR ELIXIR

Aether: EE-ther
Ananke: ah-NAN-key
Agapi: ah-GAH-pee
Apollyon: a-POL-ee-on
Atropos: ah-TRO-poes
Clotho: KLO-tho
Daimon: DEE-mun
Hematoi: HEM-a-toy
Khalkotauroi: kal-koh-TOR-oy

CHAPTER ONE

Alex clenched the titanium bars honed by Hephaestus and Apollo, amber-colored eyes burning with hate. But those eyes…they didn't belong to Alex.

Alex's eyes were warm and brown like good whiskey. I'd memorized those eyes the first time I saw them in that warehouse in Atlanta. This was a different creature entirely.

When we'd moved her to the safe house deep in Apple River, Illinois, we'd almost lost her. None of us, including me, had been ready for the full display of her power. If Apollo hadn't finagled Hephaestus—the only god who could build something that could withstand the Apollyon—into creating a room to keep Alex in, we wouldn't have been able to control her.

"If you don't let me out of here, I'm going to rip your brother's ribs out and wear them as a crown."

I showed no emotion. Perhaps I'd grown used to the intimidations over the last couple of days. Threatening to kill Deacon was one of Alex's favorites. She'd grow bored with it soon enough. It hadn't been like that at first. She'd been… almost normal, except for her amber-colored eyes. She'd talked and sounded like Alex.

Cracked jokes like Alex. Argued like Alex. And she'd reasoned like Alex.

She clenched the titanium bars. Each bar had been encased with an unbreakable chain-link net that Hephaestus had used on Aphrodite once. Not even the Apollyon could break through it.

Above her, several marks had been carved into the cement, neutralizing most of her newly discovered abilities—not fully stopping her, but enough that she wasn't a danger to herself or others.

For now.

My blood boiled at the memory of what'd happened after she'd Awakened. She'd connected with the First—Seth—and there was no doubt in anyone's mind that she'd given up her location. I'd completely understood that she needed to be moved and quickly, but I didn't agree with how Apollo had done it.

He'd hit her with a god-bolt. And I'd punched him.

I was still surprised that I was alive.

"Do you know how it's going to feel when you stand there and watch me do it?" she taunted. "Just like you stood there and watched your parents get slaughtered by daimons, but this will be much, much sweeter."

I folded my arms.

Exhaling slowly, she lowered her head and blinked back tears. "Please. Aiden, *please* let me out of here."

I closed my eyes. A muscle spasmed along my jaw. This… this tactic was the hardest.

"Why are you treating me like this? I don't feel good. I hurt. Why did you let them hurt me like this?"

My eyes flew open. Every muscle in my body went rigid. Tears spilled down her cheeks, and for a moment—just a moment—I forgot that it wasn't really Alex in there, pleading and begging.

"I thought you loved me?"

I moved so fast I startled her. My hands shot through the bars, clasping the sides of her face. My forehead pressed against the cold bars and my lips were on hers. The kiss was hard and fast. Angry. Desperate. She went still, unsure of how to respond. Several times in the past forty-eight hours it had been the only way to shut her up.

I pulled back, releasing her. "Because I love you, I won't release you."

Frustration rolled off her and threatened to tear the skin from *my* bones. The teary gaze was gone in an instant. Alex screamed and threw herself to the back of the cell. Ten feet away from the bars, she leaned against the wall, back bowed. "You can't keep me in here forever."

"I can try."

"He's coming for me."

"He'll never find you," I said, sitting down in the metal chair placed before the cell. I'd made sure she had everything she needed in there—a small bathroom off the one room, a bed that she'd destroyed and had been stripped down to just a mattress, and clothing.

Alex laughed, pushing off the wall. "You can't take him."

My gaze fell to the untouched plate of food by the barred door. "Eat, Alex. You need to eat."

"You can never be *him*."

I rubbed the growth of facial hair along my jaw as she slowly approached the plate of food and hope sparked deep inside me. She hadn't eaten in the four days since she'd

Awakened. I had no idea how she was still walking around. Picking up the plate of food, she backed away.

"Are you going to eat the food this time?" I asked wearily.

Alex smiled and then threw the plate directly at where I sat. Plastic crashed against titanium before clattering on the floor. Pieces of food—maybe mashed potatoes and some kind of meat—made it through the bars, splattering my chest and cheek. We'd stopped giving her ceramic plates after she'd tried to turn the broken shards into weapons.

Drawing on patience I was running out of, I slowly knocked the chunks of food off me. "Did that make you feel better, Alex?"

She pouted. "Not really." Then she started pacing, her movements fluid and spellbinding in spite of the fact she'd thrown her dinner at me *again*. "I can't take this any longer. Let me out or, so help me, I will destroy you."

I shook my head. "Alex, you have to be in there. I know you. My heart would not be beating if you were truly gone."

Dropping onto the mattress, she growled. "Gods, isn't that just so sweet? My heart is all aflutter."

"There he is." I stood and grasped the bars, mirroring her earlier actions. "I wondered how long it would take to bring you out. Does my love for her bother you, Seth?"

She rolled onto her side, brows pinched and face pale. "Seth's not in here, you stupid pure-blood."

"It hurts when he's connected to you, doesn't it?"

"He's not in here!" she screamed, her voice cracking.

I knew she was lying. "He's there." I leaned against the bars. "I can see him in your eyes."

Alex curled, tucking her knees to her chest. A shiver rolled through her. I knew what she was doing—retreating inside herself, reaching out to Seth, making contact with him.

"Alex," I said.

Her hands curled into fists as she lifted her head. "Go away."

My eyes met hers. "Never."

"I hate you," she hissed, and she sounded like she meant it. "I hate you!"

"That's not true. Alex loves me."

She rolled her eyes. "I *am* Alex, you idiot. And I don't love you. I need—"

"You need Seth." Fire snapped through me as I gripped the bars until my knuckles ached. Deep down, I knew it wasn't just Seth that was forcing her to behave like this. Yeah, some of what she said was Seth to the core, but it was the *need* driving her. The need to be near the First was a tangible thing—potent and real.

I could taste it.

I remembered what the oracle had told her about need over the summer. Part of me hadn't fully understood it then, but I did now. Need was destroying her, destroying me.

"Need is not love, Alex."

Before Alex could respond, the door opened. "Oh!" She unfurled her legs and clapped her hands. "More visitors for little old me? I'm just so damn lucky. I'm tired of seeing *his* face."

Marcus, Alex's pure-blooded uncle, glanced at me. "I see she's in good spirits."

I snorted.

She rose to her feet, swaying unnaturally to the far right. The mattress, the last item left in the room, floated several feet off the floor. We'd removed everything else. Elemental use now came easily to her. She seemed to just will it to happen and it did. And gods, did she ever love doing it.

Marcus and I stared, morbidly fascinated with the display. It was stronger than yesterday, which meant the protective magic was wearing off. Hephaestus would need to make another visit and soon.

"Where is here?" She pushed with those words, fueling them with power.

I stepped back as her words rippled through me, breathed inside me. Forcing myself to break eye contact with Alex, I turned to Marcus. His eyes were glazed over and vacant. He was seconds away from spilling our location. I placed my hand on Marcus's shoulder.

He blinked, and then swore. "Is it just me or is she getting better at that?"

Alex giggled, and it sounded off, reminding me of that creepy little boy in *Pet Sematary*. The one who ran around killing people with a scalpel.

"I think so. You'd think she'd grow weaker, since she hasn't eaten a damn thing." I watched her move back to the mattress. She stopped, glancing over her shoulder at us. Her eyes narrowed, and I couldn't wait to find out what she was up to now. "Anyway, we need to make sure *no one* comes down here."

Marcus nodded. The house was another piece of property owned by Solos's father, but this one had more Sentinel traffic, as some stopped in while traveling to new assignments. We had to keep the door to the basement sealed when strangers were in the house, which was often. The place was hopping with the most recent events. Many were being moved out of the west, heading either toward what was left of Deity Island or to the Covenant in New York.

"Marcus?" Alex faced us.

"Yes, Alexandria?"

One side of her lips tipped up as her gaze slid to mine.

"Does it bother you that Aiden and I have been, how do I put this? He's seen me naked? Multiple times."

Oh. Dear. Gods. Here we go again. Shaking my head, I scrubbed my hand over my eyes. "Alex..."

Marcus stiffened. "I've had time to come to terms with it. I can't say that I'm surprised, though." He glanced at me, scowling. "If there's a rule, you'll break it, Alex. But I didn't expect Aiden to be so..."

"Irresponsible?" she supplied helpfully, and I rolled my eyes. "And such a bastard to take advantage of me—your poor niece who has been through so much? He took advantage of me. Used a compulsion on me. He *forced* me."

My hand dropped to my side. Horror rolled through me, leaving me reeling. She didn't just...she had.

"He's a bastard," Marcus responded coolly, "but I doubt he took advantage of you or used a compulsion."

"Thanks," I muttered.

Alex shrugged as she drifted toward us. "He broke the rules. Shouldn't you be more upset?"

"Honestly, out of everything that is going on, that's the least of my worries." Marcus smiled, and her eyes flared a heated tawny color. "And really, if we are going to make a list tallying up how many rules have been broken, I think you top it."

"But *he* used a compulsion on a pure."

"And *you* killed one. Tit for tat, Alexandria." Although this wasn't the first time we'd had this conversation with Alex, it never failed to amaze me how calm Marcus remained through it.

"Then you should punish us." She leaned into the bars but kept her hands to her sides. "Rules are rules, uncle. Take us to the Council."

"We're not letting you out," I cut in. "Move on to something else, Alex."

She pulled her lips back and made a very real-sounding hiss. "How about you come in here?"

I flashed my teeth at her. "You'd like that, wouldn't you?"

Her hands flexed at her sides and she moved back from the bars, keeping her eyes trained on me. "I'd *love* it."

The door opened, spilling light down the concrete stairs. Marcus turned, but I kept my gaze on Alex. There was a challenge in her stare—a dare. She wanted to fight, and even with her elemental powers lagging, she'd be a hell of an opponent. More skilled than the last time I'd goaded her into fighting me. Thinking of that, I was reminded of how that fight had ended.

Alex had kissed me.

My stomach tightened, even though I knew it wouldn't end that way this time. If she got her hands on me, she'd try to kill me. I had to keep reminding myself of that. When connected to Seth, she wasn't the girl I'd admired when I'd seen her around the Covenant, or the one I'd fallen in love with.

"Marcus? Aiden?" Solos called from the top of the steps. "You guys down there?"

"Don't come down here," I reminded him, eyeing a suddenly alert Alex. Halfs were more susceptible to compulsions, and she packed one hell of a punch.

"Wasn't planning on it," he replied. "You guys are needed upstairs. Apollo's back."

Marcus shot me a look full of meaning, and then glanced at Alex before heading up the stairs. Apollo's arrival hopefully meant he'd found something to break the connection threading Alex and Seth together.

Alex shot toward the bars, gripping them. "Don't you dare leave me."

I heard Marcus's footfalls stop at the top of the steps. "I thought you were tired of my face, Alex."

Closing her eyes, she pressed her forehead against the bars. "I hate it in here. I can't take it. The silence… I hate the silence."

And I hated the razor edge of real pain in her voice.

The skin around her eyes crinkled as her brows knitted together. "Fine. Leave. I don't care. I hate you anyway."

Approaching the bars, I slipped my hand through. My fingers brushed aside the tangled mess of hair. Alex was so still I wasn't sure she was breathing as I found the chain and gently tugged it up so that the crystal rose was cradled in my palm.

She sucked in a sharp breath but didn't bolt.

"If you hated me, you would've destroyed this."

"Give me time and I will."

I laughed and let go of the rose. She opened her eyes, watching me warily. "No. You won't. As long as you wear that, I know there is still a part of you in there. That there is still hope."

Alex reached for the necklace, gripping it in a fist as she backed away. Instead of ripping it off her neck, she held onto it and retreated back to her mattress. Sitting down, she leaned against the wall and pulled her knees to her chest.

Hope grew like a fragile seedling, and I guarded it carefully. I pushed off the bars. "I'll bring you something to eat and drink later."

There was no answer, and I knew I wasn't going to get one. Pivoting around, I hurried up the stairs. Marcus and Solos waited in the narrow hallway.

"She still hasn't eaten?" Solos asked, rubbing his hand along the jagged scar that cut down his face from eye to jaw.

Walking past them, I shook my head. Her not eating was a

huge concern. Apollyon or not, she couldn't last much longer like this without lasting consequences.

Solos snapped at my heels. "We could always hold her down and force-feed her temperamental butt."

"You come within a foot of her, and she'll have you hanging yourself from the rafters in the basement." Marcus shot the half-blood Sentinel a dark look. "Don't even think it."

"Not to mention I'm sure she'd just vomit the food back up." I thrust my fingers through my hair as I headed toward the den. There was an unnatural stirring in the air, a fissure of power.

A god-like power.

"Heads up, guys, Apollo is *not* in a good mood," Solos announced, and my stomach sank. "I don't think he was successful in finding a way to break the bond. I hate to say it—"

I whirled so fast on the half-blood that he took an unsteady step back. "Then don't say it."

"Aiden," Marcus warned.

Solos held up his hands. "Look, all I'm saying is that we have to consider the possibility that we can't break the bond."

"There is nothing else to consider." I took a deep breath and searched for the patience I'd cultivated while raising my brother, but I couldn't find it. "We'll find a way."

"And if we don't?" Solos shot back, shaking his head. "Do we let her out of the cage so she and Seth can go all Bonnie-and-Clyde on the world? Or do we let her rot in the basement and starve to death?"

"Solos, I am warning you that it would be wise to stop," Marcus said.

"Don't get me wrong. I like Alex. I think she's a pretty cool kid," Solos went on. "But isn't it more humane to put her out of her misery instead—"

My fist connected with his jaw before I even knew what

I was doing. His head jerked back as he staggered to the side. I shot forward, grabbing him by his shirt, and slammed him into the wall, rattling several paintings.

"Aiden!" Marcus yelled.

"We are not going to harm Alex," I snarled, lifting the Sentinel onto the tips of his boots. "We aren't going to touch a hair on her head. Do you understand me?"

Solos's eyes bugged. "I know you love her—"

"You don't know shit. You sure as hell don't know the lengths I will go to keep her safe." I dropped him and he slumped against the wall. "And if that means killing one half-blood to make sure nothing happens to her, I won't hesitate."

"As entertaining as you going all *grrr* on Solos is, we need to talk," came Apollo's booming voice from inside the den. "So, knock it off, Aiden."

Solos straightened, cupping his jaw. "Aiden, I didn't mean—"

"Save it." I spun around and passed Marcus, storming into the den. Upon taking one look at Apollo, my eyes narrowed. "Don't say it."

"Oh, you going to hit me again? I kind of liked it that first time."

No way was I going there. I crossed the room and brushed back a heavy curtain. Night had fallen over the tall elm and oak trees. Their branches were still bare, like skeletons—a landscape I would've once found beautiful now seemed desolate and without hope.

"Have you discovered anything?" Marcus asked.

"I have, but we have bigger problems than Alex right now."

Facing both of them, I leaned against the cool windowpane. "How so?"

"Part of me is afraid to ask," Marcus said. Solos snickered, and then winced. Moving to the leather sofa, Marcus sat. "Because I really don't know what could be worse than Alex turning on all of us."

Apollo arched a brow. "Oh, this has it beat."

"Are you just dragging this out for dramatic effect?" My patience was seriously lacking.

The eerie whites of his eyes crackled, and the scent of burning ozone filled the room. Marcus shook his head, but I raised my brows, unfazed, because honestly, nothing really fazed me anymore.

Apollo's lips twitched into a smirk. "There's a war brewing."

CHAPTER TWO

Okay, I guessed it was kind of hard to top that. A dry, biting laugh escaped me as I pushed off the window. "A war?"

Now that he had everyone's attention, Apollo seemed to grow in height. "A war between the gods and those following the First."

Marcus cursed. He'd been doing that a lot lately. "The gods are going to take on Seth?"

"They're planning to take on Seth and anyone who stands with him." His lip curled with distaste. "That would include Lucian."

"There is no way Lucian could amass such a following." Solos leaned over the back of the couch. "Joining him would be insanity."

"But Lucian has the Apollyon. That alone holds an appeal." Marcus leaned back, looking as weary as I felt.

"You are correct," Apollo replied. "We have gained knowledge that many are siding with him."

"Do you have spies?" I asked, curious.

Apollo smiled, and it was just as creepy as Alex's childish giggle had been earlier. He snapped his fingers, and there was a burst of raw power that rolled through the room like a shock wave. A blue light shimmered beside Apollo, and a human shape began to take form.

A man—nearly seven feet tall, with a crop of spiky blond hair—appeared. He bore a striking resemblance to Apollo and shared the same, all-white eyes. Dressed in cargo shorts, flip flops, and a Jimmy Buffett shirt, he looked like a college dropout.

And he was a god.

Maybe one day I'd get used to gods popping in and out like there was no tomorrow, but after spending my entire life never seeing one, it was almost overwhelming to stand in the same room with some of the most powerful creatures to ever exist.

Apparently, some of the most pissed off, too.

Marcus shot to his feet quickly and bowed, along with Solos and me. Not that the god noticed. He turned to Apollo with a fierce scowl. "You snap your fingers and demand I just appear? Like I have nothing better to do?"

Apollo smirked. "Isn't that what happened?"

"I am not one of your servants, brother. Next time I will break that finger off and shove it so far up your—"

"We have an audience." Apollo gestured toward us, and I was sure we all wore the same expression of shock and awe. "And no one wants to hear about the things you like to do in your spare time, Dionysus."

The God of Wine and Nonstop Partying laughed at his brother and dropped into a chair. He stretched out his long legs and rubbed the scruff along his chin. "The least you could do is make sure I have some refreshments here."

Marcus jerked to attention. "We can get something. There's wine—"

"Not necessary." Apollo's eyes narrowed. "And the least you can do is hold a conversation for five minutes without being drunk."

"Whatever." Dionysus turned his head toward us and chuckled. Part of me wondered if he was drunk now. "Two pure-bloods and a half, but there's something much, much more in this house." His eyes flared as he sniffed the air. "Ah, yes, the little female Apollyon is here."

I stiffened at the obvious sound of interest in Dionysus's voice.

Apollo shot me a look, one that warned that no other god would be as tolerant as he'd been when it came to throwing punches. "You know she's here and you know that's not why you're here."

"Is that why you had Ananke in a tizzy this morning?" Dionysus smiled gamely.

At the sound of Ananke's name, a thousand violent emotions roared alive inside me. I started to move but stopped. Coiled tension locked up my muscles. Apollo wouldn't dare. Even Solos had paled. Everyone knew who and what Ananke presided over, and it didn't bode well for Alex. Rage rendered me speechless, and before I could recover, Marcus spoke.

"Why are you involving Ananke?"

Apollo waved him off. "Now is not the time to discuss that. Dionysus has gained information that has all of Olympus preparing for war."

Dionysus yawned. "As much as politics and blood bore me, I am of great use when it comes to gleaning information from those who are in the know."

"Wine and drink," Solos murmured.

"Loosen the tongue," Dionysus finished, grinning. "There is an encampment of sorts surrounding the movement of

Lucian and the First. Damn near the size of an army. They have moved to just outside the Tennessee Covenant. My brothers and sisters are watching them closely."

Dammit. If Seth and Lucian went after the Council there, the gods would retaliate again, and more innocent lives would be lost.

"There are over a hundred half-blood Sentinels and Guards with them," he added as an afterthought.

"Dear gods," Solos muttered, rubbing his temple.

"Whatever the two are selling, those people are buying like crack addicts." Dionysus studied his fingernails, appearing bored. "No offense, but the halfs are like idiot cousins if they truly believe siding against us is wise."

I didn't have to look at Solos to know that comment didn't sit well with him. "Lucian is probably offering them the one thing no one ever has."

"And that is?" Dionysus asked.

"Freedom." I sat on the arm of the couch. "The freedom to do as they please and to not be indebted to the pures in any form."

"But this one is free, is he not?" Dionysus gestured at Solos.

"Free?" Solos straightened. "If I may be blunt?"

"Sure," the god replied. "Why not?"

Solos took a shallow breath. "Becoming a Sentinel was the lesser of two evils. My choices were to allow myself to become indentured and have everything that I am stripped away from me, or this life, which is one that most likely ensures an early grave. How is that freedom?"

Dionysus's brows knitted. "Do you not feel that your duty is honorable enough?"

"It has nothing to do with his duty," I cut in, glancing at

Apollo. "The halfs who are Guards and Sentinels believe in their duties and will give their lives for them, but we haven't given them any choice—not the same kind of choice I had. And if Lucian is tempting them with the idea of choosing their own destinies, then can we really blame them?"

"I understand that desire, Aiden, and maybe there is a need for change, but we cannot allow Lucian to lead them to war against us," Apollo said. "And I know what you're thinking—that those following him are innocent in their naïveté, but that does not change the outcome if they go against us."

"Which is exactly what they're planning," Dionysus said, much to everyone's dismay. "A night ago, I made sure several halfs who were with Lucian were well-stocked in the whiskey department and sent in a few of my…girls. I've learned that they are planning to make a move on the New York Covenant but are waiting for Seth and his little girlfriend."

My teeth were going to break from how hard I was clenching them. Marcus leaned forward, clasping his hands together. "What I don't understand is how none of you can take out Lucian."

"We can't get near him. He is always accompanied by the First." Dionysus shrugged. "And we cannot harm *him*, but he can harm us."

"A few bruises," I said. "Without him being at full power, he can't kill you."

Dionysus's brows rose. "He killed Thanatos's furie."

"By draining Alex of her power," I argued. "Without her near, he can't tap into that."

"We won't take the risk." Apollo leaned against the seat. "He can put us out of commission. If one of us is weakened, so are we all."

"The family that—"

"Anyway," Apollo cut Dionysus off. "According to what he has learned, they're planning a full assault on all the Covenants. We cannot allow that."

"So, what does Olympus plan?" Marcus asked, shoulders bending as if the weight of this conflict rested on them.

"See, there's the pickle." Hearing the word "pickle" come out of Dionysus's mouth just seemed wrong. "We plan to go to war, but there is dissension among the fearless leaders."

"What kind of dissension?" I rubbed the heel of my palm over my temple, pressing against a dull ache no doubt brought on by lack of food.

"Six want to annihilate the problem," Dionysus said casually, as if he were discussing where he got his gaudy-ass shirt.

"Go after Lucian and those supporting him?" Solos asked. "Take as many out as possible?"

Apollo nodded. "The rest of us believe there is still hope that a full-scale war can be avoided, because if we do go to war, what happened with the Titans will have nothing on this. The body count will include mortals—possibly millions of them. There is no way that can be avoided."

There is still hope. Those four words brought forth images of Alex cradled against my chest, talking about Seth just a few short weeks ago. She'd had hope for him—right up to the moment he'd connected with her.

"Not to mention the risk of exposure," added Marcus. "Gods, this is…"

There were no words.

It sort of struck me then. None of us—not even the two gods—really had foreseen this a year ago. The prophecies hadn't predicted that the world would be on the verge of a war the likes of which had never been seen before—a war that would rip this world apart.

"We believe that the war can be stopped," Apollo continued, "but the others are doubtful, especially with the most recent events."

"Alex," I whispered, now accustomed to the pang that shot across my chest.

Dionysus stood. "Many were willing to stay out of it, even after what the First did to the North Carolina Council. Only Poseidon and Hades were quick to respond, but now that she's connected, they have no hope. And they are searching..."

Unease stirred and spread like a weed. "Searching for what?"

With a sigh, Apollo said, "A way to kill the Apollyons."

CHAPTER THREE

I worked at keeping my expression blank and my temper in check, but anger was tearing through me, shredding my control. It took everything in me not to leave the room and go downstairs to keep vigil over Alex.

Solos eyed me and cleared his throat. "I was under the impression that only the Apollyons can kill one another."

My hands balled into fists as Apollo turned to me. "You know."

Now Marcus and Solos stared at me, and I wanted to shove my hand through a wall. "The Order of Thanatos killed Solaris and the First. Somehow they know how to do it, which means wouldn't the gods?"

Dionysus laughed. "Thanatos gifted the Order with the ability—a code or something—but even Thanatos can't recall what it was. There were never supposed to be two Apollyons—never the possibility of a God Killer. Thinking it wouldn't be needed again, he didn't write it down. Idiot."

Should I feel bad for being relieved?

"The Order knows, but with Telly's death, they've scattered. Not to mention that some of the Sentinels under Lucian aren't hunting daimons anymore." Apollo paused and glanced at the door. "They've begun hunting members of the Order."

"Good gods." Marcus strode to the window. Stopping, he dragged his fingers through his hair. "I don't even know which is worse."

There was the distinct impression that there was more. After a few more barbs directed at Apollo, Dionysus vanished, and a little bit of the pressure seeped from the room. "Is he on our side?" I asked.

Apollo laughed dryly. "Yes, but not because he feels the way we do. Only because he's too lazy to engage in battle."

Well, that was good for something. I sighed. "There is more, isn't there? And it has to do with Alex."

"Yes." He looked toward the door again, eyes narrowing. Turning back to me, he nodded. The message was clear—the same look we'd shared a dozen times over the years, when he'd been known as Leon. We had spies. Hands fisting at my sides, I stalked toward the door while Solos continued to gain information from Apollo about the Sentinels hunting the Order.

Two narrow shadows crept along the wall of the hallway, and I was sure the two thought they had James Bond stealth. More like two of the Three Stooges. How long had they been standing outside the room, and was I going to strangle them both? Possibly. I stepped out.

Deacon jumped back, knocking into an equally unprepared Luke. One would think, after all Luke's training, he would've recovered a lot quicker, but things were different now. The Covenant hadn't trained their students to face what was coming.

A sheepish look crossed my brother's face as he straightened and ran a hand through his mess of blond curls. Instead of being angry over him eavesdropping, I was just relieved that he was here with me, when things seemed to be crashing down around us.

"Hey, there, brother…" he said.

I arched a brow. "Deacon, what are you doing?"

Luke's shoulders squared, and then he stepped in front of Deacon. "It was my idea, Aiden."

"Not really." Deacon rolled his eyes. "I felt the presence of another god and I told Luke—"

"But I suggested that we try to find out what's going on." Luke drew in a deep breath. "You guys have been keeping us out of the loop on everything, and this stuff involves us too."

"Probably because it's safer that way for you," I pointed out.

Luke shook his head. "Honestly, considering how screwed up everything is right now? With Evil Alex locked up in the basement and *a war* brewing, keeping us safe isn't a top priority. We should know what's going on. We could help."

My respect for the young half-blood fought to show itself in the form of a smile. "How could you two help?"

"We haven't quite figured that part out yet," Deacon replied, leaning against the wall. "But I'm sure there's something. And I think Lea's going to kick our asses if she's forced to spend one more evening with us."

I frowned. "Where is Lea?"

The half-blood had been through enough, and all of us had been keeping an eye on her. First, she'd lost her father and stepmother in a daimon attack orchestrated by Alex's mother, and then Seth had killed her sister during his attack on the Council. I knew her ties to those deaths had gotten to Alex.

"Sleeping," my brother answered, craning his neck, trying to see around me. "Which god was here?"

There was no reason to keep that a secret. "Dionysus."

"Dude? Are you serious?" Deacon looked crestfallen. "He's like my favorite god of all time."

"Why doesn't that surprise me?" Luke muttered.

And it didn't surprise me, either. Even though Deacon had substantially cut back on the drinking, he could easily be mistaken for Dionysus's soul-twin.

I had a decision to make—send them away or treat them like the adults they almost were. Luke was—or had been—months shy of graduation. Soon he would've been out in the world hunting daimons, but part of me balked at the idea of drawing Deacon into this further than he already was.

But I couldn't baby Deacon for the rest of his life. Perhaps I'd done too much of that already, which might explain some of his previous behavior and why he didn't feel comfortable talking to me about his relationship with Luke.

I nodded. "Come on."

Both of them looked like I'd just professed my love for Seth, but they shot forward as if worried I'd change my mind. Following them into the den, I rolled my eyes when Apollo arched a brow.

"Okay," Apollo said, looking around the room. "Now that everyone who is anyone is here, we have one more thing to discuss."

Luke grinned as he moved to stand beside Solos, and my brother went to the chair farthest away from Apollo. I couldn't figure out his aversion to Apollo, and dear gods, if *those two* had something going on, I might have to hurt someone.

"Alex," Marcus said, leaning against the desk. His right hand absently spun a nearby globe.

Apollo grimaced, and I knew this was going to be bad. "The only hope we have of preventing a full-scale war is if Alex comes around and agrees to take out Seth."

In the past, Alex never would've agreed to that, but now? If we could somehow reach her and break the bond, would she go after Seth? And did I even want her to? She could get hurt…die. As a Sentinel, I needed to accept those risks, but as a man, I couldn't when it came to Alex.

"We have found a way to break the bond. Temporarily," Apollo continued. He blinked, and bright blue irises appeared. I had to look away, because it reminded me of how Alex hated the god eyes and how Apollo toned them down for her. "It will give us time to find a permanent solution."

Everything centered on what Apollo had just said. A temporary break in the connection was better than nothing. The rush of anticipation couldn't be stopped and it almost knocked me on my ass. "What temporary fix?"

"You're not going to like it—none of you are going to like it—but it's the only option that we have at this point."

My hands flexed. "Just get on with it. What's the fix?"

Apollo's brows furrowed. I was pretty sure that if it weren't for the friendship we'd cultivated during hunts, he would've blasted my ass by now. "I've spoken with Ananke—"

"No," Marcus said before I could open my mouth. He pushed off the desk. "There is only one reason why you'd be speaking with Ananke, and the answer is no."

The god folded his arms and the way his entire face hardened, I could tell he wasn't used to being told no. "I know that the thought is unsavory."

A hot rush of rage twisted my insides into raw knots. "'Unsavory' isn't a word I'm shooting for," I grated out.

"Okay, I don't get it." Deacon brushed the flop of blond

curls out of his eyes and frowned. "I'm totally failing Myths and Legends. Who in the hell is Ananke?"

The fondness in Luke's voice ruined his smirk. "Besides the fact that she's the momma of the Fates and of destiny, she rules over compulsion and all forms of slavery and bondage—bondage as in imprisonment."

"Our ability to use compulsion is gifted from Ananke," Marcus explained, eyes narrowed. "She's a lesser-known goddess, practically forgotten."

"Except that she was the one to come up with the Elixir that keeps halfs in servitude docile." Solos's jaw hardened.

Deacon looked at Apollo, his nose wrinkling. "Then why are you contacting a goddess that…?" His mouth dropped open. "Oh. Shit. You want to put Alex on the Elixir."

I folded my arms to keep from hitting something. "No. Apollo, absolutely not."

"I don't even see why we're discussing this." Solos headed around the couch, wisely avoiding the area around me. I was like a geyser seconds away from erupting. He stopped beside Marcus. "The Elixir won't work on the Apollyon, right?"

"Not the kind that we give half-bloods, but Alex would be receiving something different." Apollo paused. "She'd be getting something stronger. Ananke has assured me that it would break the bond, and the effects would only be temporary. It's not the same thing that's done to the others."

"It's not? Because it sounds like it is to me." The idea of putting Alex on the Elixir turned my stomach and pissed me off. "I can't do that."

Apollo opened his mouth but seemed to be choosing what to say. "We have to break the bond, Aiden. At some point, Alex will discover where she is. Then what? Seth will come for her and transfer her power to him, and it will be all over. There will be no second chances."

"There has to be another way!" My control snapped. In that instant I was *this close* to finding out if I could actually take out a god. The only thing that stopped me was the fact that I knew Apollo was trying to help us—help Alex. I didn't doubt that the god cared for her. "We just haven't looked hard enough, checked every available resource."

"Where else can we look, Aiden?" Apollo faced me, eyes wide. "I have turned Olympus inside out looking for a way to break their bond. The only thing is the Elixir and—"

"No." I held my ground.

Apollo looked around the room for help. Solos stepped back, raising his hands. "Don't look at me—I'd like to keep my face in one piece, thank you."

I smirked.

Clearly struggling for patience, Apollo paced the den. "This is only a temporary solution, Aiden."

"That solution is unacceptable!" I yelled so loudly that Deacon jumped. He'd been on the receiving end of my anger time and time again, but the surprise flickering across his face told me he'd never quite seen me like this before. How I felt for Alex, if there was any doubt held by those in the room, was now painfully visible. "You're asking us to agree to strip away *everything* that she is! To turn her into a mindless zombie who has no control—" I broke off, sucking in a shallow breath. It was Alex's greatest fear. The thing that had kept her up at night, that had haunted her steps like a vengeful ghost. "She would have no control."

"She has no control now," insisted a soft feminine voice.

I spun around. Lea stood in the doorway, as tall and thin as her older half-sister had been. Her cinnamon-colored hair was pulled back in a tight ponytail. Dark shadows spread under her eyes and her cheeks were gaunt.

"You don't understand," I said.

She inched into the room, glancing at Apollo and then the rest of us. "I haven't seen her, but I've heard her. We've *all* heard her. And the gods know that she and I have never been friends, but Alex—she never would've said the things I've heard her yelling. That isn't her."

Pressing my lips together, I turned away, shaking my head. Lea had a point. What was down in the basement wasn't really Alex—not the girl I loved with every breath I took. And she wasn't in control of herself.

But the Elixir—that was different.

Lea sat beside Deacon, folding her small hands in her lap. "The idea of using the Elixir screams *wrong* on every level, but what choice do we have? We can't keep her down there."

"She's not eating," murmured Marcus. He rubbed his brow, face strained. "I'm not sure she's even really sleeping or if…if she's communicating with Seth, and that's what's keeping her up."

I stared at him. "Marcus, you know how terrified she was of being put on the Elixir."

Unable to hold my stare, he looked away. "I know, Aiden. Dammit, I know, but something's got to give. As much as I hate the idea of doing this to her, it will give us more time."

Refusing to believe that this was our last option, I searched frantically for another way and grasped at brittle, painful straws. "What about the Fates? Can you go to them and see what the outcome is? If she will break the connection herself? Or if there is some way for us to do so?"

Apollo shook his head. "The Fates are no fans of mine,

and even if they were and if they knew, they wouldn't tell me or you. You know how they work, Aiden. You—"

"You know what this will do to her!" I roared, flushing hot with fury.

"I know what this will do to you," he said quietly. "And I know the idea of doing this is killing you—"

"Stop—just stop," I seethed, backing up. "I will not let any of you do this to her. So help me…"

The threat hung in the air like thick smoke that choked the occupants of the room. Marcus just looked sad, almost beaten down by it all. Solos was pale, probably because he thought Apollo was seconds away from knocking me through the wall. Lea and Luke stared at the floor, faces drawn. Did the two younger halfs feel the sharp bite of guilt for agreeing that Alex needed the Elixir, knowing what it would do, what it would mean?

They were too young for this—for this shit. So was Alex.

So was I. Hell.

The only person in the room who now watched me was my brother. A faint, sad smile appeared on his face. "Alex would kick our asses for considering something like this, but I think she would understand, Aiden. I think she would understand why."

Then Marcus stepped forward, placing his hand on my shoulder. I fought the urge to shake it off. And to hit him—to hit *something*. But he was suffering, too. "There was another thing that Alex feared." His voice was so low I doubted anyone besides Apollo could hear him. "And you know what that was."

I did. Gods, did I ever know.

Alex feared losing herself to the First—to Seth. And I'd promised her, sworn that it would never happen. And it had.

I'd failed her. The sting of that festered and rotted inside me, but agreeing to the Elixir was no better. It would be just another way I'd failed her.

Stepping away from Marcus, I dragged my fingers through my hair. No one really talked for a few moments. The silence was as bad as my threat. Finally, everyone started talking, tossing around more ideas. "Take out Seth" topped their list, but it wasn't possible. "Move Alex farther away"—maybe that would lessen the connection, give her breathing room, give us time to search for more runes and spells and prayers.

The best efforts just added to the hopelessness of the situation.

Apollo finally approached me. "We need to talk in private."

I wanted him to just leave, but I nodded, and we slipped out and headed toward the empty kitchen. My steps were quick and harsh. "There is no way you'll be able to convince me that putting Alex on a souped-up version of the Elixir is the right thing to do."

He closed the door with a wave of his hand before speaking. "I know you feel strongly for her."

I met his stare. "I love her. You don't get that."

"No. I do. You forget that I was with you when you hunted down Eric. I saw what no one else did—how affected you were by what had happened to Alex. And I know what you did to that daimon."

My jaw clenched and I looked away. "He deserved it."

"I'm not contesting that."

What I had done to Eric wasn't something I was particularly proud of. "Torture" seemed too light of a word for what I'd done. I swallowed hard. "What are you getting at, Apollo?"

He tilted his head to the side. "The kind of love you hold for Alex is admirable, but I've seen this love before. It has brought down entire civilizations. Need I remind you of Troy?"

"Is this a history lesson?"

His eyes flashed. "Okay. We won't talk about the glaring elephant in the room, Aiden."

"Good."

"I haven't been entirely forthcoming with information," he said after a few moments.

I laughed darkly. "Why doesn't that surprise me? You've been a fountain of honesty."

Apollo ignored that. "Since Zeus created the Apollyon thousands of years ago, the First has always been of my lineage."

"What?" I wasn't following him. "Artemis said that *Alex* was of your lineage."

"She is." He moved to the rack of wine and popped a cork. "But throughout history, the Apollyon always has been an offspring of mine. To this day, I have no knowledge of who Solaris was descended from and I don't know who Seth hails from. This time—only this time—has been different." Pausing, he poured himself a glass. "Seth is the First, but he is not one of mine. Somehow, another god is responsible for him. And I'd bet my laurel crown that this same god was responsible for Solaris."

He offered me a drink and I waved him off. "Are you saying Alex was meant to be the First and Seth was the fluke?"

Apollo shrugged. "I don't know. And none of the gods are claiming responsibility for him."

"Well, obviously," I said dryly.

A smirk graced his lips as he placed the wine back in the rack and then took a drink. "That's not the kicker, Aiden. Whoever is responsible for Seth is not claiming him for their own reason—the same reason that Lucian would know spells to keep me out of his home."

"You think a god is working with Lucian—the same god of Seth's lineage?"

"Most likely," he said, downing the glass of wine. "But there's another reason why that god would not stand up. Because he or she would know that there is another way to kill the Apollyon."

A sheet of ice slipped over me. "What are you saying, Apollo?"

"The god linked to their bloodline is able to kill them. I can kill Alex."

CHAPTER FOUR

The floor seemed to move under my feet and the walls changed from white paint to deep brown paneling. It took me a few moments to realize that I was walking—walking away from Apollo, away from the bomb he'd just dropped.

Of course he followed. "Aiden, where are you going?"

I was heading for the basement. I needed to put myself between Alex and…and whoever came for her.

Apollo appeared in front of me, blocking my route. I stepped to the side, but he followed. "Aiden, listen to me."

"I'm done listening."

"This is not a threat, my friend. But if she is about to connect with the First, I will put her down. I have to—" He caught my fist, pushing me back. "The entire world hinges on us not going to war."

I stepped toward him, beyond thinking, and he pushed me back again. And again. Pain tore through me. Physical? Emotional? I didn't know. "You'd kill her?"

"I wouldn't want to." The blue of his eyes glowed. "And

that's why I'm doing everything to avoid that. Putting her on the Elixir gives us time, Aiden. And we need time. *I* need time, because I have six family members ready to rip into the mortal world. I cannot be here, waiting for Alex to manage an escape or for Seth to figure out a way to connect with her."

"No one is asking you to be here, Apollo. I have it covered."

He shot me a dubious look. "You're not getting it. The gods know they can't kill her, but that won't stop them from trying. And while they might not be able to kill her, they *will* harm her."

Leaning against the wall, I pressed the heels of my hands against my temples. All I wanted was to go down there, get Alex, and take her far away from all of this. "You're asking too much."

Apollo sighed. "You need to take a step back from this, Aiden. Look at this from the perspective of a Sentinel—how you were trained."

I lifted my head, pinning him with a dark look. "You're asking me to be objective now?"

He barked a short laugh. "Yes, I know I'm not the most objective god, but you have a job to do, Aiden. A job to protect mankind—and to protect the Hematoi. That is your duty. And you know what the right thing to do is."

"So, I need to choose between my duty as a Sentinel and my duty as a man? To Alex?"

"Yes and no. You need to choose both." Apollo leaned against the other wall, still towering over me, and I was a good six and a half feet. "Marcus is right. Apollyon or not, she can't last much longer like this. Not eating? Not sleeping? Has she even been drinking water?"

I closed my eyes. "Twice. She drank water twice when she thought I wasn't watching."

He cursed under his breath. "She needs to rest. She needs a break from this, Aiden. And we need time to find a way to end this."

"Or what—you will kill her?"

Apollo didn't answer.

"Gods." I listened to the feet of Sentinels on the floors above for a few moments. "Who knows about what you can do?"

"Only my sister Artemis and possibly Zeus—if he's been paying attention, which is up in the air," he said. "I have gotten the six to agree that if we put Alex on the Elixir they will back down. It's not just about her, Aiden. It's about millions of people."

I nodded, pushing off the wall, pulling myself back together. Duty and love had never really mixed well before, but there'd always been an in-between. "I need time."

"Aiden, we don't have time."

"I'm not asking for days. I'm just asking for tonight." I started toward the basement door and paused. "I need to try one more time."

"I can't fault you for that." He grinned. "I'll give you tonight. Then I'll be back tomorrow morning."

Nodding again, I opened the door. Apollo was gone when I glanced over my shoulder, and I was alone. Alone with a decision I knew I could never live with if I made it.

Alex was lying on the mattress, curled on her side, back to the door. She didn't start demanding that I let her out or start cussing me like she'd done the last three days or so. She didn't even acknowledge I was there.

Maybe she was sleeping, but my heart rate picked up as I

reached into my pocket, pulling out one of the three keys to the door. "Alex?"

Nothing. Not even a flicker of a muscle.

Hopefully, she was sleeping, but my hands shook as I turned the lock and slipped inside, quickly closing and locking the door behind me. I called her name again as I slid the key back into my pocket. There was no answer, and by now, Alex would've been all over me like a daimon after aether.

Something was wrong.

I rushed to her side and knelt on the edge of the mattress. A mess of hair hid her face. Pulse pounding, I placed my hand on her still shoulder. "Alex, are—"

Flipping onto her back, she slammed her bare feet into my stomach. Air rushed out of my lungs in a grunt. I fell back, catching myself as she popped up on her feet.

Dammit. I should've known she was like a daimon playing possum.

With a near-feral sound, she came down on me, knees first. I flipped to the side, and I could've taken out her legs, but hurting her wasn't something I would do. Hitting the floor beside me, she threw her leg over mine, locking it between her thighs.

My brows shot up. "What are you doing?"

"Shut up," she hissed, grabbing my hand closest to her.

"Really, if you wanted to hold my hand and snuggle, all you had to do was ask."

Anger flushed her cheeks as she rolled on top of me, straddling my legs. Silent and scowling, she went for my pocket.

I grabbed her wrist. "Geez, Alex, normally I'd love you being all grabby, but knock it off."

She sneered as she tried to pull her arm free. "Didn't know you were such a pervert."

Smiling tightly, I twisted my other arm free and caught her hand when she tried to slam it into my throat. "You know exactly what I am."

"Don't remind me." Using her weight and what strength she still had, she tore herself free. Scrambling to her feet, she balled her hands into fists. "Let me out of here, Aiden."

I stood. "That's not going to happen."

Alex shot forward, shoving me back a step. "Give me the key. I have to go. I need to go to him."

Hearing her say that pricked at my skin. "What you need to do is *listen* to me."

Her chest rose quickly and her eyes darted to the locked doors. She moved her left foot back an inch, and just like I'd taught her, she braced her weight on that leg and spun.

The kick was freaking perfect—knee bent at a ninety-degree angle to get the most oomph behind the extension—but I expected it. Using my forearm, I blocked the kick instead, using the momentum to send her crashing to the hard floor, hissing as hot pain jarred my bones.

Alex was incredibly fast when she wanted to be, even more as the Apollyon. Spinning around, she jabbed with her elbow and then the heel of her palm. Then she dipped, going for my legs—all maneuvers we'd played out hundreds of times. Fighting each other truly was like fighting ourselves.

Anticipating a butterfly kick, I darted behind her. She pivoted around, swinging her arm. Air rushed over my jaw as I ducked around her and wrapped my arm around her waist. I drew her back against my chest, jerking my head back to avoid hers.

"Let me go!" she screeched, wiggling like crazy. Her voice was pitched high, as if I was hurting her, but I knew I wasn't. "Let go of me!"

"Alex, you need to listen to me." Reasoning with her probably ranked right up there with insanity, but I had to give her a chance to pull out of this. "If you don't break this connection with Seth, you're not going to like what happens."

"You're not going to like what happens!" She threw her weight back, lifting her legs to her chest, but I held her easily. "Because I'm going to seriously hurt you when I get out of here. My first visit is going to be to your brother!"

"Stop it! Listen to me." I cocked my head to the right, avoiding hers again. "The gods are going to war because of what Seth is doing."

"Good! Let them bring it." She laughed, lowering her feet to the floor. "We will destroy each of them. Starting with that idiot Apollo."

I sighed, running out of patience. Yeah, I wasn't as saintly as Seth claimed. "You can't continue like th—"

Her elbow thrust into my stomach and she broke free. I sprang forward, catching her around the waist, and flipped her onto the mattress when I should've just dropped her on her head. It wasn't like she'd repay me the same kindness.

Alex reared up, trying to hook her legs around my waist to roll me. I pressed down, using my weight to trap her lower body. Her hands flew at my face, fingers curved into claws. Snatching her wrists, I pinned them down above her head.

"Look at me," I said, leaning down so that only a few inches separated our faces. "Look at me and listen."

She started to turn her head, but I pressed my forehead against hers, trapping her. Her eyes squeezed shut and there wasn't a damn thing I could do about that.

Taking a deep breath, I willed for her to understand me. Just this once… "This isn't you, Alex. You would never act like this. This *isn't* you."

"Yes, it is!" Pain broke her voice as she arched again, almost throwing me off. "You're just pissed because I don't want you anymore. You're jealous and obsessive."

I ignored her words. "You're letting Seth control you. Do you remember how afraid of that you were? How terrified that you'd lose yourself to him? What happened to that?"

She stilled except for the ragged rise and fall of her chest.

My eyes traced the contours of her face. "I swore to you that I wouldn't let that happen, and I know I've failed you, but I'm not going to just give up, Alex. I'll never give up on you."

Her lips formed a tight line and a shudder rolled through her.

"You've always been so strong—unique. Only *you* controlled your life. No one made decisions for you. But this—not even questioning or fighting what's happening—is *weak*."

Alex's eyes flew open. "I am not weak."

"Then prove it!" Dammit, I wanted to shake her. "Shut him out, just for a few minutes. I know you can. I know you worked for months on blocking him. *Shut him out*, Alex, and talk to me. Prove to me you're not weak."

Amber eyes churned, luminous and powerful. They were beautiful, like a god had placed two topaz jewels in her face, but I hated them. Hated what they meant and stood for. Hated that no matter what Alex had done—no matter what *we'd* done—she'd connected with Seth anyway and lost herself within seconds.

"I know you can do it," I said. "I know you have that strength in you, because that's what I love about you most. Your strength is admirable—beautiful. It is who you are. And what you've become is not you."

"Love?" she repeated the word as if it were foreign to her tongue.

My chest tightened and the words spilled out of my mouth

before I could stop them. And dammit, I begged—something I'd never done before. "Please come back to me, Alex. *Please.* I love you too much to lose you. And I love you too much to allow what's about to happen, but you're leaving me no choice."

Her lashes fluttered down and a heartbeat passed, then they reopened. I sucked in a breath, too astonished to feel or think anything other than the fact that her eyes were brown—warm, whiskey brown.

Her eyes were brown. "Alex..."

Face pale and lips trembling, her brows puckered. "I'm so sorry. Aiden, I lo—" A scream tore from her, and she arched clear off the mattress, eyes widening.

My heart stopped. "Alex?"

"I can't... It's everywhere. It...hurts. Aiden, please... make it stop... Please..." She slumped back, whimpering and twisting, thrashing her head back and forth.

With my heart in my throat, I started to let up, but then her eyes opened again and I wanted to rage. Golden eyes stared back into mine. I'd almost had her—almost.

Alex went wild underneath me.

The erratic mix of emotions funneling inside me made it hard to wait this out. Hope crashed and burned into barb-tipped disappointment that eventually gave way to anger. Alex was in there and she was hurting. Five seconds of catching a glimpse of her and she'd been sucked right back into Seth. I didn't know if I should be happy or sick to my soul.

Even with the lack of food and sleep, it still took a godsawful amount of time for her to tire herself out. She thrashed, screamed, kicked, and even tried to bite me.

But finally, she grew weary and was panting. "Does this

make you happy? Hurting me like this? Make you feel all big and bad?"

"I'm not hurting you." I opened my eyes, weary.

"You're killing me!" She tried to rise up but fell back. The damn girl was going to hurt herself.

"Dear gods, Alex, can you stop fighting me for a damn second?" She opened her mouth, but I placed my other hand over her lips. "Don't say something smart-ass. You have no idea what kind of shitty night I've had."

Her eyes narrowed.

"I mean it. Not one smart-ass comment."

She grew very still, and I removed my hand. The tip of her tongue darted out, wetting her lips. I could tell she had something entirely infuriating to say but was holding back.

"I need you to try again, Alex. Block him. Cut the cord, and I'll help you through it this time. I swear. I'll get you through it."

Alex stared at me for so long that I feared she'd lost the ability to speak. "You don't get it. I don't want to. I need him, Aiden. Not you. A half and a pure can't love each other. Just let me go."

Someone must have punched a hole right through my chest. The pain was that real—just as real as the pain I'd witnessed moments ago.

Aiden, please make it stop.

I focused on that instead of what she'd said. Alex was in pain when she fought him, and who knew if there were periods of time when she was fighting him and we just didn't see. All I did know was that when she'd been herself—her *real* self—she'd asked me to make it stop, begged me. And there was only one way I could make it stop.

I knew right then, as much as it tore me apart, there was no other choice.

Leaning down, I placed a kiss against her damp temple and closed my eyes. A second—only a second—passed, and I soaked up her warmth and the moment of closeness without her fighting me. Then she jerked her head to the side and said something too horrible to really even acknowledge. Lifting myself off her, I rose to my feet and backed off, leaving the cell.

Alex remained on the mattress, not bothering to rush the door as I locked it. I stood there, watching her, knowing that what I was about to do had nothing to do with my duty to humanity or to my own kind. It really didn't have anything to do with Apollo and his warnings.

Aiden, please make it stop.

There was only one way I could make it stop.

CHAPTER FIVE

The next morning, Apollo, Marcus, and I stood in the small sunroom that overflowed with plants and flowers. The sweet tangy scent reminded me of Alex. Hell, everything reminded me of Alex.

She was right about one thing last night. I was obsessed.

Apollo cut to the chase. "Have you agreed?"

I glanced at Marcus, knowing that he'd finally made up his mind sometime last night. So had I. Weary and bone-tired, I scrubbed my hand over my rough cheek. Man, I needed to shave.

"Aiden," Marcus said.

Exhaling roughly, my eyes narrowed. They didn't know that Alex had snapped out of it for a few seconds last night. The tiny glimpse of her was something I held close to my heart, but in the harsh glare of the sunlight, I wasn't sure if it had really happened, or if it had been wishful thinking.

I cleared my suddenly dry throat. The words were hard to get my tongue to form. "Give her the Elixir."

And that was it—all it took.

What sounded like a series of champagne corks shattered the silence. The air was sucked out of the room as I spun toward the crackling sound. A shimmery blue dust formed in the rays of sunlight. Each particle shined like a sapphire. They came together quickly, as if drawn to become whole. Within seconds, a woman stood before us.

Swathed in blue silk robes that clung to her curves, the goddess tipped her golden head back. Long, thick curls fell to her waist as she drifted toward Apollo with a twitch in her hips.

Marcus sucked in a breath, obviously affected by the goddess's beauty, and I felt nothing but chilled numbness as we both bowed.

There was something seriously wrong with me.

Or perhaps I was just too focused on what she held in her delicate-looking hands—an ancient-looking porcelain pitcher engraved with a hateful symbol. A circle with a slash through it—the mark of servitude.

"Ananke," Apollo said, bowing before the older goddess.

My brows shot up. That was quick. It was eerie seeing how in-the-know the gods could be when they wanted. Immediately I disliked her, but I forced my expression blank.

She handed Apollo the pitcher and then turned toward me, her lip tipping up at one corner before facing Apollo again. "You will only need to use a…shot of this. You will need to finish with the compulsion."

Hands clenching, I started to turn but stopped. I'd heard the compulsion time and time again over the years. Already it was flowing through my thoughts. My stomach rolled.

The goddess moved away from Apollo, returning to the center of the room. "It will take a few minutes to take effect. It will shut down all of her Apollyon powers, therefore breaking the bond. She will be…different."

Not liking the sound of this, I asked, "What do you mean by 'different'?"

Her lip tipped up again. "She will be more pliable to deal with—compliant in nature. The girl will know who she is on the most basic level, but no more."

"What?" I glanced at Apollo. "I didn't agree to that."

Apollo shot me a look that said *shut the hell up* and then some. Taking in a deep breath, I clasped my hands behind my back. "I apologize."

The goddess arched a brow and nodded. "I have added ma huang, which affects the memory. Her memories link her to the First. Without them, he simply does not exist. It is not perfect, but the best we can do given the situation."

A chill crept up my spine. If Seth didn't exist, then neither did anyone she cared about or trusted. Neither did I.

"She will tire easily," Ananke continued. "And will be very easy to handle while we search for a more permanent fix."

The permanent fix was in the room—Apollo—but thankfully the bulk of the gods didn't know that he could take her out.

"How long will it last?" Apollo asked.

Ananke shook her head. "There is no telling. Maybe a few days if you're lucky, but you will know when it's wearing off. She will grow restless, may start to remember things. When this happens, she will need a new dose."

"Will this harm her in any way?" Concern colored Marcus's voice.

"No." She started to shimmer out, but her voice still carried with its cold indifference. "But I would not give her more than six doses. The effects may become permanent at that point."

And then she was gone, leaving all of us open-mouthed.

Marcus exhaled loudly. "Nice of her to throw that in."

"It could become permanent?" I raised a brow, daring Apollo to look away. "Did you know this?"

His eyes narrowed. "I know the same amount as you do. At least we know not to exceed six doses. If it lasts at least four days, then that gives us nearly a month."

"If it lasts four days each time," I pointed out.

Apollo glanced down at the pitcher. "Well, we're about to find out."

I went down the stairs, detached as I could be. Knowing what I was about to take part in darkened my soul. Something like that might sound dramatic, and before, I really didn't think it was possible, but now I understood.

"It's for the best," Apollo said.

Glaring at him, I slid past him and stopped in front of the cell. Alex was sitting on the mattress, back against the wall and knees tucked close to her chest. She stared behind me, to where I knew Apollo waited in the shadows. For some reason, Alex reacted like a crazed hydra when Apollo went near her.

"Did you finally come to your senses and decide to let me out?" A smirk twisted her once beautiful lips. They were now chapped from lack of water. The bottle sat untouched by the wall.

I unlocked the door. "You know the answer to that."

Alex rose to her feet, swaying as she stepped off the mattress. Her face was as pale as the walls surrounding her. "I should've known none of you would be smart enough."

We slipped into the cell, locking it behind us. I watched Alex wearily. She was growing weaker by the day, but the girl was a fighter to her core. Marcus moved back, letting me deal with her as we'd planned.

It seemed fitting that I'd be the one who did this.

Her eerie amber gaze slid past me to what Marcus held in his hands. The liquid inside the glass was deep blue and thick. Recognition flared, and she took a step back. I moved to her side, holding my breath.

As expected, she went wild.

Shooting forward, I wrapped my arms around her, clamping her arms to her sides. Using my weight, I brought her to the floor as carefully as I could, but she thrashed and struggled. From behind her, I got my legs around her waist and locked them down over hers.

Alex was trapped.

"No! No!" she screamed over and over, each word a punch straight to my heart. "No! No!"

Pressing my cheek against hers, I forced her head back. "I'm sorry, Alex, I'm so sorry."

"You can't do this to me!" She tried to wiggle her head down but failed. Her voice was laced with hatred and power, an edge that didn't belong to her. "You'll regret this. All of you, it will be the last thing you do. I promise you."

"Do it," I urged, wanting this over with. Over Marcus's shoulder, my eyes met Apollo's. He stood just outside the cell now. Even the god looked disgusted with what we were doing.

With a pained expression, Marcus crouched in front of us and grabbed Alex's chin. His hand shook as he lifted the glass of Elixir, and he squared his shoulders. "Sorry, Alexandria. It'll be over in seconds."

Like a switch being thrown, the voice that came out of the trembling girl was one I recognized and feared. "Please don't do this," she begged. Seconds later, my cheeks were wet from her tears. "Please, Marcus, please don't do this to me."

Marcus hesitated. "Alex?"

Her body shuddered against mine. "I'll behave. I promise. I'll do whatever you ask, but please don't give me the Elixir."

I drew in a shallow breath. "What color are her eyes?"

"Gold," he grunted.

Moving both of her slender wrists to one hand, I knocked Marcus's hand away and grasped her chin. "It's not her, not really. Do it. Godsdammit, just do it!"

Alex wailed, and a part of me turned cold—forever. I forced her mouth open, bruising her jaw as her struggles renewed. Energy hummed through me, shocking me every couple of seconds. Marcus tipped the glass to her lips, and the sickeningly sweet aroma of the Elixir filled the cell.

Even after the contents of the glass were gone, Alex still fought. Screaming, rolling her hips, throwing her head back and forth until I felt her breaths turning deeper, slower.

Marcus moved back, setting the glass aside. He wiped his hands along his pants as if he could somehow wipe away what he'd just done to his niece, but it had left a mark on my soul.

I'd never be able to wipe it away, no matter how hard I tried.

I watched Marcus and Apollo as her muscles loosened and her body relaxed against mine. Her head fell back against my shoulder and to the side as she drew in a deep, long breath that sounded like a sigh.

Gazing down at her, I saw the marks again. Intricate designs bled through her skin, swirling over her cheeks and down her neck. Inked in blue, they brightened until the whole room was awash in sapphire, and then they faded out. Alex stilled.

"You have to finish this," Apollo said.

One of these days I was going to hit Apollo again. I probably wouldn't survive, but it was going to happen. Turning Alex in my arms, I cradled her against my chest and cupped her cheek. "Alexandria, open your eyes."

Her lashes fluttered against her pale cheeks, and then finally, they lifted. I sucked in a sharp breath. Her eyes were shattered—dull brown with gold shredded through them. The connection had been broken, but it wasn't Alex staring back at me blankly. It wasn't Seth, either.

She was a stranger—a young, scared girl who didn't recognize me, an empty slate perfect for compulsion.

I clamped down on the anger rising in my throat and kept my eyes locked with hers. "Το όνομά σας είναι Alexandria."

Your name is Alexandria.

She blinked slowly.

Pain sliced through my chest. "Το όνομά μου είναι Aiden..." I choked as the back of my throat burned. Wetness gathered in my eyes, clouding Alex's face. *I can't do this. I have to do this.* The words burst out of me. "Το όνομά μου είναι Aiden και είμαι ο Δάσκαλός σας."

My name is Aiden, and I am your Master.

"Θα υπακούσει μου κάθε επιθυμία, την επιθυμία, και την εντολή σε θάνατο."

You will obey my every wish, desire, and command to death.

Or until the Elixir wore off.

She breathed in the words, relaxed a little more, and became them. And I watched the shattered eyes dull even more. I let go of her hands and they fell to her lap.

"What is your name?" I asked, voice hoarse.

"Alexandria," she repeated in a soft voice I'd never heard Alex use in real life.

"And who am I?"

"Aiden." She smiled, and I flinched. "You are my Master."

CHAPTER SIX

The first thing we did was get her to eat, but it wasn't a simple process. I took Alex upstairs and sat her at the table. The entire time she kept her eyes glued to her hands, which were folded in her lap.

Alex didn't speak unless she was directly spoken to, and even then, she didn't raise her eyes. I set a plate of cold cuts and a bowl of fruit in front of her, along with a can of grape soda—her favorite.

She didn't move.

I glanced at Marcus, who remained by the door, making sure no one entered. Apollo had disappeared the instant I'd brought her out of the cell. Bastard. "You have to be hungry, Alex. You haven't eaten a thing in days."

"My name is Alexandria," came the soft whisper.

I blinked several times and then pushed the plate toward her. "Aren't you hungry, Alexandria?"

"Am I?"

It clicked then. Like most indentured half-bloods, she

would have to be *ordered*—ordered to do everything. Sitting back, I dragged my fingers through my hair. "Please eat, Alexandria."

Her lashes lifted. Those strange eyes met mine for a brief second, and then went to the plate of food. She was slow to eat at first, but once she grew comfortable—or confident in what she was doing—she finished the plate and most of the bowl. Two cans of soda later, she tugged at a limp lock of hair.

Marcus shook his head and turned, leaving us. Did he regret all those times that he'd wished Alex was more amenable? Funny thing was, even when I'd demanded that she not do something in the past, I'd secretly loved that she rarely listened.

I stood, surprised when she automatically came to her feet. "I'll show you to your room and you can shower if you want." I bit the inside of my cheek as her lashes swept down. Try this again. "You will clean up and then rest."

"Okay." She looked up, her eyes drifting over my face. "I…"

"What?" I stepped forward.

Alex moved back behind the chair as if it were some kind of shield. She shook her head. I gave her a few moments to speak again, but she'd gone mute. I wanted to reach out and touch her, comfort her, but I had a feeling it would upset her.

I led her to the bedroom I'd been staying in. A smaller room was linked with mine through a shared bathroom. Placing her in that room would enable me to keep an eye on her.

At least that's what I told myself as I showed her the shower and placed two towels and a robe on the bathroom sink. It had nothing to do with the fact I just wanted her close to me.

Yeah, I wasn't kidding anyone.

At first I thought I was going to have to undress her, and dear gods, there was no way I could do that and not, well, think and feel the things I would. Then she grabbed the hem of her sweater and started to lift. I had to force myself from the bathroom. *Saint* Delphi my ass.

Shutting the door behind me, I leaned against it and closed my eyes. The water turned on, and I pushed off, crossing the room and sitting down on the edge of the bed. Weariness seeped into my bones. Maybe I could sleep now, at least longer than a few hours.

A very small, minuscule amount of relief pinged through me. Alex was moving around, not trying to kill anyone, and no longer connected to Seth. Something to celebrate, right? No. What was walking around wasn't really Alex. She couldn't be that meek if she tried.

Fifteen minutes passed and the door slowly cracked open. A much cleaner Alex peeked out, clutching the robe's collar, eyes downcast. She stepped into the bedroom, shifting from one foot to the next.

"I'm finished."

I stood, staring at her—transported back to the day I'd brought her back to the Covenant and seen what lay beneath the grime and muck—the same maddening rush of feelings sucker-punched me.

Alex was beautiful—flawless—to me.

Her lashes lifted. Our eyes locked, and a sweet flush crept across her cheeks. My gaze dipped to her parted lips and a very different kind of hunger stirred. Before I knew what I was doing, I crossed the room, hands outstretched, reaching for her.

Alex darted back, her knuckles bleaching white. Confusion shot across her face as she sucked her lower lip between her teeth. Anxiety rolled off her as she stared back at me.

I stopped short, pulling my hands back. What was I

thinking? She was…afraid of me—afraid of her Master. I cursed.

She jumped, eyes widening.

I'd never hated myself more. Clamping down on my emotions, I gave her space. "Stay here. I'll find you some clothes."

"Yes, Ma—"

"Don't call me that." My tone was harsher than I intended and I worked to soften it. "Call me Aiden. Okay?"

Alex nodded.

Tearing myself away from her, I headed to the door and glanced over my shoulder. My brows furrowed. She stood in the same spot, hands clenching the robe and eyes on the floor as if it was some sort of beacon. What the hell was she doing?

Then it struck me. I'd told her to *stay*. And she was staying. "Alex…"

"My name is Alexandria."

"Okay." I sighed, approaching her carefully. When I was sure she knew I was beside her, I cupped her elbow. "You don't have to stand here. You can do whatever you want, Alex—Alexandria. Sleep. Or watch TV." I nodded at the flat screen in the corner as I led her to the bed. "You can do as you wish. Okay?"

Sitting down, Alex nodded and watched me. "You're coming back, right?"

"Of course," I assured her. She kept glancing around the room, growing more and more agitated. "I won't be gone long at all. I promise."

Alex nodded again. "Okay, Ma—" She flinched. "Okay, Aiden."

It didn't take me long to find clothes for her. All of her things were still in the room next to mine. Marcus had already checked in, then disappeared back downstairs, and now Deacon hovered by the door.

Gathering up Alex's clothes, I faced my brother. "What's up?"

He leaned against the doorframe and crossed his arms. "How'd it go?"

"She fought it, as expected, but it worked." I sat on the arm of a chair, yawning. "She's…she's not like she was."

"As in she's not Evil Alex…?"

I shook my head. "She's…just not—it's only temporary."

Deacon pressed his lips together. "That bad, huh?"

"I didn't say it was bad."

He arched a brow. "I know you, Aiden. Your disappointment—in yourself, not Alex—is written all over you. It's practically dripping from your grubby face."

My brows rose. "I'm grubby?"

"You're kind of gross. Might want to think about shaving, too, unless you're going for the scraggly look with no chance of getting laid."

I laughed and stood. "I'll keep that in mind."

A genuine smile, one that was so rare on my brother, parted his lips, though it quickly faded. "She's going to be okay, right? I mean, someone will find a way to break the connection and she'll be snarky-but-not-homicidal Alex in no time? They have to."

My good humor vanished. A crack broke my control, shattered the weakened wall around me. "Gods, I hope so, Deacon. I can't…"

"Live without her?"

Turning away, I didn't answer because there was no need. "Has it always been that obvious?"

"Honestly?" Deacon laughed. "I knew you had a thing for

her and her for you from the moment you came back from Atlanta and bitched me out. To me, it was obvious, but only because I know you. It's funny, because she's a half, but in a weird way she's perfect for you, don't you think?"

I smiled weakly. "Yeah, I think so."

There was a pause and then he asked, "Even if all of us make it out of this alive and the gods don't go all Godzilla on the world and she goes back to Team Aiden, how are you two going to get your happily ever after?"

"We'd leave. That was our plan. It would work. Apollo owes us."

"No shit?" He sounded incredulous, not upset. "You'd give up being a Sentinel? Run off and try to live as mortals?"

Nodding, I faced him. Sadness congealed in my chest. "Yeah, that was our plan. I was going to tell you. We'd work something out so that you and—"

"Dude, I know you'd make sure I knew where to find you," he said, blinking several times. "Damn, Aiden..."

"What?"

"It's just...wow, I'm happy for you. I think this is great. It's love—the real kind you make sacrifices for. The kind where you scream 'screw it' to everyone else. That's envy-worthy."

I arched a brow. "Not quite sure any part of my life is envy-worthy right now, considering that Alex thinks I'm her *Master*."

"Hey, you know, that could be—"

"Don't even go there."

"Okay. Okay. But it will get better." His familiar gaze flicked up, meeting mine. "You're doing okay, Aiden. Better than most would do in this...situation."

"Thank you." I smiled, shifting my bundle. "So are you."

"I know." Deacon grinned. "I'm just awesome."

"And modest." I stopped in front of him, lowering my chin. "Seriously, how are you holding up?"

He shrugged. "Been through worse, so don't worry about me. You have enough on your plate."

Not worrying about Deacon was going against nature. I'd spent the last decade of my life worrying about him—maybe a little too much. Smothering him instead of supporting him.

Deacon tipped his head back, suddenly looking much older than seventeen. "Go get some rest—shower first, though." A quick flash of a grin appeared. "We've got the watch for now."

I nodded, handing over the proverbial reins. Stopping at the bathroom door, I turned back to him. "Deacon?"

He brushed a curl out of his eyes. "Yeah?"

"I know about you and Luke, and I don't care as long as you're happy. Just do right by him, and you know what I mean."

His mouth dropped open, and for once, it was me surprising my brother and not the other way around.

I didn't even go into my bedroom, opting to place Alex's clothes on a shelf and clean up first. After a long and hard look at myself in the mirror, I acknowledged I did look...*grubby*. Digging out a razor, I showered and then shaved quickly. A pair of clean pajama bottoms was tucked back away in the shelving, but no shirt. Hoping Alex didn't freak out when she saw my bare chest, I opened the bathroom door.

And I came to a complete standstill.

Alex was curled on her side on top of the bedspread, her hands folded under her chin as if she was praying. Her lips were parted and rosy. Two curvy legs peeked out from under the robe, immediately drawing my attention. I'd always loved Alex's legs.

She was fast asleep.

Setting her clothing on a nearby chair, I went to her side and called her name. She murmured something, and I felt a damn flutter—an actual *flutter*—in my chest. Very carefully, I placed another blanket over her legs. Either exhaustion or the Elixir had taken its toll on her. I pulled the cover up, tucking it around her.

Backing away from the bed, I left the room and stalked through the quiet house. Downstairs, off the basement, was a small room that was nothing but four cinder block walls. Someone had strung a punching bag from the ceiling.

Pent-up frustration and helpless anger reared its head, and a second later, my bare knuckles crashed into the worn, tough leather. I went crazy, and while each punch brought a spike of pain across my hand, I welcomed it.

Hours passed as I jabbed and kicked. Sweat poured off me, stinging my eyes and the torn skin along my knuckles. Physical pain did nothing to dampen the torment building inside me.

In a flash, I was taken back to the past summer, when I'd seen Alex doing the very same thing, after she'd discovered the truth about her mother. She had been a fierce, beautiful creature as she'd whirled around the practice dummy. A cyclone of raw emotions had reached out across the training room, tapping into my own mixed-up feelings. When she had sensed my presence and our gazes locked, as crazy as it sounded, I'd felt what she had.

Dragging in a ragged breath, I stopped and looked over my shoulder toward the door. Why I'd been expecting to find her standing there I'll never know. Of course, the doorway was empty.

Alex was empty.

I went back upstairs, grabbed a towel from the dark bathroom and cleaned myself up. Back in the bedroom, I glanced at the oversized couch pushed up against the wall, and then grabbed a thin quilt off the end of the bed. Every cell in my body demanded to be close to her, but it seemed wrong. If she woke with me beside her, I was afraid it would upset and confuse her. That was the last thing I wanted. Easing down on my side, I spread the quilt out and watched her sleep until exhaustion pulled me under.

CHAPTER SEVEN

Alex slept for nearly twenty-four hours, waking up minutes before I caved to my growing concern. Late in the night, we went downstairs and, between the two of us, we just about cleaned out the fridge. She was still fidgety and would only do something if I told her to, but by the time morning came around, she'd loosened up enough that it was almost like being around a very calm and sedated Alex.

We moved from the kitchen to the sunroom and stayed there. She didn't talk to me unless I asked her a question. After investigating every flower and plant in the room, she sat on one of the window seats and remained there, gazing at the thick woods that surrounded the safe house.

I sat beside her, on the other end of the window seat, surprisingly content to just be there with her. I wanted to know what she was thinking and each time I asked, the answer was the same.

"Nothing," she said, not taking her gaze off the glass walls.

That was like a cut to the chest, but not as bad as when

there'd be footsteps in the hallway or voices nearing and Alex would lock up. She'd look away from the woods then, staring at the closed door. Panic would fill the brown and amber eyes. Solos came into the sunroom at one point, checking to see if we needed anything from the nearby town.

The only person she didn't freak over was her uncle. Was it some kind of leftover familial bond? But even then, she treated him the same way she treated me. Marcus had the same amount of luck that I did drawing her into a conversation. After that, I decided it would be best to keep her away from the rest of the household.

Finally, after hours of being together, her eyes focused on me. I pretended not to notice, but I was aware of her gaze traveling down.

Alex moved suddenly, slower than she normally would, and grasped my hands in hers. "Your hands…"

Stunned that she was even touching me, I couldn't respond. Like an idiot, I sat there as her thumbs smoothed over the bones in my hand, stopping short of the raw knuckles.

"You're hurt," she said. "Why are you hurt?"

As gently as I could, I pulled my hands free. "I'm not hurt. It's nothing to worry about."

Her lashes swept up as she searched my face. Then she nodded and settled back, staring down at her own hands with a frown.

She tired quickly after that, becoming lethargic before it was nine. I managed to get her to eat before I took her back upstairs. She was out the minute her head hit the pillow, and I retreated to the couch. We repeated the same action the next day, and it was like there was a giant clock over our heads, counting down the minutes until I'd need to give her another dose.

We spent the morning in the sunroom, but I coaxed her out of that room, mainly because I was going to lose my ever-loving mind if I had to look at another plant again. The den was always occupied by my brother, Lea, and Luke, but there was another sitting room upstairs that was full of books. I took her up there after grabbing a bag of chips and a grape soda for her to snack on.

I watched her move around the room, looking for signs that she was growing antsy. She stopped in front of a desk, picked up a pen and then placed it down. Her fingers roamed over the top of a notepad, and then she made her way to a bookcase. She stood there, brow pinched as she placed a finger on the spine of each book.

"Do you want to read something?" I asked.

She jumped at the sound of my voice, and then lowered her chin obediently.

I started toward her but stopped. Any unexpected movement seemed to send her fleeing. "It's okay, Alex. If you want to read something you can."

"My name is not Alex," she whispered. "It is Alexandria."

A dull burn started in my chest, under my heart. "But you like to be called Alex."

Shaking her head, she backed away from the books and slowly headed toward the TV, eyes downcast. She stopped in front of the blank screen. I picked up a small statue of Athena, and then placed it back down. I wanted to go to her, to hold her, but I wasn't sure how she'd respond. Everything between us was stilted and awkward.

"Want to watch something?"

Her chin shot up, but she didn't look at me. At her sides, her hands opened and closed. "May I?"

May I? Gods, when Alex was better, she was going to flip out. "You can do what you want."

A small, tentative smile pulled at her lips and her lashes swept up, revealing those shattered eyes. I breathed out slowly, but it did nothing to ease the pressure clamping down on my chest. Her gaze flickered away from mine. "Will you—"

The door opened and Apollo strolled in. "There you two are."

Alex froze in front of the TV, like a wild animal that had just been encroached upon. Then she dashed across the room, ducking behind me. She huddled there, clenching the back of my shirt.

Apollo stopped short, blond eyebrows shooting up. "Did she just *hide* behind you?"

I glared at the god. "She's not the same. You know that."

He blinked all-white eyes. "I know. It's just unexpected. She's like a little nymph or something."

Hearing the word "nymph" come out of *Apollo's* mouth grated at my self-control. "What do you want?"

Apollo cocked his head to the side and spoke low. "Testy, testy, Aiden."

Her fingers dug into my back. I moved to the side, shielding her completely. If Apollo had had normal eyes, I was sure they would've rolled at that point. Ignoring him, I smiled down at her. "It's okay. Apollo won't hurt you."

Or at least I hoped so.

Alex peered up at me through her lashes. For the first time since she'd Awakened, I saw trust in her expression. Warmth poured into the cold cavern where my heart rested. I'd never seen an indentured half-blood look upon their Master that way. It had to mean something.

Apollo cleared his throat. "And I see some things never change."

I frowned. "What's that mean?"

"Oh, you know, the googly-eyed looks of love. Even when someone—ahem, like me, a god—is standing right in front of you two."

I rolled my eyes, prepared to ignore that comment, but Alex tugged on my shirt. "What does he mean by that?" she whispered.

How was I supposed to answer? The fact that Alex didn't remember a lot was key to keeping her away from Seth, but I wasn't sure how much information to share with her. And she was actually asking a question, which was huge. "I'll explain it later."

Apollo chuckled. "I'd love to hear that conversation." My eyes narrowed, and he grinned. Sometimes I think his sole purpose was to get under my skin. "There's been a development I believe you should be aware of."

I doubted it was good news. I started to respond, but Alex tugged on my shirt once more and whispered, "My head hurts."

"I'll get you something for that in a few moments. Okay?" Casting her eyes down, she nodded.

I wanted this to hurry up. Shifting to the side, I shielded Alex. "Does it have to do with the other one?"

Catching that I meant Seth, he nodded. "He's not happy about not being able to make contact. Dionysus's spies have said that both he and the Minister are growing agitated."

"I bet." No one really knew how Seth would react once the bond was broken. I felt Alex peek around me. She was watching Apollo with large eyes. He grinned at her, and she gave him a hesitant smile. "Has he done something?" I asked.

"Hmm, if you count obliterating two Sentinels who refused to join their cause? Then yes."

"Gods," I murmured, shifting again when Alex moved behind me.

Apollo craned his neck to the side, following Alex's nervous movements. "They haven't moved against the Tennessee Covenant yet, but about fifty of their Sentinels have broken away and appear to be heading toward the New York one. He's with the Minister still."

"And if they make it to New York, what will happen?"

His expression turned grim. "I've let a few things out of Olympus, just in case those Sentinels are up to no good."

Dread blossomed. "What few things?"

"A few of Hephaestus's most interesting creations—namely the Khalkotauroi."

I choked on my breath. I had to have heard him wrong. The Khalkotauroi were automatons—bronze bulls that breathed fire—but they weren't what were known in the myth of Jason and the Golden Fleece. First off, there weren't just two of them. There were hundreds of them, and they walked on two legs. Like all the creatures that belong to the gods, they had been rounded up and sent to Olympus when the gods had retreated from the mortal world.

"And what happens if a mortal sees them?"

Apollo arched a brow. "The Khalkotauroi know how to stay hidden, but if New York—or any of the other Covenants—goes under siege, it will be a moot point. The mortal world will become well aware that some myths are true."

There really wasn't anything else to say to that, and my mind was already occupied with too many concerns to dedicate time to this latest development. Apollo left, but not before trying to talk to an edgy Alex who wanted nothing to do with him, much to his amusement. It amazed me that the whole world was on the brink of war and Apollo was laughing.

Granted, this probably wasn't his first time at the rodeo. When Apollo left, she stared up at me, expression pinched.

"My head…it hurts."

"I'll get you something now."

As I left to find her some aspirin, she followed, never straying too far from my side. Taking the two pills without question, I realized then how such trust could be abused—and was with many other halfs—in the wrong hands. A sick and twisted kind of fear rose with that realization.

The aspirin didn't seem to work. Alex withdrew further into herself, eyes squeezed shut through most of the movie I'd put on. A dark voice picked up in the back of my head, remaining constant even after she'd fallen asleep and I carried her to bed, her weight seeming nonexistent. Her headache was a sign.

The Elixir was wearing off. Tomorrow would be the fourth day.

The thought of giving her another dose chipped away at me. Hours passed as I lay on the couch, staring at the ceiling, watching the thin slips of moonlight reach across the darkness. The quilt twisted with my legs as I flipped onto my side. Could I do it again? Hand her something that destroyed her very core and watch her take it with that innate trust in her eyes?

I squeezed my eyes shut, folding my arms beneath my head. There was no other choice. Apollo needed to find a way because she couldn't do it on her own. Sleep finally claimed me, but it didn't last long.

I was jolted awake later. Darkness cloaked the room and the couch felt infinitely smaller than before. The scent of… peaches surrounded me. Something warm and soft pressed against my side, wiggling closer. Hands clenched the old T-shirt I'd dug up the day before.

My eyes flew open.

The top of Alex's head came into view as she placed her

cheek on my chest and let out a little sigh. Every muscle in my body locked up. Was I dreaming? I think I stopped breathing. What was she doing over here, on the couch with me?

"Alex?" My voice sounded gruff. "What are you doing?"

She lifted her head enough that I could see the shreds of amber peeking out from behind her lashes. The shattered eyes were the damndest thing to see at night. "My head hurts."

I started to sit up, but Alex shifted, throwing a leg over mine as if she was asking me not to move without saying a word.

"Uh…" I'd never been more unsure in my life, or unable to read a person. "Do you want me to get you some more aspirin?"

"No." She placed her head on my chest again, snuggling down. "It feels better now. Empty."

I swallowed. Hard. "Empty?"

"Mmm-hmm," she murmured, shivering. "It's quieter when I'm near you."

My heart stuttered. "Quieter? Are you hearing things? A person?"

"I don't know. It's like…" She yawned, splaying her hand across my chest. "It's like someone talking to me far, far away. Does that make me…?"

Seth. Anger surged through me and I fought to keep it out of my voice. "What?"

"Crazy? Does that make me crazy?"

"Not at all, agapi." I lowered one arm and reached down, tugging the quilt up so it covered most of her. "Can you make out what the voice is saying?"

She shook her head. "I don't want to know. I don't have to, do I?"

"No." I ached for her.

"Good," she said, and I wondered if she smiled. "Can I stay with you?"

"Always." Good gods, I didn't want her to be anywhere else.

Silence fell between us, and her breathing became steady and deep. So, the headaches were a sign of Seth trying to contact her, which explained the brief flashes of pain I'd seen before the Elixir and confirmed my suspicions all along. The connection hurt somehow. And now the bond was muted, but it meant she definitely needed another dose tomorrow.

A new wave of fury rolled through me, but I kept my body relaxed, not wanting to frighten her. I'd truly believed that Seth had grown to care for Alex, perhaps even love her in his own way—whatever way that was. Especially after Caleb died, he'd cared for her, protected her when I hadn't. In New York, he watched over her and would've killed without a thought to make sure no one learned that she'd killed a pure in self-defense. Had it all been a ruse? An act to ensure that Alex would live so that she could Awaken, giving him power as the God Killer?

Yeah, I'd never fully trusted the punk, those moments when I'd seen something I could never name in his cold eyes—eyes that had belonged to Alex for a period of time. Something about him set off my warning system and pissed me off like nothing else. That could've just been his interest in Alex, but still.

I'd never expected him to hurt her.

If I ever got my hands on that little bastard, I was going to kill him or die trying.

But right now, Alex was lying beside me, and hell if I was going to think about Seth. Very carefully, I lowered my left arm and wrapped it around her too-slender waist. There was another soft sigh from her. She seemed incredibly small beside me. How had I not noticed that in the past? Maybe because all I ever saw was her strength.

I could've suggested that she go back to the bed or that both of us move there, but I didn't have the heart or desire to move her. Not when she was close to me like this, pulling loose bittersweet and tender memories. I flicked through the days spent in my parents' house and the brief time in Ohio.

Alex murmured something and tipped her head back, brushing the tip of her nose along my chin and jaw. A wealth of warmth spread through me and before I knew what I was doing, I turned my head. My lips brushed her forehead.

"G'night, Aiden…"

My pulse sped up and a smile pulled at my lips—a real one. "Good night, agapi."

CHAPTER EIGHT

Alex took the Elixir and the compulsion without protest the following morning. Four days later, she did so again. Each time, I was more affected by the process than she was. Alex didn't really understand what I was giving her, only that afterward I spoke to her in Greek and she was generally tired.

But with each passing day, a little of her old self shone through while we were alone. Her typical sharp tongue was still absent, much to my dismay. Who could've known how badly I'd miss her smart-ass responses? She did smile more often and even though she rarely left my side, she didn't freak out too badly when Lea and Luke popped in on us one day. They were good with Alex, if not a little shocked by how different she was. They didn't stay too long.

I think it scared them—seeing how very real the Elixir was, what it could do to them. How it stripped Alex down to nothing more than a shell. I caught Lea staring at her once, and it was clear what she was thinking. *This could be me.* She was seeing herself in Alex's dull, shattered eyes.

By the third day, the headaches started, and each time she looked at me and mentioned the pain, I wanted to break each of Seth's ribs individually.

A sort of routine developed between us while we waited for Apollo to show, hopefully with good news. We spent the day together and at night she eventually made her way over to the couch. Admittedly it was my favorite part of the day. The bed was still off-limits. There was an intimacy to that, one I desired and had a hell of a time refusing, but with her like this, it would've crossed the line.

Alex pulled out the chessboard and placed it on the coffee table while I watched her. Gods, I loved just watching her. Sounded creepy as hell, I know, but my eyes just sought her out. There was a gracefulness about her that she'd retained, even after three doses.

"Play?" She plopped down on the floor on the other side of the coffee table.

I'd been teaching her how to play chess. When I nodded and moved to sit on the floor, she grabbed one of the pawns and placed it in the row closest to her.

Teaching her how to play wasn't really going well.

When she looked away, I reached over, replacing the pawn with a knight. Clasping her hands under her chin, she listened while I went over the rules again. Once I was finished, she went first, moving a pawn forward one space.

I tried picturing playing chess with Alex in a different time, like a month ago. Imagining her sitting still long enough and having the patience for a game like chess was impossible. Knowing her, she'd have thrown a chess piece by now. I laughed.

Alex's chin jerked up and she grinned. "What?"

"Nothing," I told her.

Still smiling, she crawled over and sat beside me, then reached across the board, moving another pawn right into position to be taken by mine. I laughed again. "You can't sit next to me and play chess, agapi."

Her shoulders lifted. "I like sitting beside you."

And I liked it, too. I moved a pawn forward, not taking hers.

"I like when you laugh too." She placed a finger to her lips, her brows furrowing as she studied the board. "I think I just like you."

My mouth opened but nothing came out.

"Sometimes I feel…I feel like I should be doing more"— she picked up a rook— "than this. With my life." She placed it back and looked up, searching my face. "With you too."

I knew I needed to say something, but there was too much I wanted to say.

She scooted closer and rested her head on my shoulder. A heartbeat passed. "I have these memories. They are like dreams. Some are really good and others are dark and red." She rubbed her cheek against my shoulder. "I know there is more…to all of this."

"There is," I whispered, watching her lashes fan her cheeks, her lips part.

"I like this. I like when you hold me at night. That feels right…real." She paused, lashes lifting. "Thank you."

"You're welcome." My voice sounded, felt heavy.

Alex raised her head, lips puckered. "I have a feeling you do not say that often."

My breath caught. A ball of emotion formed in my chest. "I don't."

"Do you like it?" She gazed at the board, her fingers now hovering over the wrong pieces.

"Of course I do, agapi." I slid an arm around her shoulders

and leaned over, pressing my lips against her temple, then her forehead. Her cheeks rose with her smile and so did my chest, and that ball tightened and tightened. I pressed my face into the mass of wavy hair and inhaled.

Apollo had said he knew what this kind of love was capable of. And I finally understood why Paris had risked his country and his blood for Helen. Selfish, yes, but I understood. I would burn down the world if that meant Alex would be safe.

"Knock, knock," came Deacon's voice. Alex stiffened.

Pulling away from her, I looked up. He stood in the door, a slight smile on his face. Withdrawing my arm, I stood, surprised to find my legs weak.

Alex's eyes bounced from my brother to me and she must've read something in my eyes, because she relaxed and went back to the chessboard.

"What's up?" I asked.

He sauntered into the room. "What's up with you?"

My lips twitched. "Playing chess with Alex."

"Stimulating." Deacon watched Alex move her chess pieces around the board in no particular order. "Luke's been in contact with Olivia. She's with her mom and they've hooked up with Laadan. They want to come here."

"If they are with Laadan, then I trust them. Clear it with Marcus, though."

"I like Marcus." Alex stood and drifted over to me.

Deacon arched a brow. "Now, that's odd…"

"Deacon," I warned.

Alex smiled up at me, holding a bishop in her hand. "Checkmate?"

He chortled. "Good gods, she's like a beta-version AI."

Anger whipped through me so fast I saw red, and then Alex frowned. "Is that a good thing?" she asked.

Taking a step toward my brother, I exploded. "Get the hell out of here before I strangle you within an inch of your life."

Eyes wide, Deacon's hands flew up. "Whoa, I was just kidding. I mean, come on, she's pretty random now."

Rage swept through me. He was my brother. I loved him, but dammit, he never thought before he spoke. Voice low, I said, "Do you even know how insulting that is to Alex?"

He blinked, his cheeks flushing. "I wasn't thinking—"

"No shit."

"I didn't mean anything by it, Aiden. I'm sorry." His gaze went behind me and he frowned. "I really am."

Taking a deep breath, I let the red-hot anger slip off my brittle skin. "I know. It's just that…" There was no need to finish. Deacon knew. "I didn't mean to…yell at you. Just let Marcus know about Laadan and Olivia. Okay?"

Deacon looked like he wanted to say more, but wisely nodded and backed out of the room.

Sighing, I turned around. "Alex—"

The spot she'd stood in was empty. Dammit. I should've known better. Yelling and threatening to choke the ever-loving crap out of Deacon in front of her hadn't been wise. I kept forgetting that this wasn't Alex.

This was a frightened girl.

My eyes scanned the room, stopping on the linen closet door. It was ajar, revealing a thin strip of darkness. She wouldn't…

To think of Alex—my strong, beautiful, and resilient Alex—hiding in a closet killed me. For a heartbeat, I couldn't move or breathe. I'd done this to her—given her the Elixir, changed her into something that ran when voices were raised. And I wanted to blame Seth for his influence, the bond he'd forged with her that'd led us to this choice, but I'd been the one who'd forced the Elixir down her throat.

There wasn't forgiveness for me.

Stamping down the whirling mix of grief and rage, I made my way to the closet and slowly opened the double doors. It was a deep closet, with several shelves on the top stocked with quilts. A few garment bags hung from a rail. My gaze dropped. Five tiny toes peeked out from behind a bag.

I closed my eyes and swore under my breath, and then I eased the bags apart. Alex's foot jerked back, and I could hear her moving deeper into the recesses. Kneeling down, I found her pressed against the wall, knees tucked against her chest and eyes wide.

"Oh, Alex."

She watched me warily. "My name is Alexandria."

And just like that, all those days of drawing her out of the Elixir-induced shell were lost.

"Okay." I sat down cross-legged and dragged my fingers through my hair, debating on how to proceed with this. Deacon used to get nightmares when he was a kid. He hadn't hidden in the closet, but he *had* screamed like a furie. I used to read to him. Somehow I doubted that would work now. "Are you all right?"

A moment passed. "I do not like yelling."

"I know. I'm sorry." And I was. "But I would never hurt Deacon. He's my brother."

Confusion flickered over her face. "You said you were going to strangle him."

I really wanted to strangle him now. "I didn't mean it. Sometimes we say things we don't mean when we're upset."

She appeared to consider that. "When you yelled, I saw something."

"What?" I inched forward, careful not to startle her. "What did you see?"

Opening her hands, she stared down at them. The bishop was in her hand, leaving behind angry red marks from how tightly she'd been holding it. "Blood—there was blood on my hands, but it was not there. Not really."

I had no idea what she meant by that, but I'd moved to her side while she'd been talking, and she hadn't seemed to notice. I sat next to her, stretching out my legs in the cramped space. My shoulder brushed hers, and her eyes shot to my face, questioning and indecisive but not scared.

"Is there still blood on your hands now?"

Alex shook her head. "I heard something, too. It was a voice," she continued softly. "It was important."

My stomach sank. I didn't like where this was going, what it would lead to. If she was starting to remember things, it meant she'd need another dose, another compulsion. And I'd just given the last dose two days ago. I sighed. "What is it?"

Her fingers twisted along the edges of the bishop. "You'll kill the ones you love." She lifted her gaze. Tears glistened in her eyes. "Have I?"

"Alex..." There weren't words for this. Her lower lip started to tremble, and my heart squeezed. My mind was made up. "No. You've never killed anyone."

She blinked and her voice was just a hushed whisper. "I haven't?"

"No, agapi mou, you haven't."

Wiping under her eyes with her sleeves, she sighed. Pain brimmed underneath the surface, as did confusion. "I dream that I have, over and over again."

I smiled for her even as I felt my chest constricting. "They're just dreams. That's all."

Several moments passed, and then she pressed against me,

wiggling until she wedged her body under my arm. She curled up, her head resting against my chest and my arms folded across hers. "You are very nice, even if you say mean things you do not mean."

I shook my head, but I wrapped my arms around her. "Did I ever tell you about the first time I saw you?"

She shivered. "No."

Closing my eyes, I felt her snuggle closer. My hand curled into the thick material of her sweater. I rested my chin on her head. "I was sixteen and you were probably fourteen."

"I can't remember fourteen."

"That's okay. I remember for both of us." I counted to ten before I continued, making sure my voice didn't give. "It was toward the end of the day and I was heading into the training rooms with a friend. Classes were still going on, and I was walking by the door—it was open—and I heard laughter. Something you don't usually hear during training. I had to stop and see what was going on."

It was the first time I'd seen her. No one could miss her. She was the smallest in the room, shorter and skinnier than all of her opponents, but that wasn't why she stuck out. There'd been this impish grin on her face, an energy that was infectious as she'd bounced around the mats, circling a tall, blond-haired boy. The Instructor had been irritated, no doubt by her and the attention she was drawing from a pure and an entire class riveted on her. But once I'd seen her, I couldn't look away. It was like being hit by lightning.

"You were training with Cal—with a friend—going through takedown moves. He kept trying to get the upper hand, but you kept laying him out, laughing the entire time. Both of you were laughing. That's why I looked."

“Did you know me then?” she asked sleepily.

“No.” I held her closer, as if I could somehow pull her inside me and keep her safe. “But I knew, in that moment, you were amazing.”

CHAPTER NINE

Apollo showed up just after Alex's fourth dosage with no news. The Sentinels hadn't reached New York. They'd stopped in Pennsylvania and scattered. The Khalkotauroi followed. Seth and Lucian were still outside of Nashville. From the look of it, their army had nearly doubled.

Having so many Sentinels willing to side with them wasn't that surprising to me. They'd been offered something none of us had ever provided, and they were willing to die for freedom.

And there was a good chance they would, according to Apollo.

"Hades, Poseidon, and Demeter." Apollo ticked the names off on his fingers, his eyes a vibrant blue. "And Ares, who is thrilled by the way, and Hermes, and Hera have all pledged war."

"Hera?" I rubbed my chin. "At least we have Zeus."

Apollo rolled his eyes. "That doesn't mean much. He's probably only siding with us to upset Hera, but we do have Athena and Artemis. That's something."

"So, they are willing to wait and see? To give us time?"

He nodded. "They do not want to see another war. Not after what happened with the Titans. So many mortals were lost during that time, and with the population now, the loss would be several times larger."

And our only hope was that Alex could somehow break the connection with Seth and defeat him. I looked at the sleeping girl curled beside me on the couch. The outlook was bleak.

"And no one's found anything to break the connection?"

Apollo sighed. "There's nothing that any of us can find, Aiden. Not in the old myths or scrolls. And if one of the other six know, they aren't telling." He glanced at Alex and fondness crept into the coldness of his voice. As did a great sadness that caused dread to explode in my gut. "I've run through all the prophecies. They haven't changed. One to destroy. One to save. Only one can live during any generation."

He leaned back, shaking his head. "I can't let my brethren go to war."

I placed my hand on Alex's shoulder. "Are you giving up on her?"

"I'm preparing for the worst." Apollo stood. "And don't hit me, Aiden, but I think you need to start preparing for it too."

My skin burned and I said in a tight voice, "You've asked me to put her on the Elixir, and I told you then that you asked too much, but I did it. Asking me to give up is unacceptable."

"It's not giving up." He crouched, meeting my stare. "I would make sure she was taken care of, even allow her to visit you. We could do a Persephone thing."

I sucked in a shrill breath that came back out sounding like a growl. "You're asking me to let you kill her."

"I would make sure there was no pain," he said, standing again. He turned his back—daring, considering I was close to shoving a dagger into it. "This isn't easy for me. I care for her. She is basically a child of mine. And I've watched over her for years, far longer than you've known her." He faced me, hands on his hips. "This would not just be your loss, but only one of them can live and I can't do a thing about Seth. Nor do I know who he's linked to."

My hand curled into a fist as I moved to stand between Alex and Apollo. "Get out."

"Aiden—"

"I mean it. Get out."

His eyes flashed to all-white. No pupils. No irises. "I only allow you to speak to me like this because I know your love and pain, because I have felt it myself. Hyacinth wasn't turned into a flower by my brethren. It was I who did it. It was the only way I could save him from them. So, I know what love does and the pain that comes from that kind of sacrifice. But make no mistake, I do not regret what I had to do. And I will do it again."

I stayed in place between them, my legs widespread, so ready for battle I could taste it. "And make no mistake, Apollo, I will not make that same sacrifice."

I couldn't stand to be in the house any longer. My nerves were stretched taut, my body ready to fight. Bloodlust had invaded my system.

I needed fresh air.

So did Alex. Once she'd woken up, she'd been all over the place, not able to sit still for longer than five minutes.

For the first time since she'd Awakened, I led her outside.

Seeing the joy light up her eyes and the cool breeze brushing the hair off her cheeks lessened the darkness growing inside me. The almost-hyper bounce in her step as she made her way around fallen branches and shrubs reminded me of the old Alex.

Especially when she stopped suddenly, spying a small stream up ahead. She spun around quickly and threw her arms around me.

Surprised by the sudden affection, I froze, then wrapped my arms around her waist and leaned back. "What's that for?"

Alex shrugged. "I wanted to."

I caught her hand as she shimmied loose. "I liked that."

She smiled. "Maybe I'll do it again." Glancing over her shoulder, excitement hummed through her. She tugged me forward.

Letting go of her hand, I stopped. She looked over her shoulder again, brows knitted. "You can go," I urged.

"Are you sure?"

I nodded, and then leaned against an old oak. Her gaze darted over my face and she seemed to find whatever she was looking for. She turned, slowly starting toward the creek bed. Her footsteps were quick but not jerky. The antsy energy she'd been feeling all day would eventually grow. Crippling pain would assault her again as soon as her tolerance to the Elixir grew and Seth started pecking away at her.

And if I didn't give her a larger dose along with a booster compulsion, the bond between them would form again.

Closing my eyes, I tipped my head back. There had to be another way. We couldn't keep doing this to her. Sooner or later, the effects of the Elixir wouldn't wear off. She'd be like this forever—forever stuck between the tenacious and strong-willed Alex and this naïve, watered-down Alexandria. To do this to her wasn't right. The wrongness of it coated my mouth and throat like bile. It was acid churning in my stomach, burning a hole through my soul.

And Apollo…he was giving up, even if he didn't want to admit it—giving up and preparing to kill Alex.

Clenching my jaw, I opened my eyes. Alex sat on a fallen log near the slow-moving creek. She held something in her hands—flowers? Her face was turned to the side and her lips were pulled down at the corners. Sadness had crept into her features.

I pushed off the tree but stopped as she picked off a petal and placed it on the log. Then another and another, until ten or so petals formed a loose circle beside her. She placed two more, completing the circle, and then two more inside the circle.

My chest tightened and, without any warning, a fissure of energy skittered over my skin. I turned, expecting to find Apollo—or worse yet, an unfriendly god. I sucked in a sharp breath.

An ethereal glow surrounded the feminine form and slowly faded, revealing a slender woman who stood taller than me. Lilies adorned the brown hair that had been piled atop her head in an intricate maze of braids. A sheer white dress covered her body and left very little to the imagination. I felt I should look away but couldn't. She was almost painfully beautiful—unreal.

A faint smile appeared. "Hello, Aiden." Her voice was a symphony, and I started to bow, but she stopped me with a raised hand. "That is not necessary. Unlike my brothers and sisters, I do not have a taste for formalities."

It took me a few moments to find my voice. "You're one of the Moirae…one of the Fates."

"I am Clotho."

Fear formed a cold, hard ball in the center of my chest. Clotho was responsible for spinning the thread of human life, but she also decided when gods could be saved or put to death. I glanced over my shoulder at Alex. Did her powers extend to god-like creatures, too? I moved to block Alex from her view.

Clotho's laugh was soft and melodious. "I am not here to harm her, and even if I were, I cannot cut her thread. Neither can Atropos."

Relieved by that piece of information, I faced the goddess. "Why are you here?"

"I've been watching you and her." She stepped to the side. Sunlight broke through the branches, cutting across her bare shoulder and over her dress. The material shimmered. "It pains you to see her like this, I know. You love her so."

I saw no reason, no point, in lying to a goddess of Fate. "More than anything in this world, and without her..." Clearing my throat, I looked away. I couldn't finish the sentence, let alone the thought.

"Going on would be like existing with a piece of you missing?" She nodded when I looked at her again. "Your threads are intertwined. Not by my doing, you see?"

I didn't see a damn thing. Now I understood Alex's frustration when she'd spoken to the oracle. I opened my mouth but closed it. Understanding slid over my skin like thick oil. "She was Fated to be with Seth, wasn't she?"

She looked at me and her smile faded. "She was, but Fate has many plans for her."

"What will happen to her?" I asked before I could stop myself. Somehow, I knew that asking a Fate that kind of question equaled poor social skills.

"You do not ask for yourself?"

Sure, curiosity was there, but my fate didn't matter. I shook my head.

Her brows rose. "Most would not pass up a chance to learn their fate, but I cannot tell you what lies in wait for your Alexandria. Some things are even unknown to us."

Disappointment seeped into me, wrapping its way around my bones like a too-tight binding. I turned back to Alex. She was watching us, eyes wide and hands stilled over the petals.

"It's okay," I called out to her.

Alex didn't move for a full minute, and then she gathered all her torn petals, tossing them one by one into the creek.

Clotho watched Alex, too. "Their threads are intertwined closely—the First's and hers."

My hands clenched. "And there's no way that can be undone?"

She tilted her head. "No. Just like yours cannot be undone. Fate is fate, you see, but there is one thing we do not take into consideration when we spin the threads of life, not even when we cut it."

Part of me didn't expect an answer, but I asked, "What is that?"

"Love. We do not take love into consideration."

I looked at her. "Seriously?"

She laughed and it carried on the breeze. "Love is such a wild and reckless creature. It cannot be planned or threaded. It cannot be controlled. Love can coexist with Fate, or it can undo it. Love is the only thing more powerful than Fate."

The words were slow to sink in as I stared at the goddess. Was this why the goddess had made such a surprise visit?

Her white eyes burned and hummed with electricity. "You want to know how to break the connection?"

My breath caught. "Yes."

Sympathy creased Clotho's brow. Stepping forward, she placed a small hand against my chest, above my heart. "There is no god or person who can break their connection, but there is still hope." She dropped her hand and stepped back, nodding. "There is the heart, Aiden. There is love, which means there is always hope."

Then Clotho shimmered out of focus and disappeared. Feeling as if my nerves were exposed, I stalked around the fallen branches and overturned trees. Reaching Alex's side, I realized I was holding my breath.

Something was building inside me, clicking together.

Alex turned to me, her shattered eyes meeting mine. The mix of brown and gold was as beautiful as it was heartbreaking. I really looked into them, seeing the trust that had always been there, devotion and love buried deep inside her. No bond—no connection—could fully extinguish that. It was why she hadn't destroyed the necklace I'd made her.

There was still hope.

Clotho had said that love was stronger than Fate. Was that really the answer we'd been searching for? Love—our love for one another?

Then I remembered what Alex had said to me. *"I won't lose myself, because...well, how I feel about you, it would never let me forget who I am."*

Somehow, I'd forgotten that. I'd believed that she'd forgotten who she was, but in reality none of us, especially me, had had hope once she'd Awakened—not that kind of undying hope that saw people through the tough stuff. Granted, this wasn't the ordinary tough stuff that most couples faced.

And what had I told her then? *"I'd never let you forget who you are."*

Lowering her lashes, she opened her hand and the rest of

the petals fell from her grasp, fluttering to the ground like thin, torn pieces of paper. "It's beautiful here…and quiet. Can we stay for a little while longer?"

I wasn't sure what I was doing when I placed my hands on her cheeks, tilting her head back. "Alex…"

Instead of correcting her name, she let it slide. Her eyes searched mine. "Aiden?"

My lips curved into a smile for her—always for her. "Do you believe in love?"

"Yes," she said without hesitation. "Do you?"

"I do." My hands slid to her shoulders and she shivered. "I believe in love."

Thick lashes fanned her cheeks again and a grin tipped her lips. "I think I am in love."

Six words stopped my heart when facing down a horde of daimons couldn't.

She bit her lip and a faint blush stained her cheeks. "I feel it in here," she said, placing her hand against her chest and then against her stomach, "and here. It's like there's not enough air or room inside me. That I may…burst out of my skin or drown in it, and that wouldn't be a bad thing. I don't know why I feel this way, but I always have…and will." She tipped her chin up and her entire face was a rosy color. "It's you. I…I love you."

Heart pounding, I swept her against me in a fierce hug, lifting her off her feet. Her giggle was smothered but light. I buried my face in her hair. "I love you, Alex, always you."

CHAPTER TEN

Determination burned through me like a righteous fire. I had a plan—I had hope—and nothing was going to stop what I was about to do. After depositing a worn-out Alex in the bedroom, I quickly changed into my Sentinel uniform. A sense of rightfulness filled me as I strapped on the daggers and laced up what Alex referred to as my "ass-kicking" boots. I smiled.

I hadn't worn the uniform since we'd left Deity Island.

Straightening, I glanced at myself in the mirror. Freshly shaven and hair brushed back, I looked and felt like a different person. The heavy weight that'd settled on my shoulders had lifted the moment I'd made up my mind.

I left the bathroom, stopped by and checked on Alex, and pressed a kiss to her temple before going downstairs. It took me a few minutes to round up the group of Sentinels who'd stopped in on their way east. I sent them packing.

Solos snapped at my heels. "What are you doing, Aiden?"

"They don't belong here."

He stared at me as I closed the door behind the last one

and stepped back. "They would come in handy if Seth finds his way here, you know."

"No, they wouldn't. No one would stop him if he finds his way here." I knelt, pulling out a Covenant dagger. "Only Alex would be able to stop him."

"And is Alex in the frame of mind to stop him?"

"Not yet."

Marcus came into the hallway behind us. "What's going on?"

"Go get Lea, Luke, and my brother. We need to talk." I cut my palm, hissing at the flash of pain. Blood welled quickly. I placed my palm on the floor and started to draw the symbol I'd seen in Lucian's house.

Marcus sucked in a breath. "Aiden, what is—?"

"Get them." I finished with the snake symbol. An instant later, a flash of bright white light filled the hallway. The walls were luminous, sealing off the property, preventing Apollo from entering the home. I stood, wrapping a rag around my hand. "I'll explain."

"Dear gods, I hope so."

Solos still stared. "Aiden has gone Rambo on us."

Everyone gathered in the den. Nervous energy surrounded Lea and Luke. Only my brother seemed relaxed. Perhaps he'd seen this version of me before and knew that nothing could change my mind once it was made up.

Nothing except Alex, and this was about Alex—this was *for* Alex.

I stood before them. "The only way for Alex to break the connection is for her to do so herself. No one—no god, no magic—can do it. *She* has to. And I believe she can if given the chance."

"Didn't we give her the chance?" Solos asked.

"Not enough," I told him, prepared to send his ass flying

out the window if he didn't agree. "But I believe in her—I have hope. And hope is what we need. I'm taking her off the Elixir."

Marcus stared at me, then nodded. "What does Apollo have to say about this?"

And here was the kicker. "He's giving up, and he's preparing himself to kill her. Only one of them can live, and she's the one he can do something about."

They didn't question what that meant, but I think they had a good idea.

Lea's eyes narrowed. "He wouldn't."

"He would. And I understand why." My jaw ached saying those words. "He has to protect humanity. That's what he does. But I'm not giving up on her. And if any of you have, I suggest you leave now."

No one moved, but I waited, giving them ample opportunity to choose. "There's no doubt in my mind Apollo's going to be pissed when he realizes what I've done and what I plan to do. If you stay here..."

The unspoken words hung in the room. They knew. On top of everything else, they'd face Apollo's wrath.

Luke glanced at Deacon and smiled. "Apollo kind of freaks me out, anyway."

"No doubt," Deacon replied, shaking his shoulders. "And hey, if you believe in Alex, so do I. You know her better than any of us."

"That is true." Marcus smiled, leaning against the couch. "I'm in."

Solos sighed. "This is crazy, but what the hell? I came here to protect Alex. Not to hand her over to be put down like a dog."

I turned to Lea, and for the first time in a long time, she

smirked. "I want to see Alex kick Seth's ass. Someone's got to do it. It wouldn't be fair that she dies for him to live."

I breathed a sigh of relief. "You guys know this could get bad, really bad."

No one moved for a while, and then Marcus strolled forward, clapping a hand down on my shoulder. "We've got your back, Aiden. We've also got Alex's."

And that was what I needed to hear. "She can do this. I know she can."

I left them then, retreating to the bedroom. I crossed the room to the bed and sat. Alex stirred, aware enough that she didn't resist when I pulled her into my arms, cradling her to my chest. I'd prepared myself, but not in the way Apollo meant.

Alex would get no more doses, and when the Elixir wore off, I would do what I felt was the worst thing possible. I'd place her back in the cell, and then I'd wait.

I'd fight.

Alex. Seth. A whole slew of gods if necessary. No one was going to take Alex. No one was going to give up on her or hurt her—not even Alex.

Apollo had changed Hyacinth into a flower to protect him. I would give Alex control back so she could protect herself instead of making the decision for her. That's how we were different from the gods.

I lowered my lips to her cheek and kept them there, holding her tighter and tighter. The gods wanted war?

They were about to get it.

READ ON FOR SPECIAL BONUS SCENES

DEITY CHAPTER THIRTY-FOUR (AIDEN'S POV)

Not going to lie to myself. Hearing Apollo say Seth needed to die made me want to hug the guy. By far, it was the smartest thing the god had ever said, but…

"What?" demanded Alex, her voice pitching in horror.

Apollo turned back to the window. "You would have to kill him, Alexandria. As an Apollyon, you will be able to."

Alex paled, and I knew the idea of killing Seth horrified her. As much as I hated to admit it or even acknowledge the fact, there was a bond between the two that even I feared I could not always breach.

"I can't do that," she said.

"You can't?" Lea sparked to life. "He killed my sister, Alex! He killed those Council members."

"I know, but it's…it's not his fault. Lucian has warped his mind." She paused, taking a deep breath. "It wasn't his fault."

Lea's lips thinned, and I moved closer to Alex. "That doesn't make what he did okay."

"I know that, but..." Alex's gaze fell to the cake. "There has to be another way."

"I know a part of you cares for him," Apollo said quietly. "You were...built to feel that way. A part of him is you and vice versa, but it is the only way."

Built to feel that way? If I could, I'd carve out that part—*in* Seth.

Alex swallowed. "Is there another way, Apollo?"

"Does it matter?" Lea slammed her hands down on the table. "He needs to die, Alex."

Alex flinched.

"Lea," Marcus said gently.

"No! I'm not going to shut up about this!" She shot to her feet, her face flushing. "I know it doesn't seem fair, Alex. But Seth killed those people—*my sister.* And that wasn't fair. And it sucks. I even thought Seth was hot, but that was up until he *incinerated* my sister. You like him. That's great. You're a part of him. Awesome. But he killed people, Alex."

"I understand that, Lea." Alex looked around the room, her gaze settling on me, and when she spoke next, I had a feeling she was directing these words at me. "Everyone keeps saying there's hope. Maybe we can save him. And Artemis mentioned something about power going both ways. Maybe there is something to that."

Pain lit up my chest, and I wanted nothing more than to back her up, but I couldn't on this. It was too dangerous.

"You loved your mom, right?" Lea asked, her hands trembling. "You loved her even after she became a daimon."

"Lea," I cut in sharply, eyes narrowing. Bringing up Alex's mom was going way too far.

"But you knew she needed to...needed to be stopped,"

she rushed on before I could silence her. "You loved her, but you did the right thing. How is this any different?"

Alex recoiled like she'd been slapped. Her mouth opened, but she didn't speak. The ache in my chest grew. Putting Alex once again in a situation where she'd have to hurt—to kill someone she loved wasn't fair. No one should have to face what Alex had and would have to.

"I think that's enough for today," Marcus interjected.

Lea stood her ground for a few more seconds, but then stormed out of the room. I was grateful when Alex didn't follow her. That conversation wouldn't end any place good.

"She's in a dark place right now," Marcus said. "She hurts. Maybe later she'll understand that this is hard for you, also."

"It's not as hard as it is for her." Alex tucked her hair back. "I just can't… The idea of killing him makes me sick. There has to be another way."

Apollo glided toward her, and I stiffened. "All of this…can wait. Today is your birthday, your Awakening."

"Yeah, well, I don't know what's going on with that." She stared at her palms, frowning. "I feel the same. Nothing's happened."

"When were you born?" Apollo asked.

"Uh, March the fourth."

I grinned.

He arched a brow. "What time, Alexandria? What was the time of your birth?"

She pursed my lips. "I don't know."

A dubious look crossed Apollo's face. "You don't know what time you were born?"

"No. Do people know that?"

"I was born at 6:15 a.m.," I said, failing to hide my grin. "Deacon was born at 12:55 p.m. Our parents told us."

Her eyes narrowed. "Well, no one told me…or I forgot."

"Marcus?" Apollo asked.

He shook his head. "I don't…recall."

"Well, you obviously have not hit your time of birth yet." Apollo pushed away from the window. "I think we have had enough serious talk for the day. It is, after all, your birthday. A time for celebration, not making plans for battle."

Alex shuddered, and in that moment, I wanted everyone in the room to stop talking. I wanted to pull her into my arms.

"You will be fine." Apollo placed his hand on her shoulder, and damn if I didn't like that, which was messed up. "You do not feel the bond from where we are, so he cannot connect with you. You will be fine."

Alex kept watching the clock, and I knew she was obsessing over every second that passed. We sat together on the couch. No TV. No music. Just us. Most would be surprised by the fact Alex could actually sit and not talk or be moving around. Sometimes that even surprised me.

"Stop it." I grabbed her hand, pulling it away from her mouth. "Since when did you become a nail-biter?"

She shrugged and then she took a little breath. "Do you think I'm weak?"

"What?" Did she really just ask that? I tugged her over so that she was in my lap, her legs stretched over the cushions. Probably not the smartest thing, considering anyone could walk in on us, but I'd been dying to hold her ever since Apollo made his announcement. "Good gods, you're one of the strongest people I know."

She stiffened as she eyed the door and then, willing to be reckless as ever, placed her cheek against my chest. My heart jumped as she pulled out the rose, fiddling with it. "I don't feel very strong."

Wrapping my arms around her, I held her tight to my chest. "Because of what everyone was talking about today?"

Her gaze fixed on the rose. "Lea had a point, you know? I faced down my mom, but I can't…do that with Seth."

Hearing that wasn't easy. As much as I loathed Seth's very existence, I would never want Alex to have to face this. I placed my chin atop her head and said the words that tasted like venom on my tongue. "Apollo was right. He's a part of you. In a way, it's different than what happened with your mom."

"It is different. My mom was a daimon and there was no coming back from that." She closed her eyes. "He's still in there, Aiden. There has to be another way. And I think Apollo knows, but he's not telling us."

"Then we'll talk to Apollo. He mentioned the oracle, and maybe something has changed." I dipped my head, brushing my lips along her smooth forehead. "But if there isn't another way…"

"Then I have to face it. I know. I just want to make sure before we decide he needs to be…killed."

I covered her hands with mine. "Maybe we need to go see this new oracle. Who knows? She may be able to tell us something, visions or not."

"That is if we can get Apollo to tell us."

"We will."

She smiled up at me, and my body and my heart responded to the curve of her lips. Gods, I could never grow weary of seeing her smile. There was a certain level of abandonment behind her smiles, a gift of a love she gave so freely and recklessly.

"You're amazing," she whispered.

I grinned. "What makes you say that?"

"You're easily the most sup—*ow!*" She yelped as she jerked her hand free from mine. "Something stung me."

I straightened, gripping her wrist in a gentle hold. Tiny drops of blood covered the top of her left hand. "Alex, you're bleeding."

Alex stared at her hand for a moment and then she sat up quickly, her gaze swinging toward the clock. "It's happening."

For a moment, I was frozen. It was happening? Why was there blood? No one mentioned blood. The words came out hoarsely. "It'll be okay."

Her face tensed as more blood appeared on her hand and then she lurched free, standing. "Oh my gods…"

I shot to my feet, my heart thumping. "Alex, what can I do?"

"I don't know. I didn't—" She gasped as blood appeared on her arm. "Oh gods, the marks—the marks are like tattoos."

No. No way. Her whole body would be covered. Bile rose in my throat.

"*Gods*," I said, reaching for her, but she backpedaled. I swallowed as my gaze locked with her panicked one. "Alex, it's going to be okay."

She kept moving backward and then she stopped suddenly. Her face flushed and droplets of blood appeared. A scream parted her lips as she dropped to her knees, doubling over, hands curling into the empty space around her face.

"Oh…oh man, this is gonna blow," she gasped.

Heart racing and throwing itself against my ribs, pure terror ripped through my insides as I knelt beside her, wanting to comfort her, but knowing I could not touch her. There was nothing I could do, absolutely nothing!

"Just…take a deep breath, Alex. Breathe with me."

She let out a strangled laugh. "I'm…I'm not having a baby,

Aiden. This is—" Her body convulsed and she screamed again, planting her hands on the floor. "Okay…okay, I'm breathing."

Gods, this…this was killing me in a way nothing ever had. I inched closer, hating the helpless feeling. "Good. You're doing really good. You know that, agapi mou. You're doing great."

Tears streamed down her face as her back bowed and then her legs gave out. Carefully, I helped her lay on her stomach. My gaze traveled the length of her, sucking in a horrified breath. Spots of blood soaked through the back of her jeans.

The door opened, and Marcus barreled in. "What the—oh, my gods, is she okay?"

"Shit," Alex whimpered.

"She's Awakening." I didn't recognize my own voice as my hands hovered helplessly above her rigid body.

"But the blood…" Marcus moved closer. "Why is she bleeding?"

Alex eased onto her side. "I'm being tattooed by a giant, mother fu—" Another strangled scream cut off her words.

"This is… Wow," Deacon said from the door.

"Get them out of here!" she screamed, jackknifing on the floor. "Gods, this sucks!"

"Whoa," Deacon murmured. "This is like watching a chick give birth or something."

"Oh my gods, I'm going to kill him." Alex's shoulders shook with each breath. "I'm going to punch him—"

"Everyone leave," I yelled, swinging toward the door. "This isn't a godsdamn show."

"And I think he's like the father," Luke said.

I rose to my feet, ready to take all of them out. "Get. Out."

They must've seen their own deaths in my glare, because a

few seconds later, the door closed. Marcus remained, holding my stare.

"She's my niece. I'm staying." He edged closer, and an almost near-feral sound came from deep in my throat. He stopped, eyes narrowing on me. "Is it…is it supposed to be like this?"

"I don't know." I turned back to her, feeling as if I couldn't catch my breath. "Alex?"

"Okay," she breathed. "Just…just don't talk. No one—" She jerked up, hands shaking.

I dropped down beside her just as her body stiffened as if steel had been poured down her spine. Her eyes—those beautiful brown eyes—were wide and unfocused. My mouth dried as a pale sheen covered her complexion. The scream faded as her body folded like paper bag. I caught her before she hit the floor, pulling her across my lap.

Alex opened her eyes and whimpered, and I would've given anything to make this stop, to take the pain away from her. Anything.

"It's okay. I'm here." I smoothed the hair off her damp forehead. "It's almost over."

"It is?" she gasped, squeezing my hand until I was sure she was going to crush my bones. "How in the fuck do you know? Have you ever Awakened before? Is there something—" A hoarse, weak scream interrupted her tirade. "Oh gods, I'm… I'm so sorry. I didn't mean to cuss at you. It just…"

"I know. It hurts." My gaze drifted over her and I forced a smile. "It can't be much longer."

She squeezed her eyes shut as she curled toward me. Smoothing the hair back from her face didn't seem to hurt her. If anything, it appeared to calm her, so I kept doing it, because it was the only thing I could do.

Dipping my head, I whispered to her, calling her my love, telling her that I loved her. She'd stopped squirming, but I had a feeling she might be beyond hearing, but I kept on. All the while, I could feel Marcus's gaze on me. There was a good chance he was going to punch me again, but it would be worth—

Suddenly, her body jerked in my arms, going straight as a board. I cursed loudly as she kicked her head back. Veins in her neck pressed forward and then…

"Oh my gods," I said.

A vibrant blue light darkened the veins in her neck, rapidly spreading across her face and her arms. The light faded and then it happened, and I could *see* it. Glyphs appeared on her skin, blue and bright. So many of them that there didn't seem to be one tiny patch of skin unmarked. They started to swirl sluggishly and then sped up, spinning in dizzying designs.

I was absolutely stunned by what I was seeing for the first time in my life and probably the last—the marks of the Apollyon. I was awed. Thunderstruck. The marks continued to glide over her skin seamlessly.

"Do you see this?" Marcus said, his voice hoarse. "My gods…"

I could only nod. Nothing—absolutely nothing—in my life could prepare me for seeing this.

"The Apollyon," I whispered reverently, smoothing my hands through her hair. Alex was the Apollyon, and she was beautiful, and she was *mine.*

The shimmery blue marks pulsed intensely bright, shining light through the whole room and then faded, seeping back into her skin.

It was over.

Thank gods, it was over. Finally.

My shoulders slumped as I gathered her close, stretching out my legs so that her bottom fit against me. Tears pricked at my eyes. Gods, I was seconds from weeping like a baby, but it was over.

But once the marks receded, Alex didn't move. Seconds ticked into minutes, and panic punched me in the gut. I tore my gaze from her, landing on Marcus. He looked as pale as I felt.

"Alex."

Nothing.

Panic quickly turned to fear and it sunk its claws into me. "Alex, baby."

Still nothing.

"Gods," I swore, turning my panicked stare to her uncle. "I don't know what to do. She's not moving."

Marcus said something, but I didn't hear him. Bending over her lifeless body, I hauled her to my chest, pressing my forehead to hers. Only then did I felt her chest move slowly.

"Come on, baby, talk to me. Agapi mou, come back," I begged. And I was so ready to get on my knees and plead. "Agapi mou, open your eyes and talk to me."

There! Movement. Her lashes fluttered once, twice, and then opened.

Air halted in my lungs. Blood turned to ice in my veins. My entire world broke apart when her eyes opened.

They were not brown.

Golden-colored eyes stared back into mine, eyes identical to Seth's. Eyes that were not warm, but were harsh and devoid of compassion.

"No." The word burst from me, from my very soul.

A popping sound filled the room, and I sensed the presence of a god—of Apollo. He was behind us, the air crackling with tension.

The god swore. "Let her go, Aiden."

Never. My arms tightened around her. I couldn't—wouldn't let her go. Ever.

"Let her go now." The door slammed shut somewhere behind the shining god. "She's connected with the First."

My arms curled around her as words turned to ashes on my tongue. I shook my head slightly, my vision blurring. This couldn't be happening. Not to us. Not to her.

Alex smiled—smiled in a way that Seth would—and in that moment, my heart shattered.

This wasn't Alex.

AIDEN AND ALEX CHRISTMAS SPECIAL

Pures and halfs didn't celebrate Christmas like mortals. We had our own super-special holiday in February—Anthesteria. Pretty much everyone partied it up like Dionysus on spring break in Cancun. It was that…wild. But no Christmas tree, Yule log, cookies, or mistletoe. No cheesy but fun songs.

Since I'd spent so many years in the mortal world, I'd grown to love Christmas and all that holiday cheer. So much so that for two straight weeks it was all I talked about when I was around Aiden or Seth. And as Christmas Eve arrived and everyone at the Covenant couldn't care less, I was entering Downersville, population Alex.

Sigh.

I shuffled into my dorm room, dropping my bag on the floor. There was a truckload of Myths and Legends homework to be done, but I went to my computer on my little desk and booted up the beast. Bringing up YouTube, I started watching clips from *National Lampoon's Christmas Vacation*. Several hours of Griswold family fun later, there was a knock on my door.

Smoothing my hands over my hair, I went to it.

Aiden stood there, hands folded behind his back, his striking features expressionless. Those eyes, they were a gunmetal gray. Cool. Focused.

"Busy?" he asked, his deep, smooth voice doing funny things to my stomach.

I glanced around my room and arched a brow. "Not really."

"Good. Come."

Normally, I would've been all like hell to the no when it came to an order of "Come" with no explanation, but this was Aiden and yeah, he got a little more leeway than most. And I was also curious as to why Aiden was searching me out. Curious. Hopeful. Warm and fuzzy...

Shutting the door behind me, I followed him down the silent hall. It was later than I realized. Cold, wet wind blew off the ocean, and I huddled down in my sweater. Back in the mortal world, everything would be covered in dazzling lights and people would be caroling.

Here, we had Guards and Sentinels patrolling the dunes. None of them were surprised to see us. Considering everything, they were used to seeing me with Aiden or another babysitter.

"So, what's up?"

Aiden glanced down at me. "You'll see."

My brows lowered. "I'll see what?"

"It's just a few more minutes, Alex."

Patience was a virtue I constantly struggled with. My mouth burned with questions I could barely hold back as we rounded the courtyard and headed toward the training facilities. My shoulders slumped.

"We're training?" Geez, I got the fact that they didn't celebrate the holidays, but it was Christmas Eve for crying out loud.

He said nothing, but there was a look to his gray eyes. Secretive with a touch of mischievousness mixed in. As he pushed opened the doors, my curiosity knew no limits. What in the world was Aiden up to? And would it involve something of the fun kind?

If so, there truly was a Santa Claus.

Now I was blushing like a goober.

Instead of swinging a left to the large rooms where all the training stuff was, he kept going down the hall dimly lit by recess lightning.

"Aiden, what's going on?"

He brushed a lock of dark, wavy hair out of his eyes and sighed. "We really need to work on your patience."

"Ha."

His lips slid into a half grin. "Have you ever heard of the saying good things come to those who wait?"

I rolled my eyes.

"Come on." He dropped a heavy hand on my back, between my shoulder blades, and my breath stalled.

I was effectively silenced by his touch. Perhaps that was why he did it. Not many people would blame him and probably wished they wielded that kind of power over me.

Aiden stopped in front of a door that had no windows, and my imagination jumped out of PG-13 territory into NC-17. He dug a ring of keys out of his pocket and unlocked the door.

Stepping aside, he motioned me into the dark room. I inched in, looking over my shoulder. "Uh, you aren't going to lock me in a dark room or something? Right?"

Aiden chuckled as he stepped in, closing the door and plunging the room into utter darkness. My eyes bugged and I stood perfectly still. I knew this room held one of the sensory deprivation chambers.

Warm air brushed over my cheek, stirring the hair around my temple. A shiver danced over my skin, and I closed my eyes. There was a sound of a switch being thrown.

"Open your eyes, Alex." Aiden's voice was tantalizingly close to my ear.

I did and my mouth dropped open.

It looked like...like Christmas threw up in the room.

And I loved it.

"Oh..." Words failed me.

Christmas lights were strung across the walls, blanketing the sensory chamber to the right. A six-foot Christmas tree was in the center of the room, draped in silvery tinsel that matched Aiden's eyes. Shiny bulbs covered the tree.

I went to it slowly, as if in a daze.

Garland was everywhere—red and green. There were huge red stockings hanging from a cabinet. On top was a lamppost with a face.

"See the red button?" Aiden said from behind me. "Push it."

I did with one shaky finger. "Rudolph the Red-Nosed Reindeer" played. I started to laugh, but it got stuck in my throat.

"It plays a bunch of songs." Aiden's lashes hid his eyes. "I wasn't sure if you had a favorite."

"It's perfect." I turned around. A dozen candy canes were piled under the tree, along with what looked like milk and cookies. My breath caught. "Aiden..."

There was even a Charlie Brown tree in the corner. The branches were skinny and bare, drooping under the weight of the glassy red and green bulbs. I managed to laugh past the lump in my throat. I had no idea how he managed to get all of this in here without a million questions being asked. It was amazing—he was amazing.

"Oh, my gods, Aiden…" I went to the little tree, blinking back tears. Gods, I was about to break down like a girlie girl watching *The Notebook* or something.

"Seth and Deacon helped, too," Aiden said, hands in his pockets.

My gaze shot to a photo of a sexy elf in a red bikini lined in white fur. I grinned. "I bet they did."

Aiden swooped down, and as he stood, he handed me a plate of cookies and a glass of milk. I grinned as I took them. "Did…did you make these?"

Aiden tipped his head back and laughed. "No. Deacon did. He broke out the red and green sprinkles just for you."

I blinked again as I bit down into the sugary goodness. Happy tears burned my eyes. "Thank you so much, Aiden. Honestly, you…you have no idea."

He shrugged. "Don't need to thank me for this."

It seemed I was never supposed to thank him, but what he'd done for me—what the other guys had helped with—had my chest swelling. Any moment I would float right up to the ceiling. I finished off the cookies and milk, trying to keep it together.

"Anyway," he said. "You can spend as much time in here as you want—are you crying?" Aiden moved to my side. His hand curved over my shoulder.

"No—not at all." I forced a laugh and sat the plate and cup aside. "I just can't believe you guys did this." I took in the room again and then looked up, meeting his eyes. "I love Christmas. I love this…"

His smile turned tender. "I know. That's why we did this. You deserve a little holiday cheer."

I wasn't so sure I deserved all of this. "It was your idea, wasn't it?"

Aiden's gaze drifted over my face. No answer. Of course, it was. This was Aiden—the kind of guy who listened to my senseless babble about a holiday he never celebrated and caught on to how much it meant to me. And then not take any real credit for it. Part of me melted.

"Thank you," I whispered.

He glanced up. "Huh, look here."

My gaze followed his and my heart flip-flopped. A leafy green plant hung from the ceiling. Two red berries glistened in the twinkling light.

Yep, now my heart stopped.

"I do believe there is some kind of custom associated with this plant," Aiden said, turning his gaze back to my own wide-eyed stare. "What do they call it?"

"Mistletoe."

His lips spread into a slow, bone-melting smile. "Hmm..."

I had nothing to say. Nada.

Aiden lowered his head. Thick lashes swept down, shielding his eyes, but I saw them flash silver before they were hidden from me. My own eyes fluttered shut as my heart raced, my legs weakened. I felt his warm breath first over my lips and then the soft-as-air kiss.

He took my hand, brought it to his mouth, and placed a kiss against the center of my palm. "Merry Christmas, Alex."

I sighed, happier than I ever remembered being. "Merry Christmas, Aiden."

ACKNOWLEDGMENTS

Short and sweet—Thank you to Kate Kaynak, Patricia Riley, Rich Storrs, and Rebecca Mancini. Another big thank you to Kevan Lyon for being an awesome agent. Thank you to Malissa Coy and to Wendy Higgins for being their amazing author/editorial selves. Each time I write these, it gets harder and harder to make sure I'm getting everyone. So a big thank you to everyone who has supported the series and has wanted to take part in Alex's journey, and who has kept me sane during the process.

ABOUT THE AUTHOR

#1 *New York Times* and #1 international bestselling author Jennifer L. Armentrout lives in Shepherdstown, West Virginia. All the rumors you've heard about her state aren't true. When she's not hard at work writing, she spends her time reading, watching really bad zombie movies, pretending to write, hanging out with her husband, her Border Jack Apollo, Border Collie Artemis, six judgmental alpacas, two rude goats, and five fluffy sheep. In early 2015, Jennifer was diagnosed with retinitis pigmentosa, a group of rare genetic disorders that involve a breakdown and death of cells in the retina, eventually resulting in loss of vision, among other complications. Due to this diagnosis, educating people on the varying degrees of blindness has become a passion of hers, right alongside writing, which she plans to do as long as she can.

Website: jenniferlarmentrout.com
Facebook: JenniferLArmentrout
Instagram: @jennifer_l_armentrout

See yourself
in
Bloom
every story is a
celebration.
Visit bloombooks.com
for more information about
JENNIFER L. ARMENTROUT
and more of your favorite authors!
bloombooks
@read_bloom
read_bloom
Bloom books

OTHER BLOOM BOOKS BY JENNIFER L. ARMENTROUT

COVENANT SERIES

Half-Blood (includes the novella "Daimon")

Pure

Deity (includes the novella "Elixir")

Apollyon

Sentinel

FRIGID SERIES

Frigid

Scorched

PURE

PURE

JENNIFER L.
ARMENTROUT

Bloom books

Cover design by Nicole Hower and Brittany Vibbert/Sourcebooks
Cover images © Lisa-Blue/Getty Images, Sybille Sterk/Arcangel, highhorse/Getty Images, Anna Kim/Getty Images, SENEZ/Getty Images, kharp/Unsplash, creativejunkie/Unsplash

Published by Bloom Books, an imprint of Sourcebooks
P.O. Box 4410, Naperville, Illinois 60567-4410
(630) 961-3900
sourcebooks.com

Originally self-published in 2012 by Jennifer L. Armentrout.

Cataloging-in-Publication data is on file with the Library of Congress.

Printed and bound in Germany.
BPG 10 9 8 7 6 5 4 3 2 1

To my family and Loki.
(Yeah, I'm dedicating Pure *to a dog).*

PRONUNCIATION GUIDE FOR PURE

Daimon: DEE-mun
Aether: EE-ther
Hematoi: HEM-a-toy
Apollyon: a-POL-ee-on
Agapi: ah-GAH-pee
Akasha: ah-KAH-sha

CHAPTER ONE

I stared at the ceiling of the gymnasium, little splotches dancing in front of me. Man, my butt hurt. No surprise, as I'd landed on it about fifty times already. The only thing not burning with pain was my face; it was on fire for an entirely different reason.

My Gutter Fighting class wasn't going well.

This style of hand-to-hand combat wasn't exactly second nature. My muscles screamed as I pulled myself off the mats and faced our Instructor.

Running a hand through his thinning hair, Instructor Romvi looked disgusted with the entire class. "If he'd been a daimon, you'd be dead now. Do you understand? Dead, not alive, Miss Andros."

Like there was some other definition of "dead" I wasn't familiar with. I gritted my teeth and managed a nod.

Romvi shot me another scathing glare. "It's difficult to believe you have any amount of aether in you, Miss Andros. The essence of the gods is wasted on you. The way you fight, you might as well be mortal."

Hadn't I killed *three* aether-craving daimons? Wasn't that worth something?

"Square off. Keep your eyes trained on muscle movement. You know the drill," he instructed.

I turned back to Jackson Manos, resident Covenant heart-throb and my current opponent. With his swarthy looks and those dark, sexy eyes, he could be quite the distraction.

Jackson winked at me.

I narrowed my eyes at him. We weren't allowed to talk during sparring. Instructor Romvi felt it took away from the authenticity of fighting. Really, even in all of Jackson's glory, he wasn't the reason I kept missing his heel strikes and spin kicks.

The source of my absolute failure leaned against the training room wall. Dark waves tumbled over his forehead, falling into gunmetal gray eyes. Some would say Aiden St. Delphi needed a haircut, but I loved the wilder look he'd been favoring recently.

An instant later, our gazes locked. Aiden returned to the stance I was all too familiar with—well-defined arms crossed over his chest, legs widespread. Watching, always watching. Now he communicated a look that said I should be paying attention to Jackson and not him.

Tight coils sprung within me—another thing I'd grown accustomed to. It happened whenever I laid eyes on him. It wasn't so much the near perfect curve of his cheekbones or the way his smile hinted at a set of dimples. Or that impossibly ripped body of his—

I snapped out of my reverie with a moment to spare. I blocked Jackson's knee with a brutal swipe of my arm, and then I went for a throat strike. Jackson countered it easily. We circled one another, delivering blows and dodging them.

He stepped back, dropping his arms to his sides. I saw my opening and went for it. Spinning around, I aimed my knee for his midsection. Jackson darted to the side, but not quickly enough. I caught him hard in the stomach.

Surprisingly, Instructor Romvi clapped. "Good—"

"Oh, crap," Caleb Nicolo, my best friend and partner in mayhem, moaned from the group of students standing against the wall.

The thing about defensive kicks—once we made contact with our opponents, we either needed to go for the kill shot or back up. I'd done neither. Jackson doubled over my knee and went down, taking me along for the ride. We hit the mat, and somehow—and I seriously doubted by accident—Jackson ended up sprawled atop me. His weight knocked my head back and the air out of my lungs.

Instructor Romvi yelled, slipping into a different language—maybe Romanian or something.

Anyway, whatever he said sounded suspiciously like cursing.

Jackson lifted his head, his shoulder-length hair shielding his grin from the class. "Always on your back, huh?"

"Yeah, that's more like your girlfriend. Get off." I pushed at his shoulders. Chuckling, Jackson rolled and stood. Ever since the whole "my mom murdered his girlfriend's parents" incident, Jackson and I hadn't gotten along. Actually, courtesy of my dead daimon mother, I wasn't getting along with most of the other students, either. Go figure.

Flushing with embarrassment, I scrambled to my feet and stole a quick glance at Aiden. His expression may have appeared blank, but I knew he'd already compiled a mental list of all the things I'd done wrong and filed it away. But he wasn't my immediate concern.

Instructor Romvi stalked across the mats, stopping in front of Jackson and me. "That was absolutely unacceptable! You move away or dispose of the opponent."

To drive his point home, he threw his arm out, hitting me square across the chest. I stumbled back an inch and clenched my jaw shut. Every cell in my body demanded that I do the same in return.

"You do not wait! And you." Romvi whirled on Jackson. "Do you plan to lie on daimons for fun? Let me know how that works out for you."

Jackson flushed but didn't respond. We didn't talk back in Romvi's class.

"Off the mats now—not you, Miss Andros!"

I stopped, eyeing Caleb and Olivia hopelessly. They stared back, their expressions mirroring mine. Resigned to what I knew was going to happen next, because it'd happened every class with Romvi, I turned to the Instructor and waited for the epic smackdown.

"Many of you aren't ready for graduation." Romvi prowled the edge of the mat. "Many of you will die the first week on the job, but you, Miss Andros? You're an embarrassment to the Covenant."

Romvi was an embarrassment to the male race, but he didn't hear me bitching.

He circled me slowly. "I am shocked that you faced down daimons and still stand before me. Some may think you have potential, Miss Andros. I have yet to see it."

Out of the corner of my eye, I saw Aiden. He'd stiffened, gaze narrowed upon us. He also knew what was coming, and there was nothing he could do, even if he wanted to.

"Prove to me that you belong here," Romvi said. "Prove

to me that you have gained reentry to the Covenant based on merit and not familial ties."

Instructor Romvi was a bigger jerk than most Instructors. He was one of the pure-bloods who'd chosen to become a Sentinel instead of coasting through life living off old money. Like Aiden, pures who chose this kind of life were a rare breed, but that was where the commonalities between the two ended. Romvi had hated me from the first day of class, and I liked to believe Aiden felt quite the opposite.

Romvi attacked.

For someone so old, Romvi sure could move fast. I backed across the mats, trying to remember everything Aiden had taught me over the summer. Romvi swung around, his booted heel aiming for my midsection. I swiped his leg away and threw a punch I really, *really* meant. He blocked that. On and on we went, exchanging and receiving blows. He was landing more on me, continuously edging me toward the end of the mat.

With each swing and each kick, Romvi's blows became more brutal. It *was* like fighting a daimon, because I seriously believed Romvi wanted to do me real harm. I was holding my own until my sneaker slipped off the edge of the mat. I made a tactical mistake.

I allowed myself to be distracted.

Romvi took it. Reaching out and grabbing a fistful of my ponytail, he yanked me forward. "You should be less worried about your vanity," he said, twisting me so my back faced the doors. "And cut your hair."

I struck out, catching Romvi in the stomach, but it didn't faze him. Using my own momentum—and my hair—he slammed me onto the mat. I rolled into the fall, half grateful that it was over. I didn't even care that he'd kicked my ass in front of the entire class. Just as long as this—

Romvi grabbed my arm and pulled it high above me, yanking me to my knees. "Listen to me, half-bloods. Dying in battle is not your worst nightmare anymore."

My eyes popped wide. *Oh, no. No, no, no. He wouldn't dare...*

He pushed the sleeve of the Under Armour shirt back until my skin was exposed to the elbow. "This is what happens to you. Take a good, long look at what happens when you fail. They will turn you into a monster."

Fire coursed across my cheeks and my brain sort of emptied. I tried, really tried, to keep the scars hidden from my classmates. I focused on anything other than the faces of the students as he continued to show the world my tags. My gaze fell over his rough, aged hand, then up his own battle-scarred arm. The sleeve of his shirt had fallen back, revealing a tattoo of a torch turned downward.

Instructor Romvi hadn't struck me as the type to be into tattoos.

Romvi dropped my arm then, allowing me to pull my sleeve down. I hoped he got eaten by hungry daimons. I might look like a scarred-up freak, but I hadn't failed a damn thing. I'd killed the daimon ultimately responsible for leaving me this way—my mother.

"None of you are ready to become Sentinels, to face a daimon half-blood trained just like you." Romvi's voice carried through the room. "I don't expect most of you to show any improvement by tomorrow. Class is over."

I fought the urge to jump on Romvi's back like a monkey and snap his neck. That wouldn't win me any fans, but the sick sense of satisfaction would almost be worth it.

On his way out, Jackson bumped into me. "Your arm looks like a checkerboard. That's real hot."

"Yeah, that's what your girlfriend said about your di—" Instructor Romvi's hand snapped out, catching my chin.

"Your mouth, Miss Andros, could also use improvement."

"But Jackson—"

"I do not care." He dropped his hand, glaring down at me. "I do not tolerate such foul words in my class. This is your last warning. Next time you will find yourself in the dean's office."

Unbe-freaking-lievable. I watched Romvi stalk out of the room. Caleb approached me, handing Olivia her gym bag. His eyes, the color of the clearest sky, shone with sympathy. "He's a prick, Alex."

I waved my hand dismissively, not sure if he was talking about Romvi or Jackson. They were both pricks in my book.

"One of these days, you're so gonna snap and kill him." Luke dragged his fingers through bronze-colored locks.

"Which one?" I asked.

"Both." Luke grinned as he tapped my arm. "I just hope I'm here to see it."

"I second that." Olivia wrapped her arm around Caleb's. They pretended whatever was going on between them was a casual thing, but I knew different. Whenever Olivia touched Caleb, which was often, he completely forgot about whatever was going on and got this stupid smile on his face.

Then again, a lot of the male halfs got that look on their faces around her. Olivia was stunning. Her caramel-colored skin was envied by most of the halfs. So was her closet. I'd kill to get my hands on her clothes.

A shadow fell over our little group, quickly dispersing them. I didn't have to look up to know it was Aiden. Only he had the kind of power to send just about anyone running in the opposite direction. Respect and fear did that.

"See you later," Caleb called out.

I nodded vaguely, staring at Aiden's sneakers. Shame over Romvi's little display made it hard to look at him. I worked hard for Aiden's respect, to prove I had the potential he and Leon believed I did back when Marcus tried to toss me out of the Covenant.

Funny how one person could ruin that in a matter of seconds. "Alex, look at me."

Against my will, I obeyed. When he spoke that way, I couldn't help it. He stood in front of me, his long and lean body tense. We were currently pretending I hadn't tried to hand my virginity over to him the night I'd found out I was going to be the second coming of the *Apollyon*. Aiden seemed to be doing really well with it. I, on the other hand, couldn't stop obsessing over it.

"You didn't fail."

I shrugged. "Doesn't seem that way, does it?"

"The Instructors are tougher on you because of the time you've missed and because your uncle is the dean. People look at what you do. They pay attention."

"And my stepfather is the Minister of Council. I get it, Aiden. Look, let's get this over with." My voice was a little sharper than I intended, but Aiden had seen how mortifying this class had turned out. Not like I needed to discuss it with him.

Aiden caught my arm and pushed up the sleeve of my shirt. It had a whole different effect on me. A flutter formed in my chest, spreading a warm flush all over me. Pure-bloods were off-limits to us halfs, which meant what had gone down between us was tantamount to feeling up the Pope or offering Gandhi a roast beef sandwich.

"You should never be ashamed of these scars, Alex. Never." Aiden dropped my arm and motioned me to the center of the floor. "Let's get this going so you can rest."

I trailed behind him. "What about your rest? Don't you have a patrol tonight?" Aiden was pulling double duty between training me and his Sentinel duties.

Aiden was special. He'd chosen to be a Sentinel, and he'd also chosen to work with me so I wouldn't be so far behind the other students. He didn't have to do either, but a sense of justice had propelled him to become a Sentinel. We shared that desire. What made him want to help me? I liked to think he was undeniably attracted to me—like I was when it came to him.

He circled me, stopping to position my arms at mid-level. "You're holding your arms wrong. That's why Jackson's hits kept getting through."

"What about your rest?" I persisted.

"Don't worry about me." He squared off, motioning me forward with one hand. "Worry more about yourself, Alex. This is going to be a tough year for you, and you're doing triple time in training."

"I'd have more free time if I didn't have to practice with Seth."

Aiden swung forward so fast I barely blocked the blow. "Alex, we've been over this."

"I know." I stopped his chop. I alternated days between Aiden and Seth, as well as every other weekend. It was like they shared joint custody of me, but I hadn't seen my *other half* yet today. Strange—he usually lurked around nearby.

"Alex." Aiden moved out of the offensive stance, studying me closely.

"What?" I dropped my arms.

He opened his mouth, seeming to rethink his words. "You've been looking a little tired lately. Are you getting enough rest?"

I felt my cheeks burst with color. "Gods, do I look that bad or something?"

He drew in a deep breath and let it out slowly. Softness crept across his features. "You don't look bad at all. It's just that…you've been through a lot and you seem tired."

"I'm okay."

Aiden placed his hand on my shoulder. "Alex?"

My heart thundered in response to his touch. "I'm fine."

"You keep saying that." His gaze flickered across my face. "You always say that."

"I say it because there isn't anything wrong with me!" I swatted at his hand, but he dropped his other one on my shoulder, effectively trapping me in front of him.

"There's nothing wrong with me," I said again, but much quieter. "I'm okay. Completely a hundred percent fine with everything."

Aiden opened his mouth, probably to say something ridiculously supportive, but he didn't say anything. He just stared at me and then his grip on my shoulders tightened. He knew I was lying.

Everything wasn't fine.

Nightmares of those horrifying hours in Gatlinburg kept me up at night. Nearly everyone at school hated me, believing I'd been the reason for the daimon attack at Lake Lure during the summer. Seth's constant stalking only added to their suspicions. Out of all the halfs, only Caleb knew I was fated to be the second Apollyon—and fated to *complete* Seth as his supernatural supercharger or something. His continuing attention didn't win me any fans among the female halfs. All the girls wanted Seth, while I just wanted to be rid of him.

But when Aiden looked at me like he did now, I forgot about the world. I couldn't read much of anything from

Aiden's expression, but his eyes…well, his eyes told me he wasn't doing so great with the whole pretending-we-hadn't-almost-hooked-up charade. Aiden still thought about it; hell, he was thinking about it right now. Maybe he imagined what would've happened if Leon hadn't interrupted—maybe even as much as I did. Maybe he'd lie awake and remember how our bodies had felt together.

I know I did.

The tension racked up several degrees, and my body warmed deliciously. These were the kind of moments I lived for. I wondered what he'd do if I stepped forward and closed the distance between us. It wouldn't take much for me to do it. Would he think I just wanted comfort? Because he would comfort me—he was that kind of guy. And then, if I tipped my head back, would he kiss me? Because he looked like he wanted to do both. Hold me, kiss me, and do all sorts of wonderful, forbidden things.

I stepped forward.

His hands jerked against my shoulders, indecision crawling over his features. For a second—just a second—I think he seriously considered it. Then his hands flattened, like a barrier meant to keep me back.

The doors opened behind us, and Aiden dropped his hands. I twisted around, wanting to punch whoever it was in the face. I'd come *this* close to getting what I'd wanted.

Leon's bulky mass filled the door, dressed in his typical, all-black Sentinel garb. "I'm sorry to interrupt, but this cannot wait."

Leon always had something important to tell Aiden. The last time he'd interrupted us had been two seconds after I'd given Aiden the green light to go all the way.

Leon had the worst timing ever.

Of course, the last time he'd interrupted, things had been pretty serious. They'd found Kain alive. Once a half-blood Sentinel, Kain had helped Aiden train me. A weekend trip to nearby Lake Lure had proved fatal for everyone involved. He'd survived the daimon attack but had come back to the Covenant as something we'd thought was impossible—a half-blood daimon.

Now Kain was dead, and I'd seen it happen. I'd liked and missed Kain, even after he'd killed a bunch of pures and knocked me around the room. That hadn't been the Kain I'd known. Like Mom, he'd turned into a terrible version of who he'd really been.

Leon moved his massive body forward, looking like the poster child for steroids. "There's been a daimon attack."

Aiden tensed. "Where?"

"Here at the Covenant."

CHAPTER TWO

Practice was officially cancelled.

"Go straight to your dorm, Alex, and stay there," Aiden said before leaving the training arena.

I went to the cafeteria instead.

There was no way I was going to hang out in my dorm while there was a daimon running amuck. I'd considered following the two for a moment, but my ninja stealth skills were subpar.

By the time I'd cut across the quad, the sky had darkened and turned ominous. I picked up my pace, because when the sky got this way, one had to pay attention. September was hurricane season around this place. Or it could just mean Seth was pissed off somewhere nearby; his moodiness had a startling effect on the weather.

In the cafeteria, everyone huddled together in little groups, their faces animated. I grabbed an apple and a soda, noting there wasn't a single pure in the lunchroom. I dropped into the seat beside Caleb.

He looked up, eyes bright. “You heard?”

“Yeah, I was practicing when Leon came to get Aiden.” I glanced at Olivia. “Do you have any details?”

“All I’ve heard is one of the younger students—Melissa Callao—didn’t show up for classes today. Her friends got worried and checked her dorm. They found her in bed, the window open.”

I sat back, squelching the unease shifting through me. “Is she alive?”

Olivia stabbed a fork into her pizza. Her pure-blood mother worked closely with the Council. Lucky for us, she kept her daughter well-informed. “She was practically drained, but she’s alive. I don’t know how her roommate didn’t know, or why she wasn’t attacked, too.”

“How in Hades is a daimon running around here?” Luke held up a hand, a puzzled frown on his face. “How could one get past the Guards?”

“It had to be a half,” Elena said from farther down the table. She looked like an extraordinarily tall Tinker Bell with her short hair and wide, green eyes.

Up until this summer, we’d believed that half-bloods couldn’t be turned into daimons. A pure was chock-full of aether, and a daimon would chew, gnaw, and kill to get at that essence like a psychotic drug addict. Once drained of their aether, the daimon could let the pure die or turn them, adding to the daimon horde. No one thought half-bloods had enough aether inside them to make the switch over to the dark side, but for a patient daimon more interested in building an army than getting a meal, we were as good as a pure.

It sucked that the only place we were equal to pures was in a fate worse than death.

“Halfs who’ve turned don’t change like the pures.” Olivia

flicked the fork between her long fingers. "They're immune to titanium, right?" Her gaze landed on me.

I nodded. "Yep, gotta cut off their heads. Gross, I know."

Or Seth could use his Apollyon mojo. He'd zapped Kain with *akasha*—the fifth and final element—and that'd done the job.

Caleb rubbed a spot on his arm where I knew he'd been tagged. He stopped as his eyes caught mine. I forced a smile.

"If it's a half, it could be anyone." Luke leaned back, folding his arms. "I mean, think about it. They don't need elemental magic to conceal what they really look like. It could be *anyone*."

When pures turned all evil and whatnot, they were noticeable to half-bloods—like, really noticeable. Empty black eye sockets, pale skin, and mouths full of razor-sharp teeth doesn't make for a look that blends into the crowd. Halfs had the wacky ability to see through the elemental magic pure-blood daimons used, but daimon half-bloods just looked the same after they turned. At least Kain had.

"Well, it would have to be a half-blood who'd been attacked by a daimon," a throaty, husky voice intruded. "Hmm, wonder who that could be? It's not like they grow on trees around here."

Lifting my head, I found Lea Samos and Jackson. It was the middle of September and the chick still sported a super tan—still so beautiful that I wanted to stab her in the eye with a plastic fork.

"Yeah, that would make sense." I kept my voice even.

Those amethyst eyes settled on me. "How many half-bloods do we know who've been attacked recently?"

I stared at her, stuck between disbelief and wanting to throw something. "Knock it off, Lea. I don't want to hear your crap today."

She pulled those full lips into a cruel smile. "I know of two."

Caleb shot to his feet, knocking his chair over. "What are you saying, Lea?"

Two Guards by the door stepped forward, eyeing the situation with interest. Olivia grabbed Caleb's hand, but he ignored her. "Come on, Lea. Just say it."

She tossed a mane of coppery hair over her shoulder. "Chill out, Caleb. You got tagged how many times? Two? Three? It takes a hell of a lot more to turn a half-blood than that." She looked at me pointedly. "Isn't that right? That's what I heard the Guards say. That the halfs have to be drained slowly, and then the daimon gives them the kiss of death."

I took a deep breath. Lea and I were enemies. There'd been a time when my heart had sort of bled for her after her parents had been murdered, but that seemed like ages ago. "I'm not a daimon, you skank."

Lea tipped her head to the side. "If it looks like a daimon, then…"

"Lea, go screw someone and tan, in whatever order." Caleb sat back down. "No one wants to hear your crap. And that's the funny thing about you, Lea. You think everyone cares what you have to say, when all they care about is how easy it is to get you on your back."

"Or how the Instructors found a bottle of Brew in your room last week," Olivia added, her lips curving into a half smile. "Didn't know you were into such freaky stuff, or maybe that's how you get guys into you."

I snorted. I hadn't heard *that*. "Wow. Drugging guys to sleep with you? Nice. I guess that's why Jackson practically humped my leg in class today."

Lea's cheeks flamed an odd shade of brown and red. "You

stupid, daimon-loving bitch; you're the reason why my father's dead! You should have—"

Several people moved at once. Olivia and Caleb darted across the table, trying to get a hold of me, but I was fast when I wanted to be.

I didn't think; I just launched my shiny red apple right at her face. A throw like that from a half-blood turned an apple into a serious weapon. It struck home with a loud cracking sound.

Lea stumbled back, clasping the front of her face. Blood gushed between her fingers, matching the color of her nails. "You broke my nose!"

Everyone in the cafeteria stilled. Even the drab-looking half-blood servants stopped cleaning tables to watch. No one screamed or seemed overtly startled. After all, we were half-bloods—a violent bunch. The servants were usually too doped up to be concerned.

Somehow, I'd forgotten about the Guards as I'd gone for Lea. I squeaked when one of them got an arm around my waist and hauled me across the table. Drinks spilled; food fell to the floor, and mystery meat smeared itself all over my gym pants.

"Knock it off, right now!"

"She broke my nose again!" Lea dropped her hands from her face. "You can't let her get away with this!"

"Oh, shut up. The docs will fix it. Half your face is plastic anyway." I struggled against the Guard until he twisted my arm back so far that any movement caused my shoulder to scream.

"She wanted to get at my aether." Lea pointed a blood-stained hand at me. "Her mother killed my parents, and now she wants to kill me!"

I laughed. "Oh, for the love—"

"Shut up," the Guard hissed in my ear. "Shut up before I make you shut up."

Threats made by half-blood Guards weren't meant to be taken lightly. I quieted down while the other Guard grabbed ahold of Lea. Blood pounded in my ears and my chest still heaved with fury, but I realized that I may've overreacted a tiny bit.

And I was going to be in *so* much trouble.

Half-bloods fighting amongst themselves wasn't a big deal. The aggression and controlled violence sometimes rolled out of the training rooms into places like the cafeteria. Whenever halfs did get in trouble for fighting, they ended up with one of the Instructors who handled disciplinary issues.

Each dorm floor had one assigned. My floor had Instructor Gaia Telis, a pretty cool chick who wasn't overly strict or annoying. But I didn't end up with Instructor Telis. Five minutes after breaking Lea's nose for the second time, I ended up in Dean Andros's office.

This was only one of many drawbacks of my uncle being the dean.

I stared at the vibrant fish zooming across the aquarium and fidgeted with the string on my pants while I waited for Marcus. Sometimes I felt like one of those fish—trapped by invisible walls.

The doors swinging open behind me made me cringe. This was going to suck daimon butt.

"If you discover anything else, notify me immediately. That is all." Marcus's deep voice filled the room. The Guards adorned the outside of his office doors like Greek warrior statues. Then he slammed the door shut.

I jumped.

Marcus stalked across the room, dressed like he'd spent

the majority of the day on a golf course. I expected him to sit behind his desk like a dean should, so when he ended up directly in front of me, grasping the arms of my chair, I was a bit shocked.

"I am sure you're aware of what has happened today." The tone of Marcus's voice was both cold and distinctively cultured. Most pures sounded that way—classy, refined. "A pure-blood was attacked at some point last night."

I strained back as far as I could go, focusing on the aquarium. "Yeah—"

"Do not look away from me, Alexandria."

Sucking in my lower lip, I faced him. His eyes were the same as my mother's had been before she'd turned into a daimon—a vibrant shade of green, like glittering emeralds. "Yes, I heard."

"Then you understand what I'm dealing with right now." Marcus lowered his head so we were at eye level. "I have a daimon half-blood on my campus, hunting my students."

"So, it's a half who's been turned?"

"I think you already know that, Alexandria. You are a lot of things—impulsive, irresponsible, and ill-mannered—but stupid is not one of them."

I wanted to hear more about this daimon half than my character flaws. "Who was the half? You've caught them, right?"

Marcus ignored my question. "Now, I'm pulled out of an investigation that will make or break my career here, all because my half-blood niece broke a girl's nose in the cafeteria...with an apple, of all things."

"She accused me of being a daimon!"

"So, your natural response is to throw an apple at her face hard enough to break a bone?" His voice dropped, deceptively soft. Marcus was Chuck Norris in an off-pink polo shirt. I'd learned not to underestimate him.

"She said I was the reason her parents were killed."

"I'll ask you one more time: So, you decided to throw an apple hard enough to break a bone?"

I wiggled uncomfortably. "Yeah, I guess so."

He exhaled slowly. "Is that all you have to say?"

I glanced around the room, my brain emptying out. I said the first thing that came to mind. "I didn't think the apple would break her nose."

Pushing off the chair, he towered over me. "I expect more from you. Not because you're my niece, Alexandria. Not even because you have more experience with daimons than any other student here."

I rubbed my forehead.

"Everyone will be watching you—everyone of importance. You will give Seth unprecedented power. We cannot afford any misguided behavior from you, Alexandria. Neither can Seth."

Irritation flared deep inside me. At eighteen, something called palingenesis would hit me like some kind of instant supernatural puberty. I'd Awaken and my power would shift to Seth. What power, I had no clue, but he'd become the god killer. Everyone cared about Seth, but me? They didn't seem so concerned with what would happen to me.

"People expect more from you. They will watch you because of what you will become, Alexandria."

I disagreed. They watched because they feared history would repeat itself. The only time there'd ever been two Apollyons in the same generation, the First had turned on the Council. Both Apollyons had been executed. Two Apollyons at one time was considered dangerous by the Council and the gods. It was why Mom had taken me from the Covenant three years ago. She'd thought she could keep me safe, hide me among the mortals.

"At Council, you cannot behave like this. You can't run around starting fights and mouthing off at people," he continued. "There are rules—rules of our society that you must follow! They will not think twice about throwing you into servitude, and it won't matter who you're related to. Do you understand?"

Exhaling slowly, I lifted my head and found Marcus by the aquarium. His back was to me. "Yes, I understand."

He ran a hand over his head. "You will leave your dorm for school, training, and dinner—dinner at the assigned time—and that is all. As of now, you have no friends."

My gaze narrowed on his back. "Am I, like, grounded or something?"

He looked over his shoulder at me, lips thinning. "Until further notice, and do not even think of arguing with me. You cannot go unpunished for this."

"But how can you ground me?"

Marcus turned around slowly. "You broke a girl's nose with an apple."

Suddenly, I didn't want to argue. I *was* getting off light. Being grounded also didn't mean anything. It wasn't like my social calendar was full. "All right, but are you going to tell me if you found the daimon?"

He stared at me a moment longer. "No. We haven't found the daimon yet."

I gripped the chair. "So…it's still around?"

"Yes." Marcus motioned me up, and I followed him to the door. He addressed one of the Guards. "Clive, escort Miss Andros back to her room."

I groaned inwardly. Clive was one of the Guards I seriously suspected of hooking up with Lea. Every single conversation spoken inside Marcus's office somehow got back to Lea. Considering Clive had a thing for young girls who wore fake Prada shoes, he was the likeliest suspect.

"Yes, sir." Clive bowed.

"Remember our conversation," Marcus said to me.

"But what about—"

Marcus shut the door.

Which part should I remember? The fact I was a disgrace to him or the fact there was a daimon running around? Clive grabbed my arm, fingers biting deep. I winced, trying to jerk my arm back, but he increased the pressure. The daimon tags still felt oddly sensitive.

"I guess you're enjoying this." I clenched my jaw.

"That would be a good guess." Clive shoved me into the stairwell. The pures were wealthy, and I mean, more money than anyone could comprehend. Yet there wasn't a single elevator in the entire campus.

"You think you can get away with anything, don't you? You're the dean's niece, the Minister's stepdaughter, and the next Apollyon. You're just so damn special, aren't you?"

There was a very good chance I might hit him, but with my fist instead of an apple. I jerked my arm free. "Yeah, I'm that damn special."

"Just remember you're still a half-blood, Alex."

"Just remember I *am* the dean's niece, the Minister's stepdaughter, and the next Apollyon."

Clive stepped up, his nose almost touching mine. "Are you threatening me?"

I refused to back down. "No. I'm just reminding you of how special I really am."

He stared a moment, then gave a short, harsh laugh. "Maybe we'll all get lucky and you'll be a daimon snack on the way back to your dorm *alone*. Have a good night."

I laughed as loud as I could and was rewarded with the door slamming shut. Hurrying down the stairs, I forgot about Clive. There was a daimon on campus and it'd already attacked one pure-blood, almost killing her. Who knew how long it would take before the daimon half needed its next fix? Mom had said a pure would keep a normal daimon going for days, but was it the same for a daimon half?

She hadn't said anything about that, but she'd talked a lot about their plans to overthrow the Council and the pures while I'd been captive in Gatlinburg. Mom and Eric, the only surviving daimon from Gatlinburg, had plotted to turn the halfs first, and then send them back to infiltrate the Covenants. Sounded like that was already well underway...or could it just be a random attack?

Yeah, I doubted that.

What I'd learned in Gatlinburg was the whole reason I'd be attending the November Council session, but my testimony seemed pointless now.

I rounded the second-floor level and came to an abrupt standstill. Apprehension trailed icy fingers down my spine, awakening the uncanny sense we half-bloods carried in our blood. I glanced over my shoulder, practically expecting a half-blood serial killer to be standing behind me...or at least Clive, about to push me down the steps.

But there was nothing.

Trained not to ignore the freaky sixth sense that alerted us to all kinds of messed-up things, I admitted that maybe I shouldn't have pissed off Clive. After all, there was a daimon roaming around. I took the steps two at a time and flung open the door to the main level.

Dread still trailed along with me, coiling around my fingers. It didn't help that the long hallway was lit only by flickering overhead lights, adding to the creepy feeling. Where were all the Instructors and Guards? It was tomb-quiet.

"Clive?" My eyes devoured every vacant inch of the hallway. "If you're messing with me, I'm seriously going to break *your* nose."

Silence was my answer.

Tiny hairs on my body stood up in warning. Up ahead, the statues of the muses cast harsh shadows over the front lobby. Scanning every nook and cranny for a possible threat, I made my way down the hall. My footsteps echoed madly, almost as if the sound was laughing at me. I came to a sudden halt, mouth dropping open. There was a new addition to the Academy lobby, one that hadn't been there when I'd been escorted to Marcus's office.

Three new marble statues had been erected in the center of the lobby. The angelic, beautiful women clustered close to one another, their arms folded close to their bodies and their wings arched high above their tilted heads.

Oh, my gods.

There were *furies* in the Covenant.

Entombed for now, their arrival was a sign from some very unhappy gods. I walked around them slowly, as if they'd break free from their shells and rip me limb from limb at any moment. I imagined they were waiting, sharpening the claws that would appear in their true form.

Furies were ancient, horrific goddesses once used to capture those who had committed evil but had not been punished. Now they appeared whenever there was a threat to the pures as a whole...or to humankind in general.

Something was about to go down, or already had.

Tearing my eyes away from the furies' serene expressions, I pushed open the heavy doors. A hand clamped down on my arm. My gasp of surprise came out as a shriek as I leaned back and brought my leg up to deliver a vicious kick. My eyes flicked up an instant before I made contact.

"Crap!" I yelped.

Aiden blocked my knee, brows raised. "Well, your reflexes are definitely getting better."

Heart racing, I closed my eyes. "Oh, my gods, you scared the crap out of me."

"I can tell." He dropped my arm, his eyes falling to my pants. "So, it's true."

"So, what's true?" I still couldn't get control over my heart. For crying out loud, I'd thought he was a daimon about to chomp down on what was left of my arm.

"You got into a fight with Lea Samos and broke her nose."

"Oh." I straightened, pursing my lips. "She called me a daimon-loving—"

"Words, Alex, just words." Aiden tipped his head to the side. "Haven't we had this conversation before?"

"You don't know Lea. You don't know how she is."

"Does it matter how she is? You can't fight everyone who says something negative about you. If I approached people the way you do, I'd be fighting all the time."

I rolled my eyes. "People don't talk bad about you, Aiden. Everyone respects you. You're perfect. They don't think *you're* a daimon. Anyway, there's a new happy family entombed in the lobby back there."

He frowned.

"There're furies in the lobby—statues of them."

Aiden dragged a hand over his head, sighing. "We were afraid that might happen."

"Why are they here?"

"The Covenant has been breached, which is something the Council assured the gods would never happen. It was part of their agreement ages ago, when the first Covenant was established. The gods see this breach as the Council not being able to handle the daimon problem."

My stomach flopped. "And what does that mean, exactly?"

He grimaced. "It means, if the gods believe the pure-bloods have lost control, they will release the furies. It's not something anyone wants. The furies will go after anything they perceive as a threat—daimon, half-blood, or…"

"Apollyon?" I whispered. Aiden didn't respond, which confirmed I was correct. I groaned. "Awesome. Well, hopefully that doesn't happen."

"Agreed."

I shifted uncomfortably, my brain unable to really process the new threat. "What are you doing over here, anyway?"

Aiden pinned me with a dark look. "I was going to see Marcus. What are you doing roaming around by yourself?"

"Clive was supposed to escort me back to the dorm, but that kind of fell through."

His eyes narrowed, and then he sighed. Tipping his head toward the dorms, he shoved his hands into the pockets of his dark cargos. "Come on, I'll walk you back. You shouldn't be out here alone."

I pushed away from the doors. "'Cause there's a daimon still on campus? And furies ready to attack?"

He glanced down at me, frowning. "I know your flippant attitude is an act. It's probably what made you turn an apple into a deadly weapon. You of all people know how serious this is."

My cheeks flushed at his reprimand. Guilt twisted my

stomach into raw knots. I stared down at the markings on the pathway. "I'm sorry."

"I'm not the person you should be apologizing to."

"Well, I'm sure as hell not apologizing to Lea. So, you can forget that."

Aiden shook his head. "I know what Lea said upset you. I can even…understand your reaction, but you have to be careful. People are—"

"Yeah, I know. People are watching me, blah and blah some more." I squinted at the shadows of the patrolling Guards. It was the time between dusk and nightfall, but the lamps hadn't kicked on yet. The largest buildings—the ones housing the school, training facilities, and dorms—slipped dark shadows over the pathway. "Anyway, do you guys have any idea where the daimon could be?"

"No. We've searched everywhere and are still searching. Right now we're focused on keeping the students safe."

We stopped at the bottom of the steps outside my dorm. The porch was empty, a sign of everyone's unease. Girls usually hung out here, hoping to get some guy time in. "Did Melissa see the daimon? Was she able to give some sort of description?"

Aiden ran a hand over his forehead. "She barely remembers anything from the attack right now. The doctors…well, they think it's the trauma. A way of protecting herself, I guess."

I looked away, grateful it was dark outside. Why couldn't I forget what'd happened in Gatlinburg? "It's probably more than just that. She's a pure. Where one of us would be trained to pay attention to details, to gain as much information as possible, she wasn't. She's just like a…normal girl. And if the attack happened at night, she probably thought it was a nightmare. Waking up to something like that? I couldn't even imagine." I stopped. He was staring at me strangely. "What?"

"It's just that you're thinking along the right lines."

I couldn't keep the goofy grin off my face. "I'm that awesome. I know."

His lips twitched as if he wished to smile. "So, how much trouble are you in?"

"Grounded basically, but I guess I got off light." I was still smiling like an idiot.

"Yeah, you did." He looked relieved. "Try to stay out of trouble and *please* don't sneak around the grounds. I doubt the daimon is still here, but you never know."

Drawing in a deep breath, I folded my arms over my chest. "Aiden?"

"Hmm?"

I stared at Aiden's boots. They were shiny, never scuffed. "It's starting, isn't it?"

"You're talking about what your mother told you, aren't you?"

"She said this is what they would do. And Eric's still out there. What if he's behind this and—?"

"Alex." He leaned toward me. We were close, but not as close as we'd been in the gym. "It doesn't matter if it's Eric or not. We'll make sure this doesn't happen again. You have nothing to worry about."

"I'm not scared."

Aiden reached out, brushing his fingers over mine. It was a brief touch, but my body tingled nonetheless. "I didn't say you were scared. If anything, you're too brave."

Our gazes met. "Everything is changing."

"Everything already has."

Later that night, I tossed and turned. My mind wouldn't shut down. The daimon attack, the apple assault, bitchy furies, the impending Council session, and everything else kept cycling in one giant, endless cluster. Each time I flipped over, I grew more irritated at the prospect of another sleepless night.

The trouble sleeping had started about a week after returning from Gatlinburg. I'd fall asleep for an hour or so before a nightmare crept into my dreams. Mom was usually in those nightmares. Sometimes I relived fighting her in the woods; sometimes I didn't kill her, and other times it was just me and Daniel, the daimon with the too-friendly hands.

Then there were the dreams where I *wanted* to be turned into a daimon.

I'd flipped onto my stomach and shoved my face into the pillow when I felt a strange tingling in the pit of my stomach—like the butterflies right before a first kiss, only much, much stronger.

I pushed up and squinted at the clock. Past one in the morning, and I felt wide awake. And hot—really hot. Thinking the temperature controls may've gone all wacky again, I got up and opened the window by the bed. Cool, damp air rolled in from the ocean, providing some relief. I didn't feel like I'd crawl out of my skin at any moment, but I still burned—like all over. I ran my hands over my face, aching in a way that reminded me of the time I'd spent with Aiden. Not our training sessions, oh no—but the night before I'd found Kain, the night I'd lain naked in Aiden's bed.

But I remembered more than the physical stuff. Words I'd never ever forget in a trillion years—*you got inside me, became a part of me*. No one had ever said anything like that to me—no one. I glanced at the clock again, sighing. Fifteen minutes went by, then twenty minutes, then half an hour. Finally, I stopped paying attention to the time. My heart pounded until I squeezed my eyes shut. I could almost see Aiden now, feel the soft brush of fingertips and hear those words again. Then, without any warning, the itchy feeling vanished. The cool air coming in from the window suddenly felt brutal.

"What the hell?" I flopped onto my back. "Hot flashes? Really?"

It was a long, long time before I fell asleep.

CHAPTER THREE

Everything did change the next day.

Olivia and I shared a trigonometry textbook in class, trying to figure out the difference between a sine and cosine.

Considering we'd be spending the bulk of our adult lives hunting and killing daimons, learning trig seemed pretty pointless, so we really didn't apply ourselves.

I drew a pair of humongous boobs on the free space above the formula and labeled them "Olivia." She immediately scratched her name out and scribbled "Alex."

I snorted, looking up just in time to see Mrs. Kateris, a pure-blood with enough degrees to be teaching at Yale, twist around and frown at us.

"Great," Olivia muttered from behind her hand. "If she picks up this textbook and asks what we're doing again, I'm going to die. Seriously."

I yawned loudly. "Whatever."

Mrs. Kateris placed the chalk down and clapped her hands. "Miss Andros and Miss Panagopoulos." She paused long enough for the entire front of the class to twist around in their seats and look at us. "Would you like to share—?"

"I like how she says your last name," I murmured to Olivia at the exact moment our classroom door swung open and a small fleet of Guards entered the room.

"What the hell?" Olivia sat up straighter.

Mrs. Kateris stepped back, smoothing her hands over the front of her skirt.

The Guards bowed in her direction, the custom when addressing pures of status, which in our world was pretty much every pure.

"We apologize for interrupting your class, Mrs. Kateris," said the first Guard. I almost didn't recognize him. He was the Guard from the bridge, the one who'd followed me around the Island—Crede Linard. Well, he must've been promoted.

Mrs. Kateris gave him an uneasy smile. "No need to apologize. How can we help you?"

"Dean Andros wishes for the presence of the half-bloods. We are here to escort them."

The halfs in the class glanced around the room, confusion and wariness on our faces. Had there been another attack?

Stepping back, Mrs. Kateris clasped her hands. Guard Linard faced the class, expression impressively blank. "Please follow us."

Olivia snapped the textbook closed as her face lost its color. "What's going on?"

I grabbed my backpack off the floor, thinking of the furies. Everyone had been talking about them this morning, thinking they looked pretty cool. No one seemed to get what a big deal they were. "I don't know."

Several halfs started asking questions as we filed out of the classroom, but Guard Linard frowned at them. "No talking."

The same thing was happening in the other classes. Doors opened as Guards led halfs in a single-file line down the corridor. Upstairs, the sound of herded footsteps followed our group. I glanced behind us, spotting Caleb and Luke.

Turning back around, I drew in a shallow breath. This was something serious, and we all recognized it. Tension rippled through the air, itching at our skin as we continued to the first floor. Getting down the stairwell took a ridiculous amount of time. Once again, I felt the desire to mention the fact that we needed elevators.

We ended up being ushered through the lobby of the school, past the administrative offices, then into the middle of the Covenant—to the indoor coliseum. It was the only place big enough to hold all of us.

Once inside the room we students referred to simply as the "gymnasium," we were ordered to take our seats and to stay with our classes. Olivia and I ended up in the third row. Caleb and Luke were at least in the eleventh, which sucked. I'd rather be sitting near Caleb when they dropped whatever bomb they were about to drop on us, and I knew Olivia felt that way, too.

I bounced my knee, scowling. The seats in here had been made out of some kind of sandstone, and they were the most uncomfortable things to sit on.

Olivia squirmed. "Do you—"

From the gymnasium floor below us, Guard Linard whipped around. "No talking."

Olivia's brows flew up, and I wondered if Linard would stroke out if I asked who was guarding the bridge. I exhaled loudly as I scanned the sea of half-bloods in green training clothes. A bunch of blue-uniformed Guards stood watch. But I didn't see many people in the black uniforms of the Sentinels, the hunters of daimons.

Then my gaze settled on a tall blond leaning against the wall, and I recognized the well-muscled arms and narrow hips. He had one long leg bent at the knee, his booted foot planted on a mosaic of a semi-nude Zeus.

Seth.

His hair was pulled back in a leather tie, but like always, shorter strands slipped free and curled around his chin. He had this golden complexion uniquely his own and a face perfectly pieced together, with those odd amber eyes holding an exotic curve. Sometimes I wondered if the gods had specially crafted those cheekbones and smug-looking lips, if they'd put the faint cleft in his chin and carved his jaw out of granite. No one else quite looked like him.

He was, after all, the First Apollyon of our generation. According to my stepfather, Seth and I were fated to be together in some weird, energy transfer way. According to me, Seth was a pain in my—

Seth inclined his head in my direction and winked. I leaned back and focused on the Guards below. Seth and I weren't getting along at the moment. In our last training session, he'd "accidentally" hit me with a blast of pure energy and I'd "accidentally" thrown a rock at his head.

Perhaps I did have a problem with throwing things.

After what seemed like forever, Marcus entered the gymnasium, and the entire student assembly shifted forward. Around two hundred of us sat together, ranging from seven to eighteen years old. The wee ones sat on the floor, knee to knee. They probably had no clue what was going on.

Marcus wasn't alone. Council Guards dressed in all white followed behind him. The Council resembled the Olympian Court, eight pures and two Ministers—one male and one female. Only the Covenant locations held a Council—here in North Carolina, upstate New York, South Dakota, and the wilds of Tennessee. The Council acted as our ruling government, establishing laws and carrying out punishments. The Ministers were the only ones who communicated with the gods, but if what Lucian had said during the summer was true, the gods hadn't spoken to the Ministers in ages.

This was a lot of pomp for just one Minister. It wasn't like the entire Council was swarming the gymnasium—just Lucian and his awesome hair. Jet black, it flowed to his waist, pin straight. Complimenting his hair was the only really good thing I could say about my stepfather. Well, that and he sent me lots of money.

The Guards bowed, straightening slowly. I noted that Seth hadn't moved an inch. Lucian stepped forward, clasping his hands together. He wore an all-white, tunic-type dress. I thought he looked ridiculous.

"A daimon attack occurred within the grounds of the Covenant yesterday." Lucian's clear voice rang through the silent room. "Such an attack is unprecedented and must be dealt with swiftly. At this time, we believe there will be no further…breaches of security."

Yeah, he must've seen the furies. I bet he hoped there wouldn't be any more breaches.

"But," he continued, "we must move forward and focus on prevention."

Like a violent tide rolling in from the ocean, apprehension swept through us. I held my breath.

"The Council and the Covenant have agreed that measures must be taken to ensure another attack does not occur."

Marcus stepped forward then, smiling in a way that sent shivers down my arms. "Several things are going to happen over the course of the next week. New rules are being put into place and these rules will be unconditional and effective immediately."

And here it starts, I thought angrily. One half-blood turned bad, so all half-bloods will be punished. I recognized the severity of the issue, but it didn't make it any easier to swallow.

Marcus scanned the crowd, meeting the gazes of the halfs. His steady eyes held mine a moment, then glided past. "A curfew of seven p.m. will begin tonight for all half-bloods"—gasps could be heard echoing through the room, and my jaw hit the floor—"unless the half-blood is accompanied by a Guard and is participating in an activity related to schoolwork. There will be no other exceptions. At no time will half-bloods be allowed into the rooms of pure-bloods unless accompanied by an Instructor or Guard. No half-blood will be able to leave the Covenant-controlled Island without permission, and then must be accompanied by a Guard or Sentinel."

"Oh, my gods," Olivia murmured, rubbing the palms of her hands over her thighs. "Can they do this?"

I didn't respond. The pures could do whatever they wanted. I had a feeling it was about to get a lot worse.

"Sentinels will be posted outside the dorms, along with the Covenant Guards. In addition to these measures, all half-bloods will be required to submit to a physical exam. These"—his eyes cut a strong look toward the upper level, where several muffled curses sounded—"these exams will be mandatory. After every half-blood has been examined, then the exams will continue based on need."

Ice rushed through my veins, settling in the pit of my stomach. Of course there would be physical exams. How else could they tell if any halfs had been turned? Their bodies, much like mine, would show the evidence of multiple daimon tags. It was the only sign of a half being turned.

I wanted to puke.

"Exams will begin tomorrow and will be done alphabetically." Marcus stepped back, allowing Lucian to take center stage once more.

"None of us enjoy the idea of limiting your freedom or imposing potentially uncomfortable situations upon you." Lucian splayed his hands open in front of him. "We care for our half-bloods, and this is as much for your benefit as it is for the pure-blooded students."

I covered my mouth, afraid I'd say something. Benefit us? Restricting our comings and goings, forcing us to submit to *physical exams*? There was no difference between us and the halfs who served them—except we wouldn't have the pleasure of being doped up and unaware of what was happening to us.

I looked away from Lucian and caught sight of Seth again. Every line of his face had hardened in disapproval and his eyes flared like the sun. I could feel his anger as if it were my own.

After going over a couple more rules regarding where we were allowed to enter and something about random dorm checks, the assembly drew to a close. I had a hard time focusing on what Marcus and Lucian had gone over. My own anger roiled inside me, and the brewing storm against the wall kept my attention.

We were ordered to exit the gymnasium the same way we'd entered: a silent, single-file line of half-bloods. Briefly, I caught a glimpse of Caleb's face. Disbelief and anger warred across his boyish features, making him seem so much older. No one had considered what this could mean for Caleb and me. They would find evidence of recent daimon attacks on both of us. Then what? Shove a bleeding pure in our face and see if we attacked? I glanced over my shoulder, searching for

Seth. He stood with Lucian, off from the white-robed Guards, and they appeared to be…arguing.

At lunch, we went over the new rules quietly. More Guards than normal hovered around the perimeter of the cafeteria, and even a few Sentinels stood post, limiting what we could say. I wondered what those half-blood Sentinels thought, knowing that they'd be subject to the exams, too.

Pures usually mingled with the halfs during this time, but today was different. Halfs took up one side of the cafeteria while the pures sat at the farthest tables possible. My gaze landed on Cody Hale and his cronies. Cody hung out with halfs sometimes, like when he had nothing better to do. There were many times during the summer when I'd wanted to hit him, but hitting a pure meant expulsion, and that meant servitude.

Right now his group had their heads bent together. Every so often, Cody would run a hand over his neatly cropped, brown hair, look at our table, and snicker. I wasn't the only one who noticed this.

Caleb's silent anger simmered around our table. Since the whole incident in Gatlinburg, I hadn't seen much of Caleb. My spare time consisted of training sessions, while his revolved around Olivia. Looking back, I kind of wished I'd made time for him. Maybe then I would've noticed the subtle changes in him, the shade of darkness that seemed to surround him, how quickly he reacted with anger.

"Just ignore them, babe." Olivia nodded toward Cody's table, forcing a causal smile. "Cody's an idiot."

"It's not just Cody." He gave a tight laugh. "Haven't you seen how the other pures have been looking at us? Like we're all about to jump them?"

"They're just scared." Olivia squeezed his hand. "Don't take it personally."

"Caleb's right." Luke leaned forward and lowered his voice. "Today in class, a pure I've known for years requested his seat to be changed. Sam didn't want to sit next to me—or any half. Hades, he looked like he didn't want to be in the same room as us."

I rubbed my fingers over my temple as my appetite vanished. "They're all scared. There's never been a daimon on campus before."

"It's not our fault." Luke's eyes met mine. "And what do they have to be afraid of? The way the Minister talked today, it sounded like the daimon wasn't here anymore."

"No one really knows that for sure." I picked up my soda, watching Caleb. He didn't speak for the rest of lunch. As we filed out of the cafeteria, I pulled Caleb aside. "You doing okay?"

He nodded. "Yeah, I'm fine."

I wrapped my arm around him, ignoring the way he stiffened. "You don't seem like it. I get—"

"You get that we're already top suspects, Alex?" Caleb pulled away. "That none of this is right or fair? I don't want them stripping you down, or Olivia, looking for some sign that we're chomping on pures during our spare time. And with you..." He paused, glancing around the hallway outside the cafeteria. Luke and Olivia went on, but two Guards eyed us—the same two from yesterday. "Lea was being a bitch yesterday, but people..."

"People have been talking? Caleb, people have been talking about me since they found out my mom was a daimon. So what? Who cares?" I squeezed his hand, just like Olivia had. "Why don't you sneak over tonight and bring a movie?"

Caleb pulled away again, shaking his head. "I got things I need to do."

"Like Olivia?" I joked.

That brought a hint of a smile. "Come on, you're going to be late for class. You have practice with Seth—"

I groaned loudly. "Please don't say his name. He throws balls of energy at my head like it's some kind of game."

"He looked pretty pissed off during the assembly."

"Yeah, he did." I thought about him arguing with Lucian. Only gods knew about what. "Anyway, sure you don't want to come by?"

"Not feeling it tonight. Besides, dodging the normal Guards is bad enough, but double the amount? Even I may have problems with that."

I pouted but relented as we parted ways. The rest of the afternoon crawled by, but I perked up when I saw Aiden enter the gym toward the end of Gutter Fighting. I tried and failed to contain my excitement.

"Where's Seth?" I bounced up to Aiden.

Aiden's eyes glittered with amusement. "He's with the Minister. Would you prefer him?"

"No!" I said a bit too eagerly. "What's he doing with Lucian?"

Shrugging, Aiden led me out to the center of the mats. "Didn't ask. You ready?"

I nodded, and Aiden handed me the dummy blades. He'd allowed me to practice with the real ones a week ago. Sadly, the thrill of finally getting to practice with them ended up overshadowed by the fact I'd already used them for real. I knew the weight of the slender daggers in my palms, the feeling of them slicing through daimon flesh. Using them in battle had killed that naïve appeal.

Aiden coached me through several techniques we'd learned in Silat training. We broke apart while he pulled out the dummies for me to stab. I twirled the plastic daggers like they were batons. "The new rules they set up for us suck. You know that, right? Physical exams and dorm searches?"

Aiden reached out, carefully tucking a strand of hair back behind my ear. He was always doing little things like that, things he shouldn't be doing. "I don't agree with all of them, but something has to be done. We can't continue as if nothing has happened."

"I know we can't continue as if nothing has happened, but that doesn't mean the pures have a right to punish every single half-blood."

"We aren't punishing the half-bloods. These rules were put into place to protect the half-bloods also."

"To protect us?" I gaped at him. "Because all I heard today were rules limiting what we can do. I didn't hear anything about the pures having to submit to embarrassing exams or being told they couldn't even visit the main Island."

"You weren't in the assembly when they laid down the new rules for the pures, were you?" A bit of frustration began to seep through, furrowing his dark brows.

"Well no, but I haven't heard any pures bitching about anything."

Aiden took a deep breath. "Then you haven't been listening. They aren't allowed to go anywhere unless they're in groups. They can't leave the Island unless they're with a Guard or a Sentinel—"

"Whoa." I laughed harshly. "Those poor pures have to have babysitters? At least they don't need to get permission to leave. We don't even have that option."

"Aren't you grounded from doing anything anyway? And preventing the halfs from leaving the Island is to keep them safe."

I clenched the dagger, squeezing it so hard I thought it would shatter. "The new rules aren't fair, Aiden. You have to see that. I know you're a pure, but you can drop the act around me. You don't have to say you agree with it because you're expected to."

"This isn't an act, Alex. And this has nothing to do with me being a pure. I agree that drastic measures need to be taken. If the half-bloods have to sacrifice a couple of weeks of partying and jumping dorms to ensure—"

"Sacrifice a couple of weeks of partying? Are you serious? Do you think that's why we're upset?"

Aiden stalked toward me. "You're upset because you're being irrational and stubborn. You're letting your emotions rule your logic, Alex. If you'd stop and *think* for five seconds, you'd see that these rules need to be in place."

I jerked back a step, unable to remember the last time he'd spoken to me like that. An icky feeling started in my chest and spread.

"So let me get this straight." My voice shook. "You think it's okay for them to restrict where we can go and what we can do? That they can search our rooms at any time? You think it's acceptable for them to subject us to *full body* searches? And it's just okay for them to launch a witch hunt the moment they think there's another daimon?"

"No one's starting a witch hunt, Alex! I agree that certain measures have to be taken, but I don't agree with—"

Anger pounded through my blood. I threw the practice blade to the floor. "My gods, you're just another pure, Aiden! You're no different than the rest of them. How *irrational* of me to think otherwise."

Aiden flinched as if I'd hit him. "I'm no different than the rest? Do you hear yourself?"

"Whatever. Who cares, right? I'm just a half-blood." I pushed past him before I did do something irrational, like cry in front of him. Turns out, I didn't make it very far. I kept forgetting how fast Aiden could move.

He blocked me, eyes flashing silver. "How can you even say I'm like the other pures? Answer me, Alex."

"Because...because you should know that those rules aren't fair to us!"

"This isn't about the damn rules, Alex. I'm like the other pures?" He gave a low, sharp laugh. "You really believe that?"

"But you think—"

Aiden grabbed my arm, pulling me right against his chest. The unexpected contact fried my brain. "If I was like every other pure-blood, I would have had you by now, without even thinking about the consequences for you. Every day is a struggle not to be like them."

I stared up at him, shocked to hear him put it out there so bluntly. Words—and I always had words—totally escaped me. *I would have had you by now.* I was pretty sure I knew what he meant.

"So don't tell me I'm like other pures."

"Aiden...I'm—"

"Forget it." He released me, a cool mask slipping onto his face. "Practice is over."

Aiden left the room, and I stood there for several minutes. I'd never really argued with him before. Not like that. Sure, we disagreed on things all the time—like favorite TV shows. He liked the golden oldies—the kind they showed in black and white. I hated them. We'd come close to knocking each other out over that, but we'd never argued over *who* we were.

To add insult to injury, Guards were searching my room when I returned to the dorm. I don't know what they were looking for. Did I have a daimon hidden in my sock drawer, or evidence I was going to pounce on the next pure and suck up their aether stashed away with my undies? I stood by—powerless to stop them—and when they were done my stuff was a mess. It took me the better part of the evening to clean my room.

After I'd showered and slipped on my pajamas, I paced the room. I kept revisiting the lovely conversation I'd had with Aiden, and my stomach did the twisting thing again. I needed to apologize, because I'd been out of line. And to hear him say what he had? That if he'd wanted to be like other pures—he would have *had* me?

So caught up in my thoughts, I banged the sensitive part of my elbow into the doorframe. I cursed and bent over, gasping. Standing there, with sharp pain shooting through my arm, I thought of Mom.

About whether or not she really did look relieved the instant before she simply crumbled away. Had I seen the glimmer of relief in her eyes because I'd wanted to see it? Because I'd wanted to believe I'd done the right thing by killing her?

Aiden believed that I'd done the right thing. And I…well, I wasn't so sure anymore.

A soft knock sounded, then it came again, and there was no denying that someone had knocked on the window in my bedroom.

Caleb? Maybe he'd changed his mind and brought some movies over. Thrilled over the prospect of hanging out with him, I went to the window and drew the blind up.

"Crap." I recognized the back of the blond head. "Seth."

CHAPTER FOUR

Seth spun, pointing to the lock on the window.

"Open," he mouthed.

I planted my hands on my hips. "Why?"

His stare became dangerous. "Now."

Against my better judgment, I unlocked the window and pushed it up. I had about a second to step back before he jumped through the window like a damn alley cat. My room was dark, but I could make out the eerie glow in his eyes.

"What do you want? Hey! Don't shut that window. You're not staying."

"Do you want me to leave it open so the next Guard who makes his rounds looks in here and sees me in your bedroom?" He shut the window and pulled the rope on the blinds. They clattered against the windowsill.

"I'll tell them you forced your way in here." I walked over to the lamp and switched it on.

Hanging out in a dark bedroom with Seth wasn't on my list of things to do at the moment.

Seth smiled. "I wanted to apologize for not being at training today."

I watched him with a general sense of wariness. He tossed a few loose strands out of his eyes as he surveyed me with almost the same look.

"Apology accepted. You can now leave."

"Do something to your arm?"

"Huh?"

He leaned over, brushing his fingers over the elbow I'd just cracked. "This."

There was a small, barely visible red spot. "How in the world can you see that? I hit it on the door a few minutes ago."

A grin slipped over Seth's lips. "You're so unbelievably graceful. Should I kiss it and make it better for you?"

I could tell he was only half-joking. His presence around the Covenant had created quite the stir. So had his…extracurricular activities. If bed-hopping ever became a major sport, Seth would go pro. Or so I'd heard. I stepped around him. "Thanks, but I'll pass."

He followed me around the edge of the bed. "I've been told my lips can make a girl forget just about anything. You should try them out."

I wrinkled my nose. "Anyway, why were you with Lucian instead of at practice?"

"Alex, that's none of your business."

Somehow, I'd cornered myself between the wall and the bed. "He's my stepfather. It's my business."

"What crazy logic you have."

My hands curled into fists. "Look, you can leave now. You apologized. Bye."

His smile increased as he looked around my room. "I think I'll stay. I kind of like it here."

"What?" I sputtered. "You can't stay. It's against the rules."

Seth laughed deeply. "Since when do you care about rules?"

"I'm a changed person."

"When did you change? Just right now? 'Cause I heard about your smackdown in the cafeteria yesterday." A mischievous grin played across his lips. "By the way, that was made of awesome."

"Really? No one else thinks it was awesome. They said I was being…irrational." I pushed away from the wall and dropped on the bed. "Do you think I'm irrational?"

Seth sat down beside me, his left leg pressing against mine. "Is that a trick question?"

I scooted to the top of the bed. "So, I'm irrational?"

He twisted at the waist and stretched out on his side. "You're a bit impulsive. You throw apples at people's faces when you're angry. You go off half-cocked half the time. It entertains me to no end. So, if you are irrational, I hope you stay that way. I love it."

I frowned. "All of that sounds really good. Thanks."

"Rational is mundane and uninteresting. Why would you want to be that?" He reached out, tugging lightly on the hem of my pj's. "You don't even have it in you."

"Have what in me?" I pushed his hand away. Of course, Seth would be drawn to the unstable part of my personality. He was a bit crazy himself. I wasn't sure if it was all the aether in him that made him that way, or if he was just plain old crazy.

"You're too wild to be balanced and normal. Or logical," he added as an afterthought.

"I'm completely logical—totally. You don't know what you're talking about."

He sent me a knowing look before rolling onto his back. "I think I'll stay here tonight."

"What?" I shot to my knees. "Absolutely not, Seth. You aren't staying here."

He chuckled, resting his hands on his flat stomach. "I haven't been sleeping well. Have you?"

"I've been sleeping great." I pushed at his shoulders, but he didn't budge. "Seth, you're not staying here, so don't change the subject."

He rolled slightly, catching my hands with his. "Look, we didn't have training tonight. I'm owed an hour of your time."

I tried to pull my arms free. "That's ridiculous."

Seth sat up in one clean motion. "And it starts now."

"What?" My fingers curled helplessly. "It's late. I have class tomorrow."

He grinned, letting go of my arms. "You'd still be up even if I wasn't here."

Scooting back once more, I kicked him in the thigh. "You're a pain in my—"

"I think we'll work on how to control your anger."

I moved to kick him again, but he caught my calf. "Let go."

Seth leaned over, voice low. "Don't kick me again."

Our eyes locked. "Let. Go."

Slowly, he released his grip and sat back. "I want all of your attention for a moment." He paused, brows lowering. "That is, if you're capable."

"Whatever."

"What do you think about the daimon attack?"

I glanced at him. Everything about him had changed in an instant. "Honestly? I think it's just the beginning. I mean, for all we know, this could have been going on long before."

Seth swiveled around and sat beside me. Once situated, he nodded approvingly. "There's something you don't know, but I don't think it would hurt if you did."

I leaned forward. “What?”

“The Council has been tracking incidents that look like daimon half attacks. The attacks have been picking up over the last three weeks, so there are now two to three attacks a week. And it’s happening all over.”

“But…they haven’t said anything.” Mainly, Aiden hadn’t said anything, and I’d thought he told me everything. “How do you know about this?”

“I have my ways. The Ministers don’t want the pures or halfs knowing right now. They’re afraid it would cause a panic.”

“So that’s why you were with Lucian? He’s feeding you this information?” Seth just raised his brows.

I fell back against the headboard, sighing. “But not knowing is stupid. People need to know what’s happening. Look at what my mother told me. It’s happening.”

“I know.” He tipped his chin toward me, but his heavy lashes concealed his eyes. “I don’t think the Council wants to believe that.”

“That’s so stupid, Seth. They need to focus on that instead of trying to control us.”

“I agree. These rules are wrong.” He lifted his eyes, meeting mine. “But you won’t have to submit to them.”

“Uh…it doesn’t sound like I have a choice.”

“The half-bloods won’t have a choice, but you’re different.”

I stared at him in amazement. “I’m not any different, Seth.”

He held my stare. “Yes, you are. You will become an Apollyon, which makes you very different from the other half-bloods. You won’t submit to those exams.”

“Is that what you and Lucian were arguing about after the assembly?”

His stare was intense, calculating. "Among other things, but it's not anything for you to worry about."

"It's not? That's pretty ballsy of you to argue with the Minister, Seth."

The look on his face faded, replaced once again with the smug amusement. "Lucian has promised me that you…will not be searched."

I slouched to the side, eyeing him suspiciously. "I didn't know you had the kind of influence to make Lucian promise anything."

"You don't need to worry about the exams. So don't."

"What about the other halfs? They shouldn't have to go through that."

He looked away, letting out a soft breath. "Can I ask you a question—a serious question?"

"Sure." I stared down at my scuffed hands. I doubted Lucian cared enough to honor that promise.

"Why do you want to become a Sentinel? Is it a sense of obligation or…?"

That question took me a few moments to respond to. "It's not about protecting pures, if that's what you're getting at. That's what the Guards are for."

"Of course, you wouldn't settle on being a Guard," Seth said mostly to himself.

"Daimons kill for no reason—even mortals. What kind of creature just kills for the fun of it? Anyway, I'd rather do something about it than sit around and wait for them to attack."

"What if you had a different choice?"

"Servitude?" I stared at him. "Are you serious?"

He rolled his eyes. "I mean, what if you had other choices not given to half-bloods? To live a normal life?"

"I already did that," I reminded him, "for three years."

"Would you do it again?"

Why was he asking this? "Would you?"

Seth snorted. "I wouldn't give up being a Sentinel for the world. Or being the Apollyon. I rock."

Laughing, I rolled my eyes. "Wow. You're so humble."

"Why should I be humble? I'm great."

I didn't even bother responding, because I felt confident he was being serious. We sat in silence for a little while. I knew he caught I hadn't answered his question, but in not-so-typical Seth fashion, he didn't push it. "Did you see the furies in the lobby?"

He nodded.

"Aiden said they're here because the gods feel the Council isn't doing an adequate job." I toyed with the hem of my shirt. "Do you think…we need to be worried about them?"

"Ah…if they get loose, then it could be a potential problem."

"Oh." I don't know what made me say the next thing that came out of mouth. "I yelled at Aiden in training."

Seth nudged my arm with his shoulder. "I'm afraid to ask."

"He agrees with the new rules." I yawned. "So, I yelled at him."

"And he said you were being irrational, huh?"

"Yeah, so I yelled at him some more. I told him he was just like all the other pures."

"Well, he is like other pures."

I shifted down, trying to ease the ache in my side. "Not really."

Seth frowned down at me. "Alex, he's a pure-blood. Just because he chose to become a Sentinel doesn't make him any different. Ultimately, Aiden will always side with the gods. Not us."

"You mean the pures, not the gods." Weary, I lay my head down on the pillow and closed my eyes. Our hour was almost up. Maybe I'd get some sleep tonight. "You don't know him, Seth."

"I don't need to know him to know what he's capable of."

My brows rose, but I ignored that. "I need to apologize to him."

"You don't need to apologize to him." He bent down, brushing my hair off my cheek. "I'm being serious. You'll be the next Apollyon, Alex. You won't apologize to him, to any pure, or even to a god."

After a few moments of silence I said, "You know you need to leave, right? Even if I fall asleep, you're going to leave?"

"Of course." I couldn't see him, but I heard the smile in his voice. Seth kept talking, bombarding me with questions, but I gave up answering them as sleep pawed at me, the kind of sleep I was almost sure I wouldn't wake up from in an hour or two. I finally gave into it, confident that when I awoke in the morning, Seth would be gone.

It felt like someone had trapped me face down on the bed. I thought I was having one of those dream paralysis things I'd read about once, but then I realized what pinned me to the bed was an arm.

And that arm belonged to Seth.

He hadn't left, and apparently, Seth was a cuddler.

His arm curled around my back, fingers balled into the comforter. His steady breath blew across my neck, almost as if he had moved my hair out of the way. Under a different circumstance, I would have enjoyed the feeling of having someone wrapped around me so closely. Because the warmth Seth exuded was nice—very nice. It was Seth, yet for a moment—a really tiny moment—I closed my eyes and drank in the warmth.

Then I wriggled out from underneath him, beat him on the chest until he woke up, and yelled at him for staying. All of this made me late for my first class, and the whole episode left me in a weird funk, which wasn't helped when I passed Lea in the hallway.

Even with the black eye and bandaged nose, Lea looked good. No one could sneer like her. I ignored her for the most part, feeling ambivalent for doing so.

In Technical Truth and Legends, which was a cross between history and English, I usually sat beside Thea, a quiet pure I'd met over the summer, but today Deacon St. Delphi slid into the seat beside me.

I liked Deacon for a lot of reasons—none of them being the fact he was Aiden's younger brother.

He tended to drink a bit too much, but he was fun—lots of it. "Hey there." Deacon dropped his book on the desk.

"Why isn't Thea sitting here?"

He shrugged and several blond curls fell across his gray eyes, the only physical trait he and his brother shared. "Some of the pures are scared of you. Thea knows we're friends. She asked to switch."

"Thea's scared of me? Since when? What did I do to her?"

"It's not you personally. A lot of us are freaked out right now."

"That's nice to know." I focused on the chalkboard. Our teacher hadn't showed yet.

"You asked."

"I did."

"Besides, you should be nice to me."

I cracked a half smile for him. "I'm always nice to you, Deacon."

"Yeah, but you need to be nicer. I'm losing a lot of cool points being seen talking to you."

I glared at him.

Deacon grinned. One dimple in his right cheek appeared. "Not just you, but any half at this moment. We pures don't trust a single one of you. Every half is a suspect. We're just waiting for one of you to pounce on us and suck away at our aether."

"Then why are you talking to me?"

"Have I ever cared what the other pures think?" His voice was loud enough for several of the pures seated around us to hear. I cringed inwardly. "Anyway, my brother thinks I need a babysitter while he goes to Council. Probably thinks I'm going to overdose or something without him being up my ass."

"That's not what he thinks. He's probably worried someone *will* suck up all your aether."

Deacon arched an eyebrow at me. "Defensive, aren't you, when it comes to my brother?"

Looking away, I felt my cheeks flush. "No. You give him a hard time when all he does is care about you."

"I don't know. He just thinks I'm a drunk little shit, which I am." He grinned, but it rang sort of false. "Anyway, his birthday is coming up. He's going to be twenty-one, yet he acts like he's thirty."

"'Cause thirty is real old," I said. Of course, I hadn't forgotten Aiden's birthday. It was the day before Halloween, and a week or so before we left for the Council.

"Anyway, I thought about throwing him a party. You should come."

I shook my head, grinning. "Deacon, I'm not allowed

to go anywhere. None of the halfs are." I also doubted Aiden would be down with a party, but I didn't say that. I think Deacon was serious in wanting to do something for Aiden, and I didn't want to hurt his feelings.

"So, you excited about going to Council? I hear they know how to party up there."

Edginess turned my tummy upside down. "Excited isn't the word I'd use."

Our teacher finally showed up and launched into a long-winded, dry lecture about archetypes and the first creation of the Council. Other than wanting to bang my head against the desk, the class was a breeze. So was the rest of the morning, once I got used to the suspicious looks. They weren't directed just at me, but at any and all half-bloods.

The pures were a paranoid bunch.

Halfway through Silat training, several Guards entered the room, bringing everyone to a halt. I sent Caleb and Luke a nervous look as the first Guard started reading out names in a flat, emotionless tone. My name was among the ten called out.

My stomach turned over as I grabbed my bag and followed the other halfs out. Their faces were pale, eyes sharp with distrust. Quietly, we trailed behind the three Guards to the med center. The sickening feeling expanded when I saw we were going to the same room Kain had been kept in. That alone was enough to make me want to flee.

One of the male nurses, a pure with salt and pepper hair, faced our group. Part of me hoped Lucian really had promised Seth that I wouldn't have to go through with the exams, but I should've known better. There was no bond between us, nothing to make him care about me.

The pure smiled, showing off a row of straight teeth. Something about his smile clenched my lungs. There were three female halfs in the group, and his mouth twisted into a greasy grin. Nausea rose up sharply.

"We will take you in one at a time. We will make this as fast as possible for you," the pure said. "Any questions?"

I raised my hand, heart tumbling over itself.

"Yes?" He sounded surprised.

"What if we don't agree to this?"

The pure's gaze darted to the Guards behind me, and then bounced back to me. "There's nothing to be worried about. It will be over within a couple of minutes."

I nodded slowly, feeling the eyes of the other halfs on me and the Guards shifting uncomfortably. "Yeah, I'm not down with this."

"But…you have no choice," he said slowly.

"But I do and I'm choosing no. And if you don't like that, then I'd like to see you try to make me do this."

That was pretty much when the Guards behind me decided they were going to try to make me do this. And that is when I decided I was going to be hitting someone again.

CHAPTER FIVE

I elbowed the first Guard in his stomach. The second Guard tried to force me into a corner, but my spin kick sent her flying into a gurney. The third and final Guard took a swing at me, and I'm not sure what happened, but I do know I kind of lost it.

A deep and terrible rage flowed through me. Time sped up incredibly fast. I caught the Guard's hand and twisted his arm backward, spinning him around. Planting my foot in his back, I knocked him into a table. The first Guard came at me again. He dodged my kick, but I spun around before he could anticipate my next move and my foot connected with his chin. The impact sent him staggering back.

The female half rushed me. I jumped the table of medical gloves and cotton swabs with startling grace. There was a second when I acknowledged that I *shouldn't* have been able to do that. Not clear a five-foot table with one jump. Especially when I hadn't even looked behind me, but then the heel of my shoe slammed into the cart, crashing it into the female's chest. The three Guards struggled on the floor in various degrees of pain.

The white walls of the med office spun as I turned around, facing the cowering pure. "I still don't have a choice?"

He edged along the wall, his face as white as his coat, hands held out in front of him as if *that* could stop me. I took a step toward him out of maliciousness. Not like I'd actually hit a pure…again. He bolted for the door yelling, "Guards! Guards!"

Several of the halfs looked shocked, like they too couldn't believe what I'd just done. Two of them looked like they wanted to join the melee.

"You don't have to do this," I said earnestly. "They can't make you if you don't—"

My words were cut off by the first Guard. Recovering, he jumped to his feet. "Miss Andros, you have made a very unwise decision. No one would have hurt you."

I wheeled around. They weren't going to come at me one at a time now. Some of the rage ebbed as I stumbled backward. Time stopped moving so fast. The three of them rushed me at once. I managed to knock one of the Guards aside, but another grabbed hold of my arm. I would have had him too, I swear, but the swarm of Guards entering the room distracted me.

So did the two halfs blocking their entrance, putting up a decent fight. I almost smiled, but a heartbeat later, I was pinned to the cold tile. Two of the male Guards held my arms down, and the female half literally sat on top of me. I bucked, trying to free myself.

"Stop." She grabbed the sides of my head and forced it back. Blood trickled from her nose. "Stop fighting us. No one wants to hurt you."

I could hear the scuffle by the door. "You're hurting me now," I gasped out. "You're busting my spleen."

The commotion caused by the fighting quickly ceased, and for a moment, all I could hear was the sound of my heartbeat slamming against my ribs painfully. "Okay. I'm done."

She glared down at me. "We'll decide when you're done."

"No. I will decide when you are done. And you are done with her," came a new voice—one that was both as cold and as hard as it was oddly musical.

The weight on my chest suddenly vanished, along with the Guard. She flew across the med room, slamming into one of the many carts lining the walls. I rolled onto my knees, drawing in air.

Seth took one step into the room, eyes simmering with anger. "You. Help her up now."

"But…we have our orders. She refused to comply," said the Guard.

"You must not have paid close attention. The Minister gave orders for all halfs to be searched, but not his *stepdaughter*. I doubt he will be pleased to know you three disobeyed him." Seth's gaze fell over me. "Why have you not helped her up yet?"

The Guard who had spoken darted forward and gently placed me on my feet.

"Apologize to her. All of you."

Surprised, I looked at Seth. He was being serious. He actually wanted them to apologize for doing their jobs. And the way he looked, well, he looked like he wanted to physically make them sorry. There was something unstable in his eyes. "Seth, that's not—"

"Be quiet, Alex. I want to hear them apologize."

My brows shot up. "Excuse—"

"I'm sorry, Miss Andros," the male Guard interrupted, as pale as a daimon. "I beg your pardon." Seth looked pointedly at the other Guards. The female Guard limped forward, apologizing profusely. When I nodded, they filed out of the room, leaving Seth and me alone for a few moments.

"You didn't have to make them apologize, Seth. They were just doing their jobs. You didn't—"

He stood directly in front of me, moving so fast I hadn't even registered it. He caught the edge of my chin with the tips of his fingers, looking me over. My cheek felt a little tender, but I doubted it would bruise. "A 'thank you' would be nice. I did stop them, you know."

I shifted uncomfortably. "Thanks."

Seth arched a brow as he tipped my head back. "You could also sound like you mean it."

"I do mean it, but you embarrassed them."

He dropped my chin, seeming pleased that I didn't screw up my face. "You beat the Guards up when they were just doing their jobs. I guess we're even."

Dammit. Seth had a point. I sighed. "Did…Lucian really order them not to search me?"

"Yes, but apparently he wasn't clear enough."

"But what about the other halfs? They shouldn't have to go through that." Instead of answering, he reached out and straightened the collar of my shirt. It must have come down during my fight, exposing the tags covering my neck. "Seth, what about them?"

Dropping his hand, he shrugged. "I don't know. I only have enough room in my head to be concerned about myself and you."

I snickered. "I'm surprised you have any room to think about anyone but yourself."

The smug grin was back. "Me too. I don't think I like it, actually." He dropped his arm over my shoulders and steered me toward the exit, past the halfs waiting outside and the cold looks of anger from the pures.

Aiden ended practice early that evening. We didn't speak much, but I could tell he had heard about what'd happened earlier. The only bright spot of the evening was when I ended up getting to eat dinner with Caleb. The news had already traveled to him and probably the rest of the Covenant.

"How much trouble did you get in?" Caleb asked.

I shrugged and dipped a fry into a glob of mayo. "None, actually. Lucian had ordered them not to search me."

Caleb cringed as I stuck the mayo-covered fry in my mouth. "You've been touched by the gods. I swear."

"Touched in more ways than one," I cracked. "Where's Olivia?"

"Can you dip your fries in something normal, like ketchup?"

I swirled my fry in the mayo gleefully. "And where's Olivia?"

Caleb leaned the chair back on two legs, sighing. "She's mad at me about yesterday. We got into an argument this morning."

"Oh. You guys fighting?"

"I guess so. It's stupid. Anyway, any news about the daimon?"

I told him what Seth had said about more half-bloods being attacked and turned. Caleb had the same reaction as I did: disbelief and anger. Sometimes I really, truly believed that the Councils would run better if half-bloods had control.

We seemed to have better critical thinking skills and more common sense.

After a few moments, Caleb spoke. "You know, I think what you did was pretty awesome."

I shrugged, thinking about how embarrassed the Guards had seemed. "Thanks. But it doesn't feel pretty awesome now."

Caleb raised his brows. "Well, it's got everyone talking and thinking. None of us want to go through with this. We think it was brave."

"It wasn't brave. Stupid maybe, but not brave."

"No," he insisted. "It was brave."

"Caleb, you know the pures will go crazy if we start really, really pushing them. One half refusing a strip search is one thing, but dozens? That's treason to them. You know what they do when you're suspected of treason."

The determined look gave his blue eyes an unfamiliar edge. "Like I said, I think things have to change around here."

I leaned forward. "Caleb, don't get in trouble."

"Why are you arguing with me about this, Alex? You stood up to them today, but you sound like you don't think any of us should. Why? Only you're allowed to, and the rest of us should just go along with whatever they want?"

"No. That's not what I'm saying at all. It's just that this is serious, Caleb. It's not about sneaking into rooms or leaving the Island. People could get expelled or worse."

"You didn't."

"Yeah, well…I'm different. And—*and* I'm not saying that to be like I'm super cool, either. The only reason I'm not in trouble is because Lucian stepped in—why, I don't know. But you guys will get in trouble."

Incredulous, he threw up his hands, shaking his head. "You're being way too…"

"Way too what?"

Caleb frowned. "I don't know, too rational about this or something."

For a moment I did nothing but stare at him, and then I busted out laughing. "Do you know you're the only person to accuse me of being *too* rational?"

A smile broke out across his face, reminding me of the younger, more carefree Caleb—the Caleb who didn't get excited about taking a stance against the pure-blooded Council. "Well, I guess there's a first time for everything."

We grinned at each other, but then my smile faded. "Caleb, you've changed."

His smile disappeared. "What do you mean?"

"I don't know. You're just different now." I didn't think he was really going to respond, especially when he stood up.

He walked around the table to sit next to me, and his lips pursed for a thoughtful moment. "I am different."

"I know," I whispered.

A brief smile appeared. "You know, I keep thinking about when we were in that cabin and I couldn't do anything to help you. I don't know what I'd thought it would be like to face a daimon. I guess I really had no idea." A muscle along his jaw ticked as he rubbed his fingers over a scuff mark on the table. "All I keep thinking is there had to be something I could've done to make them stop hurting you. I should've fought through the pain or something."

"Caleb—no." I grabbed his cool hands. "There was nothing you could do. And that whole, messed-up situation was my fault."

He faced me, lips twisting into a cynical smile. "I just never felt more…powerless in my life. I don't want to feel that way again."

"You're not powerless. You never were." I scooted over and wrapped my arms around his stiff shoulders.

Caleb responded a little awkwardly at first, but then he rested his chin atop my head. We stayed like that for a little while. "You have mayo in your hair," he murmured.

Giggling, I pulled back. "Where?"

He pointed. "You're such a messy eater."

After I got the mayo out of my hair, he studied me. "What? Do I have more mayo in my hair?"

"No." He glanced around the empty cafeteria. "How are things between…you and Aiden?"

I dropped the napkin. Usually Caleb sensed Aiden wasn't something I wanted to talk about. "I don't know. Everything is the same, I guess."

He rested his chin on my shoulder. The edges of his soft hair tickled my cheek. "Was he mad about the Guard thing?"

"He didn't say anything about it, but I'd go with a yes."

"Have you guys, you know, done—?"

"No!" I jerked back, hitting his arm lightly. Caleb shot me a knowing look.

"Nothing can happen between us, you know that. So, stop looking at me like that."

"Like not being allowed has ever stopped you before, Alex. Just…just be careful. I'm not going to lecture you—"

"Good."

He flashed a grin. "But if anyone finds out about what almost happened between you two…"

"I know." I glowered at the rest of my fries. "It's nothing to worry about, all right?"

The topic thankfully switched to less serious subjects. Way too soon, we had to head back to our dorms, and I was feeling a little bit better about things by the time I showered. But I still worried about Caleb, feared that the events in Gatlinburg had damaged him.

After I'd changed, I was hit again by that weird tingly sensation. Heat crept over my skin right before the intense ache started in my belly. Really, I tried to ignore it. I even picked up my trig book, but I couldn't focus. I turned on the television, but the force of whatever affected me made it nearly impossible to think about anything other than not having a boyfriend. Maybe this was the way my body was telling me I needed to find someone—someone who was actually available and wasn't a pure-blood.

When it finally did ease off, I fell into a restless sleep that lasted only hours before I shot straight up in bed, heart racing. I scanned the dark bedroom, trying desperately to rid the image of Daniel's face from my mind, his touch from my memories.

I rolled over and looked out the window. A second passed before my brain processed the dark shadow behind the blinds. My heart leapt into my throat. Jerking up, I threw the covers off and crept over to the window. The shadow was still there, sending shivers over me. Was it Seth trying to peep into my window?

If so, I was going to beat him over the head.

Or it could be the daimon—since they hadn't caught it yet. Hell, if it was, it wasn't going to sneak into my room.

I drew the blinds up and jumped back. A pale face—clearly not Seth's—stared back at me. In the dim light of the moon, I almost thought it was a freaking daimon.

But it was a Sentinel. I think the icy blond was named Sandra. Still, what was she doing staring into my bedroom window? Something about that creeped me out majorly. Without further ado, I unlocked the window and pushed it open. "Is everything okay?"

Sandra's eyes dropped to the tags on my bare arms before she dragged them back to my face. "I thought I heard screaming coming from this room."

I flushed as I realized I must've been dream-screaming. "I'm sorry. Everything's fine."

"Make sure this window is locked." She smiled. "Good night."

Nodding, I closed the window and threw the lock. My cheeks still felt bright red as I climbed back into bed and pulled the covers over my head. Although my childish screams had brought a Sentinel and not a daimon to my bedroom, the creeped-out feeling lingered all night.

I stumbled through the day, feeling out of it and sick. Not throwing-up-sick, but nervous-sick. I dozed off beside Deacon in class. He woke me up before the teacher spotted me sleeping. My hands trembled when I picked up my soda at lunch, which earned me a slew of concerned questions from Caleb and Olivia.

Maybe I was coming down with something. Or maybe it was the nightmares I'd had for the last two nights. I really didn't know, but all I wanted to do was crawl back into bed and sleep.

In Gutter Fighting, it was hard for me to follow the movements of my sparring partner. Luke took it easy on me, only knocking me to the floor a couple of times. And my day wasn't anywhere near over.

Practice with Aiden immediately followed, and I sucked at that, too.

I feinted to the left, but my movements felt jerky and too slow. Aiden's leg came around viciously, striking me in the calf. The impact knocked me forward, face-first into the mats. Dropping very real blades, I caught myself awkwardly. All my weight landed on my wrists, and I let out a sharp gasp.

"Alex! Are you okay?" Aiden came to my side and reached down.

Ignoring the pain, I pushed myself up. "I'm fine."

Aiden's arm was still extended, as if he'd forgotten he had been reaching for me. He just stood there, staring at me. "What's up with you today? You're going to break your neck at this rate."

Fire scorched my cheeks as I grabbed the blades off the mats. "I'm okay."

I wanted to apologize for accusing him of being like other pures while we had a few moments of downtime, but the words "I'm sorry" just wouldn't move past my lips, and then Aiden was falling back into an attack stance.

He flipped the blades over in his hands. "Again."

I attacked. Aiden brought his blades down on mine, and the sound of metal clashing rung through the training room. He pushed me back, jabbing one blade at my midsection. I caught his arm with my forearm, knocking his aim off.

"Good," he said. "Keep moving. Never stay still."

I darted under his arm, staying out of his range while I studied his moves. There was always something that gave away the move, the technique. Sometimes it was just a slight quiver of the muscle or eye movement, but it was always there.

Aiden jabbed, but it was a ploy. I saw it an instant before he dropped down, going for my legs with a low kick. I jumped out of the way and then went for the kill shot. This game would have been over for an untrained half, being caught on the mats like that.

But Aiden wasn't untrained and he was incredibly fast. He jumped to his feet in one swift movement, simultaneously tucking both blades into one hand.

I leapt, bringing the blades down. Aiden met me mid-flight, catching my arm. Within a second, he had my back pinned against him and two daggers pointed at my throat.

He bent his head down, his breath dancing over my cheek. "What did you do wrong?"

I felt his heart slamming against his chest. We were *that* close. "Um…?"

"You saw me moving the blades to one hand as a vulnerable move. You should have gone for the hand that held the blades. One clean swipe and you would have disarmed me."

Mulling that over, I saw he was right. "Well, hell's bells."

He leaned his head down farther, the longer strands of his hair brushing my cheek. Neither of us moved. I let my eyes fall shut as his warmth surrounded me. I think I could've fallen asleep standing against him. "Now you know." He released me. "Go again."

And I did. Again and again, we squared off. I blocked a series of his jabs, and he blocked all of mine. After a few rounds, I was slick with cold sweat and exhausted. All I wanted to do was sit down.

Aiden rushed me, and I pushed him back. With distance between us, I launched to the right, fingers spasming around the hilt of the blade. *Kick. Use a kick,* I ordered myself. Aiden dodged my jab, but not my kick. He lost his grip on one of the blades, and it clattered to the mat. Surprise and pride flickered across his face before he charged me with one blade. I blocked his attack, arms trembling. He dropped down, moving into position to sweep my legs out from underneath me. I saw it coming a mile away.

I just didn't—couldn't—will my legs to move fast enough.

Everything slowed down, ensuring that the lameness of what was about to occur would be perfectly captured. I jerked back toward the edge of the mat. His long leg swept around, catching both of my legs. I lost my grip on the blades and fell backward. A second later my head cracked off the floor.

I lay still, stunned and queasy.

Aiden's face popped into my vision, but his features were a bit muddled. "Alex, are you okay?"

I blinked slowly. My head hurt so bad my teeth ached. "I…think so."

"Can you sit up?"

Every part of me protested the movement, but I sat up. Aiden immediately checked the back of my head for damage with swift and gentle fingers. "That…was kind of stupid of me."

"It's not a big deal. You were doing really well. You even disarmed me." He sat back; his hands cupped my cheeks and tilted my head back. He smiled. "I don't think there's any permanent damage."

I tried to smile but failed. "I'm sorry."

A frown creased his brow. "Don't apologize. It happens. You can't always be the fastest—"

"I saw your move, Aiden. I had more than enough time to get out of the way." I lowered my eyes. "I'm just so freaking tired."

Aiden scooted forward, his knees pressing against my thigh. "Alex, look at me." Sighing, I lifted my eyes. He smoothed my hair back with a little smile. "Are these practices too much?"

"No—"

"Alex, be honest with me. You're training all the time. Is it too much?"

If he kept touching my hair, I'd admit to anything. "It's not too much, Aiden. Really, it's not. I'm…just not getting a lot of sleep."

He shifted so that he was right beside me, his other hand falling to my shoulder. I inhaled his unique scent of sea and burning leaves. With him this close, with one hand curving over my shoulder and the other continuously smoothing back my hair, I was putty in his hands. I think he knew that.

"Why are you not sleeping?" he asked, voice low and soft.

The words just kind of spilled out of me. "I have nightmares—every night and all night."

"Nightmares?" he repeated. He didn't sound like he thought it was funny, more like he just didn't understand.

I closed my eyes, taking a shallow breath. "You don't know what it was like all those hours...in Gatlinburg, not being able to really do anything. And all those tags—it felt like they were breaking off pieces of me. You don't know what I would've done to make them stop—*just stop*."

Aiden stiffened, his fingers curling around the nape of my neck. "You're right, Alex. I don't know, but I wish I did."

"You don't mean that," I whispered.

"I do." He went back to moving his fingers through my hair. "Then maybe I'd be able to help you somehow. Is that what you're having nightmares about?"

"Sometimes they're about Mom and other times it's the other two—Eric and Daniel. They're so vivid, you know? Like it's happening again." I pressed my lips together, stopping the ball of emotion from making it past my throat. Talking about that night, about what they'd done, curdled my stomach like sour milk. "So yeah, I don't get much sleep."

"How...how long has this been going on?"

I shrugged. "Since a week or so after everything happened."

"Why haven't you said anything? That's too long for you to deal with this alone."

"What was I supposed to say? It's pretty damn childish to be having night terrors—"

"They're not night terrors. It's stress, Alex. What you've had to deal with…" He looked away, a muscle working in his jaw. "No wonder you're having nightmares. She was a daimon, but she was also your mother."

I pulled back, looking into his face. Concern etched across Aiden's features, shifting his eyes to a thunderous gray. "I know."

He shook his head. "And then you've been running nonstop. You haven't had a moment to just…shut down. The daimon attack probably added to it. I don't know why I didn't think about that—why no one did. This is all too much. We have to—"

"Please don't tell Marcus. *Please.*" I started to climb to my feet, but he kept me on the mat. "If he thinks something's wrong with me, he'll take me out of the Covenant." And he would, too. If Marcus thought I was damaged, I'd be in servitude. Halfs didn't go to counseling. They didn't get post-traumatic stress. They *dealt* with things. They didn't lose sleep and screw up in practice. "Oh, gods, Marcus is going to kick me out."

Aiden caught my chin again. "That's not what I was going to say. You worry too much, Agapi. I'm not going to say anything to anyone. Not a single word of this, but that doesn't mean I'm going to forget."

"What does that mean?"

He smiled, but it seemed off and a little sad. "Well, you need to get some rest, and you need time to just chill out. I don't know. I'll think of something."

I covered his hand with mine. At once, he let go of my chin and threaded his fingers through mine. My little heart just got all kinds of happy. "What does Agapi mean?"

Aiden sucked in air. "What?"

"You've called me Agapi…a couple of times. It sounds beautiful."

"Oh. I…I didn't realize I had." He pulled his hand free. "It's the old language. It doesn't really mean anything."

That was kind of disappointing. Reluctantly, I climbed to my feet. I drew in a deep breath and watched Aiden stand. "I feel okay—"

The gym doors flew open, banging against the wall. Seth strode in like he owned the place. "What's going on?"

I glared at him. "What does it look like?"

Aiden swiped the blades off the mats. "I really need to find a way to bar those doors."

Seth shot Aiden a look. "I really wish you'd try."

Aiden lowered his arms, his fingers inching over the hilt of the blades. "Don't you have something you should be doing? I cannot believe your sole purpose of being here is to help Alex a few days a week and prowl the halls of the female dorm."

"Actually, that is my sole purpose. Didn't you know? I'm here—"

"Uh, is practice over, Aiden?" I cut in before the two choke-slammed one another.

"Yeah." His eyes stayed on Seth.

I felt there was a good chance he might stab Seth. There was also a good possibility Seth might zap Aiden. "Okay. Thanks for the practice…and everything."

Seth smirked and raised his brows at Aiden.

"No problem," replied Aiden.

Groaning inwardly, I hurried over to my bag. On the way out, I grabbed a fistful of Seth's shirt. "Come on."

"What?" Seth protested. "I think Aiden wants to hang out with me."

"Seth!"

"All right." He spun around, straightening his shirt. I didn't look back. Once outside the building, I dared a glance at Seth. "Did you need something?"

He grinned. "Nope."

"So, you busted up my training for no apparent reason? I call bullshit on that."

Seth dropped his arm over my shoulder. "You can call it whatever you want. Let's go get something to eat. You can still do that, right? Or are you grounded from showing your face in the cafeteria?"

"I'm not supposed to be hanging out with friends."

"Then I guess it's a good thing you and I are not friends."

CHAPTER SIX

After another long and boring day of classes, I waited for my turn with Seth, praying I didn't crack my head again. Last night, I'd gotten a decent night's sleep after Seth had shown up and popped in a DVD. I was feeling pretty rejuvenated.

Since I was alone for a few moments before training, I approached the wall of mass destruction. I was about to pick up the dagger Aiden favored when I realized something was off about the wall.

The weapons hung from little black hooks, and now several spots were empty. Of all the times I'd practiced in this room, I'd never seen any spot open. Daggers and blades were kept in this room for training purposes only. Each blade required a different handling technique and was used at a different time during the day. Did they remove the blades for cleaning? It wasn't like they gathered much dust in this room.

"Ready, my little Apollyon-in-training?"

I dropped my bag and turned around. Seth strolled across the mats, a cocky grin smeared across his face. Rain dripped from his hair and ran down his neck, giving him a wild look. I forgot about the missing blades at the sight of the wicked look on his face. He was *so* up to something. "Not really."

Seth cracked his knuckles. "Since it's pouring outside, I figured we could work on your grappling skills—since they are terrible. I know, I know—you're devastated by the knowledge of not being able to practice with the elements today, but look on the bright side. We get to roll around on the mats. Together."

I arched an eyebrow. "Sounds like fun."

He stopped behind me and placed his hands on my shoulders. "You up for it?"

I shrugged off his hands and ripped the hair tie off my wrist. "Yeah, I'm not damaged."

"I didn't say you were."

"Can we do this without you talking?"

Seth pouted. "But I have something you may want to know."

"Doubtful."

"Let me ask you a question: Do you feel bad about getting the halfs to refuse to submit to the exams being done? I saw five more halfs all bruised up today."

Caleb hadn't been joking when he'd said several halfs had been planning on refusing the exams. I could pick them out easily. Though there hadn't been a sign indicating that the daimon was still on campus, the pures kept up with the rules and exams. I think it had something to do with the fact no one knew how long a daimon half could go without aether.

"I didn't make them do anything," I grumbled.

"They're following your lead, and if I remember correctly, didn't you tell the ones with you that they didn't have to do it?"

My cheeks flushed with frustration. "Whatever. Shut up."

"Then let's play, Alex."

He considered grappling "playing" only because it really did involve a lot of rolling around…and at times, hair pulling. And I think Seth used it as an excuse to cop a feel. Like right now. I knocked his hand off my butt. "You're such a dog."

"And your grappling skills suck." He pinned me for the third time. Most of his hair had come loose, hanging over his face. "Most females suck at it. It's basic body strength. Males have more mass. So, you need to stay on your feet."

Rolling my hips, I managed to knock Seth off. I scrambled back to standing. "Yeah, I think I grasped that already."

Lounging on his side, he tipped his head back. "So, you slept like a little baby Apollyon last night. I wonder why."

I glared at him. "I loathe you."

He chuckled. "You reluctantly like me."

"Whatever. So, are you going to tell me why you're always with Lucian? Is he a part of your little fan club now?"

"My *fans* love to hear my war stories." He jumped to his feet, swinging at me. "They're obsessed with me. What can I say? I'm that cool. And I'm not always with Lucian."

I grabbed his arm, twisting it back in a submissive hold. "I seriously doubt that."

Seth stilled. "You know what, Alex?"

Straightening, I relaxed my hold on his arm. "What?"

He glanced back over his shoulder at me. "You really need to start resting more. The lack of sleep is clouding your judgment. I am that cool, and you just made a fatal mistake."

"Huh?"

"You should never relax your hold." Then he flipped me off his shoulder. I hit the mat with a loud grunt. "Aw, did you just fall?"

"No." I rolled onto my back, wincing. "I attacked the floor."

He dropped down, planting one leg on either side of mine. He caught my chin. "What were you and Aiden doing in practice yesterday?"

I grabbed Seth's wrist, intending on snapping it. Seth appeared to guess my intentions, because his eyes narrowed into thin slits before he slipped his hands away from my chin. "We were practicing, and why do you need to sit on me to talk to me?"

"Because I can and I like it."

I wanted to hit him. "Well, I don't like it. So, get off me."

He leaned forward instead, his face only inches from mine. "I don't like your practices with Aiden. So no, I won't get off."

My throat felt dry. "You just don't like Aiden."

"You're right. I don't like him. I don't like the way he looks at you, and I really don't like the way he looks at me."

I tried to keep my expression blank, but I felt my cheeks burn. "Aiden doesn't look at me weird. And he looks at you that way because you *are* weird."

He laughed. "Yeah, I don't think so."

Could Seth be picking up on my feelings for Aiden like he'd picked up on my fear while I was in Gatlinburg? If so, that would be really, really bad. "What are you getting at?"

Seth rolled off and sat cross-legged beside me. "I'm not getting at anything. By the way, I do have something to tell you."

As long as I lived, I'd never get used to the way Seth switched topics so frequently. He made my brain hurt. "What?"

"There was an attack at the Tennessee Covenant last night. It was a half who'd been turned. He cut up a pure, drained him of aether, and tossed him out of a seventh-story dorm window."

Horrified, I jackknifed up. "Oh, my gods! Why didn't you say something at the beginning of practice?"

He stared at me. "I clearly remember telling you I had something you'd be interested in knowing and you said it was doubtful."

"Well, you could have explained it a little better." I fell back against the mats. "Holy crap, what are they doing about it?"

"The same thing they are doing here, but they caught the daimon—it was a Guard once upon a time, and since the pure died, they're taking more extreme measures."

"Like what?"

"There's talk of segregating the pures from the halfs."

"*What?*" I shrieked.

Seth flinched and scooted away. "Ouch. Damn, Alex, I can only imagine what you sound like in the throes of—"

"Are you serious?" I sat up again, folding my legs under me. "How can they do that? We share dorms with the pures. And classes. It's the same everywhere!"

"From what I hear, they're going to put all the pures in one dorm and all the halfs in the other. And change the class schedules."

I rolled my eyes. "Oh, so they're going to make the dorms coed? Yeah, that is going to go over well. Everyone's going to be having sex."

"Sounds like my kind of place." Seth grinned. "Maybe I can get a transfer."

"Do you ever take anything seriously?" I pushed to my feet.

Seth shot to his feet, towering over me. "I take you seriously."

Eyeing him, I stepped back. "This is serious, Seth. What if they do something like that here? What if this is the beginning of everything changing?"

The ever-present—and annoying—mix of smugness and amusement faded from those eerie, golden eyes, revealing a level of gravity I didn't think Seth was capable of. "Alex, everything has already changed. Don't you see that?"

I swallowed and folded my arms around me, but it didn't stop the sudden coldness from washing over my body like I'd stepped into the freezing downpour outside.

Aiden had said the same thing.

"There are two of us," Seth said quietly. "Everything changed the moment you were born."

I tapped my finger along the edge of the keyboard. I was having one of those nights where I questioned everything that ever was, and I was getting on my own nerves.

I blamed Seth.

Everything changed the moment you were born.

I tried not to think about how the whole Apollyon business worked most of the time. Usually, I pretended like it wasn't a big deal. But that didn't mean I wasn't dealing with it; I just knew there was nothing I could do about it. It's like not crying over spilled vodka and cranberry juice or whatever. But there were times—like earlier with Seth—when the idea of becoming this *thing* that people expected something miraculous from, and were also scared to death of, terrified me.

I stared at my computer screen, forcing myself to stop worrying about the Apollyon stuff and what was happening at the Covenants. I then played about a dozen rounds of minesweeper and solitaire—anything to keep my brain nicely blank. It worked beautifully for a short while.

Another question poked at me. Why had Lucian intervened on my behalf? And why was Lucian handing over so much information to Seth? Yes, he was the Apollyon, but Lucian was the Minister and Seth was just a half-blood. Why would Lucian allow Seth to be privy to such information?

Then there was the business with the Council. I had this feeling I didn't have many fans on the Council and my time with them was going to suck daimon butt.

All of this made my brain sore.

Groaning in frustration, I dropped my head on the keyboard. An immediate, shrill buzzing filled the otherwise quiet room, but I ignored it until I had a streak of brilliance. And it had nothing to do with the Apollyon, the Covenant, or Lucian.

It had to do with Aiden.

Lifting my head, I bit my lip and opened up an internet page. For the last week, I'd been scouring the internet for the perfect gift for Aiden's birthday. Not just a birthday gift, but a peace offering, too. I figured I could get him something—I don't know—special. I'd come up empty-handed for the most part, but tonight, I had an idea.

It had to do with what I'd seen in his cottage that night—a ridiculous number of books, comics, and a colorful assortment of guitar picks. I'd thought then it'd been a strange thing to collect, but at least he didn't collect something gross like body lint. Anyway, I knew there was one color he didn't have—black. But I didn't want to get him just some crappy, old plastic pick. I wanted—needed—something special.

An hour later, I came across an online store dedicated to rare picks and I knew I'd found the perfect gift. They had one made out of onyx gemstone, and apparently it was a super extraordinary guitar pick. I had no idea why. Buying the thing would be hard, though. I hadn't been trusted with a bank account for some reason.

The next day I cornered Deacon before class started. "Can you do something for me?"

"Anything for my favorite halfy." He gave me a little nod as he eyed Luke, who was gesturing wildly at the front of the class.

"Halfy?" Only Deacon could get away with that. "Never mind. You have credit cards, right?"

He flicked a wayward curl out of his eyes and smiled. "Loads of them."

I shoved a piece of paper in his face. I'd scribbled the name of the website and the stock number of the pick on it. "Can you order this for me? I'll give you cash."

Deacon glanced down at the paper and then lifted his head, looking at me. "Do I even want to know?"

"Nope."

"This is for my brother, isn't it?"

I felt my cheeks flush. "I thought you didn't want to know."

He folded up the paper and stuck it in his pocket, shaking his head. "I don't. I'll order it tonight."

"Thanks," I murmured, feeling overexposed.

Staring at the front of the classroom while not really seeing anything the teacher wrote on the board, I hoped Aiden liked the pick—*loved* it. My muscles locked up at the idea of love and Aiden in the same sentence.

Just because I was buying him a stupid little guitar pick didn't mean anything. And just because I wanted to jump his bones didn't mean I…loved him. Halfs didn't love pures. So where had that thought even come from?

I ignored Deacon for the rest of the class and slipped into

a weird mood that lasted all day long. Not even Caleb and Olivia's hilarious bickering at lunch snapped me out of it. Not even Lea tripping in the hallway. Practice with Aiden couldn't shake me out of the funk either.

Aiden's tense and concerned gaze followed every one of my movements. I imagined he was waiting for me to fall asleep and crack my head or something.

But I didn't.

By the end of practice, some of the tension had eased off his face and a lopsided grin appeared as he picked up my gym bag. "I want to do something different tomorrow."

"Are you going to let me off my Saturday training?" I was only half-joking. The idea of lying around in bed all day did sound really nice.

"No. That's not what I was thinking. Not really."

I reached out for my bag, but he held it back. I grinned. "What were you thinking?"

"It's kind of a surprise."

"Oh." I perked up. "What is it?"

Aiden chuckled. "It wouldn't be a surprise if I told you, Alex."

"I can act surprised tomorrow."

"No." He laughed again. "That would kind of ruin it."

"All right, but it better be good." I reached for the bag again, but Aiden caught my hand. His fingers wrapped around mine. Our hands fit perfectly together. Well, at least I thought so. A swarm of butterflies stirred in my stomach. My eyes flicked up, and I was immediately snared. I could always tell what Aiden was thinking by the color of his eyes.

Generally, they were the palest shade of cool gray, but when they shifted, becoming an intense silver, I knew he was on the verge of doing something—something he probably shouldn't, but something I really wanted him to do. Like right now they'd heated to a bright quicksilver.

"It's going to be good." Aiden's gaze dropped to my lips. "I promise."

"Okay," I whispered.

"Wear something warm tomorrow, but no workout clothes."

"No workout clothes?" I echoed dumbly.

"Meet me here at nine." He carefully placed the strap of my bag over my shoulder. His fingers lingered long enough to make breathing difficult. My skin still tingled from the brief, wonderful contact long after he'd left the room.

After grabbing some food from the dining hall, Olivia and I walked back to our dorm. Neither of us had made it to the cafeteria in time to eat there. Apparently, she and Caleb had had another fight.

"I don't know what else to do." She clutched a can of soda in her hand so tightly I thought she'd crush it at any second. "One minute he's hot and the next he's cold."

I didn't know how much Caleb had told Olivia about what'd happened to him in Gatlinburg, so I was fairly limited on what I could tell her. "I know he really likes you." I decided that was the best tactic. "During the summer he totally obsessed over you."

A light breeze played with her tight curls, tossing them across her face. "I know he likes me, but he's just been so…I don't know, *off* lately. All he cares about is what Seth is doing. Gods, it's like he loves him."

I focused on how the horizon and the sky blended seamlessly together, trying not to laugh. "Unfortunately, I think Caleb looks up to Seth."

Olivia stopped walking. "I don't get why everyone is so infatuated with Seth."

"I'm not."

"Then we're the only halfs in the world that don't think he's awesome." She suddenly screeched, startling several seagulls. "I just don't understand! Seth's arrogant, rude, and he thinks he's better than everyone else!"

I stared at her, quickly ascertaining I wasn't really good at girl-talk. I had no idea how we'd jumped from Caleb to Seth. "Is Caleb with him now?"

A bit of the anger faded from her face. Olivia sighed, shaking her head. "No. We were hanging out in the rec room before dinner, and I asked him if he thought about where he would take a Sentinel post. You know, not a serious question, but a really important one."

Nodding, I shifted my soda to my other hand, trying and failing to get my hair out of my face. "I mean, I know we say it's nothing serious between us, but I think it is." She started walking again. "Anyway, we're graduating in the spring, and they give us options. I was hoping Caleb and I could pick the same place or get posted close together so we could still see each other."

"Okay...so what happened?"

"He told me he hadn't thought about it, and I was like, 'What the hell?' If I was important to him, then he would have thought about it. Right? So, I told him that." The skin on her cheeks darkened. "And do you know what he said? 'What's the point of picking a place? In the end, the Council will determine where we go.' Well, duh—thanks for the newsbreak, asshat. That's not the point. The point is we can hope that we end up together, right?"

"Olivia, I don't think it has anything to do with you. Right now..." I shifted, suddenly feeling warm even though it was an overcast, chilly day. "He told you about..."

Unable to ignore the swamping heat flooding me, I stopped and drew in a shallow breath. My entire body tensed painfully.

"Alex?" Olivia stepped closer. "Are you okay? You look really flushed."

No. Oh. No. This could not be happening during the day and in front of Olivia. This was so unfair.

On top of everything else, I was losing my—

Delighted giggling drifted out of the courtyard. Then a very male and very pleased chuckle followed. There were more sounds, sounds indicating that either someone was in a lot of pain or having a lot of fun.

"Are you kidding me?" Olivia shoved her food into my limp hands. "For the love of the gods, there are empty class-rooms and beds for this kind of stuff."

Before I could stop her, she pushed open the gate to the courtyard. I guess if she wasn't getting laid, then no one else could? "Olivia—"

"Hey!" she yelled, storming forward. "Hey! You little pervs, go get a room!"

Olivia disappeared around a thick rosebush. Rolling my eyes, I trailed behind her. Walking inside the courtyard was like being in a different world. The wild mixture of flowers and plants, all sweet and tangy, mixed with the bitterness of the herbs and assaulted my senses. There was also something unique about the plants in here. Come summer or winter, the foliage never died. Gods mojo juice, I guessed.

Greek statues lined the walkway, serving as a reminder that the gods were always watching. Runes were etched into the pathway, as were various symbols that signified the gods. Whoever had done the drawings seriously could have benefited from art lessons. But the place was kind of like the Garden of Eden.

And someone was partaking of its forbidden fruit. "You guys need to—*oh*."

Olivia stopped so unexpectedly I nearly crashed into her. She stood beside the nightshade—the plant the oracle had compared to "kisses from those who walk among the gods" or something crazy like that. I don't know why I noticed the purple hue of the petals first. Perhaps it was some kind of natural preservation instinct.

But then I saw Elena.

I'd never seen her quite so undressed before, however. Her skirt was hiked up, shirt gaping wide open, and…that was pretty much all I wanted to see. Then my gaze fell on her partner.

"Oh. My. Gods!" I shrieked, wishing my hands were empty so I could cover my eyes—or claw them out.

Golden eyes, full of amusement, met mine. "Is there something we can help you two with?" Seth asked, clearly unfazed by the intrusion.

I whirled around, squeezing my eyes shut. My face felt like a thousand shades of red. "No. Nothing at all." Olivia backed up. "Sorry to interrupt."

"You sure? There's always room for one—or two—more."

"Seth!" Elena shrieked, not sounding entirely dismayed by the prospect.

I headed back up the path, Olivia snapping at my heels. Seth's deep laughter followed us all the way out of the courtyard. We didn't speak again until we stood in front of our dorm. Shock must have dampened the weird hot flash, because it was no longer there. For a multitude of reasons, I felt grateful.

"Well," Olivia said a bit unsteadily.

"Yeah…"

Her lips pursed. "I hate Seth. I think he's an ass, but he does have a really nice butt."

"Yeah…"

Olivia's eyes were wide. "You know what? I think I'm going to go see Caleb. Like right now."

I snickered. "Yeah, you go do that."

CHAPTER SEVEN

Not surprisingly, Seth knocked on my bedroom window that night. Honestly, the curfew thing sucked—being confined to my room and not being able to sleep usually left me with a mad case of boredom—so I kind of welcomed his little visits. Especially when he just wanted to watch a movie and I'd fall asleep.

But tonight was different.

I still hadn't decided what to wear tomorrow, and that was a major deal. Aiden only ever saw me in boring gym clothes. I needed something cute—a little sexy—but I couldn't look like I was trying too hard. My entire closet was on my bed. And of course, I'd just seen some of Seth's—uh, more private parts. I kind of didn't want to see his face tonight.

The knock came again, more urgent. Groaning, I went to the window and opened it. Thankfully, he was fully dressed. "What?"

Seth loped over the windowsill, inviting himself in. "Nice jammies."

"Shut up." I grabbed a sweater off the bed and slipped it on, wishing I'd put on long pajama bottoms instead of shorts and a thin tank.

"You know, I don't care about the tag marks. Makes you look dangerous in an extremely hot way."

"It's not the marks I'm covering up, and you know that."

"Partly true and partly a lie. The scars embarrass you, because you're incredibly vain for a chick who wants to be a Sentinel. And you're uncomfortable being half-naked around me—"

"I'm not half-naked! And I'm not uncomfortable around you. *And* I'm not vain."

"You're a terrible liar." He sat down on my bed.

Okay. I was lying. Vanity wasn't the worst sin, and yeah, Seth made me uncomfortable for a lot of reasons, but that wasn't the point. "Why are you here?"

"I wanted to check on you."

My brows furrowed. "Why?"

His glanced around the room, his gaze settling on the clothes scattered around. "Can't find what to wear?"

"Uh…I was just going through my closet."

"I can tell."

I sighed, rubbing my forehead wearily. "What do you want? As you can see, I'm kind of busy."

A brow arched. "I know. What an exciting life you live, going through your closet on a Friday night and all."

"Yeah, not all of us have the exciting life you do, Seth."

His lips split into a satisfied grin. "I knew it."

"Knew what?"

"You're mad at me."

I stared at him and lifted my arms, waiting for a better explanation.

"You're upset over this afternoon." He pushed aside several potential choices for tomorrow as he leaned back. "Were you jealous, Alex?"

My jaw almost hit the floor. It took me a moment to respond. "I'm confused as to why you think I'd be jealous."

Seth gave me a knowing look. "Perhaps you're jealous of Elena?"

"What?" I picked up a cute sweater I'd bought before we'd gone into lockdown. "Me, jealous of Elena and her Tinker Bell hair—don't think so."

He stretched over and tugged the sweater out of my hand. "Oh. Catty, aren't you?"

"Not at all. If I'd only known about your Peter Pan complex, I would've introduced you two sooner." I reached for it, but he rolled it up into a ball and tossed the sweater across the room. "Ugh! You are so annoying!"

"Just admit you're jealous. That's the first step, and the second step is doing something about it."

I glared at Seth. "I couldn't care less what—or who—you do in your spare time." Then something struck me. "Wait. You know what? This is messed up."

"Do tell."

"Everyone jumps me about how every single thing I do is a reflection upon you, but you're *doing* people in the garden! How is that okay?"

"You make it sound so distasteful." He smiled much like a cat. "Don't knock it until you try it. Oh. Wait. You haven't tried *anything*, have you, my little virgin Apollyon?"

I swung out at him as hard as I possibly could. Anticipating my reaction, Seth caught my hand. His eyes flashed dangerously as he tugged me forward. My own momentum caused me to stumble. I ended up falling forward.

Seth twisted onto his side and circled his arms around me. "Always hitting," he said cheerfully. "I think we should work on your manners."

The side of my face was smashed into a pile of shirts that had gone into the "maybe" pile. "Oh, come on. You're wrinkling all my clothes, you jerk-face."

"Your clothes are fine. I want to chat."

I tried to elbow him, but his arms clamped down. "Really, you want to talk right now?"

He wriggled closer. "Yes."

"And we have to be lying like this for what reason?"

"I don't know. It makes me feel good. I know it makes you feel good. And I don't mean the way I'm sure you think I mean." He paused, and I could feel his chest rise and fall against my back. "Our bodies relax around each other."

I scrunched up my face, not buying his reason at all. "Can we talk about something else?"

"Sure." I could hear the smile in his voice. "Let's talk about the fact you haven't been sleeping."

"What?" I managed to squirm enough to get one of my arms loose and flip onto my back. "I…I sleep fine."

"You sleep for a few hours. Then you wake up. Nightmares, huh?"

I stared at him. "Why do you always have to be so creepy?"

His lips twitched. A flicker of amusement, then his expression returned to the customary smug mask. "Whenever you're upset, you suck me right in. Wakes me up every single night, and now I'm not getting any sleep unless I stay with you."

I scooted over, but his arm caught me. "Well, sorry. I don't know how to stop it. If I did, I wouldn't interrupt your precious beauty sleep."

Seth chuckled low in his throat. "I guess it's because

the connection between us is getting stronger since we're spending more time together. With you being an emotional wreck these days, I spend half my time wanting a Valium."

The urge to kick him off the bed hit me hard. "I'm not an emotional wreck."

He didn't bother responding to that. "Doesn't it strike you as odd that the only times you sleep all the way through the night are when I stay with you?"

It did strike me as odd—and annoying. "So?"

Seth leaned over. "Your body relaxes around me and you can rest. All thanks to your favorite thing—the connection we share. If you get too upset, you just need me. It will work both ways once you Awaken."

I jerked as far away from him as I could, which wasn't very far at all. "Oh, for the love of the gods, you have *got* to be kidding me."

"Alex, I'm as serious as a daimon attack."

And I knew he was being serious. I just didn't want to admit it. The idea of him sensing my emotions made me what to hurl. If I wanted to cry, he'd know. The same went for needing to punch someone or if I was in the middle of a hot make-out session, he'd know and—

My eyes widened in realization and a strange feeling unfurled in the pit of my stomach. "Wait. Wait one second, Seth. If you can feel my emotions or whatever when I'm freaking out, then I should be able to feel yours."

"Right, but not—"

I moved so fast I broke free of his embrace and shot to my feet. He stayed on the bed, half-reclined. "Oh. My. Gods. I *have* felt you."

Seth's brows rose slowly. "No way, I know how to shield

myself so that I'm not broadcasting my every wish and desire like you."

"Oh. No. You are so wrong." My cheeks burned just thinking about it. The nights I'd felt all hot and tingling—and right before I'd walked in on him and Elena—it wasn't just my overactive hormones. "Oh, this sucks."

Interest sparked in his eyes and he sat up, resting his hands on his knees. "What are you talking about?"

"I've felt you a couple of times—at night. Like when you're doing…your thing."

He gave a short laugh, and then it seemed to hit him. His mouth dropped open. "Doing my *thing*?"

"Yeah," I said, growing frustrated. Did I have to spell it out for him? "Just forget I said anything."

"No. Not likely. What did you feel?"

This really did suck. It was also mortifying and beyond freaky. "You know, fooling around. I've felt…you then."

Seth stared at me so long I thought he lost the ability to speak. Then, when I was just starting to get worried, he threw his head back and laughed. Really loudly—and he didn't stop.

I gaped at him. "It's not funny!"

"Oh, it's probably the funniest damn thing I've heard in a long time." He stopped long enough to draw in a deep breath. "This is great."

"It's not great. What kind of connection is this? A one-way hotline to Pervyville?" I took a step forward, on a roll now. "It's disgusting. Freaky—stop laughing, Seth!"

"I can't," he gasped. "Of all the times for you to connect with me, and it had to be then? Damn Alex, I didn't know you're such a peeping—"

I hit him hard on the arm. It wasn't a playful tap. It would bruise. I wanted to do more—like kick him in the head.

"Jeez. And you're so violent. Do you know how hot—"

I swung at him again, but this time Seth was prepared. He dodged my fist and caught me around the waist. Before I could even break his hold, he flipped me onto my back. This time he hovered above me, arms planted on either side of my head. A wild and beautiful smile chipped away at some of the coldness in his face. Not all of it, but some. "This is priceless."

"You are so annoying."

That seemed to amuse him even more. He laughed so hard I felt it rumble through me. Not in the way Aiden's laugh usually did. Aiden's laugh made me feel all light and fluttery. Seth's made me feel weird—flushed and weird. And a part of me wanted to hear it again—or feel it again. Which was wrong—all kinds of wrong—because I didn't think of him that way. At least my brain didn't. My body, on the other hand, had a totally different viewpoint on these things.

My body must be a sad, lonely thing.

"You know," Seth said with a grin, "you probably shouldn't have told me this. I'm going to take advantage—Alex, what are you *doing*?"

I didn't get what he was talking about at first. Then my eyes dropped and I saw my hand pressed against his stomach, my fingers curling around his shirt. How in the world did my hand get there, because surely—*surely*, I didn't do that?

Seth appeared on the verge of saying something ignorant, like always, but he became very, very still. I don't even think he breathed. Slowly, I lifted my gaze and found what I expected. Swirling glyphs spread across the left side of his face. The intricate markings etched down his neck and disappeared under the hem of his black shirt, reappearing on his left arm and coming to stop over his hand.

And Seth, well, Seth was no longer laughing. Those odd

eyes caught mine and flared a heated tawny. He lowered his head; the loose strands of hair brushed my cheeks. I jerked my hand back, but he was still close, way too close. So, I did the only thing suitable in situations like these. I shoved my knee into his stomach—hard.

He rolled off me, onto his back, laughing once more. "Crap, Alex, why did you go and do that? Actually kind of hurt, you know?"

I scrambled off the bed, putting as much distance between us as possible. "I hate you."

"No, you don't." He tipped his head back, his gaze finding me. "I guess this was bound to happen. The more time we spend together, the more we'll start connecting. It is the way of the Apollyons."

"Just go somewhere, why don't you?"

Seth flipped onto his stomach and rested his chin in his hands. "I'd love to. I could go for seconds with Elena right about now."

I let out a groan and rolled my eyes. "No one is stopping you."

"True, but then you'd fall asleep after pacing or reading some incredibly boring textbook and have another nightmare about Mommy, and then I'll be awake all night long." He arched one blond brow at me. "I do need my beauty sleep."

I glared at him. "You're not staying here again, Seth. You have a bed—several, actually. Go."

"You didn't care the last couple of times."

"Because...well, those times were different," I sputtered, running a hand over my hair. Turning around, I started grabbing clothes off the floor. "I didn't know you were staying. You just helped yourself."

Seth sighed. "You don't like any of this, do you?"

"No. I don't like not being in control. You know that." I grabbed another shirt. I also didn't like the fact that my body reacted to him even though my heart didn't. "It's about having control over—" I dropped the clothes and straightened. "Remember what you said to me during the summer, the night you were in my room?"

He looked confused. "Not really."

I took a deep breath, searching for patience I didn't have. "You promised me that you would leave if things got out of hand. Do you remember that?"

Seth's lips pursed. "Yes, I do."

"Do you still mean it?" I stepped forward, standing in front of him. "Do you?"

"Yes. I still mean that. I made you a promise. I keep my promises." Seth reached out and grabbed my hand. With a gentle tug, he pulled me down beside him. Whatever relief I felt was short-lived. "Do you know what I find interesting?"

I watched him wearily. "What?"

He turned his head toward me. "You've never shown any interest in getting to know me better. You don't know a thing about me."

"That's not true."

His lips curled into a sardonic grin as he let go of my hand. "You don't even know my last name, Alex."

Well, he didn't need a last name. Seth was just *Seth* to me.

"You don't even know where I'm from, if my mom was a pure or my dad," he continued. "I bet you don't even know how old I am."

I started to protest, but Seth was right. We'd known each other for about four months, give or take a week or two, and I didn't know anything about him. In all of the time we'd spent together, in training or when he showed up in my room, we never talked about anything personal. And I never cared to ask. I frowned. Was I truly that self-centered?

Seth sighed. "You have this one-track mind thing going on."

I looked at him sharply. "You can't read my thoughts, right?"

"No. But that doesn't mean some of what you think isn't as obvious as reading your thoughts." He turned to me. "Everything you think, everything you feel is always right on your face. You're terrible at hiding your emotions. Or what you're thinking. Like I said: one track mind. Whether it's getting back into the Covenant, fighting your Mom or fighting your fate or that…*special* person in your life."

"I don't have a special person in my life!" I felt my cheeks start to burn again. "I have no idea where you come up with these things."

One side of his lips curled upward as he met my stare. "I'm nineteen."

I blinked. "Huh?"

Seth's eyes rolled. "I'm nineteen years old."

"Oh. *Oh.* Only nineteen—wow. I thought you were older than that."

"Well, I don't know if I should be offended or flattered."

"Flattered, I guess."

A few moments passed before he spoke again. "I'm from a tiny island near Greece."

"Ah, that explains your voice—the accent. What island?"

Seth shrugged and didn't respond. Sharing and caring time seemed to be over. Why hadn't I ever thought to try to get to know Seth any better? After all, I was going to be stuck with him for a while.

I bit my lip. "Do you think I'm self-centered?"

A surprised laugh escaped him. "Why are you asking?"

"Because you said I have a one-track mind. And everything you listed had to do with me, like I don't think about anything or anyone other than me."

Seth let out a ragged sound and came to his feet. "Do you want me to be honest?"

"Yes."

Several seconds passed as he stared down at me. "Sometimes, Alex, you have more pure in you than you do half."

My mouth dropped open, shocked that he would say that about *me*.

He ran a hand over his head. "Look, I've got some stuff I need to do. I'll see you later."

I didn't say anything as he climbed back out the window. I sat on the bed; the fun of finding something pretty to wear tomorrow had lost most of its appeal.

You have more pure in you than you do half.

It was a terrible thing to say to a half-blood, like I was a disgrace who couldn't be trusted—a sellout, phony, and fake. That if it came down to choosing between a half and a pure, I'd choose the pure.

Something must've crawled into my hair and made a nest during the night, because nothing I did—no curling iron, no flat iron—seemed to make it do what I wanted. One side wanted to settle in waves, while the other looked like limp spaghetti.

Maybe I was being overly critical of myself, but I truly believed that the dark smudges under my eyes made me look like I'd entered the first stage of a zombie infection. I'd put on too much lip gloss, and then rubbed my lips raw getting it off and reapplying. The mountain of concealer I'd put on the disgustingly huge zit on my temple made it seem even bigger.

I finally tore myself away from the bathroom mirror when I made a grab for the lip gloss again. I settled on a pair of skinny jeans—not the designer kind Olivia wore, more like the Target brand. I chose a deep red sweater that dipped a little low in the neckline area, and these killer heels I'd stolen from Olivia's closet.

But before I ran out to meet up with Aiden, I was struck dumb by the cold possibility that this could be some sort of field experience. It definitely wasn't a date, so what the hell was I doing?

And if I would be training, then I'd look stupid in heels and my boobs would fall out. While that sounded pretty entertaining for the masses, somehow I doubted Aiden would appreciate it. So, with no time to spare, I slipped on a pair of checkered flats and a more sensible top—a black, cable-knit sweater.

I made it to the training room late, of course.

"Sorry," I said as soon as I spotted Aiden's dark head by the wall of things that stabbed, out of breath from running across the quad. "I…I had to do something…"

Every single excuse I'd practiced on the way over leaked out of my mouth when I got a really good look at Aiden. He wore a pair of worn jeans, the kind that looked so comfy you wanted to climb into them. He also had on this gray sweater, and gods, *oh, gods*, did it look good on him—like it'd been crafted to just fit the strong expanse of his shoulders, his chest, his arms, and so on.

I needed to get a grip.

I knew this, but I rarely saw Aiden in anything other than

workout clothes or a uniform. He'd been wearing something different the night I'd sent those spirit boats into the sea, but I hadn't been paying attention. My mind had been occupied.

It was sure as hell occupied in a totally different way now. "It's no problem," he said. "You ready?"

I nodded in a jerky motion. Suddenly, I felt as adept as a bull in a china shop. "So, what are we doing?" I asked, humiliated to hear my voice crack halfway through the question.

Either Aiden hadn't noticed or he pretended otherwise. "It's a surprise, Alex." He started walking. "Are you coming, or what?"

I hurried behind him; my suspicions were confirmed when he led me out the back way. "We're leaving the Covenant, aren't we?"

He pushed the hair off his forehead, clearly trying not to smile. Aiden reached into his pocket and dangled keys in front of my face. "Yes."

"Field experience! I knew it." Silently, I thanked every god there was that I'd developed enough common sense to change shoes.

Aiden looked at me strangely. "I guess you can consider this field experience."

I followed him to one of the black Hummers, feeling rather smug for figuring out his surprise. "So, what are we going to do? Trail some daimons back to their hive?" I climbed into the passenger side and waited until he got behind the wheel. "I have to admit, I'm not really good at the whole tailing thing. I'm more—"

"I know." He turned on the engine and eased the dinosaur-sized vehicle out of the fleet of cars. "You're more of an action girl instead of a sit-and-be-quiet girl."

I smiled in spite of the fact I doubted that was a compliment.

"Well, my quiet-as-a-ninja skill could definitely use some practice."

Another quick smile appeared. "But the other skills? Not so much. I really don't think you need much more of the additional practices. You'd definitely have more time to yourself—time to rest."

Now I really beamed…for about three seconds. No extra practices also meant no Aiden. My smiled faded as I stared at him. Suddenly, a giant clock appeared between us, quickly counting down to when there would be no more Aiden in my life.

A rather depressing thought.

"What?"

I faced straight ahead, swallowing down the lump in my throat. "Nothing."

When we were stopped by the first set of Guards, I expected them to demand what Aiden was doing with a half-blood. But they let us pass without so much as asking for an explanation. The same thing happened at the second bridge, the one leading off of Deity Island and onto Bald Head Island.

"I can't believe they just let you take me off the Island without a single question," I said as Aiden navigated the streets of the mortal island. "What happened to the rules?"

"I'm a pure-blood."

"And I'm a half-blood—a half-blood who's not supposed to step one foot off the Covenant, let alone Deity Island. Not that I'm complaining or anything. I'm just a little surprised."

"They assume we're doing field training."

I glanced at him. "Aren't we?"

Smiling, Aiden leaned over and turned on the radio. He settled on a rock station, and I stared at him. The early smugness started to flake away. He didn't give any further explanation when I asked again, and finally, I decided to stop asking and we started talking about normal things. My classes, an episode of some old TV show called *Sanford and Son*—never heard of it—but some guy apparently pretended to have a heart attack every episode, and Aiden found it hilarious. I wasn't convinced of the hilarity.

We talked about how I'd almost beaten him in practice yesterday and how he was considering buying a motorcycle. Which I was strongly behind, because really, what could make Aiden hotter than he already was?

A motorcycle.

"What kind of bike are you looking at?"

He got this dreamy, far-off look on his face—almost like the kind of look I got when I saw chocolate…or him. "A Hayabusa." He passed a string of cars without missing a beat.

"A crotch rocket?" I reached for the radio, flipping the stations. Aiden had the same thought in mind, because his fingers brushed over mine. I jerked back, flushed.

Aiden cleared his throat. "It's more than a crotch rocket. It's, well, let me put it this way. If it came down between me saving a Hayabusa or the Minister, it would be a difficult decision."

I busted out laughing. "Oh, my gods, I can't believe you admitted that."

He started to smile. "Well."

"It's awesome," I gasped.

The smile grew, exposing the deep dimples in his cheeks. For a moment, I stopped laughing, stopped smiling—hell, I stopped breathing. Then I saw the sign along the interstate for Asheboro, and I really did stop breathing for a couple of seconds.

We were thirty miles from Asheboro. "I know Asheboro," I whispered.

"I know."

I could feel his eyes on me, but I couldn't pull my gaze from the window. The trees lining the road formed an array of browns, reds, and yellows. The last time I'd been near Asheboro it had been summer, and the rolling hills had been green.

Seven years ago.

Tearing myself away from the window, I stared at Aiden. He focused on the road. "I know where we're going."

"You do?"

Excitement bubbled through me. So did disbelief. I bounced forward in my seat. "This isn't field experience."

Aiden's lips twitched. "Consider it an experience in taking a day off—a day being normal."

"You're taking me to the zoo!" I screeched, bouncing again.

The seatbelt choked me back.

He couldn't keep the smile back. It covered his face, filled his eyes. "Yes, we're going to the zoo."

"But—but why?" I swiveled around in the seat, pressing my face against the window. The smile on *my* face was absurdly huge. "I don't deserve this."

Several moments passed. "Yes, you do. I think you deserve a break from everything. You've been working so hard, pulling double—triple—duty. And you really don't complain—"

I shot around, facing him. "I complain. I complain all the time."

Shaking his head, Aiden laughed. "I stand corrected."

Shock kept pushing more stupid statements out of my mouth. "But I've been in so much trouble. I threw an apple at Lea's face. I fought Guards. I cheated on my trig exam."

Aiden looked at me, frowning. "You cheated on your math exam?"

"Uh, forget that. Anyway, wow, I'm just surprised."

"Alex, you need to get away from it all every once in a while. You need a break—a real one. Just like I do," he paused, concentrating on the road. "I figured we could get away together."

I think my heart may have exploded, right then and there. The importance of what he was doing—the implication of it—didn't pass by me unnoticed. This was huge—huge to us. Pures and halfs didn't get away together for a relaxing day. We may coexist together, but we lived in different worlds. We had to. It was the rules, the way of our society. Aiden risked a lot by doing this. If by random chance we were spotted, he'd be in a lot of trouble. Maybe not as much as me, but hell, I didn't care. I cared that he wanted to do this *for me.*

That had to mean something—something really wonderful.

Aiden glanced at me, his eyes shining—with what? I didn't know, but in that instant, I could only think about what I felt for Aiden. Until then, I hadn't been willing to admit that it was anything more than a crush or lust, because really, who didn't lust after him? But what expanded in my chest, swelled my heart until I felt sure it would burst from my chest, wasn't a silly crush. It wasn't just a physical attraction.

It was love.

I loved Aiden—I loved a pure-blood.

CHAPTER EIGHT

***I stared at him, caught up in my realization.* I loved Aiden.** I loved him, really loved him.

Oh, gods, I was so totally screwed.

Aiden's cheeks flushed under his natural tan. "I mean, all of us need a day away from our world. We need moments to take a breather and let it all go." He glanced at me, a wry grin replacing the one I'd throw pretty much anyone in front of a daimon to see. "Anyway, today is just a normal day. We aren't going to talk about training or the daimon attack."

"Okay." I took a deep, calming breath and ordered myself to pull it together. Then I saw the sign for the zoo, and I faced the window again.

"We can't stay for long—only a couple of hours—or the Guards will suspect something. We also need to keep this a secret. We can't let anyone find out."

I nodded. "Of course. I won't say a single word. I just can't believe you remembered this." I also couldn't believe I was in love with a pure-blood.

He merged toward the exit ramp, expression suddenly serious. "I remember everything you say."

I peeled myself away from the window. It was all too easy for me to recall the day I'd told him about my love of animals and zoos. It'd been in the small med office when he'd rubbed that gunk over my bruises. But I didn't expect him to actually remember that day, or any day for that matter. And if he really did remember everything I said, then…

My fingers curled in my lap. I was a big douchebag. I said mean things. A lot. I took a deep breath. "I'm sorry."

Aiden looked at me sharply. "For what?"

I stared down at my hands, guilt gnawing at my insides. How could I have not apologized sooner? "I'm sorry about saying you're like other pure-bloods. I shouldn't have said that. Because you're not—you're nothing like them."

"Alex, don't apologize. You were angry. So was I. It's in the past. Over."

The guilt eased off a little bit as I gazed out the window, but an old yearning pulled at my heart. Mom had loved it here. The sights brought forth a mix of sorrow and happiness. I sighed, wanting to be happy but feeling bad about it.

Trees dotted the winding road leading up to the entrance. Mom had known the names of the trees. I didn't. Off in the distance, I could make out the top of the main building.

"It bothered you though," I said as Aiden coasted the Hummer to a stop. The lot was full for this time of year, but the weather was still warm enough. The zoo would be packed. I undid the seatbelt and twisted toward him. "I know it did."

Aiden cut the engine and pulled the keys out. Lifting his gaze from his hands, those eyes pierced me. "Yeah, it did."

I bit my lip, wanting to apologize again.

"I don't want you to see me like that." A short, harsh laugh escaped him, and he focused on the steering wheel as he held the keys in a tight grip. "The funny thing is that what you said shouldn't have bothered me. I'm a pure. So, I should be like all the others. I really shouldn't care if you saw me like that. I should care how the other pure-bloods view me."

"I'm sure they think you're wonderful, too." I flushed after saying that, because it sounded stupid. "Anyway, screw what anyone thinks. Who cares, right?"

Grinning, he glanced over at me, and I felt my heart skip a beat. "Yeah, who cares? We're at the zoo. Screw them."

"Yeah, screw them."

Aiden tilted his head back, letting out a relieved sigh. "Does this place have funnel cakes?"

"I think so. I want a hamburger and a hot dog." I paused. "And ice cream in one of those waffle cones. And—and I want to see the big kitties."

"So demanding," he murmured, grinning. "Well, we better get started, then."

First-stop honors went to a portly, balding man who had more grease on his shirt than he did in his pan. He made funnel cakes. Aiden liked him a lot. While I waited in line beside him, I spotted a vendor flipping burgers. I darted in that direction, after which Aiden commented that he'd never seen me run that fast before.

When we finally made it past the food and into the actual park, I was overflowing with giddiness. The slight breeze carried the oddly alluring scent of animals and people. Sunlight broke through the park's dense canopy of trees, casting slivers of warmth as we made our way deeper into the attractions.

I probably looked goofy with the extra bounce in my step and the way I kept grinning at everyone we passed. I was just so happy to be out in the world again—and with Aiden of all people. And watching how the mortals responded to him was highly entertaining. It could have been his alarming height or godly looks that stopped women *and* men in their tracks. Or it could be the way he laughed, tipping his head back and letting loose that rich, deep sound. Either way, I got a thrill seeing him do his best to ignore them.

"You don't mingle with the natives a lot, do you?" I asked as we stepped into the Forest Glade and watched a gorilla sitting on a rock, picking fleas. Stimulating stuff here.

Aiden chuckled. "Is it that obvious?"

"A little bit."

He shifted closer, lowering his voice. "Mortals scare me."

"What?" I laughed in disbelief.

Smiling at my expression, he nudged me with his hip. "They do. They're unpredictable creatures. You don't know if they're going to hug you or stab you. They're ruled by emotions."

"And we're not?"

Aiden appeared to consider that. "No. They—I mean, we're taught to control our emotions. To not let them be what guides our decisions. Everything in our world—both of our worlds—is about logic and continuing our races. You know that."

I glanced over at him, noticing the way the proud lines of his face were relaxed. In these moments, he did look younger and carefree. I liked him this way—with his eyes full of light and laughter, his expressive mouth curved upward. Seeing him now, it was almost hard to believe he was far more deadly than any animal in the park.

"But you seem to be at ease around all of them." He nodded at a group at the other end of the pen. A mother and a father stood with two young kids. The little girl handed her brother a half-eaten ice cream cone. "You have more experience dealing with them than I do."

I nodded, turning back to the cage. Another hairy beast made its way to the one on the rock. Maybe something interesting would happen. "I blended in, but I never fit in. They can sense something off about us. That's why no one will get too close to us."

"I cannot possibly imagine you blending in."

"Why? I think I did a damn good job of going unnoticed for three years."

"I just can't. No one is like you, Alex."

I grinned. "I'll take that as a compliment."

"It is." He nudged me again, and my grin grew into another ludicrous smile—the kind Caleb gave Olivia when they weren't tearing each other's heads off. "You're incredibly intelligent, Alex. Funny and…"

"Pretty?" I supplied, only half-serious.

"No, not pretty."

"Cute?"

"No."

I frowned. "Well, then."

Aiden's laugh sent shivers through me. "I was going to say 'stunning.' You're stunningly beautiful."

I sucked in air sharply, cheeks flushing. I tilted my head back and our gazes locked. Somehow, I hadn't known we stood so close. And Aiden was close. Close enough that I could feel his warm breath against my cheek, speeding up my pulse.

"Oh," I whispered. Not the most eloquent of responses, but it was the best I had.

"Anyway, what is it with you and zoos?" Aiden stretched his arms above his head.

A shaky sigh escaped me, my gaze drifting over the family, settling on the little girl. She had the cutest pigtails ever, and she was smiling at me. I smiled back.

"I like animals," I said finally.

Aiden glanced down at me, eyes full of…well, full of yearning. "That's why you practically choked yourself in the car?"

I cringed. "You noticed that, huh? My mom loved animals, too. She said once that we were a lot like the ones in the cages. Well-fed and taken care of, but caged nonetheless. I never agreed with that."

"You don't?"

"Nope. Here the animals are safe. Out in the wild, they'd be killing one another or being poached. I know they've lost their freedom, but sometimes things have to be sacrificed."

"That's a strange perspective for you to have."

"You mean it's a strange perspective for a *half-blood* to have. I know. But we all have to sacrifice something to gain something else."

Aiden reached out and grabbed my hand, pulling me out of the path of a woman on a mission of pushing a stroller. I'd been so caught up in watching him I hadn't seen the woman—or heard her screaming baby. I glanced down between us. His hand was still wrapped around mine. The simple, unexpected gesture sent a crazy amount of heat through me.

Aiden guided me through the ever-increasing throng of visitors. He parted the crowd like the Red Sea. People just got out of the way for him as we left the Kitera Forest and entered the Forest Edge.

"Can I ask you a question?" I asked.

"Sure."

"If you weren't a pure, what would you be doing right now? Like, what would you want to do with your life?"

Aiden glanced down at our hands and then his gaze flicked to mine. "Right this instant? I'd be doing a hell of a lot more than what I'm allowed to do."

Heat infused my entire body, swirling my thoughts into a heady mess. I almost convinced myself I totally made up that response and that lack of sleep had finally driven me crazy. Auditory hallucinations were a bitch.

His fingers tightened around mine. "But I'm sure you were wondering more than that. What would I be doing if I was just a mortal? I don't really know. It's not something I've thought about."

I had to mentally kick myself to find my voice again. "You've never thought about it? For real?"

Aiden sidestepped a couple taking pictures, shrugging. "I never had to. When I was younger, I knew I would follow in my parents' footsteps. The Covenant groomed me to do so. I took all the right classes: politics, customs, and negotiations. Basically, the most boring classes you could imagine. Then after the daimon attack, everything changed. I went from wanting to follow my parents to wanting to do something to ensure another family didn't go through what Deacon had to."

"And what you had to," I added quietly.

He nodded. "I don't know what I would do if I woke up tomorrow and had a choice. Well, I can think of a few things, but a career?"

"You do have a choice. Pures have all the choices."

He glanced down at me, frowning. "No, we don't. That's the biggest misconception between our races. Halfs think we have all the choices, but we are just as limited as your kind is, but in different ways."

I really didn't believe that, but I didn't want to argue and ruin the moment. "So...you really don't know what you'd do?" He shook his head, so I offered my suggestion. "A police officer."

Aiden's brows rose up. "You think I'd be a police officer?"

I nodded. "You want to help people. I don't think you're corruptible. Being a Sentinel and a police officer are kind of the same thing. Fighting the bad guys, keeping the peace, and all that good stuff."

"I guess you're right." He smiled then. A mortal girl about my age stumbled as she passed us on the trail. Aiden seemed oblivious to her. "Hey, I'd get a badge. I don't have one of those now."

"I want a badge, too."

Aiden cocked his head to the side, laughing. "Of course, you'd want a badge. Hey—look what I see." He pointed around the bend.

"Cats!"

His hand curved around mine more fully, almost like some unconscious part of him was responding to me.

Several yards of empty space and fencing separated the lion pen from the visitors. At first, I didn't see him, and then he prowled up from behind a rock, tossing his mane from side to side. His orange-yellow coat reminded me of Seth's eyes. Actually, the way the lion stopped in front of the gathering crowd and yawned—flashing a row of razor-sharp teeth—also reminded me of Seth.

"He's beautiful," I whispered, wishing I could somehow get closer. I wasn't one of those lunatics who climbed into a lion's den, but I also wanted to touch one—a people-raised, totally tame one not likely to rip off my hand.

"He looks bored out of his mind."

We stayed there a while, watching the feline stroll around the grassy knoll before climbing atop a large rock and lying down, tail swishing back and forth. Finally, some of the female lions decided to show up. I told Aiden they were the real deal, recalling something I heard on *Animal Planet* about the females actually being more badass than the males. Within a couple of minutes, two of them joined the male on the rock.

I groaned as they lay down beside the male. "Ah, come on. Knock him off the rock."

Aiden chuckled. "I think he's got two girlfriends."

"Dog," I muttered.

We left the African lion habitat, wandering into the North American section. This part seemed virtually empty compared to the other. I guess the mortals were bored by the bears and other familiar critters. Aiden seemed fascinated with them, and I spotted a bobcat. I let go of Aiden's hand and went up to the outer fence. A slight breeze rolled in. We were much closer than any of the other exhibits. Close enough that the bobcat appeared to catch our scent.

She'd been stalking some unseen prey up until that moment. She stopped, though, inclining her head in our direction. A second or two passed, and I swear our eyes met. Long, thin whiskers twitched as she smelled the air.

"Do you think she knows what we are?" I asked.

Aiden propped himself up against the guardrail. "I don't know."

We weren't allowed to have pets on the Island. Some pures could use compulsion to control their actions, which meant so could a daimon. It was rare and took an extremely powerful pure to do so, but it was a risk no one ever took. I'd always wanted a pet growing up—a cat.

"Mom believed they did," I said. "She said animals could sense we were different from the mortals, especially cats."

He was silent for a few moments, and I was sure his brain

was turning. Putting together some sort of puzzle. "Did your mother like cats?"

I shrugged. "I think it had something to do with my father. Whenever we'd come here, we'd always end up here right before we left." I glanced over my shoulders, nodding at the weathered benches. "We'd sit over there and watch the cats."

Aiden shifted closer but didn't speak.

I turned back to the pen, smiling. "It was the only time Mom would talk about my father. She never really said much about him. Except that he had the warmest brown eyes. I wonder if he had something to do with animals, you know?" I curled my fingers around the wire mesh of the fence. "Anyway, the last time we were here was when she told me he was dead and told me his name. She named me after him, did you know that? I guess that's why Lucian hated it when Mom called me Alex. After a while, she started calling me Lexie instead. My father's name was Alexander."

Several moments passed where neither of us said anything.

Aiden spoke first. "That's why you like the zoo so much."

"Yeah, you got me." I laughed self-consciously.

"It's nothing to be ashamed of, to want to be close to something that reminds you of your loved ones."

"I didn't even know him, Aiden."

"Still," he said. "He was your father."

I watched the bobcat for a few more seconds. She prowled the edge of her pen, no longer curious about our presence. Her powerful muscles flexed under the spotted coat. There was something amazingly graceful about the way she moved.

"I hate to do this, but we need to head back, Alex."

"I know."

We started walking back through the park. Aiden was a lot

quieter this time around—lost in thought. It didn't take nearly long enough to reach the front gates. Thick trees gave the zoo an almost surreal quality as we strolled back to the Hummer.

Before I knew it, I was sitting in the passenger seat, and Aiden had just put the keys into the ignition, but he hadn't turned the car on. He twisted in his seat, facing me, and the expression on his face caused my heart to falter in my chest.

"I know how brave you are, Alex. But you don't always have to be. It's okay every once in a while to let someone else be brave for you. There's no loss of dignity in that. Not for you. You've already proven that you have more dignity than any pure-blood can muster."

I kind of wondered where that had come from. "You must be high off sugar or something."

Aiden laughed. "You just don't see what we see, Alex. Even the times you're being utterly ridiculous about something or when you're just standing around, doing nothing, it's hard to not notice. As a pure-blood, it's the last thing I should notice." His eyes flickered shut, long lashes fanning his cheeks before his eyes reopened to reveal intense silver. "I don't think you have a clue."

The world outside the car ceased to exist. "What don't I have a clue about?"

"Ever since I met you, I've wanted to break every rule." Aiden turned away, the muscles in his neck tensing. He sighed. "You'll become the center of someone's world one day. And he'll be the luckiest son of a bitch on this earth."

His words created a mad rush of strong emotions. I was hot—so incredibly hot. I really did think the world ended right then. Aiden glanced over at me, his lips parting. The intensity in his gaze, the hunger in his eyes left me dizzy. His chest rose sharply.

"Thank you." My voice sounded thick. "Thanks for doing all of this for me."

"You don't need to thank me."

"When am I ever supposed to thank you?"

"When I do something that is truly worth thanking me for."

Those words struck a deep chord in me, and I don't know who moved first. Who leaned over the center console—who was the first to cross the invisible line between us? Who broke the rules first?

Aiden? Me? All I did know was that we both moved. Aiden's hands were around my face, and mine fell to his chest, to where his heart beat just as fast as mine. In an instant, our lips met.

This kiss was nothing like the first one we'd shared. Its rawness left us both breathless. There wasn't a moment of hesitation or indecision. There was just want and need and a thousand other powerful, crazy things. His lips scorched mine, his hands dropping to my shoulders, sliding down my arms. My skin burned under my sweater, but oh, this was so much more than just a kiss. It was the way he touched the deepest parts of me. My heart and soul would never be the same. It was nearly overwhelming to realize something as powerful as that, and it brought a sense of urgency that pushed me into the unknown.

Aiden pulled back, resting his forehead against mine. He was breathing heavily. What came out of my mouth next was not something I'd planned. The three words just bubbled up my throat, barely even audible.

"I love you."

Aiden jerked back, eyes wide. "No. Alex. Don't say that. You can't...*you can't* love me."

I started to reach for him, but then pulled my hands back to my chest. "But I do."

His face was tight, as if he was experiencing some terrible pain. Then he closed his eyes and leaned in, pressing his lips against my forehead. He lingered there a few moments before pulling back. His chest rose and fell as I stared at him.

Aiden scrubbed the palms of his hands over his eyes and let out another ragged breath. "Alex..."

"Oh, gods," I whispered, facing the front of the car. "I never should have said that."

"It's okay." Aiden cleared his throat. "It's all right."

Okay? It didn't seem okay. And *okay* and *all right* weren't what I wanted to hear. I wanted him to say he loved me, too. Wasn't that what was said after a declaration of love? Not *okay*. I knew he cared about me and he wanted me in the physical sense, but he wasn't saying those three little words.

And those three words were so important. They changed everything.

I willed my heart to stop the aching it was doing. Maybe he was just shocked into silence. Maybe he didn't know how to say it. Maybe he felt it but thought he couldn't say it.

Maybe I should've kept my big mouth shut.

I fell asleep during the ride back, which served several purposes. I got one hell of a power nap, and I avoided what probably would've been the most awkward car ride of my life. I pretended to still be asleep while we crossed the bridges.

Aiden kept it cool, like he hadn't kissed me and I hadn't professed my undying love for him. He even hopped out and opened the door for me before I'd gotten the seatbelt off. He was such a gentleman—or he was just that eager to get rid of me.

After a half-assed goodbye, I headed back to my dorm. I

cut through the courtyard, hoping to avoid the more heavily populated areas of the quad. I kept replaying everything Aiden had done and said.

Those kisses still sent shock waves through my belly. The way he'd kissed me had to mean something, because people didn't *kiss* like that. He had wanted to get away with me, and planned the whole zoo thing. He had to feel something—something powerful for me.

But he hadn't said he loved me. He hadn't really said anything after I'd said it.

I kicked a loose pebble, sending it flying into a nearby lilac bush. There was a good chance I was overreacting. I tended to do that a lot. Tallying up everything Aiden had done in the last few hours, his actions proved he cared and totally outweighed the fact that he hadn't said he loved me.

I moved on to the rose bush and broke off one bloom by the stem. Somehow the roses were thornless here. I had no clue how they grew that way, but hell, I didn't have a clue about anything. I closed my eyes, inhaling its clean scent. Mom had loved hibiscuses, but I loved roses. They reminded me of spring and all things new.

"Child, that rose ain't going to ease your heart. Move on? Let go? Stay on the path your heart has chosen? Ain't nothing easy when the heart has laid claim."

My eyes popped open. "You have got to be kidding me."

A dry, rasping cackle that sounded like it was one step away from death confirmed who stood behind me. I wheeled around. Standing in the middle of the walkway, bent over a gnarly cane, was Grandma Piperi—oracle extraordinaire. Her hair looked like it had the last time I'd seen her, like its enormous weight would topple her over.

She smiled, stretching her way-too-thin skin. It looked a

bit grotesque and crazy. "Do you know why a heart lays claim? Survival. That heart lays its claim to ensure survival of its kind."

Once again, I was standing in front of the oracle and she was spouting the craziest crap I'd ever heard. "Why didn't you tell me my mother was a daimon?" I clenched the fragile stem of the rose in my fist. "Why didn't you tell me the truth?"

Piperi cocked her head to the side. "Child, I only speak in truths. I gave you the truths."

"You told me nothing!"

"No. No." She shook her head. "I told you everything."

I gaped at her. "You told me a bunch of crazy crap that didn't make any sense! You could have just said, 'Hey, you're the second coming of the Apollyon. Your mother is a daimon and she's going to try to turn you. And oh, by the way, she's going to try to kill your friend!'"

"Isn't that what I told you, child?"

"No!" I screamed, throwing the rose to the ground. "That's not what you told me."

Piperi clucked her tongue. "Then you didn't listen with those ears. People never do. Only ever hear what they want to hear."

"Oh. My. Gods. Woman, you're the reason my mom left here in the first place. She was turned into a damn daimon. If you hadn't told her about me—"

"Your momma wanted to save you—save you from your fate. If she hadn't, you'd be nothing but a memory and a fear long forgotten. Just like all you who mix breeds. What they want you two for, what they planned." She shook her head again and when she looked at me, sorrow etched across her face. "They fear you, fear what comes from you. I told you, child. I told you that your path was filled with dark things that must be done."

I blinked. "Uh…okay."

Piperi hobbled forward, stopping in front of me. She only came up to my shoulders, but I remembered how strong she was. I took a step back. She cackled, but this time the laugh ended in a wretched wheezing sound. Gods, I hoped she didn't keel over right here. She lifted her head, giving me a big, toothless smile. "Do you want to know about love, child?"

"Oh, come on." I groaned. "You make me want to hurt myself."

"But love, child, love is the root of all that is good, and the root of all things that are evil. Love is the root of the Apollyon."

I shifted to my other foot. "Yeah, I think this is around the time I say goodbye. I hope you have a nice trip back to whatever hut you crawled out of."

Her free hand snaked out, covering mine. Her skin felt papery thin, dry, and so gross. I tried to jerk my hand back, but she held on. Her strength was unnatural. Her eyes fastened on me. "Listen to me, child. Fate is afoot. Things cannot be undone. Fate has looked into the past and into the future. History is on repeat, but this is the time to press 'stop.' To change everything."

"I don't know what you're talking about. I'm sorry. You're not making—"

"Listen to me!"

"I'm listening! But could you speak a coherent sentence for once?"

Piperi's fingers slid over mine, and then she let go, wheezing. "I ain't nothing no more. You must see what I've shown you. Hear what I have spoken. Nothing is what it seems. Evil hides in the shadows, plotting its plans while you fear the daimons."

I scowled. "I don't fear daimons."

Her black eyes pierced me. "You should fear those who follow the old ways. Those who do not seek change and cannot allow things to continue as they are. And what a path, what a path the Powers have chosen. The end, the end is near. He," she japed at the sky, "will see to it."

I rolled my eyes. "Oh, for the love of the gods, this makes no sense."

She shook her head again. "You don't get it. Listen to me." Piperi poked me in the chest with one bony finger. "You must make a choice between what is fated and what is unknown."

"Ow!" I stepped back. She jabbed me again. "Hey! Knock it off!"

"Take the risk or suffer the consequences!" She stopped suddenly, her eyes growing wide as her gaze darted around the otherwise silent garden. "You must not accept gifts from those who seek to destroy you."

"Or candy," I muttered.

Piperi ignored my sarcasm. "You must stay away from the one who brings nothing but heartache and death. Do you hear me? He brings nothing but death. Always has. Know the difference between need and love, fate and future. If you don't, everything your momma sacrificed will be for naught."

That caught my attention—perhaps because it was the clearest thing she'd ever said to me. "Who is *he*?"

"He is not what he seems. He has them all fooled—has *him* fooled. Poor child doesn't see it. He doesn't see it, and it has sealed his fate." She sighed. "That one plays both sides. You don't know—you wouldn't know. He—" She jerked backward, the cane slipping from her grasp. The thing hit the marble sidewalk, shattering into a dozen thick pieces.

I grabbed for her, expecting her to fall flat on her face. So, I was surprised when she didn't fall over…and utterly shocked when she folded in on herself, flaking away until nothing remained but a pile of dust.

CHAPTER NINE

"The oracle has passed." Lucian whirled around, addressing each of us. He looked ridiculous as the white robes twirled around his slender body. "Another has come into power."

I had a headache.

Apparently, the oracle dying wasn't a big deal. Grandma Piperi was ancient. I just happened to stumble upon her on her dying day or something—lucky me.

Woo.

Leon raised one massive arm and pinched the bridge of his nose. This impromptu gathering of the minds had not been going well. I'd come straight to Marcus after Grandma Piperi *poofed*, and from there, Marcus had called everyone to his office. Unfortunately, Lucian had brought a very contrary Seth. And worse yet, Aiden had *already* been in Marcus's office for whatever reason.

Marcus took a deep breath. "Alex, what happened exactly?"

"I've already told you everything. I ran into her in the

garden. She was talking one second, and the next, she just sort of poofed—"

"She poofed?" Seth laughed. He lounged in the corner, arms folded across his chest and that damn smile plastered across his face. "Seriously?"

"Yes, she poofed. Like she was there one second, and the next she was a pile of dust."

"We just don't *poof*, Alex. That doesn't happen."

"Well, it did. She poked me in my chest with her bony finger and said some crazy stuff. Then she poofed!"

Seth's brows flew up and he laughed again. "What have you been doing today? Smoking something?"

Addressing Marcus, I threw up my hands. I had no idea why Seth was being such a jerk to me. He'd started in the moment he'd stepped into this room, and now I wanted to kill him. "Does he have to be here?"

"He is where I need him to be," Lucian answered instead. "And I need him here."

"Can he shut up, at least?" I missed the more charming version of Seth. This version sucked. "There's no need for him to comment on everything that comes out of my mouth!"

"I'm commenting on everything, because it sounds like you've smoked some crack," Seth countered. "Where have you been all day?"

"Seth," Aiden warned. It was the first he'd spoken since the meeting began. He had changed into his Sentinel garb, and I was having one hell of a time not looking at him. "Can you be quiet for five seconds?"

Seth's yellow eyes snapped fire. "Does he have to be here? He's *just* a Sentinel."

"He was here before any of you were," Marcus responded

with a tight smile. "And Seth, please try to contain the comments."

Seth slouched against the wall, raising his hands in surrender. "Sure. Sure. Go on, *Alexandria.* Tell us how she *poofed* again."

"I've already explained it," I said. "It's pretty easy to understand. Even for you. Or did you wake up on the wrong side of stupid this morning?"

"Alex." Aiden sighed. "Just talk to Marcus."

I stiffened. "Sorry. If he says one more word to me, I'm going to take that dagger off the wall and shove it through his eye."

Seth straightened, every cell in his body rising to the occasion. "Well, that's brave for a little Apollyon-in-training. If you want to try it, I'm game."

"Seth!" Marcus yelled, slamming his palms down on the table. Several ledgers and books shuddered.

My hold on my temper stretched to the breaking point. "You know what? I bet your mother wanted to drown you after you were born."

"Alexandria!" Marcus started around the desk. "Would you two—"

"And there's a reason why mothers turn daimon and try to kill their daughters."

I shot across the room, aiming right for the dagger behind Marcus's desk. Aiden cut me off. I considered barreling through him, but he looked like he would employ every measure possible to keep me from killing Seth.

"Don't," Aiden ordered in a low voice. "Just ignore him."

"Don't tell me what to do," I seethed. "I want the dagger so I can cut him."

"Cut me?" Seth laughed. "What are you—a street thug Apollyon about to shank me?"

Lucian sat down in one of the leather seats. "So much passion between you two," he murmured. "Can be expected, I imagine. You two are one and the same. Let them go. We can continue this conversation without any more interruptions, entertaining as they are."

I stopped. So did Seth. Actually, everyone in the room who didn't appear to be on drugs stopped and stared at Lucian. "What?"

Smiling like he knew some huge secret, he flicked his wrist elegantly. "Let them go. Alexandria has already told us what has happened. The oracle has passed and another has come into power. Let them work through their lovers' quarrel in private."

Even Seth's eyes widened at that. I had a more vocal response, one that caused Marcus to look like he wanted to shove me in a dark room and never let me out again.

"We have not yet determined what the oracle told Alexandria," Leon interjected from the corner.

I'd almost forgotten he was there.

"She's already told us what she could. What was it, dear?" Lucian simpered in my direction. My hand itched to smack him upside his head. "She said that fate can be changed? Is that not great news? The oracle was referencing our two Apollyons."

I scowled at him. "Why does everything in your head automatically go back to the Apollyon?"

Lucian waved his hand again. "Let them go."

Aiden's hard stare bounced between us. "I don't think that's a good idea at the moment. One of them may seriously injure the other."

I wondered if he really thought that or if the idea of us "handling" our "lovers' quarrel" in private bothered him.

Marcus sighed. "I think it is an excellent idea, as we aren't getting anywhere with both of them in the roo—"

"I thought Lucian needed Seth here," Aiden interrupted, eyes like chips of ice.

Something ridiculously stupid sprung alive in my chest. Aiden was jealous?

"You know what?" I shot Aiden a defiant look. "Let's go. Come on, Seth. Let's go continue our *lovers' quarrel*."

Pushing off the wall, Seth arched a brow. "Yes, *my love*, that sounds absolutely fantastic. Don't forget to grab a dagger so you can poke my eyeball out. Oh, that's right." He fixed a sympathetic look on his face. "Only a trained Sentinel can carry a dagger."

I sneered and then whirled around and stalked out of the room. My head pounded like crazy, and even though I'd agreed to leave, I didn't want to continue talking with Seth. We actually made it to the first floor before all hell broke loose.

Seth grabbed my arm and dragged me into one of the empty offices, slamming the door shut behind him. "You little brat, what the hell have you been doing all day?"

I pulled my arm free and moved to the other side of the office. Seth stalked after me, and I thought of the lion from earlier. All he needed was a swishing tail. I laughed, not able to help it. The image of Seth with a tail was kind of funny.

Seth stopped short, scowling. "What's so funny?"

I sobered up. "Jeez, nothing."

"What have you been doing all day, Alex?"

"What have you been doing?" I sidestepped him, putting some space between us. "And why don't you seem to care that the oracle died?"

"Alex, she was ancient. At least a couple of hundred years old. It was bound to happen. Lucian is right. Another has come into power and blah, blah."

"She died right in front of me! It was a bit unsettling."

Seth cocked his head to the side. "Do you want me to host a pity party for you? I'm sure I can wrangle up a few people who can help you commiserate."

"Gods, would it kill you to be a tiny bit nice? Oh. Wait. It would. So, excuse me, I have stuff I need to do." I started for the door, but Seth caught my arm. His skin felt like fire. "Seth, come on. I have a freaking headache and—"

His eyes searched my face. "What have you been doing today?"

I started to get uncomfortable. "I've been training. What the hell else could I be doing?"

"Training?" Seth laughed harshly. "Where?"

"Here," I said immediately.

Seth's eyes narrowed. "You little liar, I checked the training room for you. You weren't there." Oh, crap.

A smug smile inched across his face. "So I checked all the other training facilities, and the gym, and the beach, and finally your room. You weren't in any of them."

Oh, double crap.

"Don't lie to me." He backed me up until I hit the edge of the desk. "Your cheeks are bloodred, your pulse has skyrocketed, and you're a terrible liar."

I clenched the edge of the desk. "I have no idea what you're talking about."

Seth bent down so we were eye level. "You don't?"

"No."

"I'm going to ask you one more time, Alex. What were you doing today?"

"Or what?" I demanded. "What are you going to do? And why do you even care?"

"Because the emotions you were feeling today were outrageous."

"Gods, this day will never end," I muttered. Throbbing temples aside, I was pretty sure I had enough aggression in me to take out Seth at this point. "Who cares?"

"I care because you were supposed to be training with Aiden today, and there is no reason you'd be feeling those kind…" Seth's eyes widened. I swear, I'd never seen his pupils so dilated, and for someone who kept dragging me back to him, he sure let go of me awfully fast. "Oh. No, no, no."

Apprehension blossomed, quickly turning my insides cold. "What?"

"You wouldn't." He ran his hand down the side of his face. "Wait. What am I saying? You *would* do something so incredibly stupid."

I leaned against the desk. "Uh…gee, thanks."

Seth shot forward, grasping my shoulders. I flinched, unable to suppress the natural response. "Please tell me I'm wrong. Tell me that you are not messing around with a gods-damned pure-blood. Damn it, Alex. *Him?* My gods, it explains so much."

Anything and everything in my head sort of emptied out. My brain had this wonderful ability of doing so when I really needed to think fast.

He laughed harshly. "Now I know why he hates me, at least. Why he's always on you. I just figured it was in the figurative sense and not literal. What the hell are you thinking? What is he thinking? You're going to throw everything away! Your future—my future—and for what? To get more pure in you?"

Shrugging his hands off my shoulders for the umpteenth time, I snapped out of it. "You don't have a clue what you're talking about! I'm not messing around with Aiden."

"Don't you dare lie to me about something like this!" He shoved his finger in my face. I had the urge to break it. "You can't do this, Alex. I will not allow this to continue." Seth started for the door.

"No. No! Seth, stop! Please." This time I grabbed him, pulling him back from the door. "Please listen to me. It's not what you think!"

His eyes practically glowed he was so angry. "It's not about what I *think*. It's what I *felt* today!"

"Please. Just listen to me for a second." My fingers dug into his arms. "You can't say anything. They'll—"

"I'm not going to say anything to the Council, you little idiot. They would send you into servitude in a heartbeat." He pushed me off, swearing under his breath. "You know, I actually thought he might be different from the other pures, but he sure as hell doesn't act any different. Screw a half; enslave a half. That's what they say, Alex."

"What are you doing? You can't—"

"I'm going to have a little talk with Aiden."

I flew in front of him, plastering myself to the door. "You are so not going to talk to him! You're going to try to fight him."

"Quite possibly. Now get out of my way."

"No."

"Get out of the way, Alex," he snarled. Edges of the Apollyon marks started creasing his otherwise flawless skin.

"Okay," I breathed, pressing against the door. "I'll tell you the truth. All right—just please don't do anything...stupid."

"I don't think you should be lecturing me on not doing anything stupid."

I counted to ten. Now was not the time for me to lose my patience. "Nothing happened between Aiden and me. Okay? I do care about him, all right? I know it's wrong." I closed my eyes, wishing the words didn't hurt as much as they did. "I know it's stupid, but nothing is going on between us."

"What I felt from you today wasn't *nothing*, Alex. You're still lying to me."

"Okay. We kissed, but—stop!" I pushed Seth back as he tried to pry me away from the door. "Listen to me. We did kiss, but it's nothing. It was stupid—a mistake. It's nothing to get all bent out of shape over. Okay?"

He stared down at me, lips drawn tightly. Then he closed his eyes. Terse silence stretched out between us. "You…you love him, don't you?"

I stared at him, my heart thumping loudly. "No. No, of course I don't."

Seth nodded, running a hand over his face again. "Alex… Alex, you're insane."

Obviously, he didn't believe me. I needed to make Seth understand that nothing needed to be done about this. There was no way he could go after Aiden. Gods only knew what Seth would do, or what Aiden would do. I could see them now, brawling on the beach. One thing would lead to another, and the Council would find out. The pures would dope me up to suppress the Apollyon in me, and I'd be scrubbing floors for the rest of my life. Aiden would never forgive himself. I couldn't let that happen. And then there was the idiot standing in front of me. If Seth attacked a pure, that would be it. The Council would move against Seth, and even though I wanted to strangle him, I didn't want…well, I didn't want anything to happen to him.

Call it self-preservation.

"Nothing's going on," I said. "Just promise me you won't do anything."

Seth stared at me so long the silence that enveloped us started to get to me. Then the tattoo started to sink back into his skin and he looked surprisingly calm.

"You're not going to do anything, right?"

"No." Seth reached for me and pried my hand off the doorknob. "I'm not going to say anything."

Relief, sweet and beautiful, flooded through me. I let out my breath. "Thank you."

"You're not going to ask why?"

"No." I shook my head. "I'm not going to look a gift horse in the mouth."

"Do you even know what that means?"

"Not really," I said. "But it sounds about right."

Seth arched a brow, and then tugged me away from the door. "Come on, let's go."

I spared our joined hands a brief glance. "Where are we going?"

"We're going to do some training, since you apparently didn't do any of *that* today."

"She poofed into nothing? Damn, that's crazy."

I stared at Caleb, wishing he would poof into nothing. "What is everyone's big deal with the terminology? I swear to the gods, if one more person questions that, I'm going to lose it."

"Poof," Olivia whispered, grinning.

I shot her a death glare. "Ha. Funny."

"Sorry." She slid her arm around Caleb. Apparently, they'd made up at some point, again. That made me happy. I liked the way they looked at one another when they weren't fighting. "I bet that was freaky, though."

"Freaky doesn't even begin to describe it."

"She was old as dirt," Caleb said, "but still. The old crone was kind of entertaining."

"Entertaining" wasn't a word I'd use to describe Grandma Piperi. I leaned back in the moon chair and let my eyes drift shut as Olivia and Caleb started talking about the party they'd snuck off to last night. I felt a spark of jealousy and bitterness. I hadn't been invited. Maybe Caleb thought I had more pure than half in me, too. *Blech.*

I refocused my thoughts on Piperi. Even a few days later, I was still too wrapped up in the almost exposure of Aiden's and my nonexistent relationship to give much thought to what she'd said before she'd died.

The conversation I'd had with her didn't make much sense—no big surprise there. The only important thing I'd picked out was about the guy who wasn't who he appeared, that he had everyone fooled. If only she hadn't poofed into nothing a second later, maybe she would've said his name, which would've helped tremendously. I didn't share this part of the conversation with anyone. It seemed that whoever it was wasn't a friend of mine. Then again, I couldn't be sure. After that thought, I must've drifted off to sleep, because I jerked upright at the sound of my name.

"Miss Andros."

I peeled my eyes open and found Leon standing in the doorway to the rec room. "Yeah?"

"You're not supposed to be in here."

Odd. When had Leon been assigned to be my babysitter? I only saw him around campus when he had terrible and urgent news to deliver. "Come on," I whined.

Caleb peered over the back of the couch. "She's not bothering anyone."

Leon didn't even glance at Caleb. "Up."

Caleb twisted toward me. "One of these days, you'll be able to stay out and play. Then everything will be right in our world."

Pulling myself out of the chair, I rolled my eyes at Caleb. "Leon, can I have a playdate with my friends?" That got a giggle out of Olivia.

Leon's expression remained bland. "Perhaps you'd be allowed to have playdates if you stayed out of trouble for a whole week."

"I guess that's a no." Caleb grinned up at me. "So, now you know what to do. Stay out of trouble for a whole week, Alex. *A whole week.*"

I smacked the back of Caleb's head as I made my way past the couch. He swung out at me, but Olivia got in the way.

"Bye!" Olivia chirped, already snuggling down beside Caleb.

Giving them a little wave, I followed Leon out of the lounge. I felt a little uncomfortable walking beside him. The man was almost seven feet tall and looked like he belonged on the pro-wrestling circuit. Not to mention, I didn't know how much Leon knew. I remembered how unsurprised he'd looked when Marcus had mentioned me being the Apollyon.

I searched for something to say but came up empty until my gaze fell on a statue of Apollo. "Hey, you kind of look like Apollo. Has anyone told you that? All you need is blond hair and raging hormones. Maybe he's your great-great-great-great grandfather or something."

Leon's gaze flicked over the marble statue. "No. No one has ever said that."

"Huh. Funny. 'Cause you do. I wonder if you have anything else in common with Apollo."

"Like what?"

"You know. Didn't Apollo have a thing for pretty boys?"

I snorted. "Wait, didn't Apollo have a thing for just about everything that walked? Until they got turned into trees or flowers, that is."

"*What?*" Leon came to a complete standstill, gaping down at me. "There are some myths that are true, but most are exaggerated."

I raised my brows quizzically. "Didn't realize you were an Apollo fanboy. Sorry."

"I am *not* a fanboy."

"Okay. Never mind, then."

"Do you know what I find interesting, Alexandria?" he asked after a few moments.

"No. Not really." I shivered in the rapidly cooling air.

"How you happened across the oracle right before she died."

I glanced around the nearly empty campus, spotting only Sentinels and Guards. I hadn't realized it had gotten so late. "I have no clue. I guess I have that kind of luck."

"Twice?"

I looked at him sharply. And there was another thing I hadn't known he was aware of. "I guess so."

Leon nodded, eyes scanning the pathway to the girls' dorm. "Did you know the oracle only seeks out those she wants? That many, many pure-bloods go their entire lives without even seeing the oracle once?"

"No." I wrapped my arms around myself, wondering where summer had gone. It was almost the end of October, but usually it didn't get *this* chilly.

"Then she must have had something very important to tell

you," Leon said. "I'd assume something more than just being able to change history."

My steps slowed as the oracle's words rushed through me. *He is not what he seems. He has them all fooled. He plays both sides.* I glanced up at Leon, wary of where this conversation was going. There was nothing I knew about him except his wonderful ability to pop up when I didn't want him around—and his fanboy love for Apollo. "That's all she said."

Leon stopped in front of the steps to the dorm, folding those massive arms over his chest. "Seems rather vague."

"Piperi is—was—always vague. Nothing she ever said has made much sense to me."

He cocked his head to the side and a small smile appeared on his face. I think that was the first time I'd ever seen him smile. "That's the thing about oracles. They do tell you the truth, you just have to really hear it."

My brows inched up my forehead. "Well, I guess I didn't hear it."

Leon's gaze fell on me, heavy and hard. "I'm sure in good time you will." Then he twisted around and disappeared down the pathway.

I stood there a few more moments, staring after him. That had been the longest conversation I'd ever held with the guy and it ranked right up there with the conversations I'd held with the oracle. It made no sense.

It also filled me with a decent amount of unease. There was always something about Leon that didn't seem right—a sort of otherworldly trait I couldn't quite put my finger on. But could he be the mystery man the oracle had been talking about?

I shivered and headed up the stairs. I hoped not. There was no way any of us could take that massive hunk of flesh out in a battle.

CHAPTER TEN

I was a nervous mess of funk.

It had to do with the little box in my gym bag. Nice of Deacon to gift wrap the guitar pick, but now I felt stupid for giving it to Aiden, especially after everything that had gone down between us at the zoo.

But I had it and I needed to give it to him. If I didn't, there was a chance Deacon could make some passing comment to him about it and then I'd be even more mortified. And it was just a guitar pick. It wasn't like it screamed *I love you* or anything. Not that it mattered since I'd already blabbed that.

I went through practice with Aiden sort of numb and hyperaware. I kept missing chances to say "happy birthday" or give him the damn box. I just couldn't bring myself to do it.

What if he laughed at me? What if he hated it? What if he looked at me and said, "What the hell is this for?" and threw the box on the mat? Then stomped on it?

I couldn't stop thinking about how many ways this could go wrong. Did his reaction really matter? Since our trip to the zoo and my embarrassing declaration of love, he'd kept things perfectly cool between us. There were only a few times I'd caught him watching me with this hawkish level of interest. I always wondered what went through his mind then.

Aiden sent me another weird look, and I felt my face turn red. I'd never hated myself more.

Unsurprisingly, I ran out of time. While my heart pounded in my chest, I bent down and dug the little white box out of my bag. Deacon had even put a black bow on it. I hadn't known he was such a crafty guy.

"Alex, what are you doing?"

Clutching the box in my hand, I stood. "So, are you doing anything…um, special tonight?"

He dropped the mat he'd been rolling up. "Not really. Why?"

I shifted uncomfortably, keeping the box hidden between my hands. "It's your birthday. Shouldn't you be celebrating?"

Surprise flashed across his face. "How did you know it was today? Wait." He gave a rueful smile. "Deacon told you."

"Well, your birthday is the day before Halloween. Kind of hard to forget."

Aiden brushed off his hands. "We're going to have dinner with some people, but it's nothing big."

I smiled, inching closer. "Well, that's doing something."

"Yeah, it's something."

Just give him the stupid box, Alex. "Well…you don't have to work tonight, right?" *Give him the damn box, Alex, and stop talking. Like forever.*

Aiden flashed a quick grin as his gaze drifted toward me. "No. I got the night off. Alex, I need to tell—"

I stepped forward, shoving my hands at his chest. Well, I

shoved the box at his chest. "Happy birthday!" I looked and felt like the worst kind of dweeb.

His startled gaze dropped, and then flicked back to mine. He took the little box. "What's this?"

"It's just a small gift. Nothing big," I said in a rush. "It's for your birthday. Well, obviously."

"Alex, you really didn't have to do this." He turned it over, running those graceful fingers over it. "You didn't have to get me anything."

"I know." I pushed a few strands of hair off my face. "But I wanted to."

"Can I shake it?"

"Yeah, it won't break."

Grinning, he shook the box. The pick rattled off the sides. He glanced at me once more and then untied the black bow. Holding my breath, I watched him carefully open up the lid and peer inside. Aiden's eyes narrowed and his lips parted. I didn't know what that expression meant. Slowly, he reached inside and plucked the pick out of the box.

Aiden held the gemstone pick between two long fingers, his expression incredulous. "It's black."

I glanced around the room. "Yeppers. It's black. Um, I saw that you had every color except black." He continued to stare at the pick with this dumbfounded look on his face. I folded my arms, suddenly wanting to cry. "If you don't like it, I'm sure you can return it. I got it at this store online. They do—"

"No." Aiden looked up and his eyes met mine. They were a dark gray, bordering on silver. "No. I don't want to return it." He flipped the pick over, smoothing his thumb over it. "It's perfect."

I flushed, still wanting to cry, but in a totally good way now. "You really think so?"

Aiden took a step forward, his eyes like liquid pools. They took up his face, my entire world. I didn't know what was going to happen next. All I knew was that I was hooked on him, irrevocably so.

"There you are." Marcus stood at the entrance to the training room. "I've been searching everywhere for you."

There was a sort of grace to how fast Aiden slid the gift into the pocket of his pants and twisted around. I couldn't see his face, but I knew it was perfectly devoid of any emotion. Only his eyes would give anything away, and Marcus would never be able to tell anything from their colors like I could.

However, I was also sure my face would give everything away. I hurried over to my gym bag and became fascinated with its strap.

"What can I do for you?" Aiden asked casually.

"Practice is running a little late for you two, isn't it?"

"We were just finishing up."

"Alexandria, what are you doing over there?" asked Marcus.

Cursing under my breath, I shouldered the bag and faced my uncle. He wore a three-piece suit. No one on campus dressed as well as he did. "Nothing, just getting my stuff."

He raised a brow elegantly. "Were you running late from class and held up Aiden? You should have more respect for his time."

I shot my uncle a dirty look but managed to keep my mouth shut.

"It's fine," Aiden responded quickly. "She wasn't that late."

Marcus nodded. "Well, I'm glad I found you two together."

My brows inched up my forehead, and the urge to laugh hit me hard. Aiden looked less amused. "I've given what you asked some thought and I do agree with what you've suggested, Aiden."

The lines around Aiden's mouth tightened. "I haven't had a chance to discuss this with Alex."

Marcus frowned. "Don't concern yourself with that. You've done wonderfully with her. I must admit, I didn't think she'd be able to get caught up, but you were right. We can end the additional practices."

I stepped forward, but I didn't feel the floor under my sneakers. "End my practices?"

"Aiden feels that you no longer require these additional practices, and I happen to agree with him. You'll still be working with Seth, but this will afford you some time off and also allow Aiden to return to his Sentinel duties fully."

I stared at Marcus, hearing him but not really understanding. Then I turned toward Aiden. His face was utterly blank. I knew I should feel good about this, because it was a huge step in the right direction and Marcus had sort of complimented me, but I couldn't get past the hole opening up in my chest. Aiden and I would never see each other if we didn't train together.

"Aiden, you've spoken about this with Seth?" Marcus asked. "Discussed areas for potential improvement?"

"Yes, Seth is aware of things she can use additional work on." Aiden's voice sounded surprisingly empty and flat.

He'd already talked this over with Seth? I inhaled, but the air fled my lungs. My chest seized in a weird way and my brain tried to tell me that I'd known this day was coming. I just hadn't thought it was coming this soon.

"Well, I don't want to keep you. Enjoy your dinner tonight." Marcus paused, seeming to remember I still stood there. He turned back, smiling politely. "Good night, Alexandria."

He didn't wait for my response, which was good, because I had none. The moment I felt sure he was out of hearing range, I whirled on Aiden. "We aren't going to train anymore?"

Aiden still wouldn't look at me. "I was going to talk to you about it. I think—"

"You were going to talk to me about it? Why didn't you talk to me before you went to Marcus?"

"I went to Marcus last week, Alex."

"After…we got back from the zoo? That's why you were in Marcus's office when I got there?"

Aiden still hadn't looked at me, not once since Marcus had dropped the bomb. "Yes."

"I…I don't understand." I gripped the bag's shoulder strap like it was some kind of lifeline. "Why don't you want to train me anymore?"

"Alex, you don't need me to train you anymore." His body started to tense, to lock up. "You're caught up with the other students."

"If that's true, then why did you have to discuss areas of improvement with Seth? Why can't you just work on them?"

Aiden turned away fully, running a hand through his hair. "You need time off. You're exhausted all the time, and something has to give. You need to work with Seth a lot more than you need to work with me. He can work with you on the elements, prepare you for when you Awaken."

There was a strange buzzing in my ears, adding a surreal element to all of this. "That's not true. I don't need Seth."

Aiden's head snapped in my direction. "You don't need me, Alex."

It took me several tries to get the next words out over the huge lump in my throat. "I do. I won't see you anymore if we don't train."

"You'll see me at Council, Alex, and you'll see me around here. Don't be ridiculous."

I ignored the coldness in his voice. "But after that? I won't see you." My voice cracked. The sound was equally humiliating and sad.

"Well, I think that is…for the best."

It felt like he'd reached inside me and crushed my lungs into lifeless lumps. I drew in a deep breath and tried to calm down, but there was this raw hurt in my chest. It ached, throbbed in a way that felt so real. I could only stare at him. "Is…this because of what I told you at the zoo? Why you don't want to train me anymore?"

Aiden's lean body tensed again, and a muscle in his jaw jumped. "Yes, that has something to do with it."

A crack in my heart started. "Because…because I said I loved you?"

He made a deep sound in his throat. "And because I don't…" He paused, looking away. "I don't feel the same way about you. *I can't.* Okay? I can't let myself love you. If I did, I would take everything from you—*everything*. I can't do that to you. I won't do that to you."

"What? That doesn't—"

"It does matter, Alex."

I reached for his arm, but Aiden moved away from me. Stung, I wrapped my arms around my waist. "You're saying this—"

"Just stop." He ran a hand through his hair again.

The rawness of his words sliced through. "Then why did you tell me that stuff at the zoo? Why did you say you cared for me? That you wanted to break the rules for me? Why would you tell me any of that?"

Aiden turned gunmetal gray eyes on me, and I took a step

back. He looked nothing like the Aiden I knew. Aiden never looked at me so coolly, so detached. "I do care for you, Alex. I…don't want to see anything bad happen to you or to see you hurt."

"No." I shook my head. "It's more than that. You…you held my hand." The last bit came out a pitiful whisper.

He flinched. "That was…a silly mistake."

Now I flinched, and I couldn't stop the words from coming out. "No. You want me—"

"Of course, I *want* you," he said harshly. "I'm a man, and you're a beautiful girl. I can't help that. Wanting you in the physical sense has nothing to do with how I feel about you."

My mouth opened, but nothing came out. I blinked back hot tears.

Aiden's hands curled into fists. "You're a half-blood, Alex. You can't love me, and pure-bloods don't love halfs."

I staggered back, feeling as if he'd smacked me in the face. I was so embarrassed—humiliated. How had I mistaken how he felt about me so badly? I had *everything* wrong. Letting out a ragged breath, I turned away just as Aiden closed his eyes and lowered his head. Sick to my stomach, I walked back to the dorm in a daze. The worst part was the shame. I couldn't see past it, couldn't think around it. There was a burning in my eyes I desperately fought. Crying wasn't going to solve anything, but damn, that's all I wanted to do. My chest felt like it'd been ripped open, my heart torn apart.

When I opened the door to my room, I wasn't entirely surprised to find Seth sitting on the couch.

Not surprised, but angry. I needed to consider barring the window in the bedroom.

He didn't look up. "Hey."

"Please leave." I dropped my bag on the floor.

Seth's lips pursed as he stared straight ahead. "I can't do that."

Fierce emotion swept through me, agonizing and raw. I couldn't—wouldn't lose it in front of Seth. "I'm not screwing with you. Get out."

He looked up, eyes the color of a warm sunset. "I'm sorry…but I can't leave."

I stepped forward, clenching my hands. "I don't care what I'm throwing off right now and how it's affecting you. Please leave."

Seth slowly came to his feet. "I'm not leaving. You could use the company."

I might've hated the connection that fed my emotions to Seth more than I hated anything in my life. "Don't push me, Seth. Leave, or I'll make you leave."

He was in my face in a heartbeat. Grasping my arms, he lowered his head so that we were eye level. "Look, I can leave this room. Fine. You're still going to feel like hell, which means I'm still going to feel like hell."

I inhaled roughly, unable to escape him. Tears burned my eyes and clogged the back of my throat, threatening to choke me.

He took a deep breath. "I knew you'd lied to me when you said you didn't love him. Why are you doing this to yourself? Aiden is like every other pure, Alex. Sure, he may have moments where it doesn't seem that way, but he *is* a pure-blood."

I turned my head away from Seth, biting down on my lip until I tasted blood. An hour ago, I would never have agreed with that, but Aiden had just said the very same thing.

"And what if he did love you, Alex? What then? Would you be satisfied with being something he had to *hide*? Satisfied with lying to everyone and watching him pretend like he didn't care for you? Then, when you did get caught, would you be satisfied giving your life up for him?"

All very good questions, ones that I'd asked myself time and time again.

"You're too important, too special to throw everything away for a pure." Seth sighed, dropping his hands to mine. "Now, I brought us a movie to watch, the one that has sparkly vampires in it. I thought you'd be down for that."

I studied him silently. He looked like he always did—a living, breathing statue. Perfection without any humanity, and yet he was here. "I can't figure you out."

He didn't answer as he deposited me on the couch. He put the movie in and then returned to the couch, remote in hand. "I'm moody," he said finally, fiddling with the controls.

I stared at him and a strangled sort of laugh escaped me. Moody? More like borderline personality disorder or something. But who was I to judge? I had to be crazy, didn't I? I'd fallen for a pure-blood. That topped the list of symptoms for possible mental illness.

Thinking about Aiden brought a sharp pang to my chest. And here I'd thought my heart was somewhere in the gym, bleeding on the floor. I tried focusing on the movie, but my brain wasn't into it. Immediately, I rewound my conversation with Aiden—all my conversations with him, actually. How could he go from the guy I could spill my guts to—could trust and rely on, who could make my heart swell with the tiniest of smiles or compliments—to someone just as cold as I believed Seth to be?

Yet, Seth sat next to me.

Maybe he wasn't as cold as he appeared, and Aiden wasn't as perfect as I'd believed him to be.

Maybe my judgment was just as screwed up as my taste in guys.

Seth sighed again, this time much louder than before. Quietly and rather casually, he reached over and tugged me across the couch. I ended up with the side of my face smooshed against his thigh and his heavy arm draped over my side. "What are you—?"

"Shh," he murmured. "I'm watching the movie."

I tried to sit up but didn't make it very far. His arm weighed a ton. Several unsuccessful attempts later, I gave up. "So…uh, you're a Team Edward kind of guy?"

He snorted. "No. I'm Team James or Team Tyler's Van, but apparently neither of them won by the look of it. She's still alive."

"Yeah, seems that way."

Seth didn't say anything after that, and eventually, my body relaxed and some of the hurt eased off. It was still there but muted by Seth's nearly overwhelming presence—the Apollyon connection doing its thing. Perhaps that was why Seth had made himself available. Or maybe he'd just wanted to witness my stupidity.

CHAPTER ELEVEN

The next week of my life sucked.

It sucked in a way I wasn't entirely accustomed to. I'd had crushes before, even a few cases of mad lusting. But I'd never loved someone other than my Mom and Caleb, and that was a different kind of love.

This kind of love hurt like hell.

Not seeing Aiden after class felt wrong, like something was missing or I'd forgotten something terribly important. On the days I should've practiced with him, I tried spending time with Caleb and Olivia, but I usually retreated to my room and sulked until Seth showed up.

I missed Aiden, missed him so badly. Hurt consumed every waking second, turning me into one of those girls whose world ended when a guy rejected them. I lived in this miserable state of existence—miserable and obnoxious.

"Are you going to get out of this bed at some point today?" Caleb sat with his back against the headboard of my bed. A Classics textbook lay unopened in his lap. He'd gotten the humiliating story out of me a few days ago. Just like Seth, he hadn't been surprised by the outcome. However, he'd been pretty pissed that I'd been entertaining the idea of a relationship with Aiden this entire time. And I just felt more stupid.

He nudged me with his knee when I didn't respond. "Alex, it's almost seven and you haven't budged."

"I don't have anything to do."

"Have you even showered?" Caleb asked.

I rolled over, shoving my face into my pillow. "No."

"That's kind of gross."

"Uh-huh," was my muffled response. A second later his cell made this annoyingly shrill sound from the table next to my bed, and the textbook smacked the floor. I didn't move. Caleb climbed over me, shoving his elbow into my back.

"Gods!" I yelled into the pillow. "Ouch."

"Shush," Caleb said, still sprawled over me, his bony elbows digging into my back as he flipped his phone around and checked his messages.

I could turn my head to the side, but that was all. "Jeez, you weigh a ton. Who is it? Olivia?"

Caleb rolled onto his side, cracking my lower back in the process. Kind of felt good. "Yeah, she wants to know what the smell is radiating up to her room."

"Shut up."

"Seriously, she wants to know if you've showered." He shifted onto his stomach. "You know, you're kind of comfortable. You're getting some extra cushion, Alex."

"Am not, you douche."

He laughed. "Olivia wants to know if we want to watch a movie."

"I don't know."

"How can you not know? It's a simple question."

I managed to wiggle out a shrug.

Caleb snorted. "Look, I just sat here for the entire day while you stared up at the ceiling like an idiot. You're getting out of this bed, taking a shower, and we're going to have a movie night in *your* dorm. Then Olivia and I are going to leave and engage in wild animal sex. End of discussion."

"Ew, that's an image I never wanted imbedded in my memory. Thanks."

"Whatever. So, what do you think? You game?"

I rolled my eyes. "It's almost curfew time."

"What the hell?" He dropped the phone next to my head, and the next thing I knew, he was sitting on my back with both his hands planted on my shoulders. "We haven't done anything fun in ages, Alex. And you need fun—stat."

"You're killing me," I squeaked. "Can't…breathe."

"It's not like I'm suggesting we have a threesome. I'm suggesting we sneak over to the cafeteria, grab some drinks and food, and then watch a movie."

I lifted my head off the pillow. "Darn, you're not suggesting a threesome? My life is over."

"Pay attention to the finer points of what I'm saying. With all the rules-crap and you being grounded, we haven't been able to do anything," Caleb continued while his phone buzzed in my ear. "Besides, you're leaving next week for the Council and you're going to be gone for weeks. We need to do this. You need to do this. It's our last hoorah."

"Can you check your phone? It's annoying."

He leaned forward, pressing his head against the back of mine. "Where's the old Alex I know and love, my wild and crazy friend?"

I grunted, unable to push him off. "Caleb, come on."

"Come on, come out and play. What else are you going to do?"

What else? Lie around my room all night and feel sorry for myself, and…and that was just pathetic. Hanging out with Caleb and Olivia would do me some good. For a little while I could forget about Aiden, about how badly I loved him and how he'd rejected me.

I squeezed my eyes shut. "Do you think…Was I being stupid for, you know, the stuff with Aiden?"

Caleb leaned over, pressing his cheek against mine. "Yes, it was and is stupid. But I still love you."

I laughed. "Okay. Fine."

He rolled off me, resting on his side. "You serious?"

"Yeah." I sat up. "But I need to shower first."

"Thank the gods. You stink."

I punched his arm and swung off the bed. "Still smell better than you, but I love you nonetheless."

Caleb fell back. "I know. You'd be lost without me."

An hour later, Olivia dropped three packs of microwave popcorn overloaded with butter, a packet of Twizzlers, and a bunch of candy bars on my coffee table.

"Do you hoard food or something?" I grabbed one of the red ropes.

She giggled as she reached into the pocket of her hoodie and pulled out bags of Sour Patch Kids. "I like to be well stocked. Now all we need are some drinks."

"That's where Alex and I come in." Caleb wrapped his arms around Olivia's waist.

I gnawed on my Twizzlers, eyeing the candy bars. Gods know I'd assaulted the vending machines this past week. I didn't need more chocolate. "We need a bag." I turned around and went back into my bedroom. Digging around in my closet, I found a dark blue tote bag that would do. Holding the candy between my lips, I rolled up the bag and went back into the little living room.

It was like Caleb had fallen into Olivia's mouth; they were kissing that deeply. Rolling my eyes, I plucked the Twizzler out of my mouth and threw it at the back of Caleb's head. He turned around, running a hand through his hair. Looking down, he spotted the candy on the floor. "Gross," he said. "That's really gross, Alex."

Laughing, Olivia ducked around Caleb. "You tasted kind of sour and sweet, baby."

"Oh, gods," I moaned, twisting my still-damp hair up in a bun. "That was TMI."

She flipped me off as she hopped on the couch. Her hair was one thick braid tonight, falling over her shoulder. I suspected the distressed jeans and gray sweatshirt had cost a pretty penny. "All right. The mission, if you choose to accept it, is to return with a bag of canned liquid goodness. It will be a risky, yet fruitful one. Do you accept this mission?"

I glanced over at Caleb, grinning. "I don't know. It's dangerous. There'll be Guards and Sentinels lurking in the shadows, preventing us from reaching the ark of soda. Are we up for it, Caleb?"

He pulled a band off his wrist and secured the shoulder-length blond strands in a ponytail at the nape of his neck. "We must be brave and strong, cunning and quick." He paused dramatically. "We shall not fail in this mission."

"Oh, I like it when you're all macho and serious. It's sexy." Olivia leaned over, pressing a kiss to Caleb's cheek, which led to a full-blown make out session.

Standing there awkwardly, I tried to focus on anything but the two of them. It didn't work. "Olivia, I pray to the gods you haven't forgotten your booster shot. 'Cause you guys are *so* about to make some babies."

Caleb pulled back, his entire face flushing. "All right, any requests?"

"Anything with lots of caffeine," Olivia responded, straightening her shirt. Her eyes gleamed in the light. "Don't take too long and don't get caught."

I laughed. "Us get caught? Ye of little faith."

Olivia waved her hand and sat down, messing with the remote. I motioned Caleb to follow me back into the bedroom. I opened the window Seth used quite frequently and gripped the bag. "You ready?"

Caleb nodded, his cheeks still a pretty shade of pink. "After you."

I swung my legs over the windowsill and hung there for a moment, scanning the area. Finding it empty, I dropped the five feet to the ground, landing in a crouch. I popped up. "All clear, my dear."

He stuck his head out. "That rhymes."

"Well, yes it does. You're so observant." I stepped back as Caleb launched out the window.

Standing beside me, he shook out his shoulders. "Which way should we take?"

I turned around, facing the back of the dorm. "This way. Lots more shadows back there and no lights."

Caleb nodded, and we set off for the cafeteria. Chilly air clung to my damp hair, sending shivers down my neck.

We stayed in the shadows, edging along the building. Both of us knew better than to talk too much as Guards and Sentinels had uncanny hearing abilities when it came to rooting out students sneaking around.

At the edge of the girls' dorm, I peeked around the corner.

It was hard to make out much of anything in the darkness. I wondered how the Guards could even see a daimon creeping up on them.

Caleb stopped beside me, giving me a hand motion I couldn't decipher. He looked like a crossing guard.

"What's that supposed to mean?" I whispered, dumbfounded.

He grinned. "I don't know. It just seemed like the right moment to do it."

I rolled my eyes but smiled. "Ready?"

"Yeppers."

We took off, crossing the wide-open space between the girls' dorm and the training facilities. Halfway across, Caleb pushed me into a prickly bush. Cursing under my breath, I flew after him. Caleb was fast, reaching safety a few feet before me. He leaned against the side of the training arena, laughing softly.

I punched him in the stomach. "Douche." I started picking little needles out from my jeans.

After that, we continued to the edge and dashed to the medical building. It was kind of like a weird version of hopscotch. Next, we had to skirt around the building where they stored all the weapons and uniforms and then we'd be at the back of the cafeteria and rec rooms. From there, Caleb knew how to get in the cafeteria even when the main entrance was gated shut. He'd raided the place many times.

A shadow moved up ahead, blending in with the night sky. As the form drew closer, we flattened ourselves against the building and waited until the Guard disappeared around the corner of the med building. Almost getting caught fueled the excitement of doing something we shouldn't. I could tell it got Caleb going, too. His blue eyes seemed to glow and the devilish grin on his face spread.

A sudden sound—much like a muffled gasp—broke the silence. We looked at each other, puzzled. Caleb's grin slipped a little as his eyes met mine. Shrugging at him, I strained to hear anything else, but there was only thick silence. Slowly, I crept to the side and tried to see into the darkness.

"Looks good," I whispered.

We darted across the pathway, slowing down as we made it to the back of the dining hall, keeping an eye out for more Guards. I took a deep breath and immediately regretted doing so. The smell of rotting food filled my nostrils. Black garbage bags lay where several trash cans had toppled over. "Gods, it stinks back here."

"I know." Caleb pressed against my back, looking around. "Or it could just be you I smell."

I shoved my elbow into his stomach. Caleb doubled over, groaning. I started around the corner of the dumpster and froze. The small light at the back door used by servants flickered, casting ghoulish yellow light over the trash cans. We weren't alone in the cramped space. Another shadow moved up ahead, smaller than the Guard we'd spotted before. I held up my hand, silencing Caleb's groans.

He straightened and looked over my shoulder. "Shit," he muttered.

The shadow was moving straight toward us. I backed into Caleb, pushing him against the wall. In the seconds before the shadow reached us, I could easily picture Marcus's face when I got hauled into his office tomorrow morning. Or worse yet, they might notify him now. Oh, gods, it would be epic.

Caleb's breath sawed in and out as his fingers bit into my arm. I looked around desperately for a better hidey-hole. Our only option was to climb into the dumpster, and that wasn't happening. I'd rather face down a pissed-off uncle than do that.

The shadow came into view as it crested the edge of the dumpster. My mouth dropped open. "Lea?"

Lea jumped back, letting out a little shriek. She recovered quickly, whirling on us. Loose gravel crunched under her sneakers. "Seriously," she hissed. "Why am I not surprised to find you two hanging out with the trash?"

Caleb stepped out from behind me. "That's real original, Lea. Come up with that one all on your own?"

"What are you doing out here?" I pushed away from the dumpster and the gods-awful smell.

Her lips curled at the corners. "What are *you* doing?"

"She's probably sneaking back from hooking up with one of the Guards." Caleb craned his neck as he kept a wary eye on the darkness.

"I am not!" she screeched, startling both of us. "I hate when you guys say crap like that! I'm not a whore!"

I raised my brows. "Well, that's totally up for—"

Lea's hands slammed into my chest, knocking me back a few steps. Catching myself before I tumbled into bags of garbage, I dropped the tote bag on the dirty ground, and then threw myself at her. My fingers brushed her silky strands just as Caleb wrapped his arm around my waist and hauled me back.

"Oh, gods, come on." Caleb gritted his teeth. "We don't have time for this."

"You freaking pushed me?" I reached for her again, hands coming up empty. "I'm going to rip out every strand of your hair!"

Lea squinted as she flipped her hair over her shoulder. "What are you going to do about it, you little freak? Break my nose again? Whatever. You get into another fight, you're out of here."

I laughed. "You want to test out that theory?"

She smirked, giving me the middle finger. "That's probably what you want. Then you could go hang out with your daimon friends."

"You're such a *bitch*!" I considered knocking Caleb down just to get my hands around her skinny, tanned neck. He must have suspected as much because his grip tightened. "I'm sorry about what happened to your parents, okay? I'm sorry that my mom had something to do with it, but you don't have to be such a—"

Footsteps at the mouth of the alley silenced us. Turning in Caleb's arms, my heart sank. A female Sentinel stood there, watching us. Her long blond hair was pulled back tightly, giving her face a sharp, angular look. In the weak light, her eyes looked like two black, empty sockets. A shiver coursed down my spine, heightening my senses.

Caleb groaned, releasing me. I straightened my shirt while I shot Lea a nasty look. I held her a hundred percent responsible for us getting busted. If she hadn't been out here, slinking around, then we wouldn't have been held up. We'd already be inside, shoving my bag full of soda.

"I know this looks bad, but—" Caleb started.

"They were totally sneaking around," Lea cut Caleb off, planting her hands on her hips.

I looked at her, wanting to smack her upside the head. "And what the hell are you doing, exactly?"

The Sentinel cocked her head to the side, her lips spreading in a tight smile that showed no teeth.

I recognized her then. It was Sandra, the Sentinel who'd come to my window the night I'd screamed in my sleep.

Lea glanced at us, eyes wide. "Okay. Weird," she murmured loud enough for only us to hear. She folded her arms and cocked her head. "It really stinks back here, okay?" she said in probably her snootiest voice ever. "So can we get this over with quickly?"

Caleb choked on his laugh.

Sandra's head turned toward him as she reached down, unhooking the Covenant dagger. Her fingers circled the hilt of the blade, her eyes still fastened on Caleb.

"Uh..." Caleb stepped back. His expression told me he wanted to laugh but knew better. "No need to bring a dagger into this. We were just sneaking around."

"Yeah, we're happy half-bloods, totally daimon-free." Lea sent me a sly glance. "Well, two of us are."

"I'm going to seriously hurt you," I snapped, glaring in her direction.

Lea rolled her eyes and turned back to the Sentinel. "I have nothing to do—oh, my gods!"

"What?" I followed Lea's open-mouthed, horrified stare.

Sandra wasn't alone. Behind her stood three daimon pures, their ghoulish faces marked by dark veins and empty eye sockets. I almost didn't believe what I was seeing. My brain tried to propel me into motion. The startled gasp we'd heard earlier and the Sentinel's strange behavior suddenly made sense. There were no visible marks on her, but I knew beyond a doubt she was a daimon—maybe even the daimon behind the attack on the young pure weeks ago. But how had she not been checked? The mystery of that would have to wait.

"Oh, man," I whispered.

"We so picked the wrong night to sneak around." Caleb's lanky body tensed and coiled.

One of the daimon pures stepped forward, not even bothering to use elemental magic to conceal itself. Which was strange to me, but then again, I wasn't a daimon expert. "Two half-bloods and…" He sniffed the air. "Something else. Oh, Sandra, excellent work."

Gods, were Seth's Apollyon cooties rubbing off on me? Now they could *smell* me?

"They talk?" Lea gasped, sounding as if the knowledge horrified her. She'd never seen a daimon, let alone talked to one.

"A lot," responded Caleb.

The daimon pure cocked his head to the side. "Should we kill them?"

Sandra, who was still staring at Caleb, raised her dagger. "I really don't care. I've waited long enough, so one of them is all mine."

His laugh sounded twisted. "You'd need more than just one if you bag a half, Sandra. They're nothing like pures, but the girl is…different."

"We've already killed the Guards at that bridge." The other daimon's gaze slithered over Lea and me, his mouth spreading in what appeared to be a smile. All I saw was jagged teeth. "You could've got some aether then. Kill the boy. We'll take these two with us."

My stomach turned over in revulsion. I pulled from deep inside of me, forcing the nearly overwhelming terror down. Fight daimons without titanium? Crazy and suicidal, but there still had to be Guards and Sentinels patrolling—*there had to be.* They'd hear us and they would come.

That is, if these four hadn't already killed them all. But I couldn't let myself believe that, because I knew Aiden and Seth were out there somewhere, and they wouldn't have gone down on a night like this—not a night when Caleb and I had just wanted to grab some soda and watch movies with Olivia.

Lea bumped into me, her chest rising and falling quickly. "We are so screwed."

"Maybe." I dipped down and grabbed a lid off a garbage can. Straightening, I reached over and squeezed her arm. I heard her sharp intake of air, and then felt her body stiffen. I knew she was doing the same thing I did, calling on instinct and years of training. I let go of her arm.

Caleb shifted in front of me. "When there's an opening, make a run for it."

I didn't take my eyes off the daimons. "I'm not leaving you." As those words left my mouth, the daimon pures flew at us.

CHAPTER TWELVE

When I say they flew, I wasn't kidding.

I dipped down as the daimon swung at my head. I shot up under his arm, slamming my fist into his throat, hearing the sickening crunch as the cartilage gave way. He fell back from me, clutching his throat and wheezing.

"Dammit!" I heard Caleb yell, and then a body hit the ground. Panicked, I searched the alley and let out a sigh of relief when I saw Caleb standing over a daimon.

Lea spun on her heel, hitting the daimon in the chest. He staggered back, and she kicked him again. Hell, she was quick, sure-footed, and damn good. The daimon she fought didn't have a chance to recover from her blows. She *kept* landing them.

Flipping the trash can lid over, I watched the daimon with the crushed larynx climb to his feet. I whacked him over the head, and then inspected the nice dent his skull had left behind. Not too bad. I caught the one daimon who hadn't spoken upside the head. It was kind of like playing Whac-A-Mole.

Except the quiet one swung back, clamping down on my shoulder. He wrenched me forward.

Stumbling, I dropped the lid as I tried to yank myself free. The daimon latched onto my other arm and pulled harder, sending darts of pain through my shoulders. I dug my feet in, but I inched across the gravel.

Behind him, Lea sprinted forward and launched herself at the daimon. Wrapping her legs around his waist, she grabbed his head and twisted. Bones crunched and gave. The daimon released his hold and hit the ground, twitching in a messy heap.

"Damn, Buffy," I said, eyes wide. Part of me couldn't believe she'd intervened—and saved my life. "Thanks. I owe you."

Lea sent me a wild grin. "We need to make a run for it—"

A strong current of air hit her from behind, slamming her against the wall. She slid down, rolling onto her side and moaning.

"Lea!" I started toward her, but the daimon Sentinel cut me off. Breathing harshly, I skidded to a stop. Caleb was struggling with the daimon who had sent Lea flying, but the daimon half consumed my world. Fighting them—especially one trained as a Sentinel—was nothing like battling daimon pures.

And this daimon half knew it.

Smiling coldly, she stepped forward. "It's time to stop playing, little girl. You can't beat me."

Ice drenched my veins. Her hand struck out, catching me in the chest. I saw nothing but flashing white light when I hit the ground. Sharp gravel cut into my palms as I rocked onto my feet, lightheaded and stumbling.

Lea climbed to her feet and rushed the daimon half. I

wanted to press stop and hit the rewind button. I couldn't move fast enough. I couldn't scream loud enough. And maybe, if I'd had a do-over, I could've stopped Lea. But everything was moving and changing with incredible speed.

Lea swung at the daimon half, her fist ramming the half's chin. It knocked the daimon half's head back, but that was about all. She slowly turned back to Lea, catching Lea's second throw. She twisted Lea's arm, and the sound of bones shattering overwhelmed the sound of the blood pounding in my temples. I shot forward, but I couldn't get to her.

Time...there wasn't enough time in the world.

Lea paled, but she didn't scream. Not a sound, and I knew she had to be in pain. She didn't even fall, didn't even flinch. Not even when the half daimon raised her arm, Covenant dagger in hand.

But Caleb was like lightning running past me, full of rage and purpose. He grabbed Lea by the waist, breaking the daimon's hold and tossing her out of the path of the dagger.

And the dagger found a new home.

A boy and a girl, one with a bright and short future...

"No!" The scream tore from my throat, from my soul.

The blade sank deep into Caleb's chest, all the way to the hilt. He stared down at his chest, staggering back. The front of his shirt looked like someone had thrown black paint on it, soaking it.

I wrapped my arms around his waist just as he started to fall. "Caleb! No. *No!* Caleb, look at me!"

He opened his mouth, but no words came out. His weight carried us both to the cold, dirty ground.

Those bright blue eyes dulled, fixed on some unseen point. "No," I whispered, brushing damp strands of hair off his forehead. "No no no. This isn't supposed to happen. We were just getting soda. That's all. *Please!* Caleb, wake up."

But he didn't wake up. Some part of my brain that was still functioning told me that people who died didn't wake up. They never woke up again. And that Caleb was dead. He was gone before he even hit the ground. Pain—so sharp and so real—cut through me, taking away a chunk of my soul.

The universe ceased to exist. There were no daimons, no Lea. There was just Caleb—*my* best friend, *my* partner in dysfunction, the only person who *got* me. My shaky fingers slipped over his boyishly shaped cheeks to his neck, to where his pulse no longer beat. A piece of my world ended just then, gone forever with Caleb. I pulled him into my lap, pressing my cheek against his. I thought that maybe, if I held him long enough and wished hard enough, all of this would be just another nightmare. That I'd wake up, safe in my bed, and Caleb would still be alive.

Hands delved deep into my hair, wrenching me backward. I lost my grip on Caleb and fell onto my back. Stunned and vastly empty, I stared up at the daimon. She'd been a *half-blood*—once a Sentinel—sworn to kill daimons. Not their own kind.

She gripped my head, slamming it back against the concrete. I didn't even feel it. Dark rage filled me. It rushed through my system, so potent that I tumbled over the edge. She would die, and it would hurt.

Seizing the sides of her face, I shoved my thumbs into her eyes. She let go, shrieking and pulling at my hands. Someone was screaming and screaming…and I pushed harder. Tears and blood mingled, streaking down my face. I couldn't stop. All I could see was her shoving the blade into Caleb's chest.

Pain was everything. I had no idea if it was physical or mental.

It swamped me in waves and waves of hurt. And then the daimon flew backward and someone dropped down beside me. Firm, strong hands caught my wrists in a gentle grasp and hauled me to my feet. I caught the familiar scent of sea and burning leaves.

"Alex, calm down. I've got you," Aiden said. "Calm down."

It was me who was screaming, and making a terrible sound that was so final, so shattering. And I couldn't stop. Aiden flipped me around, pressing me against the muck-covered wall. He whirled on his heel, slamming his blade deep into the chest of a daimon.

I slid down, turning to the side. The daimon half edged along the very same wall.

Blood ran in rivulets down her face from her damaged eyes, but she could still *sense* me. Blue light erupted, briefly swallowing everything around me. The daimon half flew backward, striking the ground beside Caleb. Screams filled the air—as did the smell of burning flesh.

Then arms were around me, lifting me to my feet. The moment his hands brushed mine, I knew it was Seth. He half-dragged, half-carried me out from the narrow alley behind the dining hall and into the darkness of the quad. I fought him the entire way, throwing punches and clawing. Sentinels and Guards rushed past us, but they were too late.

They were too late.

When Seth let go, I tried moving past him, but he grabbed my shoulders. "I can't leave Caleb like that! Let go!"

Seth shook his head, his amber eyes luminous in the darkness. "We're not going to leave him there, Alex. We wouldn't—"

I punched him in the stomach. He grunted but did little else. "Then you get him! Get him out of there!"

"I can't—"

I hit him again. Seth'd had enough. He caught my wrists in one hand and held them between us. "No! You have to let me get him! You don't understand! Please—" My words broke off in a sob.

"Stop it, Alex. We will not leave Caleb's body behind the dining hall. You need to calm down. I need to make sure you're okay." When I didn't answer, he swore under his breath. I felt his fingers against the back of my head. They were quick and gentle. "Your head is bleeding."

I couldn't respond. Even though my eyes were open and Seth was in front of me, all I saw was the shock on Caleb's face. He hadn't seen it coming.

Neither had I.

"Alex?" Seth's arms eased around me.

The world started to unravel some more. "Seth?" I whispered. "Caleb is gone."

He murmured something as he brushed his fingers over my face, wiping away tears that continued to fall. I didn't speak again, not for some time.

Seth carted me off to the med center. The docs looked me over, determining that I only needed to be cleaned up and get some much-needed rest. Someone washed the gore off my hands, and concerned looks were exchanged.

When they were done, I stayed where they'd left me. The white walls blurred. Seth returned just as I'd sat back down. I stared at him, feeling nothing inside me.

He came to my side, strands of hair hanging loose around his face. "Aiden and the rest have disposed of the daimons. There were only three of them, plus the half, right?" He paused, running a hand through his hair. "They managed to kill two of the bridge Guards, and they wounded another three Sentinels inside the Covenant. You're…lucky, Alex. So very lucky."

I stared down at my fingers. There was still blood under my fingernails. Was it mine, the daimon's, or Caleb's? Seth grabbed my hand, leading me out to the hallway.

He stopped briefly. "They have Caleb's…body. He's being taken care of."

I bit down on my lip until I tasted blood. I just wanted to sit down and be left alone.

Seth sighed, his grip on my hand tightening as we walked out of the med center. I didn't ask where we were going. I already knew, but Seth felt the need to make sure I understood.

"You're in a lot of trouble." He ushered me through the dark campus. It was near midnight, and Guards were everywhere. Some were patrolling, some huddled in groups. "Just to warn you, Marcus actually threw something. Lucian was woken up, and the gods know he didn't appreciate that. They're going to want to know why you were outside your dorm."

Numbness settled into my body. Perhaps that was why I wasn't worried about Marcus. I stumbled along behind Seth, stopping when he opened the Academy doors and the statue of the three furies came into view. Why hadn't they broken free? The Covenant had been breached again.

Catching what I was staring at, he squeezed my hand. "No pures were harmed, Alex. They…they don't care."

But Caleb had died.

Seth tugged me away from the statues. I was only barely aware of the crowd gathered at Marcus's door. The moment I stepped into the room, Marcus let loose. Lucian remained standing, which was new for him. Both of them yelled at me simultaneously, and then they took turns when the other appeared out of breath or out of words. What they said was pretty much the same old: I was irresponsible, reckless, and out of control. I didn't tune them out like I normally would. I soaked up everything they said, because what they said was true.

As I sat there staring up at my uncle and seeing real emotion in his face for the first time in a long time—albeit anger—I remembered another cryptic warning Grandma Piperi had left me.

You will kill the ones you love.

I should've stayed in my room like I was supposed to. There was a reason why a curfew had been imposed. The sanctuary of the Covenant had been violated once. I'd forgotten that, or I just hadn't thought about it, or cared.

I never stopped to think.

"I don't think any of this is helping." Seth stood behind me while I sat in the chair. "Can't you see she's upset? Maybe you should let her rest and ask questions tomorrow."

Lucian whirled around. "Of course, none of this is helping! She could've been killed! We—*you*—could have lost the Apollyon. As the First, you should have been aware of what she was doing. She is your responsibility!"

I felt Seth stiffen behind me. "I understand that."

"And you?" Lucian snarled at me. "What were you thinking? You knew there had already been a daimon attack here. It was not safe for you or any student to be out there at night!"

There was nothing to say. Didn't they understand that? I'd been wrong, so very wrong, and there wasn't a damn thing I could do about it now. Closing my eyes, I looked away.

"Do not look away from me when I am speaking to you! You are just like your—"

"Enough!" Seth shot around the chair, nearly overturning it in the process. "Can't you see there's no point in talking to her right now? She needs some time to deal with the loss of her friend!"

Several Council Guards moved forward, ready to intervene. None of them looked like they wanted to. I'm sure they remembered what'd happened to the Guards in Lucian's house over the summer.

Lucian's nostrils flared with anger, but he backed down. A moment of clarity pushed through the grief. Why had Lucian backed down? Apollyon or not, Seth was just a half-blood and Lucian was the Minister. It was more than just strange, but before I could really catch hold of the realization, it slipped away as another thought pushed to the surface.

Seth remained where he was, between me and everyone else in the room. He was like a wall of fury, and no one dared to move a step closer. It struck me then why everyone was afraid of there being two of us. Seth alone was a force to contend with. They were already fearful of him. Even Marcus seemed visibly affected, but Seth after I Awakened...?

"All right." Marcus cleared his throat. He strode forward, keeping a wary eye on Seth. "These questions can wait until a better time."

"Sounds like a plan to me," Seth replied casually enough, but he watched Marcus like a bird of prey.

Sidestepping Seth, Marcus stopped and crouched down in front of me. I stared at him. "Now do you understand that everything you do, every decision you make—even the slightest one—will have great consequences?"

I did, and I also understood he was talking about more than just Caleb, but also about Seth. However, Marcus had been wrong about one thing the last time he'd lectured me. My actions didn't just reflect upon Seth—they were a catalyst for how Seth would react.

CHAPTER THIRTEEN

Grief was not something that went away when I opened my eyes and found that the sun still rose in the morning. Nor did it pass when the sun declined and stars lined the sky.

I'd been mute and emotionless until I'd returned to my dorm and seen the remnants of our movie party. Someone had gotten Olivia out of the room, but standing there, staring down at the Twizzlers I'd thrown at Caleb's head hours before, I broke apart. All I remembered was Seth picking me up and carrying me back to the bed.

Sometime in the afternoon, Seth left. Returning before dinner, he tried to coax me into eating. But I'd hit the dark abyss that followed such things. Maybe I'd never really dealt with Mom's death, and the loss of Caleb had brought everything to the surface. I really didn't know, but when I thought about her, I thought about Caleb and our spirit boats.

All I did was sleep, and it was the deep sleep where the nightmares of reality finally couldn't reach me. During the random moments I was awake and fully aware of what was going on around me, I yearned for Caleb—and for my mom. I needed one of her hugs. I needed her to tell me everything was going to be okay, but that could never happen, and my heart couldn't bear the idea of mourning Caleb, too.

Seth stayed by my side, turning into this protectively fierce creature who wouldn't allow Marcus or any of the Guards into my room. He kept me in the loop, letting me know what was going on outside my room. Halfs were being searched again, but they believed Sandra was the culprit for the original attack. She'd been a Sentinel, so she'd been on and off the Island so many times—enough times that they'd missed her when they'd searched the Sentinels and Guards. This whole time their suspicion had been on one of the students, and it'd been a Sentinel.

He also tried telling me that what happened to Caleb wasn't my fault. When that didn't work, he went with the whole "Caleb wouldn't want this" tactic. Then he relied on the one thing that usually stirred me up—insults and witty banter. I think he told me I smelled by the third day.

Eventually Seth seemed at a loss for what to do. He stretched out, wrapped his arm around me, and waited. It took a while for me to realize the heartache I felt had transferred to him. Seth didn't know how to deal with it either and by the beginning of the fourth day, it was like he, too, had lost his best friend. So, we both lay there, silent and soul-sick.

Like two sides of the same coin.

Sometime during the middle of the night, Seth leaned over me. "I know you're not sleeping." A few seconds later, he brushed the limp strands of hair off my face. "Alex," he said softly. "They're having Caleb's funeral at noon tomorrow."

"Why...why aren't they doing it at dawn?" I asked hoarsely.

Seth shifted closer, his breath warm. "The Guards who

were killed will be buried at dawn, but Caleb was only a half-blood student."

"Caleb…deserves a funeral at dawn—he deserves that tradition."

"I know. I know he does." Seth sighed deeply, sadly. "You have to get out of this bed, Alex. You have to go."

I steeled myself against the sharp pang, but it still cut through me. "No."

His head dropped to lie beside mine. "No? Alex, you can't be serious. You have to go."

"I just can't. I'm not going."

Seth continued to push the topic until frustration and anger took over. He jumped off the bed. I rolled onto my back and ran my hands over my face. My skin felt grubby.

Standing by the foot of the bed, Seth did the same thing with his hands. "Alex, I know this—all of this—is killing you, but you've got to do this. You owe this to Caleb. You owe it to yourself."

"You don't understand. I can't go."

"You're being ridiculous!" he shouted, not caring if he woke up everyone on my floor. "Do you know how much you'll regret this? Is that something else you want to eat away at you?"

There was a fine line between rage and sorrow, one that I tottered on. I tipped onto the side of rage this time. I pushed up, climbing to my knees. "I don't want to see them hoisting his body up in the air and burning it! His body—Caleb's body!" My voice cracked, along with my heart. "That's *Caleb* they'll burn!"

Just like that, the anger faded from Seth's face. He took a step forward. "Alex—"

"No!" I raised my arm, ignoring the way it shook. "You

don't understand, Seth. He wasn't your friend! You barely knew him! And you know what? You want to know the most messed-up thing about that? Caleb looked up to you. He *idolized* you, and did you even give him the time of day? Sure, you spoke to him every once in a while, but you didn't know him! You didn't care to."

Seth rubbed his jaw. "I didn't know. If I thought—"

"You were too busy fooling around with girls or being an arrogant jerk." After the words left my mouth, I immediately regretted them. I sat back down, heart racing painfully. "You can't do anything…about this."

"I'm trying to do something about this." Those eyes sparked to life, glowing amber. "I don't know what else to do! I've stayed with you—"

"I didn't ask you to stay with me!" I screamed so loud my throat hurt. I needed to calm down. Guards would rush this room if I kept it up. "Just leave. Please. Just leave me alone."

Seth stared at me for what seemed like an eternity and then he left, slamming the door shut behind him. I collapsed back on the bed, balling my hands over my eyes.

I shouldn't have said those things.

All this time I'd worried about having no control. Ironically, from day one I'd acted out-of-control. I didn't control my anger or my impulses to do whatever I wanted. How had I fooled myself this entire time? Having control meant acting in the right way, at least most of the time. But I'd acted wild—reckless. I'd let my heart decide when I'd questioned contacting the Covenant after Mom and I had left. There was no logic behind that. My heart had destroyed whatever friendship I'd had with Aiden. And my heart and my selfishness had led me to sneak around with Caleb. If we'd just stayed in my room—or if I hadn't moped around for a week—Caleb wouldn't have felt the need to cheer me up. We wouldn't have gone to get drinks.

He wouldn't have died.

I don't know how long I lay there tangled up in the blankets. My mind raced through my childhood with Caleb, the three long years without him, and every single moment I'd spent with him since I'd returned to the Covenant. Rolling over, I curled into myself. I missed him—missed Mom. Both of their deaths were linked to me, to decisions I'd made or hadn't made. Action. Inaction. Marcus's words came back to haunt me in those hours, over and over again. *Everything you do...*

On the fifth day, the day of Caleb's funeral, the sun rose early and it shone brighter than I remembered for a November morning. In less than four hours, Caleb's earthly remains would forever be lost. Five days since he'd died, one-hundred-and-twenty hours since the last time I'd touched him and heard him laugh, over seven thousand minutes of slowly adjusting to a world that didn't include him.

And only a few short hours since I realized I'd never had any control.

I sat up, threw the covers to the side and swung my legs off the bed. Standing made me woozy at first, but I went into the bathroom and stared at my reflection.

I looked terrible.

One of the daimons had left behind faint, purplish bruises along my jaw and cheekbone. My hair hung in thick, straggly clumps. Red tinged the rims of my eyes. Slowly, wearily, I peeled off the disgusting clothes and dropped them on the floor. In the shower, I leaned my forehead against the cool tile, letting my mind go blissfully blank.

Cold water bounced off my skin by the time I pulled

myself from the shower and wrapped a large, white towel around me. It was when I mindlessly tugged a comb through the tangles in my hair that something occurred to me.

In the dim light, the scars covering my neck looked shiny and uneven. I always kept my hair down and wore long sleeve shirts to hide the red patches on my arms. Those scars had never seemed to heal like they should've. I did everything and anything to hide the scars. Scars left behind from my own reckless, thoughtless actions. So ugly—

Instructor Romvi's words came back to me. *You should be less worried about your vanity.*

The big-toothed comb slipped from my fingers. Hurrying from the bathroom, I went to the small kitchen area and straight to the wicker basket beside the microwave. I rummaged through napkins, clips, and other stuff I never used. Among them I found a pair of orange-handled scissors. Picking them up, I doubted they would cut through most things, but they'd do.

I went back to the bathroom and grabbed my hair, pulling it around my shoulder. My own wide, brown eyes stared back at me. The hair, wet and thick, hung past my chest. Without thinking twice, I positioned the scissors just above my bare shoulders.

A hand shot out, snatching the scissors from my grasp. So fast—so unexpected—I shrieked and jumped back. Seth stood there, dressed in all black. I clutched the front of my towel and stared.

"What are you doing?" Seth handled the scissors as if they were a snake about to sink its fangs deep into his skin.

"I…I'm vain."

"So, you were going to cut your hair?" He sounded incredulous.

"Yeah, that was the plan."

He looked like he wanted to question that further, but he turned around and dropped the scissors on the dresser. "Get dressed. Now. You're going to Caleb's funeral."

My grip on the towel tightened. "I'm not going."

Ignoring me, Seth went into my bedroom. "I'm not arguing with you about this anymore. You're going to his funeral, even if I have to drag you there."

I didn't really believe that. So, I was shocked when I tried to shut and lock the bathroom door, and Seth whipped around. He pried my hand off the door and yanked me out of the bathroom.

Exhaustion and hunger made me slow, and I had a death grip on my towel. Those were the reasons I ended up pinned to his chest, both of us on the floor in front of the bed. I could feel his heart hammering against my shoulder and his breath against my cheek.

Seth's hands were clamped on my arms, keeping me from delivering a nasty elbow to his face. "Why…why do you always act like this? Why? Why did you do this to yourself? All of this could've been avoided."

The sudden tightening in my throat warned that the yawning emptiness was still there, lingering. "I know. Please… please don't be angry with me."

"I'm not angry with you, Alex. Okay, maybe a little." He moved slightly, pressing his head against mine. Several moments passed before he spoke again. "How could you do this to yourself? You—*you* of all people should have known better."

I felt the tears start to well up again. "I'm sorry. We didn't—"

"You could have died out there, Alex—or worse." Seth let out a ragged breath, his fingers tightening around my upper arms. "Do you know what I thought when I felt your panic?"

"I'm sorry—"

"Sorry wouldn't have done a damn thing if I'd lost you, and for what?" He grasped the sides of my face, turning my head so I had no other choice but to face him. His eyes searched mine. "Why? Is it because of what happened with Aiden?"

"No." Tears rolled down my cheeks now. "I did it because I was being stupid. We just wanted to get some drinks. I didn't think anything would happen. If I could change it, I would. I would do anything."

"Alex." Seth closed his eyes.

"I mean it. I would do anything to change what happened! Caleb—he didn't deserve that. I did know better. If we'd stayed in my room, he would still be alive. I know that."

"Alex, please."

"I know I acted stupid." My voice cracked. "And if I could go back, I would. I'd switch places with him. I would—"

"Stop," he whispered, his thumbs wiping away my tears. "Please stop crying."

Everything inside me felt like it was tensing and twisting into one giant knot. "I'm so sorry. I want to take it all back. I want a do-over because I can't do this again."

He made a strangled sound as he pulled me to his chest, holding me there until my heart stopped racing and the tears subsided. "You have to do this again and you don't get a do-over, Alex. None of us do. You can only move forward from here, and the first step is going to his funeral."

I drew in a deep breath. "I know."

Seth caught my chin with the tip of his finger, tipping it back. I think that's when he realized I wore nothing more than a towel. His eyes flicked down for a moment and then his entire body seemed to stiffen. It could have been all the extreme emotions rolling through both of us, or the connection we shared, but every inch of my body suddenly felt warm.

It was strange how the body could forget all these terrible things so quickly. Or maybe it was the soul that worked that way, seeking out warmth and touch, needing to prove that we were still in the world of living. I leaned in, resting my cheek against his shoulder. I closed my eyes.

"You're shaking," Seth murmured.

"I'm cold."

His hands slid over my shoulders. "You really need to put some clothes on. You shouldn't be dressed like that."

"You came in here. That's not my fault."

"Still. You need to put some clothes on."

I bit my lip and pulled back. Seth stared at me, his eyes unnaturally bright. "Okay. But you're going to have to let go of me first."

His hands tensed on my back, and for a second…well, he looked like he wasn't going to let me go. I wasn't sure how I felt about that. Seth did let go, but he leaned in, resting his forehead against mine. "You do smell better now. I think we're making progress."

My lips twitched. "Thanks."

Some of the tension in his body seemed to seep out. "You ready?"

I breathed in deeply, and it felt like the first time in days. "Yes."

When I was little, my mother had once told me that only in death could a pure and a half be viewed as equals. Both would stand before the River Styx, waiting for their souls to be carried into the hereafter.

Everyone had already filed into the cemetery by the time

Seth and I made it there. The pures stood up front, before the halfs, which made no sense to me. Caleb had been one of us, not them. So why should they stand closer to him? Aiden would say it was tradition.

It was still wrong.

I roamed the outer edge of the groups with Seth, dodging outright curious looks and even a few stares of condemnation. I tried to convince myself I wasn't looking for a certain, dark-haired pure as my gaze kept returning to the group at the front. Aiden was the last person I wanted to see.

Seth finally stopped, so I did, too. He hadn't spoken since we'd left my room, but he kept glancing at me. I think he worried I'd flip out again. Tucking my still-damp hair back, I looked up at him, chewing on my lip.

"You're going to thank me, aren't you?" Seth sounded amused.

"Well…I was. Not so sure about that now."

"Come on. I want to actually hear you say it. It'll probably be your first and last time."

I squinted against the sun's harsh glare. Far away, I could see the pyre, the body swathed in white linen. "Thank you for staying with me. And I'm sorry for being such a bitch toward you."

Seth unfolded his arms, nudging me with his elbow. "Did you just call yourself a—"

"Yes, I did, because I am one." I sighed loudly. "You didn't deserve it when I yelled at you…about Caleb."

He stepped closer as Lucian moved to stand before the pyre. As the Minister, he would give the parting speech, eternal life and all that. "I deserve a lot of things," Seth said.

"Not that." I tore my eyes from the scene before me. I focused on a nearby hyacinth bush. The single dense spike of flowers was a vibrant red, the blossoms shaped like little stars. They signaled grief and mourning, and they were everywhere in the cemetery, reminding all of us of the tragedy of Apollo's love for the beautiful Hyacinth. Back when the gods roamed the earth freely, people who ended up dying some tragic death became a flower if they were young and beautiful, male or female, and had earned a god's favor.

Twisted.

Seth shifted closer, his arm brushing mine. "You know, the connection between us didn't leave me with any other choice."

I rolled my eyes. "Well, thank you, anyway."

Lucian started in on the memorial speech, speaking about Caleb's spirit and strength. The ache in my chest grew and the sweetly scented air felt cool against my damp cheeks. When the pyre was lit, my insides twisted and I couldn't stop the shudder that kept running through my body. I turned halfway, pressing against the waiting warmth while the air filled with the sounds of crackling wood and quiet sobs.

I don't know what hurt more: the fact that I'd never see him again or that I'd never hear his infectious laugh. Each realization sent a sharp pang through me.

It wasn't until the crowds began to disperse that I grasped the warmth I'd sought out actually belonged to a body—and that body belonged to Seth. Cheeks flushing, I stepped out of his embrace. I'd cried on him enough to last me a lifetime. "I need to…"

"I understand." Seth stepped back. "I'll wait for you outside."

Grateful that he got it without me actually having to say anything, I watched him head back to the cemetery gates. I wiped under my eyes again and turned around.

I froze.

Olivia stood in front of me, dressed in black slacks and a sweater. Her skin was shades lighter; her eyes, usually so warm and open, were now cold and angry. Tears ran down her face unchecked.

I stepped toward her, wanting to comfort her. "Olivia, I'm so—"

"Why didn't you do something?" Her voice broke. "You were his best friend. You could've done something!" She moved forward, her arm trembling as she pointed at me.

Luke reached out and wrapped an arm around her shoulders. "Don't. It's not Alex's—"

"You're the Apollyon!" Olivia cried out, her words ending in a broken sob. "Yes, I know! Caleb told me what you are, and I've seen you fight!" She turned to Luke, eyes pleading. "You've seen how fast she can move. Why didn't she do something?"

I knew—*I knew* there was nothing physically I could've done. I wasn't the Apollyon—not yet—but to hear her say that? Well, it was like hearing Marcus's voice in my head. *People expect more from you, because of what you will become.*

"I'm sorry, Olivia. I'm so—"

"Don't say you're sorry! That won't bring Caleb back!"

I flinched. "I know."

"Olivia, come on. Let's go back to your room." Luke sent me an apologetic look as he started inching her around.

Elena came forward, taking Olivia's hand. "It's okay. It's going to be okay."

Olivia slumped against Luke, her head falling to her chest. The full weight of her loss was visible for all of us to see.

Grief clawed its way through my chest. I turned away, feeling a rush of hot tears. Blindly, I stumbled away from them, roaming deeper into the memorial grounds. It wasn't until I bumped into someone that I looked up, wiping under my eyes. "Oh, sorry—" I stopped, mid-apology.

It wasn't a person I'd run into, but a statue. A small laugh crawled out of my throat as I stared up at the striking, yet woeful face carved out of stone. The sculpture had been shaped so that he bent at the waist slightly, one hand reaching out toward something, palm open in a beckoning manner. My gaze drifted down to the base, where the name Thanatos had been scripted. Under his name was a symbol—a torch turned downward.

I'd seen it before…on Instructor Romvi's arm.

CHAPTER FOURTEEN

Sighing in frustration, I shoved my hands into the pockets of my hoodie and scanned the night sky. Stars broke up the darkness, some shining more brightly than the others. The last time I'd seen the dark sky had been more than a week ago. I'd been behind the dining hall, holding Caleb's cold body.

Caleb.

I squelched the rising tide of sorrow and regret before it consumed me again by focusing on something that had been nagging me since his funeral. Why in the world would Romvi have the symbol of the God of Peaceful Death tattooed on his arm? And wasn't he the same god that the old book had claimed was responsible for killing Solaris and the First Apollyon? I wasn't sure it really mattered, but the image kept coming back to me.

"You okay?"

Every muscle in my body locked up. I reminded myself that it was only going to take eleven hours to get to the Catskills—eleven hours stuck in a car with the guy I loved, the guy I'd practically begged to love me in return. Maybe not in so many words, but that was how I felt. This was going to be easy. Yeah, really easy.

"Alex?"

I turned around. Aiden was tucking my suitcase into the back of the Hummer, watching me over his shoulder. My gaze skittered away, unable to really, really look at him. "Yeah, I was just thinking."

"Is this all your stuff?"

Nodding, I kicked the toe of my shoe along the asphalt. I needed to act normal or this was going to be the longest car ride of my life. "How...how is Deacon?"

A few seconds passed before he answered. "He's doing okay." He shut the rear door. "He wanted me to tell you that he's really sorry about...what happened."

I faced him, keeping my eyes trained on his shoulder—which was one really nice shoulder—when I spotted a silver chain around his neck. It disappeared under his sweater. Odd—Aiden never wore jewelry. "Tell him I said thanks."

Aiden nodded as he headed around to the side of the vehicle, but then he stopped so unexpectedly that I bounced off his back. He turned and caught my arm, setting me right. Our eyes met for a fraction of a second, and then he dropped my arm.

He stepped back. "I don't know what you were thinking." He broke off, glancing toward Leon, who waited under the awning of the Covenant.

"We just wanted to get some drinks from the cafeteria." I swallowed, but the lump in my throat didn't go away. "We were going to watch movies."

"Are we ready?" called Leon. "We should be leaving now if we want to reach the Catskills before noon."

"Yeah." Aiden turned away, but then faced me again. "Alex?"

Slowly, I lifted my eyes to his. That turned out to be a mistake of epic proportions. A different kind of hurting opened up in my chest.

His gaze drifted across my face. "I'm so, so sorry about Caleb. I know how much he meant to you."

I couldn't look away, couldn't say a word.

He glanced over his shoulder and when he turned back to me, his eyes shone bright silver in the dim light. "Don't... don't ever do anything like that again. Please. Promise me."

I wanted to ask why he'd care if I threw myself in front of a daimon, but those words didn't come out. Something else did. "I promise."

Aiden watched me a moment longer, and then broke away. After that, we climbed into the Hummer. I took a seat in the back while Aiden slid into the one in front of me. Leon drove and the other Guard took the seat next to me.

Leaning my head back against the seat, I closed my eyes and wondered how I'd ended up in the car while Seth got the private jet with Lucian, Marcus, and the Council members. They'd flown out this morning. Half-bloods—even Sentinels—usually didn't get seats on the planes, but an exception had been made for Seth.

Car rides typically turned me into a bratty five-year-old, especially astronomically long ones, but I was too tired to really think about it. With all the sleeping I'd been doing, I probably should've been wide awake for days, but I drifted off quickly.

I woke up about two hours in when we stopped to get gas in Middle-Of-Nowhere, Virginia. Leon and the Guard went into the shack of a gas station, and I climbed out to stretch my legs. It was so dark out here, surrounded by woods and farms. The only sounds were the cows mooing in the distance. I strolled around the rear of the Hummer and found Aiden leaning against the bumper. He looked up when I stopped beside him. His eyes were nearly the same color as the moonlight.

"If you want to get something to eat, Leon or the Guard will get it for you." Aiden rolled a bottle of water between his hands.

"I'm not hungry." I moved past him, keeping my back to him.

"We don't want to stop unless we have to."

"I'm fine." I hopped up on the curb and proceeded to place one foot in front of another.

Mid-step, I glanced over at the convenience store—if you'd consider that place a convenience store. It looked like an old pizza shop and the blinking red sign out front read "OPE." Leon stood at the counter. "So…has Marcus confirmed that the Sentinel was responsible for the first attack?"

"There's no way to really confirm that, Alex. We believe so. Another round of searches is being conducted"—he paused when I stiffened—"to make sure she was the one."

I reached the end of the curb. "I guess now I understand why the searches were so important. They missed her and… look what happened. The Guards at the bridge, they probably didn't expect anything when she showed up."

"No. And the daimons are obviously getting smarter. She was on and off the campus a lot, making her a prime candidate. And her tags weren't visible."

I bent over backward, sprung off my hands, and landed perfectly on the narrow curb. I could have been a gymnast in a different life. Turning to face him, I found Aiden staring at me.

He glanced away as a strange, almost sad look crept across his face. Pushing off the bumper of the car, he shoved his hands into the pockets of his jeans. "You and Seth seem to be getting along a lot better."

I frowned at the change in subject. "Yeah, I guess so."

Aiden stopped in front of me. "That's a vast improvement from wanting to stab him in the eye."

Even though I stood on the curb, Aiden was still taller than me. I tipped my head back, meeting his pale gaze. "Why do you even care?"

His brows rose slightly. "It's just a statement, Alex. Has nothing to do with me caring or not."

I felt my cheeks burn as I nodded stiffly. "Yeah, I think I grasped the whole caring and not caring topic." I hopped off the curb and inched around the gas pumps.

Aiden followed behind me. "I saw you two at the funeral. He was there for you. I think that's good. Not just for you, but for him. I think you're the only person Seth cares about besides himself."

I stopped, wanting to laugh, but I felt...embarrassed. Like I'd been caught doing something wrong, but I hadn't. Confused by what Aiden was getting at, I started walking again.

"Seth cares about himself. That's about it."

"No." Aiden followed my movements, meeting up with me at the edge of the pumps. "He rarely left your side. Seth wouldn't allow anyone—not even me—near you."

I whipped around, surprised. "You stopped by to see me?"

Aiden nodded. "Several times, actually, but Seth was determined that you needed time to come to grips with everything. That doesn't sound like someone who cares only about himself."

"Why would you come see me?" I stepped toward him, hope and excitement building inside me. "You told me you didn't care about me."

He fell back a step, clenching his jaw. "I never said I didn't care about you, Alex. I said I couldn't love you."

I flinched, cursing myself for the stupid window of hope I'd allowed to open. Smiling tightly, I headed back to the Hummer and slammed the door shut behind me. Unfortunately, Aiden followed me.

He got in the seat in front of me and turned around. "I'm not trying to fight with you, Alex."

My temper and hurt feelings took over. "Then maybe you should try not talking to me. Especially when you sound like you're trying to pawn me off on another guy."

Aiden's eyes snapped alive, flaring in the darkness. "I'm not trying to pawn you off on someone. You were never mine to do so."

I leaned forward, my fingers digging into my thighs as I spoke in a whisper thick with pain. "I was never yours? You should've thought about that before you stripped me naked in your room!"

He sucked in air sharply, then his eyes shuttered to a dull gray. "It was a temporary loss of sanity."

"Oh." I gave a harsh laugh. "Did your temporary loss of sanity last several months? Did it make you say all those things to me at the zoo? Did it—"

"What do you want me to say, Alex? That I'm sorry…for leading you on?" He paused, visibly trying to rein in his anger and frustration. "I am. Okay? I'm sorry."

"I didn't want you to say that," I whispered, stomach tumbling over.

Aiden closed his eyes and shook his head. "Look, you

don't need this right now. Not after everything with Caleb and with us going to the Council. So, just stop."

"But—"

"I'm not going to do this with you, Alex. Not now. Not ever."

Before I could respond, Leon and the Guard returned, putting an end to this. I flung myself against the seat and glared at the back of Aiden's head. I knew he could feel me staring holes into him, because he sat stiffly with his eyes forced front.

Eventually I got bored with that and climbed over the back of my seat to dig out my music player. I tried going back to sleep, but my mind was too busy thinking about Caleb, the argument with Aiden, and whether or not Seth was as self-centered as I'd always thought he was.

After nine more hours of hell, we turned onto a winding road lined with towering pines and spruce trees so thick it reminded me of a Christmas tree farm. We were deep in the Catskills no-man's-land. About a mile in, a nondescript fence poked out, surrounding what I assumed was the perimeter of the New York Covenant.

I snorted. "Nice security."

Aiden turned halfway around. "You haven't seen anything yet."

I ignored him and leaned forward, seeing nothing more than a wire fence and trees. Maybe it was one of those fences that electrocuted people, because I'd really expected more than this.

Then I saw the Guards standing in front of the pitiful-looking fence, armed with what looked like semiautomatic weapons. My eyes widened as they leveled the guns at our vehicle. Leon slowed down as the four Guards approached us cautiously.

"Alex, take your hair down," Aiden said quietly.

I didn't understand why, but the seriousness in his tone told me not to fool around. I unraveled the messy bun, letting it fall around my face. Leon rolled down all the windows, and at once, the Guards peered inside the vehicle, searching each of us…for *visible* tags.

I shrank back but met the dark-skinned Guard's intense gaze as he looked me over once, then twice. The tags felt like they were burning under my mass of heavy hair. I wasn't sure what they would've done if they'd seen the scars. Shoot me?

Not quickly enough, they gestured at the one Guard who remained back. The tall gate shuddered and creaked opened. I let out the breath I'd been holding. "Am I supposed to keep my hair down the entire time I'm here?"

Aiden glanced back at me, his lips forming a hard, tight line. "No. But I'd rather you not provoke a trigger-happy Guard."

I could understand that, I supposed.

We rolled through the gate and went another half mile down the road before the trees started thinning out. I leaned on the back of Aiden's seat as the New York Covenant finally came into view.

Well, the twenty-plus-foot wall made out of white marble came into view.

After passing another set of gun-toting Guards, we finally entered the grounds. It didn't look much different than our Carolina branch. There were statues of gods everywhere, except where ours stood among the sand, theirs rose up from the greenest grass I'd ever seen.

The first building I got to see was a mansion—the kind I didn't expect to see in the middle of the Catskills. I'd once heard the Rockefellers had a house around these parts, but nothing compared to this monstrous thing. I counted six stories, several all-glass rooms, and possibly a ballroom with a skylight dome by the time the car stopped in front of the sandstone manor. I started to follow them, but Aiden stopped me.

"Alex, hold on a second."

My fingers froze on the handle. "What?"

Aiden had turned around completely and those eyes… gods, those eyes always drew me in, always filled me with such warmth that I could almost taste his lips on mine. Too bad his words kind of ruined the moment.

"Don't do anything here to draw unwanted attention."

My fingers tightened on the door handle. "I don't plan on it."

"I'm being serious, Alex." His eyes bored into mine. "No one here will be as forgiving as your uncle or stepfather. I can imagine that they won't go easy on you when you have your session. Some of the Council…well, they're not fans of yours."

An ache throbbed in my chest in response to his clipped, professional tone. I had no idea where the tender Aiden had gone, the one who'd sworn to always be there for me, the one who'd gently brought me back from the brink when I'd freaked out in training. Gods, there were so many more moments, but all of them were gone.

Aiden was gone. Like Caleb, but in a different way. I'd lost both of them. A lot of the anger leaked out of me then. I faced the window, sighing. "I didn't expect them to. I'll behave. You don't have to worry about me." I started to open the door again.

"Alex?"

Slowly, I turned to him. Aiden wasn't so guarded in that instant, and a deep, unsettling pain reflected in his gaze. There was more—almost like an uncertainty. But he pulled it together, like slipping on a well-worn mask of indifference, shuttering any and all emotions.

"Just be careful." His voice was strangely hollow.

I wanted to say something, anything, but a flurry of activity outside the car made that impossible. Servants—droves of half-blood servants—descended on the Hummer, opening doors and retrieving luggage. My mouth dropped open as one, a fair-haired boy about my age, meekly opened my car door. A black circle with a slash through it had been tattooed onto his forehead. I glanced at Aiden and saw his gaze still fastened on me. He gave me a strained smile before climbing out. I couldn't help but wonder if the doubt I'd seen in his face had anything to do with me.

I was given a room on the fifth floor, one that connected to Marcus's room. Or at least, that was what the half-blood doorman inside the mansion said before stepping back into the shadows. I really had no clue, so I just followed the blond boy. I didn't see where Aiden and Leon were carted off to, but I bet they got rooms on the bottom floors—big, awesome rooms.

We crossed the grandiose lobby and entered a glass-enclosed breezeway. To our left was the entrance to what appeared to be the ballroom, but the twinkling lights didn't hold my attention. Right in the middle of the breezeway was the very same statue that stood in the Covenant lobby in North Carolina.

Furies.

Sucking in a sharp gasp, I hurried around the statues to catch up with the half servant. Their heavy presence remained after I left the breezeway, nagging at the back of my thoughts. We went up several flights of steps, and I couldn't deal with the silence any longer.

"So…um, how do you like it here?" I asked as we stepped into a narrow hallway adorned with oil paintings.

The boy kept his eyes fastened on the Oriental carpet.

Okay…was there some sort of "no talking" rule? I glanced at the paintings, mentally listing the gods as we passed them: Zeus, Hera, Artemis, Hades, Apollo, Demeter, Thanatos, Ares—wait. Thanatos? I stopped to get a closer look at his painting.

He had wings and a sword. Thanatos looked like a pretty rocking angel, actually. But he shared the same woeful look the cemetery Thanatos had had on his face as he gazed upward. His left hand held a flaming torch turned downward. Why would Thanatos, who wasn't one of the major Olympian gods, have his picture here among them?

An opening door drew my attention from the painting. I glanced over my shoulder. The half servant held the door open, eyes downcast.

I pursed my lips, scanning the four dull-white walls within. A closet would have been too nice of a description for this… this thing considered a room. I walked in as the servant placed my luggage inside the door.

There was a bed—a twin size bed covered with an itchy-looking brown blanket and one flat pillow. A tiny bedside table offered a rusty lamp that'd seen better days. It took me two seconds to cross the room and peek inside the bathroom.

It was the size of a coffin.

My eyes fell over the scuffed-up tile, dirty mirror, and rust stains surrounding the drain in the shower stall. "You've got to be kidding me," I muttered.

"They expect you to sleep in this room—on that bed?"

Jumping at the unexpected sound of Seth's voice, my hip slammed into the washbasin. "Ouch!" I rubbed my hip as I turned around.

Seth stood at the foot of the bed, his ever-present smug expression tainted with disdain. It'd only been a day since I'd seen him, but strangely, it felt longer than that. His hair was down, curving around his chin. And he wore jeans and a plain black sweater—a rarity.

I was kind of glad to see him.

"Yeah, this room sucks." I left the bathroom.

Seth strolled to a door on the other side of the bed. He reached down, throwing the lock. "I guess that's not the closet?"

"Nope, that's the door to Marcus's room."

He arched a brow. "They gave you a servant's room?"

"Nice." I looked around, discovering there wasn't even a closet in the room—or a dresser. I'd be living out of a suitcase for my whole stay. Yippee. "Why'd you lock it?"

Seth threw me a mischievous grin. "I can't have Marcus just walking in on us. What if I want to snuggle on these cold New York nights?"

My frown increased. "We don't snuggle."

He dropped his arm over my shoulder, and the scent of mint and something wild tickled my nose. "How about we cuddle?"

"We don't do that either."

"But you're my cuddle bunny. My little Apollyon cuddle—" I punched him in the side.

Laughing, Seth steered me toward the door. "Come on, I want to show you something."

"What?"

He removed his arm and captured my hand. "The Council is starting their first session at one today. I think we should go watch it."

"That sounds boring." I let him drag me out of the room, though. It wasn't like I had anything else to do.

"We could always practice." Seth pulled me into the stairwell, taking several steps at a time. "I'm feeling froggy—haven't thrown fireballs at anyone's head lately."

"That sounds more interesting than watching a bunch of pures postulate how great they and their laws are."

"Postulate?" Seth glanced over his shoulder, grinning. "I can't believe you used the word 'postulate.'"

"What?" I scowled. "It's a real word."

Seth raised a brow at me and then continued down the steps. In the stairwell we passed several servants in drab clothing. Each of them looked down. I watched them lift their heads once they'd passed us.

Seth tugged on my hand. "Come on. We're going to miss it."

Outside, the biting wind cut through my sweater and sent shivers through me. For once, I was grateful for Seth's hand. It felt incredibly warm in mine.

"Anyway, the Council session should be interesting. It's a hearing."

"I thought mine was the only hearing?"

"No." Seth led me around the west wing of the mansion. "There are several hearings. You are one of many."

I started to respond, but we stepped around back and my lips clamped shut. A labyrinth of waist-high marble walls separated us from the Greek style coliseum. Bright flowers, all in full bloom, sprung from the vines that covered them. Thick cords of a creeping plant climbed the statues and benches, covering everything in front of us in a mass of vibrant red and green. "Wow."

Seth chuckled. "If you stay on this pathway it leads straight to the Council."

I glanced down several of the walkways that branched off the main one. "Is it a real labyrinth?"

"Yes. But I haven't checked it out."

"Looks kind of fun, don't you think?" I looked up at him. "I've never been in a labyrinth before."

A real smile replaced the smug one. "Maybe if you're good—and I mean, really good—we can come play in the labyrinth."

I rolled my eyes. "Gee, really?"

He nodded. "You have to eat your dinner, too."

I didn't even bother responding to that. I got kind of lost in the scenery for a while. How in the world did the pures manage to keep these fragile flowers alive all year round? It had to be magic—old magic. The deeper we moved down the pathway, the thicker the vines grew and when we neared the end, Seth slowed.

"We have to sneak in," he said. "We aren't really supposed to be listening to the Councils."

"And if we get caught?"

"We won't."

Trusting Seth felt strange, mainly because I did…trust him. Not in the same way I would have placed my life in Aiden's hands, but almost there—almost.

Behind several thick columns made of stone, Themis, the Goddess of Divine Justice, stood at the entrance to the coliseum. She was quite formidable with that sword in one bronzed hand and balanced scales held high in the other, but her presence seemed kind of ironic to me—the pures knew nothing of balanced justice.

The building was something straight out of ancient Greece. Hidden as the New York Covenant was, they could get away with designs not normally found in neighborhoods boasting Walmarts and fast-food joints. The closest thing we had was the amphitheater where the Carolina Covenant held sessions.

I followed Seth and we slipped through the side entrance

used by the servants. Most of the halfs we passed cast their eyes to the ground as they carried goblets and plates of tiny appetizers. I had a hard time looking at them, harder than I'd realized I would. Back home, we rarely saw so many. They were kept separate from us, as if the Carolina Covenant didn't want us to see what the other side was truly like.

What did the servants think when they saw me—or any half who wasn't in servitude? Were they even capable of thinking? If I were one of them and I had some critical thinking skills left, I'd be outright hostile toward the "free" halfs.

The icky feeling in the pit of my stomach was hard to acknowledge, so I started jabbering as Seth led me past several small doors. "Stairs—more stairs? Would it kill them to put a damn elevator in one of the buildings?"

Seth started up them. "Maybe they think the gods would be unhappy with elevators."

"That's stupid." The long car ride had made my legs feel like jelly.

"We only have to go up eight flights. I promise."

"Eight?" I eyed two more servants heading down the stairs, hands empty. One was a middle-aged female in a plain gray dress. She wore thin-soled shoes and no socks. The skin around her ankles looked bruised and red, as if it had been rubbed raw. Cringing, I glanced at the male servant behind her.

A sudden cold shiver crawled over my skin.

The older male half had dark brown hair that curled around a strong chin and cheeks weathered by the sun. Fine lines jutted out from the corners of gentle brown eyes…that were looking straight at me.

His eyes weren't the glassed-over eyes of a servant. They were keen, intelligent—seeing. There was something familiar about him, something I should *know*.

CHAPTER FIFTEEN

"Come on," Seth urged, tugging on my hand. "We're going to miss it."

With surprising effort, I refocused on Seth's back and started up the stairs again. The line of Seth's shoulders seemed unnaturally tense. At the landing to the fourth floor, I spared a second to look over my shoulder.

The half-blood servant stood below, staring up at us. Our eyes met for a second, and the half stepped back, hands balling into fists. Then he spun around, disappearing down the stairwell.

"That was strange," I murmured.

"Huh?"

Hadn't he noticed how alert that servant had been? Seth stared at me like I'd just made out with a daimon. Guess not. "Nothing."

Seth inched open a door. "You ready?"

"I guess." I was still thinking about that servant.

"We have to keep back, but we should be able to see everything from here." He motioned me through.

I stepped onto what turned out to be a balcony overlooking the Council below. I started forward, but Seth pulled me back.

"No." His breath stirred the hair around my ear. "We have to stay back against the wall."

"Sorry." I wiggled free. "Can I sit?"

He smiled gamely. "Of course."

I slid down the wall and stretched out my aching legs. Seth did the same, managing to be as close as possible. I elbowed him, but he only grinned. "So, what's the big deal?"

"Aren't you at all interested in the Council hearing?"

I faced the Council below, fiddling with the string on my hoodie. "Interested" wasn't the word that came to mind; "terrified" seemed more accurate. These pures could make or break a half-blood. Leaning forward, I scanned the crowds through the slats of the balcony railing.

A sea of red, blue, green, and white moved around the floor, taking seats with others who wore the same colored robes. I looked at the white robes and saw a coppery redhead moving with the grace of a ballerina through the throng of pures.

"Dawn Samos," I whispered. She made white sheets look good.

Seth leaned forward. "You know her?"

"Lea is her sister. Do you think she's come with Dawn?" I paused, remembering how Lea had fought beside me. "I…I'd like to talk to her."

"She didn't come, but she did stop by your room after… everything."

"She did?" Surprised, I watched the throng of pures. "That's surprising. Did…she look okay?"

"Her arm was broken and she was a little bruised up, but she'll be okay."

I nodded, watching Dawn sit down and smooth the robe out around her. She kept looking around—looking for someone. Before I could really study any more of the Council pures, I realized that non-Council members were also in attendance. Toward the back sat Marcus and a raven-haired beauty I'd only seen once.

"Laadan—the woman with Marcus is Laadan. She was the pure who pretty much came up with the deal to give me a chance to stay at the Covenant." I tucked my hair back. "I forgot she was here."

Seth nudged my leg with his. "I've heard of her. She doesn't seem too bad."

A familiar dark head slid into the seat beside Laadan. Aiden had changed into white slacks and a white buttoned-down shirt rolled up to the elbows, showing off his powerful forearms. The edges of his hair curled around the collar, giving him sort of an untamed look. I watched as he turned to Laadan and said something. She smiled and patted his arm while Marcus shook his head.

Something struck me. Marcus was dressed like he normally was—dark slacks, a suit jacket—looking more like a Wall Street stock trader than a demigod. Laadan wore a deep red dress made out of crushed velvet. I scanned the back crowd, noticing that some wore the colors that matched the robes. "Why is Aiden wearing white?"

"He's owed a Council seat."

I looked at Seth sharply. "What does that mean?"

Seth arched a brow. "Since his father's seat is still open and will remain so, he's owed a seat on the Council."

"So? He doesn't want that seat."

"That doesn't matter. Aiden still has to show his respect to the current Council members. That's why he's wearing all white. The other people dressed like that? They're either next in line or ones who will campaign for seats when others open up."

I turned back to Aiden. He'd leaned back, one arm thrown over the empty seat beside him. "He never told me that."

"Shouldn't you have known that?"

"I really don't pay attention in civics class."

Seth snickered. "He'll probably take his seat one day, when he settles down. All the pures do."

I wrapped my arms around my waist. "What do you mean by *settles down*?"

Seth's heavy stare settled on me. "I didn't mean anything."

But he did. His unspoken words hung between us. Most pures thought hunting and killing daimons below their station, but some female pures found it dangerous and thrilling—sexy. My insides twisted into raw knots. The idea of him with someone else made me want to dropkick something—or someone.

A sudden silence descended on the crowd as the Ministers from all four Covenants entered. I recognized Lucian and Minister Nadia Callao, a tall female who I'd only seen a few times in Carolina. They took their seats together, as did the rest of the Ministers. One—a man with dark hair graying at the temples, a full face and piercing blue eyes—stepped to the center of the raised dais, his green robes heavily adorned with gold thread. A golden laurel wreath sat atop his head.

"Who is that?" I asked.

"Minister Gavril Telly. The house you're staying in is his. The woman in green is Diana Elders—the other Minister of New York—but Telly is the head of the Ministers. He's the one in charge."

Telly started the opening session with a prayer in ancient Greek. I had no clue what he was saying.

The language was beautiful, almost musical, but went on for so long I leaned back and yawned.

Seth grinned. "Don't go falling asleep on me."

"No guarantees."

I didn't fall asleep, though. Minister Telly eventually started to address the crowd in heavily accented English. I couldn't place where he was from, but his voice carried the same lilt Seth's did, just with a hell of a lot more authority.

"We have several urgent issues that must be addressed during this Council session." Telly's voice rang through the building. "Most importantly, we are here today to discuss the…unsavory situation that has arisen over this past summer."

"They're going to talk about Kain, aren't they?" I perked up, eager to see how the pures would handle this.

Seth shrugged. "There are a lot of things they could talk about."

Telly paced the length of the dais, the long green robes trailing behind him. Raising one arm, he signaled to the section of the theater underneath us. I strained forward, but Seth got a handful of my sweater and held me still. Two Guards eventually came into view, escorting a woman dressed in nothing but a gray tunic that ended above the knees. She didn't even wear shoes. They brought her to stand below the center of the dais, and then forced her to her knees.

Apprehension blossomed in the pit of my stomach. The dark-skinned woman wasn't a daimon from what I could tell. She looked like a normal half-blood—perhaps a Guard or a Sentinel. Her legs were toned enough for someone who'd spent years training and fighting.

She lifted her head defiantly, and a hushed murmur carried through the crowd of pures.

"Kelia Lothos." Telly's upper lip curled. "You have been accused of breaking the Breed Order by having inappropriate contact with a pure-blood."

My eyes widened. Caleb had told me about her—and her pure-blood boyfriend, Hector. I twisted back to Seth. "Seriously? Their most pressing issue is a half having sex with a pure?"

Seth's amber gaze met mine. "So it seems."

Shaking my head in disbelief, I turned back to the drama unfolding on the floor below. "Damn Hematoi."

"How do you plead?" Telly demanded.

Kelia started to stand, but the Guards forced her to stay down. "Does it matter how I plead? You have already found me guilty."

"You have the right to tell your side." Minister Diana Elders rose, slowly approaching the center of the dais. An open kindness marked her expression, softening the set of her lips. "If you feel that you are not—"

"It is not her fault!" A voice cried out from deep within the audience as a pure in green robes came to his feet. His complexion was swarthy, much like Jackson's. "She has done nothing wrong. If anyone is to blame, then it is me."

"And so it begins," muttered Seth.

I ignored him, transfixed by this pure-blood coming to Kelia's defense. This was better than watching daytime soaps.

Telly drifted to the left of the dais. "Hector, no one here holds you at fault. Halfs can be just as beautiful as pures…and as manipulative as any daimon."

Hector—Kelia's pure-blood lover—pushed down the aisle. "Yes, she is beautiful, but manipulative? Never. I love her, Minister Telly. That is no fault of hers."

Telly scoffed as he came to the edge of the dais. "A

half-blood and a pure-blood cannot fall in love with each other. The idea is as absurd as it is disgusting. She has broken the law. Perhaps she should have thought of that before she acted as a common whore."

"Do not speak of her like that!" Hector's face flushed with anger.

"How dare *you* speak to *me* that way?" Telly drew himself up. "Proceed carefully, or your next action might be mistaken for treason."

Kelia twisted around. Concern and fear filled her eyes—and so did love. My heart twisted for her—for them. "Hector, please don't. Just leave."

Hector's dark eyes fell on Kelia, mirroring the same emotions displayed across her face. "No. I can't let this happen. You've done no wrong. I should have never—"

"Hector, please leave," Kelia begged. "I don't want you to…see me like this. Please!"

"I'm not leaving," Hector said. "You're not guilty of anything!"

"I'm guilty of loving you!" She pulled her arms free of the Guards. They seemed too stunned by the explicit outpouring of emotion to do anything. "Don't do this! You promised me you wouldn't do this!"

Promised what? What Hector was doing was heroic, romantic, and swoon-worthy. How could she not want the man she loved to stand up against the entire Council for her?

Hector rushed down the main walkway, and the Guards finally snapped out of it. They positioned themselves between the half and pure.

Hector halted, his hands clenching at his sides. "Stand down."

"Are you going to allow this to continue, Minister?"

asked Lucian, speaking for the first time since the session began.

Telly exhaled slowly. "Kelia Lothos, how do you plead?"

The crowd of pures watched, excited and horrified, eager to see how Kelia would respond. But it was Hector who did.

"She pleads not guilty."

An elderly female Minister stood. The red robes swallowed her frail body. She reminded me of the Crypt Keeper I'd faced when I was seven. "Enough. Sentence the half to servitude and remove this pure from the session!"

A clap of thunder *inside* the building sent me back from the railing into Seth. Above us, the air started to thicken and darken. As impossible as it seemed, dangerous-looking clouds began to form—and they were coming from Hector. He was using the element of earth, the electrical power creating an indoor thunderstorm.

Hector met Telly's stunned gaze. "I will not allow you to take her."

Chaos broke loose on the floor below. Hector surged forward, and the cloud above us flashed with lightning, filling the air with an electrical charge. The Ministers came to their feet, full of shock and anger.

"Please! We can discuss this civilly!" cried Diana. "Can we not—"

Another crash of thunder drowned out her words. I pressed my face into the gap between the slats for a better look at what was happening below. Unsurprisingly, the Guards who'd held Kelia back didn't look willing to attack a pure. We were trained from birth to never do so, not even in extreme cases like these. They moved back warily as Hector grabbed hold of Kelia, pulling her to his chest.

"The half-blood is found guilty!" Telly shouted. "Seize the half and send her to the Master's! Remove the—"

Hector thrust Kelia behind him as the cloud cracked, shooting streaks of lightning throughout the room. Pures shot from the benches, pushing at each other as they hurried out of the way. Worried for Aiden, I searched him out in the madness. He stood in the center beside Laadan, his expression a steely mask.

"I will kill anyone who dares to take her." Hector's voice was low and steady.

"You would stand against your own kind—for a half-blood?" Telly's face was pale with anger.

Hector did not hesitate. "Yes. I would for the *woman* I love."

Telly backed off. "You have sealed your fate."

I didn't understand those words. Pures were *never* punished for messing around with halfs. About the only thing they were ever punished for was using compulsion or other elemental powers against other pures, but...

The cloud continued to darken, and Seth pulled on my arm, but I held onto the slats of the balcony railing.

"Guards!" Telly ordered, and Guards from every corner descended in a flurry of white. All of them were halfs, except one. The pure-blood Guard had eyes the color of rich soil. He stared at Telly, his fingers wrapped around a Covenant dagger. The other Guards reached the two lovers, managing to break Kelia from Hector's hold. She screamed and fought them, breaking loose once to only be tackled to the floor.

Overhead, the cloud darkened even more. A bolt of lightning snapped from the cloud, striking the floor near Telly. "Take him down!" said Telly.

"No!" screamed Kelia. "Stop this, Hector! Please!"

The pure reached Hector before he could send another lightning bolt. A horrified scream rose in my throat, muffled by Seth's hand. The pure-blood Guard—the only one out of all of them who could strike down another pure—shoved the titanium blade into Hector's back and twisted. A sucking sound shot through the building and the ominous cloud fizzled out.

Seth jerked me from the railing. "You can't scream, okay? I doubt they're going to be thrilled if they find us here. Promise me you won't scream." He eased off after I nodded. "We need to get out of here."

I barely heard Seth. Horror and anger slammed through my heart and my fingers dug into his arm. Kelia's screams filled the air until they were abruptly cut off. All of this was impossible, cruel, and horrifying.

Seth gave a weary sigh. "I guess it's a good thing Aiden came to his senses."

Ice drenched my veins, stealing the very air from my lungs. I twisted around, facing him. "You knew this was going to happen. You brought me here on purpose!"

The tawny hue of his eyes glowed. "I didn't know it would go this far."

"I don't believe you." I pushed against his chest, feeling sick. "You knew what they were going to do!"

Seth looked away, the hollow of his cheeks flushed. "I only know what Aiden's future would've held if you two had continued with that insanity."

I pushed again, and this time, Seth let go.

I spent the rest of my first day in New York holed up in the dingy room. I didn't want to be here—or anywhere near here. Raw knots formed in my stomach, and I was furious with Seth.

But I was also furious with myself.

I plopped down on the edge of the hard mattress. *I only know what Aiden's future would've held if you two had continued with that insanity.*

As much as I hated to admit it, Seth had been right.

Aiden was the kind of man who would've done exactly what Hector had done. If Aiden had loved me and I'd ended up in Kelia's position, he would've fought an army of Guards and received a dagger in the back.

I lowered my head to my hands and drew in a strangled breath. My heart yearned for Aiden like he was the very air I needed to breathe, but at the same time I understood—really understood—that, even if Aiden had loved me in return, we could never be together.

What had he said to me that day in the gym? That if he loved me he'd take everything from me.

What I'd seen proved that I'd also take everything from him—even his life.

A soft knock drew me out of my troubled thoughts. I crossed the two feet to the door and opened it.

Seth stood there, arms folded across his chest. "Alex—"

I shut the door and locked it. Seth may've been right, but I still didn't want to see him. If I had to deal with his gloating face, I'd really punch him. I sat back on the bed and scowled at the door.

A minute passed, and then the knob turned, first left then right. Squinting, I leaned forward. There was the unmistakable sound of the door unlocking.

"What the hell?" I sprang to my feet.

The door swung open. Seth stepped into the little room. "I fried your lock."

My mouth dropped open. "You arrogant son of—"

"Shush." He shut the door behind him and surveyed the room with another disgusted look. "I still can't believe they stuck you in this craphole. I'm going to have to talk to Lucian about this."

"Why would Lucian care?"

He strode past me and bent at the waist, pressing his open palm into the mattress. "Lucian cares more about you than you realize." He straightened and smiled. "You should come to my room. You'd like it."

I rolled my eyes. "Not going to happen."

Seth looked disappointed, and then his eyes fell on my skeevy bathroom. "I have a Jacuzzi tub in my bathroom."

"Seriously?"

"Yep."

The idea of a nice long bath teased me. I shook my head, dispelling the dream. "Seth, I really don't want to talk to you right now."

He dropped down on the bed and winced. "Well, we need to talk."

I tipped my head back, groaning. "Does what I want ever matter to you?"

"What you want always matters to me." His face was serious. "By the way, I liked the other jammies you wore that one night. The thermal and flannel shirt aren't very alluring, but those little shorts were nice."

My gaze narrowed on him. "It's freezing in this room, and this"—I marched over to the bed and tugged on the itchy blanket—"is not touching me. It probably has fleas." I turned back to him. "What do you want, Seth?"

He cast his eyes down. "I'm sorry you had to see that today." That wasn't what I expected. "But you needed to see it," he continued, his gaze flicking up, meeting mine. "I know you…love him. Don't deny it, Alex, I know you do. And I know that no matter what Aiden says to you, he still cares for you more than he should."

I opened my mouth to deny that, because Aiden had told me in many different ways that he didn't, but I stopped. Did it matter if Aiden really did care for me? I whirled around and sat beside Seth, staring at the frayed carpet.

"I think you know that, Alex," he said softly. "I've said it before. Eventually you two would've gotten caught. No one—not even me—would've been able to stop the Council. You know what Aiden would have done."

"I know." I rubbed my palm over my thigh. "He would have done exactly what Hector did. I just didn't think they'd do that to their own kind."

"This place is a different world. I've been here a couple of times. It's straight old school. It doesn't take much to insult Minister Telly, and he's no fan of half-bloods…even the Apollyon."

I lifted my head, looking at him. "What do you mean?"

Seth's lips thinned. "It's nothing that I've been told, it's just a feeling I get."

"Is he going to be the one questioning me during my testimony?"

"I don't know." Seth smiled then. "He's nothing to worry about."

I really didn't believe him, but I was too tired to poke further. "I hate this place."

He leaned over, brushing my hair back off my neck, exposing my scars. "You've only been here a day, Alex."

"I don't need more than a day to know." I turned my head, startled to find our faces mere inches apart. "Do…you like it here?"

Seth's eyelids lowered, fanning his cheeks with long lashes. "It's not the worst place." He was quiet for a few moments and then his eyes flicked to mine. "You really have realized that Aiden is sort of a lost cause, haven't you?"

I blinked tightly and turned away. I suddenly wanted to cry, because it was true. "I guess that fills you with some sick sense of satisfaction, doesn't it?"

"I'm not a terrible person, Alex."

His sharp tone brought me back to him. "I didn't say you were a terrible person."

Seth smiled tightly. "Then why would you think I'd like to see you hurt? And I know you're hurting."

Now I felt guilty. "Look, I'm sorry. I'm just out of it."

He relaxed. "That's the second time you've apologized to me. Wow."

"It'll be the last."

"Maybe." He scooted back, lying down on his side. He patted the tiny spot left. "This bed really sucks. You sure you don't want an upgrade?"

I sighed. "Seth, you can't stay here."

He shrugged. "I don't see why not."

"My uncle is right next door."

"So?" He patted the bed again. "He's not even in his room. He's downstairs with the rest of the pures. They're having their opening party fest."

"It doesn't matter." I climbed over his legs and sat beside him. "This bed sharing thing has to stop."

Seth looked up at me, his face the picture of innocence. "Why? It keeps the nightmares away, doesn't it?"

A retort died on my lips. Damn him.

"You haven't had one in a while. What did I tell you about needing—?"

"Oh, shut up."

Seth chuckled, and then told me about his first visit to the New York Covenant. I told him about some of the towns Mom and I had lived in. After a while, his eyes drifted shut and there were no more stories. I watched him for a few moments. What in the world was I supposed to do with him?

I eased down onto my side, careful not to wake him. I stared at the scruffy white wall for what seemed like hours. My mind wouldn't shut down, which was strange. Usually, Seth's presence easily lured me into sleep.

Tonight was different. I missed Caleb, hated where I was, and wished more than anything that things could be different between Aiden and me. Tonight I felt more alone than I ever had before. Maybe everything seemed so much more real here, so much more cold and stark. Seeing Hector slaughtered had destroyed whatever little seed of hope I'd still carried deep inside me that there would be this wild, beautiful fairytale ending when it came to Aiden.

Beside me, Seth's breathing slowed into a deep, steady rhythm. I flipped onto my back and looked at him.

Seth was staring at me, definitely not asleep. He looked curious and even a bit confused. In this minuscule bed, lying on my back gave him little room. As it was, he already was using one arm as a pillow and his other was clamped to his side. I sucked in my lower lip and sat up. Reaching behind me I picked up the pillow and offered it to him. He took it, his eyes narrowing inquisitively. We stared at each other, and then Seth seemed to understand. I expected him to say something conceited or dirty.

But he said nothing. Quietly, he lifted up and slid the pillow under his head. Then he lay down on his back and stretched out his right arm. His chest rose sharply as he waited.

I ran a hand over my face and squeezed my eyes shut. *What was I doing?*

I didn't really know. I was tired and I hated this place. The room was cold, the coarse blanket was left on the floor, I *wanted* Aiden…and I stopped making excuses. I lay down, resting my head on the crook between his shoulder and chest. My heart pounded strangely.

Seth remained still for a minute, maybe two. Then he moved his arm down, circling my waist, pulling me closer. My body fit against his, my hand resting on his chest. Under my palm, his heart hammered as wildly as mine.

CHAPTER SIXTEEN

"Are you feeling unwell?"

"Huh?" I looked up from my untouched plate. Marcus eyed me curiously. "You haven't eaten any of your breakfast."

I glanced over at Aiden. He also watched me. So did Seth. Laadan's eyes were on me, too, except she kind of had this nostalgic look about her, as if she really wasn't seeing me.

This breakfast was a whole lot of awkward.

My gaze settled back on Aiden, and I couldn't stop the image of the pure-blood Guard stabbing Aiden in the back from flashing through my mind. I felt the blood slide out of my face.

Aiden put his glass of orange juice down. "Alex?"

"Yeah…I just didn't get much sleep last night." I could feel Seth's eyes boring through me. "It's just being in a new place and all."

"Is your room not to your liking?" asked Marcus.

"Have you seen my room?" I debated shoving forkfuls of egg in my mouth, but the way Aiden studied me over the rim of his glass, it didn't sound like a good idea. "If you can even consider that box a room."

Marcus sat back, crossing one leg over his knee. "I haven't seen your room, but I'm sure it's not that—"

"Marcus, what time are the sessions this morning?" asked Laadan.

Distracted, he glanced at his watch. "They should be starting shortly."

I sent Laadan a grateful smile, and she winked as she twirled her glass of champagne. Drinking champagne this early in the morning appeared sophisticated and cool to me, and so did the awesome green dress she wore. It was demure, with little cap sleeves.

The scratching of Seth's chair across the marble tile sounded harsh. "Alex, it's time for practice."

Aiden glanced over his shoulder at Seth. "She hasn't eaten anything."

"Then at least she'll eat her lunch," Seth replied.

Hardness crept across Aiden's face. "Or you could give her a few minutes to eat her breakfast before she starts practice."

"Hmm…I'm having this strange sense of déjà vu, except you were telling me to stay out of your training business, and I told you how weird—"

"That's funny." Aiden's full lips twisted into a smirk. "I'm having the same feeling, except I said you should—"

"Oh, for the love of baby daimons everywhere, I'm ready to start practice." I pushed up from the chair.

Aiden twisted around, his eyes narrowing into thin slits. I grabbed my glass of juice and took a healthy swallow while Laadan watched on with amused interest. "Happy?"

"Do they do this often?" she asked, taking a sip from her crystal flute.

Marcus cleared his throat. "Do you even have to ask?"

"What?" Seth scowled, turning his beauty even colder. "What do we—"

"Dean Andros, I've been looking for you. There are some things I'd like to talk about with you—oh, is this the infamous Alexandria?"

I tensed, recognizing the voice. *Minister Telly.* I met Seth's stare for an instant, and then I forced my body to turn around. Seeing him after he'd ordered Hector's death caused my stomach to sour. I smiled—probably looked more like a grimace—but I tried.

Telly's gaze drifted over me in a wholly condemning matter. "So, this is what all the fuss is about?"

That plucked the wrong nerve. "I guess so."

He smiled faintly. "Well, there has been a lot of uproar surrounding what you've accomplished. Many rumors have spread, claiming you have already killed daimons. I am curious if this is true. How many daimons have you killed?"

Vaguely, I sensed Seth moving around the table. Odd that I knew where he was in a room. "I've killed three."

"Oh." Telly's brows rose. "Impressive. And how many innocent people have you thrown into harm's way? Or gotten killed?"

Blood came rushing back to my face. Telly's smile spread, becoming genuine. He was getting off on seeing me squirm.

"Seth? Isn't it time for Alex's practice?" asked Aiden.

If Seth was humored by Aiden's sudden change, he didn't express it. "Why, yes. Excuse us, Minister Telly, but we must—"

I met Telly's icy stare. "One."

"One what, dear?"

Everyone behind me probably stopped breathing. "I've

gotten one innocent person killed, and I don't know how many I've put in harm's way—maybe dozens."

Seth swore under his breath.

Telly's eyes flared wide for a second, filled with shock. "Is that so?"

Surprisingly, it was Marcus who came to my rescue. He slid in front of me, blocking the Minister's hostile glare. "Minister Telly, there were a few things I wished to discuss with you also. If it pleases you, would now be a good time?"

Without waiting for Telly's response, Seth grabbed hold of my arm and pulled me away from the table. He waited until we were a step away from the doors. "Gods, you just cannot keep your mouth shut."

"Whatever." I yanked my arm free and stepped outside. The thermal and sweats I wore were no protection against the biting wind.

Seth seemed unfazed by the chilly air. He held his hand up as we walked toward the labyrinth, and a small ball of blue energy formed in his open palm. "He is *not* someone you want as an enemy."

The little ball bounced up and down on his palm. My inner golden retriever couldn't look away. "I don't think he liked me to begin with."

"Still, you don't need to make it worse."

His tone pissed me off. "You know what, you need to stay out of my bedroom. You have your own."

He smiled. "I know I do. I see it quite often. I just prefer your bed. It smells better."

I made a face. "It smells better? What does your bed smell like? Regret and bad taste?"

Seth chuckled. "Wherever you sleep, it smells like you."

"Gods, that has to be the creepiest thing I've heard in a long time. And that is...that is saying something, Seth."

"You smell like roses and summer." He tossed the ball a little higher. "I like it."

I choked. "I smell like summer? For real? Summer?"

"Yeah, you know. Warm. You always smell warm."

Two pures passed us, glancing over their shoulders at Seth's little display of power. I started to smile at their shared looks of shock, but remembered I was supposed to be mad. "I don't care if you like the way I smell, you freak."

"It's not like Marcus is going to walk in." The ball grew bigger, swallowing his hand. "That's why I locked the door. He can't interrupt our cuddle-fest."

"That's not the point, and would you put that away!" I snapped.

Seth was quiet for a whole minute—a new record for him. "Don't worry; you'll be able to do this one day. And you'd miss me if I didn't want to cuddle."

"That's not true."

He cast me a sideways glance that said he remembered *me* cuddling up against him last night. I groaned, wanting to smack him with every fiber of my being. But he did put the ball of energy away as we cleared the labyrinth and the amphitheater came into view. A shudder ran through me that had nothing to do with the temperature. "Where are we going?"

"Not in there."

"Well, I figured that much." I followed him around the building, refusing to look at it. Just like the servants we passed on the way refused to look at us.

Behind the Council building, I could finally see the actual Covenant. A wrought iron fence surrounded the campus grounds. While our school looked like something straight out of Greece on a good day, theirs looked like a medieval fortress with creepy turrets and towers that rose out of the fog. Behind the sprawling structure, I could see the tops of gray buildings I assumed were the dorms.

I noticed the designs in the fence as we neared it. "What's up with the torch thing?"

"Huh?"

"These downward torch things." I pointed one out on the fence. "They're everywhere here."

"Yeah, I've noticed that. They're a symbol of Thanatos."

"One of my Instructors at the Covenant has a tattoo of it on his arm."

His lips pursed. "Minister Telly has one on his arm, too."

"How in the world do you know that?" We cut across the frost-covered lawn to one of the covered walkways connecting smaller buildings to the main one. "Have you been sneaking into his room and cuddling with him, too?"

"Don't be jealous. You're my only cuddle bunny. But to answer your question, when I got here with Lucian, Telly was waving his arm around as he yelled at some servants. The sleeve of his robe slipped back and I saw the tattoo."

"I wonder if they belong to some secret society or something."

"A secret society of douchebags, maybe."

I snickered. "Sounds about right."

We passed two halfs walking to class and they came to an abrupt standstill. Eyes wide, they gawked at us. One boy elbowed the other. "That's him! And that has to be her—the other one."

The other boy's mouth dropped open. "Then it's true! There really are two Apollyons."

"By the gods." his companion ran a hand over his chest. "This is so cool."

Seth bowed at them. "Way cool."

Rolling my eyes, I pushed him to the side. The whole sensing Seth thing was getting annoying. "Where are we going?"

"Since it's freezing up here in the mornings, I figured we'd do our first session in a training room. Then move outside."

My shoulders slumped. "I have to practice with you all day?"

Seth spun around in front of me, the perpetual, cocksure grin on his face. "You have to spend *all* day with me. Every day. For as long as we are here." I stared at him.

He clapped his hands together, letting out a rather high-pitched squeal before grabbing my hand. "Oh, we are going to have so much fun! Aren't we? Fun, Alex—we will have fun."

We weren't having fun.

I spun around, blocking first his kick then his jab. Sweat poured off me and my muscles ached from the never-ending onslaught that was Seth.

Then again, I preferred these morning sessions over the afternoon ones. Over the past three days, I'd come to dread the outside training sessions. The weather didn't warm up very much by then, and the frozen ground was unforgiving, even with the magically green grass springing up from it.

Seth tossed me a bottle of water. "Five minutes."

I retreated to the edge of the mats and took a long swallow. Seth, who never seemed thirsty, decided to entertain the ever-growing crowd of gawkers. In between class changes, half students had started gathering at the doors. Seth left them open since this kind of thing stroked his ego. All the halfs were pretty cool, though, and they didn't treat me like people did at my Covenant. Somehow—and I totally blame Seth—they'd found out I'd already made some kills, which upped my cool factor into uncharted territory. We had students and Instructors watching us try to tear each other's heads off.

This, in a way, was what we really wanted to do.

It seemed the only time we didn't fight was when we slept. There hadn't been another repeat of the night I'd used Seth as a pillow, and I think that ticked him off.

I strolled across the mats, catching the tail end of what Seth was saying to the pretty little half with eons of red hair and a chest that made me feel like I wore a training bra.

"Maybe after practice I'll show you my balls of—"

I chucked the water bottle at the back of Seth's head. He spun around and caught it before it connected. Gasping, the girl stepped back and stared at me. I had a feeling that if I were anyone else, she'd pull my hair out.

"Not nice." Seth threw the bottle to the floor.

"Five minutes are up." I bounced back a few steps, grinning.

Cross, a half-blood who'd become a regular at the door, elbowed his friend. "Hundred dollars they end up in a fight to the death by week's end."

"Who do you think would win?" Will, another now familiar face, grinned.

"I'd put my bets on that one." Cross jerked his head at me.

I tossed my head back, smiling at Seth. "Me," I mouthed.

Seth looked bored.

Boobs stopped twirling her hair for five seconds. "Oh no, I'd say the First would come out on top."

My smile faded, and I decided to ignore them. I turned to Seth. "Ready, *sweetheart*?"

He moved to stand in front of me, his back to

his—our—groupies. "I'm always ready for you, *cuddle bunny*."

My hand slipped past his block, slamming hard into his solar plexus. He staggered backward, grunting. "Moving a little slow there, Apollyon?"

Not to be outdone in front of the growing fan base by the door, he tapped into the elements. *Jerk-face,* I thought. The first gust of wind missed me only by an inch, but the second was so far off that I stopped to laugh. The third punched me square in the chest. I hit the mats hard but rolled to my feet before he could pin me down. We went at it until we broke for lunch. Seth liked eating with the students. It provided more chances for his head to grow bigger.

Cross and Will invited us to a party they were throwing Saturday night. "It'd be awesome if you guys could come," said Cross. "The pures will be doing their own thing, so no one will be checking on us."

The pures had been doing their own thing every night. Even five floors up, I could hear their raucous laughter in the wee hours of the morning. Thinking about that soured my mood. I wondered if *he* was one of the pures partying it up.

Seth thought the party sounded like a great idea. So did Boobs. I wasn't so sure, because the secondhand hot flashes I'd caught from Seth had been bad enough from a distance. I really didn't want to experience them in the same room. At the end of our afternoon practice outdoors, Seth caught my hand before I could take off without him.

"What?" I desperately wanted a long, hot shower.

Uncaring of the cold mud covering every square inch of my clothes, he pulled me toward him. "You have to come to the party with me."

I arched a brow at him. "I didn't say I wasn't going."

"You didn't say you were, and you've been grumpy all afternoon."

"That's because I'm stuck with you, day and night."

"I don't believe that." Seth's gaze flicked up and behind me, and then he inched me closer. I braced myself by putting my hand on his shoulder, but he smiled down at me—a different kind of smile, one he usually reserved for girls like Boobs and Elena. Sudden wariness shifted through me, ratcheted up to the tenth degree when he reached out with his free hand and cupped my chin.

My pulse skyrocketed. "What are you—?"

Seth smoothed his thumb over my lower lip, sending a weird mix of shivers through me. His stare locked onto mine, and the yellow of his eyes flared. "You have mud on your lip."

"Oh." I wiped my hand over my mouth, twisting out of his embrace. "I have—"

Aiden stood under a statue of Apollo, appearing just as unmoving and fierce as the god. It took quite a lot for me not to turn and sock Seth in the face.

"Hey there." Seth stepped around me. "Checking out our training sessions, are you? Don't fret; I've been taking really good care of her."

I decided right then and there: the first thing I was going to do once I Awakened was zap Seth.

"I'm sure you have." Aiden's voice was cold.

Seth moved past Aiden, clapping him on the shoulder as he did so. "How are the Council sessions going? Changing the world?"

Aiden's gaze settled on Seth's hand and then slowly lifted to his face. Whatever Seth saw in his eyes must've told him to remove his hand as quickly as possible. Chuckling as if it amused him, Seth glanced back at me. "See you later, cuddle bunny."

What came out of his mouth made Aiden's eyes widen, but only made Seth laugh harder as he strolled back toward the campus.

"Hey," I said, grateful that mud *did* cover half of my flaming face.

Aiden shoved his hands into his white trousers. "I can see training with him is going as expected."

"I hate him, really I do."

"'Hate' is such a strong word."

My chin jerked up. "You'd understand if you had to spend five seconds with him."

His gray eyes settled on my face, then my lips—lips that he'd seen Seth touch. "I guess so."

"So, why are you here?" I sounded harsh, but I was bristling at the coldness in his eyes and still licking the emotional wounds Aiden had sliced open.

"I haven't seen you in a few days, so I was actually checking in on you."

I felt warm despite the brisk air and hated myself for it. "Why?"

He shrugged. "I'm not allowed to?"

Secretly, my heart was jumping around happily at the idea of Aiden searching me out. My brain, on the other hand, brutally ordered me to walk away. I stayed. "I guess so."

"Walk you back?"

"Is that okay—I mean, no one will care that a pure is walking with a half? I don't see many of them doing so here." I paused, frowning. "Actually, I never see any pures talk to halfs here."

"Minister Telly is a bit archaic in the way the Council and the Covenant are run here. He wants things to be as if centuries of change have not occurred—a complete separation of breeds and races."

We started back toward the main house, together. "So that's why I haven't seen any mortals here."

Aiden nodded. "I think Minister Telly would go completely back to the old ways, to a time when our kind devoted every aspect of our lives to the gods. He doesn't even believe we should have any contact with mortals, not even through compulsion."

"Well, how does he expect to build up his half-blood army of daimon killers?" He gave me a straight look. It hit me. "He doesn't think there should be any half-bloods, does he?"

"He thinks that pures should be able to refrain from the carnal activities that lead to little half-bloods being made, and that we should be able to defend ourselves against the daimons."

I knocked back a mud-encased strand of hair. "Then what would you all do without servants? Actually take care of yourselves?"

He stared at the cloudy sky. "There are enough half-bloods in the world now to carry the pures through several generations. After that, I don't know what Telly would do."

"So, he wants to see all half-bloods enslaved? Nice. I knew there was a reason why I thought he was a giant douchebag. My judgment isn't as bad as I thought it was."

Aiden glanced down at me, a curious expression on his striking face. "Why would you think your judgment is off?"

I looked at him pointedly.

He pursed his lips and nodded stiffly. "Got it."

We continued on in silence for a few minutes. "So…how do you like it here?"

I wet my lips, thinking about Hector. "I miss…home."

Aiden continued to stare up at the overcast sky. "I miss it, too."

I drifted closer to him as we neared the Council building. I told myself that was normal. Aiden was my friend—only a friend. "This whole place makes me uncomfortable. I just wish I could get on with my hearing and be done with it. It's stupid that I have to be here all this time, when my hearing isn't even scheduled until the end of the session. Anyway, how have the hearings been?"

"Long. The Councils spend more of the time arguing than anything else."

That didn't surprise me. "Have they talked about halfs turning yet?"

His expression suddenly emptied. "That discussion provokes the most arguments, but anyway, what are you planning to do with your evening?"

"What am I planning to do?" I tipped my head back and sighed. "Shower."

Aiden laughed, sending a flurry of warm and fluttering feelings through my stomach. It'd felt like years since I'd heard him laugh. "You are such a mess right now."

I sighed pitifully. "I know. I think I have mud in my mouth."

"Well, I might have something that'll make you feel better." He reached into his pocket and pulled out a slender black tube about four inches long.

"What is that?"

Aiden smiled as he held it out from his body. "They've been working on new weapons since the discovery of halfs being turned. This is what they came up with."

"A black tube? Wow."

His smile turned into a grin. "Just watch." His fingers moved to the end of the tube, pressing down on a small button. Titanium blades shot out from each side. Aiden shook his wrist and the blade on the right side extended and curved in.

My eyes went wide. “Whoa. I like.”

He laughed. “I know how much you like things that stab. Here.” He handed me the blade. “But be careful. The ends are wicked sharp.”

I took the weapon, holding it reverently. It was heavier than I expected, but still manageable. My fingers curved on the cool matter of the center. One end had been finished down to a sharp point, while the other reminded me of a sickle. Why had they shaped the blade this way?

Then I felt stupid for not realizing right off the bat. Cringing, I pointed to the sickle end. “This is for taking off heads, isn’t it?”

“Yeah, we can't all harness akasha like Seth. And even he can’t zap every daimon half. Using akasha soaks up energy, so he can only use it when he really needs to.”

“Oh.” I made a wide-sweeping motion, grinning in spite of the messy business it represented. “I wonder what it will be like after I Awaken. If he’ll be able to use akasha easier.”

“I don’t know.” Aiden eyed the blade warily. “Probably something you should ask Seth.”

I remembered what Lucian had said about Seth pulling from me once I Awakened. “He’s going to suck me dry, probably.” The moment those words left my mouth I froze. Mom had said that. Was that what would happen?

Aiden noted my sudden stillness. “You okay?”

I blinked. “Yeah, I’m fine.” I pressed the little button on the end of the metal tube. The sickle side straightened before both ends collapsed back into the tube. I handed it back to Aiden, forcing a casual smile. “Thanks for letting me see that.”

"No problem." We walked a while in silence before he spoke again. "You sure you're all right?"

"Yep," I said, promising myself that Seth and I would have a conversation very soon.

Aiden stepped in front of me, opening the door to the main house. Inside, we stuck to the less-traveled areas as we made our way to the stairwell. We passed another one of those damn paintings with the torch, but this one had something written in ancient Greek.

"Hey, you read ancient Greek, right?"

Aiden halted in front of me and turned around. "Yes."

I pointed one dirty finger at the painting. "What does this say?"

He stepped closer. "It reads 'Order of Thanatos.'"

"I know that from somewhere." I crossed my arms. "What's up with all the Thanatos stuff here?"

He brushed messy waves off his forehead. "I really don't know what the fascination is, but the Order was a mystic group that existed centuries ago. It's in the Myths and Legends book I gave you."

"Well, that's currently being used as a doorstop in my dorm."

Aiden grinned at that, and I realized we hadn't argued or said anything mean to each other. This was progress. "The group died out centuries ago. I don't remember much about them, but they were pretty extreme about tradition and the old ways."

I thought about the tattoos Instructor Romvi and Minister Telly shared. "What do you think it means if someone has a tattoo of Thanatos's symbol?"

"Nothing probably, since a lot of us have tattoos of various symbols."

"You don't." As soon as the words left my mouth, I regretted them.

His eyes turned from gray to silver in a heartbeat. I imagined he was remembering how I would know if he had a tattoo hidden somewhere.

"I'm sorry," I whispered.

"It's okay." Aiden stepped back, his eyes dropping to my lips again, then back up.

What passed between us in those tense moments could've caught the whole damn building on fire. A yearning—deep and powerful—sprung alive. My fingers dug into my own skin, but it did nothing to dampen the desire to be close to him, to be in his arms. I thought I saw the same look on his face.

I squeezed my eyes shut, letting the mad desire wreak havoc on my heart. Aiden was gone when I reopened them. Pressing my lips together, I headed up the stairwell used by the servants since I was sure Aiden had taken the main one, and being stuck with him in a stairwell...well, my overheated imagination supplied possible scenarios that would never happen. I rounded the fifth landing, almost plowing through a servant coming through the door to my floor.

"Sorry! I should have—"

The half-blood from the first day here—the servant with eyes that seemed so familiar, stared down at me, incredibly alert. A second passed before he jerked his chin down and hurried past me. I spun around, gripping the handrail. "Hey!"

He stopped.

I went down a step. "Do I know you from somewhere?" No answer.

"I know you can talk—you especially." I inched down one more step. "You don't look like the rest." He whipped around so fast I leaned backward. His eyes searched my face, but he still didn't say anything. I took a deep breath. "Your eyes aren't glassed over like…like most of the servants here."

His head cocked to the side, and he came up a step.

I held my hands up, my heart pounding. "I'm not going to say anything. I'm totally Team Half-Blood. Are there others like you, others that aren't all doped up?"

Probably not the best word choice, but he nodded.

I mulled that over, studying his features. He may've been handsome before the servant's life took a toll on him, but I kept going back to his eyes. They were such a warm brown. "Why won't you talk to me?" I made a face. "Why won't any of you talk to me?"

His hand clenched the rail, knuckles bleaching.

"Okay. Anyway." I swallowed nervously. Were the servants up here unstable? "You look familiar to me."

That seemed to be the wrong thing to say, because he backed off.

"Wait—just wait a second." Once again, he stopped and watched me, lips thinned into a tight line. "What's your name?"

The door opened and Marcus's voice rang out. "Alex, is that you in the stairwell?"

The servant's eyes narrowed, then he disappeared down the stairs. Groaning in frustration, I pulled myself up the last couple of steps. "Yeah, it's me."

"Who are you talking to?"

I shook my head, sliding past him. "No one."

CHAPTER SEVENTEEN

Red meat and politics didn't agree with one another.

"Marcus, things have changed, but in some aspects, things have not." Lucian twirled a glass of wine between his elegant fingers. "Minister Telly's stance on separation versus integration is gaining ground."

"Only because he believes that the gods are among us." Marcus leaned forward, voice low. "Telly's a fanatic—always has been."

Lucian sipped his wine. "I agree with you, but sadly, most do not."

"I'd like to believe that most see the error in his thinking." Laadan sat across from me, her hair pulled up into an elaborate twist. The silky, pale blue dress she wore was to die for. "We are on the brink of change. The Breed Order must also change."

I stabbed my steak, watching the juices run out of it. It sucked to sit here and be expected to not say anything. I could only imagine the words coming out of Seth's mouth if he were here, but he was MIA.

I kind of missed him.

A plate of tiramisu slid in front of me. Politics forgotten, I glanced at the gray-eyed pure sitting beside me. Whoever had designed the seating chart needed to be killed. "Thanks," I murmured.

Aiden nodded and went back to following the conversation. I dug my spoon in the bowl and tried not to read too much into his gesture.

"Nadia and I will do everything to ensure that the Breed Order is changed," said Lucian. "But I'm afraid there are many who plot against change and will stop at nothing to see that things remain the same."

I choked on my dessert, and everyone stopped to look at me.

"Sorry," I gasped, waving my hand in front of my face.

Lucian frowned. "Are you all right, dear?"

"You…you want to see the Breed Order changed?"

"Of course," he responded. "It is time that half-bloods have representation on the Council. Just a few short hours ago I was telling Seth that with you two, we are closer to that change than ever before. It will not be us, the pure-bloods, who bring up such wondrous things. It will be you and Seth."

My brows inched up my forehead.

Lucian patted my hand. "Pure-bloods like Telly believe that the gods would favor the road back to the old way."

I stared down at Lucian's pale hand, unable to let go of the innate suspicion I felt when it came to him. He patted my hand once more and smiled. "Dear, have you put any thought into what you will be wearing to the ball next week?"

"What?" I had no idea what he was talking about.

"The annual Fall Ball? You are invited, which is a great honor for you and Seth. You two will be the first half-bloods to be in attendance. You must find something decent to wear." He glanced across the table. "Laadan, would you help her?"

She nodded. "Of course."

Ball, what ball? I glanced around the table, bewildered. Aiden looked slightly amused at the idea of me attending their ball. I scowled.

"Then it is settled." Lucian turned back to Marcus, already forgetting about me. "Have you received any word from the dean at South Dakota?"

Marcus shook his head. "It was a student who'd been turned—a half-blood. The pure wasn't killed."

How in the world did they just jump from politics to a ball, and now to daimon attacks? And here I'd thought *I* had the attention span of an ant on Red Bull.

Aiden leaned forward. "So, each Covenant has had an attack, but the Council believes that none of these events are related?"

I picked up my spoon, pretending not to listen.

Lucian reclined back in his chair, studying Aiden. "We are not so foolish to believe that the daimons do not have something up their sleeves, but what? They cannot truly believe they can take on the Covenants?"

Aiden's fingers tensed around the stem of his glass. "Haven't they already tried, Minister? The only things I've heard the Council discuss are what drinks will be served at the Ball, whether or not a new Covenant should be opened in the Midwest, and other insignificant items."

Lucian eyed him over the rim of his glass. "For someone who shows no interest in his Council seat, you are very opinionated about how the sessions are proceeding."

Two bright spots appeared on Aiden's cheeks. I felt the immediate urge to defend him. "He has a point, you know."

Four sets of eyes turned on me. Crap. "Look at what happened at home. They got past our Guards and…and killed people. They are planning something—something big. Shouldn't the Council be concerned with that instead of a stupid dance?"

Marcus glared at me. "If you are finished with your dinner, you are excused."

I slammed my spoon down. "If you don't want my opinion, then maybe you shouldn't talk about these things in front of me."

"Point taken." Marcus met my furious stare. "Good evening, Alexandria."

Embarrassed at being dismissed like that, I jerked to my feet. None of the pures seated in the elaborate dining hall looked up as I passed them, and neither did the servants removing trays and replenishing drinks. I scanned the hall, but the one servant I had an interest in finding wasn't bussing tables.

There wasn't anything for me to do besides go back to my room, and I'd rather shove my head in an oven than go back there. I roamed the halls aimlessly, as unnoticed as all half-bloods were in this magnificent hellhole.

I missed North Carolina even more—and Caleb. Gods, I wished I could hop online and chat with him like we'd planned. I blinked away the hot tears and stepped into a large, musty-smelling room—a library.

Strange that I would find myself in a library, since reading really wasn't my thing. A few lonely chairs sat beside the antique lamps, but they looked like they were covered with dust. I made my way through the stacks, trailing my fingers over the spines of books. Maybe I'd find one of those smutty historical romance novels—the kind Mom used to read.

Not likely.

Nothing in the room looked like it'd been touched in years. I couldn't even begin to decipher most of the titles. But I continued on, anything to avoid the heartache that thoughts of Caleb always brought on. I tried pronouncing the titles but gave up after five. Sighing, I tucked back my hair and crouched down.

"Unpronounceable. Unpronounceable. Unpronounceable." I tipped my head to the side. "Really unpronounceable. This one can't even be a real word. Oh, come—" My fingers stilled over a thick black book with gold lettering. I had no idea what the words were, but I recognized the symbol on the spine. "Downward torch..." I wiggled the book free.

A fine shiver coursed down my body. My head jerked up and I scanned the library. There was no mistaking the feeling of being watched.

"Alexandria, are you in here?"

I let go of the book and straightened. "Laadan?"

She appeared at the edge of the stacks. In the dim light and pale dress, she looked ethereal. A tentative smile pulled at her full lips. "I'm not interrupting anything, am I?"

"No. I was just looking for something to read, but everything is in ancient Greek."

Her gray eyes dropped to the books. "I don't know why Telly stocks the library with books most of us can't read."

I stepped closer but kept a decent distance between us. "I thought all of you pures read the old language."

Laadan laughed softly. "All of us are taught it in school, but I promptly forgot it. Most of us can't."

Except Aiden, I thought. Thinking of him reminded me of the first time I'd seen Laadan, standing beside Leon and bargaining with Marcus to allow me to stay. "I never got a chance to thank you."

"For what?"

"You convinced Marcus to give me a chance. If you hadn't been there, I don't think he would've allowed me back into the Covenant." I bit my bottom lip and took another step toward the end of the stacks. "Why did you speak up for me? Did you know...what I was?"

She smoothed her hands down the front of her dress as she glanced toward the door. "Did I know you would become an Apollyon? No, but in a way, I did know you."

More than just a little curious, I walked out of the stacks.

"When I was your age, I attended the Covenant in North Carolina. Your mother and I were very close. To this day, I wish we hadn't grown apart, that I'd stayed in North Carolina. Maybe things would have turned out differently."

Surprise left me speechless. Laadan smiled again. At once, the nostalgic looks she'd get when she looked at me made sense.

She nodded. "You look so much like Rachelle did when she was your age. You're a bit wilder, but I think that's your father in you."

My chest tightened. "You—you knew my father?"

"Yes." She drifted closer, lowering her voice. "Much better choice and fit for Rachelle than Lucian, but your mother didn't really have a choice. A lot of people will tell you that she met your father after marrying Lucian, but that wasn't true. She knew your father first—she *loved* your father long before Lucian entered the picture."

"But...I don't understand. She married Lucian when she was young, and it was at least five years before I was born."

There was a far-off look in her eyes as she recalled a past I was not familiar with. "Then you can imagine the scandal when you were born, but don't let that tarnish what your parents had. Their love was the kind written about in those silly books your mom used to read. She and Alexander started off as just friends—the three of us actually—but over the years their friendship grew into something much deeper."

Hearing my father's name spoken felt strange and oddly wonderful—as if he was a real person who'd existed once upon a time.

"Rachelle tried to do the right thing. She stayed away from your father as long as she could after she married Lucian—marrying Lucian was what was expected from her. She was determined to follow the rules of our society, but love like theirs can't be denied for too long, no matter how wrong it is." She paused, eyes widening. "Alexandria, are you okay?"

"Yeah." I shook my head. "I'm sorry. It's just Mom never talked about him. Like ever. I had no idea it was this epic love affair."

She pressed her lips together and turned away. Walking off toward one of the lamps with green and gold-stained glass, she shook her head. "I think it was too hard for your mother to talk about him after everything."

I followed her. "What was he like?"

"Alexander?" Laadan glanced over her shoulder with a sad smile. "A good man, loyal to a fault, very handsome, and Rachelle was his entire world." She turned around, folding slender arms across her waist. "You look so much like her, but you have his personality. When Marcus read off your files in his office that day, all I could think of was Alexander. He's incredibly strong-willed, a bit reckless, and wild."

The way she talked about Alexander, as if he were still here, made me wonder if she'd had feelings for him. "I wonder what he'd think of me." I laughed self-consciously. "That sounded so stupid."

"No, not at all. He'd be proud of you, Alexandria. I hope you know that."

"Well, I am an Apollyon."

She reached out, patting my arm. "Not because of what you'll become, but because of who you already are."

The sting of tears hit my eyes, which seemed so weak. I pulled away, fiddling with the chain on the lamp. "I don't know about that. I should've done something when Mom left the Covenant. And I really shouldn't have gone after her when she'd turned, or at least, when Caleb showed up, I should've gone back to the Covenant, but I didn't. I mean, what was I thinking?"

"You did what you believed was right." She drifted to my side, resting her hands on the old, scuffed-up table the lamp sat on. "Rachelle probably would've smacked you for doing something so incredibly dangerous, but you made sure she had peace."

"You think so?"

"Yes."

A little bit of weight lifted off my chest, but my breath still sawed in and out. "I've messed up, really bad, a lot of times." I squeezed the chain between my fingers. "I don't think he'd be so proud."

Laadan placed her hand over mine. "He would be proud. You followed your heart when it came to Rachelle, and yes, sometimes the decisions you've made have not been the right ones, but you know that. You've learned from them. And owning up to Telly about your role in what happened to your friend? That was brave and mature."

I looked up at her—a pure-blood. This all seemed strange to me. It took me a couple of minutes to make sense of my own mixed-up thoughts and emotions over what she'd told me of my mother and father. "How did she meet him—my dad? There aren't many mortals around the Covenants. Did he work on Bald Head?"

Laadan's smile seemed off, nervous almost. She pushed away from the table, running her hands over her arms. "She met him in North Carolina."

There was more to it than that, which filled me with curiosity. So, Mom had loved a mortal for many moons. They weren't the first or last, I imagined. "What was he doing there? How did he die?"

A loud crash caused us both to jump. I whirled around, expecting to see a crap ton of books on the floor.

Laadan laughed nervously. "I forget that there are things here that move unseen."

I looked at her sharply. "What do you mean? Spirits?"

She blinked and laughed again. "Yes, spirits. I'm a bit superstitious. This library doesn't help, creepy as it is. I think one of the shelves collapsed in the stack." Laadan came to my side, scanning the rows quickly—and I thought a bit anxiously. "It happens from time to time. Anyway, if you are anything like Rachelle, you love ice cream and pie."

I swung back to her. "Vanilla—"

"And pumpkin pie," she finished, smiling. "I know where we can score some. Interested?"

My mouth watered. "I'm always interested in anything food related."

"Good." She threaded her arm through mine. "Let's go gorge ourselves until we swear off food."

At the door, I shivered and looked over my shoulder. The feeling of eyes boring into my back was uncanny, but no one was there—no one that I could see.

My father would be proud of me, even after all the stupid

things I'd done—and probably would still do? It seemed hard to believe, but Laadan had known him and she had no reason to lie to me.

"Alex, are you even paying attention to me?"

"Huh?" I blinked, glancing up from my rock. We were in a wooded area off the labyrinth, a few hours into our afternoon practice. "Yeah, I heard you. Dodge. Run. Stuff."

Seth folded his arms.

"What?" I stood and brushed off my rear.

"I think you just fell asleep. That would hurt my feelings—if I had any."

"Sorry. You're kind of boring me."

"Well, okay then. Let's get to work." Seth held up his hand, like he was going to throw a baseball. A blue ball of flames formed in his open palm. He released the tiny ball, launching it straight at my head.

I ducked easily. "Boring."

Seth let go of another ball, but this time he sent it at my feet. I jumped onto the rock and yawned loudly. A devilish grin pulled at his lips as he slowly approached me. My foot caught him in the shoulder as soon as he came within reach. He retaliated by sending two balls of flames—one at my head and one at my legs. It took some fancy footwork to avoid them, but I did and I still managed to stay atop the rock.

I stuck my tongue out. "You can do better than that."

He threw up his hands and a gust of wind hit me square in the chest. There was nothing I could do to block something like that.

"Remember to tuck and roll," Seth called out, laughter in his voice.

If I hadn't been flying through the air, I would have flipped him off. However, I did remember to tuck and roll. I hit the cool patch of grass shoulders first. I didn't give my body a chance to recognize the impact. Rolling onto my feet, I suspected Seth would be making his move.

I was right.

A ball of fire grazed my head as I darted to the side. We went at this until he hit me with the element of air, knocked me down, and didn't let go. Pinned to the dirty ground, I glared up at him.

"Get up," he ordered, standing above me.

"I can't get up. And you know that."

Seth cocked his head to the side and sighed. "This is getting old, Alex. You excel at every aspect of fighting—not as good as me, but who am I kidding? No one is better than me."

I rolled my eyes. "You like to hear yourself talk, don't you?"

"Why, yes. Yes, I do."

"That's why you don't have any friends."

"And the last time I checked, I'm *your* only friend." My jaw clicked shut. Score one for Seth.

"But that's not the topic of discussion. We are discussing the fact that you cannot break through the air element, and it's the most common element pures and daimons can wield. That's a problem."

"Gee, you think so?"

He increased the pressure until it felt like someone was sitting on my chest. I squirmed, but that was about all. "What did I tell you about the elements, Alex?"

"Something about…magic being…all in the head," I gasped.

"No. The elements are very real—obviously. You have to

force yourself through it, Alex. Push." I still didn't get what he meant by *push*, but he kept telling me to do it every time this happened. "If you can't push through it then you're going to be a daimon snack again. They're going to smell that aether in you and go crazy. You sure you want to be a Sentinel?"

Now he was just pissing me off. "Shut up, Seth."

He stepped over me, planting his legs on either side of my prone body. Crouching down, he brought his face close to mine. "Remember, you're not fast food to them; you're like the best steak this side of the continent."

"You say that…like it's a good thing."

Seth smiled like he knew some kind of private joke. "Concentrate. You need to concentrate on moving forward. Picture yourself sitting up, Alex."

I stared at him.

He sighed, rolling his eyes. "Close your eyes and picture yourself sitting up."

Cursing under my breath, I did as he asked. I closed my eyes and pictured myself sitting up. "Okay."

"Focus on that image. Hold it in your mind. Focus."

I did as he asked, but all I managed was to get one leg to bend. And that exhausted me. "This is ridiculous. A daimon would've already killed me by now."

"A daimon would've already bitten into your skin by now." His eyes fastened onto mine, refusing to let go. "But you know that, don't you?"

A ragged breath leaked from my tightly pressed lips. My skin practically burned at the reminder, and Seth knew it.

"How many times were you tagged, Alex?" Seth reached down and brushed the hair off my neck. "I can count at least three on this side of your neck."

"Stop," I hissed.

His fingers moved over the scars on the other side. "I see three more, Alex." Then his fingers dipped under the collar of my thermal, brushing over more scars. "How many here? Two or three…or even more than that? Want to add more? No? Then sit up."

I tried because I badly wanted to knock him upside the head. Every muscle in my body tensed, but I still couldn't break through the hold. "Stop it now."

Frustration flared in his eyes. "How many are there on your arms?"

"Stop it!" Something shifted in me, a sense of deep awareness. Suddenly, everything around me seemed acute and vivid. The overcast sky was more muddled, the cawing of the crows sounded closer, and the golden hue of Seth's skin became a pearly luster.

"Then sit up! Break this hold, Alex!"

A couple of things happened next.

I felt the rage snap deep inside my core—a tightly coiled ball of energy unraveled. It was so strong, so vibrant, that I imagined it looked like the cord I'd seen wrap around Seth and me the first time we'd touched.

Seth leaned in, going for my arm this time. Too close, he was *way* too close. The coil raised, my heart stopped, and something—the rock I'd stood on—blew up.

The shattering boulder startled Seth enough that he let go of the crushing wind. Every muscle in my body had been straining to sit up. So, when he let go, I flew up so fast I rammed right into him.

The impact of my body knocked Seth flat on his back. His arms immediately swept around me.

I wasn't sure what that had to do with practice.

We remained that way for a second, both of us struggling

to breathe. I couldn't process it or even begin to understand what had happened.

"Alex…?"

I pushed off his chest and stared down at him. The marks of the Apollyon shifted over his skin crazy fast. I'd never seen them move quite like that before. "Um…"

Seth's eyes were wild, practically glowing. "I didn't do that."

"Me, neither."

"Bull." His expression was full of amazement.

I swallowed. "Okay. Maybe I did."

"What did it feel like inside, when it happened?"

"I don't know, kind of like a coiling feeling in my stomach."

His lips parted, working slowly. "This can't be possible, but it is. You're Awakening already. I don't believe it, but it explains how you've been able to sense my emotions."

"What?" I started to sit up, but his hands dropped to my hips, holding me in place. "What do you mean I'm Awakening? Am I like ahead of schedule or something?"

Seth tried to laugh, but it came out more like a gasp. "No. I don't know. I mean, who knows? Right? The other two Apollyons were never around each other before Solaris Awakened. He only sensed Solaris *after* she Awakened. Maybe…maybe this is what happens. Has anything like this happened before?"

"Yeah, I blow up rocks in my spare time. Jeez. No." I started to move again. "Seth, you can let go."

He smiled the kind of smile that warmed his features. "I don't think I'm ready to. And get that freaked look off your face. This isn't a bad thing, Alex. No—nope, not at all. This is good. We can start working on your powers and…"

I tuned him out. The freaked-out look on my face had

nothing to do with blowing up rocks. I had long come to terms with the fact that I'd be some weapon of mass destruction one day. The look came from the fact our bodies were touching in all the strategic places bodies liked to touch.

"Alex, are you listening to me?"

"Yes." I stared at the runes gliding down his neck. When they reached his pulse they throbbed. I shifted my weight. A raw ache hit me hard. I wanted to touch them—needed to touch them. Something, I was sure, would happen if I did.

"You are not paying attention to me." Seth sighed. The movement brought us closer. "You know," Seth was saying, "this opens up so many possibilities. We—"

I reached out my right hand and touched the rune on his neck, where his pulse pounded, with just the tip of one finger. A burst of crackling blue light flared. The light split, one strain shooting through the tip of my fingers, the other pulsating over his neck. Pinpricks of pain burst across my hand, searing and intense.

Seth's back bowed as his fingers dug into me. Under my left hand, his chest rose and fell rapidly. His eyes snapped open, wide and unseeing. The glyphs on his face shifted shapes and changed color, becoming a shade of blue that mirrored the sky seconds before dusk.

The air popped and fizzed as the blue light spilled onto the ground, and out of that blue light, another shone much brighter, more intense. An amber cord radiated from the glyph on his neck, quickly twining itself around my finger, twisting over my hand, up my wrist...trying to connect us once again.

CHAPTER EIGHTEEN

I jerked my hand back and it followed me, an amber line arch-ing through the space between us. I needed to get up—get away, and put as much distance between us as possible, because this was weird as hell. "I—"

The amber cord vanished, as did the blue light. Seth fell back to the ground, letting out a ragged sigh.

"Seth? Are you okay?" I clutched my throbbing hand to my chest. Seth wasn't moving, wasn't talking. Fear blossomed in my chest. What if I'd killed him? I knew I'd said I wanted to kill him—I'd said it a lot—but I hadn't meant it. Not really. "Seth, please say something."

An eternity passed before his eyes opened. "That…felt wonderful."

A sudden wave of dizziness crashed over me, and my stomach dropped.

Seth's head lolled to the side, his smile lazy and faint. "I'm pretty sure I could stop a truck with my hand right now."

"Okay…" I took a shallow breath. "That tells me nothing.

And I really want to know what happened when I touched your marks—"

Seth twisted up, rolling me onto my back in one fluid motion. Hovering above me, he used one arm to support himself. Only our legs touched, but it still felt like…well, like every part of us was still touching. "Angel, that's like Apollyon foreplay right there."

"For real?"

"For real." He reached out and brushed a strand of hair off my cheek.

I swallowed. "I didn't know that. My bad, but that's kind of weird. Usually takes more with most guys." I had no idea why I just said that.

Seth's fingers trailed over my cheek, down to my chin. "Does it, Angel? Well, what does it take?"

This was probably a conversation not to have with Seth, especially when he was practically lying on top of me. "I think you of all people would know."

His hand slipped to my neck. "I have a secret to tell you. It's not Apollyon foreplay; I'm just messing with you. I have no clue what that was."

"Gods, I hate you." Flushed with embarrassment, I knocked his hand away.

Seth caught my hand and sat up, pulling me along with him. "How do you feel?"

"Fine. I'm just a little dizzy."

He nodded. "I'll tell you what, my skin still tingles. Man—that was one hell of a rush. I've never felt anything like it." He turned my hand over, palm up. "We should try it—*what the hell?*" His fingers slid over my palm as he studied it, then his eyes widened. "Oh. Wow."

"What?"

He held my hand up between us. "Look."

I squinted at my hand. "I don't see anything." Sighing, he flipped my hand over, and my jaw hit the ground. A faint blue line marked the center of my palm with a smaller line through it. It would've looked like a cross, except the horizontal line was slanted.

"Oh. My. Gods." I jerked my hand away, scrambling back. "I have a rune on my hand. It's an Apollyon rune, isn't it?"

Seth rested his hands on his knees. "I think so. I have one like that."

"But why is it still there? Why is it there at all?" I flipped my palm over several times, shook it, but the faint blue tattoo was still there. "You can see it, right? Like right now, you can see it?"

"Yes. It hasn't faded." Seth leaned forward, catching my hand. "Stop shaking it like it's a damn Etch A Sketch. That doesn't make them disappear."

I met his eyes with my own wide ones. "What makes them go away? Yours go away. They're not there all the time. I haven't Awakened, have I? Wait—what if I have? Need or want something, and I'll see if I want it, too. Go ahead. Try it."

His brows flew up. "Whoa. Alex, calm down. Take a deep breath. I mean it. Take a nice, long and deep breath."

I inhaled and let it out slowly. "That didn't help."

He looked like he wanted to laugh. "Alex, stop freaking out. You haven't Awakened. I would know, and while I do feel a somewhat different—"

"How do you feel different?"

"I feel…more charged, but you haven't Awakened."

I exhaled roughly. "Then what happened?"

Seth's face softened and all traces of smugness and coldness vanished, revealing a youthful, earnest quality I'd never seen before. "I think…it's just another product of the connection between us. Minutes before, you used the earth element—earth, Alex. That's one of the most powerful elements. And I don't know how you did that, but I think you were probably feeding off me. That makes sense."

"It does?"

He nodded. "I think so. I also think that's what happened when you touched me—by the way, why did you touch me?"

I glanced down at my mark, blushing. "I…don't know."

"You really don't know why?"

I scowled. "No."

"Whatever." Seth didn't sound like he believed me. "All right, this is nothing to freak out about, right?"

"Right."

"Nothing has changed, really, and everything is okay. You following me? Everything is okay. We're in this together."

In that instant, he reminded me of Aiden—when I'd found out about being an Apollyon and Aiden had coached me through it. I climbed to my feet. My legs felt like rubber. "Are we done with practice?"

He stayed on his knees, lifting his head. "Yes."

I nodded and turned away, but Seth called out to me. "Alex, I don't think we should tell anyone about this, all right?"

"Okay." I could agree with that. I started back to the main house, mind reeling. I looked down at my hand. I had a mark of the Apollyon already.

One that didn't seem to fade.

During dinner, I excused myself after the first course. They did the four-course meal thing and I usually stuck around for dessert, but tonight was different. My mind was on my tingling palm.

Aiden eyed me curiously but didn't remark on my lack of appetite. However, I felt Seth stand and follow me out of the dining hall.

"Are you feeling okay?" asked Seth.

My gaze flicked up to his eyes. They looked abnormally bright tonight, like two mini suns burning. "Yeah, I'm just not hungry."

He gave me a knowing look as he reached down and picked up my right hand. He turned it over. "It's still there."

I nodded. "I tried to wash it off earlier."

Seth gave a startled laugh. "Oh, Alex, you can't wash it off."

My cheeks flushed. "Yeah, I know that now."

He ran his thumb over the rune's straight line, eliciting a sharp gasp from me. I felt the butterfly touch all the way to the small bones in my fingers. I yanked my hand free and backed up.

His eyes narrowed on me. "What did you feel?"

I curled my hand, covering the rune. "It just felt weird."

Seth reached for my hand again, but I dodged him. He shot me an annoyed look. "What are you planning to do now?"

I debated on telling him it was none of his business. "I'm feeling a little keyed up. I think I'm going to work it off or something."

He smiled. "Want me to go with you?"

"No." I shook my head. "I need some time alone."

Surprisingly, Seth dropped it and went back into the dining hall. I rushed upstairs and grabbed my hoodie, then took off for the training arena.

It didn't take much for me to get worked up, swinging and kicking a dummy. Seth didn't prefer to work with them. He was into the whole contact thing.

Go figure.

I don't know how much time had passed as I beat the crap out of the dummy, but when I stopped, I was panting and covered in sweat. I rested my hands on my knees. The dummy swayed in front of me. Fighting had done nothing to get rid of the overall frustration of…*everything.*

I straightened and turned over my right hand.

The blue rune was faint but there. I stalked over to where I'd dropped my hoodie and pulled it on.

A fine shiver crept over me. Turning around, I scanned the empty training room. It was the same feeling I'd gotten the night I'd left Marcus's office. Like a warning, telling me I wasn't alone. I wasn't going to ignore it.

The overhead lights flickered once and then went out, plunging the room into darkness. I wished I had super-vision or something because I couldn't see crap. Not even where the door was, and I really wanted to get out of this room. All my senses were screaming at me to go. Something was wrong, something wasn't—

Air stirred behind me, lifting the damp hair at the base of my neck, caressing the skin with a lover's touch. I whipped around, striking out into nothing but air.

My breath came out harsh, my voice pitched high. "Who's there?"

Nothing…and then I heard, *"Alexandria, listen to me."*

The words—oh, gods, the words smoothed over my skin like the richest silk. My arms fell to my sides as my eyes drifted shut. A small part of my brain that was still working recognized the compulsion, but that thought flickered out.

I felt the air stir again. A hand slipped around the nape of my neck, a soft voice whispering in my ear. My thoughts flashed in and out until they were devoid of any meaning. Then they were filled with instructions the conscious part of me couldn't recognize, but I would follow nonetheless.

"Okay," I heard myself say in this dreamlike voice.

Vaguely, I was aware of the air stilling around me and the lights coming back on. I floated out of the training room. Outside, in the near frigid temperatures, maybe I'd just float right up into the night sky.

I think I'd like that.

I found myself standing at the mouth of the dark labyrinth. I was supposed to be here. My body knew that. I bent down slowly and untied my shoelaces. My fingers slipped over the knots a few times, but I finally got them and my socks off. I placed them side-by-side on the frozen ground. I pulled off my sweatshirt and folded it neatly. I placed that atop my shoes.

Then I entered the labyrinth, smiling as the cool air washed over my bare arms, still slick with sweat. I roamed aimlessly, having no clear purpose other than to keep walking until I was too tired to walk. That was what I was supposed to do—place one foot in front of the other.

It started snowing.

Beautiful, large flakes fell from the sky, landing on my arms. Each piece felt like it belonged there—like I belonged here. The grass crunched under my toes as I continued farther into the maze. Snow encased my hair, sticking to my cold skin. My breath puffed out in pockets of steam, eventually slowing.

Hours must have passed because each step became more difficult than the one before. I stumbled, hitting the hard ground on my knees and the palms of my hands. My skin looked strange beside the snow-covered ground. Blue? Not entirely blue, but like the veins under my skin were leaking, tinting my flesh with a faint violet hue.

It was so pretty.

I pushed to my feet and swayed off balance. I was tired, but I could make it a little farther. I kept walking. Well, tripping really. I couldn't feel my toes, and my skin felt pleasantly numb. Stumbling again, this time into an ice-cold statue, I slid down the marble, feeling the rougher edges pull at my skin. It should have hurt, but as I sat there, I realized I didn't feel anything.

Somehow, I was on my back, staring up at the winged statue. He looked down upon me, arm outstretched, palm open. I willed my arm to move, but it wouldn't lift. My gaze drifted beyond the statue as I drew in a shallow breath that didn't seem to fill my lungs. The sky was dotted with small flakes that eventually made their way down to me. My lids grew too heavy to stay open, and it was only seconds before the snow caked my lashes. I thought I heard a desolate cry in a beautiful language, but then there was nothing.

CHAPTER NINETEEN

"What was she doing out there?"

"I don't know. I find it hard to believe she somehow mistook it for summer! Why hasn't she woken up yet?"

The voices sounded familiar to me. My right palm burned. Everything burned actually—really freaking burned.

Someone moved something warm and heavy over me. It made my skin scream. "She'll be fine," a woman said. "She just needs rest."

"Needs rest?" That sounded like Seth, but he didn't sound right to me. His musical voice was pitched wrong. "She *was blue* when Leon brought her in."

Leon brought me in? From where? Why had I been blue? Blue didn't sound good.

"The girl is lucky. A few more minutes and she would have lost a finger or four, but she is fine," the woman said again, irritation lacing her words. "There is nothing more to be done."

Wait? What the hell? Lose fingers?

I heard a door shut, and then the bed dipped beside me. Someone brushed my hair back off my face. Seth. I tried to open my eyes, but they felt annoyingly heavy.

"Where did she say she was going when she left dinner?"

My heart sped up, recognizing Aiden's voice. Why couldn't I open my eyes? And why was I so damn tired?

"She said she was going to practice," answered Seth.

"And you let her go by herself?" That was my uncle speaking. Only he could sound so coldly displeased and yet cultured.

"I'm not her babysitter," snapped Seth. "She didn't want me to go with her."

"Alex shouldn't be roaming around here alone." Aiden's anger filled his voice. "Dammit, she knows better than this."

Seth snorted.

"Even though Alex is prone to idiotic behavior, I seriously doubt she's responsible for this one," said Aiden.

Gee, thanks, I thought sleepily. I kind of wished they'd all shut up so I could go back to sleep.

My skin didn't burn when I slept.

"She wouldn't go skipping through a maze dressed like it's summer and almost die from hypothermia," Aiden continued. "Someone did this to her."

"You're suggesting a compulsion?" Seth's voice lowered. "You know pures are forbidden from using compulsions on halfs who aren't indentured. Would one dare?"

"What do you think?" asked Aiden.

"I think I'm going to kill someone," Seth replied casually.

Marcus sighed. "I'll speak with Minister Telly first thing in the morning. He assured me there would be no trouble here."

They continued for a few moments, their voices drifting farther away as I fell back into the blissful oblivion where my skin felt normal. I awoke a little while later, shivering uncontrollably. The room was quiet and dark when I opened my eyes.

I wanted to get up and grab a thermal, but my muscles didn't want to cooperate. Whimpering, I fell back to the hard mattress and willed a nice heavy blanket to appear out of thin air. Too bad I didn't have any powers like that.

Suddenly, the bed shifted and a dark shadow leaned over me. If it weren't for the bright yellow eyes, I would've screamed. "How are you feeling?"

"I'm c-cold," I gasped out.

"They brought in extra blankets. You're still cold?"

"Uh-huh." My teeth chattered. I heard Seth sigh, and then I felt his hands sliding underneath me, rolling me onto my side. "W-what are you doing?"

"Getting you warm, since we already have every blanket known to mankind on this craptastic bed." He pulled me back against his chest and wrapped his arms around me. "Wow, you are cold. Like a little Popsicle."

I squeezed my eyes shut. "I wasn't s-suggesting this."

He rested his chin against the top of my head. "Do you have any better suggestions?"

"Yeah, g-go get more blankets?"

"That wouldn't be nearly as fun as this."

I didn't respond to that, because truthfully, Seth was really hot. Hot in a totally platonic, body-warming way. Then his leg slipped in between mine and my eyes snapped open. "S-Seth!"

"Just making sure you are warming up. Is it working?" Seth shifted his arms under the blanket, one hand finding the curve of my hip.

I bit down on my lip. Yes, I was warming up. "Alex?"

"Yeah?" I wiggled uncomfortably and stopped when

Seth's hand tightened on my hip. "What were you doing in the maze tonight with half your clothes off?"

"What?" I squeaked.

"You…don't remember?" Seth slipped his hand under the hem of my shirt. "Your stomach is ice cold."

And his hand was really warm. I told myself that was the reason why I didn't break his arm. "N-no, I don't k-know what you're talking about."

"Okay. Do you remember talking to me after dinner?"

What a stupid question. "Yes."

"Did you go to the training rooms?"

"Yeah."

"What happened after that, Alex?"

"I worked with the dummy for a little while and then…" I frowned. Then what? I remembered walking over to the corner and putting on my hoodie. "The lights went out."

"In the training room?"

I nodded, still concentrating. My memories floated just out of reach, like a word lost on the tip of my tongue. "I don't know."

Seth stiffened. "You don't remember anything else?"

There was a huge blank spot where nothing existed. I rolled onto my back, only making out his eyes in the darkness. "Can you fill me in on what happened?"

"I was kind of hoping you'd be able to do that, Alex. We don't know what happened. Leon found your shoes and hoodie at the beginning of the labyrinth. Obviously, that concerned him greatly. He found you in there, half-frozen."

"What? I didn't do that." I reached down and placed a hand on his creeping one. It was moving a little too far north. "Well, I don't remember doing that, and that sounds really stupid."

Seth's fingers curled beneath my ribs. "Do you remember talking to any pures?"

"No. I don't remember anything after the lights going out." I paused, feeling slightly nauseous as I picked up on Seth's suspicions. "Do…do you think a pure used compulsion on me?"

He didn't answer immediately. "Yes."

"But that doesn't make any sense. Why would a pure compel me to walk the maze? Of all the things they could compel me to do and they…" I closed my mouth. I had no idea what the pure had compelled me to do. Walking through the maze could have been just one part of it. Anything could've happened. I had no idea and that made me sick. Compulsion was a violation, pure and simple. It stripped a person's free will, and their ability to say no.

It was straight out mind-rape.

But why couldn't I remember what'd happened? I'd only been compelled once, and that had been when Aiden made me sleep the night they'd found me in the warehouse. I remembered everything about that.

"Alex?" Seth moved his hand out from underneath the blankets and cupped my face. My stomach kind of missed his hand. "Are you remembering something?"

"Do you think I was compelled to forget the compulsion? Is that even possible?"

"It is possible. A compulsion is limitless."

I swallowed. "I had clothes on, right? Just my shoes and sweatshirt were missing?"

"Yes." His voice sounded strained. "I think it's best that you don't go anywhere without someone being with you, Alex. I know you hate that idea—"

"They sent me out to freeze to death," I said, stunned by the realization. "I would've died if Leon hadn't found me."

"Like I said, I think it's best that you don't go anywhere without someone with you."

I wanted to punch someone. I also wanted to cry. I didn't like this helpless feeling, this not knowing. I drew in a breath and let it out slowly. "I want to know who did this."

"We'll find out. Trust me on that. But you need to get some rest now."

Sleep didn't seem like an option, but Seth rolled onto his back, bringing me along for the ride. I was too caught up in my own thoughts to protest his possessiveness. My head rested against his chest as I stared into the darkness.

Quiet as he was, I knew Seth didn't sleep that night either.

A few hours into light practice a day later, Council Guards arrived and stated that Minister Telly wanted to see me. Clearly only my presence had been requested, but Seth refused to leave my side.

The Council session had paused for lunch, and we were led to an elaborate office inside the Council building. I'd never seen so many gold-plated things in my life. What was left of my family was present: Marcus and Lucian. They were seated on luxurious leather chairs. I decided to stand, which meant Seth stood directly behind me.

Telly gazed out a circular window, a glass of dark wine in his hand. He turned around, his pale gaze flickering past me, narrowing on Seth. "Miss Andros, I apologize for interrupting your training, but I wanted to express my sincere relief to see that you were not permanently injured due to such a misfortunate event."

He didn't sound sincere. "Someone used a compulsion on me," I said. "I wouldn't consider that a *misfortunate event*."

"I would have to agree," Lucian said. "My stepdaughter is not given to flights of fancy."

Telly pushed away from the window, his eyes settling on my stepfather. "I would hope not, but I can assure you there is no one here who would be so audacious to use a compulsion against a guest of mine."

"Then what are you suggesting, Minister?" asked Marcus. Today he was dressed in a navy blue suit. I'd kill to see the man in jeans.

"I am as curious as you to find out how Miss Andros ended up in that predicament," Telly said. "I have my best Guards investigating the matter. Perhaps they will discover what truly happened."

"You say it like I'm somehow responsible for what happened," I said, which earned me a bland look from Telly.

"I know we are rather lax around here in regard to drinking." Telly took a leisurely sip of his wine. "Did you have anything to drink with your dinner?"

My mouth dropped open. "I wasn't drunk!"

"Alexandria." Marcus's head snapped in my direction. Turning back to the Minister, he smiled politely. "I can attest that Alexandria did not drink at dinner."

"Hmm? What about afterward?" asked Telly.

"I spoke with her afterward and she went straight to the training arena." Seth's annoyance with the whole thing radiated from him.

Telly's brows rose. "You'd cover for her, would you not? Since she is yours and your fates are so intricately tied together?"

"I'm not—"

"Are you calling me a liar?" Seth cut me off, his annoyance flipping right into fury.

Lucian stood, smoothing his robes. "Minister Telly, I trust you are taking this event seriously. If not, I cannot agree to keeping Alexandria here."

"She must give her statement at Council."

"She also must be kept safe, and that is the priority," replied Lucian. "Not her statement."

Telly took another drink, his pale gaze falling back to Seth and me. "Of course, I take her safety very seriously. After all, she is such a rarity, and we would not want anything to happen to the Council's precious Apollyon."

"*The Council's precious Apollyon,*" I spat, swinging out harder than I probably should. They hadn't been Seth's words, but he was the only target I had. He barely dodged me. "This 'precious Apollyon' is going to shove her foot so far up his—"

Seth caught my fist. "Alex, if you don't take it down a notch we're going to stop. I don't know why I agreed to spar with you when you're in this kind of mood."

Stepping back, I wiped my forearm across my forehead. "I loathe the way he speaks, the way he looks at us like he wished he could zap us into oblivion."

"And you shouldn't be practicing this hard," Seth continued as if he hadn't heard me. "You were an ice cube not too long ago. You need to take it easy."

"Stop babying me. I feel great." That wasn't a lie, even though the chilly air whipping through the clearing made me feel a little icky.

Seth sighed. He was getting really good at the sighing thing. This one said *I don't know what to do you with sometimes.*

"And he hates half-bloods. Did you know that?" I continued, lashing out with a fierce back kick. Seth deflected that. "Aiden told me so. Did you also know that he'd like to see all half-bloods enslaved? Even Lucian thinks he'd like to see things go back to the old way. Jerk-off, stupid mother—"

Seth caught my shoulders, giving me a little shake. "Okay. I get it. You hate Telly. Guess what, everyone does, but he controls the entire Council, Alex."

I was breathing heavily, sucking in cold air. "I know that!"

He smiled. "With him controlling the Council, nothing will change. The Breed Order will remain the same. If anything, the lives of half-bloods will get worse."

"Oh, well, that makes me feel so much better. Thanks."

"But—but listen to me, Alex." A look of eagerness crept over his face. "When you Awaken, we can change the Council. We have supporters, Alex. People who would surprise you." He brushed a strand of hair off my cheek.

I swatted his hand away. "Don't touch me. I don't need any more never-fading-magical-runes to appear."

Seth dropped his hands, grinning. "Still hasn't faded?"

I shoved my hand in his face. "Still there?"

"Yep."

"You don't have to sound so happy about it." I dipped around him, stopping. We had company.

Cross, Will, and Boobs stood at the edge of the field. Will held a small cooler in his hand. "We thought you guys could use some drinks since you missed the party."

Seth fell into an easy banter with them while I fiddled with the string on my pants. "Drinks" consisted of cheap wine coolers that Caleb would've laughed at, but I was so thirsty I wasn't complaining.

Once Seth shut up long enough to allow someone else to talk, Will began drilling me about the daimon battles I'd taken part in. Cross watched on with this sort of hero-worship look on his face, which was so different from the ones sent my way in North Carolina. None of them here knew the whole story surrounding my rise to fame—or the crash and burn I'd taken on my way down. I wanted to keep it that way. I relaxed on the rock eventually, sipping my drink while I answered their questions.

"So how many times were you tagged?" asked Cross, two wine coolers in hand.

Will turned to his friend slowly. "Dude, that's not a question you ask someone. You fail."

I froze. Unintentionally, I had exposed my neck by flipping my hair back. Flushing, I tipped my head so my hair fell forward in a heavy curtain. Seth, who'd been in a deep conversation with Boobs—probably about himself—pulled his head out of gods know where and twisted around to us.

Cross grimaced. "I'm sorry. I didn't mean to…offend you. It's just that I think it's awesome that you fought daimons and survived. Not that you were tagged, of course. That's not awesome. That's pretty messed up."

Will rolled his eyes, groaning. "Just shut up, Cross."

"No. It's okay." I cleared my throat, deciding if I didn't make a big deal about it then none of them would. "I don't know how many times. A couple, I guess."

Cross looked relieved, but then Seth stood, and Cross shifted farther back. I watched him stride between us and stop, blocking both Cross and Will as he faced me. I had no idea what he was doing, but what came out of his mouth wasn't even on the possibility list.

"Dance with me."

I stared up at him. "What?"

Seth bowed gracefully, extending one arm to me. "Dance with me, *please*?"

"Why do you want to dance in the middle of a field, Seth?"

"Why not?" He wiggled his fingers. "Dance with me, *pretty please*."

"With sugar on top," Will added, chuckling.

Seth's grin grew to epic proportions. "Dance with me, Alexandria."

Over his shoulder, I spotted Boobs eyeing the whole thing with a pouty, displeased look. I don't know if that made me take Seth's hand or if it was the fact he was embarrassing the hell out of me. Seth yanked me to my feet, keeping my one arm outstretched while placing my other around his back.

Then he started waltzing around the field—with no music.

It was so ridiculous that I had to laugh. We rounded a boulder, tripping over the uneven ground. Seth knew how to dance—really dance—like the kind people did in ballrooms. With one arm, he spun me out from him.

I giggled. "Did you pick this up from watching *Dancing with the Stars*?"

"You mock me." Seth spun me so my back was against his chest. "You wound my sensibilities when I'm trying to help you."

"Help me with what?"

Seth twirled me around. "You need to know how to dance without a pole if you're going to the ball."

I smacked him on the chest. "I don't dance like a stripper and I'm not going to that stupid ball."

He didn't respond. Grinning, he slipped his hand up my back and dipped me over his arm. I laughed and let my head fall back. I could see Boobs on her rock. Very slowly, when she was sure she had Seth's attention in that nanosecond he had me bent backward, she licked her lips.

Seth dropped me.

Much later, after the sun had fallen and we were covered in mud, Seth and I slipped past the dining hall. Trying not to bring attention to ourselves, we moved as quietly as possible.

I rubbed my aching rear and caught Seth watching me. "Your fault," I whispered.

"You're never going to let me forget that, are you?"

"You dropped me on my butt."

He tipped his head back, laughing softly. "I blame the wine coolers."

"I blame Boobs."

Grinning madly, Seth grabbed my hand and hurried me down the hall. We passed several quiet rooms, and then we heard Marcus, loud and clear. "I have no idea if Lucian is planning anything!"

We stopped and looked at each other.

"Are you not close with him?" I heard Telly ask.

"Lucian keeps a lot of secrets, just like every one of you does," Marcus responded angrily.

Seth pulled me under the stoop beside the room Marcus and Telly occupied, pressing me against the wall. He didn't have to get *that* close. "Come on, Seth. Back—"

"Shh." He tipped his head toward mine, strands of his hair swept against my cheeks. "This feels naughty."

I shot him a dirty look.

"I know he's up to something!" said Telly. "He thinks he can control him, but he is foolish for believing so."

Seth straightened an inch, a slight frown pulling at his lips. "Even Lucian is not that foolish," Marcus responded.

Telly made a disgusted sound. "It is my job as a Minister to protect them—my duty! If you know something—"

"I know nothing of the sort!" Marcus slapped something down. "You are being paranoid, Minister."

"You call it being paranoid, and I call it planning for the future. There are certain precautions we could take—just in case. Ways to ensure that they are never threatened."

I wondered what they were talking about. Seth also had a puzzled look on his face, which almost made me giggle. Maybe the wine coolers were still in my system. He must've felt the laugh bubbling up in me, because he looked down at me and smiled.

"What are you suggesting, Minister?"

"There are ways of eliminating the threat—ways in which no one is harmed. Some of the Council members agree that it may be best to do so."

When Marcus spoke next, his words were cold and flat. "Has the Council already acted on this?"

Telly scoffed. "What are you insinuating, Marcus?"

There was a stretch of silence. "And how would you eliminate the threat, pray tell?"

The tension that followed Marcus's question was so thick I could feel it. "We already have one here," replied Telly. "Why not keep them both here?"

There was a stretch of silence. "That is out of the question. I am sorry, but I cannot agree to that."

"Perhaps you just some need time and motivation. You want that Council seat very badly. I could make it happen."

Seth dropped his head, his breath warm against my neck. I tried to move back, but there wasn't anywhere to go. "Do you know what they're talking about?" he whispered.

For a second I had to think about what he was asking. I felt kind of out of it. "No clue."

"I do not believe my mind will change," Marcus finally responded. "It is late, Minister. And this conversation is over."

Seth's lips brushed against my neck, right under my ear. I jerked from the unexpected touch, and then socked him in the stomach. He chuckled softly.

Telly laughed mirthlessly. "My offer stands until the end of sessions."

"Good evening, Minister Telly."

We ducked into the adjoining room, shutting the door just in time. Telly exited seconds later, followed by Marcus. Seth and I stared at each other. There was something in his eyes, mischief definitely, but something else. He prowled toward me, grinning.

I put my hand up, flattening it against his chest. My pulse sped up. "Playtime is over, Seth."

He placed his hand over mine. "Sounds like a bit of bribery going on."

"That doesn't surprise me." I gave the room a brief glance. We were in another sitting room. How many of these things were there? "I'm a little surprised over how much Marcus dislikes Telly."

Shrugging, Seth went to the door and peered out. "All clear." He paused, grinning over his shoulder. "Unless you want to stay here a little while. That couch looks comfy."

I shoved past him. "Can't you think of anything else?"

He followed me out. "No. Not really."

"Wow. You're so multi-dimensional, Seth."

Chuckling, he sidled up and dropped his arm over my shoulders. "And you're such a killjoy."

CHAPTER TWENTY

Over the next couple of days, Seth consumed most of my time. I saw very little of Aiden and Marcus. Once, when Seth wasn't attached to my hip, I hung out with Laadan while she got a mani and pedi for the ball. I opted out of the indulgence.

People touching my feet creeped me out.

Seth and I had snuck into one of the training classrooms between practices and sparred with some of the halfs the other day. I think we caused more mayhem than anything else, but I'd enjoyed fighting people other than Seth. Goofing off eased some of the pent-up frustration of being in this place and the growing unease that occupied each day closer to my Council session.

But time with Seth hadn't been all fun and games. We'd spent most of our training sessions working on avoiding the use of elements in battle. Throwing balls of flame around really wasn't an indoor sport, so we were forced outside.

We also argued. A lot.

He got pissy because he claimed I'd been watching Aiden

when he'd shown up one day during our practice and worked out alongside us. Seth also claimed that I'd drooled on myself.

Not true.

Flushing with embarrassment and anger, I'd stormed off and left him standing in the middle of the field we'd practiced in. A short hour later, Seth reappeared with hamburgers and fries—my favorite—and I kind of forgave him. He had hamburgers; what else could I have done?

I still had no recollection of how I'd ended up in the maze. Not knowing what'd happened—or why a pure would do that—nagged at me. So did the conversation we'd overheard between Marcus and Lucian. I couldn't shake the feeling that those two events were connected.

But that could just be my paranoia.

Today's practice had been cut short as Seth had something important to discuss with Lucian. When I'd asked what it was, he'd told me not to worry my pretty little butt over it and to go hang out with Laadan.

I hate boys.

And I couldn't find Laadan anywhere.

Even though it irked me that no one wanted me to roam around alone, I didn't want to end up a pure's compulsion toy again. Thinking about that filled me with enough anger I could have put my fist through the wall. After checking out a million sitting rooms, I gave up on my search for Laadan. Another long and boring evening staring at the white walls in my room awaited me.

With barely restrained aggravation, I turned the corner and froze.

Up ahead, a female servant trembled on her knees. She'd dropped a stack of dishes on the carpet.

The man towering over her wore the unmistakable—and

terrifying—garb of a Master. I'd only seen one once before, and that had been when Mom had brought me before the Council when I was seven.

I'd never forgotten the bloodred tunic or how they shaved their heads and *all* facial hair.

The Master kicked one of the empty plates, shattering it. "You careless, stupid half-blood. Is carrying plates too complicated for you?"

She cowered, lowering her head and clasping her knees. She didn't speak, but I could hear her soft cries.

"Get up." Disgust dripped from the Master's voice. The girl didn't move quickly enough for his liking. He reached down and grabbed a handful of her tangled hair, yanking her to her feet. Her gasp of surprise and pain brought forth a cruel laugh from the Master and something far worse. He lifted his free hand to hit her.

I didn't even think.

Rage propelled me into action. I struck out, catching the Master's fist before it landed a blow. The Master whirled around. Lack of eyebrows gave his startled expression an almost comical aspect. He recovered quickly and tried to pull his hand free.

I held on. "Didn't your mother ever teach you not to hit a lady?"

Anger and contempt filled his eyes, sharpening them. "You dare to touch me and interfere in a situation that does not concern you? Do you have a desire for the Elixir, half-blood?"

I smiled, tightening my grip until I felt the bones in his hand rub together. His lips thinned in pain, filling me with sick satisfaction. "Oh, I'm not just a half-blood."

"I know what you are." He wrenched his hand free, lips curling with disgust. "You think that will save you? If anything, that ensures that one day you will be under the Master's control…or worse."

His words should've scared me, but they just pissed me off. "Go screw yourself, you eyebrowless freak."

The Master laughed as he twisted back to the silent girl, but then he swung around so fast I hadn't a chance to raise my hands in defense. The fist intended for the servant ended up smashing right into my jaw.

Fierce pain exploded along my face as I stumbled back into the wall. My eyes immediately filled with tears; the throbbing sent darts of dizziness through me. I held my jaw, almost certain he had broken it. And then Seth was standing in front of me, a towering inferno of fury. I don't even know where he'd come from or how he'd gotten there so quickly.

"That will be the last thing you ever do," Seth snarled. He threw back his hand. Not to hit the pure, but to *kill* the pure.

Many times in practice I had seen akasha start to build in his hand, but always as just a small ball of energy. When he'd taken down Kain, Aiden had blocked most of it, but now it was all that I could see. The blue energy shot from somewhere under the sleeve of his shirt, filling his hand, crackling and snapping blue fire.

Pain forgotten, I pushed off the wall and grabbed Seth's other arm. "No! No!"

"Get back, Alex, now."

I got in front of him, blocking the Master. The mark of the Apollyon stood out in contrast against his pale face. "You can't do this, Seth! You need to calm down."

"Do it," urged the Master. "Seal your fate, Apollyon. As your bitch's fate has been sealed." Seth's eyes glowed, his lips pulled back in a snarl. Akasha spread, spitting flames.

"Ignore him." I balled my hands in the front of his shirt.

"Please! You can't do this!" This wasn't working. He wasn't listening to me. His arm went back, readying to release the most powerful element known to man. I twisted around. "Get out of here! Now!"

The servant took off, but the Master stayed, daring Seth with his smile as if he had no sense of self-preservation. Then it struck me—he wanted Seth to do this, knowing that for a half to kill a pure in any situation meant death.

Possibly even for the Apollyon.

I turned back to Seth, hands trembling. I pressed against his chest as if I could somehow burrow my way into him and make him understand that the penalty for hitting me wasn't capital punishment. I could taste the fear in the back of my throat; panic overshadowed the physical pain.

Seth shuddered and then his arms swept around me. I almost cried out in relief. The Master's cruel laugh echoed around us, seeming to hang in the air long after he left the hallway.

He stared down at me, still furious. "I want to kill him."

"I know," I whispered, blinking back tears.

"No, you don't. I still do."

"But you can't. It was my fault. He was about to hit a servant and I stopped him. He—"

"Your fault?" he said, eyes widening with disbelief now. He reached out and caught my chin, turning my head to the side. "No. This wasn't your fault."

I swallowed, closing my eyes. Crisis averted…for now. "Is it going to bruise?"

"Most definitely."

"I think…I'm going to be in trouble." I stepped back, staring at the floor. This Seth—this hard and lethal Seth—was frightening. "You're going to be in trouble, too."

"Yes." Seth sounded as if he didn't give a crap about that.

I touched the left side of my face and winced. "Oh, crap."

Seth pulled my hand away from my face. "I think if we make it to dinner without anyone saying anything, then we're in the clear."

"You think so?"

Seth smiled, but everything about him still seemed on the verge of destroying something. "Yes."

We didn't make it to dinner.

About twenty minutes later, Marcus and crew stormed the sitting room Seth and I were kind of hiding in. Aiden was with them, his eyes immediately finding me. His gaze glided over my face, stopping on what I knew was a nasty-looking bruise. He came to a complete stop and inhaled sharply. Potent anger rolled off him in waves, nearly as overwhelming as what was still radiating from the one next to me.

"What were you thinking, Alexandria?" demanded Marcus.

I pulled my eyes from Aiden's but didn't look at Marcus. I watched Seth instead. His face was still a picture of hard lines and chilling beauty. "I know I shouldn't have stopped the Master, but he was going to beat a girl for dropping plates. I had to do—"

The door swung open, revealing Minister Telly and a slew of Council Guards. I stiffened, but Seth stood. "What is this?" he demanded, hands balling into fists.

"What is this?" Minister Telly repeated, striding across the room, tall and graceful, his green robes flowing. He stopped before Marcus and Lucian. "What is it that I hear about Alexandria attacking a Master this afternoon?"

"Attacked?" I sputtered. "I didn't attack anyone. I stopped—"

"She did interfere with a Master, but she did not attack the man," Marcus cut in, sending me a dangerous look. "However, he did strike Alexandria."

Telly spared me a brief glance. "Half-bloods know to not interfere with a Master and their treatment of servants. To do so is a breach of the Breed Order!"

My mouth dropped open. Had I expected to be in trouble? Yes. But not to be accused of breaking the Order.

"Are you serious?" Seth stepped forward, eyes narrowing into thin slits.

"Get your Apollyon under control this instant, Lucian," Telly spat. "Or my Guards will."

Lucian swung toward Seth, but I knew there was nothing that he could say or do. I grabbed Seth's arm and tugged hard. "Sit," I whispered.

He glanced over his shoulder at me, brows raised. "I'd rather stand."

Gods, he so wasn't helping matters. Not like it would stop him, but I held onto his arm. "Minister Telly, I understand that Alexandria should not have interfered, but accusing her of breaking the law?" Marcus shook his head. "I think that's a bit extreme."

"That half-blood is extreme," Telly responded. "Neither of you have any control over her. She's threatening Masters now? What will she do as an Apollyon? Massacre them in their sleep?"

I laughed. Everyone looked at me. "I'm sorry, but this is ridiculous. All I did was stop him from hitting a girl. That's it! I didn't hit him, but he did hit me." I pointed at my jaw. "And I wouldn't massacre people in their sleep."

Telly turned, facing me fully. "You, little girl, have shown no regard for the law or for rules from the moment you could breathe. Oh yes, I've seen your files."

Had everyone seen my files? Gah. I felt exposed.

"You are uncontrollable and a constant problem for the Council," Telly continued, turning back to Lucian. "She belongs here, where the Council can control her, since neither of you have been able to ingrain a sense of respect in the girl."

Fear stopped me dead in my tracks. "What?"

"That will not happen," Seth said so low that I wasn't sure anyone else heard him. But then everyone in the room froze.

"Are you threatening me, Apollyon? Threatening the Council?" Telly demanded. I'd swear he sounded happy about this, but that would be crazy, because Seth would kill him.

Seth would wipe the ground with Telly's face.

I tore my gaze from the Head Minister and saw the marks of the Apollyon swirling across Seth's face. And then I realized Aiden had moved, standing on the other side of me. I thanked the gods that everyone was focused on Seth, fearing he was about to lose it. The look on Aiden's face said he was about to rip through everyone in this room.

My heart sank as I looked between the two guys. This wasn't going to end well at all. I stood, my knees shaking. "I'm sorry."

"Don't apologize. You did nothing wrong," Seth hissed.

"But I did. I shouldn't have interfered." I met Telly's eyes and swallowed my pride at the same time. "I forgot...I forgot my place."

Seth whirled on me so quickly I thought he might actually zap *me*. I met his furious stare, willing him to just sit down and shut up.

"Minister, as you can see, Alexandria sees her error." Lucian moved in front of Seth, his hands clasped together. "She is strong-willed, stubborn even, but she broke no law today. As you know, if she had attacked the Master, I doubt he'd be well enough to spread such atrocious exaggerations."

"She thinks without acting sometimes," Marcus joined in. "She is reckless, but she never has ill intentions. As for controlling her, I can promise you that she won't even speak out of turn for the rest of her stay here."

I opened my mouth but shut it.

Telly drew another breath before turning to Lucian. "This kind of behavior she has repeatedly displayed is concerning not only to me, but the Council. But that is something you are already aware of, Lucian." He paused, scanning the room. His gaze, full of condemnation, fell on me. "I will not forget this." With that, he turned and stalked from the room. The Guards followed him, stiff and silent.

I collapsed on the couch, exhausted. I'd barely escaped the noose with that one. I felt Seth sit back down, but I didn't look at him.

"Alexandria, what have I told you time and time again?" asked Marcus.

"Enough," Lucian said. "It is in the past now. It is done."

"It just happened," Marcus retorted. "And this one here threatened the Master with akasha, for crying out loud! He is lucky that the Master didn't report him."

"What did you expect?" Lucian countered wearily. "He will defend what is his."

I sent my stepfather a death glare. "I am not *his*. Would you please stop referring to me as a possession instead of a person?"

Lucian smiled. "Either way, Seth cannot be blamed for defending her. Or would you rather he'd allowed the Master to continue to beat Alexandria?"

"That is preposterous, Lucian!" Marcus's hands balled into fists.

They went back and forth for a little while. Eventually my head ached as badly as my jaw did. On the positive side, Seth began to relax and no longer looked like he wanted to wipe out an entire village of pures. Once I'd gathered I wasn't in *that* much trouble, I slipped out the double doors and breathed in the brisk air.

I didn't roam off too far, staying just around the corner from the sitting room. I kept thinking about what the Master had said. My fate had already been sealed? Had the Master known something or had he just been taunting Seth?

"Alex?"

I turned to the sound of Aiden's voice. His eyes were a flinty silver.

"Hey," I murmured. "I know I messed up again and—"

"I'm not here to yell at you, Alex. I just wanted to make sure you are okay."

"Oh. Sorry. I'm just used to everyone yelling at me."

He tipped his head to the side, eyes a dark gray. "I understand why you did what you did. Honestly, I wouldn't have expected you to do anything differently."

"Really?" I looked around skeptically. "Are you on drugs?"

Aiden smiled, but then his eyes flickered to my jaw. The smile faded. "Does it hurt?"

"No," I lied.

He looked like he knew better. Before I knew what he was doing, he reached out and brushed his fingers around the edge of the bruise. "It's swelling. Have you put ice on it?"

I had actually, but I'd grown bored holding the ice bag Seth had rifled together. Staring at Aiden now, though? I completely forgot what he'd just asked me. His fingers were still against my cheek and that was the only thing in this world that mattered.

"You still show so much strength." A small smile appeared on his lips. Then he dropped his hand, the heady connection brief. "No other half-blood would have done what you did."

"I don't know why you keep saying that." I leaned against the smooth wall as if it could somehow ground me back into reality.

"It's the truth, Alex. And I'm not even talking about what you did for the half-blood. It's what you just did in there. I know damn well what it took for you to apologize and say what you did. That took strength."

"It wasn't strength. I was scared out of my mind, actually. Maybe a little irrational, you know?" Aiden glanced away, toward the labyrinth. From here, all I could see were the tips of the vine-covered statues.

"I was wrong."

My breath caught in my throat. "Wrong about what?"

He turned back to me, eyes silvery. "About a lot of things, but I always thought your irrational nature was a flaw. It's not. It's what makes you so strong."

I stared at him, my heart doing all kinds of crazy things in my chest. "Thank…you."

"Don't thank—"

"I know." I smiled even though it made my jaw hurt. "Don't thank you for that, but I did."

Aiden nodded. "I better get back in there. Don't wander off too far, okay?"

I nodded and watched him turn around. He got to the French doors and stopped. Turning around, the expression on his face was unreadable, but his words were precise.

"Part of me wishes Seth had killed that Master for touching you."

Dinner was served early on the night of the ball, and the mad bustle of servants drove me up to my room. My nerves were stretched tight from my impending Court session, my run-in with a Master's fist, Seth's psycho akasha killing power, and Aiden's parting words.

Part of me wishes Seth had killed that Master for touching you.

Two days later and I still couldn't forget what he'd said.

That had been a serious statement, but what could it mean? Did it matter? No, I told myself. Even if Aiden loved me as much as I loved cake, it didn't matter. There was no future there, only death and despair.

A soft knock on the door pulled me out of my thoughts. Since Seth never knocked, I knew it couldn't be him. I scooted off the bed and went to the door.

Laadan stood in the hallway, dressed in a beautiful deep green dress that clung to her hips before billowing out around her in soft, wispy material. Her hair was done up in an intricate twist, adorned by several fresh rose blossoms.

I glanced down at my sweats and shirt. Gods, I never felt more boring and ugly in my entire life.

And here I thought Lea was the only one who could evoke such feelings.

Laadan smiled faintly. "If you're not busy, which I can tell you're not, I want to show you something."

I glanced back at my bed and shrugged. It wasn't like I had anything to do. We passed several servants on the way to her room on the floor above, and Laadan smiled at each of them graciously.

Once inside her room, she circled one arm around my shoulders and steered me to an overstuffed chair by her closet.

I sat down and pulled my legs up to my chest. "You...wanted to show me your closet door?"

Laadan's laugh was throaty and infectious. I found myself smiling at her. "You're so much like your mother." She shook her head as she leaned against the doors. "The things you say—it's like hearing Rachelle speak."

My smile faded a bit, and I wrapped my arms around my knees. "My mom never said half of the stupid stuff that comes out of my mouth."

"You'd be surprised." She paused as a soulful look crept across her features. "Do you know what your mother loved most about the Council sessions?"

"No."

Laadan spun around and threw open her closet doors. She stepped back and spread her arms in a sweeping gesture. "All the dancing and beautiful dresses."

Curious, I leaned forward to get a look inside the closet and nearly fell out of the chair. "Wow. That's a lot of clothes."

She gave a saucy grin over her shoulder. "A girl can never have too many clothes. Come on. Take a look."

I pulled myself from the chair. The gowns caught my eye. Like being under a compulsion that'd turned me into a girlie girl in under two seconds flat, I stepped forward and ran a hand over the soft material.

"You like them?" She tugged on a deep purple dress in crushed velvet.

My fingers lingered on a red silk dress. I couldn't see the cut of it, but the color was divine. "These are the kinds of dresses you'd give up your firstborn child for."

She laughed, dropping the purple dress and gently unhooking the red one. She held it up between us. "Why are you so dead set against going to the ball?"

I shrugged, eyeing the sleeveless dress. It had scalloped edging around the bodice, a high waist, and a skirt cut to cling to the legs. "I don't even know why I'd be invited since halfs aren't."

"But you are different." She hung the dress on the closet door and smoothed out the silk. "Being an Apollyon sets you apart from the rest of your kind, Alex. Once you Awaken, I've been told that both you and Seth will even be able to attend Council sessions."

I hadn't known that, but I seriously doubted at eighteen I needed to be in that kind of position of power. Maturity didn't happen overnight.

My eyes and mind were fastened on *that* dress. "There's not going to be anyone there I know. And no offense, but my idea of fun isn't spending a night with a bunch of pures."

"None taken." Laadan pulled out the skirt. The hue of the red caught the light, casting a faint glimmer over the dress. "Seth will be there. So will Aiden."

I looked at her sharply. "Why would I care if Aiden will be there? He's a pure. Where else would he be tonight?"

Laadan smiled faintly. "Would you like to try it on?"

"No, thank you."

"Humor me, why don't you? Your mom wore a dress like this once, and I only have a little while before I'm due downstairs."

The yearning to try the dress on was a physical ache, but I shook my head. Laadan persisted until I found myself standing in front of a full-length mirror with the red silk dress on. She stood behind me, hands on my shoulders. "You look beautiful."

The dress was stunning. It was made to fit me—or at least altered to do so. The silk hugged from my chest to my hips before gliding out around my thighs. I twisted to the side, grinning. The back looked just as good as the front. Red was definitely my color. For a moment, I let myself drift into a dream where Aiden actually saw me in something this elegant and sexy.

And what if Seth saw me in this? Even my dirtiest imagination couldn't capture his response accurately.

"I should probably take this off before I ruin it."

Laadan pulled me away from the mirror and sat me down in front of a small table full of makeup and other suspicious-looking things. I started to stand, but she planted her hands on my shoulders again. "Alex, there is no reason for you to stay in your room tonight while everyone else is enjoying the ball. So be still and let me do something with this hair of yours."

"I don't want to go." I twisted around so I faced her.

She turned me back around and picked up a brush. "Why? Is it because you have your session tomorrow? Wouldn't that be even more of a reason to relax and enjoy tonight?"

I frowned and tried to ignore the soothing way the brush moved through the tangles in my hair. "It's not because of the session tomorrow. I just…don't want to go."

Ignoring me, she picked up a curling iron and started twisting long sections of hair around the barrel. I gave in to the primping pretty quickly, still having no real intention of going to the ball. It was nice to have someone make me pretty, even if all the hard work would be wasted on my pillow. Chattering on about my mother, she moved on to the makeup and when she was done, I barely recognized the smoky-eyed girl staring back at me.

Laadan had outdone herself.

She'd piled the curls atop my head but pulled several thick strands down to cover my neck and tease the bodice of the dress. The curls seemed strategically placed, as they hid the scars.

"What do you think?" she asked, a powder brush in her hand.

I had no idea what to say. The blush accented my cheekbones, making them appear higher than normal. She'd covered the bruise on my jaw without coating my face with makeup. The mascara and artfully applied shadow turned my eyes into the warmest chocolate instead of the dirt color they usually favored. Red stain plumped my lips in a way that begged to be kissed.

"Wow. My nose looks small."

Laadan laughed, setting the brush down. "Wait. The only thing you are missing is…" Drifting off to a dresser and opening a large velvet box, she rooted around for a few moments and pulled out a silver chain with black stones surrounding a ruby.

The necklace probably was worth more than my life, but she dropped it around my neck and clasped it. "There! Now you'll be the belle of the ball."

I stared at myself, wanting a picture of this moment. I don't think I'd ever look so…unlike me again. If Caleb could've seen this, I think he might've complimented me.

Laadan glanced at a clock gilded in gold. "And we're finished just in time. The ball has only just begun, and you will make a fashionably late entrance."

My gaze drifted down the mirror. "I can't go."

"You're being silly. You're going to look more beautiful than any pure-blood in that room, Alex. You'll belong."

I stood, shaking my head. "You don't understand, Laadan. I do appreciate all of this and it was fun, but I…I can't go."

She frowned. "Perhaps I don't understand. Would you explain it to me?"

Slowly, I turned back to the mirror. The girl staring back at me looked beautiful if no one looked *too* hard or *too* close. If anyone did, the picture of perfection would start to fall apart. There wasn't a pretty dress in Laadan's closet that could fix that.

"Alex?"

"Look at me," I said quietly. "You don't see...them? I can't go down there and have everyone stare at me."

Laadan's concerned face appeared above my head in the mirror. "Honey, everyone will be staring at you because you look beautiful."

"Everyone will be staring at my scars."

She blinked and took a step back. "No. They're not even—"

"I know they will be." I turned around, fingering the delicate chain around my neck. "Because it's what I notice first on someone. And look at my arms, they're pretty gross."

And they were. The skin had never quite returned to the original skin tone. They'd paled, like all daimon tags did, but the tiny teeth marks left behind were uneven and red, lining my forearms, starting right above my wrist and ending along the tender skin of the inside of my elbow. The skin was just as uneven and patchy as my neck, but at least the scars on my throat had faded into a shiny color a shade or two lighter than my normal complexion. The bit of cleavage the dress showed off took away from those scars, but my arms totally made up for it.

Laadan suddenly smiled, which I found really inappropriate considering she should be commiserating about how much of a freak I looked. She moved to her closet and pulled a large box off the top shelf. Taking it to her bed, her smile grew wider. "I have the perfect thing."

Doubtful, but I followed her to the bed.

She flipped up the lid and pulled out two elbow-length gloves in black silk. "Problem solved."

I took the gloves gingerly. "I'm going to look like Rogue from *X-Men*."

Her nose wrinkled. "Who? It doesn't matter. Try them on. The gloves will work now. If it were the summer, it would be a tad bit questionable."

I slid one on and it did cover the scars quite nicely, but gloves? For real? Who wore them but old grannies? "I don't know about this."

Laadan sighed, shaking her head. "This is a formal ball, Alex. Have you been to one before?"

"Um, no."

"Trust me when I say that you will not be the only girl wearing gloves. Now, come on. We don't have much more time to stand up here and feel sorry for ourselves. You look beautiful, Alex. More so than even your mother ever did."

I wiggled my fingers in the silk gloves, feeling excitement bubble up for the first time. Half-bloods didn't go to grand balls, and they didn't have pure fairy godmothers, either. So, I'd never really expected to attend anything like this, especially not in this killer dress.

But here I was.

A slow smile crept over my face. "Laadan?"

"Yes?" She stopped at the door.

"Thank you."

Her hand flew to her heart. "Honey, you don't have to thank me. I'm just glad I could do this for you."

"You had this planned ever since Lucian mentioned something at breakfast, didn't you? That's why this dress fits so well."

Laadan gave a sly smile. "Well, I always thought red would be your best color."

The ball was in full swing by the time Laadan and I made it downstairs. The soft hum of an orchestra filled the corridors as we moved closer to the ballroom. A display of dazzling candles lit the way.

My excitement quickly turned into nerves. I'd never worn anything like this before, and attending something like this just went against everything a half-blood knew. Also, orchestra music just wasn't my thing.

Would I be expected to waltz? The last time—and only time—had been with Seth and he'd dropped me. I couldn't hit the ground in this kind of dress—that would be a sacrilege. And who would even dance with me? Was I going to be hugging the wall all night?

That's when I started sweating.

Laadan grasped my hand with hers and led me forward. "You've fought daimons and the idea of a ball scares you?"

"Yes," I whispered.

She laughed, the sound reminding me of wind chimes. "You're going to do beautifully. Just remember that you belong among them. More so than any of them can even realize."

I looked at her warily. "You really do love some half-bloods, don't you?"

Her cheeks flushed a fierce red. "I…I just believe that all of us are equal and should be treated that way."

I doubted that was the main reason, but I didn't push it. She pulled me out of the soft shadows of the hallway, past the frozen furies, and right into the ballroom. I think I may've had a minor heart attack standing there, taking it all in.

The room was massive, the walls entirely made of glass. Crystal vases full of roses sat in every corner and on every table, and flower-covered vines streamed across the ceiling and hung from sparkling chandeliers in a dazzling display of light and darkness. At the far end of the room, a small orchestra sat—mortal musicians. Mortals were easy for both pures and halfs to pick out. It was more than just the physical attributes that set them apart. Their movements were jerky and slow, while the pures glided gracefully around them. Compared to the pures, their expressions were bland. They were probably under compulsion to play here and not acknowledge anything weird.

Pures could get a little freaky after a few drinks.

Behind the orchestra, Thanatos rose above the mortals to loom over them like some kind of angel of death. His wingspan had to be at least eight feet, and the ever-present sad expression had been carved into the marble. Someone had laid a wreath of roses on the god's head.

Nice touch.

Two servants appeared in front of us. One held a tray of champagne flutes and the other carried a platter of finger sandwiches and what smelled like raw fish. I had a sudden mad desire for tater tots. Laadan graciously accepted two glasses of champagne and handed me one. She caught my hand before I could down the glass. "Careful," she warned softly. "This isn't like mortal champagne. It's much stronger."

I stared down at the bubbling liquid. "How much stronger?"

She tipped her head to a table where a pure girl laughed hysterically while her companions looked on in annoyance. She had a glass of champagne in her hand. "That's probably her second. You sip this champagne."

"Advice taken."

Lucian drifted out of the throng of pures and grasped my

free hand. His eyes drifted over me in a mixture of shock and appraisal. "Laadan, you have outdone yourself. She looks just like Rachelle did when she attended this very ball."

It was official. I felt creeped out on a whole new level.

"And you can't even see her scars," Lucian continued. There was a weird sheen to his eyes, and I wondered if he was drunk. "Utterly amazing job, Laadan."

Straining back, I tried to maintain a polite smile. "Uh… thanks."

Laadan looked as put off as I felt. Smoothly, she engaged Lucian's interest. I scanned the room for friendly faces as my fingers clutched the fragile stem of the glass.

Everyone—all the pures—looked magnificent in their finery. Most of the females wore the kind of risqué dresses I'd love to, showing off expanses of perfectly smooth skin and long, graceful necks.

I didn't belong here. No matter what Laadan said, I didn't belong here.

Taking a deep breath, my gaze skittered over the crowd. Out of them, I recognized Minister Diana Elders. She wore a white diaphanous gown that reminded me of something a goddess would wear. Beside her, my uncle looked extremely interested in whatever she was saying. In awe, I watched as he actually smiled, and when they turned toward us, those emerald eyes shone like jewels.

That is, until he saw me.

Marcus stepped back, blinking. Shock splashed across his face. He reacted like he'd seen a ghost. Recovering slowly, he and Minister Elders approached us. He nodded at Lucian and Laadan. "Alexandria, you decided to join us after all."

Uncomfortable, I nodded and *sipped* my champagne.

Diana smiled warmly enough, but she looked nervous

when she addressed me. "Miss Andros, it is a pleasure to meet you."

"Same here," I murmured dumbly. I was never good at exchanging pleasantries, but the good thing was that the pures surrounding me gravitated toward each other and I was able to drift off to the side. I continued searching the crowd… well, for Aiden if I was being honest with myself. I knew he wouldn't speak to me, but I wanted him…to see me. Pathetic, yes, but I wanted that.

Go figure it was Seth I saw first.

Or he saw me first. I'm not sure. Either way, I was surprised to find both Aiden and Seth standing with another pure-blood male I didn't recognize. Several pretty pures had crowded them, possibly fascinated by the fact that an Apollyon half-blood was in the mix—or they'd just been drawn to the general hotness of the group.

Dawn Samos was one of those pretty pures. Her dress was a white sheath that ended above her knees. She stood the closest to Aiden, her slender tan arm brushing his as she spoke. I hadn't seen her since the first day of sessions and I'd forgotten about her, but there she was.

Seth stood facing Aiden and the entrance. He wore a tux like the rest of the pures, except he'd managed to find an all-white one and still look good in it. A grin pulled at my lips.

Like Seth needed any extra help sticking out.

His gaze moved around the edge of the ballroom and landed on me. The expression on his face was almost comical. His brows inched up his forehead, eyes widened with surprise. Apparently, I looked like a doofus most of the time. Me being in a dress must be a sight to behold. A smug quirk to his lips was quick to replace the startled expression. He nodded at me approvingly.

I tipped my glass at Seth.

He must've said something, because Aiden's muscles stiffened under his black tux. Then slowly, almost reluctantly, Aiden looked over his shoulder. The moment our eyes met, I felt like Cinderella.

Aiden's lips parted as his gaze drifted over me in a way that made the glass tremble between my fingers. When his eyes made their slow journey back to mine, all the air fled my lungs. The silver burned so fiercely, so hot, that a warm blush swept over my skin. My hand fell to the side, the barely touched glass of champagne forgotten as it hung from my fingertips.

Aiden turned around fully, his chest rising and falling sharply. He didn't smile. He seemed only capable of staring. Just like me, because he looked truly magnificent in the sharp cut of the black tux, the wild waves of hair tumbling over his forehead, and those soft lips still parted in surprise, eyes still full of hunger.

As if in a daze, Aiden crossed the ballroom floor, his piercing eyes fastened on me. I knew I looked good, but not *that* good. Not so good that everyone else seemed to fade and disappear to Aiden. I thought of what he'd said outside the sitting room, how he'd been wrong about a lot of things.

I think I knew one of those things he'd been wrong about.

So caught up in Aiden, I hadn't realized Seth had moved, but I felt him before he placed his hand on me, his fingers curving over my bare shoulder. Anger flashed over Aiden's face. He stalled, silver eyes dropping to my shoulder. I could almost feel it in the air—the primal jealousy, his raw urge to physically remove Seth's hand.

Seth leaned close, his warm breath stirring the hair at the nape of my neck. "People are starting to stare."

Were they? I couldn't say I really cared, which was wrong, but Aiden was staring at me—staring at me with so much passion, so much want—it was the only thing I could think about.

And then Aiden pulled it together. Halting mid-step, he clamped his jaw shut. Those eyes were still like quicksilver, smoldering in the soft light. His gaze drifted over me once more. Shivering under its intensity, I imagined that he was filing the image of me away.

Seth's hand slid down my arm, fingers tightening around mine. "You know he's not for you."

"I know," I whispered. And I did know that, and maybe that was why I felt so hollow inside.

Aiden turned away then, smiling at something Dawn said. But it was a fake smile. I knew Aiden's smiles. After all, I lived for them.

"Do you want to dance?" Seth suggested.

Coming to the ball had been a bad idea. The emptiness I felt spread, leaving a gaping hole. I didn't belong here, but Aiden did. Aiden belonged here with pures like Dawn. Not with me, not a half-blood.

I tore my gaze from Aiden and looked up at Seth. "I don't want to dance."

Seth's amber gaze drifted over me. "Do you want to stay here?"

"I don't know."

He smiled and leaned forward. When he spoke, his lips brushed my ear. "We don't belong here, Alex. Not with them."

I wanted to ask exactly where it was we belonged, but I knew what Seth's answer would be. He'd say that *we* belonged *together*. Not in the way I wanted to belong to Aiden, but in a different way. A way I hadn't figured out yet.

"Let's go," he coaxed softly.

I could stay here and continue pretending that I belonged, or I could leave with Seth. And then what? My fingers trembled as I set the glass down on the nearest table.

I let Seth lead me away from the ball. A sudden heaviness settled over me. I felt like I'd made some sort of irrevocable choice.

And maybe I had.

CHAPTER TWENTY-ONE

"Let's do something stupid."

I turned to Seth, oddly nervous. "You want to do something stupid right now?"

"Can you think of a better time to do something stupid?"

I considered that. He kind of had a good point. "Okay. I'm down with stupid."

"Good." He started off, pulling me through the labyrinth. We rounded the Council chambers and headed into the campus. Seth cut toward the dark and silent building I'd spent the majority of my waking time in.

"You want to train?"

He shook his head, jaw clenched. "No. I don't want to train."

Seth picked up his pace. I had no idea what he was up to, but I'd learned a while ago to just go with it. The door to the arena was unlocked. A wide grin broke out across his face when he spotted the double doors inside the dark corridor.

"You want to go swimming?" I asked.

"Sure."

"It's like forty degrees outside."

Seth pushed open the door. The smell of chlorine was everywhere. "So? It's not forty degrees in here, is it? More like sixty."

I pulled away from him and stepped to the edge of the pool. Glancing over my shoulder, I saw Seth kick off his shoes. He caught my eye and winked.

"You're ridiculous," I said, fighting a grin.

"So are you." He slipped off the dress jacket, dropping it on the cement. "We are a lot alike, Alex."

I started to deny it, but I stopped and actually thought about it instead of dismissing it. There *was* something about Seth that called to my wilder and yes, stupider side. We were both reckless, a little wild and aggressive, and neither of us ever knew when to be quiet. I guess there were two types of people in the world, those who sat around a fire, staring into the flames, and those who started the fire.

Seth and I started the fire, and then we danced around it. "Was it so obvious back there?" I asked quietly.

Seth had been yanking his white shirt out of his pants, but he stopped and looked up. He appeared to be choosing his words. "I don't know what goes on in your head, Alex. I can't read your thoughts. I just picked up on your emotions."

"Good to know."

"I second that." He started unbuttoning his shirt. "Anyway, I don't even need to be able to sense your emotions to know. I don't think you want to know what it looked like."

"No. I do." I shifted my weight to my other foot. These heels were killing me.

Shaking his head, Seth sighed. "You were staring at him like an ugly chick stares at the last cute guy at the bar when they make the last call."

I choked on my laugh. "Oh. Wow. Thanks."

He raised his hands in a helpless gesture, which looked so strange for him. "I told you."

"Yeah." I pushed strands of hair off my neck. "So, I looked like an idiot to everyone?"

"No, everyone saw a beautiful half-blood. That's all anyone saw." Seth glanced away, a wry smile on his face. "Can I tell you something?"

I turned back to the pool. "Sure."

"I prefer you without gloves." His breath stirred the tendrils of hair against my neck. I had no idea how he moved so quietly.

"Oh," I said, watching Seth as he moved to my side. Quietly, he peeled off one glove, and then the other, tossing them both away from the water. His fingers slid around the scars before he dropped my arm, stepping back. My tags never seemed to bother him. I looked at him through my lashes. "Better?"

"Much."

I glanced down at the beautiful gown. Laadan would be so upset if I ruined her dress. I turned slightly, catching my reflection in the windows of the pool room. It didn't look like me. I looked like a doll, a carbon copy of my mom. So much so that even Lucian had looked at me in a way that made me puke a little in my mouth. Had that been what Laadan wanted? To fashion me like her long-lost friend?

"Can you get silk wet?" I asked.

Seth made a funny noise behind me. "I'd say probably not."

"That's a shame." I kicked off my shoes. My toes immediately sighed and thanked me.

"You really are going—"

I dove in. The water wasn't as heated as I'd thought and was a shock to my system, but after a few seconds I grew used to it. Staying underwater, I swam to the opposite side of the pool.

The water immediately killed all of Laadan's hard work. Twisting around, I found Seth at the pool's edge. Amusement and satisfaction played out across his face, which made him look sort of normal.

"So childish, Alex. You've ruined her dress."

The vibrant red silk floated around me as I treaded water. "I know. Bad me."

"Very bad." He sounded more appreciative than chastising.

Grinning, I sank underwater again and closed my eyes. Under the water, it was a quiet, blissful world. I didn't have to think, or worry...or love.

I inched my way back up and caught Seth shrugging off his shirt. I saw maybe a second of his bare upper body before I hastily ducked underwater. It wasn't bad—all golden skin and hard muscles.

Seeing his chest wasn't a big deal, for crying out loud.

On the nights Seth stayed with me, he did so fully clothed—thank the gods—but it was just weird. Seth was weird—*I was weird*—and I couldn't stay underwater all night. Using my legs, I pushed off the bottom of the pool.

Seth had moved to the center of the room. His head was tipped back, arms stretched high in the air as he stood on the tips of his toes, completely at ease. "Stop staring."

I floated forward. "I'm not staring."

He chuckled. "How's the water?"

"Nice."

His arms dropped to his sides. "Do you remember the last thing I told you in training?"

I pushed through the water, coming to where he stood. "You tell me a lot of stuff in training. Honestly, I don't pay attention."

He snorted. "You do wonders for my self-esteem."

Rolling my eyes, I pushed off the cement wall and floated on my back. The dress streamed out around me as water glided over my skin. "I feel like a mermaid."

Seth ignored that. "Tomorrow, when they ask you about what happened in Gatlinburg, only answer their questions."

I sighed. "I know. What do you guys think I'm going to say? That I love daimons?"

"Just don't elaborate on anything. Answer yes or no, and that is it."

"I'm not stupid, Seth."

Seth arched a brow. "I didn't say you were. I just know you tend…to talk a lot."

"Oh. Like you're one—"

Seth dove in, sending a wave of water crashing over me, and I lost my balance. I sank under, only to find him swimming toward me. Recognizing the wild grin plastered across his face, I pushed back, but he caught the edge of my dress. I smacked his hand away and resurfaced. He came up a few feet away, shaking his head, sending beads of water flying.

I splashed him. "You talk more than I do."

He floated over to the side and swung one arm over the edge. Squinting through water and hair, he made a face at me. "You look like a drowned monkey."

"What? I do not." I ran a hand over my hair, then under my eyes. Come to think of it, I probably had brutal raccoon eyes right now. "Wait. Do I?"

Seth nodded. "Honestly, you look like a mess. This was a bad idea. What was I thinking?"

"Shut up. You don't look so hot yourself."

That wasn't entirely true. Seth looked rather…nice soaked. The whole shirtless thing probably helped. A little bit. Not much. For some bizarre reason, I thought about the day the rune had appeared.

His lips curved into a mad sort of grin as he placed his hand over the water. "Watch this."

I tried keeping the edges of my dress from floating all the way up. "Watch what?"

The water under his hand spun, much like water going down a drain. Then it shot straight up in the air, reaching for the ceiling. The cone of water twisted in midair, arced, and then came down.

I couldn't move back quickly enough.

Water funneled around me, pulsating and drowning out everything. Then it froze. I couldn't see beyond the wall of still water. I tilted my head back and smiled. Being stuck in a Seth-made typhoon was strange, but also cool. Tentatively, I reached out and poked a finger through it. Wrong move. It all came crashing down.

The weight of the water pushed me under, and when I came back up, an all-out water war ensued. We both were acting like two bored kids who'd sneaked away from their parents, but this was *fun*. It didn't matter I was sorely outmatched in the water arena and Seth seemed intent on drowning me.

I wasn't thinking about Aiden, or the Council, or *anything*.

Laughing and swallowing way too much water, I backed off while Seth pushed clumps of blond hair out of his eyes. "You're such a girl, Seth. Do we need to take a grooming break?"

"You need to give up." He reared back, sending his arm crashing against the surface of the water. "You can't beat me. Ever. At anything. Give it up."

I swam back, slipped under and resurfaced quickly. "I don't give up, Seth."

He inched closer. "Well, we all have to learn how to someday. Besides me. I'm secure in my awesomeness."

"More like you're secure in your douchiness."

"You are such a goner." He shot across the water, and I dropped underneath. I aimed for his legs, thinking that if I could take them out, I could take him out.

But it didn't quite go as planned.

I got one arm around a leg and tugged. Seth retaliated by reaching down and tugging me back up to the surface. The moment my head broke through the water, I struggled and cursed. Unsurprisingly, a long, wet gown really hindered the use of one's legs.

"That's cheating, Alex." Seth planted both hands above my hips. "You know what happens to cheaters."

I tried prying his fingers from my waist. "Don't you dare!"

He lifted me until over half of my body was out of the water. I stared down at his face. His smile went up a notch as I dangled above him. "Cold up there, huh?"

Yeah, it kind of was. "Stupid down there, huh?"

Seth's brows flew up. "For one in such a precarious position, you sure don't know how to talk yourself out of it."

"That's because it's hard to reason with idiots." I gave him a cheeky grin. "Why bother?"

"Oh? Is that how it is? Well, my little Apollyon-in-training, have a nice flight."

"Seth! I swear I will—"

Using the air element, he launched me out of the water, cutting off my words. I went up…and up another couple of feet, and back down in a mess of arms and red silk several feet away. Water went up my nose as I sank to the bottom of the pool.

Breaking the surface, I immediately started yelling things only Seth could truly appreciate. A lot of four-letter words that rhymed with other four-letter words. This resulted in me flying back through the air again and again.

"Okay. Okay," I gasped, hanging above him. "You're awesome."

"And?"

"And…you're not a douche…all the time—Wait!" I stalled as my knees came out of the water. "You're just a *great* person."

Seth frowned. "That doesn't sound very sincere."

My hands slipped off his. "Okay. You're the best Apollyon there is."

He tipped his head to the side and arched a brow. "I'm the only Apollyon there is right now."

I grinned. "You're still the best."

He sighed, but he lowered me back down. "Now you really do look like a drowned monkey."

"Thanks." I started for the shallow end of the pool, but Seth pushed through the water like a damn fish.

He circled one arm around my waist and flipped me back around. "Where do you think you're going?"

I went to push against his chest, but remembered there was literally nothing between my hands and his skin. I opted for his shoulders, which turned out to be rather pointless. "Don't throw me again."

"I'm not going to throw you."

I considered that for a moment. "Then I win the water war?"

"No."

"Damn. Well, I guess you have to be better than me at something. Congratulations."

"I'm always better than you. I'm—"

“Egotistical?” I supplied helpfully. “Narcissistic?”

He pressed forward, and I backed up, trying to keep as much space between us as possible. Not that it did any good in water. My legs floated everywhere I didn't want them to—like closer to him.

“I have some words for you, too. How about stubborn? Impudent?” he countered, slowly pushing on until my back hit the rough edge of the pool.

“Was ‘impudent’ your word choice of the day?”

He put his finger on my lips. “Well, yes it is. I could even use it in a sentence if you like.”

“That won't be necessary.”

He removed his finger and planted his hands on either side of me, effectively caging me in. I looked up and our eyes locked. An immediate level of awareness passed between us. It was powerful, almost like the charge that'd shot through us when I'd touched his rune.

Something I never planned on doing again.

The atmosphere was no longer playful or light, and as the silence grew, so did the nervousness in the pit of my stomach.

Seth had *that* look on his face—all intent and purpose-driven, and it was directed at me. He liked to flirt, liked to the push the line between us, but this—this was different. I felt *it* inside me, waking up and stirring.

Suddenly I thought of the heaviness I'd felt leaving the ball. “I think…we should head back now. I'm cold and it's getting late.”

Seth smiled. “No.”

“No?”

“I'm not done being stupid yet.” He leaned in. Strands of his wet hair brushed my forehead. “Actually, there's a lot of stupid left in me.”

At once, I placed my hands against his chest to stop him. His skin felt incredibly warm for being above the water. I opened my mouth to respond but found myself at a loss. A strange edginess swamped me. Somehow, he managed to get closer and I…I didn't push him away or move my hands. Seth seemed to read something in that, because his hands slipped away from the edge and fell to my waist.

"You know what?" His breath was warm against my cheek. "There are a lot of stupid things to do, but I really want to do the stupidest thing possible."

"What's that?"

"I want to kiss you."

My stomach hollowed. "That is crazy. I'm not Elena…or any number of girls."

"I know. Maybe that's why I want to."

I turned my head in the other direction. Or at least I thought I did. That was what I planned, but for some reason my head went the direction I didn't want it to—toward him and his warm breath. "You don't want to kiss me."

"But I do." His lips brushed against my cheek, sending shivers that had nothing to do with the cold air over me.

My hands slipped from his chest and I gripped the edge of the pool. "No, you don't."

Seth chuckled against my cheek. He slipped his fingers up my spine, curving his hand around the nape of my neck. "Are you arguing with me over what I want?"

"You're arguing with me."

"You're ridiculous." I felt him smile as his lips brushed over the line of my jaw, over the bruise. "It's such an annoying quality, yet strangely endearing."

My heart was beating way too fast. "Well…you're annoying, too."

He laughed again and pulled me against his chest. My fingers lost their tenuous grip on reality, falling into the water. "Why are we still talking?"

I rested my cheek against his shoulder and closed my eyes. "This is your one chance to talk without me telling you to shut up, because we aren't doing…anything else."

"Do you know how amusing I find you?" He shifted, pressing my back into the pool edge. His hand left my waist, smoothed down over my hip and thigh. Jerking back, I grabbed for his hand. Too late, he hooked my leg around his.

"What are…you doing?" I hated how breathless my voice sounded, confused by the need burning through me.

"Do you know why I think you're so amusing?" He slid the hand over my thigh.

"Why?"

"Because I know how badly you want me to kiss you." Seth cupped my chin, tipping my head back with his other hand.

"That's not true."

"You lie. Why? I have no idea." He pressed his lips against my cheek, then against my throat, my shoulder. The hand on my leg slipped between my thighs. My blood pounded, sending my heart into a frenzy. "I can feel what you're feeling. And I know you want me to kiss you."

I grasped his arms. "It's not…"

"Not what?" He lifted his head, brushing his nose against mine.

"I…"

"Just let me kiss you."

Gods, I needed him to kiss me. I needed him to keep doing what he was doing with his hands. But was any of this about the heart…or even the body? Or was it just what existed in both of us? The connection, the bond—whatever it was—controlling what we wanted. It sang between us, tightening until it was all that existed. But what I felt with Aiden wasn't a product of a connection, and it didn't fade away because he didn't return my feelings. I didn't even question what it was, but this? I had to question everything.

I opened my eyes. "Is this real?"

"Very real." He leaned back and brushed strands of wet hair off my face.

I did want to kiss him, and I also wanted to wrap myself around him. The ache his hands created was almost too hard to deny, but as I stared at him and saw the runes slipping down his neck, slowly reaching toward where my hands rested against his skin, I had no idea if I could trust what I wanted. There was something between us that neither of us fully understood. We didn't know what the connection actually controlled, what it could make us want.

His breath danced over my cheek, then my lips. "Angel, just let me kiss you."

With Aiden, with what I felt for him, there was nothing external—or internal—pulling me toward him except what I *felt* for him. It didn't matter that it was forbidden or that he didn't want me.

Seth dropped his hands suddenly. I hit the edge, wincing as the cement scraped my skin. The mark of the Apollyon shifted over his chest, swirling and moving. "You're thinking about Aiden."

I bit my lip. "Not in the way you think I am."

He ran both his hands over his head. Then he pushed forward, suddenly right in my face. "You know, I don't know which is worse. That I was stupid enough to want to kiss you, or the fact that you're still hung up on someone who doesn't even want you."

I blinked. "Wow. That's a little harsh."

"It's the truth, Alex. Even if he did profess his undying love for you, you can't have him."

I whirled around and hauled myself out of the pool. Standing above him, water ran off the ruined dress. "Just because I can't be with him doesn't change the way I feel."

In an instant, he was out of the water. "If you have this epic love for Aiden, why did you want to kiss me as badly as you did?"

I flushed hot with fury, the kind that only came from Seth making a point I couldn't argue. "I didn't kiss you, Seth! That should answer your question right there!"

"You wanted to. Trust me, I know you did." He smiled that smug smile. "You really wanted to."

"I don't know what I want!" I yelled, my hands balling into fists at my sides. "How do you know, Seth? How do you know it's not the damn connection between us instead of something real?"

The anger faded from Seth's eyes, replaced by surprise. "You think it's just the connection? Do you really think that's all I feel for you?"

I laughed harshly. "You say it yourself all the time! Anytime you do something nice for me, you say it's the connection forcing you to do so."

"Did you ever consider that I was joking?"

"No! Why would I? You said the connection would grow stronger between us," I said. "That's why you want to kiss me! It's not real."

"I know why I want to kiss you, Alex, and it has nothing to do with either of us being Apollyons. And apparently it has nothing to do with your common sense, either."

I narrowed my eyes. "Oh, shut up. I'm done talking—"

"I know exactly why." Seth stalked forward, backing me up until I hit the cement wall behind me and he stood inches away. "I can't believe I'd even have to spell it out for you."

Shivering in the cool, damp air, I flattened my hands against the wall. "You don't have to."

"You're the most frustrating person I know."

I rolled my eyes. "And that makes you want to kiss me? You're twisted."

His eyes burned like liquid gold. "Do you feel the connection between us right now?"

I frowned, searching for the telltale signs the connection was doing its thing. I didn't feel that swamping heat or edginess, so I was going to go with no. "Not really, but I don't know what it feels—"

Seth grasped the sides of my face and brought my mouth to his. I froze, shocked that he'd actually kiss me after all of that, but he was. Soft, tentative, questioning kisses, as if he was doing this for the very first time, and I *so* knew that wasn't the case.

I knew I should stop him, because allowing him to kiss me totally defeated the point of the argument we'd just had, but I found myself closing my eyes instead. His mouth was so warm and sweet, dizzying actually. Then it deepened, stealing my breath and sending my heart racing.

Kissing wasn't a big deal, so this kiss shouldn't be any different. But by the gods, I'd never been kissed like this before.

I looped my arms around his neck, tangling my fingers in his hair, and then I was kissing him back. Kissing him with the same wild abandonment he dove into, and gods, I liked kissing Seth.

He was really good at it.

Seth nipped at my lower lip as he pulled back just enough that I could breathe. "You can't tell me you didn't like that." He pressed his lips to mine again, soaking up my response. "And don't you dare tell me you didn't kiss me."

I let my hands slide down to his chest. I knew, if I opened my eyes, I'd see the marks. "I…don't know what that was."

He chuckled and brushed his lips across mine. "You have a choice, Alex."

I opened my eyes then. The marks stretching across his face were faint, but I still had the insane desire to run my fingers along them. It took everything in me not to. I met his eyes. "What choice?"

His hands dropped to my shoulders, then made their way to my waist. They fisted the soaked material, holding me still. "You can choose to continue wasting away for something you can never have."

I swallowed. "Or?"

He smiled. "You can choose not to."

"Seth, I—"

"Look, I know you aren't over him." He said *him* like it was some kind of venereal disease. "But I do know you like me. I'm not suggesting anything. Not asking for stupid little labels or promises. No expectations."

I took a shallow breath. "What are you suggesting?"

"You choose to see what happens." Seth let go of my dress and stepped back, running his hands through his wet hair. "Between us—you choose us."

Choose us? I shivered and wrapped my arms around me. Choose between what? Aiden was completely off-limits, and Seth and I—even though we were stuck with one another—couldn't go a day without wanting to knock each other's heads off. This didn't seem like a great choice.

Seth smiled faintly. "Think about it, at least." He turned around and went back to where he'd left his clothes.

I sagged against the wall and sighed. Seth had done some pretty nice things for me. He'd stayed with me after Caleb's death, defended me against the Master. But then there was Aiden and all that I felt for him, and the way he'd looked at me tonight.

But choosing Aiden meant choosing nothing.

Choosing Seth meant submitting to a whacked-out fate. Or did it?

My gaze fell to my hand. The rune on my palm shone an iridescent blue, as if it were pleased by Seth's suggestions. And his suggestion didn't sound so bad. No labels. No expectations. No feelings. And that was good, because my heart… my heart was somewhere else. Soon, I'd be heading home to North Carolina, where there would be no Caleb, no halfs who really wanted to be around me, and no more Aiden.

But there would be Seth.

I pushed off the wall. Seth had his back to me, head bent in concentration. *What was I doing?* I stopped a few feet behind him, my heart jumping in my throat. "Seth?"

He turned sideways, fingers finishing the last of the buttons. "Alex?"

"I…I choose you—or whatever it is that you're saying." I flushed. Gods, I sounded stupid. "I mean, I choose the whole seeing what—"

Seth's mouth cut my words off. His arms swept around me, dropping something warm and dry over my shoulders. I realized it was his suit jacket, but then I was thinking about how warm *he* felt. Before I knew it, I was gripping his shirt, arching against him, soaking up his warmth.

Then I felt it waking up like some kind of slumbering

giant, sending sparks of electricity over my skin. My palm itched—burned, really. I gasped against his lips. The kiss wasn't enough. I slid my hands under his shirt, over the hard expanse of his stomach.

He jerked back, breathing heavily. A fleeting, satisfied look shot across his face—gone so quickly I couldn't be sure what I'd seen. Then he smiled, and I knew I couldn't have seen that calculated edge to his stare. The transformation that occurred was nothing short of amazing. "You're not sleeping in that bed—in that terrible little room—tonight."

CHAPTER TWENTY-TWO

I did sleep in my bed, in that terrible little room.

And I did so alone.

It'd taken every ounce of my self-control to convince Seth that sharing the same bed wasn't a good idea, which was difficult, mainly because my body had thought it was an awesome idea. Surprisingly, my brain had won that battle.

I didn't know why I'd kissed Seth—once, then twice. Hell, I didn't even know why I agreed to *see what happens*. The smart thing would've been to punch Seth and make a run for it.

But I never did the smart thing.

"That *was* a beautiful dress." Laadan wore a slight, curious frown. "I guess there are several ways to ruin silk, and I suppose a midnight swim would be one of the more daring ways to do so."

Cringing and flushing, I ran my hands down the only pair of dress pants I owned. They were made of some thin, black material and they swallowed my feet, which sucked. Even after

I'd destroyed Laadan's dress, she'd let me borrow some sexy black pumps that made me feel tall and clever.

"I'm really sorry about the dress." I glanced back at the double doors adorned with a golden eagle. "I have some money saved up. I can pay for it."

"No. Don't worry about it." She patted my shoulder. "Although I am curious as to what provoked you to leave the ball so quickly, and then go swimming. You left with your Seth. I'm assuming you went swimming with him?"

My cheeks flamed at the mention of Seth. If *my* Seth had been here to catch that, I'd never hear the end of it, but he wasn't allowed in the Council building. "He's not *my* Seth."

Marcus and Lucian rounded the corner before Laadan could do more than give me a knowing smile. Oddly, I felt grateful to see them.

Lucian floated up to me, clasping my cold hand in his. Or maybe his hand was so warm that mine felt chilled to the bone. "Dear, you look so nervous. There is nothing to be worried about. The Council will ask you a few questions, and that is all."

I met Marcus's stare over Lucian's shoulder. He looked like there was something to be worried about. Sliding my hand free, I resisted the urge to wipe it across my pants. "I'm not nervous."

Lucian patted my shoulder as he slid around me. "I must go in and take my seat. It's about to begin."

It being the whole reason I'd come up here. Watching the Council Guards hold the doors for Lucian, I decided I *wasn't* nervous. I just wanted to get this over and done with.

Marcus's lips were drawn tight when I faced him. Passing a meaningful look at Laadan, he waited until she nodded and followed Lucian into the Council before he spoke. "Alexandria,

I expect you to be on your best behavior in there. Do not allow yourself to get drawn into any arguments. Only answer their questions—nothing more. Do you understand?"

My eyes narrowed as I crossed my arms. "What do you all expect me to do? Go buck wild and start cussing people out?"

"Anything is possible, really. You're known for your temper, Alex. Some probably expect you to lose your cool," said a deep, familiar voice from behind me.

Every cell of my skin recognized and still responded to that voice. It didn't matter that I'd chosen Seth last night. Wasn't that what I'd done? My brain screamed at my body to not turn around, but it didn't listen.

Aiden looked every inch a pure-blood. One lock of his otherwise tamed, dark hair kept falling forward, brushing against thick, sooty lashes. Dressed in that white, mafia-style getup, he appeared even more untouchable to me.

Marcus cleared his throat, and I realized I was staring.

Blushing fire-engine red, I turned to Marcus. "I know. Just answer their questions, blah, blah. I got it."

Marcus glared at me. "I hope so."

I didn't know how else to prove to them that I wasn't going to jump out of my chair and body-slam someone.

Marcus checked his watch. "We must head in. Alexandria, the Guards will call you when the Council is ready."

"I won't go in with you all?" I asked.

He shook his head and disappeared into the Council, which left Aiden and me alone with the silent Guards. Ignoring him was out of the question. "So…how have you been?"

Aiden stared somewhere over my head. "Good. You?"

"Good."

He nodded and then glanced at the doors.

The awkwardness of all of this pained me. "You can go in. You don't have to wait out here."

His gaze fell on me finally. "I do have to go in."

I nodded, biting the inside of my cheek. "I know."

Aiden started toward the door, but then stilled. Seconds went by before he pivoted back to me. "Alex, you can do this. I know you can."

Our eyes locked, and I sucked in air. Speechless, I stood there as his gaze left mine and roamed over my face. I couldn't remember if I'd put on any makeup today. Maybe some lip gloss? My hair was under control so it fell around my cheeks and covered my neck perfectly. I touched my lips, happy to find they felt glossy.

His eyes zeroed in on my movements before he broke away, running a hand over his head. He let out a ragged sound and when he spoke his voice was so low that I barely heard him. "I think…I'll remember how you looked last night for the rest of my life. Gods, you were so beautiful."

I may have stroked out.

The next thing I knew he'd disappeared beyond the heavy Council doors. He left me spinning in confusion. Hot then cold, kind and then standoffish. I didn't get it. Why tell me that…and then walk away? Like the day he'd said he wished Seth had killed the Master for hitting me. Why admit any of that?

Leaning against the wall, I let out a long, tired sigh. Now wasn't the time to obsess over Aiden's manic mood swings. I needed to focus on—

The door to my left opened, revealing a Council Guard. "Miss Andros, your presence has been requested."

Well, that came sooner than I'd expected. I pushed off the wall and followed the Guard into the Council. It looked different from what I remembered. Granted, the only time I had seen it was from the top balcony, hidden from the pures below. Titanium trim graced the curved benches that filled the ground floor of the coliseum. The symbols etched into the tiles were artfully done—nothing like the chicken scratches in the pathways back home. Things had to be bigger, better here.

Those in attendance swiveled around in their seats as I made my way down the center aisle. Openly curious stares met mine. Others were not so curious—more like downright hostile and suspicious.

Steeling myself, I focused on the raised dais ahead instead of the violent roiling in my stomach. The Ministers sat like gods about to rain down some great and terrible divine justice. They watched my progress, picking apart everything about me before I'd even reached them. Only one didn't seem bothered by me. Reclining in one of the smaller thrones, dressed in lavish white robes, Lucian stared at Telly. Or perhaps he was staring at Telly's throne, imagining himself in the seat that offered the closest thing our world had to absolute power.

An open chair faced the audience in front of the Eight, directly between two thrones occupied by Head Minister Telly and Diana Elders. I stared at the seat, unsure if I was supposed to wait until I was given the okay to sit or make myself at home.

I sat.

A hush of disapproval swept through the crowd of pures. Apparently, that'd been the wrong action. This was starting out great. Lifting my eyes, I glanced at the balcony and caught a shadow flickering back from the railing.

Seth.

I felt Telly rise behind me, but I didn't dare look. Somehow I knew that would also give rise to another murmur of censure.

Casually, I rested my hands on the arms of the chair and stared out at the crowd in front of me. I searched out Aiden immediately. He was leaning forward in his seat, eyes fastened on the Ministers behind me.

"Alexandria Andros." Head Minister Telly drifted around my chair. He stopped beside me, tipping his head to the side. With an elegant wave toward the audience, he smiled broadly, making him look like a demented cherub past its prime. "We must ask that you swear an oath to the Council and to the gods that you will answer each question today with the utmost honesty. Do you understand?"

I nodded, eyeing the Head Minister. Was it just me, or did the gray clinging to the hair around his temples appear to be spreading?

"Breaking this oath would be an act of treason not just against the Council, but also the gods. Doing so would result in your removal from the Covenant. This is also understood, I assume?"

"Yes."

"Then do you, Alexandria Andros, swear to disclose all information regarding the events that took place in Gatlinburg?"

I met Telly's pale eyes. "Yes."

His smile turned brittle as he held my gaze. "Good. How have you found your accommodations here, Alexandria? Have they been to your liking?" Telly *tsked* softly. "Look only at me, Alexandria."

The arms of the chair groaned as my fingers dug into the wood. "Everything has been *lovely*."

One dark brow arched as he glided to the other side of my chair. "That pleases me to hear. Alexandria, why did your mother leave the Covenant three years ago?"

I blinked tightly. "What does that have to do with what happened in Gatlinburg?"

"You have been asked a question—no, do not look out to the audience. Why did your mother leave the Covenant three years ago?"

"I…I don't know why." I kept my eyes on Telly this time. "She never told me."

Telly glanced at the audience while he rubbed his thumb and index finger together. "You do not know?"

"No," I heard myself say, staring at his hand.

"That is not true, Alexandria. You know why your mother left the Covenant."

Jerking my eyes away from his hand, I shook my head. "My mother never told me why. All I know is what other people have said."

"What were those reasons?"

Where was he going with this? I followed his slow, purposeful movements. He was circling me. "She left because the oracle told her I would become the next Apollyon."

"Why would that make her leave?"

I couldn't help it. My gaze moved to the balcony, to where I knew Seth watched. "Alexandria, do not look away!" he snapped.

Now I understood why Marcus had looked so worried. My entire body thrummed with the desire to plant my foot into Telly's gut. I glared at him. "She wanted to protect me."

A different Minister spoke next. The older pure woman's voice rubbed like sandpaper over my skin. "From whom would she have wanted to protect you?"

Was I supposed to continue looking at Telly or the Minister? "I don't know. Maybe she was worried about the gods getting upset over there being two of us."

"That would be a concern," she responded. "There should not be two of you in the same generation."

"What other reasons would there be?" asked Telly.

Words tumbled out of my mouth. Not good or smart ones. "Maybe she was afraid of what the Council would do."

Telly stiffened. "That is absurd, Alexandria."

"It's what she said."

"Really?" His brows rose. "I thought she never told you why she pulled you from the Covenant?"

Dammit. I could imagine the look on Aiden's and Marcus's faces. "She never told me why before she was…before she changed."

"But she told you after she chose to become a daimon?" asked a male Minister.

"My mother didn't choose to become a daimon!" I gripped the arms of the chair again, drawing in several deep breaths. "She was forced to become one. And yes, she told me that I wouldn't have lived if I'd stayed at the Covenant."

"What else did she tell you about why she left?" asked Telly.

"That was it."

"Why did you never report her during the three years you were missing?"

"She was my mom. I was afraid she would be punished."

"Rightfully so," said the elder Minister. "What she did was unforgivable. From the moment she was told of your true nature, it was her duty to tell the Council."

"That is true, Minister Mola." Telly paused, placing a hand on the back of my chair. "How is it that you did not know your mother had turned?"

Air couldn't fill my lungs quickly enough. "I found her

and I thought she was dead. I killed the daimon that…was hurting her."

"Then what happened?" Telly asked so softly I felt sure no one else could hear him.

My throat burned. "There was another daimon, and I…I ran."

"You ran?" repeated Telly, loud enough for the entire Council to hear.

"I thought she was dead." I swallowed, my gaze falling to the floor. "I was trying to get back to the Covenant."

"So, it took the perceived death of your mother for you to remember your duty to the Covenant?" Telly didn't wait for me to answer, which was a good thing. I had no answer for that. "You were found in Atlanta? With four daimons, is that not correct?"

What did any of this have to do with what'd happened in Gatlinburg? "They were following me. It wasn't like I was hanging out with them."

"Your tone is one of disrespect," snapped the elder Minister. "It would do you well to remember your position, *half-blood*."

I bit down on my lip until I tasted blood.

Telly drifted to the right of me. "Were you aware of your mother's whereabouts after you returned to the Covenant, Alexandria?"

A fine trickle of sweat traced down my spine. "No."

"But you left the Covenant in August to find her, did you not? After she took part in the Lake Lure massacre? And you did find her?" Telly's full lips twisted cruelly.

Telly had tripped me up *again*. I closed my eyes and inhaled. "I didn't know *where* she was. I didn't even know she was alive until Lucian told me."

"Ah, yes." He glanced behind me at Lucian. "What did you do once you found out she was alive?"

Punched and kissed a pure-blood, but I doubted he wanted to know that. Actually, he'd love to know that; he'd use it to send me to the Masters within the hour. "Nothing."

Telly clucked his tongue. "But—"

Anger pulsed through me, pounding in my temples. "What do these questions have to do with what my mother told me the daimons were planning? They want to overtake the Council. Turn halfs and send them back to the Covenants to kill. Isn't that more important?"

Surprisingly, Telly handled my temporary loss of sanity well. "It has everything to do with it, Alexandria. What provoked you to leave the Covenant in search for your mother?"

The need to lie was almost too great. "When I realized she'd killed at Lake Lure, I left. I figured she'd find me and she did. I felt like...she was my responsibility, my problem."

"Interesting." Telly roamed to the edge of the dais. Looking out over the audience he spoke louder. "Is it true you did not fight Rachelle when you saw her in Bald Head?"

I glared at the back of Telly's head. "Yes."

He cocked his head to the side. "Why?"

"I froze. She was my *mother*."

"Half-bloods see through the elemental magic. We cannot. How could you see past the monster she'd become?" He pivoted around, smiling at me. "This is what we do not understand, Alexandria. You left Florida, claiming that you believed she was dead. You came back to the Covenant, and your mother followed you, leaving behind a trail of slaughtered pure-bloods and Guards."

"What? There was only the attack at Lake Lure. She didn't—"

"You've been sadly misled." His smile grew wider, truer. "She was responsible for over twenty attacks across the south-eastern coast. We were able to track her progress right to the doorsteps of the North Carolina Covenant. She sent a daimon half-blood back to the Covenant. Was that to draw you out?"

Twenty attacks? No one had told me that. Not Aiden, Marcus, nor even Seth. They had to have known. Why wouldn't they've told me that?

"Alexandria?"

I lifted my eyes. "Yes…I guess she wanted to draw me out."

"It worked. You left the day after Kain Poros had returned and murdered several pure-bloods." Telly strode across the dais. "Tell me, Alexandria, a half-blood named Caleb Nicolo was also with you in Gatlinburg?"

My chest clenched. "Yes."

Telly nodded. "Did he try to stop you in Bald Head?"

"Yes."

"Is this the same half-blood who died a few weeks ago?" asked a female Minister. "In a daimon attack while he was with this one?"

"I believe so," Telly answered.

"How convenient," the Minister murmured, but it sounded like he had screamed those words. "While you were in Gatlinburg with Rachelle, what did she tell you the daimons planned to do?"

Somewhat sick to my stomach, I told the Council what Mom had planned. Remembering my instructions, I didn't tell them it was actually Eric who elaborated on the whole thing. Nothing crossed Telly's face as he watched me. Honestly, I don't even think he cared about what I was saying.

"They plan to attack the Council and bring us down?" The old Minister snorted. "This is ridiculous. All of this."

Telly chuckled then. "It is to think that a bunch of addicts could form a cohesive plan."

"Addicts? Yes, they're addicted to aether, but they are the most dangerous kind of addict," said Minister Diana Elders, speaking for the first time. "We cannot dismiss what they are capable of. Knowing they can turn half-bloods changes things. And obviously the gods are questioning our ability to rein the daimons back in."

This started a battle of wills for the next several minutes. A few Ministers didn't like the idea of ignoring the daimons' plans, while the others simply didn't take the threat seriously. Suggestions were thrown around, like increasing the number of Sentinels and sending them out to target large infestations of daimons, but the majority of Ministers didn't see any reason to do so. The talks kept coming back to *me*.

My stomach filled with dread as understanding dawned. Telly and much of the Council outright dismissed the daimons' plans. Suddenly I knew what my mother had told me was not the whole reason why I'd been ordered to attend this session. Marcus had been *sadly misled*. Or maybe he'd known all along. Distracted by the other Ministers, I was able to look out over the crowd without Telly bitching me out.

Aiden whispered to Marcus, his hands tight and white-knuckled on the back of the bench in front of him. I looked up at the balcony. I could only imagine what Seth thought of all this.

Telly finally returned his attention to me. "Rachelle planned on turning you into a daimon?"

I wanted to say *no shit*, but I decided against it. "Yes."

Telly turned his hawkish nose into the air. "Why?"

I rubbed my hand over my forehead. "She wanted me to become the Apollyon as a daimon. She thought she'd be able to control me then."

"So, she wanted to use you?" asked Telly. "To do what?"

"She wanted to make sure I didn't come after her, I guess."

"What would you do for her?"

I met Telly's stare. Somehow, I think he already knew this part. "She wanted me to take out the other Apollyon…and she wanted me to help the daimons with their plans."

"Oh yes, their plans to take out the Council and enslave the pure-bloods?" Telly shook his head, smiling. "How many times were you tagged, Alexandria?"

My entire body tensed. "I don't know. A lot."

He appeared to consider this. "Enough to be turned, you think?"

Nightmares of those hours locked away with Daniel and Eric haunted me still. I remember that last tag—the one I'd felt sure would finally darken my soul, shatter it into nothing. One more tag and I would've crossed over to the dark side. A fine sheen of cold sweat broke out across my forehead.

"Alexandria?"

I blinked, bringing his face back into focus. "Almost enough."

"Did you try to stop them? Trained or not, you had already killed two daimons by then." Disbelief coated the back of my throat. "Tagging is very painful," Telly continued, stopping beside me for what felt like the hundredth time. His face seemed fuller when he stood close. "How could you allow that to happen repeatedly? It seems that a half-blood would do everything and anything to prevent being tagged."

"I couldn't fight them."

His dark brows rose in incredulity. "You couldn't or wouldn't?"

I closed my eyes, struggling with patience. "I promised her I wouldn't if she didn't kill Caleb. I had no other choice."

"There are always choices, Alexandria." He paused, disgust curling his lip as he stared down at me. "To allow something so revolting seems suspicious. Perhaps you wanted to be turned."

"Head Minister," Lucian spoke up then. "I understand that some of these questions are necessary, but Alexandria did not submit to those atrocities willingly. To even suggest something like that seems unnatural and cruel."

"Is that so?" Telly sneered at me.

"Wait a second," I said, his words finally sinking in. "Are you suggesting that I wanted to be turned into something that evil? That I asked for it?"

Telly raised his hands haughtily. "How do you think we'd interpret it?"

I looked at the audience then, briefly catching a pained look on Marcus's face. "Do you know that sounds like a rapist's motto? She wore a short skirt, therefore she *wanted* it?"

Several gasps could be heard from the audience. It seemed the word "rapist" was unseemly. The smug look slowly slipped from Telly's face. "Alexandria, you are out of line."

My brain clicked off at that point. What Daniel had said to me before he'd tagged me filled my mind. It was like Telly thought the same thing. That I *wanted* to be tagged, that I enjoyed it. I stood. "You're telling me I'm out of line?"

"No one gave you leave." Telly drew himself up to his full height.

"Oh, I'm not leaving." All eyes were on me. I reached down and pulled my sweater up and over my head. There was a moment when no one seemed to breathe. I met the open-mouthed stares; I'd think I didn't have a camisole on underneath the sweater by the looks on their faces.

"What in the world are you doing, Alexandria?" demanded Lucian.

Ignoring him, I stepped away from the chair and held my arms out in front of me. "Does this look like something I wanted to go along with? That I asked for this?"

Against their will, dozens and dozens of eyes fastened on my arms. Most gasped and shuddered, looking away quickly. Others didn't. As if they couldn't tear their eyes from the patchy red skin and its unnatural shine. My gaze flitted across the floor as Telly looked like he was having a heart attack beside me. I saw the proud tilt to Laadan's chin. A few rows in front of her, I saw Dawn's horrified gaze. Further back, behind the Council members, Marcus paled. It kind of hit me that he'd never seen my scars, only caught glimpses of the ones on my neck. I don't think he'd known how bad they were. I felt a hot flush crawl up my neck, but the stunned look of pride on Aiden's face gave me the confidence to face the Ministers.

I wondered what Seth's expression looked like. He was probably smiling. He loved it when I was irrational, and this was *really* irrational.

Twisting around, I showed them my arms. "They look like they hurt, don't they? They did. It's the worst kind of pain you can imagine."

"Alexandria, sit down. We get your point." Telly reached for me, but I stepped aside.

A Guard moved in, picking up my sweater. He held it, his eyes nervously bouncing between Telly and me.

I glanced at the other Guards, hoping they weren't planning on body-slamming me to the ground. All but one were half-bloods and none of them seemed willing to stop me.

Tipping my head at the Ministers, I tried to keep the smile off my face. "So, do you really think I went along with my mother? That I wanted this?"

Diana paled and looked away, shaking her head sadly. The remaining Ministers reacted much like the audience had. Either way, I'm pretty sure I'd gotten my point across.

A furious shade of red covered Telly's cheeks. "Are you done, Alexandria?"

I met his scowl with my own. Leisurely, I went back to my chair and sat down. "I guess so."

Telly ripped the sweater out of the Guard's hand. I could tell he wanted to throw it at me, but with amazing self-control, he handed it over. I didn't put it back on. "Now where were we?"

"We were at the point where you were accusing me of wanting to become a daimon."

Several Ministers inhaled sharply. Telly looked seconds away from exploding. Leaning down so that our faces were inches apart, he spoke low and quick. "You are an unnatural thing, do you understand me? A harbinger of death to our kind and to our gods. The both of you."

I shrunk back, wide-eyed. "Harbinger of death" sounded extreme and crazy.

"Head Minister," called Lucian. "We could not hear your question. Would you care to speak again?"

Telly straightened. "I asked her if there was anything more she would like to add." My jaw hit the floor.

He smiled evenly. "There are areas besides the event in Gatlinburg that concern me greatly, Alexandria. Your behavior before you left the Covenant and the fighting you have taken part in upon your return have served you a great disadvantage, I'm afraid. And how is it that the night the Covenant was breached in North Carolina, you were outside your dorm after the curfew implemented for half-bloods?"

I so knew where this was going, so I cut to the chase. "I didn't let the daimons in, if that is what you're suggesting."

Telly's smile turned sour. "So it appears. Then there is your behavior since you arrived here. You accused a pure-blood of using a compulsion against you, did you not?"

"She did what?" screeched the old female Minister. "To accuse a pure-blood of such an act is shocking. Was there any proof, Minister Telly?"

"My Guards could not find anything to support the claim." Telly paused dramatically. "And then you attacked a Master who was disciplining a servant."

Several Ministers lost it then. Telly preened as they demanded to know exactly what occurred. I pictured rushing across the dais and kicking Telly in the groin over and over again.

When it calmed down a bit, Telly addressed the Council. His voice rang loudly through the coliseum. "I fear that we have a greater concern than daimons pulling together and attacking us in droves. What you see sitting before us may look like an ordinary half-blood, but we all know that is not the case. In a matter of a few months, she will become the second Apollyon. If she is even half as uncontrollable as she is now, what do you think will occur when she Awakens?"

My heart stuttered, missing a beat.

"As the Head Minister, it pains me deeply to suggest this, but I fear we have no other choice. We must protect the future of our true Masters. I petition that we remove Alexandria Andros from the Covenant and place her under the supervision of the Masters." I jerked forward blindly. I couldn't even move as the rush of fear coated my mouth and churned my stomach into raw knots.

This was what Telly wanted—the whole reason for me being here. It had nothing to do with what the daimons planned.

From above, I felt a tempest building. It drifted over my skin, raising the tiny hairs on my body.

Seth was a storm about to explode.

"Minister Telly, my *stepdaughter* has committed no crime that warrants servitude," Lucian objected. "She has to be found guilty before you can expel her from the Covenant and place her into servitude."

"As the Head Minister—"

"You have a lot of power as the Head Minister. You can expel her from the Covenant, but you cannot sentence her to servitude without due cause or by vote of the Council," Lucian said. "Those are the rules."

I looked up, my eyes meeting Aiden's. This was one of those rare moments in my life that I knew *exactly* what Aiden was thinking.

I twisted around in the chair. Telly glared at Lucian, but I saw that Lucian was right. Telly could expel me, but he couldn't send me into servitude on a whim. He would need the Council to do so, and I had a feeling if the Council agreed it would be the last thing they ever did.

"Then I call for a vote." Telly's voice was like ice.

I calculated the distance from where I sat and the door to my right. My muscles tensed as I let go of the chair and twisted sideways. My sweater fell from my lap. I didn't want to hurt the half-blood Guards, but I was going to get past them.

Then what? Run like hell.

"How do you vote?" asked Telly.

The first "yes" sent a shiver through me; the second caused the air to ripple with electricity. The audience shifted as the third "yes" skyrocketed the tension. I wanted to look at Aiden one last time, but I couldn't take my eyes off the door. It would be my only chance.

Three of the Ministers said "no," and Telly stalked toward the end of the dais. The next said "yes," and my stomach dropped. I wanted to cry out, but fear clamped my throat shut. Facing down daimons was one thing, but a lifetime of servitude was my worst fear.

"Head Minister Elders, you are the last vote." I could hear the smile in Telly's voice.

Silence filled the room, holding the pures transfixed and stretching my nerves into taut lines. *This was it... This was it.* I closed my eyes, drawing in a deep breath.

"She has proven to be...a problem," Diana said, her voice as clear as Telly's. "There are many areas which concern me greatly, but I have to vote 'no.' She has to break the Breed Order to be placed in servitude, and she has not, Minister Telly. Everything that has been provided has been circumstantial."

Sagging against the chair, the air expelled from my lungs. Violent energy pulled back, slithering from my skin as it made its way back to its host.

Telly didn't take that well, but there was nothing he could do.

He returned to my side, glaring. I wanted nothing more than to karate chop him in the neck.

"Then Miss Andros, you shall continue as you are, for now." Telly smiled tightly. "One more mistake, Alexandria, one more time and that will be it. You will be placed into servitude."

CHAPTER TWENTY-THREE

After Council, Marcus escorted me to my room with explicit instructions. "Do not leave this room unless someone is with you."

Had he seen this room? Spending the rest of "however long it took for Seth to show up or Laadan to take pity on me" felt like punishment. I hadn't done anything wrong. It wasn't my fault Telly was a lunatic, hell-bent on sending me into servitude.

But I spent the rest of the day and the better part of the evening in my room, picturing the look on Telly's face after I Awakened and lit him up with enough Apollyon juice to obliterate him into nothing. And all those pures who'd looked at my scars with such disgust? I'd give them something to freak out about. Okay. Maybe I was overreacting a tad bit. But Telly's antagonistic attitude chafed at me. I needed to get out, needed to do something.

What I really needed was to hit something.

Just when I was about to go crazy, there was a soft knock

on my door. Rushing toward it, I threw it open. Laadan stood in the doorway, two crystal glasses in her hands. Her cheeks were flushed, eyes bright.

Please be here to let me out of this room.

Her eyes weren't really focused on me as she smiled. "I figured you could stretch your legs." She stepped back. "Coming?"

Thank you, gods. I followed her graceful form down the hall and the steps. Downstairs, the pures were in full celebratory mode. From the sounds coming out of the ballroom and reception hall, they sounded trashed already. No one would be paying attention to me. They were too busy partying it up. Their blasé attitude toward everything was infuriating and frustrating.

"I thought you could use the company," she said slowly, speaking for the first time since she'd appeared outside my door.

We stopped outside the crowded reception hall. Laadan stood beneath a painting of the Goddess Hera. The resemblance between the two was striking. She offered me a glass of the luminous red liquid. "Here, you deserve this after the day you had."

The glass felt warm in my hand. "What is it?"

She smiled as her gaze drifted away. "It's something special for a special girl. You'll love it."

"Are you buzzing?" I giggled.

Laadan sighed dreamily. "It's a beautiful night, Alex. How is your drink?"

I lifted the glass and took a cautious sniff. It smelled magnificent—like wild orchids, and a hint of honey and sesame. Looking up, I saw Laadan float into the entrance of the reception hall. I trailed behind her, my gaze gliding across the crowd as I brought the glass to my lips. I saw Marcus and Diana standing super close. Once again, the smile on Marcus's face confused me. He never smiled like that, especially not when I was around.

Giggles erupted across the room, drawing my attention. Young pure girls surrounded a good-looking male, clamoring over each other to be the closest to him. Several Guards stood behind the happy little group, looking equally bored and aloof. Among them stood the pure-blood Guard whom Telly had called on during the first session. I shuddered, holding the glass tighter. Then my eyes flitted farther into the hall and settled on Aiden.

Dawn stood by his side, looking stunningly beautiful and staring at him with large eyes the color of amethyst. Seeing them together didn't bring the warm and fuzzies. He'd never showed her an ounce of interest outside of being friendly, but she was the kind of girl Aiden would be allowed to date—should date.

Maybe he'd marry her one day—or another pure like Dawn. He'd settle down and commit. *Stop*, I ordered myself. That didn't matter—not even if he had a dozen pure-blooded babies. I'd accepted I couldn't be with him. Besides, I'd kind of chosen Seth. But hurt climbed deep inside my chest, taking root around my heart. I deserved a swift kick in the butt for standing here, staring at him like some kind of obsessive stalker chick.

"Your drink, dear, are you not going to try it?"

"Oh." I glanced down. It still felt wonderfully warm in my hand. The drink burned my lips and the tip of my tongue but went down surprisingly smoothly. It actually tasted minty—a warm wintergreen. "It tastes…"

Laadan was gone.

Surprised by her vanishing act, I looked around the hall, finding Aiden instead of Laadan. He'd moved, standing at the end of the hall now. Minus Dawn, he spoke to another pure, but he appeared focused on me.

His disapproval stretched beyond where he stood and slammed into me. Was it because I was outside my room? If so, that irked me. What also irked me was the fluttering in my chest.

Aiden broke away from the pure, stepping forward and looking very, very angry. My heart leapt in my chest. He was coming to me—not Dawn, not some other pure, but *me*. The fluttering in my chest increased.

Any attention was good attention.

Suddenly, I hated that idea. Hated the fact I would be *satisfied* with that. I tipped the glass back and took a long swallow. It was either that or throw myself on the floor, sobbing and flailing.

I took another sip, expecting the burning this time. It did taste good, really good. I looked up again and found that a tall, blond pure partially blocked Aiden, but his furious gaze still found me. I quirked a brow at him and brought the glass to my lips again, taking another draft.

Aiden cut around the pure and made a beeline straight for me.

Out of nowhere, and I mean freaking nowhere, Seth appeared and whipped the drink out of my hand, splashing red drops all over my sweater.

"Jeez!" I ran my hand over my mouth. "Was that necessary?"

Seth brought the glass to his face and sniffed it. Swearing under his breath, he shoved it at Aiden. "Who gave you this?" Seth demanded.

"Why do you care? It's just a drink."

"Alex, who gave you this drink?" Aiden's quiet voice left no room for me to push his buttons.

"Laadan gave it to me. What's the big deal?"

Seth's mouth dropped open, but Aiden's reaction was far stronger. "Shit. Unbelievable."

"What?" I looked between the two. "What's going on?"

"Freaking pures," Seth spat. "I can only begin to imagine what they hoped to achieve with this."

The glass looked like it would shatter in Aiden's hand. Fury radiated off him in waves and his eyes burned, but he wouldn't look at me now. Not at all. "Dammit. Was this your first glass?"

"Yes." I stepped forward. "Aiden, what's going on?"

Seth exhaled harshly. "Half a glass is more than enough."

"There is no way Laadan would have given her this." Aiden scowled. "She knows what this drink will do."

"Laadan did give it to me. I wouldn't lie about that. Tell me what the hell is going on."

Seth ran a hand over his head. "I think I'm going to hit someone."

I shot a look at Seth. He wouldn't look at me either. Was there something wrong with my face?

I put my hand to my cheeks and the only thing I noticed was my skin felt warm.

"I can't leave now." Aiden spoke in crisp, short words. "Telly and the other Ministers want us here. She can't be left alone, Seth."

Seth nodded. "I'll keep an eye on her."

Aiden barked a short laugh. "Yeah, I don't think so."

"Then what do you suggest we do?" Seth demanded. "Let her roam free?"

My temper snapped. I reached out and grabbed Aiden's arm—a bad thing to do to a pure in public, but they were acting like I wasn't even standing there. "What is going on?"

Aiden whirled around and grasped my hand, pulling me between the two of them. "There is no way Laadan would have given you this drink freely. Did she seem strange to you? Acting different in any way?"

"Yes," I whispered. "She seemed buzzed."

His eyes snapped fire. "She was compelled to give you this drink."

"No way, that's impossible. It's completely illegal to compel another pure. You have to—"

"Someone set you up, Alex, and they wanted to badly enough to break the rules themselves. All pures know what that drink is just by looking at it. You were given Aphrodesian Brew, Alex."

"Brew? Oh. *Oh*. Oh, my gods." I felt cold and hot all at once. I'd just drunk the equivalent of an Olympian roofie. Disbelief set in. "You have to be wrong. A pure wouldn't compel another pure, and Laadan would never give me something like that. I don't care what you say."

"Alex," Aiden said gently. "There are pures who know you're close with Laadan."

"Aiden, we need to get her out of here. Soon," Seth interjected.

I glanced at him. "I feel fine. I must not have had enough."

Seth laughed dryly. "Yeah."

Aiden let go of my hand, staring at Seth. "I don't like you—let alone trust you."

A muscle feathered along Seth's jaw. "You don't have any other options at this point. I won't let anything happen to her, Aiden. And I wouldn't...take advantage of her."

I shot Seth a dirty look. "No one is taking advantage of me unless I want to be taken advantage of."

Whoa, that didn't come out right.

"Out of the question," Aiden said in a low, dangerous way.

"Guess what? I don't like you, either. But you don't have any other choice. Either you risk this or you trust me enough to know that I'll keep an eye on her." Seth paused, his gaze meeting Aiden's. "I have just as much invested as you."

I scratched my leg. "Invested in what?" They ignored me.

Aiden sort of growled. "If anything—anything happens to her—"

"I know," replied Seth. "You'll kill me."

"I'll do worse," Aiden spoke softly. "Don't take her to her room. We don't need Marcus knowing about this. Take her to…your room. As soon as I can, I will come." He turned to me and forced a smile. I hated that kind of smile. "Everything is going to be okay. Just please, please listen to Seth, and whatever you do, don't leave his room."

I stared at Aiden. "Wait. I want—"

Aiden had already turned and disappeared into the crowd. Then Seth took hold of my hand, leading me from the hall. I really didn't know what to expect. I'd heard rumors at the Covenant about the Brew, knew that Lea had supposedly had some, but I'd never seen anyone under its influence.

Seth didn't say anything as we navigated the hallways and headed upstairs. Several flights of stairs later, I still felt okay. "I really feel fine. Nothing is wrong with me. I'm sure I can go to my room. I won't leave."

Seth pulled me down the hallway.

"Look, why won't you talk to me? Especially after last night—"

He shot me a dangerous look over his shoulder. "This right now has nothing to do with last night."

I glared back at him even though I thought his hand felt incredibly smooth around mine. "Are you mad at me?"

"Alex, I'm not mad at you. But I am pissed right now. It's best I just don't speak. I might end up burning down this building." Letting go of my hand then, he pushed open the door to his room and motioned me forward. "In."

I shot him a haughty look. Really, they were making this into a bigger deal than—"What the hell?"

Seth kicked the door shut behind him. "What?"

"How come you get this awesome room?" I turned around, amazed by the cathedral ceilings, plush carpets, and a big screen television that took up half the wall. And the bed—it was the size of a boat. My current predicament was temporarily forgotten. "I've been sleeping in a closet. This isn't fair."

He dropped his key on a dresser. "I'm the Apollyon."

"So? I am, too, and I got a matchbox for a room. A coffin would've been bigger."

"You're not an Apollyon yet."

That was the extent of our conversation for several minutes. I watched him prowl around the room and then over to the window. There he stayed.

"What're you doing?"

Seth leaned against the windowsill, attention fastened on whatever he saw outside. Several strands of hair had slipped from the tie and obscured most of his expression. "Help yourself to whatever you want in the room. Watch some TV or go to sleep."

My temper stretched and snapped. "You're an ass." He didn't respond.

I shifted uncomfortably, wishing I'd thrown on a shirt

under the hoodie. The room felt steamy, nearly unbearable. I went to the bed to sit down but stopped. A strange sensation crawled up my spine. It felt different—incredible. Like an incredible rush of—of happiness. Yes. Like waves of sunshine and all things good.

Everything suddenly seemed okay—great even.

Seth turned from the window, his eyes narrowing on me. "Alex?"

I twisted around slowly. The room seemed lighter, soft, beautiful. Everything seemed beautiful.

I think I may have sighed.

"Oh, gods," Seth groaned. "It's starting."

"What's starting?" I barely recognized my own voice.

Seth looked at me pointedly. I thought he looked funny, so I laughed, and it was like a switch being thrown. I wanted to run and dance, and sing—and I couldn't sing, but I wanted to—and I wanted to…do stuff.

His slouch vanished and his expression took on a hard edge. "Go sit down, Alex."

I tipped my head back. Well, it kind of fell back, and I liked the weight of my hair falling into empty space, just hanging there. It felt good on my neck.

"Seriously, go sit down."

"Why?" I lifted my head, swaying a little. My skin tingled, like, all over—tingled like electric shocks—like when Aiden used to touch me or when I'd kissed Seth last night. I'd liked that, too, but I liked Aiden's kisses better. Seth's touch evoked something different. Gods, my brain wouldn't shut up. It just kept going and going.

He pushed away from the window. "You look ridiculous, Alex."

I stopped moving, having no clue exactly when I'd started

swaying back and forth. "Yooooou look mooooore ridiculous," I sang. "You're brooding. Brooding doesn't fit you."

He rubbed his chin as his gaze followed me with the intensity of a hawk stalking its prey. "This is going to be a long night."

"Maybe." I inched closer to him, because I wanted to be closer to something, someone. "Hey. You smiled."

He dropped his hand. "Don't."

I giggled. "Don't what?"

"Don't come any closer, Alex."

"You had no problem being close to me last night. Why, are you scared of me?"

"I'm not."

"Then why can't I?"

Amusement flickered across his face for a second before vanishing. "Alex, you need to go lie down."

I spun around, suddenly overcome by the urge to dance. When we'd waltzed in the field—that'd been fun. I wanted to do it again, and I wanted Seth to join me. Dancing alone was kind of sad.

"Alex—"

"Okay. I'm sitting down." Then I darted for him. I must've taken him off guard, because he didn't move, and come on, Seth could've moved out of the way if he'd wanted to.

But he didn't.

I wrapped my arms around his waist like an octopus, and I didn't want to dance anymore. "This feels good," I murmured, rubbing my cheek against the front of his shirt.

Seth didn't react at first, and I *knew* he thought it felt good, too. Then he grabbed my arms and untangled them from his waist. "Alex, please go sit down."

"I don't want to." I tried to reach for his neck, but he

stepped back. I frowned. "Why do you keep moving away from me? Are you scared of me now?"

"Yes. Right now, I am."

I threw my head back, laughing. "The big bad Apollyon is afraid of me? I'm hot. Can't you open up a window?"

Seth spun around and went to the window. "Why did I suggest this?"

"Because yoooou like me," I sang, turning and turning until I felt dizzy. "You really, really like me. Gods, I need to drink this stuff more often. I feel awesome."

Groaning, he looked for the window lock. "You won't later."

"Huh? You drank it before? You have! You dirty, dirty Apollyon." I threw myself on the bed. It was *so* comfortable. "I love your bed." I rolled onto my stomach, smiling. "I love it so much I'd marry it if I could."

Seth laughed out loud. "You'd marry my bed?"

"Mmm." I flopped onto my back. There was a painted mural on Seth's ceiling. Angels and other winged creatures painted in pretty pastels. "I would if I could marry, but we can't marry. Not even inanimate objects. Kind of takes the fun out of falling in love."

"Does it?" murmured Seth.

I pushed off the bed, unable to sit still. Seth was still at the window, but he'd forgotten about the lock. "Haven't you ever been in love, Seth?"

He blinked slowly. "I don't think so. Does loving yourself count?"

I laughed. "No. It doesn't. But good try. Seth?"

"Yes?"

"It's hot in here."

Shaking his head, he turned back to the window. "Yeah,

let me find the damn lock on this thing and I'll fix that for you."

It was too hot. Just too hot in here, and I couldn't stand the itchy material against my skin anymore. Seth was taking too long. I tugged the hoodie over my head and dropped it on the floor. I immediately felt a thousand times better.

Seth stiffened and let out a strangled sound. "Please tell me you did not take off your clothes."

I giggled. "No."

He ran his hands over his head. More silky strands sifted through his fingers. "I'm going to regret this. I'm so going to regret this."

"I'm not naked, you idiot." I tugged my hair off my neck and started twisting it. "And you've been trying to see me naked since I met you."

"That may be the case, but not like this."

"Naked is naked," I reasoned.

Slowly, Seth turned around and froze. His chest rose and fell unsteadily. "Oh, for the love of the gods, Alex, where is your shirt?"

I didn't understand why he was making a big deal about this. I had a bra on. It wasn't like…the thought evaporated. "I'm so hot. Just give me a shirt. Your shirt would work."

"Yes…you're hot. I can tell." His voice sounded thick and edgy.

I laughed and let go of my hair, but I was still hot…and out of control. The last time I'd felt this way, I'd kissed Aiden. That is, after I'd punched him in the face. I stopped moving, not liking the nervous fluttering in my stomach. I looked down, expecting to see my skin move. I poked my tummy once, but it felt like I'd jabbed my finger into the skin a thousand times. My heart skipped a beat.

"What are you doing?" Seth asked.

"I don't know. My stomach feels all light."

"It's the drink. You'll feel better if you just sit down. I'll get you a shirt. Just hold on a sec."

I looked up then. Seth had moved to the dresser, rummaging through the drawers. His back was to me—a vulnerable position—and he seemed to be concentrating awful hard on finding a shirt.

A new, although somewhat old, idea consumed me. I don't think I'd ever moved so quietly in my life. I was ninja stealth. Seth didn't realize until it was too late. He shot up and whipped around, eyes wide.

"Alex, just let me get you a shirt. Stay put." He moved to the left.

I followed him, shadowing his movements much like I did in training. Giving up on the shirt, he darted away from the dresser—away from me. But I was quicker. Once again, I had my arms around him. Then an even better idea took over.

"Kiss me?" I asked.

CHAPTER TWENTY-FOUR

Seth tipped his head back, sighing loudly. "Alex, you don't want this. It's the drink."

"That's not true. Nothing's wrong with me. Don't you want to kiss me?"

"It's not about what *I* want." He clasped my arms. "I'm not doing this when you're like this."

"I'm not drunk," I said indignantly.

"You were just dancing like a wood nymph five minutes ago. You took off your shirt and now you're latched onto me like a little monkey. So don't tell me you're in complete control of yourself."

Damn. When he said it like that, I had to stop and think about what I was doing. Thinking lasted all of five seconds, maybe six. Thinking was overrated. "You want to kiss me, and you liked kissing me last night."

Seth made a low sound in his throat as he grabbed my shoulders, giving me a little shake. "Do you know why you feel this way right now? It has nothing to do with me or you," he said roughly. "Someone wanted to ruin you, Alex. They wanted to get you on your back with some pure so you'd be removed from the Covenant and placed into servitude. Don't you get it? This—*this* is not you."

"No. This is me, really me. Or the connection thingy, but who cares? I want you to kiss me again. I like you, Seth. I really don't know why. You're arrogant and rude, but I like you. Don't you like me?"

"Alex." He said my name as if he was in some sort of exquisite pain. "I'm trying to be a good guy right now, and you're not helping."

"I don't want you to be a good guy."

He choked on his laugh. "You are making this really hard."

I pressed against him. "You're making this harder."

His hands slid down my arms again, sending shivers over me.

Could it be possible to be so hot and so cold all at once? "Alex."

"Seth."

"There are a lot of things I want to do to you right now, but it wouldn't be right."

I tipped my head back and looked him in the eye. Faint marks of the Apollyon started to creep across his face. "Don't you want to kiss me?" I reached up, running my fingers over his parted lips. "I know you do. I can tell."

Seth's grip tightened and his eyes fell shut. I slipped a hand under the hem of his shirt. He inhaled and tried to step back, but I followed him…a bit too closely. My leg got snared with his. For someone normally so graceful, he wasn't right then. He went down, half on his side and half on his back.

And I, well, I was right where I wanted to be. Giggling, I pressed my mouth to his neck. "Yay me," I murmured against his skin.

Seth jerked his head back, but his hands dropped to my hips, fingers digging through the denim. "Alex! Get off—"

I lowered my mouth to his. Seth pushed at me, but I had a really good hold on him and he didn't push too hard. And then he stopped pushing me and was pulling me closer—so close that I melted into nothing. Restraint and good intentions vanished when my lips brushed over his. This kiss wasn't soft or filled with tentative exploration. Seth's hands got tangled in my hair, and for a while, I got lost in that kiss, lost in all the insane sensations. Then his hands were on my shoulders, my back, and then the clasp of my bra. Seth's lips never left mine once, not even when he rolled me onto my back.

Things kind of got beautifully out of control at that point. His shirt came off. My jeans ended up clear across the room. My fingers found the button on his jeans and so on. Crazy as it sounded, Seth held back when I tugged him closer, lifted off me when I tried to wrap myself around him. And even though my body burned for more—demanded it, really—a small nagging voice picked up in the back of my mind, asking questions I didn't want to answer. Pointing out that this *wasn't* real. Or was it? I didn't know anymore. I knew I should care, but I didn't. Everything became about feeling.

Seth's lips moved across my skin. His hands cupped my cheek before drifting down. My own hands followed his lead, mimicking everything he did until the tips of my fingers no longer felt tingly, but numb instead.

Seth pulled away again, his breathing heavy and ragged as his fingers traced the curve of my neck. "I shouldn't do this. Not when you're like this, but I can't help myself. What does that say about me?"

His words confused my already jumbled thought process, but then he kissed me again. This was the powerful, deep kind—the kind I'd had little experience in handling. Only once had I been kissed like this.

Aiden.

Oh, *my* Aiden. My heart, the very air I breathed equaled Aiden. But his name disappeared in the mad rush of Seth's touch. I shifted restlessly, needing to be closer, and I thought I'd moved at first, but I hadn't moved at all. I tried to again, but my body wouldn't respond.

"We should stop here, Angel," Seth whispered against my lips, even as he slid a hand under my hip, lifting me, bringing me closer.

Closer. Hadn't that been what I wanted all along? Didn't I still want that? I just couldn't get closer.

My hands slipped off his back and then my arms fell limply to my sides.

Seth lifted his head and two bright, nearly iridescent eyes filled my vision. They were hazy, clouded with passion. I think he frowned, but then his face blurred in and out.

"Alex? What…? Oh, hell."

Concern replaced lust, passion—whatever he'd felt. He sat back, pants sliding low on his hips as he pulled me into his lap. "Alex, are you in there?" He brushed the hair off my face.

"I'm…so tired. Sorry…"

He smiled, but it rang false. "I know. It's okay."

I shivered, unable to wrap my arms around myself. Where had all that heat gone?

Seth got his other arm around me and stood, cradling me like he'd had a lot of experience carrying girls. Judging by his recent actions, I think he did. He placed me on the bed and hovered over me. "You still there?"

I blinked slowly, his face going in and out. "I'm…sleepy."

"Okay." Seth leaned in and brushed his lips over my forehead.

I squeezed my eyes shut, stomach twisting when he disappeared.

A few seconds later, he returned to my side and helped me get into a shirt that fell to my knees. Things were kind of hazy after that. Numbness settled so deep in my bones, I started to believe that my limbs weren't connected anymore. Unable to move, unable to say more than a few words at a time, I lay there and tried to figure out what was going on with my body.

Lust and all those other warm, wonderful feelings had vanished. So had the numbness, and in their place was a gods-awful feeling in the pit of my stomach. I squeezed my eyes shut again and tried to breathe through the sharp rise of nausea. It didn't help. A twisting and churning motion swept through me. Oh, gods, this wasn't going to be good. I was going to puke. I could feel—taste it—and I couldn't move. A soft whimper escaped my lips.

The bed dipped beside me, and a warm hand brushed across my cheek. "You hanging in there?"

"Sick," I gasped out.

Seth scooped me up in one swipe and carried me to the bathroom. The part of my brain that still functioned on normal Alex level noted that his bathroom was bigger than my entire room, and much nicer. So not fair. But then I stopped thinking altogether. The moment he held me over the toilet, I started heaving. Once I started, I couldn't stop.

I really don't know how long I remained latched there or how in the world Seth stomached all of it, holding me up and keeping my hair out the way. Only when my sides ached and my eyes leaked did the painful heaving subside.

"Better?" Seth smoothed the damp strands off my forehead.

"I want to die," I moaned pitifully. "I think I'm…dying."

"No, you're not." Seth shook his head. "Water will help. Just hold on to—" He tried to keep me upright, but I slipped to the floor. "Or just lie down. That works, too."

I pressed my forehead against the cool tile. It helped with the hot feeling, but my head throbbed something fierce. Moaning, I wrapped my arms around my waist and curled into a ball.

Seth cursed under his breath. I felt him stand and go back into the bedroom. I hoped he left me there. I never wanted to move ever again. I could rot there, as long as the pounding went away and the room stopped spinning.

But he returned a few seconds later and forced me to sit up. He barely got one bottle of water in me. I struggled, slapping his hands away a dozen times. Seth was halfway through forcing a second bottle when someone knocked at the door. We heard it swing open.

Seth swore again, put the bottle of water down, and eased me back to the floor. Ah, the cool floor was my friend—*friend*? I missed Caleb. I missed him so terribly.

"Where is she? Seth?" Aiden's firm voice called from the bedroom.

"Dammit," Seth muttered, standing. "She's fine," he called out. "Just needs a few more minutes to hang on to the floor."

I wanted to hit him.

Seth left the bathroom then, and the silence from the other room stretched out long, becoming ripe with tension. My mind provided the images of what the room must've looked like to Aiden. And shirtless, pants-unbuttoned Seth. Surely—*surely* Seth would've taken five seconds to button them?

I heard Seth sigh. "Look, I know all this looks really bad. It's not what you think."

"This isn't what it looks like?" Aiden growled, and I'd never heard his voice sound that way before, so hard and flat but with an edge that trembled with the promise of violence. "Really? Because I think *this* belongs to Alex."

I cringed, wishing I could sink through the floor and disappear. A mass of confusion and unease formed in my delicate stomach. Then Aiden stood in the doorway to the bathroom, and I knew I must've looked a mess. Damp hair clung to my skin; the room smelled of sickness, and I was dressed in Seth's shirt and little else.

"Aiden," I said weakly. "It's not—"

"Seth, I trusted you." Aiden's voice was filled with cold steel.

"Look, I know. This wasn't—"

The sound of a fist connecting with flesh came from the next room. A body slammed into something—a dresser? Something heavy crashed to the floor, shattering. The really sweet TV came to mind. Curses exploded from each of them.

I pushed myself off the bathroom floor, standing on wobbly legs. The white walls and gilded mirror spun in wild circles for a moment. Pushing through the dizziness, I staggered out of the bathroom and into the middle of a major throwdown between a highly trained Sentinel and the Apollyon.

"Guys, come on…you both are being so stupid." I swayed to the left. Cold sweat clung to my forehead.

They either didn't hear me or didn't care. Aiden, who looked surprisingly unscathed, backed Seth across the room. He lunged at Seth, knocking him to the floor. They rolled, each of them exchanging and receiving blows.

"Aiden! Stop it!" I lurched forward, swearing as my stomach rolled violently. "Seth—don't choke him!"

Seth had gained the upper hand, rolling Aiden onto his

back. He reared back, throwing one arm in the air. Blue light shimmered around his fist. *Akasha.* I panicked—which maybe wasn't the greatest thing to do considering my reflexes and even basic walking skills were subpar at the moment. I stumbled to them, intending on pulling Seth off Aiden, and then I planned to knock the crap out of both of them.

I wrapped my arms around Seth's waist the same moment Aiden slammed his fist into Seth's stomach. When Seth fell backward, so did I. My shoulder smacked off the edge of the bed first and then Seth's weight crashed onto me. I hit the floor for the second time that night.

Aiden popped to his feet and grabbed Seth, tossing him to the side. I turned over and there was my bra—lying right there, laughing at me. I closed my eyes, utterly mortified.

"What the hell?" another voice rang out. A clear, distinct voicc I knew belonged only to Leon. "Have you all lost your godsforsaken minds?"

Seth rolled to his knees, wiping his hand over his bloodied lip. "Oh, we're just wrestling."

Aiden shot him a dark look as he dropped down. "Alex, are you okay?" He slid his hands under my arms and helped me to sit up. "Say something."

I peered through the mess of hair covering my face. "I'm…great."

Aiden brushed the hair off my face. "I'm sorry. I should have never—"

"Aiden, I know you're pissed—"

"Pissed? You took advantage of her, Seth." Aiden rose to his feet. "You son of a—"

"Stop it!" Leon ordered. "You two are going to bring every Guard in the building to this room. Seth, get out of here now."

"This is *my* room," Seth protested, climbing to his feet. "And if this dickhead would give me five—"

Aiden growled low in his throat. "I'm going to kill you."

"Oh, that's *it*." Seth whirled around, eyes flaring. "Let me see you try."

I staggered to my feet and reached for Aiden. The room swayed off kilter, but I ignored it. "Don't. Please. This isn't Seth's…whoa." The wall spun suddenly.

"Alex?" Aiden said, but he sounded so far away, which was weird, since he was right beside me.

I reached for him, but then I think I keeled over.

When I woke up, I felt like hell and I hadn't even opened my eyes yet. A drummer lived inside my head and my mouth was a desert. I groaned and tried to roll over, but I couldn't move. Something stopped me. Slowly, I pried my eyes open and looked down.

A heavily muscled arm lay across my waist—not my arm.

Well, this was odd.

I tilted my head to the side, blinked once, and then twice. It couldn't be him… Waves of dark hair fell over his forehead and along his cheek. It was Aiden's flawless face inches from mine, but a younger version of him. At rest, he looked vulnerable, peaceful. My fingers itched to trace the smooth line of his jaw, to touch his parted lips and see if he was real. It had to be a dream, something my heart had produced, because he couldn't be here.

"Stop staring at me." Aiden's voice was gruff with sleep.

I jerked back an inch. Okay, maybe not a dream. "I'm not." He pried one gray eye open.

"Yes, you are."

Accepting that this was reality, I glanced around. We were still in Seth's room. "Where's Seth?"

"I don't know. He left a couple of hours ago." Aiden seemed to realize then that his arm was around me. Looking confused, he pulled back and sat up. "I sat down for a little while. I must've fallen asleep. How are you feeling?"

Everything seemed hazy at first. Then, slowly, the memories clicked into place: Laadan giving me the super sex cocktail drink, Aiden ordering me off with Seth, and then…everything with Seth.

"Oh. My. Gods," I moaned. "I want to die. Like right now."

Aiden hovered beside me. "Alex, it's okay."

I covered my face with my hands. When I spoke, my voice was muffled. "No, it's not. I'm going to kill someone."

"I think you're going to have to get in line for that."

"Have you found Laadan?" I asked. "Is she okay?"

"Yes, I found her in her room just before I…I checked on you. She's fine, but she doesn't remember a thing. It's just like the night Leon found you in the maze. To compel someone that strongly and to make them forget is a hell of a compulsion. And to use it against another pure is unheard of."

I mumbled incoherently against my hands. Delayed as it was, it struck me then that Aiden had spent the night with me—in a bed. And I'd been passed out for it. Gods, that royally sucked, but it didn't suck as badly as it would have if someone found out about it. "Why did you stay here? What if someone—"

"Only Seth and Leon know what happened. And Laadan. No one else knows we're here." He pulled my hands away. "I wasn't leaving you alone. The drug was still in your system, and I wasn't taking a risk on something else happening to you. You were sick again in the middle of the night. You don't remember that?"

"No," I whispered, trying to ignore the warmth his protective words brought. "I don't remember that."

"Probably a good thing, it was pretty rough."

"Great," I muttered.

A brief smile appeared. "You were…talking a lot, too."

"This just keeps getting better. What did I say?"

"You told me you wanted to marry Seth's bed, and then you told me you'd marry me if I asked. After that, you started to—"

"Enough," I groaned, wanting to crawl under the blankets.

Aiden laughed. "It was actually kind of cute."

More embarrassed than I'd ever been, I had a hard time looking at Aiden. His face didn't show any signs that he'd duked it out with Seth. Maybe I'd imagined it. "Did you and Seth…fight?"

One eyebrow arched. "Yeah, we did."

"Oh, gods, Aiden, it wasn't Seth's fault."

"I'm sorry," he said. "I'm sorry that you had to go through any of this. You have nothing to be ashamed of. You did nothing wrong, but he did."

"Don't apologize. Please. None of this is your fault." I drew in a deep breath. "It wasn't Seth's, either. Aiden, he tried. Really, he did, but I just…" I couldn't believe I was going to say any of this. "I just kept pushing him. I couldn't stop, but I knew what I was doing. I just couldn't stop myself."

"That doesn't matter, Alex. Seth should've shown restraint. He knew you were vulnerable, that it didn't matter *who* you were with." He paused, drawing in a deep breath. "Alex, look at me."

I lifted my head slowly. I expected there to be some sort of judgment or disappointment in his gray gaze, but all I saw was infinite understanding, which made the ball of conflicting emotions feel that much worse. His eyes shut briefly. When they reopened, they burned an unnatural shade of silver. "Did he…did you two…?"

"No. We…didn't do that. He stopped." I figured it was best to leave out the exact reason why he'd stopped.

We fell into silence for a little while. My mind worked through the events of last night, the implications of them. Someone had wanted me to screw up in a bad way. And to go to that kind of extreme—even the idea sickened me. What if Aiden and Seth hadn't seen me?

"You really think someone was waiting for me?" I swallowed down the taste of bile, shuddering. "Waiting to catch me with a pure?"

Aiden looked at me straight on. "Yes."

It was hard to wrap my head around that kind of tactic. I shuddered again. Aiden reached down and tucked the blanket around me, but then I jerked up, ruining his hard work.

"Are you feeling sick again?" He moved as if he would carry me off the bed.

I wasn't sure. The walls did feel like they were closing in around me, but it wasn't the effects of the Brew. "I could've lost everything."

Aiden didn't respond, because really, what could he say?

My mind raced. There were so many things I could do with the power I would have. I'd learned one thing at the Council—I needed to be able to do something to change the lives of my kind. Seth had been right; we could do something about that as long as I made it to eighteen without being forced into servitude. If I were put on the Elixir—which was what someone had intended last night by hoping to catch me with a pure—I might never Awaken. I'd lose such a huge opportunity—more than any half had ever had.

And someone had tried to take that from me at least three times in the last couple of weeks: the compulsion, the Council session, and now this? Telly had warned me if I messed up one more time, I'd be kept in New York.

Sleeping with a pure, willingly or not, would have classified as messing up. "Alex, are you okay?"

My gaze dropped to his. I don't know what I saw in his eyes. I couldn't read them anymore. "Do you think Telly did this?"

Aiden blinked. "Minister Telly? I don't know, Alex. He's a lot of things, but to do this? And why?"

"He doesn't like me."

"Not liking you is one thing, but to destroy you? It has to be more than dislike, Alex. There has to be a reason."

Aiden had a point. "Then I need to find out why."

"We will find out why."

I nodded. "Right now, I just…I just want to leave here. I want to go home."

He leaned forward and placed his hand over mine, easing my fingers off the blanket I'd been gripping. "There's a late afternoon session, and we'll leave immediately afterward."

Surprisingly, I didn't feel very relieved by that. The plus side in all of this was I now knew not to take drinks from…it hit me then. I laughed.

Aiden's eyebrows furrowed with concern. "Alex?"

I shook my head. "I'm fine. It's just that damn oracle was right again. She warned me, did you know? She told me not to accept gifts from those who meant me harm." I laughed again. "Of course, she failed to mention that it would be a secondhand gift from someone who didn't mean me harm. Gods, if that woman were still alive, I'd hit her. Seriously."

His lips stretched into a lopsided grin and his hand

tightened over mine. An old and familiar ache sprung alive at the sight of his smile, forcing me to look away. I swallowed, wanting nothing more than to climb into his arms. "Do you know where Seth is?"

"No. He left when he realized I wasn't leaving. He's around here somewhere."

I ran a hand over my face. I was surprised and kind of stung that he'd actually left me with Aiden, but I was happy that he had. Because that gave me time with Aiden—time in bed with Aiden. Which didn't make any sense. "I need to find him."

Aiden's hand left mine. "You shouldn't be worried about him right now. And I don't want you running around looking for him. It's not safe here."

"I know it's not, but I have to see him. You don't understand. Things—"

"Things are what, Alex?"

I turned toward him. He was frowning, eyes a deep and dark gray. "I don't know. Things are different with him." That was all I could say.

Aiden stared at me a moment, then straightened. "Are you two...seeing each other?" My cheeks turned several shades of red. His eyes turned silver in a nanosecond. "I thought you were against this whole *fate* thing."

"I am! But...I don't know. Things have just changed and...he's been there for me," I finished lamely.

A muscle started ticking along his jaw. "And I haven't been. So, you decided to be with Seth?"

I gaped at him, but then my temper shot to the surface. "No, you haven't been. But that's not why I'm with Seth."

"Really?" He pushed off the bed. Standing, he ran his hand through his hair. "I find that hard to believe since you told me a few days ago you hated him."

I flushed, partly because he was right and that pissed me off. "Why do you even care, Aiden? You can't—*and* don't—want me. And you even said you thought Seth cared about me. Or is this one of those creepy lines like 'I don't want you but I don't want you with anyone else?' Because that's so not cool."

He dropped his hand. "That is not what this is about, Alex. I just don't want to see you getting wrapped up in something…so serious for the wrong reasons."

My gaze flicked up, meeting his. His eyes burned so brightly, taking up his whole face. "You've told me we can't be together and—and I know. I know we can't, but—"

Aiden bent quickly, leaning down so our faces were only inches from one another. "But that doesn't mean you should settle for Seth, Alex."

I crushed the blanket in my hands. "I'm not settling for Seth!"

He quirked an eyebrow and held my glare with his own.

Then it hit me and my heart sped up. "This isn't even about Seth. This is about you! You don't want to see me with him or anyone else! Because you still care about me!"

Aiden jerked back, shaking his head. "Of course I care for you."

I drew in a deep breath, trying to quell my racing heart. "Tell me…tell me that you feel the same way I do about you, because if you do…" I couldn't bring myself to actually say it. If he told me that he felt the same way—that he loved me—then to hell with everything else. To hell with it all, because I would not—could not walk away from that. No matter how wrong it was, how I'd resolved to let him go, and no matter how dangerous it would be for the both of us. I simply couldn't.

Aiden inhaled sharply. "I won't."

"Or you can't?"

He shook his head again, eyes flickering shut. A quick grimace pulled at his lips, and then he looked at me dead-on. "I don't."

I exhaled harshly, suddenly wanting to curl up in a ball and cry. But I didn't. I'd brought this on myself. "Okay."

"Alex, I want—"

"No. I don't want to hear anything else." I pushed off the bed. "What I have with Seth is none of your—" A rush of dizziness made me stumble. I bent, grabbing the edge of the bed for support.

"Alex?" Aiden moved around the bed, reaching for me.

"Don't!" I threw up my hand. "Don't pretend you care. That takes douchebaggery to a whole new level."

Aiden stopped, opening and closing his hands. "Good point."

The room righted itself, and it felt safe to move again. Ignoring Aiden and the need to wail like a baby, I started the mortifying search for my clothes. I gathered up my jeans and hoodie, tucking them under my arm. One very important, very embarrassing item hadn't been located. I scanned the floors rather desperately.

"I think this belongs to you."

Cursing under my breath, I turned around. Aiden dangled something small, black, and flimsy from his fingertips.

Color burst across my face. I snatched it out of his hand. "Thanks."

Aiden didn't smile. "It's my pleasure."

CHAPTER TWENTY-FIVE

I went through my morning routine slowly, still feeling a bit whacked. Part of me wanted to dive under the covers; another part wanted to strangle Aiden, and I still needed to find Seth.

I also needed to deal with the fact that someone seriously didn't want me to turn eighteen. I pushed down the ball of conflicting emotions to dwell on some other day—which I felt sure would be a day very soon—and opened the door. Aiden stood there, waiting. He was there because I obviously couldn't be allowed to be anywhere by myself, but I still wanted to punch him in the face.

Our walk downstairs was awkward.

A few Guards who had been present during the Council session nodded respectfully as I passed them. That was an improvement from being ignored. Aiden left me when I stopped at the linen-covered tables. I guess he figured I was safe within eyesight.

I stared at the plate of fresh croissants and bagels, swallowing thickly. I didn't think I could ever eat again. I grabbed a bottle of water and shuffled to where Aiden sat beside Marcus. Marcus didn't look up from his newspaper when I dropped into the seat beside him.

I could feel Aiden's eyes on me, and I wanted to bang my head on the table. Instead of doing that, I twisted around and stared across the cafeteria. I pretended to be engrossed in the wall until I noticed the two servants standing by it.

It was *him*—the clear-eyed one I'd seen the first day here and tried to talk to in the stairwell. He leaned toward the other half-blood, a boy. I couldn't help but wonder how the pures—the Masters—couldn't see how alert this Brown Eyes was.

Brown Eyes must have sensed me watching, because he turned and looked me straight in the eye. Not quite a hostile look, maybe a little curious. He quickly turned back to the other servant. I don't know why I watched them for so long. It may've been how tense their conversation seemed. Half-blood servants rarely argued, even among themselves. They were usually too medicated to even hold a decent conversation, but these two were different.

"Where were you last night, Alexandria? This morning, you were not in your bed."

Marcus's question jerked me around. I said the one thing that I knew Marcus wouldn't question and was sort of true. "I was with Seth. We were talking and I fell asleep."

"Really?" He nodded at the double doors leading to the patio. Seth stood there, his back to us. "So, are you the one who gave him that black eye?"

"Uh..." I was already standing. "I'll see you guys in a little bit."

Marcus made a noise that sounded a lot like a chuckle and went back to his paper. I found it disturbing that he'd find the idea of domestic violence so humorous.

Taking a deep breath, I cut between the empty tables and followed Seth outside, not daring a look back to see Aiden's expression. Seth didn't turn around, but I knew he felt me. His shoulders tensed as he leaned against one of the thick marble columns.

I shivered in the chilly air, wondering why I hadn't brought a jacket. I stopped next to him and stared across the grounds. The top of the mammoth wall surrounding the place peeked over the tree line. I hoped he'd say something first, but the minutes passed and Seth remained silent. He wasn't going to make any of this easy.

"Hey," I said, immediately feeling stupid.

"Hey."

I rolled my eyes and stepped in front of him. Seth stared down at me coolly. Up close, the purple and blue ring around his left eye looked brutal. "Does that hurt?"

"Don't you think that's a stupid question?"

"Do you want another black eye?" I snapped.

He arched an eyebrow. "I think I prefer the drunken version of you. She's much nicer."

I stepped back. "You know what? Forget it."

Seth reached out and caught my arm. "What do you want to talk about? How disgusted you are with me?"

"No." I stared at him in surprise. "That's not what I was going to say at all."

Some of the coolness slipped from his expression, but he still regarded me warily. "Then why did you want to talk to me?"

"I want to talk about…last night." I felt my cheeks burn. "It wasn't your fault."

His brows flew up. "Not my fault?"

"No." I glanced over his shoulder, spotting the pure-blood

Council Guard who had taken out Hector. He stood by the glass door leading out to the patio, trying to appear as if he wasn't watching us. "Can we go somewhere private?"

Seth looked over his shoulder. "Let's go."

We ended up a few rows into the labyrinth. Being in here left a bad taste in my mouth, but there was really no other place that was private. Seth leaned against the stone wall and folded his arms. "So, talk."

I swallowed uncomfortably. This would be so awkward. "I wanted to apologize for...well, for everything that happened last night."

"You're apologizing to me?" He sounded stunned.

Shifting to my other foot, I nodded. "I know you tried to get me to sit down and not do what I was doing. You tried to—"

"I didn't *try* hard enough, Alex." He pushed off the wall. "Aiden's right—gods, I can't even believe I'm saying that, but he is. I knew you weren't yourself. So, I should've stopped it."

My gaze followed him. He plucked a rose off a bush next to an armless gray statue of a woman in an ill-fitted toga. "You did stop, Seth."

He shot me a bland look over his shoulder. "You and I both know why I stopped. It wasn't out of chivalry."

I didn't believe that—not entirely. "Seth, you aren't the bad guy in this. You were sort of drugged, too—through our connection. And you took care of me afterward."

He shrugged. "What else was I supposed to do?"

"You held my hair while I puked. You didn't need to do that. You could have left me in the bathroom. That's pretty hardcore."

"It was also gross. Just so you know." Seth turned around, not looking at me, but at the rose in his palm.

Irritation surged to the surface. "Why are you acting like this? I'm trying to tell you that you weren't at fault for last night, and you're being a jerk!"

Blue fire sprung from his hand, folding over the rose. It smoked a wispy blue before disappearing into nothing, leaving the rose untouched.

I dragged my eyes from his hand and struggled for patience.

Was every conversation today going to end in argument?

His eyes flicked up, meeting mine finally. "It appears you were well taken care of after I left. Were you thrilled that Aiden stayed with you? I'm sure you were."

I felt stung and confused by Seth. "I don't want to argue with you."

The blue flames licked at the rose between his fingers much slower this time. Plumes of blue smoke puffed into the air. "Then you should probably stop talking to me."

I stepped back, chafing my arms. "Why are you being so pisstastic with me?"

Seth blinked and the blue fire evaporated, leaving the rose whole. "I don't believe pisstastic is a real word, Alex."

Hiding underneath the covers for the rest of the day started to look even better. "All right, well, this was fun. I'll see you around."

Seth moved then. He reached out and caught my arm again, the rose dangling from his other hand. "I'm sorry."

I gawked at him. Seth never apologized. Ever.

The impossible happened. The mask he wore slipped off his face. Suddenly, he looked very young and unsure. "I felt you this morning. You were embarrassed and upset, and then so angry. I'm sorry for putting you through that. I should have…restrained myself."

It took me a few moments to realize what Seth referenced. "That had nothing to do with you, Seth."

"Why are you trying to make me feel better?"

"Seth, I'm embarrassed. I danced around your room and molested you. So yeah, I'm a bit embarrassed about that. But the other things you picked up on? That was because of Aiden."

"Isn't it always about Aiden?" He dropped my arm and turned away. "Did he finally profess his undying love for you?"

I laughed brokenly. "Not quite."

Seth glanced over his shoulder. "My eye socket has a hard time believing that."

"He stayed with me because he fell asleep."

His head dropped, and I wondered what he was doing. "And you believe that?"

I blinked back sudden tears. I would've risked everything this morning if Aiden had said he loved me, but he hadn't. "Does it matter?"

He turned around, studying me like he was trying to figure something out. "Does it?"

A breeze rolled through, rattling the leaves and kicking my hair into my face. I pushed the hair away, but it blew right back. "Seth, you asked me to make a choice the night before. And I did."

Seth glanced down at the rose before peering up through thick lashes. "And that choice still matters today?"

That was a good question. How could it, when an hour ago I would've given up everything for Aiden if he'd told me just once that he loved me. But he hadn't. I looked away, once again wondering what exactly I was doing. Was this fair to Seth? Because Aiden had been right, I was kind of settling for him. But Seth hadn't said he had any hardcore feelings for me. He hadn't even asked me to be his girlfriend. What he *had* suggested was for us to see what happens—no labels and no expectations. And if I was honest with myself, I did care for Seth. A lot.

I bit my lip. "I chose you. Does that still matter to you?"

He laughed suddenly and then fell silent. I could see him trying to pull the shutters back up but failing. I'd never seen him so vulnerable. Trying to give him space, I moved back to the wall and watched him.

"Yes, it does matter to me."

Something fluttered in my chest faintly. "Okay, so…um, where does that leave us?"

Silently, he handed me the rose. A small jolt ran over my fingertips. The stem felt warm to the touch and a faint trace of blue still clung to the blossom, turning the dewy petals violet. Without warning, he lifted me onto the wall. He placed his hands on either side of my legs. "Alex."

I looked around, dangling my legs. "Seth."

"Well, all of this is weird."

"Yeah, especially right now."

"It's about to get weirder. Be prepared."

"Great." I twirled the rose around with one hand and tapped my thigh with the other. "I can't wait."

Seth smiled. "I can tell you're freaked out."

My eyes narrowed. "You're doing it now? Reading me, aren't you? How in the world do you do that?"

I was surprised when he answered the question. "I just open up my mind to you, tune into the connection. It's like a two-way radio signal. Your feelings come through in waves, sometimes loudly. Other times, it's just a twinge at the edge of my mind. You probably could pick up on them now if you tried."

"Is it always going to be like this? When I Awaken, will I constantly be feeling you and vice versa?"

"You could shield your feelings."

I popped forward. "How do I do that?"

Seth laughed softly. "I could teach you, work it into your training if you want."

"Can we start now?"

A slow smile appeared as he dipped his head. "That's not what I want to do right now."

Parts of my body tingled—some parts more than others. "Seth..."

Seth kissed me. It wasn't like the heady and deep kisses from the night before. His lips were sweet, soft. His hand caressed my cheek before sliding around the nape of my neck and delving into my hair. I let my eyes drift shut, soaking up the dizzying warmth of his lips. For the briefest moment, I didn't think about *anything*. And that's what I liked most about Seth's kisses. I didn't think or want anymore. In Seth's arms, with his lips trailing kisses over mine, his presence overshadowed the hurt, eased it.

The tingling in my body suddenly grew stronger, like little sparks dancing over my skin. My palm itched, burned. I gasped as his mouth dropped to my throat, where my pulse had gone from pleasant to throbbing.

Seth pressed his lips there, inhaled deeply and pulled back, fingers trailing over my flushed cheeks. "Interesting."

"Yeah...that was different," I said breathlessly.

He chuckled. "Not the kiss. Don't get me wrong, that was interesting too, but look."

"Huh?" I followed his gaze and squeaked. The rose in my hand was on fire again. Blue flames licked over the stem, curling around the fragile petals, smoldering into thin wisps of azure. The rose shuddered once and then collapsed into itself, leaving a fine blue dust covering my hands.

"Akasha," Seth explained quietly.

"Okay." I let out a breath, relaxing for the first time in days—weeks even. "Okay. I don't know what that really means, but okay."

He hopped up on the wall beside me. We sat there for a little while, legs swinging above the ground. "What do you want to do? We have a couple of hours before you leave."

"You're not leaving after the session?"

"Nope. Lucian wants to leave in the morning, so I'm stuck here another night."

Dammit. Another eleven-hour car ride with Aiden.

Seth nudged my shoulder. "What?"

"I was kind of hoping you could convince Lucian to let me fly back with you."

He looked surprised. "You hate flying. It scares you to death, you little wimp. But you can't stay here another night. You have to leave tonight with Aiden."

"And with Leon."

"Yeah," he sighed, kicking his legs off the wall. "Want to go swimming?"

I laughed. "No."

"Damn. I was hoping you'd fall for that one again."

I stared at the moss-covered walkway, knocking my heels off the wall. "Seth?"

"Yep."

"Who do you think was responsible for slipping me that drink?"

His expression hardened. "I don't think it was the Council's decision."

"Then who could it be if it wasn't the Council?"

"I didn't say it wasn't one or more of them, but I know it wasn't something approved by the Council. Lucian would never allow something like that to happen."

I snorted. "You give Lucian way too much credit."

"Don't get me wrong, he's still a pompous ass." Seth flashed a grin. "But he wouldn't allow something like that to happen to you. I'm sure it could be a Council member, but they don't have the official backing of the Council."

"Sorry. I don't trust Lucian."

Seth twisted around. "You need to start trusting him. He wants to make sure you Awaken, Alex. There isn't a damn thing he's going to do to jeopardize that."

"And that is another thing I don't trust. Why does Lucian want two Apollyons, when every other pure is scared to death of that idea?"

"Because Lucian wants to see change—and we are the vessel for that change. You want to change this society, make it better? Lucian wants that, too."

"Since when did Lucian become such a half-blood lover?"

"You don't know your stepfather, Alex. You never really tried."

I shook my head. "Sorry. You didn't spend fourteen years with him. Lucian is cold, conniving, and has never been a fan of halfs. You're not going to get me to believe otherwise."

Seth sighed. "I'd put my bets on Telly, but that seems too obvious and he's too old school. But it's one or more of them."

I wrapped my arms around me, shuddering when I thought about what could've happened. "They didn't have to do something so vile."

He reached over and pulled me down so my head rested in his lap. It felt weird at first, but after a few seconds, I rolled onto my back and stared up at the gray clouds. "We'll figure it out once we get out of this damn place. Lucian is already—"

"You told Lucian?"

"He needed to know." He brushed a strand of hair off my forehead. "Needless to say, he was pissed."

I groaned and placed my hands over my eyes. "Did he throw something dainty? He usually throws something small and expensive."

Seth laughed. "Yes, he did actually. I believe it was a Fabergé egg."

"Oh. Sweet."

He picked up my pinky and peeked down at me. "What are you hiding from?"

I considered that. "I don't know. Everything?"

"Sounds like a plan."

I lowered my hands to my stomach, but Seth still held onto my pinky. "Childish, huh?"

He wrapped his hands around mine. "It's all right. You can hide for a little while longer, but then you've got to face… everything."

"I know."

He grinned down at me. "But for right now, just relax."

Once we got back to North Carolina, there would be classes, and Olivia now hated me, and we still needed to find out who'd set me up last night, and…crap, Instructor Romvi. I cringed. "Can we stay…here for a little while?"

"Sure." He bent down, pressing his lips against my forehead. "If that's what you want." It really didn't matter what I wanted, but I closed my eyes and smiled anyway.

The sun had set by the time the servants lugged my bag downstairs. Seth and I waited in the glass breezeway outside the ballroom. I tried to not stare at the furies, but my eyes kept going back to them.

"Do you think I'll get to see Laadan before we leave?" I asked.

Seth leaned against the wall opposite from me. "I'd think so."

I slid down the glass and crossed my legs. "I just want to see her before I leave. I hope she doesn't feel"—I stopped, glancing around me before I continued—"guilty or anything."

"Understandable." He shot an irritated look back toward the ballroom. "How long is this crap going to take?"

"Who knows?" I muttered. Telly had all the pures gathered, doing some kind of stupid closing ceremony. I stretched out my legs and eyed Seth. He had changed into his Sentinel uniform, blades and all. Squinting, I noticed the new blade attached to his thigh. "Can I see that one?"

"Hmm?" He glanced down and unhooked the blade. "This one?"

I wiggled my fingers. "Let me see it."

He walked across and handed it to me. "Be careful with it, both edges are deadly sharp when released."

"Yeah, I know. Aiden showed me one earlier." I pushed to my feet, imagining chopping a daimon half's head off with it. "You know, using this thing is going to be really messy."

Seth made a grab for the weapon, but I stepped back. He gave me a droll look. "Haven't used it yet, but I'm sure it's not going to be pretty."

I whipped the sickle blade through the air again, and then remembered what I'd realized when Aiden had showed me the blade. I peered up at Seth. "What about after I Awaken? You'll just have unlimited zapping powers, right?"

"I don't know." He watched the blade with wary eyes.

"I imagine it will be different. Could even be different now. Remember, we don't know all the fine details."

I looked at Seth, but he was still fixated on the blade. "What happens to me when you pull from my energy?"

Seth's eyes snapped to my face. "I don't know."

My fingers tightened around the blade. "I'm not sure I believe you."

His eyes bored into mine. "I've never lied to you before."

I swallowed hard. Seth had a point, but if he did know that something bad would happen, would he actually tell me?

Leon strolled into the foyer, coming to a complete stop when he saw me holding the blade. "For the love of the gods, who gave that to you?"

I pointed the sharp edge. "Seth."

Seth arched a brow at me. "Wow. Thanks."

"Please give it back to him before you do damage." Leon frowned as I twirled the blade. "You're going to cut off your hand or arm. The sickle blade is by far the sharpest."

Rolling my eyes, I stopped twirling it. But I kept it. I liked it. "Are they almost done in there? Because I'm getting really—"

A siren blasted off in the distance, starting as a low pitch and building into a never-ending loop of eardrum-breaking noise. I jumped a good five inches off the floor. The three of us looked at one another and seemed to share the same mind for a moment. Even though I'd never had the misfortune of hearing a Covenant siren, I knew they meant only one thing: security breach.

Usually, a very big and very bad security breach.

CHAPTER TWENTY-SIX

I turned to the glass wall facing the yard.

Behind me, several Guards burst into the hall, and beyond them excited voices came from the adjoining ballroom. Guards rushed past us, one of them yelling, "Secure the gates! Lock down the school!"

Then the sirens ceased their blaring, and a cold shiver ran down my arms. "False alarm?"

"Not sure." Seth whipped the blade out of my hand. "But I'll be taking this back now. Thank you."

I barely paid him any attention. The light from the scattered lamp posts outside began to dim and flicker. I glanced back, finding Leon with a sickle blade in one hand and a dagger in the other.

"Everyone calm down!" a Guard yelled over the panicked voices. "The siren has ended! Everything is fine. Everyone just needs to calm down and stay in the hall."

Marcus and Aiden brushed aside curious and frightened pures as they entered the room. My overactive imagination said that Aiden's eyes searched the crowd until he found me and that there was a flicker of relief on his face.

Aiden crossed the room, dagger in hand. He must've changed into gear before the closing ceremonies. He stopped beside Leon. "What's going on?"

"I don't know." Leon shook his head. "But I've got a bad feeling about this."

I turned back to the glass, squinting. Farther off, near the tree line, it looked like something moved—several things, actually. Guards and Sentinels, I thought.

Marcus joined our little group. "Telly is keeping all the pures in the ballroom as a precaution." He paused, glancing down at me with a little frown as if he'd forgotten about me.

"Hello." I wiggled my *weaponless* fingers.

Marcus frowned. "Alex, you're coming with me."

I scowled. "I'm not hiding in a room with a bunch of freaked-out pures."

Aiden turned to me, eyes thundercloud gray. "Don't be ridiculous."

I glared right back at him. "Can I be irrational instead?" Aiden looked like he wanted to shake me…or worse.

"Alex, do not argue with us," Marcus snapped. "You are going in that room."

My temper snapped. "I can fight if one of you would give me one of those neat blades."

Seth grabbed my arm. "All right, little Apollyon—who is not completely trained and is on the verge of becoming annoying—go with your uncle."

Pulling my arm free, I whirled on Seth. "I can—"

The lights outside shuddered off, casting the grounds in utter darkness. Temporarily forgotten, I turned back to the glass. Squinting to see through the reflection of the lighted interior, I saw the shadows of the Guards forming a line. But something looked off about the formation. It moved forward instead of away from the house.

"Uh, guys..." I started to back up.

Leon stepped forward. "Miss Andros, get into that room. Now."

Someone grabbed my arm, pulling me backward. I glanced up, expecting Seth but finding Aiden.

His eyes were trained on the glass wall. "Alex, for once in your life—"

A loud crack drew our attention back to the glass. My mouth dropped open. Glass splintered and fissured under the impact of a body.

I flinched back. "Holy crap!"

The glass exploded, shooting large shards through the air as several bodies thudded onto the marble floor. The color of their uniforms made them unmistakable, although blood stained their white shirts and pants. The Council Guards hadn't even *drawn* their weapons. All of their throats had been ripped open, revealing pink and jelly-like tissue. Some still twitched before their eyes glossed over.

Aiden pushed me toward Marcus. "Go!"

With a tight grip on my arm, Marcus rushed across the room as Sentinels entered, drawing weapons—*weapons*? I broke free and went in the opposite direction.

"Alexandria! No!" shouted Marcus.

"Give me a second!" I skidded over to one of the bodies, trying not to look too closely at it. Wincing, I unhooked a sickle and a dagger. There was no way I was going to be weaponless in a daimon siege.

A shrill, heart-stopping cry broke through all the commotion, drowning out everything else. Shivers of dread dug deep into my muscles as the soulless howls hit an intense pitch. I wrapped my hands around the blades and jerked up. Shadows descended, like a wave of death moving incredibly fast.

Daimons—buttloads of daimons.

The sight of so many pale faces—black veins throbbing under papery-thin skin and empty holes where eyes should have been—freaked the holy hell out of me. My nightmares had come alive in vivid, startling detail. There were at least a dozen of them, screeching with mouths full of razor-like teeth. But scattered among them were faces that looked no different.

Daimon halfs.

The Sentinels—Aiden and Seth included—rushed them, disappearing into the mob. Blades clattered and fell to the floor, screams and shouts mingled with the ripping and tearing of clothing and flesh.

"Alexandria!" Marcus shouted. "Let go of me! I have to get her!"

I spun around. A Council Guard pulled Marcus toward the reception hall—toward the stronghold. Another Guard appeared, helping remove Marcus to safety. Taking off after them, I reached them just as they pushed Marcus into the hall and slammed the titanium-lined door shut. Marcus beat on the door, his words muffled by the thick metal separating us.

"This door does not open again." The Guard looked me straight in the eye. He was the pure—the Guard who'd carried out Telly's orders.

"Thanks," I said through clenched teeth. Then, taking a deep breath, I turned around and faced hell.

It was a bloody mess, literally. In that instant I knew that all the smaller scale attacks on the Covenants over the last couple of months had been practice runs. They'd been testing how to infiltrate the Covenant, gearing up for a grand-scale attack on the Council. Mom had warned me, and I'd warned the pures—but they'd dismissed it.

Idiots.

I caught sight of Seth as he engaged a half-blood daimon. He slammed the half in the chest with a booted foot, knocking it to the ground. In a stunning display of brutality and grace, he whipped the sickle blade through the air.

Then there were Aiden and Leon, their backs against one another as four pure daimons circled them. They looked screwed.

Fighting was in my blood, not running. This was where I was supposed to be, and this definitely wasn't my first time at the rodeo. I bolted across the room, dodging bodies of the good, the bad, and the downright ugly. The ones closing in on Leon and Aiden didn't even see me coming. I shoved the dagger deep into the back of the daimon closest to Aiden.

Leon knocked aside one of the daimons, going blow-to-blow with it. Aiden went after the other two, trying to keep them both focused on him. "Alex, behind you!"

I whirled around, gripping the dagger in my right hand. A female daimon dove at me, but I ducked out of her grasp. Swinging around, I caught her in the chest with my sneaker just as Seth had done. She went down on one knee, and I lurched forward, jabbing the blade into her stomach. Looking through the poof of blue dust, I grinned at Aiden. "That's two."

"Five for me," he grunted, sinking his dagger into the throat of his daimon.

I flipped the dagger. "Well, la-dee—"

Hands grabbed my shoulders, throwing me backward. I hit the mess of glass and blood, skidding a few feet on my back and losing my grip on the dagger. Stunned, I stared up into the face of a daimon half.

"Alex!" yelled Aiden, sounding truly panicked.

It leaned over me and sniffed. "Apollyon…"

I could easily remember what'd happened when I'd tried to fight the last half-blood daimon. It hadn't gone well. Pushing those memories down, I scrambled across the floor. Glass dug into my palms, mixing my blood with the blood of the fallen. My hand brushed against something wet and soft. A thousand gruesome images flashed through my mind of what I'd possibly backed into.

The daimon half—a trained female Sentinel—opened her mouth and howled. She jumped in the air, swinging a Covenant dagger right at my head. There was a popping noise and then she was a ball of flames crashing down on me. I rolled out of the way as she hit the floor, screaming and thrashing. I jerked toward Aiden. He nodded at me, then lowered his hand and swung at another daimon.

Glancing back at the daimon on the floor, I winced. She slowly climbed to her feet, a charred, stinky mess of skin and cloth.

"Good gods," I muttered, wanting to yak. "Don't even touch me."

She opened her mouth, and then her head went in one direction and her body in the other. Leon stood behind her, sickle in hand. "Miss Andros," he said politely. "I do believe you were supposed to go to safety?"

"Yeah, that was the plan." I looked around the room. There were a lot of bodies on the floor—some of the halfs who'd been turned, while others were of our kind. Seth had two daimons cornered, fighting rather gleefully. I grinned, even though it was sort of twisted.

Aiden followed my gaze. "Leon, that one there counts half for me. So that's six-and-a-half." Then he pivoted around, heading toward another daimon who had a Guard pinned on the floor.

Leon shrugged. "That's okay. I have ten, loser."

A howling sound spun me around. Two daimon halfs charged, going right for Leon. It was as if I wasn't even standing there. "It's about to be twelve," Leon said casually.

"Eleven." I switched the sickle blade to my right hand.

Leon glanced down at me. "Do try not to get yourself killed."

With that, we met them halfway. The male, finally noticing me, made a grab for my arm, but I feinted to the right. He was much bigger than me, maybe the size of Aiden, and I knew I couldn't let this one get me on the ground. I got a good kick in, but he barely moved.

Not good.

I blocked his punch, but it still knocked me back a few steps. I kept my balance, whipping the blade through the air. He dipped quickly, retaliating with a vicious swing aimed to take me down. I felt the wind of the blade whizzing past my head. I jumped to the side, but the daimon half moved so damn fast. His fist came around, slamming into my stomach. I staggered back, gasping for air.

The daimon half laughed. "Ready to die?"

"Not really." I straightened. "The pale and addicted look isn't a good one. You look a little strung out. Need some aether?"

He tilted his head to the side and smiled. "I'm going to rip you apart, you stupid—"

Dipping down, I swept his legs out from underneath him. He went down—leaving only an instant to attack. Jumping up, I brought the sickle blade down on his throat. It met no resistance.

Wide-eyed, I lifted the blade. "Damn, that *is* sharp." I turned around, about to point that out to Leon when the daimon pure was suddenly right in my face.

It licked its lips. "Apollyon…"

"Oh, come on, can you all really smell it?" I flipped the sickle over and shoved it into his stomach.

"You smell like warmth and summer." Seth appeared at my side. "I told you, you smelled good."

"Well, you smell like…like…" Seth waited, brows raised.

My eyes widened. Over his shoulder, I saw at least five more daimon pures coming down the hallway. "Daimons."

"I smell like daimons?" He looked let down.

"No, you idiot, there're more daimons coming."

Seth glanced over his shoulder. "Oh. Well, damn. They must've broken through the entrances."

"That's not good."

Another cracking sound shattered through the hall, different from the breaking glass. It reminded me of an artist chipping away at marble. Seth and I turned at the same time, but I don't know who noticed it first. Both of us took a step back.

A network of fractures split the white marble encasing the furies. Chunks of stone broke off, dropping to the floor. Pink, luminous flesh appeared through the larger gaps in the marble. A fine current of electricity shot through my body.

"Oh, my gods," I whispered.

Seth's arm shot out, slamming his dagger into the chest of a daimon pure without even taking his eyes off the crumbling statues. "Indeed."

A soft, tinkling laugh overcame the sounds of battle, halting everyone and everything in the hall. Transfixed, I watched the rest of the marble slip away like a snake shedding its skin. And there they were, the three of them hovering above the makeshift battlefield. And oh, my gods, they were savagely beautiful.

The gods had unleashed the furies.

Their diaphanous white gowns stood in sharp contrast to the surrounding blood and gore. Pale, blond, and perfect, the three cast their all-white eyes toward the carnage before them. They moved through the still air on pale, transparent wings, delicate-looking and soundless. The furies were lesser goddesses, but their presence took over the hall.

I'd never seen a god before, let alone three of them, but they appeared the way I'd imagined them: compelling and beautiful. Frightening. I even took a step toward them, barely realizing that Seth had done so, too. Neither of us could help it. They were gods—freaking gods appearing before us. None of the other halfs or pures moved, seeming too stunned to do much of anything.

Around the room, the daimons backed off from their opponents, all their attention fixed on the furies as they sniffed the air. Some started to whine, others growled. It was the aether flowing through the gods, I realized. If Seth and I were steak, then the furies had to be the most succulent cuts of filet mignon.

One of the daimons, a half-blood, let out a low howl and charged forward.

The furie in the middle lowered to the floor, sinking her bare feet into blood and glass. Thick blond curls floated around her head as her noiseless wings fluttered around her. A pearly glow radiated from her skin as she tipped her head to the side and smiled. The daimon lunged at her, but she simply raised one hand and froze it mid-attack.

Her smile was innocent, child-like, and yet held a barbed edge to it that was cruel. She reached back with her other arm and slammed her hand clean through the daimon's chest. She shot straight up in the air, bringing the frantic daimon with her. Floating above us, she ripped the daimon in two.

I gasped. "Holy…"

"Shit," Seth finished.

In an instant the furies shifted, shedding their beautiful bodies. Their skin and wings turned gray and milky, their hair darkening and thinning into stringy black ropes that snapped at the air around them. Snakes, not ropes, I realized. Their hair was *freaking snakes*!

The middle one screamed, bringing several pures to their knees. I backed up, knocking into Seth. He wrapped an arm around my waist, hauling me against him. One of the furies swooped, snatching up a daimon and launching it through the air. Another arced down, grabbed a Sentinel with her clawed feet, and sliced him apart as he screamed. The third landed near a crop of daimons, one strand of her snake hair zipping out and right through the eye of a Guard as she eviscerated a daimon pure.

It didn't matter who stood in their paths—the furies were destroying everyone.

I caught sight of Leon ducking under a gray wing and pulling Aiden out of reach of one of the furies. An expression of awe and horror marked Aiden's features as he swung a blade into a nearby daimon that wasn't even paying attention to him.

A furie swept the ceiling, her all-white eyes glowing much like Seth's did when he was pissed. A second later, the furie swung toward us, shrieking shrilly. It stared straight at us, arms extended and claws sharpened into fine points.

Seth grabbed my free hand. "Come on!"

I let him pull me back. "But what about Aiden and Leon?"

"They don't have a furie gunning for their asses. Now, come on!"

We rushed toward the reception hall. The Guards still held their ground at the doors, protecting the pures. Looking back, my heart dropped; the furie was coming after us.

"Seth!"

"I know, Alex, I—" Seth stopped as we rounded the corner.

I slapped into his back. Peering over his shoulder, horror twisted my insides. The hall was choked with daimons. Half-blood servants littered the floor, necks broken or ripped open. As medicated as they were, they'd been utterly defenseless against the daimons. Guards struggled with the flood, trying to hold them back.

The furie screamed, dipping down. Seth spun around, knocking me to the floor and throwing his body over mine. By the grace of the gods, I didn't accidentally stab him with the sickle. My heart thundered and fear stuck to my skin as the furie's wings stirred the air around us. Seth tensed as the furie swooped again, but sensing a god chock-full of aether in their presence, the daimons swarmed the furie.

Jumping to his feet, Seth pulled me up and we started back down the hall. We rushed past rooms full of carnage and disaster. In the midst of the chaos, I saw Brown Eyes fighting back daimons along with the younger half he'd spoken with in the dining room this morning. He moved as gracefully as any Sentinel, taking down a daimon with a titanium candelabrum.

Seth and I reached the ballroom just as a sudden burst of panicked and terrified screams whirled the Guards around. As they yanked the door open a stampede of pure-bloods trampled the Guards, pushing and clawing to get away. Then the herd of frightened pures descended on us, tearing my hand from Seth's. The wave of red and white robes slammed into me from all sides. Trying to stay upright, I screamed, "Seth!"

Bodies rocked into me from every direction, and I was knocked to the floor by one of the Ministers. Sharp pain exploded in my head. I tried getting up, but the hysterical crowd kept pushing me down. Dropping the blade, I curled into a ball and protected my head. Feet were everywhere, stamping down on me, kicking into me. This was how I was going to die—not in battle, not from the plot of some Council member hell-bent on destroying me, but trampled to death by a bunch of pure-bloods. *Of all the ways to die.*

I was so going to haunt every last one of them.

My side throbbed, and I was pretty sure I had a broken rib. In the mad rush, daimons were running and killing right beside the pures, and I had no idea where those damn furies were. I squeezed my eyes shut, whimpering as each sandal-covered foot dug into me. Seconds after I didn't think I could take it anymore, the crowd thinned enough for me to lower my hands and grab the blade.

Shaken and bruised, I climbed to my feet. Pures cluttered the hall, smelling of smoke, sweat, and fear. I didn't see Seth anywhere. Stumbling toward the ballroom, I went against the tide of pures.

Marcus had been in that room, along with Laadan and Lucian.

Inside the once-grand ballroom, I staggered through the destruction, scanning the bodies littering the floor. Marcus and I didn't get along for longer than five seconds, but he was the only person left in this world who shared the same blood as me. I didn't want to see his body among the ones on the floor. I didn't know what I'd do. I just didn't.

Several side doors of the reception hall had been busted in, and some daimons stalked the remaining pures like prey. I watched one pounce on a pure—a coppery-headed one, super tan and beautiful.

Dawn Samos.

It sank its teeth into her arm. Screaming, she tried to wretch her arm away, but the daimon had her in a death grip. She was lucky, though. He could've gone for her throat. A small voice in the back of my head whispered, *Let her go; she likes Aiden.*

But that was all kinds of wrong—super messed-up.

Pulling on my remaining strength, I ignored the aches and rushed toward them. The only easy daimon to kill was a daimon tagging some hapless fool. Didn't I know? My eyes met Dawn's amethyst ones as I plunged the sharp edge of the blade into the daimon's back. He exploded into blue dust all over her pretty white robes.

Dawn scuttled back, face sharp with pain and terror. Dismissing her, I faced the carnage. The daimons, both half and pure, were giving into all the aether, feeding on the fallen. I started toward them, but a raw shriek stopped my heart.

I turned around.

The three furies hovered in front of the door, their snake hair nipping at the space around them. An unfortunate Guard stood between me and the furies, but not for long. The ugliest of them, her gown stained with blood, snapped his neck with a twist of her wrist.

Rage and fear swept through me, dulling the ache deep in my bones. Coiling, responsive power expanded in my stomach and spread through my limbs. A jolt of energy shot through my palm, lighting my hand on fire. It traveled up my arm, and then it twisted down to my core where it licked at a muscle never used. Maybe it was akasha, maybe it was something far stronger—far deadlier—because everything shone like a tawny jewel, as if someone had dipped a paintbrush in amber and spread it over the room.

Stepping forward, my fingers spasmed over the center of the sickle blade. One of the furies laughed. The other two tittered and brushed past the really ugly one. Behind me, I could hear the Guards fighting the daimons, but I focused on the furies.

The two glanced at one another and licked their lips. One of them spoke, "Pretty little Apollyon, siphoning off the First, are you? Or is he throwing his power to you? He better be careful doing that."

"It won't be enough," the other said. "You can't kill us."

"I can try." I clenched the blade.

The furie laughed. "Try and die."

Then they flew toward me. I wheeled around and raced toward the wall. Launching myself up, I kicked off the wall and flipped over the two furies, bringing the blade down in a wide, arcing sweep. I landed in a crouch behind them, arms widespread. The two furies staggered backward, their bodies falling forward without their heads. Blue fire shot from their necks, swamping and consuming their bodies.

The ugly furie cackled, and I whirled around, facing her. She drifted several feet off the floor, her hair wriggling. "You didn't kill my sisters, but Thanatos will not be pleased upon their return."

"Sorry to hear that."

She smiled, slipping back into the form that was so beautiful it almost hurt to look at her. "You're a threat, and we must deal with the threat. It's nothing personal."

"I didn't threaten anyone. I'm not the problem."

"Not yet, but you will. We know what you will do." She reached for the blade, striking unbelievably fast.

I lashed out, kicking her arm back. "What will I do?"

"Why fight me? You kill me and I will come back." She jumped out fast, catching the front of my shirt. I narrowly escaped her claws. "That is what we do. We will keep coming back, hunting you 'til the threat is eradicated."

"Great. You're like herpes. The gift that just keeps on giving."

She blinked. "What?"

I spun into a scissor kick, ignoring the sharp spike of pain as her claws caught my arm and pulled me forward. Using the momentum, I crashed into her. The furie was under me for a second, snarling as I gained the upper hand. I shoved my knee into her, delighting in the flicker of surprise.

She stared up at me, a picture of beauty and innocence. "What a path, what a path the Powers have chosen. You will be their tool. That is why you're a threat."

I stilled. "The oracle said that—"

The furie shifted again, her hair snapping at me. Coming up, I lopped the sickle across her neck and rolled off. Seconds later she went up in blue flames, but her laugh still lingered. For a moment I lay on my back, staring up at the ceiling. Did taking down each furie count triple? Surely they were enough that I'd blown Aiden and Leon out of the water.

Rolling to my feet, I ran the sleeve of my sweater over my cheek. I turned around, seeing so many blue piles of dust and dead halfs that had been turned. Only one Guard remained in the reception hall—the pure-blooded one. Of all the people to survive, it had to be him. I should feel terrible about that thought, but I didn't.

Sighing, I slowly approached the Council Guard. He

had a fresh bruise blooming across his jaw, but was otherwise unscathed. "That was insane."

He flipped the dagger in his hand and turned toward the two remaining pures. Dawn huddled behind a statue of Themis, her arm cradled to her chest. Blood dripped onto her white robes. A male pure several decades older than her had his arm around her, whispering something to her. The chick looked freaked out. I couldn't blame her. She'd been *this* close to meeting her end.

I wiped my hand under my nose, not surprised to see my blood smeared across my skin.

"Is she okay?" the Guard asked.

The male lifted his head. A deep, angry-looking tag bled from where his shoulder and neck met. "Yeah, I think so. We need to get her checked out." He looked at me. "You were amazing. I've never seen anything like that."

"I was, wasn't I?" I murmured, wanting to feel great about winning the fight, but the furie's words left a jolting echo in my mind. She had given me an additional part of the puzzle, finishing what the oracle had said. But it still made little sense. Who were "the Powers" and how would I become a tool?

The pure had turned back to Dawn. "It's over," he soothed her, "all over now."

It was, but I was still unwilling to put the sickle down—just in case. I kept having visions of horror movie monsters jumping out at me. I moved to the broken doors and peered out. Nothing moved, which I believed to be a good sign. But when would the furies be back? Five seconds from now? A day, a week, or a month?

"Alexandria."

I wheeled around. "What?"

The Guard pressed his lips into a smile. "You did do really

well. I saw you. You may be the first person in history to face down a furie and live. And you took out three of them? That…that was amazing."

Reluctant warmth cascaded through me. That meant something coming from a pure-blood Council Guard, even if he'd been ordered to kill Hector. A smile spread across my face. "Thanks."

He put his hand on my shoulder and squeezed. "I'm really sorry for this."

My smile started to fade. "For what?"

"The furies were right. There can't be two of you. You are a risk."

A shiver of warning went up my spine. I stepped back, but the Guard's grip tightened on my shoulder, holding me in place. I looked up with wide eyes and met his. Only one word came out. "Please."

There wasn't an ounce of regret or doubt in the Guard's eyes. "We must protect the future of our race."

Then he swung his blade at my chest.

CHAPTER TWENTY-SEVEN

He's going to kill me.

The words flashed through my mind, and I reacted out of instinct. In the back of my mind, I recognized the act of shoving the sickle into his chest was far different than shoving one into a daimon's or even a furie's. The blade felt heavier in my hand, the sucking noise the skin made when pierced by the sharpest metal seemed louder.

And the thing that was the most different? Pure-blood Guards didn't collapse into themselves and fade to nothing but a fine shimmer of blue dust. The Guard kept standing, a horrified look on his face. I think he'd actually believed he could outmaneuver me, that there wasn't a blade stuck deep into his chest.

I screamed, yanking the sharp end of the sickle out. Then he fell. First to his knees, then face-first onto the marble floor. I lifted my head, the bloodied sickle clenched in my shaking hand. I didn't even know the Guard's name…and I'd killed him.

The male pure must have risen to his feet at some point. He stared back at me, equally horrified.

He opened his mouth, but nothing came out.

"I had to do it," I pleaded. "He was going to kill me. I had to do it."

Dawn whimpered from behind the figure of Themis. The statue had been damaged during the battle. The scales had tipped—no longer equal.

So many rules governed the half-bloods. I really couldn't keep them all straight. But there were two I always remembered: never get involved with a pure-blood, and never kill a pure-blood. Self-defense didn't matter. A pure's life was and always would be valued higher than mine. Being an Apollyon didn't make me above that law. Breaking one rule had seemed bad enough, but both of them?

Well, I was so screwed.

Footsteps thundered into the reception hall, the only sound that seemed greater than the pounding of my heart. Innately, I recognized the two. How had they known where I was? Of course, Seth would know—always know—where I was.

Aiden was the first through the door. Both he and Seth halted a few feet away. I could only imagine what they saw—piles and piles of blue dust, the bodies, the broken doors, and two pures cowering under the statue.

Then they saw me, standing with a bloodied sickle in hand and a dead Council Guard lying at my feet.

"Alex, are you okay?" Aiden crossed the room. "Alex?"

He stepped around the fallen Guard and stood in front of me. A bruise shadowed under his right eye, and a scratch slashed across his left cheek. His shirt was torn, but the blade hooked to his pants didn't have blood on it.

"Alex, what happened?" He sounded desperate as his eyes searched mine. I blinked, but I kept seeing the look on the Guard's face.

Seth surveyed the mess with a cold, almost feral look to him. "Alex. Tell us what happened."

It all came out in a nervous rush. "I was fighting the furies and he told me I did a good job, Aiden. Then he apologized. I had to do it. He said there couldn't be two of us and that he had to protect his race. He was going to kill me. I—I had to do it. I don't even know his name and I killed him."

Pain and panic flared in Aiden's eyes, and then they took on a hard, steely edge. Resolve burned from them while a red-hot fury built behind him. Seth dipped down and rolled the Guard over.

"Okay." Aiden reached out to pry my fingers from the dagger. "Let me have the blade, Alex."

"No." I shook my head. "It has my prints on it. It's *mine*."

"You have to let me have it, Alex."

I shook my head, holding the sickle tighter. "I had to do it."

Aiden gently pried the blade loose. "I know, Alex. I know." He glanced over his shoulder before turning back to me. "Do not speak a word of this to anyone. Do you understand?"

"But—"

"Alex." His voice rose sharply. "Do not speak about this to anyone. *Ever.* Do you understand me?"

"Yes." My breath was coming out in sharp, little gasps.

He spun toward Seth. "Get her out of here. Take Lucian's jet to North Carolina. Use compulsion if you have to to get them to leave without him; I don't care. If anyone stops you or asks why you're leaving now, tell them the daimons had plans to take the second Apollyon. That the risk was too great for her to remain here."

Seth nodded, his eyes glowing. "What about them?"

Aiden glanced back at the pures. "I'll deal with them." His voice was low. "What happened in here will never leave this room. You can trust that."

"Are you sure?" Seth frowned. "If you change your mind, it's all over for Alex. We could just take care—"

"We will *not* kill them," Aiden hissed. "I know what I'm doing!"

Seth's eyes widened. "You're insane—as insane as Alex. If anyone finds out what you're about to do, you're—"

"I know. Go—go now. Before anyone else comes. I'll take care of this."

Would Aiden use compulsion on another pure? That alone was another forbidden act, another rule to be broken. How else would he get them to keep this secret? Especially Dawn? She was a Council member, obligated to report what'd really happened.

Aiden would compel the pures. Everything else would fall into place. The halfs who'd been turned had all used daggers. People would find the Guard and believe a daimon half had ended his life.

But if anyone ever found out the truth, Aiden would be deemed a traitor. He would be killed for it.

I shot forward. "No. You can't do this. I won't allow it. You won't die—"

Aiden spun around and grasped my shoulders. "I will do this and you will allow this. Please, for once, don't fight with me. Just do as I say." His eyes met mine and when he spoke again, he did so barely above a whisper. "Please."

I closed my eyes against the sudden rush of tears. "Don't do this."

"I have to. I told you before I'd never let anything

happen to you. I meant it." Aiden turned toward Seth. "Leave now."

Seth took my hand in a firm grip. There was so much I wanted to say to Aiden, but there wasn't time, not with Seth dragging me past the bodies and the shell-shocked pures. I did get one last glance, though.

Aiden was already setting his plan into motion. He crouched in front of Dawn, speaking low and quick—the same way he'd spoken to me that night in the warehouse.

A compulsion—he was really using a compulsion on another pure.

Seth pulled my hand. "We have to hurry."

The two of us raced through the hallways, avoiding the more heavily populated areas. We passed rooms where soft cries filled the space between our footfalls, corridors where bodies of half-bloods covered the floor. As Seth swiped a set of keys from a dead Guard, I looked into a dark chamber. Half-blood servants littered the floor, all of them dead or dying, and no one seemed to even care. No one tended to them. There were only moans and pleas for mercy. Pleas for help—help that would never come. I started toward them.

"We don't have time. I'm sorry, Angel. We just don't have time. We have to go." Seth wrenched me away from the room.

Numb—I was numb inside. So numb that I really didn't feel the bruises the hits had left behind, the ache that each step jarred out of me. Finding a Hummer wasn't hard, but ignoring the sounds of fighting all around us was difficult. Instinct demanded that I throw myself back into the fray, but I doubted Seth would appreciate that.

I scanned the dark grounds, relieved to see that Guards still held a line around the school. The daimons hadn't broken through. At least the students were safe.

But what about the servants?

On the way to the airport, Seth carried out Aiden's plan. After several unsuccessful tries, he was able to reach Marcus. I stared out the window, still numb with shock.

Seth said exactly what Aiden had instructed, telling Marcus that the daimons had tried to take me. "We need to get her out of here on Lucian's plane tonight," he finished.

It sounded as though Marcus agreed with the idea of getting me out of New York. "Lucian is among the survivors. I'll pass on the information."

Some of the tension in my body eased off knowing that Lucian and Marcus were alive, but there were still many more whose fates were unknown at this point. There'd been so many bodies, so many daimons. What about Laadan?

Seth and I didn't talk until we'd boarded Lucian's jet. I took a seat beside a window while Seth *encouraged* the pilot and the servants to take off without Lucian.

I rested my head against the cool pane, squeezing my eyes shut. My stomach felt hollow. At some point after the plane took off, I stopped thinking. I just sat there, existing in a world where I might not even have a future. So many things could go wrong at this point. What if the compulsion failed to work? If so, Guards would be waiting for us the moment the plane landed. And even if Aiden was successful, compulsions weren't guaranteed to be permanent. They could wear off after time.

Then what? Both Aiden and I would lose everything.

Seth dropped into the seat beside me. I lifted my head and glanced at him. He held two glasses in his hands, filled with something that looked a lot like liquor. "What is it?"

"It's not the brew." His joke fell flat, but I smiled weakly and took it. "It's just scotch. It should help."

I downed the glass and handed it back. "Thank you."

"You really stopped the furies?"

Nodding, I handed the glass back to him. "Cut their heads off. They said they'd be back, though."

"Only a god can truly kill another god." He paused. "Or a god killer, but if you cut off their heads I can imagine that would put them out of commission for a while."

"Seth, they said…they said I was the threat." I bit my lip, shuddering. "Oh, gods, I killed a pure."

"Shh. Don't ever say that again. You know how much Aiden is risking. Don't let it all go to waste." Seth leaned over, draping his arm around my shoulders. After a few seconds, he spoke. "He really…isn't like the other pures, Alex."

"I know," I whispered. Aiden wasn't like anyone I knew, and there was no way I could accept that his actions tonight were a sense of duty on steroids.

But there was nothing I could do about that right now.

I looked out the tiny window, out into the dark night. Below, diamond-shaped lights grew smaller and smaller, becoming insignificant and vanishing as we moved into ominous clouds. I drew in a deep breath, but it got stuck in my throat. I'd killed a pure-blood and the man I loved was down there, covering it up, risking everything for me.

What had I done?

Thinking back on those seconds when I'd seen the pure raise the dagger, I knew there'd been time to avoid the deadly plunge of the blade. I was fast. I could've moved out of the way. I could've run. I hadn't needed to *kill* him.

Seth's arm around my shoulders tightened as if he could read my mind. "You were defending yourself, Alex."

"Was I?"

"Yes. They declared war on us. You had no other choice."

"There are always choices." I pulled my gaze from the

window and looked at Seth. *There are always choices.* I just had this terrible habit of making the wrong ones, and now I had to deal with it. So did Aiden. So did Seth.

Seth reached out slowly, as if he was afraid to startle me. His hand caught my chin with the tips of his fingers. He didn't say anything. Not that he needed to—the connection between us was there, sparking alive.

I *needed* it right now—*needed* Seth.

Closing my eyes, I let him guide my head to his shoulder. And after I could take the first deep breath of air without choking on it—after I'd made my choice—I finally let the connection in completely. Seth's presence—his warmth surrounded me. Waves of comfort washed over me, easing the knots in my stomach. Not filling in all the cracks, not replacing ones that lingered back in the Catskills, but filling enough that I felt a little better, a little saner.

READ ON FOR SPECIAL BONUS SCENES

BONUS SCENE (SETH'S POV)

I watched Dawn place her hand on Aiden's arm and once again felt a wealth of gratitude that Alex had decided not to attend this ball. If she *were* here watching this, she might've ripped out every strand of the pure-blood's coppery hair.

Images of Alex going all girl-fight filled my head, and I snickered. Aiden raised his brows at me. "Doing okay over there?"

I rolled my eyes, not even bothering to answer. Just because I was standing next to him—only because he was the least undesirable option at the moment—didn't mean I was going to be chatty with him. On a good day, the animosity levels between us were usually at CODE RED. Bad days they were at CODE I'M GOING TO KILL YOU.

We had more bad days than good days.

The pure's gray eyes narrowed before he turned back to the one of the Councilman's sons, who was currently describing how thrilling yachting on the open sea was. Boredom was going to kill me. My gaze slid over to where Lucian stood, surrounded by the Ministers. Even he was looking like he'd be more stimulating company.

Aiden sighed under his breath, loud enough that I could hear him, and I almost laughed out loud.

Apparently, he and I shared more than one thing in common: our current boredom and one—

A shiver of awareness rolled over my skin, and I felt the marks tingling, responding to the presence of her. Alex.

I turned slowly, zeroing in on where she was. Now what in the Hades was she doing down…my brain pretty much emptied of all rational thought.

Alex stood just inside the entrance of the ballroom, looking as frightened as a wood nymph having earned Apollo's favor. Her anxiety hummed around her, but I wasn't feeling it. Well, I was feeling *something*.

There always was this certain beauty to her—one that was rough at the edges, making her unique to those around her. But tonight, dressed in a red gown that should've been illegal on her body? I'd seen Alex in workout clothes, in those little distracting pajama bottoms, and in regular clothes, but *damn*. That wild tangle of hair was twisted up…and those eyes…

Tonight, she was the most beautiful thing I'd ever seen.

I watched her move away from Laadan and Lucian, retreating to the side. She didn't belong there.

Hades, she didn't belong *here*.

Finally, after what seemed like forever, her eyes met mine. She lifted her glass, silently saluting me. Every muscle in my body locked up, and then I realized I was staring at her like an imbecile.

"Holy crap," I murmured.

I felt Aiden stiffen beside me, and I wondered if he somehow knew that she was here, if there was some kind of bond that coursed between those two that was far more powerful than what Alex and I shared. Impossible...but I wondered.

Then he looked over his shoulder, and dear gods, I'd never seen a man more surprised by a girl in a dress than Aiden. Okay. Lie. I had been just as surprised, and if he was thinking half of what I was thinking, I sort of wanted to hit him more than I usually did.

The look on both of their faces actually did make me want to hit—no, zap something. Right here, out in the open, they were doing the eye-screw thing.

And it was about to get worse. Aiden seriously *was* walking toward her. Clenching my jaw until I was sure my teeth would crack, I slipped away from the group, passing Lucian and Marcus. When I made it behind Laadan, she lifted her gaze.

"She's not for you," she murmured over the rim of her glass. The slight, knowing smile of hers didn't fade. I didn't even want to know how she knew. "Be penny-wise, Seth..."

"And a pound of shut-the-hell-up."

Laadan arched a brow, but said nothing else, which was fine by me. Out of all the pures I knew, she even freaked me out. I moved past her toward Alex and briefly considered grabbing a napkin off the table to help with the drool, but I doubted she'd appreciate the offer.

Sighing, I slid up behind her, placing my hand on her shoulder. She didn't even flinch, but I did. Zeus could be feeling her up right now and she wouldn't even notice. But Aiden noticed. He did nothing to hide the flash of rage contorting his usually cool expression.

My lip curled up on one side.

Aiden looked like he was going to hit me, and I sort of hoped he did. I would love nothing more than to shove my foot so far up his...but Alex—it wouldn't end well for Alex.

Leaning into her, I inhaled the scent of peaches and something mysterious and uniquely hers. "People are starting to stare."

And I knew she couldn't care less, and that made me want to throttle her, but Aiden—as always—displayed some common sense. He stopped, grinding his teeth just as strongly as I did.

I slid my hand down her arm, threading my fingers through hers, and then I said the most ironic thing of all. "You know he's not for you."

"I know," she whispered, and her desperation and pain blew back at me so strongly I struggled not to drown in them as Aiden turned around. Part of me wanted him to come back to her, just to end what she was feeling.

A very small part that I knocked the crap out of. "Do you want to dance?" I asked.

She tipped her chin back, her eyes a honey brown. "I don't want to dance."

My gaze dripped. "Do you want to stay here?"

"I don't know."

Ah, indecision—a man's best friend. I smiled and as I spoke, my lips brushed her ear. "We don't belong here, Alex. Not with them."

Her eyes flickered away from mine and she sucked in her lower lip. She was confused, which usually brought out the less than tolerable side of Alex, but then her eyes came back to mine.

"Let's go," I coaxed.

Her fingers trembled as she placed her wine glass down, and we went even though I knew her head wasn't with me. Her thoughts and her heart never were, always wrapped up in the wrong place.

Only for now, I reminded myself, *only for now*.

I led us around the building, not really giving her much of a choice but to follow. She shivered in the cool air and remained silent the entire time, which had to be a record for her. My free hand curled into a fist. Her distress ate away at me like acid, and she had no clue how much she fed through our connection.

"Let's do something stupid," I said.

She glanced at me. "You want to do something stupid right now?"

"Can you think of a better time to do something stupid?"

Her lips twitched. "Okay. I'm down with stupid."

"Good." Great. Yay. Yippee. I pulled her through the labyrinth, fighting the anger building in me.

"You want to train?"

Shaking my head, I picked up the pace. "No. I don't want to train."

The double doors weren't locked, and I grinned when I spotted the swimming pool. Both of us needed stupid right now.

"You want to go swimming?" she asked, sounding doubtful.

"Sure."

"It's like forty degrees outside."

I pushed open the door, greeted with a nose full of chlorine. "So? It's not forty degrees in here, is it? More like sixty."

Alex pulled away from me and went to the edge of the pool. Of course, I watched her as I kicked off my shoes. She glanced at me, and I winked.

"You're ridiculous," she said.

"So are you." I dropped my jacket on the cement, watching her, always watching her. It wasn't so much me, but what was inside me—inside her. It was just the way it was, I supposed.

"We are a lot alike, Alex."

She looked like she wanted to argue that, but she got that look on her face that said she was thinking real hard. Brows knitted, nose scrunched a little, and lips parted. Cute.

"Was it so obvious back there?" she asked.

It took me a moment to realize what she was getting at and then I strung as many four-letter words together as I could. They were creative. "I don't know what goes on in your head, Alex. I can't read your thoughts. I just picked up on your emotions."

She frowned. "Good to know."

"I second that." I started unbuttoning my shirt. "Anyway, I don't even need to be able to sense your emotions to know. I don't think you want to know what it looked like."

"No. I do."

Famous last words, but who was I to deny her? I sighed. "You were staring at him like an ugly chick stares at the last cute guy at the bar when they make the last call."

She let out a strangled laugh. "Oh. Wow. Thanks."

Dammit. I raised my hands. "I told you."

"Yeah. So, I looked like an idiot to everyone?"

An idiot? I wish. "No, everyone saw a beautiful half-blood. That's all anyone saw."

I glanced away, knowing it was time to change the subject. "Can I tell you something?"

She turned back to the pool. "Sure."

I moved toward her, partly because I *had* to and because I knew she hated it when I moved too fast. "I prefer you without gloves."

"Oh." She watched me warily.

I peeled off one glove, surprised that she was even letting me, and then the other, tossing them both away from the water. Give an inch, and I'll take a mile. I slid my fingers around the tags on her arms before stepping back.

She lowered her lashes. "Better?"

"Much." I folded my arms, eyeing her. Alex was always a great curiosity to me. She shouldn't be, but she was. Perhaps that was what made her such a mystery to me. Even though I knew what she was feeling half the time, I never knew what she was going to do next.

"Can you get silk wet?" she asked.

Was she seriously going to jump in with that dress? I choked at the thought. "I'd say probably not."

She removed her shoes. "That's a shame."

My eyes widened. "You really are going—"

Alex dove in, and I laughed as her shock rippled through me, joining with mine. I moved to the edge of the pool, grinning as she resurfaced. "So childish, Alex. You've ruined her dress."

"I know. Bad me."

"Very bad," I murmured, watching her sink under the water again. She stayed under the water so long I began to wonder if she had a little bit of Poseidon in her.

A tremble coursed through the marks, and I moved away from the edge. Lifting my arms, I closed my eyes and stretched, trying to ease the tension building inside me, lessen the way the marks tingled and burned.

I pried one eye open, finding Alex floating, watching me. "Stop staring."

"I'm not staring."

I chuckled. "How's the water?"

"Nice."

The marks were still driving me crazy. Power was building in them, zinging across my skin. Dropping my arms, I took in a deep breath of air. "Do you remember the last thing I told you in training?"

She swam toward the edge. "You tell me a lot of stuff in training. Honestly, I don't pay attention."

Nice. I snorted. "You do wonders for my self-esteem."

Alex pushed off the cement wall and floated on her back. The dress streamed out around her like she was some kind of water nymph. "I feel like a mermaid."

I felt a lot of things. "Tomorrow, when they ask you about what happened in Gatlinburg, only answer their questions."

She sighed. "I know. What do you guys think I'm going to say? That I love daimons?"

It wouldn't surprise me. "Just don't elaborate on anything. Answer yes or no, and that is it."

"I'm not stupid, Seth."

I arched a brow. Stupid? No. Reckless? Yes. "I didn't say you were. I just know you tend…to talk a lot."

"Oh. Like you're one—"

I dove in, going right for her. I grabbed for the dress, but she pushed my hand away. Resurfacing, I shook my head, sending water flying everywhere.

She splashed me. "You talk more than I do."

Going to the side, I swung one arm over the edge and turned to her. Good gods, water did the girl good. "You look like a drowned monkey."

"What? I do not." She ran a hand over her hair and then her eyes. "Wait. Do I?"

I nodded, fighting the nearly all-consuming urge to throw myself at her. "Honestly, you look like a mess. This was a bad idea. What was I thinking?"

"Shut up. You don't look so hot yourself."

There was a spike of interest that wasn't mine, betraying her words. I grinned, placing my hand over the water. "Watch this."

She struggled with the edges of her dress. "Watch what?"

Using the water element, I let the water spin, then shot it up, directing the typhoon toward her. This started an all-out water war, and even though she knew she was no match, Alex didn't give up. Not even when the play turned more physical, and I had her suspended in air above me, kicking and squealing like a little banshee. And for the first time in a very long time, I was actually having…fun. Childish, stupid fun, but fun nonetheless.

In the back of my mind, I knew why I'd brought her here, but by the third time I'd tossed her a good twenty feet in the air, watching her come right back to me, I started to forget the whole reason as a new, better idea took hold.

She grinned down at me.

Sighing, I lowered her back into the water. "Now you really do look like a drowned monkey."

"Thanks." She started to swim away.

I let her get only so far before I circled an arm around her waist and flipped her back around. "Where do you think you're going?" I wasn't sure what I was doing. Yeah, I flirted with her and pushed the limits, but there was always this invisible line between us. It had a name—Aiden. But right now, that line had been drowned.

She placed her hands on my shoulders, and I gritted my teeth. "Don't throw me again."

"I'm not going to throw you."

"Then I win the water war?"

"No," I said, my gaze dropping down the curve of her neck. The tags were barely noticeable.

"Damn. Well, I guess you have to be better than me at something. Congratulations."

"I'm always better than you. I'm—"

"Egotistical?" she cut in, her eyes gleaming in the dim light like whiskey. "Narcissistic?"

Tipping my chin down, I backed her up until she hit the edge of the pool. "I have some words for you, too. How about stubborn? Impudent?"

Her breath caught. "Was 'impudent' your word choice of the day?"

I put my finger on her lips. "Well, yes it is. I could even use it in a sentence if you like."

"That won't be necessary." Her eyes narrowed.

Planting my hands on either side of her, I watched the water-soaked lashes lift, her eyes met mine, and it was like being sucker-punched in the gut. The rush of confusion, tinged red with attraction, burned at the back of my throat.

There was also a great deal of nervousness radiating from her, and for good reason. She swallowed. "I think…we should head back now. I'm cold and it's getting late."

I smiled. "No."

"No?"

"I'm not done being stupid yet." I leaned in, so close that the edges of my hair brushed her forehead. "Actually, there's a lot of stupid left in me." Because this really *was* stupid.

Alex placed her hands on my chest, and a jolt of electricity shot through me. Uncertainty pinched her features, but she wasn't pushing me away. I took that as a good sign. My hands found her waist without much thought, the material thin enough that I could feel her hot skin.

"You know what?" I said. "There are a lot of stupid things to do, but I really want to do the stupidest thing possible."

"What's that?"

I inhaled her, breathed her in. "I want to kiss you."

She stiffened. "That is crazy. I'm not Elena…or any number of girls."

"I know. Maybe that's why I want to," I admitted. Alex was different. None of the other girls had my skin prickling. It might not even be her, but what lay resting inside her. Either way, I knew I wanted this, because it was what the thing waiting inside me wanted.

Alex turned her head toward mine. Another really good sign. "You don't want to kiss me."

"But I do." My lips brushed against her soft cheek.

Her hands slipped away and gripped the edge of the pool. "No, you don't."

I laughed, slipping my fingers up her spine, curving my hand around the base of her neck. "Are you arguing with me over what I want?"

"You're arguing with me."

"You're ridiculous." I smiled for a moment before recognizing that my touch had come in contact with the bruise the Master had left behind. Anger rushed through me, heightening the tension. "It's such an annoying quality, yet strangely endearing."

"Well…you're annoying, too."

I laughed again, because she was funny. Always arguing, always denying what was right in front of her. "Why are we still talking?"

Resting her cheek against my shoulder, I felt her lashes flutter. "This is your one chance to talk without me telling you to shut up, because we aren't doing…anything else."

"Do you know how amusing I find you?" I shifted closer, running my hand over the curve of her hip, down her thigh.

She went to stop me, not quick enough, and I knew Alex could be damn quick when she really wanted to. I hooked her leg around mine and bit back a groan.

"What are…you doing?" she whispered.

"Do you know why I think you're so amusing?"

"Why?"

"Because I know how badly you want me to kiss you." I cupped her chin, tipping her head back with my other hand.

"That's not true."

Such a little liar—her need beat at mine, blurring who each of us were. "You lie. Why? I have no idea." I kissed her cheek and then her throat, her shoulder as my hand on her thigh slipped further down. She jerked, and I grinned. "I can feel what you're feeling. And I know you want me to kiss you."

Her little nails dug into my arm. "It's not…"

"Not what?" I lifted my head, bringing my mouth so very close to hers.

"I…"

"Just let me kiss you."

And I knew she wanted me to—*needed* me to. It roared through the bond, and I felt the marks bleed through my skin, churning as they slid over me. Alex was fighting it, because that's what she did. And then there was the other issue, a sense of guilt I was picking up from her.

She opened her eyes. "Is this real?"

"Very real." I brushed the soaked strands off her cheek, wondering if I was lying or not and if I should care if I was. "Angel, just let me kiss you."

Her lips parted not even an inch from mine, and my stomach tightened. So close…and then I felt the guilt growing, becoming more powerful than the need. The marks stilled on my skin. She wasn't thinking of me right now—son of a bitch. I dropped her, wincing when she smacked off the pool edge. "You're thinking about Aiden."

She bit her lip, but the truth was in her eyes. "Not in the way you think I am."

Frustration whipped through me, and I knew I needed to leave before I did or said something I'd regret, but I pushed forward, getting right up in her face. "You know, I don't know which is worse. That I was stupid enough to want to kiss you, or the fact that you're still hung up on someone who doesn't even want you."

Her eyes gleamed. "Wow. That's a little harsh."

Total asshole move, but she needed to understand. "It's the truth, Alex. Even if he did profess his undying love for you, you can't have him."

Alex spun away from me and hauled herself out of the pool. Water streamed off her dress, forming little puddles around her feet. "Just because I can't be with him doesn't change the way I feel."

And that did it. Maybe at one point I would've left it alone, but not now. I was out of the water so fast she took an unsteady step back from me. "If you have this epic love for Aiden, why did you want to kiss me as badly as you did?"

Red stained her cheeks with fury, mixing with my own. "I didn't kiss you, Seth! That should answer your question right there!"

"You wanted to. Trust me, I know you did." I smiled. "You really wanted to."

She stared at me a moment, then her hands balled into fists. "I don't know what I want! How do you know, Seth? How do you know it's not the damn connection between us instead of something real?"

And that was the million-daimon question. I didn't

know, not really, but there was more than just the connection. Like when Caleb was killed, part of the reason why I'd stayed with her was because of the sorrow that was eating away at her, but the other part was because I *wanted* to be there. So much so that I'd even blocked Aiden from seeing her.

Yes, there was the connection feeding us, but that was the way it was supposed to be, how both of us had been created. There wasn't anything wrong with it. Denying it was unnatural. Explaining that to her wouldn't get me anywhere, though. She didn't understand. Not yet.

"You think it's just the connection? Do you really think that's all I feel for you?"

Her laugh was harsh. "You say it yourself all the time! Anytime you do something nice for me, you say it's the connection forcing you to do so."

"Did you ever consider that I was joking?"

"No! Why would I? You said the connection would grow stronger between us. That's why you want to kiss me! It's not real."

Dammit, sometimes I literally wanted to choke her. "I know why I want to kiss you, Alex, and it has nothing to do with either of us being Apollyons. And apparently it has nothing to do with your common sense, either."

Now she looked like she wanted to choke me. "Oh, shut up. I'm done talking—"

"I know exactly why." I stalked forward, backing her up until she hit the cement wall behind her. "I can't believe I'd even have to spell it out for you."

Flattening her hands against the wall, she shivered. "You don't have to."

"You're the most frustrating person I know."

She rolled her eyes. "And that makes you want to kiss me? You're twisted."

"Do you feel the connection between us right now?" I asked.

Alex frowned. "Not really, but I don't know what it feels—"

I don't even know why I did this. Anger? Frustration? Need? Or maybe just to prove that she did want me even though she loved someone else, which in my mind, proved that love was probably one of the most fickle, stupid things the gods had ever created. Grasping the sides of her face, I lowered my mouth to hers.

She froze against me, but didn't fight back as I deepened the kiss, rushing past the exquisite feel of the first time, delving headfirst into it. Gods, I could eat her up. She was right. It had a lot to do with connection between us fueling the desire, but I didn't care. There was a lot to that, a purpose to all of this, not that I could remember or think about a damn thing other than how soft her lips were, how I'd bet my life ambrosia tasted like her.

And finally she moved. Wrapping her arms around my neck, she tangled her fingers in my hair, kissing me back like there was no tomorrow. I loved that—loved how when Alex finally decided to do something, she threw all of herself into it—right or wrong.

Coldness lingered at the back of my mind, though. Knowledge. This was my chance, the only chance I knew I'd get.

I pulled back, catching her lower lip. The sound she made wasn't even fair. "You can't tell me you didn't like that." I kissed her again, unable to help myself after so long. "And don't you dare tell me you didn't kiss me."

"I...don't know what that was," she said.

I chuckled, moving my mouth against hers. "You have a choice, Alex."

Her eyes flew open then, and she watched the marks on my face almost obsessively. They hummed with approval. "What choice?"

I slid my hands to her waist, holding her still. "You can choose to continue wasting away for something you can never have..."

"Or?"

Huh, not an outright no. I smiled. "You can choose not to."

"Seth, I—"

And here we go. "Look, I know you aren't over *him*, but I do know you like me. I'm not suggesting anything. Not asking for stupid little labels or promises. No expectations."

She drew in a shallow breath. "What are you suggesting?"

"You choose to see what happens." I let go, stepped back and ran my hands through my hair, needing space. "Between us—you choose us."

Alex wrapped her arms around her waist, looking incredibly small. It was a risk, putting it out there like that, but it was far past time that I did. Like staking my claim, I supposed.

I smiled faintly. "Think about it, at least."

Then I left her, giving her a few moments to think, which in hindsight might not have been such a good idea. Alex had turned making wrong decisions into a hobby. My movements were jerky as I grabbed the discarded shirt and slipped it on over my shoulders. The material rasped against the now sensitive marks, but I was getting used to that sting.

"Seth?"

I turned halfway, finishing the last of the buttons. "Alex?"

A flush crept across her cheeks "I...I choose you—or

whatever it is that you're saying." She paused, her nose wrinkling. "I mean, I choose the whole seeing what—"

My mouth cut her words off, and I swept my arms around her, dropping the jacket over her chilled shoulders, and then I lifted her up against me. Fire swept through both of us, and she moved in my arms, deliciously so. The marks blasted against my skin, swirling to where her hands fisted my shirt, demanding to make contact with her, to brand her skin once again.

Then her hands slid under my shirt. *Too fast.* I jerked back, breathing heavy. I had her, but still, too fast. My lips spread in a smile that reached every part of me. "You're not sleeping in that bed—in that terrible little room—tonight."

DELETED SCENE (ALEX AND AIDEN)

Aiden threw up his hands. In such a small space, the gesture pretty much took up all the room. "Don't you think that my disappointment has nothing to do with the fact Seth was in your room, but that you would so blatantly break the rules again?"

"That is so not true, Aiden. I break the rules all the time."

"My point exactly," he said dryly.

I really have no idea what provoked the next words to come out of my mouth. Maybe it had to do with all the pent-up frustration. All those times we trained together and we were so very close, and yet so far apart from one another. Maybe I just wanted to piss him off. "You're disappointment comes from him being in my bed and not you. Anybody else could admit that."

Aiden let out a strangled breath, and I knew I went too far. He was going to yell at me. Lecture me about how I never think. Worse yet, I knew—just knew—Aiden would say I had it all wrong. That he had let go of whatever had happened between us. And I was pretty sure I might cry if he did so. Or hit him. Neither would be fun. So I had to say something to undo what I said a few seconds ago.

"You said I was beautiful once," I said in a rush. "Don't you still think I'm beautiful?"

Frustration and something else flared in his eyes. Hunger maybe? I took it and ran with it.

"I don't…I don't think you look beautiful. You look… exquisite." He placed his hand over mine. "You always do."

"Exquisite?" I smiled broadly. "I like that."

"You would," he replied with a sigh.

Wonderful warmth spread over me. "Do you think anyone else is exquisite?"

He tipped his head to the side and strands of dark hair fell against his cheek. He sighed again. "Alex, don't."

His words were more like a soft plea, but they had no impact on me. "Do you? Tell me you do and I'll stop. I'll even be quiet. For like a week. Just tell me you feel this with anyone else."

Those eyes switched from pale gray to liquid silver. An instant later Aiden pulled me right up against him. "You always push."

"I do?" I whispered, my pulse pounding through me. I was like a kid. Any attention was good attention. As long as he paid attention to me. I wanted him to touch me, to want me as badly as I wanted him.

And he did.

Our lips met. He gave no warning. His mouth was on mine, and all thought fled. Lost to the simple touch, to the act that was so forbidden, we both risked everything. Urgency burned between us, deepening the kiss. His hands slid to my waist, fingers pressing fire into my spine. A rich ache blossomed, spreading out of control. My nails dug through his thermal, and he backed me up. I knocked into a cart, spilling sheets onto the floor. He pressed closer and one hand snaked down my hip and over my thigh, and then he brought it up so my leg hooked around his.

With so very little clothing between us, I was quickly reminded of the night in his room, on his bed. The memory fueled the fervor, and my hands sunk into the strands of his hair.

His lips left me spinning, gasping for air. I couldn't get enough of him. My hips moved toward him, my hands slid to his shoulders, down his arms, and under his shirt. Things were spiraling madly. Everywhere he touched, my skin burned and my soul sung.

And even though I felt like I would come apart at any second, this was so much more than a physical thing. Desperation clung to the edge of each kiss, to the way our bodies were sealed together, chest to knees. So tightly I could feel his heart thundering. And in the midst of all these glorious sensations, I realized something so important, so powerful.

Aiden could tell me he didn't feel the same way I did. He could fight what lay between us night and day. He could speak only in lies from here on out. It didn't matter.

I would always, always know differently.

Even if space separated us, or a dozen rules were imposed to keep us apart, and we could never be together, I would always know. So why did I suddenly want to cry?

Aiden broke away, breathing heavy. His arms were still fastened around me. "I shouldn't have done that."

THE ZOO SCENE (AIDEN'S POV)

I stood beside Alex, pretending to watch the bobcat when I was really watching Alex. Ever since she'd faced her mom in Gatlinburg, the dark, far-off look in her eyes had become painfully familiar. Seeing her lips curve into the smile that always made me feel like someone reached into my chest and squeezed, and hearing her laugh proved to me that this trip had been worth the risks involved.

She'd already faced way too much—things a weaker person would've broken from—and I had a horrible feeling that whatever truly waited for her in the future wouldn't be any easier than what lay in her past.

If I knew how to prevent her from experiencing any more pain and heartbreak, I would. I would do anything.

"Do you think she knows what we are?" she asked.

I leaned against the guardrail. "I don't know."

Her eyes continued to follow the lithe movements of the predator. "Mom believed they did. She said animals could sense we were different from the mortals, especially cats."

As I watched a breeze stir the strands of her hair, it suddenly made sense—this whole fascination with zoos. "Did your mother like cats?"

She shrugged. "I think it had something to do with my father. Whenever we'd come here, we always ended up here right before we left." Looking over her shoulder, she nodded at the weathered benches. "We'd sit over there and watch the cats."

I moved closer to her, unsure if it was on purpose or not.

Alex faced the pen again, smiling. "It was the only time Mom would talk about my father. She never really said much about him. Except that he had the warmest brown eyes. I wonder if he had something to do with animals, you know? Anyway, the last time we were here was when she told me he was dead and told me his name. She named me after him, did you know that? I guess that's why Lucian hated it when Mom called me Alex. After a while, she started calling me Lexie instead. My father's name was Alexander."

Several moments passed where neither of us said anything. "That's why you like the zoo so much."

"Yeah, you got me." She laughed and her cheeks flushed.

"It's nothing to be ashamed of, to want to be close to something that reminds you of your loved ones."

"I didn't even know him, Aiden."

"Still, he was your father."

Alex fell quiet as she returned to watching the bobcat prowl the edges of its pen. Within seconds, my gaze swung back to her. Pink still colored her cheeks and her eyes seemed shades lighter. I glanced back at the pen, thinking that Alex was much like the bobcat. Powerful and graceful, but trapped by the cage of what she would become. Then again, all half-bloods were that way. They were some of the most powerful creatures to walk the mortal realm, but all of them were prisoners to the percentages of their blood.

For a brief, insane second, I considered taking her somewhere far away from Deity Island. Like I imagined some mortals wanted to do when they saw wild animals caged—they wanted to see them free. But that was impossible. The Council would find her. Hell, the gods might even find her.

Seth would find her.

Letting out a low breath, I loathed what I had to do next. "I hate to do this, but we need to head back, Alex."

"I know."

We started walking back through the park. I wondered what Alex was thinking. Did she want to go back to the Covenant? Did she still want to be a part of that world, after everything? Anger flashed through me like fire. It didn't matter what she wanted, and gods, that pissed me off. What pissed me off even more was the fact that I had told her only she had control over her destiny, and that was a godsdamn lie.

My brain shot to work, going back to the insanity of setting her free. Money wasn't an issue. Thanks to my parents, I had enough to set her up for decades. Getting her into a mortal school wouldn't be hard, either. Compulsion would take care of that. Safety was an issue, though. Daimons were bound to find her again. The Council would send Sentinels again. Seth would probably tear the world apart to locate her. But I could hide her well enough that she wouldn't be found for years and I could keep her safe from—what in the hell was I thinking?

Air punched out of my lungs as I opened the driver's door and climbed in.

I could hide her? I could keep her safe?

Sentinel—I was a Sentinel, and Sentinels like me would be

sent to retrieve her. And on top of that, taking her away from the Covenant would break so many laws it made my head spin. My punishment wasn't a concern. It would be hers, because she would take the brunt of this foolishness. I'd be stripped of my Sentinel duties, but my life would go on. Alex would most likely be put on the Elixir, Apollyon or not.

But taking her back…gods, she deserved so much better than all of this, and she didn't need to shoulder everything on her own.

Twisting toward her, pressure clamped down on my chest. The words came out before I could stop them. "I know how brave you are, Alex. But you don't always have to be. It's okay every once in a while to let someone else be brave for you. There's no loss of dignity in that. Not for you. You've already proven that you have more dignity than even a pure-blood can muster."

Her beautiful eyes widened—gods, those eyes always got to me. "You must be high off sugar or something."

I laughed and damn, I had no control over my mouth. "You just don't see what we see, Alex. Even the times you're being utterly ridiculous about something, or when you're just standing around, doing nothing, it's hard to not notice. As a pure-blood, it's the last thing I should notice." I closed my eyes briefly, telling myself to shut up, because what I said could never be taken back. And I wasn't sure I wanted it to be. "I don't think you have a clue."

"What don't I have a clue about?" she asked in a soft voice.

And since I was incapable of keeping my mouth shut, this time was no different. "Ever since I've met you, I've wanted to break every rule."

I turned toward the windshield, my entire body tensing. Gods. "You'll become the center of someone's world one day. And he'll be the luckiest son of a bitch on this earth."

The quick inhale drew my attention, and I looked at her. She was so godsdamn beautiful it hurt to look at her sometimes, and she didn't even have a clue. Muscles in my stomach tightened. That pressure increased. I sucked in a deep breath of air and it went nowhere.

"Thank you," she said, her gaze locking with mine. "Thanks for doing all of this for me."

Hunger for Alex gnawed on my insides, chewing away things like common sense and consequences. "You don't need to thank me."

"When am I ever supposed to thank you?"

Definitely not right now, I wanted to say. Not when I was seconds away from doing something neither of us could undo, when I was so close to risking her future and her freedom. "When I do something that is truly worth thanking me for."

I don't know how it happened. My brain was screaming at me to stop, throwing out warnings. But she was leaning toward me and I was leaning toward her. And my brain clicked off and my body took over.

Clasping her cheeks, my mouth found hers as her hands settled against my chest. My heart was beating like I was a sixteen-year-old kissing a girl for the first time. Ridiculous, but she had that kind of effect on me. Always had.

The kiss wasn't gentle or soft. There wasn't a questioning nature to it. I took her into me, because I wanted her. Wanted her more than I'd ever wanted anything in my life, and gods, there were so many things that I wanted, but she took the top spot and she stayed there.

Touching her, sliding my hands down her arms, to where her hands dug into my shirt, and kissing her was just a teasing glimpse of what could be, and it wasn't enough. Not when her lips tasted of cotton candy and sunshine. And what the hell did sunshine taste like anyway? But if the sun had a taste, Alex shared it.

She moaned against my mouth, and that sound shot straight through me. My grip tightened, and a shudder ran through her body, multiplied in mine. I needed to stop. I kissed her again, soaking her up. I had to stop. My lips devoured hers. I held her future in my hands. And then I did stop.

Pulling back, I rested my forehead against hers, breathing heavily. What I wanted from her was something I could never ask of her.

Alex's grip loosened and her breath was shaky, but her next words were strong and unmistakable. "I love you."

I jerked back, eyes going wide. At first my heart jumped—it actually jumped—and then reality smacked into me. Please gods, I wanted to scratch those words out of the air between us, because those three little words were a death sentence to her. "No. Alex. Don't say that. You can't…you can't love me."

She started to reach for me, but pulled her hands back to her chest. "But I do."

I stared at her, caught between so many warring emotions. Hearing her say that and defend those words was like being struck by lightning. In another world, where she and I weren't so very different, those words would've undone me in all the right ways.

Instead, those words destroyed a part of me.

Closing my eyes, I leaned over and pressed a kiss on her forehead, wishing for something—anything—other than this.

Oh, gods, this was my fault. I mentally strung words together that would've made Deacon proud. She couldn't love me—there was no way. I lingered there too long and forced myself to let go.

Scrubbing my palms over my eyes, I could feel her stare on me and my chest cracked. "Alex…"

"Oh, gods," she whispered. "I never should have said that."

"It's okay." I cleared my throat. "It's all right."

I knew that wasn't what she wanted or hoped to hear, and her sharp intake of breath cracked the fissure in my chest wide open. I glanced at her. Alex's eyes were trained straight ahead, her lips pressed so tightly together that the skin around her mouth was a shade or two lighter. But it was the misty sheen to those whiskey-colored eyes that killed me. It was the silence that settled like lead between us that threw the dirt on my grave. It was the way her hands trembled in her lap that made me want to punch something.

I'd never hated myself more than at that moment.

But it was for the best, because a love between us would only end in tragedy, and she already had her fair share of that.

THE BREW SCENE (AIDEN'S POV)

My face hurt from keeping up appearances and smiling through conversations I didn't give a damn about and introductions to other pure-bloods I'd already forgotten. This was the last place I wanted to be, but if I ran off too soon, people—important, powerful people—would start to ask questions.

A member of the Council said something, and I nodded, having no idea what he'd said. All I could think about was Alex…on the Brew and left alone with Seth. I didn't trust any man with two eyes to do right in that situation. Alex would be…I couldn't finish the thought.

I wasn't sure I could even trust myself in a situation like that. But Seth had sworn that he would look after her.

A warm hand skimmed up my arm, and I turned, finding myself staring down at a pure-blooded woman a good five years older than me. Her red-painted lips split into a wide smile as she leaned into me. "Aiden St. Delphi," she purred, placing her other hand on my chest. "You should grace the Catskills with your presence more often. Your visits are too far apart."

I had no idea who this woman was. Politely as I could, I reached down and removed her hand from my chest as I sidestepped her. She followed, blue eyes flaring with challenge. "Sorry," I said. "Not interested."

She cocked her head to the side and honey-colored hair cascaded over her shoulder. "What? Do you prefer male companionship?" Lashes lowered coyly. "I don't have a problem sharing."

I arched a brow, so over all of this. There was somewhere I needed to be. "I'm not interested in any form of companionship. Good night." Pivoting on my heel, I rolled my eyes at the rough curse that came out of the woman's lips.

Heading out of the ballroom, I nodded my goodbyes to Marcus and Head Minister Diana. Luckily they didn't stop me.

It felt like it took forever to get to Seth's floor. I knocked, hoping I didn't wake Alex if she'd passed out. Gods willing, she'd fallen asleep instead of going through the effects of the Brew. When there was no answer, I opened the door, my gaze roaming over the empty bed, and then toward the small settee.

Knots twisted in my stomach. "Where is she? Seth?"

I stepped into the room, breathing deeply. Noise came from inside the bathroom. A muffled voice and then footsteps followed. I bent down, swiping a sweater off the floor. It was Alex's. My gaze moved by the bed again.

There were jeans—her jeans and her…I dropped the sweater and picked up the lacy, black cloth. Seth entered the room. Shirtless. Jeans unbuttoned. Hair disheveled. I was going to fucking kill him.

"Look, I know all this looks really bad. It's not what you think."

Rage I'd never felt before boiled my blood and rose like a monster. My fingers clenched her shirt. I wanted to grab a dagger and shove it up under his chin. "This isn't what it looks like? Really? Because I think this belongs to Alex."

Seth just shook his head, like he didn't even have anything to say. I tossed the cloth aside and pushed past him, to the open door of the bathroom.

I'm not sure what I saw first that snapped the thin thread on my control—Alex on the floor, hair soaked with sweat and a deathly pale sheen to her pinched features. Was it the fact that I hadn't been there for her when the sickness took her? Or was it the fact that she was wearing one of Seth's shirts and that was all?

Her watery eyes met mine and her voice was thready and weak. "Aiden, it's not—"

I spun around. "Seth, I trusted you."

"Look. I know. This wasn't—"

I punched him. Dull pain flared across my knuckles. I welcomed it.

I didn't give a flying crap what he had to say. It was black and white to me. Alex was under the influence of the Brew. Seth had taken advantage of that. There was no in-between.

And Seth didn't defend himself right away. Not even when I hit him in the jaw again. He stood there. He took it, because he knew—he knew—that he had screwed up, that what he had done was horrible. I saw that flash of guilt in his eyes. Oh yeah, it mattered that it was Alex, but for him to do this with any female who had her ability to make decisions stripped away from her was repulsive.

I saw that flimsy piece of clothing again. There wasn't an ounce of control left in me. I pounced on him, taking him to the ground like a linebacker. Then he fought back, swinging his arms. Barely feeling the glancing blows, I laid into him.

Obviously, Seth had enough of the beating. He tossed

me off, and I fell back, knocking into the dresser. On my feet, I rushed him and we both went down again, swinging and kicking, beyond employing techniques we'd learned in training to be Sentinels.

This was like a cage match.

Alex stumbled into the room, swaying dangerously to one side. "Guys, come on…you both are being so stupid."

Neither of us stopped. We were past that. I forced Seth across the room, away from where Alex stood. His gaze flicked over my shoulder, landing on her, and I'll be damned if he even got the pleasure of looking at her. I lunged at Seth, bringing him down on the floor hard.

"Aiden! Stop it!" Alex lurched forward, swearing. "Seth—don't choke him!"

Seth gained the upper hand, rolling me onto my back. He threw his arm into the air. Blue light shimmered around his fist. Son of a bitch…

Alex smacked into us, her arms wrapping around Seth the same moment I shoved my fist into his stomach. Seth fell backward, taking Alex with him. Her shoulder knocked off the edge of the bed and she yelped. The sound of her pain cut through the red haze.

I popped to my feet and grabbed Seth by his ripped shirt, tossing him aside. Alex rolled onto her side, right next to her bra. Her cheeks turned red as she closed her eyes.

"What the hell?" another voice rang out. Leon. "Have you all lost your godsforsaken minds?"

Seth shoved himself to his knees, wiping a hand over his busted lip. "Oh, we're just wrestling."

I shot him a hateful look as I knelt beside Alex. "Alex, are you okay?" I got my hands under her arms and helped her sit up. "Say something."

"I'm…great."

Brushing the mess of hair back from her face, I grimaced. "I'm sorry. I should have never—"

"Aiden, I know you're pissed—"

"Pissed? You took advantage of her, Seth." Anger propelled me to my feet. "You son of a—"

"Stop it!" Leon ordered. "You two are going to bring every Guard in this building to this room. Seth, get out of here now."

"This is my room." Seth climbed to his feet. "And if this dickhead would give me five—"

I growled, "I'm going to kill you."

"Oh, that's it." Seth whirled around, eyes flaring an intense amber. "Let me see you try."

Alex staggered to her feet and reached for me. "Don't. Please. This isn't Seth's…whoa."

"Alex?" I spun around as she leaned to the right and kept on going. Dipping down, I caught her around the waist before she hit the floor. She was out. Shit. Slipping my arm under her knees, I lifted her to my chest.

Seth inched closer, thrusting both of his hands through his hair. "Is she—"

"Get out," I snarled.

"I—"

"Get. Out."

Leon stepped forward, putting his hand on Seth's shoulder. "I think you need to leave, buddy."

Seth's eyes locked with mine for a second, and then he shrugged Leon's hands off. "I'm not your buddy." Without saying another word, he stormed from the room, slamming the door behind him.

Leon sighed. "I can stay with her, just in case she wakes up again."

"No." I turned to the bed, gently laying her down. "I'm not leaving her. I shouldn't have let her come up here with Seth."

"It's not your fault, Aiden." There was a pause. "You can trust me."

I barked out a short laugh as I tucked her legs under the covers. "I don't trust anyone."

"Do you trust yourself?" Leon was suddenly behind me. I hadn't even heard him move. "Because if she wakes up, she's probably still going to be feeling it. You get what I'm saying."

Turning to him slowly, I looked at him dead-on. "I'm not leaving her."

"I am the last person you have to worry about when it comes to her."

I said nothing, because nothing in this world would convince me otherwise. I'd already failed her by allowing Seth to be with her. I wasn't making the mistake twice.

Leon held my stare and then shook his head. "Whatever. It's your funeral." He spun and stalked to the door, where he stopped. "I'll keep watch outside."

Before I could say thank you, Leon was gone. Cursing under my breath, I turned back to the bed. Alex was curled on her side, hands tucked under her cheek. Color had returned to her face and she looked peaceful. She looked…

I shook my head as I went over to the settee and dropped down on it, rubbing my aching jaw. All I could hope for was that she'd stay asleep long enough for the Brew to wear off.

Should have known I wasn't that lucky.

"Aiden," came her voice, not even an hour later. My gaze flicked up. She was sitting in bed, the blanket shoved off her long, long legs.

"Yes?"

"You're here."

"I am."

Her head tilted to the side and she smiled—a beautiful, amazing smile that reached inside my chest and squeezed. "You're here."

My lips cracked into a smile. "Yes, Alex, I'm here."

"Good." She tipped her head back and sighed. Wariness peeked. "I wanted you here. I always wanted you here." I tried not to feel anything in response to those words. She lowered her chin. "You were starting to smile and now you're not."

"I'm fine. You should probably lie down or you'll be sick again."

"I feel great." Then she flopped on her back. "Have you been in this bed? Oh my gods, Aiden, it's amazing. I'd marry it. You know that?" I couldn't help it. My laugh burst out of me. "Marry a bed?"

Alex made a disgruntled little sound. "Seth laughed, too."

My humor dried right up at the mention of him.

"If you just lie down for a few moments," she said, patting the bed. "You'd totally understand." Then she was sitting up again. "Aiden?"

My wariness went up a notch at how she said my name, like she was rolling it around in her mouth and decided it tasted good—like the woman downstairs had said it, but I had a totally different reaction to it coming out of Alex's mouth like that. My body went tight and hard in a second.

"Yeah?" My voice was way too hoarse.

She climbed onto her hands and knees and thank the gods I wasn't sitting on the bed. "I'm happy you're here."

But that shirt was way too loose around her neck. I looked away. "I'm happy…I'm happy I'm here, too."

Alex crawled forward and slipped her legs off the bed. "Is wanting to marry a bed so weird?"

That caught me off guard. "It is a little weird, Alex."

"Because it's an inanimate object and all?"

I smiled, because she looked endearingly serious. "Yeah, that would be one of the reasons."

"I'd marry you if you asked."

Words left me. I had no idea what to say to that.

"You're not an inanimate object." She stood, surprisingly steady on her feet, while my legs felt weak and I wasn't even standing. "But you'd never ask me. So I'll ask you. Will you marry me?"

A rush of warmth hit my chest. "Alex…"

She pouted…for a second. And then she skipped—literally skipped forward—stopping a few inches from where I sat. "But you're not going to ask me. So I'll take a kiss instead."

The tightness was back. "Not going to happen."

Alex's eyes narrowed. "I know you want to." My mouth opened. "Don't lie. Lies are ugly and pointless. You want to kiss me. You want to do more." She moved forward, until her legs brushed mine and her gaze dropped. I couldn't move. "I can tell that you do."

Damn her.

"Kiss me."

My hands curled into fists. "It's not going to happen, Alex."

Alex's lips curled up at the corners. "Okay. Then at least admit you want to kiss me." I shot her a bland look. Her smile spread. "That's all. I want to hear you say it. Then I'll go back to bed, like a good girl."

Having some serious doubts about that, I watched her wryly. "I don't believe you."

"Believe me," she whispered.

The words whipped through me. I knew better. I really, seriously knew better. But they were just words. "Yes."

Her lips parted. "Yes what?"

"Yes, Alex, I want to kiss you."

She let out a loud sigh, and then she moved, faster than I'd expected from her. A second later, she was straddling my legs and her hands were plastered to my cheeks, forcing my head down. The shirt…hell, the shirt had ridden up her sleek thighs, drawing my attention for far too long.

Alex grinned. "Kiss me."

I gripped her arms, holding her back. "Alex, I swear to the gods…"

Giggling, she slipped her hands down, under my shirt, over my lower stomach. My whole body jerked at her soft touch. "Swearing is bad."

"You're bad." I started to lift her off, but she was like a damned octopus, getting her arms around my neck and holding on. Her thighs clamped down on mine with startling strength, and I couldn't help but think about that and everything that came with it. "Alex…"

"Aiden," she mimicked, and finagled her head against my shoulder. Her lips moved against my neck, warm and wet. The slight touch was felt in every part of my body. "You smell so good. They should bottle you up and sell you. Make millions. Yum."

My brows shot up.

Then her teeth grazed my neck, and I was sure I was in the sweetest kind of hell. I clamped my jaw down, suppressing a groan as she wiggled around. Red-hot desire washed through me, and my hands tightened on her arms without intending to. Her lashes swept up and she bit down on her lower lip. Our eyes locked, and my breath caught. She didn't break eye contact, not once as her hips rolled against mine, pressing down and rotating. Lust slammed into my gut, made all the worse when a shudder rolled through her.

"Holy Hades in Hell," I groaned.

I shoved to my feet, taking her with me. Her lips moved against my skin, under my jaw, nearing my chin as I moved toward the bed. That direction got her all kinds of excited. The soft noises coming from her throat were heady and made what I did next so incredibly hard.

I dumped her on the bed. Alex bounced, her eyes going wide. "Hey!"

"Don't," I warned as she started to her feet.

She came at me and I caught her shoulders, pushing her back down and holding her there until she stopped struggling. She glared at me, cheeks flushed. "You want me."

The gods knew I did, probably more than I wanted anything in my life, and in a way that made me no better than Seth. The only difference was that I wouldn't act on it, no matter how badly I wanted it.

We went at this for what seemed like hours—her pouncing on me, me dumping her on the bed—over and over again until she finally wore herself out. Relief was short-lived because as soon as she settled down, she started shivering. Nothing was making her warmer. The extra blanket did no good. There were no temperature settings in the room.

"It's so cold in here." Her teeth chattered as she hunkered down, her entire body shaking.

I stood at the head of the bed, helpless and frustrated in more ways than anyone could possibly imagine. Watching her like this was torture. She shook so badly the whole bed trembled. Mind made up, I stalked around the other side of the bed. It was a risk, but I couldn't stand it any longer. I climbed into the bed and wrapped an arm around her waist, dragging her against me.

"T-thank y-you," she mumbled after a few moments.

I said nothing, because while this was a smart idea for her, it was also one of the worst ideas for me. I closed my eyes and began picturing the alphabet in Greek.

There was silence, and then she said, "I'm sorry."

My eyes opened. "What for?"

"For...for all of this." She paused, shivering. "I know you don't really want to be here."

My heart skipped a beat. "That's not true."

Alex said nothing and there was nothing more said the rest of the night. She drifted off to sleep, and all I could think about was how wrong her words were. As messed up as it was and it being the last thing I should ever want, where I was right that moment was the only place I had ever truly wanted to be.

THE ONE AND ONLY (DEACON AND LUKE)

The room was spinning like Deacon St. Delphi was hanging upside down from a Ferris wheel. Actually, why would he be hanging upside down from a Ferris wheel? That seemed stupid as shit.

He felt stupid as shit at the moment.

Closing his eyes, he focused on the breath he was taking. In. Out. In. Out. He did that on repeat until he figured the room would've righted itself, and when he reopened his eyes, he saw that it had worked.

Except he had no idea where he was.

Man, if his brother saw him now, he'd flip out. Lecture Deacon on how he needed to get his shit together. Needed to stop drinking. Needing to stop with the drugs. Needed to stop the screwing around. Focus on school. Blah. Blah. Blah.

He'd never be like Aiden, though.

Deacon frowned as he turned his head to the right. There was a painting on the wall of the Olympian Twelve. All were in their white robes, smiling down on him like they approved of his current state.

Sitting up, he groaned as his stomach tumbled like a drunken Pegasus. He shoved his hand through his hair. Blond curls fell forward, brushing his brows as he swung his feet off the bed.

A pair of black briefs that were definitely not his lay on the floor, by the nightstand. Next to a lacy red bra that also wasn't his. Huh. Looking over his shoulder, he made sure the bed he'd woken up on was indeed empty. It was. He glanced down at himself.

Shirt was on backward.

Jeans unbuttoned.

Must've been a good night.

Fixing his clothes, he stood, deciding he needed to make an exit and get back to the dorm or to the beach house before whatever went down last night caught up with him.

Or got back to Aiden.

Not like he really needed to worry about it getting back to Aiden. He was still up in New York, and Deacon had no idea what was going on. Alex and Seth had come back, and both…yeah, both weren't acting right.

Then again, Alex hadn't been acting right since Caleb died.

And Alex was totally in love with Aiden. Totally messed up considering loving Aiden would most likely end with her in servitude or dead, but he saw how Alex stared at his brother every time they were around each other. That was love. And he also saw how his brother watched Alex when he thought no one was looking.

They were each other's one and only. Shit. They had to see it. He knew Alex did, and his brother wasn't stupid. His brother had to see it too. Deacon didn't know how any of that could end well.

He really didn't want to think about that, because even though Deacon wasn't a good brother, he loved his brother and he really liked Alex. He knew where that shit would head.

Walking outside, he winced as the harsh glare of the sun reflected off the white sand. Sunglasses. He needed sunglasses stat.

Somehow, because the gods were smiling down on him still, he made it across the bridge, off Deity Island and onto the main part of the campus without lying down in the sand and calling it a day.

He passed a dozen Sentinels and Guards standing sentry. They didn't pay him any attention as he shuffled down the marble walkways, cutting across the courtyard. Rounding the corner of a high stone fence, he jerked to an abrupt stop, seconds from plowing into someone.

"Hell," a deep voice barked, and a tall form stepped back.

Deacon looked up and then continued looking up. He wasn't short, but this guy was a good head taller than him. His silvery gaze locked with a pair of vibrant ocean-blue eyes framed by dark lashes. Recognition flared inside him.

Yeah, he knew this guy.

Luke.

He hung out with Alex a lot. A half-blood, training to be a good little—er, tall—Sentinel. And he knew enough about the guy to know he wasn't into females. Deacon, on the other hand, was equal opportunity when it came to those kinds of things. Male. Female. Non-binary. Whatever. So of course he recognized this six-and-a-half-feet of hotness whenever he saw him around. How could he not? All that bronze-colored hair and muscles? Lots of muscles. Deacon's gaze dipped. The plain black shirt Luke wore, the attire of a Sentinel in training, stretched across a very well-defined chest.

Yum.

Luke blinked and muttered, "Sorry."

"No need to apologize," he replied.

He gave a curt nod and started to step to the side, to go around Deacon, but for some reason, Deacon followed, blocking him. Luke's brows rose and a puzzled frown crossed his striking face.

"I know who you are," Deacon announced with a half grin.

One of Luke's brows went down. "And I know of you."

Deacon cocked his head to the side. "You're saying that like it's something bad."

The half-blood eyed him. "You take that however you want to take that. Now I have—"

"I'll take it however you want to give it." His response was quick.

Surprise shot across Luke's face. He opened his mouth and immediately clamped his jaw shut. Those words lingered in the air between them.

Deacon had done the forbidden thing before—gotten with half-bloods. They were not off the list for him. The key was to be discreet and to not get too serious. Not because he worried about himself. Nothing would happen to him. To the half-blood? A different story. And that was where he and his brother were polar opposites. Deacon would take the risk. Aiden wouldn't.

Or maybe Aiden would one day.

Who knew?

Deacon really didn't care in that moment as he watched Luke try to work out a response and fail. The grin on his face kicked up a notch. "Was that too much?" he asked, honestly not caring if it was.

Luke glanced down at and gave a little shake of his head. "I have no words."

"I have that kind of effect," he teased.

His gaze flew up. "I'm immune to you."

He chuckled. "No one is immune to me."

The frown was back, but it lacked severity. "Whatever."

Deacon could sense that Luke was about to hightail his very nice-looking ass out of there, but Deacon wasn't…well, he was having too much fun. "I'm very charming."

"You're also very drunk," Luke retorted. "You smell like a brewery."

He widened his eyes, feigning innocence. "I'm offended."

That got a lip twitch out of the guy. "For some reason I doubt you get offended a lot."

"True," he murmured. "But I'm not drunk. Slept it off."

A look of doubt crossed Luke's face.

"And that's my cologne you're smelling. Not beer."

The blue hue of his eyes lightened. "Then you really need to think about changing that up."

Deacon chuckled. "So…where are you heading?"

"Away from here."

"Does away from here have a name?"

Luke folded his arms, drawing Deacon's attention to the biceps. Also very, very nice. "It does. It's called a cafeteria."

"Awesome," he replied. "I'm hungry."

Humor danced in Luke's gaze. "I don't remember inviting you along."

"That's okay. I know you're just too shy."

A surprised laugh coughed out of him. "Man…I'm not getting rid of you, am I?"

"Nope."

Luke sighed, but he didn't sound at all put out. "Then come on. I only have about forty-five minutes before I've got to head to class." Luke paused. "You know, that thing you're probably supposed to also be at."

"Huh," Deacon murmured.

Luke started walking.

"Hey." Deacon stopped him. When their eyes met again, he felt it—this tightening in his chest and lower, much lower. Wasn't the first time he'd felt something like that, but this time…yeah, it was stronger. Deeper. Interesting. "I think I can like you."

"I think I don't care," Luke returned.

He grinned as he stepped closer. Luke didn't back up, not even with Deacon crowding him. Nah, he wasn't the type to back down from anything, Deacon realized. His grin spread. "I think you do."

Luke's lips twitched again. "I think you're trouble."

"The good kind," he told him. "Or at least that's what I've been told."

The half-blood held his gaze, and shit, Deacon didn't believe in the whole sparks flying crap, but man, he felt it then. Like a charge of electricity hit his arm, licking over his skin. And he knew, just knew, that Luke felt it too. His pupils dilated slightly. His lips parted. That defined chest rose swiftly.

A moment passed. A damn eternity and then Luke said, "We'll see about that."

And then Luke smiled. No lip twitch. No grin. All even, white teeth. A real smile.

Oh yeah, he really could like this guy.

A lot.

READ ON FOR A SNEAK PEEK AT THE NEXT BOOK IN THE COVENANT SERIES

DEITY

CHAPTER ONE

Red silk clung to my hips, twisting into a tight bodice that accentuated my curves. My hair was down, silky around my shoulders like the petals of an exotic flower. The lights in the ballroom caught each ripple in the fabric so that, with every step, I looked like I was blooming from fire.

He stopped, lips parting as if the mere sight of me had rendered him incapable of doing anything else. A warm blush stole over my skin. This wouldn't end well—not when we were surrounded by people and he was looking at me like that, but I couldn't make myself leave. I belonged here, with him. That had been the right choice.

The choice I…hadn't made.

Dancers slowed around me, their faces hidden behind dazzling bejeweled masks. The haunting melody the orchestra played slipped under my skin and sunk into my bones as the dancers parted.

Nothing separated us.

I tried to breathe, but he had stolen not just my heart, but the very air I needed.

He stood there, dressed in a black tux cut to fit the hard lines of his body. A lopsided smile, full of mischief and playfulness, curved his lips as he bowed at the waist, extending his arm toward me.

My legs felt weak as I took the first step. The twinkling lights from above lit the way to him, but I would've found him in the dark if necessary. The beat of his heart sounded just like mine.

His smile spread.

That was all the reinforcement I needed. I took off toward him, the dress streaming behind me in a river of crimson silk. He straightened, catching me by the waist as I looped my arms around his neck. I burrowed my face against his chest, soaking in the scent of ocean and burning leaves.

Everyone was watching, but it didn't matter. We were in our own world, where only what we wanted—what we'd desired for so long—mattered.

He chuckled deeply as he spun me around. My feet didn't even touch the ballroom floor. "So reckless," he murmured.

I smiled in response, knowing he secretly loved that part of me.

Placing me on my feet, he clasped my hand and placed the other on the small of my back. When he spoke again, his voice was a low, sultry whisper. "You look so beautiful, Alex."

My heart swelled. "I love you, Aiden."

He kissed the top of my head, and then we spun in dizzying circles. Couples slowly joined us, and I caught glimpses of wide smiles and strange eyes behind the masks—eyes completely white, no irises. Unease spread. Those eyes...I knew what they meant. We drifted toward a corner where I heard soft cries coming from the darkness.

I peered into the shadowy corner of the ballroom. "Aiden…?"

"Shh." His hand slipped up my spine and cupped the nape of my neck. "Do you love me?"

Our eyes met and held. "Yes. *Yes.* I love you more than anything."

Aiden's smile faded. "Do you love me more than him?"

I stilled in his suddenly lax embrace. "More than who?"

"Him," Aiden repeated. "Do you love me more than him?"

My gaze fell past him again, to the darkness. A man had his back to us. He was pressed against a woman, his lips on her throat.

"Do you love me more than him?"

"Who?" I tried to press closer, but he held me back. Uncertainty blossomed in my belly when I saw the disappointment in his silvery eyes. "Aiden, what's wrong?"

"You don't love me." He dropped his hands, stepping back. "Not when you're with him, when you chose him."

The man twisted at the waist, facing us. Seth smiled, his gaze offering a world of dark promises. Promises that I'd agreed to, that I'd chosen.

"You don't love me," Aiden said again, fading into the shadows. "You can't. You never could."

I reached for him. "But—"

It was too late. The dancers converged and I was lost in a sea of dresses and whispered words. I pushed at them, but I couldn't break through, couldn't find Aiden or Seth. Someone pushed me and I fell to my knees, the red silk ripping. I cried out for Aiden and then Seth, but neither heeded my pleas. I was lost, staring up at faces hidden behind masks, staring at strange eyes. *I knew those eyes.*

They were the eyes of the gods.

I jerked straight up in bed, a fine sheen of sweat covering my body as my heart continued to try to come out of my chest. Several moments passed before my eyes adjusted to the darkness and I recognized the bare walls of my dorm room.

"What the hell?" I ran the back of my hand over my damp and warm forehead. I squeezed my watery eyes shut.

"Hmm?" murmured a half-awake Seth.

I sneezed in response, once, and then twice.

"That's hot." He blindly reached for the box of tissues. "I can't believe you're still sick. Here."

Sighing, I took the tissues from him and cradled the box to my chest as I pulled a few free. "It's your fault—*achoo*! It was your stupid idea to go swimming in—*achoo!*—forty-degree weather, jerk-face."

"I'm not sick."

I wiped my nose, waiting a few more seconds to make sure I was done sneezing my brains out, and then dropped the box on the floor. Colds sucked daimon butt. In my seventeen years of life, I'd never gotten a cold until now. I hadn't even known I *could* get one. "Aren't you just so damn special?"

"You know it," was his muffled response.

Twisting at the waist, I glared at the back of Seth's head. He almost looked normal with his face planted into a pillow—*my* pillow. Not like someone who'd become a God Killer in less than four months. To our world, Seth was sort of like any mythical creature: beautiful, but usually downright deadly. "I had a weird dream."

Seth rolled onto his side. "Come on. Go back to sleep."

Since we'd returned from the Catskills a week ago, he'd been up my butt like never before. It wasn't like I didn't understand why, with the whole furie business and me killing a pure.

He probably was never going to let me out of his sight again. "You really need to start sleeping in your own bed."

He turned his head slightly. A sleepy smile spread across his face. "I prefer your bed."

"I prefer that we actually celebrate Christmas around here, and then I'd get some Christmas presents and get to sing Christmas songs, but I don't get what I want."

Seth tugged me down, his arm a heavy weight that pinned me on my back. "Alex, I always get what I want."

A fine shiver coursed over my skin. "Seth?"

"Yeah?"

"You were in my dream."

One amber-colored eye opened. "Please tell me we were naked."

I rolled my eyes. "You're such a perv."

He sighed mournfully as he wiggled closer. "I'll take that as a no."

"You'd be correct." Unable to fall back to sleep, I started chewing on my lip. So many worries surfaced at once that my brain spun. "Seth?"

"Mmm?"

I watched him snuggle farther down into the pillow before I continued. There was something charming about Seth when he was like this, a vulnerability and boyishness missing when he was fully awake. "What happened when I was fighting the furies?"

His eyes opened into thin slits. This was a question I'd asked several times since we'd returned to North Carolina. The kind of strength and power I'd displayed as I'd faced the gods was something only Seth, as a full-blown Apollyon, should've been able to accomplish.

As an un-Awakened half-blood? Yeah, not so much. I

should've gotten my rosy rear handed to me when I fought the furies.

Seth's mouth tightened. "Go back to sleep, Alex."

He refused to answer. Again. Anger and frustration rushed to the surface. I flung his arm off me. "What aren't you telling me?"

"You're being paranoid." His arm landed on my stomach again.

I tried wiggling out of his grasp, but his grip tightened. Grinding my teeth, I rolled onto my side and settled next to him. "I'm not being paranoid, you asshat. Something happened. I've told you that. Everything…everything looked amber. Like the color of your eyes."

He blew out a long breath. "I've heard that people in high stress situations have increased strength and senses."

"That wasn't it."

"And that people can hallucinate while under pressure."

I swung my arm back, narrowly missing his head. "I didn't hallucinate."

"I don't know what to tell you." Seth lifted his arm and rolled onto his back. "Anyway, are you going to go back to class in the morning?"

Instantly, a new worry surfaced. Classes meant facing everyone—Olivia—without my best friend. Pressure built in my chest. I squeezed my eyes shut, but Caleb's pale face appeared, eyes wide and unseeing, a Covenant dagger shoved deep in his chest. It seemed I could only remember what he'd really looked like in my dreams.

Seth sat up, and I felt his eyes boring holes in my back. "Alex…?"

I hated our super-special bond—absolutely loathed that whatever I was feeling fed into him. There was no such thing as privacy anymore. I sighed. "I'm fine."

He didn't respond.

"Yeah, I'm going to class in the morning. Marcus will have a fit when he gets back and realizes I haven't been to class." I flopped onto my back. "Seth?"

He inclined his head toward me. Shadows cloaked his features, but his eyes cut through the darkness. "Yeah?"

"When do you think they're coming back?" By *they* I meant Marcus and Lucian…and Aiden. My breath caught. It happened whenever I thought about Aiden and what he'd done for me— what he'd risked.

Easing down on his side, Seth reached across me and grabbed my right hand. His fingers threaded through mine, palm to palm. My skin tingled in response. The mark of the Apollyon—the one that shouldn't be on my hand—warmed. I stared at our joined hands, not at all surprised when I saw the faint lines—also the marks of the Apollyon—making their way up Seth's arm. I turned my head, watching as the marks spread across Seth's face. His eyes seemed to brighten. They'd been doing that a lot more lately—both the runes and his eyes.

"Lucian said they'd be back soon, possibly later today." Very slowly, he moved the pad of his thumb down the line of the rune. My toes curled as my free hand dug into the blankets. Seth smiled. "No one's mentioned the pure-blood Guard. And Dawn Samos has already returned. It appears Aiden's compulsion worked."

I wanted to pull my hand free. It was hard to concentrate when Seth messed with the rune on my palm. Of course, he knew that. And being the tool that he was, he liked it.

"No one knows what really happened." His thumb now traced the horizontal line. "And it'll remain that way."

My eyes drifted shut. The truth of how the pure-blood Guard had died would have to remain a secret, or both Aiden and I would be in deep trouble. Not only had we almost hooked up over the summer—and then I'd had to go and tell him that I loved him, which was *totally* forbidden—I'd killed a pure-blood out of self-defense. And Aiden had used compulsion on two pures to cover it up. Killing a pure meant death for a half-blood, no matter the situation, and a pure was forbidden to use compulsion on another pure. If *any* of it came out, we'd both be totally screwed.

"You think so?" I whispered.

"Yes." Seth's breath was warm against my temple. "Go to sleep, Alex."

Letting the soothing sensation of his thumb against the rune lull me away, I drifted back to sleep, momentarily forgetting all the mistakes and decisions I'd made in the past seven months. My last conscious thought was of my biggest mistake—not the boy beside me, but the one I could never have.

ACKNOWLEDGMENTS

Acknowledgments are so tricky. I always feel like I'm forgetting someone terribly important. So I'll start with the business side of things. Huge thanks to Kate Kaynak, Rich Storrs, Kendra, Marie, Osman, Carol, and Rebecca Mancini. Without you guys, The Covenant Series wouldn't even exist.

Many thanks to my family and husband for your continuing patience and support when I ignore you while writing. Love you guys. Thank you to my agent Kevan Lyon for rocking it out, and also to my PA Malissa Coy, and my editor for this edition Wendy Higgins.

To my friends: Lesa Rodrigues, Julie Fedderson, Dawn Ransom, Cindy Thomas, Carissa Thomas, and everyone else, you know who you are, thank you for always being there for me when I need a break away from people that aren't real or when I need to brainstorm.

Speaking of brainstorming—I don't know what I would do without Lesa, Julie, Carissa or Cindy.

You guys rock my socks. You are the awesome sauce with an extra helping of sauce.

Julie—you are still my rock star.

A huge, GIGANTIC thanks to all the book bloggers/readers/BookTokers out there, spreading their love of reading and their passion for it along with discovering new authors. You guys do this for free, in your spare time and are my go-to peeps.

Without you guys, honestly, The Covenant Series wouldn't be half of whatever success it may be. You all don't nearly get the thanks you guys so very much deserve.

ABOUT THE AUTHOR

#1 *New York Times* and #1 international bestselling author Jennifer L. Armentrout lives in Shepherdstown, West Virginia. All the rumors you've heard about her state aren't true. When she's not hard at work writing, she spends her time reading, watching really bad zombie movies, pretending to write, hanging out with her husband, her Border Jack Apollo, Border Collie Artemis, six judgmental alpacas, two rude goats, and five fluffy sheep. In early 2015, Jennifer was diagnosed with retinitis pigmentosa, a group of rare genetic disorders that involve a breakdown and death of cells in the retina, eventually resulting in loss of vision, among other complications. Due to this diagnosis, educating people on the varying degrees of blindness has become a passion of hers, right alongside writing, which she plans to do as long as she can.

Website: jenniferlarmentrout.com
Facebook: JenniferLArmentrout
Instagram: @jennifer_l_armentrout

OTHER BLOOM BOOKS BY JENNIFER L. ARMENTROUT

COVENANT SERIES

Half-Blood (includes the novella "Daimon")

Pure

Deity (includes the novella "Elixir")

Apollyon

Sentinel

FRIGID SERIES

Frigid

Scorched

HALF-BLOOD

HALF-BLOOD

JENNIFER L. ARMENTROUT

Bloom books

Published by Bloom Books, an imprint of Sourcebooks
P.O. Box 4410, Naperville, Illinois 60567–4410
(630) 961-3900
sourcebooks.com

Originally self-published in 2011 by Jennifer L. Armentrout.

Cataloging-in-Publication data is on file with the Library of Congress.

Printed and bound in Germany.
BPG 10 9 8 7 6 5 4 3 2 1

For Kathy
You're missed and loved by many

DAIMON

A COVENANT NOVELLA

PRONUNCIATION GUIDE FOR DAIMON

Daimon: DEE-mun
Aether: EE-ther
Hematoi: HEM-a-toy

BEFORE

CHAPTER ONE

She smelled like mothballs and death.

The elderly Hematoi Minister facing me looked like she had just crawled out of a tomb where she'd been stored for a couple hundred years.

Her skin was wrinkled and thin, like old parchment, and each breath she took I swore would be her last. I'd never seen anyone that old, but of course I'd only been seven, and even the pizza guy had seemed ancient to me.

The crowd murmured its disapproval behind me; I'd forgotten that simple half-bloods like me weren't supposed to look a Minister in the eye. Being the pure-blood spawn of demigods, the Hematoi had huge egos.

I looked at my mother, who stood beside me on the raised dais. She was one of the Hematoi, but she wasn't anything like them. Her green eyes flashed a pleading look to cooperate, to not be the incorrigible, disobedient little girl she knew I could be.

I didn't know why she was so frightened; I was the one

facing the crypt keeper. And if I survived this poor excuse for tradition without ending up carrying this hag's bedpan for the rest of my life, it would be a miracle worthy of the gods that supposedly were watching over all of us.

"Alexandria Andros?" The Minister's voice sounded like sandpaper over rough wood. She clucked her tongue. "She is far too small. Her arms are as thin as the shoots of new olive branches." She bent over to study me more closely, and I half expected her to fall in my face. "And her eyes, they are the color of dirt, hardly remarkable. She barely has any blood of the Hematoi in her. She is more mortal than any we have seen this day."

The Minister's eyes were the color of the sky before a violent storm.

They were a mixture of purple and blue, a sign of her heritage. All the Hematoi had startling eye colors. Most of the half-bloods did too, but for some reason I'd missed the whole cool eye color boat when I'd been born.

The statements had continued on for what seemed like forever to me, and all I could think about was ice cream and maybe taking a nap.

Other Ministers had come down to check me over, whispering to each other as they circled me. I kept glancing at my mother, and she'd smiled reassuringly, letting me know that all of this was normal and that I was doing okay—great, even.

That was, until the old lady started pinching every piece of my exposed skin and then some. I'd always had this thing about being touched. If I didn't touch someone, then I believed they shouldn't touch me. Grandma had apparently missed that memo.

She'd reached out and pinched my belly through my dress with her bony fingers. "She has no meat on her. How can we expect her to fight and defend us? She is not worthy to train at the Covenant and serve beside the children of the gods."

I'd never seen a god, but my mom told me they were always among us, always watching. I'd also never seen a pegasus or a chimera, but she'd sworn they also existed. Even at seven I'd had a hard time believing the stories; it had strained my fledgling faith to accept that the gods still cared about the world they had so diligently populated with their children in a way only the gods could.

"She's nothing more than a pathetic, little half-blood," the ancient woman had continued. "I say send her to the Masters. I'm in need of a little girl to clean my toilets." Then she had twisted her fingers cruelly. And I had kicked her shin.

I'd never forget the look on my mother's face, like she'd been caught between terror and full-blown panic, ready to run between them and snatch me away. There were a few gasps of outrage, but there were also a few deep chuckles.

"She has fire," one of the male Ministers had said. Another stepped forward. "She will do fine as a Guard, maybe even a Sentinel."

To this day I had no idea how I'd proven my worthiness by kicking the Minister in the shin. But I had. Not that it meant a damn thing now that I was seventeen and had been nowhere near the Hematoi world for the last three years. Even in the normal world I hadn't stopped doing stupid things.

Actually I was prone to random acts of stupidity. I considered it to be one of my talents.

"You're doing it again, Alex." Matt's hand tightened around mine.

I blinked slowly, bringing his face into focus. "Doing what?"

"You got this look on your face." He tugged me against

his chest, snaking an arm around my waist. "It's like you're thinking about something universally deep. Like your head is a thousand miles away, somewhere up in the clouds, on a different planet or something."

Matt Richardson wanted to join Greenpeace and save some whales. He was the pretty boy next door who'd sworn off eating red meat.

Whatever. He was my current attempt to blend with the mortals, and he'd convinced me to sneak out and go to a bonfire on the beach with a bunch of people I barely knew.

I had bad taste in boys.

Previously, I'd crushed on a brooding academic who'd written poems on the back of his school books and styled his dyed, jet-black hair so it covered his hazel eyes. He'd written a song about me. I'd laughed, and that relationship had been over before it started.

The year before that was probably my most embarrassing—the bleached blond JV football captain with sky-blue eyes. Months had gone by with us barely exchanging a "hey" and "Do you have a pencil?" before we'd finally met up at a party. We'd talked. He'd kissed me and mauled my boobs, all the while smelling like cheap beer. I'd punched him and broken his jaw. Mom had moved me to a different town after that and lectured me about not hitting as hard as I could, reminding me that a normal girl couldn't throw punches like that.

Normal girls didn't want their boobs mauled either, and I wholly believed if they could land a fist like me, they would.

I smiled up at Matt. "I'm not thinking about anything."

"You're not thinking at all?" Matt lowered his head. The edges of his blond hair tickled my cheeks. Thank the gods he'd gotten over the "trying to grow dreads" stage in his life. "Nothing going on in that pretty head of yours?"

Something was going on in my head, but it wasn't what Matt hoped for. As I stared into his green eyes, I thought about my very first crush—the forbidden, older guy with thundercloud eyes—the one so far out of my league he might as well have been a different species.

Technically, I guess he was.

Even now, I wanted to spin-kick myself in my face for that one. I was like a walking romance novel character, thinking love conquers everything and all that crap. Sure. Love in my world usually ended up with someone hearing "I smite thee!" as she was cursed to be some pathetic flower for the rest of her life.

The gods and their children could be petty like that.

I sometimes wondered if my mom had sensed my budding obsession with the pure-blood guy and that was why she'd yanked my happy butt out of the only world I'd known—the only world I really belonged in.

Pures were *so* off-limits to halfs like me.

"Alex?" Matt brushed his lips over my cheek, moving ever so slowly toward my lips.

"Well, maybe something." I lifted up onto the tips of my toes and circled my arms around his neck. "Can you guess what I'm thinking about right now?"

"That you wish you hadn't left your shoes back at the fire, because I do. The sand is really cold. Global warming is a bitch."

"Not what I had in mind."

He frowned. "You're not thinking about history class, are you? That would be kind of boring, Alex."

I wiggled out of his grasp, sighing. "Never mind, Matt."

Chuckling, he reached out and wrapped his arms back around me.

"I'm just kidding."

Doubtful, but I let him lower his lips to mine. His mouth was warm and dry, the most a girl could ask from a seventeen-year-old boy. But to be fair, Matt was a pretty damn good kisser. His lips moved against mine slowly and when he parted them, I didn't sock him in the stomach or anything like that. I returned the kiss.

Matt's hands dropped to my hips, and he eased me down in the sand, supporting himself with one arm as he hovered over me and trailed kisses over my chin and down my throat. I stared up at the dark sky riddled with bright stars and very few clouds. A beautiful night—a normal night, I realized. There was something romantic about all of it, in the way he cradled my cheek when his mouth returned to mine and whispered my name like I was some kind of mystery he'd never figure out.

I felt warm and pleasant; not rip-my-clothes-off-and-do-me excited, but this wasn't bad. I could get used to this. Especially when I closed my eyes and pictured Matt's eyes turning gray and his hair much, much darker.

Then he slipped his hand under the hem of my sundress.

My eyes snapped open, and I quickly reached down, pulling his hand out from between my legs. "Matt!"

"What?" He lifted his head, his eyes a murky green. "Why'd you stop me?"

Why had I stopped him? I suddenly felt like Miss Purity Princess guarding her virginity from wayward boys. *Why?* The answer came to me pretty quickly. I didn't want to give up my V-card on a beach with sand finding its way into unseemly places. My legs already felt like they'd been well-exfoliated.

But it was more than that. I really wasn't in the here and now with Matt, not when I was picturing him with gray eyes and dark hair, wanting him to be someone else.

Someone I would never see again...and could never have.

CHAPTER TWO

"Alex?" Matt nuzzled a spot on my neck. "What's wrong?"

Using a bit of my natural strength, I rolled him off me and sat up.

I readjusted the top of my dress, thankful for the darkness. "Sorry. I'm just not into it right now."

Matt remained sprawled beside me, staring up at the sky like I had moments before. "Did…did I do something wrong?"

My stomach twisted and felt funny. Matt was such a nice guy. I turned to him, grabbing his hand. I threaded my fingers through his, the way he liked it. "No. Not at all."

He pulled his hand free and rubbed it across his brow. "You always do this."

I frowned. Did I?

"It's not just that." Matt sat up, dropping his long arms over his bent knees. "I don't feel like I know you, Alex. You know, like really know who you are. And we've been dating how long?"

"A couple of months." I hoped that was correct. Then I felt like a douche for taking a guess. Gods, I was turning into a terrible person.

A small smile pulled at his lips. "You know everything about me. How old I was when I got into a club for the first time. What college I want to go to. The foods I hate and how I can't stand carbonated drinks. The first time I broke a bone—"

"Falling off your skateboard." I felt good about remembering that.

Matt laughed softly. "Yeah, you're right. But I don't know anything about you."

I nudged him with my shoulder. "That's not true."

"It is." He glanced at me, the smile on his face fading. "You don't ever talk about yourself."

Okay. He had a point, but it wasn't like I could tell him anything. I could see me now: *Guess what? You ever watch* Clash of the Titans *or read any Greek myths? Well, those gods are real, and yeah, I'm sort of a descendant of them. Kind of like the stepchild no one wants to claim.*

Oh, and I was never even around mortals until three years ago. Can we still be friends?

Not going to happen.

So I shrugged and said, "There really isn't anything to tell. I'm pretty boring."

Matt sighed. "I don't even know where you're from."

"I moved here from Texas. I've told you that." Strands of my hair kept blowing across my face and over his shoulder. I needed a haircut. "It's not a big secret."

"But were you born there?"

I looked away, watching the ocean. The sea was so dark it looked purple and unfriendly. I pulled my gaze away and stared down the shore.

Two figures walked along, clearly male. "No," I said finally.

"Then where were you born?"

I fought the soft touch of annoyance as I focused on the guys near the shore, who hunkered down as the wind picked up, pelting them with a fine sheet of cold water. A storm was coming.

"Alex?" Matt climbed to his feet, shaking his head. "See? You can't even tell me where you were born. What's up with that?"

My mom thought that the less people knew about us the better. She was incredibly paranoid, believing if anybody knew too much then the Covenant would find us. Was that such a bad thing? I kind of wanted them to find us, to put an end to this craziness.

Growing frustrated, Matt dragged his fingers through his hair. "I think I'm just going to head back to the group."

I watched him turn around before I scrambled to my feet. "Wait." He turned around, brows raised.

I took a shallow breath, then another. "I was born on this stupid island no one has ever heard of. It's off the coast of North Carolina."

Surprise flickered across his features, and he took a step toward me. "What island?"

"Seriously, you wouldn't have heard of it." I folded my arms over my chest as goose bumps crawled over my skin. "It's near Bald Head Island."

A wide smile spread across his face, and I knew the skin around his eyes was crinkling like it did whenever he was exceptionally happy about something. "Was that so hard?"

"Yes." I pouted and then smiled, because Matt had the kind of smile that was infectious, a smile that reminded me of the best friend I hadn't seen in years. Maybe that's why I was drawn to Matt. My own grin started to fade as I wondered what my former partner in mayhem was doing right now.

Matt dropped his hands on my arms, slowly uncrossing them. "Wanna head back?" He nodded down the beach, at the group of kids clustered around the bonfire. "Or stay here…?"

He'd left the offer open, but I knew what he meant. Stay here and kiss some more, forget some more. It didn't sound like a bad idea. I swayed toward him. Over his shoulder, I spotted the two guys again.

They were almost on us and I sighed, now recognizing them. "We have company." I stepped back.

Matt glanced over his shoulder at the two guys. "Great. It's Ren and Stimpy."

I giggled at the accurate description from the old cartoon. During the few times I'd actually met the gruesome twosome, I'd refused to learn their real names.

Ren was tall and lanky, his dark brown hair so full of hair gel it could be labeled a dangerous weapon in most states. Stimpy was the shorter and wider of the two, shaved bald and built like a locomotive. The two were known for causing trouble wherever they went, especially Stimpy and his questionable weight lifting program. They were two years older than us, having graduated from Matt's high school before I even stepped foot in Florida. But they still hung out with the younger crowd, no doubt to scope out impressionable girls. There'd been some bad rumors about those two.

Even in the pale moonlight I could tell their skin was a healthy shade of orange. Their overly broad smiles were obscenely white. The shorter one whispered something, and they fist-bumped each other.

Not unexpectedly I didn't like them.

"Hey!" Ren called out as the pair's swagger slowed down. "What's up, Matt, my man?"

Matt shoved his hands in the pockets of his cargo shorts. "Nothing much—you?"

Ren glanced at Stimpy, then back to Matt. Ren's neon pink polo shirt looked painted on his scrawny frame; it was at least three sizes too small.

"We're just chillin'. Gonna head out to the clubs later." Ren looked at me for the first time, his eyes drifting over my dress and down my legs.

I puked a little in my mouth.

"I've seen you around a few times," Ren said, bobbing his head to and fro. I wondered if it was some kind of weird mating dance. "What's your name, sweetness?"

"Her name's Alex," answered Stimpy in all his shifty-eyed glory. "It's a guy's name."

I stifled my groan. "My mom wanted a boy." Ren looked confused.

"Actually it's short for Alexandria," Matt explained. "She just likes to be called Alex."

I grinned at Matt, but he was watching the two guys closely. A muscle feathered along his jaw.

"Thanks for the clarification, bud." Stimpy crossed his massive arms, eyeing Matt.

Catching Stimpy's look, I shifted closer to Matt.

Ren, still staring at my legs, made a sound that was a cross between a grunt and a moan. "Damn, girl. Is your daddy a thief?"

"What?" I'd never actually met my dad. Maybe he was. All I knew was that he'd been mortal. Hopefully he'd been nothing like these two asshats.

Ren flexed his nonexistent muscles, smiling. "Well, then who stole those diamonds and put them in your eyes?"

"Wow." I blinked and turned to Matt. "Why don't you ever say such romantic stuff like that to me, Matt? I'm hurt."

Matt didn't grin like I expected. His gaze kept bouncing between the two, and I could see his hands balling into fists inside his pockets. There was a certain edge to his eyes, to the way his lips were drawn into a tight line. My amusement vanished in an instant. He was...*scared*?

I reached for Matt's arm. "Come on, let's head back."

"Wait." Stimpy clapped Matt on the shoulder with enough force to cause Matt to stumble backward a few inches. "Kind of rude of you guys to just run off."

A rush of warm air crawled up my spine and spread over my skin.

My muscles tensed with anticipation. "Don't touch him," I warned softly.

Out of surprise, Stimpy dropped his hand and stared at me.

Then he smiled. "She's a bossy one."

"Alex," Matt hissed, staring at me with wide eyes. "It's okay. Don't make a big deal out of it."

He hadn't seen me make a big deal yet.

"The 'tude must come with the name." Ren laughed. "Why don't we go party? I know a bouncer down at Zero who can get us in. We can all have a good time." Then he grabbed for me.

Ren may have meant to do it playfully, but it was the wrong move. I still had a serious issue with being touched when I didn't want to be. I caught his arm. "Was your mom a gardener?" I asked innocently.

"What?" Ren's mouth hung open slightly.

"Because a face like yours belongs planted in the ground."

I twisted his arm back. Shock flickered over his features. There was a second when our gazes locked, and I could tell he wasn't sure how I'd gained the upper hand so quickly.

It had been three years since I'd fought anyone, but unused muscles woke up, and my brain sort of clicked off. I dipped under the arm I held, bringing it along with me as I clipped his knee with my foot.

The next second Ren ate sand.

CHAPTER THREE

Staring down at the guy sprawled spread-eagle in the sand, I realized I kind of missed fighting, especially the rush of adrenaline and the "Damn, I rock" feeling that came along with taking someone down. But then again, fighting mortals was nothing like fighting my own kind or the things I'd once trained to kill. This had been effortless. If he'd been another half-blood, I might've been the one with a mouthful of sand looking pretty damn pathetic.

"Jesus," Matt whispered, jumping back.

I looked up, expecting to see a shock-and-awe kind of look from him. Maybe even a thumbs-up. Nothing, I got *nothing* from him. At the Covenant, I would've been applauded. But I kept forgetting I wasn't at the Covenant anymore.

Stimpy's dumbstruck gaze swung from his pal to me and quickly turned to fury. "You act like a man? You better be able to take it like a man, you bitch."

"Oh." I smiled as I faced him fully. "It's on like Donkey Kong." Having the obvious body mass thing going for him,

Stimpy rushed me. But he hadn't been trained to fight from the age of seven, and he didn't have my literal god-given strength and speed. He swung a meaty fist toward my face, and I spun around, kicking out and planting my bare foot in his stomach. Stimpy doubled over, throwing out his hands as he tried to capture my arms. I stepped into him, grabbing his upper arms and yanking him down as I brought my leg up. His jaw bounced off my knee and I let go, watching him fall into the sand with a grunt.

Ren stumbled to his feet, spitting out sand. He swayed and then took a swing at me. It was way off, and I could have easily dodged it. Hell, I could've stood still, and he wouldn't have made contact, but I was on a roll now.

I caught his fist, sliding my hand down his arm. "Hitting girls isn't nice." I turned around, using his body weight to knock him off-balance.

He went over my shoulder, face-first into the sand once more.

Stimpy climbed to his feet and staggered to his fallen friend. "Come on, man. Get up."

"Need help?" I offered with a sweet smile.

Both guys scrambled down the beach, looking over their shoulders like they expected me to jump on their backs. I watched them until they disappeared around the cove, smiling to myself.

I turned back to Matt, the wind blowing my hair around me. I felt alive for the first time in…well, years. *I can still kick ass. After all this time, I can still do it.* My excitement and confidence dried up and shriveled away the moment I got a good look at Matt's face.

He looked horrified. "How…?" He cleared his throat. "Why did you do that?"

"Why?" I repeated, confused. "It seems pretty clear to me. Those guys are dicks."

"Yes, they're dicks. Everyone knows that, but you didn't have to lay the smackdown on them." Matt stared at me, eyes wide. "I just…I just can't believe you did that."

"They were bothering you!" I planted my hands on my hips, past caring about the wind smacking my hair in my face. "Why are you acting like I'm some kind of freak?"

"All they did was touch me, Alex."

That was enough reason for me, but apparently not enough for Matt.

"Ren grabbed at me. I'm sorry. I'm not down with that."

Matt just stared at me.

I bit back the string of curse words that were forming in my mind.

"Okay. Maybe I shouldn't have done all that. Can we just forget about it?"

"No." He rubbed the back of his neck. "That was too weird for me. Sorry Alex, but that was just…freaky."

My ever-tenuous hold on my anger started to thin. "Oh, so next time you want me to stand here and let them kick your ass and molest me?"

"You overreacted! They weren't going to kick my ass or molest you! And there won't be a next time. I'm not *down* with violence."

Matt shook his head and turned away from me, plowing his feet through the mounds of sand, leaving me standing all alone.

"What the hell?" I muttered and then louder, "Whatever! Go save a dolphin or something!"

He whirled around. "It's a whale, Alex, *a whale*! That's what I'm interested in saving."

I threw up my arms. "What's wrong with saving dolphins?"

Matt ignored me at that point, and about two minutes later I truly regretted yelling that. I stormed past him to retrieve my sandals and bag, but I did so with grace and dignity. Not one single disparaging remark or cuss word escaped my tightly sealed lips.

A couple of kids glanced up, but none of them said anything. The few friends I had at school had been Matt's friends, and they liked saving whales, too. Not that anything was wrong with saving whales, but some of them threw their beer bottles and plastic wrappers in the ocean. Hypocritical much?

Matt just didn't understand. Violence was a part of who I was as a half-blood, ingrained in my blood since birth and trained into every muscle in my body. It didn't mean I was going to snap and body slam someone for no good reason, but I would fight back. Always.

The walk home sucked butt.

I had sand between my toes, in my hair, and up my dress. My skin chafed in all the wrong places, and everything freaking sucked. Looking back, I could admit that I might've overreacted a tad. Ren and Stimpy hadn't been particularly threatening. I could've just let it slide. Or acted like a normal girl in the situation and let Matt handle it.

But I hadn't.

I never did. Now everything was going to be screwed up. Matt would go to school on Monday and tell everyone how I'd gone Xena Warrior Princess on the douchebags. I'd have to tell my mom, and she would freak. Maybe she'd insist we move again. I'd actually be happy about that; there was no way I could go back to school and face those kids after Matt told them what'd happened. I didn't care that school would be ending in a few weeks, anyway. I also wasn't looking forward to the major bitch-fest coming my way.

One I knew I deserved.

Clenching the little purse in my fist, I picked up my pace. Normally, the neon lights from the clubs and the sounds of the nearby carnival put me in a happy mood, but not tonight. I wanted to punch myself in the face.

We lived three blocks off the beach, in a two-story bungalow Mom rented from some ancient guy who smelled like sardines. It was kind of old, but it had two tiny bathrooms. Bonus points there because we didn't have to share. It wasn't exactly in the safest neighborhood known to man, but an iffy side of town wasn't anything that would scare my mom or me.

Bad mortals we could handle.

I sighed as I navigated the crowded boardwalk. The nightlife was a big thing here. So were fake IDs and super-tan, super-skinny bodies. Everyone looked alike to me in Miami, which wasn't very different from my home—my real home—where I'd once had a purpose in life, a duty I'd be obligated to fulfill.

And now I was pretty much a loser.

I'd lived in four different cities and attended four high schools in three years. We always picked large cities to disappear in and always lived near water. So far, we'd only attracted a little attention, and when we had, we'd run. Never once did my mom tell me why, not even a single explanation. After the first year, I'd stopped getting mad when she wouldn't tell me why she'd come to my dorm room that night and told me we had to leave. I'd honestly given up asking and trying to figure it out. Sometimes I hated her for all of this, but she was my mom and where she went, I went.

Dampness settled in the air, the sky overhead quickly

darkening until no stars shone down. I crossed the narrow street and kicked open the gate of the waist-high, wrought iron fence surrounding our little patch of grass. I winced at the screech as it swung open, scraping along the sandstone pavers.

I stopped in front of the door, looking up as I searched my purse for the key. "Crap," I muttered as my eyes roamed over the little garden balcony. Flowers and herbs grew like crazy, overflowing their ceramic pots and climbing the rusty railings. Empty urns I'd stacked in a pile weeks ago had toppled over. I was supposed to have cleaned up the balcony this afternoon.

Mom was going to be pissed for a lot of reasons in the morning. Sighing, I pulled out the key and shoved it in the lock. I had the door halfway open, thankful it hadn't creaked and groaned like everything else in the house, when I felt the most unfamiliar sensation.

Icy fingers ran up my spine, and then down. All the tiny hairs on my body stood up as the unerring sense of being watched came over me.

CHAPTER FOUR

I quickly turned, my gaze darting over the little yard and beyond. The streets were empty, but the feeling only increased. Unease gnawed at my stomach as I stepped back and reached behind me, wrapping my fingers around the edge of the door. Nobody was there, but…

"I'm losing my mind," I muttered. "I'm getting as paranoid as Mom. Nice."

I went inside, locking the door behind me. The uncanny feeling slowly eased off as I tiptoed through the silent house. I inhaled and nearly gagged on the spicy aroma filling the living room.

Groaning, I turned on the lamp beside the shabby, secondhand couch and squinted into the corner of the room. Sitting beside our TV and the magazine rack full of *Us Weekly* was Apollo.

A fresh wreath of bay laurel wrapped around the marble cast of his head. Of all the things my mom had forgotten to pack the many times we moved, she'd never forgotten him.

I loathed the statue of Apollo and his stinky bay laurel wreath my mom replaced *every* godsforsaken day of my life. Not because I had anything against Apollo. I guessed he was a pretty cool god since he was all about harmony, order, and reason. It was just the gaudiest damn thing I'd ever seen in my life.

It was only a bust of his chest and head, but engraved across his chest were a lyre, a dolphin, and—if that wasn't enough symbolic overload for the masses—there were a dozen tiny cicadas perched on his shoulder. What the hell did the annoying, buzzing insects that got stuck in people's hair even stand for? Symbolizing music and song my rosy left butt cheek.

I'd never understood my mom's fascination with Apollo or with any of the gods for that matter. They'd been on the absentee list since mortals had decided sacrificing their virgin daughters was a totally uncool practice. I didn't know a soul who'd ever seen a god. They'd run around and bred a hundred or so demigods and then let them have babies—the pure-bloods—but they never showed up on anyone's birthday bearing gifts.

Holding my hand over my nose, I walked over to the candle surrounded by more laurel and blew it out. Being a god of prophecy, I wondered if Apollo had foreseen that. Gaudiness aside, what was shown of his marble chest was pretty nice.

Nicer than Matt's chest.

Which was something I'd never be seeing or touching again. With that in mind, I grabbed the carton of double chocolate fudge ice cream out of the freezer and a large spoon. Not even bothering with a bowl, I climbed the uneven steps.

Soft light spilled out from the gap between my mom's bedroom door and the floor. Stopping in front of her door, I glanced at my room and then down at the ice cream. I bit my lower lip and debated bursting into her room. She probably already knew I'd snuck out earlier, and if she didn't, the sand covering half my body would give it away. But I hated the fact that my mom was home alone on a Friday night. Again.

"Lexie?" The soft and sweet voice called from behind the door. "What are you doing?"

I nudged open the door and peeked inside. She sat at the head of the bed, reading one of those smutty romance novels with half-naked guys on the cover. I totally stole them when she wasn't looking. Beside her on the small bedside table was a pot of hibiscus flowers. They were her favorite. The purple petals were beautiful, but the only scent came from the vanilla oil she loved to sprinkle over the petals.

She looked up, a slight smile on her face. "Hi, honey. Welcome home."

I held up my carton of ice cream, cringing. "At least I'm home before midnight."

"Is that supposed to make it okay?" She pinned me with a look, her emerald eyes glittering in the dim light.

"No?"

My mom sighed, setting her novel down. "I know you want to go out and be with your friends, especially since you started seeing that boy. What's his name? Mike?"

"Matt." My shoulders slumped, and I eyed the ice cream eagerly. "His name is Matt."

"Matt. That's right." She gave me a brief smile. "He's a really nice boy, and I understand you want to be with him, but I don't want you running around Miami at night, Lexie. It's not safe."

"I know."

"I've never had to...what do they call it? When privileges are suspended?"

"Grounding." I tried not to smile. "They call it grounding."

"Ah, yes. I've never had to 'ground' you, Lexie. I really don't want to start now." She brushed back the thick, wavy brown hair from her face as her gaze drifted over me. "Why in the name of the gods are you covered in sand?"

I inched inside her room. "It's a long story."

If she suspected I'd rolled around in the sand with the boy whose name she kept forgetting and then fought my way through two other guys, she didn't let on. "Want to talk about it?"

I shrugged.

She patted the bed. "Come on, baby."

Feeling a bit dejected, I sat and tucked my legs under me. "I'm sorry about sneaking out."

Her bright gaze dropped to the ice cream. "I believe you may be wishing you'd stayed home?"

"Yeah." I sighed, cracking open the lid and digging in. Around a mouthful of ice cream, I said, "Matt and I are no more."

"I thought his name was Mitch?"

I rolled my eyes. "No, Mom, his name is Matt."

"What happened?"

Looking at her was like staring in the mirror, except I was more like a mundane version of her. Her cheekbones were sharper, her nose a little smaller, and her lips lusher than mine. And she had those amazing green eyes. It was the mortal blood in me that watered down my appearance. I'm sure my dad must've been hotness to have caught my mom's *married* eye, but he had been very human. Hooking up with humans wasn't prohibited by any means, mainly because the children—half-bloods like me—were extremely valuable assets to the pures.

Well, I couldn't be included as an asset any longer. Now I was just...I didn't know what I was anymore.

"Lexie?" She leaned forward, snatching the spoon and carton from my hands. "I'll eat, and you tell me what the idiot boy did."

I smiled. "It's all my fault."

She swallowed a mammoth chunk of ice cream. "As your mother I am obligated to disagree."

"Oh no." I flopped on my back and stared up at the ceiling fan. "You're going to change your mind on that one."

"Let me be the judge of that."

I scrubbed my hands over my face. "Well, I kind of…got into a fight with two guys on the beach."

"What?" I felt the bed shift as she straightened. "What did they do? Did they try to hurt you? Did they…touch you inappropriately?"

"Oh! Gods no, Mom, come on." I dropped my hands, frowning at her. "It wasn't like that. Not really."

Thick strands of hair blew back from her face. Simultaneously all the curtains in the room lifted, reaching toward the bed. The book beside her flew off the bed and landed somewhere on the floor. "What happened, Alexandria?"

I sighed. "Nothing like that, Mom. Okay? Calm down before you blow us out of our own home."

She stared at me a few moments, and then the winds died down. "Show-off," I muttered. Pure-bloods like my mom could command one of the elements, a gift the gods had bestowed upon the Hematoi.

Mom had a thing for the element of air, but she wasn't very good at controlling it. Once she blew over a neighbor's car—try explaining *that* to the insurance company. "These guys started messing with Matt, and one of them grabbed at me."

"Then what happened?" Her voice sounded calm.

I prepared myself. "Well, they kind of needed to help each other off the ground."

My mom didn't immediately respond to that. I dared a quick look at her and found her expression relatively blank. "How bad?"

"They're fine." I smoothed my hands down the front of my dress. "I didn't even hit them. I mean, I kicked one of them. But he called me a bitch, so I think he deserved it. Anyway, Matt said I overreacted and that he wasn't into violence. He looked at me like I was a freak."

"Lexie..."

"I know." I sat up and rubbed the back of my neck. "I did overreact. I could've just walked away or whatever. Now Matt doesn't want to see me anymore, and all the kids are going to think I'm some kind of...I don't know, weirdo."

"You're not a weirdo, baby."

I gave her a droll look. "There's a statue of Apollo in our living room. And come on, I'm not even the same species as them."

"You're not a different species." She dropped the spoon in the carton. "You're more like the mortals than you realize."

"I don't know about that." I crossed my arms, scowling. After a few seconds, I glanced at her. "Aren't you going to yell at me or something?"

She arched a brow and seemed to consider it. "I think you've learned that action is not always the best response, and the boy called you such an ugly name..."

A slow grin pulled at my lips. "They were total douchebags. I swear."

"Lexie!"

"What?" I giggled at her expression. "They are. And douchebag isn't a cuss word."

She shook her head. "I don't even want to know what it is, but it sounds revolting."

I giggled again but sobered up when Matt's horrified face flashed before me. "You should have seen the way Matt looked at me afterward. It was like he was afraid of me. So stupid. You know? Kids like me would have applauded that, but no, Matt had to look at me like I was the Antichrist."

My mom's brows puckered. "I'm sure it wasn't that bad."

The painting of a goddess on her wall became a sole focus to me. Artemis crouched beside a doe, a quiver of silver arrows in one hand and a bow in the other. The eyes were unnerving, painted completely white—no irises or pupils. "No. It was. He thinks I'm a freak."

She scooted closer, placing a gentle hand on my knee. "I know it's hard for you to be away from the Covenant, but you'll be okay. You'll see. You have your whole life ahead of you, full of choice and freedom."

Ignoring that comment and wherever it came from, I took back my ice cream and shook the empty carton. "Boo, Mom, you ate it all."

"Lexie." Cupping my cheek, she turned my head so I faced her. "I know it bothers you being away from there. I know you want to go back, and I pray to the gods that you can find happiness in this new life. But we can never go back there. You know that, right?"

"I know," I whispered, even though I really didn't know why.

"Good." She pressed her lips to my cheek. "With or without a purpose, you're a very special girl. Don't ever forget that."

Something burned in the back of my throat. "You're like totally obligated to say that. You're my mom."

She laughed. "That is true."

"Mom!" I exclaimed. "Wow. Now I'm going to have self-esteem problems."

"That is one area you are not lacking in." She sent me a saucy grin as I smacked at her hand. "Now get off my bed and go to sleep. I expect you up bright and early. Your little butt better be out on that balcony, cleaning up that mess. I'm serious."

I hopped from the bed and shook my butt. "It's not that little."

Her eyes rolled. "Good night, Lexie."

I skipped to the door, glancing over my shoulder at her. She was patting the bed, frowning.

"Your windstorm knocked it on the floor." I went over and picked the book up, handing it to her. "G'night!"

"Lexie?"

"Yeah?" I turned back around.

My mom smiled and it was such a beautiful smile, warm and loving. It lit up her entire face, turning her eyes into jewels. "I love you."

I smiled. "Love you, too, Mom."

CHAPTER FIVE

After dumping the empty carton and washing off the spoon, I scrubbed my face and changed into a pair of old jammies. Restless, I tinkered around with the idea of cleaning my room, an impulse that lasted long enough for me to pick up a few socks.

I sat on the edge of the bed, staring at the shuttered balcony doors.

The white paint was cracked, showing a deeper layer in a pale shade of gray—like a cross between blue and silver, an unusual shade that struck an old yearning inside me.

Really, after all this time, to still even think about a guy I'd never see again was freaking ridiculous. Worse yet, he hadn't even known I'd existed. Not because I'd been some kind of wallflower wilting away in the shadows at the Covenant, but because he hadn't been *allowed* to notice me. Here I was, three years later, seeing chipping paint that reminded me of *his eyes*.

That was so pathetic it was embarrassing.

Annoyed with my own thoughts, I pushed off the bed and

went to the little desk in the corner of my room. Papers and notebooks I rarely used in class covered the top. If there was anything I loved about the mortal world, it was their school system. Classes out here were a piece of cake compared with what went on at the Covenant. Knocking the clutter to the side, I found my out-of-date music player and earbuds.

Most people had cool music on their players: indie bands or the current hits. I decided I must've been high on something—Apollo's bay laurel fumes?—when I'd downloaded these songs. I clicked through until I found Van Morrison's "Brown Eyed Girl."

There was something about the song that turned me into a walking cheeseball from the very first guitar riff. Humming along, I danced around my room, picking up discarded clothing and stopping every few seconds to flail about. I threw the pile in the basket, bobbing my head like a Muppet Baby.

Starting to feel a little better about things, I grinned as I shimmied around my bed, clutching a pile of socks to my chest. "Sha la la, la la, la la, la la, la-la tee da. La-la tee da!"

I winced at the sound of my own voice. Singing was not a personal strength, but that didn't stop me from mutilating every song on my music player. By the time my room was fairly decent, it was past three in the morning. Exhausted but happy, I tugged out the earbuds and dropped them on the desk. Crawling into bed, I flipped off the lamp and dropped down. Usually it took me a while to drift off, but sleep came easily that night.

And because my brain liked to torture me even while I slept, I dreamed of Matt. But the dream-Matt had dark, wavy hair and eyes the color of storm clouds. And in the dream, when his hands roamed under my dress, I didn't stop him.

A strange, satisfied smile pulled at my lips when I awoke. I kicked back the covers, stretching lazily as my gaze fell on the balcony doors.

Thin sheets of light broke through the creases under the shudders and slid over the old bamboo throw rug. Specks of dust floated and danced in the rays.

My smile froze when I spotted the clock. "Crap!"

I swung my legs off the bed and stood. "Bright and early" did not translate to waking up at *noon*. My mom had gone easy on me last night, but I doubted she'd feel the same if I added not doing my chores for the second day in a row. A quick glimpse at my reflection in the tiny bathroom mirror while I stripped confirmed I looked like Chewbacca. I took a quick shower, but the hot water still went cold before I could finish.

Shivering from the wrath of the evil water heater, I changed into a pair of worn jeans and a loose shirt. Towel drying my hair, I started toward my door. I stopped, smothering a yawn. Mom was probably already outside in the tiny garden in the front. It was right below my balcony, facing the apartment buildings and row homes across the street. I tossed the towel on the bed and threw open the balcony doors like some kind of princess greeting the day, all ladylike and delicate.

Except it all went wrong.

Wincing from the glare of the bright Florida sun, I shielded my eyes and stepped forward. My foot snagged in an empty flowerpot. Trying to shake it off, I lost my balance and careened across the balcony, catching myself on the railing before I could topple over it headfirst.

Death by flowerpot would be a hell of a way to go.

Underneath my arms, the rickety-ass wooden plant stand

swayed to the left and then the far, far right. Several pots of green and yellow tulips shifted all at once.

"Crap!" I hissed. Pushing off the railing and dropping to my knees, I hugged the plant stand to my chest. Kneeling there, for once I was grateful that none of my old friends had been around to see that.

Half-bloods were known for their agility and grace, not for tripping over things.

Once I got everything back to where it was supposed to be without killing myself in the process, I stood and leaned *carefully* over the railing. I scanned the flowerbeds, expecting to find Mom laughing her butt off, but the yard was empty. I even checked by the fence, where she had planted a row of flowers a few weekends ago. I started to turn back when I saw the gate was open, hanging to the side.

"Huh." I was almost positive I'd closed it last night. Maybe Mom had gone to the Krispy Kreme to get doughnuts? *Mmm.* My stomach grumbled. I grabbed the garden spade out of the mess of tools piled atop the small folding chair, bemoaning another morning eating shredded wheat if there weren't doughnuts. Who did I have to kill to get some Count Chocula up in this house?

I flipped the spade over in the air, catching it by the handle while I gazed past the yard. The row houses across the street all had bars on the windows and paint peeling off the sides. The old women who inhabited them didn't speak much English. Once I'd tried helping one of them pull her garbage bags out to the curb, but she'd yelled at me in another language and shooed me away like I'd been trying to steal it.

They were all out on their stoops right now, cutting coupons or doing whatever it was that old ladies did. Traffic packed the street. It was always like this on a Saturday afternoon, especially when it was turning out to be a nice day for a beach trip.

My gaze crawled over the townies and the tourists as I continued to toss the spade in the air. It was always easy to pick out the out-of-towners. They wore fanny packs or abnormally large sun hats, and their skin was either fish pale or sunburned.

A strange shiver coursed over me, spreading tiny bumps over my flesh. I sucked in a sharp breath, my eyes scanning the passing crowds with a will of their own.

Then I saw it.

Everything around me stopped in an instant. The air went right out of my lungs.

No. No. No.

He stood at the mouth of the alley, directly across from the bungalow and right beside the front porch where the old ladies sat. They glanced over at him as he stepped out onto the sidewalk, but they dismissed the stranger and returned to their conversation.

They couldn't see what I saw.

No mortal could. Not even a pure blood could. Only half-bloods could see through the elemental magic and witness the true horror—skin so pale and so thin that every vein popped through the flesh like a baby black snake. His eyes were dark, empty sockets and his mouth, his teeth…

This was one of the *things* I'd been trained to fight at the Covenant.

This was a *thing* that thrived and fed on aether—the essence of the gods, the very life force running through us—a pure blood who had turned its back on the gods. This was one of the *things* I was obligated to kill on sight.

A daimon—there was a *daimon* here.

CHAPTER SIX

I wheeled away from the railing. Whatever training I'd managed to retain vanished in an instant. Part of me had known —had always known, deep down—that this day would come.

We'd been outside the protection of the Covenant and their communities for far too long. The need for aether would eventually draw a daimon to our doorstep. Daimons couldn't resist the pure-blood magic. I just hadn't wanted to give voice to the fear, to believe that it could happen on a day like this, when the sun was so bright and the sky such a beautiful azure blue.

Panic clawed inside my throat, trapping my voice. I tried to yell, "Mom!" but it came out a hoarse whisper.

I rushed through my bedroom, terror seizing me as I pushed and then pulled open the door. A crash sounded from somewhere in the house.

The space between my bedroom and my mom's seemed longer than I remembered, and I was still trying to call out for her as I reached her room.

The door opened smoothly, but at the same time, everything slowed down.

Her name was still just a whimper on my lips. My gaze landed on her bed first, and then on a section of floor beside the bed. I blinked. The pot of hibiscus had toppled over and broken into large pieces. Purple petals and soil were strewn across the floor. Red—something red—mingled among the blossoms, turning them a deep violet. My gasp drew in a metallic smell that reminded me of the nosebleeds I used to get when a sparring partner would get in a lucky shot.

I shuddered.

Time stilled. A buzzing filled my ears until I couldn't hear anything else. I saw her hand first. Abnormally pale and open, her fingers clawed at the air, reaching for something. Her arm twisted at an awkward angle.

My head shook back and forth; I refused to accept the images in front of my eyes, to name the dark stain spreading down her shirt.

No, no—absolutely no. This is wrong.

Something—someone—braced half her body up. A pale hand clenched her upper arm, and her head lolled to the side. Her eyes were wide open, the green somewhat faded and unfocused.

Oh gods...oh gods.

Seconds, it had only been seconds since I'd opened the door, but it felt like forever.

A daimon was latched onto my mother, draining her to get at the aether in the blood. I must've made a sound, because the daimon's head lifted. Her neck—*oh gods*—her neck had been torn into. So much blood had been spilled.

My eyes met those of the daimon—or at least, they met the dark holes where its eyes should have been. His mouth snapped away from her neck, gaping open to reveal a row of razor-like teeth covered in blood. Then the elemental magic took over, piecing together the face he'd had as a pure, before he'd tasted that first drop of aether. With that glamour in place, he was beautiful by any standard—so much so that, for a moment, I thought I was seeing things. Nothing that angelic-looking could be responsible for the red stain on my mother's neck, her clothes…

His head tipped to the side as he sniffed the air. He let out a high-pitched keening sound. I stumbled backward. The sound—nothing real could sound like that.

He let go of my mom, letting her body slip to the floor. She fell in a messy heap and didn't move. I knew she had to be scared and hurt, because there couldn't be any other reason why she hadn't moved.

Rising up, the daimon's bloody hands fell to his sides, fingers twisting inward.

His lips curved into a smile. "Half-blood," he whispered. Then he jumped.

I didn't even realize I still held the garden spade. I raised my arm just as the daimon grabbed me. My scream came out as nothing more than a hoarse squeak as I fell back against the wall. The painting of Artemis crashed to the floor beside me.

The daimon's eyes widened with surprise. His irises were a vibrant, deep blue for a moment, and then, like a switch being thrown, the elemental magic that hid his true nature vanished. Black sockets replaced those eyes; veins popped through his whitish skin.

And then he exploded in a burst of shimmery blue powder.

I looked down dumbly at my trembling hand. The garden spade—I still held the freaking garden spade. Titanium-plated, I realized slowly.

The spade had been coated in the metal deadly to those addicted to aether. Had my mom bought the ridiculously expensive garden tool because she loved to garden, or had there been an ulterior motive behind the purchase? It wasn't like we had any Covenant daggers or knives lying around.

Either way, the daimon had impaled itself on the spade.

Stupid, evil, aether-sucking son of a bitch.

A laugh—short and rough—bubbled up my throat as a tremor ran through my body. There was nothing but silence, and the world snapped back into place.

The spade slipped from my limp fingers, clattering on the floor.

Another spasm sent me to my knees, and I lowered my eyes to the unmoving form beside the bed.

"Mom…?" I winced at the sound of my voice and the shot of fear that went through me.

She didn't move.

I placed my hand on her shoulder and rolled her onto her back. Her head fell to the side, her eyes blank and unseeing. My gaze fell to her neck. Blood covered the front of her blue blouse and matted the strands of her dark hair. I couldn't tell how much damage had been done. I reached out again, but I couldn't bring myself to brush back the hair covering her neck. In her right hand, she'd clenched a crushed petal.

"Mom…?" I leaned over her, my heart stuttering and missing a beat. "*Mom!*"

She didn't even blink. During all of this, my brain was trying to tell me there was no life in those eyes, no spirit and no hope in her vacant stare. Tears ran down my face, but I couldn't recall when I'd started crying. My throat convulsed to the point I struggled to breathe.

I cried her name then, grabbing her arms and shaking her.

"Wake up! You have to wake up! Please, Mom, please! Don't do this! *Please!*" For a second I thought I saw her lips move. I bent down, placing my ear over her mouth, straining to hear one tiny breath, one word.

There was nothing.

Searching for some sign of life, I touched the undamaged side of her neck and then jerked back, falling on my butt. Her skin—her skin was so cold. I stared at my hands. They were covered with blood. Her skin was *too* cold. "No. No."

A door shut downstairs, and the sound broke through to me. I froze for a second, my heart racing so fast I was sure it would explode. A shudder passed through my frame as the image of the daimon outside flashed through my head. What color had his hair been? The one in here had been blond. *What color?*

"Hell." I scrambled to my feet and slammed the door shut. Fingers shaking, I turned the lock and whirled around.

There were two. There were two.

Heavy footsteps pounded on the stairs.

I rushed over to the dresser. Squeezing myself behind it, I shoved the heavy furniture with every ounce of strength I had in me. Books and papers toppled over as I blocked the door.

Something slammed into the other side, shaking the dresser. Jumping back, I ran my hands over my head. A keening howl erupted from the other side of the door, and then it struck the door again…and again.

I whirled around, stomach twisting in painful knots. Plans—we had a stupid plan in place just in case a daimon found us. We modified it every time we moved to a different city, but each one boiled down to one thing: *Get the money and run.* I heard her voice as clear as if she had spoken it. *Take the money and run. Don't look back. Just run.*

The daimon hit the door again, splintering the wood. An arm snaked through, grasping at the air.

I went to the closet, pulling down boxes from the top shelf until a small wooden one fell to the floor. Grabbing it, I yanked it so fiercely that the lid ripped from the hinges. I threw another box at the door, hitting the daimon's arm. I think he laughed at me. I grabbed what my mom called the "emergency fund" and what I referred to as the "we are so screwed" fund and pocketed the wad of hundred dollar bills.

Every step back to where she had fallen ripped through me, taking a piece of my soul. I ignored the daimon as I dropped beside her and pressed my lips to her cool forehead. "I'm so sorry, Mom. I'm so sorry. I love you."

"I'm going to kill you," the daimon hissed.

Looking over my shoulder, I saw the daimon's head had made it through the door. He was reaching for the edge of the dresser. I picked up the garden spade, wiping the back of my arm over my face.

"I'm going to rip you apart. Do you hear me?" he continued, squeezing another arm through the hole he'd made. "Rip you open and drain you of whatever pathetic amount of aether you have, half-blood."

I glanced at the window and grabbed the lamp off the table. Tearing the shade off, I tossed it aside. I stopped in front of the dresser.

The daimon stilled as the glamour settled around him. He sniffed the air, eyes flaring wide. "You smell dif—"

Swinging with all my might, I slammed the bottom of the lamp on the daimon's head. The sickening thud it made pleased me in a way that would've concerned guidance counselors across the nation. It wouldn't kill him, but it sure as hell made me feel better.

I threw the busted lamp down and raced to the window. I pushed it open just as the daimon let out a string of creative cusses and threats. I wiggled into the window, perching there as I stared at the ground below, assessing my chances of landing on the awning over the small porch off the back of the house.

The part of me that had been in the mortal world too long balked at the idea of jumping from a second-story window. The other part—the part that had the blood of the gods running through it—jumped.

The metal roof made a terrible sound when my feet slapped into it.

I didn't think as I went to the edge and leapt once more. I hit the grass, falling to my knees. Pushing up, I ignored the stunned looks from the neighbors who must've come outside to see what was going on. I did the one thing I'd been trained *never* to do during my time at the Covenant, the thing I didn't want to do, but knew I had to.

I ran.

With my cheeks still damp with tears and my hands stained with my mother's blood, *I ran.*

AFTER

CHAPTER SEVEN

A deep numbness settled over me as I stood in a gas station bathroom. I turned my hands over and rubbed them together under the rush of icy water, watching the basin turn red, and then pink, and then clear. I kept washing my hands until they, too, felt numb.

Every so often a spasm shot through my legs, and my arms would twitch, no doubt a by-product of running and running until an ache had settled so far into my body that every step had jarred my bones. My eyes kept flicking to the garden spade as if I needed to assure myself that it was still within reach. I'd placed it on the edge of the sink, but it didn't feel like it was close enough.

Turning off the faucet, I picked it up and slid it under the waistband of my jeans. The sharp edges bit into the flesh of my hip, but I tugged my shirt down over it, welcoming the little stab of pain.

I left the dingy bathroom, walking in no particular direction. The back of my shirt was soaked with sweat, and my legs protested the whole walking thing. I'd take a few steps, touch the handle of the spade through my shirt, walk some more, and repeat.

Take the money and run…

But run where? Where was I supposed to go? We didn't have any close friends that we'd trusted with the truth. The mortal part urged me to go to the police, but what could I say to them? By now, someone would have called 911, and her body would've been found. Then what?

If I went to the authorities, I'd be placed in the state system even though I was seventeen. We'd exhausted all of our money in the last three years, and there were no funds left over except the few hundred dollars in my pocket. Lately my mom had taken to using compulsions to get cheaper rates whenever we'd had bills to pay.

I kept walking as my brain tried to answer the question of *what happens now?* The sun was beginning to set. I could only hope the humidity would ease off some. My throat felt like I'd swallowed a dry sponge, and my stomach grumbled unhappily. I ignored them both, continuing to put as much distance between my house and me as I could.

Where to go?

Like a sucker punch in the stomach, I saw my mom. Not how she'd looked last night, when she'd told me she loved me; that image of her escaped me. Now I kept seeing her dulled green eyes. A sharp stab of pain caused my step to falter. The ache in my chest, in my soul, threatened to consume me. *I can't do this. Not without her.*

I had to do this.

In spite of the humidity and heat, I shivered. Wrapping my arms around my chest, I barreled down the street, scanning the crowds for the horrific face of a daimon. Several seconds would pass before the elemental magic they wielded would have an effect on me. It might give me enough time to make a run for it, but they obviously could sense the little aether I had in me. It didn't seem likely that they'd follow me; daimons didn't actively hunt half-bloods. They'd tag and drain us if they happened across us, but they wouldn't seek us out. The diluted aether in us wasn't as appealing as that of the pures.

I wandered the streets aimlessly until I spied a motel that looked somewhat decent. I needed to get off the streets before nightfall. Miami after dark wasn't a place a lone teenage girl skipped around happily.

After grabbing some burgers from a nearby fast-food joint, I checked in at the motel. The guy behind the counter didn't look twice at the sweaty girl standing in front of him—with no luggage and only a bag of food—asking for a room. As long as I paid in cash, he didn't even care that I didn't show any ID.

My room was on the first floor at the end of a narrow, musty hallway.

There were questionable sounds coming from some of the rooms, but I was more disturbed by the dirty carpet than the low moans.

The bottoms of my worn sneakers looked cleaner.

I shuffled the burgers and drink to my other arm as I opened the door to room thirteen. The irony of the number didn't pass me by; I was just too tired and out of it to care.

Surprisingly, the room smelled good, courtesy of the peach air freshener plugged into the wall outlet. I set my stuff down on the small table and pulled out the garden spade. Lifting my shirt, I inched down the band of my pants and ran my fingers over the indentations the blade had left on my skin.

It could be worse. I could be like my mo—"Stop it!" I hissed at myself. "Just stop it."

But the aching pain welled up anyway. It was like feeling nothing and everything all at once. I drew in a shallow breath, but it hurt. Seeing my mom lying beside the bed still didn't seem real. None of this did. I kept expecting to wake up and find that everything had been a nightmare.

I just hadn't woken up yet.

I rubbed my hands on my face. There was a burning in the back of my throat, a tightness that made it hard to swallow. *She's gone. She's gone. My mom's gone.* I grabbed the bag of burgers and ripped into them. I ate angrily, stopping every couple of mouthfuls to take a huge gulp from my cup. After the second one, my stomach cramped. I dropped the wrapper and rushed toward the bathroom. Falling to my knees in front of the toilet, everything came back up.

My sides ached by the time I fell back against the wall, pushing the heels of my palms against my burning eyes. Every couple of seconds my mom's blank stare flashed up, alternating with the look on the daimon's face before he'd burst into blue powder. I opened my eyes, but I still saw her, saw the blood that'd run over the purple petals, saw the blood everywhere. My arms started to tremble.

I can't do this.

I pulled my knees to my chest and rested my head on them. I slowly rocked, replaying not just the last twenty-four hours over and over again, but the last three years. All those times I'd had a chance to figure out a way to contact the Covenant and hadn't. Missed opportunities.

Chances I'd never get back. I could've tried to figure out how to reach the Covenant. One call would've prevented this from happening.

I wanted a do-over—just one more day to confront my mom and demand we go back to the Covenant and face whatever had sent us fleeing in the middle of the night.

Together—we could've done it together.

My fingers dug into my hair and I pulled. A tiny cry worked its way past my clenched jaw. I yanked on my hair, but the hot flash of pain zinging across my scalp did nothing to relieve the pressure in my chest or the yawning emptiness that filled me.

As a half-blood it was my duty to kill daimons, to protect the pure-bloods from them. I'd failed in the worst way possible. I'd failed my mother. There was no way around that.

I had failed. And I had run.

My muscles locked up, and I felt a sudden rush of fury rise inside me.

Balling my hands over my eyes, I kicked out. The heel of my sneaker slammed through the cabinet door below the sink. I pulled my foot free, almost pleased when the cheap particle board scraped my ankle. And I did it again and again.

When I finally did stand and leave the bathroom, the motel room was pitched in darkness. I tugged the chain on the lamp and grabbed the spade. Each step back into the shabby room hurt after forcing my sore muscles into such a cramped position in the bathroom. I sat down on the bed, not meaning to collapse there and not get back up. I'd wanted to check the door again—maybe block it with something—but exhaustion claimed me, and I drifted off into a place where I hoped no nightmares could follow me.

CHAPTER EIGHT

Night turned to day, and I didn't move until the motel manager knocked on the door, asking for more money or for me to get out. Through a tiny crack in the door, I handed him the cash and went back to the bed.

I went on repeat for days. There was a general sense of time changing when I would get up and wobble into the bathroom. I didn't have the energy to shower, and this wasn't the kind of place that put out little bottles of shampoo, anyway. There wasn't even a mirror in here, just a couple of little plastic brackets framing an empty rectangle above the sink. Either moonlight or sunshine would break through the window, and I kept count of each time the manager visited. Three times he'd come to ask for money.

During those days I thought of my mom and cried until I gagged into my hand. The storm inside me thrashed, threatening to pull me under, and under I went. I curled up in a small ball, not wanting to talk, not wanting to eat. Part of me just wanted to lie there and fade away.

The tears had long since come to an unsatisfying end, and I just lay there, searching for a way out. There seemed to be an empty void looming up ahead. I welcomed it, rushed in, and sank into its meaningless depths until the manager came the fourth day.

This time he spoke to me after I handed him the cash. "You need something, kid?"

I stared at him through the gap. He was an older guy, maybe in his late forties. He seemed to wear the same pin-striped shirt every day, but it looked clean.

He glanced down the hall, running a hand through his thinning brown hair. "Is there anyone I can call for you?"

I didn't have anyone.

"Well, if you need something, just call the front desk." He backed away, taking my silence as the answer. "Ask for Fred. That's me."

"Fred," I repeated slowly, sounding like an idiot.

Fred stalled, shaking his head. When he looked back at me, his eyes met mine. "I don't know what kind of trouble you got yourself in, kid, but you're too young to be out here and in a place like this. Go home. Go back to where you belong."

I watched Fred leave, and I shut the door behind him, locking it. I turned around slowly and stared at the bed—at the garden spade. My fingers tingled.

Go back to where you belong.

I didn't belong anywhere. Mom was gone now and—

I pushed away from the door, approaching the bed. I picked up the spade and ran my fingers along the sharp edges. *Go back to where you belong.* There was only one place I did belong, and it wasn't curled up in a ball on a bed in a craptastic motel on the wrong side of Miami.

Go to the Covenant.

A tingle ran along the back of my neck. The Covenant? Could I seriously go back there after three years, not even knowing why we'd left? Mom had acted like it wasn't safe there for us, but I always chalked that up to her paranoia. Would they allow me back without my mother?

Would I be punished for running away with her and not turning her in?

Was I fated to become what I'd avoided all those years ago when I'd gone before the Council and punt-kicked an old lady?

They could force me into servitude.

All those risks were better than being chomped on by a daimon, better than tucking my tail between my legs and giving up. I'd never given up on anything in my entire life. I couldn't start now, not when my life seriously depended on me not losing it.

And by the way the bed looked and how I smelled, I was officially losing it.

What would my mom say if she could see me now? I doubted she'd suggest the Covenant, but she wouldn't have wanted me to give up.

Doing so was a disgrace to everything she'd stood for, and to her love.

I couldn't give up.

The storm inside me stilled, and the plan began to form. The closest Covenant was in Nashville, Tennessee. I didn't know exactly where, but the whole city would be swarming with Sentinels and Guards. We'd be able to sense each other—the aether always called out to us, stronger from the pures, more subtly from the halfs. I'd have to find a ride, because my butt wasn't walking all the way to Tennessee. I still had enough money to get a ticket on one of those buses I usually wouldn't consider riding in. The terminal downtown had been closed ages ago, and the nearest bus stop going out of state was at the airport.

That was one hell of a hike from here.

I glanced at the bathroom. No light shone through the window. It was night again. Tomorrow morning, I could take a cab to the airport and get on one of the buses. I sat down, almost smiling.

I had a plan, a crazy one that could end up backfiring on me, but it was better than giving up and doing nothing. A plan was *something,* and it gave me hope.

After waiting until dawn, I caught a cab to the airport and lingered in the near-vacant bus terminal. The only company I had was an elderly man cleaning the hard plastic seats and the rats that scurried along the darker corridors.

Neither were very talkative.

I pulled my legs up on the seat, cradling the spade in my lap while I forced myself to stay alert. After existing in the void of nothingness for days, I still wanted to climb into my favorite jammies and curl up in my mom's bed. If it wasn't for every little noise causing me to jump out of my seat, I would've fallen out of my chair in a dead sleep.

A handful of people were waiting for the bus when the sun rose outside the windows.

Everyone avoided me, probably because I looked like a hot mess. The motel shower hadn't even been working when I'd finally tried it, and my quick rinsing in the sink hadn't included soap or shampoo.

Standing slowly, I waited until everyone got in line and looked down at the clothes I'd been wearing for days. The knees of my jeans had been torn open, and the frayed edges were stained red. A sharp pang hit me in my stomach.

Pulling myself together, I climbed the steps to the bus and briefly made eye contact with the bus driver. Right away, I wished I hadn't. With a head full of bushy white hair and bifocals perched on his ruddy nose, the driver looked older than the guy who'd been cleaning the chairs.

He even had an AARP sticker on the sun visor and wore suspenders.

Suspenders?

Gods, there was a good chance Santa Claus was going to fall asleep at the wheel and we all were going to die.

Dragging my feet, I picked a spot in the middle and sat down beside a window. Luckily the bus wasn't even half full, so the body odor usually associated with these buses was below the norm.

I think I was the only one who smelled.

And I did smell. A lady a few seats ahead of me turned around, wrinkling her nose. When her gaze landed on me, I looked away quickly.

My questionable hygiene was the least of my problems, but it still made my cheeks burn with humiliation. How, at a time like this, could I even care about how I looked or smelled? I shouldn't, but I did. I didn't want to be the stinky girl on the bus. My embarrassment flashed me back to another horrendously mortifying moment in my life.

I'd been thirteen and had just started an offensive training class at the Covenant. I remembered being thrilled to do something other than running and practicing blocking techniques. Caleb Nicolo—my best friend and an all-around awesome guy—and I had spent the beginning of the first class pushing each other around and acting like monkeys on crack.

We'd been quite…uncontrollable when together.

Instructor Banks, an older half-blood who'd been injured while doing his Sentinel duties, had been teaching the class. He'd informed us that we'd be practicing takedowns and paired me up with a boy named Nick. Instructor Banks had shown us several times how to do it correctly, warning us that, "It has to be done this way. If not, you could break someone's neck, and that's not something I'm teaching today."

It had looked so easy, and being the cocky little brat that I'd been, I hadn't really paid attention. I'd told Caleb, "I so have this." We'd high fived like two idiots and gone back to our partners.

Nick had executed the takedown perfectly, sweeping out the leg while maintaining control of my arms. Instructor Banks had praised him.

When it came to my turn, Nick had smiled and waited. Halfway through the maneuver, my grip had slipped on Nick's arm and I'd dropped him on his neck.

Not good.

When he didn't get up right away and had started moaning and twitching, I'd known I'd made a terrible miscalculation concerning my skill level. I'd put Nick's butt in the infirmary for a week and had been called the "Pile Driver" for several months after that.

Up until now, I'd never been so embarrassed in my life. I wasn't sure which humiliation was worse, though—failing in front of my peers or smelling like gym socks left forgotten in the hamper.

Sighing, I glanced down at my travel itinerary. There were two transfers: one in Orlando and the other in Atlanta. Hopefully one of those stops had some place I could clean up a little better and grab some food. Maybe they'd also have drivers who weren't nearing their expiration dates.

I looked around the bus, smothering my yawn with my hand. There were definitely no daimons on the bus; I imagined they'd loathe public transportation. And—from what I could tell—I didn't see any possible serial killers who looked like they'd prey on dirty chicks. I pulled the spade out and shoved it between me and the seat. I dozed off pretty quickly and woke up a few hours in, my neck cramping something fierce.

A couple of the people on the bus had these neat little pillows I'd have given my left arm for. Wiggling in my seat until I found a position that didn't feel like I was cramped in a cage, I didn't notice I had company until I lifted my eyes.

The woman who'd sniffed the air earlier stood in the aisle beside my seat. My gaze fell over her neatly coiffed brown hair and pressed khaki pants. I was not sure what to make of her. Had I stunk up the bus? Smiling tightly, she pulled her hand out from behind her back and held a package of crackers out toward me. They were the kind with peanut butter in the middle, six to a pack. My stomach roared to life.

I blinked slowly, confused.

She shook her head, and I noticed the cross dangling from a gold chain around her neck. "I thought...you might be hungry?"

Pride sparked in my chest. The lady thought I was some homeless kid. *Wait. I AM a homeless kid.* I swallowed the sudden lump in my throat.

The lady's hand shook a bit as she pulled back. "You don't have to. If you change—"

"Wait," I said hoarsely, wincing at the sound of my own voice. I cleared my throat while my cheeks heated. "I'll take it. Thank...thank you."

My fingers looked especially grubby next to hers, even though I'd scrubbed them in the motel bathroom. I started to thank her again, but she'd already moved back to her seat. I stared down at the package of crackers, feeling a tightening in my chest and jaw. Somewhere I'd read once that was a symptom of a heart attack, but I doubted that was what was wrong with me.

Squeezing my eyes shut, I tore into the package, eating so fast I really couldn't taste anything. Then again, it was hard to savor the first food I'd eaten in days when tears clogged my throat.

CHAPTER NINE

At the transfer in Orlando, I had several hours to try to clean up and grab some food. When the bathroom was free and didn't look like anyone would be coming in, I locked the door and approached the sink. It was hard to look at myself in the mirror, so I avoided doing so. I stripped off my shirt, holding in a whimper as several sore muscles pulled. Choosing to ignore the fact I was kind of taking a bath in a public restroom, I grabbed a handful of rough, brown towels that were sure to make my skin break out. Dampening them and using the generic soap, I cleaned up as quickly as possible. Ghosts of deep purple bruises still marred the skin from my bra to my hip. The scratches on my back—inflicted when I'd wiggled through my mother's bedroom window—weren't as bad as I thought they'd be.

All in all, I wasn't that bad off.

I was able to score a bottle of water and some chips from a vending machine before boarding the next bus. Seeing the remarkably younger driver made me feel so much more relieved, since it was starting to get dark out. The bus was fuller than the one from Miami had been, and I was unable to fall back asleep. I just sat and stared out the window, running my fingers along the edge of the spade. My brain kind of clicked off after I finished the bag of chips, and I ended up staring at the college-aged boy several rows ahead. He had an iPhone, and I was jealous. I really didn't think about anything during the next five or so hours.

It was around two in the morning when we unloaded in Atlanta, arriving ahead of schedule. Georgia's air was just as thick with humidity as Florida's had been, but there was a smell of rain. The station was in some kind of industrial park surrounded by fields and long forgotten warehouses. We seemed to be on the outskirts of Atlanta, because the dazzling glow of city lights appeared a couple of miles away.

Rubbing my aching neck, I shuffled into the station. A few people had cars there waiting for them. I watched the college boy rush over to a sedan, and a tired-looking but happy middle-aged man climbed out and hugged him. Before my chest could tighten again, I turned away to seek out another vending machine to raid.

It took me several minutes to find the vending machines. Unlike the ones in Orlando, these were all the way back near the bathrooms, which I found gross. I pulled out the wad of cash and separated a few singles from the hundreds.

A shuffling sound, like pants dragging along the floor, caught my attention. I looked over my shoulder, scanning the dimly lit corridor. Up ahead, I saw the glass windows of the waiting room. After freezing to listen for several moments before I dismissed the sound, I turned back to the machine and grabbed another bottle of water and *another* bag of chips.

The idea of sitting for the next few hours made me want

to break something, so I took my meager goodies and headed back outside. I kind of liked the wet smell in the air, and the idea of getting rained on wasn't too bad. It would be like a natural shower of sorts. Munching on my chips, I headed around the terminal and past a rest stop full of truckers.

None of them whistled or propositioned me when they saw me. This, in a way, totally ruined my whole image of them.

Across from the rest stop turnoff were more factories. They looked like something straight out of a haunted house reality TV show—broken or boarded-up windows, weeds overflowing the cracked pavement, and vines trailing up along the walls. Before Matt had decided I was a giant freak, we'd gone to one of those carnival haunted houses. Come to think of it, I should have known he'd be a wuss. He'd screamed like a toddler when the guy had come out at the end and chased us with a chainsaw.

Smiling to myself, I followed a narrow path around the rest stop and tossed my empty bottle and bag into a trash bin. The sky was full of heavy clouds, and the loud purr of the tractor trailer engines was comforting in an odd way. In four hours I'd be in Nashville. Four more hours and I'd find—

The sound of breaking glass startled me. My heart leapt in my throat.

I whirled around, expecting to be faced with a horde of daimons. Instead I found two young guys. One had thrown a rock through the window of a maintenance building.

What rebels, I thought.

I moved my hand away from where I had the spade shoved into the back of my pants, studying them. They weren't much older—or cleaner—than me. One was wearing a red beanie… in May. I wondered if there was some kind of weather situation

I was unaware of. My gaze drifted to his partner, whose eyes kept bouncing from his friend to me.

And that made me nervous.

Beanie Boy smiled. The off-white shirt he wore clung to his scrawny frame. He didn't look like he was getting three square meals a day.

Neither did his friend. "How ya doin'?"

I bit my lip. "Good. You?"

His friend gave a sharp, high-pitched laugh. "We're doing okay."

Knots began to form in my stomach. Taking a deep breath, I started to edge around them. "Well…I've got a bus to catch."

Giggles shot a quick look at Beanie Boy, and damn, Beanie Boy could book it. Within a second, he was standing in front of me and had a knife pointed right at my throat.

"We saw ya with the money back at those machines," said Beanie Boy, "and we want it."

I almost couldn't believe it. On top of everything, I was being robbed.

It was official. The gods hated me. And I hated them.

CHAPTER TEN

In stunned disbelief, I lifted my hands above my head and exhaled slowly.

The one without the knife gaped at his partner. "Man, what are you doing? Why'd you pull a knife? She's just a girl. She's not going to fight us."

"Shut up. I'm running this show." Beanie Boy grabbed my arm as he leered in my face, pressing the tip of the knife under my chin.

"This wasn't part of the plan!" argued the guy who didn't seem to want to stab me. I eyed him hopefully, but he was staring at his partner, his hands opening and closing at his sides.

Great, I thought, *I'm being robbed by unorganized criminals. Someone's definitely getting stabbed, and it's probably going to be me.*

Instead of fear, I felt a hot stab of annoyance. I so did not have time for this crap. I had a bus to catch, and hopefully, a life to reclaim.

"We saw ya getting the food." He inched the tip of the knife down my throat. "We know ya have money. A whole wad of cash, right, John? Must be a lot of hooking to get that kinda money."

I wanted to kick myself in the face. I should've been more careful. I couldn't pull out a wad of cash and expect not to be robbed. Surviving a daimon attack only to have my throat slashed for a few hundred dollars? Dammit, people sucked.

"Did ya hear me?"

I narrowed my eyes, figuring I was about five seconds from going ballistic. "Yeah, I heard you."

His fingers dug in my skin. "Then give us the damn money!"

"You're going to have to get it yourself." My gaze went to his friend. "And I dare you to try it."

Beanie Boy motioned toward John. "Get the money out of her pocket."

His partner's eyes darted between his friend and me. I hoped he refused, because he was so going to regret it if he didn't. That wad of cash was all that I had. In it was my ticket for the next bus. No one was getting that.

"Which pocket?" the one holding me asked. When I didn't answer, he shook me, and that was it.

My bitch switch was flipped and, well, my sense of self-preservation went right out the window. Everything—*everything* that'd happened boiled up inside me and burst. Did these wannabe bandits actually think I was afraid of them? After everything I'd seen? My universe went red. I was going to stomp the ever-loving crap out of them.

I laughed in Beanie Boy's face.

Bewildered by my response, he lowered the knife a fraction of an inch.

"Are you freaking serious?" I wrenched my arm free and grabbed the knife from his fingers. "You're going to rob me?"

I pointed the knife at him, half tempted to prick him with it. "*Me?*"

"Whoa, now." John backed up.

"Exactly." I waved the knife around. "If you want your bal—"

A shiver went down my spine, icy and foreboding. An innate sense kicked in and every fiber of my being screamed out a warning. It was the same thing I'd felt before I'd spotted the daimon from the balcony.

Panic punched a hole in my chest.

No. They can't be here. They can't.

But I knew they were. The daimons had found me. What I couldn't wrap my head around was *why* they had. I was just a freaking half-blood.

I wasn't even a snack pack to them. Worse yet, I was like Chinese food to them—they were going to be craving aether again in a few hours.

Their time would be better spent hunting down pures. Not me. Not a half-blood.

Clearly distracted, Beanie Boy took advantage. He shot forward, grabbing and twisting my arm until I dropped the knife in his waiting hand. "You stupid bitch," he hissed in my face.

I pushed him with my free hand as I scanned the area. "You have to go! You need to go now!"

Beanie Boy pushed back and I stumbled to the side. "I'm done messing with you. Give us the money or else!"

I gained my balance, realizing these two were too stupid to live.

So was I for hanging around and trying to convince them. "You don't understand. You have to go now. They're here!"

"What's she talking about?" John turned around and

scanned the darkness. "Who's coming? Red, I think we should—"

"Shut up," Red said. Light from the moon broke free from the heavy clouds, glinting off the blade he jabbed at his friend. "She's just trying to freak us out."

Part of me wanted to bolt and let them deal with what I knew was coming, but I couldn't. They were mortals—obscenely stupid mortals who'd pulled a knife on me—but there was no way they deserved the kind of death coming their way. Robbery attempt or not, I couldn't let this happen. "The things that are coming are going to kill you. I'm not try—"

"Shut up!" yelled Red, swinging on me. Once again the knife was at my throat. "Just shut up!"

I looked at John, the saner of the two. "Please. You've got to listen to me! You need to go, and you need to make your friend go. Now."

"Don't even think it, John," warned Red. "Now get over here and get this money!"

Desperate to get them out of here, I dug in my pocket and pulled out the wad of cash. Without thinking, I shoved it at Red's chest. "Here—take it! Just take it and go while you still can! Go!"

Red looked down, his mouth dropping open. "What the—"

A cold, arrogant laugh froze the blood in my veins. Red whirled around, squinting into the darkness. It was almost like the daimon materialized out of the shadows, because the spot had been empty a second ago. He stood a few feet from the building, his head cocked to the side and his horrific face twisted into a gruesome smile. To the boys, he looked like a yuppie in Gap jeans and a polo shirt—an easy target.

I recognized him as the daimon I'd hit over the head with a lamp.

"This is it?" John looked at Red, visibly relieved. "Man, we hit the lotto tonight."

"Run," I urged quietly, reaching behind me and wrapping my fingers around the handle of the garden spade. "Run as fast as you can."

Red glanced over his shoulder at me, snickering. "Is this your pimp?"

I couldn't even respond to that. I zeroed in on the daimon, my heart doubling over as he took a slow, lazy step forward. Something wasn't right about the daimon. He was…too calm. When the elemental magic took over, amusement flickered over his arresting features. Then, when I was pretty sure I couldn't be having a crappier week, a second daimon stepped out of the shadows…and behind her stood another daimon.

I was so screwed.

CHAPTER ELEVEN

My hand was still up in the air, clenching the four hundred and twenty-five dollars along with my bus ticket. Perhaps it was shock that held me in that position. My brain quickly flipped through my lessons at the Covenant, the ones teaching us about pure-bloods who'd tasted aether and turned to the proverbial dark side.

Lesson number one: They didn't work well together. Wrong.

Lesson number two: They didn't travel in packs. Wrong again.

Lesson number three: They didn't share their food. Wrong again.

And lesson number four: They didn't hunt half-bloods.

I was so going to kick a Covenant Instructor in the face if I ever made it back there alive.

John took a step back. "Too many people—"

The first daimon held up his hand, and a gust of wind came rushing from the field behind the trio. It shot down the dirt path, slamming into John's chest and sending him flying through the air. John hit the back of the rest stop, his surprised shriek cut off by the snapping of his bones. He fell into the shrubs, a dark, lifeless lump.

Red tried to move, but the wind was still coming. It pushed him back and knocked my arm down. It was like being caught in an invisible tornado. Hundred dollar bills, a bunch of singles, and my bus ticket flew up in the air, caught and tossed by the wind. A hole opened in my chest as the rushing wind took them up and up.

It was almost as if the daimons knew that, without those things, I was trapped. Completely freaking trapped.

Lesson number five: They could still control the elements. At least the Covenant Instructors had gotten that part right.

"What's going on?" Red backed up, stumbling over his own feet. "What the hell is going on?"

"You're going to die," said the daimon in Gap jeans. "That's what's going on."

I reached out, grabbing Red's flailing arm. "Come on! You've got to run!"

Fear rooted Red to the spot. I pulled on his arm until he twisted around. Then we were running, me and the guy who'd held a knife to my throat moments before. Flat laughter followed us as our feet left the dirt path and crashed through field grass.

"Run!" I yelled, pumping my legs until they burned. "Run! RUN!" Red was so much slower than I was and he fell—*a lot.* I briefly considered leaving him there to fend for himself, but my mother hadn't raised me that way. Neither had the Covenant. I yanked him back to his feet, half tugging him across the field. Incoherent babbling came from him as I dragged him on. He was praying and crying—sobbing really.

Lightning zipped overhead and a crash of thunder jolted

both of us. Another bolt of light split the dark sky. Through the fog rolling over the field, I could make out the shapes of more warehouses beyond a cluster of ancient maples. We had to make it there. We could lose them, or at least we could try. Anywhere was better than being out in the open. I pushed harder—pulled on Red harder.

Our shoes tripped in the tangled weeds, and my chest was hurting, the muscles in my arm straining to keep Red on his feet.

"Move," I gasped as we dashed under the canopy of trees, darting to the right. It seemed better than running in a straight line. "Keep moving."

Red finally fell in step beside me. The beanie was gone, revealing a head full of thick dreads. We dipped around a tree, both of us stumbling over thick roots and underbrush. Low-hanging branches slapped at us, tearing at our clothing. But we kept running.

"What…are they?" Red asked breathlessly.

"Death," I said, knowing no better way to describe them to a mortal.

Red whimpered. I think he knew I wasn't kidding.

It came out of nowhere then, slamming into us with the ferocity of a freight train. I hit the ground face-first, inhaling spit and dirt. Somehow I kept ahold of the spade and rolled onto my back, praying we'd just gotten tackled by a chupacabra or a minotaur. Right now either would be far better than the alternative.

And I was not that lucky.

I stared up at the daimon as he picked Red up and held him several feet off the ground with one hand. Thrashing wildly, Red screamed as the daimon smiled, although he didn't see the rows of razor teeth that I could. Full of panic and terror, I rolled to my feet and rushed the daimon.

Before I could reach them, the daimon drew back his free arm and a burst of flames encompassed his hand. The elemental fire burned unnaturally bright, but the gaping eyeholes remained dark. Seemingly indifferent to the horror playing out across Red's face and his terrified screams, the daimon placed his fiery hand on Red's cheek. The fire sparked from the daimon's hand, swallowing Red's face and body within seconds. Red shrieked until his voice cut off, his body nothing but flames.

I stumbled backward, choking on a silent scream. The taste of bile filled my mouth.

The daimon dropped Red's corpse to the ground. The moment his hands left the body, the flames vanished. He turned to me and laughed as the elemental magic cloaked his true form.

My brain refused to accept reality. He wasn't the daimon from Miami or the one who had spoken behind the rest stop. A fourth. There were four of them—*four daimons*. Panic raked at me with fresh, sharp claws.

My heart pounded fiercely as I backed up, feeling a cold desperation well up inside me. I whirled around and found him now standing in front of me. Nothing moved as fast as a daimon, I realized. Not even me.

He winked.

I darted to the side, but he mimicked my movements. He shadowed each step I took and laughed at my pathetic attempts to get around him.

Then he stilled, letting his hands fall harmlessly to his sides. "Poor little half-blood, there is nothing you can do. You can't escape us."

I clenched the handle of the spade, unable to speak as he stepped to the side.

"Run, half-blood." The daimon tilted his head toward me. "I'll enjoy the chase. And once I catch you, even the gods won't be able to stop what I will do to you. Run!"

I took off. No matter how much air I dragged into my lungs as I ran, it didn't seem like I could breathe. All I could think as branches snagged strands of my hair was that I didn't want to die like that. Not like that.

Oh gods—not like that.

The ground became uneven; each step sent a spike of pain up my leg and through my hips. I broke free from the trees as another rumble of thunder drowned out every sound except that of the blood pounding in my temples. Seeing the outline of the warehouses, I pushed my sore muscles harder. My sneakers left the weed-covered earth and pounded across a thin layer of gravel. I darted between the buildings, knowing wherever I went I might have only a few stolen moments of safety.

One of the buildings, the farthest from the woods, was several stories tall while the rest looked squat in comparison. The windows on the ground floor were either broken or boarded up. I slowed down, peering over my shoulder before I tried the door. I kicked at the rust-frozen handle and the surrounding wood cracked and gave way. I ducked inside and shut the door behind me.

My eyes roamed the dark interior, searching for something to secure the door with. It took several seconds for my eyes to adjust, and when they did, I could make out the shapes of abandoned work benches, presses, and a set of stairs. I struggled to get my fingers to stop shaking as I shoved the spade back into my pants. Grabbing a work bench, I yanked it toward the door. The screeching sound it made reminded me too much of a daimon's howl, and it also seemed to send things scurrying in the shadows.

Once I'd barricaded the door, I rushed the stairs. They creaked and shifted under my weight as I took the steps two at a time, keeping a death grip on the metal railing. On the third floor, I went straight to a room with a large set of windows, dodging discarded benches and flattened boxes. A startling realization hit me as I peered out the window frantically, scouring the ground for daimons.

If I didn't make it to Nashville—if I ended up dead tonight—no one would even know. No one would even miss me or care. My face wouldn't even end up on the back of a milk carton.

I flipped out.

Leaving the room, I hit the rickety stairs and kept climbing until I reached the top floor. I raced through the dark hallway, ignoring startled squeaks. I threw open the door and tumbled onto the roof.

The storm continued violently overhead as if it had become a part of me. Lightning streaked across the sky, and a crack of thunder vibrated through my core, mocking the cyclone of emotions building inside.

Going to the edge of the roof, I peered through the fog. My eyes scanned every inch of the nearby woods and grounds where I'd just been. When I saw nothing, I rushed to each of the other sides and did the same.

The daimons hadn't followed me.

Maybe they were playing with mc instcad, wanting me to believe I'd somehow outsmarted them. I knew they could still be out there, toying with me like a cat does with a mouse before it pounces and rips the poor thing apart.

I went back to the center of the roof, the wind whipping my hair around my face. Lightning flashed overhead, casting my long shadow across the rooftop. Waves of sorrow crashed over me, coupled with anger and frustration. Each swell cut me from the inside, lancing open wounds that would never really heal. Bending over, I covered my mouth with both hands and screamed just as the thunder rolled through the dark clouds.

"This isn't it." My voice was a hoarse whisper. "This can't be it."

I straightened, swallowing down the burning lump in my throat.

"Screw you. Screw all of you! I'm not dying like this. Not in this state, not in this stupid city, and sure as hell not in this pile of crap!"

Fierce determination—so hot and full of rage—burned through my veins as I climbed back down the stairs to the room with the windows. I dropped down on a pile of flattened boxes. Pulling my legs up to my chest, I leaned my head back against the wall. Dust coated my damp skin and clothing, sucking most of the moisture out.

I did the only thing I could do because this couldn't be the end for me. With no money and no bus ticket, I might be trapped here for a while, but this wasn't how I was going to go out. I refused to even entertain the possibility. Closing my eyes, I knew I couldn't hide here forever.

I ran my fingers over the edge of the blade, preparing myself for what I would have to do when the daimons came. I couldn't run anymore.

This was it. The sounds of the storm melted away, leaving a cloying humidity, and off in the distance, I heard the roar of trucks passing in the night. Life went on outside these walls. It couldn't be any different inside them.

I will survive this.

HALF-BLOOD

PRONUNCIATION GUIDE FOR HALF-BLOOD

Daimon: DEE-mun
Aether: EE-ther
Hematoi: HEM-a-toy
Apollyon: a-POL-ee-on
Agapi Mou: ah-GAH-pee MOO
Akasha: ah-KAH-sha

CHAPTER ONE

My eyes snapped open as the freakish sixth sense kicked my fight-or-flight response into overdrive. The Georgia humidity and the dust covering the floor made it hard to breathe. Since I'd fled Miami, no place had been safe. This abandoned factory had proved no different.

The daimons were here.

I could hear them on the lower level, searching each room systematically, throwing open doors, slamming them shut. The sound threw me back to a few days ago, when I'd pushed open the door to Mom's bedroom. She'd been in the arms of one of those monsters, beside a broken pot of hibiscus flowers. Purple petals had spilled across the floor, mixing with the blood. The memory twisted my gut into a raw ache, but I couldn't think about her right now.

I jumped to my feet, halting in the narrow hallway, straining to hear how many daimons were here. Three? More? My fingers jerked around the slim handle of the garden spade. I held it up, running my fingers over the sharp edges plated in titanium. The act reminded me of what needed to be done. Daimons loathed titanium. Besides decapitation—which was *way* too gross—titanium was the only thing that would kill them. Named after the Titans, the precious metal was poisonous to those addicted to aether.

Somewhere in the building, a floorboard groaned and gave way. A deep howl broke the silence, starting as a low whine before hitting an intense shrill pitch. The scream sounded inhuman, sick and horrifying. Nothing in this world sounded like a daimon—a hungry daimon.

And it was close.

I darted down the hallway, my tattered sneakers pounding against the worn-out boards. Speed was in my blood, and strands of long, dirty hair streamed behind me. I rounded the corner, knowing I had only seconds—

A *whoosh* of stale air whirled around me as the daimon grabbed a handful of my shirt, slamming me into the wall. Dust and plaster floated through the air. Black starbursts dotted my vision as I scrambled to my feet. Those soulless, pitch-black holes where eyes should have been stared at me like I was his next meal ticket.

The daimon grasped my shoulder, and I let instinct take over. I twisted around, catching the surprise flickering across his pale face a split second before I kicked. My foot connected with the side of his head. The impact sent him staggering into the opposite wall. I spun around, slamming my hand into him. Surprise turned to horror as the daimon looked down at the garden spade buried deep in his stomach. It didn't matter where we aimed. Titanium always killed a daimon.

A guttural sound escaped his gaping mouth before he exploded into a shimmery blue dust.

With the spade still in hand, I whirled around and took the

steps two at a time. I ignored the ache in my hips as I sprinted across the floor. I was going to make it—I had to make it. I'd be super-pissed in the afterlife if I died a virgin in this craphole.

"Little half-blood, where are you running?"

I stumbled to the side, falling into a large steel press. Twisting around, my heart slammed against my ribs. The daimon appeared a few feet behind me. Like the one upstairs, he looked like a freak. His mouth hung open, exposing sharp, serrated teeth, and those all-black eyeholes sent chills over my skin. They reflected no light or life, only signifying death. His cheeks were sunken, skin unearthly pale. Veins popped out, etching his face like inky snakes. He truly looked like something out of my worst nightmare—something demonic. Only a half-blood could see through the glamour for a few moments. Then the elemental magic took over, revealing what he used to look like. Adonis came to mind—a blond, stunning man.

"What are you doing all alone?" he asked, voice deep and alluring.

I took a step back, my eyes searching the room for an exit. Wannabe Adonis blocked my way out, and I knew I couldn't stand still for long. Daimons could still wield control over the elements. If he hit me with air or fire, I was a goner.

He laughed, the sound lacking humor and life. "Maybe if you beg—and I mean, really beg—I'll let your death be a fast one. Frankly, half-bloods don't really do it for me. Pure-bloods on the other hand…" He let out a sound of pleasure. "They're like fine dining. Half-bloods? You're more like fast food."

"Come one step closer, and you'll end up like your buddy upstairs." I hoped I sounded threatening enough. Not likely. "Try me."

His brows rose. "Now you're starting to upset me. That's two of us you've killed."

"You keeping a tally or something?" My heart stopped when the floor behind me creaked. I whirled around, spotting a female daimon. She inched closer, forcing me toward the other daimon.

They were caging me in, giving no opportunity to escape. Another one shrieked somewhere in the pile of crap. Panic and fear choked me. My stomach rolled violently as my fingers trembled around the garden spade. Gods, I wanted to puke.

The ringleader advanced on me. "Do you know what I'm going to do to you?"

I swallowed and fixed a smirk on my face. "Blah. Blah. You're gonna kill me. Blah. I know."

The female's ravenous shriek cut off his response. Obviously she was very hungry. She circled me like a vulture, ready to rip into me. My eyes narrowed on her. The hungry ones were always the stupidest—the weakest of the bunch. Legend said it was the first taste of aether—the very life force running through our blood—that possessed a pure blood. A single taste turned one into a daimon and resulted in a lifetime of addiction. There was a good chance I could get past her. The other one…well, he was a different story.

I feinted toward the female. She came right at me. The male yelled at her to stop, but it was too late. I took off in the opposite direction like an Olympic sprinter, rushing for the door I'd kicked in earlier in the night. Once outside, the odds would be back in my favor. A small window of hope sparked alive and propelled me forward.

But then, the worst possible thing happened. A wall of flames flew up in front of me, burning through benches and shooting at least eight feet into the air. It was real. No illusion. The heat blew back at me, and the fire crackled, eating through the walls.

In front of me, *he* walked right through the flames, looking every bit like a daimon hunter should. The fire did not singe his pants nor dirty his shirt. Not a single dark hair was touched by the blaze. Those cool, storm-cloud-colored eyes fixed on me.

It was him—Aiden St. Delphi.

I'd never forget his name or face. The first time I'd caught a glimpse of him standing in front of the training arena, a ridiculous crush had sprung alive. I'd been fourteen and he seventeen. The fact that he was a pure blood hadn't mattered when I'd spotted him around campus.

Aiden's presence could mean one thing only: the Sentinels had arrived.

Our eyes met, and then he looked over my shoulder. "Get down."

I didn't need to be told twice. Like a pro, I hit the floor. The pulse of heat shot above me, crashing into the intended target. The floor shook with the daimon's wild thrashing, and her wounded screams filled the air. Only titanium would kill a daimon, but I felt confident that being burnt alive didn't feel too good.

Rising up on my elbows, I peered through my dirty hair as Aiden lowered his hand. A popping sound followed the movement, and the flames vanished as fast as they appeared. Within seconds, only the smells of burnt wood, flesh, and smoke remained.

Two more Sentinels rushed the room. I recognized one of them: Kain Poros, a half-blood a year or so older than me. Once upon a time we had trained together. Kain moved with a grace he'd never had before. He went for the female, and with one quick swoop, he thrust a long, slender dagger into the burnt flesh of her skin. She too became nothing but dust.

The other Sentinel had the air of a pure blood to him, but I'd never seen him before. He was big—steroids big—and he zeroed in on the daimon I knew was somewhere in this factory but hadn't seen yet. Watching how he moved such a large body around so gracefully made me feel sorely inadequate, especially considering I was still lying sprawled on the floor. I dragged myself to my feet, feeling the terror-fueled adrenaline rush fade.

Without warning, my head exploded in pain as the side of my face hit the floor *hard*. Stunned and confused, it took me a moment to realize Wannabe Adonis had gotten ahold of my legs. I twisted, but the creep sank his hands deep into my hair and yanked my head back. I dug my fingers into his skin, but it did nothing to alleviate the pressure bearing down on my neck. For a startled moment, I thought he intended to rip my head right off, but he sank razor-sharp teeth into my shoulder, tearing through fabric and flesh. I screamed—*really* screamed.

I was on fire—I had to be. The draining burned through my skin; sharp pricks radiated out through every cell in my body. And even though I was only a half-blood, not chock-full of aether like a pure blood, the daimon continued to drink my essence as though I were. It wasn't my blood he was after; he'd swallow pints of it just to get at the aether. My very spirit shifted as he dragged it into him. Pain became everything.

Suddenly the daimon lifted his mouth. "What are you?" His whispered voice slurred the words.

There was no time to even think about that question. He was ripped off me, and my body slumped forward. I rolled into a messy, bloody ball, sounding more like a wounded animal than anything remotely human. It was the first time I'd ever gotten tagged—drained by a daimon.

Over the small sounds I made, I heard a sickening crunch, and then wild shrieks, but the pain had taken over my senses. It started to pull back from my fingers, sliding its way back to my core where it still blazed. I tried to breathe through it, but *damn…*

Gentle hands rolled me onto my back, prying my fingers away from my shoulder. I stared up at Aiden.

"Are you okay? Alexandria? Please say something."

"Alex," I choked out. "Everyone calls me Alex."

He gave a short, relieved laugh. "Okay. Good. Alex, can you stand?"

I think I nodded. Every few seconds a stabbing flash of heat rocked through me, but the hurt had faded into a dull ache. "That really…sucked something bad."

Aiden managed to get one arm around me, lifting me to my feet. I swayed as he brushed back my hair and took a look at the damage. "Give it a few minutes. The pain will wear off."

Lifting my head, I looked around. Kain and the other Sentinel were frowning at nearly identical piles of blue dust. The pure blood faced us. "That should be all of them."

Aiden nodded. "Alex, we need to go. Now. Back to the Covenant."

The Covenant? Not entirely in control of my emotions, I turned to Aiden. He wore all black—the uniform Sentinels wore. For a hot second, that girly crush resurfaced from three years ago. Aiden looked sublime, but fury stomped down that stupid crush.

The Covenant was involved in this—coming to my rescue? Where the hell had they been when one of the daimons had snuck into our house?

He took a step forward, but I didn't see him—I saw my mother's lifeless body again. The last thing she ever saw on this Earth was some god-awful daimon's face, and the last thing she'd ever felt… I shuddered, remembering the body-ripping pain of the daimon's tag.

Aiden took another step toward me. I reacted, a response born out of anger and pain. I launched myself at him, using moves I hadn't practiced in years. Simple things like kicks and punches were one thing, but an offensive attack was something I'd barely learned.

He caught my hand and swung me around so I faced the other direction. In a matter of seconds, he had my arms pinned, but all the pain and the sorrow rose in me, overriding any common sense. I bent forward, intent on getting enough space between us to deliver a vicious back kick.

"Don't," Aiden warned, his voice deceptively soft. "I don't want to hurt you."

My breath came out harsh and ragged. I could feel the warm blood trickling down my neck, mixing with sweat. I kept fighting even though my head swam, and the fact that Aiden held me off so easily only made my world turn red with rage.

"Whoa!" Kain yelled from the sidelines, "Alex, you know us! Don't you remember me? We aren't going to hurt you."

"Shut up!" I broke free of Aiden's grasp, dodging Kain and Mister Steroids. None of them expected me to run from them, but that's what I did.

I made it to the door leading out of the factory, dodged the broken wood and rushed outside. My feet carried me toward the field across the street. My thoughts were a complete mess. Why was I running? Hadn't I been trying to get back to the Covenant since the daimon attack in Miami?

My body didn't want to do this, but I kept running through the tall weeds and prickly bushes. Heavy footsteps sounded behind me, growing closer and closer. My vision blurred a bit, my heart thundering in my chest. I was so confused, so—

A hard body crashed into me, knocking the air right out of my lungs. I went down in a spiraling mess of legs and arms. Somehow Aiden twisted around and took the brunt of the fall. I landed on top of him, and I stayed there for a moment before he rolled me over, pinning me down into the itchy field grass.

Panic and rage burst through me. "Now? Where were you a week ago? Where was the Covenant when my mother was being killed? Where were you?"

Aiden jerked back, eyes wide. "I'm sorry. We didn't—"

His apology only angered me further. I wanted to hurt him. I wanted to make him let me go. I wanted…I wanted…I didn't know what the hell I wanted, but I couldn't stop myself from screaming, clawing, and kicking him. Only when Aiden pressed his long, lean body against mine did I stop. His weight, the close proximity, held me immobile.

There wasn't an inch of space between us. I could feel the hard ripple of his abdominal muscles pressing against my stomach, could feel his lips only inches from mine. Suddenly I entertained a wild idea. I wondered if his lips felt as good as they looked…because they looked awesome.

That was a wrong thought to have. I had to be crazy—the only plausible excuse for what I was doing and thinking. The way I stared at his lips or the fact I desperately wanted to be kissed—all wrong for a multitude of reasons. Besides the fact I'd just tried to knock his head off, I looked like a mess. Grime dirtied my face beyond recognition; I hadn't showered in a week, and I was pretty sure I smelled. I was *that* gross.

But the way he lowered his head, I really thought he was going to kiss me. My entire body tensed in anticipation, like waiting to be kissed for the first time, and this was definitely not the first time I'd been kissed. I'd kissed lots of boys, but not him.

Not a *pure blood*.

Aiden shifted, pressing down farther. I inhaled sharply and my mind raced a million miles a second, spewing out nothing helpful. He moved his right hand to my forehead. Warning bells went off.

He murmured a compulsion, fast and low, too quick for me to make out the words.

Son of a—

A sudden darkness rushed me, void of thought and meaning. There was no fighting something that powerful, and without getting out so much as a word of protest, I sank into its murky depths.

CHAPTER TWO

Whatever my head rested on felt firm, but oddly comfortable. I snuggled closer, feeling safe and warm—something I hadn't felt since Mom pulled my butt from the Covenant three years ago. Jumping from place to place rarely afforded such a comfort. Something wasn't right.

My eyes flew open.

Son of a bitch.

I jerked back from Aiden's shoulder so fast I cracked my head against the window. "Crap!"

He turned toward me, his dark brows high. "Are you okay?"

I ignored the concern in his voice and glared at him. I had no idea how long I'd been out of it. Judging by the deep blue of the sky outside the tinted windows, I guessed it'd been hours. Pures weren't supposed to use compulsions on halfs who weren't in servitude; it was considered highly unethical since compulsions stripped people of free will, choice, and everything.

Damn Hematoi. Not that they ever cared about ethics.

Before the original demigods had died along with Hercules and Perseus, they'd all shacked up with each other in the way only the Greeks could. Those unions had produced the pure-bloods—the Hematoi—a very, very powerful race. They could wield control over the four elements: air, water, fire, and earth, and manipulate that raw power into spells and compulsions. Pures never were to use their gifts against another pure. Doing so meant imprisonment—or even death in some cases.

Being a half-blood, the product of a pure blood and ordinary old human—a mongrel by pure standards—I had no control over the elements. My kind was gifted with the same strength and speed the pures had, but we had an extra special gift that set us apart. We could see through the elemental magic the daimons used. The pures couldn't.

There were a lot of us halfs running around, probably more than the pure-bloods. Considering pures married to improve their position in our society instead of marrying for love, they tended to fool around—*a lot*. Being that they weren't susceptible to diseases that plagued mortals, I figured they assumed it was okay to forego protection. As it turned out, their half-blood offspring served a very valuable position in the pure-blood society.

"Alex." Aiden frowned as he watched me. "Are you okay?"

"Yeah, I'm fine." I scowled while taking in my surroundings.

We were in something big—probably one of the Covenant's super-large Hummers that could plow over an entire village. Pures weren't concerned with things like money and gas mileage. "The bigger the better" was their unofficial motto.

The other pure—the enormous one—was behind the

wheel, and Kain sat in the passenger seat, silently staring out the window.

"Where are we?"

"We're on the coast, just outside of Bald Head Island. We're almost to Deity Island," Aiden answered.

My heart jumped. "What?"

"We're going back to the Covenant, Alex."

The Covenant—the place I'd trained and called home up until three years ago. Sighing, I rubbed the back of my head. "Did the Covenant send you? Or was it…my stepfather?"

"The Covenant."

I breathed easier. My pure-blooded stepfather wouldn't be happy to see me. "You work for the Covenant now?"

"No. I'm just a Sentinel. I'm more on loan for the time being. Your uncle sent us to find you." Aiden paused, glancing out the window. "A lot has changed since you've been gone."

I wanted to ask what a Sentinel got accomplished on the well-protected Deity Island, but I figured it wasn't any of my business. "What's changed?"

"Well, your uncle is now the Dean of the Covenant."

"Marcus? Wait. What? What happened to Dean Nasso?"

"He died about two years ago."

"Oh." No big surprise there. He'd been old as dirt. I didn't say anything else as I mulled over the fact my uncle was now *Dean* Andros. Ugh. I made a face. I barely knew the man, but the last I remembered, he'd been working his way up through the pure-blood political world. I shouldn't be surprised he'd found his way into such a coveted position.

"Alex, I'm sorry about the compulsion back there." Aiden broke the silence that had stretched between us. "I didn't want you to hurt yourself."

I didn't respond.

"And...I'm sorry about your mother. We searched everywhere for you two, but you didn't stay in one place long enough. We were too late."

My heart squeezed in my chest. "Yeah, you were too late."

Another few minutes of silence filled the Hummer. "Why did your mother leave three years ago?"

I peeked through the curtain of my hair. Aiden watched me as he waited for an answer to his loaded question. "I don't know."

Since the age of seven, I had been a half-blood in training—one of the so-called "privileged" halfs. We had two options in life—either attend the Covenant or go into the working class. Halfs who had a pure blood willing to speak for them and foot the cost of an education were enrolled in the Covenant to train as Sentinels or Guards. The other halfs weren't so lucky.

They were rounded up by the Masters, a group of pures who excelled at the art of compulsion. An elixir had been created out of a special blend of poppy flowers and tea. The concoction worked differently in a half's blood. Instead of leaving them lethargic and sleepy, the refined poppy made them compliant and vacant, giving them a high they never came down from. Masters started indentured halfs on the elixir at the age of seven—the age of reason—and continued in daily doses. No education. No freedom.

The Masters were ultimately responsible for dealing out the elixir and monitoring the behaviors of the halfs in servitude. They were also the ones who marked them on their forehead. A circle with a line through it—the painfully visible sign of enslavement.

All halfs feared that future. Even if we did end up training in the Covenant, it took only one wrong move before we were given the drink that keeps on giving. What my mom did by pulling me out of the Covenant without so much as an explanation was a major strike against me.

I was also sure taking half of her husband's—my stepfather's—fortune wouldn't help me out any either.

Then there were all those times I should've contacted the Covenant and turned my mom in, done what was expected of me. One call—one stupid call—would have saved her life.

The Covenant would hold that against me, too.

The memory of waking up and stumbling into my worst nightmare resurfaced. Days before, she'd asked that I clean up the balcony garden I'd demanded on having, but I'd slept in. By the time I'd gotten up and grabbed the little bag of garden tools, it'd been noon.

Figuring Mom was already working on the garden, I'd gone out on the balcony, but the garden was empty. I'd stood there for a while, staring down at the alley across the street, toying with the garden spade. Then, from the shadows, a man had stepped out—a daimon.

He'd stood there in broad daylight, staring up at me. He'd been so close I could've chucked the spade and hit him. With my heart in my throat, I'd jerked back from the railing. I'd rushed back into the house, screaming for her. There'd been no answer. Rooms had blurred as I'd raced down the tiny hallway toward her bedroom and pushed open the door. What I'd seen would haunt me forever—blood, so much blood, and Mom's eyes, open and vacant, staring at nothing.

"We're here." Kain said, leaning forward eagerly.

All my thoughts vanished as my stomach did a funny twist. I turned and stared out the window. Deity Island actually consisted of two islands. The pures lived in their fancy homes on the first island. To the outside world, it looked like any normal island community. Small shops and restaurants lined the streets. There were even shops run by mortals and tailored to them. The pristine beaches were to die for.

Daimons didn't like to travel across water. When a pure turned all dark side, their elemental magic twisted and could only be accessed if they were touching earth. Being out of contact weakened them. It made an island the perfect hidey hole for our kind.

It was too early for anyone to be on the streets, and in a matter of minutes we passed over the second bridge. On this part of Deity Island, nestled among marshlands, beaches, and forests virtually untouched by man, stood the Covenant.

Rising up between the endless sea and acres of white beaches, the sprawling sandstone structure we passed was the school where pures and halfs attended classes. With its thick marble columns and strategically placed statues of the gods, it was an intimidating and otherworldly place. Mortals thought the Covenant was an elite private school where none of their children would ever have the privilege of attending. They were right. People had to have something super-special in their blood to make it this far.

Beyond the main building were the dorms, and they too boasted columns and statues. Smaller buildings and bungalows dotted the landscape, and the massive gyms and training facilities sat adjacent to the courtyard. They always reminded me of the ancient coliseums, except ours were enclosed; hurricanes could be a real bitch around these parts.

It was all beautiful—a place I loved and hated at the same time. Seeing it now, I realized just how badly I'd missed it… and Mom. She'd stayed on the main island while I'd gone to school, but she'd been a fixture around the campus, popping up and taking me to lunch after classes, swaying the old dean to allow me to stay with her during the weekends. Gods, I just wanted one more chance, one more second to tell her—

I checked myself.

Control—I needed to be in control right now, and caving in to the lingering grief wasn't going to help me. Steeling myself, I climbed out of the Hummer and followed Aiden to the girls' dorm. We were the only ones moving down the silent hallways. With it being the beginning of summer, only a few students would be running around.

"Get cleaned up. I'll return for you in a little bit." He started to turn but stopped. "I'll find something for you to wear and leave it on the table."

I nodded, at a loss for words. Even though I was trying to push the emotions down, some of them seeped through. Three years ago, my entire future had been perfectly planned. All the Instructors at the Covenant had praised my abilities in the training sessions. They even went as far as to say I could become a Sentinel. Sentinels were the best—and I'd *been* one of the best.

Three years without any training had set me back behind every half. A lifetime of servitude most likely waited for me—a future I couldn't face. Being subject to the pures' wills, having no control or say over anything—the possibility scared the crap out of me.

A possibility made worse by my nearly all-consuming need to hunt daimons.

Fighting them was ingrained in my blood, but after seeing what'd happened to Mom, the desire skyrocketed. Only the Covenant could provide the means for achieving my goals, and my absentee pure-blooded uncle now held my future in his hands.

My footsteps felt heavy as I moved around the familiar

rooms. They were fully furnished, seeming larger than I remembered. There was a separate living area, a decent-sized bedroom, and a bathroom. The Covenant offered only the best to its students.

I took a longer than necessary shower, reveling in the feeling of being clean again. People took things like showers for granted. I knew I had. After the daimon attack, I'd hit the road with little cash. Staying alive had turned out to be more important than a shower. Once I was sure all the grime was washed away, I found the neat stack of clothes left on the small table in front of the couch. Picking them up, I realized at once they were the Covenant-issued training attire. The pants were at least two sizes too big, but I wasn't going to bitch about it. I brought them to my face and inhaled. They smelled so clean.

Back in the bathroom, I craned my neck. The daimon had tagged me just where the neck sloped down to the collarbone. The tag would be an angry red color for the next day or two and then fade to a pale, shiny scar. A daimon's bite never left the skin undamaged. The nearly identical rows of tiny indentations made me queasy, and they also reminded me of one of my old Instructors.

She was a beautiful older woman who'd retired to teach basic defense tactics after a nasty run-in with a daimon. Her arms had been covered with pale, half-circle marks a degree or two lighter than her skin tone. One tag had been bad enough. I couldn't imagine what it must've been like for her. The daimons had tried to turn her by draining her of all her aether. When it came to turning a pure, there was no exchange of blood.

It was a frighteningly simple process.

A daimon placed their lips on the drained pure's, shared some of their aether and—voila!—brand spankin' new daimon. Like infected blood, the tainted aether they passed turned a pure, and nothing could be done to undo the change. The pure was lost forever. As far as we knew, it was the only way a daimon could be made, but then again, it wasn't like we hung around and talked to them. They were killed on sight.

I'd always thought that policy was stupid. No one—not even the Council—knew what the daimons thought to accomplish by killing. If we caught one and actually questioned it, we could learn so much about them. What were their plans—their goals? Did they even have any? Or was it just the need for aether that kept them going? We didn't know. All the Hematoi cared about was stopping them and making sure none of the pures were turned.

Anyway, rumor said our Instructor had waited until the very last moment to strike, thus foiling the daimon's plans. I remembered staring at those marks and thinking how terrible it was that her otherwise flawless body had been ruined.

My reflection in the fogged mirror stared back at me. This tag would be hard to hide, but it could've been worse. He could've tagged a chunk of my face—daimons could be cruel.

Halfs couldn't be turned, which is why we made such excellent fighters against the daimons. Dying was the worst that could happen to us. Who cared if a half-blood went down in battle? To the pures, we were a dime a dozen.

Sighing, I flipped my hair over my shoulder and pushed away from the mirror just as a soft knock sounded. A second later, Aiden opened the door to my dorm. All six and half feet of him came to an abrupt stop the moment he saw me. Surprise flickered over his face as he stared at the fresh version of me.

What can I say? I cleaned up nicely.

With all the dirt and overall grossness gone, I looked just

like my mom. Long dark hair fell down my back; I had those high cheekbones and full lips most pures did. I was a bit curvier than Mom's willowy frame, and I didn't have her amazing eyes. Mine were brown, homely old brown.

I tipped my head back, looking him straight in the eyes for the first time. "What?"

He recovered in record time. "Nothing. You ready?"

"I guess so." I snuck another peek at him as he headed out of my room.

Aiden's dark brown waves continually fell over his forehead, brushing against equally dark brows. The lines of his face were nearly perfect, the curve of his jaw strong, and he had the most expressive lips I'd ever seen. But it was those thundercloud eyes I found beautiful. No one had those eyes.

From the brief time he'd held me down in the field, I felt positive the rest of him was just as stunning. Too bad he was a pure blood. Pures equaled hands-off to me and every half out there. Supposedly the gods had forbidden interactions of the fun kind between halfs and pures eons ago. Something to do with the purity of a pure's blood not being tarnished—a fear a child of such a coupling would be... I frowned at Aiden's back.

Would be what—a Cyclops?

I didn't know what might happen, but I did know it was considered very, very bad. Gods got offended, which wasn't a good thing. So since we'd been old enough to understand how babies were made, we half-bloods had been taught to never look at a pure blood with anything other than respect and admiration. Pures were taught to never taint their bloodline by mixing with a half, but there were times when halfs and pures did hook up. It didn't end pretty, and halfs usually caught the brunt of the punishment.

It wasn't fair, but it was the way this world had existed.

The pures were on top of the food chain. They made the rules, controlled the Council, and even ran the Covenant.

Aiden glanced over his shoulder at me. "How many daimons have you killed?"

"Just two." I picked up my pace so I could keep up with his long-legged one.

"Just two?" Awe filled his voice. "Do you realize how amazing it is for a half-blood not fully trained to kill one daimon, let alone two?"

"I guess so." I paused, feeling the bubble of anger threatening to boil over. When the daimon had seen me standing in the doorway of Mom's bedroom, he'd launched himself at me...and right onto the spade I'd held. *Idiot.* The other daimon hadn't been that dumb. "I would've killed the other one in Miami...but I was just—I don't know. I wasn't thinking. I know I should've gone after him, but I panicked."

Aiden stopped and faced me. "Alex the fact that you took down one daimon without training is remarkable. It was brave, but also foolish."

"Well, thanks."

"You're not trained. The daimon could've easily killed you. And the one you brought down in the factory? Another fearless, but foolish, act."

I frowned. "I thought you said it was amazing and remarkable."

"It was, but you could've been killed." He walked off ahead.

I struggled to keep up with him. "Why would you even care if I was killed? Why does Marcus care? I don't even know the man, and if he doesn't allow me to resume training, I'm as good as dead, anyway."

"That would be a shame." He looked at me blandly. "You have all the potential in the world."

My eyes narrowed on his back. The sudden urge to push him was almost too great to pass up. We didn't talk after that. Once outside, the breeze played with my hair, and I sucked in the taste of sea salt as the sun warmed my chilled skin.

Aiden led me back to the main school building and up the ridiculous number of stairs that led to the dean's office. The formidable double doors loomed ahead, and I swallowed hard. I'd spent a lot of time in this office when Dean Nasso had overseen the Covenant.

As the Guards opened the door for us, I remembered the last time I'd been in this office for a lecture. I'd been fourteen, and out of boredom, I'd convinced one of the pures to flood the science wing using the water element. Of course, the pure had totally ratted me out.

Nasso had not been pleased.

My first glimpse of the office was exactly how I remembered: perfect and well designed. Several leather chairs sat before a large cherry oak desk. Wildly colored fish zoomed back and forth in the aquarium lining the wall behind the desk.

My uncle stepped into my line of sight and I faltered. It'd been so long since I'd seen him—years really. I'd forgotten how much he looked like Mom. They shared the same eyes—emerald-colored ones that shifted depending on mood. They were eyes only my mother and uncle shared.

Except the last time I'd seen her eyes, they hadn't been vibrant. The icky feeling swelled inside me, pressing on my chest. I stepped forward, pushing it all the way down.

"Alexandria." Marcus's deep and cultured voice snapped me back into the room. "After all these years. To see you again? I am at a loss for words."

Uncle—and I used the term loosely—sounded nothing

like a close family member. His tone was cold and plastic. When I met his eyes, I knew right off I was doomed. There was nothing in his stare linking me to him—no happiness or relief at seeing his only niece alive and in one piece. If anything, he looked rather bored.

Someone cleared his throat, drawing my attention to the corner of the office. We weren't alone. Mister Steroids stood in the corner, along with a female pure. She was tall and slender, with cascades of raven-colored hair. I pegged her as an Instructor.

Only pures who had no aspirations for the political games of their world taught for the Covenant or became Sentinels—or pures like Aiden who lived with super-personal reasons for doing so: say, like having his parents murdered by daimons right in front of him when he was a child. That was what'd happened to him. Supposedly it was why Aiden had chosen to become a Sentinel. He probably wanted some sort of revenge.

Something we had in common.

"Sit down." Marcus motioned to a chair. "We have a lot to discuss."

I pulled my eyes from the pures and treaded forward. Hope flared with their presence. Why else would there be pures here if not to talk about my lack of training and ways to overcome it?

Marcus moved behind his desk and sat. From there, he folded his hands and leveled a look at me. Unease made me sit straighter, and my feet dangled above the floor.

"I really don't know where to begin with…this mess Rachelle created."

I didn't respond since I wasn't sure I'd heard him correctly.

"First off, she nearly ruined Lucian. Twice." He spoke as if

I'd had something to do with it. "The scandal she created when she met your father was bad enough. When she emptied Lucian's bank account and ran off with you? Well, I'm sure even you can understand the lasting implications of such an unwise decision."

Ah, Lucian. Mom's perfect, pure-blooded husband—my stepfather. I could imagine his response. It probably had involved a lot of throwing stuff and bemoaning his poor character judgment. I don't even know if Mom had ever loved him, or if she'd loved my mortal father who she'd had an affair with, but I did know Lucian was a total priss.

Marcus continued listing the ways her decisions had hurt Lucian. I pretty much tuned him out. The last I remembered, Lucian was working to secure a spot on the pure-blood Council. Reminiscent of the old Greek Olympian court, the Council had twelve ruling figures, and, out of those twelve, two were Ministers.

Ministers were the most powerful. They ruled the lives of both pures and halfs just as Hera and Zeus ruled Olympia. Needless to say, the Ministers had huge freaking egos.

Each Covenant location held a Council: North Carolina, Tennessee, New York, and the pure-blood university located in South Dakota. The eight Ministers controlled the Council.

"Are you even listening to me, Alexandria?" Marcus frowned at me.

My head jerked up. "Yes…you're talking about how bad everything's been for Lucian. I feel sorry for him. Really, I do. But I'm sure it pales in comparison to having your life ripped away from you."

A strange look inched across his face. "Are you referring to your mother's fate?"

"You mean your sister's fate?" My eyes narrowed as I met his gaze.

Marcus stared at me, his face going blank. "Rachelle sealed her own fate when she left the safety of our society. What happened to her is truly tragic, but I cannot find it in myself to feel overly upset. When she pulled you away from the Covenant, she proved she gave no thought to Lucian's reputation or for your safety. She was self-centered, irresponsible—"

"She was everything to me!" I jumped to my feet. "She did nothing but think of me! What happened to her was *horrific*—'tragic' is for people who die in car wrecks!"

His expression didn't change. "She did nothing but think of you? I find that strange. She left the safety of the Covenant and put both of you in danger."

I bit the inside of my cheek.

"Exactly." His gaze turned arctic. "Sit down, Alexandria."

Furious, I forced myself to sit and shut up.

"Did she tell you why you needed to leave the Covenant? Give you any reason to why she would do such a reckless thing?"

I glanced over at the pures. Aiden had retreated to stand beside the other two. The three of them watched this soap opera through poker faces. A lot of help they were proving to be.

"Alexandria, I asked you a question."

The hard wood embedded into my palms as I gripped the chair arms. "I heard you. No. She didn't tell me."

A muscle ticked along Marcus's jaw as he stared at me in silence. "Well, it is a shame."

Since I wasn't sure how to respond, I watched him open a file on his desk and spread the lined papers out in front of him. Leaning forward, I tried to see what they were.

Clearing his throat, he picked up one of the papers. "As it is, I cannot hold you responsible for what Rachelle did. The gods know she is suffering the consequences."

"I think Alexandria is aware of how her mother suffered," the female pure interrupted. "There is no need to go any further."

Marcus's stare turned glacial. "Yes. I suppose you are correct, Laadan." He turned back to the paper he held between his elegant fingers. "When I was advised you were finally located, I requested your reports be sent to me."

I winced and sat back in the seat. This wasn't going to be good at all.

"All of your Instructors had nothing but glowing accolades when it came to your training."

A small smile formed on my lips. "I was pretty damn good."

"However." He glanced up, briefly meeting my eyes. "When it comes to your behavior records, I find myself… flabbergasted." My smile shriveled up and died.

"Several write-ups for issues of disrespect toward your teachers and other students," he continued. "A particular note here, written personally by Instructor Banks, states your level of respect for your superiors is seriously lacking and had been an ongoing issue."

"Instructor Banks had no sense of humor."

Marcus arched a brow. "Then I imagine neither did Instructor Richards nor Instructor Octavian? They also wrote, at times, you were uncontrollable and undisciplined."

Protests died on my lips. I had nothing to say.

"Your problems with respect didn't appear to be your only issues." He picked up another piece of paper, and his brows rose. "You were disciplined numerous times for sneaking out of the Covenant, fighting, disrupting class, breaking numerous rules, and oh yes, my personal favorite?" He looked up, smiling tightly. "You had racked up repeated demerits for breaking curfew and for fraternizing in the male dormitory."

I shifted uncomfortably.

"All before the age of fourteen." His lips thinned. "You must be proud."

My eyes widened as I stared at his desk. "I wouldn't say proud."

"Does it matter?"

I looked up. "I…guess not?"

The tight smile returned. "Considering your previous behavior, I'm afraid to say there is no way I could allow you to resume training—"

"What?" My voice turned shrill. "Then why am I here?"

Marcus placed the papers back into the file and closed it. "Our communities are always in need of servants. I spoke with Lucian this morning. He has offered you a place in his home. You should be honored."

"No!" I came to my feet once again. Panic and rage seized me. "There is no way you're going to drug me! I won't be a servant in his house or any pure's!"

"Then what?" Marcus folded his hands again and looked at me calmly. "Will you go back to living on the streets? I will not allow that. The decision has already been made. You will not reenter the Covenant."

CHAPTER THREE

Those words shocked me into silence. All my dreams of ven-geance evaporated into nothing. I stared at my uncle, hating him almost as much as I hated daimons.

Mister Steroids cleared his throat. "If I may say something?"

Marcus and I turned toward him. I was surprised he could even speak, but Marcus waved his hand for him to continue.

"She killed two daimons."

"I'm aware of this, Leon." The man who was about to bring down my whole world didn't seem too interested.

"When we found her in Georgia, she was holding her own against two more daimons," Leon continued. "Her potential, if trained properly, is astronomical."

Shocked that this pure would speak for me, I slowly sat down. Marcus still looked unimpressed, and those bright green eyes were as hard as ice.

"I understand, but her behavior before the incident with her mother cannot be erased. This is a school, not a day care center. I do not have the time or the energy to keep an eye on her. I cannot have her running wild through these halls and influencing the other students."

I rolled my eyes. He made me sound like a cunning criminal about to bring down the entire Covenant.

"Then assign someone to her," Leon said. "There are Instructors here during the summer who can keep an eye on her."

"I don't need a babysitter. It's not like I'm going to burn down a building."

Everyone ignored me.

Marcus sighed. "Even if we assign someone to her, she is behind in her training. There is no way she would be on par with those in her class. Come fall, she will be sorely behind."

This time it was Aiden who spoke. "We would have the entire summer to prepare her. It's possible she could be ready enough to attend classes."

"Who has the time for such an undertaking?" Marcus frowned. "Aiden, you are a Sentinel, not an Instructor. Neither is Leon. And Laadan will be returning to New York shortly. The other Instructors have lives—ones I cannot expect them to drop just for one half-blood."

Aiden's expression was unreadable, and I sure as hell didn't know what provoked the words that came out of his mouth next. "I can work with her. It wouldn't interfere with my duties."

"You're one of the best Sentinels." Marcus shook his head. "It would be a waste of your talent."

They battled on about what to do to me. I tried interjecting once, but after the warning glare both Leon and Aiden sent my way, I shut up. Marcus continued stating I was a lost cause while Aiden and Leon argued that I could be fixed. My uncle's willingness to turn me over to Lucian stung. Servitude wasn't a pleasant future. Everyone knew that. I'd heard rumors, terrible ones concerning how the pures treated halfs—especially female halfs.

Laadan stepped forward after Aiden and Marcus came to a standstill about what to do with me. Slowly she flicked her long hair over one shoulder. "How about we make a deal, Dean Andros? If Aiden says he can train her and still do his duties, then you have nothing to lose. If she's not ready by the end of the summer, she doesn't stay."

I twisted back to Marcus, full of hope.

He stared at me for what seemed like forever. "Fine." He leaned back in his chair. "But this is on you, Aiden. Do you understand? Anything—and I mean anything—she does will be a reflection upon you. And trust me, she will do something. She's just like her mother."

Aiden suddenly looked cautious as he glanced back at me. "Yes. I understand."

A wide smile broke out across my face and the cautious look on his face grew, but when I turned back to Marcus, my smile died under his frigid stare.

"I will be less tolerant than your old dean, Alexandria. Do not make me regret this decision."

I nodded, not fully trusting myself to speak. There was a good chance I would mess it all up if I did. Afterward, Marcus dismissed me with a wave of his hand. I stood and left his office. Laadan and Leon remained, but Aiden followed me.

I turned to him. "Thank you."

Aiden stared at me. "Don't thank me yet."

I smothered a yawn and shrugged. "Well, I just did. I really think Marcus would've shipped me off to Lucian's if it wasn't for you three."

"He would've. Your stepfather is your legal guardian."

I shuddered. "That's reassuring."

He caught my reaction. "Was it something that Lucian did that caused you and your mother to leave?"

"No, but Lucian…wasn't particularly fond of me. I'm Mom's love child, you know? He's just Lucian. What's that prick up to, anyway?"

Aiden's brows rose. "That prick is the Minister of Council."

My mouth dropped open. "What? You're kidding, right?"

"Why would I joke about something like that? So you may want to refrain from calling him a prick in public. I doubt it would help your cause."

News that Lucian was now a Minister made my stomach clench, especially considering he had a "place" for me in his household. I shook my head and pushed that implication far from my thoughts. I had enough immediate concerns other than dealing with him.

"You should get some rest. Come tomorrow, we'll begin training…if you feel up to it."

"I do."

Aiden's gaze drifted over my bruised face and then down, as if he could see the many cuts and bruises I'd racked up since I'd fled Miami. "Are you sure?"

I nodded, my gaze falling on the lock of hair he kept pushing off his forehead. "What are we starting with? I didn't start any of the offensive tactics or Silat training."

He shook his head. "I hate to disappoint you, but you won't be starting with Silat training."

That *was* disappointing. I liked daggers and all things that stabbed, and I really would like to know how to use them effectively.

I started to head toward my dorm, but Aiden's voice

stopped me. "Alex. Don't…let me down. Anything you do will come back on me. Do you understand?"

"Yes. Don't worry. I'm not as bad as Marcus makes me sound."

He looked doubtful. "Fraternizing in the male dorms?"

I flushed. "I was visiting *friends*. Not like I was hooking up with any of them. I was only fourteen."

"Well, that's good to know." He walked away.

Sighing, I headed back to my room. I was tired, but all the excitement from getting a second chance had me hyped up. After staring at the bed for an absurd amount of time, I left my room and moved through the empty halls of the girls' dorm. The pures and halfs shared living quarters only at the Covenant. Anyplace else, we were segregated.

I tried to remember what it'd been like to be here. The rigorous training schedules, ridiculous class work studying things that'd bored me to tears, and all the social games the pures and halfs had played. There's nothing like a bunch of catty teenagers who could either kick your ass halfway across the country or set you on fire with a mere thought. That alone changed who people picked fights with or became friends with. And at the end of the day, it was always good to have a firestarter in your back pocket.

Everyone had a role to play. I'd been considered cool by half-blood standards, but now I had no idea where I would stand come fall.

After roaming the empty common rooms, I left the girls' dorm and headed for one of the smaller buildings near the marshlands. The one-story square building held the cafeteria and rec rooms and surrounded a colorful courtyard.

I slowed as I neared one of the larger rooms. The laughter and crashes radiating from the room proved there were some kids still here over summer vacation. Something flip-flopped inside me. Would they accept me back? Would they even know me? Hell, would they even care?

Taking a deep breath, I pushed open the doors. No one seemed to notice me. Everyone was busy cheering on a pure who was floating several pieces of furniture in midair. The young girl was a novice at controlling the air element, which explained all the noise. Mom had used air, too. After all, it was the most common element. Pures could only control one, sometimes two if they were really powerful.

I studied the girl. With her bright red curls and giant blue eyes, she looked about twelve, especially standing next to the towering halfs in her cute jumper. I really didn't have room to talk. I came in at a whopping five and a half feet, which was short compared with most of the halfs.

I blamed my mortal father.

Meanwhile, the pure pursed her lips as another chair toppled to the floor and more chuckles erupted from her audience—all except one. Caleb Nicolo. Tall, blond, and all charming smile, Caleb had been my partner in dysfunction when I'd been at the Covenant. I shouldn't have been so surprised to see him here during the summer. His mortal mother had never wanted anything to do with her "weird" child, and his pure-blood father was totally on the absentee list.

Caleb stared at me, wide-eyed and stunned. "Holy…crap."

Everyone turned at that point, even the pure. With her concentration broken, all the items fell to the floor. Several of the halfs scattered as the couch came down, and then the pool table.

I wiggled my fingers. "Long time no see, huh?"

Caleb snapped out of it and within two seconds, he'd crossed the length of the room and pulled me into a mammoth hug. Then he picked me up and swung me around.

"Where in the hell have you been?" He put me on my feet. "Three years, Alex? What the hell? Do you even know what half of the students said happened to you and your mom? We thought you were dead! I could seriously punch you in the face, like right now."

I could barely hold back my smile. "I've missed you, too."

He kept staring at me like I was some kind of mirage. "I can't believe you're really standing here. You better have a wild story for me."

I laughed. "Like what?"

"You better have had a baby, killed someone, or slept with a pure. Those are your three options. Anything less is totally unacceptable."

"You're so gonna be disappointed, because it wasn't anything exciting."

Caleb dropped his arm around my shoulders and steered me to one of the couches. "Then you gotta tell me what the hell you've been doing and how you got back here. And why didn't you call any of us? There isn't a single place in this world that doesn't have cell service."

"I'd go with she probably killed someone."

I tilted my head back and spotted Jackson Manos in the group of halfs I didn't recognize. He looked exactly as I remembered him. Dark hair parted down the middle, a body made just for girls to drool over, and equally dark, sexy eyes. I gave him my best smile. "Whatever, you douche. I didn't kill anyone."

Jackson shook his head as he approached us. "Do you remember dropping Nick on his neck during takedown practice? You nearly killed him. Good thing we heal as quickly as we do, or you would've put him out of training for months."

We all laughed at the memory. Poor Nick had spent a

week in the infirmary after the incident. Our good time and general curiosity drew the other halfs to the couch. Knowing I had to answer some of the questions regarding my absence eventually, I came up with a pretty bland tale about Mom wanting to live among mortals. Caleb looked at me doubtfully, but he didn't push it.

"What the hell are you wearing, by the way? It looks like the guy's training uniform." Caleb plucked at my sleeve.

"It's all I have." I gave a dramatic, pitiful sigh. "I doubt I'm going to get out anytime soon, and I don't have any money."

He grinned. "I know where they keep all the training clothes here. Tomorrow, I can pick you up some extra stuff in town."

"You don't have to. And besides, I don't think I want you shopping for me. I'd end up looking like a stripper."

Caleb laughed, the skin around his blue eyes crinkling. "Don't worry about it. Dad sent me a near fortune a few weeks ago. Guess he feels bad for being a dick of a father. Anyway, I'll get one of the girls to go with me or something."

The pure—Thea was her name—eventually made her way over to where we sat. She seemed nice and genuinely interested in me, but she asked the one question I feared.

"So, has your mother...reconciled with Lucian?" she asked in a small, childlike voice.

I forced myself not to show any reaction. "No." She looked surprised. So did the halfs.

"But...they can't divorce," said Caleb. "Are they going to do the separate house, different zip code thing?"

Pures never divorced. They believed their mates were predestined by the gods. I'd always thought it was a load of bull, but the "no divorce" thing explained why so many of them had affairs.

"Uh...no," I said. "Mom...didn't make it out there."

Caleb's mouth dropped open. "Oh. Man, I'm sorry."

I forced myself to shrug. "It's okay."

"What happened to her?" Jackson asked, as tactless as ever.

Taking a deep breath, I decided to tell them the truth. "A daimon got her."

That led to another round of questions, all of which I answered truthfully. Each of their faces mirrored shock and awe as I got around to the part where I'd fought and killed two of the daimons. Even Jackson seemed impressed. None of them had ever seen a daimon in real life.

I didn't go into detail about my meeting with Marcus, but I did tell them my summer wasn't going to be all fun and games. When I mentioned I'd be training with Aiden, a collective groan sounded.

"What?" I looked around the group.

Caleb stood up from the couch. "Aiden is one of the toughest—"

"Roughest," Jackson added solemnly.

"Meanest," threw in a half-blood girl with super short brown hair. I think her name was Elena.

Unease shifted through me. What had I gotten myself into with him? And they weren't done with their descriptions.

"Strongest," another kid added.

Elena glanced around the room, her lips curving. "Sexiest." There was a round of sighs from the girls, but Caleb frowned.

"That's not the point. Man, he's a beast. He's not even an Instructor. He's a Sentinel through and through."

"The last couple of graduating classes got assigned to his area." Jackson shook his head. "He's not even a Guide, but he weeded out over half of them and sent them back as Guards."

"Oh." I shrugged. That didn't sound all that bad. I was about to point that out when a new voice interrupted.

"Well, look who's back? If it isn't our one and only high school dropout," drawled Lea Samos.

I closed my eyes and counted to ten. I made it to five. "Are you lost, Lea? This isn't where they're handing out the free pregnancy tests."

"Oh boy." Caleb moved to stand behind the couch, getting out of the way. I didn't blame him. Lea and I had a legendary history. The write-ups Marcus had gone over for fighting had usually involved Lea.

She laughed that husky, throaty laugh I was all too familiar with.

I looked up then. She hadn't changed a bit.

Okay. That was a lie.

If anything, Lea had grown more beautiful in the last three years. With her long copper-colored hair, amethyst eyes, and impossibly tanned skin, she looked like some sort of glamorous model. I couldn't help but think of my own boring brown eyes.

While my own stellar reputation had my name whispered on many lips during my time here, Lea had literally prowled the Covenant. No—she'd owned it.

Her eyes dropped the length of me as she stalked across the rec room, taking in the oversized shirt and rumpled jogging pants. One perfectly groomed brow arched. "Don't you look lovely?"

She, of course, was dressed in the tightest and shortest skirt known to man. "Isn't that the same skirt you wore in the third grade? It's getting a little tight. You may want to go up a size or three."

Lea smirked and tossed the mass of hair over her shoulder.

She sat in one of the fluorescent moon chairs across from us. "What happened to your face?"

"What happened to yours?" I retorted. "You look like a damn tangerine. You should lay off the spray tanning, Lea."

There were a couple of snickers from our impromptu audience, but Lea ignored them. She was focused on me—her archnemesis. We'd been at this since we were seven. Sandbox enemies, I guess. "You know what I heard this morning?"

I sighed. "What?"

Jackson sauntered to her side, his dark eyes devouring her long legs. He moved behind her and tugged a strand of her hair. "Lea, knock it off. She just got back."

My brows rose as she motioned him down with a flick of her little finger. He lowered his mouth to hers. Slowly I turned to Caleb. Looking bored with the display, he shrugged. Instructors couldn't prevent the students from hooking up. I mean, come on. With a bunch of teenagers thrown together, it happened, but the Covenant frowned upon it. Usually the students didn't flaunt it.

When they were done tonguing one another, Lea returned to staring at me. "I heard Dean Andros didn't want you back. Your very own uncle wanted to place you into servitude. How sad is that?"

I flipped her off.

"It took three pures to convince her uncle she's worth keeping around."

Caleb snorted. "Alex is one of the best. I doubt it took much convincing."

Lea opened her mouth, but I cut her off. "I *was* one of the best. And it did. Apparently, I have a bad reputation, and he felt I had missed too much time."

"What?" Caleb stared at me.

I shrugged. "I have until the end of summer to prove to Marcus I can get caught up in time to join the rest of the students. It's no big deal, right, Lea?" I faced her, grinning. "I think you remember the last time we sparred? It was a long time ago, but I'm sure you can recall it quite clearly."

A pink flush crawled over her tanned cheeks, and her hand crept to her nose in what looked like a subconscious move, drawing an even bigger grin from me. At such a young age, our sparring was supposed to have been an absolutely no-contact training exercise.

But one insult had led to another, and I'd broken her nose.

In two places.

It'd also landed me in suspension for three weeks.

Lea's plump lips thinned. "You know what else I know, Alex?"

I folded my arms over my chest. "What?"

"While everyone here may believe whatever ridiculous excuse you gave for your mother leaving, I know the real reason." Her eyes sparkled with malice.

Coldness settled over me. "And how do you know?"

Her lips curved at the corners as she met my stare. I vaguely noticed Jackson moving away from her. "Your mother met with Grandma Piperi."

Grandma Piperi? I rolled my eyes. Piperi was a crazy old woman who was supposed to be an oracle. The pures believed she communed with the gods. I believed she communed with a lot of liquor.

"So?" I said.

"I know what Grandma Piperi said to make your mother go crazy. She was crazy, right?"

I was on my feet without realizing it. "Lea, shut up."

She looked at me, eyes wide and unfazed. "Now Alex,

you may want to calm down. One little fight and you'll be cleaning toilets for the rest of your life."

My hands clutched. Had she been in the room, under Marcus's desk or something? How else would she know so much? But Lea was correct, and that sucked. Being the bigger person meant walking away from her. It was harder than I ever imagined, like walking through quicksand. The more I moved, the more the air around me literally demanded that I stay and break her nose again. But I did it, and I made it past her chair without hitting her.

I was a totally different person—a better person.

"Don't you want to know what she said to your mother to make her crazy? To make her leave? You'll be happy to know it had everything to do with you."

I stopped. Just like Lea knew I would.

Caleb appeared at my side and grabbed my arm. "Come on, Alex. If what she's saying is true then you don't need to fall for this crap. You know she doesn't know anything."

Lea twisted around and threw one slender arm over the back of her chair. "But I do. You see, your mother and Piperi weren't alone in the garden. Someone else overheard her conversation."

I shrugged off Caleb's grip and turned around. "Who heard them?"

She shrugged, studying her painted nails. I knew right then and there, I would end up hitting her.

"The oracle told your mother you would be the one to kill her. Considering you couldn't stop a daimon from draining her, I guess Piperi meant it in the abstract sense. What good is a half-blood who can't even protect her own mother? Is it any wonder why Marcus didn't want you back?"

There was a moment when no one moved in the room,

not even me. Then I smiled at her, right before I grabbed a handful of copper hair and yanked her out of the chair.

Screw being a better person.

CHAPTER FOUR

The way her mouth dropped open as she fell backward almost made up for her cruel words. Clearly she hadn't expected me to do anything, thinking the threat of being expelled was far too great. Lea didn't know the power of her own words.

I jerked my arm back, fully intending on undoing whatever the doctors had done to fix that perky little nose of hers, but my fist never landed. In fact, Caleb got to me before I could take another step toward her. He literally carried me out of the rec room, and then put me down and blocked my path back to Lea. There was a wild grin on his face as I tried to dart around him.

"Let me pass, Caleb. I swear to the gods, I'm going to break her face!"

"Back not even a day, Alex. Wow."

"Shut up." I glared at him.

"Alex, knock it off. You get into a fight and you're going to get kicked out. What then? Be a servant for the rest of your life? Anyway, you know she's lying. So let it go."

I glanced down at my hand and noticed several strands of red hair wrapped around my fingers. Sweet.

Caleb saw the vicious gleam in my eye and seemed to realize staying near this room wasn't going to end well. Grabbing my arm, he all but dragged me down the hallway. "She's just a stupid girl. You know she was just talking crap, right?"

"Who knows?" I grumbled. "She's right, you know? I have no idea why Mom left. She could've spoken to Grandma Piperi. I don't know."

"I seriously doubt the oracle said you would kill your mom." Unconvinced, I punched the front door open.

Caleb followed close behind. "Just forget about it, okay? You've got to focus on training, not Lea and what the oracle may have said."

"Easier said than done."

"Okay. Then you could ask the oracle what she told your mom."

I stared at him.

"What? You could ask the oracle, if it bothers you that much."

"There is no way that woman is still alive." I winced at the blinding sun. "It was three years ago when Mom would've talked to her."

Now Caleb gave me the same look.

"What? She can't be. She would have to be…like a hundred and fifty years old by now."

Pures had a lot of power and an oracle would have even more, but none of them were immortal.

"Alex, she's the oracle. She'll be alive until the next one comes into power."

I rolled my eyes at Caleb. "She's just a nutty old woman.

Communes with the gods? The only things she communes with are the trees and her bridge club."

He made a sound of exasperation. "It never fails to amaze me that being what you are—what we are—you still don't believe in the gods."

"No. I do believe in them. I just think of them as absentee landlords. Right now, they're probably hanging out somewhere in Las Vegas, screwing showgirls and cheating at poker."

Caleb jumped away from me, his feet landing on the white and tan pebbles. "Do not let me be standing next to you when one of them strikes you down."

I laughed. "Yeah, they're really watching and taking care of business. That's why we have daimons running around draining pures and killing mortals for the fun of it."

"That's why the gods have us." Caleb grinned like he'd just explained everything.

"Whatever." We stopped at the end of the stone pathway. From here, we either went to the girls' dorm or the boys'.

The two of us stared across the flooded marsh. Woody plants and low growing bushes dotted the brackish water, making crossing the mess almost impossible. Beyond that was the forest—literally a no-man's-land. When I was younger, I'd thought monsters lived in the dark woods. When I'd gotten older, I'd learned that following the marshes led to the main island, giving me a perfect escape route when I'd wanted to sneak around.

"Does the old hag still live in there?" I asked finally. What if I could talk to Piperi?

Caleb nodded. "I guess, but who knows? She comes down to the campus every once in a while."

"Oh." I squinted in the harsh light. "You know what I was thinking?"

He glanced at me. "What?"

"Mom never told me why we needed to leave, Caleb. Never once during those three years. I think I'd be...more okay if I knew why Mom left in the first place. I know it doesn't change anything that happened, but at least I'd know what the hell was so important we had to leave here."

"Only the oracle knows. But you can't go to her—she lives way back there. Even I don't venture that far into the marshes. So don't even think about it."

My lips curved at the corners. "All these years, and you still know me so well."

He snickered. "Maybe we can throw her a party and lure her out. I think she was down here for the spring equinox."

"Really?" Maybe if I talked to the oracle, she'd give me some answers—or tell my future.

Caleb shrugged. "Can't remember, but speaking of partying, there's going to be one this weekend over on the main island. Zarak's throwing it. You game?"

I stifled a yawn. "Zarak? Wow. I haven't seen him in forever, but I doubt partying is something I'm going to be partaking in anytime soon. I'm permanently grounded."

"What?" Caleb's mouth dropped open. "You can sneak out. You were like the queen of sneaking out."

"Yeah, but that was before my uncle became the dean, and I wasn't one step away from being expelled."

Caleb snorted. "Alex, you almost got expelled like three times. Since when has that stopped you? Anyway, I'm sure we can come up with something. Besides, it'll be like a welcome back party for you."

It was a bad idea, but I felt the usual excitement stirring in my belly. "Well...I won't be training at night."

"No," agreed Caleb.

A grin tugged at my lips. "And sneaking out never killed anyone."

"Or got them expelled."

We grinned at each other, and just like that, things were the way they'd been before everything had gone to hell.

Caleb and I had a little adventure in the supply room in the main school building after dinner. We swiped every possible article of clothing that would fit me, and Caleb promised once again to grab one of the other half girls and go shopping for me the following day. I could only imagine what he'd come back with.

With our arms full, we headed back to my dorm. I was only a little surprised when I spotted Aiden's formidable frame standing by the thick marble columns on the wide porch. Caleb's eyes went wide.

I groaned. "Busted."

My footsteps slowed as we neared him. I couldn't read anything from his stoic expression or by the way he bowed his head toward Caleb in a respectful manner. For once in his entire life, Caleb was struck speechless when Aiden stepped up and took the armful of clothing from him.

"Need I remind you that males are not allowed in the girls' dormitory, Nicolo?"

Caleb shook his head mutely.

He raised his brows as he turned to me. "We need to talk."

I looked at Caleb helplessly, but he backed off with an apologetic half smile. For a hot second, I considered following him. I didn't.

"What do we need to talk about?"

Aiden motioned me forward with a curt nod. "You haven't rested at all today, have you?"

I shifted my load to my other arm. "No. I've been catching up with friends."

He seemed to consider that as we made our way down the hall. Thank the gods I'd been given a room on the bottom floor. I hated stairs, and even though the Covenant had more money than I could comprehend, there wasn't a single elevator on the entire campus.

"You should've been resting. Tomorrow won't be easy for you."

"You could always make it easy for me."

Aiden laughed. The sound was a rich, deep noise that would've brought a smile to my face in a different situation. Like one in which he wasn't laughing at me.

I frowned as I pushed the door to my room open. "Why are you allowed in my room if Caleb isn't?"

He arched an eyebrow. "I'm not a student."

"Still a guy." I took my load of clothing to my bedroom, where I dropped it on the floor. "You're not even an Instructor or a Guide. So I think if you're allowed in here, Caleb should be, too."

Aiden studied me for a moment, folding his arms across his chest. "I've been told you were once interested in becoming a Sentinel instead of a Guard."

I plopped down on the bed and grinned up at him. "You've been checking up on me."

"I decided I'd better be prepared."

"I'm sure you were told wonderful things about me."

He rolled his eyes. "Most of what Dean Andros said was correct. You are well known with the Instructors. They did praise your talent and ambition. The other stuff…well, that can be expected. You were just a kid—still a kid."

"I'm not a kid."

Aiden's lips twitched as if he wished to smile. "You're still a kid."

My cheeks flushed. It was one thing being told I was a kid by any other person. Who cared? But when it was a super-hot guy telling me that, it didn't leave me all warm and fuzzy inside.

"I'm not a kid," I repeated.

"Really? Then you must be an adult?"

"Sure." I gave him my best smile, the one that usually got me out of trouble.

Aiden was unaffected. "Interesting. An adult would know when to walk away from a fight, Alex. Especially after being warned any questionable behavior could result in their removal from the Covenant."

My smiled faded. "I have no idea what you're talking about, but I would have to agree."

Aiden tipped his head to the side. "You don't?"

"Nope."

A small smile appeared on his lips. It should've served as a warning, but I found myself staring at those lips in place of paying attention to *him*. Suddenly he crouched in front of me at eye level.

"Then I should be relieved to know what I was told just an hour ago is false. It wasn't you who yanked a girl—by her hair—out of a chair in the common lounge area."

I opened my mouth to deny it, but my protests died. Dammit. There was *always* someone willing to rat people out.

"Do you understand the precarious position you're in?" His firm gaze held mine. "How foolish it is to allow simple words to lead you to violence?"

Pulling Lea out of the chair had been foolish, but she'd pissed me off. "She was talking about my mother."

"Does it matter? Think about it. It's just words, and words

mean nothing. Only action does. Are you going to fight every single person who says something about you or your mother? If so, you should go ahead and pack your bags now."

"But—"

"There are going to be rumors—ridiculous rumors about why your mother left. Why you didn't come back. You can't fight every single person who upsets you."

I tipped my head to the side. "I could try."

"Alex, you need to focus on getting back into the Covenant. Right now, you're here as a courtesy. You want revenge against the daimons, right?"

"Yes!" My voice turned fierce as my fists clenched.

"You want to be able to get out there and fight them? Then you need to pay attention to training instead of what people are saying about you."

"But she said I was the reason Mom died!" Hearing my voice crack the way it did, I had to look away. It was weak of me. Embarrassing. Weak and embarrassing were not in a Sentinel's vocabulary.

"Alex, look at me."

I hesitated before I did. For a moment, the hardness in his expression softened. When he looked at me like that, I truly believed he understood my reaction. Maybe he didn't agree with it, but at least he understood why I'd done it.

"You know there was nothing you could do about what happened to your mother." His eyes searched my face. "You do know that, right?"

"I should've done something. I had all that time, and I should've called someone. Maybe then…" I ran my hand through my hair and took a deep breath. "Maybe then none of this would've happened."

"Alex, you couldn't have known it would end this way."

"But I did." I closed my eyes, feeling a twisting in my stomach. "We all do. It's what happens when you leave the safety of the community. I knew it would happen, but I was just scared they wouldn't let her back in after leaving. I couldn't…leave her out there by herself."

Aiden was silent for so long, I thought he'd left the room, but then I felt his hand on my shoulder. I opened my eyes, turning my head so I looked down at his hand. His fingers were long and graceful looking. Deadly, I imagined. But now, they were gentle. Like I had no will of my own, I looked into his silver eyes. I couldn't help but be reminded of what'd passed between us at the factory.

Abruptly, Aiden let go. Running a hand through his hair, he looked unsure of what he was doing. "Look. Get some rest. Eight in the morning will come quick." He turned to leave but stopped. "And don't leave this room again tonight. I don't want to find out in the morning you burnt down a village while I slept."

There were several retorts I had lined up, all of them clever and snarky, but I squelched them and pulled myself off the bed. Aiden stopped at my door and glanced down the empty hallway.

"Alex, what happened to your mother is not your fault. Placing that kind of guilt on yourself will only hinder you. It will get you nowhere. Do you understand?"

"Yeah," I lied.

Even though I wanted to believe what Aiden said was true, I knew it wasn't. If I'd contacted the Covenant, Mom would still be alive. So yeah, in a way, Lea was right.

I was responsible for my mother's death.

CHAPTER FIVE

The following day was like going back in time for me—up way too early to think straight and wearing clothes made to get my butt kicked in. This time around, though, a few things were different.

Looking at Aiden, for example, it was clear he wasn't going to be like the Instructors I'd had before. They'd been Sentinels or Guards injured on the job, or the ones who'd wanted to settle down. Back then, I'd always ended up with Instructors who were either old as dirt or flat-out boring.

Aiden was neither of those things.

He wore the same style of workout pants I'd stolen from the supply closet, but where I wore a modest white shirt, he had on a tank. And boy, did he have arms to show off. His skin didn't sag, he was far from boring, and he was actually out there hunting daimons. But he did have one thing in common with my old Instructors.

The moment I walked into the gym, he was all business. From the way he coached me through several warm-up exercises and ordered me to unroll all the mats, I knew I was going to be hurting by the end of the day.

"How much do you remember from your previous training?"

I looked around, seeing things I hadn't laid eyes on in three years—training mats to ease falls, dummies with skin that felt real, and a first aid kit in every corner. People usually bled at some point in training. But the farthest wall interested me the most. It was covered with wicked-looking knives I'd never gotten to practice with. "The normal things: textbook stuff, offensive training, kicking and punching techniques." I made a beeline for the weapon wall; it was like compulsion.

"Not much, then."

Picking up one of the slender titanium daggers the Sentinels usually carried, I nodded. "The good stuff started just—"

Aiden reached around me, plucking the dagger from my fingers and placing it back on the wall. His fingers lingered over the blade reverently. "You haven't earned the right to touch these weapons, especially *that* one."

At first, I thought he was teasing, but one look at his face told me he wasn't. "Why?"

He didn't answer.

I kind of wanted to touch it again, but I pulled my hand back and walked away from the wall. "I was good at everything I learned. I could hit and kick hard. I could run faster than anyone in my class."

He returned to the center of the room and placed his hands on his narrow hips. "Not much, then," he repeated.

My eyes followed him. "You could say that."

"You should get used to this room. We'll be spending eight hours a day in here."

"You're joking, right?"

He didn't look like he was joking. "Down the hall is a gym. You should visit it…*often*."

My mouth dropped open.

Aiden gave me a bland look. "You're far too skinny. You need to put some weight on and some muscle." He reached out and tapped my scrawny arm. "Speed and strength, you have naturally. But right now, a ten-year-old could take you on."

I closed my mouth. He had a point. This morning, I'd had to tie the knot twice in my drawstrings to get them to stay up. "Well, it wasn't like I had three square meals a day. Speaking of which, I'm kinda hungry. Don't I get breakfast?"

The hard look in his eyes softened a little, and for a moment he looked like he had when he'd been in my room the night before. "I brought you a protein shake."

"Ew," I groaned, but when he picked up the plastic container and handed it to me, I took it.

"Drink up. We're going to cover some ground rules first." Aiden stepped back. "Go ahead and sit. I want you to listen."

And there went the softer and kinder look. Rolling my eyes, I sat down and gingerly placed the bottle to my lips. It smelled like stale chocolate and tasted like a watered-down milkshake. Gross.

He stood in front of me with those impossibly ripped arms across his chest. "First off: no drinking or smoking."

"Gee. That means I've got to kick the crack habit."

He stared down at me, clearly unimpressed. "You will not be able to leave the Covenant without permission or—don't look at me that way."

"Jeez, how old are you?" I totally knew how old he was, but I wanted to pick.

Aiden cracked his neck. "I turn twenty-one in October."

"Huh." I shook the bottle. "So, have you always been so… mature?"

His brows furrowed. "Mature?"

"Yeah, you sound like a dad." I deepened my voice and tried to look stern. "Don't look at me that way or else."

Aiden blinked slowly. "I don't sound like that, and I didn't say 'or else.'"

"But if you had, what would the 'or else' be?" I hid my grin with the bottle.

He glanced to the side, frowning. "Can you just not talk through this?"

"Whatever." I took a drink. "Why can't I leave the island?"

"It's for your safety and my peace of mind." Aiden returned to his original stance, arms over chest, legs spread wide. "You will not leave this island without being accompanied by someone."

"Do my friends count?" I asked, only half serious.

"No."

"Then who's allowed to accompany me?"

Aiden's eyes closed and he sighed. "Either me or one of the other Instructors."

I swished the liquid around in the bottle. "I know the rules, Aiden. You don't have to go over them again."

He looked like he wanted to point out that I could probably use a refresher, but he relented. After I was done, he took the bottle and walked it back over to where several punching bags were propped against the wall.

I stood and stretched. "So, what am I learning today? I think we should start with anything that doesn't involve you kicking my ass."

His lips twitched as if he was fighting a grin. "The basics."

"The basics." I pouted. "You've got to be kidding me. I know the basics."

"You know enough to not get yourself killed right away." He frowned as I jumped from side to side. "What are you doing?"

I stopped, shrugging. "I'm bored."

Aiden rolled his eyes. "Then let's get started. You won't be bored for very long."

"Yes, master."

He scowled. "Don't call me that. I'm not your master. Only the gods can be called our masters."

"Yes..." I paused as his eyes glinted and his jaw tightened. "*Sir.*"

Aiden stared at me a moment, and then nodded. "Okay. I want to see how you take a fall."

"I almost got one good hit on you in the factory." I felt the need to point that out.

Turning to me, he motioned toward one of the mats. "Almost doesn't count, Alex. It never counts."

I dragged myself over and stopped in front of him as he circled me. "Daimons not only use their strength when they attack, but also elemental magic."

"Yeah. Yeah."

Daimons could be ridiculously strong depending on how many pures or halfs they'd drained. Being hit by one of them using the air element was tantamount to getting hit by a freight train. The only time daimons weren't dangerous was when they were draining aether.

"The key is to never let them get you on the ground, but it will happen, even to the best of us. When it does happen, you need to be able to get back up." His gray eyes focused on me.

This was boring. "Aiden, I do remember my training. I know how to take a fall."

"Do you?"

"Taking a fall is the easiest—"

My back slammed into the mat. Pain shot through me. I lay there stunned.

Aiden loomed over me. "That was just a love tap, and you didn't land correctly at all."

"Ow." I wasn't sure I could move.

"You should've landed on your upper back. It's less painful and easier to maneuver out of." He offered his hand. "I thought you knew how to take a fall?"

"Gods," I snapped. "You couldn't have told me first?" I ignored his hand and found I could move. I stood, glaring at him.

A lopsided smile formed on his lips. "Even without a warning, you have a second before you fall. You have more than enough time to position your body correctly."

"Roll the hips and keep your chin down." I scowled, rubbing my back. "Yeah, I remember."

"Then show me." He stopped, eyeing me like I was some kind of weird specimen. "Put your arms up—here. Like this." He positioned my arms so they blocked my chest. "Keep them strong. No spaghetti arms."

"Okay."

He grimaced at my spindly arms. "Well, keep them as strong as you can."

"Hardy har har."

He grinned again. "All right."

Then he hit my arms with the broad side of his. In truth, he didn't hit me hard, but I still fell. And it was the wrong way. I rolled over, wincing.

"Alex, you know what to do."

I rolled over and groaned. "Well...apparently it's something I've forgotten."

"Get up." He offered his hand, but I still didn't take it. I stood. "Put your arms up."

I did and braced myself for the inevitable smack. Down I went, over and over again. I spent the next couple of hours on my back, and not in the good way. It got to the point Aiden went through the mechanics of landing as if I were ten.

But finally, out of the useless crap floating around my brain, I pulled out the technique I'd been taught ages ago, and I nailed it.

"About time," Aiden muttered.

We broke for lunch, which consisted of me eating alone while Aiden went off to do whatever. About fifteen minutes in, a pure blood in a white lab coat appeared in front of me. I swallowed the mouthful of food. "Hi?"

"Please follow me," she said.

I glanced down at my half-eaten sub and sighed. I dumped my plate and followed the pure to the med building behind the training facilities. "Am I getting a physical or something?"

She didn't answer.

Any attempt at conversation was ignored, and I gave up by the time I hopped up on the table. I watched her go to the cabinet and root around for a few seconds. She turned around, flicking the end of the syringe.

My eyes widened. "Uh...what is that?"

"Please lift up the sleeve of your shirt."

Wary, I did as instructed. "But what are you giving me—*dammit*!" My skin burned from where she'd jabbed me in the upper arm. "That hurt like hell."

Her lips curved in a faint smile, but her words dripped disgust. "You will be reminded in six months to receive another dose. For the next forty-eight hours, please try to refrain from unprotected sexual activities."

Try to refrain? As if I had uncontrollable animalistic urges and jumped every half in sight? "I'm not sex crazed, lady."

The pure turned her back, clearly dismissing me. I jumped off the table, tugging my sleeve down. I couldn't believe I'd forgotten about the Covenant's mandatory birth control for female half-bloods. After all, the offspring of two halfs were like mortals and useless to the pures. That had never really bothered me since I doubted I'd ever develop a parental urge. But the pure could have at least given me a heads-up before she stuck me.

When I returned to the training room, Aiden eyed me rubbing my arm, but I didn't explain. From there, he moved on to another favorite of mine: getting knocked down and jumping to my feet.

I sucked at that, too.

By the end of practice, every muscle in my back ached, and my thighs felt like someone had sucker punched them. I was a little slow in rolling the mats. So much so that Aiden eventually took over.

"It'll get easier." He looked up as I limped over to where he was piling the mats. "Your body will get used to it again."

"I hope so."

"You should hold off on the gym for a few days."

I could've hugged him.

"But you should definitely do the warm-up stretches at night. It will help loosen up your muscles. You won't be so sore then."

I followed him to the door. It sounded like good advice. Outside the training room, I waited while Aiden shut the double doors.

"Tomorrow we'll work on the jump some more. Then we'll move on to blocking techniques."

I started to point out I'd learned several blocking techniques, but I remembered how quickly the daimon had tagged me in Georgia. My hand went to my shoulder and over the slightly irregular scar.

"You okay?"

Dropping my hand, I nodded. "Yeah."

As if he could somehow read minds, he stepped forward and brushed my thick ponytail back over my shoulder. The slight touch elicited a shiver. "It's not bad. It'll be gone soon enough."

"It's going to scar—it has already scarred."

"Some would say such scars are badges of honor."

"Really?"

Aiden nodded his head. "Yes. It shows how strong and how brave you were. It's nothing to be ashamed of."

"Sure." I forced a quick, bright smile.

I could tell by the look on his face he didn't believe me, but he didn't push it. I limped off, heading back to my room. Caleb waited outside my door with a handful of shopping bags and a nervous look on his face.

"Caleb, you didn't have to do all that. And you're going to get busted over here."

"Then let me in your room before I get caught. And don't worry about the shopping. I got some hot chicks to try clothes on for me. Trust me, mutually beneficial day for me."

I snorted as I limped over to the couch and eased myself down. "Thanks. I owe you."

Caleb launched into all the things I'd missed during my *absence*—that was how I was referring to it now—while I pulled out various jeans, dresses, and shorts I doubted met the

Covenant dress code. I shook my head. Where in the hell was I supposed to wear some of this stuff?

Apparently, not much had changed. Everyone still snuck off and hooked up with everyone. Lea had successfully pitted two or three boys against one another in hopes of getting her attention. Jackson looked like the winner if yesterday had been any indication. Two halfs a year older than us, Rosalie and Nathaniel, had graduated and were now Sentinels, and I was beside myself with envy. After today's practice, I doubted Aiden still thought I had any raw potential.

Luke, a half I used to hang out with, had come out of the closet last year—not that being gay or bisexual was even remotely a big deal around here. Being the children of a bunch of horny gods who sure didn't discriminate when choosing their sexual partners left little to be shocked about when it came to sex.

It appeared I was the only virgin around here. I sighed.

"Was your training that bad?"

"I think I broke my back today," I deadpanned.

He looked like he wanted to laugh. "You didn't break your back. You're just…out of practice. In a couple of days, you'll be kicking Aiden's butt."

"Doubtful."

"So, what did he want yesterday? Man, I'll be honest. I'm waiting for him to pop in here and beat the crap out of me for being in your room."

"Then you shouldn't be in here if you're scared."

Caleb ignored that. "What did Aiden want yesterday?"

"I think Lea ratted my ass out. Aiden knew about the thing in the rec room. He really didn't bitch me out, but I could've done without the lecture."

"Damn, she is such a bitch sometimes." He sat back in the chair, running a hand through his hair. "Maybe we could burn off her eyebrows or something. I'm sure Zarak would be down with that."

I laughed. "I'm sure that won't help my cause."

"You know, I hooked up—"

"What?" I shrieked, nearly coming off the couch. Wrong move. It hurt. "Please tell me you didn't hook up with Lea?"

He shrugged. "I was bored. She was available."

Disgusted, I tossed a pillow at his head and cut him off. "I don't want to know the details. I'm just going to pretend you never admitted to that."

A grin appeared on his lips. "Well, it seems like Lea's determined to get you in trouble if she ratted you out."

I lay back down, thinking about the others in the room. "I don't know. What about the pure who was in the room?"

"Who? Thea?" He shook his head. "There's no way she would've told anyone."

"What's Thea doing here, anyway?"

It was odd to see any pure at the Covenant during the summer. They stayed during the school year, but when summer came, they went off with their parents—probably traveling the world and doing other ridiculously expensive things. Fun, totally cool things. Of course, they had Guards who accompanied them on their adventures, just in case a daimon got any ideas.

"Her parents are on the Council, and they don't have any time for her. She's really nice, but super quiet. I think she's got the hots for Deacon."

"Deacon, as in Aiden's brother?"

"Yup."

I could tell there was something behind the fact Thea liked him. "What's the big deal? They're both pures."

Caleb arched a brow at me, but then seemed to

remember I hadn't been here for three years. "Deacon has a reputation."

"Okay." I tried to work out a sudden kink in my back.

"So does Thea. And let's just say Thea wins the purity award."

Good to know I wasn't the only virgin. "And?"

"Deacon's reputation is…more of the—hmm, how do I stay this nicely?" He paused, looking thoughtful. "Deacon takes after Zeus—that kind of reputation."

"Well…opposites attract, I guess."

"Not *that* opposite."

I shrugged, and then winced.

"I almost forgot. You won't believe what I heard today in town. One of the shop owners was busy running her mouth while I was checking out, totally uncaring about who could hear her, but—oh yeah, by the way, that shop owner probably thinks I'm a cross-dresser now."

I smiled.

He rolled his eyes. "Anyway, do you remember Kelia Lothos?"

My lips pursed. Kelia Lothos—the name did sound familiar. "Wasn't she a Guard here?"

"Yeah, she's about ten years older than us. She got herself a boyfriend."

"Good for her."

"Wait for it, Alex. You must wait for it. His name is Hector—not sure what his last name is. But he's a pure from one of the other communities." He stopped for dramatic effect.

I ran a hand over my ponytail, not sure where he was going with any of this.

"He's a freaking pure blood." He raised his hands. "Remember? Not allowed."

My eyes popped wide. "Oh no, not good."

He shook his head and strands of blond hair fell over his eyes. "I can't believe they were stupid enough to even consider something like that."

The fact that we weren't allowed to have any type of romantic relationship with a pure was a rule ingrained in us since birth. Most half-bloods didn't even question it, but then again, most halfs didn't question much. We were trained into obedience from the get-go. I tried to find a comfortable position. "What do you think will happen to Kelia?"

Caleb snorted. "She'll probably be stripped of her Guard duties and sent to work in one of the houses."

That filled me with annoyance and resentment. "And Hector will get a smack on the hand. How fair is that?"

He looked at me strangely. "It's not, but that's what happens."

"It's stupid." I felt something tighten in my jaw. "Who cares if a half and a pure get together? Is it really a big enough deal that Kelia has to lose everything?"

Caleb's eyes widened. "It's the way it is, Alex. You know that."

I folded my arms, wondering why I felt so strongly about it myself. It was the way things had been for eons, but it seemed so unfair. "It's wrong, Caleb. Kelia's basically going to end up a slave all because she hooked up with a pure."

He was quiet for a moment and then his eyes zeroed in on me. "Does your reaction have anything to do with the fact your new personal trainer happens to be the pure all the chicks drool over?"

I made a face. "Absolutely not—are you insane? He's going to end up killing me." I paused, sinking down in the cushion. "I think he plans on it."

"Whatever."

Stretching out my legs, I pinned him with a glare. "You forget I spent three years out there in the normal world—a world where pures and halfs don't even exist. No one checks someone's godly pedigree before going out with them."

He stared off in the distance a few moments. "What was it like?"

"What was what like?"

Caleb fidgeted on the edge of the chair. "Being out there, away from all of…this?"

"Oh." I propped myself onto my elbow. Most halfs had no idea what it was like. Sure, they mingled in the outside world—mingled being the key word—but they were never a part of it, not for any amount of time. Neither were the pures. To our kind, the mortal life seemed like a violent one, where daimons weren't the only evil things people had to worry about.

Yeah, we had our crazies, too. The guys who didn't have the word "no" in their vocabulary, the backstabbing girls, and people who'd do *anything* to get what they wanted. But it was nothing like the mortal world, and I wasn't sure if that was a good or bad thing.

"Well, it's different. There are so many people who are different. I kinda blended in to a point."

Caleb listened with far too much excitement for his own good as I tried explaining what it was like out there. Whenever we moved around, Mom had used compulsions to get me into the local school system without transcripts. Caleb showed way too much interest in the mortal school system, but it was different than the Covenant. Here, we spent most of our days fighting in class. Out in the mortal world, I'd spent most of my classes staring at the chalkboard.

Being curious about the outside world wasn't necessarily a good thing. It usually led someone to make a run for it. Mom and I had been more successful than most of those who'd ventured out. The Covenant always found the people who tried to live in the outside world.

They'd just found us a little too late.

Caleb tilted his head sideways as he studied me. "How you doing being back here?"

I lay back down, staring up at the ceiling. "Good."

"Seriously?" He stood up. "Because you've been through a lot."

"Yeah, I'm okay."

Caleb made his way over and sat down, practically shoving me on my side. "Ouch."

"Alex, the crap that's happened has to have, you know, bothered you. It would've messed with me."

I closed my eyes. "Caleb, I appreciate your concern, but you're practically sitting on me."

He shifted but remained beside me. "Are you gonna talk to me about it?"

"Look. I'm doing okay. It's not like it hasn't bothered me." I pried my eyes open and found him watching me expectantly "Okay. It's messed with me. Happy?"

"Of course, I'm not happy."

One thing I wasn't good at was talking about how I felt. Hell, I wasn't even good at *thinking* about how I felt. But it didn't look like Caleb was moving any time soon. "I…try not to think about it. It's better that way."

He frowned. "Really? Do I need to use basic psychology on you and go with, 'it's probably not a good thing you don't think about it?'"

I groaned. "I hate psychobabble, so please don't start."

"Alex?"

I sat up, ignoring the way my back screamed, and pushed him off the couch. He caught himself easily. "What do you want me to say? That I miss my mom? Yes. I miss her. That it totally sucked seeing her get drained by a daimon? Yes, it sucked. Fighting daimons and thinking I was going to die was fun? No. It wasn't fun. That *also* sucked ass."

He nodded, accepting my little rant. "Did you get to have a funeral for her or anything?"

"That's a stupid question, Caleb." I pushed back the hair that had escaped my ponytail. "I didn't get to have a funeral. After I killed the daimon, there was another one. I ran."

His face paled. "Did anyone go back for her body?"

I cringed. "I don't know. I haven't asked."

He seemed to mull it over. "Maybe if you had a ceremony for her, it would help. You know, a little gathering just to remember her."

I leveled a hard look at him. "We're not having a funeral. I mean it. If you even think about something like that, I will risk getting expelled just to kick your ass." Having a funeral meant facing that my mother was dead. The wall—the toughness I'd built around me—would break and I…I couldn't deal with that.

"Okay. Okay." He held up his hands. "I just thought it would bring you some closure."

"I have closure. Remember? I saw her die."

This time he was the one to cringe. "Alex…I'm so sorry. Gods, I don't even know how you must've felt. I cannot even imagine it." He then took a step forward, as if he intended to hug me, but I waved him off. Caleb seemed to get I didn't want to talk about it anymore, so he switched back to safer topics—more gossip, more tales of Covenant shenanigans.

I remained on the couch after he'd snuck back out of the dorm. I should've been hungry or ready to go socialize, but I wasn't. Our conversation—the part about my mom—lingered like a festering wound. I tried focusing on the gossip I'd learned. I even tried thinking about how nice Jackson looked now—even Caleb, because he'd really filled out in the last three years—but their images were quickly replaced by Aiden and his arms.

And that was *so* wrong.

I shifted back down and went back to staring at the ceiling. I was okay. I was great, actually. Being back at the Covenant was far better than being out there in the normal world or cleaning toilets in some pure's house. I rubbed under my eyes, frowning. I was okay.

I had to be okay.

CHAPTER SIX

I wanted to curl up in a hole and die.

"There you go." Aiden nodded as I deflected one of his blows. "Use your forearm. Move with purpose."

Move with purpose? How about moving to a spot where I could lie down? That was a purpose I could get behind. Aiden launched himself at me, and I blocked his jab. Hell yeah, I was good at that. Next, he swung around, and for someone so freaking tall, he sure could move that body like a ninja.

The heel of his foot slipped past my arms and slammed into my side. The impact barely registered on my pain scale. By now, I'd gotten used to the sharp spike of pain and the throbbing that followed. I inhaled slowly and tried to breathe through the agony. Half-bloods didn't show pain in the face of the enemy. At least I remembered that.

Aiden straightened, concern flickering over his face. "You okay?"

I clenched my teeth. "Yes."

He approached me, looking doubtful. “That was a pretty hard hit, Alex. It’s okay if it hurts. We’ll take a few minutes.”

“No.” I walked it off while he watched. “I’m fine. Let’s try this again.”

And we did. Missing a few jabs and kicks was far better than having to run laps like yesterday or spend the entire afternoon in the gym.

That’s what’d happened when I’d whined about my back and sides hurting last time. Aiden went through several more blocking techniques a ten-year-old could master while I obsessively watched his movements. Over the past couple of days, I’d realized how far behind I really was, and even I was amazed that I’d managed to kill two daimons.

I couldn’t even block most of Aiden’s kicks.

“Watch me.” He circled me, his body taut. “There is always something that’ll give away my next move. It could be a fine tremor of the muscle or a brief glance, but there is always something. When a daimon attacks, it’s no different.”

I nodded and we squared off again. Aiden moved in with one swipe of the hand. I knocked his arm away, and then the other. It wasn’t his jabs or punches I had a problem with. It was his kicks—he spun around so fast. But this time, I saw his eyes drop to my waist. Twisting into the kick, I brought my arm down in a clean sweeping motion a second too late. His foot connected with my bruised back. I doubled over immediately, grasping my knees as I slowly breathed in and out.

Right away, Aiden was at my side. “Alex?”

“That…stung a bit.”

“If it makes you feel better, you almost had it this time.”

I looked up and gave a short laugh at the sight of his lopsided grin. “Good to hear.”

He started to say something, but his grin faded as his voice gave a low warning. "Alex. Stand up."

My back protested such a sudden move, but the moment I saw Marcus at the door, I understood why. I didn't need to look like I'd just gotten the crap knocked out of me in front of him.

Marcus leaned against the door, arms folded. "I wondered how training was going. I see it's moving along expectedly."

Ouch. I took a deep breath. "Would you like to give it a try?"

Marcus's brows rose and he smiled, but Aiden placed a warning hand on my arm. "Don't."

I shook his hand off. I was pretty sure I could take my uncle. With his perfectly groomed hair and pressed khakis, he looked like a poster child for yacht-club-of-the-month.

"I'm game if you are," I offered again with a bright smile.

"Alex, I'm telling you not to do this. He used to be—"

Marcus pushed away from the wall. "It's all right, Aiden. I wouldn't accept such a ridiculous offer normally, but I find myself feeling charitable."

I snickered. "Charitable?"

"Marcus, this isn't necessary." Aiden moved in front of me. "She's only beginning to learn blocks correctly."

I scowled at Aiden. *Jeez. Way to have my back there, buddy.* My ego roared back to life, and I pushed around Aiden. "I think I got him."

Marcus tipped his head back and laughed, but Aiden looked less than amused by the whole situation.

"Alex, I'm telling you *not* to do this. Be quiet and listen to me."

I looked at Aiden innocently. "Do what?"

"No. *She has this*, Aiden. Let's see what she's learned. Since she is challenging me, I assume she is ready."

I planted my hands on my hips. "I don't know. I'd feel bad for beating up an old guy."

Marcus's bright emerald gaze settled on me. "Attack me."

"What?"

He looked perplexed, but then he snapped his fingers. "That's right! You haven't learned any real attack moves. Then I shall attack you. You do know defensive blocking techniques?"

Marcus knew about defensive blocking techniques? I shifted my weight and glanced at Aiden. He did not look pleased by any of this. "Yeah."

"Then you should be adeptly trained to defend yourself." Marcus paused and the smile slipped away. "Just picture me as the enemy, Alexandria."

"Oh, that won't be too hard, *Dean Andros*." I raised my hands and motioned him forward. I was a total badass.

Marcus gave no warning other than the fine tremor in his arm right before he moved. I raised my arm, just as Aiden instructed, and blocked the jab. I couldn't fight the wild grin as I deflected another bone-jarring punch. My gaze narrowed on my uncle as he straightened and prepared for another attack.

"Back off." Aiden's voice came from the sidelines, low and harsh. "You're too close."

I pushed forward, blocking another one of Marcus's hits.

Cockiness took over. "You've got to be faster—"

Instead of Marcus following through on what I expected would be a pretty damn good roundhouse kick, he grabbed my arm and twisted. As he spun my body, he brought his other arm around my neck, placing me in a brutal chokehold.

My heart slammed against my ribs. Any movement I made only succeeded in twisting my arm to an even more unnatural angle. Within seconds, he'd rendered me helpless. In any other situation, like one where it wasn't *my uncle* holding *me* in a chokehold, I would've given him props for such quick maneuvering.

He bent his head, speaking directly into my ear. "Now just imagine if I was a daimon," said Marcus. "What do you think would happen next?"

I refused to answer, clenching my teeth.

"Alexandria, I asked you a question. What would happen if I was a daimon?" His grip tightened.

My gaze met Aiden's. He watched the whole thing with helpless anger etched into his face. I could tell there was a part of him that wanted to step in, but he knew he couldn't.

"Do we need to try this again?" asked Marcus.

"No! I'd…be dead."

"Yes. You'd be dead." Marcus let go, and I stumbled forward. He brushed past me, addressing Aiden. "If you even hope to have her ready by fall, you may want to work on her attitude and make sure she actually takes your instructions next time. If she continues this way, she will fail."

Not taking his eyes off me for one second, he gave Marcus a curt nod.

I silently fumed until the moment Marcus disappeared. "What the hell did I ever do to him?" I rubbed my neck absently. "He could've broken my arm!"

"If he wanted to break your arm, he would have. I told you to be quiet, Alex. What did you expect from Marcus? Did you think he was just some lazy pure blood who needed protection?" His voice dripped sarcasm.

"Well, he looks like one! How was I supposed to know he was secretly Rambo in Dockers?"

Aiden stalked up to me, reaching out and catching my chin. "You should have known, because I told you not to push him. Yet, you still did. You didn't listen to me. He used to be a Sentinel, Alex."

"What? Marcus was a Sentinel? I didn't know that!"

"I tried to tell you that." Aiden closed his eyes and let go of my chin. Turning away, he ran a hand through his hair. "Marcus is right. You won't be ready in the fall if you don't listen to me." He sighed. "This is why I could never be an Instructor or a Guide. I don't have the patience for this crap."

This was one of those times I knew I needed to shut up, but I couldn't. Angry as hell, I followed him across the mats. "I am listening to you!"

He whirled around. "What part did you listen to, Alex? I explicitly told you not to push him. If you can't listen to me, how can anyone—including Marcus—expect you to listen to your Instructors in the fall?"

He was right, but I was too embarrassed and angry to admit it. "He only did that because he doesn't like me."

He gave an exasperated sound. "It has nothing to do with whether or not he likes you, Alex. It has everything to do with the fact that you don't listen! You've spent too much time out there where you could easily defend yourself against mortals, but you're not in the mortal world anymore."

"I know that. I'm not stupid!"

"Really?" His eyes flashed into a furious silver. "You are behind every single person here. Even the pure-bloods who'll be attending school in the fall will have the basic knowledge of how to defend themselves. You still want to be a Sentinel? After what you've shown me today, I doubt that is the case. Do you know what makes a Sentinel? Obedience, Alex."

I felt my cheeks flush. The sudden rush of hot tears stung my eyes. I blinked and turned away from him.

Aiden cursed under his breath. "I'm…not trying to

embarrass you, Alex. But these are the facts. We've only been training for a week, and you have a long road ahead of you. You need to listen to me."

Once I was pretty sure I wouldn't start crying, I faced him. "Why did you even stick up for me? When Marcus wanted to hand me over to Lucian?"

Aiden glanced away, frowning. "Because you have potential, and we can't afford to have that potential wasted."

"If I…hadn't missed so much time, I know I'd be good."

He turned back to me, eyes shifting back to a softer gray. "I know, but you did miss a lot of time. Now we have to get you back to where you need to be. Battling your uncle is not going to help you."

My shoulders slumped and I looked away. "He hates me. He really does."

"Alex, he doesn't hate you."

"Oh no, I think he does. This was the first time I've seen him since the first morning here, and he was more than eager to prove that I'm a jackass. It's obvious he doesn't want me to be trained."

"That's not the case."

I looked at him. "Really? Then what *is* the case?" Aiden opened his mouth but closed it. "Yeah. Exactly."

He was quiet for a few moments. "Were you two ever close?"

I gave a short laugh. "Before? No. I only saw him when he visited Mom. He never paid any attention to me. I always figured he was one of the pures who weren't too fond of…my kind."

There were a lot of pures out there who looked down on halfs, seeing us more like second-class citizens than anything else. They knew they needed us, but it didn't change how they viewed us as something other than pure.

"Marcus has never felt that way about...halfs."

I shrugged, suddenly tired of talking. "I guess it's just me, then." I glanced up and forced a weak smile. "So...will you show me what I did wrong?"

"Which part?" His mouth tightened. "All of it?"

He finally smiled, but the usual banter we shot back and forth at each other during our training sessions disappeared. His direct and formal instructions made his disappointment in me clear. But what could I do? I hadn't known Marcus was Chuck Norris. I'd lost my temper. So what? So why did I feel icky?

After practice, I still couldn't shake the feeling of being an utter failure. Not even when Caleb showed up at my door hours later.

Frowning, I stepped aside and let him in. "You're really good at sneaking into this dorm, Caleb."

He smirked, but it faded as he took in my sweat-stained clothing. "It's Zarak's party. Tonight. Remember?"

"Dammit. No." I kicked the door shut.

"Well, you'd better get ready. Like now. We're already late."

I debated telling him I wasn't feeling up to it, but the idea of sulking around my room didn't seem entertaining. I figured I deserved a night of fun after the day I'd had, and it wasn't like Aiden or Marcus would know if I decided to go to Zarak's. "I need to take a quick shower first. Make yourself comfortable."

"Sure." He plopped down on the couch and picked up the remote control. "There are going to be a lot of the pures there. Ones who haven't seen you since you came back. Of course, they know you're back. Everyone is talking about it."

Rolling my eyes, I pushed on the bathroom door and stripped off my clothes. I wasn't worried about Caleb popping in on me. It'd be like walking in on his sister naked; I doubted he wanted to see my goods. As I twisted in front of the mirror, I caught sight of a smorgasbord of bluish splotches covering my back and my sides. Yuck. I turned away.

Caleb continued from the living room. "Lea and Jackson got into a huge fight today, right on the beach for everyone to see. It was fun to watch."

I wasn't so sure about that. After a quick shower, I dried my hair so it fell in somewhat manageable waves. Now what to wear?

"Are you almost done in there? Gods, I'm bored."

"Almost." I pulled out a pair of jeans and a shirt even though I wanted to wear the little black dress Caleb had picked out, but the low back would show all the bruises.

Caleb stood up as I walked into the living room. "You look hot."

I scrunched up my face. "You think this is hot?"

He laughed as he turned toward the door. "No."

By the time we met some other halfs at the edge of campus, Caleb's running monologue about who was going to be at the party had driven out the worst of my foul mood. Caleb kept sneaking looks at one of the girls who'd joined us as we trekked across the bridge to the main island. It was easy to forget about practice and all I'd missed in the last couple of years.

It wasn't hard for us to make it past the Guards. None of them recognized me, or if they did, they didn't care enough to send me back to my room. They were used to kids making their way back and forth between the two islands, especially during the summer. "Wow." One of the girls let out a low exhale as we skirted along the sand dunes. "The party's definitely in high gear."

She was right. As soon as we rounded the bend, pures and halfs spilled out from the large beach house. It'd been ages since I'd been to Zarak's house. Like Thea, his parents held seats on the Council, had a lot of money, and had little time for their pure-blood offspring. With its incredible views of the ocean, pale-blue siding, and whitewashed decks, Zarak's parents' beach house was identical to the house Mom had lived in. I assumed her house still stood on the opposite side of the island. A mixture of grief and happiness flowed through me. I saw myself as a little girl, playing on the porch, running through the sand dunes, laughing, and I saw Mom, smiling down at me. She always had been smiling.

"Hey." Caleb came up behind me. "You doing okay?"

"Yeah."

He slipped his arms around my shoulders and gave them a squeeze. "Come on, you're gonna be like some kind of rock star here. Everyone's going to be happy to see you."

Walking up to the beach house, I did kind of feel like a rock star. Everywhere I looked, someone called my name or rushed over to give me a hug and a warm, "Welcome back." For a while, I lost myself in the sea of familiar faces. Someone shoved a plastic cup in my hand; another topped it off from an open bottle, and before I knew it, I was buzzing happily among old friends.

I headed up the wide steps, hoping to find Zarak somewhere in the house. He was, after all, one of my favorite pure-bloods. Dodging around two halfs making out while still maintaining firm grips on their red plastic cups—an amazing ability by the way—I slid into the less-crowded kitchen. Finally, I spotted the recognizable head of blond curls. He appeared occupied with a cute blonde girl.

I was pretty positive I'd be interrupting, but I didn't think

Zarak would mind. He had to have missed me. I walked up and tapped my fingers along the curve of his shoulder. It took a moment for him to lift his head and turn around. A pair of startling gray eyes—clearly not Zarak's—met mine.

CHAPTER SEVEN

I took a step back. I'd never seen the boy before, but there was something oddly familiar about those eyes and the planes of his face.

"What do we have here?" He gave me a lazy smile. "A half eager to make my acquaintance?" He looked back at the other girl, then to me.

"Oh well…I thought you were someone else. Sorry."

Amusement sparkled in his eyes. "I guess I was being presumptuous, wasn't I?"

I couldn't help but grin. "Yes, you were."

"But weren't you being presumptuous by assuming I was someone else? Does it matter?" I shook my head. "Well, I should introduce myself." He took a step forward and bowed—literally, bent at the waist and bowed. "I'm Deacon St. Delphi, and you are?"

My jaw almost hit the floor. Honestly, I should've known the minute I saw his eyes. They were nearly identical to Aiden's.

Deacon's lips turned into a smug grin. "I see you've heard of me."

"Yeah, I know your brother."

His brows rose. "My perfect brother knows a half-blood? Interesting. What's your name?"

Clearly annoyed with the lack of attention, the girl behind him huffed and slipped around us. My gaze followed her, but he didn't spare her a glance. "My name's Alexandria Andros, but—"

"But everyone calls you Alex." Deacon sighed. "Yes. I've heard of you, too."

I took a sip of my drink, eyeing him over the cup. "Well, then. I'm afraid to ask."

He walked over to the counter and picked up a bottle, taking a healthy gulp. "You're the one my brother spent months chasing after and now is saddled with training."

My smile turned sour. "Saddled with?"

He chuckled, dangling the bottle of liquor from his fingers. "Not that I'd mind being saddled with you. But my brother...well, he tends to rarely enjoy what's in front of him. Take me, for example. He spends the bulk of his free time making sure I'm behaving like a good pure instead of enjoying myself. Now...he'll spend all his time making sure *you* behave."

That made little sense to me. "I don't think your brother is very fond of me at the moment."

"I doubt that." He offered me the bottle. I shook my head. Pouring himself a drink, he smiled widely. "I'm sure my brother is very fond of you."

"Why would you—"

Setting the bottle aside, he picked up a glass and placed a finger to the rim. Flames shot around the glass. A second later, he blew the fire out and downed the glass. Another damn firestarter, which was another thing I should've known. Pure's affinities toward certain elements tended to run in families.

"Why would I think that?" Deacon leaned down as if he were about to share a major secret. "Because I know my brother, and I know he wouldn't have volunteered to get any old half-blood up to par. He's not the most patient of people."

I frowned. "He's pretty damn patient with me." Except maybe for today, but I wasn't sharing that.

Deacon gave me a knowing look. "Need I say more?"

"I guess not."

He seemed to find that equally amusing. Wrapping his free arm around my shoulders, he steered me toward the porch and right into the path of Lea and Elena, the girl I'd met in the lounge my first day back. The only reason I remembered her name was because of her super short haircut.

I sighed.

Deacon looked sideways at me. "Friends of yours?"

"Not really," I muttered.

"Hey redhead," he murmured. "Looking good."

I had to give it to said redhead. Lea looked exquisite in the slinky red dress that clung to every curve of her body. She was hotness—just too bad she was a complete and total bitch.

Her gaze drifted over me and then Deacon's arm, which still hung over my shoulder. "Oh gods, please tell me you've spilled a drink on your shirt and you're temporarily walking with her to hide the stain. Because Deacon, I'd rather floss my teeth with a daimon's back hair than parade a growth like that around."

Deacon raised his brows at me. "Guess you're right about the 'not really friends' thing."

I gave him a bland look.

He turned a megawatt smile on Lea. He even had dimples, ones I was sure Aiden would have if he ever really smiled. "You have such a pretty mouth for such ugly words."

Lea simpered. "You've never cared about how I've used my mouth before, Deacon."

I gaped at Deacon. "Oh…wow."

His lips curved into a half smile, but he didn't respond. I scooted away from him and tugged Caleb back to the sprawling porch. It wasn't too crowded now. Glancing over my shoulder, I noticed that Lea and Deacon had stepped farther back into the room.

"Okay. Did I miss something while I was gone?" I asked.

Caleb's face scrunched up. "What are you talking about?"

"Are Lea and Deacon messing around?"

He busted out laughing. "No, but they like to talk a lot of smack."

I hit him on the arm. "Don't laugh at me. What if people thought they were? Lea could get in some major trouble."

"They're not messing around, Alex. Lea's stupid, but not that stupid. Even if they are trying to change the Breed Order laws, no half around here is willingly going to fool around with a pure."

"They're changing the Breed Order?"

"Trying is the key word. Succeeding is a totally different story." Caleb's eyes shot wide at the unexpected voice. I spun around, nearly dropping my cup. Kain Poros sat on the edge of the railing, dressed in Covenant fatigues.

"What are you doing here?"

"Babysitting," Kain grumbled. "And I don't care what you're drinking, so stop looking for a place to dump your cup."

Once I got over my shock at his blasé attitude toward

underage drinking, I smiled brightly. "So they're trying to change the Breed Order?"

"Yep, but it's meeting a lot of resistance." He stopped, his gaze narrowing on a half who was getting too close to the bonfire someone had decided to start. "Hey! Yes! You! Get the hell back now."

Caleb reached around me, inconspicuously sitting his cup down. "I hate that they even call it the Breed Order. It sounds so ridiculous."

"I have to agree." Kain nodded. "But that's what they've always called it."

We'd gathered a little audience at this point. "Will someone please fill me in on what the hell they're trying to change?"

"It's a petition to remove the order against the two breeds mixing." A boy with brown hair cropped close to the head smirked.

"A petition to allow halfs and pures to mix?" My eyes went wide. "What brought this on?"

The pure boy snorted. "Don't look too hopeful there. It's not going to happen. Allowing halfs and pures to mix isn't the only thing they're aiming for. The Council isn't going to go against the gods, and they sure as hell aren't going to allow halfs on the Council. It's nothing to get excited about."

The strong inclination to launch my cup at his face was hard to ignore, but I doubted Kain would stand for that. "Who are you?"

His eyes sharpened on me, obviously not liking my tone. "Shouldn't I be asking that question, half-blood?"

Caleb cut in before I could respond. "His name is Cody Hale."

I ignored Caleb and scowled at the pure. "Should I know who you are?"

"Knock it off, Alex." Kain climbed off the railing, effectively reminding me of my place in the scheme of things. If Cody said jump, I'd have to say how high. Mouthing off at him wasn't how a half treated a pure—ever. "Anyway, I overheard Council members talking about it. The halfs from the Tennessee Covenant have a strong following. They're petitioning to be on the Council."

"I doubt they'll get anywhere there," Caleb said.

"We don't know," Kain responded. "There's a good chance the Council will hear them in November, and maybe even agree."

My brows rose. "When did this all come about?"

"About a year ago." Kain shrugged. "It's picked up a lot of movement. The South Dakota Covenant is also getting involved. It's about time, too."

"What about here and New York?" I asked.

Caleb snorted. "Alex, the North Carolina branch still exists in the Greek times, and with the main Council being located in New York, they're going to hold onto all the old rules and rites. Upstate is a totally different world. It's brutal there."

"If there's such a huge movement, then why are Hector and Kelia in so much trouble?" I frowned, remembering Caleb telling me their story.

"Because nothing has passed, and I think our Ministers are looking to make an example out of them." Kain's mouth tightened.

"Yeah, a way of reminding us of where we belong and what happens when we don't follow the rules." Jackson pushed through the little group, smiling in spite of how depressing his words were.

"Oh, for the love of the gods," Kain snapped. Twisting

around, he loped off the porch. Two halfs were trying to get a dune buggy started. "You two better not even be within a mile of that thing by the time I get over there. Yes! You two!"

Talk about the petition dwindled off as more plastic cups were passed around. Apparently, political discussion was only socially acceptable before the third cup. I was still mulling over the Breed Order and what it could mean when Jackson sat down on the swing next to me.

I glanced up, smiling. "Hey."

He flashed a charming smile. "Have you seen Lea?"

"Who hasn't?" I giggled.

He didn't find that nearly as funny as I did, but my catty remark served two purposes. Jackson glued himself to my hip the rest of the evening, and when Lea reappeared, her face turned a mottled shade of red when she saw how close Jackson and I were. And we were really super-close on the porch swing. I was practically in his lap.

I tipped my cup at her.

The narrow-eyed look she sent my way said it all. Pleased with myself, I turned back to Jackson with a smug smile. "Your girlfriend doesn't look too happy."

"She hasn't been since you got back." He ran a finger down my arm. "What's going on between you two, anyway?"

Lea and I had always been like this. I imagined it had a lot to do with the fact both of us were aggressive, confrontational, and pretty damn awesome. But there was more; I just couldn't remember it. I shrugged. "Who knows?"

Zarak finally appeared and was most happy to see me. Thanks to him and Cody, everyone was keen on the idea of moving the party elsewhere by taking mommy and daddy's Porsches down to Myrtle.

Since I had my hands full with Jackson, I'd lost track of

Caleb at some point, and I hid my half full plastic cup behind the swing. I was okay with the happy buzz, but I was only a few sips away from a dizzy, fall-on-my-face buzz.

"You going with them?"

Frowning, I glanced over at Jackson. "Huh?"

He grinned, leaning in so that his lips almost brushed my ear when he spoke. "Going to Myrtle?"

"Oh." I swung my feet back and forth. "I don't know, but it sounds like fun."

Jackson grabbed my hands, hauling me to my feet. "Zarak's leaving. We can catch a ride with him."

I must've missed the part when he and I had turned into "we," but I didn't protest when he led me down the steps and across the beach. Several of the kids had left already, and I caught a quick glimpse of Lea sliding into the back seat with Deacon. I had no idea where Kain was; I hadn't seen him since the dune buggy incident. Zarak slid into the driver's seat of the only other car left—at least he seemed okay enough to be behind a wheel. The girl I'd seen earlier with Deacon was taking her sweet time deciding which car was the cooler one.

Growing bored, I leaned against the side of the house while the girl chatted with Lea. Jackson propped himself beside me.

I tipped my head back, loving the way the warm breeze caressed my cheeks. "Shouldn't you be going with her?"

He paused, looking over his shoulder. "She obviously has other plans."

"But she's staring at you," I pointed out. She had her face planted against the window.

"Let her look." He shifted closer, flashing a wicked grin. "She's made her call, hasn't she?"

"Guess so."

"I've made mine." Jackson leaned in to kiss me.

Even though I would've loved to see Lea's face in the aftermath of kissing Jackson, I darted to the side. Jackson was an equal opportunity player, and that kind of game I didn't really feel like joining.

He chuckled and made a playful grab for me. He got a good hold on my arm and pulled me back. "You gonna make me chase you?"

My happy buzz had the potential of becoming a very bad one if he kept this crap up. Pulling my arm free, I forced a smile. "You'd better get going. Zarak's going to leave you."

He reached for me again, but I dodged those too-friendly hands. "Aren't you going?"

I shook my head. "Nah. I think I'm going to call it a night."

"I can keep you company if that's what you want. We can take the party back to my dorm or Zarak's room." He started walking backward toward the car. "I don't think he'd mind. Last chance, Alex."

It took every ounce of my self-control not to laugh. I shook my head and backed off, knowing I looked like a total tease. "Maybe next time." Then I turned around, not giving Jackson another moment to sway me into that car.

Wondering if Caleb had gone to Myrtle, I made my way back across the beach and toward the bridge, passing several silent beach homes. The air around me smelled of sea salt. I loved that smell. It reminded me of Mom and the days we used to spend hanging out on the sand. So caught up in the memories, I only snapped back to reality when a fine shiver coursed down my spine as I neared the bridge.

The scraggly bushes and tall weeds swayed in the cool breeze. Odd since the breeze had been pleasant only minutes before. I took a step forward, scanning the marsh. Gloom covered the bog, but a thicker shadow pulled away from the rest, becoming more solid as the seconds passed.

The wind carried a whisper. *"Lexie…"*

I had to be hearing things. Only Mom had called me Lexie. Nothing could be out there, but fear still coiled like tight springs in my stomach.

Without warning, strong hands gripped my shoulders and pulled me back. My heart stopped, and for a moment, I didn't know who'd grabbed me from behind. Instinct to lash out kicked into gear, but then I caught the familiar scent of soap and ocean.

Aiden.

"What are you doing?" His voice held a demanding edge.

I twisted around and stared up at him. His eyes were thin slits. Seeing him rendered me speechless for a second. "I… There's something out there."

Aiden's hands slipped from my shoulders as he turned to where I pointed. Naturally there was nothing there but the normal shadows the moon cast across the marshland. He faced me. "There's nothing there. What are you doing out here by yourself? You aren't allowed off the island without supervision, Alex. Never."

Yikes. I took a step back, unsure how to respond.

Then he leaned over, sniffing the air. "You've been drinking."

"Have not."

His brows rose, lips pursed. "What are you doing outside the Covenant?"

I fidgeted with the edge of my shirt. "I was…visiting friends, and as I recall, I was told I couldn't leave the island. Technically, I'm still on Deity Island."

He tipped his head to the side, folding his arms. "I'm

pretty certain that remaining on the Covenant-controlled island was assumed."

"Well, you know what they say about assuming things."

"Alex." His voice lowered in warning.

"What are you doing out here, creeping around in the dark like some kind of…creeper?" Once that last little bit left my mouth, I kind of wanted to slap myself.

Aiden laughed in disbelief. "Not that you need to know, but I was in the process of following a group of idiots to Myrtle Beach."

My jaw dropped. "You were following them?"

"Yes, a handful of us Sentinels were." Aiden's lips curved in an uneven grin. "What? You look surprised. Do you really think we'd let a bunch of teenagers off this island without protection? They may not realize we're always trailing them, but no one gets out of here without us knowing."

"Well…that's just fantastic." I stored that little piece of knowledge away. "Why are you still here, then?"

He didn't immediately answer the question, since he was busy shuffling me back toward the bridge. "I saw you didn't go with them."

I stumbled. "What…exactly did you see?"

He glanced down at me, quirking an eyebrow. "Enough." Flushing to the roots of my hair, I groaned.

Aiden chuckled low and under his breath, but I heard him. "Why didn't you go with them?"

I debated on pointing out he already knew why but decided I was already in enough trouble. "I…figured I'd engaged in enough stupidity for the evening."

He actually laughed louder then. It was deep and rich. Nice. I glanced up quickly, hoping to see *his* dimples. No such luck. "It's good to hear you say that."

My shoulders slumped. "So, how much trouble am I in?"

Aiden seemed to consider that for a few moments. "I'm not going to tell Marcus, if that's what you're hinting at."

Surprised, I grinned up at him. "Thanks."

He looked away, shaking his head. "Don't thank me yet."

I remembered the first time he'd said that to me. I wondered when I was supposed to thank him.

"But I don't want to catch you with a drink in your hand again."

I rolled my eyes. "Jeez, there you go, sounding like a dad again. You need to start sounding like you're almost twenty-one."

He ignored that, nodding at the Guards we passed on the opposite end of the bridge. "It's bad enough I have to chase down my brother. Please don't add to my troubles."

I dared a peek at him. He stared straight ahead, a muscle feathering along his jaw. "Yeah...he seems like a handful."

"And then some."

I remembered what Deacon said about Aiden making sure I behaved now. "I'm...sorry. I don't want you to feel like you have to babysit me."

Aiden gave me a sharp look. "Well...thank you."

I twisted my fingers together, feeling tongue-tied for some reason. "It must've been hard having to raise him, practically alone."

He snorted. "You have no idea."

I really didn't. Aiden had been just a kid himself when their parents had been killed. What if I'd had a little brother or sister and I were responsible for them? There was no way. I couldn't even put myself in that situation.

A few moments passed before I asked, "How...did you do it?"

"Do what, Alex?"

We passed the bridge and the Covenant loomed ahead of us. I slowed my steps. "How did you take care of Deacon after…something so terrible happening?"

A stiff smile formed on his lips. "I had no other choice. I refused to allow Deacon to be handed over to another family. I think…my parents would've wanted me to be the one to raise him."

"But that's a lot of responsibility. How did you do it while going to school? Hell, while training?"

Graduating the Covenant didn't mean training ended for a Sentinel. The first year on the job was notoriously fierce. Time was split between shadowing trained Sentinels called Guides and still training in high-impact martial art classes and stress tests.

He shoved his hands into the deep pockets of his black, Covenant-issued uniform. "There were times when I considered doing what my family would've wanted for me. Going to college and coming back, engaging in the politics of our world. I know my parents would've wanted me to take care of Deacon, but the last thing they would've ever chosen was for me to become a Sentinel. They never understood…this kind of life."

Most pures didn't, and I didn't fully understand it until I'd seen my mother attacked. Not until then did I fully grasp the need for Sentinels. Pushing the troubling thought away, I tried to think of what I remembered about his parents.

They'd been young-looking, like most pures were, and from what I knew, they'd been powerful. "They were on the Council, right?"

He nodded. "But after their death, being a Sentinel was what I wanted."

"Something you *needed*," I corrected softly.

His step slowed, and he looked surprised. "You're right. Becoming a Sentinel was something I needed—I still do." He paused, looking away. "You would know. It's what you need."

"Yeah."

"How did you survive?" He turned the question on me.

Growing uncomfortable, I focused on the still water of the ocean. At night, under the light of the moon, it looked as dark and thick as oil. "I don't know."

"You had no other choice, Alex."

I shrugged. "I guess so."

"You don't like talking about it, do you?"

"Is it obvious?"

We stopped where the pathway split between the dorms. "You don't think it's a good idea for you to talk about it?" His voice held a serious tone that made him sound much older. "You've barely had any time to deal with what happened to your mother...what you witnessed and had to do."

I felt something tighten in my jaw. "What I had to do is what all Sentinels have to do. I'm training to kill daimons. And I can't talk to anyone. If Marcus even suspected I had problems dealing with it, he'd hand deliver me to Lucian."

Aiden stopped and when he looked at me, there was an infinite amount of patience on his face. Once again, I was struck by what Deacon had said. "You're only seventeen. Most Sentinels don't make their first kill until a year or so after graduation."

I sighed; now was a good time to change the subject. "You know what you said about your parents not wanting you to have this kind of life?"

Aiden nodded, a curious look on his face. He probably wondered where the hell I was going with this.

"I think—no, I *know* they would be proud of you, anyway."

He raised one eyebrow. "Do you think that because I offered to train you?"

"No. I think that because I remember you."

My words seemed to catch him off guard. "How? We didn't share any classes or schedules."

"I saw you around a few times. I always knew when you were around," I blurted out.

Aiden's lips tipped at the corners as he stared down at me. "What?"

I took a step back, flushing. "I mean, you had this reputation for being so kick-ass. Even though you were still in school, everyone knew you were going to be an awesome Sentinel."

"Oh." He laughed again, relaxing a little bit. "I suppose I should be flattered."

I nodded vigorously. "You should be. The halfs look up to you. Well, the ones who want to be Sentinels. Just the other day, they were telling me about how many kills you've made. It's legendary. Especially for a pure—I'm sorry. I don't mean killing a lot of daimons is necessarily a good thing or something to be proud of, but…I need to shut up now."

"No. I understand what you're saying. Killing is a necessity of our world. Each one takes its toll, because the daimon used to be a good person. Someone you may have known. It's never easy to take someone's life, but to stare down at someone you once considered a friend is…much harder."

I made a face. "I don't know if I could do it…" I saw the amusement fade from his face. That must not have been the right response. "I mean, when we see the daimon, we halfs see them for what they truly look like. At least, at first and then we see them for who they used to be. The elemental magic changes them back, so they look like they used to. You already know that, of course, even if you don't see through the dark magic like we do. I could do it. I'm sure I could kill someone I once knew."

Aiden's lips pursed and he looked away. "It's hard when it's someone you knew."

"Have you ever fought one you knew before they went all dark side?"

"Yes."

I swallowed. "Did you…?"

"Yes. It wasn't easy." He faced me. "It's getting late, well past your curfew, and you aren't getting off easy for tonight. I expect to see you in the gym tomorrow by eight."

"What?" I'd assumed I had the weekend to myself.

He simply raised his brows. "Do I need to list the rules you've broken?"

I wanted to point out I wasn't the only one who'd broken rules tonight—and that some people who weren't me were still currently breaking rules—but I managed to keep my mouth shut. Even I could acknowledge my punishment could be far worse. Nodding, I started to walk up to my dorm.

"Alex?"

I turned around, figuring he'd changed his mind and was going to order me to see Marcus in the morning and fess up to my bad behavior. "Yeah?"

He brushed a lock of dark hair off his forehead and flashed that lopsided smile. "I remember you."

I scrunched up my face. "What?"

The grin increased to a full smile. And…oh man. He had dimples. The air in my lungs died. "I remember you, too."

CHAPTER EIGHT

I was being punished. It seemed that the part from last night's conversation about not being allowed off the Covenant-controlled island wasn't an assumption. Okay. I totally knew that, but honestly, was it really that big of a deal?

It was a big deal to Aiden.

He carted my butt to the gym first thing in the morning, and we spent the better part of the day there. He showed me a few exercises he wanted me to do, a couple of weight reps, and then a whole slew of cardio.

I hated cardio.

While I ran around from one exercise machine to the next, Aiden sat down, stretched out those long legs of his, and cracked open a book that probably weighed as much as I did.

I stared at the leg press machine. "What are you reading?"

He didn't look up. "If you're able to talk while working out, then you aren't working out hard enough."

I made a face at his bent head and climbed into the machine. After doing my reps, I realized there was no graceful way of getting out of the thing. Concerned I'd look like an idiot, I stole a quick glance at him before rolling out of the machine.

There were a few more machines he wanted me to work with, and I was quiet for the next five minutes or so. "Who reads books that big for fun?"

Aiden lifted his head, pinning me with a bored look. "Who talks to hear themselves speak?"

My eyes widened. "You're in a lovely mood today."

With the obscenely large book balanced on one knee, he turned a page. "You need to work on your upper body strength, Alex. Not your motor speech skills."

I glanced down at the dumbbell and pictured it flying across the room—at his face. But it was such a nice face, and I'd hate to ruin it. Hours went by like this. He'd read his book, I'd annoy him, he'd yell at me, and then I'd hop on another machine.

Sad as it was, I was kind of having fun messing with him and I think he was enjoying it, too. Every so often, a small—and I mean *really* small—smile would grace his lips whenever I'd ask him an irritating question. I wasn't even sure he was paying attention to the book of—"Alex, stop staring at me and do some cardio." He flipped another page.

I blinked. "I hope that book of yours is on charm and personality skills."

Aha! There was that ghost of a smile. "Cardio—do cardio. You're fast, Alex. Daimons are fast, too, and hungry daimons will be even faster."

My head fell back, and I groaned as I dragged myself over to the treadmill he'd pointed to earlier. "How long?"

"Sixty minutes."

Sweet baby in Hades! Was he insane? When I asked that,

he didn't find it funny. It took me several tries to get the treadmill working at a speed I could jog to.

Five minutes later, Aiden glanced up and saw how fast I was going. Exasperated with me, he stood and walked over to where I was jogging. Without a word, he increased the speed above four—I'd been at two—and then went back to his wall and his book.

Damn him.

Out of breath and still completely out of shape, I nearly fell off the treadmill when the time hit sixty minutes and slowed to cool-down mode. I glanced over to where Aiden leaned against the wall, engrossed in his mammoth-sized book.

"What…are you reading?"

He glanced up and sighed. "Greek Fables and Legends."

"Oh!" I'd always loved reading what the mortal world wrote about our gods. Some of it was kind of correct while the rest was just bonkers.

"I got it in the library. You know, it's the place you should be hanging out in your spare time instead of drinking."

I shuddered and shook my arms out. "I hate the library. Everyone hates the library here."

Shaking his head, he closed the book. "Why is it that halfs believe there are hellhounds, harpies, and furies living in the library? I don't get it."

"Have you not been in the library, seriously? Ugh. It's creepy and you hear stuff all the time. When I was a kid, I heard something growling in there once." I stepped off the treadmill and stopped in front of him. "Caleb heard wings flapping in there near the bottom level. I'm not kidding."

Aiden laughed deeply. "You guys are ridiculous. There's nothing in the library. And all those creatures have long since been removed from the mortal world. Anyway." He lifted the book and shook it. "It's one of your textbooks."

I dropped down beside him. "Oh. Boring. I can't believe you read textbooks for fun." I paused, considering that. "Never mind. On second thought, I can believe you read textbooks for fun."

He turned his head toward me. "Cool-down stretches."

"Yes, sir!" I saluted him, then stretched out my legs and grabbed my toes. "So, what legend are you reading about? How Zeus was the most promiscuous god of them all?" That was a legend the mortals actually got right. He was responsible for most of the original demigods all those years ago.

"No." He handed me the book. "Here. Why don't you take it and do some reading? I have a feeling after today you're going to spend some long evenings in your room."

I rolled my eyes, but I took the book. After practice, I met with Caleb and bitched for the next hour about how Aiden was being totally uncool. Then I bitched about how he'd disappeared on me last night, leaving me with Jackson.

Friends don't let friends act like idiots.

Shortly after, I did go back to my room instead of sneaking off with Caleb. I had a sinking suspicion if I did, I'd get caught, and I really didn't want to spend another day in the gym. It was bad enough I had to spend a good hour or two in it every night.

Bored out of my mind, I picked up the musty-smelling book and thumbed through the ancient thing. Half of the book was written in ancient Greek and out of my ability to decipher. It looked like a bunch of squiggly lines to me. After finding the part in English, I discovered it wasn't about legends or fables. It was actually a detailed account of each of the gods, what they represented, and their rise to power. There was even a section on pure-bloods and their lesser halfs—us. Literally, it was how we were listed in this book.

No joke:

The Pure Blood and their lesser half—the Half-Blood.

I skimmed through those pages, coming to a stop on a small block of text under the name "Ethos Krian." Even I remembered that name. All of us half-bloods did. He was the first of a very select group of half-bloods who could control the elements. But…oh, he was more than that. He was the first Apollyon—the only half-blood with the ability to control the elements and use the same kind of compulsion the pures could use on mortals.

In other words, the Apollyon was one big, badass of a half-blood.

Ethos Krian, born of a pure blood and a mortal in Naples, year 2848 ED (1256 AD), was the first recorded half-blood to display the abilities of a true Hematoi. As foreseen by the oracle of Rome, at the age of eighteen, the palingenesis awakened Ethos's power.

There were conflicting schools of thought on the origination of the Apollyon and his purpose. Popular belief stated the gods who held court in Olympia bestowed the gift of the four elements and the power of akasha, the fifth and final element, upon Ethos as a measure to ensure no pure-blood's power superseded that of their masters. The Apollyon had a direct linkage to the gods and acted as the Destroyer. The Apollyon was known as "The one who walks among the gods."

Since the birth of Ethos, one Apollyon had been born every generation as dictated by the oracle…

The section then proceeded to list the names of the other Apollyons, stopping in the year 3517 in the Hematoi calendar—1925 AD.

We *so* needed updated textbooks.

I skimmed past that part and turned the page. There was another part describing the characteristics of the Apollyon and another passage I was unfamiliar with.

My breath caught as I read it once, then twice. "No way."

Throughout time, only one Apollyon had been born to each generation with the exception of what came to be known as "The Tragedy of Solaris." In the year 3203 ED (1611 AD), a second Apollyon was discovered in the New World. The palingenesis awakened Solaris (last name and parentage unknown) into power on her eighteenth birthday, setting in place a chain of startling and dramatic events. To this date, there had never been an explanation of how two Apollyons existed within the same generation or why.

I read the section again. There were *never* two Apollyons. Ever.

I'd heard legends when I was a kid about the possibility of two, but I'd chalked them up as…well, legends. Continuing on, I quickly ascertained I didn't know jack.

It is believed the First sensed the marking of another Apollyon upon her eighteenth birthday and, unaware of the consequences, joined her in the New World. The effects of their union were chronicled as vast and damaging to both pure-bloods and their masters, the gods. Upon meeting, as if they were two halves meant to be one, the powers of Solaris shifted to the First Apollyon, so the First became what has always been feared: The God Killer. The power of the First became unstable and destructive.

The reaction from the gods, particularly the Order of Thanatos, was swift and righteous. Both Apollyons were executed without trial.

"Whoa…" I slammed the book shut and sat back. The

gods, when threatened, didn't mess around. One Apollyon acted as a check and balance system, able to fight anything, but if there were two of them at once?

There was an Apollyon now, but I'd never met him. He was kind of like a celebrity. We knew he was out there somewhere, but we never actually saw him in person. I knew the Apollyon focused on daimons instead of carrying out justice against pure-bloods now. Since the creation of the Council, pures no longer thought they could take on the gods—or, at least, they didn't say so openly.

I set the book aside and turned off the lamp. Poor Solaris.

Somewhere, the gods had goofed up and created two. It wasn't like it was her fault. She probably hadn't even seen it coming.

As the excitement of the Summer Solstice bubbled through the Covenant, I settled back into the life of a half-blood in training. The thrill of my presence had worn off, and most of the students who remained at the Covenant during the summer grew used to having me around. Granted, the fact I had killed two daimons secured my awesomeness. Even Lea's bitchy comments became less frequent.

Lea and Jackson broke up, got back together, and as far as I knew, were broken up again.

During the times Jackson was a free man, I developed a routine of avoiding him. Yeah, he was pure sexiness, but he was also superfast with his hands, and on more than one occasion I'd had to remove them from my butt. Caleb was always quick to point out I had no room to complain since I'd brought it on myself.

Another sort of odd routine developed, but this was

between Aiden and me. Being that I was always crabby in the morning, we usually started off practice with stretching and some laps—basically anything that prevented us from talking. By late morning, I was less likely to bite off his head and more receptive to digging into the real stuff. He never mentioned the night he'd busted me at the party, and we'd talked about each other's need to become a Sentinel. He also never really explained what he'd meant by, "I remember you."

Of course I came up with a crap ton of ridiculous explanations. My talent was so amazing that *everyone* knew who I was. Or my antics in and out of the training rooms had made me a legend in my own right. Or I'd been so stunningly beautiful he couldn't help but notice me. That last one was the most absurd. I'd been gawky and a total dweeb then. Not to mention someone like Aiden would never look at a half-blood in that way.

During training, Aiden was stern and rigid in his methods. Only a few times did he seem to slip up and grin when he thought I wasn't looking. But I was always watching.

Who could blame me? Aiden was…hotness incarnate. I alternated between staring at those ripped arms and being envious of how he moved with such fluid grace, but it was more than just his ability to make me drool on myself. Never in my life had I met someone so patient and tolerant of me. Gods knew I was annoying as hell, but Aiden treated me as if I were his equal. No pure really did that. The day I'd embarrassed myself by challenging my uncle seemed forgotten, and Aiden did everything to make sure I was coming along as expected.

With his guidance, I was getting used to the demands of training and the toll they took on my body. I even put some weight on. The dweeb part was still up in the air. Aiden *still* wouldn't let me get within ten feet of any of the cool-looking weapons.

On the day of the Summer Solstice, I tried approaching the wall of destruction toward the end of practice.

"Don't even think about it. You'd cut your hand off…or mine."

I froze, one hand inches from the wicked dagger. Dammit.

"Alex." Aiden sounded a bit amused. "We only have a little bit of time left. We need to work on your blocking."

Groaning, I pulled myself away from what I really wanted to learn. "Blocking again? That's all we've done for weeks."

Aiden folded his arms across his chest. Today he wore a plain white tee. He made it look good, very good. "That's not all we've done."

"Okay. I'm ready to move onto something else, like practicing with knives or defense against the dark arts. Cool things."

"Did you just quote something from the Harry Potter books?"

I grinned. "Maybe I did."

He shook his head. "We've been practicing kicks and jabs, Alex. And your blocking still needs work. How many of my kicks have you been able to block today?"

"Well…" I grimaced. He already knew the answer. I'd only managed to block a handful. "A couple, but you're fast."

"And daimons are faster than I am."

"I don't know about that." Nothing was as fast as Aiden. Half the time he moved like a blur. But I stepped into position and waited.

Aiden walked me through the maneuvers once more, and I could've sworn he slowed down his kicks just a bit, because I blocked more than I ever had before. We separated, about to start another round of kicks when a whistle sounded from the hallway. The culprit—bronze-haired Luke—stood at the door to the training room. I grinned and waved.

"You're not paying attention," Aiden snapped.

My grin slipped from my face as Luke and a couple of other halfs disappeared from view. "Sorry."

He exhaled slowly and motioned me forward. I complied without argument. "Is he another boy of yours? You're always with that other one."

My hands dropped to my sides. "*What?*"

Aiden brought his leg around fast. I barely had time to block it. "Is he another guy of yours?"

I didn't know if I should laugh, be pissed off, or be ecstatic that he'd noticed I was always with the *other boy*. Flipping my ponytail over my shoulder, I caught his forearm before it connected with my stomach. "Not that it's any of your business, but he wasn't whistling at *me*."

He jerked his hand back, frowning. "What's that supposed to mean?"

I raised my brows at him and waited for him to get it. The moment he did, his eyes widened and his mouth formed a perfect circle. Instead of falling on my ass laughing like I wanted to, I struck out with a vicious kick. Aiming for the vulnerable spot under his ribcage, I almost squealed at how perfect my kick was going to be.

I never made contact.

In one nifty swipe of his arm, he knocked me to the mat.

Standing above me, he actually smiled. "Nice try."

I propped myself onto my elbows, scowling. "How come you smile when you knock me down?"

He offered his hand. "It's the little things that make me happy."

I accepted, and he hauled me to my feet. "Good to know." Shrugging, I brushed past him and grabbed my bottle of water. "So…um, are you going to the celebrations tonight?"

The solstice was a big deal for the pures. It kicked off more than a month of social events leading up the Council session in August. Tonight would be the biggest celebration, and if the gods were going to bless them with their presence, tonight would be the night. I doubted any would, but the pures got all dressed in their colorful sheaths just in case.

There would also be a ton of parties held on the main island—none of which us halfs were invited to, and I mean none. And since all the pures' parents would be home, there would be no festivities at Zarak's house. However, rumor had it there would be a beach party hosted by the one and only Jackson. I wasn't sure if I was going to make an appearance or not.

"Probably." Aiden stretched, flashing a strip of taut skin along the band of his pants. "I'm not really big on that stuff, but I need to show up at some of them."

I made myself focus on his face, which was harder than I realized. "Why do you need to?"

He flashed a grin. "It's what we adults have to do, Alex."

I rolled my eyes and took a drink. "You can go and hang out with your friends. It will be fun."

Aiden looked at me strangely.

I lowered the bottle of water. "You do know how to have fun, right?"

"Of course."

Out of nowhere it kind of hit me. I don't think Aiden *could* have fun. Just like I couldn't bear to really, really think about what'd happened to Mom. Survivor's guilt—or at least that's what I thought they called it.

Aiden reached over, tapping my arm. "What are you thinking?"

I glanced up, finding his steady gaze on me. "I was just... thinking."

He backed off, slouched against the wall, and eyed me curiously. "Thinking about what?"

"It's hard for you to...have fun, isn't it? I mean, I never really see you doing anything. I've only ever seen you with Kain or Leon and never a girl. I did see you once in jeans..." I trailed off, flushing. What did seeing him in pants have to do with anything? But that had been an *amazing* sight. "Anyway I guess it's hard after what happened to your parents."

Aiden pushed off the wall, eyes suddenly silver. "I have friends, Alex, and I know how to have fun."

My cheeks grew even hotter. Obviously I'd hit a sore spot. Whoops. Feeling very pathetic, I finished up training and hurried back to my dorm. Sometimes I wondered what I was thinking when I opened my mouth.

Disgusted, I took a quick shower and changed into a pair of shorts. Soon after, I headed back to the hub of the campus to meet up with Caleb in the cafeteria, determined to forget my awkwardness.

Caleb was already there, in deep conversation with another half about who'd gotten better scores in their field exercises at the end of last semester. Since I had yet to take part in any field exercise, I was pretty much left out of the conversation. I felt like a loser.

"You going to the party tonight?" Caleb asked.

I glanced up. "I guess so. Not like I have anything better to do."

"Just don't have a repeat of last time."

I shot him an evil look. "Don't leave me hanging while you run off to Myrtle, you douche."

Caleb chuckled. "You should've come. Lea was bitching up until the moment she saw Jackson without you. She practically ruined everyone's night. Well, Cody actually ruined everyone's night."

I pulled my legs up and leaned back in my seat. This was the first I had heard of that. "What happened?"

He made a face. "Someone brought up the Breed Order crap again, and Cody was really out of it. He started talking smack about it. He was saying stuff about us halfs not belonging on the Council."

"I'm sure that went over well."

He smirked. "Yeah, then he said something about how the two breeds shouldn't mix and all the crap about the purity of their blood." He paused, eyeing someone behind me with great interest. I twisted around, but I only caught a glimpse of light-brown skin and long, curly hair. I turned back to him with a raised brow.

"So, what happened?"

"Um…a couple of the halfs got pissed. The next thing we knew Cody and Jackson were brawling. Man, they were going at it."

My eyes widened. "What? Did Cody report him?"

"No," said Caleb, grinning. "Zarak talked Cody out of it, but he beat Cody down. It was pretty awesome. Of course, the two idiots made up afterward. They're fine now."

Relieved, I settled back in my seat. Striking a pure—even in self-defense—was a fast way to get kicked out the Covenant. Killing a pure in any situation would get you executed, even if he was trying to cut your head off. As unfair as it was, we had to be careful navigating the politics of the pure-blood world. We could knock the crap out of one another, but when it came to the pures, they were untouchable in more ways than one. And if we happened to break one of the rules…well, we were only one step away from a lifetime of servitude—or death.

Shuddering, I thought about my precarious position. If I didn't get accepted in the fall, servitude was what I had to look forward to. There was no way I could allow that. I'd have to leave, but where would I go? What would I do? Live on the streets? Manage to find a job and pretend to be a mortal again?

Pushing those troubling thoughts away, I focused on Jackson's party, which I finally agreed to attend, and a couple of hours later, I found myself there. The little party really wasn't little; it looked like all the halfs who were stuck at the Covenant during the summer had spilled across the beach. Some sprawled across blankets; others reclined in chairs. No one was in the water.

I opted for a comfy-looking blanket beside Luke. Ritter, a younger half with the brightest red hair I'd ever seen, offered me a yellow plastic cup, but I turned it down. Rit hung out with us for a little while, talking about how he was getting ready to travel to California for the rest of the summer. I was only slightly envious. "You aren't drinking?" asked Luke.

Even I was surprised by my decision, but I shrugged. "I'm not feeling it tonight."

He flicked a long strand of bronze-colored hair out of his eyes. "Did I get you in trouble today during practice?"

"No. I'm usually easily distracted. So it was nothing new."

Luke nudged me, grinning. "I can see why you are distracted. Too bad he's a pure. I'd give my left butt cheek for a piece of that."

"He likes girls."

"So?" Luke laughed at my expression. "What's he like? He seems so quiet. Like you know he'd be good in—"

"Stop right there!" I giggled, throwing up my hand. The movement pulled my sore back muscles.

Luke tipped back his head and laughed. "You can't say you never thought about it."

"He's…he's a pure," I said again, like it didn't make him sexy.

Luke shot me a knowing look.

"Okay." I sighed. "He's actually very nice and patient. Most of the time…and I just feel weird talking about him. Can we talk about some other hot guy?"

"Oh yes. Please. Can we talk about another hot guy?" Caleb snorted. "Exactly the thing I want to talk about."

Luke ignored him, his gaze flickering across the beach and settling near a couple of coolers. "How about Jackson?"

I eased onto my back. "Don't say his name."

He chuckled at my pathetic attempt to make myself invisible. "He just showed up *without* Lea. Come to think of it, where in hell is she?"

I refused to look up and draw Jackson's attention. "I have no idea. I haven't seen her."

"Is that a bad thing?" asked Caleb.

"Oh Alex, here comes your man," Luke announced.

There was nowhere for me to go, and I looked helplessly between Caleb and Luke. Neither of them did anything to hide their amusement.

"Alex, where have you been?" slurred Jackson. "I haven't seen you around."

I squeezed my eyes shut and muttered a dozen curses. "I've been busy with training."

Jackson swayed to the right, toward a distracted Caleb. "Aiden should know you need to get out and have a little fun."

Luke turned and gave me a sly wink before standing. I sat

up, but that was as far as I made it. Jackson dropped into the empty space and threw his arm around me, nearly knocking me over.

His breath was too warm and smelled of beer. "You know you're more than welcome to hang out here after the party."

"Oh...I don't know about that."

Jackson smiled and moved in closer. Normally I'd find Jackson attractive, but he just grossed me out now. Something was wrong with me. Had to be.

"You can't be practicing tomorrow. Not after the celebrations. Even Aiden will be sleeping in."

I doubted that, and I found myself wondering if Aiden was having a good time. Did he go to the celebrations and stay? Or did he show up, make an appearance, and bail? I kind of hoped he stayed and had fun. He could use it after spending an entire day holed up with me.

"Alex?"

"Huh?"

Jackson chuckled and slipped his hand over my shoulder. I grabbed it and dropped it in his lap. Undaunted, he reached for me again. "I was asking if you wanted something to drink. Zarak went on a compulsion frenzy and stocked us up for the rest of the summer."

That was good to know. "No. I'm fine. Not thirsty."

Eventually Jackson grew bored with my lack of interest and roamed off. Grateful, I turned to Caleb. "Smack me next time I even think about talking to a guy. Seriously."

He stared down into his cup, frowning. "What happened with him? Did he come on too strong?" A fierce look came over his face as his eyes narrowed on Jackson's back. "Do I need to hurt him?"

"No!" I laughed. "It's just...I don't know." I turned and

saw him standing with the female half I'd caught a glimpse of earlier. She was a pretty brunette, ridiculously curvy, and she had a smooth, light-brown complexion. "Jackson doesn't do it for me."

"Who does?" His own gaze settled on Jackson's companion.

"Who's that girl?" I asked.

He turned and sighed. "That's Olivia. Her last name is one of those unpronounceable Greek ones. Her father is a mortal; her mom's a pure."

I continued watching the girl. She wore a pair of designer jeans I would've killed for. She also kept avoiding Jackson's wandering hands. "How come this is the first time I'm seeing her?"

"She's been with her dad. I think." He cleared her throat. "She's actually...kinda nice."

I looked at him sharply. "You like her, don't you?"

"No! No, of course not." His voice sounded sort of strangled. My curiosity increased as Caleb's eyes seemed drawn back to Olivia. A red hue colored his cheeks.

"Sure. You aren't interested in her at all."

Caleb took a long gulp of his drink. "Shut up, Alex."

I opened my mouth, but whatever I was about to say was cut off when Deacon St. Delphi strolled up out of nowhere. "What the hell?"

Caleb followed my gaze. "Now, that's interesting."

Seeing Deacon on the beach wasn't at all surprising, but seeing him on the night of the solstice when all the pures hovered together was shocking.

It was so very...*impure* of him.

Deacon swept the halfs with his cool gaze and a sardonic grin broke across his face when he saw us. Sauntering over, he pulled a shiny silver flask from the pocket of his jeans. "Happy Summer Solstice!"

Caleb choked on his drink. "Same to you."

He took Jackson's empty spot, seemingly unaware of the shocked stares. I cleared my throat. "What…are you doing here?"

"What? I got bored over on the main island. All the pomp and circumstance is enough to drive a man sober."

"We can't have that." I took in the red rims around his eyes. "Are you ever sober?"

He seemed to think about that. "Not if I can help it. Things are…easier this way."

I knew he was talking about his parents. Unsure of how to respond, I waited for him to continue.

"Aiden hates that I drink so much." He glanced down at his flask. "He's right, you know."

I played with my hair, twisting it into a thick rope. "Right about what?"

Deacon tipped his head back, staring at the stars blanketing the night sky. "Everything, but especially the path he chose." He stopped and laughed. "If only he knew that, huh?"

"Aren't they going to know you're gone?" Caleb asked before I could get out a reply.

"And come over here and ruin all your fun?" Deacon's serious look vanished. "Absolutely. In about an hour, when they start their ritual chanting and crap, someone—most likely my brother—will realize I'm missing and come looking for me."

My mouth dropped open. "Aiden's still there?"

"You came here knowing they would follow you?" Caleb frowned.

Deacon appeared entertained by both statements. "Yes answers all." He brushed a sunny curl off his forehead.

"Crap!" Caleb started to stand while I mulled over the

knowledge that Aiden was still partying it up. "Alex, we should go."

"Sit down." Deacon put up a hand. "You have at least an hour. I'll give the party boys enough time to clear out. Trust me." Caleb didn't seem to hear him. He stared back down the seashore, where Olivia and another half stood close, really close together. Seconds passed while his face hardened. Leaning over, I tugged the hem of his shirt.

He gave me a broad smile. "You know what? I'm pretty tired. I think I'm going to head back to the dorm."

"Boo." Deacon stuck out his lower lip.

I stood. "Sorry."

"Double boo." He shook his head. "And the fun was just starting."

Tossing a quick goodbye to Deacon, I followed Caleb up the beach. We passed Lea coming down the wooden boardwalk.

"Like going after my sloppy seconds?" Lea wrinkled her nose. "How cute."

A second later, I wrapped my hand around her forearm. "Hey." Lea tried to pull her arm back, but I was stronger than her.

"What?"

I smiled my best smile. "You boyfriend just copped a feel. You obviously aren't doing it for him." I let go then, leaving a very unhappy Lea standing alone.

"Caleb!" I moved to catch up with him.

"I know what you're going to say, so I don't want to hear it."

I brushed my hair behind my ears. "How do you know what I was going to say? All I wanted to point out is if you like the chick back there, you could just—"

With a sideways glance, he raised his brows. "I really don't want to talk about this."

"But…I don't understand why you won't admit it. What the hell is the big deal?"

He sighed. "Something happened the night we went to Myrtle."

I tripped over my feet. "What?"

"Not *that*. Well…not really, but it came close."

"*What?*" I squealed, punching his arm. "How come you haven't said anything? With the Olivia chick? Jeez, I'm your best friend and you failed to mention this?"

"We both had been drinking, Alex. We were arguing over who called shotgun first…and the next thing I know, we're full-on making out."

I bit my lip. "That's kinda hot. So why won't you talk to her?"

Silence stretched between us before he responded. "Because I like her, really like her, and you would like her, too. She's smart, funny, strong, and her ass is just so—"

"Caleb, okay. I get the point. You really like her. So talk to her." We headed toward the courtyard nestled between the two dorms.

"You don't get it. And you should. Nothing will come out of it. You know how it is for us."

"Huh?" I stared at the intricate designs on the pathway. They were runes and symbols carved into the marble. Some represented various gods while others looked like some child got ahold of a marker and went to town. Actually it looked like something I'd draw.

"Never mind. I just need to hook up with someone else. Get this stupid whatever out of my system."

I lifted my eyes from the strange markings. "That sounds like a solid plan."

"Maybe I should just hook up with Lea again or someone else. How about you?"

I shot him a dirty look. "Gee, thanks. But seriously, you don't want to hook up with just anyone. You want something…meaningful." I stopped, not sure where *that* came from.

Clearly he didn't either. "Something meaningful? Alex you've been in the outside world too long. You know how it is for us. We don't get 'meaningful.'"

I sighed. "Yeah, I know."

"We're either Guards or Sentinels—not husbands, wives, or parents." He stopped, frowning. "Flings and girlfriends. That's what we have. Our duty doesn't allow for much else."

He was right. Being born a half-blood wiped out any chance for a normal, healthy relationship. Like Caleb said, our duty didn't allow for us to form attachments—anything we'd regret giving up or leaving behind. Once we graduated, we could be assigned anywhere, and at any given moment we could be yanked and sent somewhere else.

It was a harsh, lonely life, but one with purpose.

I kicked at a small pebble, sending it flying into the thick underbrush.

"Just because we won't have the picket fence, doesn't mean…" The skin of my forehead creased as a sudden chill brushed over me. It came out of nowhere, and by the sudden confused look on Caleb's face, I knew he felt it, too.

"A boy and a girl, one with a bright and short future, and the other covered in shadows and doubt."

The raspy, ancient-sounding voice brought both of us to a standstill. Caleb and I turned around. The stone bench had been unoccupied a moment ago, but there she was. And she was old, like should've-been-dead-by-now old.

A massive pile of pure white hair sat pinned atop her

head, and her skin was dark as coal and heavily lined. Her crooked posture aged her even more, but her eyes were sharp. Intelligent.

I'd never seen her before, but I instinctively knew who she was. "Grandma Piperi?"

She tipped her head back and laughed wildly. I half expected the weight of her hair to topple her over, but she remained upright. "Oh Alexandria, you seem so surprised. Did you not think I was real?"

Caleb jabbed me with his elbow a few times, but I couldn't stop staring. "You know who I am?"

Her dark eyes flickered to Caleb. "Of course I do." She smoothed her hands over what appeared to be a housecoat. "I also remember your momma."

Disbelief brought me a step closer to the oracle, but shock left me speechless.

"I remember your momma," she went on, nodding. "She came to me three years ago, she did. I spoke the truth to her, you see. The truth was only for her to hear." She paused, her gaze falling back to Caleb. "What are you doing here, child?"

Eyes wide, he shifted uncomfortably. "We were...walking back to our dorms."

Grandma Piperi smiled, stretching the papery skin around her mouth. "Do you wish to hear the truth—your truth? What the gods have in store for you?"

Caleb paled. The thing with truths, they usually messed with your head. It didn't matter if it was crazy talk or not.

"Grandma Piperi, what did you tell my mom?" I asked.

"If I told you, what would it change? Fate is fate, you see. Just like love is love." She cackled as if she'd said something funny. "What's written by the gods will come to pass. Most has already. Such a sad affair when children turn against their makers."

I had no clue what she was talking about, and I felt pretty sure she was certifiable, but I needed to know what Piperi had said—if she had said anything at all. Maybe Caleb was right, and I needed closure. "Please. I need to know what you said to her. What made her leave?"

She tilted her head to the side. "Don't you want to know about your truth, child? That is what's important now. Don't you want to know about love? About what is forbidden and what is fated?"

My arms fell to my sides, and I blinked back sudden tears. "I don't want to know about love."

"But you should, my child. You need to know about love. The things people will do for love. All truths come down to love, do they not? One way or another, they do. See, there is a difference between love and need. Sometimes, what you feel is immediate and without rhyme or reason." She sat up a little straighter. "Two people see each across a room or their skin brushes. Their souls recognize the person as their own. It doesn't need time to figure it. The soul always knows...whether it's right or wrong."

Caleb grabbed my arm. "Come on. Let's go. She's not telling you anything you want to hear."

"The first...the first is always the most powerful." She closed her eyes, sighing. "Then there is need and fate. That is a different type. Need covers itself with love but need...need is never love. Always beware of the one who needs you. There is always a want behind a need, you see."

Caleb let go of my arm and jabbed fiercely at the walkway behind us.

"Sometimes you will mistake need for love. Be careful. The road with need is never a fair one, never a good one. Much like the road you must walk down. Beware of the one who needs."

The lady was crazy, but her words still sent shivers down my spine. "Why won't the road be easy for me?" I asked, ignoring Caleb.

She stood. Well, as much as she could stand. Since her back hunched forward, it stopped her from standing up completely. "Roads are always bumpy, never flat. This one here," she nodded at Caleb with a tiny cackle, "this one has a road full of light."

Caleb stopped pointing behind us. "That's good to know."

"A short road full of light," added Grandma Piperi.

His face fell. "That's…good to know."

"What about the road?" I asked again, hoping for an answer that made sense.

"Ah, roads are always shady. Your road is full of shadows, full of deeds that must be done. It comes to those of your kind."

Caleb shot me a meaningful look, but I shook my head. I had no idea what she was talking about, but I was still unwilling to leave. She hobbled past me and I stepped out of the way. My back brushed against something soft and warm, drawing my attention. I turned, finding large purple flowers with bright yellow middles. I shifted closer, inhaling their bittersweet, almost acrid smell.

"Be careful there, child. You be touching nightshade." She stopped, turning back to where we stood. "Very dangerous…much like kisses from those who walk among the gods. Intoxicating, sweet, and deadly… You need to know how to handle it right. Just a little and you'll be fine. Too much…it takes away what makes you who you are." She smiled softly, as if she were remembering something. "The gods move around us, always close by. They are watching, and they are waiting to see which one is revealed to be the strongest. They are here now. You see, the end is upon them, upon all of us. Even the gods have little faith."

Caleb passed me another wide-eyed stare. I shrugged, deciding to give it one more chance. "So, there's nothing you'll tell me about my mom?"

"Nothing you haven't already been told."

"Wait…?" My skin felt hot and cold all at once. "What… Lea said is true? That I was the reason why Mom died?"

"Let's go, Alex. You're right." Caleb took a step back. "She's freaking crazy."

Piperi sighed. "Always ears around these parts, but ears don't always hear correctly."

"Alex, let's go."

I blinked and—I'm not exaggerating—in the time it took me to open my eyes, Grandma Piperi stood in front of me. The old lady moved that fast. Her clawed hand grabbed my shoulder hard enough to make me wince.

She stared up at me with eyes as sharp as blades, and when she spoke, her voice lost its raspy edge. And she didn't sound all that crazy. Oh no, her words were clear and to the point.

"You will kill the ones you love. It is in your blood, in your fate. So the gods have spoken it and so the gods have come to foresee it."

CHAPTER NINE

"Alex! Watch his hands. You're letting too many blocks get through!"

I nodded at Aiden's harsh words and squared off with Kain again. Aiden was right. Kain was tearing me apart. My movements were too slow, jerky, and distracted—mainly due to staying up half the night, replaying the bizarre conversation with Grandma Piperi.

This was a really bad time to be preoccupied. Today was the first practice that included Kain, and I was fighting like a baby. Kain wasn't going easy on me either. Not that I would've wanted that, but I also didn't want to look like a total turd in front of another Sentinel.

Another one of his brutal kicks got through my block, and I dodged with only a split second to spare. Dodging was not the point of this exercise. If it were, I'd be excelling at it.

Aiden stalked over to me then, repositioning my arms in a way that would've successfully knocked Kain's leg down.

"Watch him. Even the slightest muscle tremor will give away his attack. You have to pay attention, Alex."

"I know." I took a step back and ran my arm over my forehead. "I know. I can do this."

Kain shook his head and walked off to grab his bottle of water while Aiden led me to the other side of the room, his hand wrapped around my upper arm. He bent so we were eye level. "What is your deal today? I know you can do better than this."

I bent to pick up my water, but the bottle was empty. Aiden handed me his. "I'm just…out of it today." I took a drink and handed it back to him.

"I can tell."

I bit my lip, flushing. I was better than this, and gods, I wanted to prove to Aiden I was. If I couldn't get past this then I couldn't move onto anything else—to all those damn cool things I wanted to learn.

"Alex, you've been distracted all day." His eyes met mine and held them. "This better have nothing to do with the party Jackson held on the beach last night."

Good grief, was there nothing this man didn't know? I shook my head. "No."

Aiden gave me a knowing look and took a drink from the bottle before he shoved it back into my hands. "Drink up."

I sighed, turning away from him. "Let's go again, okay?" Aiden motioned Kain back and then clapped me on the shoulder.

"You can do this, Alex."

After collecting myself and taking another gulp of water, I dropped the bottle on the floor. I went back to the center of the mats and nodded at Kain.

Kain watched me wearily. "You ready?"

"Yeah." I clenched my teeth. Kain raised his eyebrows, like he doubted I was going to do anything different this time around.

"All right." He shook his head and we squared off again. "Remember to anticipate my moves."

I blocked his first kick, then his punch. We circled each other for a few rounds while I wondered what the hell Grandma Piperi meant by saying I would kill the ones I loved. That didn't make any sense, because the one person I'd loved was already dead, and I sure as hell hadn't killed her. You can't kill someone who's already dead, and it wasn't like I loved—

Kain's boot slammed past my defenses and connected with my stomach. Pain exploded through me, so intense and overwhelming I dropped to my knees. The way I landed put a strain on my battered back. Wincing, I reached around and held my back with one hand and my stomach with another.

I was a total mess.

Kain dropped down in front of me. "Dammit, Alex! What were you doing? You should have never been that close to me!"

"Yeah," I groaned. *Breathe through it. Just breathe through it.* Easier said than done, but I kept telling myself that. I expected Aiden to launch into a major tirade, but he didn't say a word to me. Instead he walked up and jerked Kain up by the scruff of his neck, nearly holding him off the ground.

"Practice is over."

Kain's mouth dropped open, and his normally tanned skin paled. "But—"

"Apparently, you don't understand." Aiden's voice sounded low and dangerous.

I stumbled to my feet. "Aiden, it's my fault. I leaned in." I didn't have to elaborate; it was obvious what I'd done wrong.

Aiden looked over his shoulder at me. A few terse seconds later, he released Kain. "Go."

Kain straightened his shirt while he backed up. When he turned to me, his sea-green eyes were wide. "Alex, I'm sorry."

I waved one hand at him. "No biggie."

Aiden stepped in front of me, dismissing Kain without so much as another word. "Let me take a look at it."

"Oh…it's okay." I turned away from him. My eyes burned, but not because of the throbbing pain. I wanted to sit down and cry. I'd walked right into the kick. A child wouldn't have made such a mistake. It was that pathetic.

He placed a surprisingly gentle hand on my shoulder and turned me back around. The look on his face said he understood my embarrassment. "It's okay, Alex." When I didn't move, he took a step back. "You grabbed your back. I need to make sure you're okay."

Seeing no way out of this, I followed Aiden to one of the smaller rooms where they kept medical supplies. It was a cold, sterile room like any doctor's office with the exception of the painting of Aphrodite in all her naked glory, which I found odd and a little disturbing.

"Get up on the table."

I wanted nothing more than to run back to my room and sulk in privacy, but I did what he said.

Aiden came back to me, his gaze fixed above my head. "How does your stomach feel?"

"Okay."

"Why did you grab your back?"

"It's sore." I rubbed my hands over my thighs. "I feel like a dork."

"You're not a dork."

"I am. I should've been paying attention. I walked right into the kick. It wasn't Kain's fault."

He seemed to consider that. "I've never seen you so distracted." For the last month, we'd had eight-hour training days, and I guess during that time he'd seen a lot of things from me. But I'd never been this unfocused.

"You can't afford to be so distracted," he continued gently. "You're coming along remarkably well, but you don't have time to lose. It's almost July and that leaves us about two months to get you caught up. Your uncle has been requesting weekly reports. Don't think he's forgotten about you."

Full of shame and disappointment, my eyes dropped down to my hands. "I know."

Aiden placed his fingers on my chin, guiding my head up. "Why are you so distracted, Alex? You move like you haven't slept, and you're acting as if your mind's a million miles from here. If it's not the party last night, is it a guy who has you distracted?"

I cringed. "Look. There are several things I'm not discussing with you. Guys are one of them."

Aiden's eyes widened. "Really? If it's interfering with your training, then it's interfering with me."

"Jeez." I shifted uncomfortably under his intense stare. "There is no guy. I have no guy."

He fell silent, watching me curiously. Those eyes had a calming effect, and even though I knew this was dumb, so stupid, I took a deep breath. "I saw Grandma Piperi last night."

It seemed that Aiden expected me to say anything but that. While his face was impassive as ever, his eyes seemed to deepen. "And?"

"And Lea was right—"

"Alex," he cut me off. "Don't go there. You're not responsible."

"She was right and wrong at the same time." I stopped, sighing at the dubious look on Aiden's face. "Grandma Piperi wouldn't tell me everything. Actually she told me a bunch of crazy stuff about love and need…and gods kissing. Anyway, she told me that I would kill the one I loved, but how is that possible? Mom is already dead."

An odd look flickered over his face, but it was gone before I could figure out what it was. "I thought you said you didn't believe in that kind of stuff."

Of course he would remember *that* out of the billion random comments I'd made. "I don't, but it's not every day you're told that you're going to kill someone you love."

"So, this is what's been bothering you today?"

I squeezed my thighs. "Yes. No. I mean, do you think it was my fault?"

"Oh, Alex." He shook his head. "Do you remember when you asked me why I volunteered to train you?"

"Yeah."

He pushed away from the table I sat on. "Well, I lied to you."

"Yeah." I bit my lip and looked away. "I kinda figured that out already."

"You have?" He sounded surprised.

"You stood up for me because of what happened to your parents." I stole a peek at him. He was quiet as he watched me. "I think I remind you of yourself when it happened."

Aiden stared at me for an eternal second. "You're far more observant than I give you credit for."

"Thanks." I didn't share the fact that I'd only figured this out recently.

That lopsided grin appeared. "You're right…if that makes you feel any better. I remember what it was like afterward. You always wonder if there was anything you could've done differently, as pointless as it is, but you get hung up on the what-ifs of it all." The smile disappeared slowly, and he turned his face away. "For the longest time, I used to think if I had decided to be a Sentinel earlier, I could've stopped the daimon."

"But you didn't know a daimon was going to attack. You were—are—a pure blood. So very few of you even…choose this life. And you were just a kid. You can't blame yourself for that."

Aiden faced me then, gaze curious. "Then how can you hold yourself responsible for what happened to your mom? You may have realized there was a possibility that a daimon would find you, but you didn't know."

"Yeah." I hated it when he was right.

"You're still holding onto that guilt. So much so that you're reading into what the oracle said. You can't let what she said get to you, Alex. An oracle only talks in possibilities, not facts."

"I thought an oracle talks with gods and the fates," I said dryly.

He looked doubtful. "An oracle sees into the past and the possibility in the future, but it's not set in stone. There is no such thing as a certain fate. Only you are in control of your fate. You aren't responsible for what happened to your mom. You need to let it go."

"Why do you all say it like that? No one says she died. Everyone is, like, afraid to say that. It's not *what happened*—she was killed."

The shadow appeared on his face again, but he stepped

around the table. "Let me look at your back." Before I knew what he was doing, he lifted the back of my shirt and inhaled sharply.

"What?" I asked, but he didn't say anything. He tugged my shirt up farther. "Hey—what are you doing?" I smacked his hands away.

He shot around the table, his eyes silver. "What do you think I'm doing? How long has your back been like this?"

I shrank back. "Since we…um…started blocking training."

"Why didn't you say something about this?"

"It's not a big deal. It doesn't hurt, not really."

Aiden wheeled back around, expression incredulous. "Damn half-bloods. I know you all have a higher than normal tolerance for pain, but *that* is ridiculous. *That* has to hurt."

I stared at his back as he rummaged through the numerous cabinets. "I'm in training." I forced as much maturity into my voice as possible. "We aren't expected to bitch and moan about pain. It's a part of training—a part of being a Sentinel. It happens."

Aiden wheeled back around, expression incredulous. "You haven't been in training for three years, Alex. Your body—your skin isn't used to it anymore. You cannot let things like that go because you think someone is going to think less of you."

I blinked. "I don't think people are going to think less of me. It's just a…couple of damn bruises. Some of them have faded already. See?"

He set a small jar beside me on the table. "Bullshit."

"You've never cussed before." I had the strangest urge to laugh.

"It's not just *a* bruise. Your whole back is black and blue, Alex."

Aiden paused, his hands clenching air. "Were you afraid I would think less of you if you brought this up?"

I gave a slight shake of my head. "No."

His lips pressed together. "I didn't expect your body to adapt quickly, and honestly, I should've known."

"Aiden...really, it doesn't hurt that bad." The never-ending, dull ache was something I'd gotten used to, so I wasn't really lying.

Picking up the jar, he walked around the table. "This should help, and next time, you will tell me when something is wrong with you."

"All right." I decided not to push my luck. He didn't seem like he'd appreciate any snarky response at this moment. "What is that stuff, anyway?"

He unscrewed the lid. "It's a mixture of Arnica and menthol. Arnica is part of a flower. It acts like an anti-inflammatory, and it reduces pain. It should help."

I expected him to hand me the jar, but he dipped his fingers inside it instead. "What are you—?"

"Hold your shirt up. I don't want to get this all over it. It tends to stain clothing."

Dumbfounded, I found myself lifting the edge of my shirt. Once again, there was a sharp intake of breath as he got another look at my back.

"Alex, you can't let something like this go untreated." This time, the anger was gone from his voice. "If you're hurt, you must tell me. I wouldn't have..."

Gone so hard on me? Allowed me to practice with Kain and get my ass handed to me? That wasn't what I wanted.

"Don't ever feel like you can't tell me when something's wrong. You've got to trust that I would care if you were hurt."

"It's not your fault. I could've told you—"

He placed his fingers against my skin, and I nearly jumped off the table. Not because the salve was cold—don't get me wrong, it was freezing—but they were *his* fingers moving along my back. A pure never touched a half this way. Or maybe they did now. I didn't know, but I couldn't imagine the other pures I knew seeking to ease a half's pain. They usually didn't care enough.

Aiden silently worked the thick balm across my skin and then up. Eventually his fingers brushed the edge of my sports bra. My skin felt strangely warm, which was odd to me since the stuff was so cold. I focused on the wall in front of me. There was that picture of Aphrodite perched upon a rock. She had this lusty look on her face, and her boobs were hanging out for the world to see.

That was *so* not helping.

Aiden continued quietly. Every so often my body jerked on its own accord, and then I felt hot, really hot.

"Did you ever know your biological father?" His quiet voice broke into my thoughts.

I shook my head. "No. He died before I was born."

His deft fingers slid along the side of my stomach. "Do you know anything about him?"

"No. Mom never really talked about him, but I think they used to spend time in Gatlinburg, Tennessee. We would spend Winter solstice there when she could get away from Lucian. I think…being at the cabins made her feel close to him, my father."

"She loved him?"

I nodded. "I think so."

He worked on my lower back now, moving the balm in smooth circles, and every so often the cool scent of menthol reached me. "What were you going to do if the daimons hadn't shown up? You had something to do, right?"

I swallowed. This was an easy question, but I found it hard to concentrate on anything other than his fingers. "Um...I wanted to do lots of things."

His fingers stopped and he laughed softly. "Like what?"

"I...don't know."

"Did you ever plan on coming back to the Covenant?"

"Yes and no." I swallowed hard. "Before the attack, I never thought I'd see the Covenant again. After it happened, I was trying to get to the one in Nashville, but the daimons...kept getting in my way."

"So, what were you going to do if the daimons hadn't found you?" He knew not to focus on that horrible week after the attack. He knew I wouldn't talk about it.

"When...I was really little, my mom and several Sentinels took a bunch of us kids to the zoo. I loved it—*loved* the animals. I spent the entire summer telling Mom that I belonged in the zoo."

"What?" He sounded incredulous. "You thought you belonged in a zoo?"

I felt a smile tug at my lips. "Yeah, I was a strange child. So...it was one of the things I thought I could do. You know, work with animals or something, but..." I shrugged, feeling kind of stupid.

"But what, Alex?" I could *feel* his smile.

I stared down at my fingers. "But I always wanted to come back to the Covenant. I needed to. I just didn't fit in with all the normal people. I missed it here, missed having a purpose and knowing what I should be doing."

His fingers left my skin, and he was silent for so long I thought something had happened to him. I twisted around to face him. "What?"

He tipped his head to the side. "Nothing."

I crossed my legs and let out a sigh. "You're looking at me like I'm weird."

Aiden set the jar aside. "You're not weird."

"Then...?" I let my shirt fall back down and grabbed the jar. "You done?" When he nodded, I put the lid back on.

Aiden leaned forward, placing his hands on each side of my crossed legs. "The next time you're hurt, I want you to tell me."

When I looked up, he was eye level with me, and we were only inches apart—the closest we'd ever been outside of the training room. "Okay."

"And...you're not weird. Well, I've met weirder people than you."

I started to smile, but something in the way Aiden looked at me caught my attention. It was like he was assuming responsibility for me and what I felt. I *knew* he was. Maybe it came from having to care for Deacon...and I remembered what Deacon had said last night.

Clearing my throat, I focused on his shoulder. "Does Deacon ever talk about things? You know, about your parents?"

My question caught him off guard. It took him a few seconds to answer. "No. Just like you."

I ignored that. "His drinking? I think he does it so he doesn't have to think about it."

Aiden blinked. "Is that why you do it?"

"No! I don't really do it that much, but that's not the point. What I'm saying is..." Gods, what was I doing? Trying to talk to him about his brother?

"What are you saying?"

Hoping I wasn't overstepping boundaries, I plunged ahead. "I think Deacon drinks so he doesn't feel."

Aiden sighed. "I know. So do all the counselors and

teachers. No matter what I do or who I bring him to, he won't open up."

I nodded, understanding how hard it was for Deacon. "He's…proud of you. He didn't say it exactly like that, but he's proud of what you're doing."

He said, "Why...how would you know?"

I shrugged. "I think if you keep at what you're doing, because what you're doing is right, he'll come around."

The serious look remained, and there was more to it than that. He looked worried, and for reasons I didn't even want to acknowledge, it bothered me.

"Hey." I reached out and tapped the hand that rested next to my left leg. "You are—"

The hand that I tapped reached up and clasped mine. I froze as he threaded his fingers through mine. "I'm what?"

Beautiful. Kind. Patient. Perfect. I said none of those things. Instead I stared at his fingers, wondering if he knew he was holding my hand. "You're always so…"

His thumb moved over the top of my hand. The balm made his fingers cool and smooth. "What?"

I looked up, and I was immediately snared. His stare, his soft touch along my hand were doing very strange things. I felt hot and dizzy, like I'd been sitting out in the sun all day. All I could think about was how his hand felt on mine…and then what it would feel like on other parts. I shouldn't be thinking that at all.

Aiden was a *pure*.

The door to our room swung open. I jerked back, my hand falling to my lap.

A big, hulking shadow paused at the door. Mister Steroids—Leon—glanced around the room, his eyes falling to Aiden, who had moved to a much more appropriate distance.

"I've been looking everywhere for you," Leon said.

"What's up?" Aiden asked evenly.

Leon spared at glance at me. He didn't suspect anything. Why would he? Aiden was a well-respected pure, and I was just a half-blood he was training. "Did she hurt herself?"

"She's fine. What did you need?"

"Marcus needs to see us."

Aiden nodded. He started to follow Leon out, but he stopped at the door. Turning back to me, he was all business again. "We'll talk more about this later."

"Okay," I said, but he was already gone.

My gaze went back to the painting of the goddess of love. I swallowed hard, and my grasp on the little jar tightened. There was no way—absolutely no way—I was interested in Aiden in that way. Sure, he was swoon-worthy and really nice, and patient and funny in a dry kind of way. There was a lot about him to like. If he were a half-blood, then there wouldn't be anything wrong. He didn't work for the Covenant, so there wasn't a student hooking up with a teacher kind of problem, and he was only three years older than me. If he were a half-blood, I'd probably have thrown myself at him already.

But Aiden was a freaking pure blood.

A freaking pure blood with wonderfully strong fingers and a smile that...well, made me feel like there was a nest of butterflies in my stomach. And the way he looked at me—how his eyes shifted from gray to silver in a heartbeat—affected me even now. My stupid little heart leapt in my chest.

CHAPTER TEN

Sprawled across the mats, going through the motions of the cool-down stretches a couple of days later, Aiden decided to let me in on why Marcus had wanted to see him. "Lucian is coming."

I stared up at the ceiling, disappointed. "So?"

Instead of looming over me like he usually did, he dropped down beside me on the mat. His leg brushed mine, causing a tightening in my chest. *You're being ridiculous, Alex. Knock it off.* I moved my leg away from his.

"He's going to want to talk to you."

Pushing my weird attraction to him out of my mind, I focused on his words. "Why?"

He bent his knees and dropped his arms over them. "Lucian is your legal guardian. I suppose he's curious to see how your training is coming along."

"Curious?" I kicked my legs into the air. Why? I had no clue. "Lucian has never been interested in anything that had to do with me. Why would he start now?"

His expression tightened for a moment. "Things are different now. With your mom…"

"That doesn't matter. It has nothing to do with me."

He still looked strange as he continued to watch me point my toes at the ceiling. "It has everything to do with you." He took a deep breath, seeming to choose his next words wisely. "Lucian is dead set against you returning to the Covenant."

"Good to know Lucian and Marcus share that in common."

His jaw tightened. "Lucian and Marcus share nothing in common."

There he went again, trying to convince me Marcus wasn't the douche I believed him to be. He'd been at it for weeks, talking about how concerned my uncle had appeared when my mom and I had disappeared. Or how relieved Marcus had seemed when he'd notified him I was alive. Nice of Aiden to want to repair the relationship between us, but Aiden didn't realize there was nothing to repair.

Aiden reached over and pushed my legs back down to the mat. "Do you ever sit still for five seconds?"

I grinned, sitting up. "Nope."

He looked like he wanted to smile but didn't. "Tonight, when you see Lucian, you need to be on your best behavior."

I rolled to my feet, laughing now. "Best behavior? So I shouldn't challenge Lucian to a fight, I guess? I'd win that one. He's a total wimp."

The severe frown that graced his face was a clear indication he wasn't amused. "You do realize your stepfather can overthrow Marcus's decision to allow you to stay here? His authority supersedes your uncle's."

"Yes." I planted my hands on my hips. "Since Marcus is only allowing me to stay if I prove myself capable of returning to classes in the fall, I don't see what the big deal is."

Aiden came to his feet swiftly. For a moment, I was struck by how quickly he moved. "The big deal is if you mouth off at the Minister like you do with Marcus, you won't get a second chance. No one will be able to help you."

I tore my eyes away from him. "I'm not going to mouth off at him. Honestly, there's nothing Lucian can say to me that will get me riled up. He means nothing to me. Never has."

He looked doubtful. "Try to remember that."

I threw him a grin. "You have such little faith in me."

Surprisingly, Aiden grinned back at me. It made me feel all warm and stupid. "How's your back?"

"Oh. It's doing okay. That…stuff really helped."

He stalked across the mats, gray eyes focused on me. "Make sure you put it on every night. The bruises should fade in a couple days."

You could always help put it on again, I thought, but didn't say. I backed up, keeping a space between us. "Yes, sir."

Aiden stopped in front of me. "Better get going. The Minister and his Guards will be arriving soon, and all of those at the Covenant will be expected to meet him."

I groaned. Everyone would be wearing a Covenant-issued uniform of some sort, and no one had given me one. "I'm going to look like a—"

Aiden placed his hands on my upper arms, obliterating my critical thinking skills. I stared up at him, entertaining a vividly wild scenario in which he pulled me against him and kissed me like the barrel-chested men in those smutty books my mom used to read. He picked me up and put me on the floor a few feet off the mats. Crouching down, he started to roll up the mats. There went my fantasies.

"You'll look like what?" he asked.

I ran my hands over my arms. "What am I supposed to

wear? I'm going to stick out, and everyone will be looking at me."

He glanced up at me through heavy lashes. "Since when are you bothered by everyone staring at you?"

"Good point." I grinned at him, and then bounced away. "See you later."

By the time I made it to the common lounge, everyone was buzzing about tonight.

It wasn't Lucian that had Caleb pacing the length of the room. Even Lea seemed wound up as she twisted a strand of hair around her fingers. None of us halfs cared much about Lucian personally, but as the Minister of Court he exerted a high level of control over the pures and the halfs. No one could figure out why a Minister would come to the Covenant during the summer, when the vast majority of students were absent.

I was still busy picturing Aiden as a pirate, sweeping me off my feet.

"Do you know anything?" asked Luke.

Before I could answer, Lea chimed in. "How would she know? Lucian barely claims her."

I looked at her blandly. "Was that supposed to hurt my feelings or something?"

She shrugged. "My stepmother visits me every Sunday. Why hasn't Lucian visited you?"

"How would you know?"

Her look was sly. "I know."

"You are so screwing one of the Guards, aren't you?" I frowned at her. "That explains how you always know so much."

Lea's eyes narrowed, much like a cat when it spotted a mouse.

Snickering, I placed my bet on Clive, a younger Guard who'd been present the first day I'd arrived at the Covenant. He was good-looking, liked to check out the younger girls, and I'd seen him around the dorms a few times.

"Perhaps Lucian is coming to remove you from the Covenant." Lea studied her nails. "I always thought you'd fit in better with the slaves."

Casually, I leaned forward and grabbed one of the thick magazines. I chucked it at Lea's bent head. With half-blood reflexes, she snatched it before it made contact. "Thanks. I needed something to read." She thumbed through it.

As it neared seven, I headed back to my room to get ready. Folded on the coffee table was an olive green, Covenant-issued uniform. My eyes widened as I picked up the uniform and a small note fell out. I opened it with trembling fingers:

Had to guess your size. See you tonight.

Smiling, I looked inside the pants and discovered they were my size. There was no stopping the wealth of heat spreading over me. What Aiden had done meant the world to me. Tonight I'd look like I actually belonged at the Covenant.

Instead of the black uniforms the trained Sentinels wore, the students donned green outfits of the same cut—reminiscent of army uniforms. And they had all the nifty pockets and hooks meant to carry weapons, which I really liked.

I took a quick shower and felt a rush after putting on the uniform. Years had passed since I'd worn this, and there were times when I didn't think I'd ever get to wear it again. Turning in front of the mirror, I had to say I looked good in dress greens.

Excited, I pulled my hair up in a ponytail and left to meet up with Caleb. Together, we headed over to the main campus and a funny surge of nostalgia coursed through me as we entered the largest academy building.

I'd avoided the academy section of the campus since I'd returned, mainly because that was where Marcus had his office. It also seemed unfair to subject myself to all the memories if he decided in a month or two to not let me stay.

Of course, Caleb thought things were going great and Marcus would allow me to stay, but I wasn't so sure. I hadn't even seen him since the day he'd stopped by the gym and I'd made an idiot out of myself. I felt confident that had made a lasting impression. Come to think of it, no wonder Aiden was so worried about what I would say to Lucian.

Shaking my head, I glanced around the crowd of people that filled the grandiose lobby of the school. It seemed like every Guard and Sentinel was in attendance, standing under the statues of the nine muses. The Olympian nine, daughters of Zeus and Mnemosyne, or whoever it was that he hooked up with. Who really knew? The god got around.

The Guards lined every corner and blocked every exit, looking stony and fierce. The Sentinels stood in the middle, appearing vicious and battle ready.

Not surprising, my eyes found Aiden at once. He stood between Kain and Leon. In my opinion, those three were the most dangerous looking out of all of them.

Aiden looked up then, his eyes meeting mine. He gave me a little nod, and even though he didn't say anything, his eyes spoke for him. That one glance held a measure of pride and fondness. Maybe he even thought I made the cadet uniform look good. I started to smile, but Caleb led me past them, to the left of the Sentinels where the students belonged. We managed to squeeze in next to Caleb's secret obsession—Olivia. How convenient.

She smiled. "I was wondering if you guys were going to make it." Caleb said something incoherent, cheeks flushing a ruddy color.

I turned away from secondhand embarrassment and couldn't even look to see Olivia's response. Poor Caleb.

"Looking good, Alex," Jackson whispered.

It never failed. The one guy I didn't want to notice me always did. Glancing up at him, I forced a smile. "Thanks."

He looked as if he thought I truly did appreciate his compliment, but then Lea sauntered in, and I swear, she managed to get the uniform as tight as humanly possible. I looked down at my own and noted that my legs looked nowhere near as good as hers did. Bitch.

I watched as she prowled past the Guards and curved her lips at one of them before squeezing between Luke and Jackson. She murmured something, but my attention had already been caught by something more startling than how good her legs looked.

Half-blood servants stood behind the staff, still and quiet. Row after row of drab gray tunics and washed-out white pants made them nearly indistinguishable from each other. Since I'd returned to the Covenant, I'd only caught a glimpse of a servant here and there. It was their job to be invisible, easily overlooked. Or maybe it was ingrained in us—the free halfs—to ignore their presence. Gods, there were so many of them and they all looked the same: eyes glazed over, expressions vacant, and a crudely tattooed circle with a line through it scarred each of their foreheads. Marking them so visibly ensured that everyone knew their station in the caste system. It hit me all of a sudden.

I could really become one of them.

Swallowing down the sharp spike of panic, I faced the front just in time to see my uncle stalk down the center of the room and stand with his hands folded behind his back. There wasn't a strand of brown hair out of place on Marcus's head, and the dark suit he wore looked so out of place. Even the Instructors who were present were dressed down in comparison to him, wearing Covenant-issued uniforms.

The thick glass and marble front doors swung open as the Council Guards entered. I couldn't help the tiny gasp that escaped my lips. They were an impressive sight to behold, wearing white uniforms and brutal expressions. Then the members of the Council entered. Actually only two of them floated in behind the Guards. I had no idea who the woman was, but I recognized the man immediately. Dressed in white robes, Lucian hadn't changed one bit since the last time I'd seen him. His raven-colored hair still hung ridiculously long and his face looked as emotionless as a daimon's. Undeniably, he was a handsome man—like all pures were—but there was something about him that left a bad taste in my mouth.

His air of arrogance fit him like a second skin. As he approached Marcus, his lips twisted into a plastic-looking smile. The two exchanged greetings. Marcus even bowed slightly. Thank the gods they didn't expect us to do any of that nonsense. If so, someone would have to force me to my knees with a dropkick.

Lucian was a Minister, but he was no god. He wasn't even royalty. He was just a pure with a lot of power. Oh and self-importance. Couldn't forget that. I'd never understand what Mom had seen in him in the first place.

Money, power, and prestige?

I sighed. No one was perfect—not even her.

Several more Guards followed Lucian and the woman, who I realized was the other Minister. Each of the Guards was identical to the first set, except one. *He* was different, very different from every half-blood here.

The air sucked right out the room the moment *he* stepped into the building.

He was tall—maybe even as tall as Aiden, but I couldn't be sure. His blond hair was pulled back in a small ponytail, showing off his impossibly perfect features and golden complexion. He wore all black, like the Sentinels did. Under a different circumstance—one in which I didn't actually realize what he was—I would've said he was smokin' hot.

"Holy crap," Luke murmured.

A fine undercurrent of electricity permeated the room, coursing over my skin, then through me. I shuddered and took a step back, bumping into Caleb.

"The Apollyon," said someone behind me. Maybe Lea? I had no clue.

Holy crap, indeed.

The Apollyon trailed behind Lucian and Marcus, keeping at a safe enough distance. He wasn't crowding them but could react to any perceived threat. All of us stared, affected by his mere presence. Unconsciously, I took another step back as the little group neared our side. I don't know what got into me, but suddenly, I wanted to be as far away as possible…and I needed to be right here more than anything else in this world. Well…maybe not anything, but pretty damn close.

I didn't want to look at him, but I couldn't look away. My stomach lurched when our gazes met. His eyes—they were the strangest color I'd ever seen, and as he got closer, I realized it wasn't my imagination. His eyes were the color of amber, nearly iridescent.

While he continued to stare at me, something happened. It started as a faint line inching down his arms, darkening to an inky black as it reached his fingers. Then, all at once, the thin line spread across the golden hue of his skin and shifted into a multitude of swirly designs. The tattoo shifted and changed, reaching under his shirt and stretching along his neck until the intricate drawings covered the right side of his face.

The markings meant something. What, I had no idea. When he passed by us, my breath came out as a harsh gasp.

"You okay?" Caleb frowned down at me.

"Yeah." I smoothed my hair back with shaky hands. "He was…"

"Freaking hot." Elena turned to me, her eyes dancing with excitement. "Who knew the Apollyon would be that unbelievably gorgeous?"

Caleb made a face. "He's the Apollyon, Elena. You shouldn't talk about him that way."

My brows knit. "But those markings…"

Elena shot Caleb a dirty look. "What markings? And why does it matter if I say he's hot? I doubt he'd be offended."

"What do you mean?" I pushed past Caleb. "You didn't see those…tattoos? They appeared out of nowhere. They covered his entire body and his face!"

Elena's lips pursed as she stared at me. "I didn't see anything. Maybe I was just stuck on those lips."

"And that butt," interjected Lea.

"Those arms," added Elena.

"Are you guys being serious?" I glared at each of them. "You didn't see any sort of tattoo?"

They shook their heads.

The guys, with the exception of Luke, looked pretty disgusted with the commotion Elena and Lea were making. So was I. Exasperated, I whirled right into Aiden. "Whoa! Sorry."

He raised his eyebrows. "Don't roam off far." That was all he said.

Caleb pulled me to the side. "What's that all about?"

"Ah, Lucian wants to talk with me or something."

He cringed. "That's gotta be awkward."

"You ain't kidding." I momentarily forgot the Apollyon's tattoos.

Even if I'd wanted to, I didn't get to roam very far. Our little group made it out front and into the setting sun. Everyone appeared to be talking about the Apollyon. No one had expected him to be here or knew how long he'd been one of Lucian's Guards. Since Lucian had taken up residence on the main island, it seemed like someone should've known about the Apollyon's presence earlier.

That question switched to a much more interesting one.

"The Apollyon's usually out there hunting daimons." Luke popped up on the railing. "Why would he be reassigned to guard Lucian?"

"Maybe something's going on." Caleb's eyes darted back to the building. "Like something big. Maybe Lucian's been threatened."

"By what?" I frowned, leaning against one of the columns. "He's always surrounded by a crap ton of Guards. Not a single daimon could get close to him."

"Who cares?" Lea sucked in her lower lip and sighed. "The Apollyon is here, and he's hot. Do we need to worry with anything else?"

I scrunched up my face. "Wow. You'll make an excellent Sentinel one day."

She sneered at me. "At least *I will* be a Sentinel one day."

My eyes narrowed on Lea, but Olivia's nonstop fidgeting drew my anger. "What is your deal?"

Olivia glanced up, her chocolate-colored eyes huge. "Sorry. It's just…I'm so antsy now." She shuddered and wrapped her arms around her waist. "I don't know how you guys can say he's hot. Don't get me wrong, but he's the Apollyon. All that power is frightening."

"All that power is sexy." Lea leaned back, closed her eyes and sighed. "Can you imagine what he's like in—?"

The doors behind us swung open, and Aiden motioned me forward. On the steps below, someone made a low noise. I ignored it and left my little group of enemies and friends behind.

"So soon?" I asked once I was inside.

He nodded. "I guess they want to get this over with."

"Oh." I followed Aiden up the stairs. "Hey. Thanks for the uniform." The memory of him getting it for me made me smile.

He glanced over his shoulder. "It wasn't a problem. You look good in it."

My eyebrows shot up as my heart did a cartwheel.

Flushing, Aiden looked away. "I mean…it's good to see you in the uniform."

My smile grew to epic proportions. I caught up to him and took the stairs alongside his tall frame. "So…the Apollyon?"

Aiden stiffened. "I had no idea he was going to be with Lucian. His reassignment must've happened not too long ago."

"Why?"

He nudged my arm. "There are some things I cannot disclose, Alex."

Normally, I would've balked at that, but the way he said it, in such a teasing manner, made me feel airy and funny. "That's not fair."

Aiden didn't respond to that, and we went up a couple of floors in silence. "Did you…feel anything when Seth came in?"

"Seth?"

"The Apollyon is named Seth."

"Oh. That's a boring name. He should be called something more interesting."

He gave a low laugh. "What should he be called, then?"

I thought about that for a moment. "I don't know. Something Greek sounding, or at least, something kick-ass."

"What would you have named him?"

"I don't know. Something wicked cool, at least. Maybe Apollo. Get it? Apollo. Apollyon."

Aiden laughed. "Anyway, did you feel anything?"

"Yeah…it was strange. Almost like an electrical current or something."

He nodded, still smiling. "It's the aether in him. It's very powerful."

We neared the top floor, and I wiped a hand over my forehead. Stairs were a bitch. "Why do you ask?"

"You looked a little out of it. It's a bit unsettling the first time you're near him. I would've warned you if I'd realized he was going to be here."

"That wasn't the most disturbing thing."

"Hmm?"

I inhaled deeply. "The…tattoos were more unsettling." I watched him closely. His reaction would tell me if I was crazy or something.

Aiden came to a complete stop. "What?"

Oh man, I was crazy.

He came down a step. "What tattoos, Alex?"

I swallowed hard at the sharp look in his eyes. "I thought I saw some markings on him. They weren't there at first, but then they were. I…guess I'm seeing things."

Aiden exhaled slowly, his eyes on my face. He reached out, smoothing back a strand of my hair that had come loose. His hand lingered against my cheek, and in that moment, there was nothing more important than him touching me. In a daze, I stared up at him.

All too quickly, his hand dropped to his side, and his eyes met mine. I could see there were several things he wanted to say, but for whatever reason, he couldn't. "We have to get going. Marcus is waiting. Alex, try to be as nice as you can be, okay?"

He started back up the stairs, and I hurried to catch up with him. "So, was I seeing things?"

Aiden sent the Guards at the end of the hall a meaningful glance. "I don't know. We'll talk about it later."

Frustrated, I followed him to Marcus's office. Lucian hadn't arrived yet, and Marcus sat behind his big, old desk. He looked as he had in the lobby minus the suit jacket.

"Come. Have a seat." He motioned me forward.

I trudged across the office, relieved Aiden wasn't leaving me alone. He didn't take the seat next to me but remained along the wall in the same spot he'd stood the first time I'd found myself across from Marcus.

The whole scenario didn't bode well, but I didn't have a lot of time to dwell on it. Even with my back to the door, I knew when Lucian's group approached the office, but he wasn't the one causing the small hairs on my arms to stand up. The moment the Apollyon entered the room with my stepfather, all the oxygen evaporated.

Fighting my body's almost overpowering need to turn around, I clenched the arms of the chair. I didn't want to acknowledge Lucian, and I didn't want to look at the Apollyon.

Aiden cleared his throat, and my head snapped up. Marcus stared down at me with narrowed eyes. *Oh...crap.* My legs felt oddly numb as I forced myself to stand.

Out of the corner of my eye, I saw Seth take up position

alongside Aiden. He gave the pure blood a curt nod, which Aiden returned. Because I didn't see those tattoos, I allowed myself to lift my head.

Instantly our eyes met. His gaze wasn't a flattering one. He was checking me out, but not the way most guys did. Instead, he studied me. As close as we were, I realized he was young. I hadn't expected that. With all that power and reputation, I'd expected someone older, but he had to be close to my age.

And he really was…beautiful. Well, as beautiful as a guy could be. But his beauty was cold and hard, like he'd been pieced together to look a certain way, but the gods had forgotten to give him a touch of humanity—of life.

I felt the other stares, and when I looked at Aiden, he wore a perplexed expression as he watched me and Seth. Marcus… well, he looked expectant, as if he were waiting for something to happen.

"Alexandria." He nodded toward Lucian.

I suppressed the impulse to groan loudly and lifted my hand, wriggling my fingers at the Minister of Council. "Hi."

Someone—either Aiden or Seth—sounded like they swallowed a laugh. But then the unreasonable happened. Lucian stepped forward and wrapped his arms around me. I froze, my arms stuck awkwardly at my sides as the smell of herbs and incense assaulted my senses.

"Oh Alexandria, it is so good to see you. After all the years, and through all the fear and worry, you're standing here. The gods have answered our prayers." Lucian pulled back, but he kept his hands planted on my shoulders. His dark eyes scanned every inch of my face. "By the gods…you look so much like Rachelle."

I had no idea what to do. Of all the reactions I'd expected, this hadn't been a possibility. Whenever I'd been around Lucian in the past, he'd always looked at me with such cool disdain. This bizarre display of affection knocked me speechless.

"The moment Marcus notified me that you were found safe, I rejoiced. I told Marcus I had a place in my home for you."

Lucian's eyes settled back on mine, and there was something I didn't trust in that warm gaze. "I would have come sooner, but I was attending to Council business, you see? But your old room…from when you stayed with us...is still intact. I want you to come home, Alexandria. You do not need to stay here."

My mouth dropped open at that point, and I wondered if he had been replaced by a nicer pure blood in the last three years. "What?"

"I'm sure Alexandria is just overcome by her happiness," Marcus commented blandly.

There was that choked sound again, and I began to suspect that Seth was the culprit. Aiden was too well-trained to slip up twice. I stared at Lucian. "I'm…just confused."

"Confused? I can imagine. After all that you have been through." Lucian released my shoulders, but then he grabbed my hand. I tried not to let my cringe show. "You're far too young to suffer as you have. The tag…it will never go away, will it, dear?"

My free hand went to my neck self-consciously. "No."

He nodded sympathetically, and then led me to the chairs. He let go of my hand, readjusting his robes as he took a seat. I slumped into the other chair.

"You must come home." Lucian's eyes bored into mine. "You don't need to struggle to catch up with the others. This life is no longer necessary for you. I've spoken with Marcus at great length. You can attend the Covenant in the fall as a student, but not one in training."

I couldn't have heard that right. Halfs didn't attend the Covenant as students. They trained or they went into servitude.

Marcus sat down slowly, his bright gaze fastened on me. "Alexandria, Lucian is offering you a chance for a very different life."

I couldn't stop it. The laugh started in my throat and bubbled out. "This…this is a joke, right?"

Lucian exchanged a look with Marcus. "No. This is no joke, Alexandria. I know we weren't always close when you were younger, but after all that has happened, I have seen where I have failed you as a father."

I laughed again, earning a disapproving glare from Marcus. "I'm sorry." I gasped as I pulled myself back under control. "This is just so not what I expected."

"You do not need to apologize, my daughter."

I choked. "You're not my father."

"Alexandria!" Marcus warned.

"What?" I looked at my uncle. "He's not."

"It is all right, Marcus," Lucian's voice filled with velvet-covered steel. "When Alexandria was younger, I wasn't much of anything to her. I let my own bitterness rule everything. But now, it all seems so very shallow." He turned to gaze at me. "If I had been a better father figure, then maybe you would have called for help when your mother took you away."

I ran a hand over the side of my face, feeling like I'd stepped into a different world—a world where Lucian wasn't a giant douche, and where I still had someone who was technically family and actually cared for me.

"But that is in the past, my dear. I've come to take you back home." Lucian gave me a thin-lipped smile. "I've already spoken with Marcus, and we agree that—considering the circumstances—it would be for the best."

I snapped out of my haze of dumbness. "Wait. I'm catching up, aren't I?" I whirled around in my seat. "Aiden, I'm catching up, right? I'll be ready in the fall."

"Yes." He looked past me at Marcus. "Quicker than I would've thought possible, to be honest."

Thrilled that he hadn't thrown me under the bus, I turned back to my uncle. "I can do this. I have to be a Sentinel. I don't want anything else." My voice rasped with desperation. "I can't do anything else." For the first time since I'd met Marcus, he actually looked pained, like he was about to say something he didn't want to.

"Alexandria, it's not about the training. I'm aware of your progress."

"Then what is it?" I didn't care that I had witnesses to my panic.

The walls were closing in, and I didn't even understand why.

"You will be taken care of." Lucian tried to look reassuring. "Alexandria, you can no longer be a Sentinel. Not with such a horrific conflict of interests."

"What?" I looked back and forth between my uncle and stepfather. "There's no conflict of interests. More than anyone, I have a reason to be a Sentinel!"

Lucian frowned. "More than anyone, you have a reason *not* to be a Sentinel."

"Minister—" Aiden stepped forward, his eyes narrowing on Lucian.

"I know you've worked hard with her and I appreciate that, St. Delphi. But I cannot allow this." Lucian held up a hand. "What do you think will happen once she graduates? Once she leaves the island?"

"Uh, I'll hunt and kill daimons?"

Lucian turned to me. "Hunt and kill daimons?" His face turned paler than normal—which was saying something—as he turned to Marcus. "She doesn't know, does she?"

Marcus eyes closed briefly. "No. We thought…it would be for the best."

Unease slid down my back. "Know what?"

"Irresponsible," hissed Lucian. He lowered his head, pinching the bridge of his nose.

I shot to my feet. "Know *what*?"

Marcus looked up, his face drawn and colorless. "There's no easy way to say this. Your mother is not dead."

CHAPTER ELEVEN

Nothing existed but those words.

Marcus stood and edged around his desk. He stopped in front of me. The pained look had returned, but this time it was also mixed with sympathy.

The clicking of the wall clock and the gentle hum of the aquarium motors filled the room. No one spoke; no one pulled their eyes from me. I had no idea how long I stood there staring at him while I tried to piece together what he'd said. Nothing made sense to me at first. Hope and disbelief crashed together, then a horrifying realization as I understood the sympathetic look that had crossed his face. She was still alive, but…

"No…" I pushed away from the chair, trying to put distance between his words and me. "You're lying. I saw her. The daimon drained her, and I touched her. She was so…so cold."

"Alexandria, I'm sorry but—"

"No! It's impossible. She was dead!"

Aiden was at my side, placing a hand on my back. "Alex—"

I twisted out of his grasp. His voice—*oh gods*—his voice said it all. And when I looked at him, saw the sorrow etched across his striking face, I knew.

"Alex, there was another daimon. You know that." Marcus's voice carried over the sound of rushing blood that filled my ears.

"Yes, but..." I remembered how freaked out I'd been. Sobbing and hysterical, I'd shaken her and begged her to wake up, but she hadn't moved. And then I'd heard someone else outside.

Panicked, I'd barricaded myself into the room and grabbed the money. Things had been blurry then. I'd needed to run. It was what Mom had prepared me to do if something like that ever happened. My heart stuttered and missed a beat. "She... she was still alive? Oh—oh my gods. I left her." I wanted to puke all over Marcus's polished shoes. "I left her! I could've helped her! I could've done something!"

"No." Aiden reached for me, but I backed away. "There was nothing you could do."

"The other daimon did it?" I glared at Marcus, demanding an answer.

He nodded. "We assume so."

I started to tremble. "No. Mom wouldn't become... It's impossible. You—you're all wrong."

"Alexandria, you know how it could have been done."

Marcus was right. The energy the daimon passed on was tainted. She would've been addicted from the first moment on. It was a cruel way to turn a pure blood, robbing them of all free will.

I wanted to scream and cry, but I told myself I could handle this. The burning in my eyes told me I was a liar. I turned back to Marcus. "She's...a daimon?"

Something akin to pain flickered across his otherwise stoic face. "Yes."

I felt trapped in this room with virtual strangers. My eyes skittered across their faces. Lucian seemed bored with this, surprising considering his earlier outpouring of affection and support. Aiden looked like he was having a hard time keeping his expression blank. And Seth...well, he was watching me expectantly. Waiting for me to break down into hysterics, I assumed.

He might get that. I was one step away from a full-blown freak-out.

Swallowing against the thick lump in my throat, I tried to slow the wild beating in my chest. "How do you know this?"

"She's my sister. I would know if she were dead."

"You could be wrong." My whisper held a tiny shard of hope. Dead was better than the alternative. There was no coming back once a pure turned into a daimon. No amount of power or begging—not even the gods could fix it.

Marcus shook his head. "She was spotted in Georgia. Right before we found you."

I could tell this hurt him—possibly as much as it hurt me. She'd been his sister after all. Marcus wasn't as emotionless as he made himself out to be.

Then the Apollyon spoke. "You said her mother was seen in Georgia. Was Alexandria not in Georgia when you found her?" His voice was oddly accented, almost musical in quality.

I slowly turned to him.

"Yes." Aiden's dark brows furrowed.

Seth appeared to consider that. "Does it not strike anyone as odd? Could it be her mother remembered her? Was actually following her?"

A strange look crossed Marcus's face. "We're aware of the possibility."

It didn't make sense. When pures were turned, they didn't care about things from their previous lives. Or, at least, that was what we believed. Then again, it wasn't like anyone took the time to question a daimon. They were killed on sight. No questions asked.

"You believe her mother is aware of her. Possibly even looking for her?" Seth asked.

"There's a chance, but we cannot be sure. It could have been a coincidence that she was in Georgia." Marcus's words rang false.

"A coincidence that she was in Georgia in addition to the two other daimons following her?" Aiden asked. Marcus's scowl deepened, but Aiden continued, "You know how I feel about this. We don't know how much of their previous lives daimons retain. There's a chance she's looking for Alex."

The room tilted, and I squeezed my eyes shut. Looking for me? Not as my mother, but as a daimon. For what? The possibilities startled me…sickened me.

"It is all the more reason to remove her from the Covenant, St. Delphi. Under my care, Alexandria will be protected by Council Guards and the Apollyon. If Rachelle is hunting her, then she will be safest with me."

When I opened my eyes, I realized I was standing in the middle of the room. Each breath I took hurt. The need to give in to the tears was there, but I forced it down, all the way down. I lifted my chin and looked Marcus straight in the eye. "Do you know where she is now?"

Marcus raised his eyebrows as he turned to Lucian, who took a moment before he responded. "I have a dozen of my best Sentinels hunting for her."

I nodded. "And you all—all of you think that knowing

that my mother…is a daimon will get in the way of me being an effective Sentinel?"

There was a pause. "Not all of us agree, but yes."

"I can't be the first person to face that."

"Of course not," said Marcus, "but you are young, Alexandria, and you…"

My breath got caught in my throat again. "I'm what?"

Illogical? Distraught? Pissed off? Those were a few things I was feeling right now.

He shook his head. "Things are different for you, Alexandria."

"No. They're not." My voice rasped. "I'm a half-blood. My duty is to kill daimons no matter what. This won't affect me. My mom—she's dead to me."

Marcus stared at me. "Alexandria…"

"Will you force her from the Covenant, Minister?" Seth asked.

"*We* will not force her to leave," Marcus interjected, his eyes on me.

Lucian swung toward Marcus. "We agreed on this, Marcus." His strained voice was low. "She needs to be placed under my care."

I knew he was saying a hell of a lot more. I watched Marcus consider whatever that unspoken thing was.

"She can remain at the Covenant." Marcus kept his gaze steady. "Nothing will be jeopardized if she stays here. We can discuss more of this later, don't you agree?"

My eyes widened as I watched the Minister submit to Marcus. "Yes. We will discuss this in great detail."

Marcus nodded before turning to me. "The original deal still holds, Alexandria. You will have to prove to me you are ready to attend in the fall."

I let out the breath I'd been holding. "Is there anything else?"

"No." I turned to leave, but Marcus stopped me. "Alexandria…I'm sorry for what has happened. Your mother…didn't deserve this. Neither do you."

A sincere apology, but it meant nothing to me. I was numb inside, and I wanted nothing more than to be away from all of them. I left the office with my head high, not seeing anyone. I even made it past the Guards, who'd probably heard everything.

"Alex, hold up."

Struggling to control the cyclone of emotions building in me, I whirled around. Aiden had followed me out. I warned him off with a shaky hand. "Don't."

He flinched back. "Alex, let me explain."

Over his shoulder, I saw we weren't alone. The Guards stood by the closed doors to Marcus's office—and so did the Apollyon. He watched us with casual indifference.

I forced my voice low. "You knew this entire time, didn't you? You knew what'd really happened to my mother."

The muscle in his jaw ticked. "Yes. I knew."

Hurt exploded in my chest. Part of me had hoped he hadn't known, that he hadn't kept this from me. I took a step forward. "We've spent every day together and never once did it cross your mind to tell me? Did you think I didn't have a right to know the truth?"

"Of course, I thought you had the right, but it wasn't in your best interest. It still isn't. How can you focus on training—focus on preparing to kill daimons—when you know your mother's one of them?"

I opened my mouth, but nothing came out. How could I focus now?

"I'm sorry you had to find out this way, but I don't regret keeping it from you. We could've found her and disposed of the problem without you knowing any different. That was the plan."

"That was the plan? To kill her before I found out she was alive?" My voice grew louder with each word. "You preach to me about trusting you? How in the *hell* can I trust you now?"

Those words struck home. He took a step back, running a hand through his hair. "How does knowing what your mother is make you feel? What does it make you think?"

Hot tears burned in the back of my throat. I was going to break right here in front of him. I started backing up. "Please. Just leave me alone. Leave me alone."

This time, when I turned away, no one stopped me.

In a daze, I climbed into my bed. A sickening feeling settled over me. Part of me wanted to believe everyone was mistaken and that Mom wasn't a daimon.

My stomach churned and I curled into myself. Mom was out there, somewhere, and she was killing people. From the moment she'd turned, the need to feed on aether would've consumed her. Nothing else would matter to her. Even if she did remember me, it wouldn't be in the same way.

I scrambled from the bed, barely reaching the bathroom in time. I fell to my knees, clutched the sides of the toilet, and gagged until my body shook. When I was done, I had no strength to stand.

My thoughts whirled into a heady mess. *My mother's a daimon.*

Sentinels were out there, hunting her down. But I couldn't

replace her warm smile with that of a daimon's. She was my mother.

I pushed away from the toilet and rested my head against my knees. At some point, there was a knock at the door, but I ignored the sound. There was no one I wanted to see, no one I wanted to talk to. I didn't know how long I stayed there. It could've been minutes—or hours. I willed myself not to think and to just breathe. The breathing part was easy, but the not thinking part was impossible. Eventually I crawled to my feet and stared at my reflection.

Mom stared back at me—all except the eyes, the only thing we didn't share. But now...now she'd have those gaping sockets and her mouth would be full of jagged teeth.

And if she did see me again, she wouldn't smile or hug me. She wouldn't brush my hair back like she used to. There would be no tears of happiness. She might not even know my name.

She would try to kill me. And I would try to kill her.

CHAPTER TWELVE

By Sunday evening, I couldn't hide in my room anymore. Sick of thinking, sick of being alone, and sick of myself. Somewhere over the past day, my appetite had returned and I was starving.

I managed to make it over to the cafeteria before it closed its doors. Thankfully, it was empty, and I was able to eat three slices of cold pizza in peace. The food settled into a dense ball in my stomach, but I managed to get a fourth slice down.

The thick silence of the cafeteria engulfed me. With nothing going on, the endless chatter of my thoughts picked up again. *Mom. Mom. Mom.* Since Friday night, she was all I could think about.

Was there something I could've done differently? Could I have prevented her from turning into a monster? If I hadn't panicked after the attack, maybe I could've fended off the other daimon. I could've saved my mother from such a horrific fate.

Guilt turned the food in my stomach sour. I pushed myself from the table and headed outside just as one of the servants entered to close up for the night. A few kids moved across the quad, but no one I knew very well.

I don't know why I ended up in the main training room. It was past eight, but they never locked these rooms, although the weapons were secured after training sessions. I stopped in front of one of the dummies used for knife practice and the occasional boxing match. Restlessness itched through me as I stared at the lifelike figure.

Tiny nicks and grooves marked the neck, chest, and abdomen. They were the areas where halfs were trained to strike: the solar plexus, heart, neck, and stomach.

I ran my fingers over the indentations. Covenant-issued blades were wickedly sharp, designed to cut through the daimon's skin quickly and do maximum damage.

Eyeing the strike zones marked in red—places to hit or kick if I had to engage a daimon in hand-to-hand combat—I pulled my hair up into a messy twist. Aiden had allowed me to practice with the dummies a few times, probably because he'd gotten tired of me kicking him.

The first punch I threw knocked the dummy back an inch, maybe two. Blah. The second and third blows jarred it back a couple of more inches, but still did nothing for me. The swirling blur of emotions pressed up within me, demanding I cave into it. *Give in. Take Lucian up on his offer. Never risk facing Mom. Let someone else deal.*

I stepped back, resting my hands on my thighs.

My mother was a daimon. As a half-blood I was obligated to kill her. As her daughter I was obligated to…what? That answer had eluded me all weekend. What was I supposed to do?

Kill her. Run from her. Save her somehow.

A frustrated shriek escaped me as I swung my leg around

and connected with the center of the dummy. It swung back a foot or two, and when it came rushing back at me, I attacked—swinging, punching, and kicking. My anger and disbelief grew with each explosion.

This wasn't fair. None of this was.

Sweat poured off me, dampening my shirt until it clung to my skin and stray hairs stuck to the back of my neck. I couldn't stop. The violence poured out of me, becoming a physical thing. I could taste the anger in the back of my throat—thick like bile and heavy. I tuned into it. I became it.

The rage flowed through me and into my movements until my kicks and jabs became so precise that, if the dummy had been a real person, she'd be dead. Only then was I satisfied. I stumbled back, wiping my hand over my forehead and turned around.

Aiden stood in the doorway.

He came forward, stopping in the center of the room and taking the same position he normally did during our training sessions. He wore jeans, something I rarely saw him in.

Aiden didn't say anything as he watched me. I didn't know what he was thinking or why he was there. I didn't care. Fury still boiled within me. Somehow I imagined it was what being a daimon must feel like, like some kind of unseen force controlled my every move. Out of control—I was out of control now. Without saying a word, I crossed the distance between us. A wary look flickered across his eyes.

There was no thought behind this, just overwhelming anger and raw hurt. I cocked back my arm and punched him right on the side of his jaw. Fierce pain exploded across my knuckles.

"Dammit!" I bent, bringing my hand back to my chest. I didn't think it would hurt that much. Even worse was the fact I'd barely made an impact on him.

He turned back to me as if I hadn't just punched him in the face and frowned. "Did that make you feel better? Change anything for you?"

I straightened. "No! I'd like to do it again."

"You wanna fight?" He stepped to the side, tipping his head down at me. "Then fight me."

He didn't have to ask me twice. I launched myself at him. He blocked the first jab, but my anger made me quicker than he'd realized. The broad side of my arm slipped past his blocks, cutting him across the chest. It didn't faze him—not one freaking bit. But the pleasure spiked inside me, propelling me forward. Burning with rage and another near feral emotion, I fought harder and better than I ever had in practice.

We circled each other, exchanging blows. Aiden didn't go all out on me, and it only pissed me off. I attacked harder, moving him backward across the mats. His eyes flared a dangerous silver as he caught my fist inches from connecting with his nose. Bad form to aim above the chest but screw it.

"That's enough." Aiden pushed me back.

But it wasn't enough. It would never be *enough*. I went to use one of the offensive moves he'd taught me days ago. Aiden moved so he caught me midflight, bringing me down on the mat. Once he had me down he rocked back on his heels.

"I know you're angry." He wasn't even out of breath. I, on the other hand, was gasping for air. "I know you're confused and hurt. What you're feeling is unimaginable."

My chest rose and fell rapidly. I started to sit up, but he pushed me down with one hand. "Yes, I'm angry!"

"You have every right to be."

"You should've told me!" The burning in my eyes increased. "Someone should've told me! If not Marcus, then you should have."

He turned his head away. "You're right."

His softly spoken words didn't ease me. I still heard how he'd said he didn't regret not telling me, that it was for the best. He lowered his hands to his thighs after a few moments.

Wrong move.

I reared off the mat, reaching for his silky hair. Total girl move, but somewhere along the way, I'd lost myself to the anger.

"Stop this!" He captured my wrists easily. Actually it was embarrassing how quickly he subdued me. This time he pinned me to the mat. "Stop this, Alex," he said again, much lower.

I threw my head back, ready to plant my foot somewhere when our eyes met. I did stop then, with his face inches from mine. The atmosphere changed as one of the wild emotions swirling through me managed to break free and rear its head.

His lean torso and legs pressed against mine in a way that made me think of other things—stuff that wasn't fighting or killing, but did involve sweating, lots of sweating. Breathing became difficult as we continued to stare at one another. His dark waves had fallen forward into his eyes. He wasn't moving, and I couldn't even if I'd wanted to. I didn't. Oh gods, I didn't want to move *ever*. I saw the moment he recognized the change in me. Something shifted in those eyes of his and his lips parted.

This was just a harmless, stupid crush. Even as I lifted my head, bringing my lips mere inches from his, I kept telling myself that. I didn't want him. Not this badly—not more than anything I'd ever wanted in life.

I kissed him.

At first, it wasn't much of a kiss. My lips just brushed his, and when he didn't move away, I pushed harder. Aiden seemed too stunned to do much of anything for a few seconds. But then he released my wrists and his hands slid up my arms.

The kiss deepened, full of passion and anger. There was also frustration, so much frustration. Then Aiden pressed down, and I wasn't the one doing the kissing. His lips moved against mine, his fingers pressing into my skin. After only a few seconds, he broke off the kiss and sprung away from me.

From several feet away, Aiden crouched on the balls of his feet. His heavy breathing filled the space between us. Eyes wide, they'd dilated until they were almost black.

I sat up and scooted back. What I'd done made it through the thick haze clouding my thoughts. Not only had I punched a pure blood in the face, I'd also kissed him. Oh...*oh man.* My cheeks flushed; my entire body flushed.

Aiden stood slowly. "It's all right." His voice rasped. "These things happen...when you're feeling a lot of stress."

These things happened? I didn't think so. "I...can't believe I did that."

"It's just stress." He remained at a safe distance. "It's okay, Alex."

I jumped to my feet. "I think I should go now."

He started forward then, but stopped short, wary of coming any closer. "Alex...it's all right."

"Yeah, damn stress thing, huh? Whoa. Okay. Everything is totally okay." I backed up, looking everywhere but at him. "I needed that—not the last thing! Or the thing when I punched you! But the things when I was...you know, working out my aggression...and stuff. All right...see you tomorrow." I fled the room—then the entire building.

Outside in the thick, humid night air, I smacked my forehead and groaned. "Oh my gods." Somewhere behind me a door opened, so I started down the pathway again.

I really wasn't paying attention to where I was going. Shock and embarrassment didn't adequately describe what I was feeling.

Mortification was too boring of a word. Maybe I *could* blame it on stress. I wanted to laugh, except I also wanted to cry.

Would I be able to live this one down? Gods, I couldn't believe I'd actually kissed him. Nor could I believe there'd been a moment where he'd kissed me back, that he'd pressed against me in a way that said he'd wanted it just as badly as I had. That had to have been a figment of my imagination.

I needed a new trainer. I needed a new trainer pronto. There was no way I could ever face him again without keeling over and dying. No way at all and—

Someone stepped in front of me. I moved to the side to avoid whoever it was, but the person blocked me. Pissed I couldn't sulk in privacy, I fired off without looking up. "Gods! Get the hell out of my—" The words died on my lips.

The Apollyon stood in front of me.

"Well, good evening to you." His lips curled in a casual smile.

"Um...sorry, I didn't see you." Or *feel* him, which was weird considering both times I'd felt him before by just laying eyes on him.

"Obviously. You were staring at the ground as if it had done something terrible to you."

"Yeah, I'm kinda having a bad weekend...that just won't die." I sidestepped him, but he moved in front of me again. "Excuse me." I used possibly my sweetest voice *ever*. He was, after all, the Apollyon.

"Could I just have a few minutes of your time?"

I looked around the empty courtyard, knowing I

couldn't refuse him. "Sure, but I need to get back to my dorm soon."

"Then I will walk you there and we can talk."

I nodded, having no freaking clue what he could possibly want to talk to me about. I motioned him forward wearily.

"I've been looking for you." He fell into step beside me. "Apparently, you've holed yourself up in your dorm, and your friends have advised me males are not allowed in the dorm. I'm no exception, which I find strange and very irritating. Silly little Covenant rules shouldn't apply to me."

I frowned, not sure what to be skeeved out about more: that he knew who my friends were or that he was looking for me. Both things were equally creepy to me. He could snap my neck like a twig. He was the Apollyon—someone *no one* wanted looking for them.

"So, I've been waiting for you to reappear."

Now this *was* creepy. I felt his stare, but I kept my eyes trained ahead. "Why?"

Seth easily fell into step beside me. "I want to know what you are."

I froze, and I had to look at him. He was pretty close, not touching. Frankly he looked like he didn't want to. Caution played across his arresting features as he watched me. "I'm a half-blood."

He arched a blond brow. "Wow. I had no idea you were a half-blood, Alexandria. Color me shocked."

My eyes narrowed on him. "Call me Alex. So why did you ask?"

"Yes, I know. Everyone calls you by some boy's name." His upper lip curled and frustration filled his voice. "Anyway, you know that is not what I'm asking. I want to know what you are."

Pissing off the Apollyon probably wasn't the smartest thing to do, but my mood was somewhere between crappy and really crappy. I folded my arms across my chest. "I'm a girl. You're a boy. Does that clear things up for you?"

One corner of his mouth quirked. "Thank you for the gender lesson. I've always been confused when it comes to boy and girl parts, but once again, not what I'm asking." He stepped forward, tilting his head to the side. "Around May, Lucian requested my presence at Council. They found you around the same time. I find that strange."

My instincts screamed for me to take a step back, but I refused. "Okay?"

"I don't believe in coincidences. Lucian's order has to do with you. So it begs a very important question."

"Which is?

"What is so important about a little girl whose mother is a daimon?" He circled around me. I twisted, following his movement. "Why would Lucian want me here now, but not before? You were right in your dean's office. You would not be the first half or even pure to face down a loved one or a friend in battle. What makes you so special?"

Irritation twitched within me. "I have no clue. Why don't you go and ask him?"

Several short strands escaped the leather thong and fell around his face. "I doubt Lucian is being truthful."

"Lucian doesn't have to be truthful."

"You would know. He is your stepfather."

"Lucian is nothing to me. What you saw in that office was bizarre. He must've been high on power or meth."

"Then you would not be upset if I said he was a pompous ass?"

I bit back my laugh. "Nope."

His lips curved into a half smile. "I intend to figure out why I was pulled away from hunting to guard a girl—"

My brows rose. "You're not guarding me. You're guarding Lucian."

"Is that so? Why would Lucian need me as a Guard? He rarely leaves the Council and is always surrounded by several layers of protection. A fledging Guard could assist him. This is wasting my time."

He had a good point, but I didn't have any answers for him. I shrugged and started walking again, hoping he wouldn't follow, but he did.

"So, I'll ask you again. What are you?"

The first two times he'd asked the question, it had just annoyed me, but the third time poked around inside my brain and pushed a memory loose. I thought of the night in the factory. What had the daimon said after he'd tagged me? I stopped, frowning as the words floated to the surface. *"What are you?"* My hand went to my neck, brushing over the ultra-smooth skin of the scar.

Seth's eyes narrowed on me. "What is it?"

I looked up. "You know, you aren't the first person to ask me that. A daimon asked me…after he tagged me."

Interest flickered over his face. "Maybe I just need to bite you to find out."

My hand dropped to my side and I cut him a look. He was joking, but it still weirded me out. "Good luck with that."

He smiled this time, flashing a row of perfect white teeth. His smile was nothing like Aiden's, but it was nice. "You don't seem afraid of me."

I took a deep breath. "Why, should I be?"

Seth shrugged. "Everyone is afraid of me. Even Lucian—even daimons are afraid of me. You know, they can sense me, and even though they know I am Death to them, they come running right up to me. I'm like fine dining to them. They can't pass me up."

"Yeah...and I'm like fast food," I murmured, recalling what the daimon in Georgia had said.

"Maybe...or maybe not. Want to hear something strange?"

I glanced around, looking for an escape. My stomach did the icky twisty thing again. "Not really."

He tucked the loose strands of hair behind his ear. "I knew you were here. Not you, so to speak. But I knew someone—someone different. I felt it outside, before I entered the lobby. It was like a magnetic pull. I zeroed in on you immediately."

The longer I talked to him, the more off I felt. "Oh?"

"That has never happened before." He unfolded his arms and reached for me. I jumped back. Annoyance pulled his lips down at the corners.

There were a multitude of reasons why I didn't want him to touch me. Alarmed that he was actually going to, I blurted out the first thing that came to mind. "I saw your tattoos."

Seth froze, one arm outstretched toward me. Surprise shone on his face before his arm fell and he suddenly looked wary. Hell, he no longer looked like he wanted to touch me—or be in the same zip code as me. He backed off this time.

I should've been happy, but it only increased the bundle of nerves forming in my belly. "I...have to go. It's late."

The sudden rush of air caused my head to jerk up. Seth moved fast, possibly faster than Aiden, and now he was back in my personal space. "Did you mean what you said in the dean's office? That your mother was dead to you? Do you really believe that?"

Caught off guard by the question, I didn't answer.

He leaned in closer, his voice low but still melodic. "If not, then you better hope you never face her, because she will kill you."

CHAPTER THIRTEEN

Practice was epically awkward the following day. Aiden spent the time pretending I hadn't kissed him, which created a conflicting set of emotions in me. Part of me was glad he didn't bring it up. And the other part…well, that part felt stung. Although it totally made no sense, I wanted him to acknowledge what'd passed between us.

But I did bring the anger to practice. I fought better and blocked more than I ever had. Aiden praised my technique in a truly professional manner, which irked me. When we rolled up the mats at the end of practice, I felt all kinds of confrontational.

"I ran into Seth…last night." The words "last night" probably carried a lot more weight than anything else I said. Aiden stiffened, but didn't respond. "He wants to know why Lucian ordered him to Council."

Aiden straightened, brushing his hands across his thighs. "He shouldn't question his orders."

I arched a brow. "He thinks it has something to do with me." He looked at me then, face impressively blank.

"Does it?" No answer. "Does it have something to do with what happened to my mom?" My hands curled into fists at his continued silence. "You said last night I had every right to know what happened to my mother. So I think I have every right to know what the hell is going on. Or are you going to lie to me again?"

That got a response. "I never lied to you before, Alex. I omitted the truth."

I rolled my eyes. "Yeah, that's not lying."

Irritation flared across his features. "Do you think I liked knowing what happened to your mother? Enjoyed seeing how hurt you were when you found out?"

"That's not the point."

"The point is I'm here to train you. To get you ready to attend classes in the fall."

"And nothing else, huh?" The hurt that sprang forth fueled my anger. "Not even the common courtesy of telling me what's going on when you so obviously know what's happening?"

Uncertainty darkened his expression. He shook his head and ran a hand through his hair. The dark waves tumbled back to his forehead like they always did. "I don't know why the Minister ordered Seth to the Council. I'm just a Sentinel, Alex. I'm not privy to the inner workings of the Council, but..." He took a deep breath. "I don't entirely trust your stepfather. His display in Marcus's office was...abnormal."

Out of all the things I expected him to say, I was shocked he would admit that. It defused some—not all—of my anger. "What do you think he's up to?"

"That's all I know, Alex. If I were you...I'd be careful around Seth. Apollyons can be unstable at times, dangerous. They've been known to lose their tempers, and if he's angry about his relocation..."

I nodded, but I wasn't really concerned about that. Aiden left without saying much of anything else. Disappointed, I left the training room and ran into Caleb outside.

The two of us stared at each other.

"So…I'm assuming you've heard?" I tried to sound nonchalant.

Caleb nodded, his sky-blue eyes sorrowful. "Alex, I'm sorry. It's not right—not fair."

"It's not," I whispered.

Knowing how I was with these kinds of things, he left it alone after that. We didn't bring it up again, and for the rest of the night it was like things were normal. Mom wasn't a daimon, and she wasn't out there draining pures. It was easier to go on, pretending that everything was normal. It worked for a while.

A couple of days later, I got my wish for a new trainer. Well…almost. When I opened up the double doors to the main training room, Aiden wasn't alone. Kain stood beside him, looking like he clearly remembered our last training session.

My steps slowed as my eyes bounced between the two. "Hey…?"

The look on Aiden's face was unreadable—a common expression since I'd kissed him. "Kain is going to be helping us train three days a week."

"Oh." I felt torn between being excited about learning whatever Kain could show me and disappointed someone else was encroaching on *my* time with Aiden.

I really did have a lot to learn from Kain. He wasn't as fast as Aiden, but I'd come to anticipate the moves Aiden used. With Kain, it was all new. By the end of practice, I felt a little better about the changeup in our training, but there was still a nagging worry Kain's reappearance had something to do with the kiss.

Kain wasn't the only one who kept popping back up. Over the following week, Seth lingered around campus, showing up in the rec room, the cafeteria, and the training room. It made avoiding him—which had been my plan—impossible. Trying to hold my own against Kain with just Aiden watching was bad enough, but having the Apollyon in the mix totally sucked.

Thankfully, today was Kain's off day. He'd accompanied some group of pures on a weekend getaway. I felt bad for him. Yesterday, he'd spent the majority of practice bitching about it. He was a born hunter, not a babysitter. I'd be pissed too if I'd gotten saddled with that assignment.

In practice, we'd finally moved beyond blocking techniques and were working on different types of takedowns. Even though I'd face-planted Aiden several times throughout the day, he was super-patient with me. Besides lying to me about my mom, the guy had to be a saint of some sort.

"You've done really well this week." He gave me a hesitant smile as we headed out.

I shook my head. "Kain kicked my ass in practice yesterday."

Aiden pushed the door open and held it for me. Normally, he left the doors wide open, but lately he'd taken to closing them. "Kain has field experience on you, but you were holding your own against him."

My lips curved upward. As sad as it was, I lived for those moments when he complimented my improvement. "Thanks."

He nodded. "Do you think it helps to work with Kain?"

We stopped at the doors leading outside. I was kind of stunned he would even ask for my opinion. "Yeah...he has different tactics than you. I think it helps that you can see what I'm doing wrong and walk me through it."

"Good. It's what I hoped for."

"Really?" I blurted out. "I thought it was because—never mind."

Aiden's eyes narrowed. "Yes. Why else would I want Kain to help?"

Horrified and embarrassed that I had unwittingly gone *there*, I turned away. "Uh…forget I said anything."

"Alex." He said my name in that soft, infinitely patient way. Against my will, I turned back to him. "Bringing Kain in has nothing to do with that night."

I wanted to run and hide. I also wanted to find a muzzle for myself. "It doesn't?"

"No."

"About that night…" I took a deep breath. "I'm sorry about hitting you and…the other thing."

His eyes deepened, turning more silver than gray. "I accept your apology for hitting me."

I hadn't realized it until then, but we were standing close enough that our shoes touched. I don't know if he had moved, or if I had. "What about the other thing?"

Aiden smiled then, flashing those deep dimples. His arm brushed mine as he reached around and opened the door. "You don't have to apologize for the other thing."

I stumbled into the bright sunlight. "I don't?"

He shook his head, still smiling, and then simply left. Confused and a bit obsessed over what *that* could mean, I joined my friends for dinner and found our newest addition was once again at our table. My smile faded as I saw the open wonder splattered across Caleb's face—the look he got whenever he talked to Seth.

They didn't even look as I sat down at the table with them.

Everyone appeared consumed by whatever Seth was telling them. I seemed to be the only one not impressed by him.

"How many kills have you made?" Caleb leaned forward.

Hadn't they already had this conversation? *Oh yes. Yesterday.* I bit back a sigh of annoyance.

Seth reclined in the plastic chair, one leg propped against the edge of the table. "Over twenty."

"Wow." Elena sighed, a look of pure admiration glossing over her eyes.

I rolled my eyes and took a bite of the dry pot roast.

"You don't know the exact number?" Caleb's brows rose. "I'd keep a list with dates and times."

I found that morbid, but Seth grinned. "Twenty-five. Would have been twenty-six but the last bastard got away from me."

"Got away from the Apollyon?" I took a sip of my water. "Embarrassing."

Caleb's eyes grew to the size of saucers, and honestly, I don't know what had provoked me to say it—probably that little piece of advice he'd given me the last time we'd talked privately. Seth seemed to take it in stride. He tipped his bottle of water toward me. "How many have you killed?"

"Two." I shoved a forkful of meat into my mouth.

"Not bad for an untrained girl."

I smiled brightly. "Nope."

Caleb shot me a warning look before turning back to Seth. "So...how does it feel to use the elements?"

"Amazing." Seth's eyes stayed on me. "I've never been tagged."

I stiffened, hand halfway to my mouth. Ouch.

"What does that feel like, Alex?"

I forced myself to chew the food slowly. "Oh…it felt wonderful."

He moved, leaning close enough I could feel his breath on my neck. My entire body locked up. "Nasty little scar you got there."

The fork fell from my fingers, slopping mashed potatoes across the table. I mustered my best "ice princess" look and met his gaze.

"You're in my personal space, buddy."

A playful smile graced his lips. "So? What are you going to do about it? Throw your mashed potatoes at me? I'm consumed by terror."

Punch you in the face. That's what I wanted to say and do, but even I wasn't that stupid. Instead I returned the smile. "Why are you here? Aren't you supposed to be doing important things, like *guarding* Lucian?"

Caleb and the rest of the kids didn't catch my dig, but he did. The smile slipped from his face and he stood. Turning to them, he nodded. "It was nice talking with you all." On his way out he brushed past Olivia. The poor girl looked like she was going to glitch out.

"Oh my gods, Alex. He's the Apollyon," hissed Elena.

I cleaned up my mess of mashed potatoes. "Yeah. So?"

She dropped a napkin over the bulk of the potatoes. "Uh…you could be a little more respectful toward him."

"I was being respectful. I just wasn't kissing his ass." I raised my brows as I looked at her.

"We weren't kissing his ass." She frowned, scooping up the mess.

I pursed my lips. "Not what it looked like to me."

"Whatever." Caleb exhaled with a whistle. "I mean, wow. He's killed twenty-five daimons. He can wield all four elements plus the fifth—the *fifth*, Alex. Yeah, I'll kiss his ass all day long."

I stifled my groan. "You should start a fan club. Elena can be your vice president."

He smirked. "Maybe I will."

Thankfully, we moved past talking about Seth once Olivia sat down at our table. Caleb was all too happy to see her, and my gaze bounced between the two of them.

"Have you guys heard?" Olivia's coffee-colored eyes widened.

I was half afraid to ask. "What?"

She cast a nervous glance at me. "There was a daimon attack in Lake Lure late last night. The Council just found out. They couldn't get ahold of the group of pures and their Guards."

The information wiped everything else from my thoughts. I wasn't thinking about my rude behavior toward Seth or what Aiden could've meant earlier. I wasn't even thinking about Mom.

Elena gasped. "What? Lake Lure is only four hours from here."

Lake Lure was a small community where several of the pures liked to get away. Just like the place in Gatlinburg where my mom used to take me, it should've been well guarded. Safe. At least, that was what we'd been told.

"How's it possible?" I hated the way my voice squeaked out.

Olivia shook her head. "I don't know, but several of the Council Guards left with the group this weekend. They had at least two trained Sentinels."

My mouth went dry. No. It couldn't have been the same group—the group Kain had been bitching about babysitting.

"Anyone we know?" Caleb leaned in.

She glanced around, lowering her voice. "Mom couldn't say much more. She was leaving to go investigate the scene, but she did say Kain and Herc were the two Sentinels. I haven't heard anything about what's happened to them, but..."

Daimons didn't leave halfs alive.

Silence fell across the table as we processed the news. I swallowed against the sudden tightness in my throat. Kain had been kicking my butt and joking around with me just yesterday. He's good and fast, but if he was missing, it meant he'd been taken for a later snack. Kain was a half, so he couldn't be turned into a daimon.

No. I shook my head. *He got away. They just haven't found him yet.*

Caleb pushed his plate away. Now I wished I hadn't eaten so much. The news was doing gross stuff to the food in my stomach, but all of us pretended we weren't *that* affected. We were in training.

In a year or so, we'd be facing this stuff in person.

"What about the pures? Who were they?" Elena's voice trembled.

The look crossing her face filled me with unease. Suddenly I understood it wasn't just Kain we'd lost.

"There were two families." Olivia swallowed hard. "Liza and Zeke Dikti, and their daughter Letha. The other family was...Lea's father and stepmother."

Silence.

None of us moved. I don't even think we breathed. Gods, I hated Lea. Really I did, but I knew what this felt like. Or, at least, I used to.

Finally, Caleb found the ability to speak. "Were Lea or her half sister with them?"

Olivia shook her head. "Dawn stayed at home and Lea is

here—*was* here. On the way over, I saw Dawn. She'd come to get her."

"This is so terrible." Elena's face paled. "How old is Dawn?"

"She's around twenty-two." Caleb bit his lip.

"She's old enough to take her parent's seat, but who…" Olivia trailed off.

We all knew what she was thinking. Who would want to take a Council seat that way?

Back in my dorm, I found two letters stuck to my door. One was a folded piece of paper and the other was an envelope. The paper contained a scribbled message from Aiden calling off practice tomorrow due to unforeseen events. Obviously, he'd been called to investigate the attack.

I folded up the note and placed it on the table. The envelope was something else entirely; it was from my phony stepfather. I didn't read the card. However, there were several hundred dollar bills folded inside it. Those I kept. The card went in the trash bin.

After spending the rest of the evening thinking about what'd happened in Lake Lure, I had trouble sleeping and woke up way too early, filled with an itchy agitation.

By lunch, I'd found out Seth had also taken the four-hour drive with Aiden. More information drifted back to the Covenant as the day progressed. Olivia had been correct. All the pures who'd been in Lake Lure had been massacred. So had the half-blood servants. They'd searched the lake and the grounds, but only four of the Security team had been found. They'd been drained of all their aether. The other two, including Kain, had not been discovered.

Olivia, who'd become our main source of information, filled us in with what she knew. "Some of the dead suffered multiple tags. But the half-bloods they found…they were covered in daimon tags."

I read the same, sickening question in the pale faces around the table: *Why?* By birth, half-bloods had less aether in them. Why would daimons repeatedly drain a half when they had pures who were full of aether?

I swallowed hard. "Do you know how they got past the Guards?"

She shook her head. "Not yet, but there were security cameras around the cabins, so they're hoping the video footage will reveal something."

Some of the halfs tried for some sort of normalcy as the day wore on, and none of us wanted to be alone. But the activity at the pool tables lacked the normal laughs and the game systems sat untouched in front of the televisions.

The sullen atmosphere started to get to me. I retreated to my dorm room after dinner. A few hours later, there was a soft knock on my door. I got up, expecting Caleb or Olivia.

Aiden stood there, and my heart did a weird flip I was beginning to hate.

I asked the stupidest question. "Are you okay?" Of course he wasn't. I mentally kicked myself as he stepped inside and closed the door.

"You've heard?"

No point in lying. "Yeah, I heard last night." I sat down on the edge of the couch.

"I just got back. News travels fast." I'd never seen him so exhausted or grave. His hair looked as if he'd run his hands through it many times, and now it went every which direction.

The need to comfort him nearly overpowered me, but

there was nothing I could do. He gestured at the couch. "May I?"

I nodded. "It was…really bad, wasn't it?"

He sat down, resting his hands on his knees. "It was pretty bad."

"How did they get to them?"

Aiden glanced up. "They caught one of the pures outside. Once the daimons got in—the attack surprised the Guards. There were three daimons…and the Sentinels—they fought hard."

I swallowed. Three daimons. The night in Georgia, I'd been surprised by how many were together. Aiden was thinking along the same lines. "The daimons are really starting to work in groups. They're showing a level of restraint in their attacks, an organization they never had before. Two of the half-bloods are missing."

"What do you think it means?"

He shook his head. "We're not sure, but we'll find out."

I had no doubt he would. "I'm sorry you have to deal with this."

A hardness settled across him. He didn't move. "Alex… there's something I need to tell you."

"Okay." I wanted to believe the seriousness in his voice was due to all the heavy stuff he had been dealing with all day.

"There were surveillance cameras. They let us get a pretty good idea of what happened outside the house, but not inside." He took a deep breath and lifted his head. Our eyes met. "I came here first."

My chest tightened. "This…this is gonna be bad, isn't it?"

Aiden didn't mince words. "Yes."

The air caught in my lungs. "What…is it?"

He twisted his long body toward me. "I wanted to make

sure you knew before anyone else did. We can't stop people from finding out. There were a lot of people there."

"Okay?"

"Alex, there's no easy way to say this. We saw your mother on the surveillance cameras. She was one of the daimons who attacked them."

I stood, and then I sat right back down. My brain refused to process this. I shook my head as my thoughts went on repeat. *No. No. No. Not her—anyone but her.*

"Alex?"

It felt like I couldn't catch my breath. This was worse than seeing dullness in her eyes as she'd lain on the floor, worse than hearing she'd been turned. This…this was worse.

"Alex, I'm so sorry."

I swallowed hard. "Did…did she kill any of them?"

"There's no way to know unless we find either of the halfs alive, but I'd assume so. It's what a daimon does."

I blinked back hot tears. *Do not cry. Don't do it.* "Have you seen Lea? Is she okay?"

Astonishment flickered across Aiden's face.

The laugh that came out of me was shaky and broken sounding. "Lea and I aren't friends, but I wouldn't…"

"You wouldn't want her to go through this. I know." He reached over and took my hand in his. His fingers felt remarkably warm, strong, and grounding. "Alex, there's more to this."

I almost laughed again. "How could there be more?"

His hand tightened around mine. "It can't be a coincidence she is this close to the Covenant. It leaves no doubt that she remembers you."

"Oh." I stopped there, unable to go any further. I turned away from Aiden, staring at our hands. Silence stretched out between us, and then he leaned over and wrapped his other arm around my shoulders. Every muscle in my body locked up. Even in a time like this, I could recognize the wrongness of this situation. Aiden shouldn't be offering me any sort of comfort. He probably shouldn't have even come to tell me. Halfs and pures didn't comfort one another.

But with Aiden I never felt like a half-blood, and I never thought of him as a pure blood.

Aiden murmured something I couldn't make out. It sounded like ancient Greek, the language of the gods. I don't know why, but the sound of his voice ripped through the barriers I was trying and failing at stitching together. I sunk forward, resting my head against his shoulder. I squeezed my eyes against the harsh stinging. My breath came out in short, shaky gasps. I don't know how long we stayed like that, his cheek against the top of my head, our fingers wrapped together.

"You show amazing strength," he murmured, stirring the hair around my ear.

I forced my eyes open. "Oh…I'm just saving all of this up for years of therapy later."

"You don't give yourself enough credit. What you've had to face? You're very strong." He pulled back, his hand brushing across my cheek so quickly I truly believed I'd imagined the touch. "Alex, I have to go check in with Marcus. He's waiting for me."

I nodded as he let go of my hand and stood. "Could… could there be a chance she didn't kill them?"

Aiden stopped by the door. "Alex, I don't know. It would be highly unlikely."

"Will you let me know if they do find either of the halfs alive?" I knew it was pointless.

He nodded. "Yes. Alex, if you need anything, let me know." He pulled the door closed with a click behind him.

Alone, I slid to the floor and pressed my head against my knees. There could be a chance Mom hadn't killed anyone. She could be with the other daimons because she didn't know what else to do. Maybe she was confused. Maybe she was coming for me.

I shuddered, pressing farther down. My heart hurt. It felt like it was shattering again—all over again. There was the smallest, tiniest chance she hadn't killed anyone. Even I knew how stupid it was to really hold onto that chance, but I did. Because what else did I have? Grandma Piperi's words became clearer to me—not just what she'd said, but what she hadn't.

For whatever reason, Mom had left the safety of the community to pull me away from the Covenant, setting all of this—this huge mess—into motion. During those three years, I'd never once called out for help, never stopped the insanity of living unprotected among mortals.

The countless times I'd done nothing flashed before me. In a way, I was responsible for what'd happened to her. Worse yet, if she'd killed those innocent people, I was responsible for their deaths, as well.

My legs didn't shake when I stood. Certainty filled my mind—maybe it'd been made up the night I heard what'd really happened to her. There was a small chance she hadn't committed horrific crimes, but if…if the daimon who had been my mother had killed someone, then one way or another, I was going to kill her. She was my responsibility now—my problem.

CHAPTER FOURTEEN

I pretended nothing was wrong the next day in practice. It worked well until we took a break and Aiden asked how I was doing.

I kept my voice even. "I'm fine."

Then I beat the crap out of the dummy.

Toward the end of practice, a surge of energy shimmied down my back right before Seth showed up. He stood by the door, watching quietly. I had the sinking suspicion he was there for me. Groaning, I took my time rolling up the mats.

Aiden nodded in Seth's direction. "Is everything okay?"

"Who knows?" I scowled.

Aiden straightened, coming to his full height. "Has he been bothering you?"

A huge part of me wanted to say yes, but in reality, Seth hadn't really bothered me. And if he had, what could Aiden do about it?

Aiden was a badass Sentinel warrior, but Seth was the Apollyon. Where Aiden controlled fire—*pretty awesome*—and he could fight, Seth controlled all four elements—*pretty scary*—and could wipe the floor with Aiden's face.

Aiden stared at Seth in a way that said he had no problem confronting Seth on my behalf. As stupid as it seemed, I felt a smile tug my lips.

So wrong.

Forcing the smile off my face, I skirted around Aiden. "I'll see you later, okay?"

He nodded, eyes still trained on Seth. *Okay then.* Grabbing my bottle of water off the floor, I trudged across the room. I nodded at Seth as I passed him, half-hoping he was there to partake in the epic stare down with Aiden and nothing else, but he turned and immediately fell in step with me.

Seth's smile looked self-satisfied. "Your trainer does not like me."

"He's not *my* trainer. He's a Sentinel." I kept walking. "And I doubt he's even concerned with you."

Seth chuckled. "Your trainer, who is also a Sentinel, barely spoke to me while we were in Lake Lure. And when he did, I would say it was quite coldly. It hurt my feelings."

I doubted that. "He probably wasn't up to making friends considering what was going on."

"Considering your mother was a part of the attack party?" He raised a casual eyebrow. "He seemed abnormally affected when we reviewed the recordings and saw her."

His words were a well-placed smack in the face. Stopping, I faced him. "Seth, what do you want?"

He tipped his head back. A dark cloud rolled in overhead, casting a gray gloom over the quad. It was going to storm. "I wanted to see how you were doing. Is that so wrong?"

I thought about that. "Yes. You don't know me. Why would you care?"

He looked down, meeting my eyes. "Okay. I don't really care. But you're the reason I'm stuck in this hillbilly rathole, babysitting a self-righteous prick."

My eyes widened. The lilt of his voice made those words sound classy. It was almost funny. "You know, I really don't care about that right now." I stopped as several halfs passed us. They looked at us—looked at *me*. I did my best to ignore their stares.

"Of course you don't. Your mother murdered a classmate's family. My mind would be elsewhere, too."

"Gods!" I gaped. "Really, that was great." I walked off ahead.

Seth followed. "That wasn't...very nice of me. I've been told I'm painfully blunt. Perhaps I should work on that."

"Yeah, perhaps you should go do it right now." I tossed the words over my shoulder.

Undaunted, he caught up with me. "I asked Lucian, you know. I asked why I was here."

I gritted my teeth and kept walking. The ominous looking clouds continued to roll in. The sky looked like it was going to split open any moment.

"Do you know how he responded? He asked what I thought about you."

I was only half-curious to hear his response.

"He was eager to hear what I had to say." Lightning shot across the sky, striking off the coast. A fraction of a second later, thunder silenced the conversation. I picked up my pace as the girls' dorm came into view. "Don't you want to know?"

"No."

Another flash of lightning lit the sky. This time it struck inland, somewhere beyond the marshes. It was close, too close. "You lie."

I spun around. My smart-ass response died before it fully took form. Inky marks broke the golden tone of his skin on every piece of exposed flesh. They twisted into designs, held for a few seconds, and then moved into another form. *What were they?*

I tore my eyes from his arms, but the tattoos stretched across his otherwise flawless cheek, etching toward the corners of his eyes. An urge to touch them slammed into me.

"You see them again, don't you?" There was no point in lying.

"Yeah."

Anger and confusion flared deep in his eyes. Lightning shrieked across the sky. "That's impossible."

Thunder sounded so loud I flinched. It clicked into place. "The storm…you're doing it."

"It happens when I get moody. I'm pretty irritable right now." Seth took a step forward, towering over me. "I wouldn't be so temperamental if I knew what was going on. I need to know how you can see the marks of the Apollyon."

I forced myself to meet his eyes. That was a mistake—a huge, stupid mistake.

Power surged, raw and intense. I felt it crawl over my skin and slither down my spine.

And at once, my head emptied of everything except the need to find the source of the crazy power. *I need to get away as fast as possible.* Instead, in sort of a daze, I stepped forward. It had to be what he was. The energy coursing through him had this kind of pulling effect, one that gripped pures, halfs… even daimons.

I was feeling those effects now. The wildness that lingered in me reared its head and urged me forward. It urged me to touch him, because I was pretty sure whatever was happening would somehow be exposed the moment our skin touched.

Seth didn't move as I gazed up at him. He looked as if he was working to put together a puzzle and I was one of the pieces. The lazy smile faded and his lips parted. He inhaled sharply and reached out with one hand.

It took a lot, but I ducked away. Seth didn't follow. As soon as I stepped inside the dorm, the sky ripped open, and another flash of blinding light cut across the dark sky. Somewhere, not too far away, it struck once again.

Later that night, I confided in Caleb as we stood together in the back of the packed rec room. The rain had driven everyone inside, and our privacy wasn't guaranteed for long.

"Do you remember what Grandma Piperi said?"

His brows rose. "Not really. She said a lot of crazy stuff. Why?"

I played with my hair, twirling it around my finger. "Sometimes I think she isn't so crazy."

"Wait. What? You're the person who said she was crazy."

"Well, that was before my mom turned all dark side and started killing people."

Caleb glanced around the room. "Alex."

No one was listening, although people looked over every once in a while and whispered. "It's true. What did Piperi say? 'You'll kill the ones you love?' I thought it sounded crazy, but that was before I knew Mom was a daimon. We're training to kill daimons. Seems pretty obvious, doesn't it?"

"Look. Alex, there is no way you'd ever be put in that situation."

"She's about four hours from here. Why do you think she ended up in North Carolina?"

"I don't know, but the Sentinels will get her before you…" He trailed off at the look on my face. "You won't have to deal with it. You're in the Covenant for the next year, Alex."

In other words, a Sentinel would kill her before I graduated, eliminating the chance of our paths ever crossing. I really didn't know what to think about that.

"Alex, are you doing okay?" He tipped his head, watching me closely. "I mean…really doing okay?"

I shrugged off his concern. "Aiden said they couldn't be sure Mom was actually a part of the attack. She was on the camera, but…"

"Alex." Understanding and sadness grew on his face. "She's a daimon. I know you want to think she's not. I understand that, but don't forget what she's become."

"I haven't!" Several kids by the pool table looked up. I lowered my voice. "Look. All I'm saying is there could be a chance, a small chance she is—"

"That she's what? Not a daimon?" He grabbed my arm, pulling me around one of the arcade games. "Alex, she was with the group of daimons who killed Lea's family."

I pulled my arm free. "Caleb, she came to North Carolina. Why else would she come here if she didn't remember me, want to see me?"

"She could want to kill you, Alex. That's for starters. She's already killed."

"You don't know! No one does."

His chin came up. "What if she did?"

My anger faded into determination. "Then I'll find her and kill her myself. But I know Mom. She would fight what she has become."

Caleb ran a hand through his hair and clasped the back of his neck. "Alex, I think you…*oh*."

I frowned. "You think what?"

His expression took on the awed look he got whenever he saw Seth.

Twisting around confirmed my suspicions. Seth stalked through the doors, immediately surrounded by his groupies. "You know, you keep getting that look on your face whenever he comes around, people are gonna start to talk."

"Whatever."

I changed the subject. "By the way, what's up between you and Olivia? Did you talk to her about Myrtle?"

"No, I didn't. Nothing's up between me and her." Caleb faced me, his expression curious now. "What's up with you and Seth? Wait, let me rephrase that: What's up with you when it comes to Seth?"

I rolled my eyes. "I just don't…like him. And don't change the subject."

He made a face. "How can you not like him? He's the Apollyon. As half-bloods, we're obligated to like him. He's the only one who can control the elements."

"Whatever."

"Alex. Look at him." He tried to turn me around, but I held my ground. "Oh wait. He's looking over here."

I pushed him back farther. "He's not coming over here, is he?"

He grinned. "Yes—*No.* Wait. Elena cut him off."

"Oh, thank the gods."

Caleb's brows furrowed. "What's your deal?"

"He's weird and…"

He leaned closer. "And what? Come on. Tell me. You have to tell me. I'm your best friend. Tell me why you hate him." His eyes narrowed. "Is it because you're undeniably attracted to him?"

I giggled. "Gods. No. You'll think the real reason is even crazier."

"Try me."

So I told him about Seth's suspicions considering why he'd been ordered here and about the tattoos being real, but I left out that part about me wanting to touch him. That was too embarrassing for me to even speak out loud. He looked utterly mystified...and excited.

He practically bounced. "The tattoos are real? Only you can see them?"

"Apparently." I sighed, glancing over my shoulder. Elena stood awful close to Seth. "I have no idea what it all means, but Seth isn't too happy about it. The storm earlier? The rain? That was him."

"What? I've heard of some of the pures being able to control the weather, but I've never seen it." He sneaked a glimpse at him. "Wow. That's amazing."

"Would you get the awestruck look off your face for two seconds? It's creeping me out."

He chucked me in the arm. "Okay. I need to focus." It took visible effort for him not to look at Seth. It wasn't because Caleb was attracted to him. Honestly, Seth was just chock-full of aether. None of us could help it. "Why would Lucian's order have something to do with you?"

"Good question." Then it hit me. "Maybe Lucian fears I'm a risk. You know, because of Mom? Maybe he brought Seth here just in case I'd do something."

"Do what? Let her in here? Hold a welcoming party for your mom?" Disbelief filled his voice. "You wouldn't do that, and I don't even think Lucian would consider that."

I nodded, but my new idea carried a lot of weight. It would explain why Lucian didn't want me returning to the Covenant. At his house, I'd be under constant surveillance, but here I pretty much roamed around freely. The only flaw in that idea: Did Lucian really think I'd do something that terrible?

"It's probably nothing." Caleb chewed on his lower lip. "I mean, what could it be? It can't mean anything."

"It has to mean something. I have to figure it out."

Caleb stared at me. "Do you think you're focusing on this because of…everything that's happened?"

Well, of course I was, but that wasn't the point. "No."

"Maybe stress is making you read more into it."

"I'm not reading into anything," I snapped. He didn't look like he agreed. Exasperated with him and the conversation, I looked over the rec room. Elena still had Seth cornered, but that wasn't what drew my attention. Jackson was in the room.

He leaned against one of the pool tables beside Cody and another male half. His swarthy complexion seemed unusually pale, and he looked like he hadn't slept recently. I couldn't blame him. While I didn't know the current status of his relationship with Lea, he had to be worried about her, upset over what'd happened to her parents.

My gaze shifted to Cody. For a second, our eyes met from across the room. I didn't expect a smile or anything, but his icy stare and disgusted look still cut through me. Confused, I watched as he bent down and said something to Jackson.

I took a shuddering breath. "I think they're talking about me."

"Who?" Caleb turned. "Oh. Jackson and Cody? You're just being paranoid."

"Do you think they…know?"

"About your mom?" He shook his head. "They know

she's a daimon, but I don't think they know she was at Lake Lure."

"Aiden said people would find out." My voice tightened.

Caleb seemed to grow taller as he picked up on my fear. "No one will blame you. No one will hold it against you. They can't because it has nothing to do with you."

I nodded, wanting to believe him. "Sure. I guess you're right."

Over the next week, the whispers increased. People stared. People talked. At first, no one had the guts to say anything to me directly, but the pures…well, they knew I couldn't touch them.

On the way back to the training rooms after lunch, I passed Cody in the courtyard. I kept my head down and barreled past him, but I heard his words anyway. "You shouldn't be here."

My head jerked up, but he was already halfway down the walkway. I headed back to training, his words replaying over and over again. I couldn't have misheard them.

Aiden gave me a puzzled look when I entered the training room. As training neared the end, I finally said something. "Do you think there's a chance…my mom didn't attack those people?"

He dropped the mat and faced me. "If she didn't, then it would change what we know about daimons, wouldn't it?"

I nodded solemnly. Daimons needed to drain aether to survive. Mom would be no exception. "But they could drain without killing, right?"

"They could, but daimons rarely see the point in not killing. Even turning a pure requires an amount of restraint most daimons don't have."

None of the pures had been turned in Lake Lure. The attacking daimons had shown no restraint.

"Alex?"

I looked up, not surprised to see that he was standing in front of me. Concern lined his face. I forced a smile. "Part of me hopes that she's still in there somehow. That she isn't all evil, and she's still Mom."

"I know." His voice was soft.

"That part in me, it's so pathetic, because I know—I *really* know she's bad and needs to be stopped."

Aiden stepped forward, his eyes were so bright and so warm. I wanted to forget about everything and fall into those eyes. Carefully, he reached out and tucked back the strand of hair that always ended up in my face. I shivered, unable to help it.

"There is nothing wrong with hope, Alex."

"But?"

"But you have to know when to let hope go." He brought the tips of his fingers across my cheek. His hand dropped and he stepped back, the connection broken. "Do you remember why you said you needed to be in the Covenant?"

The question knocked me off guard. "Yeah…I needed to fight daimons. I have to."

Aiden nodded. "And do you still need that? Even after knowing that your mother is one of them?"

I thought about that for a moment. "Yes. They're still out there, killing. They have to be stopped. I still need that even though Mom's one of them."

A small smile played over his lips. "Then there is hope."

"Hope for what?"

He brushed past me, stopping only long enough to give me a knowing look. "Hope for you."

I watched him leave, confused by his words. Hope for me? Hope that the kids would forget my mother was a daimon who quite possibly had slaughtered a classmate's family?

Later that night, I felt the stares in the common lounge. Eventually word did reach me. Some of them—pures and halfs—didn't think I could be trusted. Not with Mom so close and so deadly. It was stupid.

But it got worse. Now people questioned why we'd left three years ago and why I'd never returned to the Covenant during that time. Rumors circulated. My favorite? Mom had become a daimon long before that terrible night in Miami. And some people believed it.

Days passed, and only a few halfs spoke to me. None of the pures did. Seth wasn't helping matters either, and damn, he made it impossible to steer clear of him. He was everywhere: in the courtyard after practice and eating dinner with Caleb and Luke. He even showed up randomly during practice, always watching quietly. It was annoying and creepy.

A certain look would cross Aiden's face whenever Seth stopped by.

I liked to tell myself it was a mixture of dislike and protectiveness. Though today we made it through practice without Seth showing up, so I didn't get to further examine the look. What a shame. I watched as Aiden grabbed one of the dummies we'd been practicing with and dragged it toward the wall. The thing weighed a ton, but he moved it around like it weighed nothing.

"Need any help?" I offered anyway.

He shook his head and placed it against the wall. "Come over here."

"What's up?"

"You see this?" He pointed at the dummy's chest. There

were several indentations in the flesh-like material. When I nodded, he ran his fingertips over them. "These are from your jabs today." His voice filled with pride, and it was better than any look he could give Seth. "That is how strong your hits have become. Remarkable."

I beamed. "Wow. I have the fingers of death."

He chuckled softly. "And this is from your kicks." He brushed his hands over the dummy's hip. Part of the material had been knocked in. And part of me was envious of the dummy. I wanted his fingers to touch me like that. "There are students your age who've gone through years of training and can't inflict that kind of damage."

"I'm amazing. So, what do you say? Am I ready to play with the grown-up toys?"

Aiden glanced over at the wall, the one I badly wanted to touch. "Possibly."

The idea of training with the knives made me want to do a happy dance, but it also reminded me of what the knives were used for. "Can I ask you a personal question?"

He only looked a bit weary. "Yes."

"If...your parents had been turned, what would you have done?"

Aiden paused before he answered. "I would've hunted them down. Alex, they wouldn't have wanted that kind of life, to lose all their morals and ideals—to kill. They wouldn't have wanted that."

I swallowed, my eyes still trained on the wall. "But they were your parents."

"They *were* my parents, but they wouldn't have been once they'd turned." Aiden stepped beside me, and I felt his eyes on me. "At some point we have to let go of the attachment. If it's not your...mother, it could be any other person you know or love. If that day comes, you'd have to face that they're not the same person they used to be."

I nodded absently. Aiden was technically right, but in the end, his parents hadn't been turned. They'd been killed, so he'd never really faced something like this.

He steered me away from the wall at that point. "You're stronger than you realize, Alex. Being a Sentinel is a way of life for you, not just a better option like it is for some of the others."

Once again, his words brought a wealth of warmth. "How do you know I'm so strong? I could be breaking down in my room every night, for all you know."

He gave me a weird look, but shook his head. "No. You're always…so alive, even when you're going through something that would darken the souls of most." He stopped there, becoming aware of what he'd said. The hollows of his cheeks flushed. "Anyway, you're incredibly determined—to the point of stubbornness. You wouldn't stop until you succeeded. Alex, you know what's right and what's not. I'm not worried about you not being strong. I'm worried about you being *too* strong."

My heart sort of swelled. He…*cared* for me, and he'd hesitated before answering the question about his parents. Somehow it made me feel better about my own conflicted emotions, and he did bring up a valid point. No matter who I faced out there, if they were daimons, it was my duty to kill them. It was why I was training now. In a way, I was actually training to kill her.

I took a deep breath. "You know…I hate when you're right."

He laughed as I made a face at him. "But you've been right when you don't even realize it."

"Huh?"

"When you said I didn't know how to have fun—the day of the solstice? You were right. After my parents were killed, I had to grow up real fast. Leon says my personality got left behind somewhere." He paused, chuckling softly. "I guess he was right, too."

"How would Leon know? He's like talking to a statue of Apollo. Anyway, you're funny when you want to be. And nice, and smart, really smart. You have the best personality I've—"

"Okay." Laughing, he held up his hands. "I get it, and I do have fun. Training you is fun and definitely not boring."

I murmured something incoherent, because my chest, well, it was doing that fluttery thing again. Practice was over, and even though I wanted to stay with him, there were no other reasons for me to hang out. I headed for the doors.

"Alex?"

My stomach tightened. "Yeah?"

He stood a few feet away. "I think it would be a good idea…if you don't wear *that* to practice again."

Oh. I'd forgotten what I was wearing. It was a pair of questionable shorts Caleb had picked up for me. I hadn't even thought he'd noticed. Looking at Aiden now, I realized he *had* noticed. I fixed an overly innocent look on my face. "Do you find these shorts distracting?"

Aiden gave me one of his rare smiles. Every cell in my body warmed. I even forgot about the terrible thing I was training for. His smile had that kind of impact.

"It's not the shorts I find distracting." He brushed past me, stopping at the door. "In our next practice, I may let you train with the daggers if we have time."

My distracting shorts and everything else were forgotten for the time being. "No way. You're being serious?"

He tried to look serious, but his grin looked a bit

mischievous. "I think it wouldn't hurt, but only for a little bit. I think it will help you get a feel for how to handle them."

I glanced back at the wall of weapons. I wasn't even allowed to touch them, and now he was going to let me actually practice with them. It was like graduating kindergarten. Hell, it was like Christmas Eve.

Without thinking, I closed the distance between us and hugged him. Aiden immediately stiffened, obviously caught off guard. It was just a simple hug, but the tension racked up several degrees. I suddenly wondered what it would feel like if I rested my head against his chest like I had when he'd come back from Lake Lure. Or if his arms came around me and he held me, but not out of comfort. Or if I kissed him again like I had that night…would he kiss me back?

"You're far too pretty to be dressed like that." His breath stirred my hair. "And you're entirely too excited to be working with knives."

I flushed, stepping back. *What?* Aiden thought I was pretty?

It took me several moments to work past that. "I'm bloodthirsty. What can I say?"

Aiden's eyes dropped, and I decided I needed to go to the store and find as many pairs of minuscule shorts as I could get my hands on.

CHAPTER FIFTEEN

Just before dawn, the funeral for those murdered at Lake Lure began and…well, it sucked in the way all funerals did. Following ancient Greek tradition, the funeral consisted of three parts. All of the bodies—the ones recovered—were laid out before the funeral began. I stayed in the back of the funeral home, refusing to go anywhere near the dead. I paid my respects from a healthy distance.

The three bodies of the Dikti family, Lea's father and step-mother, and the Guards were wrapped in linen and draped in gold. From there, the funeral procession began, and it was long. The bodies were lifted onto pyres and carried through the main street. All tourist activity had been cut off to Deity Island, and the streets were filled with pure-blood and half-blood mourners.

The students who remained at the Covenant stood out from the crowd. We were the ones dressed in black sundresses or party dresses. None of us really had anything appropriate to wear to a funeral. I had on a black tube dress and flip-flops. They were the best I had.

I stayed close to Caleb and Olivia, and I only caught a quick glimpse of Lea and Dawn at the cemetery. The sisters shared the same coppery red hair and impossibly thin bodies, and even with puffy eyes, Dawn was absolutely stunning.

Hematoi didn't bury the dead. After burning the remains, they erected massive marble effigy statues. The artist's rendering of the one that would honor the Samos family depicted their images set on a pedestal carved with a Greek verse about immortality among the gods. The round pedestal already occupied the site.

The jewels and gold were removed from the bodies and placed on the pedestal. I really wanted to leave at that point, but it would've been the height of disrespect. I turned away as they lit the pyres, but I still heard the crackling as the fire ate away at their shrouded corpses. I shuddered, hating the finality of it, hating that these were quite possibly my mother's victims.

Slowly, the mourners broke apart. Some headed back home; others went to small receptions held in the homes of the families. I trailed behind Caleb and Olivia, going back to the Covenant, away from all the death and despair.

As we passed the pyres, my eyes found Aiden. He stood with Leon, a few feet away from Dawn and Lea. He looked up—almost as if he'd sensed me—and our eyes met. He made no other acknowledgment, but I could tell he approved of my presence. Yesterday, before the talk about hunting loved ones and the shorts incident when he'd said I was pretty, I'd mentioned I was unsure if I should come or not, considering Mom had been one of the daimons.

Aiden had looked at me with that serious frown. "You'd feel more guilty for not going and paying your respects. You deserve to do that. Just as much as anyone else, Alex."

He was right, of course. I hated funerals, but I would've felt bad if I hadn't come.

Now, he nodded slightly before turning to Dawn. He reached out and touched her arm. A lock of dark hair fell over his forehead as he bent his head, offering his condolences. I turned my attention to the large iron gates separating the town from the plot of meaningless statues. Seth stood there, dressed in his black uniform. There was no doubt he was watching us. I ignored him as we left the cemetery.

For the rest of the day, I tried to forget that we'd lost so many innocent people.

And that Mom had been responsible.

I didn't get to do anything with the daggers in the next practice. When I pitched a fit about this, Aiden watched with amused patience.

"Come on." I pushed the mats off the floor. "How am I supposed to get caught up when I can't even touch a dagger?"

Aiden nudged me out of the way and took over mat duty. "I need to make sure you know how to defend yourself—"

"She hasn't practiced with Covenant blades at all?"

Seth leaned against the door frame, arms folded across his chest. He watched us with a lazy expression, but his eyes were extraordinarily bright.

Aiden straightened, barely bothering to look at him. "I could swear I shut and locked that door."

Seth smirked. "I unlocked and opened the door."

"How'd you do that?" I asked. "The door locks from the inside."

"Apollyon secrets. Can't give them away." He winked at me before turning those amber eyes on Aiden. "How can she be prepared to fight if she doesn't know how to wield the only weapon she will have against a daimon?"

Seth gained cool points in my book with that question. I looked at Aiden expectantly The cold, distasteful expression *he* wore earned way more cool points.

"I was unaware that you had any say in her training." Aiden arched a coal black eyebrow.

"I don't." Seth pushed off the wall and sauntered across the training room. He plucked one of the daggers off the wall and faced us. "I'm sure I could convince Marcus or Lucian to let Alex have a few rounds with me. Would you like that, Alex?"

I felt Aiden stiffen beside me, and I shook my head. "No. Not really."

A slow smile crept across Seth's face as he flipped the dagger in his hand. "Really, I'd let you play…with the grown-up toys." He stopped in front of me, offering the blade handle first. "Here. Take it."

My gaze fell to the shiny metal in his hand. The end had been sharpened to a brutal point. Like I was under a powerful compulsion, I reached for it.

Aiden's hand clamped down on Seth's, pulling the dagger and Seth's hand out of my reach. Startled, I looked up at Aiden. His furious silver eyes met and held Seth's. "She will train with the daggers when I decide so. Not you. Your presence here is not welcome."

Seth's eyes flicked to Aiden's hand. His smile didn't falter once. "Awfully controlling, aren't you? Since when do pures care so much about what a half-blood touches or doesn't touch?"

"Since when would an Apollyon concern himself with a half-blood girl? One would think he had better things to do."

"One would think a pure blood would know better than to fall for—"

"Okay." I stepped between the two, cutting off only the gods knew what Seth was about to say. "Time to play nice, boys." Neither of them seemed to hear *or* see me. Sighing, I grabbed Aiden's arm. He looked at me then. "Practice is over, right?"

Reluctantly he let go of Seth's wrist and backed off. Even he looked surprised by his response, but he watched Seth intently. "For now—yes."

Seth shrugged and flipped the blade over again, his gaze centered on me once more. "I actually don't have anything better to do than concern myself with a *half-blood girl*."

There was something about the way he spoke that gave me the chills. Or it could have been the skill with which he handled the blade. "I think I'll pass."

After that, Aiden and I left the training room, neither of us speaking. I wasn't sure why Aiden had reacted as strongly as he did or why Seth felt the need to push Aiden like that. But by the time I met up with Caleb, I pushed it to the far corners of my brain to dwell on later.

Caleb decided we needed fun, and fun existed on the main island at Zarak's weekly movie night. He always got his hands on movies just released in the theater, and since none of us got to go to places like that very often, it was a big deal to watch whatever the mortal world currently obsessed over. I was surprised he was still holding it after the funerals yesterday, but I assumed everyone needed to let loose a bit and remind themselves they were still alive.

But as soon as we arrived at his house, I knew things weren't going to be fun. Everyone stopped talking when we walked down into the basement that'd been converted into a mini theater. Pures and halfs alike stared at me, and the moment Caleb followed Olivia upstairs, people started whispering.

Pretending like I wasn't at all bothered, I sat down on one of the unoccupied love seats and focused on a spot on the wall. Pride kept me from fleeing the room. After a few minutes, Deacon broke free of the cluster of kids and joined me.

"How're you doing?"

I slid him a glance. "Great."

He offered me a drink out of his flask. I took it and swallowed a mouthful, watching him out of the corner of my eye. "Careful," he chuckled as he pried the flask out of my fingers.

The liquid scorched my throat and made my eyes burn. "Jeez, what is that stuff?"

Deacon shrugged. "It's my own special mix."

"Well…it's certainly special."

Someone from the other side of the room whispered something I couldn't make out, but Cody burst into laughter. Feeling paranoid, I tried to ignore him.

"They're talking about you."

Slowly, I looked at Deacon. "Thanks, buddy."

"Everyone is." He shrugged as he flipped the flask over in his hands. "Frankly I don't care. Your mom's a daimon. So what? It's not like you can help it."

"It really doesn't bother you?" Of all people, I thought it should bother him.

"No. You're not responsible for what your mother did."

"Or didn't do." I bit my lip, staring at the floor. "No one knows if she did anything."

Deacon raised his eyebrows as he took a long drink. "You're right."

The group across from us erupted in snickers and sly looks. Zarak shook his head, turning his attention to the remote in his hand.

"I think I hate them," I muttered, wishing I hadn't decided to come here.

"They're just scared." He gave a pointed look at the knot of people across the room. "They all fear being turned. The daimons have never been this close, Alex. Four hours isn't that far away, and it could've been any of them. It could've been their deaths."

I shivered and yearned for another drink from Deacon's flask. It was really warming. "Why aren't you afraid?"

"We all got to die sometime, right?"

"That's dark."

"But my brother would never allow something like that to happen to me," he added. "He'd die first...and he'd never let that happen either. Speaking of my brother, how's he been treating my favorite half-blood?"

"Uh...good, really good."

Cody's loud voice rang out. "The only reason she's still here is because her stepfather is the Minister and her uncle is the dean."

All week I'd been ignoring the snide whispers and awful stares, but this—this I couldn't ignore. There'd be no saving face if I did. I leaned forward in my chair, resting my arms on my knees.

"What's that supposed to mean?"

No one dared to speak as Cody lifted his head toward me. "The only reason you're still here is because of who you're related to. Any other half would've been thrown into servitude."

Taking a deep breath, I searched my memories for something calming. I came up empty. "Why would that happen, Cody?"

Deacon shifted away from me, flask in hand.

"You brought your mother back here. That's why. Those pures died because your mother's out there looking for you! If you weren't here, they'd still be alive."

"Crap." Zarak stood, clearing his chair from my path. Just in time, too. I flew across the room, stopping in front of Cody.

"You're going to regret saying that."

Cody's lip twisted into a smirk. He wasn't afraid of me. "Wow. Threatening a pure will get you kicked out the Covenant. Maybe that's what you want? Then you can be reunited with your mother."

My jaw hit the floor and my fist was about to hit his. Deacon intervened, wrapping one arm around my waist. He picked me up and set me in the opposite direction.

"Out." He didn't give me much of an option with his hand on my back, pushing me toward the glass doors.

Being outside didn't calm the rage in me. "I'm going to kill him!"

"No, you're not." Deacon shoved the flask in my hand. "Take a drink. It will help."

I unscrewed the lid and took a healthy swallow. The liquid scorched my insides, and it only fueled my anger. I tried inching past Deacon, but for someone so slender and untrained, he proved a viable roadblock.

Damn him.

"I'm not letting you go in there. Your uncle may be the Minister, but if you beat up Cody, your ass is a goner."

He was right, but I smiled. "It'd be worth it."

"Would it be worth it?" He stepped to the side, blond curls falling into his eyes as he blocked me again. "How do you think Aiden would feel?"

The question hit me in the chest. "Huh?"

"If you get kicked out, what would my brother think?"

I unclenched my hands. "I…don't know."

Deacon tipped his flask at me. "He'd blame himself. Think he didn't train or counsel you well enough. Do you want that?"

My eyes narrowed. I didn't like his logical reasoning. "Just like he counsels you not to be drunk all the time? And yet you are. How do you think that makes him feel?"

He slowly lowered the flask. "Touché."

A few seconds later, backup arrived. "What the hell happened?" Caleb demanded.

"Some of your friends aren't playing nice." Deacon tipped his head back toward the door.

Caleb frowned as he walked to me. "Did one of them do something to you?" Anger flashed across his face when I told him what Cody had said. "Are you kidding me?"

I crossed my arms. "Do I look like I'm kidding?"

"No. Let's just head back to the other island. Those assholes in there don't understand."

"No one understands," I shot back, anger still flooding my system. "You can stay here with *your* friends, but I'm heading back. This was a terrible idea."

"Hey!" Caleb's eyebrows shot up. "They're not my friends. You are! And I do understand, Alex. I know you're going through a lot."

I whirled on Caleb. I knew I was being unreasonable, but I couldn't stop. "You *understand*? How in the hell could you possibly understand? Your mother doesn't want to be around you! Your father is still alive! He isn't a daimon, Caleb. How in the hell can you understand?"

He held out his hands as if he could somehow physically stop my words. Pain flickered across his face. "Alex? Gods."

Deacon shoved the flask in his pocket, sighing. "Alex, try to calm down. You have an audience."

He was so right. People had come outside at some point, loitering on the sprawling deck, watching with anticipation. They'd wanted a fight earlier and had been denied it. I took a deep breath and tried to rein in my anger. I failed. "Every stupid person here thinks I'm the reason why those people died!"

Disbelief shone on Caleb's face. "That can't be true. Look. You're just stressed out. Let's go back—"

My restraint broke. Closing the distance between us, I wondered if I would hit my best friend. Quite possibly, but I never got to find out. Out of nowhere, Seth appeared at my side, dressed in black like he always was. Did he never take that uniform off?

His presence not only stunned me into immobility, it also had a quieting effect on everyone around us. He took one long, hard look at me and then spoke in that lyrical, accented voice of his. "That is enough."

I would've told anyone else to screw off, but this wasn't a normal situation, and Seth wasn't a normal person. We stared each other down. Clearly he expected me to heed his warning, or else.

With visible effort, I backed off. Caleb took a step toward me, but Deacon grabbed his arm. "Let her go."

And I went. I made it past several houses before Seth caught up to me. "You let a bunch of pures get you that upset?"

"You're such a stalker, Seth. How long were you standing there?"

"I am *not* a stalker, and I was standing there long enough to realize you have no self-control and you're unstable. I kind of like that about you—mainly because I find it entertaining. But you have to know that you are not responsible for what your mother did. Who cares what a bunch of spoiled pures think?"

"You don't know if my mom did anything!"

"Are you serious?" His eyes searched my face. He found what he was looking for. "You are! Now I can add stupid to my list of adjectives for describing you."

I wondered what the other adjectives were. "Whatever. Just leave me alone."

Seth cut me off. "She's a daimon. She kills—*kills* innocent people, Alex. That's what daimons do. There is no reason behind it. That's what she is doing, but it is not your fault."

I really wanted to kick or punch him, but neither of those things would be smart. See, I did have self-control and intelligence. I sidestepped him, but Seth wasn't having it. He reached out, his hand closing around my forearm. Flesh against flesh.

The world exploded.

A surge of electricity shot through my body. It was like the feeling I got whenever he was near, but a hundred times stronger. I couldn't speak, and the longer Seth held on, the more powerful the rush grew. What I was feeling was insane. What I was *seeing* was insane. Intense, bright blue light wrapped around his hand. It twisted like a cord, crackling and twining itself around my arm and his hand. Instinctively I knew it was connecting us—binding us together.

Forever.

"No. No, this isn't possible!" Seth's body had gone rigid.

I really wished he'd let go of my arm, because his fingers dug into my skin and something...something else was happening. I felt *it* move inside me, twisting and wrapping itself through my core, and with each coil I knew it was linking us together.

Emotions and thoughts that weren't my own raced at me.

They came in a blinding light, followed by vibrant colors spinning and shifting until I was able to comprehend and make sense of some of it.

This isn't possible.

This is going to get us both killed.

I gasped for air. Seth's thoughts slithered around mine, and his emotions rolled and tumbled through the both of us. Abruptly it all stopped as a door slammed shut in my mind. The colors receded, and finally the blue cord shimmered into a faint glow before disappearing.

"Uh...your tattoos are back."

Seth blinked as he stared down at where his hand was still around my arm. "This can't be happening."

"What...did happen? Cuz if you know, I'd really like to be filled in on this."

He looked up, his eyes glowing in the darkness. The bewildered look faded, replaced by anger. "We're going to die."

That wasn't what I wanted to hear. "I—*what*?"

Whatever he knew finally clicked into place for him. His lips thinned, and then he started walking, dragging me along behind him.

"Wait! Where are we going?"

"They knew! They knew this entire time. Now I understand why Lucian ordered me to Council when they found you."

My feet slipped in the sand as I stumbled to keep up with him. I lost a sandal in the process, then lost the other one a couple of steps later. Dammit, I liked those sandals. "Seth! You're going to have slow down and tell me what's going on."

He shot me a dangerous look over his shoulder. "Your pretentious stepfather is going to tell us what is going on."

I didn't like to admit it, but I was scared, really freaking scared. *Apollyons can be unstable—dangerous even.* No joke. Seth picked up the pace, dragging me behind him. I slipped. My knee caught the hem of my cotton dress, ripping it. With an impatient groan, he hauled me to my feet and continued.

Lightning zipped through the sky as he continued to drag me across the island. It struck a docked boat only a few yards away. The light stunned me, but Seth ignored the mess his anger had created.

"Stop!" I dug my feet into the sand. "The boat's on fire! We have to do something!"

Seth whirled around, his eyes luminous. He yanked me against him. "It's of no concern to us."

Heavy breaths heaved within my chest. "Seth, you're scaring me."

His expression remained hard and fierce, but his grip around my arm loosened a bit. "It's not me you should be scared of. Come on." He pulled me past the burning boat and up the silent coastline.

Seth turned when he spotted Lucian's house, taking the wide porch steps two at a time. Clearly, he didn't care if I could keep up with him or not. He let go then and started banging on the door like the police did on television.

Two fearsome-looking Guards opened the door. The first one spared me only a quick glance before fastening narrowed eyes on Seth.

Seth's chin came up. "We need to see Lucian now."

The Guard straightened. "The Minister has retired for the evening. You will have—"

A brutal burst of wind rushed from behind us. For a second, I couldn't see past the mess of hair blowing in my face, but when I did, my heart stopped. The near hurricane force gust hit the Guard in the chest, slamming him back and pinning him halfway up the wall of my stepfather's opulent foyer. The wind quieted, but the Guard remained up against the wall.

Seth stepped in through the door and looked at the other Guard. "Go get Lucian. Now."

The Guard peeled his eyes off his coworker and hurried off to do Seth's bidding. I followed Seth in, my hands shaking so badly I held them together. "Seth? Seth, what are you doing? You need to stop. Like right now. You can't do this! Busting into Lucian's house—"

"Be quiet."

Retreating to the farthest corner of the foyer, I stared at the Guard. The air crackled with tension and power—the Apollyon kind of power. I pressed against the wall as it crawled over my skin and inched its way deep inside me.

A decent amount of commotion and movement at the top of the stairs drew my attention. Lucian came down the winding staircase, clad in pajama bottoms and a loose shirt. Seeing him like that made me giggle, but it came out kind of short and hysterical.

Lucian noted my semi-petrified position in the corner, and then glanced at the Guard suspended up against the wall. Finally, he gave Seth a strangely calm look. "What is this about?"

"I want to know how long you were going to continue this madness before the both of us were slaughtered in our sleep!"

My mouth dropped open.

Lucian's voice remained level and cool. "Let the Guard down, and I will tell you everything."

Seth didn't look like he wanted to, but he dropped the

Guard, and not very gently. The poor man crashed to the floor. "I want to know the truth."

Lucian nodded. "Why don't we move into the sitting room? Alexandria looks like she could really sit down."

Seth glanced over his shoulder with a frown, as if he'd forgotten about me. I must've looked pretty pitiful, because he nodded. I debated making a run for it, but I doubted I'd get very far. Besides, beyond the fear, I was also curious as hell as to what was going on.

We went into a small room with glass walls. I practically collapsed in the white wicker chair. The Guards followed us, but Lucian waved them off. "Please notify Dean Andros that Seth and Alexandria are here. He will understand." The Guards hesitated, but Lucian assured them with a dismissive nod. When they left, he faced Seth. "Sit?"

"I prefer to stand."

"Um…there's a boat on fire outside." My voice sounded tight and too high. "Someone might want to check it out."

"It will be taken care of." Lucian sat in one of the chairs beside me. "Alexandria, I have not been entirely forthcoming with you."

A tiny scoff huffed out of me. "Really."

He leaned forward, resting his hands against his checkered pajama bottoms. "Three years ago, the oracle told your mother that, on your eighteenth birthday, you would become the Apollyon."

I laughed out loud. "That. Is. Ridiculous."

"Is it?" Seth turned to face me. He looked like he wanted to shake me.

"Um, yes!" My eyes widened. "There's only one of you guys…" My voice trailed off as I remembered what I'd read in the book Aiden had loaned me. All at once, I felt hot and cold.

"Before Rachelle left, she confided in Marcus. He didn't agree with her decisions, but she felt she needed to protect you."

"Protect me from what?" As soon as those words left my mouth, I already knew the answer. *Protect me from what'd happened to Solaris.* I shook my head. "No. This is just too crazy. The oracle didn't tell Mom that!"

"You are referencing the other part, the one where she said you will kill the ones you love? That is not the important part. What is important is you will become another Apollyon." He turned to Seth, smiling. "Having Seth here was the best way to discover if what the oracle had said was correct."

Seth paced the length of the sitting room. "It makes perfect sense. Why I sensed you the first day. No wonder your mother left here. She probably thought she could somehow hide you among the mortals." He turned and eyed Lucian. "Why would you want to bring us together? You know what will happen."

"We do not know what will happen." Lucian returned his gaze. "There have not been two of you in over four hundred years. Things have changed since then. So have the gods."

My eyes bounced between them. "Guys…I know what you're saying, but you're wrong. There's no way I'm what *he* is. There's no way."

"Then how do you explain what happened outside?" Seth glared at me.

Taking a deep breath, I ignored him. "It's not possible."

"What did happen?" Lucian sounded curious.

Lucian's eyes danced between us as Seth explained about the blue cord and how, for a few seconds, we'd heard each other's thoughts.

It was clear he wasn't surprised.

"It is really nothing to be concerned about. What you

experienced was just a way of recognizing one another. This is the reason I assigned you here, Seth. We had to see if she was the other half. The possibility—it was too great an opportunity to pass up. I just didn't expect it to take this long for you two to come together."

"Is it worth the risk?" Seth frowned. "If the gods didn't know about her before, they will soon. You could have just let this be. Is her life nothing to you?"

My stepfather leaned forward, his eyes meeting Seth's. "Do you understand what this means? Not just for you, but for our kind? Two of you will change everything, Seth. Yes. You're powerful now, but when she turns eighteen your power will become limitless."

That seemed to perk Seth's interest. "But the gods—they won't allow that to happen."

Lucian leaned back. "The gods…have not spoken to us in ages, Seth."

"*What?*" Seth and I both shouted. That was some serious stuff right there.

Lucian flicked his wrist in a dismissive manner. "They have removed themselves, and the Council does not believe they will intervene on anything. Besides, if the gods are curious or concerned, they already know about Alexandria. If the oracle has seen it, then the gods already know. They *have* to be aware of her."

I didn't believe Lucian. Not for one second. "They weren't aware of Solaris!"

Both of them looked at me. A line formed between Lucian's brows. "How do you know of Solaris?"

"I…I read about her. They killed both of the Apollyons."

Lucian shook his head. "You do not know the whole truth behind that. The other Apollyon attacked the Council, and

Solaris was obligated to stop him. She did not. That is why they were executed."

I frowned. The book hadn't said anything like that. Seth finally sat. "What do you have to gain from this?"

Lucian's eyes went wide. "With you two, we can eliminate the daimons without risking so many lives. We could change the rules—the laws surrounding half-bloods, the marriage decrees, the Council. Why, anything could be possible."

I wanted to punch him in the gut. Lucian didn't care about halfs.

"What rules of the Council do you wish to see changed?" Seth asked, watching Lucian's face.

"These are things best discussed later, Seth." He waved his hand at me, smiling that weird, icky smile again. "She's fated to be your other half."

Seth turned and gave me a long look. "Could be worse, I suppose."

Okay, that creeped me out. "What do you mean by *that*?"

"You two are like puzzle pieces. You fit together. Your power will feed his…and vice versa." Lucian smiled. "Really, it is amazing. You are his other half, Alexandria. You are fated to be with him. You belong to him."

It felt like something heavy sat on my chest. "Oh. *Oh*. No."

Seth frowned at me. "You don't have to sound so disgusted."

The other day I'd felt compelled to touch him. I'd thought it was just because of what he was, but could it be because of what *we* were? I shuddered. "Disgusted? It's…revolting! Do you hear yourselves?"

Seth sighed. "Now you're just being insulting."

I ignored that, ignored *him*. "I don't belong to anyone."

Lucian met my stare, and I was struck by the intensity. "But you do."

"This is insane!"

"When she turns eighteen." Seth pursed his lips. "The power—her power shifts to me."

"Yes." Lucian nodded eagerly. "Once she goes through the palingenesis—the Awakening—at eighteen, all you have to do is touch her."

"Then…" He didn't need to say it. We all knew. Seth would become a God Killer.

He turned to Lucian. "Who knows about this?"

"Marcus knows, as does Alexandria's mother." My heart dropped.

Seth glanced at me, his expression unreadable. "It explains why she has come so close to the Covenant when most daimons wouldn't dare, but why? A half can't be turned."

"Why else would a daimon want to get their hands on an Apollyon? Even now, the aether in Alexandria could feed them for months." Lucian gestured at me. "What do you think will happen if her mother has her after she goes through the palingenesis?"

I couldn't believe what I was hearing. "You think she's here so I can be like some sort of meal plan for her?"

He glanced up. "Why else would she be here, Alexandria? It is why I was against you being in the Covenant, as was Marcus. It had nothing to do with the time you've lost or your previous behavior. There was a chance we could not stop Rachelle by the time you would graduate. The risk was too great that you would come face to face with her and falter in your duty. I cannot allow a daimon to get their hands on an Apollyon."

"But now it's different?" I asked.

"Yes." Lucian stood, placing his hands on my shoulders.

"With her so close, we will be able to find her. You will never have to face her. This is a good thing, Alexandria."

"A good thing?" I gave a harsh laugh and shrugged off his hands. "This is all twisted and…sick."

Seth whipped his head in my direction. "Alex, you can't just ignore this. Ignore what you are. What *we* are—"

I threw my hand up between us. "Oh, don't even go there, buddy. We aren't anything! We will never be anything! Okay?" He rolled his eyes, clearly bored with my protests.

I started backing out of the room. "I seriously don't want to hear about any of this again. I'm just going to pretend this conversation didn't take place."

"Alex. Stop." Seth stepped toward me.

I glared at him. "Don't follow me! I mean it, Seth. I don't care if you can throw me through the air. If you follow me, I'll jump off a freaking bridge and take you with me!"

"Let her go." Lucian gave an elegant wave of his hand. "She needs time to come to grips with this."

Surprisingly, Seth listened. I left then, slamming the front door behind me. My thoughts bounced around my head in a chaotic mess on the way back to the island. I barely noticed the air was no longer thick with smoke. Someone had taken care of the boat fire. The Guards at the bridge looked bored when they waved me through.

Minutes later, I crossed the campus and the section of sandy beach separating the faculty and guest lodging from the rest of campus. Under no circumstance was I—or any student, for that matter—allowed to wander around their housing, but I needed to talk to someone.

I needed Aiden.

Aiden could make sense out of this. He would know what to do.

Since most of the little houses were empty for the summer, it was easy to figure out which one was his. Only one of the nearly identical cottages had a light on inside. I stopped in front of the door and hesitated. Coming here—not only would I get in trouble, but so would Aiden. I couldn't even begin to wonder what they'd do if I were discovered in a pure-blood's cabin at this time of night. But I needed him, and that was more important than consequences.

Aiden answered after a few seconds and took seeing me standing at his door remarkably well. "What's wrong?"

It wasn't late, but he stood there dressed as if he'd been in bed. The low-slung pajama bottoms looked better on him than Lucian. So did the tank top. "I need to talk to you."

His gaze dropped the length of me. "Where are your shoes? Why are you covered in sand? Alex, talk to me now. What happened?"

I looked down dumbly—my sandals? They were lost somewhere on the main island, never to be seen again. Sighing, I pushed the tangled strands of hair back. "I know I shouldn't be here, but I didn't know who else to go to."

Aiden reached out and took hold of my arms in a gentle grasp. Without saying a word, he led me into his cottage.

CHAPTER SIXTEEN

As Aiden guided me to his couch and sat me down, he had this look about him. It was sort of dangerous and comforting at the same time.

"Let me get you a glass of water."

My gaze crawled over his living room. It wasn't much bigger than my room back in the dorm, and much like mine, it was devoid of anything decorative. There were no pictures, favorite paintings, or artwork cluttering the walls. Instead, books and comics lay scattered across the coffee table, lined the numerous bookshelves, and sat stacked on his small computer desk. No television. He was a reader—probably even read the comics in ancient Greek. For some reason, that made me smile.

Then my eyes wandered to the corner of the room where a guitar leaned against the wall between the bookshelf and the desk. Several colorful guitar picks formed a line on one of the shelves—every color except black. I knew it—those hands were used for something graceful and artsy. I wondered if I could ever get him to play for me. I'd always had a thing for guys who played guitars.

"You play?" I tipped my chin toward the guitar.

"Occasionally." He handed me a glass of water, and I downed it before he sat beside me. "Thirsty?"

"Mmm." I wiped a few drops off my lips. "Thanks. What's up with the picks?"

He glanced at the guitar. "I collect them. A weird habit of mine, I guess."

"You need a black one."

"I guess I do." Aiden took the glass and set it on the coffee table, frowning when he noticed the tremble in my hands. "Alex, what happened?"

My laugh hitched in my throat. "It's going to sound crazy." I stole a quick peek at him, and seeing the concern for me on his face was nearly my undoing.

"Alex…you can tell me. I won't judge you."

I kind of wondered what he'd thought happened.

His hand came out and wrapped around mine. "You trust me, right?"

I stared at our hands, those fingers. *You are fated to be with him.*

Those words had a shattering effect on me. I pulled my hands free and stood. "Yes. I did. I do. This is just so crazy."

Aiden remained seated, but his eyes followed my erratic pacing. "Try starting at the beginning."

I nodded, smoothing my hands over my dress. I started with the party. The look on Aiden's face hardened when I told him what Cody had said and turned even more dangerous when I explained how Seth had destroyed someone's boat. I told him everything, even the skeevy part with Seth, and how we were "two halves" or whatever.

Aiden was a remarkable listener. He didn't ask any questions, but I knew he caught everything I threw down.

"So it can't be true, right? I mean none of this is real." I returned to prowling the length of his living room. "Lucian said it was why Mom left. The oracle told her that I was the second Apollyon, and she was afraid that the gods would… kill me, I guess." My laugh sounded a little shrill.

Aiden ran a hand through his hair. "I suspected something strange when Lucian wanted to bring you back to his house. And when you said you'd seen Seth's markings… I can't believe I've been around someone so rare this entire time. When do you turn eighteen, Alex?"

I slid my hands down my sides nervously. "March fourth." Less than a year from now.

Aiden rubbed his chin. "When you spoke to the oracle, did she say anything like this?"

"No, she only said I would kill the ones I love. Nothing about this, but she said so much crazy stuff." I swallowed, hearing the blood rushing in my veins. "I mean, looking back, some of the things she said made sense, but I just didn't understand."

"How could you understand?" He came around the small wooden table. "Now we know why your mother would take such a risk in leaving the safety of the island. She wanted to protect you. The story of Solaris is truly tragic, but she stood against the Council and the gods. That's what sealed her fate. Not what was written about her in the books."

"Why would Solaris do that? Didn't she know what would happen?"

"Some say she fell in love with the First. When he stood against the Council, she defended him."

"That's so stupid." I rolled my eyes. "She basically committed suicide. That isn't love."

Aiden gave the briefest of smiles. "People do the damnedest things when they're in love, Alex. Look at what your mother did. It's a different kind of love, but she left everything because she loved you."

"I never understood why she left." My voice sounded young and fragile. "Now I know. She really did leave to protect me." The knowledge sat like curdled milk in my stomach. "You know, I kinda hated her for pulling me away from here. I never understood why she would do something so risky and stupid, but she did it to protect me."

"It must bring you some sort of peace to know why, doesn't it?"

"Peace? I don't know. All I can think is if I wasn't some kind of giant freak, she'd still be alive."

My words caused a flicker of pain to cross his face. "You can't blame yourself for this. I will *not* allow it, Alex. You've come too far for this."

I nodded, looking away. Aiden could believe whatever he wanted, but if I hadn't been the second coming of the Apollyon, then none of this would've happened. "I hate this. I hate not having control."

"But you do have control, Alex. What you are gives you more control than anyone else."

"How so? According to Lucian, I'm Seth's own personal electrical outlet or something. Who knows? No one does."

"You're right. No one knows. When you turn eighteen—"

"I'll be a giant freak."

"That's not what I was going to say."

I raised my eyebrows and looked at him. "Okay. When I turn eighteen the gods are going to kill me in my sleep? That's what Seth said."

Anger turned his eyes silver. "The gods have to be aware

of you. I know this doesn't make you feel better, but if they wanted to…get rid of you, they would have already. So, when you turn eighteen, anything will be possible."

"You're acting like this is a good thing."

"It could be, Alex. With two of you—"

"You sound like Lucian!" I moved away from him. "Next you're going to be telling me I'm Seth's super-special other half and I belong to him, as if I'm some sort of object instead of a person!"

"I'm not saying that." He closed the distance, putting his hands on my shoulders. I shivered under the weight of his hands. "Do you remember what I said about fate?" I shook my head. I remembered how he'd found my shorts distracting. I had that wonderful subjective memory feature. "Only you have control over your future, Alex. Only you have control over what you want."

"You really think so?"

He nodded. "Yes."

I shook my head, doubtful that I could believe in anything at this point, and started to slip away, but Aiden's hands tightened around my shoulders. An instant later, he gathered me close to him. I hesitated, because being this close to him was possibly the sweetest kind of torture.

I needed to break away…move as far away as possible, but his arms circled my shoulders. Slowly, carefully, I rested my head against his chest. My hands fell to the curve of his back, and I inhaled deeply. His scent, a mixture of the sea and soap, filled me. The steady beat of his heart under my cheek warmed and comforted me. It was just a hug, but gods, it meant so much. It meant *everything*.

"I don't want to be this Apollyon thing." I closed my eyes. "I don't even like being in the same country as Seth. I don't want any of this."

Aiden smoothed his hand down my back. "I know. It's overwhelming and scary, but you're not alone. We'll figure this out. Everything is going to be okay."

I pressed closer. Time seemed to slow down, allowing me a few moments of the simple pleasure of being in his arms, but then his fingers sifted through my hair, finding their way to my scalp, and from there, he guided my head back.

"You don't have anything to worry about, Alex. I'm not going to let anything happen to you."

Those forbidden words wrapped around my heart, forever etching into my soul. Our eyes met. Silence stretched between us as we stared at each other. His eyes shifted to fierce silver, and his other arm slid to my waist, tightening. His fingers drifted from my hair and slowly traced the curve of my cheekbone. My pulse thrummed through me as his intense stare followed his fingertips. He moved them down my face and then over my parted lips.

We shouldn't be doing this. He was a pure blood. Everything could come to a crashing end for us if we were caught, but it didn't matter. Right now, being with him seemed worth whatever consequence could come from it. This was right, like it was meant to be. There was no logical explanation for it.

Then he leaned forward and rested his cheek against mine. Hot tingles spread through me as his lips moved against my ear. "You should tell me to stop."

I didn't say a word.

Aiden made a deep sound in his throat. His hand slid up my back, leaving a trail of fire in its wake, and his lips moved across my cheek, stopping to hover above mine. I forgot how to breathe, and most importantly, how to think.

He moved, ever so slightly, and his lips brushed across

mine once, and then twice. It was such a soft, beautiful kiss, but when the kiss deepened, it wasn't a shy one. This was one of dangerously pent-up need, a desire that'd been denied far too long. The kiss felt fierce, demanding, and soul burning.

Aiden pulled me to him, pressing me right up against his body. And when he kissed me again, it left both of us breathless. Our hands tangled with each other's bodies as we made it back to his bedroom. My hands found their way under his shirt and over the taut skin of his sides. We separated long enough for me to get the shirt off, and gods, each hard ripple was as breathtaking as I'd imagined.

Easing me down on his bed, his hands glided from my face to my arms. Next his hand traveled over my stomach, then my hip, and under the hem of my dress. Somehow the top of my dress ended up at my waist, and his mouth moved over my body. I melted into him, his kisses, and his touch. My fingers dug into the tight skin of his arms, and my insides were in tight coils. Every place our bodies touched, sparks flew.

Aiden pulled his lips away from mine, and I made a sound of protest, but then his mouth trailed across my throat and to the base of my neck. My skin burned and my thoughts were on fire. His name was barely a whisper, but I felt his lips curve against my skin.

His gaze and fingers followed some unseen path as he rolled me on top. "You're so beautiful. So brave, so full of life." He guided my head down and dropped a sweet kiss against the scar on my neck. "You have no idea, do you? You have so much life in you, so much."

I tipped my head and he kissed the tip of my nose. "Really?"

"Yes." He brushed my hair back from my face. "Since the night I saw you in Georgia, you've been under my skin. You got *inside* me, became a part of me. I can't shake it. It's wrong." He shifted us, rolling me across the bed until he leaned above me. "Agapi mou, I can't..." He brought his lips down to mine once more.

There were no more words. Our kisses hardened, his lips and hands took on a purpose that could only mean one thing. I'd never gone this far with a guy before, but I knew I wanted to be with him. There was no doubt, only certainty. Everything in my world hinged on this moment.

Aiden lifted his head, staring down at me with *that* question in his eyes. "Do you trust me?"

I ran my fingers over his cheek, then his parted lips. "Yes."

He made a deep sound in his throat and caught my hand. Bringing it to his lips, he pressed a kiss against each fingertip, then my palm and then my lips.

And that was when someone knocked on the door.

We both froze against one another. His eyes, still cloudy with hunger, met mine. A second passed, and another. I thought he was going to ignore it. Gods, I wanted him to ignore it. Badly. Deeply. My life depended on it. But the knock came again, and this time a voice accompanied it.

"Aiden, open this door. Now." Leon.

Crap. That was all I could think. We were so busted. I didn't know what to do. I just lay there, wide-eyed and naked. Totally freaking naked.

Never taking his eyes off me, Aiden slowly lifted himself and stood. Only when he bent to retrieve the shirt I'd tossed aside did he break eye contact. He left the bedroom without a sound and closed the door behind him.

I stayed there for a few moments, caught in disbelief. The mood was completely ruined—obviously, and I was still naked. Anyone could bust in here, and here I was, sprawled across the bed. *His* bed… Freaked out more than I ever could've imagined, I jumped up and grabbed my dress. Throwing it on, I looked for a place to hide, but Leon's words froze me.

"I didn't mean to wake you, but I figured you'd want to know this immediately. They've found Kain. He's alive."

I listened, my stomach in my throat, as Aiden managed to convince Leon that he would meet him in the infirmary while I absolutely refused to look at his bed. My head came up as Aiden opened the door. "I heard."

Aiden nodded, his gray eyes filled with inner conflict. "I'll let you know what he says."

I stepped forward. "I want to come. I have to hear what he says."

"Alex, it's past your curfew, and how would you know to be in the infirmary?"

Dammit. I hated it when he was right. "But I can sneak in there. The rooms are just separated with partition walls. I could stay behind them—"

"Alex." Loverboy was gone. Shoot. "You need to go back to your dorm. Now. I promise I'll tell you everything he says, okay?"

Seeing no way to win this argument, I nodded. We waited a couple more minutes before we left his house. At the door, Aiden paused, his fingers curling at his side.

My brow furrowed. "What?"

Aiden's gaze settled on me, and the air left my lungs. Passion slammed into me, hard and hot. The look on his face—in his eyes—sent shivers through me. Without saying a word, he cupped my face and brought his lips to mine. The kiss took whatever air I had left in me. It was heady and deep, heart-stopping. I never wanted it to end, but it did. Aiden pulled back, his fingers slowly trailing away from my cheeks.

"Don't do anything stupid." His voice sounded thick. Then he disappeared into the darkness outside of his cottage.

I stumbled back to my dorm on rubbery knees, replaying what'd happened between us. Those kisses, his touch, and the way he'd looked at me were forever branded in my mind. Two seconds from losing my virginity.

Two freaking seconds.

But that last kiss—there was something in it, something that filled me with nervousness and heartache. Once inside my room, I paced back and forth. With learning that I'd become a second Apollyon on my birthday, what'd happened between Aiden and me, and Kain's unexpected reappearance, I was wired. I took a shower. I even straightened my room, but nothing could wear me out. Right now, Aiden and the other Sentinels were questioning Kain—getting the answers I needed. Was Mom a killer?

Hours went by as I waited for Aiden to come by with news, but he never did. I fell into a restless sleep and woke way too early. I had about an hour before training would begin, and there was no way I could wait any longer. The plan formed in my mind. I threw on my gym clothes and hurried outside.

The sun had just crested the horizon, but the humidity made the air murky. I avoided the Guards on patrol, skirting the sides of the buildings as I made my way to the infirmary. Cool air greeted me inside the narrow building. I moved through corridors lined with smaller offices and a couple of larger rooms equipped to handle medical emergencies. The pure-blood doctors lived on the main island and only staffed the infirmary during the school year. This early on a summer morning, only a few nurses would be in the building.

I already had excuses ready if I ran into one of those nurses.

I had killer cramps. I'd broken my toe. I'd even say I needed a pregnancy test if it meant I could get to where they had Kain, but I didn't need any of my excuses. The medical compound was tomb-silent as I prowled down the dimly lit hallway. After checking several of the smaller rooms, I stumbled into a ward used to accommodate several patients at once. Instinct led me past the empty gurneys and beyond the pea-green curtain.

I froze, the papery-thin fabric fluttering behind me.

Kain sat in the middle of the bed, dressed in loose jogging pants and nothing more. Dull locks of hair hid most of his downturned face, but his chest… Swallowing down the sudden rise of bile, I could only stare.

His chest, incredibly pale, was covered with crescent-shaped tags and thin slices that looked like they'd been made by one of our Covenant-issued daggers. There wasn't much space on him that wasn't marked.

He lifted his head. His blue eyes stood out against a corpselike pallor. I inched closer, feeling something in my chest tighten. He looked so bad, and when he smiled at me, he looked worse. His skin was so washed-out that his lips looked blood red. A tiny bit of guilt flashed inside me. Maybe I could've waited to question him, but in typical Alex fashion, I jumped in.

"Kain? Are you okay?"

"I think so."

"I wanted to ask you some questions if…it's okay with you?"

"You want to ask about your mother?" He looked down at his hands.

Relief crashed through me. I wouldn't have to explain myself. I stepped closer. "Yes."

He was quiet as he continued staring down at his hands.

He was holding something, but I couldn't see what it was. "I told the others I didn't remember anything."

I wanted to sit down and cry. Kain had been my only hope. "You don't?"

"That's what I told them."

An odd sound came from behind the green curtain on the other side of Kain's bed, like cloth dragging across a smooth floor. My brows knitted as I looked past him.

"Is…is someone back there?"

The only answer was a low gurgling. Dread came out of nowhere, inching down my spine, demanding that I flee this room now. I pushed past the bed and threw back the curtain. My lips parted in a silent scream.

Three pure-blood nurses lay sprawled on the bloody floor. One still clung to life. An angry red line ripped across her throat as she pulled herself across the small distance. I reached for her, but with one last bubble of a noise, she was gone. Rooted to the spot, I couldn't think or breathe.

Throats slashed. All dead. "*Lexie.*"

It was Kain's voice, but no one but Mom called me that—no one. I turned around, my hand fluttering to my mouth. Kain remained on the opposite side of the bed, staring down into his hands as he spoke.

"I think the nickname Lexie is far better than Alex, but what do I know?" He laughed, and it sounded cold, humorless. Dead. "I didn't know anything until now."

I bolted.

Kain moved surprisingly fast for someone who'd been tortured for weeks. He was in front of me before I made it to the door, Covenant dagger in hand.

My eyes froze on the dagger. "Why?"

"Why?" His voice mimicked mine. "Don't you get it? No.

Of course you don't. I didn't get it either. They tried it on the Guards first, but they drained them too fast. They died."

Something was so, so wrong with him. The torture could have done it; all those tags could've driven him crazy. But it didn't really matter why he'd gone insane, because he was most definitely a lunatic—and I was cornered.

"By the time they got to me, they'd learned from their mistakes. Gotta drain our kind slowly." He glanced down at the dagger. "But we aren't like them. We don't change like them."

I backed up, swallowing down the fear. My training vanished. I knew how to deal with a daimon, but a friend driven crazy was a different story.

"I was hungry, so hungry. There's nothing like it. I had to."

Horrifying realization set in. I took another step back just as he launched himself at me. He was so fast, faster than he'd ever been. Before I could even fully register the swing, his fist connected with my face. I flew back, crashing into one of those little tables. It happened so quickly I couldn't break my fall. I landed in a messy heap, dazed and tasting blood in my mouth.

Kain was on me immediately, yanking me to my feet and flinging me across the room. I hit the edge of the bed hard, and then the floor. Scrambling to my feet, I ignored the pain and faced the one thing that could not be.

Beyond reason or explanation, I had no doubt that Kain was no longer a half-blood. Only one thing moved as quickly as he did. Impossible as it was, he was a daimon.

CHAPTER SEVENTEEN

Besides being abnormally pale, Kain looked like...Kain. It explained how none of the other half-bloods had sensed it in him. Nothing about him gave off a warning that something was horribly wrong. Well, except the pile of dead bodies behind the curtain.

I reached for what looked like a heart monitor machine, hurling it at his head. Not surprisingly, he knocked it aside.

He laughed that sick laugh again. "Can't you do better than that? Remember our training sessions? How easily I got the best of you?"

I ignored that painful reminder, figuring it was best to keep him talking until I had a better option. "How is this possible? You're a half-blood."

He nodded, switching the blade to his other hand. "Weren't you paying attention? I already told you. They drain our kind slowly, and gods, did it hurt like hell. I wanted to die a thousand times, but I didn't. And now? I'm better than I ever was. Faster. Stronger. You can't fight me. None of you can." He lifted the dagger and wiggled it back and forth. "The feeding part is messy, but it works."

I glanced over his shoulder. There was a small chance I could make it to the doorway. I was still fast and not badly hurt. "That...has to suck."

He shrugged, seeming like the old Kain—so much so it stole my breath. "You get used to it when you're hungry."

That was reassuring. I inched to my left.

"I saw your mother."

Every instinct in me screamed not to listen to him. "Did you...talk to her?"

"She was frenzied, killing and taking great pleasure in it, too. She was the one who turned me." He licked his lips. "She's coming for you, did you know that?"

"Where is she?" I didn't expect him to answer, but he did.

"You leave the safety of the Covenant, and you'll find her...or she'll find you. But that's not going to happen."

"Oh?" I whispered, but I already knew. I wasn't stupid. Mom wasn't going to get a chance at my aether, because Kain was going to cut me and drain me.

"You know the one thing that sucks about being a daimon? I'm always so damn hungry. But you? I'm certain you'll feel like nothing else. It's a good thing you came to me. Trusted me." His blue eyes dropped to my neck—to where my frantic pulse beat. "She'll keep killing till she finds you or till you're dead. And you are going to die."

That was my cue to make my move. I pushed with all my strength, but it was no use. Kain blocked my only route of escape. With no other option but to fight him, I squared off, weaponless and out-skilled.

His too-red lips quirked. "Do you really want to try that?"

I forced as much boldness in my voice as possible. "Do you?"

This time, when he grabbed for me, I kicked out and caught the hand holding the dagger. It flew from his grasp, clattering against the floor. Before I could celebrate the small victory, his meaty fist lashed out, and it appeared he remembered how poor my blocking skills were. The punch got me in the stomach, doubling me over.

A rush of air stirred my hair, giving me only a second to straighten myself. I was a goner—no doubt about it. But as I lifted my head, it wasn't Kain standing in front of me.

It was Aiden.

He didn't say anything to Kain. Somehow he just *knew* as he forced me backward, away from the daimon half-blood. Kain turned his attention on Aiden. He let out a howl, eerily similar to the one the daimon had made in Georgia. They circled one another, and with Kain weaponless, Aiden had the upper hand. They exchanged vicious blows—no longer partners, but enemies to the core. Then Aiden made his move. He thrust the titanium dagger deep into Kain's stomach.

The impossible happened—Kain didn't fall.

Aiden stepped back, revealing Kain's startled face. He looked down at the gaping wound and started to laugh. It should've been a kill shot, but as cold understanding set in, I realized we had more to learn about daimon half-bloods.

They were immune to titanium.

Aiden kicked out at Kain, who blocked and whirled to deliver a kick of his own. A medical machine crashed against the wall. I gaped at them, frozen in place. I couldn't just stand here. I went for the dagger on the floor.

"Get back!" Aiden yelled as my fingers wrapped around the cool titanium.

I looked up, seeing the reinforcements—and the Apollyon.

"Move back!" Seth's voice thundered through the chaos.

Aiden jumped forward, pushing me against the wall and shielding me with his body. My hands fell to his chest. I turned my head as Seth stepped in front of the Sentinels, one arm stretched out in front of him.

Seconds later, something I could only describe as a lightning bolt erupted from his hand. The flash of blue light—so intense and brilliant—obscured everything in the room. *Akasha*—the fifth and final element: only the gods and the Apollyon could harness it.

"Don't look," Aiden whispered.

I pressed my face into his chest as the air filled with the crackling sound of the most powerful element known to the Hematoi. Kain's horrific screams rose above it as *akasha* crashed into him. I shuddered, pushing farther into Aiden. The screams—I would never forget those screams.

Aiden's hold tightened around me until the agonized screeching stopped and Kain's body thumped to the floor. Aiden pulled back then, the tips of his fingers brushed over my split and swollen lip. For the briefest second, his eyes latched onto mine. In one look, there was so much. Pain. Relief. Fury.

Everyone rushed into the room at once. In the chaos, Aiden quickly checked me over before handing me off to Seth. "Get her out of here."

Seth pulled me past the Sentinels as Aiden turned his attention to the crumpled body. In the hallway, we passed Marcus and several more Guards. He spared us a brief glance. Seth led me down the hallway, silent until he shoved me into another room at the end.

He closed the door behind him and then slowly approached me. "Are you all right?"

I backed up until I pressed against the wall farthest from him, breathing heavily.

"Alex?" His eyes narrowed.

In a matter of hours, everything had changed. Our world—*my world*—was no longer the same. It was too much. Mom, the crazy stuff with Seth, last night with Aiden, and now this? I cracked wide open. Sliding down the wall, I sat with my knees pressed against my chest. I laughed.

"Alex, get up." His voice carried that musical lilt, but it sounded strained. "This is a lot, I know this. But you have to pull yourself together. They are going to come in here—soon. They will want answers. Last night, Kain was normal—as normal as Kain could be. Now he was a daimon. They're going to want to know what happened."

Kain had been a daimon then, but no one knew that. No one could have known last night. I stared at Seth blankly. What did he want me to say? That I was fine?

He tried again, crouching down in front of me. "Alex, you can't let them see you like this. Do you understand me? You cannot let the other Sentinels or your uncle see you like this."

Did it matter? The rules had changed. Seth couldn't be everywhere. We would go out there and die. Worse yet, we could be turned. I could be turned. Just like Mom. That thought brought forth a flicker of sanity. If I lost it, what good would I be? What about Mom? Who would fix this—fix what she'd become?

Seth glanced back over his shoulder at the door. "Alex, you're starting to worry me. Insult me…or something."

A weak smile stretched my lips. "You're a bigger freak than I could've ever possibly imagined."

He laughed, and my ears must've been fooling me, because he sounded relieved. "You're just as big a freak as I am. What do you have to say about that?"

I cringed, my fingers tightening around my knees. "I hate you."

"You can't hate me, Alex. You don't even know me."

"It doesn't matter. I hate what you mean to me. I hate not having control. I hate that everyone has lied to me." On a roll now, I straightened my legs. "And I hate what *this* means. The Sentinels will die out there, one after another. I hate that I still think of my mother…as my *mother*."

Seth leaned forward and grasped my chin. The shock of his touch wasn't as shattering as before, but the bizarre transfer of energy still shimmied through me. "Then take the hate and do something about it, Alex. Use the hate. Don't sit here like there is no hope for them—for us."

For us? Did he mean for our kind or for him and me?

"You saw what I can do. You will able to do that. Together, we can stop them. Without you, we cannot. And dammit, I need you to be strong. What good are you if you end up a damn servant because you cannot deal?"

Well…I guess that answered my question. I smacked his hand away. "Get out of my face."

He leaned in closer. "What exactly are you going to do about it?"

I shot him a warning look. "I don't care if you can shoot lightning from your hand. I will kick you in the face."

"Why doesn't that surprise me? Could it do with the fact that you know I will not hurt you—that I cannot?"

"Probably." I really wasn't sure about that. Twenty-four hours ago he'd dragged me clear across an island.

"That doesn't sound particularly fair, does it?"

"This whole stuff with you isn't fair." I poked his chest with my finger. "You have the control in this."

Seth made an exasperated sound. He reached out and

clasped the sides of my head. "*You* have all the control. Don't you get it?"

Annoyed, I grabbed his wrists. "Let go."

He twisted his hands and grasped mine. Those amber eyes flared, like he was up for the challenge. After a few terse moments, he broke away and stood. "There's the attitude I have come to know and loathe."

I flipped him off, but the bad thing was, his general annoyingness had somehow reached me. Not that I'd admit it. Ever.

He grabbed a towel off the shelf. After dampening it, he tossed it to me. "Clean yourself up." He sent a devilish grin my way. "I can't have my little Apollyon-in-training looking like a mess."

My fingers clenched around the towel. "If you ever say something that stupid again, I will smother you in your sleep."

His golden brows rose. "Little Alex, are you suggesting that we sleep together?"

Stunned by how he came to *that* conclusion, I lowered the towel. "What? No!"

"Then how could you smother me in my sleep unless you were in bed with me?" He gave a sly grin. "Think about it."

"Oh, shut up."

He shrugged and glanced at the door. "They're coming."

I was only half-curious to know how he knew that, but as I dabbed the cloth under my swollen lip, the door swung open. Marcus entered first, and Aiden appeared behind him. His gaze swept to me, checking me over once more. The look on his face said he wanted to come to me, but with Marcus and half a dozen Sentinels present, it was impossible. I fought down the need to be in his arms and turned my attention to my uncle.

Marcus met my eyes. "I need to know exactly what

happened." So I told them everything I remembered. Marcus remained impassive through all of it. He asked the appropriate questions, and when it was over, I wanted to stumble back to my room.

Reliving what'd happened to Kain had drained my soul.

Marcus gave me permission to leave, and I climbed to my feet while he gave orders to Leon and Aiden. "Notify the other Covenants. I'll take care of the Council."

Aiden had followed me out into the hall. "Didn't I ask you to not do something stupid?"

I winced. "Yes, but I didn't know—didn't think Kain would be like that."

Aiden shook his head, running a hand through his hair. Then he asked the one question no one else had thought to ask. "Did he say anything about your mother?"

"He said she killed them." I inhaled sharply. "That she took great pleasure in it."

Sympathy shone in those cool eyes. "Alex, I'm sorry. I know you hoped that wasn't the case. Are you okay?"

Not really, but I wanted to be strong for him. "Yes."

He pressed his lips together. "We'll talk later, okay? I'll let you know when we'll have practice again. Things will be chaotic the next couple of days."

"Aiden…Kain said she was looking for me. That she was coming for me."

There must've been something in my voice because he was in front of me so quickly. He reached out and cupped my cheek, his voice so unyielding I didn't doubt a word he said. "I won't allow that to happen. Ever. You will never face her."

I swallowed. His closeness, his touch, evoked so many memories; it took me a moment to respond. "But if I did, I could do it."

"Did Kain say anything else to you about your mother?"

She'll keep killing till she finds you—

"No." I shook my head as the guilt ate a hole in my soul.

His hand dropped to his chest, where he rubbed a spot above his heart. "You're going to do something stupid again."

I smiled weakly. "Well, usually I do that about once a day."

Aiden raised a brow, his bright eyes amused for a moment. "No, that's not what I meant."

"Then what did you mean?"

He shook his head. "It's nothing. We'll talk soon." He passed Seth on the way back to the room. For a moment, both of their expressions hardened to stone. There may've been mutual respect in their faces, but there was definitely mutual dislike, as well.

I left before Seth could stop me. By the time I made it back to the girls' dorm, several of the students were on the porch. News traveled fast even though it was still early, but the most shocking part was that Lea stood among them.

Seeing her caused my heart to clench. She looked terrible by Lea standards—meaning she looked like the rest of us on a good day. I wasn't sure what to say to her. We weren't friends, but what she was going through was unimaginable.

What could I say? No amount of apologies or words of condolence would make anything better for her, but as I got closer to her, I saw the red look to her eyes, the tight line of her normally plump lips, and the overall air of desolation surrounding her. It provoked a memory of how I'd felt when I'd thought my mom had died. Now, take that and multiply it by two; that was how Lea felt.

Our gazes locked and my pathetic apology rolled out of my mouth. "I'm sorry…for everything."

Surprisingly, Lea nodded as she passed me on the way in.

I trailed behind her, wishing she'd called me a bitch or made fun of my face. That would have been better than this. Weary and sore, I pushed down the hallway and passed a group of girls. There were whispers, and they were right. My mother was a murderous daimon.

In my room, I crashed. Still dressed in my clothes, I slept the kind of sleep that only comes after facing something vast and life-changing. Somewhere, in that half-lucid state before I was completely out of it, I realized that when Seth and I had touched in the medical room, there'd been no blue cord.

Aiden sent a note the following day saying practice was still canceled. He didn't mention when he'd contact me again. Over the hours, a nagging worry developed. Did Aiden regret what'd happened between us? Did he still want me? Were we ever going to talk again?

My priorities were pretty messed up, but I couldn't help it. Since I'd woken up, all I could think about was what'd almost happened between the two of us. And when I did, I felt hot *and* embarrassed.

I stared at the mammoth book he'd loaned me. I'd left it on the floor next to the couch. An idea popped in my head. I could return the book to him—innocent enough reason to seek him out. My mind was made up before I knew it. Grabbing the book, I yanked open the door.

Caleb stood there, one hand raised as if he was about to knock and the other holding a pizza box. "Oh!" He stepped back, startled.

"Hey." I couldn't meet his eyes.

He lowered his hand. Our almost-fight lingered between us like bad blood. "So, you're reading Greek fables now?"

"Um…" I glanced down at the damn thing. "Yeah, I guess."

Caleb sucked his lower lip in, a nervous habit carried over from childhood. "I know what happened. I mean…your face kinda says it all."

Absently my fingers went to my cut lip.

"I wanted to make sure you were okay."

I nodded. "I am."

"Look. I brought food." He held up the box with a grin. "And I'm gonna get caught if you don't let me in or come outside."

"All right." I dropped the book on the floor and followed him out.

On the way to the courtyard, I opted for a safe topic. "I saw Lea yesterday morning."

He nodded. "She came back late the night before. She's been pretty low key. Even though she's a complete bitch, I feel sorry for her."

"Have you talked to her?"

Caleb nodded. "She's hanging in there. I'm not sure if it's really hit her, you know?"

I understood more than he probably could. We found a shady spot under some large olive trees and sat. I picked at the pizza, arranging my pepperoni slices into a gross-looking smiley face.

"Alex, what really happened to Kain?" His voice dropped to a whisper. "Everyone's saying he was a daimon, but that can't be possible, right?"

I looked up from my food. "He was a daimon."

The sun peeked through the branches, catching the strands of Caleb's hair and turning them a bright gold color. "How did the Sentinels not know that?"

"He looked just like he always did. His eyes were fine, his teeth normal." I leaned back against the tree and crossed my legs at the ankles. "There was no way to tell. I didn't know until…I saw the pures." An image I could never erase.

He swallowed, staring down at his pizza. "More funerals," he murmured. Then louder, "I can't believe this. All this time and there's never been a daimon half. How is it even possible?"

I told him what Kain had said, figuring there was no reason to keep it a secret. His reaction was typical: heavy and deep. Falling in battle meant death for us, and we'd never had to consider anything else.

Caleb frowned. "What if Kain wasn't the first? What if other daimons figured it out and we just didn't know?"

We looked at one another. Swallowing, I dropped my pizza back onto the plate. "Then we picked a hell of a time to be graduating in the spring, huh?"

The two of us laughed…nervously. Then I returned to rearranging my pizza, thinking about everything else that had happened. Images of shirtless Aiden flashed before me. The way he'd looked at me and kissed me. The touch of Aiden's fingertips was slowly replaced by Seth's and the blue cord.

"What are you thinking?" Caleb inched closer and continued when I didn't answer. "What do you know? You have that look on your face! The one you got when we were thirteen and you walked in on Instructor Lethos and Michaels totally making out in the storage room!"

"Ew!" My face scrunched up at the memory. Damn him for remembering the grossest things. "It's nothing. I'm just thinking…about everything. It's been a long couple of days."

"Everything's changed."

I glanced over at Caleb, feeling for him. "Yes."

"They're going to have to change the way we're trained,

you know?" He continued in possibly the softest voice I'd ever heard him use. "Daimons always had the strength and speed, but now we'll be fighting half-bloods trained just like us. They'll know our techniques, moves—everything."

"A lot of us are going to die out there. More than ever before."

"But we have the Apollyon." He reached over and squeezed my hand. "Now you've got to like him. He's going to save our butts out there."

The need to tell him everything almost overwhelmed me, but I looked away, training my eyes on the bushy, bitter-smelling flowers. I couldn't remember what they were called. Nightsoot or something? What had Grandma Piperi said about them? Like the kisses from those who walk among the gods…

I turned back to Caleb and realized we weren't alone anymore. Olivia stood beside him, arms wrapped tightly around her waist. He told her what happened, and he didn't act like a love-struck idiot, which was good. Finally, she sat down and sent me a sympathetic look. I guessed my face was pretty messed up, but I hadn't really looked at it.

Caleb said something funny and Olivia laughed. I laughed, too, but Caleb glanced at me, catching the false tone of it. I tried to pull myself into their conversation, but I couldn't. Each of us spent the rest of the day trying to forget one thing or another. Caleb and Olivia focused on anything besides the cold reality of halfs being turned into daimons. And me? Well, I tried to forget everything.

When dusk settled around us, we headed back to our dorms, making plans to meet up for lunch tomorrow. Alone, Caleb stopped me before I headed up the porch steps. "Alex, I know you've been going through a lot. On top of everything else, school is going to be starting in two weeks. You've got a lot of stress on you. And I'm sorry about what happened the night at Zarak's."

School was starting in two weeks? Holy crap, I didn't even realize. "I should be the one apologizing." I meant it. "I'm sorry for being such a bitch."

He laughed and gave me a quick hug. Pulling back, his smile faded. "You sure you're okay?"

"Yeah." I watched him start to turn around. "Caleb?"

He stopped, waiting.

"Mom did kill those people at Lake Lure. She was the one who turned Kain."

"I…I'm sorry." He took a step forward, his hands coming up and then falling to his sides. "She's not your mother anymore. It's not her doing this."

"I know." The mother I'd known wouldn't take pleasure in killing bugs. She never would've harmed another living, breathing person. "Kain said she'd keep killing until she finds me."

He looked like he didn't know what to say. "Alex, she'd keep killing no matter what. I know this is going to sound terrible, but the Sentinels will find her. They'll stop her."

I nodded, toying with the edge of my shirt. "It should be me who stops her. She's my mother."

Caleb frowned. "It should be *anyone* but you since she *was* your mother. I—" The frown faded from his face as he stared at me. "Alex, you wouldn't go after her, would you?"

"No!" I forced a laugh. "I'm not crazy."

He continued to stare at me.

"Look. I wouldn't even know where to find her," I told him, but Kain's words came right back at me. *You leave the safety of the Covenant, and you'll find her or she'll find you.*

"Why don't you sneak back with me? We can download a crap ton of movies and watch them. We can even break into the cafeteria and steal a bunch of food. How about that? Sounds like fun, right?"

It kind of did, but… "No. I'm really tired, Caleb. The last couple of days have…"

"Sucked?"

"Yeah, you can say that." I backed off then. "I'll see you for breakfast? I doubt I'll have practice."

"Okay." He still looked worried. "If you change your mind, you know where to find me."

I nodded and headed inside the dorm. There was another white envelope shoved in the little crack. When I saw Lucian's sprawling handwriting, there was a weird sinking feeling in my chest. Nothing from Aiden.

"Gods." I opened it up and quickly discarded it without reading it. I was collecting a rather large sum of money. This one contained three hundred, and I stashed it with the rest of the cash. Once things calmed down, I was going to do some serious shopping.

After changing into a pair of cotton pajama bottoms and a tank, I picked up the book of Greek legends and brought it back to the bed, thumbing to the section about the Apollyon. I read the passage over and over again, looking for something that could tell me what was going to happen when I turned eighteen, but the book told me nothing I didn't already know.

Which wasn't much of anything.

I must've fallen asleep, because the next thing I knew I was staring at the ceiling in my dark bedroom. I sat up and pushed back a tangled mess of hair. Disoriented and still half asleep, I tried to remember what I'd dreamed.

Mom.

We'd been at the zoo in my dream. It was just like when I was a kid, but I was older and Mom…Mom had been killing all the animals, ripping their throats out and laughing. The whole time, I'd just stood by and watched her. Never once did I try to stop her.

I swung my legs over the edge of the bed and sat there as my stomach twisted. *She'll keep killing till she finds you.* I stood, my legs feeling strangely weak. Was that why Kain had come back here?

Had Mom somehow known I would seek him out, and he would relay this message?

No. It wasn't possible. Kain came back to the Covenant, because he was…

Why had he come back to a place full of people ready to kill him? Another memory stood out, brighter than the rest. It was of Aiden and me standing in front of the dummies in the training room.

I'd asked him what he would do if his parents had been turned.

"I would've hunted them down. They wouldn't have wanted that kind of life."

I squeezed my eyes shut.

Mom would rather have been killed than become a monster preying on every living creature. And right now, she was out there, killing and hunting—waiting. Somehow I ended up in front of my closet, my fingers drifting over the Covenant uniform.

Then I'll find her and kill her myself. My own words burned in my mind. There was no doubt what needed to be done. It was crazy and reckless—stupid even—but the plan took form. Cold, steely determination settled over me, and I stopped thinking.

I started acting.

It was early—way too early for anyone to be roaming the grounds of the Covenant. Only the shadows of the patrolling Guards moved under the moonlight. Getting to the secure warehouse behind the training arenas wasn't as hard as I thought it might be. The Guards were more concerned with possible weaknesses in the perimeter. Once inside, I found my way to where they kept the uniforms. My hands snatched one that fit, and my heart raced as I quickly changed into it. I didn't need a mirror to tell me how I looked—I'd always known I'd look damn good in a Sentinel uniform. Black was a very flattering color for me.

The Hematoi used the earth element to glamour the uniforms so the mortal world wouldn't suspect we were some paramilitary organization. To a mortal, the uniform looked like plain old jeans and a shirt, but to a half-blood, it was a sign of the highest position a half-blood could obtain. Only the best wore this uniform.

There was a good chance this was the first and the last time I'd ever wear it. If I made it back…I'd probably be expelled. If I didn't make it back, well, that was something I couldn't think about.

You're going to do something stupid. My feet tripped up when I remembered what Aiden had said. Yeah. This was pretty stupid. How had he known? My heart turned over. Aiden always knew what I was thinking. He didn't need a blue cord or a crazy oracle's word to know me. He just did.

I couldn't think about him right now or what he'd do if he found out what I was up to. I grabbed a cap off the top shelf, twisted my hair up under it, and pulled it down so it shadowed most of my face.

Then I turned my attention to the weapons room—

one-stop shopping for knives, guns, and just about anything that stabbed and decapitated. As sick as it was, I was kind of excited to be in here. I wasn't sure what that said about me as a person, but then again, killing was part of being a half-blood, just like it was for a daimon. Neither of our kinds could escape that—only the pures could.

I opted for two daggers. One hooked onto the side of my right thigh, and the other collapsed from six inches to two with a mere touch of a button on the handle. I put that one in my pocket along the seam of my pants. I grabbed a gun and made sure it was loaded.

Titanium-encased bullets. Deadly stuff in there.

With one last look at the room of death and dismemberment, I gave a little sigh and did what both Caleb and Aiden probably had feared. I left the safety of the Covenant.

CHAPTER EIGHTEEN

Holy crap. My disguise worked.

I stayed in the shadows for the most part, refusing to let myself think about my actions. As I crossed the first bridge, the Guards simply nodded. One even catcalled, obviously mistaking me for someone legal.

While I navigated the empty streets of the main island, I thought about the times I'd killed. I had two daimon kills under my belt. I could do this. Mom would be no different.

She couldn't be any different.

Being a young daimon, she would have speed and strength, but she'd never had any serious training. Not like the kind I'd had. I'd be faster and stronger than her. Aiden had practically beaten into me the fact young, newly turned daimons would be concerned about one thing only: draining. At three months, she'd be considered a newbie—a baby daimon.

I would just have to strike while she still looked like a daimon…before the elemental magic settled over her and she looked like…Mom.

The main bridge proved to be a little more difficult to cross, but thankfully, those Guards didn't have a lot of contact with the students. None of them recognized me, but they wanted to chat. It slowed me down enough to make my confidence waver.

Until one said, "Be safe and come back, Sentinel," and stepped aside.

Sentinel. It was what I'd always wanted to be upon graduation, taking the more proactive route of dealing with daimons instead of guarding pures or their communities.

Once again, I stuck to the shadows as I made my way around the fishing and cruising boats. The townsfolk on Bald Head Island were used to the "intensely private" people from Deity Island, but there was something about us they sensed. They didn't know what it was that made them back off at the same time they wanted to be close to us.

Living among mortals for three years had been a truly craptastic experience for me. The teenagers had wanted to be close to me while their parents had said I was "one of *those* kids" they needed to stay away from. Whatever that meant.

I wondered what those parents would think if they knew exactly what I was—an almost-trained killing machine. I guess they'd been right to order their offspring to steer clear.

When I left the docks, I stuck to the sides of the buildings. I wasn't sure where to go, but I had a feeling I wouldn't have to go far. And I was right. About ten minutes into what I lovingly referred to as the normal world, I heard quick footsteps behind me. I spun around to face my would-be attacker, gun drawn and leveled.

"Caleb?" I felt something halfway between disbelief and relief.

He stood a few feet behind me, blue eyes wide and arms

raised. He wore pajamas, a white shirt, and flip-flops. "Put your gun down!" he hissed. "Gods. You're gonna accidentally shoot me or something."

I lowered the gun and grabbed his arm, dragging him into an alley. "Caleb, what are you doing here? Are you crazy?"

"I could ask you the same question." He glared at me. "I was following you, obviously."

I shook my head and shoved my gun back into the waist of my pants. I'd forgotten a holster—go figure. "You need to go back to the Covenant. Now. Dammit, Caleb! What were you thinking?"

"What were *you* thinking?" He glowered as he threw the question back at me. "I knew you were going to do something incredibly stupid. That's why I couldn't sleep at all. I sat by my damn window and waited. Low and behold, I see your crazy ass sneaking across the quad!"

"How in the hell did you even get past the Guards in your *Super Mario Bros.* pajamas?"

He glanced down at them, shrugging. "I have my ways."

"Your ways?" I didn't have time for this. Stepping away from him, I pointed in the direction of the bridge. "You need to get back there, where it's safe."

He folded his arms across his chest stubbornly. "Not without you."

"Oh, for the love of the gods!" My temper snapped. "I don't need this right now. You don't understand."

"Don't start with the 'I don't understand' crap. This isn't about understanding anything! This is about you getting yourself killed! This is suicide, Alex. This isn't brave. It isn't smart. This isn't about duty or some misguided guilt you—"

His eyes widened again as *something* landed a couple of feet behind me. I whirled around, and at the same time, Caleb grabbed the dagger from my pants as I pulled the gun.

It was her.

She stood there, in the center of the alley. It was her… except it wasn't. It had her long, dark hair that fell in soft waves, framing her pale, ghastly white face—those high cheekbones and familiar lips. But darkness existed where her eyes should have been. Inky veins covered her cheeks, and if she smiled, there'd be a row of nasty, sharp teeth in her mouth.

It was my mother…as a daimon.

The shock of seeing her—seeing her beautiful, loving face twisted into such a grotesque mask—caused my arm to waver, my finger to twitch over the trigger. It was her…but it wasn't.

I knew from where she stood, there was no way she could defend herself against a gunshot to the chest. I had the upper hand with my gun filled with titanium bullets—a full clip of them, actually. I could light her up right here and all of this would be over.

She hadn't moved, not an inch.

And now she looked like Mom. The elemental magic cloaked the daimon in her, and she stared at me with those bright, emerald-colored eyes. Her face was still pale, but no longer riddled with thick veins. She looked like she had the night before she'd turned—smiling at me, holding my gaze with hers.

"Lexie," she murmured, but I heard her loud and clear. It was her voice. Just hearing it did wonderful and awful things to me.

She was beautiful, stunning, and very much alive—daimon or not.

"Alex! Do it! Do—!" Caleb cried out.

A quick glance behind me confirmed Mom wasn't alone. Another dark-haired daimon now had a hand around Caleb's throat. He didn't move to kill him or to tag him. He simply held him.

"Lexie, look at me."

Unable to deny the sound of her voice, I turned back to her. She stood closer—close enough that a bullet would leave one hell of a hole in her chest. And close enough that I caught the scent of vanilla—her favorite perfume.

My gaze flickered over her face, each line of it familiar and beautiful to me. As I stared into her eyes, I remembered the strangest things. Memories of our summers together, the day she'd taken me to the zoo and told me my father's name, the look on her face when she'd told me we needed to leave the Covenant, and the way she'd looked sprawled across the floor in her tiny bedroom.

I faltered. I couldn't catch my breath as I stared into those eyes. This was my mother—*my mother!* She had raised me, treated me like I was the most precious thing in the world. And I had been her everything—her reason for living. I couldn't move.

Do it! She's not your mother anymore! My arm trembled. *Do it! Do it!*

A scream of frustration tore through me and my arm dropped to my side. Seconds, only seconds had passed and yet, it felt like an eternity. I couldn't do it.

Her lips curved into a smug smile. Caleb gave a yelp from behind me, and then pain exploded alongside my temple. I slipped into the sweet darkness of oblivion.

I woke up to a splitting headache and a dry, bitter taste in the back of my mouth. It took me a few minutes to remember what'd happened. A mixture of horror and disappointment jerked me upright, on alert despite the throbbing ache radiating down the side of my face. I touched my head gingerly, feeling a knot the size of an egg.

Woozy, I looked around the lavishly furnished room. The cedar log walls, the large bed covered in satin sheets, the plasma television, the handcrafted furniture, all of it appeared familiar to me. It was one of the bedrooms in the cabin we used to visit, the one I'd slept in a half dozen times. A pot of purple hibiscus flowers sat beside the bed—Mom's favorite. She had a thing for purple flowers.

Shock and dismay set in. I remembered this room. Oh gods.

This wasn't good. Nope.

I was in freaking Gatlinburg, Tennessee—more than five hours away from the Covenant. Five hours. Worse yet, I didn't see Caleb. Creeping over to the door, I paused and listened. Not a sound. I glanced at the glass doors leading out to the deck, but there was no way I could leave. I had to find Caleb… if he was still alive.

I clamped down on that thought. He had to be alive. There could be no other way.

Of course my gun was gone and Caleb had taken my dagger. There was nothing in this room I could use as a weapon. If I started breaking stuff apart, it would draw attention, and it wasn't like any of this stuff could be converted into a weapon. Anything that might've been made of titanium had been stripped away.

I tried the doorknob and found it unlocked. I inched the door open and looked around. The sun rose outside, pushing the shadows out of the living area and kitchen. A large round table sat in the middle of the room, surrounded by six matching chairs. Two of the chairs had been pulled back, as if they'd been occupied. Several empty beer bottles rested on the carved oak surface. Daimons drank beer? I had no clue. There were two large couches, nice ones covered in luxurious brown fabric.

Across the room, the television was on but muted—one

of those big ones, mounted on the wall. I went to the table and picked up a beer bottle. It wouldn't kill a daimon, but at least it was a weapon.

A muffled scream drew my attention to one of the back rooms. If I remembered right, there were two more bedrooms, another living area, and a game room. All of the doors were closed. I crept closer, freezing as the sound came again from the master bedroom. I clenched the bottle in my hand and murmured a soft prayer.

I wasn't sure what god I was praying to, but I really hoped one of them answered. Then I kicked the door. The hinges creaked and gave way as the wood around the knob splintered. The door swung open. My breath caught in my throat at the nightmare unfolding before me. Caleb was pinned to the bed. A blond daimon was on him, his rough hands covering his mouth and holding him down while he tagged his arm. The sounds the daimon made as he drained Caleb's blood to get at the aether horrified me.

At the sound of my rage-fueled scream, the daimon lifted his head. His empty stare bored straight through me. I launched myself away from the door, bottle raised high in the air. It wouldn't kill him, but I was going to make it hurt.

Except it never happened.

So caught up on what the daimon was doing to Caleb, I didn't check the room. Stupid. But dammit, these were the kind of things I'd missed out on when I'd left the Covenant. I just knew to act and fight. Not to think.

Someone snatched me from behind. My arm twisted back until I dropped the bottle to the floor. The two chairs pushed back from the table flashed before me. Should've seen this one coming. Struggling proved useless from this position, but I still kicked out and tried to wrench my body away. It only succeeded in causing the daimon to tighten his grip until it became painful.

"Now, now, Daniel isn't going to kill your friend." The voice came from behind my ear. "Not yet."

Daniel smiled, flashing a row of bloodstained teeth. In a blink he stood in front of me, tilting his head to the side. The glamour took over, revealing the pure-blood characteristics. He would've been beautiful if it weren't for the rivulets of blood dripping down his chin.

Caleb's body jerked every few seconds. Aftershocks of the tag—I would know. His bare arms revealed not one but two daimon tags. Furious, I screamed at the daimon in front of me. "I'm going to kill you!"

Daniel laughed and wiped the back of his hand over his chin. "And I'm going to love tasting you." He sniffed me—*literally* sniffed me. "I can almost taste you now."

I kicked out, catching him in the chest. He staggered a couple of feet back, hitting the bed. Caleb groaned and tried to sit up. Daniel coldcocked Caleb. I cried out, struggling like a rabid animal, but the daimon knocked me to the floor.

And then I was flying up, but no one was touching me. I hit the wall so hard the plaster cracked, along with what felt like every bone in my body. There I stayed, pinned with my feet dangling several feet off the floor. The daimon controlled the air element—something else I hadn't learned how to defend myself against.

"You need to learn to play nice. Both of you." The other daimon held his hand up. He had a Southern accent—smooth and deep. He stepped up to where I hung, leaned in, and patted the top of my foot. It was the daimon from the alley, the dark-haired one who'd been with Mom. "We do get hungry, you know? And with you here…well, it gnaws out our insides. It's like a fire inside of us."

I tried to pull away from the wall, but I didn't move. "Stay away from him!"

He ignored me, walking over to Caleb's motionless frame. "We aren't new daimons by any means, but you…make it hard to resist the lure of the aether. Just a hit. That's all we want." He ran his fingertips down Caleb's face. "But we can't. Not till Rachelle returns."

"Don't touch him." I barely recognized my own, low voice.

He glanced back at me and waved his hand as if it were an afterthought. I hit the floor feet first, and then fell to my knees. I ignored the way my stomach muscles pulled and pushed to my feet. Without thinking about anything other than getting him away from Caleb, I rushed him. The dark-haired daimon shook his head and simply threw his arm up. My body slammed into the wall, knocking several framed paintings to the floor. This—*this* was nothing like training.

And this time I didn't get up.

Clearly annoyed, he pushed away from Caleb. He advanced on me, and I screamed, swinging on him. He caught my arm and then my other, hauling me to my feet.

With both arms rendered useless, I had only my legs. Aiden had always praised my kicks, and with that thought in mind, I pushed my upper back against the wall. Using the daimon's arms and the wall for support, I pulled my legs up to my chest and kicked out.

I caught him right in the chest, and by the startled look on his face he hadn't expected it. He fell back several feet, and I hit the floor once again.

Daniel shot away from the bed and dug his hands into my

hair, wrenching my neck back. For a moment, a sick sense of déjà vu hit me, but there was no Aiden to save me now—no cavalry would be arriving.

As I struggled with Daniel, the dark-haired daimon dropped down in front of me. With his hands resting on his knees and the lazy smile splayed across his face, he looked like he was about to talk about the weather with me. He was that casual.

"What's going on here?"

Daniel released me at the sound of my mother's sharp and angry voice. I struggled to my feet, twisting toward her. I couldn't help the mixture of terror and love coursing through me. She stood in the doorway, surveying the damage with a critical eye. I only saw the glamour. I couldn't see her true form.

I was so screwed.

"Eric?" She directed her scowl at the dark-haired one.

"Your daughter...she's not happy with the current state of things."

I couldn't pull my eyes off of her as she stepped over a piece of broken wood. "My daughter better not have one hair on her head missing."

Eric glanced over at Daniel. "Her hair is perfectly fine. She's fine. So is the other half-blood."

"Oh. Yes." She turned to Caleb. "I remember him. Is he your boyfriend, Lexie? Sweet of him to tag along either way. Stupid, but sweet."

"Mom." My voice cracked.

She turned to me with a smile—a big, beautiful smile. "Lexie?"

"Please..." I swallowed. "Please let Caleb go."

She *tsked* and shook her head. "I cannot allow that."

My insides twisted. "Please. He…just, please."

"Baby, I can't. I need him." She reached out and brushed back my hair, the way she used to. I flinched, and she frowned. "I knew you would come. I know you. The guilt and the fear would eat at you. What I didn't plan on was him, but I'm not mad. See? He's going to stay."

"You could let him go." My chin trembled.

Her hand drifted down my cheek. "I can't. He's going to ensure that you cooperate with me. If you do everything I tell you to do, he'll live through this. I won't let them kill him or turn him."

I wasn't stupid enough to be hopeful. There was a catch, probably a big and terrible one.

She stepped away, turning her attention to the two male daimons. "What have you told her?"

Eric's chin came up. "Nothing."

My mother nodded. Her voice was the same, but I realized as she talked, it lacked what actually had made it hers. There was no softness in it, no emotion. It was hard, flat—not hers. "Good." She faced me once more. "I want you to understand one thing, Lexie. I love you very, very much."

I blinked, backing against the wall. Her words hurt more than any physical blow could. "How can you love me? You're a daimon."

"I'm still your mother," she replied in the same flat tone, "and you still love me. That's why you didn't kill me when you had the chance."

An act and truth I was already regretting, but looking at her now, I could only see her—Mom. I closed my eyes, willing myself to see the daimon, the monster inside of her. When I opened my eyes, she was still the same.

Her lips twisted into a smile. "You can't go back to the

Covenant. I cannot allow that. I have to keep you away from there. Permanently."

My gaze fell to Caleb. Daniel inched his way closer to him. "Why?" I could keep my cool as long as the bastard didn't touch him again.

"I need to keep you away from the Apollyon."

I blinked, not expecting that. "What?"

"He will take everything from you. Your power, your gifts—everything. He is the First, Lexie. Whether he knows it or not, he will drain everything from you so he can become the God Killer. There will be nothing left of you when he is done. The Council—they know this. They don't care. All they want is the God Killer, but Thanatos will never allow that to happen."

I backed up, shaking my head. Mom was utterly crazy.

"They don't care what it will do to you. I can't allow that. Do you understand?" She stalked forward, coming to a stop in front of me. "That's why I must do this. I must turn you into a daimon."

The room spun and for a moment, I thought I would pass out.

"I have no other choice." She caught my hand, pulling it to where her heart beat. She held it there. "As a daimon, you will be faster and stronger than you are now. You will be immune to titanium. You will have great power... When you turn eighteen you will be unstoppable."

"No." I pulled my hand back. "No!"

"You have no idea what you are saying 'no' to. I thought I lived before, but now I am truly living." She held her free hand in front of my face, wriggling her fingers once, then twice. A tiny spark flew from her fingertips, and then her entire hand was on fire.

I jerked back, but her grip increased on my hand.

"Fire, Lexie. I could barely control the air element as a pure blood, but as a daimon, I can control *fire*."

"But you're killing people! How does that make it okay?"

"You get used to it." She shrugged dismissively. "You'll get used to it."

My blood froze in my veins. "You sound…freaking insane."

She looked at me blandly. "You say that now, but you'll see. The Council wants everyone to believe the daimons are soulless, evil creatures. Why? Fear. They know we are far more powerful, and in the end, we will win this war. We are like gods. No. We *are* gods."

Daniel practically licked his lips in anticipation as he eyed me. Sickness and fear clawed through me, and I shook my head.

"No. Don't do this. Please."

"It's the only way." She turned away, glancing back at me over her shoulder. "Don't make me force you into this."

I looked at her, wondering how I could've hesitated in the alley. Nothing about this thing in front of me was my mother. Nothing. "You're freaking insane."

She whipped around, expression hardening. "I told you not to make me force you into this. Daniel!"

I pushed off the wall as Daniel grabbed for Caleb, who groaned as he started to come around. Mom caught me before I could reach them. The daimon bent his head to his arm.

Horror twisted through me. "No! Stop!"

Daniel laughed a moment before his teeth cut into flesh. Caleb jackknifed across the bed, eyes going wild as his terrified screams filled the cabin. I pushed at my mom, but I couldn't get past her. She was strong, so unbelievably strong.

"Eric come here."

Eric seemed to be more than happy to oblige. His dark eyes flared with hunger. Revulsion and fear filled me, and my struggles renewed.

Mom's hold tightened around my waist. "Remember what I told you, Eric. Small bites, every hour and no more. If she fights you, kill the boy. If she complies, leave the boy alone."

I turned cold. "No! No!"

"I'm sorry, baby. This is going to hurt, but if you don't fight them, it will be over soon. It's the only option, Lexie. I'd never be able to control you any other way. You'll see. It will be for the best in the end. I promise you."

Then she shoved me at Eric.

CHAPTER NINETEEN

Just like that.

What a bitch.

I screamed and twisted back to her as Eric pulled me into his arms. "Don't let them do this!"

She raised her hand. "Eric."

The daimon flipped me around. I kicked and I threatened every possible method of death and dismemberment, but it didn't stop him. The daimon smiled at me through my rant. Then his fingers squeezed, and in a millisecond, his teeth sank through the soft flesh of my arm.

Red-hot fire shot through me. I reared back, trying to escape the burning, but it followed my movements. Over my screams, I heard Caleb yelling and begging for them to stop. Neither Mom nor the daimon paid any attention to him. The pain slithered through every part of my body as Eric continued to drain. The room tilted, and there was a pretty good chance I was going to pass out. "Enough," she murmured.

The daimon lifted its face. "She tastes divine."

"It's the aether. She has more in her than a pure does."

Eric let go of me then, and I fell to my knees, shaking. There was nothing—absolutely nothing that felt like that. Even the aftershocks of the tagging stole my breath. Gasping for air, I stayed there until the fire dulled to nothing more than an ache.

Only then did I realize Caleb was silent. I lifted my head and saw him staring at me. There was a dazed look to his eyes, as if somehow he'd managed to remove himself from this place, left his body or something. I wanted to be wherever he was.

"Now, that wasn't too bad?" Mom grasped my shoulders and forced me back against the wall.

"Don't touch me." My words came out weak and slurred.

She gave me a cold smile. "I know you're upset, but you'll see. We'll change the world together."

Daniel returned to Caleb's side, but he didn't move. The way Daniel looked at him made me think he wanted to do bad things to Caleb. Abruptly the oracle's words came back to me.

One with a bright and short future.

Caleb would die. Horror forced me toward the bed. This couldn't be happening! In an instant, Eric had me pinned back against the wall. Blood—*my* blood—still stained his lips. Once he was sure I wouldn't move again, he let go and leaned back with a smug half smile.

Sickened, I pushed down my own pain and fear. "Mom... please let Caleb go. Please. I'll do anything." And I meant it. There was no way I was going to let Caleb die in this godforsaken place. "Please, just let him go."

She studied me silently. "What would you do?"

My voice broke. "Anything. Just let him go."

"Would you promise not to fight me or run?"

The oracle's words kept replaying over and over, like some

sick chant. There was no telling how much more of this he could take. Caleb's color was chalky, sickly. What was about to happen was fated, wasn't it? Had the gods already seen this? And if I chose not to fight, I would be turned into a daimon.

I swallowed down the taste of bile. "Yes. I promise."

Her gaze flickered over Caleb and the daimon. She sighed. "He stays, but since you made a promise, I'll make you one. They will not touch him again, but his presence will make sure you keep your promise."

Snapping out of his daze, Caleb frantically shook his head at me, but I agreed again. I wanted him out of here, but for now, this was the best I could do. I sat opposite the bed with my back pressed against the wall, eyes trained on Caleb and Daniel. Eric took up position beside me. All I could do was hope someone had checked on us by now. Maybe Aiden finally had come to talk to me or start practice again. Maybe someone had checked on Caleb, and someone at the Covenant put two and two together. If not, in a horrible twist of fate, the next time I saw Aiden, he would try to kill me.

And I doubted he would falter like I had.

Daniel turned from Caleb and stared at the fresh tag on my arm. I squeezed my eyes shut and turned my head. Next was Daniel's turn, and I had a feeling he was going to make it as painful as possible. My eyes burned as I pushed against the wall, wishing I could somehow disappear into it.

An hour came and went, and my body tensed as Daniel knelt down and pried my other arm from my chest. This was wrong, so wrong. There was no way to prepare for this, and when Eric placed his hand over my mouth, Daniel bit into my wrist.

I sagged against the wall, reeling after it was over. Like clockwork, Daniel and Eric took turns tagging me. Mom blabbed on and on about how we would eradicate the Council members, starting first with Lucian. We would then sit on the thrones, and even the gods would bow before us. The tables would turn, she said, and the daimons would rule over not just the pure-bloods, but the mortal world, too.

"We'll have to take down the First, but when you're a daimon Apollyon, you'll be stronger than him—better than him."

Mom was really, absolutely nuts.

I learned about their draining. Maybe she was trying to prepare me for my new life? Pures kept them wired for days, halfs only for a few hours, and mortals, well, they killed them for the fun of it. Too bad there wasn't a pure I could hand over to the daimons now. That may sound terrible, but my arms were covered in crescent-shaped bites, much like my old Instructor had been scarred. And I'd pitied her—ironic.

The draining continued. Pieces of who I was disappeared with each tag. I no longer pressed away when Daniel dipped down or Eric leaned over. I didn't even scream. And the whole time, *she* stood by and watched it all. I was losing myself to this sick madness, and my soul turned dark and desperate.

Eventually she left to go check the roads. Not once did she feed off me. I supposed she'd bagged herself a pure earlier, but when she left, I immediately wanted her back. With her gone, Daniel got bold, and though it made me want to vomit, I let him get close. Every so often, he would run the tips of his fingers over my arms, around the bite marks. At least it kept his attention off Caleb.

"I can already feel it," murmured Eric.

I'd forgotten he was still there. Even though he was tagging the hell out of me, I preferred him to Daniel. "Feel what?" My voice sounded sleepy.

"The aether, I'm buzzing from it. Almost like I could do anything." He reached over and poked one of the bites, causing me to wince. "Do you feel it leaving you? Going into me?"

Refusing to answer him, I lowered my head to my bent knees. He sounded high…and I felt sick—my soul felt sick. By the time Daniel tipped my neck back, I was exhausted and near delirious from the pain. Caleb hadn't moved in a while, and Eric didn't need to cover my mouth anymore. I only whimpered as the teeth pierced the skin at the base of my neck.

Eric made soothing noises as Daniel drained me, his thumb tracing the wild pounding of my pulse. "It'll be over soon. You'll see. Just a couple more tags, and it will be over. A whole new world is waiting for you."

After Daniel was done, I slumped to the side. The room spun, tilted. I had a hard time focusing on what Eric was talking about.

"We're going to change the half-bloods first. They can't be spotted like us. They don't need elemental magic. All over the world, we will launch our attack. It will be beautiful." Eric smiled at the thought. "The Covenants will be infiltrated… and then the Council."

It was a good enough plan, one that could easily become a scary reality. Eric didn't seem bothered by the lack of conversational input. He continued on, and I found it hard to keep my eyes open. Fear and anxiety had ridden me hard. I dozed off. For how long, I didn't know, but something jarred me awake.

Weary and confused, I lifted my head in time to see Daniel standing in front of me. Had it already been another hour? Was this it? I couldn't help but wonder if they were preparing for the last bite, the last drop of aether and the last of my soul.

"Daniel, it's not time."

"I don't care. You're getting more than I am. You're practically glowing. Look at me!" Daniel scowled. "I don't look like you."

Eric wasn't glowing, but his skin had taken on a healthy infusion. He looked…like a normal pure blood. Daniel, on the other hand, was still sheet-white.

Eric shook his head. "She'll kill you."

Daniel dropped down in front of me and shoved a hand through my hair, wrenching my head back. "Not if she doesn't know. How would she? I just want one more."

"Don't…let him." My weak voice held a pleading edge, but if Eric was concerned with Daniel's fate, he sure didn't show it or try to stop him.

There was a spare spot on my neck still bite-free. I silently begged that he wouldn't go for that. I don't know why I cared at this point, but dammit, I still had some smidge of vanity left.

"She probably likes it," Daniel said. A stuttered heartbeat later, he sank his teeth into that one little spot and his lips moved against my skin. The pain shot through me, causing me to go rigid. His one hand tightened in my hair and his other got friendly, slipping over my shoulder and down farther.

Out of everything that was happening, this—*this* was too much.

With every ounce of strength I had in me, I lifted my hands and dug my nails into the sides of his face.

Daniel reared back, howling. My shirt ripped in the process, but the sound—the look on his face filled me with a sick sense of satisfaction. Deep and angry-looking welts formed on his face, beading with fresh blood. Blindly he lashed out and caught me in the eye, toppling me into Eric.

"Hell!" Eric leapt to his feet as I ate the floor.

I curled onto my side and into a fetal position. Above me, I felt Eric push Daniel back, yelling in his face, but I wasn't listening. Something long and thin dug into my thigh. I slowly rolled over, inching my fingers down until they closed over the object hidden in the seam of my pants.

The knife—the retractable one.

Suddenly Eric lifted me up and straightened me so that I looked at him. Something wet and warm ran down the side of my face, dripping into my right eye. Blood. Not like I had much more I could afford to lose.

Over his shoulder, I saw that Caleb was awake. He stared at me, and I tried to send him a message, but as it was, Eric was doing a good job of blocking him. From the front of the house, we heard the door open, and the click of my mother's heels resonated through the cabin. Eric let go of me and backed clear across the room. My lips curved into a sad little smirk. He knew. I knew.

Mom was going to be pissed when she got a look at my face.

She stepped into the room, and her eyes narrowed on me. In a second, she was kneeling in front of me, tipping my head back. "What has happened here?"

Blood loss and exhaustion addled my thoughts. Moments went by as I stared at her. I couldn't remember where I was or how I got there. All I wanted to do was press my face against her, have her to hold me and tell me everything would be okay. She was my mother, and she would stop them. She had to, especially something this vile, this horrendous. "Mom? Look...look at what they've done to me."

"Shh." She smoothed my hair back from my face.

"Please...please make him stop." I gripped her in a weak hug, wanting to climb into her arms, wanting her to hold me. She didn't. As she turned away from me, I cried out and reached for her.

No. This—this *thing* in front of me wasn't my mother. My mother would never have turned her back on me. She would've held me, comforted me. I snapped out of it, blinking slowly.

"Who did this to her face?" Her voice was so cold, so deadly and so unlike Mom, but at the same time I heard the edge in her words. I recognized her tone from the many times she'd yelled at me for getting in trouble—it was the tone that happened right before she launched into a major bitch-fest. Eric and Daniel didn't know. They didn't know my mother like I did.

"Who do you think?" Eric sneered.

She pressed cool lips against my forehead, and I squeezed my eyes shut. She wasn't my mom. "I gave you both explicit orders." She straightened, her eyes falling to Daniel.

Reality settled around me once more, and I came to my knees. I couldn't think about her anymore, couldn't see her as my mom. I made my decision. *Screw fate.* My eyes met Caleb's, and I nodded at Mom's back and mouthed the words, "Get ready." I could only hope he understood.

"That is simply unacceptable." That was the only warning she gave. She launched herself at Daniel, knocking him over Caleb. The two daimons crashed to the floor, swinging and tearing at one another.

I seized the opportunity. Scrambling to my feet, I grabbed for Caleb.

Thankfully, he got the message. He slid off the bed as Eric went after Daniel, too. I staggered to my feet just as Mom pulled Daniel to *his* feet. He was a good foot taller than her, but she threw him around the room like he was nothing.

There was a moment when I couldn't move. Her strength was shocking, unnatural.

Dizzy and nauseous, I stumbled away from the room with Caleb in tow. We raced through the cabin and out the front door. Rain pounded on the roof of the deck, almost but not quite silencing the wet, sloppy crunch from inside the house. The sound propelled both of us over the railing. Forgetting how high the decks were, I hit the ground hard, falling to my knees.

"Lexie!"

My mother's voice pushed me to my feet. Glancing beside me, I saw Caleb do the same. We ran, half sliding and half falling down the muddy hill. Branches slapped me in the face, pulled on my clothing and hair, but I kept running. All that gym time paid off. My muscles pushed past the pain and the lack of blood.

"Alexandria!"

We weren't fast enough. Caleb's startled yelp spun me around. My mom plucked him up from behind, tossing him sideways. Shock flickered over his face right before he slammed into a thick maple tree. I screamed, backtracking to where he'd fallen.

A barrier of flames went up, pushing me back. The fire destroyed everything in its path as it spread. Caleb rolled to his side, barely escaping it. I stumbled backward as the world burned in red and violet colored flames. The rain did nothing to beat down the unnatural fire.

And there she stood—tall and straight, like a terrible goddess of death. Twice now, I'd failed to see that. In the alley in Bald Head and moments earlier in the cabin, right after I'd realized I had a Covenant dagger in my pocket.

"Lexie, you promised me you wouldn't run." She sounded surprisingly calm.

Did I? My hand slipped into the side pocket. "I lied."

"I took care of Daniel. You won't have to worry about him." She edged closer. "Everything is going to be okay now. Lexie, you should sit down. You're bleeding all over the place."

I glanced down at myself. Running had gotten my blood pulsing. I could feel it trickling down my arms and neck. I was kind of surprised I had any left in me. Out of the corner of my eye, a shot of dark blue darted between the flames.

"Just do it, Rachelle. She's weak." Fury and impatience colored Eric's words. "Take care of it and let's get the hell out of here!"

That was so true. Light-headed and off-balance, a bunny rabbit could get the best of me right now. "Don't come any closer."

My mother laughed. "Lexie, this will be over soon. I know you're scared, but you have nothing to worry about. I'm going to take care of everything. Don't you trust me? I'm your mother."

I backed up, stopping when I felt the heat from the flames. "You're not my mother."

She moved forward. Somewhere in the distance, I thought I heard my name being called. His voice—*Aiden's.* It had to be a hallucination because neither Eric nor my mom reacted to the sound, but even if it was just a sad manifestation of my subconscious, it gave me strength to keep standing. My fingers slid over the slender dagger. How had they missed this? "You're not my mother," I said again, my voice sounding hoarse.

"Baby, you're confused. I'm your mother."

My thumb brushed over the release button. "You died in Miami."

Her eyes held a dangerous glint. "Alexandria…there is no other option."

Wait, a voice whispered in my head, *wait until her defenses are down*. If she saw the blade, it would be over. I needed her to believe she'd won. I needed her vulnerable. Though the strange thing was, I was almost a hundred percent certain the voice didn't belong to me. But that really didn't matter right now.

"There's another option. You could just kill me."

"No. You will join me." Her voice sounded like it had in the room, right before she'd killed Daniel for touching me. How messed up was that? "And since you broke your promise, I will have to kill your little boyfriend over there. That is, if he hasn't been burned alive yet."

Everything came down to this moment. Die or kill her. Be turned into a monster or kill her. The breath I drew in wasn't enough.

"You're already dead," I whispered, "and I'd rather be dead than become what you are."

"You will thank me later." Moving inhumanly fast, she wrapped her hand through my hair and jerked my head back.

The handle of the dagger felt awkward, wrong even. Sucking in air, I pushed the little button. There wasn't a lot of space between us, but I still got my arm in between us. It wouldn't be a precise hit, not at this angle, but it would kill.

You will kill the ones you love.

Fate had been right about that.

My mother jerked back, her mouth gaping open in surprise. She looked down. So did I. My hand was flush with her chest, and the blade had sunk through her skin like titanium did when it met the flesh of a daimon.

She stumbled backward as I withdrew the dagger. Her face contorted and blurred. Bright, beautiful eyes met mine, and then they disappeared. Like a switch had been thrown, the fire circling us ceased to exist.

Her scream filled the forest, and my screams overcame hers. She slumped just as my legs refused to cooperate. We both folded into ourselves at the same time, except I collapsed into a messy heap and she buckled into herself. There was a moment—it was quick—but I saw the glimmer of relief cross her face. In that instant, she was Mom. She really was. And then she started to flake apart, fading until there was nothing left but a fine layer of blue dust.

I sagged forward, resting my head against the damp ground, vaguely aware of Eric running and the rain hammering me. Months of grief and loss swirled inside me, invading every cell, every pore. Nothing existed but the raw pain of a different kind of hurting. The tags and the bruises faded in comparison to it. Anguish consumed me. I wanted to die—to just cave in like Mom had. I'd killed her—my mother. Daimon or not, I'd killed her.

Time stopped. It could've been minutes or hours, but eventually there were voices. People called my name, called Caleb's, but I couldn't answer. Everything sounded far away and unreal.

Then strong hands surrounded me, lifting me up. My head fell back and cool rain splattered off my cheeks. "Alex, look at me. Please."

Recognizing the voice, I opened my eyes. Aiden stared down at me, face pale and drawn. He looked stricken as his gaze roamed over the many bite marks. "Hey," I murmured.

"It's going to be okay." His voice held a panicked, desperate edge. He ran wet fingers over my cheeks, catching my chin. "I need you to keep your eyes open and talk to me. Everything's going to be okay."

I felt funny, so I doubted that. There were so many voices, some I recognized and some I didn't. Somewhere I heard Seth.

"Where's…Caleb?"

"He's okay. We have him—Alex, stay with me. Talk to me."

"You were…right." I swallowed, needing to tell someone—to tell him. "She was relieved. I saw it…"

"Alex?" Aiden stood, cradling me to his chest.

I felt his heart thundering under my cheek and then I felt nothing at all.

CHAPTER TWENTY

I woke up staring at the soft glow of fluorescent ceiling lights. I wasn't sure what'd woken me or where I was.

"Alex."

I turned my head and met his pale gray eyes. Aiden sat on the edge of the bed. Dark waves of hair fell over his forehead. He looked different to me. Shadows bloomed under his eyes.

"Hey," I croaked.

Aiden smiled that wonderful full smile that was so rare, so beautiful. He reached over and, with just the tips of his fingers, he brushed a few strands of hair off my forehead. "How are you feeling?"

"Okay. I'm…thirsty." I tried clearing my throat again.

He leaned over, the bed dipping slightly as he grabbed a glass off the bedside table. Helping me sit up, he waited while I gulped the cool water. "More?"

I shook my head. Sitting up, I got a better view of the unfamiliar room. I was hooked up to half a dozen tubes, but I wasn't in the Covenant. "Where are we?"

"We're at the Nashville Covenant. We couldn't risk the

time it would've taken us to get you back to North Carolina." He paused, seeming to choose his next words. "Alex, why did you do this?"

I leaned back and closed my eyes. "I'm in a lot of trouble, aren't I?"

"You stole a Sentinel uniform. You also stole weapons and left the grounds without permission. Untrained and unprepared, you left to hunt down your mother. What you did was so reckless, so dangerous. You could've been killed, Alex. So yes, you're in trouble."

"I kinda of figured that." I sighed, opening my eyes. "Marcus is going to expel me now, isn't he?"

Sympathy shone on his face. "I don't know. Marcus is very upset. He would've come here, but he's been with the Council. Everyone's in an uproar over what happened to Kain and the implications."

"Everything's changed," I murmured to myself.

"Hmm?"

I took a deep breath. "Caleb shouldn't be in trouble. He tried to stop me, but… Where is he?"

"He's here, in a different room. And he's been awake for the last day, asking for you. He has a couple bruised ribs, but he'll be okay. He's going to head back later today, but you'll need to stay for a little while longer."

Relief washed through me. I relaxed back against the fluffy pillows. "How long have I been asleep?"

He fiddled with the blankets, adjusting them around me. "Two days."

"Whoa."

"You were pretty bad off, Alex. I thought…"

I looked at him, my eyes finding his and remaining there. "Thought what?"

Aiden exhaled softly. "I thought I—*we* thought we'd lost you. I've never seen so many tags on a person still…living." His eyes fell shut briefly. They were a startling color when they reopened—a beautiful silver. "You scared me. You really did."

There was an odd pain in my chest, sort of a dull aching. "I didn't mean to. I thought—"

"What did you think, Alex? Did you think at all?" Aiden lowered his chin. A muscle feathered along his jaw. "It doesn't matter now. Caleb told us everything."

I was sure what he meant by "everything" was her crazed ranting, the daimons, and those horrible, terrible hours in the bedroom. "Caleb shouldn't be punished. He really did try to stop me, but we got caught in an alley…and I saw her. I should've…killed her then, but I couldn't. I failed, and I could've gotten Caleb killed."

Aiden faced me again. "I know."

I swallowed. "I had to do it. She was going to keep killing, Aiden. I couldn't stand around and wait for the Sentinels to find her. Yeah, it was stupid. Look at me." I lifted my bandaged arms. "I know it was stupid, but she was my mother. I had to do it."

Aiden was quiet as he stared at me. "Why didn't you come to me instead of running off and doing this?"

"Because you were busy with what happened with Kain, and you would've stopped me."

Anger flared behind his eyes. "Damn straight I would've stopped you—prevented *this* from happening to you!"

I flinched. "That's why I couldn't come to you."

"You never should've faced what you did. None of us wanted you to go through this. What you must be feeling…"

"I'm dealing." I clamped down on the sudden pressure in the back of my throat.

He ran a hand through his hair. It looked like he'd done that several times in the last two days. "You're so foolishly brave."

His words brought back the memory of the night in his… bed. "You've said that before."

"Yes. And I meant it then. If I'd only known how foolishly brave you truly were, I would've locked you in your room."

"I also kinda figured that, too."

He didn't say anything to that, and we sat in silence for a long time. Then he started to stand. "You need to get some rest. I'll check in on you in a little while."

"Don't leave. Not yet."

Aiden stared at me as if he could read what was going on inside me. "I know what you want to talk about, but now is not that time. You need to get better. Then we can talk."

My fingers tightened around the blanket. "I want to talk about it now."

"Alex." His voice was soft.

"Aiden."

His lips twitched at my response, but then his eyes met mine and held them in their depths. "The night—what happened between us was… Well, it shouldn't have ever happened."

Ouch. It was a struggle to keep my face blank and not show how much those words hurt.

"Do you…do you regret it? What happened between us?" If he said yes, I thought I'd die.

"As wrong as this is, I don't regret it. I can't." He looked away then, drawing in a deep breath. "I lost control, lost sight of what's important to you—to me."

"I wasn't complaining."

He looked at me wearily. "Alex, you're not making this easy."

I sat up more, ignoring the way the tubes pulled on my arms. "Why should I? I…like you. I like being around you. I do trust you. I'm not naïve and dumb. I wanted you. I still do."

His hands clenched against the blanket tucked around my legs. "I'm not saying you're naïve or dumb, Alex. But… dammit, I nearly destroyed both of our futures in a matter of minutes. What do you think would've happened if we'd been caught?"

I shrugged, but I knew what could've happened. It wouldn't have been pretty. "But we weren't caught." Then something occurred to me. Maybe it had nothing to do with the actual rules. "Is it because I'm Seth's freakier half? Is that why?"

"No. It has absolutely nothing to do with that."

"Then why?"

Aiden stared at me like he could somehow get me to understand by his stare alone. "It has nothing to do with you being the Apollyon. Alex, you know that I don't see you as anything different than me, but…the Council will."

"Pures do this—they do it all the time and don't get caught."

"I know that there are some pure-bloods who break the rule, but they do it because they don't care about what happens to the other person, and *I* care about what happens to you." His eyes searched mine intently. "I care about you more than I should and that's why I'm not going to put you in that situation and jeopardize your future."

Desperate, I searched for a way we could make this work. We had to, but the look on Aiden's face stole my breath, my protests.

He closed his eyes and took another deep breath. "Both of us need to be Sentinels, right? You know why I have to do this. I know why you have to do this. I lost control, forgetting to see what could come of this. I could've ended whatever chances you had of becoming a Sentinel, but worse than that, I could have stolen your future. It doesn't matter what you are or what you'll become when you turn eighteen. The Council would ensure that you were removed from the Covenant, and I…would never forgive myself for that."

"But the Breed Order—"

"The Breed Order hasn't been changed, and with the knowledge that halfs can turn, I doubt it ever will. Whatever ground the halfs have gained was lost the moment the daimons discovered that your kind can be changed."

Well, that was depressing, but not as crushing as this. Everything about the moments we'd shared had been magical, perfect, and so right. There was no way I could've mistaken the look in his eyes or the way he'd touched me. Looking at him now, I knew I still wasn't mistaking that look of near desperation, of lust and something far stronger.

I tried to joke. "But I'm the Apollyon. What can they really say? At eighteen, I can just zap anyone who gives us a hard time."

His lips twitched. "That doesn't matter. These rules have been in place since the time the gods walked among mortals. Not even Lucian or Marcus would be able to stop what would happen. You'd be given the elixir and placed into servitude, Alex. And I couldn't live with myself knowing what that would do to you. To see you lose everything that makes you who you are? I couldn't bear that. I couldn't live seeing you like the rest of the servants. You have too much life for that, too much life to lose for me."

I shifted closer, my legs brushing his hands and my face only inches from his. I knew I looked a mess, but I also knew Aiden saw past that. "Don't you want me?"

Groaning low in his throat, he pressed his forehead against mine. "You know the answer to that. I still...want you, but we can't be together, Alex. Pures and halfs can't be together in that way. We can't forget that."

"I hate rules." I sighed, feeling the burning in my throat again. I'd wanted him to hold me ever since the moment I'd woken up. And our blood wouldn't even allow that.

He sounded like he wanted to laugh but knew it would only provoke me further. He sighed. "But we have to follow them, Alex. I can't be the reason you lose everything."

Rules could suck it. There were only a few inches between us, and if I moved just a little bit more, our lips would touch. I wondered what he would think about our future then. If I just kissed him, would he care about the rules? About what people would think?

Almost like he sensed what I was thinking, he murmured, "You are so reckless."

The last time I'd been awake, I thought I'd never smile again, but I did smile. "I know."

Aiden shifted and pressed his lips against my forehead. He lingered a few seconds, and before I could do anything—which sucked, because I *was* feeling pretty damn reckless—he pushed himself away. "I...I will always care for you, but we won't do this. We can't. Do you understand?"

I stared at him, knowing that he was right, but he was also wrong. He wanted this as much as I did, but he was too concerned by what could happen to *me*. Part of me liked him even more for that, but my heart...well, it was cracking. The only thing that kept it from shattering completely was the fleeting look of desire and fondness that flickered over his face as he backed toward the door.

"Get some rest," he said when I didn't answer. "I'll check on you later."

I scooted back down, but then something else occurred to me. "Aiden?"

He stopped, turning around. "Yes?"

"How did you all find us?"

His face hardened. "Seth."

Confused, I sat up again. "What? How?"

Aiden shook his head slightly. "I don't know. He showed up real early in the morning—the morning you left—and said something was wrong and you were in danger. I checked your room and saw that you were gone. Once we got on the road, he knew where to find you. Somehow he could sense where you were. I don't know how, but he did. Seth was the reason we were able to find you."

Two days later, I returned to the Covenant, pumped full of blood and fluids. As soon as I arrived, I was taken to the infirmary to be checked over again. Aiden sat beside me as the doctor removed the white gauze that covered every piece of exposed skin.

Needless to say, I looked torn up. Several crescent-shape bites marked each arm. They were still pretty red-looking, and while the doctor made some herb mixture that "should" help minimize the scarring, I rummaged through the cabinets.

"What are you looking for?" Aiden asked.

"A mirror."

He knew why. Sometimes, as annoying as it could be, it was like we shared the same brain. "It's not that bad, Alex."

I shot him a look over my shoulder. "I wanna see."

Aiden tried again to get me to sit back down, but I refused

to listen until he got up and found a small plastic mirror. Without saying a word, he handed it to me.

"Thank you." I lifted the mirror and nearly dropped it.

The deep purple that covered my right eye and spread toward my hairline wasn't bad. It would fade in a couple of days. A black eye wasn't a big deal. I liked to think I looked sort of badass with it. However, the tags on each side of my neck were horrendous. Some of them looked deep, almost as if patches of skin had been ripped out and fused back together, the flesh uneven and crimson in color. The redness would fade, but the scars left behind would be deep and obvious.

My fingers tightened around the plastic handle. "It—I look horrible."

He was immediately by my side. "No. They'll fade, and before you know it, no one will even notice."

I shook my head. I couldn't hide this—not all of these.

"Besides," he said in the same gentle voice, "these are scars to be proud of. Look at what you've survived. These scars will make you stronger, more beautiful in the end."

"You said that before—about the first one."

"The same still stands, Alex. I promise you."

I placed the mirror slowly down on the little counter and…I broke.

It wasn't the scars or what Aiden had said. It was that those scars would forever be a reminder of losing Mom in Miami. All the terrible things she'd done and allowed to happen. And what I had done—killing her. They were big, powerful sobs. The kind I couldn't really breathe or think around. I tried to pull myself back together, but I failed.

I sat down in the middle of the doctor's office and cried. I wanted my mom, but she would never answer, never comfort me. She was gone, really gone this time. The yawning hole opened up in me and the grief, it just poured out, and it kept coming and coming.

Aiden knelt beside me, placing his arms around my bent shoulders. He didn't say a single word. He just let me cry it out, and after months of forcing myself to just push through it, all the pain and hurt had built up into a massive knot that finally unraveled.

Once I'd cried myself out, I wasn't sure how much time had passed. My head hurt, my throat felt raw, and my eyes were puffy. But in a weird way, I felt better, like I could finally breathe again, really breathe. All these months, I'd been slowly suffocating and hadn't realized it until that moment.

I sniffled and winced at the dull pain in the back of my head. "Remember what you said about how your parents wouldn't have wanted a life like that?"

His fingers moved soothingly over my taut shoulders. "Yes. I remember."

"She didn't. I saw it just before she…was gone. She looked relieved. She really did."

"You released her from a horrible existence. That's what your mother would've wanted."

A few minutes passed. I still couldn't look up. "Do you think she's in a better place now?" I asked, my voice sounding small.

"Of course she is." Man, he really sounded like he believed it, too. "Where she is…she is no longer suffering. It's paradise—a place so beautiful that we can't even begin to imagine what it must be like."

I assumed he was talking about Elysia—a place very much like heaven. I took a deep breath and wiped under my eyes. "If anyone deserved it, she really does. I know it looks bad since she became a daimon, but she would never have chosen that."

"I know, Alex. The gods know that, too."

Slowly I pieced myself back together and climbed to my feet. "Sorry to…unload all of that on you." I stole a quick peek at him.

Aiden frowned. "Don't ever feel sorry for this, Alex. I've told you before, if you ever need anything you can come to me."

"Thanks for…everything."

He nodded, stepping aside as I shuffled past him. "Alex?" He picked up a jar from the counter. The doctor must have come in at some point. "Don't forget this."

I took the jar and murmured my thanks. Bleary-eyed, I followed him out and into the vivid sun. It hurt my head and my eyes, but in a way, the sun still felt good on my skin. I was alive.

We stood for a moment on the marbled pathway, both of us staring out across the courtyard and the ocean beyond. I wondered what he was thinking.

"You going back to your dorm?" he asked.

"Yeah."

We didn't talk about our conversation in Nashville or about that night at his place, but it lingered in my mind as we made our way to the dorms. Walking as close as we were, it was hard not to think about it, but when I thought about Caleb, all thoughts of romance—or lack thereof—fled. I really needed to see him.

"See you around?"

Aiden nodded as he stared across the quad. A few halfs lounged on the benches between the dorms. A pure was with them. She was making it rain over one spot. Kind of cool.

I sighed, stalling. "All right…"

"Alex?"

"Yes?"

He stared down at me, a soft smile tugging at his lips. "You're going to be okay."

"Yeah…I am. I guess it takes more than a couple of hungry daimons to bring me down, huh?"

He laughed, and the sound nearly knocked the air out of my chest. I loved the way he laughed. I looked up at him, a small smile tugging at my own lips. Like always, our eyes met and something deep flared between us. Even out here, out in the open as we were, *it* was still there.

Aiden stepped back. There was nothing left to say. I gave him a tiny wave and watched until he disappeared from view, then I cut across the courtyard and headed to Caleb's room. I wasn't worried about getting caught going into the boys' dorm. We hadn't gotten a chance to talk since everything had gone down. He opened the door after the first knock, wearing sweats and a loose shirt.

"Hey," I said.

He smiled and pushed the door open farther. The grin immediately turned into a grimace as he clutched his sides. "Crap. I keep forgetting not to move a certain way."

"You doing okay?"

"Yeah, my ribs are just a little sore. You?"

I followed him back to the bedroom and sat cross-legged on the bed. "Good. Just got checked out by the doctor here."

He eased himself down on the bed beside me. A frown crossed his face as he studied me. "Those tags? Why haven't they healed like mine?"

I glanced down at his arms. Four days later and the only reminder were the bruised ribs and a couple of pale scars dotting his arms. "I don't know. The doc said they would fade in a few days. He gave me a jar of stuff to rub on them." I patted my pocket. "It's pretty bad looking, isn't it?"

"No. You kinda look like...like I should be afraid of you kicking my ass or something."

I laughed. "That's because I *can* kick your ass."

He raised his eyebrows. "Alex, I was kind of out of it in the woods, but I heard you..."

"Killed her?" I leaned over and grabbed an extra pillow. "Yeah, I did."

My bluntness caused him to flinch. "I'm...really sorry. I wish I knew what to say to make it easier for you."

"You don't need to say anything about it." Stretching out beside him, I stared up at the little green stars all over the ceiling. At night, they glowed. "Caleb, I'm sorry I dragged you into that mess."

"No. You didn't drag me into anything."

"You shouldn't have been there. What Daniel was doing—"

His hand clenched beside me. I don't think he saw me notice, but I did. "You didn't—"

"You shouldn't have been there."

He waved his hand, cutting me off. "Stop it. I made the decision to follow you. I could've gone to one of the Guards or the Sentinels. Instead, I followed you. It was my choice."

I stared at him and saw he was actually serious. He looked like he hadn't been sleeping well. I looked away. "I'm sorry you had to go through this."

"It's okay, all right? Look. What are friends for if they can't share a few hours with psychotic daimons? We can look at it as a bonding experience."

I snorted. "Bonding experience?"

He nodded and started telling me about all the halfs who'd visited him since he came back to the Covenant. When he mentioned Olivia, he got that dopey look on his face.

Suddenly I wondered if I got the dopey smile on my face when I thought of Aiden. Gods, I hoped not.

"So, a skunk humped my leg earlier," Caleb went on.

"*What?*"

He laughed, and then winced. "You haven't been listening to me."

"Sorry." I blinked. "I kind of spaced out there."

"I could tell."

I then had an evil case of word vomit. "I almost hooked up with Aiden."

Caleb's mouth dropped open. It took him a couple of tries to say something coherent. "You do mean you almost hooked him like, say, with a fishing pole or something?"

My brows furrowed at that imagery. "No."

"A right hook to the jaw, then?"

I shook my head.

He stared at me, his face draining of all color. "Alex, what in the hell are you thinking? Are you out of your mind? Do you want to end up in servitude? Wow. Oh my gods, you're insane."

I cringed. "I said we *almost* hooked up, Caleb. Chill out."

"Almost?" He threw up his arms, then winced. "The Council—the *Masters* don't care about almost. Man, here I thought Aiden was cool. Freaking pure-bloods, they don't give two shits about what happens to us. Risk your entire future to just get between—"

"Hey. Aiden isn't like that."

Caleb looked at me blandly. "He isn't?"

"No." I rubbed my eyes. "Aiden's not going to risk my future. Trust me. He's nothing like the rest of them. I'd trust him with my life, Caleb."

He considered that silently. "How did it happen?"

"I'm not going to go into details, you perv. It was something that…just happened, but it's over. I just had to tell someone, but you have to promise me you won't say anything."

"Of course I wouldn't. I can't believe you'd even have to worry about that."

"I know, but I feel better saying it. Okay?"

"Alex…you really care about him, don't you?"

I squeezed my eyes shut. "Yeah, I do."

"You do realize how wrong that is?"

"Yes, but…he's so different from any pure we know. He doesn't think like them. He's kind, and he's really funny once you get to know him. He doesn't put up with any of my crap, and I kind of like him for that. I don't know. Aiden just gets me."

"And you do realize that all of that means nothing?" Caleb said. "That it can't go anywhere?"

That knowledge hurt more than it should. I sighed. "I know. Can we…talk about something else?"

Caleb lapsed into silence, thinking only gods know what. "Have you seen Seth?"

I propped myself up on one elbow. "No. He didn't stop by when I was in Nashville, and I haven't really been anywhere today. Why?"

He did his best to shrug. With his bruised ribs, it came off a bit lopsided. "I figured you'd see him since…"

"Since what?"

"I know I was in and out of it back in the cabin, Alex, but your mom said you were another Apollyon." He watched me closely.

My stomach turned over, and I flopped back on the bed, silent. Caleb still watched me. Waiting. I took a deep breath and told him everything in one big rush, stopping for a breath right before I told him Seth would become the God Killer. When it was over, Caleb stared at me as if I had three heads.

"What?"

He blinked and shook his head. "It's just…you shouldn't *be*, Alex. I remember my *History and Civilization* class last year. We talked about the Apollyons and what happened to Solaris. This is…wow."

"Wow isn't the word I'm aiming for." I pushed myself up and crossed my legs. "I mean, it's pretty cool. Right? At eighteen, I'll either be obliterated or sucked dry by Seth instead of legally buying cigarettes."

"But—"

"Not that I *would* smoke. I guess I could pick up the habit. Maybe, just maybe, I'll be all energized long enough to use *akasha*, because I saw Seth use it and it was damn cool. I'd like to hit a daimon or two with that."

Caleb scowled. "You're not taking this serious at all."

"Oh, I am. This is what I like to call coping with the impossible."

He wasn't impressed by my strategy. "You said Solaris was killed because the First Apollyon attacked the Council, right? Not because of what she was?"

I shrugged. "So as long as Seth doesn't go crazy, then I guess I'm okay."

"Why didn't Solaris stand against him?"

"Because she fell in love with him or something boring like that."

"Then don't fall in love with Seth."

"I really don't think that'll be a problem."

He didn't look entirely convinced. "Thought you guys belonged together or something?"

"Not in that way!" I forced my voice calmer. "It's like our energy responds to one another. It's nothing more than that. I'm just made to…I don't know, complete him. How freaking pathetic is that?"

He gave me a concerned look. "Alex, what are you going to do about this?"

"What can I do? I'm not going to stop living…or give up on my life because of what *might* happen. Something really bad may come out of this or something really good or…nothing at all. I don't know, but I do know I'm going to focus on being one…" I stopped, surprised by my own words. Whoa. It was one of those really mature, really rare moments in my life.

Dammit. Where was Aiden to witness this? "Focus on what?"

A wide smile crept across my face. "Focus on being one kick-ass Sentinel."

Caleb still didn't buy it, but I brought up Olivia and he was successfully distracted. Eventually, I got up to leave. On the way out, I had an idea. It kind of came out of nowhere, but the moment it popped in my head, I knew I had to do it. "Can you meet me tomorrow night around eight?"

His gaze met mine. Somehow I think he knew what I was going to ask, because he was already nodding. "I want to have…something for my mom." I squeezed my arms around my waist. "Like a memorial service or something. I mean, you don't have to."

"Of course I'll be there."

Flushing, I nodded. "Thanks."

Upon returning to my room, I found two letters stuck in the door—one from Lucian and one from Marcus. I was tempted to trash both of them, but I opened up the one from my uncle.

It was a good thing I did. The message was simple, loud, and clear.

Alexandria,

Please come see me immediately.

Marcus.

Crap.

I tossed both of the letters on the small table in front of my couch and closed the door behind me. My thoughts swirled with what Marcus could want to talk to me about. Gee, the possibilities were endless. The stunt I'd just pulled, my future at the Covenant, or the whole Apollyon thing. Good gods, I could really be expelled and sent to live with Lucian.

How could I've forgotten about that?

When I finally did make it over to his office, the sun had started its slow descent over the waters, and the hazy light sent a rainbow of colors shimmering over the ocean. I tried to prepare myself for our meeting, but I didn't know what Marcus was going to do.

Would he expel me? My stomach twisted uncomfortably. What would I do? Live with Lucian? Go into servitude? Neither of those were options I could live with.

The Guards gave me a curt nod before they opened the door to Marcus's office and stepped aside. My smile was more of a grimace, but elation swelled inside me when I recognized who stood beside the massive bulk that was Leon.

Aiden gave me a small, reassuring smile as the Guards closed the door behind me, but the moment I turned to Marcus, my skin turned cold.

He looked furious.

CHAPTER TWENTY-ONE

It was possibly the first time I'd ever seen him show any extreme emotion. I settled in for what I assumed would be a giant bitch-fest.

"First and foremost, I'm glad to see that you're alive and in one piece." Then his gaze dropped to my neck and finally, my arms. "Barely in one piece."

I bristled, but I managed to keep my mouth shut.

"What you did showed you have absolutely no regard for your life or the lives of others—"

"I have a regard for other people's lives!"

Aiden shot me a warning glare that said *shut up*.

"Going after a daimon—any daimon—untrained and unprepared is the height of reckless and idiotic behavior. Of all people, you should know the consequences. With what you are, what you will become, I cannot stress how irresponsible your actions were..." Marcus continued, but I tuned out at that point.

Instead I wondered how long Leon had known what I

was. Lucian had said only he and Marcus had been aware of what Piperi had told my mom, but a thought struck me. Leon had been the first to come to my defense when they'd brought me back to the Covenant. Had he always known? I looked up at my uncle, not really paying attention to what he was saying. There was always the chance they hadn't been honest with me about who knew. Hell, Lucian and Marcus hadn't been honest about a lot of things.

"If it hadn't been for Seth, you'd be dead or worse. And your friend Mr. Nicolo would have met the same fate."

My attention perked a bit. Where in the hell was Seth, anyway? I'd half expected him to have weaseled his way into this meeting.

"Do you have anything to say for yourself? "

"Um..." I stole a quick glance at Aiden before answering. "It was really stupid of me."

Marcus arched a perfectly groomed brow at me. "Is that all?"

"No." I shook my head. "I shouldn't have done it, but I don't regret it." I could feel Aiden's eyes boring through me. Swallowing, I leaned forward and placed my hands on Marcus's desk. "I regret that Caleb got hurt and the other daimon got away, but she was my mother—my responsibility. You don't understand, but I had to do it."

He leaned back in his chair as he studied me. "Believe it or not, I do understand. It doesn't make your actions justified or intelligent, but I do understand your motivation."

Surprised, I fell back in the chair in silence.

"Alexandria, a lot of things have changed. With the daimons able to turn half-bloods, it's altered the way we must face every situation." He paused, the tips of his fingers resting under his chin. "The Council is calling a special meeting during the November sessions in New York to discuss the ramifications. Since you were an eyewitness to their plans, you will be attending. Your testimony will help decide how the Council will act against this new threat."

"My testimony?"

Marcus nodded. "You were privy to the daimons' plans. The Council needs to hear exactly what you were told."

"But that was just Mom..." I trailed off, unsure of how much Leon knew.

My uncle seemed to understand. "It is highly doubtful Rachelle discovered that half-bloods could be turned. It's more likely that she witnessed another daimon doing it. She wanted you...for her own reasons."

He had a good point. Based on what she'd said, it did seem like there was some big master plan—more than just her merry band of psychos. And then there was Eric; he was still out there, hyped up on Apollyon aether. The gods only knew what he was getting himself into.

"There is something else we need to discuss." He had my attention again. "I've met with Aiden and have reviewed your progress."

He really had my attention. I tried to sound brave and confident.

"Lay it on me."

Marcus looked amused, if only for a second. "Aiden has advised me that you have progressed enough to continue at the Covenant." He picked up the dreaded file and opened it. I sank in my seat, remembering the last time he'd taken a gander at it. "You have a strong handle on the techniques of defense and offensive combat, but I see here you haven't started Silat training or defense against the elements, and you're extremely behind on your studies.

You haven't even taken a class on recon or basic guarding technique—"

"I don't want to be a Guard," I pointed out. "And I can catch up on the class stuff. I know I can."

"Whether or not you want to be a Guard or a Sentinel is not even a concern at this point, Alexandria."

"But—"

"Aiden has agreed to continue your training"—Marcus closed the file—"throughout the school year. He believes with his help and the time you spend with the Instructors, you will be able to fully catch up."

I tried my hardest not to look at Aiden, but I almost came out of my seat. Once school began, Aiden didn't have to continue training me. He was a Sentinel full-time. Giving up his free time for me *had* to mean something.

"I have to be honest, Alexandria. I'm not sure it will be enough, but I do have to take into consideration all you have recently accomplished. Even without all the training and classroom experience, you have proven that your ability is... beyond some of our seasoned Sentinels."

"But—*wait*. What?"

Marcus smiled, and it wasn't fake or cold. In that one moment, he reminded me so much of Mom I couldn't fight the way the proverbial wall between us cracked. But his next words blew that barrier to pieces. "If you can graduate in the spring, I am confident you will make an outstanding Sentinel."

Stunned, I stared at him. I'd expected him to try to send me back to Lucian so I'd be under the Council's thumb well before I turned eighteen, but it was the fact Marcus had actually complimented me that knocked me over.

Finally I found my voice. "So...I can stay?"

"Yes. Once classes start up, you will need to spend extra time getting caught up."

A tiny part of me wanted to jump up and hug the man, but that reaction would be so uncool. So I managed a totally calm, "Thank you."

Marcus nodded. "I've worked out an agreement with Aiden to split training with Seth. We both agreed that would be for the best. There are things that Seth will be…better suited for as time progresses."

I was too happy about being allowed to stay to care about spending mandatory time with Seth. After three years of being in limbo when it came to my future, I could barely contain the relief and excitement rushing through me. I nodded eagerly as Marcus outlined a plan for me to get caught up on my studies and how I would alternate days between Aiden and Seth.

When my meeting with Marcus was over, I still wanted to hug him. "Is that all?"

His emerald gaze settled on me. "Yes…for now."

A wide grin broke out across my face. "Thank you, Marcus."

Marcus nodded, and still grinning, I shot to my feet. On the way out, Aiden and I exchanged relieved looks before I shut the door behind me. I bounced out of the main building and all the way to my dorm. I couldn't wipe the smile off my face. Such terrible things had happened, but out of all the misery, things were starting to look up.

Once inside my dorm room, I kicked off my shoes and stripped off my shirt. My tank got stuck in the shirt during the process. Turning and tugging on my shirt, I—

"Please don't stop with just the shirt."

"Holy crap!" I clutched my chest in surprise.

Seth sat on my bed, hands folded in his lap. His hair hung

loose around his face. There was a devious smirk on his face that said he'd totally gotten a glimpse of my lacy bra.

"What are you doing in here?" Almost as an afterthought I added, "And on my bed?"

"Waiting for you."

I stared at him. Part of me wanted Seth to leave, but I was also curious. I sat down beside him, running my hands over the tops of my thighs. I wasn't exactly nervous, but I kind of felt like I wanted to crawl out of my skin. Seth was the first to break the strange silence that spread between us.

"You look terrible."

"Thanks." I groaned and held up my arms. The purplish-red splotches covered every portion of my arms, but I knew my neck…well, it was bad. For a few minutes I'd forgotten about it. "I really appreciate you pointing it out."

Seth tipped his head at me and shrugged. "I've seen worse. There was a Sentinel who got cornered once in New York City. Really was a pretty girl—a little older than you—and just had to be a Sentinel instead of a Guard. A daimon took a bite out of her face just to prove a—"

"Ugh. Okay. I get what you're saying; it could be worse. Try telling me when I don't look like I went to third base with a vampire. So why are you here?"

"I wanted to talk to you."

"About?" I stared at my feet and wiggled my toes.

"Us."

Wearily, I lifted my head and looked at him. "There's no—"

He reached out and placed one finger over my lips. "I have something really important to say about that matter, and after you give me a chance to say it, I'm not going to push or ever bring it up again. Okay?"

I should've knocked his hand down, demanded he leave, or at least leaned back. Instead, I gently brushed his fingers away. "Before you go any further, I want to say something."

Seth's brows rose curiously. "Okay."

I took a deep breath and stared down at my toes again. "Thank you for doing whatever…it was you did to find us. If it wasn't for you then I'd probably be dead—or slicing and dicing someone right now. So…thank you."

He was silent for so long I checked out what he was doing. Seth just stared at me with this dumb look on his face. To keep from smiling, I looked away. "What?"

"I think that's possibly the nicest thing you have said to me. Ever."

I laughed. "No, it's not. I've said nice things to you before."

"Like what?"

There had to be another situation when I'd said something nice. "Like…when…" I couldn't think of anything. Jeez, I was a bitch. "Okay. That *is* the first nice thing I've said to you."

"I think I need a moment to recognize and cherish this."

I rolled my eyes. "Moving on, what did you want to talk about?"

Seth turned serious. "I wanted to be up front on a few things with you."

"Like what?" I scooted back against the pillows lining the top of the bed, moving my legs so they weren't touching him.

His brows furrowed. "Like what the future has in store for us."

I sighed.

"Seth, nothing is going to happen between—"

"Aren't you even a little bit curious as to how I found you? Don't you want to know how I did that?"

"Yeah, come to think of it, I would like to know."

Seth leaned back on one arm, twisting onto his side. The movement sent locks of golden hair forward, sliding over his jaw. His hip was far too close to my curled toes. Not that he seemed to care. "I was having a really good dream about this chick I met in Houston and we were—"

I groaned. "Seth."

"All of a sudden, I was hurled out of the dream. I woke up, and my heart was racing, sweat pouring. I had no idea why. I felt sick—sick to my soul."

I pulled my knees to my chest. "Why?"

"Getting there, Alex. It took me a while to realize nothing was wrong with me, but the feeling wouldn't go away. Then I felt it—the first tag. It was like I was on fire and the pain—it was something real. For a second, I actually thought I had been tagged. It struck me then. It was *you* I was feeling. I went to Aiden—"

"Why did you go to him?"

"Because I figured if anyone knew where you were, it would be him. Lot of help he proved to be, though. He had no clue."

How did he come to that conclusion? That was something better left untouched for now. "So you felt what I was feeling?"

Seth nodded. "Every. Single. Tag. Like it was my skin being ripped into and my aether being drained. I never felt anything like it." He looked away. A few moments passed before he spoke again. "I don't know how you…dealt with it. It felt like my soul was being torn apart, but it was *your* soul."

Sort of struck dumb by what he was explaining, I listened quietly.

"Once we realized you weren't in your room, Aiden figured out what you had done. We left immediately, and I can barely explain how I knew where to go. It was like something was leading me. Instinct maybe?" He shrugged, staring down at his hand. "I don't know. I just knew to head west, and when we got close to the Tennessee line, Aiden said you once mentioned Gatlinburg. As soon as he said that, I knew where you were."

"But how? Did any of this happen before? When I was fighting Kain?"

He looked up and shook his head. "I don't think so. Whatever changed did so after then. The only thing I can come up with is that the longer I'm around you, the more… connected we are, and since I've already gone through the change, I can tune into those kind of things better."

I frowned. "It makes no sense."

"It will." He sighed. "When Lucian said we were two halfs made to be a whole, he wasn't kidding. If you had hung around that night at his house, you would've learned some interesting things. It would make things…so much easier."

Ah, damn. That night only made me think of one thing: Aiden. It was a struggle, but I managed to push him into the furthest corner of my mind. "What kind of things?"

Seth sat up and faced me in one fluid motion. "The gods know you are going to hate this, but oh, what the hell. The longer we are around each other, the more connected we will become—to the point neither of us will really know where one begins and the other ends."

I sat up a bit straighter. "I don't like the sound of that."

"Yeah…well, me either. But this is what's going to go down. I know how you are with control. You're kind of like me in that sense. I don't like not being able to control what I'm feeling. Just like you. But it's not going to matter. Even now, it's already affecting me."

"What's affecting you?"

He seemed to struggle for the right words. "Being around you is already affecting me. I can tap into *akasha* easily, sensing you when you're hurt, and even now, I can feel it." He paused, taking a deep breath. "It's the power in you—the aether. It calls to me, and you haven't even changed yet. What do you think it's going to be like when you do? When you turn eighteen?"

I didn't know, and I really didn't like where any of this was heading. "You know what will happen, don't you?"

Seth nodded again and looked away. "Once it happens, it will be a thousand times—no, a million times stronger. What I want, you will want. We will share the same thoughts, needs, and desires. Supposedly it works both ways, but I'll be stronger than you. Whatever you want may end up being skewed by what I want. I am the First, Alex. All it takes is one touch and that power shifts to me."

Panic reared and I failed at pushing it down. I started to rise, but Seth placed his hands on my knees. Thank the gods I was wearing jeans because if his skin touched mine and that goofy swirly crap started happening right now, I'd probably lose it.

"Alex, hear me out."

"Hear you out? You're saying I'll have no control over anything." I shook my head frantically. The wild movement stretched the tender skin on my throat, but I ignored the sting. "That can't happen. I can't deal with that. I don't believe in being fated to someone—or even fate."

"Alex, calm down. Look. I know this is probably up there with the worst things that can happen to you, but you have time."

"What do you mean I have time?"

"None of this affects you now. You won't want anything I want right now." He let go of my knees and leaned back—away from me. "But it doesn't work that way for me. Being near you means the connection is choking the crap out of me. Like right now, your heart is racing. So is mine. Being this close to you is like...being inside your head. But you still have time."

Processing all of this wasn't easy. I mean, I got what he was saying. Since he'd gone through the whole palingenesis thing, whatever it was between us was already wrapping its super-special cord around him, but not me. Not until I turned eighteen. Then? "Why didn't Lucian tell me any of this?"

"You didn't stick around, Alex."

I made a face at him. "I don't like any of this, Seth. We're talking seven months here. In seven months, I'll be eighteen."

"I know. Seven months of me helping you train, so try to imagine what the hell I'll be feeling this whole entire time."

I tried but couldn't. "This isn't going to work."

He leaned forward and tucked a strand of blond hair behind his ear. "That's what I'm thinking. I came up with an idea. Now hear me out on this. I can deal with this for right now, because even though it's strong, it's not that strong. It's doable—for me, but after you Awaken, things will change. If we can't handle it—if *you* can't handle it, then we'll separate. I'll leave. You won't be able to because of school, but I can. I'll go to the other end of the Earth."

"But the Council—Lucian—he wants you here, with me." I rolled my eyes. "For whatever reason. He's ordered you here."

Seth shrugged, and then he flopped down onto his back. "Whatever. Screw the Council. I'm the Apollyon. What the hell can Lucian do to me?"

Those were dangerous, rebellious words. I kind of liked them. "You'd actually do that for me?"

He turned his gaze to me, smiling slightly. "Yes. I would actually do that. You seem surprised."

One of my legs dropped off the side of the bed as I leaned over him. "Yes. Why would you? It sounds like everything comes up rosy for you."

"Do you think I'm a bad person or something?" He continued to smile up at me.

I blinked, a bit taken aback. "No...I don't think that."

"Then why would you think I'd force this upon you? Being apart won't stop the connection from growing stronger, but it will stop the shifting of power. Things will be intense once the transfer happens. If I leave, we will each still be our own person."

Out of nowhere, it struck me. "This is for you. You don't think you'll be able to handle it."

He only acknowledged my words with a sardonic twist to his lips.

This connection thing must actually bother him if he really thought he wouldn't be able to handle it down the road. Wrong as it may be, it kind of made me feel better about the situation. In the end, if things became too much, there was a way out. I still had control. So did Seth.

"What are you thinking?"

Snapping out of my thoughts, I looked down at him. "The next seven months are really going to suck for you."

Seth tipped his head back and laughed. "Ah, I don't know about that. This—*this thing*—has its benefits."

I sat back, folding my arms. "How so?"

He smiled.

"What are *you* thinking?"

"That we've actually held an entire conversation without

insulting one another. Next thing you know, you'll consider me a friend."

"Baby steps, Seth. Baby steps."

He turned back to staring at my ceiling. There were no stars that glowed, just ordinary old, dull white paint. Without thinking, I moved again, reaching out and touching the hand resting near my thigh. Call it an experiment, but I wanted to see what would happen.

Seth's head whipped in my direction. "What are you doing?"

"Nothing." And nothing was what happened. Confused, I wrapped my fingers around his.

"Doesn't look like nothing." His eyes narrowed on me.

"I guess so." Giving up on my impromptu test, I lifted my hand. "Shouldn't you be—" Whatever I was about to say died on my lips. Incredibly fast, Seth grabbed my hand and threaded his fingers through mine.

"Is this what you wanted?" he asked, ever so casually.

It happened. Being so close to him this time, I could see where the markings came from. The thick veins in his hand were the first to darken, branching out before spreading up his arm. Mesmerized, I watched the inky tats cover every piece of exposed skin. Before my eyes, they shifted away from his veins, swirling around his skin. Breaking off into different designs as he—we—continued to hold hands.

"What do they mean?" I looked up. His eyes were closed. "The markings?"

"They are...the marks of the Apollyon." He answered slowly, as if he were having trouble forming words and sentences. "They are runes and spells...meant to offer protection...or in our case, alert each other to our presence...or something. They mean other stuff, too."

“Oh.” The runes glided down his skin, toward the tips of his fingers. Call me crazy, but I was confident that those markings were reacting to where our skin touched, and for a split second, I really believed those glyphs would jump his skin and spread across my flesh.

“Will…I look like this one day?”

“Hmm?”

I pulled my gaze from our hands and looked up. Seth’s eyes were still closed, his expression relaxed. Actually it was more than that. He looked…content. Pleased. I’d never seen him so calm. “Is this one of the benefits?” I meant it as a joke, but the realization smacked me upside the head before he could respond. It *was* because he was close to me. Something as simple as that did affect him. *I* affected him that way.

I recalled what he’d said after my run-in with Kain. “I really do have all the power in this.”

His eyes opened, and they shone like two giant, tawny jewels. “What?”

My fingers tightened around his, and his lips parted, allowing a sharp sigh to leak out. Then, slowly, carefully, I loosened my hold on his fingers. Interesting. “Nothing.”

“I never should have told you the truth about that.” His voice held a certain rough edge to it. “You do, at least for now.”

I ignored the last part and pulled my hand free before the marks could touch my skin. We didn’t say anything for a couple of minutes. I leaned back against the pillows, and Seth closed his eyes once more. During that stretch of silence, I watched the steady rise and fall of his chest. He almost looked like he was sleeping. Relaxed as he was, the beauty of his face didn’t look so cold or methodical. This time, I was the first to break the silence.

“So…what are you doing?”

"Now?" He sounded sleepy. "I'm making up plans. Things I'm going to show you—in training, of course."

My brows rose. "I don't see how there is anything you can show me that Aiden can't."

Seth laughed then, and when he spoke, his voice was smug and knowing. "Oh Alex, I have a lot to show you. Things that Aiden will never be able to teach you."

Staring down at him, I admitted to myself that there was a teeny tiny part of me that actually looked forward to whatever it was that he planned on showing me. I felt confident that it would be entertaining, if not fruitful.

We really didn't talk after that, and all too soon, the excitement of everything faded, leaving me exhausted. My eyelids started to get too heavy to keep open, and I wanted nothing more than to kick Seth over, so I could lie down. As it was, he took up quite a bit of space sprawled across the middle of *my* bed.

Not surprisingly, Seth opened his eyes then and looked at me. When he gave a little half smile and pushed himself to his feet, I wondered if he'd sensed he was about to get a roundhouse kick in his side.

There went the element of surprise.

"You leaving?" I asked, because really, I had no idea what else to say.

Seth didn't answer. He lifted his arms above his head and stretched, showing off a row of taut muscles as the black shirt rode up his stomach. The image of a cat flashed before me. That was how he moved, feline and predatory. It was a subtle grace, neither human nor half.

"Do you know what your name means? Your real name—Alexandria?"

I shook my head.

He smiled slowly. "It means 'Defender of Man' in Greek."

"Oh. That sounds cool. What does your name—?"

Suddenly he bent at the waist and swooped in. He was so damn fast I didn't even have a chance to jerk back, which by the way, is totally a natural reaction when the Apollyon comes at someone *that* quickly.

He brushed his lips over my forehead, lingering just long enough that I could be positive he'd placed a gentle kiss against my skin before straightening.

"Good night, Alexandria, Defender of Man."

Stunned, I mumbled something along the lines of good-bye, but he was gone before I could fully get the words out. I reached up and brushed my fingers over the spot his lips had touched. His gesture was weird, unexpected, wrong, and… sweet.

I eased down and stretched out my legs. Staring up at the ceiling, I wondered what the next couple of months held in store for me. For the most part, I came up empty. Everything had changed—I had changed, but the one thing I could be sure about was that, between Aiden and Seth, I'd be learning lots of things.

The following afternoon, I remembered the card from Lucian I'd dropped on the table. I slipped my finger under the crease and tore it open. I slid the money out, and for the first time, I actually read the note.

It wasn't bad or too fake, but still, nothing stirred in my chest as I stared down at his elegant handwriting. No matter how much money he sent me or how many letters he personally wrote, he couldn't buy my love or erase the suspicion surrounding him like a thick cloud.

But his money was going to buy me some pretty sweet shoes soon.

With that thought in mind, I showered and found something to wear that covered the worst of the tags. Keeping my hair down helped with the neck situation, but it didn't cover all the splotches.

To my surprise, the Guards didn't stop me when I crossed the bridge to the main island, but as I prowled the main street, I had a feeling of being watched. A quick glance over my shoulder confirmed my suspicions. One of the Guards had broken away from his partner on the bridge and kept a discreet distance behind me. Perhaps Lucian or Marcus worried I'd make another run for it...or do something else incredibly irresponsible.

I tossed the Guard a saucy grin before darting into one of the boardwalk's tourist shops owned by the pures but run by mortals. The one I dove into featured an assortment of homemade candles, mosaic tiles made out of crushed shells, and sea salt baths. Smiling to myself, I sensed I'd be spending some of Lucian's money here.

Excited by all the girl stuff I planned on indulging in, I considered the simple pleasures of life often overlooked when preparing to kill daimons. Bubble baths were usually a low priority. I grabbed a few white votive candles in little pinewood spirit boats and a handful of big, chunky ones—the kind that smelled like they'd overdosed in a Bath & Body Works.

At the checkout counter, I ignored the way the obviously mortal clerk kept staring at my neck. Pures used compulsions on the mortals who lived near the Covenant, convincing them that all the weird things they saw were actually normal. This chick looked like she could use another dose.

"Is that all?" She stuttered over the last word, forcing her gaze away from my scars.

I shifted uncomfortably. Was this going to be how people acted until the damn tags faded? My eyes dropped from her to a set of ocean-themed stationery next to the register. "Can I add that?"

The girl nodded, sending highlighted hair across her face.

Unable to look at me directly, she rang me up pretty quick.

Once outside the store, I sat on one of the white benches lining the street and scribbled a couple of lines. After sealing the envelope, I headed across the street and cut between a bookstore and a novelty shop.

I didn't need to look behind to know the Guard still trailed me. Ten minutes later, I climbed the wide steps to Lucian's beach house and slid the note through the crack under his door.

There was a good chance he wouldn't even get it, but at least I'd attempted to thank him. I'd feel less guilty about spending my mini-fortune on my back-to-school wardrobe. After all, I couldn't wear dress greens and workout clothes all year long.

I rushed off his porch just in case he was actually home and caught me there. With my bag of smelly goodness, I started back to the Covenant-controlled island. "Miss Andros?"

Letting out a huge sigh, I turned and faced the Guard turned stalker. He stood by his partner now, a bland look on his face. "Yeah?"

"The next time you wish to leave the Covenant, please gain permission."

I rolled my eyes but nodded. I'd come full circle since I'd returned to the Covenant. I still needed a babysitter.

Back on the campus, I made one more stop before I met up with Caleb: the courtyard. Hibiscuses had been Mom's favorite flower, and I found several in bloom. I liked to think they smelled like the tropics, but I could never really catch any scent from them. Mom had just liked how beautiful they were. I snatched about a half of dozen and left the garden.

As I neared the girls' dorm, I spotted Lea sitting on the front porch with a few other half girls. She looked a lot better than the last time I'd seen her.

She tipped her chin when I passed her, using one über-tanned hand to flick her gloriously shiny hair over her shoulder. Silence stretched between us, and then she opened her mouth.

"Don't you look lovelier than normal?" She pushed away from the thick columns and bit her plump lower lip. "Well… at least the tags draw the attention away from your face. Guess that's a good thing, huh?"

I didn't know whether to laugh or punch her in the face. Either way, as ridiculous as it sounded, it felt good to see Lea back to her bitchy self.

"What?" She narrowed her eyes in challenge. "You have nothing to say?"

I thought it over. "I'm sorry…you're so tan, I thought you were a leather chair."

She smirked as she strutted by me. "Whatever. Freak."

Normally those words would have started a never-ending battle of insults, but this time, I let it slide. I had better things to do. Inside my room, I separated the candles and the little boats, which reminded me of the ones used to guide spirits into the afterlife. The meaning was totally symbolic, but since I didn't have a body or a gravesite, it was the best I could come up with.

I took my time getting ready. I wanted to look nice—well, as nice as I could look with half my body covered in tags. When I felt satisfied my hair didn't look like a frizz ball and the dress I'd worn to the earlier funerals wasn't covered in lint, I picked up a light cardigan. Slipping it over my arms, I gathered up my stuff and headed off to meet up with Caleb.

He was already down by the water, near the edge of the marshlands and where the staff cottages sat. It was the best, most private place to do such a thing, and I felt glad for that. Seeing Caleb in his nice clothes felt like a punch to my chest.

He must've dug a pair of black trousers out of the bottom of his closet, as they were a couple of inches too short for him. Even though Mom had tried to kill Caleb, he'd dressed up out of respect for her memory and for me. Something stuck in my throat. I swallowed, but the sensation didn't go away.

Sympathy radiated from Caleb as he stepped forward and took the flowers out of my hand. Quietly, he set up the little boats, and I plucked off the soft petals and sprinkled them in the boats. I thought she…would've liked the extra touch.

Staring down at the three boats, I swallowed again. One for Mom, one for Kain, and one for all the others who had died. "I really appreciate this," I said. "Thank you."

"I'm just glad you're doing this."

The burning in my eyes increased, and my throat tightened.

"And you wanted to include me," he added.

Oh gods. He was going to make it happen. I was going to cry.

Caleb edged closer to me and wrapped his arm around my shoulders. "It's okay."

A single tear snuck out. I caught it with the tip of my finger before it made its way down my cheek, but then came another fat tear…and another. I wiped at my face with the back of my hand. "I'm sorry," I sniffled.

"No." Caleb shook his head. "Don't be sorry."

I nodded and took a deep breath. After a few moments, I reined the tears back in and forced a wan smile.

We were kind of lost in each other's arms for a while. Both of us had something to mourn—something we'd lost. Perhaps Caleb needed this, too. Time seemed to slow down until we were ready.

I looked at the candles. "Shoot." I'd forgotten a lighter.

"Need a light?"

We turned toward the deep, rich voice. I recognized the sound all the way down to my soul.

Aiden stood a short distance from us, his hands shoved deep into the pockets of his jeans. The setting sun created a halo effect around him, and for a tiny moment, I almost believed he was an actual god and not a pure.

I blinked, but he didn't disappear. He was really here. "Yes."

He stepped forward and touched each vanilla candle with the tip of his finger. Abnormally bright flames sparked and grew, unfazed by the breeze coming off the ocean. When he was done, he stood and looked at me. Pride and reassurance filled his gaze, and I knew he approved of what I was doing.

I swallowed back more tears as Aiden retreated back to where he'd been standing. With effort, I tore my gaze from him and picked up my little boat. Caleb followed suit, and we walked to where the water turned to white, wispy foam, licking at our knees—far enough out that the surf wouldn't carry the boats back in.

Caleb set the two boats down first. His lips moved, but I couldn't hear what he said. Possibly a prayer? I couldn't be sure, but after a few moments, he let go of his boats and the waves carried them off.

So much stuff ran through my head as I stared down at my

boat. I closed my eyes, seeing her beautiful smile. I pictured her nodding and telling me it was okay, okay to let it all go now. And I guess, in a way, it was okay. She was in a better place. I really believed that. There'd always be some sort of guilt. Everything she'd done from the moment the oracle had spoken to her had led to this, but it was over—finally over. Bending down, I set the spirit boat on the water.

"Thank you for everything, for all you gave up for me." I paused, feeling the slick wetness running down my face. "I miss you so much. I'll always love you."

My fingers lingered around the boat for a second more, and then the foamy waves carried the boat from me. Farther and farther out, the three boats went, their candles still glowing. The sky had darkened by the time I lost sight of the boats and their soft light. Caleb waited for me on the sand, and beyond him stood Aiden. If Caleb thought anything about Aiden's presence, it didn't show on his face.

Carefully, I made my way back to the beach. The distance between Aiden and me seemed to evaporate, and it was only the two of us. A small smile crept over his lips as I approached him. "Thank you," I whispered.

Aiden seemed to understand I was thanking him for more than just a light. He spoke in a low voice so only I could hear him. "When my parents died, I never thought I'd find peace again. I know you have, and for that, I'm happy. You deserve it, Alex."

"Did…you ever find peace?"

He reached out and brushed his fingers over the curve of my cheek. It was such a quick gesture I knew Caleb never saw it. "Yes. I have now."

I inhaled sharply, wanting to say so much to him, but I couldn't. I like to think he knew, and he probably did. Aiden stepped back, and with one last look, he turned and headed home.

I watched until Aiden became nothing more than a faint shadow. Returning to where Caleb sat, I dropped down beside him and placed my head on his shoulder. Every so often, the salt water would tickle our toes, and I'd catch the scent of vanilla from the breeze rolling off the ocean. The air felt warm and pleasant, but the edge of the gentle wind held a soft chill, signifying autumn was on its way. But for right now, the sand felt warm on the island off the Carolina coast, and the air still smelled of summer.

READ ON FOR
SPECIAL BONUS SCENES

BONUS ALEX AND AIDEN SCENE

Saturday morning was just way too freaking early for practicing takedowns and other get-your-butt-kicked moves. Actually practicing on a Saturday was just wrong on so, so many levels. Unconditional. Sacrilegious. Pathetic. Borderline—

"Alex." Aiden's deep voice broke through my mental tirade, and I looked up, giving my best don't-mess-with-me-I-might-bite scowl. His full, expressive lips—lips I really needed to stop staring at—spread into a half smile. "Dragging your feet won't speed this up."

He had a good point, but I so wasn't going to admit that. Stomping across the mats, I tried—and failed—not to stare at him like a stalker-in-training. But gods, he made black sweats and a white shirt look like a million bucks. It probably had something to do with the way the material stretched over his broad shoulders and chest. Yeah, that was probably it…

Aiden arched a brow. "What are you staring at?"

Heat zinged across my cheeks. "Uh, nothing…?"

The look on his face was part knowing and the other half

was something I couldn't dare put into words. Without saying a word, he reached out and with just the tips of his fingers, he brushed a loose strand of hair behind my ear. Such a simple touch, really, but a shiver rolled down my skin and my breath caught.

Aiden dropped his hand quickly and turned his head. Several locks of wavy dark hair fell across his forehead. "All right, let's get this show on the road."

As we went through several warm-up stretches, my mood improved substantially. Well, at least I was starting to respond in complete sentences. Mornings were so not my thing.

We started with takedowns, which consisted of sweeping the enemy's legs out from underneath them if you happened to be lucky enough to be behind them or standing next to them. But since a daimon most likely wasn't going to stand there and eat cement, the takedowns we were running through consisted of Aiden coming at me like a linebacker.

"Remember," he said, dropping his hands on his narrow hips. "You are going to use the weight and momentum of the opponent against them."

"Uh-huh." This wasn't my first rodeo. Sometimes Aiden forgot that.

His eyes narrowed. "Is this boring you?"

Trick question. "Possibly...?"

Aiden cocked his head to the side. "Then let's do this."

I opened my mouth, but Aiden took off like a heat-seeking missile that had my name stamped all over it. Bracing myself for the impact, I forced my body forward, meeting him halfway. Technically, I should aim for his midsection, using my shoulder and lifting up. Like Aiden had said, his own weight and momentum should finish him off. But considering the fact that he'd probably had abs of steel since kindergarten, I just might break my shoulder.

I slammed into Aiden.

Yep, he didn't budge.

Backing off, I rubbed my shoulder as I frowned. "Well, that didn't go as planned."

He chuckled. "You hesitated at the last second."

Flipping my ponytail over my shoulder, I sighed. "I didn't want to hurt you."

Aiden stared a moment, then laughed again. Louder—much louder than before. "So glad you find that amusing," I muttered, knowing how ridiculous it sounded.

"Ah Alex, you're not going to hurt me." He walked backward, grinning so that one dimple popped in his cheek. "I think you were more afraid of hurting yourself."

"Whatever." Silly me for not wanting to go through reconstructive clavicle surgery.

"Do it again, and this time, don't hesitate." There was a pause. "If you do, you can run the dunes."

My mouth dropped open. "What?"

A sly look crept into his gray eyes. "For the next hour."

Oh, screw that. The pure blood was so going down. Tightening my ponytail, I glared at him. "Bring it."

He shook out his shoulders and then came at me again. This time I went straight for his midsection. Something went terribly wrong. My legs were in his path of destruction and before I knew what was happening, a thigh that reminded me of a tree trunk took mine out.

Down I went, and because I had mad skills, I took him down with me. Smacking off the mat wasn't what knocked the air out of my lungs. It was the moment Aiden's body went flush with mine. Wide-eyed, I stared at him, afraid to move, to breathe.

His hands were planted beside my head, and I had to think that if he really, truly wanted to avoid this, um, intimate position, he could have.

But he didn't. And he didn't move.

Aiden's cool, gray eyes flared and then deepened to an intense silver that sent my already racing heart into massive coronary arrest territory. His breath seemed to quicken. "Alex..."

I swallowed hard. "Aiden?"

Aiden shifted his weight onto one arm. His large hand made it to my face, covering my entire cheek. The fingers were elegant, I knew, because I stared at them way too much, but the skin was rough, calloused. I loved his hands.

Forcing myself to remain still and quiet, I waited knee-deep in an almost painful anticipation for him to do something, anything. And I knew if I made any move, he'd bolt, because that was the kind of guy Aiden was. Part of me sort of loved him for that. The other part was a ball of frustration that demanded he let go of his good, chivalrous side.

Not sure what that said about me. Nothing good, I was sure.

But I didn't care, not right now, not when Aiden was where I wanted him.

Aiden's eyes were so silver, they were like liquid as they slowly moved from my eyes and across my face, finally stopping on my parted lips. My skin flushed wherever those eyes went.

Gods, I wanted him to touch me, to kiss me more than anything I ever wanted.

Aiden made a low sound in the back of his throat that made my toes curl in my sneakers. "You really need to stop thinking what you're thinking."

"How...how do you know what I'm thinking?"

His fingers slid off my cheek, under the high collar of my shirt. I shuddered, and his lips quirked. "I can see it your eyes."

"Is that so?"

Aiden didn't bother answering, because I think he was seriously lost to this madness. Because this was crazy—the door was closed to the training room, but anyone could walk in on us, and this would be kind of hard to explain.

Then his hand was on the move again, running over my shoulder, down my boneless arm, and oh gods, his hand, it just kept going. He gripped my hip and then his fingers curved around my thigh.

I wanted, needed, to say something, but there were no words.

He lowered his head, pressing his forehead against mine, and he shuddered, just like I had a few seconds ago. His lips, they were so close I could almost taste them.

"This is insane," he murmured, tilting his head so that his lips brushed the corner of mine as he spoke. "Completely, utterly insane..."

"Yeah," I whispered. This was the good kind of insanity—dangerous, but oh-so fun.

Aiden pressed his lips against my cheek, and my eyes fluttered shut. He repeated the sweet gesture on the other one, and a great sense of sorrow rose up. He was going to stop. This was his way. Cooling the heat with something so sweet, so innocent that—

His lips brushed against mine, and like the first time we'd kissed, my entire world seemed to implode. Raw sensations shot through me, and I felt his hips roll, his entire body shake against mine. Every nerve in my body felt exposed.

I moved then, reaching up and sinking my fingers into his soft hair.

"Dammit," Aiden said, drawing in a ragged breath. "This..."

"I want this."

Not like he didn't already know that, but I guess hearing me put it out there like that broke the spell. In a flash, Aiden was off me and on his feet, backing away as he ran his hands through his hair, breathing deeply.

In a daze, I sat up and placed my fingers against my lips. I still could feel his kiss, the weight of his body.

Aiden cleared his throat, and when I looked up, he was all the way over by the edge of the mats. As if putting space between us really stopped anything. His throat worked. "Well, I guess that's one way to take down the opponent."

Yeah, I guess it was.

HALF-BLOOD CHAPTER ONE (AIDEN'S POV)

The first body we'd found at the bus station in Atlanta had at least 100 of his 208 bones broken in his body. The kid couldn't have been much older than my brother, and that made me sick. Another life wasted, and for what? Mortals had no aether. It was just the joy—the thrill of the kill.

Kneeling beside the street kid's body, I glanced up at the hulking form cast in silvery moonlight. The dude was built like a steamroller. "Find any more bodies, Leon?"

The pure-blood Sentinel shook his head, eyes narrowing. "No."

Leon was a man of few words, but I was used to it. Turning back to the body, I knew what I had to do. I hated it with every fiber of my being, but this was a mess. Sentinels just didn't hunt daimons.

We cleaned up after them.

Off in the distance, lightning struck and the last of the late spring storm rolled out. Jaw clenched, I rested my hand on the kid's arm and let one of the most powerful elements wash away what had been the horrific last moments of his life. Sparks flew from my fingertip, fueled by the very gods themselves, and traveled up the lifeless arm. Within seconds, the unnatural fire consumed the body. Nothing but ashes remained. It was like the boy never existed. And I couldn't help but wonder if he had parents out there to notify, or if they even cared.

And I thought of Deacon again.

"Hey Aiden, look what I found," Kain called out, excited.

Standing, I wiped off my hands and turned. Kain was grinning. Gods, Kain was always grinning. He could be facing down a horde of daimons and still be smiling.

"What?" Leon demanded, arms folded across his chest.

Kain waved a slip of paper. "One bus ticket to Nashville, plus there's money everywhere back here."

Leon made an exasperated sound in the back of his throat. "This is a bus station, Kain. There will be tickets scattered around."

"Yeah, thanks for pointing out that." Kain rolled his eyes. "This ticket was from Miami to Nashville, with a stop in Atlanta."

"She's been here," said Leon in a low, grave voice.

A ticket. Loose money. Dead mortals and daimons. She had most definitely been here.

"Crap." Kain pocketed the ticket and dropped the money for someone else to find. "You guys should've listened to me in Florida. We should've been watching the bus stations and not the airports."

"That's not really helping right now." I stalked down the alley, scanning for something—anything to put us in the right direction. I needed to get back to the Covenant. Gods only knew what Deacon was doing.

"All I'm saying is that—"

"Shut up, Kain," warned Leon. It was amazing that he hadn't killed Kain yet.

Kain quieted.

With a grim smile, I moved to the edge of the alley. There was a field and woods separating the truck stop from an industrial park. I felt Leon move up behind me and turned slightly. "Do you think we're too late?" I asked.

He stared straight ahead, eyes distant. "I don't think so. She made it this far after..."

After what we'd seen and learned in Miami, the girl would've had to be resourceful to keep going. But there were daimons here. They'd killed. It didn't look good. She may be only a half-blood—a very well connected half-blood—but the idea of her dying out here alone sliced through me. The injustice of it all wasn't right.

"Look," Leon said. "Someone's been in this field, running. See how sections are trampled down."

He was right. The three of us headed forward, following the trampled field grass until we reached the woods. It wasn't easy then. We split up, each of us going in a different direction. I headed down the middle, eyeing the tops of the building in the distance. Another pulse of lightning split the sky, and the following thunder shook my bones.

I'd taken a few more steps when I heard Leon call out. Following his voice, I found him by the charred remains of another mortal. It was fresh. "Daimon?"

He nodded. "Don't know what else could burn a mortal up like that and not take out an entire forest."

"She's got to be around here somewhere." Alive...or dead, but either way, we would find her. We'd bring her back like we'd been ordered to do from the Minister himself. I glanced at the buildings again, and an uncanny feeling rolled down my spine. "Let's check them out."

Sending Kain back to the Hummer with orders to meet us at the park, Leon and I headed out. It didn't take us long to cross the woods and tread quietly over cracked pavement. Kain parked at the edge of the lot, joining us quickly as we moved between the buildings.

"Okay, I've got to ask this." Kain pulled out a titanium blade. "Why in the world would daimons go through this much trouble to munch on a half-blood?"

Leon exhaled loudly.

"Don't get me wrong. Being a half-blood and all myself, I like to think I'm important, but to a daimon? No way. Something is wrong about this."

As much as I hated to admit it—because whenever Kain was right, I never heard the end of it—he had a point. Daimons didn't care about half-bloods at all. There wasn't enough aether in them. "I know," I said finally.

"I mean, what's going on that we don't—"

I stopped, hearing the sound of metal grinding. Holding up a hand, I silenced Kain as I turned to the squat building in front of us. Motioning toward it, I pulled out my blade and headed forward.

One of the rusted-out doors had been kicked in. Anticipation swelled and my adrenaline kicked into overtime. This was it. I knew it deep in my bones. After months of coming so close, this was going to be the end, one way or another. Moving quietly I eased open the door and let my eyes adjust to the darkness of the abandoned factory.

Scattered benches and broken beams lay everywhere. The place smelled of rot and decay. Heart pumping fast now, I crept around the forgotten work tables.

Then I heard it—I heard her.

"Blah. Blah. You're gonna kill me. Blah. I know."

A reluctant, amused smile pulled at my lips. From everything I'd heard about Alexandria Andros, that had to be her. When the Minister had dumped the orders to find her in my lap, I felt like I should've remembered her, but the memory was vague and unreachable.

A daimon's shriek cut through the air and then a male yelled for the female to stop. The sound of pounding feet propelled me into action. I sprung forward, racing for the gap in the wall. Not knowing how many daimons had the girl cornered, I needed a distraction.

I threw up my free hand and blew out a small breath. A wave of fire rolled over the factory floor, burning everything in its path. There was a sudden shriek from the other side. Releasing the other blade into my hand, I walked through the fire, untouched by the heat.

In an instant I saw her. She looked too tiny to be standing there, clutching…a garden spade in her small hand? From beneath the tangled mess of her hair, our gazes locked. A flicker of familiarity went through me.

The female behind her looked like any pure blood to me, but I wasn't taking the risk. I'd found her. "Get down."

Thank the gods she hit the floor as I threw out another stream of elemental fire. It slammed into the daimon, and she fell, shrieking and rolling. My senses were telling me there were more, at least two more.

I lowered my hand, hearing the popping sound as the flames went out. Leon and Kain rushed in. With his keen and sometimes freaky ability to root out daimons, Leon zeroed in on the other daimon and disappeared. Kain went to the downed female daimon, driving the titanium blade deep into her chest.

Out the corner of my eyes, I saw Alexandria struggling to her feet. Irritation flared. She needed to stay down, out of the way until we knew where the rest of the daimons were. I turned for a second—a damn second—and I heard her yelp.

Spinning back to her, a blond had her trapped, pulling her back by her hair. In a split second, horror raced through me as he struck like an angered cobra. Alexandria screamed—the sound dragged me back so many years ago. I'd heard that shrill, pained sound too many times since the first time I'd awakened to it. My stomach lurched.

The daimon lifted his gory mouth. "What are you?"

Shooting forward, I grabbed the daimon by his throat and ripped him away from her. He hit the floor, rolling onto his feet. Smiling, I spun out and caught him in the stomach with my booted foot. Then I dropped, taking his legs right off from underneath him. I could've killed him then. I could've ended it quickly.

With mercy.

But he'd tagged her.

And, well, that deserved a little payback. Mercy not included.

The daimon climbed to his feet just as I caught him by the throat, slamming the creature into the nearby wall. Bones crunched. I didn't flinch. Not even as I slammed him again… or when I finally drove the blade into him. The daimon collapsed into itself. I turned away before he was even fully gone, my gaze going straight to the girl.

She was on the floor, curled up into a tiny ball, making sounds that pecked at my chest. I'd never been tagged before, but I'd heard that Hades had nothing on the pain. Putting the blades away, I went to her.

Carefully, I reached down and rolled her onto her back.

Her hands were clutching the space between her neck and shoulder. Needing to see the damage, I pried her hands away. It didn't look too bad. No major arteries or big chunks of skin missing. But she wasn't talking. She was just staring up at me through strands of hair, her eyes wide and standing out against her pale, dirtied cheeks.

It was her.

"Are you okay? Alexandria? Please say something."

"Alex," she choked out. "Everyone calls me Alex."

I gave a short, relieved laugh. "Okay. Good. Alex can you stand?"

She nodded. Every few seconds a shudder rolled through her, but she held it together. The girl was strong. "That really...sucked something bad."

Wrapping an arm around her waist, I lifted her onto her feet. She swayed as I brushed her hair back to look at the tag again, just to be sure. "Give it a few minutes. The pain will wear off."

Leon returned, along with Kain. His eyes were fixed on the girl, and I had a sudden urge to shield her. Pure-bloods weren't known for their kindness toward halfs. A fact I hated about my own kind. I didn't know where Leon stood with that. "That should be all of them," he said.

I nodded. "Alex, we need to go. Now. Back to the Covenant."

She looked at me again, but she didn't see me as she backed up, her thin arms trembling. Like a caged animal that saw no way out. In a flicker of a second, I knew she was going to do something rash, something not fully thought out and born of residual fear. I only hoped that it was me she went after, and not Leon. I wouldn't hold it against her, but if she attacked a different pure blood, all of this would be for nothing.

I made a small step toward her, raising my hands in what I hoped came across as harmless.

She shuddered, like a sheet of glass stretched too thin.

I took another step toward her, and she threw herself at me in mass of kicking feet and clawed hands. There was some talent in there—some leftover training, but her movements were jerky with fear and exhaustion.

Catching one of her hands, I spun around and clamped her arms to her sides. She bent forward, trying to kick me. No good deed goes unpunished… I moved out the way. "Don't," I warned, speaking directly into her ear. "I don't want to hurt you."

Her breathing was harsh, broken, as she struggled like we were the bad guys. The string of curses she strung together was actually quite impressive and would've been entertaining if it hadn't been directed at me.

"Whoa!" Kain yelled from the sidelines. "Alex, you know us! Don't you remember me? We aren't going to hurt you."

"Shut up!" she screamed, gathering up the last of her strength, breaking free of my grasp only because I hadn't held her tight enough to hurt her.

Alex dodged Kain and Leon, who'd stood by, looking equally shocked and amused. Her long, stringy hair flew out from behind her as she picked up speed, heading for the exit.

Kain smirked. "Well, this has gone as expected."

I sighed. "I'll get her."

"Make sure you don't break her or anything," Leon said. "I doubt her stepfather would appreciate that."

Yeah. Yeah. I took off after her, knowing she wouldn't get anywhere. Not now. Rounding the side of the building, I saw her under the moonlight, streaking across the field. The girl could run when she wanted to. Was that how she stayed alive? Just running? Kind of sad.

Catching up to her, I wrapped my arms around her waist and took her down, twisting so I took the hit in the itchy grass. For a heartbeat, she was on top of me, stunned and silent, but if the few moments of being around her had taught me anything, I knew that wouldn't last. Tilting my hips, I rolled her under me, pinning her down.

"Now?" she screamed, voice cracking. "Where were you a week ago? Where was the Covenant when my mother was being killed? Where were you?"

I jerked back, more affected by those words than she'd ever realize. "I'm sorry. We didn't—"

She went off like an atomic bomb. Screaming. Kicking. Clawing. Someone was going to get hurt, and it wasn't going to be me. And the last thing I wanted to do was hurt someone who'd obviously been through too much, seen too much. I let my weight press her down, holding her immobile.

And finally, Alex stopped fighting. I think she stopped breathing. Or maybe it was me, because I could feel every part of her. Soft where I was hard, curved where I was straight lines. I stared down at her, sharing the same air, our lips only inches apart.

In her eyes, there was a storm of emotions. The look was shattering, deep. The soft brown irises churned in a battle with fear, rage…and something much more. I almost didn't see it, but her lips parted in a pliable exhale.

Oddly enough, I found myself wanting to know what she looked like under all the dirt. How she sounded when she wasn't cussing or screaming at me. How she moved when the actions weren't born out of instinct or fear.

All of that curiosity was highly inappropriate, wrong even. She was a half-blood.

I lowered my head, and she inhaled so sharply that her

chest pressed against mine. A primal rush went through me, really hard to ignore and push down when she looked at me like that. Like if I wanted to do something, anything crazy, she'd be down for it.

This was insane.

Placing my hand on her forehead, guilt chewed through me with tiny, razor-sharp teeth. This had to be done. If not, she'd only hurt herself. Meeting her stare, I packed a hell of a mental punch with my next words. "Go to sleep. Now. Go to sleep and do not wake up until you feel safe. Now."

Alex stiffened and then her entire body went lax, limp and compliant. I had the distinct impression this would be one of the few moments she'd ever be like that. Remorse for using a compulsion against her slithered through me as I gathered her in my arms and stood.

It was over. At least, it should be. We'd done what we'd been sent to do. We found Alexandria Andros, and yet, I knew deep in my soul that this was only the beginning.

CHAPTER TWO (AIDEN'S POV)

Alex liked to snuggle. That became apparent from the moment I placed her in the back of the Hummer and climbed in after her. Not even a minute went by before she wiggled closer, placing her head on my shoulder. It couldn't be a comfortable position, and I wanted to move my arm to give her more room, but that wouldn't go over well. The fact that she was using my shoulder as a pillow was bad enough.

I should've pushed her away, but I didn't have it in me. Every couple of minutes, she would make these little sounds, a soft whimper or moan. I glanced down at her, only able to see the top of her nose poking out from her hair. I wondered what she was dreaming.

My eyes lifted, finding Leon watching me in the rearview mirror. He raised his brows. "Eyes on the road," I grunted.

Leon snorted.

Kain hadn't said a word to me since I'd appeared with Alex in my arms. He was ticked over the compulsion. Couldn't blame him. Compulsions were a sore subject with halfs.

Shifting closer, Alex sighed deeply, drawing my attention back to her. The moment she woke and became aware of what she was doing, I braced myself.

Alex jerked back quickly, smacking her head on the window. "Crap!"

Wincing, I turned to her. "Are you okay?" She didn't answer me for several minutes. "Alex. Are you okay?"

"Yeah, I'm fine." She scowled as she looked around the Hummer. "Where are we?"

"We're on the coast, just outside of Bald Head Island. We are almost to Deity Island."

She jumped a little. "What?"

"We're going back to the Covenant, Alex."

Rubbing the back of her head, she sighed. "Did the Covenant send you? Or was it my…stepfather?"

I wasn't sure how to answer that. It all seemed complicated. "The Covenant."

"You work for the Covenant now?"

Surprised that she even remembered me from her time there, I shook my head. "No. I'm just a Sentinel. I'm more on loan for the time being. Your uncle sent us to find you." I glanced out the window. "A lot has changed since you've been gone."

She asked a couple mundane questions as I watched her closely. She fidgeted. A lot. Not a moment went by without her moving in her seat. A grin pulled at my lips until I remembered what I'd done.

"Alex, I'm sorry about the compulsion back there. I didn't want you to hurt yourself."

Not surprisingly, she didn't forgive me. I glanced up front, relieved to find that Leon wasn't watching us. "And…I'm sorry about your mother. We searched everywhere for you two, but you didn't stay in one place long enough. We were too late."

"Yeah you were too late." Her voice wavered.

A pang hit me in the chest. Part of me wanted to tell her that I knew how she felt, but I wasn't supposed to relate to her. Ever. Seeking a way to change the subject, I asked a question that had been gnawing at me. "Why did your mother leave three years ago?"

She peeked at me from behind the curtain of hair. What in Hades did her face look like? "I don't know."

Unsure if I should believe her, I let it drop. No one knew why her mother, a pure blood, had pulled her away from the Covenant. And if they did, they weren't talking. We didn't talk again, not until we crossed the bridges and Leon dropped us off in front of one of the dorms rising up between the sand and sea.

She was quiet as I led her through the halls, and I should be grateful for that. But unrest tugged at me for some reason. "Get cleaned up. I'll return for you in a little bit." I started to turn, but stopped. "I'll find something for you to wear and leave it on the table."

Not waiting for her response, I left her in the dorm and went back to the main island. Each step I took, I prepared myself for what I would no doubt find when I opened the door to what used to be my parents' house.

The stench of alcohol overshadowed that of the sea and nearly knocked me over. Anger rushed through me like a ball of fire. Stalking down the hallway, I didn't even bother to be quiet as I glanced into a sitting room.

Several pure-blood teenagers were passed out in various positions. Some I really didn't want to see. My irritation knew no limits as I continued on. Making sure that the one room was still locked, I headed for Deacon's bedroom. I shoved the door open, slamming it against the wall.

Thank the gods Deacon was alone. If I walked in on him one more time half-naked, I was going to have to let a Furie gorge my eyes out.

My younger brother was sprawled across the bed, face down, clothing rumpled and a flask beside him, seeping only the gods knew what he'd been drinking into the mattress.

Without further ado, I kicked the post on the bed. Hard.

"What?" Deacon mumbled into the blanket. "The bathroom is down the hall…or go outside. Whatever."

"I know where the bathroom is, asshat. This is my house."

Deacon froze and then let a loud sigh as he rolled onto his back, squinting up at me. He smiled—actually smiled at me. The only trait we really shared was the eyes, but his gray ones were muddled. "Hey, bro, welcome back."

I wanted to take him outside and dump him in the ocean. Hold him under until Poseidon kicked us out. "Is this what you've been doing the whole time I've been gone? Drinking? Partying?"

"No." Sitting up, he swayed from side to side as he winced. "Okay. Maybe just a little."

Taking a step forward, I bent so that we were at eye level. "Is this how you're going to spend your whole life? Is this what I have to look forward to every time I leave here?"

He tilted his head back, his smile wobbly. "You're not my babysitter, bro. You're not my dad. Gods…you act like you're fifty. You're only twenty. Live a little. Have a drink." He handed me the flask. "Chill out."

I knocked the flask out of his hand when I really wanted to knock him upside the head.

"Whoa," he murmured. "Not cool."

Drawing on patience I really didn't have, I took a deep breath. "I know you drink because you miss our parents. I know it's some deep-rooted trauma and grief. I get that, but this isn't the way to deal with it."

He blinked. "It's not, all-wise one?"

By the gods, I was going to physically harm him. "I just picked up a girl who saw her mother drained by a daimon. Who had to fight every day to survive, Deacon. She could've done what you're doing. She could've just given up."

"Maybe she should have." He flopped onto his back, closing his eyes. "Easier that way."

There was so much I wanted to say to him, but I'd probably regret every word in an hour. Or not, but I didn't have time for this. Marcus was waiting. "Get them out of this house in an hour."

"Yes sir!" He gave me a one-finger salute.

Spinning around, I left the house before I did hit him. Back on the Covenant-controlled island, I reined in my anger and went to retrieve Alex. Kain intercepted me just as I rounded the courtyard.

"What do you think they're going to do with her?" he asked, falling in step beside me.

Good question. "I have no clue."

"She missed too much time to get caught up." He ran a hand through his blond hair, agitated. "They'll send her into servitude. Put her on the elixir."

Coldness whipped through me. Servitude equaled slavery, the fear of all half-bloods. Not wanting to delve too deeply as to why the idea of the little spitfire being placed on the elixir bothered me, I shook my head. "I doubt they would've gone to all this trouble to do that."

"I'd work with her if they need someone to get her caught

up," he suggested. "That's all she really needs. I remember her, Aiden. The girl can fight. And she's quick. Gods, she got away from you."

I rolled my eyes. No doubt Kain was never going to let me forget that. "You graduated less than a year ago. You can't train someone."

"Then what? You'll do it?" Curiosity colored his tone. "You're not known for your patience."

That was true. Whenever the Covenant sent fresh out-of-school Sentinels to me, I sent over half of them back for minor infractions. I'd rather be known as a prick then be responsible for a handful of dead half-bloods. "Hopefully, it doesn't come to that."

I seriously had enough to worry about without adding a half-trained half-blood to the mix. I left Kain outside the dorm, heading straight for the room I'd taken her to. I knocked once and then opened the door. Briefly, I thought I should've waited a moment. The girl could be naked for all I knew.

Alex was standing in the middle of the little living room. She jumped when she saw me, but I was more surprised to actually get a good look at her without dirt covering her.

I remembered her.

But she wasn't the little tomboy I recalled from the times I'd seen her. Some of the features were the same. She hadn't grown much in height, but my gods, she was…

Long, thick chestnut-colored hair fell past a chest that had grown in the last three years. Her face was oval shaped with lips full like a pure blood's. Cheekbones high and eyebrows delicately arched over two wide brown eyes. Even with the faint purplish bruises marring an otherwise flawless complexion, she was…unbelievable.

Beautiful.

My entire body tensed as we locked eyes. Something most halfs wouldn't even dare do, but oh no, she did. She stared back, the same appreciative stare I was giving her. A liquid feeling, like when I called on fire, simmered in my veins.

A feeling I shouldn't have.

Alex tipped her head back. "What?"

I snapped out of it. What in the Hades was I thinking? "Nothing. You ready?"

"I guess so."

She followed me out of the dorm, and I was acutely aware of her eyes on me. I glanced over my shoulder, wondering what she was thinking. She had the strangest look on her face, like she was trying to work a puzzle. "How many daimons have you killed?"

"Just two." She picked up her pace to walk beside me.

"Just two?" Awed, I stared at her. "Do you realize how amazing it is for a half-blood not fully trained to kill one daimon, let alone two?"

"I guess so." Her face scrunched up with anger and then fell. "I would've killed the other one in Miami…but I was just—I don't know. I wasn't thinking. I know I should've gone after him, but I panicked."

I stopped, facing her. "Alex, the fact that you took down one daimon without training is remarkable. It was brave, but also foolish."

"Well, thanks."

"You're not trained. The daimon could've easily killed you. And the one you brought down in the factory? Another fearless, but foolish act."

She frowned. "I thought you said it was amazing and remarkable."

"It was, but you could've been killed." I walked off ahead. Amazing? Remarkable?

"Why would you even care if I was killed? Why does Marcus care? I don't even know the man, and if he doesn't allow me to resume training, I'm as good as dead anyway."

"That would be a shame." I didn't know why I cared, but I did. "You have all the potential in the world."

And I knew then, even when her eyes narrowed like she was imagining planting her foot in my face, I wouldn't let them cart her off into servitude. My gods, I had to be the stupidest pure blood alive, but I knew this wasn't going to end when I deposited her in her uncle's office.

Like I'd realized in the field, I was struck again by the sense of knowing. This was far from ending.

CHAPTER SIXTEEN
(AIDEN'S POV)

"I'm not saying that." Against common sense, I closed the distance between us and placed my hands on her shoulders. Her bare skin was warm, smooth, and so damn soft.

Alex shivered, and I knew I should've pulled my hands back then, but instead I allowed my fingers to curve over the delicate bones. Focus—I needed to focus. I was only trying to comfort her. And she needed comfort right now, reassurance that everything was the same as it was the day before. The last thing she needed was me feeling her up. Not that I was doing that.

"Do you remember what I said about fate?" When she shook her head, an odd expression crossed her face, and I wondered what she was remembering. "Only you have control over your future, Alex. Only you have control over what you want."

"You really think so?"

I nodded. Nothing could force Alex into something she didn't want. She was so incredibly strong, and I couldn't fathom how she didn't know that. "Yes."

Alex shook her head again, as if the simple gesture could fool me. Her eyes flicked up, a warm whiskey brown, before darting over my shoulder. The pain and confusion in her gaze was a sucker punch to the gut. I couldn't stand it, knowing what she'd been through already. My hands tightened on her shoulders. And a part of me—all of me—wanted to take her away, from all of this.

Without really thinking, I pulled her against me and tried to come up with something to prove to her that she was going to be okay. But then she placed her head against my chest, and I stopped breathing.

Oh gods, what in the hell was I doing?

Being this close to her, holding her, was wrong on so many levels. Alex's entire future was in my hands right now. What I needed to do was pat her on the back, tell her everything would be fine, and send her on her way.

"I don't want to be this Apollyon thing." Her eyes closed. "I don't even like being in the same country as Seth. I don't want any of this."

But like a true SOB, instead of pushing her away, my hand smoothed down her back. The thin cotton of her dress was a pitiful barrier.

"I know," I said, struggling to remember what was going on here. This wasn't about me or my out-of-control desire for something I could never have. "It's overwhelming and scary, but you're not alone. We'll figure this out. Everything is going to be okay."

And now I needed to gently push her away, but Alex pressed closer. Lightning jolted my body. And gods, everything changed in that instant. Intentions of comfort, no matter how true they were in the beginning, were gone. Right out the window, along with my self-restraint and common sense.

Alex felt right in my arms.

I ran my hand through her silky hair, tilting her head back. Her eyes were so wide, mirroring a dangerous mixture of innocence and temptation. "You don't have anything to worry about, Alex. I'm not going to let anything happen to you."

The moment those words left my mouth, I knew I'd crossed some invisible line that I could never, ever go back from. They weren't just words. They were an oath that I'd keep true to the end of my days.

Our eyes locked. Her chest rose unsteadily against mine as she sucked in a breath I wanted to share. An unfamiliar thing happened. My heart stuttered and then skipped a beat. The room seemed to shift, and I pulled her closer, because she wasn't close enough. Could never be close enough.

My hand drifted from her hair, across the curve of her cheekbone. Gods, she was so beautiful. Pure temptation. My thumb smoothed over her lower lip, and I felt her answering shudder under my skin.

Too caught up, I leaned in, pressing my cheek against hers. "You should tell me to stop."

Alex said nothing.

And I stopped thinking. With a growl more animal than civilized, I moved toward her mouth with only one thing in mind.

I kissed her. Savoring her mouth, soaking up her response, I was fueled by her desire for more. And though I needed more, in the back of my mind, I already knew that more could never be enough. That if I didn't stop, I'd never be satisfied. Like a daimon after its first taste of aether, I'd just keep coming back and back.

As I fitted her body to mine, the kiss deepened, shocking me to the core. Gods, I wanted this, as bad as that was, I wanted this.

Sliding my hands down her shoulders, I followed the curve of her stomach, the subtle flare of hips. Before I knew it, I was taking her to the bedroom. Never breaking contact with her mouth…or her body.

And brave, beautiful Alex threw herself into this madness like she always did. Head first, questions and concerns later. Reckless, but admirable. Dangerous, but so tempting. She slid her hands under my shirt, and I jerked at the touch of her fingers. Pulling back, I let her strip me of my shirt.

I smiled at Alex's sudden inhale.

Then I was on her, easing her down. And as I loomed over her, I don't know what got to me more—that she wanted this so badly or how much she trusted me.

Trust? I stilled. Alex trusted me and I was seconds away—

Alex's hand glided down my chest, farther south, and dammit, if I wasn't lost. Found. Whatever. She was wearing too many clothes. I kissed her again, dragging her breath into me, sliding the top of her dress down and then off. And I took my time finding her lips again, committing each dip and curve to memory. My lower body sank into hers, and little, surprisingly sharp nails dug into my arms.

She kept whispering my name, over and over again as I explored her, relished her. She was breathing in short gasps when I rolled her on top of me.

"You're so beautiful. So brave, so full of life." I sounded—felt drunk as I guided her head down so I could kiss the scar on her neck. "You have no idea, do you? You have so much life in you, so much."

Alex dipped her head, and she grinned when I kissed the tip of her nose. "Really?"

"Yes." I brushed her hair back from her face. "Since the night I saw you in Georgia, you've been under my skin. You got inside me, became a part of me. I can't shake it. It's wrong." I shifted us, rolling Alex across the bed until I towered over her. Damn, she was one hell of a fighter, who would one day become something that would crush her enemies, but she felt so small under me. So perfect.

"Agapi mou, I can't…" There were no more words. I brought my lips to hers, leaning my full weight onto her. Everything took on a near frantic edge. Our kisses. The touching. The way our bodies moved against each other.

I lifted my head, unable to wait any longer. "Do you trust me?"

Alex ran her fingers over my cheeks, then my lips. "Yes."

There had been no hesitation. I brought her hand to my lips, kissing the tips of each of her fingers. Then I looked at her, taking in her flushed cheeks, fevered eyes. Time stopped. I wanted—needed this to be perfect for her, to be—

Someone knocked on the door.

I froze.

No. No freaking way. We stared each other, possibly both of us praying for the same thing. That someone wasn't at that door.

But the sound came again, along with Leon's booming voice. "Aiden, open this door. Now."

Son of a bitch.

Never in my life did I hate someone as much as I hated Leon at that very moment. And there was no ignoring him. He'd break down that damn door and Alex…

My gaze swept over her as I lifted myself off the bed and grabbed a pair of pants and the shirt she'd tossed clear across the room. The girl had an arm on her. She'd probably throw a dagger like a—

It struck me then. And I could barely breathe.

Spinning around, I left the room and shut the door behind me. Holy crap, I'd…I'd been so, so close to taking everything from her. Most importantly her freedom…

"Shit," I muttered, stalking toward the door. What the hell had I been thinking? She didn't deserve this—because this was nothing. It couldn't ever be anything.

Halfs and pures did not mix.

But she was in my bedroom, on my bed, glorious…

Leon's impatient sigh penetrated wood. I briefly entertained the idea of grabbing a dagger and throwing it through the door.

I yanked the door open, running a hand through my hair. "What?"

He cocked his head to the side, but his gaze went over my shoulder, to my bedroom. My stomach dropped. Leon was a cool guy, but if he knew Alex was here—in there—he'd be required to report her.

Her. In the end, Alex would be the only one who'd suffer for this. The good oleboys would probably applaud me. Gods, I hated my own race sometimes.

Leon's expression remained impressively blank. "I didn't mean to wake you, but I figured you'd want to know this immediately. They've found Kain. He's alive."

I blinked, unsure I heard him right. But I had. Kain was alive. I rubbed my jaw. Crap. This could be good. Or this could be real, real bad for Alex.

Somehow I managed to convince Leon that I'd meet him over in the med center and went back to Alex.

She was waiting by the bed. Dressed. Part of me was relieved. Another part of me wanted to take the dress off. Again.

"I heard," she said, eyes wide.

I nodded. "I'll let you know what he says."

She stepped forward. "I want to come. I have to hear what he says."

Oh yeah, that's not going to work. "Alex, it's past your curfew, and how would you know to be in the infirmary?"

Her eyes narrowed. "But I can sneak in there. The rooms are just separated with partition walls. I could stay behind them—"

"Alex. You need to go back to your dorm. Now. I promise I'll tell you everything he says, okay?"

For a moment I thought she was going to argue, but she nodded. We waited a couple more minutes. At the front door, I closed my eyes and drew in a deep breath.

When she stepped out of this door…that was it. This could never happen again. We'd come within inches of being caught, within seconds of her losing everything and because of what?

"What?" Alex said.

Because I was lost in her.

I faced her, and she suddenly looked a little scared. And she wasn't the only one. What I was feeling at that moment disturbed the hell out of me. Without saying a word, I cupped her face and kissed her.

I kissed her like I was never going to see her again, because in a way, I wasn't. Not this way, and as much as that killed me, I knew the difference between what felt right.

And what was actually right.

"Don't do anything stupid," I warned her, voice hoarse. Then I left her, disappearing into the darkness.

ACKNOWLEDGMENTS

Short and sweet—thank you to Kate Kaynak, Patricia Riley, Rich Storrs, and Rebecca Mancini. A big thank-you to Kevan Lyon for being an awesome agent. Thank you to Malissa Coy and to Wendy Higgins for being their amazing author/editor selves. Each time I write these, it gets harder and harder to make sure I'm getting everyone. So a big thank you to everyone who has supported the series and has wanted to take part in Alex's journey, and who has kept me sane during the process.

ABOUT THE AUTHOR

#1 *New York Times* and #1 international bestselling author Jennifer L. Armentrout lives in Shepherdstown, West Virginia. All the rumors you've heard about her state aren't true. When she's not hard at work writing, she spends her time reading, watching really bad zombie movies, pretending to write, and hanging out with her husband and their two Border Collies, Jack Apollo and Artemis, six judgmental alpacas, two rude goats, and five fluffy sheep. In early 2015, Jennifer was diagnosed with retinitis pigmentosa, a group of rare genetic disorders that involves a breakdown and death of cells in the retina, eventually resulting in loss of vision, among other complications. Due to this diagnosis, educating people on the varying degrees of blindness has become of a passion of hers, right alongside writing, which she plans to do as long as she can.